# CONQUERED

## HIGHGATE PREPARATORY ACADEMY

ROSA LEE

DIRTY LITTLE PUBLISHERS LTD

Cover design provided by Jodilock Designs

# FOREWORD

Dear Reader,

Firstly, thank you so much for taking a chance on me and reading *Conquered*. I hope you enjoy it!

Also, as you may already know that I am British and so *Conquered* is written in a mix of British and American English. This has been done on purpose, to reflect the different characters and their cultures, so some words will be spelled differently throughout depending on who's speaking or thinking! If you see some unfamiliar words, know that they are there intentionally and I hope you enjoy discovering new phrases!

As mentioned in the blurb, *Conquered* is a dark romance. There are many subjects explored that some readers may find disturbing.

For a full list of triggers please visit www.rosaleeauthor.com/trigger-warnings

Also please visit my website for a list of all the playlists that accompany my books.

Also a small word of caution. My books have a lot of BDSM vibes in them, and if they inspire you to dive into that kinky world, please do your research and educate yourself before trying out anything new for the first time. Take care my little smut bunnies!

PREQUEL

# HUNTED

HIGHGATE PREPARATORY ACADEMY

ROSA LEE

# CHAPTER ONE

Pregnant.

I sit on the toilet, the test shaking in my hand, making that one word jump and dance around, as if taunting me. A gasping sob falls from my lips, my other hand coming up quickly to cover the sound.

Funny how one small word can change the course of your life so completely that it becomes unrecognisable.

*Shit. I can't have a child with him.* I think, panic flaring in my chest as images of flying fists flash across my mind.

A bang on the door makes me jump, dropping the stick which goes skittering across the expensive black marble tiled flooring.

"Coming!" I shout, standing and pulling my knickers back up my legs, letting my midnight blue silk evening gown fall to the floor. My hand traces over my stomach, as if I can feel the life growing inside of me, which of course is impossible as according to the test, I'm only a few weeks along.

"Violet," a deep voice sounds on the other side of the door, and I shudder at the dark tone. "You'll make us late."

"Just washing up, Ace," I call out, turning the tap on, then picking up the test and frantically looking around for somewhere to hide it. He can't see it, not until I've decided what I'm going to do. Spotting the under sink cupboard, I quickly stash it behind all of the cleaning products.

*I'll have to come back for it later.*

After washing my hands, I take a final look in the mirror. My dress has a high neck and back, and you can only just see a faint purple mark peeking out from under the collar. The rest of the dress hugs my figure, with rhinestones covering down to my hips and glittering like stars in the night sky. They lessen as the skirts flare out around my feet in a swishing mermaid tail.

I take a deep breath to steady myself, wincing as my bruised ribs twinge.

*Just get through this evening, then think about what to do next.*

I plaster a smile on my face, grabbing my matching beaded purse off the counter, and open the door to find Ace, my fiancé, standing in a full black tuxedo and looking devilishly handsome. His hair is thick and a dark chocolate brown slicked back from his arresting face. His jaw is sharp, his nose straight like a Roman emperor's, and there's a neat, dark beard covering his jawline.

It's a beautiful face, but a hard one, and right now, his thick brows are pinched over his dark brown eyes. Had I looked closer when I first met him, I might have noticed the deadness lurking just beneath the surface of those shadowy orbs. Not that it would have made much of a difference, I suppose. This is an arranged match, one both our parents decided when we were in the cradle. Contracts signed and sealed before our first birthday.

Those sable eyes take me in; starting at my lightly made up face, moving down my silk-clad body, assessing my appearance for any flaw, and leaving unpleasant tingles in their wake. Finding none, he nods and holds out one arm for me to take. I rush in my heels to do so, knowing that any infraction will be paid for later behind closed doors.

"I don't like to be kept waiting, Violet." He admonishes as we leave the house, walking towards the waiting black SUV, and Tom, our driver. "You know they'll try and steal any advantage they can. Bunch of ignorant jackals." His lip curls, tone scathing, and I wonder, not for the first time, why he went into business with the others if he finds them so distasteful. We all went to high school together, and they always seemed pretty tight knit.

Ace and I went to school here in Colorado, and Highgate Preparatory Academy is one of the best in the world, especially for meeting future business associates and leaders. The teaching is second to none, but it's the connections and networking with the top one-percenters that is the real draw. It surprised me when my English parents suggested it, but then again, since Ace is American and was coming here, it only made sense for me to come as well given our betrothal.

Once we'd graduated, I wanted to go on and study something artistic, history of art in New York perhaps, but Ace had other plans so we ended up at Yale School of Management earning our MBAs there. I should have known then what sort of man he was, but I was too meek, too desperate for affection, after a lack of any sort from my stiff and emotionally distant parents.

We graduated this summer and moved into a large mansion about twenty minutes from Brompton Lakes, back near Highgate Prep. It's got more rooms than we need and is secluded in the woods; nice and private just as Ace likes. No nosy neighbours to interfere with his pleasures.

Tonight, we're on our way to the official opening gala of Black Knight Corporation, the multifaceted company that Ace has set up with Julian Vanderbilt, Rafe Griffiths, Stephen Matthews, and Chad Thorn. All rich, entitled brats with pretty faces that hide their twisted and depraved personalities.

The SUV stops, snapping me out of my musings, and Tom gets out and comes to open Ace's door.

He turns to me, dark eyes almost black and boring into my very soul. "Best behaviour, Violet. Don't show me up tonight." He doesn't wait for an answer, just steps out of the vehicle, and then leans back to hold a hand out like the perfect gentleman.

---

A plan starts to formulate in my mind as I sit through dinner followed by rounds of self-congratulatory speeches. Over the past couple of years, I've perfected the art of smiling like I'm engaged whilst my mind wanders. No one really cares, women are just arm candy to these fat cats and corrupt leaders.

I open my purse, looking around to make sure that no eyes are on me. As usual, they're too focused on themselves to notice as I slip some powder into Ace's champagne flute whilst he's in the bathroom. I've got about fifteen to twenty minutes before the effects kick in, so I've made sure we're getting towards the end of the evening.

It's Rohypnol, and until recently, he was using it on me without my knowledge. Some mornings I'd wake up with new bruises and an ache between my thighs, yet have no clue how they got there until I saw him drugging my drink a few months back.

We were at a function, not dissimilar to this one, with rich men trying to line their pockets and Ace schmoozing his way around. I'd popped to the bathroom, returning sooner than he clearly expected, and saw him slip something into my glass. I managed to ditch the drink when he wasn't looking, only to face his puzzled anger later on in the evening once we'd arrived back at the house.

It didn't take much to put two and two together, and realise what he'd been up to and why I had gaps in my memories.

A few days later, when he was away for a business meeting, aka a prostitute orgy, I stole his stash. Black Knight Corp has a pharmaceutical arm, run by Rafe Griffiths, which explains how Ace managed to get a hold of the drug in the first place. Bunch of bloody criminals hiding behind lily white family reputations, bought of course. I knew I couldn't just take the drug without risking his notice. I'd need to replace it with something, so I replaced it with a placebo, that way I was at least aware of what was happening.

I've used the Rohypnol on him a few times; he gets especially aggressive after these sorts of events, so I pretended he just drank a lot and passed out. It seems to have worked so far, even with his control freak tendencies.

Ace gets up after he finishes his glass, indicating it's time to head back to the house. He stumbles as we walk through the tables, his already tight grip on my arm tightening further, and I know I'll have more bruises tomorrow.

"Must have drunk more than I thought," he mumbles as we step into the cool fall air. Tom is already waiting and helps me get Ace into the SUV, his hand brushing mine as he pulls away, sending pleasurable shivers down my arm.

"Home?" he asks me quietly. His blue eyes boring into mine then flicking to Ace.

"Yes please, Tom," I whisper back. His gaze flits to my neck, likely noticing the bruises peeking out of my collar. His whole body hardens, and his chiselled jaw clenches as he starts to reach out towards me.

"Don't," I plead, which stops him in his tracks. A look of frustration comes over his face, then he huffs out a breath, looking ahead as I climb in next to Ace, Tom shutting the door behind me.

The journey is short, Ace unconscious the whole time. He should be out for several hours which gives me plenty of time to put my plan into action.

We pull up outside of the house, and I look up, seeing Tom's blue gaze in the rearview mirror, his dark blond hair pushed off his forehead. A sudden image of me running my hands through its softness, and feeling his stubbled jaw under my lips, flashes through my mind. My breath hitches at the memory.

"Can you help me with him please, Tom?" I ask, voice quiet. I don't dare utter my other request until Ace is tucked up into bed.

"Of course," he practically growls, getting out of the car and opening Ace's door.

Tom grabs him, cracking Ace's head on the frame as he pulls him out of the car. Hoisting Ace up over his shoulder, he walks up the path as I follow behind, stepping up to open the door. Tom carries him up the stairs, going to Ace's bedroom, and throws him onto the bed before turning to face me.

I put a finger to his lips before he can utter a word, shaking my head. He indicates the door, and I pull my hand back, turning around and leaving the room. I walk to my bedroom, opening the door, and stepping inside. Tom is quick on my heels, leaving the door slightly ajar as he, too, steps inside.

"Let me see," he asks, voice firm and eyes pained.

I reach behind me and undo the collar, letting the dress slink down to the floor in a whisper of jewels. Tom lets out a hiss as he catalogues all the new bruises littering my torso. Before now, I've tried to keep the worst of the bruising from him, it's not like we get a lot of time together so it hasn't been too difficult to do.

"I'm going to fucking kill him," he fumes, making a move to step back through the door. He could take him too, they are evenly matched in stature and muscle. But Tom lacks Ace's cruelty, and that would be his downfall if they ever came to blows.

"No!" I rush over, gripping his muscular bicep tightly to stop him. "Tom, please, I need your help," I beg quietly. That pulls him up short, but I can see his chest heaving, and he's vibrating with anger. "I need to leave tonight, and I need you to help me."

"Why now?" he asks. It's a fair question, he's pleaded with me to leave Ace before, and I've always been too scared, so I refused. But it's not just me anymore. I take his hand and place it over my stomach. His eyes widen in the darkness, and I feel his warm hand flex as he lightly caresses me there.

"What do you need?" he murmurs, hand still splayed over my stomach protectively.

"You mentioned before that your new brother-in-law, Enzo, has connections and can get things in and out of the country without a trace?" I question a brief flicker of hope flaring to life inside of me.

He nods, understanding straight away what I'm asking.

"And I need a new identity that no one knows." He nods again, his brows pinching a little.

"He can do that, I think," he replies, his voice deep and soothing to me as it always is. My breath whooshes out of me as relief floods through my body, leaving my knees weak.

"Right," I say shakily. "I need to change and grab a few things."

I head towards my closet, stopping in the doorway. I have no idea what to take with me. As I dither, wasting precious seconds, I feel his warmth at my back. I want to lean into the comfort, but I manage to hold back, remaining upright. "I don't know what to take," I confess in a whisper, a lump in my throat.

"Comfortable clothes to travel in, things you can easily sell," Tom says decisively, stepping into the closet and reaching for a duffel bag on a shelf. It spurs me into action, and I start grabbing underwear, jeans, and tops from various drawers and stuffing them into the bag. When it's full, I turn to leave but stop as his warm hand lands on my bare waist.

"You might want to get dressed, Vi." Tom chuckles from behind me, his breath tickling the back of my neck.

"Oh, yes," I mumble, my cheeks flaming. I step past him and quickly dress in some dark jeans, a long-sleeved top, a cashmere sweater, and my comfy leather boots. Grabbing my warm winter coat, I turn back, smiling at him.

"Ready," I announce, voice still low. I know that Ace is out for the next four to six hours, but I can't help feeling like he's going to wake up any minute.

We head out of the bedroom then down the stairs, and Tom starts to head towards the front door.

"I'll be there in a minute," I softly tell him as he looks back when he notices that I'm not following. He frowns but waits by the door as I make my way to Ace's office.

I step inside and head straight to the desk, fear of even being in here hastening my steps. Behind the desk is a safe, and I crouch down, the moonlight lighting the keypad just enough for me to see. I discovered the code one day when Ace made me stand behind the desk for twenty-four hours with no food or drink for accidentally shrinking one of his cashmere jumpers in the wash.

I still breathe out a sigh of relief when the door clicks open. It's not that full as far as safes go, and there's a reason as to why his family wants mine. I find the stack of papers that I need, bonds for the company that were purchased using an advance of my dowry. *Yes, I've got an honest to god dowry!*

The next thing I take is an ornate wooden jewellery box. It contains old heirloom pieces all belonging to my family and now me. It's mine by rights anyway, and I can maybe exchange the pieces for my passage.

Closing the safe, I stand up and head out of the room, hurrying to Tom who just looks at the items then takes them from me and puts them into my bag. He opens the door, letting in the refreshing night air, and I take a deep breath as I step through.

Freedom tastes like falling leaves and damp earth, and I can't stop the smile tugging at my lips as we drive away.

# CHAPTER TWO

We arrive on the other side of town, the streets dark and empty as we drove. Pulling up outside a squat concrete building, I notice the windows are black, yet there's someone waiting for us in front of the plain wooden door as we step out of the car.

Tom gets my bag from the boot, then takes my hand and leads me up to what I now see is a man who is maybe ten years older than us, around mid-thirties. He's got swarthy Italian looks, black hair greased back, and deep brown eyes. Although unlike Ace's, there's a warmth and kindness in their depths.

Even though it's the middle of the night and autumn, he's wearing a black wife beater that shows off his arms that are covered in colourful, old school style tattoos. They're beautiful and a stark contrast to his all black outfit.

He smiles wide as we approach. "Brother, *fratello mio!*" he whispers jovially, his Italian accent strong. He opens his arms and embraces Tom, who doesn't let go of my hand, so it's slightly awkward. "*Che piacere*...Good to see you, although I wish it were under better circumstances...*purtroppo*."

He turns to me, his eyes softening with sympathy. "You must be Violet?" He asks me gently, and I nod, holding my free hand out to shake his.

He surprises me by grasping it and pulling forward, forcing Tom to finally let go with a growl, while kissing both of my cheeks continental style.

"Pleased to meet you, *molto piacere*." He grins, and he has such an aura of safety and warmth that I can't help but grin back. "I'm Enzo, Tom's brother by marriage. Although, I think he already told you that, *si? Forse?*" He asks, still grinning and not waiting for my answer. "Let's get you inside and see what's to be done...*prego*."

He ushers us inside, Tom grabbing my hand once again, where I see a couple of others waiting around what looks and smells like a boxing gym. Tom's hand tightens around my grip, pulling me back slightly. I hear Enzo chuckle as he looks back at us.

"These are my cousins, and I'd trust them with my life, *cari veramente*," he tells Tom, who gives an imperceptible dip of his head, but still keeps a firm grip on my hand.

Enzo takes us to what I assume is his office and hands me a brown packet. I open it to find a British passport, Canada Air flight tickets, and other documents all with the name Laura Darling on them. My eyes prick with tears as I look up at him, gratitude washing through me.

"Thank you," I whisper, and his eyes go even softer.

"No problem, *cara mia*," he says gently back, smiling softly at me. "*Allora!* We have a shipment leaving tonight for Toronto, so you'll get there around ten tomorrow evening. I've booked you a flight to Dublin for six AM the day after, your tickets are in the pack. There will be someone to collect you from the airport and drive you across the border to Belfast, then you will take the ferry to Liverpool...*a posto*," he tells me, face serious.

I can't say anything, overwhelmed at his kindness. I didn't realise people like this existed. People who do things for others because it's the right thing to do.

"From there, *cara mia*, it's up to you to disappear." His brown eyes cloud a little with sadness, as he looks briefly to Tom whose jaw is clenched tightly.

My heart starts pounding in my chest, and my breath catches in my throat. In the rush to escape and the relief of finally starting my journey towards freedom, I didn't consider that I'd have to leave him behind. I suddenly feel lost at sea, as if my one security net has been severed. Tom is the only thing I've ever chosen for myself, and I suddenly realise that he's my safe haven, my rock, and now I have to let him go.

This is like no other pain I've ever known. All of Ace's beatings, humiliations, and sexual assaults can't even begin to compare to the crushing hurt inside my soul at the thought of leaving Tom behind.

It's not safe for him to come with me. Ace would know immediately, and Tom's family would suffer terribly. His sister Rosa would be a target, regardless of Enzo's connections. I shudder at the thought of what Ace will do in his rage. Who he might hurt...

Tears fill my eyes as I look up into Tom's blue ones. They're usually so light and full of laughter, but tonight they are swirling, like a sea raging with Poseidon's wrath.

"Tom..." my voice breaks on a sob, and all of a sudden, I'm in his arms and they're banded around me so tightly I can hardly breathe. I welcome the embrace, the twinge of my bruised ribs as I sob against his chest, leaving a wet patch on his shirt.

"It'll be okay, Vi," he murmurs in my ear, voice rough and broken, stroking my back. "I'll find you one day, I swear it." I can hear the finality in his voice, like his promise is carved in stone. He knows as well as I do that he can't come with me right now.

"You need to go, *cara mia*," I hear Enzo say softly.

I take a huge gulping breath, somehow finding the strength to let go even though my world is crumbling down around me. I look up once more into his beautiful blue eyes.

"I love you, Tom," I whisper, unable to stop my tears from falling.

"I love you, Violet," he whispers back, lowering his lips to mine and kissing me. It's a kiss full of heartbreak, longing, and shattered dreams. We both know that there may never be a time that is safe for us to be together.

Our kiss ends on a shuddering breath, then he lowers his arms, jaw working once more as he takes a step back. Then another. And another until he turns and walks away, out of the office. I hear his footsteps echo across the silent gym floor, then the main door opens and shuts. Then finally, the sound of a car driving away.

Another breath catches in my throat, and I close my eyes, gathering my pieces up off the floor before opening them again. I meet Enzo's kind brown gaze, giving him a watery smile.

"Prego, this way, *cara mia*," he indicates the doorway, and we walk out, his hand on my lower back.

He guides me towards another door at the back of the building, where his two cousins are waiting for us. He says something to them sternly in Italian, and they nod once before bowing their heads in respect.

Then he turns to me, placing both hands on my upper arms.

"*In bocca al lupo*. All the luck in the world, cara mia," he says warmly, but I don't miss the glint of sorrow in his eyes.

"How can I ever repay you, Enzo?" I ask, knowing that I can never fully pay him back. He's helped me in my first steps towards my freedom. A shudder of unease runs through my whole body when I think back to Ace, his prone form lying on the bed. *Please let the drug work. I only need a few hours.*

"No payment needed, *cara mia*," he assures me. "*Abbiamo tutti diritto di Essere liberi di volare come gli uccelli.*" I look at him questioningly. "We all deserve to be free, to fly like birds."

As I clutch the packet in my hands to my chest, I remember the gaudy engagement ring that Ace gave me. It's obscene, and he took great pains to tell me of its value.

"Take this," I plead, taking the bauble off my finger and handing it to him. "It's worth over three million dollars, and I can't take it with me. I don't want to."

"*Cara...* " he starts, and I can see he wants to refuse so I cut him off.

"I insist. Give the money to Rosa." I hold it out to him, begging him with my eyes to take it.

He sighs, but eventually relents and pockets the jewellery.

"Just be careful where you get rid of it. He will recognise it." I tell him and he nods, with a slight roll of his eyes as if to assure me he's not a rookie in situations such as these.

I grin at him, then press up to my tiptoes and place a soft kiss onto his cheek. I notice his cheeks darken slightly in the moonlight as I pull away.

"*Buon viaggio*, safe journey, cara mia," he whispers, taking my hands in his warm grip and kissing both my cheeks.

"Thank you." I smile back, taking a deep breath of crisp autumn air.

Turning my back to him, I step up to the open door of the car that'll take me on the next step to freedom. I get in while one of Enzo's guys places my bag next to me before shutting the door quietly behind me.

A strange mix of desperate sadness, fear, and elation churn within me as we drive away. My hand goes to rest on my stomach, and I know that this is the right decision. That I would do so much more to keep the life blooming inside me safe.

# CHAPTER THREE

I spend the next few days in a permanent state of anxious exhaustion. The route Enzo picked out isn't the quickest or easiest, but it's thorough and I'm fairly confident that Ace won't be able to track me down, even with his endless resources.

As a precaution, once I arrive in Liverpool, I head to a pawn shop near the docks and sell some of the jewellery for cash, then go to the nearest salon. I emerge a fiery redhead, instead of my usual brunette, a colour admittedly, I've always wanted to be.

I decide to take the coach to London. I grew up in Surrey, and we visited the London house a few times so I know it well enough to feel comfortable there. I also like the idea of getting lost in the big city; there's a comfort of being around so many people. I know that it might be risky, it's one of the places that Ace may look for me, but if I avoid any of my previous haunts, I should be able to blend in with the throng.

The journey from Liverpool takes six long hours. Luckily, I bought a phone before I boarded the coach, and downloaded Spotify so I could at least listen to music and podcasts. I arrive at Victoria Coach Station just before ten in the evening, weary but glad that I'm almost to my new home.

It's still pretty busy, even for this late at night, and lucky for me it's not raining, as it so often is in England. My next task is to find somewhere to stay for tonight. I spy an open café across the street that looks like a good place to work out how I'm going to do that and grab a drink.

The sound of a bell tinkles as I push open the door, and I'm immediately engulfed in the warm smell of coffee and bacon. There's an empty table in the corner of the room next to the window, so I head there and take a seat. The whole place has that quaint vintage vibe about it, with mismatched chairs and old china plates, cups, and saucers. What sounds like wartime songs are playing in the background, alongside the hiss of the coffeemaker.

There are a few patrons, travellers like myself for the most part, all nursing steaming cups, and despite the late hour, one or two even have plates of a full English breakfast in front of them. There's a group of stunning women in the back, laughing and talking loudly, dressed in glittering party dresses that sparkle under the lights. I must admit, it's nice to be surrounded by the familiar sound of English voices again after hearing the American twang for so long.

One of the women, a busty brunette with green eyes, catches my gaze and gives me a blinding smile. I tentatively return the gesture, then look quickly down at the menu. I can't help the flinch as a shadow falls across the table, but breathe a sigh of relief when I look up to see a middle-aged waitress in a flowery fifties-style dress smiling down at me.

"What'll it be, luv?" she asks, her accent pure East End.

"Earl Grey tea, please. And maybe some toast and jam?" I ask timidly.

"Sure thing, luv," she answers with another smile before turning and heading back towards the counter.

Taking my phone out, I'm relieved to see that I've got a 4G signal and start looking up cheap hotels for the night. I figure I'll stay in one tonight and start flat hunting tomorrow.

A shadow falls across the table again, and I look up with a smile, placing my phone down and expecting to see the waitress with my order. My smile freezes as I meet the bloodshot eyes of a skinny man, with dark greasy hair and a lecherous grin.

"Hello, beautiful," he coos, and a shudder of revulsion passes through me at the state of his blackened teeth.

"Please leave me alone," I reply firmly, although there's a tremor in my hands now.

"Aw, there's no need to be like that," he says, leaning down so I can smell his rancid breath. "I was just bein' friendly like. And it looks like you're all alone and need a friend, eh?"

"I'm fine, thank you," I retort dismissively, hoping that he will leave me be.

Suddenly, his hand shoots out and grabs my wrist, his grip tight and painful. I try to snatch my hand back, but his hold is like a vice.

"Let go," I order through gritted teeth, panic starting to claw its way through me.

"You best let her go, Kol." A husky female voice sounds, and I crane my neck to see the beautiful brunette behind him, hands on her voluptuous hips. "This isn't your patch, and you wouldn't want Grey getting wind of this now, would you?" One of her perfect brows is raised, and there's a smug look on her face, like she knows she's already won.

Kol's upper lip curls, holding my wrist for a second longer before letting go with a snarl. He turns around and storms out, letting the door slam behind him. The effect is ruined somewhat by the cheery tinkle of the bell, and I can't help a small chuckle escaping my lips.

"Thanks," I say gratefully, rubbing my wrist.

"No worries, gorgeous. Kol is a disgusting shit face pimp, and he was over-stepping," she informs me, insinuating herself into the chair opposite mine. There's no other word for the movement, she's so graceful with a sensuality about her it would be impossible for her to move any other way. "I'm Lexi," she tells me, holding out a manicured hand for me to shake.

"V-Laura," I say, tripping over my new name. *Dammit!* "Laura Darling. Pleased to meet you." I let go of her hand, dropping mine onto my lap nervously.

"Pleased to meet you, Laura." She beams at me. "Would I be right in assuming that you're new to London?" she asks tentatively, ducking her head to catch my lowered gaze. I nod, my nerves making my heart race. "Do you have a place to stay tonight, Laura?" she asks gently, and there's something so honest about her that I want to trust her.

My gut tells me she's good people, but then my gut didn't warn me about Ace so it doesn't exactly have a great track record.

"No," I whisper quietly, and all she does is smiles kindly at me.

"Well, I have a spare bed that you're welcome to, although we're on our way to Grey's so it would need to be after that." She pauses as if in thought, then snaps her fingers. "Do you have a job yet, Laura?" she asks, and I can hear the excitement in her voice.

"No." I sound like a broken record.

"Grey is looking for a new waitress if you're interested?" She looks so hopeful, like she truly wants to help me.

"I-I've never done waitressing before..." I hesitate.

"Oh, that's not a problem." She laughs, the sound like cigar smoke caressing me. "Leave Grey to me."

"I-I'm not sure..." I reply, not wanting to look a gift horse in the mouth, but how can I trust someone I've only just met?

It's at that moment, the waitress comes back with my order.

"Babs will tell you I'm alright, won't you, Babs?" Lexi assures me, looking up at her.

Babs, chuckles. "Lexi's a good 'un, luv," she assures me. "She'll see you right as rain." Setting down my order, she pats my shoulder then heads off again.

I chew my lip, trying to decide if I dare take the risk. My eyes snap up to Lexi's, who looks so encouraging, I decide to throw caution to the wind.

"Okay," I manage before she claps her hands in glee and hollers to the others in the back.

"Ladies! This is Laura, and she'll be joining us tonight!" They all cheer, and their enthusiasm is infectious, causing my lips to split into a wide grin. A fissure of excitement runs through me.

"Finish your tea and toast, gorgeous," Lexi commands me jovially. "Then we'll take you to Grey's."

# CHAPTER FOUR

We head out of the cafe, and there's a big black stretch limo with blue neon lights underneath it waiting for us out front. It's got a grey smoke design across the doors, which I assume is the logo for Grey's.

I hesitate slightly, but I've agreed to come this far and don't really have many other options so I figure what the hell.

There are five of us in total; myself and Lexi, plus Coco who's a stunning dark-skinned woman with deep chocolate eyes, an awesome afro, and legs for days. Then, there's Anastasia, a beautiful leggy blonde with captivating green eyes full of saucy mischief and high cheekbones that any model would envy. Finally, there's Domitille, or Dom as she told me in a seductive French accent. A stunning redhead, with a beautiful hourglass figure and a wicked sense of humour.

The inside of the limo is lit up with LED strip lighting, and *Sex on Fire* by Kings of Leon is blasting out of the speakers as we step in. The girls start singing along, laughing as Coco grabs a bottle of champagne from somewhere and starts pouring glasses. She indicates the bottle to me, and I'm about to nod when I remember my condition and shake my head instead.

She just shrugs and puts the bottle away. I catch Lexi's shrewd green gaze, panic flaring in my stomach for a moment before she gives me her gorgeous smile and takes a sip of her drink. I sit back in my seat, soaking up the joy and happiness that fills the car. It's like I can finally take a deep breath after drowning for so long, and I've surfaced to find myself on a tropical island, the hot sun shining down on me.

The song finishes and *Beautiful Girls* by Sean Kingston comes on, accompanied by girlish squeals from the others. Anastasia half gets up and starts to do an impressive body roll, her gold dress twinkling in the lights. We soon pull up to a stop, and the door next to Lexi opens, letting in a rush of cold autumn air.

"Thanks, Tony," I hear her sensual voice say, but I miss his gruff reply.

I'm the last to get out, and they're all waiting for me with excitement in their gazes. A tingle of nervous anticipation races through me as I look up at the old, light coloured stone building.

There's nothing on the outside to suggest it's a restaurant or a business of any sort. It's an end of terrace townhouse, with steps leading up to a huge, shiny black front door. A black metal railing borders the front with neat box hedging behind it and a spiral metal staircase leading down to, presumably, the basement level. It's three stories high, with high windows facing the street, all with curtains drawn.

"Is this Grey's? I thought it was a restaurant." I comment, confused, and eliciting a chorus of feminine giggles as I continue gazing up at it.

"Yep, this is Grey's, " Lexi replies, with amusement in her tone.

"So, it's not a restaurant then?" I ask, looking at her warily. She bursts out laughing, the sound wrapping around me like silk.

"No," she tells me, still chuckling as they lead me around to the side of the building where I can see another shiny black door. "It's a club, sugarplum," she says before turning to rap her knuckles on the door. "Open up, buttercup!"

*A club?* I think as the door swings open, and there's a guy in a suit standing in the doorway. He's built like a brick shit house! He's huge, taking up almost the entire space. I'm surprised that he could even get a suit in his size, although by the looks of it, I wouldn't be surprised to learn it was made in Savile Row, where the best tailors in England have their shops.

"Evening, Lexi," he greets her, and I can't help the shiver that tingles across me. His voice is like warm whiskey on cold nights. He steps back, nodding at the others as they pass. I go to step in and find my way blocked by his massive bulk.

"This is Laura. She's with us, Ryan," Lexi assures him, stepping forward and placing a manicured hand on his enormous bicep.

I look up into his eyes, noticing that they're a beautiful hazelnut brown colour. His brows are drawn down, assessing me, and I can't help the hitch in my breath as he takes me in. Something softens in his eyes before he steps aside. As I pass, I smile my thanks, able to see him in the light better. His chestnut hair is buzzed short on the sides and slightly longer on top, and I can just see tattoos peeking from under his collar.

"Thank you, Ryan," I say softly, captured in his gaze once more.

He nods, then I see his gaze slip down to my neck, eyes hardening like sharp stones. Before he can say anything, Lexi grabs my arm and tugs me away.

"Looks like you've already got yourself a fan, gorgeous," she whispers conspiratorially in my ear.

"What?!" I choke out.

"He can't take his eyes off you, girl," Coco adds from in front of me, and I glance back to see Ryan looking after me intensely. I shake my head at them and scoff.

We come to another doorway that is opened at our approach, a second big suited guy behind it. Stepping through, I see that we're in a lobby of sorts. It's gently lit with a chandelier and wall lights, the floor covered in black and white tiles. The walls are painted a soft grey, and I can see a dark wooden staircase against one wall, leading to what I assume are the upper levels.

It still doesn't look much like a club to me, but then I guess I've had little experience of anything like that. I only went out with Ace to places that he approved, so I've never actually been in a club, but I did imagine them to be louder.

There's a dark wood reception desk with a very smartly dressed blonde receptionist behind it, who smiles warmly at our approach.

"Good evening, ladies," she grins. She's incredibly well-spoken, like a newsreader.

"Hi, Sami," Anastasia says, her voice definitely has a Russian lilt to it.

"And who is this?" Sami questions, turning her blue eyes to me.

"I'm Laura," I reply, feeling slightly bolder after having met so many new people tonight.

"Pleasure to meet you, Laura," she replies warmly, and I can't help but smile back.

"Is Grey upstairs?" Lexi asks, stepping up to us.

"Yes, he is. Shall I call up to let him know you're back?" Sami enquires.

"Tell him I'm on my way up," Lexi orders as she grabs my hand and leads me towards the wide staircase.

I hear Sami's voice speak softly into the phone as we make our way up. The stairs have a thick, plush Persian rug running down the middle of them, and my boot-clad feet sink in with every step. This place screams exclusivity and money with its tasteful gentlemen's club vibe. *What kind of club is this exactly?*

We reach the first floor, and a faint whiff of cigar smoke tickles my nose before Lexi is dragging me up the next flight. The walls are still painted the same soft grey colour, but there's no panelling up here, just the dark wood of the stairs. We come to the final landing, which has three dark wood doors coming off of it. This must have been the old servants' quarters.

Lexi strides up to the door opposite the staircase, knocking on the panelled wooden door.

"Come in, Lexi," a deep voice commands, and a shiver runs through me at the sound.

Lexi opens the door, walking in as if the voice doesn't affect her at all. I follow behind, slightly more reticent. The room we're in is large, with a fairly high ceiling that slopes at the sides like this was once the attic. It's painted a darker grey than the hallway, but it doesn't feel cold. There's even a small fireplace with a cheerful fire burning behind the grate.

"Ah, you must be Laura," the deep voice sounds from across the room, and my gaze catches the grey eyes of a man sitting in a leather wing-back chair behind a dark wooden desk. There are two smaller leather chairs in front of it, both unoccupied.

He's exceptionally handsome, with classical features, salt and pepper hair that's slicked back, and is wearing a dark charcoal grey suit, a white shirt, and silver tie. There's a twinkle in the tie, which looks like a diamond tie pin. He stands up and comes around to our side of the desk, and I can see that the suit is tailored to perfection, fitting his lean form perfectly.

He holds out a hand, a warm smile drawing up the corners of his mouth.

"I'm Grey, and it's a pleasure to make your acquaintance," he assures me in cultured tones.

I take his hand and discover it's warm and dry, not sweaty, and he gives a firm but not overbearing handshake before releasing his grip.

"Shall we?" he asks, indicating to the chairs, and we all take a seat, myself and Lexi in front of the desk and Grey behind it.

"Can I get you something to drink, Laura? Lexi?" he asks us politely.

"No, thank you," I smile weakly at him, butterflies dancing in my stomach.

"No thanks, Grey darling," Lexi answers with a cheeky grin.

"Now," he smiles warmly at me, and I feel a sense of safety around him that confuses me. "How can I help you, Laura?"

Before I can say anything, Lexi butts in. "Laura is going to be our new waitress, and she'll be staying with me." Grey doesn't say anything, just raises a perfect dark brow and smiles indulgently at her.

"I see," he replies.

"If-if that's okay with you?" I stutter out, cursing my new nervousness.

"Do you know what type of establishment this is, Laura?" he asks me, not answering my question. I shake my head in response. "Well, we are an exclusive gentlemen's club that caters to our members' *needs*."

I nod, thinking that to be the case from what I've seen so far.

"I take care of all my girls, no one is forced to do anything they are unhappy with, but there are opportunities for those who want them." He continues, gesturing with his hand. "Can I suggest that Lexi show you around tonight, then you can start a trial run tomorrow, provided you're happy to do so, of course?"

"That would be wonderful, thank you," I reply, tears stinging my eyes at my good fortune.

"Excellent," he grins. "Lexi, I'd like to have a word with Laura alone. Please wait outside." And all of a sudden, the butterflies are back.

"Before I go, Kol was at Maxine's." She tells him, and the skin around his eyes tightens slightly, the only indication of his displeasure. He gives her a sharp nod.

Lexi squeezes my arm reassuringly before getting up and leaving, closing the door quietly behind her.

"I don't expect you to tell me who left those bruises on your neck, trust needs to be earned, after all. But know that if you ever need whoever it was taken care of, you just say the word." He is absolutely serious, eyes boring into mine until I nod, and then he smiles kindly at me.

"As I said, I take care of my girls," he reiterates.

"Thank you," I whisper, meaning it. How can a stranger show such kindness when my own family couldn't care less?

"Now, go with Lexi, have a look around, then get some sleep. Tomorrow, you can go to the tailors and get your uniform, then start tomorrow evening," he tells me, and I feel my head already beginning to spin with a mixture of relief, and the speed at which this is all progressing.

Nodding again, I'm like one of those nodding dogs people put in the back of their cars at this stage, I get up and head towards the door.

"Oh, and Laura?" I hear him say behind me, and I turn to look at him. "Welcome to Grey's."

# CHAPTER FIVE

I wake up with a start, sweat covering my trembling body as I sit up looking frantically around the darkened room. It takes me a beat, but then I remember where I am; Lexi's house, spare bedroom, North London.

Taking a few deep breaths, I try to calm my racing heart as I remember everything that happened yesterday. The cafe, meeting Lexi and the girls, Grey's, looking around the club...I put my head in my hands with a groan as I remember the tour of Grey's.

As Lexi describes it, it's a gentlemen's club with strippers. Super exclusive, members are invite only, and anyone stepping out of line finds themselves out on their arse sharpish. It's where people take business associates, people who they want to impress, but you basically have to be in the top one percent to gain an invitation. A moment of worry flashes through me, the thought that Ace or any one of the founding members of Black Knight Corporation could potentially walk through the doors.

The door swings open, startling me out of my thoughts, and Lexi bounds in wearing short shorts and a vest top that does nothing to support her ample tits. She leaps on the bed with a squeal, bouncing her boobs up and down.

"Good morning, sunshine!" She shrieks with excitement, and I can't help but laugh in return. It's amazing to think that I've never really had a close female friend before. I didn't know what I was missing!

"Good morning," I smile back and feel lighter and full of hope this morning. Like things may finally be going alright.

"So, we've got breakfast first, then Schmidt's, then I thought we could go shopping!" she lists off excitedly.

"What's Schmidt's?" I ask, my brow furrowing.

"Why, the tailor for your uniform, silly!" she replies, smacking me lightly on the arm.

"Oh," my heart sinks. I can't afford to waste money on a tailored uniform, or go shopping. Although, I suppose window shopping would be okay.

"Don't look like that! Grey pays for the expenses, dummy! And the uniform is an expense," she shakes her head like I'm an imbecile.

"Oh," I say again, like a broken record.

"So, come on! Get your arse out of bed and into the shower!" She pushes me until I almost tumble out of bed, catching myself just in time. Straightening up, I go to walk towards the bathroom when a crack lands on my bum making me shout out.

"Get a move on, slowpoke!" she shouts while laughing. Rubbing my sore buttcheek, I chuckle to myself as I head out of the bedroom door.

---

Lexi's riverside apartment really is gorgeous. It's a modern open plan affair, with two bedrooms and a huge bathroom, plus stunning views overlooking the River Thames and the city. Apparently, Grey owns the entire building and houses all his girls here, like one big sorority house.

As we exit the building, I notice there's a black SUV with that same smoke motif waiting for us. I shiver as the wind whistles around me, the day overcast and grey. Lexi said we wouldn't need coats, but I'm regretting my choice of a loose long-sleeved dress, and cardigan with tights, and flat knee-high boots.

We climb into the back, Lexi saying hello to our driver, Sean. It really surprises me how much Grey takes care of his girls, and I can't help the fissure of worry that sparks inside of me.

"Just spit it out, Laura," Lexi demands in a joking, exasperated tone when she notices my worries.

I decided to just bite the bullet. "Is Grey your pimp?"

She chokes with laughter, her whole face going red. I even hear gruff chuckles coming from Sean up front.

"Our pimp?!" She pats my leg condescendingly. "No dearest, Grey is not our pimp." She wipes under her eyes, checking for smudged makeup. She looks particularly stunning in a deep green Ralph Lauren wrap dress.

"So, what's this all about?" I ask, indicating the car, the apartment, and the expenses.

"He likes to take care of us. That's it. No hidden agenda, no surprise cost," she tells me, and I can see the admiration in her eyes. "Rumour has it that something happened to his mother when he was younger, and he vowed that he'd look after any woman from that day on," she tells me dreamily.

Sean scoffs from the front. "They also say his cock is made from twenty-four karat gold, so I wouldn't go believing everything you hear."

"Sean!" Lexi scolds him, but I can see the laughter in her eyes.

Shortly after, we pull up outside a sweet little café, and I can see we've reached Savile Row by the black and white street sign on the side of the building.

"Breakfast, m'dear," Lexi explains proudly as we get out of the car. Sean assures us he'll park nearby, so we just have to call when we're done.

The café is beautiful, with a red awning and plants tumbling from pots and window boxes. There's a burgundy sign that reads Brushh in gold letters and several tables are outside. But as it's grey and looks like it could rain, something I haven't missed about England, we decide to sit inside.

As soon as we open the door, a gust of wind comes in with us, and I'm hit by the wonderful smell of freshly baked bread and other baked goodies.

"Maxine makes the best pastries in London," Lexi tells me, and I must say by smell alone I think she might be right.

"Ah, Lexi! So good to see you! And who's your beautiful new friend?" A short lady bustles over to us. Her accent is most definitely French, and I can feel a blush spread across my cheeks at the compliment.

"Maxine, this is Laura. She starts at Grey's today, and this is her first day in London so I knew where we had to go for breakfast!"

"Well, welcome, Laura!" Maxine beams at me and hustles us over to a table near the window. "Shall I bring two continental specials?" she asks.

"Yes please, love. And two juices of the day as well." Lexi orders for both of us. It should irk me; Ace would order for me all the time and dictate what I could eat and even how much I could eat. But it's different with Lexi. I know she's just doing it out of kindness, not control. Maxine smiles kindly and heads back the way she came, presumably to sort our order.

"So," Lexi turns her intelligent green gaze to me, and by the twinkle in her eyes, I know that she's up to no good. My heart races, I'm not ready to talk about my past yet. "What did you think of Ryan?"

"Ryan?!" I splutter out. I didn't see that coming. "What about him?" I ask, heat warming my cheeks once more.

"Oh come on, Laura! I saw him checking you out last night at the club. He couldn't take his eyes off of you, and he was meant to man the side door but swapped so that he could keep looking," she informs me with a smirk. "And, he has that whole delicious protective Alpha vibe about him."

I busy my hands with a napkin, tearing small pieces off of it. My mother would be horrified at my bad manners.

"Ryan is very attractive, but, well, I'm not after anything like that at the moment," I reply, my gaze darting up to hers and seeing that damn smirk on her lips.

"Uh-huh," she mumbles, unconvinced.

Luckily, I'm saved from further conversation by Maxine bringing over our drinks. Taking a long slurp through the straw, I'm hit with the fresh taste of oranges, apples, carrots, and a hint of ginger. It instantly wakes me up and refreshes me.

Lexi seems to get that I'd rather not talk about it and talks for the rest of breakfast, telling me all about her less than stellar upbringing on a rough council estate before Grey discovered her and offered her a job at the club. He really does sound like a Knight in shining armour, or perhaps slightly tarnished armour given the fact that fundamentally he owns a strip club and lord knows what else. He must have his fingers in many pies to be able to spend what he seems to.

After breakfast, we walked down the road to Schmidt's Tailors. The shop looks exactly how I remember a Savile Row tailor to look; a wooden counter with lots of drawers behind a curtained off portion, and presumably a back-room or upper floor where the clothes are made.

As we enter, a wizened old man approaches us looking rather stern. He has on a grey waistcoat with a shirt and tie and dress trousers. Around his elbows are those things that they used to wear in the fifties to keep their sleeves in place. There's a tape measure dangling around his neck.

"This way," he commands in a rough voice, indicating the curtained off area. I look at Lexi who leans in.

"That's Schmidt. He's a little rough around the edges, but he's the best," she whispers.

I follow him, stepping through the drawn red velvet curtains into a space that is almost entirely surrounded by mirrors. There's a woman waiting with what looks like some garments already half made over one arm. She must be in her late forties, with mid-brown hair and kind brown eyes. She smiles warmly at me, and my lips lift in return. "Undress," Schmidt orders, and I baulk at the command, remembering the bruises that decorate my body.

"It's okay, Laura," Lexi says softly behind me.

I take in a deep breath, deciding that I won't be ashamed of what I've been through. Remembering that what doesn't kill you only makes you stronger as they say. I take my clothes off, straightening up, and cringe at the sight I'm confronted with in the mirrors. My body is a watercolour of purples, greens, and yellows, littered with the remains of Ace's violence, and I'm thin to the point of being able to see the outlines of my ribs. I used to be quite curvy, but Ace thought I was fat so he put me on a strict diet.

I hear a sharp intake of breath and look up to see the pitying gaze of the woman holding the garments before she can school her features. My eyes meet Lexi's in the mirror. She gives me a sad smile, but there is no pity in her gaze. It's the look of shared experience, of someone who's been there and gotten out. It gives me the strength to stand a little taller and face my demons staring back at me.

# CHAPTER SIX

We arrive back at Lexi's with so many bags I've lost count. Poor Sean even had to carry some up to the apartment for us. Apparently, according to Lexi, I needed a lot of new clothes, so after Schmidt's, we headed west to Oxford Street and spent a small fortune there as well, which also counts as expenses according to Lexi. She whipped out a Grey's company card no less, so she must know what she's talking about.

It's late afternoon, so we basically have to dump our bags and head straight to Grey's for my training before the evening begins.

Pulling up outside of the club, it looks even more inconspicuous in the daylight, just like any other building on what appears to be a residential street. We head to the side door, and once again, Ryan opens it; his eyes go straight past Lexi to lock with mine.

"Good afternoon, Laura," he says in that deliciously deep voice of his.

"G-good afternoon, Ryan," I stutter back, blushing furiously.

"Good afternoon, Ryan," Lexi teases him, smirking when he squirms a little, realising that he totally ignored her.

"Hi, Lexi," he replies, and his cheeks flush.

"Can we come in, or are you gonna make us stand out on the street all night?" she sasses back, and he hurriedly moves aside, stumbling out an apology.

She links her arm through mine, pulling me inside and leaning her head so close I can smell her expensive perfume. “Oh girl, he’s got it bad,” she laughs, and I look back to see Ryan still looking after me, an intense look in his brown eyes.

My heart does a little flutter, which is promptly squashed by guilt. I left Tom behind not a week ago, and here I am starting to crush on another guy. Never mind the fact that I’m pregnant! A bubble of worry is added to the guilt at that thought. I won’t be able to hide my pregnancy forever, and then what will I do?

*I just can’t worry about that right now*, I think to myself, shaking my head. We continue on to a side room that’s been set aside as a dressing room of sorts for all of the girls. This, too, is guarded at all times by a burly security guy who nods at our approach. Stepping inside, we’re engulfed by feminine chatter and a cloud of different perfumes all merging together in an overwhelming fog.

“Ladies!” I hear the camp tones of Justin, to whom I was introduced to last night, call out and see him hurrying towards us. He’s Grey’s dresser and sources all the costumes and anything else that Grey’s girls need whilst they're here.

He air kisses both of us, and I take in his outfit. He’s wearing a sharp collared floral shirt, a silk scarf, fitted trousers, and killer black patent heels. His straw-coloured blond hair is styled to perfection in a quiff, and he has a wonderful moustache that he curls upwards so that, with his goatee, he looks like the character from the KFC adverts.

“Lexi darling, I’ve laid the Westwood red sequins out for you tonight,” he tells her, shooing her over to her dressing table, rail, and mirror. Yep, that’s right, Vivienne Westwood designs all the girl’s outfits.

“Laura, Schmidt just delivered your uniform so chop chop!”

He rushes me over to an empty dressing table where I can see a rail with a white shirt, grey pencil skirt, and grey fitted waistcoat hanging. There’s a pair of shiny black heels resting on the floor next to the rail, and as I approach, I see that they’re Jimmy Choo brand. No expense spared, I guess. On the table is a push-up red lace bra, matching thong and suspender belt, and sheer stockings with a seam running up the back of them.

He stands by whilst I get changed, not batting an eye at the bruises that I expose for the second time today. He does help me clip the back of the stockings in place but leaves me to wiggle into the pencil skirt. Luckily, the back has a modest split, otherwise, I'm not sure I'd be able to walk in it. Slipping my feet into the heels, grateful that I'm used to wearing ones of a similar height, I straighten up to see a frown marring his brow.

"What?" I ask, looking into the floor-length mirror on the wall beside me. The bra has made the most of my bust and combined with the skirt and fitted waistcoat, I look like I've got more of an hourglass figure than I actually have. My eyes float to my neck, and I see what Justin's problem is. There's a ring of purple bruises that look exactly like what they are; fingerprints.

As I'm staring at my reflection, I see Justin whip off his colourful silk scarf, then he wraps it around my neck a couple of times and ties a little knot to one side. I look like a fifties air hostess, but it's pretty hot if I do say so myself.

"There," he says with a nod and a smile before his attention is caught by one of the others, and he rushes off to help her.

I gaze at my reflection once more, amazed at the girl staring back at me. She looks confident and beautiful, with her stunning figure and made up face, and you'd never know that just days ago she was in a place far away and full of darkness.

"Stop admiring your beautiful arse, and let's show you the ropes!" Lexi calls out from the other side of the room.

*Courage,* I tell myself, taking a deep breath and heading into the unknown.

---

Hours later, I throw myself down on my bed with a whoosh of breath. I don't even know what time it is, two maybe three AM? It's late, or I suppose early depending on how you look at it, and I'm cream crackered!

The night was...interesting? Eye opening? It was both and so much more. The bar work wasn't difficult, taking orders down in the basement, then going to the bar at the back and bringing the drinks to the tables. Each table has a pole and is surrounded by four dark leather wing-back chairs so each table has a dancer.

And the girls are phenomenal dancers...who happen to take their clothes off. There are women of every race, colour, and dancing to suit every taste. Interestingly, many of the patrons, or members, seemed more interested in talking with each other than ogling the girls. They're great tippers at least. I don't know what the girls made tonight, but I must have made around five hundred pounds in tips.

They were all on their best behaviour, no touching allowed. That is unless you get a private room upstairs, then a contract is written, dictating any boundaries and signed by all parties. There's also a smoking lounge on the upper floors and another bar that I may work at some nights.

My first night flew by, and before I knew it, Lexi and I were being driven back by Sean to Lexi's riverside apartment. After taking a quick shower, I'm snuggled in the comfy bed, my eyelids drooping, yet my mind whirling with all that has happened over the past few days.

I can't believe how different my life is in such a short space of time. I never dreamed that not only would I break free from Ace and his toxic hold, but I'd find friends for the first time in my life. The girls are all so nice, especially Lexi, and I can see myself being happy here.

A bubble of anxiety bursts in my stomach. I've no idea what I'll do once I start showing. I mean, I doubt they'd want a pregnant waitress, and I've never heard of a pregnant stripper, or if that would even be an option?

*Stop it! Stop worrying about what is yet to come!* I internally scold myself. One day at a time.

# CHAPTER SEVEN

A few weeks pass with the same tiring routine. Waitressing at the club in the evening, sleeping most of the day, and getting up at lunchtime. Often myself, Lexi, and some of the other girls go into town, Lexi insisting that she show me the sights of London. I don't have the heart to tell her I've seen many of them before, and anyway, going with her and the others is like seeing London for the first time. They all have such life and vitality about them, it's as if I'm waking up from a deep slumber and seeing the world in all its technicolour.

Luckily, I've not suffered from any morning sickness, although I've had a couple of episodes of vomiting that I managed to easily explain away. What I can't do anything about is the tightness of my high-waisted uniform skirt around my middle. It's becoming more obvious that I'm getting bigger, and I've finally gotten my curvy figure back. Although I have put on weight by eating properly for the first time in years, it can't explain the roundness of my stomach.

One evening, just before I'm due to start, Sami tells me that Grey would like a word with me in his office. I can't stop the nervous butterflies that flutter in my stomach as I climb the stairs to the top floor. Or they could be my baby, I'm sure I've started feeling it move a bit.

Reaching the upper landing, I stop outside his door, knocking lightly.

"Come in, Laura," his deep voice invites me in from the other side, and I open the door to find Grey sitting behind his desk smiling warmly at me. Lexi is also in the room, and I feel myself hesitate as my flight mode kicks in.

"Please take a seat, Laura," Grey gestures to the other empty chair next to Lexi, taking away my decision to flee with the kind way he makes the order almost a request.

I can feel my chest rising and falling with shallow pants as I sit on the edge of the chair, looking down at my hands which are wringing in my lap. Lexi's hand reaches over to grab one of mine, stilling the movement and giving it a reassuring squeeze.

"You're not in any trouble, gorgeous, no one is angry," she assures me softly, ducking her head and catching my gaze, giving me a smile.

"Lexi is right, Laura, please don't worry. You're not in any kind of trouble. We just want to help," Grey says kindly, making me look up at him.

"O-okay," I stammer out, trying to calm my racing heart by taking deeper breaths.

"Am I correct in assuming that there will be a happy occasion in a few months' time?" he asks gently. There's genuine warmth in his eyes, and it gives me the courage to nod my head in confirmation. "Congratulations my dear, what wonderful news." He beams at me, his handsome face becoming even more devastating than before.

Tears prick my eyes as my breath rushes out of me in relief. Lexi squeezes my hand again, and I look into her green eyes only to see a touch of excitement there as well as happiness.

"Do you know how far along you are, babe?" she asks me.

"Um, maybe about three months, I think. I've just started feeling flutterings."

"Well, may I suggest we get you seen by someone as soon as possible to check you and baby over and get a scan?" Grey proposes in his business-like manner. "I know an excellent consultant and midwife on Harley Street who I can call in the morning."

"Oh, um, I'm sure I can see a local doctor. I don't want to be a bother."

"Nonsense." he assures me. "I told you before that I look after my girls, and I meant it."

"Your girls? I thought once you..." I trail off when I see him shake his head grinning, like I'm amusing him.

"You thought that when I found out, I would terminate your employment?" he asks kindheartedly.

"You're not?" I'm so confused. *Why wouldn't he?*

"No, Laura. I'm not going to terminate your contract. Although, I can't have you serving drinks in your condition, especially with the stairs," he tells me, and I nod, still a little puzzled as to what exactly I'll be doing.

"Have you ever considered dancing, Laura?" he asks, fingers steepled.

"Dancing?" I repeat, still none the wiser.

"Like Lexi and the others do," he prompts me, and I just sit and stare at him.

"But...I'm pregnant! Surely no one would want to see a pregnant stripper?" I question. *He can't be serious, can he?*

"On the contrary, my dear. A great many men find pregnant women incredibly attractive. It's a primal urge. You see, many men will seek out women who are fertile, it's an evolutionary tactic, and none are more so than a woman who is already carrying a child," he informs me, and I must confess I'm in shock. I had no idea this was even a thing men would find so attractive.

"You don't need to decide right now, take time to think about it. And be assured that I'm having a maternity package drawn up as we speak so that you can have plenty of time off to prepare before and after the baby arrives," he says, and my head reels.

I'm lost for words. I can't find any to express my delighted surprise at this turn of events.

"Excellent. Now, take the night off. I'll have Ryan drive you back so you have time to think. Let me know what you decide, say in a week, but Laura," he looks at me seriously, "there's no pressure if you don't want to dance. We will find something else for you to do."

"Th-thank you," I say around the lump in my throat. Getting up, I head towards the door with Lexi by my side.

My mind swirls with questions. *Would I want to dance like Lexi and the others? Take my clothes off for men to admire my body. My changing body? I'm not sure I would want that. Yet, why am I a little excited by the thought?*

---

I step out into the brisk evening breeze, wrapping my coat around myself. It's late October, and it's gotten chilly with the dropping temperature. It's getting darker earlier too, and winter is definitely on the way.

Shivering, I walk over to the waiting black SUV, and get into the passenger side, figuring there's no point sitting in the back by myself when I could sit next to Ryan.

Over the last few weeks, I've noticed him. A lot. He's always watching me, not in a creepy way, but like he can't take his eyes off of me. It's intoxicating and makes my cheeks burn. I can't help seeking him out if he's nearby, and the small smiles he gives me set my heart racing in my chest.

At the same time, I feel guilty. I left Tom behind, and I can't help but feel like I'm cheating on him somehow, even though it's unlikely we will see each other again. I loved him, still love him. So how can I also have feelings for Ryan? *You can't love more than one person at a time, right?*

"Penny for your thoughts?" his gruff voice sounds, breaking me out of my confused thoughts.

"Oh," I reply, flushing and squirming at the question, my hands fidgeting in my lap. "Um, well, I was considering an offer that Grey made me."

"And what was that?" He growls, and I look up to see his hands tighten on the steering wheel and his jaw clenched.

"Well, he suggested that I might consider becoming a dancer at the club," I admit, watching for his reaction.

"Will you?" he asks, brown eyes flickering to me then back to the road. I can't read his facial expression, whether he's happy or angry at the suggestion. And that bothers me. I realise with a start that I want to know what he thinks, whether he approves or not. This desire for his approval bothers me. I've had a lifetime of pleasing others at my own expense, yet I still wanted to do just that for him. "There's good money to be made in tips, so the girls tell me," he adds.

"I hadn't really considered it before now, however, I think there must be something freeing about taking your clothes off and being watched like that," I tell him, and his brows dip in confusion.

"How so?" he enquires, like he's genuinely interested in what I've got to say.

"Well, society expects women to cover up, to conform to certain standards. To be beautiful but not vain, to be admired but not to revel in it. Getting up on a table and taking your clothes off for the sole purpose to be, well, worshipped and to have your body lusted after, it's kind of like a big F-you to society and its rules. Don't you think?" I ask back, not realising that I actually felt so strongly about it. Although, it's not surprising given the way my parents and then Ace tried to repress me and force me to conform to their ideals.

I look at Ryan as we pull up outside mine and Lexi's building and can see that he's really considering what I've just said.

"I've never thought about it like that before," he tells me, "but I guess you're right. I don't look down on any girl who dances, it's nothing to be ashamed of."

He brings the car to a stop and parks while we sit there for a minute in silence.

"So, are you going to dance?" he asks me, his tone curious but not judgemental as he turns the full weight of his chocolate brown gaze onto me.

"I don't know. I mean, I didn't think it would be an option considering..." I trail off, realising that he's going to find out sooner or later but not quite able to make myself say it.

"Considering?" he queries with a raised brow, and I take a deep breath.

"Considering I'm pregnant," I say, staring him straight in the eye like I'm ripping a plaster off. Both his brows go up, his eyes falling straight to my stomach as he chews on his full bottom lip in the most distracting way.

"Ah," he starts, releasing his lip. "And Grey knows and wants you to dance anyway?" he questions me, and I nod in confirmation. "Well, pregnant birds are hot as hell," he mutters, and I can't help the bubble of laughter that escapes my lips.

"That's what Grey said," I chuckle, and he smiles in return. It's a smile so full of warmth that I can almost feel it seep into my skin, heating me from the inside out until it feels like the sun is inside me. *Damn, he really is pretty.*

"Would you like to come up?" I offer. "You know, if you don't have to rush back?"

"I'd love to," he responds, his blinding smile firmly in place as he switches the engine off.

We get out and head up to the apartment, the chilly night surrounding us as we walk towards the building. We're both quiet as we get the lift up to Lexi's floor, and it's only then do I realise how awkward things are between us. It's like I've invited him up for coffee, which I guess I have, but you know, like *coffee*. As in, well, sex. Or, maybe, just making out? *Gah! Even my brain is nervous rambling.*

"So, the weather has gotten colder recently..." I start, wanting to smack my hands over my face. *The weather?! Really?!*

He lets out a deep rumbling laugh that helps break the tension.

"That was..." I say cringing.

"Terrible?" he spits out in between bouts of laughter, and this time I join in with him.

The lift pings our floor, and the doors open. It's a short walk down the hallway; there are only maybe five apartments on each floor. Letting myself in using the spare key that Lexi gave me, I turn on the lights. Ryan follows behind me, closing the door softly and cocooning us in the quiet.

I turn around to offer him, well, coffee or something, but end up finding him standing so close that I'm enveloped in his comforting scent. He smells like cardamom and spicy cinnamon, like safety and warmth and comfort. My breath catches on an inhale, trying to keep his scent inside of me. His hand reaches out to brush my now red hair behind my ear.

"I want to kiss you so badly, Laura," he rasps out, and a shiver travels over my body at his words. I desperately want him to place his lips on mine, I ache with the need to feel them against me. It may be pregnancy hormones or sheer attraction, but it's taking everything inside of me to hold back in this moment.

"I-I can't get into anything serious, Ryan," I tell him, closing my eyes as his fingertips glide down the side of my face. I feel a warmth along the front of me and raise my eyelids to see that he's stepped up to me and is so close my breasts are brushing his hard chest. "But I need..."

"What do you need, baby?" he asks me quietly, cupping my jaw and tilting my head so that I'm looking up at him. My cheeks flush at what I want to say, and a knowing sexy as sin smirk crosses his lips.

"Oh baby, I've got you," he croons, lowering his lips until they are brushing against mine. A needy moan escapes me at the light caress. "Nothing serious," he states right before he closes the distance.

Our kiss starts off slow, an exploration of each other's mouths and tongues. It quickly turns heated, burning, as weeks of pent up attraction come to the surface. He strips off my coat, and I do the same to him, marvelling at how hot his body is. I can feel his body heat through his shirt.

His hands tangle in my hair as he guides me backwards until the backs of my knees hit the leather sofa. He breaks our kiss to gently push me back until I'm sitting down and looking up at him. There's a fire in his eyes that burns me from the inside out, and he's panting, his chest heaving. He gives me another devastatingly sexy grin and he undoes his tie, throwing it aside, and unbuttoning his white shirt. As the fabric parts, it reveals dark tattoos covering his entire ripped torso, starting at his collarbone and disappearing into his suit trousers, which have a definite bulge in them.

I gasp audibly as he pushes the shirt down his arms, and I see that the beautiful drawings on his skin go all the way down to his cuffs. They are in a kaleidoscope of colours, like a beautiful rainbow, chasing across his body. Looking back up into his face, I see he has a self-assured grin on his lush lips. I like this side of him, this confident swagger. He toes his shoes off, kicking them to one side as he kneels down in front of me.

Grabbing one of my legs, he slowly unzips my knee-high leather boot, pulling it off before doing the same to the other one. He reaches underneath my checkered miniskirt, grabs the waistband of my tights and knickers, and pulls them over my hips and off my legs. My heart is racing, my breaths shallow as his fingertips brushing over me leave trails of fire in his wake. Grabbing behind my knees, he pulls me to the edge of the sofa and spreads my thighs wide. He growls in appreciation when he sees how wet I am for him, licking his lips as he moves his head towards my core.

I'm panting, my chest rising and falling rapidly with each breath as his head disappears underneath my skirt. I feel his hot tongue on my inner folds, and I almost come off the sofa. I would have too had his arm not clamped down across my hips, holding me into place. It feels incredible, tingles of pleasure racing across my whole body as his tongue works me like I'm his last meal on earth and he's savouring every mouthful. My head tips back with a guttural groan as the pleasure starts to build to a crescendo, lightning racing across my skin.

"Ryan," I gasp as he picks up speed, sucking and nibbling my clit. Two fingers tease my entrance, coating themselves in my juices before they push inside me and start fucking me, hitting my G-spot every time. My climax crashes over me like a wave as I scream out his name and grip the leather of the sofa tightly.

When I open my eyes, it's to see him looking up at me from his kneeling position, his chin glistening with my release and a satisfied smirk on his face. Bracing his hands on my knees, he leans up and into me, kissing me hard, and I can taste myself on his tongue.

"Perhaps we should take this to your bedroom?" he asks, pulling back. I nod, unable to form words.

He picks me up under my thighs, giving me a second to wrap my arms around his neck and my legs around his waist as he stands up, taking me with him. My bare, wet pussy touches his hot skin, and I groan at the contact, grinding into his hard abs and creating a delicious friction. He growls at me, nipping my neck and heading towards the only hallway in the place.

"The last on the right," I manage to croak out.

Somehow, he is able to use one hand to open the door, kicking it shut behind him and striding across to my bed. He places me down onto it, before straightening up, his hands going to his belt. My eyes rapturously follow his movements as he undoes the buckle, then the button, and finally the fly on his trousers. He pushes them over his hips, along with whatever underwear he's wearing, and steps out of them. I take a sharp breath at the sight before me.

He is simply huge, hung like a horse! And I had no idea you could get a tattoo, well, *there*. Across his upper thigh and hip is a stunning Japanese style scene, with rolling blue-grey clouds, and floating pink cherry blossoms. This beautiful artwork extends over his balls, and up onto the other hip, interspersed with red peonies. Above his impressive length is a green double-headed dragon, one head looking up towards his torso, and the other...the other is *his* head. Like his dick. His cock is tattooed completely, from base to tip, his tip being the second dragon head! He's clean shaven down there, so the picture is completely uninterrupted.

"Like what you see, baby?" his gruff voice asks, sounding amused and pleased at the same time.

"Um...I'm not sure you'll fit!" I blurt out, then clap my hands over my traitorous mouth. *Hello! Brain to mouth filter, anyone there?*

"Oh trust me, baby, it'll fit." A deep chuckle sounds from between his kissed swollen lips. I see him reach down to the floor, taking his wallet out of his trouser pocket, and pulling out a foil packet. He opens it, rolling the condom on with ease which surprises me a little given his size. *Maybe he buys extra large ones?* He kneels onto the bed, crawling towards me with a wicked look in his eyes.

"You are wearing too many clothes, Miss Darling," he informs me, reaching out to unzip my skirt and pull it down off my hips. My black long-sleeved top is next, and I'm so grateful that all the bruises have long faded. I'm sure he's heard the rumours that have no doubt spread around the club, but at least he won't see the evidence. I can't help feeling a twinge of shame that I let someone do that to me for so long. I know it's not my fault, but I'm starting to slowly realise that I am worth more than someone's fists. I deserve so much more, and it took getting pregnant for me to see this. Ryan then takes off my soft bra, I can't stand to wear normal bras at the moment, my breasts are just too tender.

Once we are both naked, he gently pushes me down until I'm lying before him. He's still kneeling above me on the bed and looking down at me with such desire that I feel the flush spread over my skin. I've always been quick to blush.

"You are so beautiful, Laura," he tells me, admiration clear in his voice. His hands reach out and gently caress my slightly rounded stomach in reverence.

"It doesn't bother you?" I ask him, curious but suddenly worried that it will.

"Far from it," he tells me softly, still stroking my abdomen, sending tingles across my skin.

His gaze meets mine, and I see the truth in his words. He really doesn't care that I'm carrying another man's child. He leans down over me, capturing my lips with his as he settles in between my legs, his tip nudging my slick opening.

"You tell me if you want to stop or if anything is uncomfortable, okay?" he asks and waits for my nod before he starts to push inside of me.

My hands come up and grip his shoulders, the stretch of him entering me is so exquisite I can't stop the deep moan that leaves my lips.

"Shit, Laura," he growls out as he finally bottoms out, fully seated deep inside of me. He's up on his elbows, and he uses the leverage to slowly pump in and out, gyrating his hips so that he's massaging my clit too.

"Ryan! Yes!" I rasp out as he picks up speed, sending blissful tendrils of pleasure shooting all over my body.

"Laura, you feel. So. Fucking. Good," he groans out, every word punctuated with a thrust of his hips until he's practically slamming into me. I tip over the edge, falling into another mind shattering orgasm, and I hear him cry out his own release moments later.

He rolls off me, pulling me in his arms so that my head is resting on his sweat covered chest. It rises and falls with his panting breaths, and I can feel his heartbeat racing like my own as we both come down from our high.

"Feeling better, baby?" he asks me, and I can hear the smile in his voice.

"Much, thank you," I reply primly, then burst out laughing. He huffs out a chuckle too, and we lie there wrapped in each other's arms, and surrounded by our happiness.

# CHAPTER EIGHT

Ryan leaves early, kissing me tenderly on my forehead before he goes, leaving me in the warmth of the bed. A couple of hours later, I wake up with a wonderful ache between my thighs. I feel revitalised and refreshed, not bothering to stifle the giggle that escapes my lips as I relive the previous night.

"You finally had your wicked way with Ryan then?" I hear Lexi drawl from the doorway, startling me out of my memories.

I look up to see a feline smirk on her beautiful face, and I return the smile even though my cheeks are flushing.

"Come on, you hussy. Get out of bed, and make yourself presentable. You've an appointment in an hour," she tells me, casually sauntering off.

It takes a second to register what she's said, and when it does, I leap out of bed, throw a robe on, and head to the bathroom.

Half an hour later, I emerge from my room, clean and dressed in loose navy blue corduroy trousers and a cream blouse with a navy silk scarf, courtesy of Justin, and black ankle boots to complete the look.

"What's my appointment?" I ask her as she passes me a croissant in a paper bag with Maxine's on the front. I've no idea why but it's only just occurred to me to ask. I probably should take charge of my life a bit more.

"Your midwife appointment, silly!" she mockingly scolds me.

"Oh." That's when I remember what Grey had said about calling someone he knew in the morning.

We head out of the apartment building into a brisk autumn wind that whips both of our hair around us. Luckily, there's a car waiting for us at the curb, so we quickly hop into it and out of the cold. I see the driver is Sean again, and after a brief hello, we drive off.

About thirty minutes later, Sean pulls up outside a tall brick mid-terrace building with a shiny red front door. As we get out and walk up the few steps, I see a brass plaque that reads 'Dr. Phillip Evans MD'. The door opens as we approach, and in the doorway stands a woman in her mid-forties, her blonde hair in a neat bun, and wearing rose pink scrubs.

"Welcome," she greets us, smiling warmly. "You must be Laura Darling?" she questions me politely, and I nod in response. "Excellent. Follow me please, Doctor Evans is ready for you."

She leads the way into the building, past a small reception area, and down a bright corridor. Pausing in front of a white painted door, she knocks once then enters.

"Laura's here, Doctor," she says cheerfully.

I notice an older distinguished looking gentleman sitting behind a wooden desk. He's wearing a light blue shirt with a navy blue patterned tie and a white lab coat. Dr. Evans looks up as Lexi and I walk in, a broad reassuring smile on his face, he gets up and holds out his hand for me to shake.

"Laura, a pleasure, and congratulations," he beams at me in cultured tones. "I'm Dr. Evans, and I'll be your consultant for the duration of your pregnancy. Although, you'll mostly see Sally here, your midwife, unless any complications come up. Which, given your age, I highly doubt. Now, take a seat. You can tell me what you know, and we shall take it from there."

The next twenty minutes or so is taken up with form filling and relaying my medical history. The nurse takes some blood and a urine sample, then it's time to hop up on the bed and have the examination part of the consultation. Nervous butterflies flutter around in my stomach as I pull my trousers to below my hips.

Once I'm settled, Dr. Evans takes out some kind of monitor, squirting some cold jelly onto my lower stomach.

"Let's have a look, shall we?" he says as he puts the wand onto the jelly and starts moving it around.

Within moments, I hear the fast sonic sounding beat of my baby's heart, and tears rush to my eyes. For the first time, this feels real; there's actually a life growing inside of me.

"Lexi," I quietly whisper and glanced up to see her right beside me, her own eyes misted with happy tears.

"Oh love, that's your baby," she murmurs back, voice thick as she grasps my hand and squeezes.

I lay there, letting the rhythm surround me like a magical blanket, soothing my soul. All too soon the doctor pulls the wand away, passing me some tissue to wipe the gel off.

"Heartbeat is strong and good, so all is well," he declares, and I feel a rush of relief flood through me. I didn't even realise that I was worried, but I feel elated to discover that everything is okay and that my baby is safe and growing.

"That's it, so if you want to get dressed then Sally here will sort out your next appointment," he informs me kindly, turning and heading out of the room.

---

I feel as though I'm on cloud nine the whole journey back home, and even Lexi can't stop smiling.

"Have you thought more about Grey's offer, hun?" she gently asks as we walk into the apartment.

"I think," I say, biting my lower lip in apprehension, "I'd like to give it a go." She squeals, grabbing my hands and spinning me around, then apologising and saying something about being careful of the baby.

"Although, I'm not sure about taking my clothes off," I tell her, an idea that came to me this morning bubbling up to the surface of my mind as I speak. "But when I was in boarding school, we had a drama teacher, Mrs. Sin, who taught us belly dancing."

"Belly dancing?" she quirks a brow at me in confusion. "But, hun, Grey's is, well, a strip club."

"I know, but this kind of dancing is pretty sensual, and I've seen YouTube videos of pregnant women doing it and they're pretty hot," I justify, and I can see the cogs starting to turn in her mind as a twinkle enters her eye.

"Oh! Justin can dress you as a kind of fertility goddess! Dark makeup, green silk, and headdresses!" she enthuses, getting more excited as she speaks.

"Sure," I chuckle back, also warming to the idea now that I've spoken it aloud.

I feel a flutter in my stomach, and it takes me a moment to realise it's not the usual butterflies but my baby. My hand flies to cover my stomach, trying to feel anything on the outside, but it's not quite strong enough yet.

"Looks like the baby approves!" Lexi laughs.

*Looks like baby does*, I think with a smile, my hand stroking my slightly rounded stomach.

# CHAPTER NINE

A week later, I'm regretting my decision whilst Justin puts the finishing touches on my fertility goddess outfit. As Lexi suggested, I'm wearing a moss green silk skirt that is basically a collection of scarves attached to a waistband of gold that sits on my hips underneath my stomach and accentuating the slight roundness. There's a matching bra, with sheer tendrils of fabric that hang down and tickle my torso. My makeup is dark, and my freshly dyed red hair is up in an elaborate updo with a sort of gold crown in the shape of twigs and leaves nestled into it. Hanging from the crown is another sheer scarf that covers my face from under my eyes, down to my chin. That addition was mine, just on the off chance anyone from my past comes in.

"You look like a fucking goddess!" Lexi squeals, taking me in as I stand in front of the mirror whilst Justin fixes the small anklet of bells around my ankle. I'm barefoot, which is a relief as I doubt I'd be able to wear the high heeled shoes the others do.

"T-thanks," I manage to stammer out, feeling a little queasy. I do feel pretty attractive, and there is something sexy about the hint my slightly rounded stomach gives.

"Showtime," I hear Grey say from the doorway, and I catch his gaze in the mirror. “You look beautiful, Laura,” he tells me with a kind and appreciative smile.

“Thank you, Grey,” I whisper back, taking a steadying breath and turning around to walk out the door.

I head towards the back staircase, which is for staff use only, leading down into the basement. The whole room is soundproof, so it’s not until the door at the bottom is opened that I can hear all the chatter. The others go ahead of me, taking up positions on their various tables around the room. We decided that we’d all dance to the music suited to belly dancing, but that I would come in as the music starts, dancing my way to my table.

The music begins, and I step through the door, nerves fluttering in my stomach. A hand stops me, and I look up to see Ryan’s chocolate brown eyes staring down at me.

“You look fucking gorgeous, Laura,” he rasps out, his eyes scorching me as they slide down and then back up my body. “Dance for me tonight,” he orders, and I give him a nod then start my routine.

Rolling my hips in time with the music, I dance my way up the steps that lead to the table’s surface. I move in a slow circle, taking in the men sitting around me, and see hunger and appreciation in their eyes which widen as I move my hands in such a way as to highlight my rounded stomach.

One, in particular, a dark haired man in a suit, sits up straighter, his nostrils flaring as he takes me in. He’s completely ignoring the suited gentleman beside him who is trying to talk to him about something. I don’t hold his gaze for long; there's an intensity to it that leaves me feeling unnerved. Like I am a prize to be taken home and locked up.

I look up and seek out Ryan’s gaze as I twist and turn, doing a couple of stomach rolls and turning my hands in circles above me in time to the beat. It feels incredible being up here and so openly admired, and I get lost in the dance and the freedom that I’m feeling down to my very soul. It’s unlike anything that I have ever experienced before and gives me such a heady rush that I understand why the others enjoy dancing like this.

The song draws to a close, and I end my dance, out of breath but elated. I make my way down the steps to find Mr. Dark and Intense waiting. He bows his head, handing me a wad of banknotes.

“Until next time, Aphrodite,” he whispers, his voice deep and dark like wind whispering around gravestones on a moonless night.

I shudder but take the cash, and I swear I can feel his eyes follow me as I head towards Ryan and the stairs.

# CHAPTER TEN

The next few weeks continue in the same way, me dancing a couple of times over the course of the night, all while my stomach gets rounder with the baby growing inside of me. I've started to feel more movements, and the first time Lexi felt my baby kick, we both ended up in tears at the sheer magic of it.

I've also had both my scans and seeing my baby on the screen, watching the baby wriggle around and knowing that it's healthy and where it needs to be, created such a wealth of happiness in my chest, I thought that I might burst. I decided not to find out whether it's a boy or girl. We get so few surprises in life, I wanted this to be one of them.

I've entered that glowing phase that everyone talks about, and I really do feel great. My hair is thicker, my boobs are getting bigger and rounder, much to Ryan's appreciation on the nights he's had *coffee*. I generally feel well, and I'm grateful that the need to pee every two seconds has passed. I also no longer seem to have any queasiness at all, not that I had much but it was miserable when I did. It's a strange feeling having your body no longer be your own, although there's a comfort in knowing that no matter what, I am no longer alone in this world.

My now obvious pregnancy seems to draw more members my way. Grey really was right when he said that a lot of men would find it attractive. The table I dance on is always full, with some members requesting a seat specifically. Lexi jokes that she needs to get knocked up and that they've all been missing a trick all these years!

I bring in a huge amount of tips, it's crazy really what the rich will spend their money on, and my best tipper is the brooding mysterious guy from that first night. He's always at my table, watching me with his dark, predatory gaze, his intense eyes fixed on my body the whole time. I asked Lexi about him, and apparently, he's some kind of billionaire who uses the club for business meetings mostly, though no one is quite sure what his business actually is. His name is Mr. Black; each member is given an alias in the form of a different colour, and no one but Grey knows who they really are.

I'm not sure whether or not I should be worried by his unwavering attention. He never steps out of line, only touches me to help me down from the table and to place his wad of cash into my hand. He's not done anything to warrant the feeling of uneasiness that he inspires in me, yet I feel it all the same.

Ryan doesn't like it, although he's trying to keep his possessiveness in check. He's staying with me a lot in my bed, always leaving before I'm up. He says seeing me dance night after night gives him dickache, like a headache but with his dick, so it's my own fault really. *Cheeky bugger!*

I've just finished getting ready for my dance tonight, grateful that I'm in the dry and warm club, with the cold December wind blowing and sleet falling from the sky outside.

"You're up, doll," Justin tells me, then rushes off to help a new girl who's in a muddle with her suspenders.

The baby gives me a little kick as if to tell me to hurry up, and I chuckle to myself at its seeming impatience. I make my way downstairs to the basement, seeing Ryan as usual once I step past the doorway. He trails his fingers across my stomach sending flutters of pleasure skittering across my abdomen and into my core. I see him smirk in a satisfied male way as he hears my breath hitch.

My song comes on, a sensual piece with the rhythmic pounding of drums so I make my way to my table, rolling my hips in time with the beat as I walk. Dancing up the small steps to the table, I take note of Mr. Black who is here as expected. I give him a small nod, which he returns with a tilt of his lips, an almost smile. There are three other men around the table, all in dark suits, one of whom is seated next to Mr. Black, turned to face him as they speak.

My steps falter as he registers where Black's attention has gone and faces me. *Shit! Fuck!* It's Julian Vanderbilt, CEO of Black Knight Corporation and one of Ace's associates. I've met this man on countless occasions, spoken to his wife, and sat down to dinner at their house. His eyes alight with appreciation but not recognition, at least, I don't think they do but my panic is colouring my judgement.

My heart pounds in time with the drums, and I see Ryan heading in my direction, his face wreathed with concern. I look at him and shake my head, taking a deep breath and continuing to dance. My eyes catch Black's, and I can see he's sitting stock still, his own eyes tumultuous and full of what looks like anger which confuses me.

The song comes to an end, and I hurry over to the steps to find Black waiting, as usual, to help me down. My hand shakes as it clasps his, and when I reach the bottom, he leans in close to my ear, keeping hold of my hand.

"Apologies, Aphrodite, he will not come here again," he whispers darkly before handing me the usual wad of bills and releasing his grip.

I don't say anything in return, my mouth unable to utter a word, then I walk off, trying to appear casual whilst my insides churn with worry and fear.

As I go to step past Ryan, he grabs my upper arm, stepping through the door with me and closing it behind us.

"What happened? Are you okay?" he asks, cupping my jaw, worry shining in his brown eyes. "Is the baby okay?"

"Just a misstep, nothing to worry about." I try to assure him by smiling, but my heart still pounds in fear of being discovered. I know my smile falls short when he doesn't look reassured and, if anything, looks more concerned.

"One day, I hope you trust me enough to tell me about your past. You're not alone anymore, Laura, and I can protect you," he tells me vehemently, not giving me a chance to answer before he presses a light kiss on my lips then heads back out the door.

*It's not me that needs protecting the most*, I think as I stare after him, holding my stomach and feeling the life inside me move.

# CHAPTER ELEVEN

Christmas and New Year come and go. Black is true to his word, and I don't see Julian at Grey's again. As the weeks roll by, I start to relax when there are no apparent repercussions, so I can only hope that means that he didn't recognise me.

Lexi and I spend a wonderful Christmas at the apartment, stuffing our faces until we can't move, not that I can move with any speed these days anyway. We don't get dressed all day, slobbing out and watching sappy movies. We exchanged gifts; I got her a sexy little leopard print romper and matching eye mask from Agent Provocateur. I got Ryan, well, myself I suppose, a little lacy teddy for me to wear the next time he's over, also from Agent Provocateur.

We spent New Year's Eve working at Grey's. It's one of the biggest parties of the year for us, and we both make a fortune. I even get a kiss at midnight from Ryan when he pulls me to a dark corner and steals my breath away, devouring my lips and mouth.

I still haven't committed to him, which I feel terrible for. I'm not seeing anyone else, neither is he as far as I can tell, but I just don't feel like it's safe to be together officially. I mean, everyone knows we are sleeping with each other, but that's it. If Ace does find me, which admittedly is looking less likely the more time passes, he would destroy Ryan, hurting him horribly, and I can't risk that. I care for him too much. Plus there are my lingering feelings for Tom...and the guilt whenever I think about him when I'm with Ryan.

Spring is finally here, and I'm officially as big as a whale! I'm actually considering if I should stop dancing, as I feel so cumbersome and like it's time to focus on the impending arrival of my baby. There's less than a month until my due date, and although I know that babies aren't always on time, Grey did say I could take maternity leave, so I think maybe I should.

I feel lighter having made that decision. The next morning, I'm woken early by a strong pain tearing across my stomach, ending with a dull ache in my pelvis. Groaning quietly so as not to wake Ryan who's asleep next to me, I get up and head to the toilet. When I wipe myself, I see the evidence of what the midwife called my plug; basically, slightly bloody goo.

"Lexi!" I shriek, staring down at the tissue. Moments later the door bangs open, Lexi standing there dishevelled, her hair wild, and I hold it out to show her. "Look!"

"Okay, gorgeous," she says, eyes wide and voice shaky. "Let's keep calm and call Sally."

We discussed having a home birth at the apartment with her, which she was very supportive of. Lexi goes off to make the call whilst I clean up, going back into my room to find Ryan sitting on the edge of the bed wide awake.

"Will you stay with me?" I ask him, suddenly needing his strong presence around me as I go through this.

"Of course," he says immediately, getting up and enfolding me in his big arms, holding me tightly. Another pain flashes across my abdomen, but it's manageable. "Want me to run you a bath?" he asks, leaning back to look at me.

"That would be perfect," I whisper gratefully, suddenly a little scared and unsure now that the day has come.

He takes my hand and leads me back into the bathroom, turning on the taps and running me a bath that is the perfect temperature. As I'm getting in, Lexi comes back, telling me that Sally said to give her a call when I'm having roughly three contractions within ten minutes. I nod, then soak in the tub for a while, letting the hot water soothe my body and calm my nerves. Ryan doesn't leave my side, chatting gently to me and successfully keeping my mind occupied.

Getting out, he helps me dry off, wrapping me in my big fluffy dressing gown and cashmere socks that Lexi got me for Christmas. We walk towards the rest of the apartment, and I gasp as I see what Lexi has done, tears filling my eyes. The whole place is darkened with only dim lamps and fairy lights casting a soft glow on the main living space. There are cards with positive messages everywhere and soft classical music is playing. I can see on the kitchen countertop is an array of healthy snacks, some chocolate, and vitamin drinks.

"Lexi..." I choke out, lost for words.

"I hope it's okay?" she gently asks, her tone unsure. "I looked up online about calm home birth spaces, and all these things were suggested," she tells me.

"It's...it's beautiful and perfect. Thank you." I take her hands in mine and squeeze them. She beams back at me, her own eyes glistening. I gasp as another pain hits, causing me to squeeze her hands a little tighter.

"Right," she says after the pain has passed. "Remember, Sally said to keep moving. Do you want to have something to eat then go for a walk and get some fresh air?"

I nod, thinking that sounds exactly like what I need.

---

We come back from the walk when I have to keep stopping to breathe through the ever increasingly painful contractions. I get changed into loose PJ bottoms and a tank top, continuing to walk around the apartment with Ryan supporting me. The contractions have picked up. I'm not sure how frequent they are, but Lexi decides to call Sally who says she'll be over in about half an hour.

A couple of minutes after that, the pain changes and becomes a lot more urgent. I keep breathing, although it feels harder now as there's very little let up. I feel the immediate need to squat down like something is coming.

"Lexi!" I manage to gasp out, and she rushes towards me looking at me hunched over, gripping Ryan's arms tightly.

"Are you pushing, Laura?" she asks, and I don't know how to answer that as another pain hits because I do feel the urgent need to push down.

Not fully aware of what I'm doing, my body has taken over. I pushed my PJ bottoms down and kicked them off, then got onto my knees in front of the sofa. I vaguely hear someone curse as I scream out, pain tearing my body into two, my opening burning. I move one hand between my legs, and I can feel something round emerging from between my thighs. *I can't be ready! Firstborns take longer, that's what everyone said!*

I feel a strong grip on my other hand, and I look up into calming chocolate brown eyes. I don't have time to register more than that. I can hear Lexi on the phone right behind me when another searing pain tears through me. The hand between my legs comes up and I grip Ryan's other one with my own, changing position slightly. With a scream, I feel my baby slide out with a rush of wetness.

"Come here, little one," I hear Lexi coo over my rushing heartbeat and panting breaths.

A second passes, then I hear the wonderful wail of a newborn baby, angry at leaving the warmth of the womb. A part laugh, part cry escapes my lips as I let go of Ryan's hands and Lexi passes a wriggling towel-wrapped bundle between my legs, I'm still on my knees, and into my waiting arms. I look down at a bright pink screaming face, and my eyes fill with tears of joy.

I look up at Ryan to see his eyes wet as well. "Boy or girl?" he rasps out, and I unwrap the towel to see that I have a daughter. A beautiful baby girl. I cuddle her to me, feeling a rush of slickness between my legs as Lexi declares the afterbirth has come away.

A few minutes later, I hear the door buzzer go off, and Ryan gets up to answer it. I'm still kneeling on the floor; luckily, Lexi put down waterproof coverings with towels on top over the carpet.

"What's her name?" I hear Lexi say softly from beside me, and I look up from my baby who has settled down a little now.

"Lilly, her name is Lilly Darling."

# CHAPTER TWELVE

## 18 YEARS LATER...

"Fuck you!" Lilly screams at me, the sound of our front door slamming closed as I stand, leaning my hands on the kitchen counter and trying to calm my anger and terror.

My hands clenched in fists of anger and concern, one shaking around the newspaper clipping I'm clutching tightly. It's an article about an award for a creative writing competition that Lilly won. It's already two weeks old, and she had it hidden in her room. I hate that she felt like she had to hide it, knowing that I would freak out, but it's for the best that there are no images of her anywhere. She's not allowed any social media accounts, which we've fought over, and I can never give her a good enough answer. She looks so much like me, and although it's been almost seventeen years since I ran, Ace's reach is endless.

I've tried to keep us safe, by being anonymous, but of course, Lilly just sees an overbearing and controlling mother who's trying to ruin her life, as most teenagers think when it comes to their parents. How can I tell her that her father is not absent, but a monster that I had to escape from? It's been the hardest thing to keep from her, but it's what keeps her safe and that is my priority.

We've been fighting so much recently, and not just about my refusal to let her get Facebook, or Tik Tok, or whatever it is she wants to post pictures of her life onto. She hates that I won't commit to Ryan fully, I still can't bring myself to put him in that kind of danger. He knows something happened, I've never fully divulged my past, but I'm sure he can make an educated guess from the little that I have told him. We're good friends, with a few benefits when Lilly is away for the night at a friend's, which isn't often as I need to know who she's with to make sure that she's safe.

It's all such a mess!

I stay there for what feels like hours but is probably only thirty minutes or so, just breathing, listening to the radio and trying to calm down, when I hear the front door open again. Turning to face her, an apology springs to my lips.

"Lilly, I'm so sor..." I come to a shuddering halt, my whole body flushing with a white-hot terror that freezes me like the burn of ice running through my veins. My heart pounds, and it feels like the whole world has paused on its axis.

"Hello, Violet," his voice is just as dark as I remember from my nightmares, and although older, he's just as devastatingly beautiful, too. His eyes have not changed, if anything they look deader than they used to, like the small shred of humanity that used to be in there is completely snuffed out and gone.

"Ace," I manage to whisper out, my voice broken. "How did you find me?"

"Now, that's just ill-mannered, Violet, not even asking after my well-being, and I know you were brought up better than that. Although, you were also brought up not to steal, whore yourself out, show your body to others..." he trails off like my litany of sins is just too much for him to remember them all. Or like he no longer cares.

His body is loose, like a hunting tiger, as he stalks over to our small kitchen table and sits down, straightening the cuffs of his dark suit jacket like he's at a business meeting. His dark eyes look back up, locking with mine, another chill sweeping over me at the way he looks at me. Like I'm no longer a person, *I wonder if I ever was to him?*

"H-how are you, Ace?" I ask, voice shaking as I slip back into old habits of shrinking into myself and trying to appear small.

He nods his approval. "Well, considering you stole my share in Black Knight Corporation sixteen years ago, not to mention hiding my heir from me, I am not too happy with you, Violet." His eyes cut to me, slicing into me like a honed blade. "It's a shame she's a girl when the others all have male heirs, but some things can't be helped," he adds, almost to himself.

"What?" A fresh wave of terror washes over me. *He knows! How does he know?!*

"Don't be coy, Violet. You left the evidence behind, and you never leave evidence behind," he tells me, anger flashes in his eyes at my refusal to acknowledge Lilly out loud to him.

"I-I don't know what you're talking about," I stammer, flinching when he slams his hands down on the tabletop, his calm disintegrating.

"Don't lie to me, Violet!" he hisses out, suddenly standing up, and I flinch again from the vitriol in his voice and the wild look in his eyes. "You left the test behind, and I found it that night. You never were the smartest woman," he sneers, his hands sliding down the front of his jacket, smoothing out any wrinkles as he sits down again.

*Oh god, the test.* I'd completely forgotten that I'd hidden it in the cleaning cupboard. And of course, he found it, he always was methodical and thorough.

"I see you've finally remembered," he smirks at me, straightening his tie. "Now, the important thing is you will tell me where the bonds that you stole from me are, and we can maybe put all this unpleasantness behind us." I swallow as his eyes flit back up, boring into me like he can dig the information out of my brain.

"No," I reply, my eyes flitting around to try and find my phone. If I could only call Lexi or Ryan, I may be able to get help. Thank god Lilly is out with friends, even if I don't know where exactly.

"No?" he questions, tone sharp and a tic twitching next to his right eye.

"I-I won't give them to you. They're Lilly's," I say more firmly, standing up a little straighter. He bullied me for years, and I don't have to take it anymore. I have a life now with people who care about me, and those bonds are mine by right. My money was used to purchase them after all. And they're Lilly's future.

"They are not Lilly's," he spits, standing up once again and taking menacing steps towards me. "They are mine, and you stole them from me. Enough with this little game, Violet. You'll give them back to me, now!"

I hear *Every Breath You Take* by Chase Holfelder come on the radio in the silence as he reaches me, standing so close I can see the slight stubble on his cheek.

"No," I say again, knowing that if I give in, he will have won and running would have been all for nothing. They are Lilly's security, something to ensure her comfort in life. "I'll never give them to you, and you'll never find them."

"It's my fucking business!" he screams, and he's so close that I feel spittle land on my cheek. "You stole it from me, you worthless bitch. I earned it, I fucking earned it! I took the risks! I took the paths no one else dared to!" His eyes are wild, his veins bulging in his neck. "Do you want to know why I'm so successful? I am like a fucking surgeon, Violet; clinical, detached, precise. I take what doesn't work and cut it away, dispose of it. How dare you question me? Steal from me? Take what is mine?" he's panting, and I watch as he seems to calm himself down, taking in a great lungful of air.

He laughs then, and it's a cruel sound full of shards of broken glass and poison. It makes me wince. It's so cutting. His cheeks are flushed, and his hands clench and unclench into fists.

He leans in so that his lips are next to my ear. "Oh, I'll find the bonds, Violet, just like I was able to find you," he whispers in a lover's caress that leaves me queasy and shaking. He leans back, his eyes looking away from me.

"You'll never get your hands on them, Ace, I can guarantee you that," my voice is firm, and I realise that I'm not scared of him. Not anymore.

I see the glint of silver in the corner of my eye seconds before a line of fire races across my chest. Gasping, my hand flies to the pain only to come away stained with red. I look up at Ace to see the silver of one of my kitchen knives in his hand, dripping with blood. My blood. I watch with frightened eyes as it comes down towards me, as if in slow motion, unable to stop it as it enters my stomach smoothly. I grunt with the impact, but there's no fire this time, just a sort of fascination as he pulls it back out, blood pouring out of me and splattering the floor.

My knees give way, and I land on them on the lino tiles that I'd only cleaned that morning. Vaguely, I hear the haunting tones of Akine singing *Devil Like Me. I love this song,* I think as I sink down onto my side, then roll onto my back. The sunlight coming in from the window waves and undulates as it's filtered through the trees outside, creating beautiful patterns across the ceiling.

Vaguely, I register another impact on my body, then another and another, but there's no more pain. I think there should be, and for a brief moment, my body panics but the comforting numbness soon returns.

*Oh Lilly*, I think with sorrow. *My beautiful Lilly flower. I'm so sorry for leaving you.* I know a moment of true regret with the realisation that I'm leaving her all alone. *Not completely alone*, I remember as my mind supplies Lexi and Ryan's faces flashing before me. I feel my lips pull into a smile before they disappear to be replaced with the face of the devil.

"I'll be sure to keep a close eye on our daughter," he says, voice soft, and I think that I should feel terror at that statement. But all I feel is the darkness coming to wrap me in its comforting embrace.

Want to know what happens to Lilly next? Read Captured, Highgate Preparatory Academy, Book 1.

And to keep up to date with all my news, sign up for my newsletter at www.rosaleeauthor.com/newsletter-sign-up

WHO OF US ISN'T A LITTLE BIT OF A MONSTER TOO?

BOOK ONE

# captured

HIGHGATE PREPARATORY ACADEMY

ROSA LEE

# CHAPTER ONE

LILLY

*Well, this sucks hairy goat balls.*

I continue walking up the long arse gravel drive, my muscles quivering and feet stomping. Luckily, I'm wearing flats, even if my feet are soaked through because it's pissing down. My nostrils flare as I recall that my bags are also fucking drenched from being thrown in a puddle, all because the Uber guy thought he'd try to take liberties. I dick punched him for his troubles, the only light in an otherwise shitty situation, which he didn't take kindly to, so he tossed my luggage out and dumped me by the side of the road.

*I might be new to this country, but fuck him and his misogynistic belief that just because I've got tits and a vag, I must be interested!*

There is literally a river running down the drive, soaking my feet even more, and for a moment, the clear water is replaced with streams of scarlet, and I flinch as painful memories flood my mind from six months earlier...

*Red.*

*A whole room painted in shades of red.*

*Ribbons of dark crimson flow across the white lino floor, unstoppable in their path. I watch, fascinated, as the glistening ruby touches the toes of my yellow TOMS when I take a step, like a blotted ink spill.*

Damn, these shoes were favourites of mine. *The thought darts across my mind like a bird, flying away before I can grasp it.*

*My eyes follow the river to its source, lying there so still, in a pure white peaceful serenity. I walk towards her, swallowing with difficulty as a sour taste fills my mouth. I leave sticky cardinal footprints behind me, like some kind of macabre breadcrumb trail.*

*Time stops as a sharp pain hits my knees when I fall to the floor, breaking the crusty skin of the pool of blood, like custard left out too long. I'd expect it to feel hot against my leggings, but it's cool, as if it was never warm at all.*

*My mind refuses to believe what it's seeing, my eyes frenzied and watering as I try to take in the scene before me. Here is the woman who was there for me my whole life. Who gave birth to me, loved me, even when we fought like cats and dogs.*

*A strange sense of numbness settles over me like a cape, shielding me from the maelstrom of my anguish. The searing pain and hurt that I can sense lies just below the surface.*

*Nausea rolls round in my stomach as I break out in a sweat, and my muscles start to cramp, but I can barely feel the pain. Reaching out with trembling fingers, I brush her once shiny dyed red hair away from her pale face. My eyes search her body, trying to find the source of the blood leaking out of her, to see if it can be plugged. My hands frantically press into the cold liquid, lips trembling when they come away stained with the claret of life.*

*As I study them, my chest feels tight when a line that Lady Macbeth says flits into my mind, fluttering round like a butterfly demanding to be noticed.*

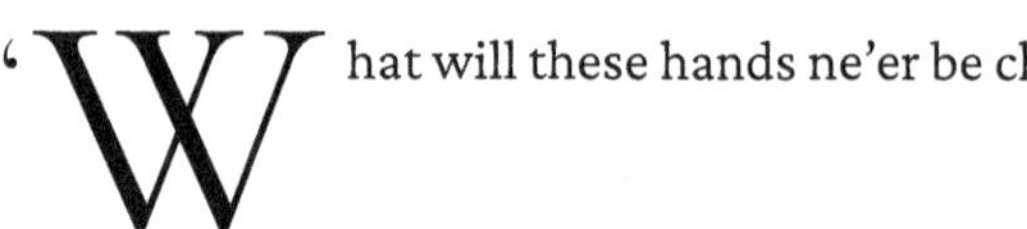

'What will these hands ne'er be clean?'

. . .

*I always thought red was such a warm colour before. But now it's as cold as ice, burning my skin where it touches it.*

*My eyes squeeze shut and I want to run, to flee, to escape from what's in this room. I beg any god that exists in this world to release me from this torment.*

*I can hear frantic voices far away, someone sobs and vomits behind me, but the wind rushing past my ears makes it impossible to hear anything clearly at all.*

*I breathe deeply through my nose, shaking my head to try and clear it, but the tangy scent of old copper pennies overwhelms me, and suddenly the wind is howling round me so viciously, my eyes fly open and I'm surprised the room isn't being torn apart in its violence.*

*Black starts to creep in round the edges, the blissful dark of ignorance welcoming me in its comforting embrace. I fall into it gladly, accepting the oblivion with open arms until I am nothing. No one.*

*And the red ribbons no longer exist.*

I stop my walk, hanging my head, and take a moment, trying to catch my breath and blinking away the vision.

*A fresh start, remember?*

A new beginning and a chance to become a new person, not just the girl that found her dead – I shut the thought off, feeling heavy inside, and continue my way up the drive in this godforsaken rain.

Finally I arrive outside the stone facade of Highgate Preparatory Academy, apparently the best high school in the west. *Snort.* It's nestled on the edge of the Rockies, surrounded by forests and amazing views, according to their website. None of which I can currently appreciate given that it's dark. I'm soaked to the bone from the pouring rain, and fucking exhausted from a long arse journey.

*We're certainly not in Kansas anymore; well, London if we're being really pedantic,* I think, rolling my eyes at myself as I walk up the smooth stone steps and knock on the huge wooden panelled front doors, the sound echoing in the darkness.

"You can do this, Lilly," I whisper under my breath, a rolling feeling in my stomach as I try to gather courage when I hear ominous footsteps on the other side, growing louder as they approach me.

*Why does it feel like I'm waiting outside the gates of Hell?*

It's just a high school, the same as many others, I'm sure. Well, perhaps not exactly the same. Highgate is a private high school for the rich, privileged, and no doubt, arseholes of the western world. And this is my senior year. *Dear lord.*

One of the impressive wooden doors opens with a sinister creak—*could this be any more like an old school hammer horror film?!*—and a tall skeletal man with a hook nose and small beady eyes peers down at me. His thin lips are downturned, like I just washed up from a stagnant swamp, and not just got soaked in an autumn downpour.

*Shoulders back, stiff upper lip, and all that.*

"Lilly Darling, I presume?" he sniffs in a nasally voice, posture unwavering. "You're late," he sneers, eyes cold, before I've even had a chance to answer.

*What a prick!*

"M–My flight was delayed..." I stammer.

*No!* I think to myself. *Don't let this crow make you feel like shit. Pull up those lady balls and stare him the fuck down.*

I straighten my spine, stand taller, and give him my best bitch glare.

"Hmph..." he scoffs cruelly. "Follow me."

Wow. His mother clearly gave up on teaching him manners. Perhaps she left the nest he was born in when she saw his ugly maw. I mean, it's not even a face a mother could love.

He turns sharply on his heels and walks away, back ramrod straight, expecting me to follow like the twatwaffle that he clearly is. I quickly grab my holdall and small suitcase, step inside, and gape.

*Jesus wept.*

This place is insane. Remember that great TV show a few years back called Downton Abbey? It's like that, but bigger. I'm standing in a huge entrance hall with a sweeping central staircase that Crow the Cuntmuffin, as he shall forever be named, is already halfway up. I can't see much else because it's so dark, although I do notice marble floors sparkling in the moonlight from the windows, and so many wooden doors I lose count.

Scrambling to catch up, I briefly notice the dark wood doors that are running along the ground floor on either side of me are carved, although I can't quite see what the images are. I moan aloud as my shoes touch the Persian rug, it's so thick I swear I sink several inches. *How awesome would this feel barefoot?* I cringe when I realise I'm probably leaving wet footprints on it, then shrug. If Crow the Cuntmuffin has to clean them up, then it's not so bad.

"Ahem."

I look up, and Crow is at the top of the stairs, peering down at me like I'm dog shit. My cheeks flush a little with embarrassment at being caught ogling the carpet. Straightening my shoulders once again, I decide to screw him and his priggish ways by not hurrying.

*This wanker and I are going to have a falling out soon. Fuck him and his opinions seven ways to Sunday.*

I notice he keeps glancing dismissively down his beak nose at me, his upper lip curling and giving me a 'hurry the fuck up' look. So I slow down my assent even more, making sure my soaked suitcase bangs loudly against each step, 'cause I'm petty like that.

"Hey, I hear ginger, honey, and lemon are great for sore throats. Sounds like you've got a doozy of one." I smile sweetly at him, although it may be more of a baring my teeth type of grin.

His lips tighten and become so thin, they almost disappear. He clears his throat again, the snarky bastard.

As he continues on, he addresses me derisively without bothering to look back, "You were supposed to have your guide show you the way round this establishment today, then join us all in the Dining Hall for a welcoming feast. But as you couldn't bring yourself to be on time, your guide has gone to bed."

It's fascinating really. It's like he's dead inside and just waiting for good ole Grim to whisk him away. "I'm to show you to your dormitory, and you must report to the office tomorrow morning. Eight o'clock sharp."

The look he gives me over his shoulder is one of such dismissal, it's like I don't exist. Like I'm not even a mote of dust. *Fucking Cockwomble.*

We carry on along the lavish hallway, and I notice that all of the portraits lining the duck egg blue walls are of stuffy old men. All in formal clothing with severe looks on their faces, and some even have hooked noses.

*Wow. Looks like Crow here is in good company.*

He pauses outside a single, dark door, carved with some sort of biblical scene. I raise a brow at what I think is Lucifer being thrown out of heaven. *That's...aspirational?*

"This is your dorm," he indicates coldly as he takes out a keychain with two beautiful scrolling old-fashioned keys on it. "You share it with four others." He's almost smirking...*hmmm*...mustn't be anything good if it brings him joy. Maybe the other girls I'm sharing with are as uptight as this wanker?

Crow unlocks the door and waits beside it. As I pass, he suddenly thrusts out his arm, holding out the keys, almost hitting me in the face with them. *Dick.* I grab them from him, and he turns his back, fucking off back down the hall.

*Guess I'll figure this shit out alone then, huh?* With a fuck you shrug, I face the room.

*Wowzers!*

My brows raise to my hairline, my eyes widening as I take in the scene before me.

On the wall opposite me, there's a gorgeous, large stone fireplace, embers still glowing and giving off a delicious heat that elicits a sigh of contentment from my lips. Three big comfy looking sofas are in a U shape round it, and what looks like an epic TV screen is hung above it. To the right of the fireplace is a floor-to-ceiling bay window covered in red velvet curtains. Nestled in the window is a dark wood oval dining table with a window seat bench covered in, yep, you guessed it, red and gold silk cushions. With fucking tassels! There are three extra chairs in dark wood and red leather on this side. In fact, the whole room is shades of red and gold. *I always knew I belonged in Gryffindor!*

"I guess it's good to stick to a theme, right?" I mumble, snorting to myself.

Directly to my right, there is a small modern kitchen, and I can see a door ajar just after the island/breakfast bar that looks like a bathroom. *Halle-fucking-lujah!*

I'm in desperate need of a piss, the urge becoming painful as the possibility of finally being able to pee presents itself. I unceremoniously dump my bags on the ground, and head in to relieve myself. Pausing briefly at the door, I admire the clawfoot tub in the middle of the floor, along with the biggest shower that I've ever seen against the wall in the corner, all with a wide grin on my face. The shower has got so many heads and jets it's almost obscene.

I'm definitely up for playing with those jets, especially round certain sensitive areas, *wink wink*. "It will be *obscene* once I'm done," I chuckle to myself.

After I've finished, I wash up and wander over to said shower, discovering shelves full of products and thick, fluffy grey towels on a heated rail next to it. Fuck it. I'm taking a shower now. Those jets are calling to me like a siren song.

I scroll through the music on my phone—*who doesn't listen to music in the shower*—internally fist pumping when I find the perfect song for this cluster-fuck of an arrival. Setting my phone on the counter, I hit play, and *Get Off My Dick* by Ilira starts playing, making me smile genuinely for the first time in what feels like days.

I start to sing along, not caring if my new roommates hear me after the night I've had so far. Stripping out of my damp clothes, dancing as I go, I leave them in a pile on the floor with my black ballet flats, then hop in the shower enclosure.

It takes a while to work out how the damn thing works, but once I figure it out, I can't suppress the orgasmic groan that passes my lips as the hot water hits my aching body. *This. Is. The. Bollocks.*

I keep shaking my tail feather along to the beat as the divine water cascades down my body, warming me up from the inside out with a heat that radiates down to my toes.

Looking back at the shelves, I spy so many products I'm almost at a loss as to where to begin. I mean, they all belong to the students I'm sharing a dorm with, but I'm sure they won't miss a little until I can buy some of my own. I'd thought about bringing some, but that would have taken up precious book space in my bags, so I figured I'd just buy them when I got here.

My eyes land on a bottle of shampoo, which I discover has a spicy ginger scent, so I pour a healthy dollop into my hands and lather up. After I rinse, I use it for a second time. Always double shampoo, bitches.

After rinsing once more, I follow with the same scented conditioner, using the bottle as my microphone when I get to the chorus of the song, singing loudly and loving the shower acoustics.

Finishing my solo, then bowing to the imaginary applause, I search for a body wash that'll go nicely with the scent of the hair products, because you can't just mix scents willy-nilly like some sort of perfume heathen. I come across one that smells like vanilla cookies, a warm feeling settling in my chest at the homely smell.

*Bingo!* Once done and fully rinsed, I switch the shower off, squeezing my wavy brunette hair out, and step out of the shower to grab a towel.

"Nice shower?" a deliciously deep voice asks.

Obviously, I play it cool, and I definitely don't screech like a fucking banshee whilst jumping about five feet in the air. Nope, not at all terrified, no siree!

Whipping round to face my peeping Tom, I'm wobbling on my feet as my heart pounds loudly in my ears. I'm naked as a newborn, completely forgetting to grab a fucking towel in my panic. *Fuck. My. Life.*

My eyes alight on the doorway to discover who the stranger is and...*holy Mary, mother of all things hotness!* Leaning against the doorframe with his muscular arms crossed over a simply glorious naked chest is the most exquisite specimen of the male species I have ever seen.

I moisten my parted lips, my skin flushing as I take him in.

He's like a fallen angel, with gently curling, fiery red hair that falls over one stunning emerald eye and a firm chiselled jaw, which is relaxed and tipped up in a lopsided grin. He's staring at me with bright eyes full of mischief, and a smouldering smile on his full come-bite-me lips.

And his ink. *Oh, be still my fucking beating heart!*

He's got tattoos on his arms, covering a good portion of them and highlighting their powerful form. As he uncrosses them, I can see that he's got a beautiful black chest piece that makes me suck in a breath, and my thighs clench. It's of the painting in the Sistine Chapel. I think it's called The Creation of Adam. On his throat is a neck piece of a stunning dragonfly, also black.

My gaze slips down to spy a nipple bar twinkling in the light, my hands twitching with the need to feel it under my fingertips. On his right hip, just above the waistband of his low-slung grey sweats—which should be fucking illegal, by the way—is a bright red lipstick tattoo. I can feel my core tingle at the sheer arrogance of that one.

"Ahem," he chuckles, and my eyes snap up to meet his.

I can see the laughter in them, they're practically sparkling with it, and I've totally been busted for checking him out. My body flushes once more when I notice that there's also a banked fever in his green depths, which sets my pulse racing.

His eyes caress all over my nude body, the green heating even further as they gloss over slightly.

*Yep. I'm still naked. In front of a hot as fucking sin stranger. Cue facepalm.*

He casually strolls in, smirking playfully, whilst I'm frozen to the spot, and stops just in front of me, my wet hardened nipples almost touching his bare chest. He's so close I can feel the heat of his body radiating out to mine, embracing me in a delicious warmth and making me shiver with pleasure.

His smirk is firmly in place as he keeps me trapped in an intense gaze, reaching over my shoulder with a long, beautiful tattooed arm. He brushes it, sending an electric current across my whole body, and I flash white hot at the touch. *Fuck me.*

Grabbing a towel from the rack behind me, he starts to dry me off with slow teasing strokes that send my pulse rocketing to new heights. I'm still unable to move so much as an inch, as this angel of a boy dries my arms one at a time, then my collarbone. He skims the towel over each breast, and I inhale sharply, filling my nose with his mouth-watering vanilla cookie scent, reminding me of the shower gel that I just used.

Instead of passing me the towel, which he really should have done from the beginning, he drops to his fucking knees in front of me, making my stomach flutter and my body feel overheated enough to combust.

*Jesus! What on earth is happening? He's a complete fucking stranger! Maybe I ought to...*

Before I can make a decision on what I really should do, he looks up with a devilish grin that's so irresistible on his angelic face, my brain just ups and leaves the building, letting Her Vagisty take over.

He proceeds to towel me from my feet, up my calves, and to my thighs. He pauses as he gets to the apex — *thank goodness I had a Brazilian wax a few days ago!*— and...*did he just sniff me?!* A low growl escapes him, and my breath hitches as I swear I can feel my core dripping, my pussy pulsing at the animalistic sound.

He stands up, pressing his front against me, and there is definitely something hard poking me in my lower stomach.

"Arms up," he orders in a dark as black treacle voice, which is a little husky now.

He's clearly as affected by me as I am by him. Thank fuck, otherwise, this would be awkward.

I'm so shocked by what has happened, what is still happening, that I do as he commands without question. He wraps the towel round me and tucks the end in so it stays shut, covering me from breasts to knees.

"Nice ink," he whispers, his hand trailing along my right side where I have a watercolour galaxy tattoo. My side tingles even though I can't possibly feel the touch through the towel.

"You too," I breathe back, swallowing hard and licking my suddenly dry lips, my eyes travelling over his chest.

When I look up, the green of his beautiful eyes is almost entirely swallowed up with black, his pupils blown with lust, and I shiver, my nipples pebbling under the towel. Taking a step back in a bid to rein in Her Vagisty who's about to go rogue, I can feel my body flush pink.

"Darlin...I–I mean Darling. That is, I am Darling. My name. My name is Lilly Darling," I manage to choke out, my whole body alight with embarrassment. *God smite me the fuck now and save me from myself. Real fucking smooth, Lilly. Jesus.*

I realise that *Get Off My Dick* is still playing on repeat when his eyes flash to my phone on the counter, then back to me. He looks at me amused, laughter dancing in those gorgeous orbs of his.

His gaze changes slightly, the heat flaring in it brighter than before, like he wants to do naughty bad things to me, and Her Vagisty perks up at the thought. *Christ on a cross. For fuck's sake, woman!*

"Boys!" he suddenly hollers, eyes still holding mine and startling me out of my dirty angel fantasies with a jump. "Our new roomie is here!"

Then, he turns round, tented sweats and all, and walks out.

## CHAPTER TWO

LILLY

B*oys? What does he mean by boys?*

My brain is still completely fried from that little performance. Frankly, I'm surprised it's not dribbling out of my ear. However, that one word, 'boys', sinks in and plays on repeat, whirling round my head until suddenly I awaken from my lusty haze, coming to with a start.

*Surely I can't have been put in a dorm with all guys...can I?*

I guess there's only one way to find out. I pull up my big girl panties, obviously, those metaphorical ones as I'm still naked as fuck under this towel, throw my shoulders back, and stride out. Yep, in just my towel. *Own it, girl*, my inner self tells me.

Because, of course, my bag is not in the bathroom, it's in the living room with all my probably soaking wet clothes inside. I'm just that lucky. *Fucking cuntflap Uber driver*.

I come to a sudden jerking halt. My heart rate picks up and my tongue darts out to trace my lower lip when I see who these 'boys' are.

*Sweet baby Jesus. Where do guys like this even come from?* This is enough to make even Dorothy throw those beautiful red shoes away and live forever in Oz.

Before me stand four boys, though men is a better descriptor. Saying that, they didn't make boys, men, or even fucking gods like this back home. *Holy fuck with a waffle on top!*

They are exquisite, indescribably beautiful, and sinful in every way that counts. My breath quickens as I drink them in.

The fallen angel to my right has that smouldering smile still plastered on his face, as well as his tented sweats. It's like he gives no fucks that he's got a raging hard-on right in front of his dorm mates.

Next to him is a guy so broad that I wonder how he even fits through the door. *I bet he could pin me down real good.* My nerve endings tingle with the image of his huge hands doing just that to me. His shoulder length blonde hair has a slight wave to it and is mussed and loose, down round his face, highlighting a closely cropped blonde bearded jaw. His eyes are a piercing blue and hold a predatory look that reminds me of being in a wolf's gaze, and I shift with excited unease.

He's leaning his arse on the back of one of the sofas, staring at me, his predator's gaze turning calculating, and his massive arms crossed over his equally huge chest. He has some sort of black tribal tattoo sleeve down one arm and spilling across one pec, my eyes narrow as I try to focus and make sense of the shapes. I can see from his long black shorts that the opposite leg also has a similar design wrapped round it.

Overall, he gives the impression of a viking warrior, ready to set sail and pillage new lands, shed blood and take what he wants. There's an almost visible aura of violence that surrounds him, colouring the air in shades of black. I shiver, not just from fear, but with a longing that begins to stir in my chest.

I briefly wonder if it's a longing for his body in a sexual way, or the protective vibe that rolls off him in waves that I desperately want extended to me. Either way, it's enough to make me take a small step towards him before I can catch myself and stop the movement.

To his right and standing a little ahead of the others is what can only be described as Lucifer himself. You know, like the one from that TV show, all dark virulent looks and black suits with a wit sharp enough to cut. *I wonder if his words hurt, too?*

His hair is so black, it's as if a moonless night has descended, kissing his head. It's neat and slicked back from his face, despite the late hour, and I get the impression it would never be otherwise. Perfectly arched black brows lend a cruel look to his devastatingly beautiful face, his cutting steel grey eyes are wholly bared and slicing into me like a honed blade, leaving me wounded. Yet my eyes feast on him all the same whilst a slight tremble comes over me.

He's in a red and navy long tartan PJ bottoms with a navy tank top that showcases his beautiful muscular arms, which are covered in simply stunning black ink. My gaze follows it as the tattoos swirl and eddie down his arms like patterned sleeves, right over the backs of his hands. The pictures spread up his neck right to his jawline in a repeated geometric pattern, and my heart pitter-patters at the sight, my breath leaving my lips in a rush.

It's so fucking hot it's unreal. I mean, he's nowhere near He-Man to his left in terms of bulk, but he definitely works out and could certainly hold you down in all the right ways. *Ahem! Head out of the gutter, Lilly!*

Finally, on the end is a guy who's smaller than the others, and although he has more of a gymnast's body, he is still drool worthy as fuck. He's the epitome of a sexy boy next door geek, yet there's also a darkness about him, like how I imagine the poet Byron would look. Beautiful but not entirely wholesome and with the glint of a tortured soul peeking through his eyes. *It's always the quiet ones you have to watch out for, right?*

His dark, chestnut brown hair is tousled, sticking up in all directions like he rakes his hands through it all the time, his thoughts consuming him. My fingers ache and tingle with the need to run them through it and mess it up even more.

He's got beautiful amber eyes, like liquid honey full of sweetness, and they're outlined by thick black frame glasses that heighten his hot nerd look. He, too, is wearing PJ bottoms, but his are plain shiny black which looks a lot like silk. *I know, right? Silk!*

He combines these with a black t-shirt that does nothing to hide his ripped torso, muscular arms, or the six pack that I want to cover in chocolate sauce and lick. *What do they feed these guys for them all to be so fucking gorgeous?*

"So, you're the new student," a low voice drawls, disdain and dismissal clear in his tone.

My eyes snap back to Lucifer, and I catch him giving me a once over...finding me lacking if the tilt of his head and his hard jawline are any indications. *What the ever loving fuck?*

He raises an ebony eyebrow haughtily, not dissimilar to the way Crow looked at me earlier, his face blank. My nostrils flare, and my eyes narrowing in response, heat flushing through my body for a completely different reason than it did moments ago.

"Yes," I say quietly. Then, I clear my throat and raise my chin, deciding to not let him get to me. *Fucking twatwaffle.* I cross my arms over my chest and say in my haughtiest tone "Lilly Darling, and you are?"

I raise one of my own brows, face blank like his. If the narrowing of his gaze is anything to go by, I am at least marginally successful in pissing him off. *Serves you right, smeghead!*

He stares at me for a second longer than is comfortable, clearly trying to make me squirm. He obviously doesn't realise who he's up against.

"Asher. Asher Vanderbilt," he drawls, carving into me with his gaze once again until it feels like he can see right into my tarnished soul. Like he's picking it apart and drinking all the light from inside me.

"Kai Matthews," the guy to his right murmurs, purposely interrupting our glare off, and making my gaze turn to his honey eyes, which are shifting and trying desperately not to stare at me in my towel. He fails and then blushes. *Cute.*

"Jax Griffiths," comes a deep rumble of thunder, and my head whips to look at He-Man. My god, that man could make a fortune in the phone sex industry. Or reading audiobooks.

I shiver before I can help myself, and am rewarded with an almost imperceptible smirk. *Oh, hell's bells. There's a dimple.*

"And I'm," the fallen angel steps forward, arms wide like a showman, a gleam in his eye and a playful smile on his lips, "your next orgasm," and then he fucking bows.

It's so ridiculous that a delighted laugh escapes me, my hand coming up to cover my mouth, and causing said angel to raise his head and give me a brilliant smile.

"Cut it out, Loki!" Asher snaps, turning his annoyed slate gaze onto his friend.

"Loki? As in the Norse trickster god?" I question the beautiful redhead, ignoring Grumpy McGrumpface.

"Yeah," his smile dims as he rubs the back of his neck. "My parents are mythology nuts."

"I like it." I smile. "It suits you," I add, a little of that heat from earlier in the bathroom returning to enter my voice. He grins back.

"So..." I begin, turning to look back at Lucifer–I mean Asher. "Why am I in a dorm with all guys?"

Again, his steel eyes cut me to the quick, and he waits before responding. This guy...he definitely is the king of all Hell, intimidating peons with only his glare.

*Ugh, I bet he's fucking mind blowing in bed. Wait, what?! Always gotta lower the tone, Lilly!*

"I have no fucking idea," he grumbles, almost to himself as he looks to Kai.

"It's the first I've heard of co-ed roommates," Kai pipes up, then blushes and quickly breaks eye contact when I look at him. *So adorable.*

"Well, if you guys show me to my room tonight, I'll see the administration in the morning and try to sort it out." I turn my head and notice a spiral staircase leading up to the floor above. *Nice.*

"That won't be necessary," Asher bites out, his tone as razor-sharp as those incredible grey eyes.

"Oh?" I question, turning my narrowed gaze back to him, my brow furrowed in confusion.

"You see," he begins, strolling towards me like a tiger stalking its prey, stopping a hair's breadth away. I have to crane my neck to look up at him. *Fucktrumpet.* "No one gets that room. Ever. So you'll need to find somewhere else to sleep tonight." He smiles like the Cheshire Cat, a malevolent grin pulling those pretty, plump lips up.

*Why are the pretty ones always such arseholes? Because you know they hold you down in all the right ways and make you come the hardest.* My mind argues smugly. *Bitch.*

"Excuse me?" I ask, my voice raised as my mouth drops open.

"I'm not in the habit of repeating myself, Rose, was it?" he replies, looking at his nails like he's bored of this conversation already.

"It's Lilly, arsehole," I snap back. *Can you believe this guy? Like, what the fuck?* I take it back. I bet he's shite in bed.

His slate eyes flit back to mine, darkening and then narrow to slits.

"Well, *Lilly,* you will not be staying in that room now or ever. Did you get that, or do I need to write it down?" he snarks, looking down at me with cold hard eyes like I'm the shit that's dared to get on his shoe.

"Where the fuck am I going to sleep then? It's the last room in the dorm," I ask, voice low, one arm sweeping round the room.

The others' gazes bounce between us, like a tennis match at Wimbledon, their faces full of interest at the outcome of this showdown.

"Frankly, my dear," he drawls, flashing me a frigid smile to match the coldness in his eyes. "I just don't give a fuck."

"Fine," I seethe, a plan forming in my mind.

I head to my holdall and snatch it up roughly to take with me to the bathroom, hoping something is dry. Just before I go in, I turn and stare at Asher straight in the eyes.

"By the way, Clark Gable was a hundred times more of a gentleman than you'll ever be. So I wouldn't attempt to emulate him again. At least have some originality so everyone knows what a prick you really are." With that, I walk in and slam the bathroom door.

# CHAPTER THREE

LILLY

Seething at Asher's rudeness, I slam my holdall down on the counter just as I hear the braying laugh of Loki from the other side of the door, and I smile to myself. *One point to me, zero to twatwaffle.* I start to rummage in my bag. *Bingo!* You see, I may have a slight addiction to lingerie. If it's lacy and racy, I've got to have it!

*I'll ease them in gently,* I think, pulling out a dusky rose silk teddy with black lace trim, that luckily is dry. I slip it on, a small moan of pleasure at the feel of the silk sliding across my body escaping my lips. Towelling dry my hair then finger combing it, I look in the mirror. A smirk curves my lips, and I jut my chin out as a puffed-up feeling radiates through me. My hazel eyes are sparkling, full of mischief.

I can hear faint talking as I open the door, leaving my bag where it is because fuck Ash, he can move it if he doesn't like it. When I step out, I see they're all lounging on the sofas. Four pairs of jewelled eyes snap to me, and the flare of heat that enters each pair is enough to rival the burning embers in the fireplace. They watch like hawks, I swear they're not even breathing, as I sashay out of the bathroom and cross to the stairs.

"What do you think you're doing?" Asher's voice cracks over me, although there's definitely an edge of arousal to his tone. *Arsehole, or should I say Ash-hole, snort.*

I pause on the bottom step, twisting my upper body slightly and looking at him over my shoulder.

"You said I couldn't have my room." His right eyebrow raises. "So, I figured I would sleep in someone else's," I say, wide-eyed. My pulse picks up and I bounce slightly on my feet, adrenaline surging through me.

I look at Loki. "May I share your bed for the night?" I ask, batting my eyelashes, my voice breathy.

It comes out huskier than I'd intended, my mouth a little dry. I'd be a liar if I said I wasn't a bit excited about snuggling up to the sinful angel. I'm also not ashamed to admit a breath of relief at the idea of not sleeping alone. I've struggled to sleep a whole night through since—*nope! Still not going there!*

He jumps over the back of the sofa he's sitting on, like a fire has just been lit under his arse, and beams as he walks towards me.

"Always happy to lend a *hand* to a damsel in distress." He smiles. "Or a tongue...or cock..." he adds, lowering his voice, and flashing me such a panty melting smile that has my thighs instantly clenching.

"Loki..." Asher warns, voice deep and stern, like the cockblocker he is.

Loki shrugs, in a 'what can I do' way.

"Ash, dude. She's right, ya know. You did say she couldn't sleep in *that* room. Nothing about sleeping in one of ours..."

Asher, or Ash, growls low, and fuck me if I don't clench my thighs a little tighter. Loki notices and smirks. *Wanker.*

Loki turns away with a shit-eating grin on his face, swaggering ahead of me, and I let out a gasp of surprise. On his back, he has an incredible inked angel, who is down on one knee, head bowed over crossed arms, and hands resting on his knee. His folded wings cover both of Loki's shoulders, curling over with an air of such desolation that my heart fractures in my chest like ice on a lake in spring.

*He really is a fallen angel.*

As I follow the wings that cascade down his body, I notice broken feathers littering his lower back. I can't help myself, I reach out and trace my fingers along those broken wings, causing Loki to pause, and a slight shiver to travel across his skin.

He doesn't say anything but turns back around to me, my fingers falling away, and the pain and sorrow that's in his green eyes makes my own fill with moisture, and my heart cracks even more.

We stay like that for a few moments, gazes locked and filled with hurt. Then he, once again, turns away from me and treads up the stairs. There's an ache in my chest as I watch him.

I follow him up, my steps heavier than before. Once we reach the top, there's a hallway with one door at the end and two on either side, so five in total. As we pass the first door on the right, I notice a little brass plaque on it, with a name, *Jax Griffiths*, engraved onto it. I see the other doors all have plaques with the guys' names on it as well, except for the one opposite Loki's which has nothing at all.

*Well, that's useful to know who is where.*

As Loki reaches for the brass doorknob, he looks at me over his shoulder. His eyes rake slowly up and down my silk clad body, causing my nipples to pebble, even though these dorms are toasty warm. The emerald colour of his gaze shines and sparkles as he takes in my hardened nubs, and a feline grin spreads across his lips.

"I sure hope you know what you're doing, Pretty Girl," he states in his low, smooth as honey voice.

I swallow hard and audibly, and his eyes flash to my throat, the flame in his gaze getting hotter.

*You can do this, Lilly,* I repeat to myself. *Take the comfort that's offered. Numb the pain for a little while.*

With that thought, I throw my shoulders back, putting my best breasts forward, *lols.*

"You gonna let me in or what, Angel?" I sass, one brow raised.

Loki throws his head back and crows with laughter.

"I think you'll do just fine here, Pretty Girl." He grins, looking at me appreciatively once again, then turns to open his door. He stays in the doorway, one arm held out, indicating I go ahead like a real gentleman.

"Mi casa es su casa. What's mine is all yours, Darlin'." He tells me, waggling his damn eyebrows like some sort of old man comedian.

I chuckle, relieving some of the sexual tension, and any lingering apprehension that was threatening to drown me.

As I pass him in the doorway, I'm suddenly engulfed once again with his warm vanilla scent when I take in a deep breath, and I can feel the heat from his delicious body all down my side.

I mentally lament my hardened nipples that are practically screaming for that delectable tongue of his to sweep across them. *I'm smuggling fucking peanuts here!*

*Bloody hell, Lilly! How many fucking times do we need to drag your head out of that gutter? You may as well take up residence there at this rate!*

I take another deep breath in a bid to calm myself down and look round the room, trying to distract my mind from fallen angels and the oblivion that their clever tongues can give.

His room is tastefully decorated in navy and cream with dark wood furniture. The walls are covered with a floral patterned wallpaper in the same colours, which should look feminine, but doesn't.

*Wait, is that fucking fabric on the walls?* I shake my head at the pretentiousness of it.

Opposite the door, there are floor-to-ceiling curtains in a sumptuous navy velvet that are drawn against the dark storm that is raging outside. To the right, sitting against the wall is a large dark wood desk, topped with navy leather and one of those industrial looking lamps. There's a comfy navy blue leather desk chair in front of it.

Next to that is a huge, dark wood wardrobe with a mirror in the door. I can see the reflection of what must be the biggest bed in Christendom. My head jerks to the left to look at it in the flesh.

*Devil's teeth!*

The wooden frame is dark, mahogany maybe, and it's got huge, thickly carved wooden posts draped in what must be silk curtains given the shine, which have the same pattern that the walls do.

*Definitely silk on the walls then,* I inwardly scoff. The bed is covered in navy and cream bedding, which is all deliciously rumpled like it wasn't vacated long ago.

He steps up behind me, so close I can feel the heat of his body warming my back like a furnace and I can't help leaning into the heat. A split second later, hot, sweet breath whispers in my ear.

"Like what you see?" His voice sends shivers of desperate longing down my spine, causing a cascade of tingles to trail to my extremities, right down to the tips of my toes.

*Hello, nipples. Long time no see. Not.*

"Pretty Girl, I'm hoping you weren't joking back there in front of the others. You're wrapped up so nicely, like a present just for me," he murmurs softly, still not touching me. I can't say a thing, my breath caught in my chest. I'm utterly under his spell.

"I'm very good at sharing; generous, too," he says breathily, as his finger finally makes contact and plays with the back of my waistband, leaving my nerve endings tingling. The digit then drops down to the black lacy hem, causing a soft moan to escape my lips and my eyes to close, revelling in his touch.

"You'd look exquisite on my bed, and I'd bet you come so prettily all over my sheets," he purrs against my ear, his voice like dark chocolate, decadent and sinful. "Can I make you come, baby? Can I touch you?"

I never knew the meaning of insta-lust until now. I mean, sure, I've seen guys that make my breath hitch a little, but the way Loki is speaking to me, touching me, I want to give him permission to do all the bad naughty things to me his heart desires. And I don't care what his motives are, or why he wants me so badly. I just need him not to stop.

"Yes," I beg, trembling, my legs slightly parting. I'm unable to stop this exquisite torture, even though I know I should. *For fuck's sake, I've only just met the guy!*

He steps closer, eliminating any distance between his front and my back, and I gasp at the contact, at the sudden hardness between us. His finger reaches round to the front of my knickers, slowly sliding underneath the silk, and he discovers just how wet I am. A low moan escapes my lips, my hand wrapping around his wrist tightly and holding on for dear life.

A deep groan leaves his luscious lips. Lips that have started to nibble my earlobe, causing me to burn hot with need, and desperate shivers to wrack my body. My head falls to the side to allow him better access.

"Such a good girl, so responsive," he praises as his fingers slide along my wet heat, fire radiating from his touch and my hips buck seeking more contact. "Look how wet you are for me already."

His other hand comes round my waist, supporting me as his fingers find my clit. I whimper in his arms, my unoccupied arm reaching up behind me and pulling him closer by his neck.

But I'm powerless, a slave to his clever, beautiful fingers as they play me like an instrument. A throaty moan leaves me as he continues to thrum the bundle of nerves, driving me fucking wild, and sending waves of exquisite pleasure rolling over my body. My fingers find his thick hair, tangling in it. I can't keep my eyes open, the pleasure is too intense.

*Fuck.*

"When you come, Pretty Girl," he whispers, kissing my neck, "you're going to scream my name in that sexy British accent of yours, aren't you?"

He pauses, and his hand stills too, waiting, tormenting me with its inactivity.

"Yes," I part groan, part whisper. "Please."

I'm beyond caring that I'm begging this beautiful stranger, my hips thrusting forward and my hand around his wrist gripping so tightly I'm amazed that I haven't cut off the blood flow.

"Please, what?" he taunts, still not moving his fucking fingers.

"Please, Loki!" I cry baring my teeth.

"Good girl."

I hear the smirk in his voice for a second until he slams two fingers inside me whilst the heel of his hand grinds into my clit. He crooks his fingers in a come-hither motion, and my knees buckle, his other arm banding round my waist to keep me upright.

I. Fucking. Shatter.

And of course, I'm screaming his name as I fracture into a thousand pieces and am scattered to the four winds.

---

## ASH

*"Loki!!!"*

We all hear her scream her release. I bet the fucker didn't even shut his door. *Asshole.*

I'm not the only one who adjusts himself, gritting my teeth hard enough to crack, and trying to pretend that I'm not painfully hard.

When she stepped out of the bathroom, damp from the shower, hair dripping and covered in my scent, her towel clinging to all those mouth watering curves...fuck me, I almost came in my pants like an inexperienced kid.

Her pixie features have an innocent yet wicked naughtiness about them, like a succubus who fucks you with a beautiful smile while draining the life out of you. The fact that she's shorter than us, even Kai, by a few inches, just adds to her harmless fairy vibe. Though clearly, she's got some fight in her and a tongue as sharp as a knife. My dick twitches at that thought, leaving me mentally cursing.

Jax's rumble is like thunder, and Kai is the shade of a ripe tomato. I let out a growl, my fists tight, and fingernails biting into my palms. Yet at the same time, my mind imagines me in Loki's place, making her scream my name instead of his.

*Goddammit!*

"Do you think..." Kai stutters, looking up at me with wide eyes full of longing and blown with lust, glancing up from the iPad he's been busily tapping away on. That thing is fucking stuck to his hand, and I swear he even sleeps with it. Lucky for us, as he's our tech guy and can find out anything we need to know.

*Jesus fucking Christ, the siren has us all in her thrall. She needs to be gone, pronto!*

"What?!" I snap at him, instantly feeling my stomach knot with regret at my harsh tone.

These guys are like my brothers. We've known each other our whole lives, our parents forcing us together at every turn from the moment we were born, our intertwined destinies carved in stone.

But joke's on them, because we chose each other early on by becoming closer than family, our bond stronger than anything that blood dictates. We became each others' support, a part of our very souls melding until we were several parts of a whole. We've been through the fires of Hell together and are still traveling through the scorching depths. I would do anything for these guys. I have done everything for them, sold my soul to the devil to keep them at least a little free from the blackness that eats away at me.

As leader of our group, it's my job to make the hard decisions, to take the punishments when things go wrong. I've taken beatings meant for them, and I'd take them a thousand times over if it keeps them safe.

Kai looks me in the eye, raising his chin. *Good, he's come a long way from the shy, scared kid he used to be thanks to his fucking cunt of an uncle.* He clears his throat.

"Do you think it's a good idea to, you know, let her sleep in there...with him?" he asks, his eyes traveling back towards the stairs.

I growl again, and for an instant, I almost wince, feeling a twinge of regret at my choice to deny her a room. Then I remember the reason why she can't be in there, and the feeling passes, leaving a taste of ash in my mouth and making my hard-on soften.

"I'll speak to the administration tomorrow," I scowl.

I rule this fucking place just like my father before me, and they'll bend over backwards to do as I say. No one wants to piss me off.

*Except a certain pixie faced, hazel eyed brunette...*

I look back at Kai, my brow furrowing and my muscles tingling with tightness.

"What do we know about her?" I demand, rolling my neck in a bid to ease the tension in my shoulders.

"Not much..." he sighs and looks down to the screen. "I can't seem to find much intel on her. Her application mentions a mother, Laura Darling, now deceased, and that she's British and lives, or I supposed lived, in Islington, London. She's eighteen, nineteen in May." He looks up at me again, pushing his glasses back up his nose, a frown on his face.

"And her father?" I question.

"No one listed on the birth certificate," Kai muses, gazing back down. "Although, it seems she was adopted by her uncle after her mother's death. A Mr Adrian Ramsey," he adds.

"And what do we know about Mr Ramsey?" I prod, my lips pinching at the lack of information on our little British flower.

"*Mr Adrian Ramsey, billionaire recluse who lives in the wilds of Wiltshire near Stonehenge,*" Kai reads. "*Not much is known about him, or his fortune, although we do know he's one of the world's richest bachelors. According to urban myth, he was involved in a huge scandal in his younger days, but no one knows what, and had his heart broken which caused him to shut himself away in his glorious mansion, never to emerge and never to love again.*" Kai makes a sound in the back of his throat. "Fucking gossip writers, vultures all of them," he mutters.

"And that's it?" I ask, my mind scrambling to understand how there could be nothing else.

"Oh, hang on..." Kai says, sitting up. "Here's a newspaper article on her mother's death, which happened in February this year." His eyes scan the screen rapidly, his face going deathly pale as he reads.

"What?" Jax asks in that gruff voice of his, obviously noticing Kai's pallor.

Gulping, Kai looks up at us, eyes wide and full of horror.

"It says that her mother died in an aggravated burglary gone wrong. Apparently, she was stabbed forty-seven times. Culprit unknown."

"Jesus," I whisper, my hand rubbing over my mouth.

"That's not all," he rasps. He looks sick. "Lilly found her when she came home from shopping with friends."

"Fuck!" Jax growls, punching the cushion next to him.

"Anything else?" I ask, a cool calmness descending over me until I become what everyone calls me, *The Ice Knight.*

"There's a police report. It confirms that the culprit has never been found; it's an open case..." he trails off, curses, then drops the iPad on the rug like it's burnt him.

On the screen is what I recognize as a police photograph of the crime scene, showing a pile of butchered meat, in a pool of blood, with a face incredibly similar to Lilly's. It's the only thing that's recognizable...It's what Lilly came home to.

*Fucking Hell.*

The ice surrounding me cracks a little as I sit there, staring at what used to be Lilly's mom.

"That's it," he sighs, taking his glasses off and rubbing his own hand across his face.

Taking a deep breath, I look up at them. My brothers in all but blood.

"This doesn't change anything," I coldly say. "She can't stay here. She doesn't belong here. And we need more intel, Kai. So see what you can dig up about the uncle." Kai nods then bends to pick up his iPad. "It's all too fucking mysterious for my liking," I finish, the black wings of panic at all the unknowns fluttering in my peripheral vision.

There's a mystery here, and I fucking hate mysteries. *Who the fuck is Adrian Ramsey? And how the fuck do we know nothing about him?*

*But most importantly, who is Lilly Darling?*

# CHAPTER FOUR

LILLY

I gradually wake up floating on a cloud wrapped in a cocoon of epic snuggliness. I've not slept so well in a long time. It feels like years, but really it has only been months since...*nope! I'm not going there today either!* Heat rises behind my closed eyelids as I shove the memories back down, locking them up tight.

Stretching, I feel a delicious ache between my thighs and a firm hot body to my right.

*Ah, yes. I'm in Loki of the magical fingers' bed. At Highgate Prep.*

I turn my head, finally opening my eyes, and my breath catches as I drink my bed partner in. He sleeps on his front with the sheets tangled low on his back, that glorious, devastating fallen angel tattoo on full display in the light coming from the slightly ajar curtains.

*He's so beautiful it hurts my heart.*

There's a fluttering in my chest, my mouth becoming moist as I gaze at his sleeping face and that mop of thick curly red hair. He smells even better than he did yesterday, like freshly baked vanilla shortbread, and hot chocolate by the fire when it's snowing outside, all mixed in with a manly musk that has my nostrils flaring to take in more.

I have to fist my hands into the sheets to stop myself from reaching out and touching him, or claiming his lush, full lips and disturbing his slumber. My eyes catch again on that tattoo, remembering the drowning pain in his emerald gaze last night.

"One day, I'll tell you about it," he rumbles in the sexiest purr, his voice rough, sending wonderful shivers skittering over my skin.

My eyes flick up to meet his, seeing a seriousness that looks at odds on his face, which has mostly been cocky arrogance thus far. He blinks, and the serious look is gone, replaced with that shit eating grin I'm becoming quickly addicted to.

"Morning, Pretty Girl. Sleep well?"

His eyes take in my dishevelled hair and rumpled silk teddy, heat burning in them as he makes his way down to where the covers are pooling at my waist. Normally, I'm a blanket hog, but these rooms are toasty as fuck!

"Very." My smile unfocused as I replay the night before in my mind. "I was incredibly relaxed, and I don't even remember dropping off." My tone teasing, but with an edge of hunger.

*Those fingers. Good lord!*

"You were definitely *sated,* and I had to pretty much carry you to bed," he drawls, his grin also turning naughty.

"Oh, I don't know." I stretch again, deliberately pushing out my breasts and smirking when his eyes land on them. "I could definitely be more *sated,*" I purr, licking my lower lip and feeling an anticipatory flutter in my stomach.

"Naughty, Pretty Girl," he chuckles, leaning over and reaching for me.

"But first, I've gotta pee," I sass as I slip out of bed, and he lands on his face with an oomph.

I chuckle as I make my way out of the bedroom and down the stairs to the bathroom. I'm so lost in my own fallen angel fantasy that I only notice someone stepping out of the shower once I've sat down, silk teddy round my ankles, and started to pee.

*Cue facepalm. Again. And why is there no lock on the fucking door?*

I stop mid-flow, and my mouth drops open. Like literally, it's almost hitting my knees as I take in the unbelievable sight before me.

Jax stands there, stark bollock naked, frozen in place reaching for a towel. His body is so ripped, huge, and dripping wet that I'm rendered speechless.

*Eyes above the waist, Lilly.* Of course, I fail at this abysmally as my eyes trace the valley of his abs, that lickable adonis belt, and...

*Jesus fucking Christ on a cross!*

My face heats and I must be bright red, but he's huge every-fucking-where! Like dude is packing some serious man meat. *Man meat?! Really?!* I cringe at my inner monologue. Although, I mean, I'm not wrong on the size front.

"Enjoying the view, Pretty Girl?" A drawl comes from the doorway, and I startle as my head whips round to find Loki, the bastard, grinning at me. It seems to surprise Jax too as he finally grabs a towel and covers up.

"It's huge," I whisper, looking at Jax's towel covered crotch. "I mean, how does he even fit it in his trousers?" Not realising I've said this last part out loud until I hear a deep rumbling cough that makes my eyes dart up to see Jax, an almost smirk on his face. Of course, Loki throws his head back and crows with laughter.

"I don't know whether to be offended or amused," Loki chuckles, not looking annoyed in the least as he grins at me.

"Although," he says slowly, "it's not what you have but what you do with it that counts, right?" He winks at me like the trickster that his name suggests.

"'Scuse me," Jax grumbles, shoving Loki out of the way when he goes through the door, sending the smaller man crashing into the doorframe.

"Hey, dude! I'm not doubting you know what to do with your...man meat," Loki teases as I groan, covering my face with my hands, and dying of embarrassment realising that I must have said the phrase out loud.

I'm also still sitting on the fucking toilet with lingerie round my ankles and my tits out. *Real fucking classy, Lilly.*

"I'll leave you to your...what do you British say? Ablutions," he cheekily says, whilst making no bones about staring at my exposed tits. He shuts the door, and I hear him chuckling whilst saying "man meat" as he walks off.

*Ablutions? Are we in a fucking Jane Austen novel?*

I take a deep breath, before a grin completely takes over my face.

*Fucking man meat!*

---

After I've finished on the toilet, I decide to have a shower, because why the fuck not, right?

I emerge, wrapped in a fluffy white towel and smelling like a zingy lemon from the shower gel I've just used, to find all four guys sitting round the dining table. The wonderful smell of bacon, pancakes, and eggs wafts in the air, making my stomach growl.

I groan aloud, who doesn't like breakfast all drizzled in syrup? *One of America's culinary achievements, in my opinion.*

All eyes snap to me, and it's like looking at a sea of jewels, if jewels could look hungry and sinful. Loki's eyes are a stunning green, light jade round his pupil, then darkening to emerald round the rim. Jax's are a piercing blue, like a glacier encapsulated in a diamond, and have a thin rim of navy round the edge. There are a myriad of different blues streaking through them, and his gaze reminds me of a wolf's, ready to devour you. Ash has eyes the colour of steel, like darkest moissanite that are shot through with grey and black diamonds. They're so unusual that I get lost in them, and am surprised to find that they aren't cold like I first thought last night, but full of molten heat.

The unbidden idea that I want to keep them all suddenly comes to mind.

*Wait...what?! Where the fuck did that come from? You've been reading too many reverse harem books, Lilly Darling!*

"We made enough for you," a soft, melodic voice invites, my eyes finding a beautiful honey brown gaze, like the finest amber full of warmth staring back at me. The final gemstone to add to my collection. Kai's cheeks are slightly pink as he talks, indicating the seat on his right with his hand. He clears his throat.

"We usually eat breakfast up here, even though there's the dining hall," his voice cascades over me like soothing water on stone. "You're welcome to join us. If you want to, that is?" An edge of vulnerability enters his tone, and as I walk towards him, I notice he has the thickest eyelashes on a guy that I've ever seen. I can see them better now that he's not wearing his glasses.

I head to sit down when Loki's familiar drawl caresses over my skin.

"Not that I object, Pretty Girl. But do you think you might want to get dressed first? Poor Kai looks like he's about to have a heart attack. And it is a little distracting." He chuckles, and I notice Kai's cheeks staining a deeper pink.

"Oh. Yes, of course. I'll just be a minute," I say, my own face heating in response. I look around for my bags, but don't see them.

"I took them up to my room," Loki smirks.

"That was very presumptuous, Loki. I may be in someone else's bed tonight," I tease without thinking—*brain meet filter!*—and even though my ears feel hot, a satisfied grin tips my lips when I see a frown mar his beautiful face.

I gasp, my skin tingling when I hear a deep, rumbling chuckle from the other side of the table that does naughty things to my core. My eyes catch Jax's blue ones, his blond hair up in a delicious messy man bun that begs to be gripped whilst I ride his face.

*Down girl!* I admonish my vagina.

"After all," my eyes swing back to Loki, "you did say you were good at sharing," I wink.

Poor Kai splutters his orange juice, and when I look at Ash, I can see he has a white knuckle grip on his knife and fork. *Interesting.*

With that, I turn and sashay my way up the stairs to find some clothes, making sure to swing my hips more than usual.

Once in Loki's room, I lay out my outfit for the day and drop my towel. On the bed lies a bright red lacy bra and knicker set, Run & Fly rainbow corduroy pinafore mini dress, a white long-sleeved crop top, white knee high socks, and my red gingham Irregular Choice heels with fake cherries on the toes.

Suddenly, the door crashes open, making me yelp and spin round. In walks Loki, a teasing grin on his face.

"Let's make one thing clear, Pretty Girl," he states darkly as he stalks towards me, and I back up until the back of my knees hit the bed. "I'm happy to share," he smirks, running a finger down my naked side, "but I get the first taste."

With that, he drops to his knees in front of me, then grabs my right leg and slings it over his shoulder. I have to grab the bedpost with my hand for support as he licks me from opening to clit, my sharp intake of breath audible in the room as my core floods with a sudden needy heat.

"Fucking delicious," he groans in that deep voice of his, sending further tingles across my pussy. "And dripping already. Such a good girl."

"Loki..." I breathe as fire races up from my core.

"Oh, you'll be doing better than that, Pretty Girl," he commands. "By the time I'm done, there'll be no doubt who claimed you first."

He lowers his head back down to my aching cunt and licks and sucks like I'm a drink of water, and he's lost in the desert and parched.

*Fuck me.* I grab his hair with my right hand, tangling my fingers in those red curls, and pull him closer, a satisfied growl vibrating across my wet folds as he goes deeper, tongue fucking me until I feel ready to explode.

"Yes! Fuck yes, Loki!" I cry out, and my eyes open to see our reflection in the mirror of the wardrobe. Him on his knees, worshipping me with that clever tongue.

As I gaze at the erotic sight, he sucks hard on my clit, then nibbles it. The edge of pain is my undoing, and my orgasm is so fast and hard, I almost black out. My knees wobble, the pleasure so intense that I see stars.

"Loki!" I scream my release, not caring that the others can hear me. Again.

He drinks my release like it's ambrosia from the gods, giving me a few leisurely licks that leave me twitching, before standing up and wiping his mouth with his thumb, licking that as well like he can't miss a drop.

"Like I said, fucking delicious," he drawls.

Then he turns round and saunters off like the arsehole that he is.

# CHAPTER FIVE

LILLY

Once my legs have stopped shaking, *I swear one day I'm gonna walk out on him in a quivering heap of post orgasm*, I get dressed, grab my leather satchel, and head downstairs with a pep in my step and humming under my breath.

As I reach the bottom, I see the guys waiting by the door for me. It amazes me how different they are, yet even in the short time that I've known them—twelve hours, maybe?—I can see how strong their bond is, that they are a unit. There's an aura about them, one that feels dark and dangerous, and tells everyone here is a brotherhood, forged in fire.

Loki's grinning, his lips still glistening. *Did he even wash up?* My breath hitches as I recall those lips on my lower ones, his tongue dancing inside me.

He's wearing light blue denim low-slung jeans, a green faded band t-shirt, and a black leather jacket. He looks every inch the fallen angel I've pegged him to be, his flaming hair all mussed up, probably from my fingers which twitch with the memory, and his clothes slightly dishevelled. He carries himself with a lazy insouciance, like a big jungle cat waiting for its prey to walk past.

Kai's sporting a sexy geek look, with mustard yellow chinos, a black and white gingham shirt all buttoned up and complete with a cheeky red bow tie, and a charcoal knit cardigan left open. His black framed glasses are back in place, and his thick chestnut hair is sticking up as if he's been running his hands through it, my own hands itching to feel its softness. He may be the smallest, but he still has buff biceps; the cardigan is tight and clings to his arms, confirming that he definitely works out.

Jax simply looks like a wet dream, my hands clenching and opening as I gaze at him. He's in bootleg black jeans, a black t-shirt that's so tight it looks like it's ready to burst, and kick-ass boots, also black. His tattoo sleeve flows effortlessly down his arm, highlighting all those lickable muscles, and as if desperate to enact that thought, my tongue darts out to touch my lips. At first, I thought his ink was tribal, but in the daylight it looks Norse, with Celtic knots and runes interlocking and running all the way down, covering the back of his hand. His blond locks are tied up in that delicious man bun, and his short beard is neat and tidy.

Then we have Ash. He may be an Ash-hole, but even Lucifer himself would be proud. He's in a navy suit—*like, what eighteen year old wears a fucking suit?* —with a grey pinstripe waistcoat, crisp white shirt, and dark blue tie, complete with an oak leaf motif in gold. His jet black hair is slicked back and tamed, and his face is set in an arrogant scowl which doesn't detract one bit from his beautiful perfection. My lips part just looking at him, and I catch myself leaning forward towards him.

Gorgeous or not, he's still an utter ballbag, which he proves seconds later.

"Glad you could deign us with your presence, Princess,"

His voice drips with condescension as he gives me a once over, top lip slightly curled and almost sneering. If I didn't know better, I'd say there was a touch of jealousy in his grey eyes.

*Princess?* I raise one brow in response.

"Let's get to the administration office, shall we, and sort this clusterfuck out." He turns on his highly polished, no doubt extraordinarily expensive heel, and storms out.

As I reach the others, Kai holds out something wrapped in foil, that dusting of pink on his cheeks.

"I made you a pancake wrap to go," he tells me, avoiding my eyes.

"You are a legend and officially my new favourite!" I smile and kiss him on the cheek, seeing his ears go red, and leave a red lipstick mark there. It's by

Urban Decay called Alpha, in Mega Matte and I love how badass it makes me feel.

"What the fuck, Pretty Girl?" Loki splutters, his hands splayed in the air. "I just fucking rocked your world up there! How am I not your favorite?" He looks at me like I just kicked his puppy, and I can't help but laugh.

"I'm sure you can make your way back up there again, Loki," I tease as I turn away and head in Ash's direction, the others following closely behind.

Twenty minutes later, I have a shiny, new, school issued iPad—*this place is bonkers!*—with everything I need to know about my classes, a map of the school, and a whole load of stuff I am completely overwhelmed by on it.

Back home, I'd only be taking four classes at this stage, but here I have like thirteen. To be fair, I get to take cool subjects like Botany and Yoga, so I can't complain too much.

Alongside my new things, I also have a silent—at least for now—fuming Ash, complete with a jaw tick, who was told in no uncertain terms by the nice lady behind the oak desk, that there simply wasn't anywhere else for me to go as all rooms had been allocated. Apparently, I was a late addition to the year group, even though this is everyone's first day of classes.

We turn away from the office as a group and start to make our way to our class.

"Don't fucking think this means you get that room," Ash snarls at me, pointing a long finger in my direction. There's such venom in his tone that I'm taken aback and quite literally stops me in my tracks. I blink, at a complete loss for words, stunned by his instant...*hate?*

I feel a warm arm land across my shoulders and am surrounded by the scent of vanilla and cocoa.

"Chill, dude," Loki's familiar drawl wraps round me like a warm blanket, providing comfort. "She's in *my room*, *my bed*, so she doesn't need it anyway."

The two guys lock gazes and stare at one another, Loki all casual arrogance, Ash practically vibrating. Neither bows down until finally, Ash growls, in a really fucking sexy way, and once again storms off.

"What is his problem?" I ask as I look up at my angel. *Wait! My angel?* "Why does he hate me?"

His emerald gaze meets mine and softens.

"It's not you, Pretty Girl," he speaks softly, hand tracing my jaw, "something...happened last year and he's still..."

"Loki," Jax rumbles, a warning note in his voice.

I swear every time that man speaks, somewhere a fairy orgasms.

The guys exchange an intense look, one I can't interpret. Then Jax follows the direction Ash took, glancing back with an ever so slightly apologetic look in his eyes. Kai turns to me, a definite look of sorrow in his honeyed depths.

"Catch you later, Lilly," he says, smiling softly at me, then follows them down the hall.

"Forget about him." Loki turns to me, panty melting grin firmly back in place. "Let me show you round. We both have free periods now according to your schedule."

"How do you know that?" I ask, my eyes widening, because even I don't know my fucking timetable.

"Oh, I sent it to myself from your iPad when I was helping you set it up."

---

Loki is a very thorough tour guide, showing me all of the places where secret trysts happen, and where they smoke weed. He also shows me where the dining hall is and the classrooms, which is probably more useful at the present time.

Our next stop is in front of enormous double wooden doors with, '*Once you learn to read, you will be forever free'* written in the scrolling script above them.

"Pretty Girl," he states in his deep, sexy voice. "There's something I wanna show you. But first, you have to close your eyes. It's a surprise."

"Okay..." I reply, raising my brows, wondering what he's up to.

I close my eyes, then hear him opening the door. He takes my hand and leads me into the room. I'm immediately surrounded by the musky smell of old books.

"Can I open them now?" I ask, my stomach fluttering.

"Yes," he laughs.

Opening my eyes, I am confronted with my very own Disney Princess moment. Floor to epically high ceiling bookcases surrounds me, absolutely filled chock-a-block with books.

"Did you just..." I start, staring at him, completely stunned and feeling giddy. "Did you just fucking Beauty and the Beast me?" I'm knocked for six.

"My little sisters are crazy obsessed with the movie, and I watched it like a million times over the summer. So when I saw all the books you had in your bag..." he grimaces slightly, looking a little bashful all of a sudden, and rubbing the back of his neck.

With a delighted squeal, I launch myself at him and climb that boy like the fucking tree he is, ignoring the fact that he went rifling through my things. I wrap my legs around his hips, kissing him soundly on the lips. Luckily, he catches me, hands cupping my arse. He groans as he traces my lace knickers with his fingers.

"Christ, Lilly," he moans. "You make me fucking wild for you," he murmurs, kissing me back hard whilst walking us towards the stacks.

He finds a dark alcove, fuck knows how, and pushes me up against the cold stone wall, nibbling my neck, those clever fingers tracing my aching slit through my knickers and finding my clit.

"Loki..." I whisper, trying to clear my head of this haze he always seems to create whenever he's near.

"What?" He grins saucily as he slides his finger under the lace and finds me fucking soaked. "I fucking love it when your cunt drips for me," his voice is husky, lips smeared in red from my lipstick.

"Now, Pretty Girl, I'm gonna make you come first with my hand, then as your beautiful pussy is still fluttering, I'm gonna fill you up with my cock and fuck you until you see stars," he promises as I whimper beneath his touch.

"But here's the thing," he continues in that delicious purr, his fingers still teasing me. "This time you can't scream my name, you have to be quiet because we're in a library, and the books deserve respect." He's building me up so slowly with his words and teasing touch, I'm almost weeping with the need for release, my heart pounding painfully in my chest. "Can you manage that, Pretty Girl?"

I nod, incapable of speech as his fingers play me like he's a master musician.

"Good girl," he croons, slipping two fingers inside me, pumping them in and out, and grinding his palm against my clit.

My thighs tremble under his touch, my breath panting and he builds the pace.

"What about the librarian?" I manage to choke out, gasping as he applies more pressure to the bundle of nerves.

"Ah, don't worry about her, Pretty Girl," he drawls between shiver-inducing nibbles. "She's probably flicking the bean in the fantasy section," he scoffs.

"Loki!" I admonish, snapping my head up to look at him.

"Ahem," a feminine cough sounds behind Loki, and I freeze, my eyes going wide with panic.

"Busted," Loki grumbles under his breath, his fingers stilling as he rests his forehead against mine.

"I'm not sure that this is the best use of the library, Mr Thorn," the female voice continues.

I move my head slightly to peep over Loki's shoulder to see an older woman in a twin set and pearls standing a few feet away.

Her greying hair is in a severe bun at her nape, and she has a perfectly plucked eyebrow raised as she looks at us with wry amusement. She's clutching several books tightly to her chest, her lips pursed, but not in anger. If I didn't know better, I'd say she's trying not to laugh. I decide then that I like this librarian.

Loki chuckles, his fingers still inside of me, and I try not to groan with the slight movement. My face is bright red with heat, and it flares hotter as my gaze catches hers over his shoulder.

"Ah, Miss Darling, our new British student," she says, not missing a beat, a warm smile on her lips. "Pleased to make your acquaintance."

"Uh, yeah, you too," I stammer out, wriggling out of Loki's hold, his hand slipping away as my feet hit the ground.

*I can't believe I met her with his fingers knuckle deep inside me!* I surreptitiously try and pull my dress down as I continue to hide behind him.

"My name is June, June Buck," she tells me, not moving any closer which is a fucking relief, and still with a look of mirth on her face.

"Lilly, Lilly Darling," I reply, finally somewhat presentable, although my hands tremble slightly as they smooth down my dress. I step away from Loki to face June.

"A pleasure, Lilly. Now, it may have escaped your attention, but it's lunchtime, so you might want to make your way over to the dining hall," she informs us, her tone teasing and full of suppressed laughter.

"Sure thing, *June*," Loki drawls in that way of his, completely nonplussed by the whole encounter, like he didn't just get caught fingering me in the library!

He takes my hand in his, not the one that was bringing me such pleasure, and starts to lead us away, an arrogant swagger to his step as he makes a show of bringing his other fingers to his mouth and sucking them. *Floor swallow me now, please.*

June steps aside as we pass, making room for us to walk past.

"Oh, and Mr Thorn?" I hear June say behind us, making us both pause and turn to look back at her. "I much prefer Science Fiction to Fantasy," she deadpans, but I swear there's a twinkle in her eye.

*Fucking crushed it!*

Loki barks out a laugh, and I don't bother to hide my own chuckle at that awesome one-liner, then we both cringe slightly, the mental image obviously hitting him the same time it does me.

We turn back towards the doors, and I'm sure I hear a wicked chortle behind me, as we make our way out of the library, hand in hand and laughing as we go.

---

## LOKI

I grip Lilly's hand tightly as we head down the hall, pulling her so close that I'm breathing in the lemon scent of Jax's fucking body wash. *I'll make sure she uses mine again tomorrow. I'll fill the whole fucking shower with bottles of the stuff if she keeps smelling like me.*

Underneath, I can smell Lilly's own natural perfume. It's like spring and new beginnings, fresh starts, and a hope so sweet that I want to weep, run, and pull her closer all at the same damn time. She's like a breath of fresh air, light after the darkest night, the warmth of spring sunshine after a freezing cold winter.

*She's turning me into a fucking poet.*

And I couldn't give less of a shit. I'm already fucking addicted. I can't get enough of her, and whenever she's near me, I want to touch her, taste her, and get lost in her smile and warm curves.

I don't know why I did that dumb Disney shit at the doors, I guess I thought that it would make her smile. And I want to make her smile because damn, when she does, my whole world fucking lights up like the Fourth of July. And when she screams my name...fuck, I'm gone.

I've had plenty of girls before, shit, I've fucked hundreds. I just take them wherever and whenever I like, not bothering to remember their names or faces. They help to take away the darkness a little, and getting lost in soft bodies is my addiction.

My brothers and I all have things that help us to get through the day. To face the monsters that we've had to become.

But I've never felt like this before with any of the others. Like the shadows and pain disappear when she's nearby. Like I can finally take a big breath of pure fresh air when I touch her. She makes me forget that I'm damaged, a devil, filled with a black soul and rotten on the inside. When I'm with her, I feel like there might just be a glimmer of light hiding beneath the pitch black.

I don't know what this is, what we might be. Hell, I've known her for less than twenty-four hours. And these feelings scare the shit out of me. But I'm not giving her up. Or the freedom that she brings with her.

I know that she's what we all need, especially after last year. After everything we've done, and will continue to do. I'm also pretty damn sure that we're no good for her. We give pain and suffering, what else can we offer her besides that?

But I'm too selfish to let her go, not after spending so long in the dark. I need her light, we all do. Even if it means that she becomes a little tainted along the way.

We are the Black Knights after all.

# CHAPTER SIX

LILLY

As we make our way to the dining hall, a sudden flare of apprehension comes over me, making me halt in the middle of the corridor, an empty feeling in my stomach.

*Oh lord! Have I missed any classes?* I panic, letting go of Loki's hand and searching in my bag for my tablet to try and work out what I may have missed.

"Don't worry, Pretty Girl," Loki assures me. "I got passes for us and I've let your teachers know I was showing you round."

"How?" I ask, frowning and stopping my frantic search, looking up at him.

"The teacher message app." He rolls his eyes like it's obvious.

Which it's not, not to me at least. I mean my mum and I were comfortable, we could buy nice things and afford the odd shopping splurge. But when I went to a state school, we didn't have school issued iPads, or apps, or dining halls, or a hundred other things these rich kids take for granted. I guess, considering my uncle gives me a more than generous allowance, I'm now one of them. *I shudder*.

Loki notes my confusion, a questioning look on his face.

"We didn't have any of this at my old school," I say, shaking my head and gesturing around me. "We had to carry round textbooks, write notes by hand, speak to teachers," his brow pinches in a frown with every word I say.

"Huh," he replies with a shrug, as if the concept of actually having to carry a textbook or write anything by hand is so foreign to him he can't even compute it. "So, what brings you here, Pretty Girl?"

I can't help it. A laugh bursts out from my lips, effectively dissipating the slight resentment I was starting to feel towards the wealthy elite of the school, Loki included. *What a line!*

"Really? That's the line you chose to go with?" I chuckle, and he smiles ruefully, his cheeks colouring a little.

"I just want to know more about you is all," he responds, slinging his arm across my shoulders, and we carry on walking.

"You want to know more about *me*...?" I question, one eyebrow raising, and my words trailing off when I see the serious look in his eyes.

"I want to know *everything* about you, Pretty Girl," he encourages.

"Okay..." I begin, a tingling sensation starting up in my chest as I look round. I don't know why, but I'm hesitant to share too much of myself. He has seen me naked at least twice now so I feel a little foolish, but there it is. "Let's see. To answer your earlier question, my uncle suggested I come here as this is where he went to school, and I wanted a bit of a fresh start so thought, fuck it, why not?"

"Ah, so you're a legacy. Like us," he informs me, a genuine interest in his tone.

"A what?" I enquire, looking up at him.

"A legacy, you know, our parents came here so now we do too. Is that not a thing back in England?" he asks me, and my heart skips a beat at the sight of those beautiful green eyes so close.

"Not really. Although, never having gone to a posh school like this one before, maybe it is?"

"Posh school or not, we now have at least two things in common," he replies with a mischievous smile.

"What's the other thing we have in common?" I query, almost dreading his answer if that look in his eye is anything to go by.

"Getting great satisfaction when you come," he tells me, in complete seriousness that it's ruined slightly by the smirk on his beautiful lips.

I roll my eyes and shake my head at him, but at the same time, I feel the heat in my cheeks at the mention of what this man can do to my body.

"Tell me more," he orders after a moment.

I chuckle and take a deep breath.

"Well, my favourite colour is rainbow. I'm allergic to cats. I love dark chocolate. My favourite novels are reverse harem..."

"What the fuck is reverse harem?" Loki interrupts me, an eyebrow arched.

"You know, one girl, three or more guys?" I shoot back, looking at him then quickly glancing away, feeling my cheeks flame again and my palms go a little sweaty.

"Oh! Like a gangbang!" Loki grins, a salacious look in his green eyes.

"No!" I yell, stopping to glare at him and drawing the attention of a couple of students walking past who probably think I am into gangbangs now. *Fucking great.* "*Not* like a gangbang," I correct him, lowering my voice, looking ahead, and carrying on walking. "There's a story and everything."

"But there's sex in the book. Between more than just one guy and the girl?" he asks, and when I glance at him he looks all too happy to see me squirm in embarrassment.

"Yes...but...I'm not getting into this with you!" I huff out as his shoulders start to shake with repressed laughter.

"Oh, Pretty Girl, don't be mad! I'd love to read one of your 'not a gang-bang' books," he teases, chuckling harder when I whack him in his hard as a fucking rock abs. *Ow! Stupid man muscles!*

"Tell me something else," he demands, still smiling like the arsehole he is. "What about your parents?"

The blood drains from my face, and I hear a wind begin to whistle in my ears.

"I never knew my father, and, well, my mother died in February this year." I say in a rush, swallowing, as my eyes start to fill, the wound of her death still fresh and bleeding. The guilt from that day still claws at me, and I'm left breathless for a moment.

"I had a sort of stepfather, well, Mum's long term boyfriend Ryan, but he kinda bailed after she passed away," I add sadly, the pain of his disappearing act adding to the hurt I feel in the centre of my being.

I realise that we've come to a standstill in the middle of the hallway, and

Loki pulls me into him, surrounding me with his warm, comforting body and rubbing circles on my back. I breathe in his vanilla cookie scent and relax in his arms. He smells like...*home*. I feel so safe in his strong arms and wish that I could stay here forever.

"I know it's not worth a damn, and won't change anything, but I'm so sorry she died, Pretty Girl," he says gently and kisses me on the head.

I take another deep lungful of air and look up, his image wavering a little with the unshed tears marring my vision. One slips free, and he catches it on his finger, bringing it to his lips and tasting my sorrow.

"Thank you, Loki," I whisper hoarsely, clearing my throat, and falling into those stunning emerald depths of his as we stand there.

"Anytime, baby," he whispers back huskily, his own eyes glistening with what looks like a pain similar to my own.

"LOKI!!!"

A screech like a female fox in heat interrupts us, assaulting my ears and I feel Loki's arms tightening round me, a soft curse sounding under his breath. I cringe at the sound, and turn to look behind me, keeping his strength wrapped round me.

A girl is hurrying down the corridor, her artfully tousled, blonde wavy hair flying behind her. She's wearing a faded pink 'save the turtles' baggy cropped t-shirt, a shell necklace, light blue cropped denim jeans, and white trainers. In her hand, she carries a metal water bottle covered in stickers and has a backpack slung over one shoulder.

*Oh, my giddy aunt! Is this...is she...a VSCO girl?!*

Don't know what a VSCO girl is? Basically, a teenage girl who spends twenty minutes making her messy bun look just so, and spends a small fortune on her casual outfit, all while spouting about 'saving the whales,' yet buying plastic stickers to stick on her reusable water bottle. Yeah, that kind of girl.

She comes right up to us, totally ignoring my presence, and is flanked by two girls dressed very similarly, both carrying the same metal water bottles. One has dark brown hair, the other black, but basically, they are all clones of each other.

"How was your summer, Loki?" she purrs, fluttering her eyelash extensions and twiddling her hair.

*I didn't know girls actually did that. And how fucking rude is this eco warrior cumbubble to just ignore me? Are we in some fucked up teen romance movie?*

I roll my eyes and chuckle at my own joke, turning round in Loki's arms so that I can face the she-wolf head on.

"Oh, hey, Amber," Loki replies in a bored tone, keeping his eyes on me and not even looking at her before stepping to my side and tucking me under his arm once again. "Have you met, Lilly?" he adds, gesturing to me with his other hand.

Her blue gaze flits over to me, her upper lip curling slightly, ruining her pretty features as she takes me in. *Cue the Mean Girl cliché.*

"Oh. You must be the Brit," she sneers, looking at me like I've just offered her turtle soup. "Charmed, isn't that what you British say?" she asks with a titter as her flunkies laugh behind her. *Yep. I officially hate the bitchtits.*

"You must be one of those VSCO girls I've heard about," I reply sweetly, flashing her a cold smile. "Tell me, how are the turtles doing here in the mountains?" *Silly cumdumpster! Teach her to be rude!*

She scowls even more, and I just can't resist poking the hornet's nest again.

"I hear the best eyelash extensions are made from mink, who suffer greatly on breeding farms and are ultimately killed for their fur. Did you go for the best, or did you get cheap plastic ones?" I blink innocently as Loki roars with laughter beside me, and Amber's eyes narrow, setting said extensions quivering.

"And on that note..." Loki chuckles once more as he leads me away from the scowling trio, towards what I assume is the dining hall.

---

As we enter through the double doors, I halt in my tracks, my eyes widening and my mouth becoming slack as Loki's arm drags across my shoulders when he keeps walking a few steps. He pauses and turns to look at me, a questioning red brow raised.

*Holy shit.*

I'm surrounded by light. Glorious, brilliant sunshine pours through the walls, two of which are entirely made from glass and held up by what looks like elegant black metal trees. The ceiling soars above us and is also made of glass so that it feels as though we are standing outside. Round Swedish design beechwood tables fill the space with matching chairs, and along the right hand side are counters filled with food to go, reminiscent of Harrods food hall in London.

"You coming, Pretty Girl?" Loki's increasingly familiar drawl comes from ahead.

I emerge from my daze to see his eyes full of amusement, causing my own to narrow back at him.

*Fucktwollop.*

We head to join the other guys at a table, my eyebrows lowering to see it's occupied by them and no one else.

"Where are, like, your cronies, minions, or probably in Asher's case, slaves?" I ask, puzzled by the lack of hangers-on. "Aren't you guys like...popular?"

I hear a low, rumbling growl that could also be a chuckle come from Jax as Ash's eyes narrow and he glares at me from across the table. He doesn't even bother with a reply, just gives me a once over, no doubt noticing my dishevelled appearance. A slight twitch in his cheek appears briefly, then he goes back to looking down at his phone.

Of course, Loki crows with laughter and is the one to reply, pulling me onto a seat next to him.

"We are popular, Pretty Girl. I mean, of course we are. Just look at us," he preens, getting a napkin thrown at him by Kai. "But we don't wanna be surrounded by ass kissers, we've got the rest of our lives for that," he sighs, his eyes dulling.

Then his face brightens, a mischievous grin on his lips. "And Ash keeps his slaves in the dungeon, only letting them out after dark, or when he wants to do terrible things to them."

The man in question snaps his head up, and his eyes turn to slits, swimming with danger. I should be afraid of that look, but all it does is start a burn between my thighs, and cause my nipples to tighten under my bra.

*Damn, get it under control, Lilly!*

Before Ash can do or say anything else, I shit you not, a waiter dressed in a black tailcoat comes to the table to take our orders.

*Where am I?*

I look round but can't see a menu, then hear a sigh from my left as Loki leans in.

"The day's menu is on your iPad, Pretty Girl," he says, tickling my ear with his breath and causing a shiver to cascade down my body.

"Oh," I reply in a breathy tone, my hand coming to my throat as my cheeks grow hot. Of course, Loki smirks, but I can see Kai, who's on my right, start to flush pink.

"Ummm…" I begin as I fumble in my bag trying to find my iPad.

"For fuck's sake!" Ash snaps from across the table, making my head jerk up and my lips press into a white slash. "She'll have what I'm having, Gerald," he continues, not even looking at me, and I flood with embarrassed outrage, my hands curling into fists. I'm also a little surprised that he actually knows the waiter's name. I thought rich pricks didn't bother with details like that.

Before I can tell Gerald that I don't eat the same as fucktrumpets, he's rushed off in a flurry of tails. I look back to Ash, who has a single jet black brow raised, cold eyes boring into mine, waiting to see what I'll do next.

*Your time will come, thundercunt.*

I ignore him, crossing my arms and turning to Kai. "How was your morning?"

Poor guy blushes berry red and stutters out, "F–f–fine, thank you," then buries his head back into his iPad.

I sigh, glancing round the room and catching the eye of The Cumdumpster, aka Amber, sitting at another table. Her eyes narrow—I seem to be inciting that reaction in a few people recently—then they flit to Loki.

I turn to him, with a devilish smirk on my face, and lean in close, my breasts brushing his arm. He smells like vanilla and days spent naked by a fire, and it's no hardship to lick the outside of his ear, sucking his earlobe into my mouth and gently tugging on it with my teeth. He abruptly stops his conversation with Jax, and from the corner of my eye, I can see his hands clench as they rest on the table, his knuckles turning white.

My gaze flits back up to Amber's, noticing with a warmth that spreads through my body, that her face is reddening more by the second, and her teeth are bared in a snarl.

*That's right. Mine, bitch. I'll hump his leg if I have to stake my claim!*

Without moving, Loki whispers, "If you keep doing that, Pretty Girl, I'll have to bend you over this table and fuck you so hard in front of everyone that you'll walk like a cowgirl for days."

His words distract me from my petty revenge, and I gasp at the thought of being watched, my thighs clenching and breath quickening.

"Ah," he smirks, noticing the movement. "I see you like the idea of an audience." His shit-eating grin is now positively sinful. He leans in closer, lips brushing my ear and sending delicious tingles racing across my jaw. "I'm sure we can convince one of the others to join us, if you like?"

I can't stop the small involuntary moan that escapes, causing three more sets of jewelled eyes to swing my way.

"Who would you like most, I wonder?" Loki continues in his deep, delicious voice, "Jax and his...*man meat*?" He gives a husky chuckle at that which does naughty things to my lady parts. "Or maybe Kai and his...toys? Although, fair warning, he's much less sweet in the bedroom than you've seen so far," he teases. "Or perhaps Ash and his penchant for ropes?"

My whole body goes white hot as I take in a sharp breath, imagining being at Ash's mercy, tied down and vulnerable.

As if he heard his name, or my dirty thoughts, the tosser in question looks up at me and holds my gaze in his cutting one, his brows a downward slash.

"Seems like Pretty Girl here likes the idea of being all tied up," Loki drawls, loudly enough for the grey eyed prick to hear. Molten heat flashes in Ash's eyes, liquefying them into swirling pools of slate and freezing me completely.

"Looks like Ash likes the idea of tying you up in knots too, Pretty Girl," Loki snickers playfully, his tone heated.

"Loki, enough!" Ash snarls, practically gnashing his teeth, just as Gerald comes back with our lunch, breaking the thick sexual tension in the air that I'm almost drowning in.

Loki chuckles evilly, and at the same time gives Ash a virtuous look, palms pressed together, as if to say '*what?*' How he manages to be evil and innocent at the same time is one of life's great mysteries, I'm sure. Must have been that fall from heaven.

Gerald sets down the plates before us, and I immediately notice this is no ordinary school canteen food. On my plate—and Ash's—sits a slab of beautifully slow cooked beef, alongside some creamy mash potato. There is a side of blanched buttery carrots and green beans. It smells divine, and I look up to find Ash with a smug arsewipe smile on his face, leaning back in his chair, arms crossed.

Being the mature person that I am, I stick my tongue out at him. He rolls his eyes, although there's definitely a hint of a tilt to his lips. Then he focuses on his own plate and starts meticulously eating so that not a drop of gravy spills on his still pristine suit.

I look over to see not one, but two plates in front of Jax, piled high with what looks like a very fancy chicken kebab. I guess big guys have big appetites. Kai seems to have some kind of stir fry noodle dish, and Loki has gone for a gourmet burger and chunky chips, or, as they're called here, fries. Of course, I reach over and grab one, I mean, chips are life! He lets me with an indulgent smile on his biteable, plump lips. *Good man.*

I turn back to my plate of deliciousness, unfortunately catching Amber's gaze along the way. She's still livid. Like I can almost see steam coming out of her ears, she's so angry. Serves her right, the jizzmuffin. I ignore her, having already wasted enough of my time on that bitch, and pile my fork with a little beef and mash, bringing it to my mouth and moaning out loud as it hits my tongue.

"Oh my god! This is...amazing!" I groan, eating more and not at all delicately. I look up to discover all four guys have paused, and are staring intently at my mouth with looks I can't decipher in each jewel-like gaze.

"What?" I ask, panicking slightly as none of them are even fucking moving.

Loki leans in, lips so close his breath tickles my ear, sending another pleasurable shiver across my body.

"Pretty Girl...those noises... Every guy at this table, hell, in this room, is imagining you making them while we're buried deep inside you," he growls huskily, voice filled with heat and causing an answering warmth to build between my legs.

*I'm going to die if this keeps up. My gravestone shall read; 'Here lies Lilly Darling. Died from horniness.'*

I look down at my plate, toying with my food, thinking about what he just said.

"It's bad manners to play with your food, Princess," Ash barks, making me jump and my fork clatter on the china.

"S–s–sorry," I whisper, face aflame and looking down again.

I hear the sound of cutlery as the guys resume eating when I feel a warm palm land on my thigh. Loki's vanilla scent wraps round me as he once more leans in.

"Don't worry, Darling. It's one for the spank bank," he sniggers, drawing a smile from my lips, which I bite down on. Then a bread roll hits him in the chest, making him laugh harder and wink at me.

*Fucking cuntbandit.*

# CHAPTER SEVEN

ASH

As Highgate Prep royalty, it's traditional for us to hold a party in the woods that surround the campus on the first Friday night of the new semester. It's been like that since my father's days, and far be it for us to renege on our duties.

God, I hate that fucking word, *duties.* My mouth fills with bile at the mere thought of it. I've done so much in the name of duty. If they were to carve me open, they would find it stamped across my blackened heart.

It's still warm in the evenings, although once the sun goes down, there'll be a chill in the air, so I make sure to keep my suit jacket on. Not that I'm often seen without it. Can't disappoint daddy dearest by looking like a mess. I know the guys rib me about it, wearing suits like I'm an old man, but it does lend a certain stay-the-fuck-away-from-me air.

As dusk approaches, Jax, Kai, and I head out of the Academy's back doors towards the forest. It really is beautiful at this time of year, the evening bird-song accompanying the faint music that's playing. Loki is behind us, his arm wrapped around Lilly like a possessive asshole. I don't know why he doesn't just piss on her and mark his territory properly.

My heart fucking leaped in my chest earlier when she came out of his room, proving the organ is not as dead as I would like. She is wearing a striking mini dress, in kaleidoscope colors that make me think I'm tripping on LSD, and hurt my damn brain. The dress skims her delicious curves and ends just under her pert ass.

*Fuck, I want to bite that ass until she begs me to stop. Though I'd not admit that little weakness out loud. You never know when it might be used against you.*

I had to hold in the growl that wanted to escape my throat as Loki reached for her, pulling her close, and kissing her like he was eating her pussy. He's still got her lipstick smeared across his lips, uncouth bastard.

I hear her giggle behind me, and I grit my teeth so hard I'm sure one will crack, my fists clenching at my sides. I don't want to admit that I might be jealous of him, that a small part of me might want to bathe in her light too.

Shaking those thoughts away, I take a deep inhale and look around to see that we've reached the woods. There are strings of bare bulbs lighting our pathway, to a clearing where the party is. The decorators have done well. The brief was A Midsummer Night's Dream, which I changed from what had previously been discussed because, if I'm being truthful, I heard a certain English girl comment that it was her favorite Shakespeare play in our class this week.

It does look like a fairyland, with glittering lights hanging from the trees in glass jars, colorful blankets, rugs, and pillows all arranged in groups, and surrounding low wooden tables. Tables which are groaning with delicious delicacies, the best that money can buy. Our fellow students are already lounging around them, talking and laughing as more nymphs bring them wine and food, like this really is the fairy court.

There's even a folk band playing reworks of popular songs, and a circular dance floor edged with flaming torches.

When we arrive, a guy dressed as a nymph, chest bare and sparkling with glitter, passes each of us silver goblets of chilled white wine, Rhenish, I believe. A scantily clad female, wearing some sort of silk scarf that exposes one glittering breast, steps up to Lilly, who's now beside me, and pins a crown of silk flowers in her tumbling brunette hair.

Somehow, they match her garish dress perfectly, and as I look at her, I'm taken aback, the hair rising on my arms and nape by how utterly spellbinding she looks, and the wonder in her eyes. She thanks the woman and takes in the scene.

“It's beautiful,” she whispers in awe, looking around us, her eyes wide and sparkling.

She's practically fucking glowing in the twilight, the candles and fairy lights shining gently on her beautiful face. She is exquisite. I can admit that much. And she seems to belong in these woods, surrounded by fairies and nymphs.

Turning her hazel eyes on me, I’m captured in her gaze, unable to look away, holding my breath.

“Ash organized it just for you, Pretty Girl,” Loki tells her with a smirk, breaking the spell she had woven around me.

“I thought you said that you always host the first party of the year?” she asks him, her eyebrows squashing together, her voice soft and turning to face him.

“We do. It was meant to be a Saints and Sinners party, but Ash changed the theme yesterday when he heard A Midsummer Night’s Dream was your favourite play,” Loki answers back like a fucking douche. This time, I don’t stop the growl from escaping my lips. *Fucking Loki and his big mouth.*

“Well, in that case,” she says, turning her gaze back to me, and I can see a delicate flush in her cheeks. “Thank you, Ash. I love it.”

I give Loki a smug look over her shoulder, trying to hide the sudden warmth pooling in my gut at her statement.

“Shall we?” she asks, taking me by my arm in her soft grip, and making my heart race.

“Of course,” I reply, clearing my throat and leading the way to a table that has been left clear just for us.

---

## LILLY

As Ash leads us to our table, I am filled with wonder at the sight of the most beautiful party that I’ve ever seen, a sense of giddiness coming over me. It’s like a magical wonderland, full of twinkling lights, and with soft melodic music wrapping round us like a fairy’s spell.

I’m astounded that he did this for me. Why? Up to this point, he’s mostly been in arsehole mode, so why would he suddenly change the party theme just because I like a certain play?

He surprises me further by guiding me to a tasselled, colourful cushion, helping me to sit down like a perfect gentleman, and my heartbeat picks up at the gesture, even as my eyes narrow up at him and his suddenly gentlemanly manner. I'm sure that I don't look like a lady with my arse hanging out of my micro sixties mini dress, but looking round, at least I'm not the only one almost flashing her lady garden.

Loki passes me my goblet of wine, and I take a sip, my lips tingling with the rich fruity flavour. He sits to my right, Ash on my left, with Kai and Jax opposite us. The low table is positively bursting with all sorts of food that looks fucking amazing. Silver platters with fruit, tarts, cured meats, and a hundred other delicacies cover the surface.

"Here, try this," Loki says, his fingers coming before my lips, holding what looks like a piece of pear that has been soaked in some kind of sticky sauce.

I open up my mouth, looking him dead in the eye as he places the fruit on my tongue, his pupils wide and his touch lingering. A burst of spicy sweetness erupts in my mouth as I chew, my eyes rolling and a moan sounding from my lips at the same time.

My eyes open to see his fingers, a drop of sauce making its way down his thumb, so before he moves his hand away, I wrap my lips round the digit, sucking the drop off. Passion flares in his eyes, making the emerald shine like the brightest of gems. I'm sure that I hear a groan or two from the other guys at my move.

I release it from my lips with an audible pop and a cheeky lopsided smile.

"Delicious, thank you," I tell him, our stare off interrupted by Ash offering me a silver tray of canapes.

We settle into eating and chatting about the first week of classes. I'm not going to lie, it was crazy intense, but I loved it. I was so busy and so tired after each day that I didn't have time to think about anything else. And with sleeping in Loki's bed every night, him beside me, the nightmares seem to be kept at bay too.

We haven't taken it further than, I think they call it, third base. Basically, fingers, hands, and tongues. Well, his fingers, hands, and tongue. I've not got so much as a glimpse of the crown jewels. He distracts me with multiple orgasms until I basically pass out. It surprises me, his lack of wanting anything in return, especially if the rumours I've heard about his promiscuous ways are true. But so far, it's been all about my pleasure.

My thoughts are disrupted by one of the servers presenting us with another gleaming tray, this time with rows of colourful pills on it. I look round to see the other tables being offered the same platters.

"What's this?" I question, a flare of adrenaline rushing through my veins at the opportunity of a new oblivion.

"This, Pretty Girl, is tonight's high, brought to you by the Black Knights of Highgate!" Loki announces, raising his voice and standing up, throwing his arms wide to cheers from the crowd. I can't help but laugh at his antics, bouncing in my seat.

"Made by the finest chemists in Israel, we give you our own personal high. Choose blue for a giggle, orange if you want to expand your mind. Pink is for if you're feeling naughty, and red," he turns his gaze to me, an understanding look in his eyes. "Red is if you require complete oblivion."

My breath hitches and my heart rate picks up at this. *How does he know?*

He settles back down, still looking at me. "What'll it be, baby?" he asks, one brow raised.

"Red," I whisper, my eyes locked with his.

He pauses for a second, and I can hear Ash behind me, muttering under his breath.

"Allow me," Loki says, taking the little red pill off the tray and placing it on the tip of his tongue, a daring look in his eyes. So, accepting the challenge with a wide grin, I lean closer and suck it off. Then he hands me my wine to swallow it down, watching me with an intensity to his gaze that I struggle to fully interpret.

As I set my goblet down, I notice that none of the guys have taken anything off the trays for themselves. I turn to Ash, intending to ask if he isn't going to imbibe tonight. My words get stuck in my mouth when I see him staring at me, his grey eyes ablaze with fury.

"What's the matter?" I ask, drawing in a sharp breath and taken aback by how pissed he looks.

"Those pills are strong, Lilly. So no more tonight," he orders, jaw clenched and getting up.

*I see we're back to being Ash-hole again!*

Before I can rip him a new one for being an overbearing jizzstain, he storms off.

"Why is he always such a twat?" I muse aloud, hearing Jax's gruff hoot from across the table.

"He's right though, this is no playground shit," Jax tells me in his sexy, deep voice, his blue eyes troubled.

I roll my eyes, waving my hand. "I know what I'm doing, I've taken Molly before."

"Not quite like this, I don't think," Kai adds, pushing his glasses up the bridge of his nose, and shifting in his seat, tugging his shirt cuffs into place even though he's as neat as a pin.

*Whatever.*

About twenty minutes later, I start to feel the buzz spreading over my body like a wash of warm water. It's incredible. The lights become brighter, glowing like stars all around me, and a delighted laugh rings out from my lips, sounding like the finest music to my ears.

"You buzzing, baby?" I hear Loki's amused drawl sound to my right, and I turn to look at him, gasping as my eyes find his green ones glowing.

"Your eyes are so beautiful, Loki," I tell him dreamily, leaning forward to get closer. "They're like emerald fire."

"Yep, she's buzzing alright," I hear Jax laugh, his deep voice causing a shiver to take over my body, my eyelids closing, and I groan aloud at the pleasurable sensation.

"I would fuck your voice if I could, Jax," I moan, this time hearing Loki barking with mirth, and Kai's melodic chuckle.

I listen to their laughter and let it wrap round me like a warm, comforting blanket. The sound of the music starts to filter into my eardrums, the sound of the drums beating along in time to my heartbeat. It's a sensual version of *Tainted Love* by Love, Alexa. I find myself swaying along, opening my eyes when a warm hand grasps mine.

"Let's dance, Pretty Girl," Loki says, voice low and husky, pulling me up to my feet.

He leads the way to the dance floor, drawing my back to his front as we dance to the slow and bacchanalian rhythm. Everywhere he touches me, even through my clothes, burns with electric fire until I feel as though sparks must be flying off me. I look down, gasping when I see that they aren't.

My gaze gets lost in the moving colours of my dress, until I feel Loki's hand on my waist pulling me closer, guiding my arms up and round his neck behind me. I can feel how happy he is to be there, his hardness grinding into my arse.

"Loki," I gasp out, pushing my hips back into him, desperate to feel more.

He growls low into my ear, then nips my earlobe and starts kissing my neck. I tilt my head back, giving him better access, feeling his kisses like lightning bolts shooting across my body.

They weren't lying. This Molly is unlike anything I've ever taken before. Everything is so much brighter, so much...more than it usually is. It's like I can feel every touch and caress a thousandfold. I'm made of pure sensation with no pesky thoughts and worries trying to break through.

The song comes to an end, and our grinding slows, both of us panting.

"Jesus, Lilly," Loki rasps in my ear, his fingers digging into my side.

We stand there whilst the next song starts up, him still behind me, his dick as hard as stone. I giggle, wiggling my arse, and hearing another groan leave his lips.

"Naughty girl," he admonishes, nipping my neck, finally letting me go and taking a step back.

"Don't worry, Loki baby. I'll sort that out later," I turn to face him, then wink. "But now, I need to pee."

He laughs, but I don't miss the fever in those fiery beryl eyes of his. I remember seeing a posh set of mobile toilets on the way in, so I head in that direction.

Once I'm finished, I wash up and step out of the portacabin, only to be confronted by Amber and her smiling crew of merry cuntbandits. The Molly does not improve her appearance at all. In fact, it makes her look a little like a gargoyle, all twisted and snarly. They all look ridiculous in their jean shorts and Birkenstocks. It's a fucking party, guys! *Twats.*

"I hear they still haven't caught your mom's killer," she snidely says, my heart stopping at the statement. "That must really suck..." she continues, but I don't hear anything else as I am assaulted by memories of red rivers flooding my mind, the crimson shining like the brightest rubies.

"W–what...?" I stammer out, my vision flickering between the bloody scene I came home to that day and the glittering party round me. Sweat breaks out all across my body, cooling in the chilly night breeze, and I start to shiver uncontrollably.

I stumble away from the group, my feet tangling as I try to run away from the memories. My eyes alight onto a silver dish, held by an ethereal nymph, my focus drawn to the little red pills lying atop it.

*Oblivion.*

Before I know what I'm doing, my hand has taken a pill, popping it into my mouth, and swallowing it dry. I breathe a sigh of relief, knowing that soon it will go away again. The rivers of blood, the pain, and heartache will all disappear again. At least for a little while.

Suddenly, a strong hand grips my upper arm painfully, turning me until I'm looking into blazing grey eyes.

"What did you just do?" Ash roars, shaking me.

"Ow!" I shout back at him, wriggling. "You're hurting me, Ash!" I try to struggle, but it's futile. His grip is too strong.

"I should put you over my fucking knee and spank you like a naughty child!" he growls back, causing more than a few sets of students to turn towards us, quickly looking away when he bares his teeth at them. He points a finger right in my face.

"I told you to only take one. Why did you take another?!"

He's shaking, and as I look deeper, I can see a flash of panic in his wide eyes, his hands trembling and breath coming in pants.

"Fucking cuntmuffin said..." I start, stopping and shaking my head, as the memories try to push through what's left of my high again.

He looks over me, which is really fucking easy given how tall the guy is. What he sees, which I assume is Amber and her crew, makes the skin around his eyes and mouth tighten, and his grip turns even more painful. His gaze comes back to me, still fuming with that edge of fear.

"What did she say?" he asks, voice deadly and cutting.

"She...she mentioned my mum and..." I can't finish the sentence, begging him with my gaze not to make me. The grey softens slightly, and I see a sorrow so deep that my breath hitches.

"You can't escape it forever, Lilly," he tells me, his grip on my arm loosening a little, his other hand coming up to stroke the side of my face. "You'll have to face your grief sooner or later, Princess. We all do."

I briefly wonder what grief he's had to face, but before I can think any more about it, Loki comes storming over, shoving Ash so hard that he has no choice but to let go of me.

"Take your fucking hands off her!" Loki snarls, his nostrils flared and the vein in his neck pulsing. I never imagined he'd get so angry over me.

Ash gets right back in his face, chest jutted out and eyes hard as flint, sneering back at him. They remind me of two male lions, all ferocious danger and about to tear each other apart. Before it can descend into violence, Jax and Kai rush up to the pair, Jax using his bulk to get in between them.

"Cool it, guys," he growls, pushing them farther apart, a hand on each torso. There's quite a crowd gathered round us now, all desperate to taste blood.

Loki and Ash stare at each other for another moment before Ash leans over, saying something to Loki, whose head immediately snaps in my direction, his brow wrinkled as he takes me in from head to toe.

Loki walks towards me, reaching out and pulling me close, wrapping his strong arms round me. I inhale deeply, feeling his pounding heart as I breathe in his warm vanilla scent, taking the comfort it gives me.

"Let's get you back to the dorm," he murmurs in my ear, kissing the top of my head softly.

Tucking me under his arm, he leads me away. As we pass Ash, I look up to see Jax with his hand on Ash's shoulder, saying something to him in low tones with Kai close on his other side. Ash meets my gaze, and the desperate sorrow is there, alongside a drowning grief that matches my own.

# CHAPTER EIGHT

LILLY

After a weekend of relaxing with Loki, and avoiding Ash, Monday rolls around, and we all have homeroom first. Then Ash and I have Shakespeare Studies, which I'm kind of dreading after the party in the woods.

Although we walk to class together, and sit next to each other, he ghosts me the whole fucking time, and won't say a word, even when I try to make conversation. Then, when the class finishes, he hightails it out of there, like his arse is on fire. *Wanker!*

My next lesson is Calculus, which, unfortunately, is also with Ash, but at least Jax and Loki are there too, so I've got people who'll talk to me. Kai is on all these advanced programs, given that he is a bloody genius, and is already doing some college level classes, so we only have Yoga together. Although, that does mean I get to see just how flexible the guy is, and imagine how all that flexibility can be put to good use.

After Calculus, I've got Botany, then Mythology with Jax, followed by lunch. After lunch, it's Creative Writing with both Ash and Loki, and finally, French with just Loki. It's so different from what we do in England. I have a lot more classes here than I did back there. But then, they're way more interesting too, so I can't complain.

I must confess, I am surprised by the amount of English classes Ash and I share. I don't know why, especially given how eloquently he speaks, but I still find it hard to believe that the thundercunt is soft enough for prose.

I share most of my classes with the guys, there's always one or more of them with me which is nice. I'm especially glad of their company after the other night with Amber and her malicious words. I don't want to be anywhere near her or her merry band of cuntflaps. Unfortunately, it's a small school, being private and all, so I can't avoid them altogether, although they leave me alone when one of the boys is there.

Monday afternoon passes quickly, thank god. By the end of the day, I feel exhausted, still catching up from the weekend, and my comedown makes me feel a million years old as I make my way to our dorm.

When I reach the door, I can hear heated arguing inside, so I pause and press my ear against wood, trying to listen to what's being said.

"You can't have her in your bed every night, Loki!" Ash's distinct arsehole tone scoffs, sounding exasperated. A flush creeps over my cheeks at his words. *Why not Ash-hole?*

"I can if she wants to be there, you jealous asshole," Loki drawls back, the grin clear in his voice. He sounds cool, calm, and collected.

"I am not fucking jealous," Ash replies, voice full of danger and darkness.

I'm holding my breath in case I miss anything, pressing closer to the door, desperate to see where this is going and to hear more.

"Oh, yeah? Tell me you don't get rock fucking hard when you hear her screaming my name most nights?" Loki challenges.

I can picture the arrogant smirk on Loki's face; he's so sure of himself. I don't know whether to be turned the hell on or irritated by him most of the time. *Perhaps both?*

"Fuck off!" Ash retorts after a pause, but not denying the accusation, which makes my pulse pick up, sounding in my ears.

"That's what I thought," Loki replies in an amused tone. "You know, I'm happy to share. I've actually come around to the idea. You could even join us. She seemed to like the idea of you tying her up. Just think, she'd be completely at your mercy," Loki teases, and I gasp, fumbling with my key to get the damn door open and rip him a new one.

I manage to open the door just in time to see Ash storm off up the stairs with Loki looking after him, a pleased grin on his face.

"I heard that, dickhead," I seethe at him, throwing my bag down and kicking off my heels. They're an iridescent petrol colour with sequins and bows on the toes, and of course, made by Irregular Choice. *Sigh.* They're so pretty that I forget my train of thought and stare at them, a feeling of pure happiness filling me up. *Whoever said money can't buy happiness obviously never came across Irregular Choice shoes.*

A snort sounds next to me, and I startle out of my shoe-fest.

"What?!" I snap as I look up, and I'm met with eyes that remind me of pictures I've seen of the aurora borealis, full of limitless possibilities. Another deep sound comes from his perfect lips, and I'm once again awoken from my reverie.

*Damn, this guy is way too dangerous.*

"Bollocks! I can't remember what I was annoyed about now," I grumble, crossing my arms and narrowing my eyes at him. Loki throws back his head and laughs, causing me to scowl even more.

"Oh, Pretty Girl," he chuckles. "You are so adorable. Especially with that beautiful pixie face and those rosy cheeks," he adds, caressing the side of my face with his fingertips and making my breath catch, my brief anger gone at his touch.

We stay that way, gazing into each other's eyes with his fingers on my face for several moments. There's something so...melancholic about Loki. On the surface, he's a joker, happy-go-lucky and always laughing, but once he stops, there's a sense of sadness, almost a resigned devastation, that calls to me.

Shaking my head at my own foolishness—*I've only known him for just over a week, for Christ's sake!*—I step to the side, letting his hand drop, and he looks crestfallen. I pause, my heart skipping painfully at the idea of having caused him any pain.

"Loki? Will you come to dinner with me?" I blurt, without thinking, then inwardly cringe, biting my lower lip as I wait for his answer.

A cocksure grin spreads his plump lips, eliminating all traces of hurt.

"Are you asking me out on a date, Lilly Darling?" he drawls in that sinful voice of his. I love the way he says my name. I want him to say it again when he's balls deep inside of me.

*Head out of the fucking gutter, woman!*

"Uh...yes?" I say, almost as a question. Right now, I'd love the floor to just swallow me up. I'm sure there's a blush staining my cheeks.

His grin grows wider, and he waits just a beat longer before giving me an answer, putting me out of my embarrassed misery.

"Pretty Girl, I'd love to take you to dinner. But we have to dress up like it's a proper date," he looks at me with mock seriousness, his eyes twinkling.

"Of course." I grin, my breath whooshing out of me in relief. "I wouldn't have it any other way."

---

I take a shower whilst Loki gets ready, using his vanilla shower gel and scrubbing myself all over until I'm pink. I don't wash my hair this time, preferring my natural hair oils to not be stripped away all the time. I style it in loose barrel curls so that it's tumbling down my back.

I make to leave the bathroom in just my towel as all my stuff is in Loki's room; after that first night, all of my dresses and skirts were hung up in his wardrobe. My other clothes have all been put away in his drawers. He even had a bookshelf put in there for my paperback RH collection. *Don't read too much into it, Lilly, it's just practical given that I'm staying in his room.*

Opening the bathroom door, I see that Loki is just reaching the bottom of the stairs, and I stall, my hand gripping the door handle, and my body flashing with warmth. *Holy shitballs!* I mean, I knew the guy was hot, but fuck me, he scrubs up nice.

He's wearing navy straight leg jeans that he's rolled up a little at the hem, his brown boots and a white t-shirt with a stonewash denim shirt open on top of it. He's rolled the arms of the denim shirt to his elbow, and I don't know what it is about a guy's forearms, but fuck me if it's not one of the hottest fucking things I've ever seen. It's made even sexier by the silhouette of trees tattooed around his left wrist, reaching his elbow in a forest of black ink. He's also wearing a massive gold watch round the same wrist, and some beads on the other, including what looks like pink plastic ones.

He looks up and sees me staring, my mouth open and almost fucking drooling. His trademark insolent, panty destroying grin pulls at his lips.

"It's almost a shame for you to get dressed really," he remarks, eyes slowly taking me in, and when his tongue darts out to lick his lips, I feel like I might self combust on the spot. “We could just stay here?” he asks, voice low and a brow lifted, clearly implying that we spend all night in his bed. *I mean, I'm probably going to do that anyway, but I want my date first.*

“I'll be down in a few,” I say, clearing my throat and ignoring his suggestion. As I sweep past him, his hand comes out, brushing his fingers down my arm. The touch makes me draw a breath sharply and builds the fire between my thighs. I continue on, somehow ignoring the need for now, and head up the stairs.

Soon, it's my turn to descend the staircase dressed to the nines. I'm wearing one of my favourite original nineteen-fifties cotton dresses. It has a fitted bodice, is pinched in at the waist, and has a huge flared skirt with a red net petticoat underneath, making it stick out more and giving it a wonderful swish. It's covered in red, orange, and yellow flames, and I've paired it with what I call my Dorothy shoes; red sequined heels, with a cute crimson satin bow on the front, and made by Irregular Choice. *I may have a slight addiction to a certain shoe brand....*

I've put a couple of clips in my hair to sweep it back from my face, leaving it to tumble down my back, and my makeup is subtle fifties, with black cat eyes and bright red lips.

Loki's waiting with Jax, chatting as I make my way down, but as he sees me, he abruptly stops talking mid-sentence. His mouth literally pops open, and I have to suppress a squeal of delight at seeing him so lost for words, although I can’t stop the wide grin that comes over my painted lips.

I catch his gaze, which is a raging inferno of jade fire, as he takes me in. My eyes flick briefly to Jax, and what I see there makes my steps falter a little so that I have to grab the bannister. His piercing blue gaze is also swirling with an intense heat as he admires me. I get caught up in the blue flames until Loki steps up in front of me, blocking my view when I reach the bottom of the stairs.

“Damn, Pretty Girl! I didn't think you could get any more beautiful,” he groans, licking his lower lip and rubbing his jaw with a strong manicured hand. *What is it about a well kept hand on a hot man that makes you go weak at the knees?*

As usual, I feel my cheeks flush pink with his compliment.

“Are you ready to go?” I manage to get out, squirming under his scrutiny.

Which is fucking ridiculous seeing as he's seen me naked and had me screaming his name, coming apart under his fingers and tongue.

"Abso-fucking-lutely!" He beams, holding out his arm for me to take.

We head in the direction of the dining hall, his forearm warm under my palm. The school has a no going off campus Monday to Friday rule so our dinner date has to take place here.

As we enter the hall, my breath is taken away and I look round with wide eyes. I am blanketed by stars. All the lights are off, bar one that highlights a single table next to one of the window walls. As most of the walls and ceiling are made of glass, and given that we are in the middle of nowhere so light pollution is minimal, the night sky sits above us, full of pinpricks of light.

"Loki," I breathe, glancing back at him. "It's beautiful. How..." I'm at a loss as to how he organised everything so quickly. And also, why are there no other students here?

"I have my ways," he boasts with a wink, leading me to our table and pulling out my chair. "I hope you don't mind, but I ordered dinner for us."

Gerald, the waiter who always serves our table during the day, brings our plates over, setting them down in front of us. Loki is sitting by my side so that we're facing the window, but can still turn to speak to each other.

I see that we have a bowl of orange coloured soup to start, and I moan aloud as I take a spoonful. It's carrot and coriander, which happens to be one of my favourites. I look up to see Loki grinning at me once again.

"You like your food, don't you, Pretty Girl?" he teases. "I like that you're not afraid to show it, like many of the girls that go here are."

He takes his own spoonful to those lush lips of his. *Damn, I've never been jealous of a spoon before!*

"So, tell me more about yourself? I still don't know everything," he asks me, smiling that beautiful smile of his which makes my heart race.

"Well...I was born in North London, a place called Islington, and lived with my mum. I loved the city. It's so vibrant and full of life and bursting at the seams. And there are so many different people and cultures." I smile fondly at the memories, seeing all my favourite places in my mind. "I guess you've maybe been there?" I ask him, remembering that everyone in this school is as rich as Midas, so obviously well travelled.

"Once or twice. But I want to hear more of what you loved about it," he invites, a soft expression on his face as he gives me his rapt attention.

So, I tell him. I talk about all of the wonderful museums, the parks, and the green spaces. About growing up in the city, how we used to smoke weed outside the old town hall and go to a dingy club called The Dome in Tufnell Park when we were fourteen. I describe the time I stole my mum's whiskey and got rat arsed—I had to explain that this means I was very drunk. I share the story of when I went to the theatre in the West End with Mum and a friend to see Grease, and the street performers at Covent Garden market we used to see.

"Sounds like a great way to grow up," he remarks, a distant empty stare in his eyes.

"But you must have had an amazing childhood?" I ask, ducking my head to meet his gaze, ready to discover more about him. "I mean, I'd never even gotten on a plane before coming here." I look at him, and he seems to have clammed up, his arms crossed and a flush creeping across his cheeks.

"Yeah. I mean it was great," he starts, hesitantly, meeting my gaze. "We had some amazing nannies and some hideous ones! This one woman, Edna, used to feed us cod liver oil every day," he reminisces, mouth pinched and nose crinkled, which I can completely sympathise with. That stuff is fucking disgusting!

"Mostly, it was me and the girls, my kid sisters. My parents were always off on business of one sort or another, so we only saw them at Christmas really," he trails off, looking away, but not before I catch a longing in his beautiful eyes that is so strong it takes my breath away.

He stays quiet, then Gerald brings our dessert; a divine smelling chocolate melt in the middle cake with custard and ice cream, successfully interrupting the sombre moment.

"Custard and ice cream?" I tease, gently nudging him with my elbow. "Only someone with a body like yours would come up with that combination."

Relief fills me as the sad, lost look leaves his face, and is replaced with his signature grin.

"You like my body, Pretty Girl?" he drawls in a tone that makes my breath quicken, and I find myself gripping my spoon hard.

Heat banks in his gaze as he takes a deliberately provocative spoonful of his dessert, slowly licking it off with that clever tongue of his. I'd be lying if I said I didn't clench my thighs a little, remembering his tongue in other more intimate places.

He looks over at me, smirking, and then gets another spoonful, only to offer it to me this time. *Tit for tat, Angel!* I copy him and oh so slowly, take the mouthful, licking the spoon until it's clean. I even raise the bar by moaning a little, all whilst holding his gaze. *Checkmate, motherfucker!*

"I think we're done here," he rasps, letting the spoon clatter to the plate.

Grabbing my hand, he pulls me up beside him, and then drags me away.

# CHAPTER NINE

LILLY

"You owe me dessert, fucker!" I admonish, laughing once we reach our dorm, and only then noticing that his trousers are tented, straining with his impressive length pushing against them.

*Jesus, I'd forgotten how well endowed he looks.*

My pussy clenches and my mouth starts to water as I pray that I'm finally going to see the size of him sans clothes. Hopefully, tonight I'll get to feel it too.

He slams me up against the door, my heart racing in the best way when he pins my arms above me, swallowing my gasp as he kisses me senseless. His kiss is full of its usual fire, but also a heart wrenching longing, and somehow, it feels...hopeful. Like I might be exactly what he's been waiting for, for so long. Everything fades from around us as he leans into me more, tongue stroking mine, playing with me, and nipping my bottom lip.

"Fuck, Lilly," he groans sexily, his pelvis grinding into me and letting me feel just how hard his cock is. "You're so fucking perfect," he whispers, nibbling my neck in that sweet spot between my neck and shoulder, making me moan and squirm, desperate for more.

Suddenly, the door swings inwards, and it's only Loki's fast reactions and strong grip that keep me from toppling backwards. I turn my head to see Jax standing there, his mouth parted and his rippling muscles rigid as he gazes at us.

"I'm going to the gym," he rumbles out in his dark as night's sky voice.

My spine tingles at the sound, then I experience a flash of guilt given that I'm in his friend's arms with his rigid dick pressed up against me.

"We're going to bed," Loki taunts, a devilish grin on his face which is comical as my lipstick is smeared all over his mouth.

I turn to look at Jax and see a moment of pure rage in his piercing gaze, my head jerking back at the intensity of it before it disappears. The two boys stare at one another in a sort of standoff, Loki with a roguish twinkle in his eyes, before Jax moves aside to let us pass with a huff.

Loki reaches round and picks me up, hands under my arse, leaving me little choice but to wrap my legs round him as best I can. Not easy in a fucking full nineteen-fifties dress and net petticoat.

I can see Jax narrow his eyes as Loki takes me up the stairs, and I hear the front door slam hard, jumping in Loki's arms from the sound when we reach the top.

"Loki!" I tell him off, only partly joking, and smack his bicep as he sets me down on my heels.

"Don't worry, Pretty Girl, he just needs a little nudge is all," he grins, my brows dip in confusion at his words as he goes to sit on the bed, leaning back on his arms and looking every inch the fallen angel that he is.

He presses something on his watch, and James Bay's acoustic version of *Wild Love* begins to play, effectively making me forget my train of thought. *This guy is so smooth he'd give Casanova a run for his money.*

"Now. What pretty lace are you wearing for me tonight?" he asks, his gaze an emerald fire as he takes me in from my sparkly shoes to my flowing hair.

"How do you know I'm wearing anything?" I tease, lowering my tone and popping a hip out, making his auburn eyebrows raise and the heat build in his eyes.

"I guess we'll see, won't we?" he responds cockily, giving me a little nod. *Arrogant arsehole.*

I pause for a moment, wondering if I should make him suffer for that, then decide fuck it with a shrug as I walk over to him, turning round and looking over my shoulder through my lashes.

"Zip, please," I ask, shivering when I feel his fingers brush my exposed shoulder blades as he reaches for it. He undoes it slowly, building the tension between us higher.

I step away once he's finished, taking my arms out of the cap sleeves and letting it fall down to my waist. I then do a totally sexy shimmy, pushing my dress and petticoat down over my hips and letting it pool on the ground in a sea of flames and frothy red net.

I'm left wearing my red sheer panelled corset with plunging cups and thin straps to keep the girls in place. A matching thong and high lace topped stockings, with a red seam down the back, complete the set. I step out of the pile of fabric at my feet and sway towards Loki on the bed, keeping my red sequin heels on.

His eyes are a raging inferno, and he's no longer lounging back, but sitting bolt upright, his hands clenched in the sheets.

"Fucking hell, Lilly," he gasps out, and a shiver breaks out all over my body, pebbling my nipples to hard points under the fabric, with the way he chokes out my name. "Just...fucking incredible," he murmurs as I reach him.

His hands instantly go to my waist, fingers splaying as he starts to explore every inch of me. He groans when his fingers spread over my bare arse, palming each cheek with enough force to leave bruises on my skin, and have me gasping in pleasurable pain. The idea that he's marked me sends another pleasurable shudder down my spine.

He pulls me closer, and in one smooth move, he flips us so that he's lying on top of me on the bed, hips between my thighs, and I can feel his hard length pressing against my clit. I squirm, trying to increase the pressure and ease the ache that has started to build there.

He makes a tsking noise before smiling, looking deep into my eyes.

"You are a goddess, Lilly Darling, and I intend to worship at your altar all fucking night."

He starts to move his way down my body, giving me little nips through the lace fabric as he goes. When he reaches the apex of my thighs, he lifts one leg and drapes it over his shoulder, and then does the same with the other. Slowly, he pulls my thong aside, and a low growl tumbles from him as he sees how wet my core is.

"Such a fucking goddess," he mumbles as he lowers his head to my aching pussy, and I feel his hot breath fanning along my folds.

In one long stroke, he licks me from my slit to my clit, my hips bucking up and eyes closing with the excruciating pleasure that courses through me at the contact.

"Loki..." I moan, my hands reaching down and tangling in his red hair, pulling him closer, desperate for more. He chuckles, and I swear I feel the vibrations in my very centre.

Then, he begins to lick, suck, and basically destroy me with his tongue. Like his kiss, it's as if he's a starving man and I'm the first meal he's had in years. He lavishes my clit with his clever tongue, nipping it with his teeth until the sensitive bundle of nerves is firing off electric pulses all over my body. Just when I think that I can take no more, he moves to my opening and starts tongue fucking me, thrusting in and out and driving me wild.

I manage to crack my eyelids open and look down to see his auburn locks tangled in my fingers, his head rocking with the movement of eating me out. It's so fucking sexy, I can feel myself tipping into nirvana. My fingers tighten their grip, making him growl, which sends me hurtling off the edge into the blissful abyss.

When I come back to the land of the living, I look up to see him kneeling, naked, dick hard and dripping precum. I catch a glint at the tip, and yep, it's fucking pierced. He's got an honest to god Prince Albert. *Fucking yum!*

His beautiful, plump mouth is glistening with my juices, and as I watch, his tongue comes out, licking his lips, savouring the taste of me.

"Best fucking dessert ever," he says smugly, whilst I relearn how to breathe. He leans over to grab the foil packet of a condom from the drawer next to us, and opening it, slides the rubber onto his length.

He crawls back up my body, hovering above me, his cock nudging my entrance, teasing. He stays that way, staring into my eyes with a look that sets my pulse racing. His arms are on either side of my face, his flaming hair falling down round his forehead. I reach up to push it back, loving how soft it is, like the finest silk.

I hear *Mine* by Joseph Vincent start to play, and as he pushes into me, he starts to sing along in a sexy, raspy voice that sets me alight.

*Oh. My. Fucking. God!*

You'd think it would be awkward and cheesy as fuck, someone singing to you whilst they fuck you. But it's not. Not at all. In fact, it feels like he's...making love to me, gazing into my eyes and singing about not wasting time and making me his. *You're just imagining things, Lilly.*

His pace is slow, leisurely pumping his hips in time to the music whilst he sings along. He's still looking intensely into my eyes, and I'm just fucking melting, my hands grasping his hair, his biceps, his body as he sends the best kind of chills cascading all over me.

His voice is so beautiful, deep and gravelly, caressing my body, and sending goosebumps pebbling across my skin. He's winding me up so tight, like a coil ready to explode as he pumps in and out of me, undulating his hips in the most delicious way, and hitting my g-spot with his piercing every damn time.

I start to feel the burn of another orgasm as it sweeps over me, and I cry out, raking my nails down his back and arms. He doesn't pause or even slow down, causing shockwaves to ripple through me and keeping my orgasm tingling.

"Loki, fuck!" I gasp out as he grabs a leg and hooks it over his shoulder, going deeper and pounding harder until I'm seeing fucking stars, a third orgasm hitting me like a fucking tsunami.

His thrusts become jagged and disjointed as he comes with a roar, releasing my leg then collapsing on top of me, breathing hard, and I can feel his heart pounding like a freight train.

"Jesus, Lilly," he breathes out after a few minutes, still sheathed inside me. He lifts his head and nuzzles my neck, then moves up to my lips and I can still taste myself on him.

"That was..." he starts, still panting and holding me tightly, looking into my eyes like he's trying to fuse our souls together. "That was fucking incredible!"

His smile is so blinding it leaves me speechless, lost in his brilliance. He's so beautiful, I just can't believe that not only does he exist, but I'm in his bed. That he actually likes me. At least, I think he does with all the attention he's been giving me, and his demands to know all about me.

"So...you can sing, huh?" I smile back, teasing him. "Any other hidden talents?" I ask, eyes going wide as I feel him getting harder whilst still buried inside me. *No fucking way! How is that even possible?!*

"I can think of a few more." He smirks cockily as he starts to gently thrust inside me, making even my fucking teeth tingle.

I barely register the song ending and *Idea 686* by Jayla Darden beginning. *I wonder if this is his sex playlist?*

"Loki!" I gasp as he suddenly pulls out and flips me over so I'm on my hands and knees, the errant thought about the playlist disappearing.

I hear the rustle of another condom packet before he literally rips my thong off, and then slams back inside of me. The sting of the thong snapping, combined with his hard dick pounding inside me again has a fourth climax tearing through me and I scream his name as my pussy clamps down hard on him. He follows soon after, growling my name between clenched teeth.

I collapse with him on top of me, then he rolls us so he's spooning me from behind, his softening cock slipping out of me. I mourn the loss of the connection, feeling him get out of bed presumably to get rid of the condom. Then the bed dips as he gets back in, pulling me back so close that there's not a single inch between us.

As the darkness overtakes me, I can't help feeling that I don't ever want to sleep any other way.

---

I'm pulled from a delicious slumber in what must be the early hours of the morning. I can just see faint watery light filtering round the edges of Loki's curtains, highlighting our discarded clothing littering the floor.

Warmth flushes over me as I remember the night before, and how many times Loki used his *talents*, my pussy throbbing at the memory.

I have the feeling that something woke me up, and as I come out of my dream state, I start to hear faint music. Climbing out of bed, I grab Loki's discarded shirt and pull it on, suddenly surrounded by his vanilla scent. I could snuggle into his smell all day, wrapping it round myself like a blanket. The same could be said of the man himself.

I open the door and can hear that the music is *Ghosts* by Nathan Wagner, his gruff melodic voice haunting the darkness. Looking round, I see that the door opposite Loki's is standing ajar, the door to what is meant to be my room, and the music seems to be coming from there.

Intrigued, I step out of Loki's room and head towards it, peering in. The curtains are open, the faint light of predawn casting everything in a dull yellow glow, leaving huge menacing shadows across the floor.

I walk farther in, looking round me. The room is pristine, nothing is messy or out of place. Yet, it doesn't look empty. A glint catches my eye from where the desk is, and I see a silver picture frame sat atop it. I pick it up, bringing it into the light to see that it's a photograph of all four guys, arms around each other laughing, and a smile comes to my face.

It's then that I notice a fifth figure on the end. I bring the picture closer, biting my lip and squinting when I see that it's Ash, which is confusing because Ash is also at the other end of the group. Their clothes are slightly different, one's in a sky blue t-shirt, the other in a light grey.

*What the hell? Two of Ash?*

Startled, I spin round clutching the frame to my chest when I hear a noise behind me.

"What are you doing in here, Princess?" Ash's cold voice washes over me, and I tremble. His face is in complete darkness, his back is to the window, so I can't make out any expression, and I can hear my heartbeat in my ears, my scalp prickling with unease.

Taking a deep breath, I pull my big girl ovaries up, figuratively speaking, and stand a little taller. I will not be bullied or intimidated by some upstart rich boy. Regardless of how hot he might be. Or scary.

"I heard music and thought I'd come and take a look in what should be *my* room," I sass back, pursing my lips. It's so difficult to gauge his reaction without seeing his face, but he appears to stiffen.

"And what are you holding?" he asks in a deadly calm.

"Oh, this?" I say, one brow raised as if it's nothing really and I'm not that interested. I hold it up for him to see. "It's a picture that you appear to be in twice. Care to explain?"

My eyes dart to his fists, which are now clenching at his sides, his arm muscles straining and the veins popping, like he's holding back from snatching the frame right out of my hands. I hear him take a deep inhale through his nose.

"Isn't it fucking obvious, Princess?" he drawls cruelly. "One is me, and the other is, well, I suppose *was*, Luc, my identical twin brother."

"W–what?" I ask stupidly, completely dumbfounded, my grip relaxing on the frame. "Where is he?" I say, looking round with raised brows as if he's been hiding in this room all along.

Ash reaches out and carefully takes the picture from my limp hand, like it's very precious to him.

"Dead." My stomach plummets at the word. His voice is devoid of any feeling and emotion. It's as cold and sharp as broken ice. "Now, get the fuck out," he barks, stepping up to me, right into my personal space. He keeps advancing until I'm forced to back up towards the door.

"Ash...I'm..." I start, my hands raised as if to ward off his anger, but he interrupts me.

"I said. Get. The. Fuck. Out. Don't make me say it a third time, Princess."

"Back the fuck up, Ash." I hear Loki's voice, rough with sleep but hard as stone, sound behind me.

With a soft curse, I turn my head to see him limned in the light from the hallway, dressed only in boxers and his hair sticking straight up.

"She shouldn't be in here, Loki. Keep her on a fucking leash if she can't be trusted not to wander where's she's not allowed. Fuck, try tying her down."

My head snaps back to Ash, my eyes narrowed and lips pressed in a thin line. I can see his haughty expression and cold eyes now that the hallway light shines on his face.

"Listen here, you rich prick..." I start, taking a step forward so that we are almost toe to toe. I poke my finger in his hard chest, only serving to hurt my finger. *Fuckface!*

Before I can finish what I was going to say—*and let's be honest here, I'm not entirely sure what that was as who doesn't like a bit of rope play?*—I feel Loki grab me by the waist and haul me back against him.

"Just leave the asshole alone, Pretty Girl. He doesn't know how to play nice."

I grumble and give a half-arsed attempt to get away from him before he pulls me in tighter, my back to his chest, his heat radiating through my body. His hand dips to the hem of the t-shirt that I'm wearing, and his fingers slide up to find my bare pussy already a little slick. I'm denying it has anything to do with the thundercunt standing in front of me and his suggestion of being tied up.

"Tying up is your kink, brother," Loki says to Ash, his fingers sliding along my opening, making my breath catch. "But maybe one day I'll let you join us, and you can tie her to the bed yourself." I can hear the teasing in his tone. He's such a shit stirrer. Still makes my heart beat faster though.

"Would you like that, baby?" he whispers against my ear, and I have no control over the moan that escapes my lips, or the liquid that escapes my lower ones. "I think you do."

I can see a fire flare in Ash's eyes, and his breathing begins to quicken as he watches Loki basically fingering me in front of him, rubbing circles around my clit in a maddening way that sends pulses shooting out from his touch. It's almost impossible to keep my hips from moving, seeking more friction.

Before I can get too close to release, Loki stops abruptly, pulling his fingers away. I see his hand come up, towards what must be his mouth, then he utters, "Delicious as always, *Princess*."

A flash of anger flies across Ash's eyes and his nostrils flare wide.

"Come on, Pretty Girl. I'll give you one more orgasm to help get you back to sleep. We've got Women's Studies first period, so we need to be up bright and early."

A shock of laughter peels out of me, breaking through my lust haze. "*You* are in Women's Studies?" I ask with a giggle.

"I'll have you know, Lilly Darling, that I am a staunch feminist. I love all women equally," he says jokingly with an eyebrow waggle.

"I'm not sure you understand what feminism means, Loki," I respond back dryly, rolling my eyes at him.

"Sure I do. Ladies first, right? Now, come on, and let me show you," he urges, herding me out of the room.

I look over my shoulder to see Ash, still standing there looking after us, with an unreadable expression in his eyes.

# CHAPTER TEN

JAX

I head to the gym, my muscles tense.

I need to burn off this...whatever the fuck this is since a certain brunette with haunted hazel eyes walked into our lives fourteen fucking days ago, wearing nothing but a towel covering those delicious curves.

She was full of fire and sass, but there was a pain in her eyes, one that made my own beast sit up, sniff the air, and take notice.

My dick stirs in my black shorts, pressing against the fabric as I think about her sitting on the toilet, her glorious rosy tits out, staring at me with a look of slight fear, yet pupils blown with lust.

The fucked up asshole that I am, it's that edge of fear that really makes me hard. Imagining my big hands wrapped around her throat, and squeezing as I pound hard and fast into her tight cunt...

*Fuck!*

I start walking faster, I'm practically jogging at this point. I desperately need the release that only working out can give me. Nothing else comes close to the freedom I feel when I'm pushing myself to get bigger, to become stronger. It's an addictive pain; building bulk, tearing muscles. Getting bigger hurts like a motherfucker sometimes, but I need to be strong. Powerful. Able to defend those that I love.

Reaching the locker room, I scan my ID card across the keypad on the door to gain access, and then step through to be engulfed with the sweet smell of sweat and hard fucking work.

A relieved sigh escapes my lips as I breathe it in, comfort washing over me and relaxing me like nothing else. Excited anticipation pulses through me as I reach my locker, using my card again to open it.

A box of unused hypodermic needle syringes fall out, scattering across the floor with a clatter, some landing a few lockers away.

“Shit,” I curse under my breath, bending down and picking up the ones at my feet. Turning to reach for the few that landed a couple of feet away, I see a muscled hand, not anywhere near as big as mine, grab them and hold them out to me.

“You dropped these, bro,” he says, a slight tremor in his hand. *Pussy. Kyle? Karl? Some shit like that, I think.* “How’s it going?” he asks, trying to catch my eye.

“Yeah, good, I guess,” I grunt, looking at him, not really wanting to talk.

“Hey, can you hook me up with some more juice? Your dad gets us the best shit,” he replies, a touch of envy in his voice as he hands me the packet of hypos. His eyes are wide and hopeful, with a touch of hero worshipping. *Fucking pathetic.*

“Sure,” I mumble, facing my locker, clenching my fist and almost breaking the needles as thoughts of the cumstain who calls himself my father flashes across my vision. He’s such a cuntish waste of oxygen.

I stuff the syringes back into the box, placing them into my locker. Taking my earbuds out of their case, I pop them in, discouraging further conversation.

Exiting the locker room, leaving him standing there like a fucking douche, I hit play on my phone, and *Scared of the Dark* by Lil Wayne and Ty Dolla $ign comes on. The lyrics flow over me as I wrap my hands and walk over to the punching bags, laying into one and making it swing violently. The dull thud of my fists hitting the bag sounds to the beat of the song.

*I’m not fucking weak, and I’m not scared. Not anymore.*

---

## LILLY

I emerge from the library on Friday night, bleary-eyed from all of the reading that we're expected to do, and the tough first two weeks we've just had.

*They don't fuck round here, do they?* I think wearily as I make my way down the dark corridor towards my dorm. A shadow steps in front of me, and I freak the fuck out, jumping about six feet in the air and screaming like...well, like a girl.

"Jesus fucking Christ on a cross!" I shout as the light hits his face, and I recognise him as one of the guys that hangs out with the Save the Whale Crew. He's even got on a blue stone washed t-shirt with 'Keep the Beaches Clean' written on it. I must admit, the surfer vibe does suit his dark blonde hair, which is longer on top reaching to just above his ears. But there's a coldness in his blue gaze that leaves me feeling the need to run, and run far away.

"Sorry, babe," he chuckles, reaching out to steady me with his hand. I take a step back, but feel his sweaty palm through my top as it alights on my arm. *Eww, back off, perv.*

"No worries..." I trail off. I can't for the life of me remember his name.

"Robert," he prompts with a charming smile. Although it seems a little off, like the smile Hook gives Peter Pan before he tries to stab him. I mean, don't get me wrong, I would stab that brat too. Fucking chauvinistic twat.

"No worries, Robert." I smile tightly and go to move down the hall. But he doesn't let go of my arm, if anything, his hand tightens. A shudder runs through me.

"Was there...something you wanted to say?" I enquire, looking up from his hand to see his smile widen a fraction. Alarm bells start to ring in my head matching my beating heart.

"Well, I heard you were...good friends with Loki, so I wanted to see if you'd like to go for a walk? I'd love to be friends with a girl who has your...experience."

*Wow! Someone smacked him a little too hard with the charming stick and ended up at fucking bellend.*

"I'm gonna go with a hard no on that one. Thanks, but no thanks," I deadpan as I turn to walk away. His grip becomes bruising, enough to cause a sharp intake of breath to escape me, which only makes him tighten it more, his eyes sparkling with a hint of lust and excitement.

"I thought we could go this way," he guides us down the hall, still oozing boy next door charm, if one could be a boy next door type with a malicious glint in his eyes. *What a straight up cunt.*

He gives me the shivers, but not the good kind. He starts dragging me down the corridor when I begin to resist in earnest, trying to pull my arm out of his bruising grip.

"Get your fucking slimy hands off me!" I shout, my heart pounding as I try twisting in his grip.

All of a sudden, I hear a rumbling growl behind me, my body sagging in relief at the same time that my nipples harden.

*Firstly, what the fuck kinda reaction is that? We should be shitting ourselves. Secondly, give me a break, nips! You girls have been like a fucking standing ovation since we came here.*

Robert pauses to look behind him, the colour draining from his face and leaving him paler than a corpse. One second I'm looking into his white pasty complexion, the next a sharp pain stings my arm, and Robert the fuckface is no longer holding onto me. He's been ripped off and is literally being pinned by his neck to the wall by a hulking Norse god who's vibrating with rage.

Robert's face is no longer as pale as Casper's, in fact, it's slowly turning purple. His eyes are bugging out in the most unattractive way, like a frog that's being squeezed.

"You ever touch her, or fucking look at her again," Jax snarls, teeth bared. His voice is like dark shadows, full of warning as if he's a beast about to rip this guy's throat out with his teeth. "I will tear your fucking balls off with my bare fucking hands."

*Called it.*

An acrid smell fills the air as Robert, like the pathetic wanker that he is, pisses himself. *Ewww.* Jax gives him a small shake then lets him go, leaving him a gasping heap on the floor, covered in his own urine. *Fucking disgusting.*

"Get the fuck out of here," Jax sneers in that delicious growl, and Fucktard —*he doesn't deserve his own name*—struggles to his feet and stumbles down the corridor.

"Jax?" I whisper, his back towards me. His whole body is shaking, his fists are tightly clenched, and his breathing is laboured.

"Jax?" I say again softly, approaching him like I would a wounded wild animal. I give him some space, walking round his side. I'm cautious, but my compass must be screwed because suddenly, my core is aching with need even as my heart races with more than a little fear.

"Jax, hey, I'm okay," I assure him, feeling so protected when I'm in his presence, like nothing will ever hurt me again. I know in my very bones that he'll never harm me. That I'm safe. Which is batshit crazy as I barely know the guy. I should be terrified of his barely controlled rage, but I'm just...not.

I finally reach him, coming round to that beautiful broad chest of his. His eyes are now closed, his nostrils flared with the effort of his breaths. He looks like he's about to explode, danger and barely suppressed violence rolling off him in intoxicating waves.

Hesitating for a beat, I take a deep breath and step closer until I'm surrounded by his wonderful citrus musk—*ah, he's the lemon body wash*—and my hand makes contact with his impossibly hard pec, which is burning with his body heat. I can feel the beat of his heart through his tank top, pounding so hard and fast that I'm amazed it's still trapped inside his chest.

"Don't touch me yet," he says roughly, my hand immediately stilling. "I don't want to hurt you." His voice is like velvet covered boulders sliding across my skin.

"I trust you, Jax. You won't force me to do anything I don't already want with you," I whisper, surprised at how quickly my fear has given way to lust.

His eyes snap open, the blue piercing like icicles, slicing straight through me, and I gasp.

"Baby Girl..." he starts through clenched teeth, his jaw so tight his short beard bristles with tension. "I don't have the control..."

His words have the opposite effect on me, and rather than scare me, they make my thighs clench tighter and my heart pound. My fingers tingle and I'm left feeling breathless, the want I can see in his gaze setting my nerves on fire. I need the risk he poses. I'm like the rabbit that needs the chase to feel alive.

"So lose control," I breathe, my fist bunching in his tank, my mouth a hair's breadth away from his.

There's a shift in his eyes as the blue sharpens to a razor point, and he takes in a mammoth breath, his chest getting even bigger.

Suddenly, he picks me up, one burning hot hand under each thigh and a squeal leaves my throat. He hoists me in his strong arms like I weigh nothing, pulling me flush against his rock hard body, and I nuzzle my face into his neck, breathing him in. I can feel his heat seeping through my lace knickers, my core burning with the contact, and I'm dripping with aching need and gasping. His hands are tight enough to bruise, and I revel in the edge of pain, wrapping my arms around his thick neck even tighter.

I have a flash of uncertainty. *I thought this kind of thing, being with more than one guy, only happened in my reverse harem novels? I've spent the week in Loki's bed, in Loki's arms. Will he be okay with this? He did say he didn't mind sharing...*

We get to our dorm, and Jax unlocks the door one handed, carrying me inside and ignoring the other guys who are sitting on the sofas. I see their faces, Kai's blush—*he is just too cute*—and Ash's narrowed gaze and compressed lips. I flip him off, smiling sweetly.

My eyes alight on Loki's emerald ones, and I bite my lower lip nervously until I notice that he's smirking.

"Don't do anything I wouldn't do!" Loki calls as we reach the bottom of the stairs, giving me a saucy wink.

*Huh, so I guess he is okay with this then.*

Jax growls, and I swear I almost come from the delicious vibrations that travel through my core. I squirm and grind against him, desperate for more friction. Jax growls at me again and holds my thighs even tighter, sending sweet tendrils of pain from his fingertips. They just add to the pleasure of his hard, hot body pressed against my lace-covered pussy.

He gets to his bedroom door and flings it open, making it crash loudly against the wall, and I'm sure I hear something fall off and land with a thud on the carpet, but don't have it in me to care right now.

"If you want to stop this anytime, just say 'red,' okay, Baby Girl?" he cautions, pulling back, and looking directly into my eyes, his demons just underneath the surface of his own sapphire ones.

I nod, incapable of speech and shivering with pent up arousal, wetting my lips. He slams the door shut with his foot and carries me over to his bed, which I notice is in various shades of blue. I can't take in much more as he flings me onto the mattress with such force that I bounce, landing in a mound of pillows with a squeak.

"This won't be gentle," he rumbles, violence still surrounding the air around him as he rips off, like literally tears in half, his tank.

I'm frozen to the spot as he begins to undress, watching with greedy eyes, my body filled with breathless anticipation and heated arousal. He toes off his trainers, and his gym shorts are next, showing me that, like Loki, he forgoes underwear. My mouth drops open as his hard erect cock jumps out.

*Fucking hell with a waffle on top!*

His hammer—*snort*—is even bigger standing to attention, and a thread of doubt runs through me as I genuinely wonder if it'll fit in Her Vagisty.

*A shower and a grower? Jesus.*

As if reading my mind, he smirks in a cocksure way, going to his bedside drawer, and pulling out a bottle of lube and a condom packet, which he throws down beside me.

I squirm and moan at the sight of him as he kneels on the bed, gasping when he grabs my legs and yanks me down towards him. He pulls off my red suede heels, leaving my knee-high lace edged socks on, rubbing his huge palms up my legs. I'm breathless and tingling all over, desperate for more.

His hands dip under my tartan mini skirt, hooking his fingers in the navy lace knickers I chose today, and agonisingly slowly, he pulls them down my thighs, then over my knees, and finally along my calves and off my feet.

I'm squirming on the bed, I can feel myself dripping onto his sheets. He brings the lace to his nose, and whilst keeping his gaze locked on mine, he takes a huge inhale, growling deep, his cock jumping as he takes in my scent.

"Ever since that first night, when we heard you cry out Loki's name, I've wondered what you'd smell like, taste like, fucking feel like," he groans, his words leaving me so turned on I'm surprised I'm not glowing fucking neon. "I've gripped my dick more times over the last week with your cry ringing in my ears than I have in the past year," he admits in that ocean deep voice of his.

"Had I known, I would have happily gripped it for you," I sass back breathily, and one side of his lips lifts in a smirk.

*Fuck. Me.* I'm literally panting with need here, unable to take my eyes off this god of a man.

He throws my knickers over his massive shoulder, his eyes darting to my soaking wet cunt, and licking his lips as he lowers himself down before grabbing each of my thighs on the inside and spreading me wide for him. Then he licks me from my opening to clit in one smooth stroke of his tongue. My hips buck, and I throw my head back hard.

*It feels so fucking good.*

He brings that wicked tongue back to my opening, using the same move and licking me over and over, with slow torturous passes like he has all the fucking time in the world. It's maddening, and leaves me writhing round, desperately seeking out more friction. More connection.

“Stop fucking teasing me, Jax!” I grind out, looking down at him and panting hard. I'm so fucking wired, I feel like a spring that's ready to burst.

“So impatient, Baby Girl,” he chuckles, and I thrash like a stormy sea as the vibrations of his laughter combine with his warm breath on my swollen pussy. His grip on my inner thighs tighten, his large fingers digging in.

“You want more?” he asks like an arsehole, giving me another slow lick, like I’m a bowl of fucking cream and he’s a cat.

“Yes!” I all but scream at him, causing another mischievous chuckle to tumble out of his glistening lips.

Letting go of one leg, he brings his hand up and taps my aching pussy in warning, right over my clit and sending a zing of electricity through me. I can’t say that I dislike the little bit of pain.

“Please, Jax,” I beg, practically crying with need.

“Good girl,” he utters as he lowers down again and takes my clit in his mouth, sucking hard as three of his massive fingers slam into me and start fucking me hard.

“Jax! Shit, Jax!” I yell out as I feel the burn of an orgasm beginning in my core, sending shockwaves all over my body.

He sucks even harder, grazing the bud with his teeth, and I explode, liquid gushing out of me. My eyes roll, and I see fucking galaxies as the intense orgasm rips through me.

“Fuck, Baby Girl. That was so hot.” I hear him rumble with appreciation while I come to.

I look up to see his beard dripping with my juices just as he wipes an arm across it. He reaches over, and I hear the foil of the condom wrapper tearing, then watch him slide it down his impressive length. *He must have to get extra bloody large!* Squirting some lube in his hand, he slathers it over his huge cock, giving it a few pumps with his fist clenched tightly round it.

I lay there, completely boneless, as he crawls up and over me before nestling himself between my thighs. I can feel his hard cock poking my entrance, causing another shiver to travel up my already sensitive body as my legs wrap around his hips.

He traces his fingers along my throat, and then with both hands grips my t-shirt and, I shit you not, tears it in half down the middle, just like the way he ripped his.

“That's better,” he grins cheekily.

*Prick!* And I'm just about to rip him a new one for desecrating my clothes when he asks, “You ready, Baby Girl?”

He doesn't even give me a chance to respond as he begins to nudge his hard length inside me, inch by delicious inch.

*Fucking Nora!*

I can feel myself stretching in the best possible way, and there’s a slight burn as he pushes all the way in. My eyes are practically rolling as he pushes in further, and I feel my walls clenching at his invasion.

“So goddamn tight,” he groans, finally bottoming out as his hips meet mine. I feel so full, like there’s not a millimetre of vacant space.

“Jax!” I gasp, clawing at him, desperate for him to move and give me the pleasure that I’m craving.

He starts to slowly withdraw, giving me time to get used to his size, but I'm done with him teasing me. I want him to let go, to lose control, and come out the other side. It feels important for him to see that he can't hurt me.

“I thought you were gonna lose control?” I say saucily, and his eyes flick to mine.

He hovers above me, his dick just an inch or two inside my wet heat. Something snaps in the blue orbs at my words, like an icicle breaking off a porch roof, and then he's slamming all the way into me, his pelvis hitting mine with a smack. I scream in anguished pleasure as he fills me so completely, I'm surprised there's room to breathe.

The bedposts hit the wall with a thud, and I swear I hear the headboard crack with the force of his thrust.

*Whoops!*

He keeps pounding into me, making animalistic sounds come from deep within my throat, and it feels like he hits my fucking cervix every damn time! He's working so hard there’s sweat beading on his temple, and his beautiful chest gleams with it.

I'm basically just holding on for dear life, my nails biting into his huge shoulders, leaving red crescents in their wake.

I start to feel the familiar burn of another orgasm, building fast into an uncontrollable raging fire under my skin. One of his hands reaches up and grasps my throat, not hard enough to cut off my air supply completely, but enough to show me that he very easily could.

"JAAAXXX!!" I scream as I shatter into a million pieces, seeing white for a moment.

He pounds into me even harder, once, twice, then he stills, roaring his release and filling the condom with his hot seed.

Somehow, he manages to collapse half off of me so that I'm not crushed underneath him, his softening cock still inside me. We lie there for a long while, relearning how to breathe and putting our pieces slowly back together.

Opening his eyes, he looks at me with that penetrating blue gaze, something hard to decipher swimming in their depths. *Gratitude? Relief?*

"Baby Girl..." he starts, that beautiful deep voice rubbing all over me, and I tingle from the sound. There's a feeling of awe in his tone as he pulls out and I wince slightly at the ache he leaves behind. "Did I hurt you? Fuck, are you okay?" he rushes out, pushing up, and I smile warmly at his worry for my well being.

"Only in the best fucking possible way, Jax," I reply huskily, reaching with my fingers to stroke his face, feeling his rough beard as I brush his chin.

His smile is so blindingly beautiful and full of joy, that my breath hitches. Taking the condom off and wrapping it in a tissue which he leaves on the bedside cabinet, he shuffles closer to me, putting his forehead against mine, and whispers, "Thank you, Baby Girl," then kisses me gently, melting me completely.

I smile, my eyes feeling heavy and already closing. Just before I drift off, I feel him pull me to him so that all space between our bodies is eliminated.

"Thank you for taking the rage away," he breathes, warmth caressing my ear. Then the darkness overtakes me, leaving me feeling the safest I've felt in a long time.

# CHAPTER ELEVEN

LILLY

I wake up feeling a delicious heat engulfing me, and surrounded by the smell of lemon drizzle cake, fresh from the oven. *Yum!* I stretch into the heat, snuggling in more.

There's a huge, heavy arm flung across my waist, pulling me in tight to the toasty hard body spooning me from behind. I can feel a tickle of breath along my neck, and my body tingles as it races along my skin causing goosebumps to erupt all over me. Everywhere our naked bodies touch feels hot, almost burning, as if I'm standing too close to an open flame.

*Someone has woken up happy.*

I chuckle to myself, feeling Jax's impressive length poking into my arse, and I can't help grinding a little against it, teasing myself and starting up an ache in my core for more. A deep, rumbling growl comes from behind me, sending exquisite vibrations straight to my aching pussy.

"Ready for more, Baby Girl?" he teases, his voice low and raspy, and so damn sexy from having just woken up.

*I wonder if he's ever thought of a career in audiobooks?*

He slides his large hand down my naked stomach, causing waves of pleasurable anticipation to roll down over me and my breath to hitch, before he finds my folds already slick with arousal. I moan as two thick digits leisurely enter me, pumping slowly in and out. I'd be lying if I said I wasn't a little sore from the pounding he gave me last night, but damn if I don't want more!

"Always so nice and wet for me," he whispers in my ear, then nips it, causing a gasping moan to escape my lips which gets louder as he picks up the pace, finger fucking me faster.

My hand reaches up behind me and tangles in his blond locks, pulling him closer towards me, in a bid to eliminate any gaps between us. I can feel his rock hard cock, slick with precum and thrusting in between my rear cheeks.

"Jax," I whimper, already feeling the burn of an impending orgasm building and opening my thighs wider for him.

"I'm gonna make you come so hard on my fingers, Baby Girl. Then I'm going to fuck you until you can't breathe, and the rest of those assholes downstairs will hear you scream *my* name this time," he growls, and I fucking come undone with his dirty talk, shouting his name just as the door is flung open and a fallen angel strolls in, butt naked and standing to full attention. Of course he leaves the door open as well. *Fucking exhibitionist.*

"The fuck you want?" Jax barks, a spark of anger in his voice. He's still leisurely thrusting his fingers inside me, making ripples flow through my body and chasing away any embarrassment I might feel at being caught like this.

"Obviously, I have an issue that I need Pretty Girl's help with," Loki sarcastically replies, indicating his raging hard on and rolling his emerald eyes at Jax.

"Loki!" I admonish, my cheeks colouring, now that my orgasm is fading.

*I'm naked in bed with his friend, for fuck's sake!*

"I'm sure you could have taken care of the issue yourself," I sass, raising one brow at him, a teasing smile coming over my lips, which is quickly replaced with a moan when Jax hits a particularly sweet spot inside me.

Loki walks in until he's standing next to the bed, his glorious cock standing proud and practically in my fucking face. *The rug really does match the drapes!*

I lick my lips at the sight, causing Loki's smirk to get even bigger.

"Nah. I'd much rather you dealt with it. After all, you caused it. And anyway, you want to help me, don't you, Pretty Girl?" he cajoles, looking directly at me. My gaze shoots up to meet his heated one, my whole body flushing and zinging with electricity.

"You want him to join us, Baby Girl?" Jax asks curiously in that sinful voice of his.

My gaze is locked on Loki, seeing every shade of green in his beautiful eyes, like dappled sunlight through leaves. The curtains are cracked, and a sunbeam shines directly onto him, lighting him up like the angel he resembles.

"Yes," I say in a whisper. A burning heat like I've never felt before races across my body, tightening my nipples and leaving me breathless.

*I can't believe I've just admitted that out loud. I'd be embarrassed if I wasn't so turned on right now.*

"Good girl." Loki smiles smugly, and without waiting for Jax's permission, he throws back the covers, letting our delicious warmth escape, and then pauses to admire the view of me sweating and naked, my thighs parted, with Jax's fingers still inside me.

"Shit, Pretty Girl. You're so fucking gorgeous, especially with your pussy wrapped around Jax's fingers," he enthuses, his emerald eyes aflame and biting his lush bottom lip. *Why is that so fucking sexy?*

"Are you getting the fuck in or what?" Jax challenges, voice rough with an undercurrent of violence that only makes me wetter. Loki gives us his signature cheeky grin, then climbs into bed, laying his head on his bent arm next to mine on the pillow.

*We're really fucking doing this?!* I feel a surge of adrenaline suffuse my limbs, and butterflies burst to life in my stomach.

"Good morning, Pretty Girl," Loki says softly, looking into my eyes whilst cupping my face with his palm. I can't help nuzzling into the warm touch, closing my eyes for the briefest of seconds. "I missed you in my bed last night and slept terribly." A hint of vulnerability enters his gaze, making my heart crack and ache.

It's difficult to think with him so close, looking at me like...like I'm the only thing standing between him and the hellish abyss. That can't be right, we've only known each other what, a couple of weeks? I mean, I know I've spent every night near enough in his bed, but still, that was just fucking. *Wasn't it?*

Before I can think of a response, his teasing grin is back in place, and I just know that what's about to come out of his mouth is gonna piss me off a little.

"My cock's not used to being so cold at night. He was lonely."

*Annnnd there it is. Fucking arsegoblin.*

I go to slap the fucker, mostly in jest, but he catches my hand first, and in one quick move squeezes a dollop of lube into it—*when the fuck did he pick that up?* He brings my hand down and wraps it tightly round his rock hard length, keeping his hand over the top of mine and moving both up and down.

"Fuck, Lilly," he groans as we pump his cock together, and I won't even bother to deny the rush of wetness that floods between my legs.

"Don't forget about me, Baby Girl," Jax growls behind me, nibbling my neck just shy of causing pain. "Remember my promise?" I whimper in response as he withdraws his fingers from my slick pussy.

There's the familiar rustle of a foil wrapper, and then he uses his hand to drape my leg over his hip, opening me wide. I can feel the cool air of the room on my bare cunt, adding another layer of sensation to my already sensitised body.

"Jesus fucking Christ, that's a sight to behold," Loki moans huskily as Jax starts to nudge his way inside me, my cream acting as lube and helping him to ease in.

The stretch feels so fucking good, my eyes already wanting to roll with the exquisite burn. At that moment, Loki shifts so the pierced tip of him rubs against my clit, sending an electric current zapping across me.

"Yes!" I exclaim, completely lost to all of the pleasure coursing through me, my eyes closing so I can feel it all better.

Jax starts to fuck me in earnest, just the way I like it, pounding into me from behind, his large hand gripping my hip hard enough to bruise. It feels so good, almost too much, as he touches every part of me inside. Loki keeps a steady pace with our hands, kissing me full on, and exploring my mouth with his expert tongue. He tastes like wicked mornings and sinful indulgence, and I can't get enough, meeting him stroke for stroke and moaning into his mouth. My free hand is grasping at his chest, no doubt leaving red scratches all over it.

I'm so close I can feel myself starting to fall, burning like I'm on fire. Loki pauses in his devastation of my mouth, leaning his forehead next to mine, and whispers, “Next time, Pretty Girl, I'll be inside you too, fucking that pretty ass of yours.”

At his words, I groan and clench round Jax's dick.

“Fuck, Loki! Whatever you just said, she's like a fucking vise around my cock,” he hisses. His pace picks up, becoming frenzied as he starts to chase his release.

Loki matches Jax's thrusts by pumping our hands along his length harder and faster, hitting my clit with each turn, making my body sing and alight all at the same time.

“I just told her,” he grinds out, voice deep and husky, “that next time, we will both be inside her, fucking her so hard she won’t be able to walk for a week.” His filthy words set off a chain reaction, and I come hard with a scream, my inner walls contracting and milking Jax.

I hear Jax shout as he climaxes, stiffening up behind me, buried to the hilt. Seconds later, Loki cries out my name as he orgasms, shooting ropes of his hot seed all across the front of my pussy, coating it and marking me as his in the most primal way.

We lay there, in a hot fucking sweaty mess, panting.

“Jesus, Pretty Girl. You look even better with my cum all over that pretty cunt of yours,” Loki sighs appreciatively, still breathing heavily, but looking at me like he wants to throw me over his shoulder and go caveman.

“If I had the energy, you'd get a smack for that comment, you Neanderthal,” I rasp out breathily, making Jax chuckle in that deep voice of his, which in turn makes me groan and clamp round his softening cock that’s still inside me. Of course, that makes him growl and thrust his hips, already beginning to harden once more.

“How the fuck are you ready to go again?!” I gasp out, although Her Vagisty seems to be open to the idea, quite literally fluttering round his cock like a fucking butterfly on a dick flower.

“Oh, you have no idea of my stamina, Baby Girl,” he smugly boasts in that deep voice of his, and I can hear the smirk as he starts to gently thrust his hips in and out of me, getting harder and harder by the second.

“Jax...” I warn, although there's a hint of a moan in my tone. “I need a shower!”

“Oh, why didn't you say so?” he replies, pulling out abruptly and leaving me gaping.

He pulls off the condom, dropping it and the one from last night into the bin nearby, then kneeling on the bed, scoops me up bridal style, and I clutch at his thick neck with a squeal.

"I can fuck you just as good in the shower," he mutters cheekily.

He walks out of the room with me in his arms, both of us completely naked and his hard cock no doubt bobbing for all to see. I look over his shoulder at Loki, sprawled on the bed looking every inch the fallen angel in his glorious nakedness.

"Don't look at me, Pretty Girl," he laughs, his emerald gaze alight with mischief. "I'm sure Jax will take real good care of you."

"Unhelpful wanker," I grumble half heartedly as we leave the room and head down the stairs.

When we get to the bottom, I can see Kai sitting on a sofa, his laptop in his lap with his iPad next to him. He looks up as we reach the last step, his eyes going wide behind his glasses and his mouth popping open as he takes us in.

Ash is making himself a coffee in the kitchenette. I can smell the deliciously warming scent, and even though I hate the drink, I love that smell. His brow furrows and his eyes narrow as he watches us, and I catch his gaze darting down to my bare pussy just as I feel Loki's cum drip down my inner thigh. His top lip curls in a sneer, but not before I see his steel eyes blaze, liquefying them to molten silver.

"You're going to get cum all over the floor," he drawls in that arrogant tone of his, and I blush bright red.

Jax doesn't miss a beat, continuing our journey towards the bathroom, throwing over his shoulder in his sexy, deep rumble, "Lucky we're taking a shower then, huh?"

I see Ash's eyes become almost slits, but Jax just walks through the doorway, turns round, and slams the door shut, all whilst still carrying me like I weigh nothing.

"Jealous ass," he mumbles as he finally sets me down on my feet and starts up the shower.

"Jealous?!" I exclaim, my eyes wide and slack-jawed as I look at him.

"Baby Girl. Trust me on this. He's all sore because he wishes it was his cum dripping off that sweet fucking pussy," he mumbles, stalking towards me like I'm his prey. I bite my lip and close my eyes, images of Ash doing exactly what Loki just did, flashing across my vision.

My thighs clench with the dirty pictures filling my mind, my eyes snapping open as I hear the rumble of Jax's laughter from right in front of me.

"He'll come around eventually. Especially if you keep walking around like that." He smirks, reaching out to brush the back of his fingers along the curve of my breast, and I shiver.

"Come on, Baby Girl. Time to get clean so we can get dirty again," he beckons, giving me another cheeky smile as he tugs me towards the shower and my next few orgasms.

---

By the time we finish and get ready for the day, it's lunchtime. As I make my way down the spiral staircase, I can smell something so delicious my stomach growls, and Jax chuffs with laughter behind me.

"Work up an appetite, did you, Baby Girl?" he asks, chuckling.

"Shut up!" I reply, though there's no heat behind it. We reach the bottom, and my stomach growls loudly again.

*Damn! I really am starving! Not surprising given all of the sexercise I've been doing lately. Snort.*

I look over to see Kai plating up what looks like homemade chicken ramen. *Fucking yum!* I walk over to help carry the bowls to the table, but Loki and Jax beat me to it, refusing to let me carry even my own. My inner feminist rolls her eyes, yet Her Vagisty approves of the chivalry and takes it as her due.

"Kai, this smells amazing," I say, taking a big inhale as we sit down to eat. I look round and realise that Ash isn't here. *Strange.* Although, maybe the stick up his arse stops him from relaxing and he's plotting world domination upstairs.

I pick up my chopsticks and grab some chicken, blowing on it before putting it in my mouth and...*holy fuck balls!* An embarrassingly loud moan escapes my lips, and my eyes close. An explosion of tastes erupts on my tongue; there's the earthy chicken stock with a hint of spicy ginger and refreshing lemongrass.

I open my eyes to see three hungry gazes staring at me, chopsticks poised over their bowls. I suddenly realise that I've had sex with two out of the three that are seated at the table, and I can feel my cheeks heating again.

"Kai, this is really fucking good!" I say, trying to break the tension in the air. It works as they all blink, like they're coming back up for air and start to eat. Kai blushes adorably, as he does a lot when I talk to him.

"Thanks, Lilly. I love to cook," he answers, quickly looking down at his bowl and beginning to eat.

"Who taught you? I mean, it doesn't exactly seem like a rich boy's pastime, if you get my drift?" I ask with a smile. I'd love to find out more about the guys.

"My nanny taught me," he replies, still looking into his steaming ramen bowl. "She used to take me into the kitchen and say, 'Right, Master Kai. It's time you learned how to cook so that you can feel the joy of feeding others.' And she showed me how to make all kinds of foods, from all over the world. I loved it, mixing the different flavors and figuring out what works well together. She was right. There is great joy to be found in feeding others, I love to give people what I make. It makes me happy to see them enjoying my food." He's become animated as he speaks, more so than I've seen so far, and there's a glow in his eyes, a warmth that I haven't seen before. *He loved her,* I think, a little surprised that a rich kid would feel such affection for a servant.

*Judgemental much, Lilly?*

"Do you still see her? Your nanny?" I ask as we continue to eat the yummy noodles. The light goes out of his gaze at my question, making the amber brown of his eyes dull and sad.

"Uh, well, when my uncle discovered that she was teaching me to cook, he fired her and wouldn't tell me her address or anything. So, no. I don't see her anymore." He sighs sadly, looking back down to his bowl, and placing his chopsticks down beside it.

My heart aches for him. *It's official, his uncle is a dickhead of the highest calibre.* Being able to cook is a valuable life skill and to punish someone for teaching a child?! *What the ever loving fuck is wrong with these people? And what about his parents? Where are, or were, they?* A twinge of pain stabs me in the gut at that thought, so I decide not to pursue it.

"So, where's Ash today? Off to torture unsuspecting kittens?" I joke, seeing it falls a little flat as the guys all seem to wince and cringe. *Goddammit! Foot meet mouth.*

Loki clears his throat, "Ash goes home for the weekend," he tentatively tells me.

I've never seen him so...sombre before. *What's that about?* I wonder. None of the others elaborate, all avoiding my gaze which is shifty as fuck.

"Okay, cool. So..." I start, hoping this time I don't make a tit of myself, "what do you guys do on the weekends?" I nervously glance at them to see what their reactions are, hoping it's not another tricky subject.

"I'm hitting the gym," Jax drawls whilst wolfing down his ramen.

"All weekend?!" I exclaim, although looking at his drool-worthy muscles that his black tank shows off to perfection, and remembering the feel of restrained power and violence he exuded when he was on top and inside of me, makes me appreciate the time he spends working on his body.

Shivering with the memories, it's like Jax can read my mind, and he gives me that devilish smile of his, the one that so far I've only seen aimed at me, and tenses his huge biceps, making them even bigger.

"These guns don't get this big with no work, Baby Girl," he cheekily replies, earning an eye roll from me before getting up from the table and taking his bowl to the dishwasher, then grabbing his gym bag, giving me a hard peck on the lips, and heading out.

"Jeez, Pretty Girl. I know how delicious that pussy of yours is, but I didn't realise it had magical powers too!" Loki teases. *Fucking cockwomble.* I throw my napkin at him, but I'm curious as to what he means.

"What on earth are you waffling about, Loki?" I ask.

"Waffling?" he queries, a perfect auburn brow raised and a very cute look of confusion on his beautiful face.

"Yeah, waffling. Like talking about, but with a healthy dollop of bullshit and a side of nonsense," I tell him, smiling sweetly and tipping my head to one side.

"Ah. The British speak again. You guys have some crazy sayings," he says, a wide grin on his face.

"Pot and kettle, Loki. Now, back to my magic vagina?" I ask again, crossing my arms and raising a brow of my own, whilst desperately trying to hold in my smile.

"Ah, yes," he smirks, giving me that panty melting grin and making Her Vasgisty perk up like a fucking dog waiting for a treat. *Greedy bitch!* "I was 'waffling' about the fact that not only does Jax remain silent most of the time, even with us, but usually, he never smiles and he never sleeps with a girl. I mean, sure, he fucks them, well, those that can handle his 'meat,'" he teases, winking at me, and I groan. I'm never going to live that down. "He never sleeps in bed with them afterwards or hooks up with them again."

My mouth falls open. I am gobsmacked. Okay, so he mostly frowned when I first arrived, but he has been smiling at me a lot recently, especially since last night. He gives me this devilish grin that makes me squirm, and butterflies dance in my stomach. I hoped that it was something just for me, but I never imagined that the act of smiling was something he didn't usually do, even with his close friends. Plus, he didn't let go of me all night, holding me close in those strong arms, letting me know that I'm all kinds of safe and protected there.

"Oh," I say, my forehead furrowing and biting my lip. I'm at a loss as to what to think, or even feel. *It's just sex with Jax and Loki, right?*

"Oh, indeed, Pretty Girl," Loki teases in a terrible British accent, breaking into my troubled thoughts, his emerald gaze sparkling. I hear a chair scrape back as Kai gets up, taking our empty bowls, and walking to the dishwasher.

"I was planning on heading into town, if you'd like to join me?" he enquires in that melodic voice of his as he straightens up, cheeks going pink as he speaks.

"I'd love to join you, Kai," I say, beaming at him, his face going even redder.

As I get up, I hear Loki retort, "See, magic pussy." And this time I playfully smack him on his shoulder when I walk past. He captures my wrist and pulls me into his lap, kissing me soundly on the lips, leaving me breathless and aching.

He looks into my eyes, his gaze heated, whispering against my lips in that sexy deep voice of his, "Go add to your harem, Pretty Girl. But tonight, you're in my bed." Then he licks my bottom lip, releases my wrist, helping me off his lap as he stands up, and heads upstairs.

My brain feels fuzzy with lust, and it takes a moment for what he's said to sink in. *Harem? Now there's an idea. If only Kai and Ash were on board...*

"Ready?" Kai asks softly, waiting by the door and looking at me with his beautiful honey gaze, once again bringing me back to the present.

"Uh...yes. Sure. Absolutely." I smile brightly as I try to shake myself out of my stupor, and head out the door with him by my side.

# CHAPTER TWELVE

LILLY

Kai leads me down to the student car park—or parking lot as he calls it—which is on the edge of campus, just past the tennis courts. Ironic, keeping cars and all their fumes so close to where people exercise.

I haven't been this way before, not having a car of my own or my American driver's licence, and as we come round the corner, I stop dead and gape in horror.

*Jesus wept!*

Before me lies millions of pounds, or dollars I suppose, worth of cars. I'm pretty much a car newb, but even I can tell that these are the best money can buy, what with all the black horse and gold bull logos.

"Bloody Nora!" I exclaim, causing Kai to turn and look back at me, his brows raised and a look of bemusement on his face.

"Bloody who?" he asks with a small chuckle.

"Oh, never mind!" I say back, flapping my hands in the air. "Are these...*student* cars?" I ask, a little aghast at the displayed wealth.

"Uh, yeah. Why?" Kai asks back, clearly having no idea how most students, or even people, live.

Like, the cars here cost more than many people's houses. Certainly more than most people's yearly salaries. It's insane, and I start to truly realise the world that I've become a part of since Mum...My mind shies away from the word.

"They're so..." I'm actually at a loss as to how to describe it to Kai, who's lived with privilege his whole life, why this is so wrong. He's never had to go without, or not put the heating on because it costs too much. It's not his fault, I guess, it's just the world he grew up in. Doesn't make it any less fucked.

"Never mind, Kai. It doesn't matter." I sigh and start to catch up with him. He puts a slender hand on my arm, stopping me once I reach him.

"No, Lilly. It does matter," he urges seriously, locking his honey brown gaze with mine. I take a deep breath, trying to figure out a way to explain what I know inherently.

"These cars...they're..." I bite my lip then think, *fuck it!* "They're everything that's wrong with this world," I rush out, causing his eyebrows to raise.

He remains silent, waiting for me to explain further. I've noticed that about him in my short time here. He's the quiet one of the group and I bet he gets overlooked for it, but he's always watching. Observing and taking in all the minute details round him.

"Growing up with Mum," my voice hitches, the pain of losing her still raw, like an open wound that just won't heal. It's as if thinking about her, talking about her reopens it, like her death has only just happened, even though it was almost nine months ago now.

I take a deep, steadying breath, letting the birdsong and other sounds filter in until my mind stills and I'm able to talk again.

"She did everything she could for me, to provide for us. She worked long hours at the club, late at night to put food on the table and clothes on my back. We were okay moneywise, we could afford nice things and shopping sprees. The odd spa day too." I remember, smiling fondly at the memory. "But I had friends who weren't as comfortable as us. Who thought we were well off. And this," I say, gesturing round us at all the shiny metal. "This is obscene! These cars are worth more than most people earn in a year. And they're owned by, what, eighteen year olds?!" My voice is a little raised with anger threaded through it as I think about how unfair it all is. "Tell me how it's right, how it's okay for some people to work so fucking hard all for a pittance when you lot don't have to lift a finger, yet can own a car worth the cost of an expensive house?" I stare straight into his eyes, pleading with him to give me answers. His hand drops from my arm, and I instantly miss the small comfort it gave.

"I...I...I don't know. I'm sorry, Lilly," he stutters, his gaze dropping and head bowing as if in shame. "I guess...it's not fair. And this world is...hard for most of us, just in different ways," he says, turning away, but not before I can see genuine pain in his eyes.

Suddenly, I feel like an arsehole. It's not his fault his family are rich one-percenters. And he's right, we all have our crosses to bear, regardless of how much we have in the bank. This time, I reach out and touch his arm, ducking my head a little trying to capture his gaze.

"Hey. I know it's not your fault, Kai. And I'm sorry for being such a prick about it all. Can we forget I said anything, please?" His lips tilt upwards, and fireflies start to dance in my stomach.

"You are not a 'prick,'" he declares, and I huff out a laugh at his use of the word. "Your feelings are totally valid, and although I can't say I've experienced going without, for what it's worth, I agree, and I try to help where I can."

He leaves it at that, not elaborating, and I notice that my hand is still on his arm at the same time he does. His lips turn up more, in a smile that almost reaches his eyes, then he grabs my hand, tucks it in the crook of his arm like an old fashioned gentleman, and leads me towards the front of the lot.

We stop in front of an admittedly gorgeous little silver vintage looking car, like something out of a Bond film.

"Your carriage, m'lady," he jokes, cringing only slightly given our recent conversation.

"She's beautiful," I say, admitting to myself that I'm not above admiring a gorgeous car. "What is she?" I ask him.

"She's a 1954 Mercedes SL 300 Gullwing with red leather interior." He grins proudly as he reaches down and opens my door upwards, so it indeed looks like a bird's wing. I get in, and he shuts it, jogging round to the driver's side and getting in himself.

"Wow," I exclaim, running my hand along the bright cherry red leather seat. The whole car smells like Kai, like fresh woods after the rain scent, mixed in with leather and beeswax polish.

He turns the key in the ignition, and I swear to the god of orgasms that I almost come from the deep purr of the engine. My thighs clench together, and I'm not sure whether I'm seeking relief or trying to stave off an oncoming orgasm. Kai gives me a knowing, Loki-worthy smirk as he puts the car into drive and pulls out of the lot, speeding down the gravel tree-lined drive and making my heart flutter like I'm on a rollercoaster.

We emerge from the scrolling metal front gates, the guards letting us pass with barely a glance, and onto the main road. I arrived so late that I didn't get to take in much of the surrounding scenery, and I'm delighted to find that Highgate Prep appears to be nestled in a forest full of what looks like pine trees. Today the sun is shining, the sky a deep beautiful blue, and its rays reach out through the gaps in the trees, like it's trying to touch us as we speed along.

The road is winding, and as we turn one particular corner, I gasp aloud, sitting up and clutching at the door. Before me is the most spectacular view. Majestic snow-capped mountains appear at the end of the road, which twists out of view. To either side of us golden grass and trees line the tarmac, in colours ranging from crimson red to deepest amber and palest yellow. It's breathtaking. Utterly spellbinding. And so far removed from the greys and hustle of London, that I might as well be on another planet.

"Like the view?" Kai teases in that melodic voice of his, sending shivers skating across my body. I turn to look at him, mouth still agape.

"It's...wow," I say, lost as to how to convey what I'm feeling right now. "It's so different from London, yet it feels familiar too. Like, I've just stepped into a favourite dream. There's so much colour here, so much life. But it's not crazy busy or noisy. It just is. Does that make any sense?" I'm trying to put into words this...peace I suddenly feel. As though this is where I was always meant to be. Which is madness, I know.

"Yes it does. I love seeing things anew from your eyes," Kai responds softly, eyes on the road and his cheeks that adorable pink colour.

---

KAI

Seeing Lilly's beautiful hazel eyes filled with wonder does something to me.

It's like she's the sun, and my soul leans towards her, desperate for any light. The moment she walked into our lives, in that towel, I was lost.

The way she challenged Ash was perfection, I've never seen someone stand up to him before, let alone looking as fiercely beautiful as she did. Especially wearing only a towel. And later, her cries of passion, screaming Loki's name in ecstasy, well, it had awoken a long dormant passion inside of me that I was beginning to think would never resurface. For the first time in a long time, I had to seek relief for the ache that she created, painting my bedsheets with my release, while images of her underneath me moaning my name played over and over in my mind.

I shift in my seat, hoping she doesn't see the evidence of my arousal, and try to focus back on the road. On the view that I feel like I'm seeing for the first time. It really is beautiful. I guess growing up near here makes you take it for granted.

"'If gravity is love of earth, the mountains teach us how to fly, and bring us back as rivers flow,'" I quote at her, the poem coming to mind as we drive along the winding road.

"That's beautiful, Kai. Who wrote it?" she asks, a touch of something in her voice that I can't puzzle out.

"It's called *Colorado* by David Mason. I can't remember the rest of it, but I always used to think of those lines when seeing the mountains around here," I tell her, noting the wistful tone of my voice.

*Gone are the days when poetry was important to me.*

"And now?" she asks softly. "Now, what do you think?"

A feeling of being trapped, of being all alone, isolated, and terrified sweeps through me with such force my breath catches and my heart pounds hard. And then to my surprise, it's followed by a slight softening, like sunlight filtering through a cave showing a way out.

"I think I'm beginning to see their beauty again," I respond, and I can feel the flush on my cheeks. It's one thing we have in common, Lilly and I, blushing like schoolgirls.

The rest of the journey is silent, but not uncomfortable. It's the quiet of longtime friends who are comfortable in each other's company. I prefer it over lots of people and loud noises, liking my own company better, or hanging out with the guys. Although, I can see the benefits of hanging out with a certain hazel eyed brunette too.

As we pull onto Main Street, I can't help but see it through her eyes afresh. The wide boulevard with its nineteenth century buildings, all leading to a backdrop of the majestic mountains that make this area so popular with the powder chasers come winter. An idea springs to mind, and for once, I don't overthink it.

“Do you like hiking?” I ask her, pulling into the parking space in front of one of the many boutiques the small town has to offer the fashion addicts of Highgate Prep.

“I used to love walking in Hampstead Heath?” she tells me, a little unsure and ending it like a question.

“Great.” And a smile takes over my face as I begin to plan. “Would you like to come for a hike next Sunday? With me? We could explore the forest around Highgate, and there's a pretty awesome lake about five miles away where we could stop for a picnic. You know, if you'd want to?” I ask, uncertainty in my tone. I mean, would she want to spend time with me? Especially as she clearly already has Loki and Jax, and I doubt Ash will hold out for much longer. Not with the way he looks at her.

“I'd love that!” she beams, and as I look into those stunning eyes of hers, I swear she eclipses the sun outside the car window.

“Great. It's a date,” I say, smiling back and feeling that fucking blush return to my cheeks.

*Real cool, asshole.*

# CHAPTER THIRTEEN

LILLY

Kai and I spent a wonderful afternoon wandering about town and looking at what the high-end shops had to offer. He didn't mind window shopping at all and was a great companion, happy to talk about anything and everything. He shied away from talking about his childhood, but then so did I, so we mainly stuck to Highgate Prep. He filled me in on all the gossip, which I must say is hilarious. When I questioned him about how he knew so much, he just shrugged and told me, a little cryptically, that he keeps an ear out for these things.

We stopped for tea in this beautiful, authentic British tea room run by an Englishwoman, named Sally. I got to enjoy a proper cup of fragrant Earl Gray tea with a slice of buttery Victoria Sponge cake, which made me tear up a little with a pang of longing for home. Although, I don't miss it quite as much as I thought I might, and that surprises me. I suppose given what happened...*nope! Still not going there! Not again today, Satan!* I know it's cowardly of me to not face what happened, but I just can't. I'm not sure that I'll ever be able to.

After tea, we went to the supermarket to pick up a few bits and pieces for dinner. Kai explained that he usually orders shopping online and gets it delivered to the dorm, but had forgotten a few key ingredients for tonight's meal. I do love how excited he gets about cooking for us all, and he really does take great joy in feeding people. Perhaps I'll make something for him one day, a typical English roast dinner. Or maybe I'll see if he'd like to cook it together?

We head back to campus as it's getting dark, the sun setting behind those breathtaking mountains with the stunning image reflected in my wing mirror. I feel so at peace here, like there's a calming breeze constantly playing over my skin. This place, it's something else.

I feel at ease for the first time since Mum died, like I can finally breathe and live again. I don't know whether it's the guys or the setting, maybe both? Mum was always a great believer in following gut instincts, and mine is telling me that here is where I'm meant to be. At least, for now.

As I open the door to our dorm, I hear the beautiful voice of Joseph Vincent singing *Mine,* and I come to a complete standstill, stalling just inside. Kai knocks into me, grabbing my arms from behind to help steady me, but I hardly notice when I see the sight before me.

I lock eyes with Loki who's lounging on the sofa looking entirely too pleased with himself, like a smug cat. No, a tiger. He's much too primal and dangerous for a mere moggy. He slowly licks his full bottom lip then captures it between his teeth, making my heart stutter, my breath catch on a sharp inhale, and my core ache fiercely. Kai's fingers tighten on my biceps, which just seems to fuel my lust and I feel my knickers getting damper by the second.

Loki looks decadent, lounging there, arms thrown along the back of the sofa and one leg up over the arm. An angel waiting to be worshipped. Or a devil waiting for his sacrifice.

He's wearing a navy blue dress shirt unbuttoned and open, displaying his delicious torso, covered in all that beautiful ink. His jeans are slung so low on his hips, I can see his happy trail, which is auburn like his hair.

*Fuck me.*

I can't even form a coherent thought as that song plays with him looking like he's seconds away from the best orgasm of his life, devouring me with that emerald gaze of his. There's a banked heat in his eyes, and I know I'm not the only one remembering him fucking me senseless whilst he sang this very song to me.

*Jesus fucking Christ.*

Curling up, he stalks over to us, not taking his predatory gaze off mine, and when he reaches me, we are so close my hardened nipples brush his bare chest. I gasp quietly at the contact, and hear a low growl from behind me, which Loki raises a perfect red brow at. A mischievous smirk crosses his lips as Kai pulls me closer, my back now flush with his front. Having them both caging me in is destroying what little sanity I had left, and I'm so close to the edge I could tumble off with the slightest nudge.

"You've a little drool there," he teases, chuckling as he uses the pad of his thumb, wiping at the corner of my mouth.

*Twatterdick. Two can play that game!*

Before he takes his thumb back, I capture it between my teeth, biting down slightly before sucking it all the way into my mouth and using my tongue to caress it. My fingers tease along his hard abs, finding every ridge and line.

A breath hisses out of him, an inferno raging deep in his eyes as I continue to caress his digit with my mouth. In all fairness, I'm not faring much better and if the hard length pressed against my back is any indication, neither is Kai. Ironically, I can hear *Swalla - Acoustic Version* by Missy & Blonde and Julia Ross come over the speakers, and I smirk as I let go of his thumb with a pop.

I can see his chest rising and falling with how hard he's now breathing, his pulse jumping in his throat. My own heart rate matches his, beat for beat as arousal floods my veins, getting me all hot and bothered.

"How long til dinner, Kai?" he growls out, gaze still locked with mine.

"Ummm...about an hour I guess. Why?" I hear Kai huskily respond back, his breath caressing the shell of my ear, sounding a little confused as his grip loosens from my arms.

"Great." Loki winks, with a wickedly sinful smile back on his luscious lips.

Without another moment's hesitation, he picks me up, tearing me from Kai's loosened hold, and throws me over his shoulder fireman style, heading in the direction of the stairs.

"Loki!" I screech as I kick my legs, and he practically bounds up each step, bouncing me against his body.

"Dick move, Loki Thorn!" I hear Kai shout as we reach the top. Loki chuckles evilly in return but doesn't falter as he walks down the hall.

He crashes his door open then deposits me on my feet, not even out of breath, the fucker. The look he gives me burns me up from the inside, like a wildfire out of control, consuming everything in its path.

Grabbing the back of my neck with one hand, he slams his mouth on mine, devastating me with a soul searing kiss. The fingers of his other hand tangle in my hair, giving just an edge of pain which makes my knees fucking buckle. I would fall to the floor if he didn't have such a tight grip on me.

"Fuck, Lilly. What have you done to me?" he whispers over my lips, our foreheads touching as he walks forward, guiding us to his bed. "I'm an addict, and you are my. Fucking. Perfect. Drug," he murmurs in between savage kisses.

Before he makes another move, I switch our places and push him onto the bed. Holding his gaze in mine, I smile teasingly at him as I sink down to my knees on the floor, my head level with his crotch.

The fire flares even brighter in his jade depths as I slowly pop each button on his jeans, opening them just enough to let him spring free. I look down to admire his beautiful, hard length, the tip glistening with a bead of precum that's caught on his piercing.

Leaning down, I lap at it, tasting the saltiness and cool metal, before hearing a deep groan sound above me.

"Lilly, that naughty fucking tongue of yours..." Loki starts, cutting off mid-sentence when I lick the underside of him, from balls to tip.

I came across a website the other night, *How to Give A Great Blowjob*, and decided that there's no time like the present to practice some of the suggested tips.

Rolling my eyes up, I hold the base of his cock in one hand licking the tip all over like it's my favourite ice cream. I watch the pleasure roll over his beautiful features, his mouth open as he pants.

I focus my gaze back down, and he groans loudly as I begin to flick my tongue over the frenulum, again and again, causing his hips to buck wildly.

"Fucking hell, Lilly!" he cries, his hand coming to grip my hair tightly.

I take the head of him into my mouth, giving a gentle suck, then use my tongue in a circular motion round the top, playing with his piercing, speeding up then slowing down. Loki curses again as I take more of him into my mouth before slowly coming back up.

Bobbing my head, I repeat this a few times, taking him all the way in then pulling away. I feel spit dribbling out of the corner of my mouth as I work to take him deeper each time.

Looking back up, I hold his lust filled gaze as I take him fully into my mouth, making sure to moan out loud with pleasure. This time, I take him right to the back of my throat, holding him there for a few seconds.

He's groaning and cursing, the hand in my hair a punishing grip, and I can feel him start to get even harder right before his balls draw up and tighten.

"I'm so fucking close, Lilly," he gasps out. So the next time, I take him all the way in and hum, pausing to swallow. At the same time, I use my hand to cup his balls and massage that sensitive spot just behind them.

His cock becomes a solid steel rod seconds before I feel hot cum scorch down my throat and he yells his release, his eyes rolling. I swallow every drop, then release him with an audible pop like I did his thumb downstairs.

I lick my lips with a satisfied smirk, sitting back on my heels, his hand letting my hair go. He's sweaty and breathing hard, his eyes closed and a look of pure bliss on his face.

"That was," he pants in between breaths, "fucking epic."

A cough sounds behind us, my head whipping round to see Ash standing in the open doorway, face flushed and eyes dark with lust. There's a definite bulge in his grey slacks. Looks like he came back early.

"You left the door open, Loki," he tells us, his voice rough, but surprisingly, given his words, he's not chastising. His eyes take us both in. Me on my knees, and Loki with his pants open. Ash's nostrils flare. "I think there's time before dinner for Lilly to have a treat for that, wouldn't you agree, Loki?"

"Abso-fucking-lutely," Loki replies, still a little breathless, leaning up on his elbows. "What would you suggest?"

Ash pauses, rubbing his chin with his thumb and index finger.

"Loki, lie back. Lilly, take your skirt off and sit on his face, facing me," he commands. My breath hitches at the authority in his tone, and my pussy gets even wetter.

"Yes, sir," Loki teases, and I catch a flare of heat in Ash's gaze.

I stand up, unzipping my pleated cotton nineteen-fifties style skirt, dropping it to the carpet, leaving me in my lace topped stockings, a blush pink suspender belt, and lace thong set.

"I swear, you wear this shit to torment me and make me fucking cream my pants like a thirteen year old seeing pussy for the first time," Loki growls out looking up at me, and I chuckle.

He lies back on the bed, legs dangling off the edge.

"You heard the Captain, Pretty Girl. Come sit on my face," Loki tells me cheekily. I look behind me at Ash, whose gaze is all kinds of intense, then turn back and walk to the other side of the bed, climbing on.

I crawl over to Loki, keeping eye contact with Ash the whole time. I manoeuvre myself so that I'm on my knees, my pussy hovering over Loki's face.

Loki's hands smooth up each thigh, playing with the lace of my stockings and pinging my suspenders, then growling under his breath when he finds my thong.

"This is in my way, wouldn't you say so, Ash?" he asks.

"Rip it off," Ash orders, and before I can even make a sound of protest, Loki takes it in his hands and snaps one side then the other until it falls off and he tosses it away.

*The fucker!* I open my mouth to reprimand Ash when he speaks again.

"Not a peep, Princess. Or Loki stops," Ash drawls, a perfect black brow raised. I snap my mouth shut.

"Good girl," Ash praises, still standing in the doorway, his eyes full of ravenous hunger.

My breath quickly turns to a stifled moan as Loki's hot tongue finds my dripping wet cunt. He starts lapping at me, swallowing every drop that I'm giving him.

"Eyes on me, Princess." Ash's voice is hard with a slight strain.

My eyes open, I hadn't even realised that they'd closed. I'm looking directly into Ash's steel grey ones from across the room.

My breath stutters at the look of desperate longing that I see in his eyes. It's there for just a moment, but feels like a lifetime, then Ash's gaze changes, the tumultuous emotions disappearing to be replaced with hard unfiltered lust.

"Touch your clit, Princess," he commands. Loki groans, a shudder cascading over me at the combination of Ash's words, and the vibrations of Loki's noise.

My hand travels down over the front of my body to find my clit, and I start rubbing the sensitive bud, sending shockwaves running through me like an electric current.

"Ash...I...I need..." My eyes still locked with his, pleading with him for more.

"More, Loki," Ash demands, voice full of tension, not chastising me for speaking against his orders.

Loki starts licking and sucking so hard, his tongue thrusting inside me, that I'm screaming his name, then Ash's along with my own release within minutes. My lids close, unable to stay open, and my body going rigid before turning to jelly.

Panting, I crack open my eyes to see that Ash is gone, the doorway now empty. I can't help but feel a pang of loss at his departure.

I swing my leg over and off of Loki, looking down to see his chin glistening with my juices and a cocksure smile on those beautiful, biteable lips.

We hear Kai calling to us that dinner is ready, and Loki huffs out a laugh.

"Come on, Pretty Girl." He sighs, curling up to a sitting position.

I just stare at him, confused.

"What's up?" he asks casually as he walks across the bedroom and finds an old t-shirt to wipe his face.

"Ash being here didn't bother you?" I ask, looking into his green eyes and seeing heat and amusement.

"It was hot as fuck, Pretty Girl," he says simply with a shrug. "I'm always open for a bit of role play. And you know my views on sharing."

He walks back towards the bed, one hand holding my skirt, the other held out towards me. I take it, letting him help me up and put my skirt on without knickers.

"You owe me new underwear, bastard," I say, and he laughs.

"What makes you think that I want you to wear panties at all, huh?" he questions, looping his arm over my shoulder and leading us out of the room. I feel a devious smile cross my lips.

"You could get me some crotchless ones," I suggest, looking up at his flushed face under my lashes, and he groans out loud.

"She's trying to kill me," he moans dramatically, leading us downstairs to the delicious smell of tacos.

# CHAPTER FOURTEEN

LILLY

I spend the rest of the weekend cooking with Kai; I show him how to make shepherd's pie, and he shows me how to make those delicious ramen noodles. It's so nice just hanging out with him, Loki, and Jax. Even Ash isn't being such an arse, and spends time relaxing with us all.

My relationship with Loki and Jax is crazy and intense, and we can't get enough of each other, fucking like rabbits. The thing that frightens me is, it's not just about sex. They make me feel things in a way I've never felt before. We haven't really openly talked about it, but I'm just taking it as it comes. I don't want to ruin what we've started by questioning it and putting a name to the feelings or a title to what we are.

Monday soon comes round again, and it's back to the grindstone of classes and studying. I'm a little surprised to find the guys taking it so seriously, only missing a couple of study evenings a week to do their 'training,' aka working out. At least, that's what I assume they do as they all come back hot and deliciously sweaty. I'm desperate to go and watch, but Loki or Jax always seem to distract me! Not that I'm complaining.

Class is finished for the day, and as I open the door to our dorm I hear a stranger's voice. A deep baritone sound and I look up to see a tall man in a tailored black pinstripe suit turning to face me.

"Ah, you must be Lilly," he says, his tone cultured, and face wreathed in smiles. He walks towards me, his manicured hand outstretched.

Something about him makes me hesitate, a cold shiver running up my spine, causing the hair on the back of my neck to stand on end.

He's older, maybe in his fifties, with black hair that's just starting to grey at the temples. His jaw is firm and chiselled, and he looks to be in pretty good shape, though not as stacked as the guys. When my gaze reaches his steel grey eyes, I make the connection.

*This is Ash's father.*

I briefly look past him to see all the guys sitting stiffly on two of the sofas. They look pretty tense, backs ramrod straight, and there's a muscle in Ash's jaw ticking, like he's furious and trying to keep it in check.

My eyes flit back to the man who's taken another step towards me, and I realise I've been silent for longer than is polite. Blinking, I quickly shut the door, walking towards him with my own hand outstretched.

"Yes. I'm Lilly. Lilly Darling. Pleased to meet you..." I trail off, not knowing his name.

He takes my hand in his, but doesn't shake it like I expect. Instead, he brings it to his lips and places a kiss on my knuckles. I have to suppress a cold shiver, and I swallow thickly, feeling all kinds of revulsion. He looks at me like I'm an interesting toy to him, something to be played with then discarded when he grows bored.

"Julian," he says in that deep voice of his. It's not an unpleasant sound, in fact, it's quite the opposite, but I feel uneasy all the same. "Julian Vanderbilt, and it's a *pleasure* to meet you." He emphasises the word 'pleasure' and it's so creepy that I can't stop the shudder this time.

Instead of looking offended or embarrassed, he looks...*excited?* at my reaction. His eyes flash with what looks suspiciously like lust, but unlike when the guys look at me that way, now I feel dirty, like I need to scrub myself clean.

"We'll see you later then, Father." I hear Ash say, and I don't miss the flash of annoyance that flares in Julian's eyes. Ash comes up next to his dad, breaking the spell that Julian's gaze held me under.

I look up and see Ash's jaw is clenched, as he takes in my hand still in his father's grip.

Julian gives it a little squeeze, drawing my attention back to him.

"Until next time, Miss Darling," he purrs out, placing another kiss on my knuckles before letting go. It takes everything in me not to wipe my hand along my side to get rid of the feel of his lips.

"Don't be late, boys," he says, his voice stern, and straightening up, he walks towards the door, Ash following behind him. As soon as they close the door behind them, Loki is next to me, pulling me into his arms and engulfing me in his vanilla scent.

I don't miss that he takes the hand that Julian kissed and rubs his thumb over it.

"He seems..." I trail off, not knowing how to finish. How do I describe the way he made me feel, like I was his prey, and he was a creature of the darkness, a snake ready to strike.

"Like a complete asshole, Pretty Girl," Loki says in that delicious drawl of his. It's completely different from Julian's which was cold, lacking any human warmth.

The door opens before I can think of a response, and Ash walks in, looking at me held in Loki's arms. He walks right up to me with something like concern in his grey eyes. They're the exact same colour as his father's, yet couldn't be more different.

I always thought Ash was the 'Ice Knight,' but meeting Julian shows me that Ash has a fire which burns in the depths of his grey orbs that his father lacks. He feels things passionately, even when it was just his dislike of me, or getting so cross when I'd taken too much Molly at the party in the woods. He may keep his feelings hidden from outsiders, but those he lets in, see how deeply he cares.

"You okay, Princess?" he asks gently, scanning me from top to bottom.

"Of course. Why wouldn't I be?" I question back, my brow furrowed as I lean back from Loki's grip. *Why is he so...worried?*

"Because his dad, Mr CE-fucking-O, just hit on you, the motherfucker," Loki interjects angrily before Ash can say anything, and I can feel a slight tremble in his muscles, like they're itching to go after Julian.

Ash glares at him but doesn't argue with what Loki's just said.

"What?! No!" I splutter out, stepping out of Loki's arms to look him in the eye.

*Why would he hit on me? And ewww!*

"He did, Baby Girl," I hear Jax rumble before he pulls me into his chest. I can feel his rapid heartbeat through my palm, and it's instinctual for me to snuggle into his warm embrace.

"Why are you guys acting so strange?" I ask, looking up into his blue eyes. "His behaviour was a little odd and creepy, but harmless. Right?"

I hear a cruel bark of laughter sound out behind me and turn my head to see Ash shaking his own.

"My *father* is anything but harmless," he practically spits the word out, like he can't stand him. "He's fucking dangerous, and you won't be meeting him again," he says in a hard voice, determination in his gaze that lets me know that his will is law as far as he's concerned. "We have to go out tonight, Princess, business stuff," he continues. "Don't forget to lock the door." And with that, he heads off upstairs.

"Well, that wasn't cryptic at all," I say sarcastically, stepping away from Jax. "What time do you guys need to leave?" I ask.

"Oh, not until after dinner," Kai answers, getting up from his seat and coming towards me. "Wanna help me make lasagna?" he asks, a smile on his face.

"I'd love to." I smile back. Before I can take a step towards Kai, Loki has grabbed me again and spun me round, his arms wrapping round my waist.

"You'll be okay by yourself, Pretty Girl?" he asks with genuine concern in his voice, his own forehead creased with wrinkles.

"I'll be fine," I say, my own hands smoothing up his bare arms. *Why are guys' arms so fucking sexy? All the better to pin you down with, duh.*

"Anyway, the next book in this crazy awesome series I'm reading has just come out," I continue, getting excited. "It's about a girl and four guys, who are all epic as fuck dancers. They've spent years apart, and I'm hoping they are *finally* getting back together. I hear the sex scenes are hot as sin, so I think I'll take my Kindle and have a long soak in the bath," I tease, grinning wickedly, the tension inside me releasing as his gaze turns lustful.

Loki groans and I hear Jax growl, stepping up behind me and caging me in between them.

"Tell me you're not gonna touch yourself in the bath," Loki pleads huskily.

"I can't make any promises, *Pretty Boy*," I sass back at him as I feel Jax moving closer from behind. They're both growing hard against me, and my smile turns evil.

"Uh uh, boys," I say, stepping out from between them. "I've got to help Kai with dinner."

"You're seriously gonna leave us with blue balls, Pretty Girl?" Loki whines, an incredulous look on his beautiful face.

"Yes," I say. "It's punishment for leaving me all alone with only my fingers for company," I tell him, wiggling my fingers as I step backwards. Heat flares in their eyes as they stand shoulder to shoulder, looking a little like they're thinking about just hauling me upstairs.

"But you can relieve them as soon as you get back and find me warm, naked, and wet in Loki's bed." I smile sweetly, laughing at the matching looks of frustration on their faces.

---

## LOKI

The meaty sound of Jax's fist hitting Brandon Franklin, CEO of Florence Pharmaceuticals, in the jaw sounds loud in the bright underground room at the cabin. An arc of crimson blood splatters across the floor, the contrast to the white tiles fascinating me for a moment.

"What do you want with me?" Brandon whimpers, whipping his head back to face us, his jaw already bruising.

There's blood dribbling down his chin from a split lip, staining his very nice powder blue shirt. Unfortunately for him, he's tied to the chair so he can't wipe it off.

"You've become a person of interest to us, Mr Franklin," Ash drawls out, in a bored tone, examining the back of his hand.

It's the role that he plays. We all have one. Ash, the cold as ice questioner; Jax, the one that coaxes answers out of them with his fists, whilst Kai uses his tech expertise to hack into their digital lives, and destroy them. Me? I'm usually the good cop. With maybe a little crazy sprinkled in to unnerve them just enough. Like now as I hit play on my phone, and *Cradles* by Sub Urban starts to play, filling the basement with eerie sounds.

"What the fuck is going on?!" Brandon shouts, looking around at us all, his blue eyes wide, his lips and chin trembling.

“Well, in layman's terms,” Ash says, walking towards him, “you have something that we want.”

“What? What do you want, you little punk?” Brandon sneers back, clearly finding his backbone. *Oh shit.*

Ash nods, and Jax steps forward, pulling back his fist and punching Brandon again in the face. I wince slightly at the sound it makes. Damn, he definitely cracked something that time.

“What the fuck is wrong with you?!” Brandon shouts, tears streaming down his cheeks and spitting out a tooth that clinks on the tiles and skitters across them.

“It’s rude to call people names,” Ash deadpans, and I don’t bother to suppress a laugh.

“Now, now, boys,” I say, stepping forward and cutting off what Brandon clearly wanted to say back. “Brandon here is a smart man, aren’t you, Brands?” I ask the man in question, stepping up to him and crouching down, slinging my arm over his shoulders. He shrugs it off with a glare, but keeps his mouth shut, thank fuck. I want this to be done quickly so I can get back to Lilly.

“Good man. See? When you play nicely, no one needs to get hurt,” I tell him condescendingly.

“What do you want?” he asks again, looking back at Ash.

“One day in the near future, you’ll be receiving a phone call, detailing instructions on what you will do next. You just need to follow those instructions. Simple.”

Brandon barks out a laugh. “Why the fuck would I do that?”

“Because,” Kai interjects, turning the screen of his tablet around where we can see a picture of Brandon in flagrante with Summer, his current mistress, who also happens to be an employee of Black Knight Corporation. “If you don’t, then this will go out to the worldwide media, plus your wife on the same day.”

“So? Who cares who I fuck?” Brandon counters, obviously still not understanding that we hold all the cards in this situation.

“Did you know that Summer is only fifteen years old?” Ash informs him. There’s disgust in his face, but also a kind of glee at being the judge, jury, and executioner.

“W–what?” Brandon stutters, face going ashen.

"That's right, you sick fuck," Jax growls, fists clenched. He finds it difficult to switch the rage off once it's started. It makes him a great punisher, but is hard for him to live with. "She's underage."

"And then there's that pesky prenup you signed before getting married, the one with the adultery clause. It would mean you'll be left destitute," Ash says, cool as a fucking cucumber.

"H–how do you know about that?"

"There's also the small matter of child porn on your computer," Kai adds, pushing his glasses up the bridge of his nose, and ignoring Brandon's question.

"What child porn?" Brandon's sweating now, visibly shaking as he finally starts to realize that he's backed into a corner.

"This is your work desktop screen, is it not?" Kai asks, turning the iPad around again and showing us a picture of an attractive middle aged woman with two young blue eyed, blonde children, with folder icons running down the side.

Brandon stays silent as Kai hits an icon, and a horrific image pops up. We all wince at this, bile rising in my throat at the picture. Kai quickly turns the screen back, but I don't miss the haunted look in his eyes. He hates this aspect as much as the rest of us. Ironically, the song changes to Ruelle's acoustic version of *Monsters*.

"Th–that's not..." Brandon starts, voice going quiet as he sees our stony stares. "Those are not my pictures. I swear."

He's telling the truth. We, well, Kai, put them there.

"That's not our concern. But I'm sure the federal police would be interested to see them," Ash replies, inspecting his nails, then looking back up into Brandon's eyes.

There's a look of resignation in them, and a twinge of guilt flashes in my gut. The small shred of humanity that's been growing in size lately, feels unease at what we're doing.

"Okay," he whispers, hanging his head. "I'll do it."

"Excellent." Ash flashes him a wolfish grin. "Jax."

Jax steps closer, full of dark black violence and barely contained rage. There's a manic look in his blue eyes, his monster is in full control.

"W–w–wait! I said I'd do it!" Brandon cries out, trying to move back in his chair.

"Yes, you did," Ash agrees, giving Jax a nod. "But don't worry. Jax spent a summer training as a medic in South Africa, so he knows how to leave you alive."

Before Brandon can say anything more, Jax pulls his fist back and hits him so hard in the chest that the chair topples over. Brandon lets out a scream of pain, but Jax just hauls him back up and keeps going, his fists becoming splattered with blood. Brandon's screams eventually turn to moans and gurgles, soon stopping completely.

Ash, Kai, and I stand sentinel, witnesses to the rage that lives in our brother.

"That's enough, Jax," Ash commands.

The sound of fists hitting meat stops and is replaced with Jax's panting breaths. I watch as blood drips off his still clenched hands, leaving drops of red on white, creating another pattern on the tiles.

"Let's untie him. I'll call clean up and tell them to dump him outside Brompton General," Ash orders, and we follow like the good soldiers that we are.

---

LILLY

I toss and turn in Loki's bed until the sun kisses the sky and I finally drift off into a fitful sleep.

*I'm running in the dark, bare trees all round me, their branches reaching out to scratch at me and tangle in my hair. I'm utterly lost, and I just can't find them; the ones that keep me safe. My heart starts pounding as raw panic takes over. I call out their names in desperation, not caring if the creatures of the night hear me. Tears pour down my icy cheeks as I run, the cold seeping into my veins.*

*I stumble, my naked feet, sore and bleeding, but I can't stop. I must find them. I trip over a rock and fall down, only I don't hit the ground like I expect. Instead, I'm engulfed in a warm sticky liquid, the colour of rubies. I realise with a jolt that I'm in a churning sea of blood. I frantically kick my legs in a bid to reach the surface, my lungs burning with the need to breathe. Just as I feel the cool air brush my fingertips, something wraps round my ankle dragging me back down.*

*I open my lips to scream, tasting copper, as my mouth and lungs fill with warm blood. I can't breathe. I always thought drowning would be a peaceful way to die, but this burns like there's a fire raging inside me, charring and blackening my insides...*

"Lilly!" I hear a familiar voice shout as someone shakes me. "Lilly, baby, breathe!" the voice commands, and I take in a huge rasping breath. The sweetness of pure air replacing the copper taste.

Gasping, my eyes snap open, and my vision is filled with the stunning green of emeralds. As I take another deep breath, the scent of copper evaporates to be replaced by warm vanilla cookies and cold nights spent by the fire.

"Loki!" I rasp, my throat sore and burning like I've been screaming for hours.

He's kneeling on the bed next to me and I throw my shaking arms round his neck, holding him tightly to me whilst I try to blink the nightmare away. His own arms band round me, pulling me close.

"You wouldn't breathe," he says, his whole body trembling. His heart is pounding hard underneath his t-shirt. "I couldn't get you to breathe." His voice wobbles as he draws me even closer, eliminating any space between us.

"I was drowning," I rasp out. "In a sea of blood. I was trying to find you all. I was so lost, Loki," I choke out, knowing that I'm not making any sense.

"Shhhh, it's okay, I'm right here, Pretty Girl," Loki soothes as his hands stroke my back and hair in a bid to calm me down, and I think, to assure himself that I'm okay.

"I couldn't find you. You were gone," I sob, feeling the heart wrenching terror of my nightmare all over again. Tears trace down my hot face, and I'm powerless to stop them.

Loki pulls away, using one hand to grip my chin and bring my gaze to his, which is full of fire. There's also a haunted look in his eyes, and a flash of unease runs through me.

"We will never leave you," he says fiercely. "We will always find you."

My lips crash into his in a messy kiss, full of passion, and the need to discover for myself that he truly is here. He kisses me back just as savagely, his hands pulling me to his hot body again, gripping me hard.

He pushes me down, lips locked with mine until I'm lying on my back and he's nestled between my legs. I'm naked like I promised, so I can feel his dick growing hard against my bare pussy, the thin fabric of his sweats the only barrier between us.

He gently brushes the hair back from my face with his long fingers, looking into my eyes with such intensity I shiver.

"Lilly Darling," he starts, biting his lower lip, which is ridiculously sexy. He seems...nervous, which is so unlike him that the nightmare melts away as I wonder what he's thinking. Then something steels in his gaze.

"Lilly Darling, I'm so fucking in love with you it hurts. I've been in love with you since the moment I saw you buck ass naked in that shower, singing *Get Off My Dick*." He chuckles, and his cheeks have an adorable pink flush to them.

I'm speechless. I mean, I knew he felt strongly about me, but I had no idea that he felt *this* strongly.

"I fucking love everything about you. I love your fierceness, your bravery; I mean, shit, you've taken us on, and that is not something for the fainthearted. I fucking love your quirky style and the way you come all over my dick." He smirks, thrusting his hips, rubbing my pussy with said dick, and my eyes flutter with the contact. "I know it's too soon, and we've only known each other for a few weeks, but this life is too fucking short not to grab it by the balls. So, there it is. I. Fucking. Love. You."

And without giving me a chance to think, let alone answer, he slams his lips against mine in a searing kiss. It's red hot, full of all the love he just spoke about. It fills me up from the inside out until I'm overflowing, and I can't help squirming against him, seeking more. His tongue dominates mine, stroking my own in a way that leaves me burning.

He breaks the kiss and sits up, ripping his grey t-shirt off over his head, and tossing it to the floor. He's so beautiful, his chiselled abs, chest, and that gorgeous adonis belt, all covered in beautiful ink.

His bright green eyes take me in with a look of awe, like he can't believe how lucky he is.

"Loki..." I start, not knowing what I want to say, but feeling ready to burst with everything that's swirling inside of me, combined with the desperate need I always feel for him. He chases the darkness away, makes me feel more alive than I ever have before.

He reaches past me, opening his bedside drawer, and grabbing a condom before straightening up. I watch him, filled with sweet anticipation, as he pushes down his sweats one handed, whilst he opens the packet using his teeth, then rolls the condom on and throws the packet away. He leans over me once more, capturing my lips in another scalding kiss, the tip of his dick is teasing my slick entrance, his piercing driving me crazy.

My legs come up round his waist as he surges forward inside of me, his lips not relinquishing my mouth for a second. I bring my hands up, raking my nails through his hair, grabbing fistfuls of the fiery auburn locks as he bottoms out, our pelvises meeting. It feels so fucking good, almost too good, having him buried to the hilt within me.

And he's right. It may have only been a few short weeks but this...this connection we have is the stuff of fucking fairytales.

I groan loudly as he starts to slowly move his hips, his piercing rubbing my inner walls in a deliciously maddening way. He finally relinquishes my lips to rest his forehead against mine, breathing in my air, until I've no idea whose breath is whose.

His hips undulate in a slow, provoking motion, like he needs to prolong this sweet torture for as long as possible. I can feel wave upon wave of pleasure roll through and over me until I'm lit up like a fucking Christmas tree.

"Jesus, Lilly. Your cunt was made to grip my dick," he rasps, his fingers interlocking with mine and bringing my hands above my head, holding them there. I love his dirty talk, it always winds me tighter, driving me higher.

He picks up the pace, grinding his pubic bone into my clit every damn time his hips meet mine, sending shockwaves of exquisite sensation over my entire body.

Suddenly, he kneels up, taking my hips with him so that he's holding my lower end up off the bed as he pounds into me. The new angle allows him to go deeper, hitting my g-spot hard until I'm gasping, moaning out his name.

"Loki..." I feel the tingle of my impending orgasm begin to build in my core. "Loki..." I breathe out again, needing to tell him before the light of my orgasm bursts over me.

"Yes, Lilly, my love?" Loki asks, a bead of sweat slowly dripping down his temple as he picks up the pace even more, starting to thrust deeper and harder. His emerald eyes catch onto mine, boring into me, searing my soul, and branding it with his love.

"I. Fucking. Love. You," I gasp out, just as the intense wave of my release crashes over me, pulling me under, my fingers gripping the sheets tightly as I come, squirting liquid all over him.

His pace turns jerky, and he roars out his own climax, his whole body going rigid before he collapses heavily on top of me, pulling out.

I can feel his pounding heartbeat begin to slow as we lie that way, feeling the world turn as we bask in each others' light. My eyelids become heavy and start to droop when I feel him shift us, rolling onto his back, pulling me to him so my head is resting on his firm chest.

"I fucking love you too, Lilly." I hear him whisper, right before darkness washes over me once more, and I drift away on the steady rhythm of his heart that belongs to me.

# CHAPTER FIFTEEN

LILLY

Thankfully, the guys don't have any more jobs from their families' company, Black Knight Corporation. The nickname, The Black Knights, that the other students have given them makes a lot more sense now.

I asked Kai what it was called so that I could look them up, which I did one evening. Black Knight Corporation pretty much have fingers in every pie, from pharmaceuticals to security, import and export to tech and lots in between. It's worth billions, and I now understand why the guys are so revered here. They're basically worth the GDP of a small country, hell maybe even a big country!

I can't help but look at them slightly differently. They are going to be world leaders one day.

A few days later, Loki and I are sitting on one of the sofas, snuggling in front of a roaring fire. He's wearing an open Hawaiian shirt, which allows me to run my hands up and down his torso. He's literally purring, like a big jungle cat. It's been a week of intense classes, they don't hang about here, wanting us all to 'be our best possible selves' or some shit like that. Each subject is full on from the get go.

Kai is on one of the other sofas, tapping away at something on his tablet, a look of concentration on his face.

"Fuck!" he suddenly shouts, making me jump in Loki's arms, and breaking the spell the fire and his warm body had cast on me.

"What's wrong, Kai?" I ask, concerned. I don't think I've ever heard him swear before.

"Just some stock that should have gone down, hasn't," he replies, brows furrowed, looking up at Loki. They exchange a hard look, and I don't miss the flash of worry that's mixed in with the annoyance that crosses Kai's features.

"Stock?" I question.

"Kai here has a portfolio of stocks and shares in various concerns, Pretty Girl," Loki tells me, all traces of the hard look from a moment ago gone, his hand trailing down my arm and making me shiver.

"A portfolio?" The term is a little alien to me, although I'm guessing that it has something to do with business.

"I buy parts of companies so that we own a share in them, and get a share of the profits that they make," Kai explains.

"We?"

"Kai does the same on behalf of myself, Jax, and Ash too," Loki clarifies.

"Oh. But, why would you want the stock to go down?" My own brows are lowered as I'm struggling to see what I'm missing here.

Both boys look away, shifting in their seats. "Well, if shares go down, we can buy more before they go up." Kai finally says, rubbing the back of his neck.

"And that makes quite a bit of money?" I ask.

"It can," he replies. "But it can also be a little risky, at times."

Loki places a kiss on the top of my head, distracting me from my questioning.

"There's a party tonight, Pretty Girl, on account of it being Ash's nineteenth birthday," he drawls in that deep, sinful voice of his. I shudder, and my nipples harden. *I am so fucked with this one.* "Will you be my date?" he asks, giving me one of his signature panty decimating grins.

"I didn't realise that it was his birthday!" I exclaim, sitting up, feeling terrible. "I don't have a gift for him," I add, worrying my lip and wondering if I can rustle something up last minute. "What time does it start?"

"Don't worry, baby, he's a fucker who has everything anyway," he says as if he's not the same. "And it doesn't start till later, so plenty of time for dinner. And dessert." Loki grins wickedly at me, and I swear I almost moan aloud.

*Lord have mercy on my poor ovaries! No wonder god threw him out of heaven, he must have made all of the lady angels spontaneously come with a single look!*

"Cool," I say lamely, still feeling a little bad about the lack of a gift. Loki chuckles as he gets up, moving his body like a big cat and making those distracting beautiful muscles bunch and stretch.

Loki cooks tonight, making a delicious pasta dish that's creamy and has me groaning in appreciation, much to his delight, and Kai's and Jax's amusement. After we've eaten, I head to Loki's room to get ready for the party. Yep, my clothes are still in there, thanks to fucking Ash, the prat.

Loki is still downstairs because according to the fallen angel himself, "There's no improving perfection, Pretty Girl."

I decide to wear my nineteen-sixties tight denim playsuit. It's capri pant style, with three quarter length sleeves, and a sharp as all fuck collar. Oh, and a zip all the way down the front, that I leave open just enough to see my red lace bra peeping out. Red sequin heels and a splash of cherry on my lips, and I'm good to go.

"Jesus, Baby Girl." I hear Jax rumble as I turn round after closing Loki's door. "I'm gonna be hard as fucking steel all night with you dressed like that," he groans, rubbing his chin, devouring me with his gaze. I feel my cheeks flush, and heat flares between my thighs, which is becoming an all too familiar situation round these guys.

"You look pretty good yourself," I say back huskily, eyeing him up and down.

He's wearing all black, as is standard for him, but he's swapped his usual workout tank for a form-fitting black muscle shirt that shows off his mouth watering body. He's also wearing tight black jeans, and kick ass black boots, with his hair in a messy man bun.

Basically, he's fucking sex on legs. I meet his gaze once again, then sway over to him, placing my hands on his broad, hard chest and leaning in. Pressing my lips to his neck, a shiver sweeps over him as I leave a perfect red lipstick print.

"There." I smile, satisfied. "That's better," I say, linking my arm through his.

"Staking your claim, Baby Girl?" he asks me with a smirk as we start to head down the stairs.

"Maybe...is that okay?" I suddenly feel unsure and a little silly.

"It's absolutely fucking perfect," he replies, giving me one of his rare genuine grins, his blue eyes sparkling like a tropical sea in the sunlight.

"What's perfect?" Loki asks, coming towards us with his gorgeous smile in place as he takes me in. "Apart from Pretty Girl here, of course," he finishes, his eyes devouring me top to bottom.

"Baby Girl staking her claim," Jax responds, leaning his head to the side so that Loki can see my mark. Loki's brows raise then he turns to me, bending his own head to the side.

"Me too, gorgeous," he commands. "I am your official date after all," he teases like the arsehole that he is. I roll my eyes at him, although I'm stupidly pleased that he too wants me to mark him.

Letting go of Jax's arm, I sashay over to him, wiggling my arse a little for Jax's benefit. Like with Jax, I place my hands on Loki's bare chest. He's so hot under my palms, it's like his blood is molten lava. I lean in and place a kiss on his neck too.

"There. Happy?" I ask as I step back, needing a little room to gather my thoughts. Being close to these boys is like coming into earth's orbit, and being pulled down by an invisible force.

"Very," he drawls back. "Shall we?" he asks as he holds his arm out for me to take. I swear I hear Jax growl behind me, Loki's grin getting wider. It's then that I notice Kai is absent.

"Where's Kai?" I query, looking round.

"Parties aren't really his thing," Loki tells me, leading us out of the door. "Unless it's the first one of the year, which we all have to attend, or he's forced. Otherwise, he usually just stays home," he continues as we head down the hall.

"Oh," I say, my brow furrowed. "Why would he be forced?" I ask, a little confused.

"Oh, you know, family shit. Being rich as kings is not all fun and games, Pretty Girl," Loki replies as we head down the main staircase. He has a resigned irony in his tone that makes me glance his way, and I don't miss the look of unhappiness that sits on his face.

I want to ask more, but we reach the doors and I hear the low rumbling purr of a car engine. Looking up, I see a cherry red car sitting on the drive, its engine running. A young guy in a smart navy blue uniform comes towards us, looking me up and down with a gleam of appreciation in his gaze.

*Creep.* As he holds the keys out to Loki, Jax's hand darts out and grabs his, squeezing, and I swear I hear a pop. The guy's eyes widen in pain and he squeaks, his gaze darting from me to Jax, who's now at my side.

"Look at her again, and your hand will be the least of your fucking worries," Jax rumbles darkly, sending shivers of desire swirling through me, along with a touch of fear.

"S–s–sorry," The guy stammers out, voice high and definitely in pain.

"Jax," I say under my breath, reaching out and grasping his arm. He doesn't immediately let go, eyes still locked on the boy who's probably shitting himself.

Not that he doesn't deserve being a little scared, he did ogle me after all and why the fuck should women have to put up with that everytime we dress up?

"Jax," I say again, more firmly this time. He takes another moment, then releases the dickhead's hand, snatching the keys out of it.

"Now, fuck off," he growls out, sending the valet scurrying away into the darkness.

"Was that really necessary?" I ask, turning to him, hands on my hips.

"I didn't like the way he was looking at you," Jax grumbles back, looking a little sheepish now that he's getting told off. Violence still wafts off him like an expensive perfume, and I can't say that it doesn't get me a little hot. *Fuck, what have these guys done to me?*

"I'm with the big guy on this one, Pretty Girl," Loki pipes in. "He saw you were with us and still decided to test it, so he deserved what Jax gave him. More if you ask me." Jax snarls at him.

I look at Loki with a 'can you stop fucking baiting Jax' look, which I know he understands, yet chooses to ignore when he walks over to the car instead.

I roll my eyes, grab Jax's arm, and pull him with me.

"I'll drive," Jax mumbles, Loki pumps his fist in the air with a whoop. "As long as Baby Girl sits up front," Jax finishes with a slight tilt to his lips.

"Ugh! Fine, asshole," Loki relents, opening the door, and pulling the tan leather seat back to get in.

"Alright with you, Baby Girl?" Jax turns to me, an unsure look in those beautiful, piercing blue eyes of his. You'd think the colour would be cold, but it's not. Instead, it's scorching hot, like the deepest part of a flame. Always banked and ready to flare into an inferno.

I come to when I hear him clear his throat, realising that I got lost in the depths of his gorgeous eyes.

“Uh...what did you say?”

He chuckles at me, stepping closer until my back hits the car as he presses me up against the rear passenger window. He's so close that I can see the pulse beating in his thick neck, the front of our bodies pressed so tightly together, I can feel his hardening cock pushing up against me.

“I asked if riding up front with me was okay with you?” he asks gruffly, his voice sending a cascade of shivers down my spine, making my core tingle.

“Yes,” I whisper, trying and failing not to get lost in those blue eyes again. I'm surrounded by his warm lemon scent until it's all I can taste. I feel light-headed, and my breathing is so shallow, it's a wonder I don't pass out.

He reaches out a finger, trailing it down the side of my face, using it to tilt my chin up, his eyes focused on my red lips. Leaning in, he surprises me by bypassing my lips and placing his own warm ones on my neck. At the same time, his knee comes between my legs, his huge thigh pressing up into my suddenly aching pussy, with a delicious pressure that has me grinding down.

“Jax,” I moan on a breath, groaning in pleasure as he begins to suck and nibble at the column of my throat, electric currents skittering across my body at his touch. I rock on his hard thigh, working myself into a feverish pitch.

The fact that he's caging me in, surrounding me completely, and shielding me from the brisk night-time breeze, as well as any onlookers, just drives me higher.

I'm so lost to the glorious sensations that he’s creating, I soon grind myself into a gasping orgasm, my nails digging into his shoulders as I come, biting down on my lips to hold my cries in.

He holds me up for a few moments until my breathing evens out a little and I can stand steadily on my own two feet. Lifting his head, he looks at me with a satisfied possessive smirk on his handsome face.

“That's better.” He grins as he gestures for me to get into the car. It takes until I'm sitting down and buckled in for what he did to click, so I pull down the mirror to see a giant hickey on my neck.

"You wanker!" I shout at him, aghast. He just rumbles with laughter in that way of his as Loki outright brays in the back.

"That was hot as fuck!" Loki exclaims as we begin to drive off, gravel flying behind us and pinging off the bottom of the car.

---

We arrive at a set of modern iron gates a short while later, pausing for the security guard to let us through.

"Blimey!" I exclaim, as we make our way up a tree-lined drive, stopping outside a huge modern mansion.

It's all glass, wood, and straight lines, and although not ugly, it's not got quite the same impact as Highgate has. It is beautifully elegant in its simplicity, not to mention fucking enormous.

"Who lives here?" I ask the guys as we walk up the front steps after Jax has thrown the car keys to another valet, who wisely keeps his eyes down.

"I do," comes the familiar, dark clipped tone of Ash as he steps into the open doorway.

His hard grey gaze sweeps me up and down, and I don't miss the second of desire that flares in those eyes when they pause on my neck, before he tamps it down. He's looking positively sinful in fitted black slacks, with a fine pinstripe, and a dove grey shirt, the top two buttons open. It's the most casual clothing I think I've ever seen him wear, and I have to swallow hard to keep my mouth from gaping a little.

"Happy Birthday, Ash," I breathe, holding his stare and getting a nod in return.

Loki leans in, wrapping one hand around my waist whilst the thumb of his other wipes the corner of my mouth. "Your lipstick was a little smudged," he drawls, a look of mischief in his eyes. "Come, let's grab you a drink, and then you can grind on my dick on the dancefloor," he follows up as he leads me inside. I hear two growls behind me, which can't be right.

*Why would Ash growl at that?*

I roll my eyes at Loki as I walk beside him, loving the feel of his arm around my waist, staking his claim for everyone to see. *Why is this caveman bullshit such a fucking turn on?*

We walk through a short entranceway, into a huge open plan space. It's got walls of glass that are currently pitch black and reflecting the low purple mood lighting, plus all of the bodies of all the teenagers filling the space. My ears are full of the pounding beat of *Champagne & Sunshine* by Tarro X PLVT-INUM, that the DJ is playing over the hidden sound system. There are so many people here; it must be the whole school. There's the sweet scent of weed in the air, and I can see several tables with lines of white powder on them, as well as hundreds of black and grey balloons, and a matching banner that says 'Happy 19th Birthday, Ash.'

Loki sees me staring, an amused smile taking over his beautiful features. "Ash always throws the best parties. They're not to be missed, so everyone, of course, turns up hoping for the scraps he may throw at them." He says the last part with a sneer curling his top lip, his voice full of disdain. A serious look crosses his features all of a sudden.

"What is it, Loki?" I ask.

"The party in the woods..." he begins, and I cringe at the memory of getting so wasted.

"I–I won't...I won't be stupid again, Loki," I assure him. "Ash was right that night, I can't run forever," I add in a whisper, and when I look up into Loki's eyes, they are full of sympathy and understanding.

We reach the bar, complete with a handsome bartender, because heaven forbid anyone would have to get their own drink or one from someone unattractive.

"What's your poison, Pretty Girl?" Loki asks me, his sexy grin firmly back in place.

"Something soft, please," I say.

Loki looks at me for a moment, and I'm sure there's a hint of pride in his eyes. Then he turns to the bartender. "One virgin passion fruit daiquiri, and a bourbon on the rocks," he orders.

"Please," I add, causing him to smirk.

"Please," he repeats, outright smiling at me now.

"Fuck off," I say, smacking his arm playfully. "Manners don't cost anything."

"True, Pretty Girl," he concedes as the bartender places our drinks on the bar. "Thank you," he makes a point of saying, one brow raised whilst staring right at me. *Knob.*

Ash and Jax make their way over to us and order drinks too. A beer for Jax and scotch for Ash, who's frowning.

*Señorita* by Shawn Mendes and Camila Cabello comes over the speakers, and I grab Loki's arm.

"I love this song! Dance with me." I smile up at him, putting down my drink, although I guess I really should be dancing with Ash given that it's his party. *You're a coward, Lilly Darling.*

Giving Loki just enough time to set his own drink down, I pull him into the space that has been created for a dance floor, I turn my back and start to grind my ass into him, hands above my head. His palms slide up my arms, placing them behind his neck, then move down my sides to settle at my hips, pulling me even closer so that I can feel his hardness poking into my arse. Without the heels, it'd be in my lower back, all the guys are taller than me by several inches.

"You trying to make me come in my pants, Pretty Girl?" he asks huskily, his warm breath caressing my ear.

I can smell the bourbon on it, that sweet, sticky scent. Fuck me, I love that smell on him. I twist in his arms, needing to taste it on his tongue, and bringing his lips to mine, I kiss him fiercely. We're still moving, grinding against each other, lips locked and tongues tangled, when I feel a heady warmth at my back and large hands grip my waist from behind. I look and see that Jax has joined us, grinding into me, his hands caressing up and down my torso.

*Fucking hell.*

One of my arms goes back over his neck, the other still around Loki as I live my best fucking life, dancing between these two beautiful, hot men. I look over to the bar to see Ash, standing stiffly, his eyes like molten metal as he watches us. He's clenching his glass so tightly, I'm surprised it doesn't crack, and his firm, sharp jaw is full of tension. His other hand goes down to adjust himself, and my eyes widen as I realise he's fucking hard. A moan escapes me as thoughts of a similar, yet different, scenario flit across my mind, one with less strangers, and fewer clothes. Loki leans in further, lips brushing my ear again.

"Would you like him to watch while we fuck you, Pretty Girl?" he teases, causing that inferno to come roaring back over me. "Grasping his cock like a schoolboy while Jax and I are inside you, making you scream?"

*Jesus Christ on a cross.* I'm not sure how much more I can take of this before I burst into flames. Or melt into a puddle on the floor. I hear a throaty chuckle at my back, vibrating through my body.

"I'm game," Jax rumbles next to my other ear, his hand sliding up to encase my throat. I take a sharp inhale of breath, my already damp knickers getting wetter at the contact, I just hope they don't soak through the denim. *How the fuck is a girl meant to function under this pressure?!*

If anything, Ash's scowl gets deeper at the move, and he sets his glass down, as if he, too, thinks it might break with the force of his grip. The song fades into *Savages* by Kerli, and as it plays, the words are clearly the straw that breaks Ash.

He storms over, grabbing one of my wrists, pulling me into him sharply. A surprised gasp escapes me, and I'm not sure if I'm in pain or even more turned on. Jax snarls, but Loki just chuckles, clearly finding this situation amusing.

I'm surrounded by a spicy ginger scent, and it dawns on me that it's Ash's shampoo I've been using this whole time. *I wonder why he hasn't said anything?*

"If you're quite finished *fucking* her in the middle of my living room," Ash hisses, practically spitting. "You need to go and mingle. Remember we need to remind these fuckers who's in charge. And I need a word, *Princess.* Alone." With that, he's dragging me away, causing me to stumble in my heels as I try to keep up.

"Hey, fucktard!" I exclaim as he yanks me towards the floating wood stairs.

At the base, they are being guarded by two beefy guys in black who completely ignore the fact that I'm clearly being dragged up here against my will. *Nice to see money can buy anything!*

We reach the very top, bypassing a floor, which opens out onto another open plan space that seems to span the whole footprint of the house. This one has a bed and desk in it, plus two doors to one side. Opposite the stairs is a wall made entirely from glass, and I can see the moon bright in the sky, illuminating the forest surrounding us. None of the lights are on, so the room is filled with the blue light of the moon and nothing else. I can still hear the party going on downstairs, although it's faint.

"What the fuck was that for, you prick?" I ask as he lets me go, rubbing my wrist where he gripped it.

He's facing away from me, breathing hard, although I don't think it's from the climb. He's as ripped as the others, bar Jax who is just ridiculous. I know that he works out and trains several times a week. Suddenly, he whirls around, the moon at his back casting his face in shadows.

"On your knees, Princess," he orders, hands clenching at his sides.

"W–what?" I ask, my forehead creased, confused as all hell. This was not what I was expecting from him at all.

"I said. On. Your. Knees," he grits out. "Don't make me tell you again."

My core throbs at his demand, but my mind balks for a second. He was such a dick to me when I first came to Highgate, and is being an absolute cunt right now with his alpha commands. But there's something about him...I can't deny that he brings out the bratty submissive in me.

"Or what?" I question. He takes a menacing step towards me, and curious to see where this is going, I slowly sink to my knees, excitement flooding my system and making my centre pulse again.

"Good girl," he praises, stalking over to me whilst undoing his belt. The clink it makes as he opens the buckle winds me up tighter with sweet anticipation for what will happen next.

"I will not let you, or anyone else for that matter, come between me and my brothers," he begins in that disdainful voice of his.

I go to say something, but he puts his finger to my lips, shushing me. "I didn't say you could speak," he growls. "So, the question is, Princess, can you handle all of us?"

He asks this rhetorically, like he's asking himself and not me at all. I remain silent, the control he exerts over me is absolute. The anticipation is getting me so excited, I think I may explode.

He takes his finger away from my lips, undoing the button, and then the zipper on his slacks, pushing them to the floor along with his black boxer briefs. *Far be it for him to ever go without underwear like Jax and Loki.*

I hum at his already hard cock, which he grabs in his hand and squeezes hard, like he's punishing himself for being so weak, and giving in to this attraction between us. His dick is surrounded by black ink that swirls and eddies in a beautiful pattern, covering every inch of skin.

"I guess we'll find out," he muses, then snapping his hard steel gaze to mine, he presses his member to my lips. I feel the precum on the tip but don't lick it off yet, keeping my mouth shut until he orders me to open it. If he wants to play the dominant role, he'll have to work for it.

"You will take my cock deep in that filthy, pretty mouth of yours until I come down your throat. You may use your hands. You are not to seek relief for yourself. Do you understand?" he commands, and I nod my consent and understanding, whimpering with the heady rush of need that fills me all of a sudden. I want to please him, I want to feel him inside my mouth.

Opening up, I take his length in all the way until he hits the back of my tonsils, choking me on his hard length and making me gag slightly, my own hands clenching at my sides. My core floods with warmth, and I'm wet and aching all over again.

"Such a good girl," he praises as he twists my hair tightly in his fist, using his grip to pull me back up, finally letting me take a breath.

I let him take control, keeping my hands beside me, letting him fuck my mouth slowly, yet never making me wait too long to breathe. I get the sudden urge to make him lose that tight control he always has. I want to see him raw and uncontrolled. I want to do that to him.

My hand comes up and starts massaging his balls, rolling, gripping, and releasing them, and a deep groan escapes his lips, his hips starting to jerk out of rhythm, bucking wildly.

"Fuck, Lilly," he moans, his grip on my hair tightening.

I keep massaging, hollowing out my cheeks to create even more friction. He's so close to losing it, and my knickers are now even wetter, the ache between my legs so intense, it just makes me pump and suck him harder.

Spit drips down my chin as I work him into a frenzy. I start to feel that tell-tale sign of his imminent climax when his dick grows rock solid, so I move my hands from his balls to the space just behind them and massage hard. He thrusts his hips, and I gag again as he shouts my name, shooting hot cum down my throat. I lap up every drop of his hot release, causing him to shudder and twitch, panting like he's just run a marathon.

I finally release him with an audible pop, sitting back on my heels, my hair running through his now relaxed grip. Looking up into his shadowed face, I can just make out that his eyes are closed, but the rest of his face looks completely at ease as he stands there breathing hard.

His eyelids lazily open, and I wish I could make out the expression in them, but it's just too dark. He reaches out and caresses my face tenderly with his fingertips. Not saying anything, he bends down to pull up his boxers and trousers, doing them up, then his belt. He once again looks down at me.

“Remember. You're not to relieve that ache between those pretty thighs until I or one of the boys says otherwise.”

And with that, he walks over to the stairs, leaving me kneeling and aching on his bedroom floor.

# CHAPTER SIXTEEN

ASH

F*uck.*

*Fuck.*

*FUCK!*

That was not supposed to happen! Where the fuck is my hard won control? It literally fucks off when that girl is around. God, she's like a fucking temptress, a siren whose call I'm helpless to resist.

When I saw her dancing with my boys, my brothers, her cheeks flushed and eyes heavy-lidded, I almost came in my fucking pants right then and there. I had to set my glass down after I'd heard it crack, nearly breaking it with the sheer fucking lust that raced through me.

I meant to just talk to her, convince her that she couldn't handle all of us, especially me and my...dominant needs. I meant to scare her off. Instead, she submitted beautifully, after a bit of sass, and I got even harder than I've been in a long fucking time. Then, when she wrapped those plump lips around my cock, letting me fuck her warm wet mouth like I deserved it...*shit!*

I've got a semi just thinking about her on her knees for me, ready for round two. She makes me fucking wild. No longer encased in ice, but wreathed in flames burning hot enough to fucking kill.

I pound down the stairs, my thoughts whirling around my head like a maelstrom. I'm brought to an abrupt halt when someone steps in front of me.

Fuck's sake! It's that cunt Amber, and I inwardly groan. She considers herself the queen bee of Highgate, and as the king, or at least leader of the Knights, naturally, she thinks we belong together, like this is some kind of fucking teen movie. Regardless of the fact that she fucked Loki last summer.

Flipping her hair over one shoulder, she looks at me from beneath long blonde lashes, batting them like it's attractive. To be honest, it just makes her look like she's got something in her eye.

I plaster a slight smile on my face, I am the host after all. "Amber. Nice of you to stop by," I drawl in my usual bored tone.

I should be playing nice. My dad has a hard on for her dad's shipping ventures, and basically commanded me to fuck the girl. A frown creases my brow as images of a certain pixie-like brunette with cherry red lips flit across my vision, tied to my bed and begging for more.

I realize that Amber has been talking to me and I've no fucking idea what she's said. I spot Loki and Jax leaning against the railing outside and decide I've played nice enough.

"Enjoy the party," I interrupt whatever mindless drivel she's spouting and walk away, heading to the open French doors. This is my house, my sanctuary away from all the bullshit. I hate having people in it. It's also a place to escape my father. *Cunt.* I can't stand the man. I only stay in the dorms because it's more convenient for class, and helps to keep the plebs in line and remind them who owns their asses.

I reach the guys, breathing in the weed scented air as Loki smokes a joint.

"Here," he says in his familiar tone, passing me the joint and blowing out smoke rings. "You look like you could use it." He laughs, but then stops as something catches his eye.

I turn, joint raised to my lips, just in time to lock eyes with the very pixie that's haunting my thoughts.

*Fuck me.*

If possible, she looks even more fucking gorgeous than usual with her hair all mussed up from my grip and her cherry lips swollen, lipstick a little smeared from the pounding my cock gave them. My dick twitches in my slacks like we didn't just come down her throat less than half an hour ago. She looks freshly fucked and more than one set of eyes follow her hungrily as she makes her way towards us, hips swinging and red heels clicking.

I'm not the only one of us who growls and death stares anyone eye fucking her right now. I can feel the tension rolling off Jax as his beast rears its head, out for blood. He must be on a steroids cycle for the violence to be that close to the surface, although given his past, and his future with Black Knight Corp., bloodshed is a part of him.

*Mine*, the animal inside me roars. Although, he doesn't seem to mind sharing with my brothers, but anyone else sends him into a fucking rage, needing to tear limbs from bodies and bathe in our enemies' lifeforce. *I am so fucked.*

"Or maybe you're more relaxed than I thought, brother," Loki drawls, amusement clear in his voice.

I glance at him, tearing my eyes away from the approaching siren, to see a look of bemused surprise come over his face. I get the surprise, it's not that I don't fuck girls, although never at parties, and never with someone who's so...close.

Lilly marches up to us and stands right in front of me, eyes ablaze, cheeks flushed, and panting. She's never looked more stunning; freshly fucked in a way that has my balls tightening as an image of me deep inside her warmth flashes across my mind. I lazily look into those beautiful eyes that are full of fire and practically sparking.

"You fucking wanker!" she hisses, hands on those delicious hips.

"I trust you followed my command?" I drawl, feigning disinterest while noticing her nostrils flare and the unmistakable heat of lust that flashes in her eyes.

"Command?" Loki asks, clearly intrigued.

"Yes. Tell him, Princess, what my command was," I order, my gaze locked on hers.

Her nostrils flare again in what is clearly frustration, naughty minx, and I feel one side of my lip tilt up slightly. She waits another moment, then still holding my gaze, calmly replies, "I'm not to come until either Ash, the Arsehole, you, Jax or Kai say I can," she deadpans, still staring me down.

*Good girl*, it'll be so much sweeter if she fights me. I still doubt she can handle all of my requirements, or Kai's for that matter, but time will tell. Perhaps, we shall start gently, working up to what we truly desire.

"Oh, Baby Girl." Jax comes up behind her, wrapping her up in those big ass arms of his and burying his face in her neck. It's strange as he never does PDA, yet it's like he can't keep his paws off her. *You and me both, brother.* "I'll make you come so fucking hard later you'll forget all about Mr Ice over here." *Fucker.* But my lips turn up in a full smirk anyway.

"Knight," I drawl. "That's Mr Ice *Knight.*"

"You're so full of shit," Jax chuckles, nuzzling her neck further, making her eyes finally close as she relaxes into his hold.

It's funny that I don't mind seeing them together. Or Loki and her for that matter. The thought of any other fucker touching, even fucking looking at her makes me want to start stabbing people. But these two and Kai, my brothers, I don't mind. We've never shared before, but it's an interesting idea...

The music suddenly stops. My head jerks up as I hear Amber declare it's time to play truth or dare. *Fucking juvenile.* I roll my eyes, but see that Lilly's are open and she has a look of excitement in them.

"Can we play?" she asks us, looking from Loki to Jax, and then me. "It'll be fun..." She smiles at each of us, and I swear I'm not the only one leaning into her light, like she's the motherfucking sun or some shit.

"Fucking fine," Jax grumbles, surprising me. "But if anyone tries to touch you or kiss you, I'll fucking choke them to death." The arch of her perfect brows goes up, but then her gaze softens, almost as if she likes his caveman bullshit.

"Deal. And the same for any of you," she responds, looking into each of our eyes, her own gaze deadly serious. I seem to be in a state of permanent fucking surprise tonight. My dick twitches once more at the thought of her fighting another girl, unleashing the beast within her soul. The one that calls to mine, and lurks just beneath the surface.

"Yes! Let's do this!" Loki crows, pulling her from Jax's arms and bringing her inside as she giggles in his arms.

*I guess truth or dare it is,* I sigh as my eyes meet Jax's, and we too, head indoors.

---

LILLY

Loki and I make our way inside, Ash and Jax following behind us like dark, grumbling shadows. You'd think I'd asked them to, I don't know, listen to a lecture on knitting. *Plonkers.*

I feel wild tonight, like something is stirring beneath my skin waiting to be set free and howl under the moon. I feel reckless, like I could do anything. Be anyone. And this feeling of freedom is heady and way too addictive.

I'm practically vibrating with pent up energy as we make our way over to the group playing the game. Loki still has my hand in his, pulling me gently along. His normal vanilla scent has the addition of sweet weed and smoky bourbon mixed in. He smells decadent, like a night full of sin and debauchery. I inhale deeply, wanting to roll round in it and coat myself in his musk.

He looks back at me with that playful smirk and must see the heat in my eyes and the raw need on my face because suddenly, his nostrils flare as he takes me in, scenting me, and his own eyes blaze with emerald fire.

"Pretty Girl..." he gasps as I press closer to him, desperate for his touch. My clothes feel too tight all of a sudden, my skin needing his fingers, his lips, his tongue to travel across it. *What's happening to me? What have these boys done?!*

Our bubble of lust bursts when I hear the nasal tones of Amber Cumdumpster ask in an attempt at a seductive tone, "Are you playing, Loki?"

We both blink back the haze and come up for air, chests heaving. Loki shakes his head as if that'll help, then clears his throat.

"Pretty Girl wants to play, so, yes, we're playing," he tells them as we move into the group, Loki sitting down on one of the sofas and pulling me into his lap. Jax and Ash sit down on either side of us.

"But no one fucking touches her," Jax rumbles, giving everyone a full look with the promise of violence if anyone steps out of line. Alpha vibes roll off him in potent waves, and I'd be lying if I said I wasn't turned all the way on right now.

"That's not really..." one of Amber's clones begins, voice drying up as she comes under the intense gaze of Jax, Loki, and...Ash? *Guess we're really doing this sharing thing, huh?* A quiver runs up my thighs at the thought of all three of them. Together. *Jesus.*

"Are you questioning Jax?" Ash's voice is low and like ice, so cold it burns.

His eyes are the grey of a hurricane, right before it rips your house away and destroys your life.

"N–n–no," she stammers, looking down and blushing furiously, hands trembling in fear.

"Good. Anyone else unclear?" he whips out, taking them all in as his head turns lazily, surveying his subjects.

There's a chorus of 'no' which seems to appease him. It hits me then, how powerful he is, actually, all of the guys are. They are the alphas of the school. The undisputed kings. And woe betide anyone who goes against their decree. I had *no* idea this was even a thing outside of novels and teen movies.

"Good. You may begin." His arrogant entitlement is astounding, but the game starts all the same.

"I'll go first," Amber declares, malice in her blue gaze as it alights on me. "Lilly, truth or dare?" she asks, her tone full of fake sweetness, like the candy covered in sugar that is sour as hell when you place it in your mouth.

I don't let my gaze waver, realising this for the battle of wills that she's clearly made it. *Bring it on, jizzstain!* I feel all three guys stiffen.

"Dare," I say, oozing confidence. *Never show weakness,* my mum used to say.

"Hmmm..." she says, considering. I bet she's trying to think of something humiliating, something to make the guys laugh at me and make me look like a fool.

"I know!" she exclaims, snapping her fingers, delight coming over her features. "I dare you to strip in front of everyone!" she bursts out with glee.

Jax leaps up, growling, Ash goes still as stone, and Loki, well, he looks amused as usual, like life is one big game. But I can see by the tightness of his eyes that he's not happy.

"No fucking way," Jax growls out, all contained violence and barely suppressed aggression.

I place my hand on Jax's huge bicep, drawing his swirling ice blue gaze to my own. "I've got this, Jax. Trust me. Please?" I hold his gaze, until acceptance shifts in those blue depths, and he sits back down.

I walk over to the DJ and put in my song request asking him to wait for my nod, then walk back and stand in front of the guys, facing them.

I smile, then wink cheekily at Loki. I've no intention of stripping in front of basically the whole school, but I can give them a show, and prove Amber to be the twat that she is. What she doesn't realise, what none of them realise, is that Mum danced at Grey's, an exclusive gentlemen's club in Soho, London, with the best dancers and strippers in the U.K. I spent many a day there, watching rehearsals and copying their exquisite gravity defying moves. I even managed to convince her to let Lexi, her best friend and fellow dancer, teach me properly a few years ago.

Confusion and hurt run through me at the thought of Lexi. I've not heard from her at all since Mum passed. Not a text, email, or phone call. Nothing. She was like an aunt to me, she was even there when mum had me, helping with my birth.

Pushing those thoughts aside, I nod, and the beginning beat of *Heaven* by Julia Michaels starts playing.

A sexy as fuck chuckle rumbles from Loki's lips, and Jax curses whilst rubbing his thumb over his lower lip in a very distracting way. I see a fire light in Ash's eyes, smouldering and just waiting to consume me.

I start to do a sexy walk, one foot in front of the other, pausing between each step to roll my hips, one hand in my hair. Then I let go and follow the beat, caressing my body, and showing these three guys how fucking horny they make me.

I flit my gaze between them, locking eyes with each in turn as I dance for them. I sensually make my way down to the wooden floor, hands planted as I spread my knees and grind into the ground. I come back up onto my spread knees, body rolling. I catch Ash's grey gaze briefly, his eyes aflame.

I smile as I slowly crawl towards him, placing my hands on his knees and undulating my body so my head hovers over his crotch as I flip my hair back. I can see his hard dick straining against his slacks when I bring myself back up onto my feet, arse in the air, and my head still over his crotch.

Standing up, I roll my arse, then do a half twist, slapping my hips. I bring my leg round so that I'm now in front of Loki, arse in his face as I bend over touching my foot then gyrate, rolling my hips and shaking my arse coming back up, my back arched.

I go back down on my knees, using my hand to roll over so that I'm now sitting on the floor, legs spread in front of and facing Jax. In a single smooth move, I get back onto my spread knees, my hands caressing down my body and going between my own legs, teasing the guys and myself. A second later,

I'm back on my feet, grabbing Jax's head, rolling my hips and bringing my aching pussy right up to his face.

"Everyone get the fuck out. Now!" he roars as he grabs my hips, stilling my movements.

I'm panting, both with the exertion from my dance alongside red hot burning desire. My eyes are closed, my head tipped back and I take deep ragged breaths, but I hear movements behind my lids. Several minutes later, the front door closes as everyone appears to have done what he's ordered as the song comes to a close.

# CHAPTER SEVENTEEN

LILLY

"Well, that was rude," Ash drawls, trying and failing for a neutral tone. I can hear a rasp to his voice, a strain that's not usually there.

"Fuck off," Jax simply says, finally tilting his head and looking up at me.

Jax looks raw, possessed, and filled with a need that I have created. It's a potent look, and my breath catches.

*Bad Intentions* by Niykee Heaton, Migos, and OG Parker comes over the speakers, surrounding us with all of our desires, giving me the chills as the lyrics flow over me.

Jax reaches up and unzips my jumpsuit, fully revealing my red lace bra. I take my arms out of the sleeves, then push the denim over my hips and thighs, stepping out of it and my heels. I hear Loki curse as I straighten up when he sees that my matching red lace knickers are crotchless.

"You've been wearing crotchless fucking panties all night?" he asks with a groan, covering his face with his hands.

I smirk at him. "No need to rip them off now."

Jax groans, his hands coming up to grab my hips, bringing my attention back to him as he digs his fingertips in hard enough to bruise. His eyes bore into mine, a fire raging in their blue depths, warming my skin with their heat.

Moments later, I feel a warmth at my back as Loki steps up behind me, his hands coming over my shoulders to skate over my lace-covered breasts, and I moan aloud with pent up need.

My skin feels so hot it's like I've got a fever running through my veins. I burn everywhere he touches, sparks racing across my skin. I feel his lips on my neck, his breath hot and heavy as he nips and sucks playfully. My head drops to his shoulder to allow him better access, finally breaking eye contact with Jax.

I feel Jax's hands push my hips back a little, moving me closer to Loki, and I look down to see him sink down to his knees in front of me, his warm breath caressing my exposed pussy lips. I'm fucking drenched, my juices sliding down my inner thighs.

“Please...” I beg them. Ash left me wanting so badly earlier and I need a release or I might explode.

Jax's tongue flicks out and finds my clit, making the barest contact before he grabs one of my legs and hoists it over his massive shoulder, opening me up to him. Loki steadies me from behind, bringing up one of my arms to wrap round his neck.

“Look at what you do to us, Pretty Girl,” Loki commands in a whisper, thrusting his hips into my lower back so that I can feel his hard length pressing against me.

I lift my head to see Ash still on the sofa behind Jax, trousers unbuttoned, palming his cock in a tight fist, and watching us with an intense gaze. A whimper escapes me at the sight.

Jax chooses that moment to lower his head and feast on me as if he’s just found the elixir of the gods. It's so hard and fast that I cry out, eyes rolling, and would have fallen to the floor had Loki not had a firm grip on me.

“Fuck!” I moan loudly, grabbing Jax's hair in a clenched fist, bringing his head in closer as I grip the back of Loki’s neck with my other hand, sinking my nails in.

“Such a naughty, dirty mouth. I'll have to put it to good use later, Pretty Girl,” Loki dirty talks in my ear, winding me up tighter. “You’d like to choke on my cock wouldn’t you, baby?”

I.

Fucking.

Shatter.

Feeling the hungry gaze of Ash, and in Loki's trusted embrace, my release explodes, coating Jax's face. It's an orgasm so powerful, so earth shattering and mind blowing, that stars blind me, and I scream as the pulses run through me.

"Fucking delicious," Jax says with a feral grin. I crack my eyes to see his bearded chin and the top of his t-shirt soaked as he stands up and wipes his chin on the back of his hand.

I'm a hot mess, Loki holding me up and supporting my body weight. Jax walks to the sofa, his tight arse shown to perfection in his black jeans.

Ash has gotten up, leaving his hard dick still out, and he's done something to the sofa so that the back is folded down and it's become a bed of sorts. Jax rips his t-shirt over his head, showing me his beautiful, muscular back. He turns to face me and unbuttons his jeans, pushing them down his legs, and steps out of them and his boots, letting his huge cock spring free. He holds out his inked arm towards me.

"Come here, Baby Girl," he rasps in that gruff voice of his.

Movement catches my eye, and I look to the side to see Ash settling down in a plush armchair, dick once again palmed, hand slowly pumping up and down. The sight makes my mouth water, remembering the feel of him as he came down my throat.

I step out of Loki's hold and make my way over to Jax, who's now sitting naked on the edge of the sofa bed. When I reach him, he pulls me to him so that I'm between his splayed knees. Reaching behind me, he unclasps my bra, letting it fall to the ground.

"You've got the best fucking tits, Baby Girl," he compliments as he grabs them in his huge hands, squeezing hard and making me gasp.

He then takes one of my nipples in his hot mouth and sucks hard whilst pinching the other. I'm still so sensitive from my orgasm, it's almost too much, but I don't stop him, moaning instead, and grabbing his hair again. He lets go with a pop, then scoots back on the sofa bed so that he's in the middle.

"Ride Jax's cock, Princess," Ash commands from the side, a thread of steel in his voice. "Then, when you're nice and warmed up, Loki is going to fuck your tight ass."

I gulp at the visuals his words create, quivering with anticipation and taking in a sharp lungful of air. I've never done anything like this before, been with more than one guy at a time, but I am so fucking here for it.

I climb onto the sofa bed, crawling over Jax until my knees are on either side of his wide hips. He's so huge, it's a bit of a stretch, my thighs spread to their limit. I grab the base of him, noticing the condom already in place, as I lift myself up and align his tip with my wet entrance. Oh so slowly, I sink down, taking him inch by glorious fucking inch, until finally, I'm flush with his hips. We both let out a groan of pleasure when he bottoms out.

It's almost too much at this angle, filling me up so completely, and I don't know how Loki will fit as well. I push that thought to the side to be dealt with by future Lilly, as I start to move, much like I did during the dance. I place my hands onto his pecs and simultaneously gyrate and lift my hips, before torturously sinking down. Over and over again, making Jax lose his control, his face set in a grimace of pleasure.

"Shit, Baby Girl! Just like that," Jax exclaims, his large hands holding my hips and helping me move.

I feel the bed dip behind me seconds before Ash issues another command.

"Lean over Jax, Princess."

I do as he says, butterflies taking flight in my stomach, and adrenaline flooding my body. I feel the tug of my knickers, then hear a ripping sound as Loki tears the opening of them even more to allow better access to my arse. *Fucking boys are always tearing my underwear!* Before I can call him out, a cold wetness slides between my arse cheeks that makes me gasp and tense slightly, which causes Jax to groan.

"Just some lube, Pretty Girl," Loki reassures me, his fingers following the lube and rubbing round my puckered hole.

"Oh, fuck," I moan, as I feel Loki's finger enter me, my hips bucking at the intrusion. Nuzzling into Jax's neck, I let the intense sensation of fullness wash over me. *It feels so fucking good.*

"Shit, I can feel him inside you, Pretty Girl," Loki rasps out as he starts to pump his finger in and out of me, slowly at first then picking up speed. My inner muscles clench round Jax, who curses again. Another finger joins the first, stretching me wider still.

"Loki..." I moan in a voice so husky and deep I don't recognise it as my own.

"I've got you, Pretty Girl," Loki replies as he moves up behind me and replaces his fingers with the head of his cock, carefully and gently pushing the tip in. I gasp at the slight burn, which disappears as Jax wiggles a hand between us and starts rubbing my clit.

"Fucking hell!" I cry out as Loki pushes further in.

I feel so full I can hardly take a full inhale, and his piercing is rubbing me in all the right places. Jax must feel it too, as he hisses out a breath, the fingers of his hand on my hip digging in.

Finally, Loki's hips meet my arse as he goes balls deep with a low moan.

"Pretty Girl...you feel so fucking incredible," he groans as he starts to slowly draw back out.

"Fuck, dude, I can feel you inside her," Jax moans deeply, his hands on my hips squeezing tight, keeping me in place.

Jax also starts to draw out of me, in tandem with Loki, and the feeling of both of them inside me, hitting every nerve, leaves me shaking and tingling all over. They keep this slow place, allowing me time to adjust, but I'm ready for more.

"Fuck me harder...please," I moan out, my nails digging into Jax's shoulders. I want, no, need, to be dominated by them and feel them pound into me, using me for their pleasure.

"You sure, Baby Girl?" Jax asks me, looking into my eyes and pausing his movements. I can see the restraint in his gaze and can feel it in the tension of his muscles. He's holding back. "We don't want to hurt you," he says, voice tinged with concern.

"I trust you," I gasp out, looking back at him with no fear.

He may look big and scary, and I might have only known him a short while, but I do trust him. I trust all of them. I know that none of them would ever hurt me. He holds my gaze for a second longer, then looks over my shoulder at Loki, giving him a slight nod.

I feel Loki wrap my hair round his hand, pulling me upright a little so my palms are resting on Jax's pecs.

"We're gonna bury our cocks in you so deep, and fuck you so hard you'll be coming for fucking days," he whispers in my ear. I whimper, and my inner muscles clench round them both, deep groans escaping their lips.

They both begin to slowly withdraw again, only to slam inside me seconds later, and I scream and claw at Jax at the wave of sudden pleasure.

"Yes! Fuck yes!" I cry out as they move in synchronicity, pounding in and out of me as one.

"Shit! I'm not gonna last long, bro. Her ass is so fucking tight," Loki hisses out, voice strained. Jax's fingers rub my clit furiously, sending wave after wave of pure unadulterated pleasure rolling over me.

"Jax! I'm so close..." I cry, and seconds later, he pinches the bud hard.

I detonate into hundreds of tiny pieces.

I feel liquid spurt out of me as I come, and I can't make a single sound. My whole body lights up, clenching, and I hear Loki roar his own release behind me, his grip on my hair tightening. Jax follows shortly after, a curse hissing from his lips as he orgasms, squeezing the globes of my arse tight, keeping them spread for Loki.

I fall boneless onto Jax's chest, my whole fucking body tingling, as I try to relearn how to breathe. Opening my eyes, I'm just in time to see ropes of cum shoot out of Ash's hard dick, as he too, finds his own pinnacle.

"Well, fuck me, Pretty Girl," Loki gasps out on the edge of a laugh.

He slowly pulls out and flops down onto the sofa bed, arm over his eyes, chest slick with sweat and heaving. I feel Jax tap my shoulder, so I look up at him, still lying along his torso with his softening dick inside me.

"Are you okay, Baby Girl?" he rumbles out, a hint of concern in his blue gaze.

I manage to get my arm moving enough to stroke the side of his face. I can't believe this giant of a guy is so attentive, so mindful of how I feel.

"I'm better than okay," I whisper, voice a little hoarse from all the screaming that just went on. "A little sore, but in a good way," I rush to add as I see him frown at the mention of being sore.

He leans in, placing the gentlest of kisses on my lips, his touch reverent like I am the most precious thing in the world to him.

I lower my head and snuggle into his sweaty chest, my body rising and falling with every breath he takes. I feel weightless, my whole body alight. Fuck, my teeth even tingle! And I can't quite believe that that just happened.

It's so unlike me, I'm not usually so...free with my affections. Sure, I've slept with guys before, but they've always been my boyfriend. We've always been in a steady relationship. I mean, me and Loki are more than just casual, especially after our confessions the other night. But Jax, Ash, and Kai? I don't know what those guys are to me. Or what I am to them. I just know that I feel safe and secure and don't want to be without any of them, even Ash, the arsehole that he is. *Surely, I can't feel the L-word with all of them? Can I?*

I almost drift off to sleep, still on top of Jax, lulled by his strong heartbeat, when he strokes my arm.

"Come on, Baby Girl. Let's get washed up, then we can go to bed," he says gently. "I don't think a cloth will cut it this time." The amusement is clear in his voice.

"I don't think I can move," I whine, although I definitely think a shower is needed. I'm wet and sticky in all sorts of fun places!

With that, Jax just curls up, me still on top of him, although his dick has slipped out now that it's no longer hard. He shuffles to the edge of the sofa bed and then stands up, holding me by my thighs and walking us over to the stairs with my arms around his neck and my head nestled in the crock. I notice that both Ash and Loki have disappeared, presumably to clean up themselves.

Jax walks up the steps, still carrying me like I weigh nothing. We don't go up the second flight that leads to Ash's room, but instead, veer off down a corridor and enter a room on the right. I can hear the shower, and although the room itself is dark, there is light coming from an open door opposite the one we came in.

He walks us over to it, pushing the door open further to reveal Loki in the enormous shower singing. Fuck, he looks gorgeous all naked, inked up, and wet, covered in bubbles. I must make a noise as Jax whispers in my ear, "Did we leave you unsatisfied, Baby Girl?"

Loki still hasn't spotted us, so when Jax lowers me down to my feet, I take off my crotchless knickers and step into the shower. Coming up behind him, I glide my hands over his slicked up torso and wrap my arms round him in a hug from behind. His song stops as he chuckles.

"Wondered when you'd arise, oh fair maiden," he jokes as he turns round, lifting one perfect brow as Jax steps into the shower behind me.

"What?" Jax grumbles out as he turns on a second shower head, then steps under it. "I could feel your dick pressed against mine inside her, I think it's okay if we shower at the same time," he says as he reaches out for the shower gel.

I grab it before he can reach it, squeezing a dollop into my palm then rubbing my hands together to lather up. I step towards him and begin to wash him, my hands trailing all over his massive chest and down his abs.

"You keep touching me like that, and we won't be sleeping anytime soon, Baby Girl," he huskily grumbles out, capturing my smaller hands in his large one, stilling my movements. My eyes widen as I look down to see his dick starting to get hard again.

I let out a gasp as I feel Loki's soaped up hands caress my own body from behind. *How is this even possible?!* I literally exploded like half an hour ago, yet now I want to go again? And by the look of it, I'm not the only one.

I look into Jax's eyes and give him a naughty smile, loosening my hands from his, then wrap my right one round his now fully erect cock. He groans at the contact.

"You're gonna be the death of me, Baby Girl," he moans out, thrusting into my grip. I feel Loki step closer, his own dick hard as he aligns our naked bodies. His hand reaches round and starts playing with my clit, and I moan and pump Jax harder and faster.

"Such a naughty, wicked thing," he teases as his clever fingers get to work, building me up again. *Can someone die of too many orgasms?*

I can feel Loki's other hand start to stroke himself, using my arse crack to nestle his dick into.

"Jesus, Baby..." Jax gasps out, his dick becoming even harder as I pump him faster. "Yes! Fuck yes!" he shouts as ropes of his cum coat my stomach. The sight brings on my own orgasm, and moments later, I feel Loki cum all over my lower back.

We stand there panting, leaning on each other as the shower water comes down on us. I have a momentary pang of longing for Ash and Kai to be here with us too. *When they're ready, Lilly.*

"Now, it really is time to wash up and go to sleep," Jax grumbles, but not unkindly, as he once again steps under the shower to rinse.

This time, we actually wash our damn selves!

# CHAPTER EIGHTEEN

KAI

I open the door to Ash's place, impressed with the job the cleaners have done given the early hour. Only the best for the Black Knights.

I'm not surprised to see Ash already up, making coffee at the island bar that I'm sure was filled with alcohol last night. If he gets more than a couple of hours of sleep a night, it's a miracle.

"Fun birthday party?" I ask, noticing that his shoulders are slightly looser than usual.

"It was...memorable," he says, his forehead creasing slightly as he pours himself an espresso. He indicates to me wordlessly asking if I'd like one. I shake my head at his offer.

"Memorable good?" I query, unable to help prying and wondering if this has anything to do with the beautiful English girl who's now in our lives.

"Hrumph," he responds, not looking at me, but a slight pink tinging his cheeks. *Interesting*. "How was your night? Did everything go to plan?" he questions back, finally looking up at me. This is part of the reason that I love my brothers by choice. He doesn't care that I wasn't at his birthday party, his nineteenth. He knows that I hate large groups, and so he won't force me to attend.

I sigh in frustration, taking my glasses off and rubbing my eyes. "I can't find out any more about Adrian Ramsey," I tell him, looking towards the stairs to make sure Lilly isn't coming down to overhear our conversation.

"Don't worry, she's tucked up with the boys and we kept her up quite late last night," he tells me, a slight tilt to his lips. I don't miss the way he said 'we' either.

"Adrian Ramsey is like a fucking ghost." Ash's brows raise at the curse falling from my lips. "All the records are there, but nothing else apart from rumors and speculation. It's like he doesn't exist in the real world."

"How so?" he questions, taking a sip of his drink.

"Well, he's got a birth certificate, driver's licence, all the usual. But, I can't find anything about his family, or about him having a sister." I tell him pointedly, and his frown deepens.

We're both lost in our own thoughts for several minutes. I know Ash hates mysteries. He needs the security of knowing everything that goes on. Controlling bastard.

"Perhaps we need to take a step back from her," he starts.

His words send my stomach plummeting to my feet, and my pulse racing.

"You think that she can't be trusted?" I ask him, taking a step closer to lean on the island.

"I don't fucking know," he says, his hand running through his jet black hair. There's a tremor in the movement. "Loki and Jax have already lost their fucking heads, and dicks. What happens if she's a snake? Another test?" He looks up at me, his eyes pleading with me to give him answers that I don't have. I do know one thing though.

"She's not a snake. And she's not a test from your father either. Her story is solid. And she doesn't give a shit about our money or status." My voice is filled with a rare passion. I know that deep in my bones, Lilly is everything that we need, if we can just let her in. *And keep her safe.* "Remember how your dad was with her? He's interested in her. He would have ignored her if she was here to test us."

I can see him mulling over my words, his eyes darting with his thoughts.

"And as for Loki and Jax, they need her, man. We all do," I say softly, his head snapping up and his gaze zoning into mine. "Loki has been starved of love and affection his whole life, apart from his little sisters. And every one of the girls he's been with before, they've all wanted something from him. His money, his name. Lilly? She just wants his love in return." I say, interrupting him before he can argue with me about us all needing her.

"And Jax?" he asks, his gaze hard like flint.

"Jax needs her nurturing side. You know his addiction, he needs her to break the cycle his dad got him into. And he needs to see that he can protect her without it." I can see him agreeing with me, nodding his head once, albeit reluctantly.

"And me?"

"You've been hurt by those that are meant to love you most, meant to protect you. You and Lilly share the same pain, you understand each other on a level that none of us do. You need her to shine a light on that darkness inside of you, to break those chains you've wrapped so tightly around you. To show you that you are not a monster." My voice is entreating him to believe me.

His jaw clenches, his fingers clasped tightly around his cup.

"And what about you, Kai?" he lashes out, as he always does when someone hits a nerve. "Or are you above the rest of us fucked up assholes?"

"I need her to feel alive," I tell him, our gazes locked. His softens slightly, a hand reaching out to me.

"Kai..." he says, his voice broken.

"Why don't you go and wake her up? Tell her I'm here," I clear my throat, unable to hold his gaze now that I've exposed myself so fully.

I hear him heave a sigh, and as he walks past me, his hand comes out to squeeze my shoulder before letting go and heading up the stairs.

My chest rises and falls with my own deep inhale.

I can't deny the truth of my words, even if they took me by surprise. Lilly makes me feel more alive than I've felt in a long time. She has breathed life into me, waking me up as if from a deep slumber.

And I need her breath, like a dying man needs the kiss of life.

---

LILLY

I wake up with two hot bodies pressed close on either side of me. Memories of the night before flash across my vision, making my toes curl and my breath quicken.

*I can't believe that happened!*

I squirm with delight, only to get growled at in stereo. I can't help but giggle out loud. I feel so happy. Full of joy, and for a moment, completely free of everything that happened earlier in the year. Before morbid thoughts can overtake my peace, I get double poked with morning wood by the arseholes on either side of me.

"If you're gonna squirm all up on my wood," Jax growls out, his voice is so deep this morning Her Vagisty starts panting, "then you'll have to deal with him," he says as he slowly grinds his hard dick up against my inner thigh. I shiver at the contact and feel the wetness of precum smear across my leg.

"Couldn't have said it better myself, brother," Loki drawls from behind me, his voice husky and delicious too. "Never too early for a bit of DP in my opinion."

"Loki!" I admonish, which turns into a groan as his hands begin to wander over my stomach.

Just then, the door crashes open, hitting the wall, and I squeal and sit upright. The guys leap up, hard dicks bobbing. I look up to see Ash framed in the doorway, wearing his familiar slacks, in soft grey today, and white shirt, no tie. *Must be the weekend,* I snort to myself.

"Kai's here." The familiar bored tone of Ash's voice travels over to me and pisses me off instantly.

His steel grey gaze meets mine, full of arrogant insolence, a perfect jet black brow raised. I don't miss the sudden flare of lust as his eyes dart down, then back up again. I look down and realise that, of fucking course, I didn't cover myself and am naked and exposed from the waist up. Nothing he hasn't seen before I guess. With that, he turns on his heels and leaves, saying nothing of the fact we are all naked in the same bed.

"Fucking asshole," Jax grumbles, heading in the direction of the bathroom.

Loki begins to say something, and it's only then I remember that I'm meant to be going on a hike with Kai today. I scramble out of bed and rush after Ash, heading down the stairs. I see Kai leaning against the makeshift bar, talking to Ash, his eyes going wide when he spots me.

"Kai! I'm so sorry! I completely forgot about our hike!" I gasp out, noticing his face getting redder by the minute. "Kai? Are you okay?" I ask, concerned that maybe he's angry with me about forgetting.

It's then that Ash turns round, his own steel eyes widening, and suddenly, the penny drops.

"I'm still naked, aren't I?" I cringe, tipping my head back as my whole body flushes with embarrassed heat.

"As the day you were born, Pretty Girl," Loki chuckles out, slapping my arse hard as he walks past.

"What the fuck was that for?" I glare at him, rubbing my buttcheek.

"Kai likes a little pain, don't you, Kai?" Loki innocently asks. "Or more specifically, likes to give a little pain," Loki finishes with a wink.

My head whips to Kai whose face is crimson, his mouth hanging open, completely lost for words. To be fair, I'm also speechless, not knowing whether to be turned on or embarrassed anymore.

Kai seems to find his voice and walks over to me. With his eyes on the ground, he holds out a black holdall to me.

"I–I brought over some of your clothes and things. I thought we could go from here," he says, finally meeting my gaze with his honey brown one. His wonderful, fresh woodsy scent surrounds me as he hands me the bag.

"Thanks," I smile. "I'll be ready in two shakes of a lamb's tail!" I call as I turn and head back up the stairs, feeling three sets of eyes following my movements.

Twenty minutes later, I'm coming back down the stairs, washed and ready to go. Kai packed my most sensible clothes; high-waisted nineteen-fifties style slim leg blue jeans, long-sleeved red striped top, tucked in at the waist obviously, and a soft as butter red cashmere jumper. *Seems he likes the vintage look,* I muse. He's also brought my brown leather utility style boots, the most like walking boots-type shoes that I own.

I wonder if I should be pissed that he went through my stuff...it seems that the dominant behaviour of the others is definitely turning me submissive because I find, with some surprise, that I don't mind.

He looks up from where he's sitting on the sofa, I think it's the one that we.... At least it's been neatly folded away, although surely it needs cleaning after last night's activities? A shudder runs through me at the thought of some poor cleaner having to deal with that clean up. It's then that I look round and realise that the whole place is spotless. You wouldn't be able to tell that a party took place last night.

He stands up as I approach, honey brown eyes roving my body, heat entering his gaze.

“You look lovely, Lilly,” he says in that soft melodic voice of his. “We won't be going over any rough terrain so your boots should be fine,” he assures me, handing me a lightweight crimson waterproof jacket that still has tags on it.

“What's this?” I ask, looking at the cherry red jacket in my hands.

“Uh, I saw you didn't have one, so I got it for you,” he says shyly, flushing pink once more and rubbing the back of his neck.

“Really? That's so kind, Kai! Thank you.” I lean over and kiss his cheek, making him go even redder. I pull the tags off and slip the jacket on. It’s a perfect fit and doesn't look too bad either.

“Ready?” he asks, clearing his throat.

“Yep,” I say, popping the P. I smell the sweet lemon scent of Jax before huge arms go round me from behind, and he nuzzles my hair.

“See you later, Baby Girl,” he rumbles in my ear, and I shiver. “Stay safe, and don't go off the path,” he adds, looking up to Kai, who just rolls his eyes as if he's not being stared down by a giant.

“Hey, big guy! Quit hogging our girl!” Loki says, bounding up to me, and literally snatching me out of Jax's arms, making Jax growl.

*Hang on, our girl? They really are happy to share me?* My thoughts are still whirring as Loki's lips descend on mine, kissing me soundly and leaving me breathless.

“Laters, babe,” he says teasingly, giving me his usual grin and a wink.

“Uh...bye,” I manage to stumble out, looking round and catching Ash's serious grey gaze. *Does he ever lighten up?* He just nods then turns away, dismissing us. *Wankstain.*

Kai opens the front door on a beautiful, sunny autumn day. The trees, now that I can see in the daylight, are a riot of colour. From a deep amber to a brilliant red, and every autumn colour in between. The sky is a gorgeous cloudless blue, and the sun is warm, but not too hot. I take a deep breath of sweet air, marvelling at how I ended up here. After everything that happened, I never dreamt I would feel happy again. Or so at peace. But that's what I feel here, with the guys, surrounded by all this beauty.

Kai hands me a foil wrapped package that's still warm. “I made you some breakfast to go,” he tells me, and I open it to find an egg and bacon roll.

"Thanks," I say, tucking in straight away and moaning my appreciation. I'm starving! Or Hank Marvin, as Mum used to say, which is cockney rhyming slang for starving. A familiar pang hits me at yet another thing about her that will live in my memory. But it doesn't overwhelm me as it would have done a few weeks ago.

Kai leads me into the trees, taking a path that is small, but well worn.

"Do you walk here often?" I ask, loving the crunch of leaves under our boots.

"Every chance I get," he replies. "I love the outdoors. I feel so...free here. Like there is nothing I can't do, and no weight dragging me down."

His solemnly cryptic answer makes me pause, looking at him. He's so reserved, and I know next to nothing about him. About any of them, really. The thought makes me frown. Given how intimate we've been, I ought to know more about them. And they me.

"I find the same sense of peace here," I reply, filing away the urge to find out more about him. "I didn't think I would ever feel that way again. But I do here."

"Is that because of what happened with your mom?" Kai asks me softly. We're side by side, but I come to a halt, feeling suddenly cold, like I've been dunked in ice cold water.

He stops and turns back, a pain so stark in his honey eyes I gasp. It's the same pain as mine, the one I see in the mirror when I can't sleep. When the nightmares and the images of drowning in blood keep me awake.

"My parents died in a car crash when I was young," he begins, still holding my gaze. "I, like you, went to live with my uncle. I thought I'd never smile again, never laugh or dream. But I had the guys, and soon I was able to do all those things and not feel guilty doing them."

He reaches for my hand with such understanding in his gaze that I feel a tear slip down my cheek. His hand changes course, fingertips brushing the tear away.

"It'll get easier. Promise," he says with a sad smile. "And I'm always here if you need to talk," he adds as his hand captures mine. He gives a gentle squeeze, then we start walking again, hand in hand.

We walk all morning and stop by a beautiful lake for a break at about midday.

Kai takes off his backpack, dropping it by his feet, and proceeds to empty it. He pulls out a picnic blanket and an array of foil or paper wrapped packages. There's even a couple of plastic Tupperware dishes.

"I did a bit of everything," he says as he begins to unwrap them. There's a whole load of food, from golden fried chicken legs to a selection of deli meats and creamy coleslaw. There's even what looks like yellow cornbread, and the fudgiest brownies I've ever seen.

"Kai, this looks amazing!" I say, my mouth is already salivating just looking at all the delicious food. We sit down and tuck in, me moaning out loud much to Kai's amusement.

By the time we've finished, I'm absolutely stuffed, and definitely need a little rest before we start to head back. I lie down on my back, groaning.

"That was fucking awesome, Kai," I say, closing my eyes and feeling the warm sun on my face. "Thank you."

"Anytime, Lilly," he says softly. "It's nice to have some company for a change."

I crack one eye to see him leaning on one elbow, smiling down at me, his brown hair sticking up all over the place, as usual. He's haloed by the sunlight, and his beauty takes my breath away. These guys, they're all so beautiful, yet so unique. Kai with his hot nerdy vibes, Loki with his fallen angel looks, Jax with his gruff Viking feel, and even Ash and his cold, yet stunning beauty. No wonder they are the rulers, the Knights of Highgate Prep.

"Tell me more about you and the guys. What were you like as kids?" I ask him, suddenly desperate to know more.

"Well, our parents all grew up together, and now own a joint business, so we've basically been friends forever," he starts with a grin. "We used to get up to all sorts of mischief, especially Loki, he used to lead us into so much trouble." He laughs outright then, and it's a beautiful, joyous sound. "One time, he got us to rig up all the toys in his sisters' room so that when they opened the door, they all flew off the shelves and landed on them. Only, it wasn't his sisters that opened the door, but their nanny Martha! I've never run so fast in my life as I did that day, running away from her screaming at us, threatening all kinds of punishment." He chuckles, eyes alight with remembered mirth.

I giggle with him, imagining them all tormenting poor Martha, unsurprised that Loki was the mischievous one.

"Ash managed to sweet talk her out of it, as usual, he was always the peacemaker," he muses. "Still is, I guess." I frown a little, *Ash the fucktrumpet a sweet talker?*

He tells me other stories, like the time when they were all thirteen, and Loki convinced them to drink a bottle of vodka he'd stolen from his parents, who were never there so wouldn't have noticed. According to Kai, they were so sick that none of them have been able to touch the drink since.

Or the time when they were fourteen, Ash decided to run away and become a concert pianist. According to Kai, Ash was an extraordinary piano player. His music was apparently so full of emotion that you were swept away and transformed into someone new. *Ash the Ice K?*

He'd convinced them all to tag along, but they were caught by Mr Vanderbilt, trying to catch the bus and taken promptly home.

His eyes darken then, a haunted look entering into them.

"We didn't see Ash for weeks, or Luc, Ash's twin, either. And when we next saw them, well, Ash no longer played piano, and Luc, he had an anguished look in his eyes that I'll never forget." His own eyes are full of sadness mixed in with rage, a combination I've not seen in them before.

My heart breaks for Ash. What terrible thing happened to not only keep him from his friends, but stop him from doing something he loved? And I'm more than a little intrigued about Luc, Ash's twin.

Not knowing what to say, I reach out and grasp his hand, interlocking our fingers and squeezing. I hate the sadness, the hopelessness I can see in his eyes. I can't help feeling there is something more here, and although I feel so comfortable and safe with the guys, I can't seem to find the words to ask more.

I can't stand the tormented look in his eyes, and I'm racking my brain for something to take it away when inspiration strikes.

"When I was seven, we had a talent show at school," I begin, "and I decided to dance like my mum. She danced at Grey's, a club in London..."

"Wait. Your mom danced at Grey's? Like *the* Grey's? In Soho?" Kai asks, his tone impressed and eyebrows raised.

"Yep. I practically grew up there, watching them all dance. I used to think they were beautiful ballerinas, who, you know, happened to take their clothes off." I chuckle, the memories flooding back over me. The soft lighting, the sound of the sensual music wrapping round me as the dancers moved with a grace that defied gravity. The memory doesn't hurt like I expected, and that surprises me.

"Anyway, I stole one of my mum's costumes, her routine was based on belly dancing, and I remember the beautiful turquoise silk outfit that was the softest thing that I'd ever touched. I hadn't told her what my talent was, I wanted to surprise her.

"Cue the night of the show, and I darted onto the stage when the music started playing. I'd danced like I'd seen the girls at the club do, like I'd seen my mother do, starting to remove some of the silk scarves that made up the skirt, just as Mum did. She definitely was surprised, that's for sure!" I tell Kai with a laugh as I remember my mum's face and that of the other parents as I basically started stripping. Kai joins me, and his laugh is music to my ears.

"Did you get into trouble?" he questions, wiping his eyes.

"Surprisingly, no. Mum and Lexi, who came to watch, just cheered and then took me out for pizza and ice cream afterwards." I beam at him, and even though my heart twinges at the memory, I'm not crippled by it.

Kai's eyes soften, his laughter fading away as he looks at me. Reaching out his hand, he cups the side of my face in his palm, stroking my cheek with his thumb.

"Your mum sounds like an extraordinary woman, Lilly," he murmurs, and tears spring to my eyes. "And she brought you up to be the rarest flower."

He leans over, his lips brushing mine in the softest of caresses. I moan softly, my hand coming up to tangle in his thick hair and pull him closer, fusing my lips to his. A deep growl escapes his throat, surprising the shit out of me as he lets go of the hand he's holding, grabbing my wrist and pulling my hand away from his hair, pinning it behind me.

The hand that was on my face moves up into my hair, grasping a handful and tugging sharply, angling my head to allow him deeper access. I moan in earnest this time, as he plunders my mouth, holding me immobile as he takes what he wants. It's not the gentle kiss it started out as. It's full of possession, fire, and passion and I realise that Loki hasn't been lying when he's mentioned Kai's dominant tendencies.

Abruptly, he releases me, his eyes a little wild and his breathing as hard as my own.

"We should start heading back," he says, his voice a little gruff. I just nod, my heart racing with the remnants of our kiss.

He starts to pack away the picnic stuff, and I help him gather it all up and put it in his backpack. I can't miss the bulge in the front of his trousers. Shouldering it, he turns to me.

“I'm really glad you came here, Lilly,” he says, his voice now soft and a blush rising on his cheeks. “I think you're exactly what we all need.”

He reaches for my hand, looking deep into my eyes, his own honey coloured ones full of hope. Finally, after some soul searching moments, we start to walk back, hand in hand.

# CHAPTER NINETEEN

LILLY

My fourth week at Highgate is mostly uneventful. The guys and I settle into a routine of sorts, having breakfast and dinner in our dorm, which Kai usually makes, and lunch in the dining hall.

Things between Kai and I have changed since our hike, and that kiss. He's certainly not shy anymore, stealing touches and dominating kisses that leave me breathless and weak kneed.

We spend a lot of time cooking together, with Kai teaching me all that he knows. Earlier in the week, when I was helping him make fajitas for dinner, he came up behind me, placing his hands over mine and showing me how to chop the peppers correctly, into thin even slices. Ordering me to keep chopping, and not make a sound, which would alert the guys who were sitting on the sofas a couple of feet away, his own hands left mine to dip into my leggings, his fingers proving to me how skilled he is with them, and not just for cooking.

Every time he shows me his dominant side, and I embrace it wholeheartedly, it's like he opens up more with the acceptance I give him, becoming firmer in his demands the next time.

On Wednesday morning, I made French toast and bacon, drizzled with maple syrup for them all.

Loki and I happened to have a free first period, which is lucky, as Loki felt like he hadn't had quite enough maple syrup. So once the others had left, he'd stripped me down, laid me on the table, and indulged in his sweet tooth.

Suffice to say, we both ended up very sticky and needed a shower, which meant we had to practically run to get to our first class on time.

#soworthit.

It's now Thursday, and I'm making my way to the dining hall for lunch with the guys when my way is barred by the Save the Whales Crew, led by Amber the Cumdumpster.

"You listen up, you English bitch," she spits out, getting so close to me that I can see the individual hairs on her fake lashes. "Loki may be enjoying your whore cunt now, but he'll soon grow tired of the novelty and come back to me."

Her pretty face has been transformed with her vitriol, her lips thinned in a sneer and her eyes narrowed until she resembles a haggard witch. Or maybe a harpy. *That's a little harsh on the harpy.*

"You mean Loki and Jax," I correct her, crossing my arms and raising my eyebrows, a smile on my face as she looks at me in confusion.

"Wh–what did you say, slut?" she splutters out, taking a step back.

*Bitch needs to learn some more inventive curses.*

"Loki *and* Jax have been enjoying my 'whore cunt'," I say sweetly back, tilting my head to one side and lowering my voice conspiratorially. "Sometimes together."

My grin gets wider as she starts to turn red, rage filling her blue eyes.

*I can't believe she tried to Mean Girl me. Fucking harpy cumdumpster.*

"Why you little fucking..." she begins to screech, stepping forward but stopping her tirade abruptly when a huge hand comes down on her shoulder, squeezing hard, and making her wince.

"You okay here, Baby Girl?" Jax's deep voice washes over me, and I shiver.

"Just correcting a mistake Amber here made," I reply, smirking and stepping to one side away from her.

"Shall we go to lunch?" I ask him, taking another step past Amber who is now almost purple with hate, her eyes practically spitting fire.

"Jax?" I ask, laying a hand on his outstretched arm. It's as hard as stone, if stones vibrated with tension.

His own hand is still gripping Amber's shoulder and I can see the indents his fingers are making into her shirt, his eyes drilling into her now wide ones. Slowly, his head turns as he looks at me. His blue eyes are wild, like it's taking everything in him to not explode and beat Amber to a pulp.

I step closer to him, my breasts brushing against his arm. "Let's go to lunch, Jax," I say softly, encouraging him to let her go with my eyes.

His breathing is shallow, and he's staring at me like he's slipping away but desperate to hold on. Yet, outwardly you can't tell the battle that's raging within him. Amber has no idea how close he is to losing his shit.

I can hear murmuring behind me, but all I can see is the rage in Jax's beautiful eyes. I need to get him out of here now, or he will do something that I know he'll regret, so I do the only thing I can think of.

I crush my lips to his, hearing Amber squeak as he pushes her roughly away to grab me by the throat and slam me up against the wall.

Everything else, everyone else, Amber and her crew of bitches, all melts away until I'm submerged in Jax. He surrounds me completely with his huge body, and his warm lemon scent fills my nostrils until I'm breathing in nothing but him.

My hands go up into his blond hair, releasing it from his sexy as fuck man bun and raking my nails down his scalp. He groans in that low sensual voice of his, sending vibrations running through me.

His strong hand tightens a little, drawing me closer as his mouth ravishes mine, his tongue plundering until I'm a hot fucking mess.

His other hand glides up over the top of my t-shirt, palming my breast, and squeezing it hard. I whimper, loving the dominantly rough gesture, completely forgetting where we are until I hear someone clearing their throat behind Jax.

"As much as this is turning me all the way on..." Loki's familiar drawl reaches my ears, and I pause. "Perhaps you'd like a less public location for your make out session?" he teases, a note of amusement in his tone.

We stop kissing, and Jax presses his forehead to mine, his chest still heaving. His blond hair falls round our faces, creating a little cocoon for us. He's panting hard, taking in deep gulps of air as he strives to calm down.

"Are you okay?" I whisper, smoothing my hands down his arms.

"Yeah," he rumbles back after a moment. "Are you okay, Baby Girl?" he asks in return, pulling his head back and looking into my eyes, his forehead furrowed in a frown. His own eyes are clearer now, the rage having drained away. Although, there's definitely lust in there now, as well as concern.

"I'm fine, Jax." I smile back, pushing some of his gorgeous hair back off his face.

He takes another moment, clearly gathering his thoughts, then steps back, letting go of my neck and adjusting himself in his black jeans, not giving a flying fuck who sees him do it. I straighten my own clothes and hair, pulling my navy corduroy mini skirt down where it had started to ride up a little.

"What was all that about?" Loki asks us, turning to Jax. "You don't usually go in for so much PDA, dude."

"I'll tell you what that was, you dickweed." I narrow my eyes at the beautiful boy, taking a step towards him, my index finger pointed accusingly at him.

I take another step closer to Loki, so that I'm all up in his business, poking the finger in his hard chest. *Damn! Now I have a sore fucking finger!*

I'm aware that there's still a bit of a crowd gathered round us, although thankfully Amber and her cronies have gone, so I lower my voice.

"Your fucking bitchtit of an ex started a pissing contest that she didn't have the ladyballs to finish."

"And..." he prompts, raising a perfect auburn brow, a lopsided smirk on his handsome face.

"And I corrected her, that it wasn't just you enjoying my 'whore cunt' as she so eloquently put it. I said both you *and* Jax have been enjoying it. Together. That seemed to piss her off." I smile again, thinking about the colour of her face when I revealed that little tidbit.

Loki throws his head back and roars with laughter, clapping his hands, and causing more than one set of eyes to glance our way. I even hear Jax huff out a laugh as he comes up next to me.

"I bet that ticked her off," Loki says, wiping his eyes as he tries to get himself under control. "She's been trying to get us to have a threesome with her for years!"

"You're the only one who would ever tap that crazy ass bitch," Jax grumbles as we begin to walk off. He takes my own much smaller hand in his huge grip.

"It was once!" Loki hisses back, holding up a finger. "And I was fucking wasted so I thought she was someone else. Anyone else to be honest."

"Well, she thinks you'll get bored of me and go back to her," I say, my voice quiet and small as I look down. That thought bothers me. A lot.

Both guys stop dead in their tracks, Jax's grip pulling me up short. I turn back, wondering why we've stopped in the middle of the hallway.

Before I can ask, Loki steps up to me, hand cupping my face. His palm feels so warm, I can't help but lean my cheek into it, closing my eyes briefly at the comfort I find, before opening them to gaze into his.

"I may have been...free with my attention before..." Loki begins, his usually mirthful green eyes serious. I hear Jax snort behind me. "Fine," he rolls his eyes. "I may have been a bit of a man whore, but I won't get bored with you. Ever."

My breath hitches as he leans down and kisses me on the lips. It's a kiss full of sweetness and days filled with sun and laughter. It's a kiss full of a promise, one that I'm scared to believe in.

I know he loves me, and I love him back so much that sometimes it makes my heart ache. But do I dare believe that this is forever?

He ends the embrace, dropping a soft kiss on my nose that melts me completely.

I'm then turned round to face Jax, who looks me deep in the eyes too. He doesn't say anything, just nods and kisses me gently.

*I guess we're going public*, I think ruefully as he releases me, interlocking our fingers once again, just as Loki puts an arm across my shoulders, and we walk towards the dining hall.

# CHAPTER TWENTY

LILLY

The next couple of weeks pass by in a rapid blur of intense studying, and mind blowing orgasms with Loki and Jax, sometimes separately, but often together. They're insatiable, and I can't help the feeling that they are trying to find escape in my arms, as much as I am in theirs.

Not to be outdone, Kai regularly invites me to cook with him, taking me by surprise when his fingers cause me to lose focus. Like with Loki in the beginning, he won't let me reciprocate, just leaves me sated and my knickers damp. We've not managed any other hikes, although I can't deny that even with a chill in the air I wouldn't say no to getting hot and heavy outside with him.

Nothing has happened with Ash, not since the night of his party. Though his heated eyes follow me round the dorm, and I can't forget the look on his face as he watched me, Loki, and Jax together. *Smeghead!*

I don't talk to my uncle, it still feels so strange calling him that. I'm not used to having any family other than Mum, and now the horrible irony of gaining an uncle only to lose her cuts me to the quick.

He has sent me precisely two emails. One after my first week of being here, asking how I'm settling in, to which I get no response when I reply. The other was the week before autumn—sorry, fall—break. Apparently, I won't be able to go back to England, so he asked me to make alternate arrangements.

Although he still feels like a complete stranger, I can't deny the flash of hurt that runs through me at his casual rejection. It's compounded by the fact that neither Lexi; my mum's best friend, or Ryan; Mum's boyfriend, have contacted me at all since Mum died. I've known them both my whole life, I even used to hope that Mum and Ryan would get married one day, and yet nothing. Not a text, an email, shit, even a letter.

Lounging on the sofas with my feet in Loki's lap, I sigh as I read the email from Adrian again. *I'm sure he doesn't mean it, Lilly,* I try to reassure myself.

"What's up, Pretty Girl?" Loki asks, grasping my foot and beginning to massage it, causing a moan to slip through my lips.

We're all alone as Jax is at the gym, *again*, and Kai is in his room doing something technical with his stocks. I still can't get over the fact that he has a stock portfolio and makes obscene amounts of money.

Ash is out, probably making someone miserable.

"My uncle says I can't go back to England for the break." I sigh, "I guess I'll be staying here for the week."

"Fuck that!" Loki exclaims, and I jump a little at his raised voice. "You can stay at my place, that is, if you want to?" he says, uncertainty in his tone. I look up to see him concentrating back on my feet. "I mean, my parents are never there, and I'm sure my sisters would love to meet you. Usually, the boys stay a few nights over fall break, so it should be fun."

"I dunno..." I can't help teasing him, trying to hide a smile. "I was kinda looking forward to wallowing in self-pity all week. And Mr Twinkles has been feeling left out recently, so I was gonna show him some attention," I joke, desperately trying not to laugh as his head snaps up, a low growl leaving his lips as his hands still.

"Who the fuck is *Mr Twinkles?*" he sneers, his eyes ablaze with jealousy. I can't help it, I sit up and grab his hand, pulling him upstairs after me.

"I'll introduce you," I say, giggling.

We enter his room, my stuff is still in here and looks like it will be for the foreseeable future if Ash keeps getting his way. Which he always does, the bastard.

I go to the top drawer of his—I guess our—chest of drawers and rummage round in the lacy underwear until my hand alights on a pink satin bag.

Opening it, I pull out my sparkly pastel rainbow vibrator, holding it aloft as I spin round to face Loki once more.

His eyebrows hit his hairline as I brandish the silicone member at him.

"Loki, this is Mr Twinkles. Mr Twinkles, meet Loki," I say, bursting out laughing at the look of arrogant amusement on Loki's face.

"Well, pleased to meet you, Mr Twinkles," he drawls as he casually strolls towards me, and my laughter stops, knowing he's up to something. "But your services are no longer required."

Suddenly, he snatches the vibrator off me, goes over to the window, opens it, and throws poor Mr Twinkles out into the grey October afternoon whilst shouting "Timber!"

"Loki!" I screech, running up to the window to see my vibrator nowhere in sight. "You owe me a new, improved Mr Twinkles!" I hiss, poking him in his solid chest with my finger and only succeeding in hurting myself. *You'd think I'd learn to stop poking them in their hard chests!*

"Baby," he drawls, "I got all the speeds you need right here," he tells me cockily, grabbing his dick through his grey sweatpants—which should be classed as male lingerie in my opinion!

I turn to face him and smile evilly. "Guess you'll never know how good it feels to be pounding into my arse, whilst feeling the vibrations in my pussy from the future Mr Twinkles The Second..."

I see raw heat flash in his eyes as I turn and start to walk away, heading out of the door. Just as I reach for the handle, he calls out to me. "So, are you coming to mine for fall break?"

"I guess, without Mr Twinkles to catch up with, I suppose I've nothing better to do," I sass back, making sure to add some more sway to my hips as I leave the room.

---

## LOKI

As we drive up my family's gravel driveway, I can't help the feeling of butterflies dancing in my stomach. *Why am I so fucking nervous?* I'm never, ever, nervous around girls.

But Lilly...she keeps my attention like no other has before. And I don't even mind sharing her. Shit, seeing Jax pound into her has got to be one of the hottest fucking things I've ever seen. And when we're both inside her...annnd now my dick is fully straining against my jeans.

*Fuck, this girl makes me horny!* I think to myself, turning my eyes back to the road before we crash. I don't know what it is about her that draws me in, but I can't even look at another girl anymore. I'm usually the kind of guy who has a flavor of the week, hell, sometimes even a flavor of the day!

Pulling up outside my parents' house, it's like seeing it with fresh eyes having her next to me. God, this place is so fucking pretentious. With its four white columns holding up what is basically an ostentatious porch, its massive wooden front doors, and like fifty-odd windows on the front alone, it's the epitome of rich America. *Shame the people who own it are such assholes. And there goes my hard-on.*

I stop as the front doors open, and my sisters come barrelling down the marble steps, red hair flying. I just about manage to get my door open and step out of the car when both of them fling themselves at me, talking a million miles an hour.

"Loki! What took you so long? We were expecting you earlier," Heather scolds, eyes narrowed, her arms still wrapped around my neck.

"We made you cupcakes!" Julie shouts with joy.

"Hey, ladies." I grin, kissing them each on the cheek. "That sounds awesome, thanks."

"Who's that?" Heather asks, looking behind me when we hear the passenger car door open. Both girls instantly go shy, peering around me, but not stepping fully away.

"Ladies, this is Lilly. She's staying for fall break," I tell them, a mischievous grin on my lips. "She's our new..." before I can finish my sentence, Lilly jumps in.

"Roomie!" she quickly says. "I share a dorm with the guys at Highgate." She gives me a 'behave' type of look. I, of course, smile innocently back, pretending I have no idea what she's talking about.

"Yes, our new...'roomie'," I say, emphasizing the word. "Lilly, this is the Misses Heather and Julie Thorn."

Lilly smiles at them, her eyes full of warmth, and for a split second, I feel jealous of my little sisters. I want all that warmth directed at me.

"I have a present for you girls, if you'd like it?" she asks them, walking round to the trunk and waiting for me to pop it open.

I look at her with surprise. I didn't know she'd gotten them anything. The girls glance at me, and I smile encouragingly, so they quickly follow behind as I walk over.

I open the trunk to see the two deep green dress bags that she'd placed in there earlier, lying on top. Interesting...

"Loki, can you take those inside for me, please?" Lilly requests a twinkle in her hazel eyes as she looks at me.

"Of course, m'lady," I say, bowing and making the girls giggle. I hear Lilly's sexy chuckle in there too, so I call that a win all around.

Grabbing the dress bags, we head inside, turning left into the sitting room. *Still boring as hell, I see.* It's decorated in shades of beige, or shit coffee as I like to call it. Beige walls, beige curtains, beige leather couches, even beige fucking rugs.

I glance over at Lilly, who looks fucking breathtaking in a short golden yellow dress, fishnet pantyhose, and these sparkly green heeled shoes with a cute little bow on the front. She needs to keep those on later, the thought of them digging into my ass, as I pound into her makes my dick twitch in my jeans. *Down boy!*

I lay the bags over the back of the couch, the girls coming to stand beside me, clutching either arm, and looking at them like they're desperate to see what's inside, but are also a little worried about it.

"Go on, ladies. Don't be shy," I say with a smile, leading them forward a little. They hesitate for another moment, then both step forward and unzip the plastic zipper of each bag at the same time.

I'm nearly deafened by the squeals that erupt from their mouths, wincing, as frothy yellow silk fabric bursts from the opening.

*What the...?* I think as they tear off the rest of the bag, pulling out matching yellow princess dresses, that look a lot like the one from Disney's *Beauty and the Beast.* She must have remembered what I'd said in the library on her first day, about them being obsessed with the movie. My heart skips a beat at the awesomeness of this girl.

They both turn and look at me, then Lilly, with shining eyes.

"You like them, then?" Lilly asks, laughing as they launch themselves at her, wrapping their spindly arms around her.

"Ohmygoshtheyaresobeautiful!" Heather squeals out all in one breath.

"I love it!!" Julie shouts, dancing on the spot and clutching the dress in front of her.

"What do we say, ladies?" I prompt, feeling a grin almost splitting my face.

"Thank you, Lilly," they say in unison.

"You are most welcome," Lilly beams back.

"Loki. Can we go and play princesses? Please?" Heather asks. Being older, at seven and a quarter, she's braver than Julie, who's only just five.

"Of course," I begin, but they dart off before I can finish. "But where's..." I trail off as I hear heeled footsteps approaching.

---

## LILLY

Loki's voice trails off as a tall, very attractive woman walks into the room. She's dressed in low black heels, sheer tights, a black pencil skirt, and a white blouse with a pink silk scarf tied round her neck, sixties style. Her hair is in a chic chignon, and her makeup is tasteful and subtle. She looks to be in her late thirties, maybe early forties.

I glance over to Loki and see that although he has a smile on his face, he's gone absolutely still, like a mouse when a hawk flies overhead. His visceral reaction confuses me and I can feel my forehead crease.

"Loki!" she exclaims, smiling with what looks awfully like attraction, and lust, on her face. She even licks her lower lip. *Gross!*

His answering grimace is tight, almost pained. It's a look I've never seen on him before. He's usually so easygoing, but he seems tense now, his fists clenching and unclenching at his sides.

"Clarissa," he responds, his voice lacking its usual warmth.

I edge closer to him, placing my hand on his arm and squeezing gently. I can feel the tension in him ease a little, so I step even closer, our sides brushing. *What is going on here?*

Her head snaps to me, blue eyes sharp and cutting. Her smile, however, is still in place, yet it lacks any of the warmth that it held moments ago.

"And who is this?" she asks with a tightness to her voice, immediately raising my hackles.

"Clarissa, this is Lilly Darling," Loki responds with a slight growl, as if she's annoyed him. "Lilly, this is Clarissa, the girls' nanny." My brows raise. *The nanny? Then what the fuck is this about? And why is she looking at Loki like she wants to eat him?*

She stares at me like I'm some kind of leper.

*Oh, that cuntpuddle has just pissed me right off!*

Turning to Loki, I mould my body to his side. I dismiss her like she no longer exists. I'd never usually be so rude, but something about this jizzstain rubs me up the wrong way.

"Loki, baby," I say breathily, running my hand down his chest and batting my lashes at him, drawing his gaze to me. "Why don't you show me to your room," I tease, biting my lip and forgetting all about said jizzstain for a moment, lost in a rush of lust.

His eyes flare with fiery lust as he stares down at me, and I'm relieved to see his usual cocksure smile back on his face, even if it's edged with a little confusion.

"Sure thing, Pretty Girl. I'll just grab our bags," he says, going to make a move away from me. I clutch his arm a little tighter, feeling his muscles bunch and flex under my fingertips.

"Oh, honey. I'm sure...*Melissa?*" I say like I can't even be bothered to remember her name, looking at the woman in question. "Anyway, I'm sure she can grab them and bring them up? Just leave them outside the door," I order whilst starting to lead Loki away out of the room and towards the stairs.

I don't miss the flash of rage in her icy blue eyes and can't help but smile smugly at her. *Check, bitch.*

I turn to face Loki who's looking slightly bewildered, but also turned the fuck on if the semi that he's sporting is any indication. I smile brightly at him and gesture with my head for him to lead the way.

He takes me up the wide staircase, then we turn right at the top, and go down the hallway to the last door on the left. He opens it and ushers me inside, closing it shut behind us. I only get the chance to register the forest green colour of the walls before he's coming towards me.

"I don't know what the fuck went down out there, Pretty Girl," he starts, walking towards me and pulling his t-shirt off in that sexy way that guys do, "but it was hot as fuck."

He grabs me round the waist and pulls me to him, grinding the evidence of just how hot he found it against me. My hands roam his beautiful chest, pulling his nipple bar slightly when I reach it, and loving the moan that leaves his lush lips.

"I didn't like the way she looked at you," I say, leaning forward and bending slightly, catching his other nipple in my mouth and sucking hard. His hips buck, and he hisses out a breath.

"Jealous, Pretty Girl?" he teases, my head snapping up at his words, eyes narrowing. I pause in whatever I may have said when I look into his eyes and see...they're wet, and his cheeks are flaming. Something about this isn't right.

I can't stand that he's hurting. I need to chase it away. So I don't say anything, but lean up and capture his plush lips with mine, telling him how I feel with my kiss. It's soft and loving, trying to soothe the hurt away, whatever it is.

A sound escapes him, almost like a sob, as he deepens the kiss, one hand tangling in my hair. He starts to move us backwards, towards the huge bed that I spotted when I walked in.

His hands try to get my pinafore mini dress undone, and he growls when he can't work it out. Breaking our kiss, I chuckle against his lips, taking a step back. I look into his eyes, a breath leaving me to see they are no longer full of pain as I unzip the dress, loosen the straps, and then whip it over my head.

The emerald of his irises are almost completely swallowed up with black as he watches me take off my long-sleeved rainbow cotton top until I'm left in just my underwear.

Today, I decided to go with pretty and flirty. I've got on a black bra and thong set with delicate lace all over that tickles my shoulders and hips. I've also gone for a matching suspender belt, known over here as garters. And thigh-high fishnet stockings. All finished off with my emerald green sparkly heels.

"Fucking hell," Loki curses, slowly raking his eyes up and down my body, the hunger growing in them.

"Your turn." I nod to him, indicating that he needs to show me the goods.

A lazy grin spreads across his lips as he steps out of his already untied boots. Apparently, it's fashionable to never tie them up. His hands go to the front of his deep blue jeans, grabbing a condom packet out of the pocket, then slowly popping each button open, until I can see that he's not wearing any underwear as usual. He pushes the denim over his hips, letting his impressive manhood spring free, the pierced end glinting in the light.

Tearing the packet open with his teeth, he slides the condom over his hard length, then he steps out of his jeans in just a pair of white socks and I giggle at the sight. I raise an eyebrow, nodding my head towards his feet.

“You keeping your socks on, *baby*?” I tease, emphasising his new nickname.

He walks towards me, a devilish grin on his face.

“I thought we could both keep our socks on,” he says, pinging one of my suspenders when he reaches me.

The sharp sting makes me gasp, anticipation flooding my veins, thoughts of his socks all gone. His fingers toy with the front edge of my thong, whilst his head descends to my throat.

“You are.” Kiss. “So.” Kiss. “Fucking.” Kiss. “Gorgeous,” he tells me, kissing his way down my neck until my head is spinning and my pussy is aching.

I grab a fistful of his wavy red hair when his mouth closes over one of my nipples through the lace fabric of my bra. He sucks and teases my nub until it’s hard and I'm quivering.

“Loki, please!” I gasp out, needing release like I need my next breath.

He comes up for air, lips swollen and cheeks flushed with desire. He turns me round, pushing my upper back so that my hands are on the bed.

“Fuck, that's a beautiful sight,” he says seconds before a sharp crack lands on my arse, and I gasp and moan.

“You like that, Pretty Girl?” he asks, soothing the hurt away with his palm. I make a groaning sound as my hands fist the sheets.

“I didn't quite catch that?” He leans down a little, and I can feel his cock teasing my fabric covered entrance.

“Yes!” I gasp out as he pushes my thong aside and inch by inch, starts pushing inside me. This time, a deep groan leaves his lips when he’s in balls deep.

“Shit, Pretty Girl,” he says huskily. “Your pussy is like a fucking clamp, it’s so tight.”

And he stays there, filling me up with his hard cock, which feels so fucking unbelievable.

I don't get any warning as another hard smack lands on my other arsecheek, my inner walls squeezing round him, a whimper spilling from my lips.

Loki starts to pull out, then slams back inside me as his hand comes down to whack me again and again, and I cry out with the waves of pleasurable pain sweeping through me.

In next to no time, my core is tightening round him as I scream my release and claw at the bed. I collapse down as Loki's rhythm becomes jerky, and he roars his own release, stilling above me.

I can feel him panting hard, then hear the thump of what must be our bags landing outside the door. A smug, satisfied smile spreads across my lips.

*Checkmate, nanny jizzstain!*

# CHAPTER TWENTY-ONE

LILLY

After we've regained our breath and cleaned up a little, we get dressed again, bring in our bags, and Loki takes me for a tour round. I desperately want to ask him about Clarissa, but I can't stand the idea of bringing that wounded look back into his beautiful eyes.

This house is crazy bonkers! God knows how many bedrooms there are, all with en-suite bathrooms and walk-in closets. Loki and his sisters' rooms are on opposite ends of one floor, luckily for us, with his parents' suite of rooms on the floor above.

Downstairs there is a library, games room, and two sitting rooms; the one where I gave the girls' their dresses in, and another one just as decoratively bland. There's also the huge open plan kitchen and dining room, plus another more formal dining room. And then his dad's office, which is out of bounds and locked.

It's a rhapsody of beige, cream, and caramel. In fact, so far Loki's and the girls' are the only rooms with any colour.

Loki stops by another wooden door that has a keypad next to it. He turns to me grinning with excitement.

"This is my domain. My sanctuary," he tells me, opening the door with a flourish to reveal a set of dark wooden steps heading down to the basement level.

The walls are painted a soft grey, with dark wood everywhere and muted lighting. We get to the bottom step and are immediately in what looks like a mini cinema, with a huge screen taking up most of the wall on the left. There are comfy, dark grey sofas and bean bags surrounding the TV, and a pool table to the left of the screen, with a fully stocked bar on the far right.

"The guys and I hang out here when they come over," Loki explains, walking over to the bar and passing me a cherry cola from the fridge. "We've also got an outdoor pool and hot tub out back, but we pretty much stay in here when they come over during fall and winter."

"Wow. This is amazing," I say, looking round. I mean, my uncle's place back in England is impressive too, with its old English aristocratic feel. But these Americans, they go all in for next level shit.

"What's through there?" I ask, pointing to the door coming off the bar. It's solid dark wood, with a slight Japanese feel to it, and I can just make out a soft green glow coming from underneath it.

"Ah." Loki gives me his panty melting grin, making butterflies erupt in my stomach. *Every damn time!* "That is the indoor pool, hot tub, sauna, and gym," he tells me whilst opening the door.

My breath stills as I walk over, open the door and look through. There's a huge, glowing green pool, entirely surrounded by soft cream stone. The walls and ceiling have dark wooden beams criss-crossing over them until the space looks like an old Japanese style barn.

Along the edges of the room are loungers and wide chairs covered in pillows, all made from what looks like bamboo, and I can just see some bamboo screens towards the back left edge that separate off an area.

"Loki, it's beautiful here," I gush, understanding why he called this place his sanctuary. "Although, I did forget my swimsuit," I lament, walking towards the pool.

"That's okay, Pretty Girl," Loki assures me in his beautiful, deep voice. "I usually don't bother with one."

He winks at me as he hits a pad on the wall, and *In for the Kill*, the Billie Martin version, begins to play, filling the room with a beautiful melody.

"What if your sisters decide to go for a swim?" I ask as he begins to undress me. It's easier this time as I'd just thrown on leggings and one of his soft graphic t-shirts. This one is a soft sky blue and has a picture of an eye, a heart, and a beaver. *Snort.*

"The door down here has an access code which they don't have, so we should be all good," he answers as he slides my leggings down, kneeling and helping me to step out of them. He kisses my thigh whilst he's down there, and I shiver in sweet anticipation, as well as from the cool air hitting my skin, causing goosebumps to rise.

I unhook my rose pink silk bra, throwing it in the pile of clothes, then step out of my silk French knickers and do the same with them.

There's something about being naked in a space that's not your own which is so exhilarating. It sends a thrill right through me, and I can't help but breathe a little faster, my nipples pebbling as the song and intimate space heightens the feeling.

I look down at Loki, still on his knees before me, looking every inch like the fallen angel that he is. I can't help but reach for his hair, running my fingers through the auburn locks. In this light, they look like the flames of sunset.

"Now you," I whisper, holding his emerald gaze.

He gets up, a smouldering look on his beautiful face. He's so gorgeous, he takes my breath away every time I look at him. It's like he's stepped out of an Italian Renaissance painting, his face enough to make angels weep with envy.

My gaze devours him as he, too, gets undressed, pulling his t-shirt off by grabbing the back of the neck and revealing those drool worthy, inked up muscles. He smirks at me with his sexy as fuck smile, toes off his boots, and then sliding his jeans down his hips and legs, he steps out of them.

"This time the socks too," I command, a smile teasing my lips.

He reaches down and takes them off, and that's when I notice he's got a new tattoo just above his ankle. It's a stunningly lifelike open pink lily, with green leaves swirling round it.

"Do you like it?" he asks, voice husky as he walks towards me completely, gloriously naked.

"It's..." I start at a complete loss for words. Surely this means something serious. I mean, I know we confessed our feelings a while ago, but tattoos are for life, right? Is that what he's saying about us?

I look up into his eyes trying to read him. His gaze is so full of intense emotion, they're practically swirling, like a whirlwind ready to snatch me up and never let go.

"When did you get it?" I question, wondering how I've not noticed it up until now.

"A week or so back," he tells me, stepping so close that I can feel the heat of his body caress mine.

He traces my jaw with his fingers, sending shivers down my spine, making my nipples harden more and almost brush his chest.

"Let's go for a swim, Darling," he suddenly says, moving his hand to tangle our fingers, and stepping towards the pool.

With a deep exhale, I let him tug me along, my mind still churning with what's happening, and not just with Loki, but the others too. I come to with a jolt when he taps my temple, tsking.

"No thinking," he says calmly, smiling at me. "Don't question it."

He turns back round, giving me a perfect view of his biteable arse when he walks down the steps into the glowing green water. He ducks under, coming back up some feet away, and then swimming to the end underwater. I see his auburn head turn once he reaches it, and he makes his way back towards me.

I follow down the steps, and the warm water swirling round my ankles helps me to just let it go, as Elsa would say.

After what happened back in February to my mum, I vowed that I would live in the moment, enjoy life, and dive in—*snort*—head first. If the events of that awful day prove anything, it's that life is too short not to live every minute of it to the fullest.

Ignoring Loki, I swim a length of the green pool too, relishing in the release it gives my muscles and mind.

As I swim back, I see that Loki's sitting down on what looks like a long bench seat built into the corner of the pool. His arms are splayed along the back, like a king on his throne, as he leisurely watches me make my way towards him.

Unable and unwilling to resist him, I swim across, straddling his lap so that my legs are on either side of his. My hands roam the hard muscles of his pecs, tracing his chest ink. His own hands come up to grasp my hips, kneading them like he can't not touch me when I'm near.

"Do they have meaning to you?" I ask as my fingers move to the dragonfly that takes up the front of his throat. I see and feel him swallow as he thinks about what I've asked.

"Did you know that dragonflies moult several times throughout their lives, leaving their old selves behind and starting a fresh chapter each time?" he asks me back, my eyes flitting up to his which stare right back at me. "I like to think that every day, every moment is a new beginning. A chance to start anew. This reminds me of that if I forget."

His words still the movement of my fingers, and unbidden tears spring to my eyes, making it feel even more like a magical underwater world that we've stepped into, as it waves and wobbles.

"I like that," I whisper, voice rough round the lump in my throat. "And this one?" I question, brushing my fingers over his chest piece yet again.

He chuckles darkly.

"Ah, The Creation of Adam. That one was to remind myself that, although I may like to think I'm God, I'm not. I'm always reaching, trying, but never quite managing it."

It's hard to describe the look on his beautiful face, it's almost one of self-loathing. *That surely can't be right, can it? He can't hate himself, can he? He's Loki.*

Needing to see his usual arrogance back, I drop my fingers to his hip, stroking the lipstick mark, making his already hard cock jerk between us.

"And this one?" I ask in a sultry tone, a flirty smile on my lips and one brow raised.

His own eyes flash with want, and his cocksure grin is back in full force.

"That's my second favorite place to be kissed," he teases, his smile sinful and full of deeds done late at night between lovers.

"And your favourite place to be kissed?" I watch as his sinner's grin deepens.

He takes my hand, wrapping it round his dick, pumping our joined hands a couple of times. He releases his grip, moving his hand back to my hip, leaving me to continue moving my own hand up and down his hard shaft. I add in a corkscrew motion, knowing that's what he likes, and his head tips back, his eyes closing, and a long, low groan leaves his lush lips. I love giving him pleasure. It makes me feel powerful that I can bring this fallen angel, this god, literally to his knees.

His hands move down, grasping the globes of my arse, his fingers digging in and adding that little bit of pain I've become so addicted to. He's pulled me closer so that the tip of him rubs my clit, sending spirals of pleasure shooting through me.

His eyes open and lock with mine, and although blown black with lust, there's an intensity in them that leaves me reeling. I lean my head down so that our foreheads are resting together, my eyes closing with the rush of emotion that is taking over me completely.

"How can it be like this?" I whisper. "How can we feel so...right together?"

I can hear the bubbling water of the hot tub nearby, and *Wicked Game* by Daisy Gray is playing in the background, her haunting voice caressing us and saying what seems to be between us.

"I don't know," he says after a moment, voice husky. "But I'm too fucking selfish to let you go, Lilly." A thrill runs down my spine at the sound of my name on his lips. "I love you so fucking much, Pretty Girl."

Before I can say it back, he grabs a fistful of my hair, pulling enough to make me whimper, then slams his lips against mine.

His tongue forces past my lips whilst he holds me hostage, seeking to dominate my mouth and tear me apart. His kiss destroys me, breaking me down, then building me anew.

We break apart, breathless and panting. I feel like we're in the eye of a storm, winds swirling round us with all of the feelings that are desperate to take flight and overpower us.

Suddenly, the door to the pool bangs open, and in strides Lucifer himself.

# CHAPTER TWENTY-TWO

LILLY

"Loki!" Ash calls as he walks in. "That cunt Clarissa said you were down here with Lilly."

Ash's disdainful voice sounds over the music, breaking us out of our intense moment. My head snaps up to see Ash stride in, with a scowl on his face and looking sinfully handsome in his black shirt, tie, and slacks.

I'm facing the door, so I see the moment he spots us. He stops, his steel grey eyes widening a fraction as they meet mine. His nostrils flare, and I can't tell whether he's pissed as all hell, or turned the fuck on at the sight of us.

"Here you are," he says, voice as cold as ice and I can't suppress the shudder that runs through me.

Just then, Jax and Kai step through the door, laughing about something, but coming to an abrupt halt and falling silent as they take us in. Me in Loki's lap. Clearly naked. Clearly playing with his dick.

My cheeks flush with heat at having all of them here, seeing us like this. I'm still full of the maelstrom of emotions that Loki created with that kiss, those words. It's almost too much with them watching as well, and my heart starts racing.

"Would you like them to join us, Pretty Girl?" Loki whispers, lips brushing my ear, and I swallow hard, taking in a sharp breath. I feel my inner walls tighten down, wanting to be filled. "I take that as a yes."

Chuckling, he tips his head to the side.

"Why don't you guys join us?" he says, raising his voice. "Lilly wants to fuck us one by one, while we all watch," he adds, and I gasp aloud, my eyes snapping to his and seeing in them a mix of mischief and lust.

I narrow my eyes at him, but I can't deny that the idea of all of them together, makes me hot as hell, fire racing across my skin at the thought. He arches an auburn brow, daring me to contradict him.

Ironically, *Dirty Mind* by Epic Boy starts playing.

"Don't need to ask me twice," Jax rumbles, deciding for me, and shedding his black gym shorts and tank top, leaving them in a pile on the stone.

His beautiful Viking and Norse tribal tattoos look like they're twisting and seething in the dim light of the room. *One day, I must ask him about them*, I muse as he makes his way over to us, grabbing a folded towel on the way. I can see that he's already hard and standing to attention, his huge cock almost pointing straight up. Jax, my He-Man, erect is a sight that always causes butterflies to come to life in my stomach.

As he reaches us, he drops a foil packet and the towel next to Loki, then he slips in the water, not bothering to use the steps. He leans forward and captures my lips in a searing kiss, and I rock against Loki who groans when my grip around him tightens. Jax releases my mouth with a satisfied smirk, then moves to sit next to us on the bench seat.

My eyes flit behind him to see Kai is now taking his clothes off. I've yet to see Kai fully naked, we've literally just kissed and fooled round a little, but never taken it any further. To say I'm excited would be the understatement of the year.

I watch, biting my lip, as he first takes off his deep red t-shirt, sexy boy style. It's got some math equation on it, which he told me is a joke, but fuck if I know what it's supposed to mean. My eyes eat up every detail of his beautiful torso, my pulse beating faster. He may be the geek of the group, but the boy still works out and is hot as fuck. He's not as big as Loki, but he's got a beautiful chest, with *both* nipples pierced through with nipple bars that glint in the low lights, and my mouth waters at the sight of them.

He toes off his boots, which are untied like the others wear, and then drops his jeans. Unlike Loki and Jax, he is wearing underwear, plain bright orange boxers which make me smile. I can see his hard-on pressing against them, and I'm all kinds of breathless.

He looks me straight in the eye, with a sweet and sexy smile on his lips. There's no hint of the shy guy I first knew, as he drops his underwear down to the floor.

My gaze unashamedly goes down, following his gorgeous six pack and dark happy trail, until I reach the jackpot. *Is that...*Glints of silver sparkle along the underside of his rapidly hardening dick, catching my eye. I whimper when I realise exactly what it is that I'm seeing.

"I take it you've spotted Kai's jewelry?" Loki asks wryly, and pumps his hips a little, hitting my clit again, a moan slipping out of my lips.

I don't take my eyes off Kai as he leisurely strolls towards me, completely naked and with a confident grin on his face. His 'jewellery' happens to be a Jacob's fucking Ladder piercing along the top of his impressive dick, creating a ridge that I am just dying to feel inside me.

*I don't know what they feed these boys, but whatever it is, gives them perfect cocks!*

He comes down the steps on the side of the pool into the water and makes his way over. When he reaches us, he stops beside me, and like Jax, he kisses me full on the lips. Unlike Jax's claiming kiss, Kai's is a slow and sensual exploration of my mouth, his tongue massaging mine, making my toes curl and a moan sound low in my throat.

He pulls away, ending our connection, but keeps his amber eyes locked on mine, a fire within his setting them alight. He's not been with all of us like this before, never been present when it's been myself, Loki, and Jax, and wasn't at the party that night with Ash.

As if reading my mind, he smiles gently, yet with a fierce look in his eyes, saying in a husky voice, "I'm all in, Lilly." He holds my gaze for a moment longer, then settles on the other side of Loki and me on the bench seat.

Three down...I look up to see Ash still fully clothed.

"Ash?" I ask, somehow feeling that this moment is what it comes down to. This is important if we're to explore... whatever this is between us.

He stands there, holding my gaze in those inscrutable steel eyes of his, not giving anything away. After what feels like a lifetime, he starts to unbutton his shirt, revealing his gorgeous ink covered chest. I slump in Loki's arms, which tighten round me as if he knows how important it was for me that Ash joined us too.

As Ash turns to set his now folded shirt on one of the loungers, I gasp, my breath stilling in my lungs. His entire back is covered with the face of a skull, and it's the most beautiful thing I've ever seen. It reminds me of the Day of the Dead sugar skulls, as it's covered in black patterns and mandalas. It's impossible to trace all of the swirls and whorls of black ink, but in moments he's turned back round and is facing me again.

I'm left reeling as he unbuckles his black leather belt, and unzips his pressed slacks, stepping out and laying them on the lounger with his shirt. His dress shoes are already there on the tiles in front. His pants and socks are next, again neatly placed on the pile.

When he straightens up I get a view of his beautiful, sinful body. Unlike Loki's angelic beauty, Ash never fell from Heaven. He's always ruled over Hell, with a cruel beauty and an iron fist. *What I wouldn't give to see him lose a bit of that control.*

Like the others, he makes his way over to us, stepping in and wading through the water to just behind me and to one side. He grabs my chin in a tight grip, forcing my head to bend at an awkward angle to meet his.

"I hope you know what you've got yourself into, Princess," he warns in a voice as dark as the night's sky. "We don't always play nice, and we've never shared before, so here's hoping you can handle us." His bright grey eyes are searching mine, seeking out an answer.

I give a brief nod, as much as his fingers allow. He holds me trapped in his gaze for a moment longer before leaning down and devastating me with his kiss.

Ash kisses me like I'm the answer to all of his prayers, and as if he's been searching his whole life for me. At the same time, it's almost as if he's trying to drink in my soul, and absorb all my light, leaving only darkness. He leaves me wrecked and shaking as he steps away and sits down further away but still on the bench seat.

Loki gently guides my face back to him, bringing me back with his tenderness. "You okay, baby?" he asks, and I know he would stop, hell, all of them would if I said so.

I nod, unable to speak as excitement and pure sizzling lust rushes through me. They're all here, we're all together like this, and it feels so fucking right, like it was always meant to be this way. I can't explain it, but I know deep down that this is where I belong. Where we all belong.

"Good," Loki says, his smile making my insides tighten and reminding me that he's been patiently waiting. "Now ride me, they're all watching," he commands, a hint of laughter in his eyes.

"Yes, sir," I say cheekily, noticing the flare of heat in his gaze at the submissive term.

He urges me off his lap, using the seat to get out of the pool, then holds a hand out to help me up too.

He places the folded towel Jax bought over on the edge of the pool, then sits back down on it, his feet dangling in the water. He pulls me down into his lap once more, my knees on either side of his hips and cushioned by the towel.

Grabbing the condom packet that Jax so kindly left for us, he opens it and slides the rubber along his still very much erect cock. The contrast of his hot, warm body in front of me, with the cool air of the room, has my nipples pebbling to hard aching points.

I grab the base of him, lining him up to my already slick core and sinking slowly down, taking him all the way inside with a groan of pleasure. Once my body is flush with his, I begin to move my hips, teasingly grinding down on him, whilst my hands rest on his shoulders for support. His fingers are grasping my hips, digging in and showing me exactly how he likes it, as he begins to move me up and down making us both moan loudly.

"Fuck, Loki," I gasp as he hits a particular sweet spot inside of me again and again.

I can feel the burn of my orgasm begin already, filling my body with flickers of electric fire. Having the others here and watching is a major turn on. It's this knowledge that makes me come harder than I thought was possible. I scream my release, digging my nails into Loki's shoulders, as wave upon wave of blissful pleasure tears through me, leaving me weightless and floating.

"Oh...goddamn, Lilly," he huskily groans.

I feel Loki's hands tighten on my hips as he pounds into me hard from below, then he too finds his climax, roaring my name, his head bowing to rest on my shoulder.

We stay that way, gripping tightly to each other as we come down from our high.

"My turn," Jax rumbles behind me, his voice so deep and gruff, it causes shivers to run down my spine, and Loki groans when my inner walls clench round him.

I look up at the sound of swishing water, to see Jax pulling himself out of the pool next to us. He lifts me off of Loki, my lips making a sound of protest at the loss of Loki's still semi hard length. Turning me in his arms, he carries me bridal style across the tiles.

The cool air hits my overheated, exposed skin now that I'm out of Loki's embrace, and goosebumps pebble across the surface as I hear Loki call, "Where are you taking her, asshole?"

"To the lounge, dickhead. You know pool water isn't the best lube," Jax responds, and I chuckle as he carries me to the screened off area at the back corner of the room. I look over his shoulder to see the others following.

We go through the screens, which are an open lattice work so that you can see into the pool area. Jax gently sets me down on what can only be described as a lounger-bed. A *huge* lounger-bed.

I look up at him quizzically. "This is handy," I tease, lying back and stretching like a cat.

It has a firm, yet comfy foam mattress and the back part is propped up slightly so that you can relax and say read a book without craning your neck. Or, you know, have an orgy. *Cue excited horny butterflies.*

"Isn't it?" Jax says in that rough voice of his, sending tremors running across my body. He has a slight tilt to his lips as he climbs up, kneeling between my spread legs, capturing my gaze in his piercing blue one.

I can hear *Kiss Me* by Lola Jane beginning to play, which just feels perfect for this moment. I'm completely lost in these boys, and it's like nothing I've ever felt before.

Jax crawls up to me, reaching over to the drawer set beside us, and pulling out a bottle of lube and another condom packet. I can't help but giggle, I mean, come on!

"Something funny, baby?" Jax asks, a teasing warning to his tone.

"Awfully convenient bottle of lube you've got there, Jax," I giggle out, raising a brow.

"You know me, I always like to be prepared," he quips back, eyes sparkling as he rolls the condom on, then squeezes a dollop of lube into his palm, coating his enormous cock.

My thighs clench at the sight, like they always do, though I'm still not sure whether it's with anticipated excitement, or in a bid to protect my poor kitty cat from the pounding she will be getting. *You know we love it!* Great, now Her Vagisty is talking to me.

"A regular Boy Scout," I whisper, when he sets the bottle aside, coming to rest over me with a feral grin.

"Nah," he says, nuzzling my neck, making my back arch, and taking my wrists in his huge hands. "Ash is the one who knows all about knots."

My widened eyes flit to the side to see Ash lounging on, well, a lounger, watching us. There's a hunger in his steel grey eyes that I've not seen before, reminding me of a trapped tiger waiting to pounce.

"Eyes back on me, Lilly," Jax growls, raising my hands above my head, and pinning them down in just one of his. "Ash will get his time later. It's just you and me now, baby."

My body lights up at his words, both at the mention of Ash, and the thread of possessiveness in Jax's tone.

He holds my gaze in his piercing blue one as his other hand reaches between us, lining his wide tip to my soaking entrance.

"Fuck, Jax!" I exhale as he slowly begins to push in, the slight burn of the stretch to accommodate his size familiar, yet new every time.

"Open your eyes, baby," he growls. I hadn't even realised I'd closed them, the pleasure of him filling me so exquisite that I was lost to the sensation.

My eyelids flutter open, and immediately I'm drowning in a sea of blue, churning with possession, want, need, and something so intense, I daren't even think it.

"Jax," I moan as he finally bottoms out, fully encased inside me.

"I know, Baby Girl," he says hoarsely, lowering his head so that our foreheads are touching, in the same way mine and Loki's were not so long ago.

He begins to move slowly, undulating his hips in a way that has me wrapping my legs round him, pulling him closer, and crying out for more.

"Shit, you feel so fucking good, Baby Girl," he gasps out, and hearing how much he's coming undone, knowing I'm the cause of it, starts the delicious burn of another orgasm deep inside me.

My arms are still pinned above me in one of his big hands, and he leans down, kissing me so thoroughly, that I forget whose air I'm breathing. Then, his other hand comes up to wrap round my throat and squeeze just shy of cutting off my air supply.

Drawing back a little, he looks into my eyes again as he thrusts harder, pounding into me.

"Come for me now, baby," he commands in a rough whisper and tightens his grip so that for a single earth shattering moment, I can't breathe.

I come so hard that my whole body lights up, and even my teeth tingle. My inner walls clamp down on him in a vice grip, my hips bucking, making him curse out his own release on a roar.

I vaguely feel his weight drop down onto me, but I'm so lost to bliss that I barely register it. We stay locked together, breathing heavily, until I hear Ash.

"Kai, you next," he orders, like the arsewipe that he is.

*God, he's so fucking arrogant!* But my thighs clench all the same.

My eyes snap open, and I'm about to rip him a new one for interrupting my post orgasm high by being such a cunt, when I see him hand Kai his belt and I go completely still.

Jax rolls off me with a grunt, and I gasp as his dick leaves me.

Kai is waiting at the end of the lounger-bed, the belt folded in half with the buckle end in his right hand. My heart begins to flutter wildly in my chest, like a trapped bird wanting to be freed.

My eyes meet Kai's honey brown ones, which contain a hardness I've not seen before. Instead of scaring me, it leaves me all kinds of excited with breathless anticipation.

"Do you trust me?" he asks in that soft melodic voice of his, soothing away the rough edges his hard eyes had created.

"Yes," I whisper after a moment's hesitation. "I trust you, Kai."

"If it becomes too much or you want to stop at any time, I want you to shout the word 'red.' Okay?" he instructs, and I nod. Excitement, and a thread of fear running through me. My nerves feel alight once again, gone is the lazy satisfaction of moments ago.

"Come to the end of the lounger, and turn around so that you're facing away from me on all fours," he orders, and there's a core of steel running through his voice that makes me shiver and my nipples harden.

I vaguely register that *Sucker For Pain* by Lil Wayne, Imagine Dragons, et al. is playing as I do what he says, and I crawl to the end of the bed, my limbs shaking. I glance up at him and lick my lips, turning round so that I'm looking at Jax, who is still lying on the bed, his eyes boring into mine.

"You okay, Baby Girl?" he asks, brow dipped and face concerned. He seems ready to beat the shit out of Kai if I say I'm not. Kai fucking growls back at him, like a wolf who doesn't want to share his meal.

I like this Kai, this alpha that's come out to play.

"I'm okay," I assure Jax in a soft voice, quivering and a slight tingle coming over my limbs at what will happen next.

Kai strikes my arse gently with his palm, and I jump at the unexpected contact.

"I'm going to use Ash's belt on your ass three times. Once on your left cheek, once on your right, and once across both. If you take it like a good girl, then, and only then, will I give you my cock. Understood?" he asks, his voice rough, full of desire and lust.

My eyelids flutter as I reply.

"Yes," I can feel myself already getting wet at his words.

"Yes, what?" he says, tone full of command, winding me up even tighter.

"Yes, sir," I answer, fulfilling my role as a sub and loving every minute.

"Good girl," he praises back, giving my arse a final gentle caress, the warmth lasting for a moment after he withdraws his hand. I'm so tightly wound up, I feel like I'm about to explode with pent up need.

I feel the slight whoosh of cool air milliseconds before the sharp sting of leather on my bare backside. I gasp loudly as the shock of it reverberates through me, the pain immediate and intense. My hands clench in the fabric of the cushion, my breathing shallow. My whole body goes tense, yet, I've never been wetter, the combination of pain and pleasure a heady mix that leaves me reeling.

"You took that so prettily, my darling Lilly. Such a good girl," Kai croons with approval, soothing the hurt with a gentle rub of his palm, the pleasure of his touch eliciting a low whine from my lips.

Seconds later, another explosion of pain cuts across my other arse cheek, and this time I cry out, hearing a growl of appreciation sound behind me. I barely get a chance to catch my breath before the third hit cracks across both cheeks.

I'm sweating and shaking, my heart is racing, and I can feel my pussy pulsating like it has its own heartbeat. I'm so turned on right now I'm almost keening, needing Kai inside me so badly.

I hear the belt drop to the floor, the buckle clanking on the stone tiles. Kai strokes my sore throbbing arse, and I hiss in pleasure and pain whilst my body tries to get away and move into his touch at the same time.

"Such a good fucking girl, Lilly," he says softly. "Look, Loki. See how she's dripping for us."

Panting, I glance over my shoulder with hooded eyes to see Loki make his way over from one of the other loungers.

"Jesus fucking Christ," he curses in his low sexy voice, reaching out and swiping a finger along my dripping slit. I moan low and loud as he puts it in his mouth sucking the juices off.

"Kai," I beg, my voice breathy, and making his head snap back to me, his eyes sharp.

"Naughty, Lilly," he scolds. "I didn't say you could speak. And now, you'll have to be punished."

He sighs, but there's that flash of heat in his eyes that tells me he'll like this punishment. Probably as much as I will.

He turns back to Loki. "You fill that naughty mouth of hers. Make sure she can't speak out of turn again," he orders, his voice firm and unyielding.

"Yes, sir," Loki teases with a smile and a salute, and Kai's dick twitches as Loki turns to come to my side of the bed, then climbs on. He kneels in front of me, his hard dick proud, his round piercing glinting in the low light.

"You heard the man, Pretty Girl. Open up," he says, a devilish smile on his face.

I do as he says, knowing that I'm going to enjoy this punishment very much. He looks up and behind me as if waiting for a signal that I can't see, before starting to push his way into my mouth.

"Fuck, I forgot how good your mouth around my cock feels," he groans as he holds still, eyes closed. He wraps my hair round one fist, tugging slightly. The slight pain skittering across my scalp, coupled with my throbbing arse is almost too much, and I groan round him, making his hips jerk.

"That's better," I hear Kai say as I hear the rustle of foil, then I feel his hands grip my hips tightly, his tip lining up with my aching pussy entrance.

Without a moment's warning, he slams into me hard.

I'm wound up so tightly from the belt and his sheer dominance, that I fucking shatter round him, my pussy pulsing and gripping him hard as I come, groaning round Loki's cock.

Kai gives me no respite, pounding hard into me, his Jacob's Ladder piercing adding an extra sensation that is making my orgasm roll on and on. Both of his hands have a death grip on my hips, holding me exactly where he wants me in a bruising hold.

Not to be forgotten about, Loki starts moving in and out, giving me a little time to adjust before he starts fucking my face, a tight grip on my hair.

I will my throat to relax as I take him deeper, his auburn curls tickling my face as I suck and lick him like he's the best fucking lollipop I've ever had.

Kai's sending waves of such intense pleasure through me from my core, that I briefly wonder how I'm going to survive when his movements become jerky, and I feel him get harder right before he thrusts a final time, and with a shouted curse, stills as he orgasms. Seconds later, Loki pours his hot release down my throat with a grunt, and I swallow every salty drop.

He pulls out of my mouth, tugging my head up by my hair, so he can kiss me on the lips, uncaring of the taste of himself that lingers in my mouth. It's short and sweet before he releases me to flop on the bed, next to Jax, his breathing laboured.

"You are so. Fucking. Sexy," he pants, arm over one eye.

I can't even make a coherent thought, let alone say anything in response. My body feels used, spent, and I'm just fucking liquid.

Kai pulls out, and I groan as I try to breathe normally again. He comes round and leans over, kissing me tenderly on the shoulder, my sensitised skin tingling at the touch. His lips come to my ear, "Thank you, Lilly," he whispers before he goes to sit down on a lounger nearby.

*These boys sure know how to melt a girl's heart.*

I see Ash, still lounging like a lazy cat, and raise my eyebrow in challenge. I may be a hot fucking mess, but I said I could handle all of them. I meant it. His gaze sharpens as he sits up.

"You think you can handle me? After all that?" Ash waves his hand in our direction, scoffing. But I can see the desire, the desperate need swirling in his steel eyes.

And suddenly, it hits me. He let his friends, his *brothers*, go first even though he thought that I may be too spent to please him too. He loves them so much that he's willing to put himself and his needs last. He is a true leader in every sense of the word. I may be liquified, and fucking orgasmed out, but I won't leave him wanting.

I blink, pushing up to my knees with a small groan, then allow my eyes to go heavy and a sassy smirk to pull up my lips.

"Of course I can handle you, Ash. You're only a pussy cat after all." My lips twitch with suppressed laughter when his grey eyes intensify with the gauntlet that I've just thrown down.

The music changes to *Sanctify* by Years and Years as he curls up, all perfected elegance, even though he's stark bollock naked. He stalks towards me, like a jaguar who's spotted its prey, and is getting ready to pounce. His slate eyes stay on mine, and suddenly, my heart is beating wildly in my chest, my flight, fight, or fuck mode switching on all the way.

Without missing a step, or taking his eyes off me, he grabs the bottle of lube from the bed.

"I think I'm wet enough for you already, wouldn't you say?" I sass as he comes to stand behind me.

I hear a sinful chuckle leave his lips, then one of his hands comes in between my shoulder blades, pushing down hard so that my arse is up, and my cheek rests on the soft mattress.

My natural instinct with Ash is to play the brat, fight him a little, which I know he enjoys. But I'm too fucking spent, my limbs still feeling like I can barely hold them up. So I comply with a low grumble, provoking another deep chortle from him that sends a shudder through me.

"If you think I'm having sloppy seconds," he says in a low husky voice as I feel a cool glob of lube slide between my arse cheeks, "or I suppose sloppy fourths, then you don't know me as well as you claim," he finishes.

His words make me bristle, and I look over my shoulder narrowing my eyes at him. *Fucking cockwomble!*

My ire is short lived, as he reaches down and begins to rub the lube round my puckered hole sending tendrils of heady pleasure reaching over me. I squirm and groan, my head falling back down and my eyes rolling. I'm so sensitive after the others, it's almost too much. I never used to enjoy anal play, but with these guys, I can't get enough.

I push back as his thumb starts to enter me, the intrusion feeling so damn good a low keen leaves my lips and my fingers curl into the mattress. He pumps in and out a few times, his other hand reaching round, his fingers circling my over sensitive clit.

I'm mewling like a fucking kitten under his touch, and when he pulls his thumb out and starts pushing his lubed up dick into me, I groan like an animal, my knuckles going white.

"Jesus fucking Christ," he hisses as he bottoms out, hips flush with my sit bones. "The boys said you were tight, but, fuck. Your ass is like a fucking vise."

He starts to move in and out of me, and the sounds that I make, well, I'd be embarrassed if it didn't feel so good. Like an electric pulse deep inside my very being is sparking. Moving one hand from my hip, he wraps his fingers round my hair and pulls me upright so my back is arched, against his front, my tits pushed out.

His pace speeds up, as he plays with my clit relentlessly, and I buck, crying out, my nails carving lines into the arm holding my hair. The pleasure is overwhelming in the best way, and I begin to shake with the force of my impending orgasm.

"Ash..." I plead, almost crying with the need to come again. One of my hands tangles in his hair, holding hard as he keeps up a punishing pace.

"Open your eyes, and look at them, Princess," he growls out. "Look at what you do to them."

And I do as he says, opening my eyes to see Loki, Jax, and Kai in front of us, watching with hungry eyes, all with hard dicks in their hands, seeking their own release.

The sight of these beautiful guys coming undone whilst looking at me, tips me over the edge, into a breath stealing, earth shattering orgasm. My vision whites out, and my whole body goes rigid, as wave upon wave of pleasure washes over me, until I can barely hold myself upright.

I feel the warm liquid of my release gush out of me, soaking the mattress underneath, as Ash pulls out and coats my arse with ropes of hot cum.

"Lilly, fuck!" he exclaims roughly, before we both collapse, his hard body covered in sweat and draped over mine. I hear the other guys curse as they, too, find their climaxes, but I'm too boneless to even lift my head to see.

We lay like that panting, whilst the universe rights itself once more. I can't move a single muscle, my eyes closed, so I don't protest when strong arms pick me up, cradling me against a warm, firm chest. I manage to lift my head enough to look up and am surprised to see that it's Ash carrying me.

"Told you I could handle you all," I croak out, my voice hoarse from my pleasure filled screaming.

He pauses, his grey eyes meeting mine as he looks down at me, and I get lost in their spiralling depths. There are so many emotions churning in them, it's hard to see what he's feeling. What he's thinking.

"It's not just our dicks you have to handle, Princess, though you did that beautifully," he adds, a rare smile lifting his lips. It transforms his cold beauty into something awe-inspiring and my breath hitches at the sight. "We're all broken, fucked up, in one way or many. None of us are going upstairs when we die. I just..." he trails off, and there's frustration in his gaze and the skin round his beautiful lips is tight. "I just don't want to drag you down too."

He looks away, his face pained, all hard lines and sharp angles.

"Hey," I whisper, my hand coming to cup his chiselled jaw, turning his gaze back to me. "I'm broken too. I've been to Hell, and I'm not sure I ever left. I don't need angels, or knights in shining armour. And you don't need a sheltered innocent princess."

His churning gaze stays on mine, and I try to let him see the pain that lives in my soul, the shattered pieces slowly turning to ash. Well, they were before I came here...I let the jagged edges show in my eyes so that he can see that I'm just as fragmented as them.

He brings his forehead to mine, heaving a sigh, his warm breath tickling my face.

"Let's get you cleaned up, Princess," he eventually says, raising his head and walking us into a waterfall shower. Being true to his word, he cleans me up, lavishing me with all of the care and attention as if I am in fact the princess he calls me and he is my very own dark knight.

# CHAPTER TWENTY-THREE

LILLY

The next few days pass by in a blur of messing round with the guys in the pool and hot tub, watching movies, and playing card games, which I officially suck at. I also have some epic Disney marathons with Loki's sisters, which are made funnier by the guys joining us, then getting told off for groaning at the admittedly ridiculous princes.

It is the early hours of Thursday morning, and I wake up in a cold sweat, shaking with a bone deep fear. Red ribbons twirl round my mind as I sit up, and looking round, I notice that the bed is cold and empty.

*That explains the nightmare then*, I think, rubbing my eyes with trembling hands. Before arriving at Highgate, I couldn't go a night without waking up screaming, visions of drowning in a sea of blood swirling in my mind, and a soul destroying terror taking root in my heart. Apart from one night, when the guys were away and Loki woke me up from my nightmare, I've not slept by myself without Loki or Jax by my side, since arriving. I'd be a fucking idiot not to make the connection between that and my dreams coming back to haunt me.

Swinging my legs over the side of the bed, I scoop up a huge black t-shirt from the floor, slipping it on over my naked body. I'm engulfed in the warm citrus scent of Jax as it falls all round me, ending at mid-thigh. The guy is seriously big, and wearing his clothes is like a comforting hug, and I can't help wrapping my arms round myself, even though the heating is obviously on as the air is warm.

I head to the door, planning to go downstairs and find the guys, there's no way I'm getting back to sleep without one of them holding me close. I'd be scared of that, of how dependent it feels, but I promised myself a fresh start. A new me. And I refuse to be scared of these feelings.

I pad down the stairs on bare feet, intending to make my way to the basement, when I see light coming from one of the sitting rooms. I can hear *Devil Like Me* by Akine playing softly, the lyrics haunting and my heartbeat becomes sluggish with a sense of dread as I creep closer and peer round the doorway. I see Loki, Ash, and Kai sitting there, dressed head to toe in black and all sporting glasses filled with amber liquid.

*What the...*

They're just sitting there, not speaking, and there's such an air of desolation about them, their gazes vacant, that I can feel my chest begin to tighten and chills run down my spine, making me shiver.

Ash is staring into his glass like it holds all the answers. His beautiful brow is marred with a frown, his lips pursed. He looks so cold, like all of the humanity inside him is gone, and has been replaced with something dead and unfeeling.

My gaze flits over to Loki, who has a look of such self-loathing on his angelic face that I take an involuntary step forward, my hand reaching out, feeling the overwhelming need to erase the pain, and see his beautiful smile. He swirls his liquor round and round in his glass, lost in his own clearly hellish thoughts.

Kai is harder to read, his glasses reflecting the lamplight and hiding his honeyed eyes. His grip on his glass is tight, knuckles white. Like Ash, he looks detached, like he's not really here and his brow is deeply furrowed.

"Did we wake you?" I hear the deep rumble of Jax behind me, and I spin round, my heart pounding.

"I–I had a bad dream," I stammer out, suddenly nervous at being caught spying. I look him over, taking in his all black attire, which is not unusual for Jax, but something just feels off. "Why were you not..." I begin to ask, but come to an abrupt stop as I suddenly notice his hands. He holds them by his side, but in the low light, I can see that his knuckles are split and bleeding.

He tries to hide them behind his back, but I lurch forward, grabbing one to inspect, wincing at the sight of how raw they look.

"Jax! What on earth happened to your hands?" I gasp. "What's going on, Jax?" I ask, my eyes boring into his blue ones. Sharp butterflies take flight in my stomach when he remains silent, not even flinching at my touch on his bleeding knuckles.

He sighs heavily, looking heavenward, then indicates the sitting room with a nod. "You better come in, I guess," he grumbles out, and I drop his hand as he moves past me into the room with the others.

I hesitate a beat, knowing that whatever I discover beyond the doorway will change things irrecoverably. I take a deep inhale, heart pounding, and step forward.

The others look up as I walk in, a range of emotions flashing across their faces. Kai looks dismayed, and he sighs, taking off his glasses and rubbing his eyes with his thumb and forefinger. Loki's gaze is filled with horror, his eyes wide, like this is his worst nightmare come true. And Ash. Ash has a look of sad resignation on his face, his jaw sharp and hard, yet his eyes burn with a rage so bright, it makes me stall.

"What's going on?" I ask them, panic clawing at the edges of my vision. I start to sweat, and fear sizzles down my spine in a white hot line. I look directly into Ash's grey eyes, staring down his rage.

"Whatever it is, I can handle it," I assure him, lifting my chin and reminding him of my promise the other day, even though I'm quivering inside. "Whatever it is, it can't be that bad."

Still, no one answers me. They all look as though they're awaiting their fate at the gallows.

"Did you get into a fight?" I ask, looking round, but none of them will meet my gaze, and that fact alone turns my skin clammy and makes my stomach churn.

"You're making me nervous with the silence. What's going on?" I ask again. I'm shaking with the spine tingling terror that this is bad. Really fucking bad.

"What if I told you we'd hurt someone tonight," Ash finally says back, voice devoid of all emotion, yet his steel grey eyes are seething and roiling. I hear Loki curse in the background and a glass smash, but I can't tear my eyes away from Ash's hateful gaze.

My heart stops. I feel my stomach plummet, like I've just come down a rollercoaster, and black dots dance at the edge of my vision. "W–what?" I whisper, voice shaking yet unable to look away from him. "Why?"

He stands up, his body radiating barely controlled violence, trembles racking his frame.

"I told you we were fucked up. I warned you we were bad people, destined for Hell. What the fuck did you think I meant?" he scathingly asks, his eyes are so cold, I feel hurt at his words as tears spring to my own, unbidden.

"It's what we do, Princess," he spits, panting and more out of control than I've ever seen him before.

His hair is out of place, sticking up like he's been running his hands through it constantly. His eyes are wild, pupils blown so that only a sliver of mercury shows. My desire to see him lose his rigid control comes back to haunt me. This is not what I wanted. Not at all.

"Loki and I interrogate and question the targets. When they don't tell us what we want to know, which they never fucking do, we hold them down, and Jax beats the ever loving shit out of them. Kai, being the tech genius that he is, destroys their lives, leaving child porn on their laptops, and emptying their bank accounts."

His chest is rising and falling, he's breathing so hard, taking in ragged gasps, it's like he's just run a marathon. He's standing so close to me that I can see his pulse jumping in his throat, his hands clenching and unclenching by his sides.

"Jesus fucking Christ, Ash!" I hear Loki exclaim, but my attention is all on the inked up bastard in front of me, and what he's saying. I can't look away, however much I wish I could.

"Why?" I choke out. "Why do you do it?"

I'm shaking, my body cold, and my mind full of so many emotions that I can't even begin to untangle them. They're like a hurricane inside me, twisting and swirling, ripping me apart. And they're the colour of red ribbons trying to pull me back into memories that I can't face right now.

"We have no choice," Kai whispers. His voice is so low I almost miss what he says. My head turns in his direction, taking him in my wild gaze.

"Not good enough," I snap, roaring anger sweeping everything else away.

"There's always a fucking choice, Kai!" I practically scream, images flashing across my vision of me leaving the kitchen that day, in a fit of pathetic anger, only to come home later and find my life irrevocably changed.

The song has changed to *Empty Crown* by Yas, the beat hitting me in the gut as the desperate lyrics wash over me. It's too much with what's happening right now, the words too poignant, that I snap, throwing my arms out. "Can someone turn the fucking music off!"

"Hey, Pretty Girl," I hear Loki say gently, reaching out to touch me.

I instinctively jerk back, regretting the move instantly as I see the desolate look in his emerald eyes. My heart cracks, yet I don't step closer, I can't with the past and present blurring right now, and his hand drops to his side, breaking me a little more.

"Just tell me why?" I sob, tears making hot tracks down my cheeks at the thought that these boys are capable of such brutality. Have maybe hurt people like my mum was hurt before death claimed her that day.

My eyes look round frantically, then finally settling back on Ash. His gaze softens a fraction, although it feels like he's preparing for a blow as he almost cringes.

"Princess..." he starts, looking suddenly bone weary, his whole torso caving in as his shoulders round. "It's too dangerous for you to know everything," he says pleadingly, scrubbing his hands over his face and leaving his usually pristine hair in even further disarray.

"Tell me," I demand, standing straighter even though every fibre of my body is shaking. "Please, Ash. Just tell me what is going on."

I feel so numb, like I'm not really here. I'm fucking floored by the fact that they hurt someone. That they've done it more than once. That they'll probably do it again.

*Rivers of red ribbons...*

The image sears my retinas, as if I'm in that room once more, and I force it down with a shake of my head before it can take root.

Ash sits down heavily, elbows dropping to his knees and hands dangling between them, like he's just too exhausted to stand up anymore.

"As Kai told you, our families are all in business together. Sometimes, someone oversteps the line and needs to be dealt with."

"Dealt with?" I ask, wrapping my arms around myself, but finding no comfort. "What do you mean?"

I see Loki jerk towards me, and I can't deny how much I want his strong arms wrapped around me right now, holding me tight. But, I just can't. I need a clear head. I need to understand. So I shake my head, and once again fracture into pieces as he looks heartbroken, rubbing his chest as if he's in physical pain.

"I thought I made that pretty fucking clear earlier, Princess," Ash says, his voice full of cold arrogance as he looks up at me, jaw hard. "We interrogate them for intel, we hurt them if they don't give it to us, or we teach them a lesson if they cross us." He says all this so casually, like he's talking about calculus and not the fact that they injure people.

"And you have to...deal with them? Like the way my mum was dealt with?" I ask, my voice cutting and only hitching slightly at the end. Ash flinches like I've struck him, and I hear curses behind me.

"We have to prove ourselves, Baby Girl," Jax rumbles from his place behind me, and I spin round.

A part of me notices that none of them deny the inference that things may go further than just bodily harm. My stomach threatens to revolt at that thought.

I can see his arms are crossed over his chest defensively, and he's leaning against the mantelpiece. A fire burns in the fireplace sending out a warmth that I can't feel, whilst I stand here with what feels like despair wrapping its cold fingers round my heart.

"It's our legacy," he tells me, and he's completely closed off, withdrawn from me and giving me the bare facts. But there's a pleading look in his blue eyes, begging me to understand. "We must show that we are worthy to take over our roles in the company one day."

I just gape at him. *This is all about business?*

"I don't understand," I reply, looking into his sharp blue eyes, silently asking him to explain it to me. To tell me this isn't just about money and lining their pockets.

"A few years back, we were all taken to a cabin in the Rockies," Loki begins out of the blue, his low voice making me ache to be surrounded by his warmth. I look over to him, still standing nearby, arms at his sides, like he can't bear to be too far away from me.

"Loki..." Ash growls out, standing up, his whole body bristling.

Loki spins towards him. "She deserves to know the whole fucked up story,

Ash!" Loki shouts, getting up in Ash's face. They stay like that for a few moments, chests heaving and gazes locked.

"Fine," Ash snaps out, turning his back on Loki, and grabbing his drink before sitting back down.

"We thought it was some team building shit that they, our fathers, kept putting us through. I guess it was in a way." Loki lets out a cruel chuckle. It's a sound I've never heard from him before, and I hate it. "We arrived, and they took us down to the basement." He closes his eyes, tilting his head back, hands running over his hair. "There was a...mark, a target in the basement. Tied and gagged." He looks at me then, and the pain and loathing in his eyes takes me aback, my pounding heart stuttering in my chest. "They told us that now that we were older, and if we ever wanted to take over the business, we needed to learn what had to be done when someone got in our way. When someone knows too much, or tries to cross us." He stops, his eyes hard, yet asking me to understand why they've committed such atrocities. But I don't. Not yet.

"What happened?" I whisper, not wanting the story to continue, but needing to know the truth about these guys. "What did you have to do?" I ask, dreading the answer, but desperate for the truth.

"We each took turns beating the shit out of him," Kai's soft melodic voice sounds out. Only, it's got a hard quality to it now.

"You could have refused," I counter quietly. "You could have said no."

"Pretty hard to say no with a gun to your head, *Princess*," Ash scoffs.

"Wh–what?" I ask, shocked, my gaze flitting to his sharp one. I seem to be asking this question a lot tonight, like a broken fucking record.

"Our *fathers,"* Ash spits the word out like it leaves a bad taste in his mouth. "Or in Kai's case his uncle, held guns to our heads, saying that if we couldn't prove that we were men enough to do what was best for the company, then we didn't deserve a seat at the table. Jax and I protested loudly, calling their bluff." Ash doesn't finish his sentence, but Kai steps in.

"But then my uncle clicked off the safety and shot me in the shoulder," he says quietly, and I turn my gaze on him. He looks tired, and there is a guilt in his eyes as he briefly looks at the others. *Does he blame himself for that night?*

"He shot you?!" I all but screech, my eyes travelling over him as if I can see the wound.

*How could their own families do this to them?*

“He said next time he wouldn't miss,” Ash adds, his face full of pain.

“Unbeknownst to us, they filmed the whole thing. They have proof and use it against us at every fucking opportunity,” Loki finishes, and he looks so hopeless, his arms loose at his sides, that my heart breaks anew for these guys.

“B–but, they're your family! What kind of fucked up shit is that?” I ask, no one answers, as we all know it's above and beyond fucked. I can't fathom having the people who are meant to love you, protect you at all costs, be willing to destroy you. To hurt you. To kill you.

I look at Loki who's still standing close to me, and the bleakness on his face breaks my heart and makes my very soul wail. Yet, how can I reconcile the fact that they badly hurt people, with the guys who I have feelings for? Who I’m falling for?

I feel so churned up, full of anger, sorrow, and betrayal. It's like they've ripped my beating heart right out of my fucking chest, devouring it and leaving me an empty shell. It’s all so overwhelming, and I don’t know how to process any of it. And it’s all tied up with fucking crimson ribbons that bind me so tightly, there’s no hope of escape.

Dizziness washes over me, my limbs cold and my breaths shallow as panic flares brightly inside me.

“I...I will go sleep in one of the spare rooms,” I say haltingly, starting to back away, as my flight mode screams at me to run.

“Lilly, please don't run away,” Loki asks desperately, a look of sorrow in his eyes that rips my soul apart even more until there is nothing left.

He takes a step towards me, and again I step back, flinching and putting distance between us. His face falls further, and he slumps against the side of the sofa in defeat.

“You know we'd never hurt you, don't you, Baby Girl?” Jax asks, his deep voice that usually soothes me, raspy as he takes a step away from the mantle in my direction.

My eyes flit from Jax, to Loki, to Kai, and finally to Ash, who has become cold and distant again.

“I...I know,” I say, still backing up, my movements jerky and body tense. “I just need some time. I–I need to think, to process everything you just told me.”

*Run! Get out of there!* My mind begs me.

And then I turn tail and flee up the stairs, my heart racing, my pulse drumming in my ears. I hear Jax roar, the sound making me jerk in my flight, my steps coming faster. Then the crash of furniture and smashed glass sounds behind me, as I finally throw open the door to a spare room, slamming it shut once I'm inside. Sliding down to sit on the floor, I break into a million pieces that scatter out into the darkness.

---

KAI

I watch with a heavy heart full of agony as Lilly flees the living room, leaving hopelessness and destruction in her wake.

I look up as my brothers fall apart around me, feeling utterly hopeless. There's not a single thing I can do about it. Nothing I can do to help, or ease the pain that is tearing through all of us at her rejection.

Jax reacts with his usual violence, throwing his glass in the fireplace, making the flames roar up the chimney, before he upends a table, smashing it to pieces all the while bellowing like a wounded lion.

Loki looks after her, his whole body shaking, and I can see the glisten of unshed tears in his eyes. On his face is a lost look that breaks my heart more, and a flash of worry dries my mouth at what path he will go down now. Things weren't great before Lilly came here. He was taking too many drugs, drinking until he passed out and coming home with a different girl almost every night. I don't want to see him like that again. I can't bear it.

And Ash. Well, Ash retreats into himself as he tends to do, his body stiff and his face hard as stone. It's only then that I realize with a jolt, that he'd begun to emerge at all.

I sit here, not knowing what to do to fix it. I am usually good at fixing things, but I'm all out of ideas. And hurting just as much as my brothers.

"Shouldn't we have told her the full story?" Loki asks the room, still staring up the stairs. His voice is rough, scratchy with sadness.

"Why?" Ash sneers, his upper lip curling. A classic defensive move for him and I ache to see it. "You saw her, she could barely fucking look at us as it was. It wouldn't have made any fucking difference, Loki." He ends on a sigh, like he's given up already.

“We were fucking fourteen! Still kids! And we had no fucking choice!” Loki, the calm playful one of us, suddenly roars. He's gotten up in Ash's face again, squaring off against him, and at least he’s shed some of the hopelessness, even if he’s replaced it with rage. I can see Ash bristle, his fists clenching by his sides.

“Well, go on then,” Ash says in a deadly calm voice, that lets me know he's close to losing it. “Go upstairs, and tell her that we're murderers too. I fucking dare you.”

“We had no choice,” Loki bites back, and I can see that they're moments away from trading blows.

“Doesn't matter. We still killed a man, the rest is semantics,” Ash counters in that same unemotional tone.

Just as I think Loki is gonna go for him, and I’m wondering if I’m going to need to stop him, Jax gets between them.

“Enough,” he says in that gruff voice of his, placing a hand on each of their chests. “Us fighting doesn't help anything.”

“Well, what do you suggest, *big guy*?” Ash asks Jax scathingly, his eyes narrowing to slits. He's lashing out because he's hurting. It's how he copes with pain. And he’s had more than his fair share of that over the years.

“We give her time,” I say simply, but loud enough that everyone hears and turns to look at me. “She'll come around.”

“How do you know?” Loki asks me, voice small and uncertain, yet there’s a shred of hope in there. A dim light in his eyes.

“Because she needs us as much as we need her,” I reply, hoping with my whole being that I’m right.

# CHAPTER TWENTY-FOUR

LILLY

I don't sleep at all that night, tossing and turning, covered in sweat with visions of blood soaked hands, and monstrous devils plaguing my dreams.

I'm still reeling from the news the guys shared with me. About what they are forced to do for their company. What the hell kind of company expects that from its own children?!

How can I get past the fact that these guys, my guys, have hurt people so brutally?

The fact that they've spilt blood...it's barbaric. I'm suddenly awash with anxious apprehension all over again, bile touching the back of my throat.

A piss. I need a piss. And a shower. Definitely a shower. I'll think about this all later.

I head to the en suite, gently shutting the door. I don't want them to know I'm awake. Not yet. *Hurts Like Hell* by Fleurie plays on my phone that I've left on the counter. It suits my sombre mood, and the searing pain in my heart at the thought that I've lost my guys, lost parts of myself that I didn't know were no longer inside of me.

After taking care of business, I turn the shower on, setting the temperature to scorching. It's another walk in, all singing and all dancing affair, like showers back at Highgate. Stepping under the hot spray, I hiss, yet I feel the tension in my shoulders begin to ease. I stand there, head bowed, torn between my feelings for these guys, and what they've done. What they will continue to do.

I drop to the floor of the shower, curling my arms over my knees and sob, tears mixing with the water as it cascades over me.

The song switches to *Lovely* by Billie Eilish and Khalid, and I'm instantly transported back in time, gasping as I'm sucked into the horror of finding my mum carved up and bleeding all over our kitchen floor.

*The scent of copper surrounds me. I'm drowning in it as I gaze at the ruin before me. Her face is untouched, still so beautiful. Her hazel eyes are unseeing, but forever open, staring through me. Her body is unrecognisable in the carnage of blood, and parts of her are exposed that never should have seen the daylight.*

I blink, coming back to the here and now. Some time after her murder, I read a newsletter article that said she was stabbed forty-seven times, the number filling me with horror at what she'd gone through before her last breath left her.

Just as I think the flashback is over, that fucking song keeps playing, like it did that day on the radio, sending me hurtling back into the nightmare.

*I'm kneeling beside her, her blood on my clothes, covering my hands, and staining everything with her lifeforce. Lifeforce that had spilled its vitality and essence all over the tiled floor, like a dropped glass of juice. It's true what they say, 'there's no use crying over spilt milk.' And I don't cry. I can't cry.*

. . .

I come back to the present with a gasp this time, my eyes searching for a handhold, something to keep me here, but it's no use.

*I'm blinking, my eyes scratchy and sore, to see a hospital room, a strange man and woman standing before me, talking in hushed tones.*

*I sit up, confused, and catch their attention.*

*"Lilly," the woman says gently, taking a step towards me. "My name is Carol, and I'm your social worker."*

Social worker? Why do I need...*my thoughts are cut off as memories of blood come flooding back, and I hear a keening noise, only to realise it's me as I curl up into a ball on the bed.*

*I hear the faint sound of the door opening, as if from far away, before a sharp prick to my neck turns everything black once more.*

I open my eyes to find myself curled in a similar ball in the corner of the shower, still feeling the phantom sting of that needle.

They kept me sedated for three weeks. Three weeks of bliss, where I didn't have to face what had happened.

When I finally emerged from the haze of drugs, it was to find myself in a strange mansion, with an older lady in a nurse's uniform, sitting near the huge bed that I was lying in.

Turns out it was my long lost uncle's house in Wiltshire, and she was Teresa, the nurse he had hired in order to bring me 'home.' Ironic really, a nurse called Teresa.

I'd never met Adrian before. Mum had a falling out with her parents, which she'd briefly mentioned one night years before. She hadn't mentioned a brother, but then again, perhaps they'd never been close and she was always so cagey about her past. It doesn't surprise me that some things were missed.

He was an extremely handsome man, with the darkest eyes that I'd ever seen. There was something...odd about him. He was too charming, too caring. Like he was trying too hard. But then, I suppose having finally found his sister, only to find her brutally...murdered, took its toll on him too.

It took a further three months before the flashbacks from that day lessened enough that I could function without ending up curled in a ball and rocking. The nightmares never stopped though.

Then one day, Adrian suggested that I might like to get away from it all. To have a fresh start in a new place. He told me that he went to school in Colorado, America. Hence the accent as he spent most of his childhood and early adulthood out there getting the best education money could buy. He told me all about Highgate Preparatory Academy, and how great it was. How much fun he had here, and what good lifelong friends he made.

I was reluctant at first, not wanting to leave England, the only country I'd ever known. But then I realised that this was no longer my home. My mum was...gone, and her best friend, practically sister, Lexi hadn't been in touch once. Neither had Ryan, mum's long-term boyfriend, although she'd never committed fully to him, lord knows why.

I had no ties keeping me in England, nothing to stay for. So I came here, hoping to escape the tragedy of my past.

After I've picked myself up off the floor, then washed and rinsed, I wrap a towel around myself, wiping the steam off of the mirror to look at my reflection. I look like death warmed up.

I stare into my churning eyes, willing the answer to be in them. It's not, and I'm left feeling just as lost, just as heartbroken as before.

Sighing, I turn and open the door. Looking up, I see Kai sitting stiffly on my bed.

My heart stutters in my chest as my gaze devours him. I can see the sadness draped over him like a shroud, and tears spring to my eyes when I know that it's because of me.

"You don't need to say anything, Lilly," Kai says, his voice melancholy, yet there's a thread of hopefulness in it too. "Just, please, don't give up on us. Give us a chance."

His honey eyes beg mine, yet I have no idea what to say, so I just nod.

His features flood with relief, and he practically sags on my bed. He gets up, walking over to me, and reaches out, brushing my hair away from my face with a soft touch of his long fingers that sends shivers skating across my skin.

"We need you so badly, Lilly," he whispers, leaning in and kissing my forehead so tenderly that fresh tears spring to my eyes, before turning around and leaving the room, shutting the door quietly behind him.

---

I get dressed in my favourite sailor blue Lucy & Yak corduroy dungarees, called overalls in the U.S. apparently. I've paired them with a red and white striped t-shirt, an oversized red knitted jumper, or sweater I should say, and my blue and red plaid Irregular Choice heeled boots. I hoped that the outfit would make me feel better, giving me some strength to face the day. Instead, I'm left feeling unbearably empty.

I go downstairs to find my bags being loaded into the car by Loki himself. The others are nowhere in sight.

*Deep breaths, Lilly. Deep fucking breaths.*

He looks up as I come out of the house, and the despair in his beautiful emerald eyes utterly destroys me. My already bleeding heart cracks even more, my breath hitching and stuttering in my chest.

"Loki..." I gasp, but I have no idea what I'm going to say next.

His eyes shutter, becoming hard and cutting, and a painful lump forms in my throat.

"Are you ready to leave?" he asks, jaw clenched and voice cold, missing all its usual warmth and colour, until it's become dull and lifeless.

I bob my head, afraid that I'll break down if I speak a single word. He looks away, walking around to the driver's door, opening it and getting in, leaving me to sort myself out.

Taking another deep inhale, I walk down the stone steps, but don't get far before I hear a girlish shout behind me.

"Lilly, wait!" Heather calls out. I turn around to see both girls running towards me, hair flying behind them.

Seconds later, they collide into me with an oomph, wrapping me in a tight hug and it feels so good to be held that my eyes moisten.

"We're gonna miss you," Julie says, a slight whine in her voice as both girls pull back and I quickly choke back tears.

"Promise you'll come back soon?" Heather asks with such an earnest look on her face that I couldn't refuse her, even if I wanted to. Which I'm not sure I do.

"Of course," I manage to get out around the lump in my throat that's grown even bigger. "I'll see you both soon."

"Promise?" Julie asks, eyes hopeful.

"Pinky promise," I say, remembering when Mum used to say the same to me. Pinky promises were sacred, not to be broken.

They both beam as we hear the window wind down.

"Girls, we've got to get back," Loki's hard voice says, and both girls roll their eyes at him.

"He woke up grumpy and has been like a bear all morning," Heather says, giggling.

I kiss the top of both their heads and disentangle their arms just as Clarissa comes to the door.

"Girls!" she calls, not even bothering to look at me.

They roll their eyes again, the sassy minxes, then step away, waving as I get in the car. Loki starts the engine and then speeds off in a shower of gravel.

"Your sisters are lovely," I say, glancing at him from the corner of my eye, my heart beating so fast I'm afraid it'll burst out of my chest.

It's agony sitting so close to him, yet it's like a huge chasm lies between us. I can see he has a death grip on the steering wheel, his knuckles white, and his forearms corded.

Even in anger, he's so fucking beautiful it takes my breath away. And then I remember what he's done, the blood he's spilt, and I feel sick, glad I didn't eat any breakfast.

He says nothing, doesn't even acknowledge that I've spoken, just clenches his jaw so tightly that I'm surprised his teeth don't crack.

We stay that way for the rest of the drive, sitting in complete silence, my heart hurting so much I can barely suppress the tears that threaten to fall.

---

LOKI

*I watch, my chest heaving, as the light leaves his chocolate eyes, a dribble of dark burgundy oozing between them. Smoke from the barrel of my gun rises up and obscures the sight of his broken body, adding to the feeling of a soul rising to the heavens. Of a soul finally being at peace. A peace I'm beginning to ache for.*

*Except for the ringing in my ears, for the first time tonight, there's a beautiful cathartic silence. Lost in thoughts of taking flight, of freedom from this life, I startle with a gasp when a hand lands on my shoulder.*

*I look up to see Ash's pain filled eyes, my hands dropping at my side, the gun still locked in my grip. He's started doing what he can to protect us from all this shit, even though I can see it tormenting his soul. The darkness is slowly eating him from the inside out, and soon nothing will stop him, us, from becoming the monsters that they've started training us to be.*

*I hear a thunderous clap mocking the peaceful silence, and I look up to see my father gliding from his seat in the corner, striding closer to me, a look of pride on his face. A warmth runs through me at the look of approval and I suddenly feel sick.*

*"I'm impressed, son," he says in his gravelly voice. "To be honest, I didn't think you had it in you." He laughs cruelly, clapping me on the back. "I'd even considered having to train up one of your sisters when the time came, but a shot right in the middle of his forehead! Beautifully done." He's smiling at me, and I think it might be the first time that he has smiled at me and spoken nicely to me my whole life.*

*"Good work, boys," Julian Vanderbilt says, before turning on his heel and going towards the basement stairs, the other three men following behind like loyal sheep.*

*"What do we do with..." Ash asks his back, indicating the body.*

*Julian pauses. "I expect you to clean up your own mess. Take out this trash, and do it right. If there is any evidence left...there will be consequences," he tells us sharply, his eyes cutting before heading up the stairs with the rest of them.*

*I'm still holding the gun, my hand shaking slightly. My head whips up when I hear Kai's groan. Jax has stripped his shirt off, pressing it to the bleeding wound in Kai's shoulder, Luc standing there helping him apply pressure.*

*My eyes flit back to the dead man in the chair in front of me. I feel a sense of relief that it's done. That he's free from pain. That I was the one to free him. Then I remember that he's someone's father, husband, or brother. Bile rises up my throat, my knees go weak, and I stumble forward.*

*Ash catches me, and when I look up at him, I can see the mantle that settles on his shoulders. He's the oldest of us all, yet still only fourteen. Ghosts haunt his eyes, and his responsibilities age him, making him seem so much older.*

*"Jax, Luc, help Kai upstairs and call our doctor. Wait with him, and make sure he understands the term confidentiality," he orders, and they both start helping Kai up.*

*His grey gaze turns down to me. "Loki. Give me the gun." I automatically snap to his command, my hand holding it out to him before my brain registers the movement.*

*He takes it, then goes over to the shelving on the back wall, and picks up a bottle of spray. I see the words 'DNA safe' on the front. Ash sprays the gun fully, then places it in a zip-lock plastic bag which he seals after.*

*"Ash..." I croak out, my voice sounds far away like I'm miles from this cursed basement. "What about..."*

*I can't bring myself to finish the sentence. Ash knows what I'm referring to, his hard eyes looking past me to the guy in the chair.*

*"We need a clean up crew..." he says, thinking aloud, biting his bottom lip.*

*"I've overheard my dad talking about his crew once..." Jax suggests, pausing at the base of the stairs.*

*"No, we need our own," Ash responds firmly. "We can't leave it to chance with those cunts." We know who he's referring to. Our fathers, Kai's uncle.*

*"I could call Enzo from the gym?" Jax asks. Enzo runs the boxing gym downtown. It's rough, but clean, and Enzo has been more of a father to Jax, to all of us, than ours will ever be. We trust him with our lives.*

*Ash thinks for a moment, then nods.*

*We hear Kai's sharp inhale as they head up the stairs. I'm still standing there, feeling a sense of unreality, the whole room in hyper focus. Like, this can't be actually happening. I can't have just shot a guy after we beat him to a bloody pulp.*

*"Hey," Ash says gently, and I look up. "Loki, I'm...shit...what a fucking birthday," he says, his grey eyes full of concern.*

*Yep. Happy fucking fourteenth.*

I wake up with a jolt, gasping and covered in sweat from the nightmare. Only, is it still classed as a nightmare if it's a memory? I don't fucking know.

I lay there in Kai's bed, trying to breathe normally, when a feminine scream rents the air in two, making my heartbeat skyrocket again.

Kai sits up with a start, rubbing his eyes before reaching over and putting his glasses on. We then hear the soul destroying sobs, and my heart shatters into thousands of sharp, tiny pieces.

"I don't know how much longer I can take this," I say into the dark, my voice breaking. I feel on the verge of tears myself.

"Me either," Kai says back, his own voice desolate.

The sobs subside to whimpers, then eventually stop.

"When she hurts, I hurt, Kai," I say softly, just above a whisper.

Sometimes it's easier to say things in the dark, even if it's to someone you've known your whole life. My hand rubs at my chest, trying to ease the dull ache inside.

"I know. Me too," he confides back and lays his head on my shoulder seeking comfort. We sit there for a time, in our shared pain.

"I had another nightmare," I admit into the silence.

"The cabin?" he asks gently.

Although we told Lilly about that night, she doesn't know the full truth. She doesn't know that she's been my light, chasing away the demons that have tried to consume me ever since my fourteenth birthday. She blazed into our lives with her quirky humor, sharp tongue, and beauty, both inside and out.

Before her, Kai was there. Every time I was plagued by my doubts, and the devils reared their ugly heads, he was there. This guilt, this dark depression claws at me like a parasite. Anytime I feel it crawling under my skin, he helps me. He knows that there are worse ways I could try to drown them. Have tried to drown them.

"Yep," I say, reaching for my phone that's on the bedside cabinet, scrolling through my playlists until I find the song I'm looking for.

*Demons (Philosophical Session)* by Jacob Lee sounds over the Bluetooth speakers in Kai's room, and a breath of relief eases through me.

"Loki..." Kai says, his voice pained.

I know he thinks that this isn't healthy, but it's the only way I know how to stop the pain, the guilt from eating me alive. Other than having Lilly by my side.

"Please, Kai. I need you to," I beg, looking into his eyes imploringly. My mind starts to panic, my thoughts tortured. He knows my struggles and knows how to quiet them.

"Fine," he sighs, turning away from me and switching on the bedside light.

He gets out of bed, his back to me, that wonderful Koi tattoo looking alive in the dim light. Going over to a cupboard that's up against a wall, he uses a small key to unlock it, opening the doors to reveal an array of whips, paddles, and restraints.

He takes out a pair of thick leather cuffs and a red and black leather flogger. My breath hitches at the sight, it's a favourite of mine. I already feel the heady anticipation of escape that it'll bring me.

Standing up, I walk around to the end of the four poster bed and hold my wrists out. As I'm just in a pair of boxer briefs, there's no need to strip above the waist. Kai slowly comes over to me, buckling the cuffs onto my wrists one at a time. There's a chain that links them, which he takes and places onto a hook in the frame of his bed so that my hands are held aloft and my back exposed to him.

"I'm going to strike you five times, Loki," he tells me, his voice husky and low. My dick twitches as it always does, but there isn't going to be a release of that kind for me tonight. This will be something so much sweeter.

Although we've been doing this same thing for years, it's never gone further than the liberation I find in being punished. I know Kai gets hard while giving out the lashes, and I get hard receiving them, but we've just never gone there. We're not into each other in that way, although I wouldn't be objectionable if it would turn Lilly on...

My thoughts fly out of my mind, a gasp leaving my lips as the first hit strikes. It sends sweet agony across my back, never deep enough to break the skin, but enough to chase those demons back to Hell.

The second strike hits before I've taken a full inhale, then the third, fourth, and fifth, until I'm shaking and panting.

I smile as my mind is finally quiet, finally free. I feel Kai come over, gently caressing my back.

"Better?" he whispers next to my ear. I shiver as his breath tickles me.

"Yes," I say simply.

He unhooks my hands, the blood rushing to my fingers and making them tingle. Gently, he unbuckles each cuff, then takes them and the flogger back to the cupboard.

I stand there, my chest rising and falling, basking in the glow that the pain has bought me. The deliverance it has given me. I close my eyes and smile, the demons finally quiet, my thoughts blessedly still.

# CHAPTER TWENTY-FIVE

LILLY

A week goes by, then two, and in all that time the guys have completely avoided me. They're gone before I come down in the morning, and are absent when I get back at night. Loki gave me his bed, and I think he sleeps in with one of the others, as I've not seen any blankets or pillows in the living room. It's a mixed blessing being surrounded by his heavenly vanilla scent all night.

It's not enough to stop the darkness from taking over, and I've gone back to having my nightly night terrors, like I used to before coming here. I wake up with a raw throat, a wet pillow, and the taste of copper in my mouth.

Kai always leaves me some breakfast in the morning, and it reminds me of his plea from the morning after that awful night.

*Please don't give up on us. Give us a chance.*

It plays on repeat, swirling around and around my head until it's all I can think about.

*Was I too harsh on them? What right do I have to judge them?*

Yes, they hurt someone, they still hurt people, but none of it is their fault. They are being forced to do atrocious things by their families. They tried to resist the first time, and look at what happened. Kai got shot for Pete's sake!

The fog suddenly lifts, and it's as though a ray of glorious sunshine beams down on me.

*I need to get them out of this!*

Somehow, some way, I need to help them throw off the shackles that have been placed on them.

*But how?*

That's the million dollar question. How can they get out? And do they even want to? I think they do. That night, they all looked so desolate and ashamed when I walked in.

But first, I need to get them to talk to me, which almost feels harder than actually getting them away from their awful families and that toxic company.

As I head to my first class of the day; Works of Shakespeare, these tumultuous thoughts fill my mind, whilst *War of Hearts, Acoustic Version*, by Ruelle plays in my headphones.

I share the class with Ash, my heart fluttering at the thought of seeing him. Although the guys are in most of my classes, they've been leaving as soon as it's over, not walking with me like they used to.

Their silence, their icing me out, hurts; but I'm not sure I can blame them. I ran away when they opened up to me, when they showed me their darkness. I judged and rejected them when they needed me most, so it's no wonder they've turned away from me.

*I have some serious apologising to do*, I think as I open the door, taking my headphones out, and my eyes meet steel grey ones making me pause in the doorway. They are as hard as the metal they share the colour with, and just as cold.

Walking in, I let the door swing shut behind me, not taking my eyes away from his. My chest is rising and falling with my heavy breaths as I take my seat next to Ash, my hands slightly clammy.

I don't register anything around me, it's all noise that's unimportant as we continue to stare into each other's eyes. I can see pain in the depths of his, a sharp ache that cuts me to the quick, knowing that I am responsible for some, if not most of it. I hope he can see the regret in mine, the sorrow and heartache that fills me until I'm overflowing with it.

"Asher and Lilly, please read Act One, Scene Five for us." I hear Mrs Jones say, breaking into our bubble.

I grab my copy of the play we're currently studying from my bag, *Romeo and Juliet*, and turn to the right page.

Ash begins reciting in his deep, beautiful voice, and it sends shivers up my spine, my breath leaving my lungs in a gasp.

*"'If I profane with my unworthiest hand*
*This holy shrine, the gentle fine is this:*
*My lips, two blushing pilgrims, ready stand*
*To smooth that rough touch with a tender kiss.'"*

And as he reads, he reaches across and grabs my hand, bringing it to his lips, placing the barest of kisses upon my knuckles and causing a riot of butterflies to take flight inside me. He looks up at me whilst he does it, a look so intense in his eyes, my heart stops, and I have to clear my throat before I can start my lines.

*"'Good pilgrim, you do wrong your hand too much,*
*Which mannerly devotion shows in this;*
*For saints have hands that pilgrims' hands do touch,*
*And palm to palm is holy palmers' kiss.'"*

I lick my dry lips as I look back up to see his gaze locked on mine, my hand still in his warm one. He looks down then reads the next part.

*"'Have not saints lips, and holy palmers too?'"*

He looks to me again, his eyes unreadable, yet there's a fire there too. I'm just not sure if it's meant to hurt or heal me.

My heart is pounding, my breath short as I read my next lines.

*"'Ay, pilgrim, lips that they must use in prayer.'"*

*"'O, then, dear saint, let lips do what hands do;*
*They pray, grant thou, lest faith turn to despair.'"*

A darkness enters his gaze then, and I'm hit again with the hurt that I've caused him.

*"'Saints do not move, though grant for prayers' sake,'"*

I read, barely above a whisper, looking back up at him as he starts to lean in, still clutching my hand in his tight grip.

*"Then move not, while my prayer's effect I take.*
*Thus from my lips, by yours, my sin is purged,"*

He whispers back as his lips close on mine, and he kisses me.

It's a kiss that defies the ages, full of pain and longing and despair. But also hope, and something so sweet and pure, I dare not even think of its name.

I vaguely hear the class whistling and catcalling as Mrs Jones clears her throat loudly.

Ash breaks away, his breathing as heavy as my own, both our chests rising and falling in tandem. He stares into my eyes once more, his grey ones swirling like a storm.

Then, abruptly he lets go of my hand, stands up, his chair scraping across the floor, and strides out of the room.

"Mr Vanderbilt!" I hear Mrs Jones shout, but I'm just frozen with my hand to my burning lips.

---

It's the end of the day, and I head to the library, putting off going back to the dorm, especially after what happened with Ash this morning. I want to make amends, to make things right between us. But I don't know how, so I take the coward's route and postpone the inevitable.

I study for hours, the library empty and the windows dark when I look up bleary-eyed, realising how late it is. I pack my things in my bag and go to head out when I see someone step from the shadows.

For a moment, my heart leaps thinking it's one of the guys, and then I realise it's not. It's that creep, Robert. Goosebumps erupt all over me like a warning, my instincts telling me to get out of there pronto.

"Hi, uh, Robert," I say, starting to slowly back away, instinctively looking for an escape. The hair on my nape and arms lifts, my stomach rock hard. I have a terrible feeling about this. How long has he been waiting there? How did I not notice?

"Hi, Lilly," he says back mildly, taking a step towards me, and it's then that I realise with a sinking feeling he's blocking my easiest way out. "I'm glad I found you," he adds, still advancing with a predatory grin. I could go round the table, and hopefully, make it before he cuts me off.

"Oh yeah?" I ask as I keep backing away, my heart beginning to pound. I'm clutching my bag in front of me like a shield. I may have to use it as a club if he keeps coming towards me.

"Yeah," he answers, still smiling. It's a smile full of entitlement and malicious intent. "I thought seeing as how you, Loki, and Jax don't appear to be an item anymore, we could go for that walk."

My heart is beating wildly in my chest, like a bird trapped in a room and frantically trying to find a way out, even if it ends up bleeding, beating against a window. My brain is screaming at me to run and run fast.

"Ah, it's kinda late, so maybe another time," I respond, proud of how firm my voice is even though I'm a quivering mess inside. I finally reach the end of the table and slowly ease around it, all the while keeping eye contact. My shoulders are tight, my body tense as I prepare to flee.

"I was thinking now," he tells me, dropping the smile, his face reddening and his eyes hard as flint. My heart jumps painfully. "And didn't your whore mother ever teach you it's rude to walk away when someone is talking to you?" he asks viciously as he lunges for me.

I spin on my heel and run in the direction of the door, but I'm too fucking slow. I feel him grab the back of my hair, pulling me back towards him, a scream of pain leaving my lips as he rips some strands clean out of my scalp. I stumble and fall, landing on my spine hard, and knocking my head on the edge of a chair, making stars dance in my vision and my stomach roil.

When my eyesight clears, he's already kneeling on top of me, ripping open my shirtwaister dress, the buttons flying and scattering across the floor as he exposes my navy lacy bra. My hands come up, clawing and trying to bat his own away from me, but he must have hit me hard because I feel so weak and he easily grabs both of my wrists, pinning them above my head in a bruising grip, grinding my bones together.

I make to scream, desperately hoping that someone will hear, when a clammy hand comes over my mouth hard, so that only a muffled sound can be heard.

*No. No, no, no. Please, God, no.*

"Shut the fuck up, you bitch, and spread your fucking legs!" he snarls, his lips curling and spittle flying.

Biting down hard I taste blood and hear him yelp and curse. His fist suddenly collides with my jaw in a brutal punch that snaps my head to the side and white hot pain bursts across my cheek.

I must blackout for a few seconds because when I come to, he's got my knickers off, and is lowering himself between my spread legs, lining up his repulsive veiny erect dick with my opening. His other hand on my inner thigh is holding me open for him like he has all the right to be there.

Screaming like a fucking banshee, I rake my nails down both sides of his face, taking him by surprise as he rears back. Using his momentary distraction to my advantage, I bring my knee up hard, catching him in the balls, and causing him to roar in pain and roll off me. Getting to my feet unsteadily, my head and face pounding, and my vision wavering, I take off at a run, glad my heels have fallen off at some point.

I leave my bag and all my things behind, not caring what happens in my desperation to escape.

Panicking as I hear him try to follow, relief floods me as I realise that he must get tangled in his trousers, because seconds later a crash and grunt sound behind me and I thank all that is holy for the sensitivity of men’s nuts.

The library is completely empty, as are the hallways, and as I race down them, I start to shiver at all of the what ifs that fill my head. I don’t stop running until I reach our door, pounding on the wood and screaming incoherently.

“Let me in! Please, let me in!” I'm sobbing, tears and snot dripping down my face as I continue my assault on the door.

It suddenly flies open, and I look into Kai's wide eyes, which flash with confusion as he takes me in.

“Lilly...” he says, brows pinched, but that's all I see as I push past him with a whimper, knocking him aside.

My frantic eyes alight on Jax, who is standing near the kitchen, his hand poised as if reaching for something on the countertop. I don't think, I just rush towards him, throwing myself in his arms, wrapping my own around his strong neck in a vicelike hold. He's my safe harbour, my protector, and my panicked mind somehow knows this.

He catches me in his massive arms, wrapping them around me tightly as I cry convulsively into him, almost hyperventilating, the neck of his black t-shirt screwed up in my hands as I grip him tight.

“Baby Girl?” he asks, his voice broken and rough with concern.

I can't speak. My head is buried in his chest, trying to breathe in his familiar lemon scent and take comfort from his embrace. But all I can do is relive clammy hands, pain, and the violation that just happened.

“She's bleeding,” I hear Kai say in a worried tone as I feel the others start to close in, making my breath speed up further and I shrink more into Jax. I feel a soft touch on my shoulder, and I jump so hard even Jax almost stumbles.

"Give her some fucking space," he growls as I sink deeper into his arms.

"Princess," Ash's deep voice says from near me, but not too close. There's a catch to it, like he's terrified of what has happened to me. "Kai says you're bleeding. We need to see how badly you're hurt."

I whimper as I feel the blows to my head and face again, experiencing the moment afresh.

"Please, Pretty Girl. Please, let me see," Loki's voice sounds so distraught from near my face, and he hasn't called me that for so long that it breaks me out of my turmoil, and I look up at him.

His eyes go wide and then become hard, full of a rage that I see him try to get under control. It should scare me, but all I can feel is the claws of my own panic receding a little now that I'm here. With them.

"Oh, Darling," he gasps brokenly, his hand coming out to touch me then stopping short. "Please, can I touch you?" he asks, his eyes shattered and desperate.

"Loki?" I whisper, blinking, feeling as though I've come out of a nightmare. Only, a part of me knows that this is no land of make-believe.

"I'm here, Pretty Girl. We're all here, and you're safe," he tells me, stepping towards us, his hand brushing my cheek and making me hiss a gasp at the sharp pain his touch elicits.

"Safe?" I question, lifting my head further to look around me at the other guys.

As I meet Kai's eyes, I can see the glisten of tears, and he's visibly shaking. I catch Ash's gaze, and there is terror, pain, and a blinding rage in the grey depths. He's practically vibrating with it.

I finally turn to meet Jax's piercing blue eyes. The banked rage in his is intense and should be terrifying, yet Loki is right. I'm safe here.

"Baby Girl..." Jax rasps, his voice rough and filled with the need for violence. His whole body is trembling, his muscles tense as he holds me. "What happened?" he asks me gruffly.

One minute, I'm standing wrapped in Jax's arms, and the next, it's hard hands grasping and pulling and hurting me.

"I'm going to be sick," I manage to blurt out, tearing out of his arms and rushing for the toilet.

I make it just in time and heave my guts out until my stomach is empty, my head pounding even more. I sit back, away from the toilet. My head thumps and my eyes are closed, so I smell vanilla before I feel the warmth of a body in front of me.

"I need to take care of you, Pretty Girl. Can I do that, please?" Loki's deep voice begs, cracking at the end.

I nod, not ready to open my eyes yet. I feel the soft press of a cool cloth against my forehead, and I moan whilst leaning into it. A glass is pressed into my hand. I open my eyes to see that Loki is crouched down beside me, his face creased. I drink all the water in the glass, then hand it back to him. He passes it up to Kai, who gives me an anguished smile, then heads out of the doorway.

Loki scoops me up in his arms, and I wince at the pain that fills my body. He looks down and gives me an apologetic look, then walks us out of the bathroom, sitting down on one of the sofas with me nestled in his lap. His arms come around me as he pulls me in for a tight hug, being mindful of my injured head. As I'm pressed against his chest, I can feel how hard his heart is beating.

Ash is pacing in front of the lit fire, but he stops and looks at me, coming over to sit next to us.

"Can you tell us what happened, Princess?" he asks gently, reaching out a hand to hover over my lip. It feels like it's split, and my jaw throbs with pain. His eyes dart to my ripped dress, his hand clenching into a fist then lowering to his lap.

Jax walks over, crouching in front of me with a bowl of water, some dressings, and other first aid bits on a tray. He also takes in the state of my clothing, and a low angry rumble sounds from his throat.

I stiffen in Loki's lap, instinctually not wanting him to touch the sore parts of me, then relax a little as Loki's hand comes up, rubbing soothing circles on my back.

"I'll try," I whisper, my voice croaky. My hands worry at my dress skirts until Ash's hand reaches out to still them, taking one in his own grasp. I notice there's blood under my nails, and I swallow hard.

"I–I was at the library studying when I realised how late it had gotten," I begin, my voice small and almost unrecognisable. "I saw someone come out of the shadows, and I thought that it was one of you." I feel Loki tense underneath me.

"Who was it, Baby Girl?" Jax asks, his voice deep and full of the darkness in the dead of night. He reaches out with a warm wet cloth, wiping at my temple, and I cringe at the sharp sting.

I look him in the eye, and I see the moment it dawns on him. His whole body stills, like a snake ready to strike.

"That cunt Robert?" he asks in a growl. I nod.

"He's a fucking dead man walking," Loki bites out, his whole body rigid.

"What happened next?" Kai asks softly, and I turn my head to see him on my other side, his hand coming to rub my back too.

I swallow again and close my eyes.

"H–he came at me. Started saying about how now that I wasn't with Loki and Jax, it was his turn. I–I tried to run."

My breath hitches and I feel hot tears begin to trickle down my cheeks. A hand holding a soft piece of fabric wipes at them, and I look up to see Ash with a white handkerchief.

"B–but he grabbed my hair and pulled me down. I hit my head, I think, and then he was pinning me beneath him." I swallow again, feeling like I'm experiencing it all over again, my heart rate picking up and my breathing becoming shallow.

"I tried to scream, but he put his hand on my mouth, so I bit it, hard." I'm looking into Ash's eyes, and I see the barest hint of a smile at that, like he's proud of me for fighting dirty.

"Good girl," he praises gently when I pause. "And then?" His fingers start rubbing over the knuckles of the hand he's still holding.

"He punched me, here," I say, hearing growls behind me as I lift my other hand to my throbbing jaw.

I hiss as Jax presses an ice pack gently to the area. The cold feels so good on my heated skin, a breath of relief leaves me. I start to smile at him in thanks, then wince at the movement. His blue eyes flare with anger, which he's somehow still managing to hold in check.

I look away from Jax. I can't bear to meet any of their eyes as I recall the next part.

"I must have blacked out for a few moments because when I came to, he...he was on top of me, his pants down, my knickers gone, and...and..." I stutter, unable to continue. My hand has Ash's in a death grip, his own gripping back just as hard.

Loki's arms are so tight around me it hurts, but I don't tell him to loosen his grip. I need to feel him anchoring me, or I'll slip away.

"Did he..." Ash takes in a breath but holds my gaze. "Did he rape you, Lilly?" I've never heard him stutter before, or his breath hitch like that.

I shake my head, fresh tears running down my face.

"No..." I whisper. "But he was almost there," I admit, hanging my head as I feel an itchy uncomfortable shame flush through me.

"Hey," I hear Kai say as he gently lifts my chin. He's come around to my side, next to Jax, and is staring deep into my eyes. "You have nothing to be ashamed of, Lilly. None of this was your fault."

"I–I know. It's just... if I hadn't run away from you guys that night..." I sob, unable to continue. But I see the shame flash brightly in his eyes.

"This. Is. Not. Your. Fault," Jax says between gritted teeth, the first aid stuff abandoned by his feet as I look at him. "We should have taken better care of you." His voice is filled with anger and self-loathing.

I glance at the others, and they all have the same guilt-ridden look on their faces. They truly believe my...attack is their fault.

"No," I say firmly, anger flooding my veins and helping to straighten my spine a little. "This is not your fault either. None of you." I look them each in the eye, one by one. "It's..." I swallow. "It's h–his fault."

I can see the rage transform the guys as it sweeps over each of them. And I realise that they may be monsters, but they are beautiful monsters. And they're mine. They will burn down the entire world and everyone in it for me.

"What happens if I report this to the police?" I ask, turning back to Ash. I may be new to this world, but I'm not stupid. These kids, their families, have immense power, and I know that things like this can easily be made to disappear.

"His father is the Governor of Colorado," Ash tells me, still gripping my hand like I'm his lifeline instead of the other way around. "I doubt the police would even show up."

I take a deep breath, closing my eyes, hating that the world is like this. That people can do what they please with no consequences. Although, perhaps, that can work in my favour.

My eyes snap open, and I stare into Ash's swirling steel grey ones.

"Then I want you to make him bleed. Make him hurt so bad that he will never be able to do this to anyone else." My voice is hard and as sharp as glass.

*Perhaps, in order to beat the true monsters of this world, you need to first join them?*

A smile so wicked that even the devil himself would cower lifts Ash's beautiful lips.

"Your wish is our pleasure, Princess."

Then he lifts my hand, and just like in class earlier today, places a gentle kiss on my knuckles.

# CHAPTER TWENTY-SIX

LILLY

A little later, I head to the shower, needing to wash off the feel of rough, clammy hands.

I look at myself in the mirror, gasping aloud at the sight. My jaw is already starting to mottle purple with a bruise, my bottom lip is swollen where it's split, and there's dried blood all down the left side of my face. Jax checked the wound, luckily it's not deep enough to need stitches. I can see small marks littered across my chest where he ripped my dress open.

A sob catches my throat, and I have to lean my hands on the counter to steady myself, taking deep gasping breaths of air.

"Please, can I help you, Pretty Girl?" I hear Loki's deep voice behind me, and looking up, I see his reflection in the mirror, his brow wrinkled and his gaze pained.

I nod then turn around, feeling fresh tears sting my eyes at being brought so low in front of him. *I'm so sick of crying.*

He walks towards me, then gently peels my torn dress down, leaving it to pool on the tiles at my feet. His eyes take in my torn bra and missing knickers, a growl sounding in his throat when he sees the red welt on my hip where they were ripped off. I see him catalogue every bruise or cut on me, like he's making a list of my hurts so that he can return them tenfold to my abuser.

His eyes come back up to mine, and there is rage in the emerald depths, along with a guilt so strong, it cracks my heart further and takes my breath away. I take a step towards him, my arm outstretched, wanting to give him comfort. He looks away, but not before I see the glisten of tears.

I run my fingers through his silky auburn hair, and for a moment, get lost in its texture, realising just how much I've missed it.

“Loki, look at me.” I gently tug so that his eyes meet mine. “Hey. This isn't your fault.” I look deep into the myriad of greens, willing him to believe me.

He swallows hard, and I can see his Adam's apple bobbing with the movement.

“If I hadn't...” he begins, closing his eyes briefly before opening them and looking at me. “If we hadn't iced you out. If we'd taken better care of you...” I'm shaking my head and interrupting before he's even finished.

“Loki, no. By the same token, if I hadn't run away, judged you so harshly, without thinking it through...”

“You needed time,” he replies firmly, then softer, almost a whisper, “you broke my heart that night, Lilly.” And the anguish in his gaze shreds my soul in half.

“I broke my own too,” I say quietly back, more tears beginning to track down my face. “I'm so sorry, Loki.”

“I'm sorry too,” he gently responds, wiping my tears with the pads of his thumbs.

I close my eyes, but rather than Loki's gentle touch, it's Robert’s painful one. My eyes snap back open as I jerk back with a gasp, breaking contact with Loki.

“Shit, did I hurt you?” Loki asks frantically, his eyes searching my face, fresh guilt in them.

I shake my head. “Every time I close my eyes, I see him. Feel his touch. I can't make it stop,” I choke out, my voice thick.

“What can I do, baby?” Loki asks, looking helpless and angry, all at the same time as he stands with his fists clenched at his sides like he’s scared to touch me.

“Replace his hands with yours,” I beg, my eyes pleading with him. “Chase his touch away, Loki, please.”

I know this is probably so unhealthy, but as I think about it, I know that it's what I need.

"Lilly...I'm...I'm not sure that's such a good idea," he says hesitantly, but I can see lust starting to replace some of the helplessness in his eyes. I can see his primal need to mark me as his own. To reestablish our bond.

I undo what's left of my bra, letting it fall to the ground as I step up to him, reaching out for his hand then placing it on my bare breast.

"Please, Loki. I need you." And those words seem to be his undoing as he squeezes the globe, a gasp escaping me as he pulls me in for a searingly hot kiss.

It's a kiss full of pain, heartache, and longing. We both groan as our tongues meet, and we taste each other again for the first time in two weeks. I feel the sharpness of my split lip, and taste copper as it reopens but I don't care. I need Loki, need his lips on mine more than my next breath.

I can feel the memories try to creep in, try to taint this, so I pull him closer, undoing his jeans and pushing them down his hips.

I palm his beautiful cock, relishing in the silky soft feel of it as I start to pump slowly up and down, adding the twist of my wrist that I know drives him wild.

"God, Lilly," he rasps, breaking our kiss. "You keep doing that, and I won't last long."

I feel a surge of satisfaction at his words. There's power in giving someone pleasure. In bringing a man such as Loki to his knees with your touch.

He starts to slowly back us up to the counter, kissing me senseless the whole way.

"Fuck, Lilly, I missed you," he says in between kisses.

I kiss him deeper, like I'm trying to forge our beings into one. His vanilla scent surrounds me, and I feel such a sense of relief at being safe in his arms again that the darkness is chased away a little.

"Loki, please..." I moan, needing more. I need all of him.

He grabs me under my thighs, lifting me up onto the countertop. The cold marble surface makes me gasp as it touches my fevered skin. I take the opportunity to pull his t-shirt up and over his head, dropping it to the tiled floor.

My eyes devour his nakedness, like I'm starving and he's my feast. My hands reacquaint themselves with the hard planes of his chest, my gaze following their movement, then I pull his nipple bar, making him groan long and low.

Reaching in between my legs, I open a drawer beneath me, and pull out a condom packet, tearing it open and taking the rubber out. My right hand goes between us, grasping his hard cock and rolling the condom on, then lining him up with my already soaked entrance.

He pauses just outside of me, and I look up to see worry etched on his face.

"Are you sure, Pretty Girl?" he asks me, and I know he's ready to stop if I say so.

"Yes," I assure him softly. "I need you to chase his touch away, Loki."

He begins to slowly push in, his pierced tip pressing into me, sending delicious shivers rolling through me. His serious eyes are locked onto mine, searching my gaze for any sign of hesitation.

We both groan, my head falling backwards and eyes heavenward as he bottoms out, fully seated to the hilt and my inner channel clamps around him, remembering the feel of him.

"I'd almost forgotten how your pussy fits like a fucking glove, Pretty Girl," Loki rasps huskily.

He starts to withdraw, slowly kissing and nibbling my exposed neck, sending tingles of pleasure shooting all over my body.

"Loki..." I groan. "You feel so good."

He pauses, his tip just inside of me, teasing me. He threads his fingers through my hair, guiding my head back so that I am once again looking at him. For a split second, other rough hands are pulling my hair painfully.

I blink and see intense emerald eyes staring at me, full of want and need and something so much deeper.

"You're ours, Lilly. You're ours forever, and there's no way we're letting you go."

He holds my gaze as he thrusts hard, our pelvises slapping together. My eyes roll as I gasp at the exquisite sensations lighting up my body.

I didn't realise how much I'd missed his closeness, his touch and taste. It's like I've been dormant these past two weeks, and Loki, he's bringing me back to life. Every touch lights me up, every thrust filling me with colour.

"Fucking hell, Lilly. No one has ever felt as good as you," he moans out, before bringing his lips to mine and kissing me hard, matching the movement of his tongue with that of his undulating hips.

He's grinding into my clit every time he's fully inside me, one hand gripping my hip, the other still tangled in my hair. I'd say that I'd forgotten how much of an amazing lover he was, but I'd be lying. He knows just the right spot to hit until you're weeping with the need for release.

“Lilly, baby, I need you to come all over my dick,” he says against my lips as his hand leaves my hip and captures one of mine, sliding both our hands between us.

Using my fingers and his own, he starts to rub circles around my clit, applying just the right amount of pressure to make my hips buck wildly, both seeking and trying to hide from the contact.

“Loki! Oh my God, Loki, I'm gonna come!” I scream, just before I feel my liquid release shoot out of me, coating his dick.

“That's it. Such a good fucking girl,” Loki praises as my pussy walls convulse around his hard cock, which is still pounding in and out of me.

Suddenly, he pulls out, and I cry out loud as he drops to his knees, starting to lick and suck me like I'm his favourite dessert. He's relentless, circling his tongue around my overly sensitive clit as I squirm. His hands clamp down hard on my hips to hold me still, licking me in long strokes, from my opening to my clit, swirling his tongue when he gets to the bundle of nerves.

“I fucking love how your tongue feels on my clit, Loki,” I gasp out, and he groans at the dirty talk.

My hands come to his head, gripping his hair and tugging, making him growl. I open my eyes and see that Jax is standing in the doorway, his blue eyes like the deepest part of a flame.

My mouth drops open, and I can’t suppress the moan at the look of desire on his face. He steps in, closing the door softly behind him.

Loki pauses, looking over his shoulder, and then turns back with a wicked grin.

“Come and help me take care of our girl, Jax,” he orders, then settles his head back in between my thighs.

Jax walks over, and I can see his hard on tenting his black sweats. He's not dropped eye contact with me, and there's so much swirling in his gaze I can't even begin to unpack it. Guilt, regret, lust and a love that would burn down the world are just a few emotions that flit through their depths.

“Jax...” I murmur when he reaches me. “Please, Jax.” I'm panting, my body shaking with the pleasure that Loki's tongue is giving me.

His hands grip my face gently as he leans in.

"I'll always take care of you, Baby Girl," he whispers, taking my mouth in a hot kiss, showing me that I've not lost him either.

A sob sounds in my throat, a mixture of relief and terror at what could have been, what could have happened tonight. What life would have been like if I'd lost them for good. I revel in the scratch of his short beard on my chin, showing me that he's really here. I've missed him so fucking much.

He breaks our kiss, looking deep into my eyes once more before he too drops down onto his knees. He spreads my legs wider, throwing one over his left shoulder. Loki copies him, throwing my other leg over his right shoulder until I'm stretched open completely to them.

Jax starts to kiss up my inner thigh, nipping and sucking along the way. Seconds later, Loki does the same with the other thigh, and I begin to shake with breathless anticipation, my head thrown back, eyes closed.

When they reach the apex of my thighs, one of them blows on my bare dripping pussy. The cool air feels incredible against my inner heat, and I sigh, only to moan seconds later as a tongue licks up my open slit. A second tongue is quick to follow until I can't tell them apart.

I look down to see blond and red hair mixing, both their tongues working me into a frenzy. I moan at the sight of these guys on their knees for me, my hands reaching down to grasp their hair in tight fists.

One tongue enters me, curling upwards and licking my inner wall, whilst the other begins slow teasing circles around my clit. They switch over, meeting in the middle, and the idea of their tongues touching has me screaming my release as I tug at blond and auburn locks.

They don't relent, prolonging my orgasm until I'm a fucking twitching, whimpering mess. I can feel my whole body tingling, and all painful terror filled thoughts from earlier have fled my mind, leaving me languid and sated.

Loki's the first to sit back on his heels, a satisfied look on his face. His lips and chin are glistening with my juices. He gets up, leaning over to give me a kiss on the lips, and I moan at the taste of myself in his mouth.

"Get your dick out of my face," Jax grumbles, and I giggle.

"I've missed your laugh so much, Pretty Girl," Loki whispers seriously against my lips. "So fucking much."

We stay together, lips and foreheads pressed until I hear the shower turn on. I look up and see a gloriously, now naked Jax holding his hand out to me. I swallow at the sight of him.

*How could I have forgotten how beautiful he is?*

Loki helps me climb down, my legs still shaking from that orgasm.

Jax grabs my hand when I reach him, pulling me into his embrace and holding me tight. I nuzzle into the crook of his neck, breathing him in. I'm instantly calmer, my body and mind knowing that I'm safe, that nothing can hurt me whilst I'm in his arms.

"I'm so sorry, Jax," I say softly into his neck. "I'm so sorry for running away. For judging you."

Fresh tears sting my eyes, tears that have nothing to do with what happened in the library, and everything to do with almost losing these guys.

"I was wrong, Jax. So wrong, and I shouldn't have run. When I came through the door tonight," his arms tighten around me, "and I saw you standing there, I knew instinctively that you would keep me safe. That nothing could hurt me, as long as I was with you. All of you," I add, opening my eyes and looking into Loki's emerald ones as he makes his way over to us, stepping into the shower.

Leaning back, I look up into Jax's face. My arms are still wrapped around him, and I meet those piercing eyes of his. The blue is swirling and churning with a myriad of intense emotions. I reach out to cup his bearded cheek.

"Jax, you are my home, where I belong and where I'm safe. The thought of losing you, any of you...I'm not sure I would survive it."

His hands tighten where they're now resting on my hips. I can see him swallowing, and when he talks, his voice is thick with emotion.

"You're ours, Lilly," he says simply. I feel a warmth at my back when Loki steps up to me, his hands coming to my waist.

"We're right here, and we're not going anywhere. None of us," Loki says into my ear, his voice serious. "Lilly, we need you. We need your light to temper our darkness and make us believe we're worthy. That we're not completely bad. That we're not just monsters."

"Loki..." I reach a hand back around his neck and pull him closer. "You've done bad things, do bad things because you have to. And I don't care if you're monsters, as long as you're *my* monsters."

"We're yours," Jax rumbles out, fingers pressing hard into my soft flesh.

"You're ours," Loki purrs behind me. I can feel them both hard again, pressed into my stomach and lower back. “Let's clean you up,” he says softly, placing a gentle kiss on my shoulder.

I need these guys, and no matter what they've done or what they’ll do, they're good guys.

*Who of us isn't a little bit of a monster too?*

We gently untangle ourselves, then Loki and Jax wash me so tenderly, so reverently, that fresh tears spring to my eyes. They wrap me up in a huge, fluffy towel, shepherding me out of the bathroom, where we see Ash and Kai sitting on the sofa, who look up as we exit.

Ash gets up and walks towards us, then stops short in front of me. He looks torn, torment churning in his grey eyes. Before he can say a word, I step forward and wrap my arms around his waist, nuzzling my nose into his neck and taking a deep breath in.

His spicy ginger scent floods my senses as he hesitates for a beat, then wraps his own arms tightly around me. I can hear his heart pounding in his chest, and his body is shaking all over.

“I'm so sorry, Ash,” I whisper, feeling him stiffen in my arms. “I was wrong that night, and I just got scared and ran. But I shouldn't have.” I can feel more tears stinging my eyes again. Crying is all I seem to do tonight.

He pulls back to look into my eyes, his own full of a thousand emotions.

“This life is so fucked up, Lilly, it's not safe, and now we've dragged you into it too,” he replies. He looks desolate and full of guilt, his jaw tight. “We should have stayed away from you. We shouldn't have gotten involved in the first place.” He hangs his head, and my heart stutters.

*Does he regret being with me?*

Taking a deep breath, he looks back up at me. One hand cups the side of my face, his thumb gently caressing my cheek.

“I'm sorry, Princess,” he murmurs, leaning down and pressing his lips to mine in a bittersweet kiss before stepping out of my arms, turning his back on me, and walking away.

I feel sick and numb, my heart so sore I'm surprised it's still beating. I hear Loki, Jax, and Kai in the background arguing, but all I can do is watch as Ash walks out the door.

A sob escapes me, my hand covering my lips when Kai steps in front of me, his hands capturing my face.

“Hey, Lilly, he just needs time,” he says gently, and I look into his eyes. “He's hurting and feels like he's failed you tonight.”

“Kai, I've lost him.” My voice is small and lost. Fresh tears track down my cheeks, which Kai brushes away with his thumbs.

“Not forever,” he says back, pulling me into his embrace, holding me whilst I gently cry into his chest, my tears wetting his t-shirt. His hands are soothing down my back, and his lips place gentle kisses on my head until a wave of exhaustion washes over me.

The events of tonight have wrung me out until I feel like a damp rag. Boneless, and like there's no more tears left.

He must feel my body droop because he scoops me up and carries me upstairs, taking me to Loki's room. I hear the others come in as Kai carefully sets me on my feet, removing my towel and picking me up again, then lying me down in Loki's bed.

He tenderly kisses my forehead before straightening up. I crack my eyes open a slit to see Loki and Jax climb in naked on either side of me, the bed dipping with their weight.

“Sleep now, Pretty Girl,” Loki mumbles, pulling me close to him, my back to his chest. “It'll all be okay.”

Before I can utter a word of protest, darkness overtakes me, and I fall into a blissful, dreamless sleep.

# CHAPTER TWENTY-SEVEN

JAX

I watch as sleep overtakes Lilly's beautiful features, a deep furrow in between her brows that I hate seeing there.

Loki told Lilly it'll be okay, but how can it be? That cunt, that dead man fucking walking, touched her. He hurt her, tried to take what didn't belong to him. She's fucking ours, and no one, no motherfucking one, gets to lay a finger on her but us.

I reach out, my hand falling on her soft waist, and she sighs in her sleep.

My heart stopped in my chest when she ran into the dorm, bleeding and eyes wild, full of panic like a deer who's been caught by a hunter. Our beautiful, strong girl was broken, and we'd done it to her just as much as that bastard. Guilt slithers over me, sticky and viscous as tar when I recall how we iced her out, taking the pain of her supposed rejection out on her.

It was bullshit! She's a normal fucking girl, and our lives are anything but normal. How could we have just expected her to have been cool with it? With what we have to do? Especially after what happened to her mom.

And look what fucking happened because of our stupid fucking reaction. This is as much our fault as that fucker's, *Robert*. We may as well have thrown her to him, abandoning her like we did. I feel sick with the knowledge that we're to blame. We didn't protect her when she needed us most.

And I'll spend every damn day for the rest of my cursed life making it up to her.

---

## LOKI

I pull Lilly in closer, holding her so tightly I'm surprised that she can still breathe. Tears prick my eyes when I remember how she ran straight into Jax's arms and broke down earlier. I look up over her head and see Jax's eyes in the low light. They reflect the self-loathing and crippling guilt that I feel inside.

We failed our beautiful girl, the only girl I've ever loved in my miserable life. And I let her down. At the first sign of trouble, I quit, not realizing that she just needed time to adjust. Not for us to just drop her like a bag of garbage.

Sure, we were hurting, but she was confused and frightened, and we just walked away like fucking children.

I tighten my grip even more, I've fucking missed holding her in my arms. It's like a piece of me has been gone these past couple of weeks. And when I think about what could have happened to her tonight...My blood boils, searing my insides, and making me feel like I want to vomit, all at the same time.

Robert will hurt so badly he will wish he was dead, long before we do him the mercy of ending his pathetic life.

I've never wished for faith as much as I do now, just so I'd know for sure that he will be tortured in Hell for all eternity.

As I hold her, I silently vow to seek revenge. Then to spend every waking moment loving her with my whole heart.

My whole fucking soul and everything that I am, or ever will be, belongs to her now.

---

## KAI

I close the door softly and take a deep breath, placing my forehead on the wood.

Then another.

Then another.

It doesn't help. Rage, like I haven't known for years, burns my insides, blackening them until I feel like my whole being is darkness incarnate. Most people see red when they feel uncontrollable anger. I see black. The black of endless night, and monsters that'll devour your soul.

Blinking, I come back to myself. I head downstairs to wait for Ash. He's hurting badly and has never been good with his emotions. Like I told Lilly, he feels like he's personally responsible for what happened tonight.

He's not wholly wrong, we are all culpable. We abandoned her and opened her up for this sort of thing. It just never occurred to us that someone would be stupid enough to touch her after we'd claimed her.

More fool us.

I tidy the bits and pieces of first aid that Jax got out to tend to her wounds. I have to pause and focus on my breath several times, as the black once again threatens to consume me.

Once I'm back under control, I go to make some Bi Luo Chun tea. I find the ritual calming; heating the water to exactly two hundred and five degrees, measuring out the leaves into the warmed gaiwan, leaving the leaves to steep, then pouring the tea into the saucer.

I breathe out a sigh as the first slightly bitter sip enters my mouth, calming me instantly. Going to sit on the couch, I pick up my discarded iPad with my free hand, opening a new window on my dark web browser.

I won't take part in whatever harm we cause Robert physically. If I'm let loose on him, there would be bits of him all over the floor while his heart still beats, his blood bathing me in delicious crimson. My dick twitches at the thought of Lilly, naked and also covered in his blood, her hands bound as I pound into her.

Time for that in the future. *We will have the rest of our lives to make it up to her,* I think as I begin to systematically destroy Robert's life, one click at a time.

---

## ASH

Once I'm outside in the crisp night air, I place my earbuds in, selecting *Suffocate* by Nathan Wagner to play. It suits my dark mood.

I fucked up.

We all did, but I messed up the worst. I'm meant to protect them, and along the way, Lilly became part of those included on that list. But I let her down. I wasn't there when it mattered, and it feels like a fucking knife has gone through my gut, cutting my insides to shreds.

Like my father, I'm the leader, the alpha, the top dog. But unlike that cunt, I actually give a shit about the people under my care. Those guys, and now it seems Lilly, are like family to me. More so because I fucking chose them, over a father who's an evil son of a bitch, and a mother too doped up on tranquillizers to notice a fucking thing.

The song plays on, reminding me how badly I messed up.

My mind flashes back to when she burst through the door, broken, bleeding, and terrified. My hands clench at the thought of that cumstain laying his hands on her. Trying to take something that doesn't fucking belong to him.

A menacing growl escapes my lips when I think of how close he came.

How dare he even look in her direction! Let alone touch her. White hot rage fills me up until every atom of my being is burning with the need for violence. For vengeance.

Jax is right. Robert is a dead man walking, and his days are fucking numbered. We're coming for that asshole, and he'll be so broken by the time we're done, there won't be enough pieces to put him back together.

# CHAPTER TWENTY-EIGHT

LILLY

For the next seven days, I stay in our dorm, with at least one of the guys with me at all times. Well, except Ash, who seems to be avoiding me like the plague.

The other three take care of me so tenderly, my heart repairs a little more each day. Kai makes me all my favourite foods, like chicken ramen and triple chocolate brownies, and I get breakfast in bed every morning.

Loki runs me epic bubble baths, often joining me in them, and although we make out, I'm the only one who ever comes.

We've not gone further than kissing, or them eating me out like I'm their last meal, since the night of the attack. I want to feel them inside me so badly, to feel that connection, but I just can't. Any time we've tried, I get horrendous flashbacks or start to panic. And they're so sweet about it, saying it's all about my pleasure, and taking care of me.

Jax makes it his mission to show me some basic self-defence moves, often ending with me pinning him down, or with my legs wrapped around him. I can feel him getting hard, but like Loki, he keeps it strictly about me and my release.

Some sessions, certain positions cause horrible flashbacks to that night.

But Jax helps me through the panic, with soothing words and his comforting embrace, holding me until the tremors subside and my breathing evens out.

Every night, Loki and Jax leave me exhausted in bed with multiple mindless orgasms before falling asleep on either side of me, wrapping me up in their arms. They hold me when I wake up screaming, nightmares now featuring clammy hands, alongside the visions of drowning in a sea of blood.

The bruise on my jaw begins to fade from the deep purple of a plum to a rather sickly yellow, which I suppose is better, as I can now hide it with makeup.

It's October thirty-first, All Hallows' Eve, and my first day back to class. I'd told my teachers that I was sick with a stomach bug, not wanting everyone to see the marks that were painted on my face and body.

As I get dressed, I look over to the burgundy dress bag that's hanging on the front of Loki's closet. It's the school Halloween party tonight, which is being held in the ballroom.

*I know, right?! What fucking school has a ballroom? Pretentious twats.*

I'm not sure what the guys are dressing up as, but I have a killer dress that I bought a while back. I can't wait to show them and have a night to let my hair down after everything that has happened recently.

I never really bothered with school discos back in England, shite doesn't even begin to cover how lame they'd been. Apparently, here at Highgate Prep, it's a different affair, with amazing decorations and entertainment, a themed buffet style banquet, and the rules on alcohol consumption are relaxed.

*Money may not be able to buy you happiness, but, apparently, it can enable underage drinking.*

I add the finishing touches to my makeup, making sure that every bruise is covered. Luckily, I don't have PE today, and even though I have chosen Yoga and Pilates as my electives, which I can wear leggings and long-sleeved tops for, I'd still have to get changed in front of the rest of the girls. They'd definitely see the bruises, and I'm not up for Cuntflap Magee, aka Amber, to start shite over them.

I look myself over in the full length mirror, deciding that I'm looking fierce as fuck. I've chosen my red tartan Run and Fly dungarees, rolled up at the hem, with a black roll neck sweater underneath. On my feet, I've gone for white lace ankle socks, paired with my red snakeskin Irregular Choice heels that have super cute sparkly heels and bows on the toe.

Dark smoky eyes and bright red lips finish off the punky look. Grabbing my leather satchel, I head out of the door and down the stairs to find all of the guys waiting for me.

Loki, of course, wolf whistles before grabbing me around my waist, pulling me towards him, and whispering in my ear.

"Those heels are staying on later, Pretty Girl," he says, nipping my earlobe, and I flush with heat as I feel my core tingle. I love him that little bit more for keeping the flirty banter up. It's definitely helping me to heal.

"Are you ready to go?" Ash asks, his voice cold but not unkind.

I start a little, I haven't heard him say a word since that awful night and I'd almost forgotten his deep beautiful voice, sliding like the finest silk velvet across my skin.

"Yes," I reply quietly, looking into his tumultuous eyes.

Ash gives me a brisk nod, then opens our door and heads out. Kai looks at me with a smile, then turns to follow him.

I take a deep breath, nervous butterflies fluttering in my stomach.

*What if I see Robert?*

I shudder at the thought, then a flash of anger runs through me. I'll not let that cumstain scare me into hiding.

*At the very least, I owe him a dick punch. Fucking fucktrumpet.*

Squaring my shoulders, I look up to see Jax studying me, a look of pride in his blue gaze.

"No one will fucking touch you," he promises darkly.

He may not be a knight in shining armour, he's more like the dragon who protects his princess from the fuckers who try to kidnap her by setting the world alight.

He steps up to me, grabbing the front of my throat just shy of painfully, giving me a searing kiss full of possession and darkness. After looking me in the eyes, his own churning with fierce emotion, he steps away and follows the others.

A flutter of excitement and lust transforms the flying insects into sensuous silk winged creatures, and I must admit that I'm surprised. I'd expected rough handling to scare me or cause a flashback. But it doesn't. Not with Jax anyway.

Loki slings his arm around my shoulders, pulling my body in tight to his.

Even after the time I've spent with him, it still feels like a live current is running through me wherever we touch.

"Come on, Pretty Girl," he says, grim determination in his tone. "Let's show them you're not afraid." And he leads me from the safe haven of our dorm.

Everything goes well until we approach homeroom, where just my fucking luck, standing by the door is Queen Cumdumpster herself and her fawning sycophants. She's draped all over Robert, stroking him like a fucking cat, as though she's some kind of Bond villain, and the sight makes bile rise to my throat.

I stiffen under Loki's arm, but keep moving alongside him and his stride doesn't pause. Robert has clear nail marks tracked down his cheeks, still red with scabs.

*I wonder what he's told everyone about how he got those? Rogue tiger?*

I hear Jax growl in front of us, stepping right up in Robert's face, harshly whispering something that makes the other boy turn ashen and pale, and shake like a leaf in the breeze. Jax steps away and towards me, wrapping his arm around my waist so that I'm sandwiched in between him and Loki.

"I hope your *stomach* is feeling better, Lilly?" Amber asks, mock sincerity clear in her voice and a nasty smile pasted on her face.

"Much, thank you, Amber," I reply, my own voice sweetly scornful. My smile is just as fake.

Dismissing her, I turn back to look at Robert, and for a moment, I'm transported back to that night. His clammy hand on my face, his disgusting dick lining up with my...I blink, and I'm back in the hall again.

"Those scratches look bad. You should probably get something for them. Wouldn't want them to scar," I say, proud that my voice doesn't shake, and not taking my eyes away from his shit coloured ones as I speak. His gaze darts away, like he's afraid to look at me. *Interesting.*

Loki roars with laughter beside me.

"Let's head inside, beautiful," he says, kissing me on the cheek.

Jax does the same to my other cheek, making it clear to everyone watching that I am once more theirs. I'd be pissed that they've basically, well, just pissed all over me, but there's something so hot about being claimed publicly. Especially in front of those wastes of oxygen.

Amber's blue eyes narrow, and I see a flare of annoyance flash in her gaze. *I wonder if she had anything to do with the other night?*

My gaze flits to Ash, who's just standing there, a dangerous, calculating look in his eyes as he looks at Robert, and then Amber. He's definitely planning something.

*I hope it's fucking agonising.*

Kai is standing next to him, and the look of pure hate on his face is so shocking I almost stumble. This is Kai. I know he likes a little pain in the bedroom, but I've never seen him look so much as cross before, let alone murderous like he does now.

Loki gives me a gentle tug, and we head into class, Jax only letting go at the last minute so that we can actually fit through the doorway.

*Possessive arsehole.* I smile, loving it.

---

We finish our last class of the day, French with Loki, who spent the entire time telling me, in French, what he plans to do to me later. I only managed to translate a few sentences, but fuck, if they didn't make me all hot and bothered, flushing red as a tomato.

After class, Loki and I head back to our dorm, and he carries my bag like a true gent. As we open the door, we hear low voices. Ash, Jax, and Kai look up at us from the table. It's hard to describe the look on their faces. The closest I can come to is that they look like they're readying for battle, excited yet also sombre, angry yet controlled.

"What's going on?" I hesitantly ask, gazing at them each in turn, and then up to Loki. Whatever it is, he's in on it. I can see it in his face.

"Loki?" I ask, anxiety rolling through me and I bite my lip, my heart rate speeding up.

"You asked us to make him bleed. To make him hurt so bad that he can't do what he tried to do to you, to anyone else," Ash states, getting up and walking towards me.

His grey eyes are boring into mine, and it's then that it dawns on me. They're preparing to take vengeance. For me.

I nod, unable to say anything, my throat is dry, and my heart pounding hard in my chest.

“That's what we will be doing tonight. The question, Princess, is whether you want in?” he challenges, and I hear the others curse and start to argue.

“I want in,” I say softly, not taking my eyes off Ash's.

“Are you sure, Princess? Once you go down this road, there's no going back,” he says, voice devoid of any emotion, but his eyes are churning.

It's not just about my revenge. Or even justice, to stop this happening to anyone else. If I want to be with these guys, truly with them, and accept them for who they are, I need to see who they are. I need to know all of them, the good and bad. The monstrous and angelic.

If that means I have to wash my hands in the blood of our enemies, then so be it.

I also need to make sure they don't take things too far.

“I'm sure,” I reply, and something like relief flits across his eyes for the briefest of moments as he gives me a single decisive nod.

“Ash, I don't think...” Kai begins, stepping up next to Ash.

“The decision has been made, Kai,” Ash says simply. Then he turns and walks upstairs.

“Lilly...are you sure?” Kai asks, stepping up to me, his hands coming up either side of my face. “You don't have to be there. Let us be your monsters.” He's almost pleading with me.

“Kai...” I say gently, stepping into him and bringing my hands up to rest on his chest. I look at him in those gorgeous honey brown eyes. “I need to do this. I want to do this. If I want to be with you, *truly* with you, then I need to see who you really are. All sides of you, the beautiful and not so beautiful,” I tell him, willing him to understand.

He stares into my eyes for a beat longer, then sighs, leaning in to rest his forehead to mine, our eyes closed.

“I just don't want to lose you, Lilly. Not again,” he says softly, and my heart lurches.

I don't really know what to say to him. If I don't pass this test, if I can't handle it, then how can I be with them?

# CHAPTER TWENTY-NINE

LILLY

I put the finishing touches to my makeup, admiring the pretty damn good job I've made of it. My face is painted as a Day of the Dead sugar skull, all white with blacked out eye sockets, colourful swirls, and flowers in an intricate pattern across my whole face.

*Thank fuck for YouTube!*

My costume is a stunning full length, figure hugging, off the shoulder halter dress, covered entirely in sequins. The best part? The sequins are in a white skeleton pattern on black, and there's a red organza tiered train, as well as red organza frothing across the top of my arms and my neckline. It's sexy as fuck, especially as it looks like it's about to fall down at any moment.

Of course, it wouldn't be complete without my signature Irregular Choice heels. I've got on a pink pair with black lace over the top, black sparkly heels, and black roses across the front. Nestled amongst the roses is a silver skull. Classy, yet appropriate for the theme.

I haven't seen the guys' outfits yet. I guess they wanted to surprise me, too. I head out of Loki's room, I really ought to start thinking of it as mine given that all my stuff is in here.

Walking down the stairs, I notice them all standing around the breakfast bar, and I pause to drink them in. They are panty-exploding gorgeous. I see them every day, sleep in a bed with one or more of them every night, and they still take my breath away on the regular. They spot me and I can see a fire in each of their gazes, and suddenly I'm glad that my face is painted white because I'm sure underneath it's beetroot red as I flush from head to toe with raw desire.

Loki is the first one to reach me, looking like he's going to grab me, throw me over his shoulder, and head back upstairs.

"Jesus, Pretty Girl," he rasps out, eyes devouring me. "You look fucking exquisite." His hand brushes across the top of my exposed breasts, which, thanks to the lace corset I'm wearing, have been pushed up until it looks like they'll topple out.

"You look pretty hot yourself," I say, taking my time looking him up and down.

He's got on a white shirt, with lace on the cuffs and down the unbuttoned front, which shows off his beautiful inked chest. On top of that, he's wearing a gorgeous emerald green velvet jacket that makes his eyes pop. Dark black jeans tucked into knee high black leather boots encase his muscular legs. And around his neck is an old fashioned looking locket. I reach out and open it to see a hideous painting of Loki, looking wizened and almost zombie-like.

"Dorian Gray, I presume?" I ask, meeting those beautiful eyes of his with a smile on my lips.

"Charmed," he replies in a terrible British accent, giving me a rakish smile in return, and taking my hand. He brings it up, but instead of kissing it, he leans in and places a kiss on the exposed globe of my breast, making my breath stutter.

He straightens up, gives me a wink, and then saunters off. *God, I could bite that arse of his! Maybe I will later...*

Jax steps up next, and I can't help the delighted laugh that escapes me.

*He's dressed as fucking He-Man!*

All he's wearing is a pair of dark red y-fronts, a gold belt, red boots, and some sort of sword holder strapped across his chest, with a legit sword on his back. I mean, it looks real and wicked sharp.

I'm having to hold back tears of laughter, and I can see the annoyance at my reaction to his costume in his gaze.

"What's so funny, Baby Girl?" His voice is dark, and it helps to calm my laughter, making lust flare through me, which isn't hard as all of his drool worthy muscles are on display.

"Jax, I'm sorry, it's just..." I say, still giggling. "When I stepped out of the bathroom that first night, before I knew your name, I called you He-Man in my head," I say, smiling at him.

His lips twitch to my relief. I really didn't want to offend him. I step closer to him and can't help but run my palm up his arm appreciatively.

*That's a fine piece of real estate right there!*

I hear snorts of laughter and look back at Jax to see him smirking at me.

"A fine piece of real estate?" he questions with a blond brow raised, and I realise I said that out loud.

"You broke my filter," I pout, my hand still rubbing up and down his arm. "Although, you are far, far sexier than He-Man," I purr. I don't mean for it to come out in a husky voice, but damn, this boy is ripped, and that makes me all hot and horny.

"Careful, Baby Girl. These pants don't hide much," he rumbles out, his own voice more gravelly than usual, and I can't help looking down and admiring the growing bulge between his legs. "And you're already testing my control with that dress." He runs his fingers across the neckline, and I shiver and ache, my thighs clenching together.

I take a step back before things can get any more heated between us. Looking up, I see Kai, who looks devastatingly handsome in a grey suit, white shirt, and thin black tie. He also has a pair of handcuffs dangling out of one pocket.

"I see the other Mr Grey has joined us for the evening," I smile, arching a brow at him.

He smiles back sheepishly, a blush coming to his cheeks. "He's a little vanilla for my tastes, but well, I had to dress as something," he says, his voice low and melodic.

It's then that I remember he doesn't really like parties. I go around Jax, sliding up so close to him that my breasts brush his jacket front, and smooth down his tie.

"Maybe later you can show me that neat tie trick I keep seeing on TikTok, sir?"

Obviously, I just can't help myself around these guys. Kai's honey eyes flare with lust, and I see him swallow before giving me a nod.

"You look beautiful by the way, Lilly," he says simply, taking me all in.

"We should get going," Ash drawls from near the door, and I look up, my breath hitching when I see his costume.

It's not that different from what he usually wears, yet it's the small details that make my heart race.

He's wearing his normal tailored to perfection suit, yet this one is a shiny coal black, giving the impression that it has been poured on. He's got a black shirt underneath, the top two buttons undone, which is unheard of for Ash and so damn sexy I feel wetness seep into the crotch of my knickers.

There's an air of decadent debauchery about him tonight, and my heart aches anew at the distance there is now between us. We didn't get as close as I got with the others, but we were on the way before that night during fall break. I just hope it's not too late to get back there.

He opens the door and gestures the guys through, taking hold of my upper arm in a gentle grip as I move to pass him. I look up at him, our eyes meeting. His are filled with such fire, the grey is molten and swirling with emotion.

*"'Did my heart love till now? Foreswear it, sight! For I ne'er saw true beauty till this night.'"*

I'm utterly spellbound, unable to utter so much as a single syllable.

*Did he just...? Did Ash just tell me...? No. He was just saying I look nice.*

My mind churns with conflicting thoughts, eyes locked with his when he suddenly lets go and walks ahead of me. It's then I notice that on the back of his jacket, a pair of matte black angel wings are printed.

*Ah! He's Lucifer tonight,* I think. Apt, given the turmoil he's just left me in.

Sighing, I shut our door and head after him.

We walk towards the ballroom, a room I had no idea even existed until I found out about this party. Apparently, it's used for school functions, award ceremonies, and graduation, but not much else.

There was, of course, a design committee for the party, and I heard all about them and their plans during my Interior Design classes. But unfortunately, as Amber Cuntflaps heads it up, I couldn't get involved.

We approach the huge wooden double doors to find two men wearing red velvet jackets, top hats, and white gloves waiting for us. Their faces are painted all white, with dark lines around their eyes and highlighting their cheekbones.

"Welcome," they say in unison, voices deep yet emotionless.

They open the doors to reveal an extraordinary sight. The room no longer looks like a ballroom, or any kind of room at all. Jewel coloured silks drape across the ceiling and down the walls, creating a tent like appearance.

There are fantastically dressed aerial performers, twirling on hoops and dangling from ribbons. Servers dressed in glittering costumes with ghoulish masks walk around, serving what looks like sparkling cocktails.

There's a DJ on the stage, his body painted to look like an Aztec skeletal demon glowing under ultraviolet light. As we step in, the song quickly changes to *Heaven Knows* by The Pretty Reckless. It seems a little too coincidental, and as I look around at the guys, who are either side of me, I see Loki's self-satisfied smirk.

"Loki, did you just get the DJ to play this as we walked in?" I ask, narrowing my eyes, lips twitching.

He full on grins at me, and I can see the excitement bouncing in his eyes. "It's fucking epic, right?!" he says, practically pulling me over as we walk in and head towards the long tables.

They, like the walls, are covered in jewel coloured table cloths, which you can barely see underneath plates groaning with food of every description. There must be every type of canapé here. From sushi rolls, to small pastries, to cut up fruit on tiny kebab sticks. There are small glasses full of colourful desserts, and so many things that I have no idea what most of them are.

The amount of food is obscene, far too much for those in attendance. I shudder at the waste, knowing much of it will be thrown out when the night is over.

The guys descend on the spread, piling plates high whilst I stand there overwhelmed. I feel a warm hand on the small of my back and look to the side to see Kai, his kind eyes looking down at me. He may be the smallest, but he's still got a few inches on me.

"Want me to fix you a plate?" he asks, and I notice Jax and Loki look up and give him a dirty look. It reminds me of the barbecue scene from *Gone With the Wind*, where they all fight to bring Scarlett O'Hara desserts at the barbecue, and I smile.

"Do I get to pretend to be Scarlett O'Hara, having all the men fawn over me?" I tease, and his eyes light up as he gets the reference.

"Well, we all know who Rhett would be," he sighs out as we see Ash stalk over to a round table, sitting in one of the golden chairs, facing the room.

He sits as a king would on his throne, like it's his right and woe betide anyone who dares to question it. Then, the arrogant arsehole that he is, he clicks his fingers at one of the servers who comes hurrying over to deposit a tray of cocktails on the table.

I find myself sighing too. Ash is so beautiful, I used to think that it was a cold hard beauty. Now I know that underneath, he burns with the purest flame. A fire that protects those he loves. His darkness is what helps to keep them safe.

*But who keeps him safe?* I can't help but wonder.

"Come on, Pretty Girl," Loki says in his familiar drawl. "Let's eat so you can grind on me on the dance floor," he says, winking, and then giving me a lascivious grin for good measure.

*Fucking turnip.*

I look around to see that Kai has indeed filled a plate for me and is carrying it to the table Ash is seated at. I follow him, taking a seat with Loki and Jax on either side of me. Kai and Ash are on the other side, and although there are vacant seats, no one else tries to sit down, even though I can see people glancing our way.

I often forget how untouchable these guys are. How the other students, all of whom are rich as royalty, leave space for them and keep their distance. And I'm not sure whether it's out of fear or respect. Maybe a bit of both?

We sit and eat, not really talking. I don't know how the guys are feeling, but I'm full of a nervous energy that's leaving me feeling tightly coiled and tense. I don't know what the plan is for later tonight, but I can imagine we will all be bloody by dawn.

My ears prick at the familiar notes of *Siren*, by Kailee Morgue. I smell vanilla before I feel Loki's lips against my ear.

"I dare you to dance for Ash," he whispers seductively, the spot that his breath caresses tingles.

He's such a shit stirrer, but I can't seem to back down from the challenge he's issued. I look over to Ash, who is scanning the room with dark eyes, his chair pulled out as he lounges back in it.

"What do I get if I do?" I whisper back, my eyes still on Ash.

I'm definitely going to do it because I want to ruffle the Ice Knight's feathers as much as Loki does. I just want to see if I can get anything out of Loki first.

"I'll take you behind one of those curtains and get on my knees for you, making you come so hard with my tongue, the whole school will hear your cries." His voice is deep and husky, sending shivers down my spine.

Smiling, I get up and sway over to Ash, standing in front of him, but still slowly undulating my hips. Bringing my hands up my body, caressing my curves, I take them over my head, rolling my wrists so that my hands do a sensual dance of their own.

Our gazes are locked, and there's an intense look in his grey eyes. It's like looking into the eyes of a wolf, you know it's going to pounce and devour you, you're just not sure how much time you have left. Or, if you mind all that much.

Turning my back on him, I look over my shoulder as I roll my hips, smiling seductively at him, before turning back to face him and stepping right in between his splayed legs.

I can see a bulge in his crotch that just makes my smile grow wider as I realise what this is doing to him. I mean, I'm not unaffected by his undivided attention, my knickers are getting damper by the second.

His hands are clenched into fists on his thighs, like it's taking a gargantuan effort not to grab me and pull me down onto his lap.

*I wonder if I can tip him over the edge...*

Leaning forwards, I place my hands on his shoulders and move my torso in a wave towards him so that my barely covered breasts are practically in his face.

*Bingo!*

His hands clamp down on my sequinned hips, squeezing just this side of painfully. He leans forward, his lips brushing my ear just like Loki's did and eliciting the same tingles.

"Are you sure you wanna play, Princess? You seemed to have trouble handling it last time," he says, his voice dark and cruel, aimed to inflict maximum damage.

My eyes narrow, my body stopping its movements. We're still pressed together, his hands on my hips and mine on his broad shoulders.

*Fucktrumpet.*

I smile as an idea forms in my mind.

"I think I can handle you, *Vanderbilt*, just fine," I whisper back in his ear before I lick up the side of his face.

He's so stunned that his hands drop, and straightening up, I laugh at the look of surprise on his face. I hear Loki's roar of laughter, and even Kai and Jax snort.

"Did you just lick me, Princess?" he asks incredulously.

"Yep," I say, popping the 'P.' "And now you're mine."

I wink at him just as the song ends, and *Killer* by Valerie Broussard starts to play.

I feel my hand being tugged and turn to see Loki pulling me onto the dance floor.

"Come on, Pretty Girl. This is our song," he says, laughing at my raised brow. I follow him anyway, but can't help the shiver of trepidation that runs down my spine.

*By the end of the night, will I be a killer too?*

# CHAPTER THIRTY

LILLY

I spend the rest of the party dancing with Loki, Jax, and even Kai, who is surprisingly adept and pulls me so close that I can feel his hardness against my arse.

Loki spirits me away at one point, to a dark corner behind the curtains, and pays his debt. Luckily, the music is loud, so I don't think too many people hear me shatter on his tongue.

Of course, Amber Cuntmuffin and her merry band of Pissflaps are here, they did decorate the ballroom, after all. She keeps her distance, just glaring at me as I grind on the guys. In a way, it makes me more wary of her. I don't trust the bitch, and it feels like she's plotting something.

Loki, Jax, and I have just come off the dance floor when the clock strikes midnight, and I see Ash give the others a nod. My heart rate picks up.

"It's go time, Cinderella," Loki murmurs, grabbing my hand and interlocking our fingers.

He looks excited, yet I can see a bone-deep weariness in the depths of his gaze. Like what is about to happen is not something he relishes, but something that has to be done. And I feel a pang of guilt at being the cause of another stain on his soul.

"You ready, Baby Girl?" Jax rumbles from my other side, and I look up into his face to see violence swirling in his blue eyes. He's definitely more excited than anyone else. He craves bloodshed and vengeance.

I swallow, my mouth suddenly dry. All I can do is nod, my eyes wide and my breaths shallow.

"You can still stay here, Lilly," Kai offers, and I see concern and worry in his honey gaze and his lowered eyebrows. He knows this is not easy for me, and I know he wants to spare me any pain and heartache.

But I need to do this, not just for myself, but also for them. These guys. *My* guys. If I want to be with them, fully and completely, I need to know them inside and out. The good and the bad. The men and the monsters.

"I'm ready," I whisper in a hushed tone, hoping my voice sounds more confident than I feel.

"Let's go then," Ash orders, his tone sharp and commanding.

I look up into his unreadable, sharp steel gaze. The butterflies dance frantically in my stomach, desperate for release. I feel like I'm on the edge of a cliff, about to jump off, and I've no idea if I'll survive the fall.

We all follow Ash, the party still in full swing around us. The teachers have all gone to bed, leaving everyone to their own devices, and it's as if Lust himself has walked through the room spreading his debauchery. There are couples out in the open, practically fucking on tables. We pass several orgies, one with a naked server in the middle, mask still on, whilst girls and boys snort snow off her body. She looks happy enough, so I hope she's not been forced.

As we're leaving, I see Amber on her knees whilst a guy fucks her mouth relentlessly, making her gag and spit fly everywhere. She's moaning and touching herself, *gross*, so I assume she's having a great time and living her best cuntflap life.

Blinking the image away, although let's be honest, it's seared on my retinas for all time, I walk through the double doors that are still being manned by the men in top hats.

We head straight for the front doors, where there is an all black truck waiting, that same valet from the party in the first week standing beside it. He doesn't even acknowledge my presence, *good lad*, as he hands the keys to Jax and then walks away.

“Nice ride,” I admire, knowing the car is worth a fortune, but deciding not to get on my soapbox this evening.

He grins wolfishly at me. “Thanks. She's an all black Ford Raptor...” he starts to say, then stops as he sees my *I'm totally interested but have no idea of what you speak* look. “You're in the back, Baby Girl,” he smirks, with a *there, there, don't worry your pretty little head about it* look. *Bastard.*

He opens the door for me, and I climb in, which is pretty fucking hard in a full length dress given how high the damn truck is! I see Kai is already sitting on the other side, and as I sit down, Loki gets in behind me so I am once again in between the two of them. Not that I’m complaining.

Kai leans over to buckle me in, his hand brushing my hip slightly as he pulls away. It distracts me momentarily from my swirling thoughts about what is about to happen. He gives me a sad smile, not saying anything, but laces our fingers together, bringing our hands onto his lap.

I'm so nervous I can feel my hand shaking both of ours in his firm grip. Fingers trace the side of my face and down my neck, as Loki's vanilla scent washes over me. It's mixed with fresh sweat from all of the dancing, making the smell even more intoxicating and I take a deep inhale, letting it calm me a little.

“Relax, Pretty Girl,” he breathes against my ear, increasing my tremble. Now I'm nervous and horny. *Fucking great!*

I hear the deep rumble of the engine, reminding me of Jax's voice, and my thighs clench. *Do It For Me* by Rosenfeld blasts over the speakers, the bass adding another layer of vibration that I feel in my core.

When my shaking doesn't subside after a few minutes, Loki leans in again.

“Let me help you, Lilly,” he purrs softly into my ear, nuzzling my neck and gently nipping and caressing it with his tongue, sending pleasurable shivers cascading all over my skin. I hum aloud at the sensation, which goes straight to my clit, making it burn. “Can I touch you, baby? Just my fingers and you tell me to stop at any moment if it's too much,” he pleads in low tones.

I swallow hard. I want him so badly, but what if it triggers memories I'd rather forget? Loki just waits patiently until I nod my head.

A breath of relief whooshes out of him, then he leans forward, sliding a hand under the hem of my dress. He slowly brings it up my leg, lifting the dress with him, the train making it loose enough to allow the movement. His trailing fingers send electric pulses zinging over my body, and my hand tightens in Kai's grip. He looks down and curses softly.

"Loki..." he hisses in a warning tone as Loki's hand reaches the top of my thigh, exposing my stocking clad thigh to the cool air inside the truck. We were all so overheated that we didn't turn the heater on, which I'm doubly glad for now.

"She needs relaxing, so stop whining, and do something useful," Loki snaps back, not at all chastised, his hand continuing to move upwards.

Kai takes a second, huffs out a breath, then uses the hand not gripped in mine to undo the bow of my halter, pulling the fabric away from my breasts. Both boys exhale loudly when they see the red lace strapless corset I'm wearing underneath, my nipples peaked and visible through the sheer fabric.

"Jesus fucking Christ!" I hear Jax curse from the front, my eyes snapping up to his blue ones in the rearview mirror. The truck jerks slightly as his own eyes flit back to the road. "I'm gonna turn up with a fucking hard on," he grumbles, continuing to drive.

I look down to see Ash gripping his armrest so tightly his knuckles are white. Loki must see this, too.

"Don't you wanna see, Ash?" he teases, just as he moves his hand up higher, caressing the edge of my lace thong, and I groan, my eyelids becoming hooded.

Ash's knuckles get even whiter, then he turns in his seat, his eyes trailing up my exposed leg, to where Loki has his hand between my thighs. His gaze travels further up my body to my lace covered breasts. Finally, his eyes come up to meet mine, and I gasp at the raw longing and potent desire in their grey depths.

He holds my gaze as Loki's fingers slip inside the lace that's covering my aching cunt, grazing my lower lips. At the same time, Kai brings his head down, placing his mouth over the lace of my corset and sucking hard on my nipple. I gasp, writhing on the leather seat, my other hand clutching Loki's thigh. Being watched by Ash has heightened things before, and this time is no different.

"Okay, Pretty Girl?" Loki asks huskily.

"Yes," I rasp out, as Kai swirls his tongue around my nipple before blowing on it, the cool air making it harden more.

"Good."

Loki's hand slips in more, his finger using my own wetness to help glide around and over my clit, sending shockwaves through me. My hand tightens in Kai's grip as they start to work me into a frenzy, Loki at my clit, and Kai on my nipple until I'm thrumming with the need for more.

"Loki..." I plead, not knowing what I'm asking for, but hoping that he does.

"I got you, Pretty Girl," he whispers, before sliding one long finger down to my opening, slowly pushing it inside me. "Still okay?" he asks, and I can only nod. It feels so good to have him inside me, even if it's only his finger.

Loki starts moving the digit in and out of me, crooking it in a come hither motion, and hitting my g-spot every damn time. His palm grinds into my clit, the intense pleasure the bundle of nerves brings, making me squirm in my seat.

"Look at me, Princess," I hear Ash command, his voice deep and strained. My eyelids crack open to find his steely gaze on me and an intense look of desire in them. "Good girl," he praises, and I can't help the satisfaction I get from pleasing him. "Add another finger, Loki," he orders, and I whimper in ecstasy as Loki complies. "Now. I want you to come all over Loki's fingers, soaking the seat underneath you, understood?" he commands, his voice husky and low.

He's unable to help taking charge and issuing orders, but I am so here for it.

The thing is, I'm powerless to disobey, and I can feel the exquisite burn of an orgasm begin in my core at his words.

"Kai!" I gasp, gripping his hand tighter, and praying he knows that I need a little edge of pain to tip me over. Without warning, Kai bites down, hard, his mouth wide over my nipple.

It sets off an explosion inside me, and I cry out my release, throwing my head back and feeling the gush between my legs, coating Loki's hand.

I sit there, legs spread, panting, as my whole body tingles in the aftermath of my climax.

"There should be a clean towel in the gym bag down there," I hear Jax grumble. He sounds so pissed, and I'm too spent to stifle a giggle.

I moan as Loki withdraws his fingers and hand, then seconds later, I hear the zip of a bag, before I feel a soft towel between my legs.

"I fear the dress needs a dry cleaner," I groan out, managing to muster enough energy to unbuckle my seatbelt, then turn my back to Kai, wordlessly asking him to unzip me. He complies, brushing his fingers down my spine, sending more shivers skittering over me.

I manage to wiggle out of the dress, leaving it in a shimmering pile on the floor at my feet, and leaving me in my lace corset, thong, red stockings, and heels.

Loki groans, his head thumping the headrest.

"She's trying to fucking kill us, I swear," he laments, eyes closed.

"Pass me that bag, you numpty," I say with a smile, still kneeling on the seat. I feel hands wrap around my hips and look behind me to see Kai holding onto me.

"You're not buckled in, Lilly love," he tells me, and my heart skips at the endearment.

"Why the fuck isn't she..." I hear Jax start, then stop abruptly. I look up to see his gaze once again in the mirror. His blue eyes burn with a fire so intense my breath hitches.

"Eyes on the fucking road, Jax!" Ash shouts as the truck swerves, Ash's hand on the wheel. "Lilly, put some fucking clothes on," Ash admonishes, turning to look at me.

He can't hide the heat that is still there in his gaze. Feeling playful, I stick my tongue out at him, and his eyes narrow in response.

"Naughty, Lilly," Loki chuckles, holding the bag open for me to look inside. My choice is limited as it's Jax's gym bag.

*Ah, this'll do nicely!* I think as I take out a black tank top with a white skull printed on the front. Pulling it over my head, it falls to mid thigh, just exposing the tops of my red lacy stockings. The armholes are huge, gaping down to my waist and flashing my lace corset, but it'll do.

"Better?" I ask Ash, an eyebrow raised.

"Marginally," he quips back, nostrils flared and turning to face the front once again.

"Not fucking better," I hear Jax grunt from the driver's seat.

I sit back down and buckle myself in, just as we pull off the main road and down a dirt track. Luckily, the truck's suspension is pretty good, and the road isn't too bumpy. We drive down the track for about ten minutes, before the headlights swing over a wooden cabin standing in a clearing.

It's two stories, in what looks like an L shape, though it's hard to tell in the dark. There's a front door under a porch that's made up from the overhang of the first floor. I can see windows, but they're all dark. The place looks in good condition, but not like it's used that often.

We park up in front, everyone sitting still for a moment in silence.

"Last chance to back out, Princess," Ash mocks like the arsehole that he is, turning to face me once more.

I just shake my head, unable to utter a word. The butterflies are back, only now it feels like they've got barbs on the end of their wings, scratching and digging into my insides.

"You all know the drill," Ash states cryptically, unbuckling his seatbelt and opening the door, which lets in a blast of cold air that travels across my skin, pebbling my nipples to hard points, and I shudder.

"Anytime you want to leave, just say the word," Kai insists, bringing my gaze to him. Again, I just nod. I can't seem to speak, my mouth as dry as the desert.

He stares into my eyes for a moment longer, then reaches over to unbuckle me, and then himself. He opens his door and gets out, holding out his hand for me to take.

I inhale deeply and place my hand in his, letting him help me out of the truck, letting go of his hand and then shutting the door behind me. Before I can take a step towards the house, Jax is in front of me, still just wearing his He-Man costume, looking fucking delicious. He backs me up against the side of the truck, his eyes devouring me in his tank, and my cherry red underwear.

His knuckles tickle down the open armhole of the tank, caressing the side of my breast.

"It looks better on you," he rumbles, his hand wrapping around the front of my throat with a growl. Slamming his lips against mine, he leaves me no choice but to open to him. His tongue plunders my mouth, possessing me completely and totally, and I can feel his massive hard on pressed against me.

Pulling away, his blue eyes are locked on me, churning with lust. We're both breathing hard, our breath fogging in the cool night air. I do a full body shiver with cold, as well as a healthy dollop of lust, and that seems to break the spell.

"Let's get you inside," he says, in that gorgeous deep voice of his.

He takes my arm, helping guide me to the door in the darkness. There's no moon tonight, so although the stars look incredible, there's not a great deal of light to see by.

My heels clack up the timber steps as I walk up them onto the porch. The wooden door looks suspiciously sturdy and reinforced, and there's a small black screen where you'd expect to see a lock. Loki and Kai walk up behind me as Ash lifts his thumb to the screen. A second later, there's a click, then the door swings open and Ash goes through it, holding it open for me to enter.

As we step inside, gentle lights come on casting a soft glow around the space, and the whole place feels warm. The decor is what I can only describe as a hunter's wet dream. The walls are exposed wood, as is the floor, and along the left hand side wall is a rustic wooden staircase, leading to the floor above, which has a balcony and doors that come off of it.

There's a stone chimney breast at the end opposite us, a roaring fire inside the grate, brown leather sofas and big armchairs in front of it. I can see what looks like a dining area to the right, behind a wooden bar. There are animal pelts thrown over the furniture, and animal heads mounted to the walls, which, to be honest, is a little creepy.

To the right of the chimney is a wooden door, and it's in this direction that Ash leads us. He stops in front of it, scanning his thumbprint again, before grasping the brass handle and opening the door, revealing a set of stairs going down. Ash goes first, then Jax, myself, Loki, and finally Kai follows.

There are wall lights that cast their glow on the staircase so that we can see where we are going. It feels like any other converted basement, however, dread still pools in my stomach as we head down.

We reach a metal door at the bottom, which has yet another fingerprint scanner, and as Ash opens the door, our ears are assaulted with *I Love You* from Barney the Purple Dinosaur, blaring out at a deafening volume.

*What the...*

# CHAPTER THIRTY-ONE

LILLY

"What the fuck is this shit?!" Ash shouts, walking over to a panel on the wall to turn it off.

"Hey!" Loki hollers back, pushing past us in a bid to reach the panel first. "They use this song in Guantánamo Bay as part of their PSYOPS. I thought it would help Robert pass the time."

And that's when I fully look into the stark white room and see Robert, lying on a metal surgical table. He has a thick leather band with a buckle around his waist, as well as cuffs at the wrists and ankles pinning him down.

My nose wrinkles as I see that he's naked and lying in his own piss. There's a blindfold over his eyes, and as Ash turns off the God awful song, he starts thrashing and shouting out.

"Where the fuck am I?! Let me go! You'll be hearing from my father about this!" he spits out, saliva coating his chin.

I look at him, prone and vulnerable, and I feel numb. Like, this should freak me the fuck out, but it just doesn't. He hurt me, tried to fucking rape me, and I'm glad he is now in the position he put me in. At someone else's mercy. Only his situation is far worse, as he's unable to escape the nightmare of his reality.

"I'm just gonna put my playlist on. I've been working on it for the past couple of days, and I must say it's the best one I've come up with yet," Loki tells the room, a wild look in his eyes as he does something with the panel on the wall, and *Raging on a Sunday* by Bohnes comes over the speakers.

"You've got a fucking playlist?" I ask incredulously, arching a brow.

"Music is the soundtrack to your life, Pretty Girl," he winks at me. I just roll my eyes back at him.

"Loki, is that fucking you?" Robert shouts, my eyes dart back over to where he is at the sound of his voice. "I'll fucking kill you for this!" he threatens, which just makes Loki laugh maniacally.

Jax makes his way over to Robert and in a rough move, pulls off the blindfold.

"Happy Halloween!" Loki shouts, then howls like a wolf as he moves over to the table to stand on the other side of Robert. The sound raises the hair on the back of my neck, and goosebumps shiver across my skin.

Jax leans down, getting right into Robert's face.

"What did I promise you if you ever looked at, or touched Lilly again?" Jax asks, his voice so cold it burns, and full of the darkness of deeds done in the deepest part of the night.

"Fuck off!" Robert snarls, his face contorted with rage.

"Wrong answer," Jax replies menacingly before straightening up.

He steps up to where Robert's wrists are shackled on either side of his head. I hear a crack, which makes me jump, as he casually breaks one of Robert's fingers, making Robert scream in pain. Jax doesn't even break a sweat. Loki laughs again, but it's not his usual joyous laugh. It's cruel and cuts to the bone.

I feel like I should be more horrified, appalled at what they are doing to another human. But I'm not.

I once saw an episode of QI where they debated a supposed George Orwell quote:

*'People sleep peaceably in their beds at night only because rough men stand ready to do violence on their behalf'.*

Although, it was surmised that Orwell didn't actually say this, the quote comes to mind now as I watch these guys, my Black Knights, seek vengeance on my behalf. And I don't feel horror, or revulsion or whatever it is I'm meant to be feeling. Instead, I'm full of gratitude that these warriors will do what is necessary to keep me safe.

"You can't do this to me! My father will fucking murder you all and leave your corpses to rot!" Robert screams out, snot and spit flying as he fruitlessly tries to escape.

"Ah, that's not quite accurate," Kai interjects, voice devoid of all emotion. Kai steps up next to Jax so that Robert can see him, his iPad in his hand. "It seems that your father, Governor Michaels, was arrested tonight for having a laptop full of child pornography, alongside several accusations of sex with minors. So, I'm afraid he won't be of much help."

He turns the screen so that Robert can see it. It shows a live news program with video footage of what I assume is Robert's father. He's being led away in handcuffs, from what looks like a swanky Halloween party, dressed in a tux with devil horns. *Gotta love irony.*

"What the fuck did you do?!" Robert squeaks as Loki laughs once again.

"Your father did it to himself. I guess the apple really doesn't fall far from the tree," Ash drawls in a bored tone, going over to stand near the table.

I'm still standing not far into the room, my eyes locked on the scene unfolding before me.

*Come on, Lilly, you can do this.*

I take one step towards the centre of the room, then another and another, until I finally approach the table. Ash hears me step up towards him, so he moves to one side, leaving a space for me in between him and Jax.

I clasp my hands into fists at my sides, to stop them shaking as nerves start to creep back into me, breaking through the numbness. Robert's head turns to the side, his brown eyes landing on mine. I see them widen a second before they fill with scornful loathing.

"What the fuck is this whore doing here?" he snarls, and I hear Jax growl before another snap fills the room, which makes me flinch as Robert screams again.

"You don't look at her," Jax barks, and I look up to see that I've lost him to the violence that's running through his veins, filling his blood with the need to hurt. He should look ridiculous in his He-Man outfit, but he doesn't. He looks like an avenging God, full of wrath and with the kiss of death on his lips.

The song fades to be replaced by *Oh Lord* by In This Moment. I shiver at the words, creating a sense of unease inside me.

"Oh, you're pissed because she's a fucking teasing whore?" Robert asks, voice filled with pain, but also the arrogance of someone who has never had to face the consequences of his actions before. "She was fucking begging for it, saying how your cocks were too small to keep her satisfied," he taunts, goading the guys, which is pretty fucking stupid.

Another crack fills the room followed immediately by Robert's hoarse scream, as Jax snaps a third finger.

"No, you tried to rape her, you piece of shit," Loki snarls at him, pulling his fist back and punching Robert in the face, making his head snap to the side, blood dripping from his now split lip. Loki's panting, his chest rising and falling with angry breaths. I ache to go to him but I'm rooted to the spot.

"And from these buried reports, it looks like you've been getting your rocks off by raping women for quite some time," Kai adds. I look at him in shock, catching his gaze, and the hardness in his honey amber eyes softens slightly.

*This cuntface is a real piece of work.*

"Where the fuck did you get those?" Robert asks, voice raspy and pained, his head turning to look at Kai.

Kai just smiles back at him. Robert is actually starting to look a little unsure, like he's suddenly realised that he's not coming out of this basement with only a few broken fingers.

"So you see, Robert, we know all of your dirty little secrets. And those of that paedophile daddy of yours. Now that he's been taken care of, the question remains, what to do with you?" Ash states, his head tilted to one side, like a cat contemplating its prey, and trying to decide on the best way to play with it before devouring it. "I believe Jax already told you what your punishment will be?"

"I–I–I can get you anything you need. I h–have funds of my own," Robert stutters out, and the memory of when Jax helped me in the school hallway floats to my mind.

*"You ever touch her, fucking look at her again, I will tear your fucking balls off with my bare fucking hands."*

My wide eyes snap to Jax, who has an awful smile on his face as he gazes at Robert strapped to the table. It's the smile of vengeance, of violence and bloodshed, and I briefly wonder why it doesn't terrify me. I look to Loki, who has a similar sinister smile stretching his beautiful lips, which sits at odds with his angelic features. My eyes find Kai next, whose face is set in grim determination. However, there is a fire in his eyes, something that tells me he is enjoying this. Finally, my head turns to look to my left and tilts up to meet Ash's gaze. His is the most frightening, as there's nothing there. It's like his humanity has fled, and all that's left is an empty shell. His eyes meet mine, and a flicker of something enters them, before disappearing again.

"We don't need your money, Robert," Ash turns back to the guy pinned down and helpless, sounding bored. "You have nothing that we want or need."

Ash looks up and nods at Loki, who goes and collects an instrument tray, wheeling it over next to Jax.

Robert's head turns at the noise, and his eyes go wide, the whites showing as he catalogues the instruments on the tray. Black latex gloves, a scalpel, some kind of metal clamp looking thing, and a tube of superglue.

The song finishes and *The Law* by Reach begins to play. I swallow hard, looking back up at Ash as he clears his throat.

"Robert Michaels, you have been found guilty of being a rapist and all-around cunt. You are hereby sentenced to castration without anaesthesia. May God have mercy upon your fucking soul, because we sure as hell won't." His voice is devoid of any feeling or emotion. He's not even angry and I feel myself breathing shallowly, my heart pounding, my hands cold and shaking slightly.

Instinctively, I reach out and grasp Ash's warm hand, interlocking our fingers. His nostrils flare, then he turns his head to look down at me. I have to suppress a gasp when his grey eyes meet mine. There's a look of intense sorrow in them as he gazes down, the likes of which I've never seen on his face before.

I don't think it's sorrow at what is happening before us, but more that I am having to witness it and see their true nature. Like he would save me from this if he could. I can't smile to reassure him that I'm okay, because honestly, I'm not sure if I am. I will never be the same after this night, more than the blood of my mother's death will be on my hands, and they will never be clean again.

Jax moving breaks my stare off with Ash. Jax comes around the head of the table, walking down to stand next to Robert's crotch. Robert is thrashing and crying, angry hopeless tears trailing down his face.

"I'd be still if I were you," Loki leans down to whisper threateningly in Robert's ear. "You wouldn't want Jax to cut off your dick by mistake," he chuckles darkly.

I feel a little sick and lightheaded, my breaths coming faster, and although I'm trying to control them, I can feel panic start to claw at the edges of my vision as Jax snaps the gloves onto his hands.

Suddenly, hands grasp my upper arms, and I'm turned to the side.

"Look at me, Princess," Ash commands, and I obey immediately, lifting my head up and looking into his grey eyes in desperation. "That's it, good girl," he praises, his tone soothing, and completely at odds with how he was moments ago.

The wounded scream of an animal in pain rends the air, and my head goes to turn, but is stopped by a gentle hand on either side of it.

"Eyes on me, Princess. Don't look anywhere else," his voice coaxes, and I keep my eyes locked with his. They are full of anguish, yet also some emotion that I can't, or don't, dare to name. "Now breathe with me, darling, that's it," he encourages as I follow his deep inhales and exhales.

Tears start to fall from my eyes as the screaming turns to whimpers, so full of agony my soul weeps. The sounds stop, and all I can hear is that the song has changed to *Monsters*, by Tommee Profitt and Xeah, the beat matching my heartbeat.

"Loki, adrenaline shot," Ash calls out, eyes never leaving mine. Seconds later, the whimpering starts again.

"Ash..." I whisper, not knowing what to say, just knowing that my heart hurts, my soul lamenting.

Not for Robert, he deserves to face the consequences of his abhorrent behaviour. My heart hurts for these men, these boys who have had to do this, and probably a thousand other horrible and depraved things in their lives so far.

"Shhh...it'll be over soon, darling, I promise," he says in that calming voice of his, surprising me as he wraps me up in his strong arms, enveloping me in his spicy ginger scent. I breathe him in, absorbing his strength and wrapping my own arms around his waist, burying my head into his chest.

What feels like hours later, Jax speaks.

"All done," he says in a rumble. I lift my head from Ash's chest, noticing the mess my makeup has made of his black shirt, leaving smudges of white and other colours on the cloth.

Keeping my arms tight around him, I look up and catch Jax's eyes. His hard gaze softens as he meets my eyes. "You alright, Baby Girl?" he asks gently, and I nod.

"Is she alright?!" Robert screeches, his voice broken and raspy from screaming. "The fuck does that whore have to be worried about?" he spits as I hear several growls, including the rumbling growl of Ash that I feel vibrating against my chest.

My gaze turns to look at Robert. Blood still trickles from his lip, he's slick with sweat and shaking. His brown eyes are crazed, pupils blown. I realise that for the first time, the blood doesn't send me spiralling into a flashback of the day my mother died. That I'm actually glad to see it dripping down from him, and a slow smile spreads across my face. Robert sees this, and his eyes flash with pure undiluted rage.

"I should've fucked you until your cunt was bleeding, and choked you out, watching the life fade from your eyes, my dick still inside you," he snarls at me, eyes full of loathing like this is all my fault.

All hell breaks loose before I can even register what's happening. The guys are cursing him out, Loki grabbing the bloody scalpel and lunging for Robert's neck, Jax pulls out a dagger from somewhere, and Kai's eyes flash dangerously. Ash is deathly still underneath my arms, like he's turned into a marble statue.

I know that Robert's words have tipped them over the edge, and if I don't do something, they will kill him here and now.

"Stop!" I cry out in a sob. Surprisingly, they all do as I ask and freeze. "If you kill him, his death will be on me. On my conscience. Please, I can't have another death on my hands," I beg them, looking into each of their eyes as I speak, pleading with them.

I look up to Ash last, who is still wrapped in my arms as I am in his. "Please, Ash," I ask, imploring him with my eyes to stop this.

His own have darkened to a slate grey, filled with hatred. Is it just for Robert, or for himself too? They bore into me, digging down into my very soul.

"Jax." his deep voice sounds out. I hear Jax dropping his knife with a clatter, and then the sound of fists hitting flesh, and grunts of pain as Ash leads me away.

None of the others follow as we head up the stairs, and I don't dare look back. I can't bear to see them mete out further punishment. Perhaps that makes me a coward. Perhaps it's just self-preservation. Or that I just don't care what they do to that evil man.

These guys, my guys, might be monsters, Black Knights with the souls of demons.

But they're mine, and I belong to them completely.

# CHAPTER THIRTY-TWO

LILLY

Ash and I wait upstairs, a fire roaring in the fireplace. I notice now that although it looks like logs, it's actually gas. Regardless, the heat wafting from it does nothing to warm the chill that has settled over me, seeping into my very bones.

Some time later, the others come up, and although they're clean, I can see the evidence of what has transpired downstairs. Loki's shirt cuffs are stained pink, and Jax has a couple of splatters of blood that he's clearly missed when cleaning up.

"Let's head home, Pretty Girl," Loki mumbles, not meeting my eyes as he leads the way out of the cabin. I want to assure him that it's okay, but he's gone before I can.

We arrive back at Highgate just as the sun breaks into the sky. I can hear the dawn chorus fill the air as I exit the car, and it's so at odds with what just happened, my brain is struggling to compute. The air is fresh and pure, and I take in a great lungful, as if its purity will spread through me and wash me clean from the inside out.

We walk up the stone steps to the huge front doors, and it feels like years, not weeks ago, since I first approached them. I feel even more bone-weary than I did back then, like my whole body can't go another step. I falter, and Ash catches me before I faceplant into the stone. He must see something in my gaze because he suddenly sweeps me up into his arms and carries me bridal style over the threshold and up the stairs to our dorm.

"Ash, I can manage from here, thank you," I say quietly as we walk through our door.

He just grunts at me, taking a leaf out of Jax's book, and heads to the bathroom. He sets me down next to the shower, reaching in to turn it on. Turning back to me, I can see conflict in his eyes.

Taking another moment, he lifts his phone from his pocket and taps the screen. All of a sudden, *Lonely* by Nathan Wagner starts to play from speakers somewhere in the room.

*Damn! I had no idea they had Bluetooth speakers in here!*

His grey eyes meet mine, and for a second, vulnerability shines through them making my heart skip a beat.

Before I can say anything, he drops to his knees and reaches for my shoe.

"Ash, I can manage," I murmur again softly, my eyes filling with tears as the lyrics of the song sweeps over me.

*Is this how he feels?*

"I know you can," he whispers back, then proceeds to undo the buckle on my shoe, encouraging me to step out of it.

He does the same with the other, then moves his hands up my stocking-clad leg to unhook one suspender, then the other. Grasping my hips in a firm grip, he turns me around to do the same to the back. Taking the top of my red lacy stocking in his fingers, he slowly rolls it down my legs. Then he repeats this with the other one.

Even with everything that has happened tonight, and despite all that has happened between us, my breath hitches as his touch burns my skin. My nipples harden to points, and desire for this beautiful, broken man floods through me with the force of a meteor.

Next, he reaches for my thong and glides it over my hips and down my legs. I'm practically shaking with all of the emotions that are running through me, my weariness all but fading away. I step out of the lace, and his hands glide back up my legs to grasp my hips once again, turning me back to face him.

His hands tighten their grip, and I can see that he's almost gasping, his chest rising and falling with each hard breath. He stands up, his hands moving upwards and taking Jax's tank top up and off of me, leaving me in just my red lacy corset. His nostrils flare, and his eyes flood with pure lust as he takes me in, palms coming to rest on my waist.

Leaning forward, he rests his forehead against mine.

"I should walk away and leave you right now," he growls out, his grip tightening painfully. "But I can't, Lilly, I can't leave the only light to have ever come into my life. I'm not strong enough, and I'm too selfish to deny myself."

His words set a fire inside me, my heart racing at what he's saying.

"So don't leave, Ash," I whisper back.

He inhales sharply, then his lips come down hard onto mine in a kiss that defies gravity. His tongue presses along the seam of my mouth seeking entry, and I open up gladly, letting him in as my hands come to the lapels of his suit jacket, pushing it off of his shoulders to land with a soft thud on the tiles.

Vaguely, I register that the song has changed to <3 by Vi, her voice weaving its way over and inside me, the lyrics so perfect for this moment between us, that moisture stings my eyes. I've known that Ash wanted me, that he felt the overwhelming need for me the same way that I've felt it for him. But having him finally give in, finally close that distance that we've had between us this whole time...It's like nothing on this earth. I feel complete, like all the parts of me are where they belong, and although I'm a little nervous about having a flashback of that awful night in the library, I couldn't stop this even if I wanted to.

My trembling fingers unbutton his shirt, exposing his glorious inked chest, as his hands come off my waist for a moment to help me take it off, our lips still fused. Once the shirt is on the floor, he pulls me into him, and I gasp into his mouth at the feel of his hard, hot body pressing into my lace covered breasts.

His fingers come around to my back, and start to unhook the many hooks that fasten my corset. Releasing my mouth, he starts to kiss and nuzzle down my neck. I moan aloud, grasping his ebony hair in my fingers.

Finally, the lace falls to the floor, and almost immediately, his mouth comes over my nipple sucking hard. It's the side that Kai bit earlier and is still a little sore, but the flash of pain only drives me wilder.

"Ash, please..." I beg him, needing more to ease the ache that he's created.

He gives my nipple one last suck, then drops back down to his knees. He looks at my bare pussy for a moment, his warm breath tickling me. Slowly leaning forward, he takes an exploratory lick, swirling his tongue around my clit, and I moan low and loud. He makes a satisfied noise in the back of his throat at my response, before he suddenly buries his face in my cunt.

Pleasure explodes across my whole body, lighting me up from the inside out. My hand grabs his hair once more as my hips start to move against his face, urging him deeper and harder. I can hear his satisfied groans, like I'm his favourite meal and he just can't get enough.

"Ash!" I gasp out as I feel the familiar rush of an orgasm begin to sweep over me. He inserts two long fingers inside me, thrusting them in and out as his tongue continues to pulse against my clit.

"I'm so close, Ash," I whimper, feeling the orgasm start to burn.

At that moment, he crooks his fingers and sucks hard on my clit, nipping it with his teeth, sending me over the edge into the abyss. I scream my release, my whole body flashing white with a lightning bolt.

After a few moments, Ash gets up, and I can't help but giggle, making him raise a perfect black brow.

"I think you'll need a shower too," I chuckle.

His mouth and chin are not only glistening with my release, but also smeared with my face paint, until he looks like some kind of debauched clown.

He looks up into the mirror behind us, and his lips lift up in a smile that takes my breath away with its beauty. This is the smile he would give all the time if his life was different. If he didn't have to do what he does.

"Get in," he tells me, his voice unusually soft.

As I turn to step into the shower, I see his hands go to his belt buckle, undoing it. I step under the hot spray and groan, letting the delicious jets do their work, and loosen my tight muscles.

I feel the brush of cool air across my back seconds before his strong hands alight on my waist, gripping tightly, long fingers indenting my soft skin. Turning me around to face him Ash holds up a face cloth and proceeds to wipe the makeup off my face, before doing the same to his own.

He looks glorious, his hard, toned, inked body covered in droplets of water that sparkle under the lights. He makes me think of Poseidon, all restrained violence and ill-tempered, yet tonight there's also a vulnerability to him that makes him more man than god.

My eyes trace along the valleys and furrows of his mouth watering abs, deciding to ask about all the pictures that cover his skin later as my gaze follows those gorgeous v muscles down to his erect cock, which is so hard it's almost lying flat against his stomach. Like the others, he's definitely above average in the size department, and the image of him thrusting his hard length inside me leaves me breathless.

"Lilly," he warns, his voice husky and dark. "I can only hold back for so long, especially if you keep looking at me like that."

My eyes flit up to his grey ones, his pupils blown with lust and his nostrils flared.

"So don't hold back, Ash," I whisper, feeling a sense of rightness settle over me.

"Are you sure?" he questions, and it's that, if nothing else, that tells me he's no monster.

"Yes," I simply say, my eyes still locked on his. The heat in his grey orbs flares to an inferno as he takes me in, wet and naked under the shower.

Slowly and with a control that is maddening, yet endearing all at once, one of his hands leaves my waist to cup the side of my face, his thumb stroking my cheek tenderly.

*You're The One That I Want,* the Lo Fang version, begins to play as he leans in and presses his lips to mine once more. His kiss is slow and leisurely, his mouth exploring every inch of mine as he draws us closer. Breaking our kiss, his lips go to my neck once more, kissing and nipping down it, sucking at the point where it meets my shoulder.

"Jesus, Lilly," he rasps out. "You're everything I never knew I fucking needed." His words are a balm that soothes my soul.

"Ash," I gasp out as he moves to the other side of my neck, lavishing the same attention onto it. "Since I met you, all of you, I've never felt so alive. I need you to make me feel, to make me live," I confess, becoming a little shy as he stops and straightens up.

His eyes meet mine again, and the look in them is so intense, so full of everything, that I can barely grasp what it all means. There's lust, and possession, fear, and even perhaps, dare I say, love.

Suddenly, he swoops down, grasping me under my thighs and lifting me up so that my legs come up and wrap around his waist as my arms come around his wet shoulders. Stepping out of the still running shower, he walks over to the open door and strides out, heading towards the lit fire. Both of us are still naked and dripping, Ash leaving wet footprints in the carpet.

I notice the other guys on the sofas, who all sit up as Ash takes me right in front of the fire, the warmth of the flames licking over my damp skin. I can still hear the song as he gets to his knees, lying me down on my back, the soft rug tickling my skin.

His eyes burn into mine, rendering me unable to look away.

"Loki," he says, confusing me until a foil packet lands next to him.

A giggle escapes my lips, his own lifting ever so slightly as he opens the packet and rolls the rubber on. Lowering onto his hands, he leans over me, his body covering mine, and everywhere he touches burns with a delicious heat.

"Is this okay?" he asks, and I nod, my gaze flitting to the sofas to see Kai, Loki, and Jax all with similar heated looks in their eyes.

"Look at me, Princess," Ash commands as he shifts his hips, and I feel him nudge my entrance. For a second, I'm back in that library, Robert pinning me down, and I can't help stiffening up.

"It's me, Princess. It's Ash," I hear Ash say, his soft voice bringing me back to our dorm.

My eyes fill with tears, and I have to choke back a sob.

*Will I never be free of him?*

"Do you want me to stop?" Ash asks, body frozen above me, his grey eyes pained and full of concern.

"No...I need him gone," I manage to say, my voice full of the frustration I'm feeling.

"Get on top, Pretty Girl," I hear Loki suggest, making my head turn to look at him. "Pin Ash down and take back control."

I look back to Ash who gives me a rueful smile. "You can have control," he says, leaning down to nuzzle my ear. "This time," he can't help but add. *Dickhead.*

In a move that makes me squeal, he flips us so that he's now lying on his back, and I'm on top of him, our chests pressed together. A thrill runs down my spine.

I lean even closer, placing my lips next to his ear. "Hands above your head, *Lucifer*," I whisper, then nip his earlobe. "And keep them there."

Straightening up, I see his mouth set in an indulgent smile. Slowly, he lifts his hands, bringing them above his head and crossing his wrists. My breath catches, and I have to take a minute to appreciate the sight before me, of Ash doing my bidding. Ash is giving me power over him to help me heal. And maybe, just maybe, to help himself heal a little, too.

“Good boy,” I can't resist but tease, earning a flash of heat from Ash, and chuckles from the others. Rising up onto my knees, I grasp his hardness in my hand, lining him up and sinking down slowly, until my opening is flush with his pelvis.

Both of us groan with how fucking good it feels for him to be finally, fully inside me. I can see his arms straining, wanting to reach out and grab me. Vaguely, I register the groans of the other boys, and looking over, I can see that they all now have their hard cocks in their hands. The sight winds me up even tighter, knowing how much I affect them is its own potent aphrodisiac.

The song changes to *Power* by Isak Danielson and the opening words flow over me in perfect sentiment for this moment.

I start to move on Ash, slowly at first, relishing the feel of him inside and underneath me. The sounds coming from his throat are music to my ears, encouraging me to go faster, and I begin to use my thighs to bounce up and down on his cock, riding him hard.

Looking down, his eyes are on my body, devouring me with his gaze. Moving one of my hands down, my fingers find my clit and start to rub circles around and over it, sending exquisite tingles shooting across my skin.

“Jesus, Princess,” Ash growls out, his voice strained as he watches me touch myself with fire in his eyes.

“Fuck, Ash!” I gasp, feeling the burn of another orgasm begin. I start to slam down on him, one hand reaching out and using his hard abs for balance.

My orgasm detonates, sweeping over and through me with a force that leaves me shaking and seeing stars. Ash roars his release moments later, as I fall forward onto his sweaty chest. We're both panting hard, when I hear a chorus of groans from the others, as they too find their own climaxes.

We all just stay there, not speaking, breathing each other in. The crackle of the fire, and the shower that’s still going, are the only sounds in the room. Ash's playlist must have finished because I can't hear any music.

Ash brings his hands to wrap around me, holding me close to him whilst he's still buried inside me.

“You okay, Princess?” he asks softly, rubbing my back gently.

"Mum-huh," I manage to mumble out, my eyes drifting shut as I'm lured to sleep by the warmth of the fire and Ash's soothing hands.

---

## ASH

I lie there, naked, with Lilly on top of me, my spent dick still inside her, the fire tickling my hot skin. I can feel her body relaxing, getting heavier as I rub circles on her bare back, relishing the feel of her smooth skin.

I can't not touch her, it's like my hands have a mind of their own and just lose control. It's a control I've worked so hard for, shed blood, sweat, and tears for, and this girl tears it away as if it's a spiderweb in her way.

I can't deny there was something freeing about relinquishing myself to her, of letting her take her pleasure from me, pinning me with her delectable body. It was a pleasure I'd not experienced before. Usually, I'm the one in full dominance, taking what I want with little thought to the pleasure of others. Don't get me wrong, they always come screaming, but with Lilly, it's like a fucking competition to see how many times I can make her orgasm before I seek my own release.

I look up to see my friends, my brothers, looking over at us. Their eyes are soft as they gaze at her, caressing her skin with a tenderness that our fathers, and Kai's uncle, have tried their hardest to beat out.

The thought reminds me of the time she met my father, of the way he looked at her as if she was a new toy, a toy he'd love to break. My arms tighten around her, making her sigh out and shift closer.

"We have to keep her safe," I whisper out, but I know they've all heard me when each pair of eyes goes hard. "They can't know her involvement tonight." I look back down at the top of her head and can't help but place a gentle kiss there.

"How will we explain Robert? And his dad?" Loki asks, a tinge of concern in his voice.

"We say they were trying to undermine Black Knight Corp," Kai says, his voice low so as not to wake the sleeping beauty on top of me. "Governor Michaels was trying to cut a deal with Glow Worm Pharmaceuticals, so we play on that," he explains, and we all nod. His intelligence gathering astounds me regularly.

"Good," I respond, nodding at Kai, taking up the mantle of leader again. Sometimes the load is so heavy, I don't know how I'll carry on. But I have to. For them, if nothing else.

*Maybe also for her now?* A voice in the back of my mind whispers like an autumn breeze.

"Loki, Jax, why don't you clean up and go to bed," I say, more of an order than a suggestion.

So used to following my orders, they get up and head to the bathroom.

I look at Kai and see that he's staring at me, a soft look on his face. *Bastard is too observant for his own good.*

"You need her, just as much as the rest of us, Ash," he states gently.

I say nothing, unable to deny the simple truth of his words.

Ordinarily, as their leader, I look out for their welfare over my own, seeing to their needs first. But, I'm feeling selfish tonight, especially with her warmth seeping into my soul. Kai's right, I need her light, and I'm not ready to give it up just yet.

Loki and Jax come back, breaking our stare. I curl up, my dick finally slipping from her wet folds causing her to softly groan out, but not awaken when I tighten my arms around her as I carefully move her across my lap. Settling my arms under her knees and back, I stand. She really is like a pixie, and I hardly notice her weight as I make my way to the stairs, the others trailing behind.

When I get to my door, a broad hand reaches past me to open it, allowing me to step in. Jax goes around to the bed, pulling the covers down for us as Loki dims the lights to a faint glow. Kai places a glass of water on one of the bedside cabinets, whilst Loki draws the curtains.

I place Lilly on the bed, careful not to wake her, and as I straighten up I once again catch the gazes of the others. My brothers. No words pass between us, but I can feel the love they have for me as strongly as my own for them.

With a final searing look, they turn and leave, shutting the door softly behind them. I gaze down at Lilly and realise that the strength of feeling I have for those men, is not dimmed when I look at her. If anything, it's almost stronger and mixed in with a fierce need to protect her and eradicate all and any danger.

Heaving a shaky breath, I walk around to the other side of the bed, take off the used jonny and throw it in the trash can before wiping myself with a towel flung over my chair. Then I get into bed, pulling her so close that there's not a single atom of space between our bodies. She lets out a contented sigh, her body relaxing in my arms.

Taking another inhale, breathing in her scent of fresh starts and new beginnings, my eyes drift closed, and for the first time in a long time, I drift off into a dreamless sleep.

# CHAPTER THIRTY-THREE

LILLY

I wake up to a room filled with darkness, yet I feel calm and rested.

My mind wanders to the night before, the Halloween party, dancing with the guys, the car journey, the cabin...

My breathing starts to speed up as images flash across my vision like a movie; the stairs leading to the basement, the surgical table, the black latex gloves, Ash's grey eyes...

I take a deep breath in, trying to soothe my erratic thoughts, and am flooded with the scent of spicy ginger. The comforting smell washes over me, calming my frantic heartbeat. Looking to the side I see Ash, sleeping on his stomach, one arm under his pillow. He looks so peaceful, so beautiful, every inch a tempting devil with his ink covered skin and sharp features. I reach out to push some of that midnight hair away from his brow, but my hand stills, not wanting to wake him.

Deciding to leave him and get something to drink, as quietly as I can, I go to slip from the bed, but a tattooed hand grabs my wrist, making me gasp and turn around.

"Going somewhere, Princess?" His voice is deliciously rough with sleep.

Before I can answer, he tugs, and pulls me back down so that I'm lying underneath him.

"Ash!" I exclaim with a breathy laugh as he nestles between my legs, already growing hard. "I wanted to get a drink."

His lips lift in a positively sinful smirk, then he abruptly kneels up, reaching for a glass of water that is on the bedside drawers. Looking directly into my eyes, his own shining, he takes a drink, leaning over once more to place the glass back. I quirk my brows as he comes to rest on top of me again, his hands on either side of my head, propping him up. Lowering himself down, he places his lips over mine, just barely touching. Suddenly having an idea of what he's doing, I part my lips and a trickle of water passes from his mouth to mine.

I drink it down, and once I'm done he swallows the rest, then licks my lips.

"Better?" he asks softly, our faces so close that even in the low light I can see every shade of grey in his beautiful irises.

"Yes," I whisper back, my hand coming up to run through his hair which is a mess. I love him like this, debauched and rumpled.

"Good," he replies, his lips quirk in a lopsided grin, full of wicked thoughts. "Now that you're sufficiently hydrated," he tells me, leaning in so that his lips are against my ear. "It's time I take control back. Don't you think, Princess?" he tells me, thrusting his hips slightly so that I can feel his hardness pressing against my core.

"Yes, sir," I answer, my breath quickening and my pulse beginning to race at this game we're playing. His length jumps at the word 'sir'.

"Excellent," he says back, a definite rasp to his voice.

He kneels up again, a breath of cool air whispering over my heated skin.

"Hands above your head, Princess, crossed at the wrists, and keep them there," he commands, quoting my own words from earlier back at me. His eyes flare and his dick twitches when I immediately obey. "Good girl." Heat floods my body with the praise.

I watch as he grabs a condom from the drawer, opening the packet and rolling it on, before he comes back down in between my legs, resting on his elbows. His hand comes between us, and he looks down as he lines himself up with my already slick entrance.

"It's not going to be gentle, and I'm not holding back, okay?" he asks, pausing and waiting for my confirmation.

"Okay," I murmur back.

His eyes flood with something like relief, then go hard a second before he thrusts inside me. I cry out with the pleasure-pain it causes, my back arching and it takes every ounce of strength I possess to keep my arms above my head. My legs wrap tightly around his waist, pulling him closer to me.

"Such a good fucking girl," he rasps and he grabs my jaw in one hand, slamming his lips onto mine in a messy kiss that drags my soul from the depths of my being.

His hips move in a punishing gyration, hitting my g-spot and clit simultaneously and sending waves of burning electricity running through my entire body. Breaking our kiss and releasing my jaw, his hands move up my arms to clasp mine, keeping them above my head. It's like he can't help himself, he needs to be touching me everywhere, inside and out.

"Look at me, Lilly" he orders roughly, not breaking his rhythm. I open my eyes, gazing into his and gasping when I see the grey swirl and flicker with luminescent fire. "When I think about you, I burn inside, Princess. My entire being, everything I am and ever could be is yours." I gasp, my eyes filling with moisture, but before I can say anything he continues. "I love you, Lilly Darling, and I will love you until I draw my last breath and my soul descends into the depths below. And when the stars fall from the sky, and the earth shatters into a million pieces my love for you will be in every fucking atom of the galaxy."

"Ash..." I gasp, my hands gripping his so tightly, I can feel the crests that my nails are leaving. A tear escapes the corner of my eye, and he leans down and kisses it, pausing his movements, waiting.

"You're the piece of me that was missing, Ash," I whisper into his ear, and his body sags into mine, his hips moving again and making it difficult to focus on what I want to say. "Even if they were to cut me open, they would find you there. All of you are fused to my very cells, and nothing can ever truly separate us."

He pushes up again, transferring his grip to holding my wrists in one of his hands but keeping them above my head. His weight bearing down on my wrist bones causes a pain that only drives my release closer, and I moan his name loudly.

"Jesus fucking Christ, Lilly," he gasps. His thrusts get harder, the sound of our hips slapping filling the room alongside my gasping breaths and his deep groans.

"Come for me now, Princess. Come all over my dick," he orders, and I'm helpless to resist as his other hand comes between us, pinching my clit so hard, my hips buckle and my inner walls clamp down around him as I scream my climax, coating us both in my juices.

His pace becomes frenzied, then he curses as he reaches his own pinnacle, stilling above me as every muscle goes rigid. Moments later, he releases his grip, my hands tingle slightly with the return of blood flow as he collapses down on top of me, our sweaty bodies sticking together.

We lie like that, putting our fucking souls back together, hearts pounding in perfect synchronicity, our breathing matched.

"Ash," I mumble, and he turns his head to look at me. "I love you."

The smile he gives me is so beautiful, so rare, and precious to me, it's like finding treasure at the end of the rainbow.

"I love you too, Lilly," he replies, leaning close and placing a trembling kiss on my lips.

---

Deciding that I really do need to wash up, I get out of bed, leaving Ash all rumpled and decadent looking, already half asleep with a soft smile on his face. Padding across the room on bare feet and completely naked, I open the door, heading out into the hall and down the stairs.

I pop to the toilet, and after cleaning myself up, I come out of the bathroom and walk over to the kitchen, finding a glass and starting to run the tap.

There's a change in the air, then a warmth at my back as huge, strong arms come around my waist.

"Are you scared of me now, Baby Girl?" Jax's gruff voice sounds in my ear. There's a note of worry in his tone. "After seeing what I'm capable of?"

Leaning back into him, I can't help it, I seek comfort in his powerful embrace. It feels so good to be here in his arms.

"No," I whisper. "I'm not scared of you, Jax. I could never be scared of you," His arms tighten around me, pulling me even closer. "You keep me safe," I add on a breath.

"But?" he asks, his deep voice rumbling across my skin, my nipples instinctively pebbling to hard aching points.

Sighing, I try to gather my thoughts. I bring my hands along his muscular forearms and down to the backs of his own hands, tangling our fingers together.

"But, how can these hands," I bring them up in front of us, "that bring me so much pleasure, that make me feel so safe, be capable of such..." I trail off, unable to bring myself to say the word.

*Pain,* my mind taunts, and for a moment, Jax's hands are dripping red with the blood of his victims. I blink, and they're back to being clean again.

"My mind can't unknow the fact that you've hurt someone with these hands. That you have all hurt people. Badly. Hell, I saw just what you can do last night, and with what happened to my mum..." I sigh, feeling tears prick my eyes. I close them and bring our hands back down, wrapping myself up in his safe arms again. "But, Jax, I'm...I'm in love with you, all of you, and my heart hurts so badly thinking about everything that you've had to do to survive."

Tears are tracking down my cheeks, I just can't stop them. It's true.

"Baby Girl, please don't cry," he says, his own voice made even rougher than usual with emotion.

He turns me around in his arms, wiping my tears away. Ducking his head, he raises my chin, looking into my eyes with his.

"Lilly, baby, I can't speak for Ash and Kai, but, well...ah, fuck!" He takes a deep breath, rubbing the back of his neck with a huge palm and glancing away. "I feel the same. That is..." He looks back to me, meeting my eyes with his beautiful, piercing blue ones. "I'm in love with you, too. And I don't mind that you love them as well."

His confession is awkward as fuck, but even more adorable because of it. This is the most I've ever heard him say in one go, and he's rendered me completely speechless.

"Jax..." I say, reaching out, gliding my fingertips down the side of his face and along his rough bearded jaw.

He's so gorgeous, all the guys are in their own way. Jax takes my breath away every time I look at him with his stunning viking-like colouring and looks, which are heightened by his black tattoos. He exudes strength and violence in equal measure, but I've seen and known him to be so tender and caring. He's the protector of us all.

"And as for what we've done, what we do," he continues, anger lacing his tone. "Lilly, we were kids. Barely fourteen when they took us to the cabin that first time."

My heart aches for them, a flash of hatred for their families runs hot through me, my hand stilling against his cheek. They were just boys when they were forced to do something so abhorrent, it begs belief.

"It doesn't excuse what we did, what we still do, and I don't know if it makes any difference, but there it is."

"Oh, Jax," I gasp out, the burn of more tears stinging my eyes.

Jax begins to turn away from me, his arms starting to drop from around me. I lay my hand on his broad, naked chest, right over his heart, stopping him from leaving. His blue eyes meet mine, and I can see that he's already preparing for rejection.

"Jax, I love you," I say, holding his gaze and willing him to believe me. "And I'm not going anywhere. I'm staying right here. Like I told Ash, since I met you, since I met all of you, I've never felt so alive. And life is always fucked up. Even without psycho families." I smile gently, causing a rueful smile to tug at his plush lips. "I don't regret a single moment, and I'm not leaving." I give him my best badass bitch look, which is rewarded with one of his rare, genuine smiles that melts my heart.

"Now, show me how you love me, Jax," I command, looking directly into his eyes. He hesitates.

*How can they think they're monsters when they behave like this?*

"I need you, all of you, to help take the feel of him away, Jax. Please," I say, knowing that I need his help, all of their help to get through what happened and to fully heal.

Staring into my eyes for a beat longer, his own are swirling pools of blue. Suddenly, he reaches down, hauls me up, and grips my arse tightly. I wrap my legs around his waist, my thighs spread impossibly wide as he's just that stacked. My arms come up, going around his thick neck in a tight embrace that brings us closer.

I start grinding my bare pussy on his hard abs as he carries me over to the kitchen island and sets me down on the edge.

His lips come down onto mine, devouring me with his burning kiss. One of his hands leaves my arse to grab a fistful of my hair, pulling tightly. For a moment, I'm back in the library, my hair being ripped out whilst clammy hands touch me. My body stiffens, preparing to fight, when I hear Jax's rough voice.

"Come back to me, Baby Girl."

I look up, blinking, and stare into his searching blue eyes.

"Jax...I'm sorry..." I start to say, but stop when he growls at me.

"Don't you dare blame yourself for that cunt's actions," he rumbles out. Then he takes a deep breath, closing his eyes for a moment. "You did nothing wrong, baby," he assures me softly, resting his forehead against mine.

I know he's right, but a part of me still thinks that it's my fault somehow. That I did something to make it happen.

"Do you want to stop?" he asks, opening his lids, his eyes full of understanding and worry.

"No," I say quickly. I can't explain it, but I know that if I don't do this, if I don't take back control and baulk at having sex with my guys, Robert wins. "Please, don't stop, Jax."

He gives a brief nod, staring intently into my eyes, the hand in my hair letting go as his other hand leaves my arse to snake between us. Finding me already wet, he rumbles in appreciation as he teases my clit, rubbing circles around the sensitive nub until I'm squirming and gasping, my eyes closing in pleasure.

I hear a drawer open next to us, then the rustle of a foil packet.

*These guys have condoms every-fucking-where! Always be prepared, right?*

Opening my eyes, I see he's pushed his sweats down, has rolled the condom on, and is lining up the head of his hard cock with my slick opening, all whilst still playing with my clit. My eyes roll as he starts to push his way inside me.

"Look at me, Baby Girl," he orders, his tone so gruff it sends shivers down to my core.

I'm captured in his gaze as inch by glorious inch, he glides inside me, until he's all the way in, our pelvises flush.

"This pussy is ours," he growls out possessively, and hearing Jax talk dirty is so fucking hot, my inner walls clench and flutter around him. "No one but us will ever touch you again, Baby Girl." His eyes are fierce with the fire of his promise.

Holding my gaze, he starts slowly moving in and out of me, teasing me. My gaze flits over his shoulder to see Loki standing there, rubbing lube over his erect dick, and my breath catches at the sight.

Jax turns his head to see what's caught my attention. Looking back, he gives me a wolfish grin, before picking me up and turning us around, so that his back is to the counter, both hands back under my arse, holding me up as I'm speared on his huge cock.

His hands spread my cheeks apart, just as I feel Loki come up behind me, one of his lubed fingers rubbing over my puckered hole.

"This ass belongs to us," he says against my ear, one finger dipping inside my tight back hole.

An animalistic sound leaves my lips as Jax starts to move again. Loki pushes a second finger in, and I gasp at the fullness, my nails digging into Jax's neck. Loki's fingers pump in and out in time with Jax's movements, sending delicious shivers across my body.

Jax stills when Loki pulls his fingers out, and my pussy clenches around his cock at the withdrawal, a deep groan sounding in his throat. I feel the pierced tip of Loki's dick as he starts to press inside me, and my eyes feel like they roll to the back of my fucking head with how incredible it feels. I love this fullness, of having them both inside me at once. I've missed it so much.

"We own you, Pretty Girl," Loki tells me in a strained whisper, once he's fully seated, his hips flush with my arse cheeks.

"Ours," Jax growls out, squeezing my arse hard enough that I know I'll have bruises come the morning.

"Yours," I gasp out in agreement as they both start to move in perfect unison.

Loki's hands are on my waist, holding me still as he and Jax take their pleasure, whilst giving me mine in return. It's almost too much, I can barely breathe through the intense sensation of having both of them thrusting in and out of me.

One of Loki's hands leaves my waist, gliding up my body. He pauses at my breast, pinching my nipple hard, and I cry out, my inner walls fluttering around Jax.

"Now open your eyes, Pretty Girl, and look at Jax while I wrap my hand around your throat," Loki commands in a husky tone.

I do as he says, watching Jax as I feel Loki's hand come up around my throat, squeezing just this side of painfully. Jax's piercing blue eyes rage with a lust crazed fire, and he starts pounding hard into me, the sight of his friend choking me undoing him.

"See what you do to him, Lilly?" Loki asks teasingly, tightening his fingers a little more until I'm struggling to breathe. It tips me over the edge, and I spiral into a soul stealing orgasm, raking bloody furrows down Jax's arms.

Jax curses as my cunt clamps around his dick in a vice like grip, milking his release from him.

"My turn, Pretty Girl," Loki coos in my ear, and then he starts pounding hard into my arse, soon pushing me into another screaming climax.

"Fuck! That's it! Keep coming for me, baby," he orders, his other hand leaving my waist and rubbing my over sensitive clit, leaving Jax to support my weight while I whimper and cry out.

"Loki, I can't..." I beg, the waves of pleasure becoming too much.

"Yes, you can," he says as he keeps pounding into me, leaning his head down and using the hand still wrapped around my throat, he tips mine to the side. Without warning, he bites down, the pain flashing through me before pleasure sears my insides, and I explode once more.

Seconds later, I hear him curse my name as his dick hardens even further and he comes, buried to the hilt in my ass, and filling me with his hot release.

We stay connected together, breathing each other in, and my heart mends a little bit more, my soul beginning to stitch back together.

# CHAPTER THIRTY-FOUR

LILLY

I wake up sandwiched between two hot bodies, surrounded by the smell of vanilla cookies, lemon drizzle cake, and musky man.

*God, I've missed this!*

I lie there for a few moments, eyes blinking, as I recall all of the events of the past few days and nights. I feel at peace, like I'm exactly where I need to be, with exactly who I need to be with. I should feel all kinds of fucked up, but I don't. Not anymore.

Gently extracting myself, *a girl has to pee*, I elicit a small grunt from Jax as I climb over him. Grabbing a t-shirt from the floor, Jax's by the size and smell, I throw it on and head out of the door, padding down the hallway.

The delicious smell of bacon wafts up the stairs, and walking down them, I see that Kai is making breakfast. Or I guess, brunch.

He turns and smiles at me, and I can't help but smile back. He's not necessarily as devastatingly beautiful as the others, but he's got that Disney prince look down. You know, the geeky one with the boy next door charm who is an animal in bed.

"Good morning," he says as I walk up to him. He's making pancakes by the looks of it, one hand holding a whisk and the other a bowl of pale batter.

"Good morning, Kai," I say, leaning in and kissing him full on the lips.

I think I take him by surprise as his own lips don't move for a second, then I hear the clatter of the whisk and bowl dropping on the countertop, right before his hands come up either side of my face, deepening the kiss. His tongue demands entrance, which I give willingly, morning breath be damned!

Pulling back slightly, he looks deep into my eyes, his honey brown ones full of lust, longing, and a touch of relief.

"Thank you for not giving up on us," he whispers whilst his thumb strokes my face.

"Thank you for not giving up on me either," I say softly back, and we both smile, sharing this sweet moment.

The smell of slightly burning bacon has Kai leaping towards the hob, pulling the pan off before cursing, and I giggle. He ends up laughing too, and it's such a wonderfully free sound, I wish I could bottle it up and listen to it whenever I was feeling down.

"Come for a hike with me today, Lilly? I'd like to show you something," he asks, looking into my eyes once again.

"I'd love nothing more," I beam at him, and it's true. A hike sounds perfect. "Just let me grab a shower, and I'll be good to go."

"No rush," he says ruefully, indicating the pan of charred meat. "I'll make us breakfast to go."

---

Half an hour or so later, I'm ready to go, Ash, Loki and Jax still fast asleep upstairs.

As Kai and I walk out of the Academy's back doors, the warm sunshine hits my face, and I pause, closing my eyes and soaking it in. There's a definite chill in the air, but the sun goes some way to make up for it. A smile lifts my lips, this truly is a remarkable place.

Opening my eyelids, I find Kai standing in front of me, a look of almost wonder in his gaze.

"What?" I ask, smiling up at him. My lips seem to be permanently tilted upwards today, I can't stop the expression.

He reaches out, cupping my jaw in his warm, dry palm. I nuzzle in, loving the feel of it.

"You have no idea how precious you are, Lilly," he says, his voice melodic and soft. "You are full of a light that draws us in like moths to a flame, and we would willingly burn in the depths just for a single taste."

His words send my pulse skyrocketing, and I melt in his hands as his thumb traces my lips before he leans in, placing a gentle kiss on them. He pulls back before it can get deeper, giving me a knowing smile that's more suited to Loki.

"Let's go," he says, taking my hand in his.

We head off campus into the surrounding woods, the calm and tranquillity just what I needed after the last couple of days. Hell, the last couple of weeks have been crazy, and my hand tightens on Kai's, thinking about that dark time when I was all alone without their comfort.

A thought occurs to me then, and although I hate to break the peace that surrounds us, it won't go away, buzzing in my head like a wasp.

"Kai?" I ask tentatively as he leads me up the trail. He's slightly ahead of me, but still has a firm grip on my hand.

"Yes, Lilly?" he says, looking back at me.

"Can I ask you a question? About you guys and...the cabin?" I see his shoulders stiffen slightly, and his steps slow so that he's by my side.

He sighs. "I will answer anything you want to know, Lilly. If it's in my power to do so, and if it's my story to tell," he replies.

I take a deep breath. "Last night, you all acted so in tune with each other, like you've done that sort of thing a million times before..." I taper off when I see the pained look in his eyes, his hand now gripping my own tightly.

"That's because we have done that sort of thing before. We've done terrible things, Lilly," he tells me, his tone weary. "But we've had little choice," he adds quietly, and I stop us, turning to face him. I use my hand to bring his face up so that he is once more looking at me.

His eyes are full of pain, and shadows of a past that have left scars on his soul. I know in another life, a kinder life, Kai would be the same gentle soul he is, just without the nightmares in his eyes.

"Hey, I know you guys had no choice. That you still don't have much of a choice. I don't blame you for what you've been forced to do, Kai," I say, and a flicker of hope and relief enters his gaze.

"You are too good for us, Lilly," he breathes.

"No, I think we're just right for each other," I say with a gentle expression, and the smile that lights up his face causes fireworks to explode in my heart.

We stay staring into each other's eyes until Kai breaks the contact, resuming our walk and tugging me gently along with him.

"How...how did you learn how to do it?" I ask, needing to understand more of how they came to be the guys I see today.

Another sigh leaves his lips. "That night, when Loki turned fourteen..." he begins, but I interrupt him.

"It was Loki's birthday?!" I exclaim. I know he's referring to the night their fathers and his uncle took them to the cabin.

"He's the youngest of us and turned fourteen that day," Kai says sadly, and my eyes fill with tears, my heart breaking once again for what these boys have been through.

"Well, think of that night as the kick start of our training," Kai continues. "After that, we were expected to learn our various roles and crafts." Kai's nose wrinkles at this. "We would be taken to the training camp, which is at the back of the cabin, every weekend and school holidays and put through our paces both physically and mentally. Jax even spent time in South Africa learning how to be a medic so that he could keep people alive while he..." he trails off, but I know what he is referring to. So Jax could torture people better, longer.

"Mentally?" I ask, dreading the answer.

"Have you noticed how the others are always playing music?" he queries, turning to look at me.

I nod. It was definitely something I'd spotted, but not thought too much about, as I love listening to music too.

"One of the ways we were conditioned was to be put in isolation. A white, padded, soundproof room with no windows. We'd be kept in there for hours, sometimes days. Poor Loki was once in there for over a week when his parents went abroad and forgot about him." Kai's eyes are full of anger as he recalls the memory. "The guys were left in utter silence the whole time, so now they can't bear it."

My soul aches at hearing this. *How can their parents be so cruel?*

"And you?" I ask softly as we make our way along the path, still side by side. "You don't listen to music as much as they do."

"My uncle went the opposite way with me and played only very loud thrash metal," he says with a shiver. "I still can't listen to it after all of this time."

Suddenly, I feel freezing, as if the sun is no longer in the sky. I can see it shining through gaps in the trees, but this is a cold that is on the inside, and I'm not sure it'll ever warm up.

"Oh, Kai," I say in a choked voice. My heart bleeds for them all.

"Hey," he says, stopping and taking my other hand in his. "It's okay, Lilly."

"It's not okay. How can it be okay?" I almost sob, and I feel hot tears tracking down my face.

His thumbs come to brush them away, then he pulls me in close, surrounding me with his fresh woodsy scent. It's different from the forest that surrounds us. He smells like grass and leaves after the rain, and it soothes me, despite my heart still hurting.

"I wish I could get you away from them," I murmur into his chest, my hands grasping his thick padded jacket.

"You don't need to worry about that, Lilly," Kai says. "We won't be under their rule forever. Trust me." And I look up into his eyes, realising that I do trust him. I trust them all unequivocally.

I nod, too full of sadness for the boys that lost their early teens to monsters, to be able to speak.

We head off again, and soon approach a clearing in the trees. My mouth hangs open as we get nearer. Surrounded by trees all around is a rocky pool that looks like it's steaming.

I look at Kai who's smiling broadly now, his gaze on me.

"Welcome to Highgate Springs," he tells me, dropping his backpack and undoing his jacket.

"Kai! What are you doing?" I ask. I mean, I know what it looks like he's doing. It looks like he's taking his clothes off.

"Getting in, of course," he says with a boyish grin, laying his jacket on a large rock.

"Kai, it's fucking freezing!" I say, pointing to our feet. "And there's snow on the ground!" We had a small flurry last night that was melted by the Academy, but obviously, the sun hasn't reached it here in the middle of the forest.

"Yes, there is," he agrees calmly as he pulls off his black jumper. He's still in his jeans, hiking boots, and a grey t-shirt, which he pulls off next, in that sexy guy way, and my breath hitches.

It's then that I realise his glasses are missing. "Kai, where are your glasses?" I question, my brow furrowing when he reaches into his bag, pulling out what looks like lengths of red silk. He tucks these into his back pocket then walks towards me.

"Don't worry, Lilly," he says with a devilish smile that I'm not used to seeing on his face. "I've got contacts in, so I can see you perfectly," he tells me, continuing to stalk towards me with a predatory gleam in his eyes.

"Do you remember your safe word?" he asks, standing in front of me, his voice dropping an octave lower, and I shiver inside my big coat.

"Yes," I breathe, anticipation lighting in my stomach.

"Yes, what?" he probes, raising one of his brows.

"Yes, sir," I say obediently. I love this side of Kai, and it gets me hot as all hell.

"Tell me what it is, Lilly," he whispers, a long finger tracing down the side of my face.

"Red," I reply, licking my bottom lip. His gaze catches on the movement, his nostrils flaring.

"Good." He reaches for the zip on my coat, undoing it, then takes it off me, lying it on a rock next to us, before reaching for my red wool jumper.

"Kai, what..." I begin, stopping when his head snaps up, and he looks at me with a frown.

"Did I say you could speak?" he asks, his voice hard, making my thighs clench. I shake my head. "Arms up then," he orders, and I obey so that he can pull the garment up over my head, placing it with my jacket.

He untucks my long-sleeved top from my high-waisted fifties-style jeans, before pulling that over my head too. Goosebumps erupt over my skin as the cold air caresses it, my nipples hardening to points in my pink lacy bra.

Reaching into the back pocket of his jeans, he takes out one length of silk.

"I'm going to put this around your eyes, Lilly. If at any point it gets to be too much, say 'red' and we stop," he tells me, waiting for my nod, before stepping around me so that he's facing my back.

Anticipation makes me breathless as he lifts the silk over my head, placing it in front of my eyes and plunging me into darkness. I gasp as suddenly my other senses are heightened tenfold. I can hear the bubble of the spring, some birds chirping nearby, and the creaking and groaning of the trees all around us. I can feel the cold breeze dancing across my skin, and I shiver, even though

I feel like I'm burning on the inside. The feel of the knot at the back of my head being tightened makes me moan aloud.

I startle slightly when Kai's fingers alight on the clasp of my bra, unhooking it and helping to guide it off me. I feel his warm body move, leaving my back exposed to the frigid air as he comes around to my front. Seconds later I feel the button on my jeans pop open and hear the zipper being undone.

He reaches for my hands, placing them on his muscular shoulders, then he brings my foot up onto his knee, and starts unlacing my boot. Taking it off, then my thick sock, he carefully places my bare foot back on the cold stone before doing the same to the other foot. I feel a tug on my hips as he takes my jeans down, leaving me wearing nothing but a pink thong and a red blindfold. I hear a sound of appreciation, before feeling his warmth along the front of my body once again.

He grasps my wrists, bringing them together in front of me.

"Hold them there," he orders.

The brush of silk makes me gasp as he wraps a length around my wrists a couple of times. It then feels as though he's knotting the silk, gliding it between my wrists before tying it off.

I'm fucking panting. *Who knew being blindfolded and tied up was so hot?!*

"You okay, Lilly?" he asks. He still hasn't given me permission to speak, so once again, I nod. "Good girl," he praises, and I swear I feel a drip slide down my inner thigh at the pleased tone he uses.

Letting go of my wrists, I hear the thud of what I think are his jeans and boots, then the rustle of a condom packet opening. Moments later, his warmth is back, burning me everywhere our naked bodies touch.

"Arms up, Lilly, and place them around my neck," his voice commands.

It's deeper than usual, telling me just how much he is enjoying this. I do as he says, his hands guiding my arms, then feel his arm sweep under my knees as he picks me up, bridal style.

He starts walking, and I begin to feel warm tendrils of air caressing my body as we move closer to the spring. I can't help squirming in his arms, trying to get closer.

"Keep still," he orders firmly, and I do as he says, stilling at once.

I hear the gentle splash of his feet as he wades into the water, gasping as he goes deeper and I feel the warmth against my own skin. It's at the point where it's almost too hot, perfect with the cold air playing across my exposed skin. He gently sets me down on a flat rock so that the water is just tickling the underside of my thighs, leaving my torso above the hot water.

"Do you feel the cold air playing across your skin?" he asks in a low melodic voice. "You can speak."

"Yes, sir," I whisper, groaning as I feel his fingers start to tickle over and around my breasts, avoiding my nipples, leaving me squirming and panting.

I gasp loudly as I feel a hot mouth cover one nipple, and he pinches the other hard between his fingers, sending tendrils of pleasure spiralling to my core, and my cunt flutters. He releases his assault to bite up my breast and the column of my neck, claiming me and marking me as his.

I can feel him hard and naked in between my legs, pressed up against my lace covered centre and the almost contact is driving me wild, making me buck against him in a bid for more.

"I want to mark every inch of this perfect skin, Lilly," Kai says, voice raspy, as if it's taking a great effort to hold back.

"Please, sir, I need more," I beg, and I would laugh at the *Oliver* reference, but I'm wound too tight for that shit.

Maddeningly slowly, I feel his fingers tickle up my inner thigh, taking the edge of my thong and moving it to one side to expose me. I can feel the very tip of him at my opening, the bubbling hot water caressing my sensitive clit.

"You would test a monk's sanity," I hear him grumble as he starts to push inside me.

His piercings rub my inner walls in the most delicious way, and I'm already crying out before he's even fully seated.

"I'm no fucking monk, Lilly," he groans, and hearing him curse winds me even tighter, it's so unusual for him. I love the effect I have on him, on all of the guys.

"This is going to be hard and fast," he warns milliseconds before he pulls almost all the way out, and then slams back inside me being true to his word, and I scream his name.

He keeps up this punishing pace, his hands gripping my hips for purchase. The water churns around us, and the mix of hot and cold on my skin, plus having my eyes covered and wrists bound, brings my orgasm on so suddenly, and so forcefully, that I can only scream wordlessly into the open air.

His pace doesn't falter, keeping my orgasm going until I feel wrung out and spent. Before I come down completely from my high, I feel his teeth graze my neck, then bite down hard, sending me into another soul destroying orgasm. Seconds later, I hear him groan out loud, finding his own release inside me.

He reaches up to untie the silk around my eyes, the daylight blinding me for a moment when I open them.

“I take it you enjoyed that and didn't get too cold?” Kai asks me, a relaxed smile on his lips. I chuckle, making him groan as he's still inside me.

“Abso-fucking-lutely!” I smirk back, the endorphins making me feel a little giddy.

“Good,” he says, finally pulling out of me, making my breath hiss just a little. “Next time, I'll tie you to my bed. I have a feeling you'd like that even more.” His voice is husky, and even though I've just orgasmed twice, Her Vagisty clenches at the thought.

*There's just no satisfying some vaginas.*

His fingers go to the silk binding my wrists, which has gotten a little wet, and looks like it may have to be cut off because the knot appears unmovable. He tugs one part, and the whole lot comes undone, leaving me gaping.

“How the fuck did you do that?!” I exclaim, moving my wrists now they're finally free.

There's a faint red mark where the silk was tied, and I find that I like it. A lot. I like being marked by them. Looking down my chest, I can see his teeth marks in a line snaking up to my throat, which no doubt has a set of teeth marks in it too, if the throbbing is anything to go by.

“They look very beautiful on you,” Kai says, his hand coming into view and brushing the marks with his long fingers. “Dip under the water, it’ll help ease the throbbing of the one on your neck,” he orders gently.

“Yes, sir,” I say cheekily, seeing heat flare in the depths of his eyes. The sun hits them so that I can see a spectrum of browns, from the darkest molasses to the lightest of wild honeys.

He steps from between my legs, turning around to let me off the stone ledge and wade deeper into the water. I gasp as his back comes into view, and I see a magnificent black and orange koi carp tattoo that covers him from his shoulder right down over one arse cheek.

“Kai, how did I not know that you had such a beautiful tattoo?” I ask, in awe of the piece.

It ripples like it's actually moving in water, and I can't help but reach out and touch it. Kai stiffens as my fingers brush it, and I realise too late my mistake. Tears prick my eyes as I guide my hand over his back, feeling ridges and furrows that have nothing to do with art.

"Kai..." my voice catches on a sob, "what happened?"

Although, I can take a pretty good guess given all that he has told me. His chest heaves as he takes in a breath.

"My uncle thought that I was too soft. That I needed toughening up," he confides, voice devoid of any emotion. "That was his solution."

I can't help the sob that escapes me. Their story just keeps getting worse, and I don't know how they lived through it. How they keep living through it.

Kai turns back around, the water swirling around him, pulling me to his naked body, and holding me as I weep into his chest. He makes soothing noises, saying platitudes until my tears stop.

"I'm so sorry, Kai," I say, my voice rough as I look up at him. "I wish there was something I could do to take it away or to make it better." I feel so useless.

"You have a soul of pure light, Lilly Darling. It's why we're all drawn to you, we are desperate to bathe in your goodness and cover ourselves from head to toe in your brilliance." He looks intently into my eyes as he says this, his own eyes full of need.

"I would give it all to you to take the pain away," I whisper. "My soul is yours, Kai. Every part of me belongs to you, the light and the dark. I love you."

Tears track down my cheeks as I bare myself to him completely. I mean every word, I would give my very soul if it would help to free them from the binds that their families have wrapped around them. I know that it sounds insane, but I feel like they are it for me. We were made for each other, all five of us, and it's crazy and unconventional, but it's also as natural as breathing.

"Lilly," he replies, his voice choking. "I was lost until you walked into our lives like a spring breeze after the harshest winter. From that first night, I knew my life would never be the same again. You make all of the shit, everything we've been through, worth it. And I'd go through it all again, just to get to this point and have you here in my arms."

My heart feels so full, I don't know how my body is still containing it.

"We've belonged to each other since the moment of our conception, Lilly Darling. And we are never letting you go."

# CHAPTER THIRTY-FIVE

LILLY

The next morning after breakfast, Jax, Loki, and Kai tell me that they're going to Enzo's gym and ask if I'd like to join them. Ash is at his parents' again.

I figure that I've got nothing else to do, well, I've got a whole load of homework, but I'm putting that shit off, because a girl needs a break from trying to work out where commas go in creative writing!

I go upstairs to get ready, excited to try my new activewear from Pru Apparel. It's a gorgeous matching set of tight shorts and a sports bra, in turquoise stretch fabric, with printed purple flowers that are reminiscent of African waxed cloth.

I placed an order with Lucy & Yak a couple of weeks ago, which has just arrived this morning. So I wear my brand spanking new red berry corduroy dungarees on top, grabbing one of Loki's hoodies and my heeled boots to complete the outfit. Might as well spend the money Adrian gives me.

I've not heard them mention Enzo before, or his gym, so I decide to ask about him as we all get into Jax's truck, and head down the drive. *In Hell I'll Be In Good Company* by The Dead South comes over the speakers, and I chuckle a little at the irony given the boys...occupation. *I call that progress.*

"Who's Enzo?" I ask Jax, turning to gaze at him next to me in the driver's seat.

"He's my unofficial trainer," Jax says, his voice a delicious rumble that always makes me a little wet between the thighs and leaves me breathless.

"Trainer?" I question. "Trainer for what?"

"Didn't you know, Pretty Girl?" Loki says from the back, and I glance over my shoulder to see an evil smirk on his face that tells me he's stirring shit somehow. "Big guy here is an underground MMA champion."

My brows raise at this. "How am I only just finding out about this? Jax?" I turn to glare daggers at the man in question, who looks a little sheepish.

"Why do you think he's so, well, ripped?" Loki asks, and I shrug.

"I dunno...to pin me down real good?" I tease, and I jump in my seat when Jax roars out a laugh that startles us all.

"Oh, Baby Girl," he says, his voice dropping an octave and becoming husky, looking over to me. "That's just an added bonus."

I rub my thighs together, to try and ease the ache that's started up there at his words and my dirty mind. Jax smirks at the movement.

"Eyes back on the road, big guy," I say, voice mock scolding and he turns back to look out of the windscreen with a cough.

A few moments pass while I think about what I've just found out.

"So, can I come to your next fight?" I ask Jax, and he lifts a brow.

"Um, it's not really a place nice girls go to," he tells me, and I scowl.

"Who says I'm a nice girl?" I growl out, trying to sound fierce, but eliciting chuckles from them all which just pisses me off. Then a naughty idea pops into my mind. "Please, Jax," I whine, trying not to sound petulant as I reach over and grab his hard thigh. "I'll kiss all your wounds better afterwards," I offer, lowering my own voice seductively, moving my hand upwards and eliciting a hiss from his mouth.

The leather on the steering wheel groans as he grips it hard.

"Fine," he growls out, and I squeal, letting go and planting a kiss on his cheek. "But you'll stay with one of the others at all times. It's not until after Christmas anyway."

We drive along the beautiful road that I took with Kai, heading into town, and then carrying on through, turning off Main Street onto a smaller, more worn looking street. Pulling up next to the pavement, I look up at the squat grey building to see a red sign that reads Enzo's.

Jax parks the truck, he shuts off the engine, and we all get out, Kai grabbing our bags from the trunk. It's another beautiful sunny day, but it's freezing cold and I shiver as we head towards the double doors in the front. A warm arm settles over my shoulders, the smell of vanilla washing over me.

"I'll warm you up real good when we get inside," Loki whispers against my ear, and I shiver for an entirely different reason.

The heat hits me like a slap in the face as soon as I walk through the door. Followed by the smell of sweaty man, and the tang of blood, all mixed with the rich scent of leather. My nose crinkles and Loki laughs at me.

"Too much like slumming it for you, *Princess*?" he asks, using Ash's nickname for me.

"Loki, you wouldn't know what 'slumming it' was, if it came up behind you and bit you on your peachy arse!" I scoff at him, rolling my eyes.

"Pretty Girl, you can bite my *ass* anytime you want," he quips back, nuzzling my neck and I shiver again.

*Her Vagisty is in fine form I see, the hussy!*

I look around the space, seeing that it's a pretty standard setup. At least, I think it is, but what the fuck do I know, never having been in a gym before I started Highgate Prep. There's a ring in the middle of the space, where two guys are already sparring. I notice both of them are smaller than my boys, and a sense of satisfaction washes over me.

There's a weights area in one corner, another section with loads of punch bags hanging from the ceiling, and along one wall, mats are laid out in front of a mirror. There are a couple of guys in each area, which surprises me given it's still early on a Sunday, so it must be a popular place.

An older guy with salt and pepper hair comes towards us, his handsome face full of smiles as he takes in the guys. His grin widens as he sees me standing with Loki on one side, his arm still around my shoulders, and Jax standing on the other, his hand in mine. Poor Kai is left to fend for himself next to Loki.

"Boys!" he says in a slight Italian accent, opening his arms wide and engulfing Kai in a full on man hug, kissing both cheeks. He's wearing some loose gym shorts and a black tank top that shows off his buff arms, which are covered in colourful old school style tattoos. "So good to see you all again, *che piacere*!" he tells them, moving on to hug Jax, who wraps his own huge arms around him in return. I assume this is Enzo.

"*Come stai? Tutto bene?*" Enzo asks, pulling back but keeping Jax at arm's length. Jax nods in his usual silent way, but there's a warmth in his eyes that's not often there with anyone outside of our group.

Enzo skips me with a wink as he grabs Loki, pulling him off me to squeeze him and kiss his cheeks too.

He turns his gaze towards me, letting Loki go, and his brown eyes are full of kindness, as well as a little mischief.

"*Principessa*, you must be Lilly. The boys neglected to tell me how beautiful you are, *bella come la primavera*," he says, making a blush rise to my cheeks as he takes my hand and places a kiss on my knuckles.

Jax growls which makes Enzo laugh out loud. "Oh, don't worry, *figlio mio*, I'm not trying to steal her away! I'm old enough to be her father! And Rosa, Mrs Russo," he turns to me with another wink, "would never forgive me...*sti ragazzi*," he says, shuddering. I hear Jax grumble which makes him chuckle more.

"You must be Enzo," I say back, a warm smile spreading across my lips. "And the boys neglected to mention anything about you to me," I say teasingly, narrowing my eyes at the guys, and causing Enzo to raise an eyebrow at them in mock severity.

They all rush to defend themselves, talking over each other, and their worry that they've upset him is actually kind of sweet. I can see how much he means to them in the way they behave towards him. I can't say that I'm that surprised, given how their own parents act. Enzo seems to truly care about them.

"Don't worry, boys, I'm sure I'll forgive you all for your negligence, *mannaggia*," he says with a smile, to show them he's kidding. "Now, I want you all to do your warm up, then three rounds on the punch bags, then weights, yes? *Andate, forza!* " he orders, clapping his hands and dismissing them.

"Are you sparring today, Jax?" he asks my viking, who just nods. Enzo pauses, searching his gaze for a moment, then sighs before nodding back. "I'll show Lilly around and get her settled, *prego*." He holds out his arm for me to take and starts walking away.

He shows me the equipment whilst telling me all about how his father came over from Italy when he himself was a teenager, bringing his family with him. His father set up the gym, teaching and coaching semi and professional boxers. He points to grainy pictures on the walls of a gentleman who looks very similar to himself, alongside younger men wearing boxing gloves and holding huge belts.

"So, what would you like to do today, *cara mia?*" he asks me.

"Um, well, I was thinking maybe some yoga to warm up, and then perhaps practise some self-defence moves with one of the guys. Jax has been teaching me since..." My voice trails off, realising that I'd just started to open up to a complete stranger about what happened with Robert.

Enzo's eyes go hard, and his grip on my elbow tightens. "He deserved what he got, *quel disgraziato*. My boys know how to take care of things and protect their own," he says fiercely, and I gasp.

"How do you..." I begin, confused at how, and why, they would have told him. I mean, I know they're close with the man, but still, surely it puts them in danger if anyone else knows.

"Me and my guys, we help them to...clean up," he replies, and suddenly, I understand who helped take Robert away.

"Thank you," I whisper, and his hand tightens once more as we stop outside what looks like an office.

"*Senza problema,* of course," he leans, kissing my cheek gently, and I can't help the emotion that clogs my throat.

*This is what having a father must feel like.*

"Now," he says, turning to open the door of the office. "You can get changed in here, as we don't have anywhere else suitable for a young lady. *Prego*," he smiles so kindly at me, that I can't help but lean over and kiss his cheek. His cheeks flush a little, whilst I smile.

A few minutes later, I emerge from the office, having left my clothes inside, neatly folded in a pile. I head over to where the guys have left our bags, seeing a few heated glances aimed my way. I'm just taking out my Bluetooth earbuds and phone to set up some calming music to practice to, when I hear the growl of Jax's voice behind me.

"Not fucking happening, Baby Girl," he huffs as I straighten up, turning towards him.

Seconds later, I'm encased in darkness as a soft cloth is placed over my head, smelling of lemons. My head pops through a hole in the top, and I realise that Jax is now standing before me minus his tank top, which is now on me.

He gives me a nod before turning and striding away, and although I'm a little pissed at his caveman attitude, Her Vagisty is practically drooling at all the muscles now on display and the public claiming that just went down. *Fucking traitor!*

"Is this really necessary?" I ask his retreating back. It is a gorgeous back. *Sigh*. He turns around, narrows his eyes at me, growls and then stalks off. *Possessive bastard!*

Accepting defeat, I pull my arms through the armholes, tying a knot in one side, so that at least it's a little bit out of my way. I select the music, pop the earbuds in, and make my way over to the mats in front of the mirrors.

For a time, I just lose myself in my practice. I love the flow, and synchronising my movements with breath. The burn of the stretch, and the shake of prana feeling so good. I'm winding down, my eyes closed as I breathe deeply, when I feel a warmth before me, smelling woods after the rain and fresh sweat. My lips lift up in a smile as I open my lids, to find honey brown eyes smiling back at me.

Taking my earbuds out, the sounds of the gym come rushing back in; the hissing out of breath as guys hit the punch bags, the bell that sounds every three minutes. Leaning over, I place my lips against Kai's, surprising him.

All of a sudden, his hand comes up to grip my hair as he deepens the kiss, his tongue exploring mine. Sparks fly between us as I get lost in the feel of him, my hands running over his sweaty arms as his tongue destroys me in the best possible way. I hear catcalls and whistles when we finally break apart, both of us panting and blushing at the attention.

Of course, Loki's voice is the loudest. "Come on, love birds!" he shouts, and I look over to see Jax getting ready to go into the ring.

My gaze returns to Kai's, his pupils blown and nearly swallowing his irises.

"What's going on?" I question him.

He takes a deep breath. "Jax is going to spar, and it's a sight not to be missed," he replies, getting up from his crouch and holding out his hand to help me up from the floor. I can't help but notice that he adjusts himself, trying and failing to be discreet about it.

We walk over hand in hand to where Loki and Jax are, and I hear *Believer* by Imagine Dragons start to play in the background.

"I think the big guy deserves a good luck kiss don't you, Pretty Girl?" Loki teases, a shit eating grin on his angel face.

I turn to Jax more than happy to oblige. Before I can take a step, however, he grabs the front of my throat and pulls me to him, slamming his lips to mine and demanding entry with his tongue. I open to him, matching him stroke for stroke, and as he begins to pull away, I bite his bottom lip hard, tasting copper and earning a low rumble from his throat which does all sorts of things to Her Vagisty.

*I was never the best at playing sub.*

His eyes are like blue fire as he steps away, a drop of blood dripping down his chin, and a promise of retribution in his gaze, which I am one hundred percent behind.

"That was hot as fuck, Pretty Girl," Loki purrs in my ear, pulling me close for a searing kiss.

"Your girl fuck anyone, Jax? Does she charge?" I hear a voice sneer from the direction of the ring.

I break the kiss snarling, intending to rip this arsehole a new one, but I see Jax stepping into the ring, practically charging the other guy in there.

"Oh shit!" I hear Loki say as Jax aims a brutal high kick to the guy's head.

The shitstain's head snaps to the side, the crack audible, but he keeps his feet. Jax doesn't even pause, landing punch after punch on his opponent's torso. The dull thuds of fists hitting flesh, sound like the noise of the tanks firing near my uncle's house in Wiltshire, where he lives on the edge of the Salisbury Plain Army training zone.

The guy manages to land a few punches that just fucking bounce off Jax, not even slowing him down, as Jax kicks him again in the side of the head. My pulse races with excitement, and far from being repulsed by the violence, I can feel my core become slick as I watch.

I hear Enzo's voice as he steps up beside me. "He still juicing, Loki?" he asks, and I hear Loki's sharp inhale.

I tear my gaze from the fight to look at Enzo.

"Juicing?" I ask, thoroughly confused. His eyes soften a little.

"Steroids, *cara mia*," he says softly, eyes sad. This time Loki curses, and although I can still hear the sounds of the fight and the song, it's as if from a distance.

"Steroids?" I repeat, still not quite sure what he's talking about.

"*Si, cara mia.* Jax has been taking anabolic steroids since the beginning of the year. His *father* gives them to him and supplies others at the school through Jax, *che padre!*" Enzo spits the word father out, and I'm inclined to agree.

I flush with anger, going white hot for a moment. *That motherfucking shitbag of an excuse for a father!*

Looking back at the fight, I see Jax deliver a final punch, knocking the other guy out cold. He lands with a resounding thud, and before I really think through what I'm doing, I pull myself up into the ring and storm over to a panting Jax.

I vaguely hear Loki and Kai shout out, but I'm so angry that I'm not thinking straight, reaching out to grab his shoulder and force him to face me and my wrath. Only, it backfires slightly as Jax spins around, eyes wild, and clearly not seeing that it's me as his own hand shoots out, grabbing me by the front of my throat, whilst tackling me to the ground.

All the breath rushes out of me as I land on my back hard, with him on top of me, knees either side of my hips, and his hand wrapped around my neck, squeezing. I can feel blackness starting to creep in around the edges, my hands clawing at his hand until suddenly his eyes clear.

"Lilly?" he questions, his grip immediately loosening, allowing sweet air to rush into my lungs.

Before he can say anything else, I lift my hips in a move he taught me, making him fall forward onto his palms. I hug tight to his torso, then pull myself up his body, and in a lightning quick move, I wrap my arm around his, pulling it underneath him and rolling him, so that I am now on top, pinning his wrists to the ground.

I hear a cheer from outside the ring, but my focus is all on Jax.

"What the fuck, Lilly!" Jax practically roars at me, not fighting my hold, and I can see the panic in his eyes, the worry that he really could have hurt me.

"What the fuck?" I ask, my voice raspy and my throat a bit sore from his hand. I'm still seething. "I'll tell you what the fuck! Why the fuck are you filling your body with fucking poison, Jax? Do you know how bad regular steroid abuse is for you?!" I hit his hands on the ground in my rage. I know it's not his fault, not really, but I'm so mad, and his cuntflap of a father isn't here to feel the sharpness of my rage.

His gaze softens more. "Baby..." he begins, but I interrupt him before he can say another word.

"Don't you 'Baby' me! Taking pills at parties is one thing, Jax. Taking this shit day in, day out...it'll fuck you up so bad that you might not recover." The thought of possibly losing him to this, makes my heart race, and panic fills my chest. "From this moment on you won't take them, do you hear me?" I lean down so that I can whisper in his ear. "Otherwise you can kiss this goodbye." I roll my hips which just so happen to be right over his crotch. I feel him starting to harden at the movement. "Did you know that steroids can shrink your dick, and I like it the monster size that it is," I say, rolling my hips again, forgetting our audience and making him groan out loud. I hear a chuckle that sounds like Enzo.

Licking the shell of his ear, I bite down on his lobe, hearing another delicious moan escape his lips. I let go of his wrists, get up, and stand over him, looking down.

"No pussy until that shit is out of your system," I tell him, deadly serious. His blue eyes widen.

"Baby Girl..." he starts as I turn to walk away. I look back at him.

"Lucky for you, your arms are the size of tree trunks. I'm sure they'll manage the extra exercise that your hand will get," I say, my tone laced with fake sweetness.

Then, turning on my heel, I head to the edge of the ring, where Loki is holding the rope open for me.

"That was vicious, Pretty Girl," he tells me, an evil smile on his face. "And so fucking hot," he adds as he helps me down.

Kai is right there, tilting my head and looking at my neck. He brushes his long fingers across my throat, and I wince before he puts an ice pack against it, the cold like a soothing balm.

I look up and see Enzo standing behind him. He just grins, giving me a nod, respect and what looks like relief in his eyes. I hear Jax step down, and suddenly Kai is gone, and I turn around in time to see him punch Jax square in the jaw, making his head snap to the side.

"Be more fucking careful," Kai hisses, before coming back to me. I'm standing there in shock, mouth open.

*Kai just fucking punched Jax! And Jax took it!*

"Come on, Lilly," Kai says, wrapping an arm around me and leading me towards the office and my clothes. "Let's get you back, and I'll make chicken ramen for lunch."

We go to pass Enzo, who stops me with a hand on my arm, then pulls me into a tight embrace.

"You were made for them, *cara mia, lo credo veramente*," he whispers, before kissing both cheeks, giving me a slightly quizzical, considering type of look, then letting me go.

# CHAPTER THIRTY-SIX

LILLY

It's a silent journey back to the dorms, all of us lost in our own minds. I can't stop thinking about Jax and his drug abuse.

*Did the guys know? Why did they not stop it? And did he start taking them in the first place because his father made him? Or is there another reason?*

I look over at Jax, once again in the driver's seat. His brow is deeply furrowed, and I can see him practically vibrating, his shoulders tense and his nostrils flared. I wonder if I could have reacted a little better back at the gym, and a stab of guilt runs through me. I was so angry, so blinded by my rage, that I didn't stop to think about the fact that I was taking out my fury on Jax.

Pulling up into the student lot, we all get out and hurriedly head back towards the Academy. The temperature has dropped now it's November, and we've already had a couple of small flurries of snow.

Arriving in our dorm, I quickly shower, then help Kai prepare a delicious ramen for lunch, whilst Loki then Jax wash up. I love cooking with him, he makes it so fun, and his passion is intoxicating. Not to mention the small teasing touches that leave me panting and breathless. As we sit down to eat, the atmosphere is still a little tense, and I know that I am partly, maybe mostly, to blame. Biting my lip, a thought springs to mind.

"Why don't we watch a film together after lunch?" I suggest, thinking that what we all need is to curl up on the sofas in front of a funny movie.

After much debate, we decide on Deadpool. I wait for Jax to sit down on one of the sofas, Loki next to him, and then curl up on his lap, eliciting a grunt of surprise from his lips. I look up into his slightly startled blue eyes and try not to get lost in their depths. There's a fear in them, a fear that I'm pretty sure I caused, and that I'm desperate to erase.

"I love you, Jax Griffiths," I say softly, willing him to believe me. "And I will help you to get through this. You've got me now, and I'm not going anywhere."

His hands tighten on my waist before he wraps his massive arms around me, pulling me even closer to him. I love his fresh warm lemon scent, I don't think that I'll ever get enough of it.

*These guys are definitely turning me sappy.*

"I love you too, Lilly Darling. And I'd give up the world for you," Jax confesses in a rumble above me, my head tucked tightly under his chin.

I can feel his heart beating in his chest, its sound a soothing melody. Jax has a way with words, he says things so simply, but with such a depth of feeling that I can feel their truth in my bones. In my very soul, like he brands me with each word that falls from his lips.

The lights are dim and the film starts, and I can't help asking him, "Why did you start taking them, Jax?"

His body stiffens underneath me for a moment, he knows what I'm asking about. Then a long breath leaves his lungs on a sigh.

"My dad is a weak, pathetic man," he starts his deep, rumbling voice a whisper, and I can hear how much he hates him. "But unfortunately for me and my mom, he was also a strong man. When I was a child, I vowed to one day be stronger than him," he tells me as the opening credits begin to roll. "And now I am."

Once again I'm appalled at the guys' parents. Although, why I am surprised by anything they do anymore is beyond me.

"I'm so sorry, Jax," I whisper, hating the useless words. His arms tighten around me and I burrow closer.

"The roids helped to get me bigger quicker, and I guess I became addicted to that feeling, of being the biggest," he explains into the darkness. I can see Loki and Kai paying attention, their bodies still as they listen to our hushed conversation whilst watching the film. His jaw is tight, fists clenched.

"Oh, Jax," I murmur, my heart bleeding out for him, and what he's done to himself in order to keep those he loves safe. My hand caresses his chest, my palm gliding over the bare skin and tracing the tattoos on his firm pec.

"I'm scared that I won't be able to protect everyone if I stop," he admits, voice barely above a whisper, and my heart shatters.

I sit up and move so that my knees are on either side of his hips, my hands gripping his face, lifting it up to look into those stunning eyes.

"Jax, we protect each other. You don't have to do it alone. Not anymore"

His eyes are swirling with so many emotions, it's hard to keep track of them all. He lets out another deep breath, closing his lids.

"I don't know how to get off them. To let go," he says, hanging his head, his voice tired, like he is exhausted by it all.

"I'll help, and I'm sure the others will, too." I bring his head back up, his eyes opening again, and this time, there's a shred of hope in the blue depths.

"You're too good for us, Baby Girl," he sighs out as his hands come up around me, pulling me close and placing a kiss over my heart. "But we're too selfish to let you go."

We hold each other for a time, our hearts beating to the same rhythm, our breathing synchronised. Eventually, I snuggle down in Jax's lap, my feet resting in Loki's, and I drift off surrounded by their warmth and love.

---

## ASH

"Again!" my father's voice barks out from across the room, his voice stinging like a whip.

Sweat drips into my eyes as I bounce on my toes, fists raised, not daring to let them droop, even though we've been at this for hours now.

John gives me a slightly apologetic look, before nodding to his guys that surround me. He knows the drill as well as I do, we've been training together at my father's behest for years now.

I feel the rush of air to my left and duck, just as one of the guys throws his fist at my head. The next several minutes are lost to the violence that surrounds me, the swing of fists, the meaty sound of those same fists making contact.

"Enough!" my father roars and we come to a sudden halt.

I sway slightly on my feet, breathing hard. I didn't do too badly considering the odds are five to one.

"Pathetic. Just like the waste of space your brother was," he sneers at me, his lip curled. My fists involuntarily clench at my sides, the only outward sign of the rage that his comment elicits in me.

He's perfectly put together, in slacks and a turtle neck cashmere sweater, and even though it's hot in our home gym, he doesn't have a single drop of sweat on him.

He's a fucking devil in disguise. An evil motherfucker who hides behind smiles and charm. But he'll gut you and play with your innards just the same.

"You can go, John," he commands. "Bring better men next week."

Only my father would be arrogant enough to insult ex-Marines. But he'll get away with it. For now anyway.

John gives me a slight nod, my father distracted by something on his phone, as the others all follow their leader out.

I'm still standing there, my breathing settling and my heart rate finally coming down. There's a fine tremor in my limbs, exhaustion washing over me. I can't show it to him, though. He can't know how fucking tired I am. Tired of it all.

Looking up from the screen, his top lip curls again and it transforms his handsome face into something ugly. "Go get showered, I have a call to make," he orders me like a fucking dog, and I have to bite my tongue on the growl that wants to leave my lips.

He heads across the gym towards the door, already bringing his phone up to his ear. Good. I want him to turn his back on me. That way, he'll never see me coming when I make my move. And trust me, that day is coming.

"Good evening, Ace," I hear him say, waiting for a beat before continuing as if in response to what this "Ace" has said. "Everything is in hand. Our little flower is being well taken care of, don't you worry."

My heart beats a frantic rhythm again as panic floods my veins, making me go cold all over. This must be about Lilly, it can't be a coincidence with that nickname.

"We've got the boys on it, Ace. There's really nothing for you to worry about," he replies, stepping out of the door before I can hear any more.

*Fuck!*

*Why is Julian so interested in Lilly? And what the fuck did he mean he's got us on it?*

My hands itch to grab the weights beside me and hurl them at the mirror in frustration. I rein the desire in, the ironclad control over my emotions having been instilled in me since birth.

My father is right. I'm so fucking pathetic, so useless that I can't even protect those that I love. I couldn't with Luc.

Terror floods my entire body, making me stumble a step, as I think about what may happen to Lilly. What I might be unable to save her from.

I can only pray that together, we can shield her from the monster that is Black Knight Corporation. From my father and all of his depravity and evilness.

A shudder runs through me, remembering the doubt that crept into my mind when I first saw my father's interest in her. And now this.

*What if we can't?*

# CHAPTER THIRTY-SEVEN

LILLY

I wake with a start as the front door slams open, jolting upright with a squeak. The hot bodies on either side of me leap up, fists clenched up in front of them, and face the door where we see Ash storming past us, heading up the stairs.

Seconds later, we hear the crash of a door upstairs, shortly followed by the sounds of loud pounding music.

"For fuck's sake!" Loki exclaims, running both hands over his face and through his hair, grimacing.

"Must have been bad if he's back early," Kai muses from his place on the other sofa, his face troubled as he looks after Ash.

Jax grunts at this, but his hands are still curled into fists, although down by his sides now, and his chest is heaving.

"What's going on?" I ask, looking at them each in turn, my brow pulling down in concern.

They all release a sigh, almost at the same time.

"It's not our story to tell, Pretty Girl," Loki tells me, looking torn and eyes pleading for me to understand that they can't tell me everything.

"Ash's father is CEO of Black Knight Corporation," Kai begins, and I see Jax and Loki stiffen. "So he expects Ash to follow in his footsteps. To prepare him for the role, his training has... been the most ruthless." His amber eyes have a haunted look in them. "Go to him, Lilly. He needs you more than he'll ever say," Kai urges me.

His words set off a panic inside me, like he's lit a fuse, and it's only a matter of time before the whole world blows the fuck up.

With hurrying steps, I head straight up the twisting staircase and down the corridor towards the door on the end. I can hear the song better now, it's *Popular Monster* by Falling In Reverse, and I press my forehead against the cool wooden door, my heart lurching in pain at the thought that this is how he feels.

*Oh, Ash.*

Taking a deep breath in a bid to steady myself and to give me courage for what's on the other side of the wood, I wrap my hands around the brass doorknob and twist, pushing it open and stepping into the room. There's just a single lamp lit next to the bed. The rest of the room is in complete darkness, the curtains shut.

My eyes alight on Ash, the light from the lamp highlighting his hunched over position, as he's sat on the bed wearing black boxer briefs and a white vest. He's stripped out of the suit he was wearing when he stormed in, it's cast all over the floor, which is so unlike him that warning bells ring inside my head. He's facing away from me, and I realise that he hasn't heard me come in because the music is so loud.

Walking towards him, I come around the bed, seeing something glinting silver in his hand, leaving a red trail in its wake as he slices it across his thigh. It takes a second for my brain to make sense of what my eyes see. To compute that Ash is using a razor blade to cut himself.

"Ash?" I whisper, my voice sounding distant and broken in my ears, my body tingles all over and there's a slight rushing in my ears.

The song stops at that moment, and his head whips up, his face full of agony, alongside sweet release, and an edge of panic at seeing me here.

"Lilly...I–I..." he stutters, so unlike his usual arrogant self. "You shouldn't be in here," he sighs, but there's no heat to his voice. No anger or hardness.

Only, perhaps, a resigned sadness. And maybe a touch of relief at being caught?

"Oh, Ash, my darling," a sob catches in my throat as hot tears fill my eyes and spill over. I furiously wipe them away.

*Now is not the time to break down, Lilly. Pull your fucking self together!*

"Can I see, please?" I ask gently, taking a step towards him, and indicating his leg.

He just nods his head, so I take another step until I'm in front of him, between his legs, and I go down on my knees, taking a look at the cuts. They're bleeding, but are not too deep, and it's then that I notice that underneath so much of his beautiful ink, are the raised lines of hundreds of scars.

They're all over his body, he's covered in them, and I can't believe that I haven't noticed before now.

I can hardly breathe through the pain that these marks, his scars, cause me. He must have felt so alone, and full of so much hurt for years.

It takes a couple of tries, but I clear my throat enough to ask, "Do you have a first aid kit in here?"

He nods and reaches over to the bedside drawer, pulling out a red bag with a white cross on the front and handing it to me.

"Thanks," I whisper as I open it and get out antiseptic wipes, bandages, and tape.

I set about my task, wiping the cuts with the wipes and bandaging them up. I sit back on my knees for a moment, just trying to breathe, and failing to stop the tears from falling down my cheeks.

"Please, don't cry, Princess," he asks in a pained voice, his hand reaching out and lifting my chin. His grip pulls me up so that I'm raised up on my knees, our faces close together. Both hands come up to cup my face, bringing us closer still. "I'm not worth your tears."

I pull back slightly so that I can look deep into his stunning grey eyes, which are full of darkness and shadows tonight.

"Ash, you are worth every tear, every smile, every fucking thing, and if I need to spend my entire life making you believe that, I will do so gladly." I will him to believe the words, to see what he means to me.

"You are too good, too pure, for the likes of me, Lilly Darling," he says back, his voice husky, and I can see the glint of tears in his own eyes, making the steel swim.

"I am exactly right for you as you are for me, Asher Vanderbilt," I whisper back vehemently as I place a gentle kiss on his luscious lips. Tonight, all I can taste is sadness, hopelessness. I pull back before the kiss can get deeper, and look into his eyes.

"I had a friend back in England who, when we were younger, used to self-harm. We had a code word for when she was feeling the urge, and I would help distract her until it passed. It gave her time to then feel comfortable enough to talk to me about what had triggered her."

"What was your code word?" Ash asks me softly, and I can't help a small grin.

"Rubber duck," I say with a slight giggle at the incredulous look on his face.

"Rubber duck?" he repeats, brows raised, and I nod.

"Would you like to do the same thing?" I ask him seriously. He thinks for a moment and then nods, a slight smile on his face. "And do you want to talk about what happened today to trigger you?" I ask gently.

He sighs, taking his hands from my face and rubbing them over his own, looking away from me. "My father is a sadistic asshole of the worst kind. He takes great pleasure from hurting others, he fucking gets off on it, and the thing that really gets him hard is taking control. He's been training me to take over from him in every aspect of Black Knight, from the moment Luc was...gone," he tells me, his voice tight and face full of anger, hitching painfully when he mentions his brother. "He first needs to break me to build me back up in his image. I'm just so tired, Lilly, so exhausted from it all. The responsibility, the lack of control, the not knowing if I'll be enough to save my brothers. To save you."

He looks at me as he says the last part, and my heart stops dead at the look of despair on his face.

"Why do you need to save me, Ash?" I can't help asking, my heart pounding with dark premonition and my mouth has suddenly gone dry.

"He's interested in you, they all are, and I don't fucking know why, Lilly!" he says, his voice rising with frustration and his eyes going a little wild searching the room as if he'll find the answers in here. His hands are flexing at his sides, like he wants to wrap them around his father's throat.

"Hey," I say, bringing him back to face me. "It'll be okay. You have us to help with whatever you need. You're not alone, Ash, we will get through this together."

"You don't know that, Lilly. How can you know that?" he asks, almost angrily. His grey eyes are full of fire, a fire built of a crippling lack of confidence.

"Because I love you, Ash, and I'm not leaving you," I retort back, my own conviction matching his. "You're mine, and I've claimed you, and I'll destroy anyone who hurts any of you," I tell him, deadly serious, my chest rapidly rising and falling with my almost panting breaths.

He stops, staring at me with an intense look over his beautiful features that makes his face sharp and savage. We're both breathing hard, and I can see in his eyes that he's not in the right place to believe me, to believe what I'm saying yet.

Before he can say another word, I cut in. "Would you like a distraction, Ash? Would you like your control back?" I ask, and I don't miss the way his nostrils flare, and his pupils start to widen, his anger transforming into lust.

I stand up, seeing the crumpled heap of his trousers on the floor. He really was in a state to leave them like that. Leaning over, I pick up his phone from the nightstand, and find *Use Me* by PVRIS, hitting play and feeling the beat wash over me. I walk over to his discarded trousers and bend down, taking his black leather belt out of the belt loops.

I thread the tail end through the buckle, leaving a loop big enough for one wrist before taking the tail back through creating a figure of eight. I then take the end through the buckle, framing both loops once more.

*Thank you, hot guys of TikTok!*

Placing my hands through the loops so that the cuffs now sit on my wrists, I look up to catch Ash's grey molten gaze.

"Place your hands with your wrists facing each other, Princess. Wouldn't want you to get permanently damaged. Otherwise, who will jack me off later," Ash says with a smirk on his face.

I adjust my hands according to his instructions, resisting the urge to roll my eyes as I bring them up to my mouth, grasping the end with my teeth and pulling.

"Not too tight," he orders. "Make sure you can move your hands." I wriggle them to check, earning a satisfied grunt.

Holding his gaze, I sink down to my knees, my wrists now bound before me. Lowering my eyes, I break our stare, giving him the ultimate act of submission.

I'm panting, my heart racing, and my silk shorts damp at the crotch. I love to submit to Ash, handing him complete control frees me in a way that nothing else does. I'm unshackled from the pain that lives in my heart, from the thoughts of my past that try to plague my mind. And he needs the control more than ever tonight.

His bare feet come into view of my lowered gaze, and even the top of them are tattooed in stunning tribal patterns.

"You will come to me exactly like this when I use our code word," his low voice sends shivers down my spine. "I'll provide better restraints."

"Yes, sir," I say softly back, loving this game.

"Good girl," he praises. "Now, Princess, look up at me, and open that pretty mouth of yours."

I don't bother to suppress a moan of desire, heat flooding through my entire body like a wave crashing against the shore. I do as he orders, slowly raising my head, and taking in every gorgeous inch of his tattooed body. My eyes alight on his now naked crotch, his hard dick standing proud from a nestle of black curls. I can see the white of the bandage on his thigh in my peripheral vision, but I try not to think about that, just focusing on the here and now.

Licking my lips, I open my mouth as instructed and wait for his next command.

He brings his tip to my mouth, painting my lips with his precum, and my tongue darts out to lick the salty fluid.

"You're going to take me all the way in until you're choking on my cock and your eyes water. Put that sharp tongue of yours to good use. I'm going to fuck your mouth and fill you up with my hot cum," his voice is low and raspy, filled with need, and his dirty talk makes a groan leave my lips as he starts to push his big dick into my mouth, pausing when he's hitting the back of my throat, and then pushing in some more.

He holds there, staring down at me as I struggle to breathe around him. My pussy drips with how much I'm enjoying this. I whimper around him as he starts to pull back out, and I can finally take a full gasping breath.

My bound hands start to make their way to my silk-clad core, and I'm not surprised to find I'm dripping wet, my shorts soaked. A groan of pleasure escapes me as I start to rub my clit through the fabric teasingly.

I swirl my tongue in the same motion as my fingers, a deep moan escaping his lips, as one of his hands comes up to tangle in my hair. He uses it to hold on, yet unlike Jax and Loki, Ash is all about control of the mind, and he wants me to follow the letter of his command totally, so he doesn't force my head down.

I start to take him back in, pausing when he reaches the back of my throat again, before coming back up. My tongue plays around, swirling and flicking in time with the fingers I'm trying to use on myself.

"Fuck, Lilly, yes, that's it," Ash moans out, his hand gripping my hair tighter as I pick up my rhythm, bobbing my head up and down along his shaft, saliva dripping down my chin as I work his length.

I'm so close to coming myself, it's torture. A wicked idea pops into my mind, and I love the rebellious nature of it. Managing to push the silk aside, I coat my fingers in my own juices. Then, reaching up between his legs, my index finger circles his puckered hole.

"Lilly..." he growls out as I take him all the way into my mouth, and at the same time, gently start to push my finger into his hole. I hear him gasp in pleasure so I keep going, crooking my finger, massaging his perineum from the inside, whilst sucking his dick.

Within moments, his cock becomes as hard as steel in my mouth seconds before he climaxes with a roar, pouring his hot release down my throat. I greedily swallow his whole load, sucking every last drop from him.

Tugging on my hair, I release his dick with a pop and withdraw my finger, causing another gasp to leave his lips. He keeps pulling me up until I'm standing in front of him, both our chests heaving.

"Naughty, Princess," he pants out, his grip angling my head so that he can press his lips against mine, in a searing hot kiss that merges our fucking souls together. And damn if the thought that he's tasting himself doesn't make me drip a little more.

He breaks away, and I can't help but sass him.

"But you liked it, didn't you?" I say with a cheeky grin, a brow raised cockily.

His steely eyes narrow, then he suddenly picks me up and throws me over his shoulder, in a move that reminds me of Jax, walking us over to the bed.

"Ash!" I screech as he throws me down onto the covers, and I land with a bounce, my wrists still bound with his belt.

*Devil I Know* by Allie X starts to play, making Ash smirk.

He walks to his bedside cabinet, opening the bottom drawer, and takes out several neatly tied bundles of thin black rope. Getting onto the bed, he straddles my hips, his naked skin burning every part of me that it touches. I can see that he is already semi hard—*seriously, there must be something in the water here that gives guys the ability to become erect on command!* Unbuckling his belt from around my wrists, he carefully sets it aside, before grabbing one hand and stretching my arm out.

Taking one of the bundles, he unravels the rope and starts to wrap it around my wrist, face intent as he begins to tie a series of complicated knots. I'm still able to move until he begins to tie the ends to one of the bedposts. There's a beauty to his movements, and I can feel myself getting wetter with each pass of the rope until I'm vibrating with unadulterated need.

He does the same with the other wrist and then moves down the bed to do the same with both ankles, until I'm spread eagled for him and pinned down. I give an experimental tug, discovering that although the rope doesn't tighten, it does hold me in place completely, rendering me pretty much immobile.

He looks down at me from his position at the end of the bed, a satisfied gleam in his eyes as he takes me in, open before him. I'm still wearing my navy silk shorts and cami, the feel of the fabric against my overheated skin almost unbearable, and I shift squirming and trying to find relief.

I look down at him, my breathing shallow. His inked beauty makes my breath catch every fucking time my eyes alight on him, my heart fluttering. I watch as he gets fully hard again from just looking at me. His eyes meet mine, and the look of desire and need in them, causes my heart to skip a beat inside my chest, my body flooding with excited anticipation.

"Now remember, Princess," he begins in that deliciously sinful voice of his. "If your hands or feet start to tingle, or go numb, you tell me straight away. And your safe word is red. Tell me what your safe word is?"

"Red, but, Ash, please," I beg, trying and failing to ease the ache between my thighs.

A sardonic smile lifts one corner of his lips as he continues to take me in, looking like he plans to leave me in this agony.

*Looks like you can't take the bastard out of the boy after all.*

Getting off the bed, he walks across the room to his desk, opens a drawer, and takes out a huge fucking knife that looks wicked sharp. My heart rate picks up at the sight of him walking back towards me with it, a thread of excitement laced with fear running through me.

Climbing up onto the bed, he settles himself between my spread legs.

"Probably should have stripped you before tying you up..." he mutters, but not like he cares much about the oversight, as he brings the knife to the lacy hem of my shorts.

"Ash, don't you fucking dare!" I warn him, as I realise what he's planning on doing. The fucker just smiles, lifting my shorts up with the blade.

"Don't move, Princess," he orders as he starts to cut the silk from hem to waistband. I stay still, fuming as he finishes that side and starts on the other, cutting my shorts off my body.

"You boys owe me some new fucking PJs," I grumble when he whips the pieces of silk from under me.

He then looks to my cami top.

"I'll buy you a thousand sets, Princess, but I'll just keep cutting them off," he promises like the arsehole that he is.

He then cuts right up the middle of my top, in between my breasts. He finishes by slicing the straps so that I'm completely naked and tied up underneath him.

"Perfect," he sighs, leaning over and jamming the knife into the wooden headboard, leaving it sticking out and bobbing with the force of his thrust.

I can't help it, I reach up and bite one of his nipples, hard. Any normal person might squeak, or shout. Not Ash. He moans in pleasure, rubbing his now fully erect cock along my lower stomach, and I can feel the wetness of precum smearing across my skin.

I release him and am satisfied to see indents of my teeth marking him.

"Naughty girl," he whispers, rubbing his thumb along my lower lip as he looks down on me.

Then he crawls off the bed, walks across the room, opens the door, and walks out.

*What the ever loving fuck?!*

# CHAPTER THIRTY-EIGHT

LILLY

As I curse Ash every name under the sun, I hear footsteps coming up the hall, back towards me.

*That sounds like more than just one person...*

My suspicion is confirmed when Ash walks back through the door, followed by Loki, Jax, and Kai. I take in a sharp inhale as they fan around the bed, all looking down at me with matching expressions of hunger and appreciation on their faces.

"Black certainly is your colour, Pretty Girl," Loki drawls, his emerald eyes practically on fire as he takes me in, naked and tied up in the black ropes.

My nipples harden to points under their gaze, my pussy throbbing with the need for release, which only they'll be able to give me considering my current predicament.

Ash stands at the foot of the bed again, the white bandage on his thigh stark against his tattooed skin, a condom already covering his hard member. He starts to crawl up the bed until his lips are level with my aching cunt. Holding my gaze, and lowering down, his wicked tongue comes out to lick me from opening to clit. My hips buck off the bed at the warm contact, and I moan loudly as I almost climax from that touch alone. His hands come up to my pelvis, holding me in place as he starts to feast on me, licking and sucking with such devastating precision, that within mere minutes I'm screaming and coming all over his face.

I look around the bed with hooded eyes, to see the others have all stripped down, hands wrapped around their rock hard members, condoms already on, and their eyes ablaze with desire.

Ash draws my attention back to him when he begins to climb back up my body, holding himself above me, his dick poised at my entrance.

He leans down to kiss me, devouring my mouth like he did my pussy, and tasting myself on his lips and tongue sets me alight all over again.

Pulling back, he looks me straight in the eyes as though he's trying to steal my very soul from my body.

"We're each going to fuck you, to claim you, and you're going to take it like the good girl I know you can be," he instructs, his voice low and demanding and I can't stop the full body shudder at his words. "You are ours, Lilly Darling, and will be ours until we're dragged kicking and screaming from this world into the flames. And when we're all in Hell, we will take on Lucifer himself if he dares to keep us from you."

Not giving me a moment to process his declaration, he slams into me up to the hilt with a deep primal groan, causing a pleasure filled shriek to issue from my parted lips. The way he starts to fuck me is not gentle, or soft and sweet. It's as he said, a claiming. He's branding me as his, as theirs, with every hard thrust of his hips and every grind of his pelvis into my clit. He's practically snarling, and sweat beads his brow, his grey eyes swirling with a kind of frenzied animal madness.

I'm utterly helpless, unable to move, so I give myself over to the intense sensations that he's eliciting from my body. It's euphoric, giving someone complete control over you, and just letting go. Everything fades away, apart from his hardness pounding into me, stoking the flames higher, until I'm burning all over.

"Ash!" I gasp out as he keeps hitting the same spot inside me, over and over again, driving me wild.

"Come for me, Princess. Paint me with your release," he orders, his voice strained, letting me know that he's close, too.

As if knowing I need a little nudge, he brings one hand between us and pinches my clit, which tips me over the edge, howling my climax as I fall. I hear him roar, reaching his own pinnacle whilst I'm still floating, and he stiffens above me as he comes. His face transforms when he finds release, and for a brief moment, he looks utterly relaxed and at peace.

We lie together, him still deep inside me for several heartbeats, breathing each other in like we need the other to keep existing. He leans down, kissing me tenderly on my lips.

"Thank you, Princess," he whispers against them, before pushing up and out of me. I mourn the loss, missing his heat already.

He kneels up between my legs, looking like a satisfied jungle cat, languid yet full of danger.

"Kai," he declares, getting off the bed, stripping the used rubber off his semi-hard cock, and going to sit in the big armchair that's to the side of us, which is shrouded in darkness.

My attention snaps to Kai, who's now coming around to the other side of the bed. I notice he has something long in his hand, and when he steps into the circle of light, my breath catches. He's holding a thin black whip with a red leather tip.

"What's your safe word, Lilly?" Kai asks me, his voice low and melodic.

"Red," I whisper back, a rush of excitement sweeping over me.

"Good girl," he praises, and I fucking preen at the approval. "Do you know what this is, Lilly?" he quizzes, and I nod. "You may speak," he instructs, his voice firm and commanding, and I can feel my core tighten with the authority in his tone.

"It's a whip," I say softly, my eyes darting back up to his, seeking approval.

"It's actually called a crop, but you were very close, well done," he congratulates, making my body flush.

I take in a sharp breath as he brings the leather tip along my side, teasing me with a light touch starting at my waist, then running it around the side of my breast, my underarm, and up to my closed fist.

"Open your palm, Lilly," he commands, and I immediately obey, feeling a rush of anticipation as to what he will do next. I try to crane my head up to look at my open palm, but it's too awkward of an angle, so I close my eyes and wait.

I hear the whistle of parting air milliseconds before I feel the sharp sting of the crop on my palm. Gasping, my hand involuntarily closes, and my back arches with the unexpectedly exquisite sensation.

"Open your eyes, Lilly," he orders. I look into his honey orbs which are blazing with ravenous hunger, the only sign of what he's thinking, as he appraises me. "I'm going to use the crop on your beautiful breasts now. Five times on each."

The fire in his eyes rages to a blazing inferno as he brings the crop to start caressing all over my boobs, my nipples peaking with the tickling sensation. Suddenly, he brings the crop down on one globe with a crack. I cry out at the pain, yet my centre clenches, and I feel a bead of liquid drip down my inner thigh.

He moves to the other side, teasing me with the leather tip of the crop, tracing it all around my breast before bringing it down sharply on my flesh. I shriek time and again as he catches me unaware, my cries turning to moans the longer it goes on. I'm sweating and shaking by the time he's finished, my body tingling.

"Look how beautiful she is, painted with red stripes," he admires out loud, and I hear the others murmur their agreement. My eyes open to see his face set in an expression of intense gratification as he looks at his handiwork.

He drops the crop to the floor with a dull thud, climbing onto the bed and coming to hover over me, lining up his hard, pierced cock with my weeping opening.

"Such a good, beautiful girl," he mumbles, cupping my face.

Slowly, torturously, he pushes inside me inch by inch, the metal of his piercings already rubbing over my g-spot. I'm shuddering by the time he's all the way in, panting as he starts to move in earnest, surging into me harder with each thrust, until the sounds of our bodies slamming together are all that I can hear.

He moves his body up, seeking to go even deeper, and I curse as he hits the right spot unrelentingly, my climax ripping through me, my back arching, and my head thrown back as I see stars. There's a rush of liquid between my thighs as I orgasm, my inner muscles convulsing around Kai's hard length.

He pumps his hips hard once, twice, then plunges deep, growling in ecstasy, and biting down on my neck, which sends me over the edge again.

"So beautiful," he rasps out, rubbing his nose along my throat, sending shivers skittering across my body, and my pussy flutters around him.

"Jax," I hear Ash command from the chair, and I open my eyes to find his intense steel gaze on me, taking in my prone position and Kai above me.

Kai kisses me sweetly, before pulling out and climbing off the bed, taking one final look at my flushed skin, and the red stripes that decorate my chest.

The mattress dips beside me, my head turning to the side as Jax climbs on. He hesitates, one knee on the bed and looking down at me frowning, biting the inside of his cheek. I can't bear the thought that my threats from earlier may have made him doubt my feelings for him.

"Jax, I know what I said earlier about not sleeping with you, but I shouldn't have threatened you with withholding myself. That was wrong, and I'm so sorry. I love you. Please, make love to me."

His whole body droops with relief, and I'm treated to one of those rare smiles that light up his entire face. Looking me over once more, still tied up and flushed from the attentions of Ash and Kai, he growls his approval.

"They warmed you up nicely for me, Baby Girl," he rumbles out, and I whimper when his hands trace my skin with a feather light touch, setting my nerve endings alight.

He settles in between my spread legs, lining up his impressive length with my soaked entrance, and with one smooth thrust, he's fully seated inside me. My toes curl, and my fists clench the bedclothes as he starts to fuck me so hard, the bed frame shakes and groans, hitting the wall behind us.

"Still so fucking tight," he rasps, his thrusts getting even harder. He's practically hitting my cervix every damn time, he's so fucking huge, and the edge of pain helps to build a wildfire inside me, waiting to be released.

He brings one big hand up, his palm caressing my breasts, and I hiss at the delicious sting left by Kai's crop. Supporting himself on one arm, he reaches with the other and wraps his strong fingers around my throat, squeezing. He's doing an impressive one arm push-up, still pounding hard into me, as his grip on my throat tightens, restricting my airway, so I'm struggling for each breath.

I turn my head to find Loki stroking himself slowly next to us, his Prince Albert piercing glinting and glistening in the low lights.

"Look at me when I'm fucking you, Baby Girl," Jax growls out, and my head snaps towards him at his commanding tone.

His eyes are wild, like a stormy sea churning with lust, as he thrusts even harder into me, squeezing my throat so that I can't breathe at all let alone make any noise.

The lack of air sends me spiralling higher, detonating an explosion inside me that's so intense, I blackout entirely, only coming to when I hear a lion's roar above me as Jax finds his own release. His grip loosens enough that I take a huge gasping breath, the air tasting sweet and burning slightly, as it hits my lungs.

*I will definitely have a necklace of bruises tomorrow*, I ruefully think with a satisfied smile as I lie there panting and tingling, feeling spent and exhausted.

"Loki!" Ash barks from his seat, his throne.

Jax kisses my lips tenderly, then my throat, and he climbs off of me, leaving me groaning as he leaves my body.

"Hey, Pretty Girl," Loki drawls softly, and for a second, I get lost in emerald eyes that shine with desire and love. I see him nod to Ash, and then *Earned It* by The Weeknd starts to play. *He's such a Cassanova!*

I manage a weak smile, but I genuinely don't know how I'm going to have another orgasm, I'm completely wrung out and my body is totally jellified.

Starting at my toes, he kisses my sweaty body in between singing along to the song, crawling up to me, and leaving delicious tingles in his wake. He gently kisses the red stripes that Kai left on my breasts, with a featherlight touch that leaves me squirming on the sheets. He teases my nipples with his tongue until they're pebbled and rock hard. He then moves onto my throat, kissing and sucking, until I'm writhing underneath him, his lips moving to hover over mine.

"Loki..." I breathe against them, feeling the pierced tip of him begin to push inside me. "I don't know if I can..." I whimper, shaking as he goes deeper.

"Of course you can, Pretty Girl, you're such a good girl," he croons, and gently keeps pushing until he bottoms out, letting out a deep contented sigh.

He begins to gently undulate his hips in time with the music, picking up the lyrics, singing to me like he did on our date night all those weeks ago. My breathing speeds up as he moves inside me, gasping every time he grinds his pelvis into my clit.

I can feel the flicker of an orgasm come to life inside me as he slowly builds me up, his body aligned with mine, not an inch of space between us. His hands tangle in my hair, as he sings in my ear, and it's so sensual and hot that the flames turn into a bonfire, and before I know it, I'm seeing stars as he draws another shuddering climax from my aching, spent body, tears springing into my eyes.

My inner walls convulse around his cock, my nails biting into my palms with the force of my release.

"Lilly!" he cries out moments later as he reaches his own crescendo, his body going completely rigid, a look of bliss on his angelic face.

His weight settles on top of me, and I relish the crush as we both relearn what gravity feels like.

I'm so exhausted, I can barely open my eyes, and I lay there fucking glowing. I feel a tug on my wrist, then the sweet release of the bindings being undone. Through slitted lids, I see Ash moving to untie my ankles.

"Loki, get off her," Ash demands. "Take her downstairs, and clean her up. Kai, find her fresh PJs, silk ones, then bring her back here. Jax and I will remake the bed," Ash directs, his voice firm yet not unkind. He leans over to brush my hair off my face as Loki complies with a grumble. "You're staying with me tonight, Princess," he utters under his breath next to my ear, placing a soft kiss on my cheek.

Loki takes my hand, encouraging me to the side of the bed, then scooping me up in his arms and carrying me out of the room, which I'm fucking grateful for as I doubt I could walk. I hear Jax grumble, "Fucking show off," as we pass him, which makes Loki shake with laughter.

He brings me down the stairs and into the bathroom, turning on the shower and taking me inside. My legs are like jelly, what with being tied and the multiple orgasms, unable to support my weight, so he keeps ahold of me as he sets me on my feet, washing me, then towelling me dry. Kai walks in with fresh PJs, dusky pink silk with cream lace, as per Ash's instructions, and helps me into them as Loki finishes drying himself off.

Then, Loki sweeps me back up into his arms and carries me upstairs with Kai following behind us. He sets me down gently onto the freshly made bed, pulling the covers up over me and giving me a sweet kiss on my lips.

"Goodnight, sweetheart," Loki whispers into my ear, stroking the side of my face tenderly. Moving away, he's replaced by Kai, who kisses me gently too, before wishing me a good night. Jax playfully barges Kai out of the way, leaning down to do the same.

My eyelids start to droop as I hear the door click shut, plunging the room into darkness. The bed dips some minutes later, just as I'm drifting off, and I'm surrounded by the scent of fresh ginger. Ash pulls me tight into him, my back to his front, wrapping his arm around my waist.

. . .

*"'I love thee with a love that shall not die, till the sun grows cold and the stars grow old,'"*

He quotes in hushed tones, and I vaguely register it's from A Midsummer Night's Dream, before the darkness of sleep enfolds me in its warm embrace.

# CHAPTER THIRTY-NINE

LILLY

Monday rolls around, and I'm a little sore between my thighs and pleasurably exhausted, but alas, it's back to classes for us all. I haven't seen Robert around, rumour is that after his dad's arrest, he and his mum have had to move states to escape the hounding by the media. *Good riddance to bad rubbish, I say!*

It's the second to last week before winter break, and we're preparing for a full five days of exams next week. I'm pretty much studying every spare minute, with one of the guys always by my side revising, too. I don't know why I'm so surprised at how studious they are. Even Jax, whose focus is sports, takes his theory subjects very seriously.

We all sit down for dinner on Wednesday evening in our dorm. Kai has made an incredible Pad Thai dish that has my mouth watering. There's also these little dumpling-bun things, filled with duck, and some teriyaki marinated chicken skewers.

"Kai, this smells amazing!" I gush, piling my plate high, and stuffing half a dumpling-bun into my mouth, moaning at the incredible flavours. All the guys chuckle, even Ash, used to my table manners, or lack thereof, by now.

Turning to Jax, I swallow my mouthful, slightly nervous butterflies fluttering in my stomach.

"So, I've been looking into the best way for you to come off the steroids," I inform him, twirling some noodles on my fork. "We have to be careful because sudden withdrawal can cause all sorts of unpleasant symptoms, including depression, suicidal thoughts, and reduced sex drive." Jax spits his water out at this, and Loki barks out a laugh.

"Don't worry, Pretty Girl, the rest of us can pick up the *slack*," Loki emphasises, then grunts as someone kicks him under the table.

"Unhelpful, Loki," I roll my eyes at him, then look back to Jax. "Anyway, the best course of action is to seek a medically assisted detox, usually as an inpatient in rehab," I gently suggest, taking his hand in mine. Jax's brow is furrowed, and he's stopped eating. "I know it sounds extreme, but then you can get the best treatment, and any medicine or hormone replacements that you need, plus access to a therapist, Jax," I entreat him.

"It's too public," Ash remarks, and I glare at him. "Oh, don't get your panties in a twist, Princess. They say that in England, right?" he smirks at me. *Fucking shitpouch.* His gaze turns back to Jax. "We'll go private, hire a team, and Jax can stay at our private island house over winter break."

"Your fucking what?!" I exclaim, disbelieving the words that I'm sure he just said.

"We own an island near Bali, so Jax can stay there and get clean," he explains with an eye roll. "Will your parents miss you over Christmas?" he asks Jax, and I'm still stunned and speechless. *Fucking rich arseholes.*

"Nah. Doubt the cunts will even notice," he scoffs gruffly, and I squeeze his hand, feeling a pang in my heart for him. I was so lucky to have Mum. She would have ripped me a new one if I'd suggested spending Christmas apart.

"I could spend Christmas with you if you'd like, Jax?" I ask softly. "My uncle has said that I can't go back to England, so I'm free."

His hand tightens on mine. "I'd love that, Lilly, it's just," he hesitates, "I don't know how I'll be, and I'm not sure I want you to see me like that," he admits quietly, his piercing blue eyes serious and uncertain. I feel crestfallen at his words, although I try to keep my smile in place. This isn't about me, it's about what is best for him.

"Hey, Pretty Girl," Loki interrupts my pity party and I turn my gaze to him. "My folks aren't home again, so how about you spend Christmas with me and the girls, and if Jax is up for a visit, we can go see him?" he suggests, and I feel some tension drain from Jax next to me.

"I'd love to spend Christmas with you, Loki," I grin, looking back at Jax. "Is that okay with you?"

"That's perfect, baby," he replies, leaning over to kiss my cheek softly.

---

The rest of the week is filled with more frantic studying, and Ash makes arrangements for Jax's rehab. Soon, it's Friday night, and after getting a stack of boxed pizzas from the dining hall, we sit down on the sofas, Jax and Kai on either side of me, eating them without plates. I laugh to see that Jax has three fucking boxes in front of him. *Three!*

I moan aloud at the cheesy melted goodness of my good old fashioned margarita pizza, licking my fingers when I look up to see four heated gazes turned my way.

"Keep eating like that, Pretty Girl, and you won't get the chance to finish your meal," Loki threatens, his voice a purring rumble. I hear Jax growl out his approval so I snatch my box and clutch it to me.

"Touch my pizza, and see which part I cut off first. Don't think I don't know how to do it. Jax taught me," I boast playfully. Loki throws his head back and roars with laughter, and I hear Jax chuff a chuckle beside me.

"That's my girl," he praises, giving me an approving grin.

"Let's play a game!" Loki suddenly cries like an excited puppy, bouncing up and down.

"Fuck's sake," Ash groans, wiping his hands on a napkin. "Fine. But no strip poker. You're shit, and I don't want to see your hairy balls tonight," he points a finger at Loki in warning.

*One of these days I'm gonna bite that finger.*

"Spoilsport," Loki teases, "let's play truth or dare." He has an evil grin on his face, and I get the feeling clothes will be shed anyway. I bet none of these fuckers will back down, they're so competitive it's ridiculous. "You can go first, Lilly," he offers sweetly.

"Truth or dare?" I ask him, one brow raised.

"Dare," he replies, a provocative smile on his lips.

I narrow my eyes, thinking for a moment, then the perfect idea comes into my mind and I bite my lip, wondering if he'll take it.

"Loki, I dare you to kiss Kai. With tongue," I challenge, smirking. His emerald eyes widen a fraction with surprise. I don't shift my gaze from his, not even to look at Kai to see his reaction.

"That's your fantasy, is it, Lilly Darling?" he asks, a lascivious smile on his plush lips and his voice dropping an octave. "Would that make you wet, Pretty Girl?" I swallow hard, regretting my life choices right about now, but nod anyway. He chuckles darkly, getting up, and sauntering over to Kai, who is on the other side of me. "Far be it for me to deny our girl her darkest fantasy."

He drops to his knees in between Kai's spread legs, giving me a front row seat as he reaches to tangle his hand in Kai's thick chestnut hair. My breath turns shallow, my gaze captivated as Kai smiles, not objecting when Loki leans forward. Loki's eyes close and he presses his lips lightly to the other boy's, teasing the seam with his tongue. Kai's own eyelids flutter shut as he opens for Loki, letting him dominate the kiss.

My breathing picks up, and I gasp as they deepen the kiss, their tongues tangling. My core begins to ache, and I rub my legging clad thighs together to try and ease the throbbing that's started up. The kiss comes to an end, and Loki playfully nips Kai's lower lip as he releases his grip on the other guy's hair.

"How was that, Pretty Girl?" Loki asks huskily, his pupils blown with lust, and there's a definite bulge in his sweats. I look at Kai who seems to be in a similar state. *Now that's a manwich I need to be inside!*

"Perfect," I breathe, my voice husky.

He gives me one of his panty-incinerating grins, getting up, adjusting himself, then leans down to capture my lips in a scorching hot kiss that leaves me even more breathless. I moan as I taste Kai on his tongue. *Oh, that is so happening again, preferably with less clothes on.*

Straightening up, he turns to Ash. "Truth or dare?" he asks, his tone goading.

"Dare," Ash's grey eyes are hard with provocation, even if his face looks utterly bored.

"I dare you to get a dick piercing over Christmas," Loki smirks, looking entirely too pleased with himself.

"Loki!" I screech at him, aghast. *Fucking hell!*

"Any particular one?" Ash questions, a brow raised and ignoring my outburst, like it's no big deal that he seems to be agreeing to get his knob pierced.

"You can choose. As long it's something our girl will enjoy," Loki grins patronisingly, winking at me, then walking over to Ash and holding out his hand.

"Deal." Ash grasps it in a hard grip and shakes to close the deal.

"Did that just happen?" I question aloud, shaking my head as I look at the two guys. *These boys do take this shit seriously!*

"My turn," Ash declares, looking straight at me with his steel gaze. I swallow hard, butterflies taking flight in my stomach as a shiver of premonition comes over me. "Truth or dare, Princess?" he asks.

"Truth," I decide, hoping that he goes easy on me, but knowing that he won't. He's Ash, after all.

His eyes soften slightly, and I just know it's going to be bad.

"Tell me how you found your mother."

Those seven words stop my heart, the world ceases spinning, and it's like the blood has frozen in my veins. My gaze latches onto his, pleading with him not to do this. Not to make me relive that day. But he holds firm.

"What the fuck, man!?" Loki snarls, and I hear Jax growl low beside me. "You don't have to answer that." Loki turns to me, anger and desperate sadness making his emerald eyes churn and froth, like a violent sea.

"Yes, she does," Ash commands, voice unwavering and firm, yet not unkind. "She needs to face this, Loki."

They start to argue, getting in each other's faces, but it's as if they are far away, or I'm underwater, because all I can hear is the rush of blood in my ears as the memories assault me one after the other.

"It was my fault," I whisper, unable to stop the words from spilling from my lips.

"What was your fault, baby?" Jax asks gently, taking my hand in his larger one. Ash and Loki stop and look at me, Kai shifting closer to me, his warmth comforting me as he rubs my arm.

"My mother's death. It was all my fault," I answer him, already feeling the burn of tears at the back of my throat.

Loki starts to say something, but Ash puts a hand on his arm to stop him.

"How?" Ash prompts, and like a dam has burst, the whole sad story comes pouring out of me.

"W–we were meant to go out shopping together, but we fought about something that was so trivial, I can't even fucking remember what it was now. So I left, and met up with a friend instead," I tell them, taking a shaky breath to steady me for the next part. "When I got home, I remember opening the door to our flat and being hit by this metallic smell, like copper pennies." I hesitate, and the scent comes rushing back, filling my nostrils as bile hits the back of my throat.

Leaning over, I take a sip of water from my glass on the side table. "I called out, but there was no answer. The radio was on in the kitchen playing *Lovely* by Billie Eilish, I used to love that song. Anyway, I headed in that direction, ready to apologise for earlier." I take another desperate breath, closing my eyes as I relay the next part. "There was so much blood, my mind didn't realise what it was at first, and it soaked into my favourite yellow TOMS." I can see the crimson river as if I was back in the flat, looking at the scene again. I blink my eyes open, and I'm back in the dorm, Jax gripping my hand tightly, Kai rubbing soothing circles on my back, and Loki at my feet. I look up and see Ash is still across the room, a devastating sadness in his eyes.

"I tried to stop the bleeding, but it was no use, she was already...gone." I taste salt as tears flow freely down my face, dripping off my chin until Jax starts to wipe them with his thumb. "After that, I passed out, and woke up in a hospital, with what I later discovered was my uncle standing nearby."

"Oh, Baby Girl, it wasn't your fault," Jax rumbles out, pained. He scoops me up and places me onto his lap, and I sob against his chest, my fists clenched in his hoodie. He strokes my hair as Loki massages my feet, and Kai keeps rubbing my back.

Finally, my tears dry up, and I'm bone tired, yet a little lighter at the same time. More at peace. Ash was right. I needed to face what had happened, instead of running away from it. I look up with a watery smile, gazing into the faces of these boys who are my family now. We belong to each other so completely, nothing will ever separate us.

I turn to seek out Ash, wanting to thank him for forcing me to finally confront my grief, only to find him gone.

# CHAPTER FORTY

LILLY

It's finally the last week of term, or semester as they say here. We're called into the school's chapel on Monday for a special service. Highgate is all about showing off its good, upstanding Christian students.

*What a load of shit. Did they not see the orgies at Halloween? Oh yeah, no, they didn't, because they'd just left, turning a blind eye.*

We all file into the carved wooden pews, facing the front, and I can see Headmaster, sorry, Principal Robertson standing up front with a group of five others.

*Holy shit! Is that...Pentatonix?!*

"Today we have some special guests, who are going to perform for us," he informs us in a self-important tone. "They will start with *Amazing Grace*."

Outside I'm cool as a motherfucking cucumber, but inside, I'm fangirling so hard I'm surprised I'm not throwing my knickers at them!

I hear an amused snort from my right as I'm surrounded by the vanilla scent that is all Loki.

"Bit of a fan are you, Pretty Girl?" his familiar drawl whispers in my ear, his breath caressing my neck as he speaks. *Zing, there goes my nipples!* I don't know what it is about that boy's voice, but I swear he could talk me into an orgasm. Or sing me into one.

"Oh, shut up, Loki!" Ash snarls nastily on my left. I see he woke up on the wrong side of the bed again this morning. He's been in a funny mood since we played Truth or Dare, avoiding me. I can't pretend that it doesn't hurt a little, his withdrawal. After all, he's the one that forced the issue.

Loki interrupts my train of thought by running his hand along my upper thigh, my legs opening instinctively, my left one brushing Ash's. For a brief moment, an image of Ash and Loki naked on either side of me, four hands caressing me, and two cocks moving inside me, flashes across my mind, and I gasp aloud at its intensity as heat floods over me in a rush.

I look up at Ash, confusion on his face, his perfect ebony brow dipped in a frown. I turn my gaze to Loki, to see amusement once again dancing in those green depths, as well as a flicker of heat.

*Surely he can't know what I was just thinking? Can he?*

"Naughty Girl," he teases, whilst giving me that panty melting smile of his and stroking his long fingers up and down my thigh. *How the fuck did he know?* I wonder, and as if I asked that thought aloud, he replies in a deep, husky whisper

"I know all of your deepest darkest desires, Pretty Girl," he purrs, his fingers teasing higher, delving underneath my red Run & Fly tartan pinafore dress.

"Loki!" I hiss, trying to ignore the fire that he's started, and the tingles racing to my core. "Behave!"

"Nope," he shrugs nonchalantly. "I don't feel like behaving today," he whispers, his hand going higher, those long clever fingers of his dancing along the edge of my lace knickers.

"Oh, for fuck's sake," I hear Ash mutter, and a second later, a tanned hand grabs Loki's wrist and halts its movement. I look up and see them, eyes locked and faces tense, and I can't help feeling like a fucking bone between two alpha wolves, neither willing to give up his prize.

Just as I'm about to tear them a new one about the fact that I'm not a fucking dog toy, I hear the dulcet tones of Pentatonix begin to sing, and the guys, the church, the fucking world, just melts away.

*Amazing Grace (My Chains Are Gone)* is one of my favourite covers of theirs, and like most of their songs, it starts slow and then builds to a crescendo of voices, lifting you up alongside them. It's the type of music that you feel in your soul.

I come back down to earth when I feel Ash go completely stiff next to me, so solid it's like he's made of granite. I turn to look at him, and see he's almost vibrating with...*fury?* My brows furrow as I wonder why he's so cross, when all of a sudden, he stands up and marches down the aisle and out the door.

"What the fuck?" I whisper, completely bewildered as to his strange reaction.

"Go to him, Pretty Girl. After hearing your story the other day, he needs you," Loki urges, also looking in Ash's direction, concern flashing in his eyes, all hints of lust and playfulness gone.

I get up in a slight daze, confused as hell, and quietly make my own way down the aisle, still hearing the music behind me. As I exit the carved wooden doors into the winter sunshine, I see Ash, doubled over with his hands on his knees. His back is rising and falling rapidly with his panting breaths, his eyes closed tight, like he's trying to keep the monsters at bay.

"Ash...?" I query, concern flooding me, taking a step closer. Ordinarily, I'd go to him, but the past few days have left me feeling uncertain.

I've never seen him so emotional in public. So unstable. Vulnerable. It's as if the world is closing in around him, and he's powerless to stop it. His eyes snap open, his head whipping towards me, and the desolation in his steel gaze robs me of my breath. He looks broken, and like nothing in the world will ever put him back together.

"Ash!" I gasp, horrified, my heart aching for the sadness I see in his eyes, my eyes filling with tears as I see the moisture in his.

Before I can take another step in his direction, he stands up and stalks towards me, vibrating with anger and loathing, and I've no idea if it's towards me...or himself.

"It's all fucking bullshit!" he screams at me, arms flailing at his sides. I flinch. There's a wildness in his eyes, making their grey depths churn.

I once saw a tiger at London Zoo, pacing in front of the glass, then clawing at it as if it was desperate to flee. Ash reminds me of that tiger in this moment, desperate and wild.

"They're lying!" he sneers, flinging his arm back towards the church and the beautiful music that we can hear drifting out of the open doors. "I will *never* be fucking free! My chains are here for fucking life and beyond!" he says, pounding his chest, then looking at his wrists as if he could feel the cold metal digging in.

"Why?" I whisper, knowing that the answer will break me, carve me up. I can see it in the sharpness of his eyes, as he looks back up at me, cutting me already.

"Why?" he snarls, his face so close, I'm drowning in his ginger scent and molten eyes. They are boring into mine, digging into my soul with sharp claws, and leaving me bloody and torn. Something changes in his gaze, almost as if thick darkness takes over, and I'm left staring into an abyss so deep that there's no end.

"You know I had a brother, my twin brother, Luc. We were complete opposites in every way, yin and yang, you might say. He was the lightness to my darkness. The better half of me." A pinprick of light enters his eyes, a spark of pure joy, and the effect is astounding. And then, the light goes, like a candle snuffed out by a careless breath.

"It was the end of summer semester last year, and exhausted as we were, neither of us was looking forward to going back to the shitshow that we call home. My father is....well, you know." His gaze shutters and sharpens until it's like the edge of a blade. His whole face transforms into something hard and unfeeling, like a statue sitting over a grave.

"My father enjoys setting people against each other, another of his wonderful traits," he mocks. "He fancies himself a God, playing with people like you play a game of chess. He always set me and Luc against each other, made us compete to see who was stronger, smarter, more ruthless. When we were younger, it was innocent things, like races, or who could carry more. As we got older, it became more...damaging. Who could hold their breath the longest in the pool, who could last longer without eating, who could take the most punches." He's no longer looking at me, looking instead into a childhood that's full of pain and suffering, and I feel each revelation like a blow. It takes everything I have not to flinch.

"He hated if we ever got along and would punish us if he discovered us laughing together, or even fucking smiling at each other. He's a fucked up bastard that's for sure. So, Luc and I weren't close, not as twins should be anyway. But...I never hated him, and he didn't hate me. At least, I don't think he did." He looks wistful, with a despairing kind of hope.

"That morning, I'd finished packing all my shit up and went to Luc's room to see if he was ready to head downstairs. His door was locked, but I could hear music pounding, that fucking song by Anson Seabra, *I Can't Carry This Anymore*. No matter how hard I pounded, he wouldn't answer." His breath hitches, and it's like watching a car come towards you, but being unable to get out of the way. You see the headlights, yet you're frozen to the spot, staring your death in the face.

"Loki came out of his room, asking what the fuck all the noise was about. He'd gotten wasted the night before, so he was pretty hungover, the fucker. Jax came too, and Kai wandered up the stairs at the same time. That fucking song started up again, it was on repeat, and I just knew something wasn't right."

My heart is pounding, and my palms are sweaty like I've been running for my life. I feel sick, nausea rolling in my stomach. *Please don't let it be what I think it is. Please.*

"After what felt like hours, but was probably only around five minutes, Jax kicked the door in, and all I could see was red. A sea of red covering the bed and pooling on the floor. Luc..." He closes his eyes, swallowing hard, "Luc was lying in the middle of it. He was so pale, whiter than the sheets, and he looked so...peaceful. Like he'd finally come home after a long journey. I remember feeling envy, I was fucking jealous that he didn't have to deal with this shit anymore, with our father and his mind games. I was so angry at him, for giving up, for not fighting. For leaving me." Ash's head is bowed, jet hair covering his face.

I taste salt, and I realise that tears are streaming down my face and I can't stop them. I don't want to stop them. I remember the red blood splattered on the walls, the smell of shiny pennies. There was no peace, though, only horror. I blink the memories away, now is not the time to get lost in them.

My hand reaches out to push his hair back, feeling its softness which is so at odds with the hard man it belongs to. He leans into the touch and sighs softly. He opens his eyes, that molten gaze on me once more, and the guilt I see in those steel depths is paralysing.

"Ash..." I breathe, at a complete loss as to what to say. I know nothing helps, not really. "It wasn't your fault," I tell him, desperately wanting him to know that, to believe that.

An almost smile lifts up one corner of those full lips. It's not a nice smile though. It's a smile of hopelessness, a smile of despair.

"That's where you're wrong, Princess. It's entirely my fault. He even left a note telling me so." His long finger comes up to caress the side of my face, from forehead to chin, like he can't help but touch me back.

"Wh–what?" I stutter, unbelievingly.

*"Dear Ash, I can't fight you and dad anymore. I don't want to, and I don't want what he's offering. I just want peace, so I'm taking myself out of the game. The crown is all yours. Luc"* he recites, obviously having memorised the note.

"Oh, Ash," I choke, my eyes filling up and spilling over once again.

Before I can say anything else, he tears away from me, his eyes cutting and narrowing once more. This must have been why he bailed the other day, our experiences are so similar, both finding our loved ones in a pool of blood too fucking late.

"Don't you dare fucking pity me!" he spits, pointing a long finger in my direction, then spinning on his heel and storming off. Before he's out of earshot, I hear him mutter, "I don't fucking deserve it."

# CHAPTER FORTY-ONE

LILLY

I emerge from our Calculus exam, blurry-eyed yet full of relief and excitement. Autumn term, or as the guys say, fall semester, is finally over! Calculus was our last exam, on the final day, and as I look around at Loki, Jax, and Ash, I see similar expressions on their faces. Kai should have finished his much harder college level exam around about now too.

"Fuck yeah!" Loki suddenly shouts, jumping up and pulling Jax into a headlock, ruffling his hair and making his man bun even messier. He lets go and darts to my side before Jax can react, laughing, and slinging an arm across my shoulders.

"Fucker," Jax rumbles with a smile, untying and retying his bun.

"You ready to go, Pretty Girl?" Loki asks me, pulling me closer and placing a kiss on my cheek.

We'd packed our bags last night, loading them into his car first thing this morning, so that we could be ready to leave straight away.

"Yep," I say.

A pang of sadness runs through me at the thought of being separated from the rest of the guys over the break, as Kai joins us from his exam, and we head to the student lot.

Loads of other students are heading to the lot too, and I can hear excited whoops and chatter all around me. They give us a wide berth, not getting too close to our group. I've noticed that more than once about the guys. The other students look in awe of them, not daring to approach, as if they, we, are royalty.

We walk towards the entrance, the boys have spaces right next to the road that comes in and out, and I hesitate next to the cars. Turning around in Loki's grip, I notice that the mood has turned sombre. Jax's brows are furrowed, Kai looks a little nervous, and Ash has a scowl marring his beautiful face. Even Loki is unusually silent next to me.

I step out from under his arm, going up to Jax, and use my thumb to smooth out his frown.

"Hey, big guy, I'll see you in a couple of weeks, okay?" I ask softly, trying to capture his gaze. He nods, then wraps a big hand around my throat, pulling my mouth to his, devouring my lips in a blistering kiss that leaves me panting and needy.

He pulls away, a small tilt lifting one side of his mouth, in an almost grin. *Cocky bastard.*

He steps back, releasing me. I turn to Kai next, who gives me a sweet smile, and opens his arms for me to step into. I'm surrounded by his fresh woodsy scent as he hugs me tightly and breathes me in, kissing the top of my head, my hands fisted into the front of his shirt. I look up, offering him my lips which he takes in one of his melting kisses. It's so different from the possession of Jax's, but it's no less devastating to my heart. It's full of calmness, an acceptance, yet also a desperate need, a wish, and I kiss him back just as achingly. I hate that he's going back to his uncle, that he'll be all alone there, after everything that he suffered at his uncle's hands.

I know it won't be long, we all agreed to meet up on Boxing Day, December twenty-sixth. And if Jax is up for it, we will fly out to spend the rest of the break with him. But the days ahead of us until we meet up again are going to feel like a lifetime apart.

Tears spring to my eyes as he ends the kiss and drops his arms, giving me a sad smile.

I take a steadying breath and face Ash, knowing that in a way, this will be the hardest goodbye. I feel like I'm signing his death warrant, sending him back to his abhorrent father. Especially after the story of Luc's death. He's been reserved since that day, but surprisingly he hasn't withdrawn like he did after I told them about finding Mum. I can see him shutting down now though, his grey eyes going hard and unyielding, like he's preparing himself for the ordeal ahead. I reach up, stroking the side of his face tenderly. A tear slips out of my eye, trailing down my cheek unbidden. His gaze softens, and he catches it on the tip of his finger, bringing it up to his mouth.

"Rubber duck?" he asks with a slight smile, bringing a watery one to my own lips.

"Any time, day or night," I vow in a whisper, stepping closer.

His hands come up into my hair, pulling me so close, there's not an inch of space between our bodies. The rest of the students, the sounds of cars, all fade away as we stare at each other, before he lowers his lips down to mine. I gladly open for him, his tongue teasing my own and tasting me until I'm not sure whose air is whose anymore. It's a kiss to merge two souls until they become one entity, emerging stronger than before.

A small sob leaves me as he breaks away, steel eyes still locked onto my own.

"I love you, Ash," I breathe. A fierce look takes over his face, his grip tightening in my hair.

He holds me for a moment, staring into my eyes, like he would set fire to the world in my name.

"Come on, Pretty Girl," Loki whines, breaking the tension between us. "Let's hit the road like a donkey cock," he jokes, ruining the moment entirely, and Ash reluctantly lets go of my hair, allowing me to turn around.

I roll my eyes as I walk towards Loki's car, taking one last look behind me, before stepping into the passenger side. My breath catches at the sight of the three beautiful, broken boys I'm leaving behind.

A tremble of premonition passes over me, and I have to shake off the feeling that things are changing, and won't be the same after the break.

*Don't be a twat, Lilly!*

My phone pings as we drive off, and I look down to see a message flashing on the screen.

**Ash: I love you too, Lilly Darling x**

---

Loki and I spend the first week chilling out watching movies, swimming, and hanging out with his sisters. Loki seems to have a burning desire to have sex in every room in the house. He tells me it's his goal for the rest of the year, so we end up in all sorts of positions all over the mansion.

We don't see Clarissa much, apparently, she takes most of the holidays off, but whenever she is around, Loki clams up, and I've never seen him quite so...scathingly cold towards someone before.

There's a story there that I'm determined to uncover one day, but I don't want to ruin our little bubble of happiness so I keep quiet for now. Clarissa gives me the creeps, she looks at me with such loathing, like Loki is somehow hers, and I'm the other woman. *Ewww!*

We spend one evening talking about Christmas traditions. It's mostly me talking, as it turns out Loki's parents are often away over the holidays, and so Loki doesn't really have many things that he does every year. I tell him about always making a Christmas cake with my mum, and about the time when I was ten, that I misread the instructions and put in one pound of salt instead of a pinch.

When I ask what he does for Christmas lunch, he replies that his parents get it sent in by some fancy restaurant. I'm determined to make him and his sisters a homemade English roast this year, and I make a list of all of the things I need, ordering it online to be delivered a few days before the twenty-fifth. I tell Loki to let his parents know that lunch is taken care of this year.

The next day waking up, I realise that I'm alone in Loki's bed. I look over to the clock and notice that it's mid-morning. Loki kept me up way too late last night, insatiable bastard. I grin to myself, stretching and feeling every delicious ache. Getting out of bed and grabbing one of Loki's band t-shirts from the floor, I head to the bathroom to take care of business.

I emerge with still no sign of Loki, so I decide to go downstairs and grab something to eat. Approaching the kitchen, I hear *White Winter Hymnal* by Pentatonix playing, which makes me smile, knowing that he's put it on for me as it's one of my favourites.

Walking into the room, I stop when I see Loki leaning against the counter, with his panty melting grin firmly in place. He's wearing an apron that reads 'Redheads, setting your world alight', and I would laugh because it's just so

Loki, except that it looks like that's all he's got on. He confirms my theory when he stands up and slowly turns around, flashing his peachy arse.

"Loki!" I admonish him with a laugh. "What will your sisters say?"

"They're at a friend's for the day, Pretty Girl," he purrs, sauntering towards me, and I swallow at the heat in his eyes. "It's just you and me today."

When he reaches me, he grabs me around my waist and pulls me close, growling with approval when he realises that I'm only wearing his t-shirt and silk knickers.

"That will have to wait," he muses, his hand caressing my arse, sending tingles racing over me.

"Wait?" I question, brows lowered in confusion. Loki never waits to get in between my thighs.

He takes a step back, indicating the worktop, which is covered in packets, and a very expensive looking mixer.

"We've got a Christmas cake to make, baby," he grins.

I throw myself at him with a squeal, wrapping my arms and legs around him, his hands gripping my arse, as I pepper his face with kisses.

"I fucking love you, Loki Thorn," I enthuse, a deep chuckle vibrating over my body, as he walks us across the floor.

"I fucking love you back, Lilly Darling," he tells me, his voice full of warmth, as he deposits me on the counter to stand in between my spread legs.

I can feel him growing hard, pressing against my core, heat flashing through me at the contact.

"Fuck waiting. You drive me fucking wild, Lilly," he growls, bringing his hands against my bare skin, lifting my t-shirt up and off me. Then his warm mouth closes over my nipple, my back arching as he sucks, offering him more, which he takes greedily as my hands grip his fiery red hair.

He lets go of the now sensitive bud, blowing on it, and the cool air hardens it to a point. Taking his time, he kisses his way over to my other breast, capturing that nipple in his mouth, and sucking.

"Loki..." I whimper, pulling his hair tighter. He chuckles at the action, the vibrations tickling over me.

"Yes, Lilly, my love?" he asks, and I can hear the self-satisfied smirk in his tone.

"Fuck me now, Loki," I order him, desperate to feel him move inside me and fill me up until I'm a mindless mess.

"What's the magic word?" he teases, grinning as he pulls away from me, one perfect auburn brow raised.

"Please," I growl. *Fucking dickhead.*

"Good girl," he says approvingly. He takes a small foil packet out of his apron pocket, moves the garment aside, as he tears the packet with his teeth and rolls the condom on. Then he unties the apron and lifts it off, dropping it to the floor.

My breath comes sharply at the sight of him naked and erect. It never gets old, never ceases to amaze me, that this beautiful man is mine, and I can have him whenever I want.

He steps back into me, his cock brushing up against the inside of my thigh, and I shudder with anticipation. Using his fingers he moves the crotch of my silk knickers aside, rumbling out an appreciative growl at how wet he finds me.

"Look at you so slick and ready for me," he hums out, lining up his pierced tip with my slick opening.

I let out a low moan when he starts to push forward, soon filling me completely. His hands gently push me down, until my back hits the cold marble countertop, my breath hissing out as my fevered skin makes contact with the frigid stone.

He drives into me, a bruising grip on my hips holding me in place as he thrusts his hips hard and fast. It's like he can't get enough of me. A feeling that I return wholeheartedly.

My arms come up overhead, trying and failing to find some purchase as he keeps up his relentless pace until I'm screaming my climax, my pussy quivering and fluttering around his hard cock. He doesn't slow down, if anything my orgasm spurs him on more, and I can see the sweat dripping down his chiselled abs as he works.

"Touch yourself, Lilly," he orders, voice strained as he keeps relentlessly pounding into me.

My hand snakes down my body, and he falters slightly as his eyes track the movement. I start to rub circles around the bundle of nerves, sending zings of pleasure skittering all over my skin. His pace picks up even more, encouraging me to go faster, and I can feel another orgasm building.

"Loki, I'm so close," I gasp out in a moan. "Come with me, Loki," I beg, feeling the sparks of another release begin.

"Fuck!" he growls, then suddenly pulls out, whipping the condom off and shooting hot ropes of spunk all over my stomach and breasts. His withdrawal triggers my second mind shattering orgasm, as I scream his name, clawing at the countertop.

I lie there, my whole body liquid, panting, and my heart racing. I watch Loki as he walks over to the sink, switches on the tap, and gets out a clean cloth from underneath. He comes back to me and cleans me up, sighing as he wipes his seed off of my abdomen.

"You look so pretty covered in my cum," he admires as he wipes it all off. He helps me off the counter, kissing me breathless. "Right, now let's go shower, and we can get baking!" he orders, swatting my arse as I turn my back on him.

*Arsehole*, I chuckle as we head up the stairs.

---

We spend the rest of the day making the Christmas cake. Loki even got me an apron to match his, only mine says, "My favourite boyfriend is a redhead." The others are gonna go ape shit when they see it, which is probably why he got it for me. *Bastard.*

We leave the cake to cool, we'll ice it in a few days after we've fed it copious amounts of alcohol. Usually, you do this over a number of weeks, but I'm sure this way it'll taste just as good.

The next day, I tell Loki I really must go into town, as I've not bought a single gift yet, and Christmas is only a week away. I know we won't be seeing the others for a little while, as long as Jax is up for it, and I know they all have everything they could ever want, but I want to get them each a gift anyway.

We take Loki's red Lamborghini and head into Brompton Lakes. It's another stunning day, although the temperature has dropped quite a bit now. We've had a few bouts of snow over the past week, but nothing that has settled too much, although apparently, the mountains are more covered, and ski season is upon us.

We pull up and park in town, and I can't help feeling a little nervous. I have literally no idea what to get any of them. I mean, they're rich entitled brats that have pretty much everything they want stuff wise. *What do you get boys who have everything?*

I've made them a playlist on Spotify that has all of our songs on it. The songs that we've danced to, played to, made love to. I was going to add them to it so that they can listen to it whenever they like. But I want to get them something else, I just don't know what.

We get out, and I convince Loki to split up so that I can wander around, hoping that something genius comes to me as I gaze in shop windows. My uncle gives me a generous allowance, so I don't need to worry too much about the cost.

I pass by a combat sports shop when like a lightning bolt, inspiration strikes.

*Fucking perfect!*

I emerge thirty minutes later, with four huge bags, containing four black gift boxes. Luckily, Loki sees me struggling up the street, and races to take them off me.

"What's in the bags?" he asks curiously, starting to bring them up to his face.

"Good things come to those who wait, Loki," I tease, lightly smacking his chest to discourage his investigation.

"But I hate waiting," he whines like a small child, pouting, and I can't help but laugh at him.

"Oh, poor baby," I coo, pinching his cheek. "Don't worry, I have something extra for you for Christmas Eve." I wink, and he perks up as we walk back to his car.

We're a few cars away when I spot Ash walking towards us, a scowl on his beautiful face. I smile wide and take a step to run up to him, when I stop, noticing the two people walking behind him. One of them I recognise instantly as Ash's father, and my smile freezes as he meets my eyes, a feline grin tugging his lips up.

"Ah, Lilly Darling, what an unexpected pleasure," he purrs in his dark voice, so much like Ash's, and yet totally different. His is like the cold whisper of a crypt, there's no warmth or life in it.

Ash's head snaps up, something like panic rushing across his face before he schools it again into a blank expression. I hear the rustle of bags next to me, then feel Loki's warm hand firmly grip mine, tugging me closer to him.

"Julian," he says, his voice almost a growl.

"Loki," Julian nods, keeping his steel grey eyes locked on mine. I shudder at the attention, and I can't help but feel like I've caught the gaze of a predator.

*What a fucking creep.*

We stand there, the silence just this side of awkward.

"You must be Ash's mum," I suddenly blurt, shifting my gaze to the dark haired woman next to Julian. She's stunning, tall with raven hair, the colour of Ash's. "Pleased to meet you..." I trail off as she turns to look at me. Her blue eyes are dull, vacant, and lifeless, like she's somewhere else entirely.

"This is my wife, Samantha," Julian's dulcet tones interject, before Ash's mum, Samantha, can say a word.

I risk a glance at Ash, his brow is even more pinched, and he won't look at me at all.

"Well, we best get back," Loki tells them, tugging my hand and stepping past their group.

"I'll see you soon, Ash," I murmur gently as I pass him. I wish I could just kiss him, or grab his hand, anything to take that blank look away.

He looks up, and his eyes soften minutely as he gives a quick nod.

My gut churns as we start to walk away.

"Don't be a stranger, Lilly," I hear Julian call out after us, and I can't repress the shiver that cascades through me, leaving me cold in its wake.

# CHAPTER FORTY-TWO

LILLY

It's Christmas Eve, and for dinner we have Christmas themed pizza, which apparently is the one and only Christmas tradition of Loki's. He makes snowmen shaped pizza bases, topped with turkey mince, cranberry and mozzarella, and they're seriously good, even if the snowmen are more snow blobs.

Loki, the girls, and I are sitting in the living room, a cheerful fire burning in the fireplace, as we digest our meal, staring at the Christmas tree all lit up.

Loki and I went out and bought it today, and it was like all those American Christmas movies I watched as a kid, with a forest of trees to choose from in a parking lot. We spent ages there, with me insisting that we get the perfect tree and Loki humouring me until he got bored, and dragged me into the back of the lot for a quickie. The thought of being caught at any moment had me coming so hard and fast, Loki had to cover my mouth with his hand to keep everyone from hearing my cries. That only made me come harder, as he fucking knew it would.

We finally found the best and biggest tree there, Loki strapping it to the roof of his Lambo. *I know...rich brat, remember?* We spent the whole day with the girls decorating it. It looks a little like Santa went on a bender, and then threw up on it, but Heather and Julie are so happy, I don't have the heart to change a thing.

"Let's play guess the Disney song!" Heather suddenly cries, clapping her hands. Julie readily agrees, and they both pounce on a groaning Loki.

"Fine! Fine!" he laughs, shoving them off.

He turns to me, giving a helpless shrug as he gets up to leave the room. He comes back, holding his guitar and grinning at me.

"You ready?" he asks us, sitting down, guitar across his lap, and looking all too delicious in a tight t-shirt and jeans.

"Yes!" the girls and I shout with a laugh.

He starts strumming, and as soon as he begins singing, I can't help laughing.

"Part of Your World! The Little Mermaid," Heather shrieks, as Loki keeps singing, and giggles tumble from my mouth as the girls start singing along and leaping around.

Damn! Even singing songs sung originally by Disney Princesses, he's still hot as fuck holding a guitar and strumming with those magical fingers of his. My thighs clench at the thought of what else his fingers can do.

He looks up as he begins the next song, catching my eye and giving me a devastating grin. My breath catches in my throat and tingles spread over my body.

"I See the Light," I whisper, my heart swelling as he serenades me, staring deeply into my eyes. "Tangled."

I drown in his emerald gaze, his husky voice caressing every inch of me. I swear, I hear the girls giggle, and then sigh dramatically, like we're actually in a fucking Disney movie of our own. But I don't care, I'm embracing all the warm and fuzzies that he gives me.

The tempo changes to a jazzy tune.

"Everybody Wants to Be a Cat!" Julie hollers at the top of her voice, both girls jumping up and grabbing my hands, pulling me with them. We dance until I'm breathless with laughter, as we shimmy and sway our hips to the tune. I look over to see Loki grinning so widely as he gazes at us, he looks like he may just burst, and my heart melts.

---

## LOKI

I spend the rest of the evening playing Disney songs, while Lilly and the girls guess what they are, then I switch to random pop songs while they dance. The pure joy on my sisters' faces makes my chest so tight, it's hard to take a deep breath.

My parents are absent fuckers, who give no shits about their children, other than what they can use us for. The girls have struggled over the past couple of Christmases, not understanding why Mom and Dad don't want to spend the holidays with us. I try my best, but shit, I'm not their parent, although, most days it feels like I do a better fucking job.

My gaze moves over to the girl who brings light and laughter wherever she treads, and I give thanks to whatever gods have finally smiled down on me that I found her. I know it sounds corny as fuck, but she really is like the first flush of spring, after an endlessly dark cold winter. And I, for one, will drink every drop of sunshine she offers me and bathe in her glow for however long I have left on this godforsaken earth.

The girls start rubbing their eyes and yawning widely, no longer dancing, and I share a look with Lilly.

"Time for bed, sleepyheads," I tell them gently, putting my guitar to one side as I get up. "Otherwise, Santa won't come tonight..." I caution them, interrupting their protests before they can even utter them.

I take them upstairs, Lilly following behind, then we help them get ready for bed. Once they're tucked in, Lilly steps forward with a book in her hand.

"Would you like me to read you *The Night Before Christmas*? My mum used to read it to me when I was a little girl every Christmas Eve," she offers, and they nod their heads enthusiastically.

I stand back, leaning against the doorframe, watching her read the story, and I think my heart might explode with how full it feels. My hands itch to grab her and kiss her, merging our fucking souls together, then I want to worship her body with my own until dawn. My dick twitches with that thought as she finishes up with the poem. She leans down and kisses their sleepy heads, my heart thumping hard in my chest again at the sight.

I grab her hand as she goes to walk past me, tugging her out of the room and shutting the door, then pushing her up against it. Slamming my mouth onto hers, I quiet any protests she might have made. God, I'm addicted to her sweet taste, the way she opens up for me, and caresses my tongue with her own.

She lets out a breathy moan when I grind my hardening cock into her pelvis.

"Loki..." she mumbles, gasping and arching her back as I nibble her neck. "Stockings," she rasps out, planting her hands on my chest, probably in a bid to push me away.

I curse, resting my forehead on her shoulder, trying to calm my breathing down and rein in my dick, remembering that we need to put the stockings out tonight.

"You go and put them out, and I'll meet you in your room," she tells me, her voice husky, which makes me all kinds of happy, knowing that I affect her as much as she does me.

I practically sprint down the stairs, to the coat closet, and grab the huge red stockings out from the back that we hid behind a whole load of ski stuff. I set them down either side of the fireplace, drinking some of the milk, and taking a bite of the cookie that they left out for Santa.

I rush back upstairs, and opening my bedroom door, I can hear *Play with Me* by Rendezvous at Two as I take a step inside. When I catch sight of Lilly on the bed, all of the breath rushes out of me, my jaw drops, and my dick instantly stands to full attention, like a dog desperate for a treat.

"Jesus fucking Christ," I whisper, stepping further into the room and shutting the door quietly behind me with trembling hands.

She's wrapped like my very own present, wearing a red silk bow that just about manages to cover her sweet pussy and rosy nipples. Her beautiful hair tumbles around her shoulders, and an image of my hand tangled in it whilst I pound into her tight cunt flashes through my mind.

"Merry Christmas, Loki," she whispers, licking her lips.

I'm across the room in two strides, looking down at her reclined on my bed, ready to be devoured. *Fucking genius idea!*

Kneeling on the bed, I gently push her down, until she's lying flat on her back, legs open. Lying down on my stomach, my face hovering over that delicious mound, I look up at her body to find her gazing back at me, chest heaving. I give her my best panty melting smile, then lower my face and gaze down, moving the ribbon aside to bare her to me.

*Fuck!* She's already dripping, pussy lips glistening. My tongue flicks out, tasting her from opening to clit, and her back arches with a beautiful moan coming from her lips. *God, she tastes fucking incredible!*

I keep up my slow pace, leisurely licking her like a cat with a bowl of cream. Looking up, I can see her eyes are closed, an almost pained look on her face as the pleasure my tongue gives her sweeps across her body. She looks so damn beautiful like this.

"Loki..." she growls. Clearly, she's had enough of me taking it slow. Our girl does like it rough.

"Mmhmm," I mumble, smirking as I keep licking. I know what she wants, but I love it when she begs. *Blame the asshole in me.*

"More, Loki," she begs. "I need more. Please."

"As you asked so nicely," I tease, and then without warning, I push two fingers deep inside her, and she cries out, back arching off the bed, and her hands gripping the sheets. A flood of wetness coats my fingers and I growl in approval.

I keep up my tongue movements, flicking her clit over and over, as my fingers thrust and move inside her. I add a third finger, and the noise she makes is fucking music to my ears. I start to finger fuck her in earnest, loving the wet sounds it makes with the backdrop of her gasps like the best symphony.

"Loki...I'm gonna come..." she gasps out, and I push a fourth finger in at the same time as sucking her clit, grazing it with my teeth.

She screams as her release pours over my tongue, and I drink every fucking drop of her sweet nectar. My dick is straining against my pants, desperate to bury himself in her slick folds.

I push up to my knees, admiring her flushed skin as I strip my t-shirt off, and unbuckle my pants, taking out a condom from my pocket, then pushing them down my hips, and taking them off fully.

I open the foil packet, rolling the rubber on, then grab her gorgeous legs, kissing her ankles. I place them on my shoulders so that when I lie on top of her, they are up between us and she's folded in half.

Keeping hold of her beautiful hazel gaze, I seat myself to the hilt in one thrust, groaning loudly as I feel her inner walls encase me. I have to close my eyes for a moment and breathe deeply, I swear I could come like a randy teenager as soon as I enter her. This angle is so deep, I know that I'm not gonna last long, especially if her pussy keeps fluttering like that around my cock.

I start to pound harder, going even deeper as I chase my orgasm. Sweat drips down my brow when I pick up speed even more, Lilly writhing and cursing underneath me, her nails raking down my arms. My balls start to draw up and tighten, that familiar burn beginning at the base of my spine.

"You're gonna come for me again now, Pretty Girl," I order her gruffly, going up on one arm so that my other can snake between us. My fingers find her clit, and she cries out as I start to rub and pinch it.

"Shit! Loki!" she shrieks, her pussy clamping down on my dick like a vise, as she climaxes for a second time, drawing my own thundering orgasm from me.

Groaning, I collapse on top of her, my heart clamouring in my chest. Our sweaty bodies are pressed so closely, that I can feel her own heartbeat reverberating through me until it matches the pace of mine. Her hands come up to stroke my hair, and I swear I purr like a fucking cat at the touch.

It's such a soothing gesture that I find my eyelids growing heavy, and they begin to close as I drift off into a blissful sleep, still buried inside her.

---

## LILLY

I wake up with a start, rubbing my eyes, and realise that I'm all alone in Loki's bed.

Sitting up and looking towards the door, which is slightly ajar, I can see a faint light coming from beyond it. There are the sounds of what I think are the gentle strains of an acoustic guitar, so I decide to get up and go investigate.

Pulling on my long black silk robe, I make my way towards the door, the music getting louder and I recognise the song as *Lovely,* the acoustic cover version by Thomas Daniel. Walking down the stairs, pausing to look through the spindles, I can just make out Loki sitting on one of the sofas in the living room, playing.

I sit down on the top step and just watch him, mesmerised. His voice is rough and smooth like cigar smoke, and goosebumps erupt on my skin at the sound. The song is so sad, tears sting my eyes, a lump forming in my throat as

I listen to him sing. I can't help feeling he's singing about desperately wanting to escape from his obligations to their company, from his parents. He sings with such emotion, such feeling that the tears spill over, tracking down my cheeks.

When it's finished, he looks up at me and without missing a beat, tilts his head to indicate that I should come down and join him. He begins playing another song, waiting until I'm standing in front of him before starting to sing, a gentle smile on his face, his eyes locked onto mine. As the opening verse begins, I recognise it as *Perfect* by Ed Sheeran, but the Matt Johnson acoustic version.

I just melt and explode all at once.

He holds my gaze as he sings, and I can barely breathe. It's so romantic it's ridiculous. As with many things Loki does, it should be corny as fuck, but somehow he manages to pull it off. I mean it helps that he's only wearing grey sweatpants, his glorious tattooed chest and arms on full display.

The song ends, and his hands rest on the strings. He's staring up at me, his beautiful emerald eyes full of laughter but also love. Despite what Loki has been through, he wears his heart on his sleeve, and he's never hidden his feelings for me.

"I love you, Loki," I whisper. "So much."

His smile turns beatific, and I swear I hear angels fucking weep at the sight.

"I love you, Lilly. So much," he whispers back as he sets his guitar aside and stands up.

I have to look up at him, I love that all the guys are taller than me. There's something that makes me feel so safe when I'm with them, like they can protect me from the world. My inner feminist cringes at that, but she can shut the fuck up.

He captures my face in his hands, leaning in and placing his lips on mine.

The kiss starts softly at first, tentatively, as we explore each other's mouths as if for the first time. Our tongues caress, our embrace deepening until every inch of space is eliminated between us. I can feel his hot body through the thin silk of my robe, burning where it makes contact with my skin until it's like I'm on fire.

Our soul altering kiss ends, leaving us both panting, foreheads pressed together.

"Never leave me, Lilly," Loki begs in a rasping tone, his hands still cupping my face. "Promise me you'll never leave."

He sounds so desperate, like everyone who has come before now has abandoned him without a second glance. A pang of guilt flashes through me remembering that I ran, leaving him and the others, even if only for a short time.

His fingers tangle in my hair, pulling my head back and forcing me to look into his verdigris eyes, which are churning like a storm.

"I promise. I'll never leave you, Loki," I reply fiercely.

My hands reach up and slip into his flaming hair, in a grip that matches his. "Swear to me you won't either."

"I swear, Lilly. I'll never leave you. Your soul is mine, and you'll never be free of me," he promises vehemently.

# CHAPTER FORTY-THREE

LILLY

We wake up to the sounds of girlish squeals, and it takes me a moment to remember that it's Christmas Day and I'm with Loki in his house. I hear a deep, pained grunt come from behind me, and my lips pull up into a smile, as I snuggle back into a warm, hard chest, our nakedness setting my skin on fire everywhere we touch.

"Merry Christmas, Loki," I whisper as I begin to turn in his arms.

"Merry Christmas, Lilly," he replies, his face splitting into a wide grin. He looks sexy as fuck, with his hair all mussed and his face relaxed from sleep.

Leaning in, I gently place my lips against his, screw morning breath! He deepens the kiss, his tongue seeking mine, and I readily grant him entrance. His hardness comes between us, and a chuckle escapes me.

"Loki," I admonish, pulling away. "The girls are up, and we should go downstairs," I say, gasping as he hooks my leg over his hip and pushes inside me in one move.

"Shhh," he mumbles sleepily.

His piercing hits all the right spots as he starts to make love to me, kissing and holding me close. He has me in ecstasy within moments, gasping and humming out his name, as my core ripples and twitches around his shaft. He thrusts a final time with a rumble, burying himself inside me.

"Loki! Lilly!" Heather calls from the other side of the door, the handle rattles as she tries to open it and I tense for a second.

*Thank fuck it's locked.*

"Be there in a minute!" Loki shouts back, not moving away from me in the least.

"We should get dressed," I tell him, a pout crossing his beautiful lips that are even more plush after all our kisses.

"Fine," he huffs out, like a child, pulling out of me and curling up to get out of bed.

I sit up, and it's only when I feel a trickle escape my lower lips, cold dread washes over me.

"Loki," I say, and my tone must be full of panic because he whips around, his face creased in concern.

His eyes travel to the apex of my thighs, then widen a fraction later, obviously realising our mistake too.

"Shit, Lilly...fuck, I was half asleep and not thinking," he murmurs, scrubbing his face with his hands and coming back onto the bed to sit next to me. "It'll be okay, Pretty Girl. We'll get the morning after pill, and I'm clean, I swear. I'll take care of it, baby," he tells me, holding my hand and rubbing my knuckles, then pulling me to him.

"Loki," I say softly, pulling away, and he looks at me with a question on his brow. "I love you so fucking much, and one day I would love to carry your child. Just maybe not right now." His whole face lights up, brighter even than the lights we hung on the tree downstairs.

"I fucking love you so much, Lilly," he grins, his hand passing over my flat stomach, before he stands up and stretches, giving me an uninterrupted view of his perfect peachy arse.

Back in February, I thought that I'd never be happy again. My whole world had caved in with my mother's death, and I was so full of grief I couldn't see straight.

Yet, here I am, spending my first Christmas without Mum, but far from alone, and with someone who loves me and cares about me. I'm happier now than I think I've ever been, and, although I feel a stab of guilt at being happy without her, it's less than what it once was. These guys have changed my life completely, and I think that I might be changing theirs, too.

"Coming?" Loki drawls, reverting back to his joking self, breaking into my thoughts, and I look up to see a shit eating grin on his angelic face. "Again?" he winks, and I laugh joyously, getting up and heading into the shower with him.

---

It's a magical day, full of joy and laughter. I never expected my first Christmas without Mum to be so wonderful, but I can't help the guilt that tries to creep in when I realise how much fun I'm having. Apparently, according to Kai, it's survivor's guilt, and it's perfectly normal. It still hurts like a bitch when I remember that she's not here, and the fact that I've forgotten my grief for even a second, makes me feel worse. Not to mention the slight worry about what happened this morning.

"I never met your mom," Loki says gently from beside me on the sofa, whilst the girls play with their new things upstairs, "but I'm sure she would have wanted you to be happy and not spend Christmas alone and sad." He pulls me in closer, tucking me under his arm and placing a gentle kiss on my head.

"I know," I sniffle out, a single tear rolling down my cheek. "I just hate that I forget about her at some moments, you know?" my voice trembles out.

"Yeah, I know," he replies. "I used to feel the same about Luc. We were really close, more so than me and Ash were, and after he died, I thought that I'd never be happy. That I shouldn't be happy," he tells me, his voice gruff, and this time I wrap my arm more firmly around him.

"But then a certain sexy as fuck brunette was standing naked in my bathroom, singing and shaking her ass, and I thought that I just might have found what was missing." I look up into his eyes that are alight with emerald fire, getting drawn into their depths.

I can see his pain, like a wound that hasn't yet fully healed. It reminds me of my own hurt, always there, yet not as sharp as it was a few months ago. There's also love in his gaze, and it astounds me to know that it's love for me.

*Maybe fate isn't as much of a bitch as I first thought? Soz Fate. My bad.*

Loki's phone rings, interrupting the intense moment, and we both breathe out a chuckle. He grabs it, and I can see it's a FaceTime group call from the guys. I squeal and grab the phone, swiping to answer.

"Merry Christmas!" I practically shout, bouncing up and down on the seat. Loki laughs at my antics, pulling me back into him, and I see the others grin, then they wish us a Merry Christmas too.

My gaze drinks them in, as if we've been apart for months, and not just over two weeks. I search out Jax, who, to be honest, looks like shit.

"Bro, you look like shit!" Loki observes, voicing my thoughts aloud. I elbow him in the gut, eliciting an oomph sound. *Twat.*

We hear Jax's deep, rumbling laugh come over the speaker as he rubs his hands over his face, "Yeah, I feel like shit."

"Can we come and see you tomorrow?" I blurt, unable to hold back any longer, and Jax chuckles again.

"Doc says it's okay, so I guess so, Baby Girl," he teases, and I shriek, dropping the phone to the amusement of Loki, and by the sounds of it, the others too.

"We need to get tickets," I begin, picking up the phone. I hear Ash's derisive laugh, and I look at his picture on the screen. "What? You just gonna call up your private jet, Vanderbilt?" I sass him, my joke falling flat when he gives me a self-satisfied smirk. "Fuck off!" I turn to Loki, seeking confirmation.

He at least has the sense to look a little sheepish, his cheeks flushing slightly, "Yeah, he has a private jet."

"You rich, entitled knobjockey!" I yell at Ash, who just smirks wider at me.

"Be there at ten sharp, Princess," he orders me, then leaves the group chat, without so much as a goodbye . *Dickhead.*

"I'll see you tomorrow, Lilly," Kai says, grinning at me. I can't help but notice the strain around his eyes, but I just about manage to keep the frown off my face. "Merry Christmas."

"Merry Christmas, Kai," I smile back, happiness, anticipation, and a thread of worry making my chest feel tight.

"See you tomorrow, Baby Girl," Jax rumbles out, he does sound tired, and I feel the frown tip my brows. "Don't look at me like that. I can still place you over my knee," he growls, and I feel my core tingle at the thought.

*Oh, hello, your Vagisty!*

Loki chuckles behind me, "Thanks for the idea, asshole," he teases Jax, who growls and ends the call.

"Do you always have to be such a wanker?" I ask, putting down his phone then yelping as he drags me over his knee and gives my arse a hard smack. "Loki!"

"You're right," he replies, confusion filling me. *Right?* Standing up, he sets me on my feet briefly before throwing me over his shoulder. "You really need less clothes for this," he says as he starts to stride towards the stairs.

"Loki!" I exclaim again, laughing and pounding his back, earning another sharp crack on my behind.

*You would fall for alpha-holes, Lilly.*

---

We wake up wrapped up in each other on Boxing Day morning, my arse smarting a little from Loki's smacks the day before. Stretching, I reach for my phone and see that it's already eight in the morning.

"Loki! We need to get up!" I cry out, receiving a growl in reply as he snuggles deeper into the blankets.

Getting out of bed, a wicked idea crosses my mind, and I know the smile on my face is evil. Grabbing the glass of water on the nightstand, I go into his en-suite to refill it with cold tap water after running the tap for several moments. Coming back into the bedroom, I stand next to his side of the bed and gaze down at him. He truly is beautiful.

Taking a corner of the duvet in one hand, I flip it back, letting the cold air rush over his naked body. He growls and cracks an eyelid, looking up at me. His eye widens a second before I throw the water over him and then run into the bathroom.

"Lilly!" I hear him roar, and I turn to see him striding towards me, dripping wet, a scowl on his face. I giggle nervously, and my heart starts pounding in anticipation of what form of revenge he will take. I place the glass on the countertop, my fingers trembling.

"Naughty girl," he scolds, a smile playing on his lips. I stand still, shaking with repressed laughter as he steps past me and turns the shower on behind me.

I squeal as I'm suddenly picked up and tossed into a freezing cold fucking shower. He steps in behind me, with an evil smirk on his face.

"L–L–Loki," I chatter, shivering in the cold water. He takes pity on me, reaching to turn the temperature up until delicious warm water cascades over us and I sigh as it warms my frozen body.

"That was a rude way to wake me up, Pretty Girl," he tells me off, standing so close my breasts brush his chest.

"Sorry," I smile, looking up into his eyes, and seeing amusement and lust in the emerald orbs.

"No, you're not," he replies with a grin, and I chuckle.

"Nope," I admit. "Not even a little bit."

He leans down, his hand cupping the side of my face.

"No regrets?" he asks me, face serious and eyes intent on my own.

"Not a single fucking one," I beam back, closing the distance between our lips. Our kiss is full of new discoveries, and a passion so strong, it changes the stars.

---

After we've showered, *okay fine, after we've showered, fucked, then showered again*, we head downstairs, bags packed and ready to go. Heather and Julie were picked up by their friend's nanny this morning whilst I was getting ready. Apparently, none of the rich look after their own kids so she was on hand to take them.

Leaving our bags by the door, Loki has a car coming to collect us in twenty minutes, so we head towards his parents' office to grab his passport. I did point out that surely he's old enough to be in charge of his own personal documents, but he just rolled his eyes at me and shrugged as he unlocks the door.

It's a room I've not seen before, and on Loki's list of 'rooms he still needs to screw me in'. He opens the wooden door, to reveal a study painted a forest green and panelled in dark wood. *Could this be any more cliché?* I wonder as I gaze around at the shelves full of leather bound books, which clearly have never been read, I may add.

Loki heads to the huge dark wooden desk that sits to one side of the room. It's got a dark green leather top and screams entitled arsehole. I follow to see him open what looks like drawers, but is really a false front to cover a safe. He taps in a combination code, and the door pops open. Inside are two shelves, and there's an internal light which highlights the bundles of cash in various currencies, all sealed in plastic. There also seems to be tubes of gold coins, and a couple of moleskin notebooks, as well as some sort of digital device. A revolver sits at the front top shelf. On the bottom shelf, there looks to be passports, and other documents, as well as a weird miniature bronze statue.

"What's that?" I ask, pointing to the lump of metal.

"Huh? Oh, I think it's a Matisse or some shit," Loki casually replies, grabbing out his passport, whilst I stand there mouth agape.

*Jesus.*

He gets up, closing the safe with a wicked look on his face.

"Loki..." I warn, knowing that he's up to something by the gleam in his green eyes.

"We really should cross this room off our list before we leave, don't you think?" he purrs, backing me up against the desk.

"Loki," I moan as he dips his head and starts kissing up my neck, his hands going to the hem of my dinosaur print pinafore dress.

I gasp at the sizzling contact as his fingers tease the lacy edge of my fishnet stockings. I know it's winter and impractical as hell, but we're headed to an island near Bali for Christ's sake, and I wanted to look nice for the others. Maybe even join the mile high club.

He keeps up his teasing caress on my neck, nipping and sucking until I'm putty in his hands and my legs are wobbling beneath me. His hands move to the back of my thighs, lifting me and setting me down on the top of the desk, mouth never faltering. His hand starts to travel higher up my thigh, toying with the edge of my silk knickers.

I feel burning hot need pooling low in my core, he always has this effect on me. If Loki was a superhero, his power would be to incinerate panties and make women, and probably men too, spontaneously orgasm, just by looking at them.

My eyes open on a gasp as he dips his fingers underneath the silk.

Then it's as if a bucket of ice cold water has been thrown over me.

"Loki," I say, squinting, and trying to make sense of the picture on the wall as my heart starts to pound.

"Hm?" he mumbles, still kissing my neck, although I can't feel the touch anymore.

"Why is there a picture of my mum on your wall?"

*LET NO MAN PUT ASUNDER...*

BOOK TWO

# BOUND

HIGHGATE PREPARATORY ACADEMY

ROSA LEE

# CHAPTER ONE

LILLY

*What was Mum doing in that picture? And why was it hanging in Loki's dad's office of all places?*

The drive to the private airstrip is quiet, both myself and Loki lost in our thoughts as the scenery flashes past our window.

"Hey, Pretty Girl," Loki's familiar drawl washes over me like a gentle breeze, bringing me back to the present. "Penny for your thoughts?" he asks in a terrible British accent, and a groaning giggle escapes me as he takes my hand in his warm one, squeezing it. As always, butterflies dance in my stomach at his touch, my body heating at his nearness.

I stare into his beautiful emerald eyes, and although there's laughter there, there is also a genuine concern for my well-being, and it makes me love him that much more.

"I can't stop thinking about that picture, Loki," I confess, desperate for him to give me answers that I know he doesn't have, but I can't help voicing my worries anyway. "Why was she with all of your mothers? What was she doing at that Black Knight gala?"

He sighs, rubbing his fingers over my knuckles, soothing me with his gentle caress as he scoots closer. We're riding in style, in a black limousine with glasses of bubbling champagne sitting in door holders, and the soft sounds of *Sacrifice* by Black Atlas and Jessie Reyez, coming over the speakers.

"I don't know, Lilly. But Adrian went to Highgate, and you said he had friends here, so perhaps it was something to do with that?" He ends on a question, and although I wish otherwise, I know that he only knows as much as I do. I can feel a headache beginning to form behind my eyes, and I lower my head, rubbing my temple with my free hand.

I don't know why it's bothering me so much. It just doesn't feel right. Mum never told me that she spent any time here, even to visit Adrian. But, then again, she didn't tell me about Adrian either, so what the fuck do I know? A flash of anger towards her flares within me, my jaw clenching with the effort it takes not to lash out.

I'm unnerved by all the secrets, the lies. I didn't even know I had an uncle for fuck's sake! And when I think back on it, she told me nothing about her past, where she came from. About her family, *my* family. I had a right to know.

"Hey, where'd you go, baby?" Loki whispers as his other hand comes to my face, his fingers turning my head up and towards him so that I'm looking at his face once again. My fingers fall away from my temple, landing in my lap. His eyes soften at whatever he sees in mine. "Don't be pissed at her, Pretty Girl. I'm sure she had a good reason for not telling you about her past," he assures me gently.

"How do you know that?" I question, not even surprised anymore that he can read me so easily. For all of his carefree attitude, he's incredibly empathetic, especially where I'm concerned.

"Because she raised you, and I know that you would do anything to protect the ones that you love," he tells me, his fingers caressing the side of my face and causing my breath to hitch. One second, I am looking at the sweetest, most understandable man alive, and the next, a decidedly devious gleam enters his eyes.

"Loki..." I start to scold when he leans in, his luscious lips hovering over mine until I can taste him on my next inhale. And boy, do I take a deep breath of him, breathing in his taste of naughty deeds, and passionate kisses at sunset.

"What you need, Pretty Girl, is a distraction," he informs me, his mouth caressing mine in the barest of touches that sends tingles skittering all over my body, my nipples pebbling in my bra. I'm reminded of Halloween night, in the back of Jax's truck, my nerve endings stirring at the memory.

"Loki..." And I truly mean it to be another reprimand, but it comes out as a moan when the hand that is holding mine moves to my inner thigh, bringing both our fingers up to dance at the edge of my knicker line under the pinafore dress I foolishly chose to wear today. Talk about easy fucking access.

"Shhh..." he murmurs against my lips. "Stop thinking, and just feel, Lilly," he orders me in a husky tone.

"The driver, Loki," I manage to choke out as he brings our fingers underneath the silk, running them along my slit, which admittedly is already slick with arousal. A groan slips out of my lips, try as I might to hold it back, I can't. Not with him.

"Can't hear or see us, baby," he tells me, and I glance over to see that the blacked out divider is up. A second later, his hand leaves my jaw, and the music turns up, *PILLOWTALK* by Zayn blares over the speakers. "Now, spread those pretty thighs for me."

I whimper as I obey, helpless to resist. His breath hisses out between his teeth at the same time mine does when our fingers dip inside my inner lips and find me fucking soaked.

"Shit, Pretty Girl," he groans, slipping both of our middle fingers inside me, moving them in tandem, and rubbing at the rough spot inside that makes me squirm.

All thoughts fly out of my head as pure delicious pleasure ripples through me, my juices sliding down both our hands.

"Loki..." I moan, knowing that I sound like a broken record, but giving no shits as he picks up the pace. Zings of electricity shoot through me as we finger fuck my pussy in earnest, the wet sounds almost as loud as my moans, which are rivalling Zayn right now.

"That's it, come all over our fingers, baby. I want you to coat both our fucking hands with how hot I make you," he whispers huskily in my ear, then moves down to start sucking and nibbling my neck.

"Fuck!" I exclaim, the nails of my other hand digging into my palm as the crest crashes over me, dragging me with it, and obeying him to the letter as I cover both our hands in my liquid release.

"Fuck me. I need to be in you now, Pretty Girl," he groans, removing our hands and pushing me down so that I'm lying on the plush leather seat with him kneeling in between my spread thighs.

Looking down at me with hooded eyes, he unbuttons his jeans, his thick, pierced, rock-hard cock springing free unencumbered by any underwear, as is his preference. Taking out a condom packet from his back pocket—*this man is always prepared to fuck. Well, when he's fully awake that is*—he opens it, taking the rubber out and rolling it over his hard member. Her Vagisty clenches at the sight, desperate to have him fill us. *We agree on that, at least!*

He looks back up at me, a devilish smirk on his beautiful full lips as he grabs the leg that is pressed up against the seat, and places it over his shoulder, doing the same to the other one, making the skirt of my pinafore dress bunch around my waist.

Loki leans down so that I am basically folded in half—*yay for yoga!*—he moves the silk of my knickers aside, lining up his tip with my opening. He looks back up, captivating me with eyes full of emerald fire, as he slides torturously slowly inside me, making us both groan aloud with intense pleasure.

"Fucking hell, Pretty Girl," he groans, his hands coming up on either side of my face. "You feel so fucking good." Thrust. "Every." Thrust. "Damn." Thrust. "Time."

He moans, beginning to move in and out of me with a rhythmic undulation of his hips, lowering down onto his forearms, his lips hovering over mine. The deeper angle makes me gasp, my hands grasping his biceps as wave upon wave of sublime pleasure rolls over me. If fucking was an Olympic sport, Loki would win the gold every time.

I'm so wet that there's no resistance as he starts to thrust harder, driving into me, the sounds of our fucking competing with our moans and gasps.

"Loki...Fuck, Loki. I'm going to come," I rasp as I feel the burn of another orgasm start in my core. Loki moves his head, his lips next to my ear.

"That's it. Come all over my dick, baby," he growls out, pounding harder, and then biting my neck seconds later, triggering another release. Stars flash across my eyes, my body tightening around him as I self-combust with a husky yell, uncaring at this point if the driver hears us. He follows me into oblivion moments later, groaning out his own climax, buried to the hilt inside me.

He lets my legs down, not letting his cock slip out, placing gentle kisses on my neck, throat, and lips. We lie like that, rumpled and spent, for what feels like hours, but in reality can only be twenty minutes at most, until the car begins to slow down. Loki rolls up and out of me, kneeling and staring down at me, his expression one of pure male satisfaction.

"I must look like a hot fucking mess!" I laugh out, still feeling a little boneless, and not really that worried about my freshly fucked appearance.

"You look fucking hot, Pretty Girl," he says licking his lips. "I would fuck you again right now if we didn't have places to be."

Leaning back and opening one of the many compartments the limo has in its interior, he grabs out a warm damp cloth—*don't even ask why they have those in here, ignorance is bliss, my friends*—and reaches down between my legs, wiping it along my still sensitive folds. My breath hisses out at the contact, which only makes him chuckle. *Bastard.*

"We've arrived, sir," a male voice says over the speakers.

"Thanks, Tom," Loki replies, but there's a shit eating grin on his face as he holds my glower. It takes me a second to realise that he didn't move from his position kneeling above me. My eyes widen and he chuckles. "Whoops. Looks like I forgot to turn off the two-way speaker."

*Fucking exhibitionist donkeycock ballbag!*

---

I'm still grumbling at the wanker as we get out of the car once we've straightened our clothes, which just makes him laugh openly at me. Tom, our driver, holds the door open and the blush on his cheeks is nothing compared to mine, which feel like glowing red beacons. He's handsome for an older guy, his blond hair peppered with grey, as is the scruff covering his jaw, and bright blue eyes. Apparently, he's been a driver for Black Knight Corporation since the beginning, before even the guys were born.

"Thanks again, Tom." Loki chuckles like a cockgobbler, but I see him slip some folded bills into Tom's hand as he shakes it—*hopefully not with the fingers that were inside me!*

"No problem, sir," Tom replies in his gravelly voice. "I hope you have a nice trip, sir, miss," he tells us without looking at me, then closes the car door and heads to the boot to grab our bags.

"You're a shitstain, you know that?" I tell the naughty redhead next to me, looking up into his mischievous green eyes. He grins in response, no shits given, proving my words correct.

"You're late," I hear a smooth, low voice say, my head whipping round towards the sound as my heart flutters in my chest, like a bird trying to escape its cage.

My gaze drinks in the dark angel as he stalks towards us, from his custom-made shiny black shoes to his tailored black suit, complete with waistcoat and tie, with all that glorious ink peeking through at his neck and on the back of his hands. My whole body tingles as I take him in, as if for the first time, then in a sudden decisive moment, I rush towards him, throwing myself into his arms. He catches me, just like I know he always will, and pulls me into a tight embrace, engulfing me in his spicy ginger scent as he lifts me off my feet for a moment.

I breathe him in like he's my oxygen, sagging into him with weak knees as I wrap them around his waist.

"Hello, Princess," he says gruffly, and I tilt my face to look up into those swirling grey eyes of his, the hint of a soft smile on his plump lips.

His whole body relaxes around me, and I feel him take a deep inhale, as if it's the first proper breath he's taken in weeks.

"Hello, Ash," I whisper, swallowing, my throat tight with emotion. I've missed him, and the others, so fucking much.

I can't bear to be parted from them again. It feels as though pieces of me have been taken away, and I won't be whole until I get them back. We are all irrevocably bound, so intrinsic to one another that we can never be truly separated, and any physical distance hurts.

He leans his face down, his lips hovering over mine for an agonising second before he closes the distance, my feet settling back on the tarmac. One of his hands comes up to palm my cheek, tilting my head back further as he deepens his kiss, his tongue demanding entry. Ash tastes like moonless nights, and exquisite sin, like the darkest chocolate that at first is bitter, and only sweetens the longer you hold it on your tongue.

My own hands grip his lapels, uncaring if I crease them all to buggery, just needing him closer. Deeper.

A growl sounds in his throat when I nip his tongue, and he pulls away, sucking my bottom lip before he releases me from his thrall.

"You smell like sex, Lilly Darling," he tells me gruffly, his words falling over my lips and making me quiver. "You have two minutes to get on that plane, or I'm adding to the scent right here on the runway."

I take in a sharp breath, my thighs clenching as I pull back, looking into the swirling vortex of his eyes, seeing only primal need and truth there. He really will claim me like an animal for all to see if I don't get a wriggle on. Her Vagisty practically drools at the idea, as if we weren't just satisfied twice. Yes, twice.

*Greedy bitch!*

"Hello, Lilly," I hear Kai's melodic voice sound behind Ash, and I tear my gaze away from Ash's to meet comforting honey brown eyes, although there's an edge of something in them that hasn't been there before.

"Kai!" I squeal, ripping out of Ash's grip, a snarl leaving his lips as I launch myself at Kai.

Luckily, he catches me too, folding me in a hug, nestling his face into my hair, and breathing me in deeply. My arms wrap around him, pulling him close so that no space is between us. We hold each other for a few moments, his scent of fresh woodland after the rain surrounding me, until the need to feel his lips against mine becomes overwhelming.

He must feel it the same time as I do, for his lips are suddenly on mine in a blistering kiss, full of desperation and white hot need. I meet him stroke for stroke, groaning when he grabs a fistful of my hair and tugs sharply.

Kissing Kai is like coming home, a taste of peaceful serenity coating my tongue, his domination grounding me.

We break away at the sound of a cough behind us, both of us panting and unable to look away from one another.

"We should get on board," Ash tells us, and even though I know he's not being an arsehole, Kai actually growls at him. "We can resume this once we're in the air," Ash snaps in response.

*Well, looks like the alphas have come out to play.*

Kai wraps his arm around my shoulders and leads me towards the stairs that lead up to the door of the plane. He helps me up them, my heels clattering against the metal.

Stepping inside, my steps falter, and I gasp, my eyes going wide.

*Jesus fucking Christ on a cracker!*

This place looks nothing like a plane on the inside. There's not a straight line to be seen, with curved seating leading to a curved bar against the front of the plane. There's a door to one side that I assume leads to the captain's cabin. I turn my head to look in the other direction, and see that there's a partial wall in the middle, with cut out panels that have what looks like bubbles floating in tanks set into them. Everything is in soft grey and turquoise, and there is a light fixture that looks like a constellation in the ceiling. The small windows are all running along the sides of the plane, letting in winter sunshine and making everything glow.

"Come on, Pretty Girl," Loki says as he brushes past me, grabbing my hand and pulling me away from Kai. *See, shithead behaviour right there.* "Let's give you the grand tour."

He leads me towards the bubble wall, and I see that there are wooden panels on either side, jutting out of the plane's interior sides. They're set back so that when you look head-on, it looks like a solid wall, and what's behind is not immediately obvious. We walk through the gap, and I stop dead in my tracks.

Before me is a full size super king bed. Complete with crisp white bedding and turquoise scatter cushions.

"This is the most important part of the tour," Loki whispers in my ear from behind, having taken advantage of my stupor to press himself to my back, pulling me to his chest. I see the others come up either side of us in my peripheral vision, their footsteps silent on the thickly carpeted floor.

I shiver as Loki licks up the edge of my ear, undoing the zip on the side of my dress. Ash steps in front of me, my eyes landing on his silver hungry ones, my breath stilling in my lungs at the intensity. He reaches up with long fingers, loosening the buckles of my shoulder straps and pushing them down my arms. Loki pushes the dress the rest of the way off, letting it fall to my heeled feet. Leaving me in my T-shirt, silk knickers, stockings and heels.

I look down as I feel hands running up my stockinged legs to see Kai on his knees, the others having successfully preoccupied me up until this point. I'm momentarily distracted when hands grasp my T-shirt and start pulling it upwards, my arms lifting as they pull it over my head. I feel the tug of my damp silk knickers and look back down again to see Kai pulling them down my legs, helping to guide my still heeled clad feet out of them.

There's a breath of cold air against my back, then the sounds of *Feel It* by Michael Morrone starts to play over speakers. Seconds later, Loki's warmth is back, his hands sending cascades of shudders flying across my skin, his fingers tickling up my sides until they reach my bra line. Moving to the back, he easily unhooks it, Ash helping to guide the straps down my arms, looking directly into my eyes.

I feel like I'm on fire, having their hands on me all at the same time, building something within me that's desperate for release.

"We're ready for takeoff, sir," a female voice sounds from the other side of the bubble wall behind us. I freeze, my heart thudding as if I've been caught doing something naughty, appalled that I didn't even hear her approach.

*Well, if the shoe fits, Lilly...*

"Excellent, Alisha. See that we're not disturbed," Ash tells her, not taking his stare from mine.

"S–shouldn't we, like, buckle up or something?" I ask, a full body shiver taking over me as Ash's fingers graze the side of my breast at the same time that Kai's tickle my inner thigh and Loki's pushes my hair to one side, his lips teasing my neck. A moan escapes my lips, my own fingers flexing at my sides with the exquisite sensations rolling over me.

Ash smirks as I feel the plane begin to move.

"Rules are made to be broken, Princess."

Loki's hands come to steady my hips, gripping tightly as the plane begins to tilt upwards, my heart beating wildly in my chest at the thought of not following the rules. *Shit, I'm sure it's the law.* His mouth fastens onto the base of my neck, and I moan again loudly when he starts to suck, no doubt leaving a hickey, all thoughts of seat belts literally flying from my mind. A hot tongue runs along my slit, Kai's mouth sealing over my clit and mimicking Loki's sucking. My knees buckle, and I would have fallen if Loki didn't have such a tight grip on me.

"S–shit..." I gasp, my palms alighting on Kai's head, gripping his soft hair in my fingers and pulling him closer. A soft, satisfied grunt feathers over my cunt, making me tingle even more.

"Open your eyes, Princess," Ash commands, the plane tilting further, but I almost don't notice the movement, lost as I am to what Loki and Kai's mouths are doing to me.

I do as he directs, seeing him bring up his thumb and placing it against my lips.

"Suck," he orders, pushing the digit into my mouth. "It'll help stop your ears popping," he tells me, a devilish grin on his face that turns heated as I suck his thumb deeper, swirling my tongue around it.

He brings my own thumb up to his lips, kissing the tip before taking it into his mouth and copying my movements.

*Fucking hell.*

Shockwaves of electric pleasure zing from my neck, clit, and thumb until I feel like I'm a ball of energy, pulsing and sparking, ready to electrocute everyone on this damn aircraft. As the plane starts to even out, Kai chooses that moment to push two fingers inside me, crooking them to rub against my G-spot.

I cry out, letting go of Ash's thumb as I fracture into a thousand pieces, liquid rushing out of my lower lips, which Kai drinks up like it's the finest wine. My free hand grasps Ash's forearm, my nails digging into his suit clad forearms as I come all over his friend's face.

I stand there, shuddering and twitching, my eyes closed, whilst I come down from the Heavens.

"Good girl," Ash huskily whispers, having let my thumb drop from his mouth. I crack my eyes when he steps away, and see him take off his tie. "Hands out, Princess."

"W–what?" I question, still lost in my orgasm high, my voice coming out a little rough.

A sharp tap lands across my pussy, making me gasp in pain and pleasure, my thighs instinctively clenching. I look down, and Kai is resting back on his heels, a hard look in his eyes, his hand hovering over my dripping cunt.

*Sir is in the room, I see.*

"You were not given permission to speak or question our orders," he tells me sharply, his voice threaded through with heated disapproval. "Now, apologise to Ash, and do as he says."

I look back up into Ash's smug face, waiting until his eyes narrow, knowing that he loves the brat in me. I think I may push it today.

"Make me," I challenge, raising a brow and tilting my head, my own smirk tugging my lips up.

# CHAPTER TWO

LILLY

Ash's nostrils flare, but excitement lights a fire in his eyes as he roughly grabs my wrists, bringing them in front of me lightning fast, and tying them together with his tie in one of his signature complicated knots. It's so quick that I don't have time to argue, let alone stop him. Okay, who am I kidding? I don't exactly try to stop him either.

Yanking me so hard that I stumble in my heels, he sits on the end of the bed and pulls me down so that I'm lying across his knees, my bare arse in the air, my bound hands hanging down in front of me. His suit trousers are of the finest quality fabric, but even so, they chafe my sensitised nipples as I squirm against his hold.

My face heats with a mixture of anger and lust as he strokes and caresses my backside.

"Naughty, disobedient princesses are taught their manners when they forget them," he tells me, his voice a husky growl, threaded with arousal that sends a shudder running through my body, ending at my pulsing mound. "And how to follow orders."

His hand leaves my rear, and I look to the side to see Kai and Loki standing there, hunger written across their faces, their eyes devouring my submissive position. Both boys have tented trousers, their hands held rigidly at their sides, fists clenched.

Loki uncurls one fist, taking his phone out of his pocket, his eyes lowering as his fingers fly over the screen. *Do I Wanna Know?* by the Arctic Monkeys comes over the speakers, the beat resounding in the pit of my stomach.

Suddenly, a loud crack sounds in the room, and I gasp at the sharp pain that spreads across my lower left cheek. I squirm in Ash's lap, my nails digging into my palms as desire starts to replace the anger within me, although not fully.

Another hit lands on the right globe, and this time, I almost rise to meet it, relishing in the pleasure-pain that it gives me. A third punishing smack makes my arse cheeks burn, and I moan, hanging my head, heady acceptance flooding my veins as I give myself over to the punishment.

I'm panting, my heart racing in time to the beat of the song as Ash continues his assault on my arse, his palm landing time and time again until my buttocks are burning and throbbing, and my cheeks are wet with tears.

His hand stills, after more hits than I could count, resting on my hot smarting backside.

"Ready to apologise, Princess?" he asks in a rasping voice. He's breathing hard, and the evidence of his arousal is pressing against my waist. I'd be lying if I said that it didn't make me even wetter, moisture dripping between my thighs.

*I hope it stains his trousers.*

Guess he didn't quite beat the brat out of me. But then again, that's our game. He enjoys the challenge as much as I do.

"I–I'm sorry, sir," I gasp out, my voice croaky.

"Good girl," he replies, eliciting a hiss from my lips as he caresses my tender behind. "I'm glad to see that you've learnt your lesson well, Princess. Loki, Kai," he says gruffly, and the snick of a drawer opening soon follows after his words.

"You took that so beautifully, Lilly," I hear Kai say in my ear, a touch of awe in his tone. He brushes my sweaty hair aside, and I raise my head slightly to look at him. "Drink, my darling," he instructs caringly, holding a glass of iced water with a metal straw in it. He brings the straw to my lips, and I sigh as the cold water hits my mouth. I hadn't realised how thirsty I was.

"You're such a good girl, Princess," Ash praises. "I'm just going to put some Arnica gel on you, then you can have your treat, okay?" he asks.

"Yes, sir," I whisper once Kai takes the glass away, placing a brief kiss on my lips and brushing the tears from my cheeks away with a cloth napkin. I hiss when the cool gel hits my overheated skin, sighing as Ash rubs it in, the throbbing immediately dulling.

"You look so beautiful, Pretty Girl," Loki tells me, and I turn my head to see him ravenously staring at Ash's hand, which has stilled on my arse, his erection straining against his jeans.

"All done, Princess," Ash informs me, with one last caress. "Now, get your feet under you, and we'll help you up.

I awkwardly obey, managing to get to my feet with their help, and swaying slightly with my hands still tied in front of me. I'm standing before Ash, who's sitting with his knees wide, a small space between us.

"What's my treat?" I ask him, and a jet black brow lifts, even as he smirks. "Sir."

His grin turns feline as he gets up, shrugging his jacket off, then starts to unbutton his cufflinks, diamonds glinting in them of course, all while looking me in the eye. I can't resist looking down as he exposes his forearms, and my breath hitches at the sight of his inked flesh against the crisp white shirt. *Why are guys' forearms so fucking sexy?*

"The boys will show our appreciation at the same time, Princess. You can handle them, can't you?" he questions me, a twinkle in his grey eyes. I'm reminded of the time in Loki's house, by the pool, when I told him that I could handle them all.

"Yes, sir," I say, willing to tone the brat down to get what I'm hoping he's offering. Kai and Loki inside me at the same time. For a second I wonder why not Ash too, he's yet to join in a threesome, yet I know he enjoys watching and ordering us around. Although this will be Kai's first multiplayer—*snort*—event too...

"Such a beautiful, good, Pretty Girl," Loki murmurs behind me, and I take my eyes off Ash, my thoughts distracted, to see that he and Kai are both stripping.

My breath comes in a sharp inhale as I look my fill. The sight of them, their glorious bodies coming onto display. These guys, my guys, are so stunningly gorgeous it hurts. And I still can't believe that they're all mine. I lick my lips as sweet anticipation trickles through my centre.

"*Our* beautiful, good girl," Kai whispers, stepping up to me, naked and hard. He cups my face in his palms, leans in, and presses his lips to mine in a gentle, worshipping kind of kiss that leaves my toes tingling.

I give in to him freely, opening up fully as I'm caged in his embrace, my hands trapped between us. He breaks the kiss, rubbing his nose against mine in such a sweet gesture, that a lump forms in my throat.

"I'm so glad to be with you again, Lilly," he reverently confesses against my lips.

"Me too, Kai," I choke out.

"Get on the bed, Princess," I hear Ash say from across the room after a moment. My head snaps in his direction; he's lounging on a white leather swivel chair, facing the bed. *All the better to direct us, I guess.* Though, a pang runs through me at the thought that he won't be joining in.

Kai lets his hands drop away, and I turn to see that Loki is lying naked on the bed, propped up on his elbows, his dick hard and already rubbered up lying against his firm abs, the piercing glinting in the light.

"Come ride me, Pretty Girl," Loki says with a lopsided grin, folding his hands behind his head. "And leave your heels on."

I huff a laugh, Loki really has a thing for fucking me in heels. I mean, these are gorgeous glitter mermaid rainbow shoes, so I can't blame him.

Swaying over to the bottom of the bed, my butt is still smarting but the rush of arousal that floods my body is helping to mask the ache, alongside the soothing gel. I crawl up the bed on my knees, my hands held in front of me, making me a little wobbly as I position myself so that my thighs are on either side of his hips.

"God, I love it when you're on top, baby," Loki groans, one of his hands coming to my hip, the other holding his erect cock up, helping guide me down onto his shaft.

We both moan when my opening is flush with his pelvis, his dick buried deep inside me and feeling fan-fucking-tastic. He was right earlier; it feels incredible every damn time!

"Jesus fucking Christ," Loki hisses out when I start to move my hips, both of his hands now on my hip bones, his fingers gripping me tightly, indenting my soft flesh.

The song changes to *I Want To*, by Rosenfield, and I gyrate my hips to the rhythm, rising up and sinking down, riding him like he commanded, my tied hands resting on his tight abs for balance. The pleasure is exquisite, almost unbearably so, combining with my throbbing rear to send sweet tendrils of pleasure-pain skittering across my whole body.

The bed dips behind me, and my movements falter. Turning my head, I look over my shoulder to see Kai kneeling on the end, lubing up his hard pierced dick, and my breath stutters, my pussy clenching around Loki, leaving him groaning.

"Bend forward, Princess, and let Kai fuck that pretty asshole of yours," Ash orders gruffly, and I obey without question, Loki helping me as my bound hands make it tricky.

I'm desperate to feel Kai's fully pierced member inside me along with Loki's. My hardened nipples brush Loki's chest, sending a shiver over my skin, adding to the hypersensitivity that I'm feeling. Loki's hands move to the globes of my arse, and I gasp sharply as he grabs them none too gently and spreads them wide for Kai.

"Shhhh," he hushes in my ear when I squirm against him, my arms above his head as I simultaneously try to escape the biting sting, and push into it. "I just need to open you up nice and wide for Kai's hard dick."

A gasp escapes my lips at his words, a sharp inhale leaving me as I feel a cold dollop of lube run down my crack, followed by a deep moan when Kai's thumb starts rubbing it around my puckered hole.

"Kai!" I hiss when he pushes the digit in, feeling a delicious fullness as he starts to pump it in and out of me.

Shudders rack my body as the heady sensation sweeps through me, and I can't help rocking and clenching around Loki, causing deep groans to leave his plush lips.

"Kai, please," I beg, needing more. I need him inside me too.

He's obviously in a forgiving mood, ignoring my lack of addressing him as 'sir,' because he pulls his thumb out and replaces it with the tip of his hard length. I look under one arm to see his knees on either side of Loki's thigh as he presses forward.

"That's it, Lilly. Relax for me, darling," he coos as he pushes in, the piercings on the underside of his cock eliciting desperate animalistic noises from my throat.

"Fuck, dude," Loki moans as Kai keeps thrusting forward until his hips are flush with my arse cheeks. "I can see the appeal of all that metal."

I'm shaking and panting like a fucking dog at how full I now feel. Having the two of them, both with piercings in their dicks, is overwhelming to say the least. Kai gives me no chance to adjust as he starts pounding hard into my arse, Loki following from underneath, until they are both fucking me so hard, with alternating thrusts, that the slaps of our bodies can be heard over the music.

"Oh god, oh god, oh god..." I moan loudly, uncaring if the fucking pilot can hear me, as wave upon wave of pleasure rips though my entire body.

Suddenly, Kai leans forward, grabbing my bound wrists and pulling me sharply. He brings them above my head, holding them so my elbows are bent and my hands are behind my head. My back is arched almost uncomfortably as he continues his hard, frantic thrusts.

"Fuck, Kai," I cry out, just as Loki, clearly feeling left out, starts to rub and pinch my clit, making me fucking squirm. "Loki..." I pant, feeling the delicious burn of another orgasm building in my core.

"That's it, Pretty Girl. Come all over us," Loki orders, and I'm helpless to disobey when his other hand leaves my hips and slaps my breasts hard, the sound as loud as the noise of our pelvises rocking together.

I scream as I tumble into Wonderland, flashes of bright light blinding me as I climax all over them. My body goes boneless, the guys using me for their own pleasure, seeking their own release, which they achieve one after the other, growling as they come.

After a few minutes of tranquil oblivion, there's a tug at my wrists; Kai loosening the tie. My hands fall into my lap, unable to hold them up, I'm that fucked out.

I whimper when Kai pulls out, feeling his cum seep out of my back hole and slide down my arse crack, shuddering and causing Loki to groan below me when my inner walls clench around him.

"Let's get cleaned up, sweetheart," Kai offers, holding his hand out for me to take.

I grasp it, getting up on shaking legs. He pulls me to him, his arms wrapping round my waist, and my own settling round his neck. Lowering his lips, he kisses me affectionately, setting my body tingling all over again.

"I love you, Lilly Darling," he whispers on an exhale, and a smile tugs at my lips.

"I love you, Kai Matthews," I tell him back, my fingers playing with the hair at the back of his neck, warmth suffusing my whole body at his words.

Sighing in contentment, he turns, keeping one arm round me as he leads me to the side of the bed. What I thought was wood panelling to either side, turns out to be more partial walls, and there's a full on shower room behind the bedroom, complete with a large shower, sink with vanity, and full length mirror on the back of the wall that the bed rests against.

"There is a toilet behind that door," he tells me, letting me go and walking over to the shower, opening the glass door and turning it on.

I head to the loo, taking care of business, then step out to find him already in the shower alongside Loki. I stand there, dumbstruck, watching as they soap themselves up under the spray. *Too fucking hot! How's a girl meant to function?*

"You gonna keep staring like a pervert, Pretty Girl, or are you hopping in?" Loki teases with a smirk.

I roll my eyes at him, walk towards the shower and join them, closing my eyes and letting the hot water run over my body and relax my muscles. Soapy hands caress the front of my body, washing me, and a sigh falls from my lips at the soothing touch.

"Can I ask you guys a question?" I say, my eyes still closed as it's the only way I'll feel brave enough to ask. A second pair of hands joins the first, washing my back. My nipples pebble under their ministrations.

"You just did, baby," Loki tells me. *Shithead.*

"Fuck off, Loki," I sass back, cracking my eyes to glare at him, then closing them again.

"Ask your question, Lilly," Kai offers over my shoulder. I take a deep breath.

"Would you two, ever, you know, be up for some...sword crossing. Outside of my body that is."

Both sets of hands still, and I hold my breath, desperate to see their faces but a little afraid too.

"Open your eyes, Pretty Girl," Loki commands gently, and I do as he says. His smile is gentle, but also lascivious at the same time. "Would that turn you on? To see me with Kai's cock up my ass? Or mine in his mouth?"

My breath stutters, my eyes widening at the mental image that gives me.

He chuckles. "I guess that gives me your answer," he says, his hand tightening its grip on my waist. "You up for a bit of experimentation, bro?" he asks Kai over my shoulder, and I turn my head to look back at him.

Kai's eyes are serious, considering. There's darkness in their depths that's not all heat. It makes my brows dip in worry.

"Kai? It's okay if you're not, truly," I assure him, turning to face him fully and stroking my arm down his.

"I'm not sure about anal, but maybe other stuff. I think I'd like to be top, though," he tells us honestly, looking between Loki and I.

"We can work with that, can't we, Pretty Girl?" Loki states, his hand dipping in between my still tender arse cheeks. "I'm up for your dick in my chocolate starfish."

"Loki!" I chastise, my nose wrinkling as my head whips round.

"What? Would you prefer my ham flower? Or maybe the Hershey highway? The brown puckered eye?"

Tears of laughter are streaming down my face, even as I cringe, and I look to Kai, finding him in a similar state, the darkness of moments ago gone, as he laughs at his friend.

"I can't even with you, Loki," I tell him in between gasps as I step out of the shower and reach for a towel.

"What about Gary?" he asks, and even he can't hold back the chuckles.

*And now, I'm officially dead.*

# CHAPTER THREE

LILLY

Once I've gotten over the fact that Loki just called his arsehole Gary —*fucking snort*—I get dressed in some navy lacy French knickers, soft colourful harem pants, and a dark red vest top sans bra. Luckily for me, Tom brought in my hand luggage whilst we were otherwise—*ahem*—occupied, and I'd packed some comfy flight clothes knowing that we'll be in the air for over eighteen hours.

I walk out of the bedroom to find Ash lounging on one of the curved sofa type seats, a drink, whisky on the rocks by the look of it, in his hand.

"Better, Princess?" he asks with an indulgent smile, and I sit right next to him, snuggling under his arm, and feeling all kinds of languid from my many orgasms.

"So much better," I tell him, sighing and wrapping my arm around his chest. He has also changed into something more casual; soft grey linen trousers, a white linen shirt, sleeves rolled to the elbow, and black flip-flops that showcase his beautiful inked feet. "I missed you, Vanderbilt."

He pulls me in closer, his arm around my shoulders, and I take in a deep inhale of that spicy scent that is all Ash.

"I missed you too, Princess," he whispers, placing a gentle kiss on the top of my head.

"You didn't..." I start, trying to tread carefully with what I'm about to say. "That is, I didn't get any texts from you?"

I feel him stiffen ever so slightly underneath me, but as I make a move to sit up so that I can look into his eyes, he holds me tighter to him.

"Rubber duck was not needed," he tells me in a low voice, and I exhale a long breath at his words, grateful that he didn't feel the need to cut himself whilst back at home.

Just then, what I assume is Alisha, walks over in stiletto heels and a navy flight attendant uniform. She's an attractive blonde with a perfect hourglass figure, sparkling blue eyes, and plush lips. Someone who looked like her would have intimidated me previously, leaving me feeling inadequate. But not so much anymore. She's carrying a tray of drinks, ice clinking in the glasses, looking at us with a broad smile and not spilling a single drop.

"Here you are, Mr. Vanderbilt," she says, setting the drinks aside on a low table in front of us, and giving me a quick glance.

"Thank you, Alisha," Ash replies. "May I introduce Lilly Darling," he says, not moving his arm, clearly staking his claim.

"Pleased to meet you, Ms. Darling," she says, her American accent husky as she gives me a quick smile, a slight blush stealing over her cheeks.

"You too, Alisha," I respond, feeling my own face heat with embarrassment.

"Will that be everything, sir?" she asks, turning to face Ash, being the consummate professional that she is, and not acknowledging the DP that went on earlier, which she clearly heard.

"Just dinner in about an hour, please," Ash replies in a business-like tone, and I get a flash of the man he is becoming, a leader of a multibillion dollar corporation.

"Of course," she says and walks away.

I groan, slapping my palm to my forehead once she closes the door to presumably the cockpit. Ash just chuckles, the muff tickler.

We hear Loki and Kai laughing as they walk in, Loki's gaze zeroing in on me snuggled next to Ash, and then the drinks.

"Perfect. Fucking always makes me thirsty," he claims, reaching over and grabbing his bourbon whilst passing me a fruity looking cocktail. *Yum!*

Kai grabs his wine glass, which is filled with clear liquid.

"What's that you're drinking, Kai?" I ask, curious.

"It's Yaegaki Mu, a junmai daiginjo sake," he tells me as he takes a seat opposite us, next to Loki. He takes a small sip, savouring the flavour and heaving a contented sigh as he swallows.

"I thought sake was served warm?" I enquire, taking a sip of my own drink, the tart raspberry bursting on my tongue as I watch him swirl the liquid round in the glass.

"This is a premium quality sake, and it's best to serve it chilled like a white wine. Regular sake is served warm to uncover the flavours in less complex brews."

*Learn something new every day!*

"So, are there any pharmacies where we land?" Loki interrupts, and I choke a little on a sip of my raspberry cocktail. Fuck, I'd forgotten all about that, what with the picture of Mum, and the sex.

"Why?" Ash questions, his voice containing a hint of warning that makes me sit up a little.

Loki's face flushes, one of his hands rubbing the back of his neck.

"I need to get Lilly the morning after pill," he admits, almost cringing.

Before I can even blink, Ash is launching himself across the small table, and I hear the thud of a fist hitting flesh followed by a groan of pain.

"Ash! What the fuck!" I shout, leaping up, setting my drink on a side table to rush over to Loki, who looks like he didn't even defend himself.

As I reach him, Loki makes another grunting sound as Kai's fist connects with his ribs.

"Kai!" I scold, seeing Kai pull his fist back and pick up his glass, taking a large sip. His face is set in a scowl, glaring at Loki.

"When did this happen? Why the fuck didn't you wrap up?" Ash practically roars in Loki's face, his chest heaving and his hands clenched into fists at his sides. Loki just sits there, looking ashamed, his lip starting to swell and bleed. I sit down next to him, turning to glare at Ash.

"Hey, it's not just his fault. It takes two to tango, cunt whiskers," I snark at Ash, and his lips twitch slightly at the insult, although he's clearly still pissed as all hell, his cheeks flushed and his nostrils flaring.

"It was Christmas morning and I fucked up. I'm sorry, okay?" Loki tells them, his hand running through his hair and not looking at me.

"Hey, it'll be fine, Loki. We'll grab a pill, and it'll all be gravy," I try to assure him, placing my palm gently on his cheek, and turning his head to face me. I wince at his split lip, grabbing one of the napkins that Alisha left to dab at the blood trickling from it.

"Well, by the time we get to Bali, that'll be over forty-eight hours. The morning after pill becomes less effective the longer you wait, going down to around fifty-eight percent chance of success," he tells us, his fingers dancing over the screen of his phone.

Ash growls and looks like he's about to hit Loki again.

"Fucking cool it, Vanderbilt," I tell him firmly, narrowing my eyes. "It'll be fine. Chances are I'm not in that part of my cycle anyway."

"Where are you in your cycle, Lilly?" Kai asks with no hesitation, looking up at me.

"Fuck's sake, Kai! I don't know." I can feel the blush returning to my cheeks, which is ridiculous given that he was in my arsehole less than an hour ago. *Fucking stupid patriarchial society making women feel embarrassed about periods.* "It can be a bit random, and I don't really check, so..." I trail off.

"Well, I've got someone meeting us when we land with the pill, so let's hope it works," he says gently, then turns to glare at Loki.

Desperate for a subject change before it turns violent again, I blurt the first thing that comes into my head. "So, there was a photo of my mum, with all of yours in Loki's dad's office."

*Really?! That's what you choose to go with? FML.*

"What?" Ash yells, grabbing my hand and pulling me away from Loki, dragging me back to the sofa opposite like some cave dwelling Neanderthal. Or, like Loki can't be trusted not to try and impregnate me. *Sigh.*

"Yeah, Lilly's mom was standing with all of ours, at some Black Knight Gala or some shit," Loki tells him, taking a sip from his glass which he somehow managed to keep from spilling when Ash punched him.

He pulls his phone from his pocket, scrolling a bit, and then leans over to hand it to Ash. On the screen is the picture. Mum's dressed up in a midnight blue beaded evening dress, holding a champagne flute and smiling for the camera, surrounded by four other women, all in similar states like that of my mum.

My gaze flits back to my mum, who looks so young but no less beautiful than when I knew her. As I stare at the photograph, I can't help feeling that although she looks happy and is smiling, there was something that was not quite right. Maybe it was because of the tightness around her eyes, and the death grip she has on the glass in her hand.

"Did she ever mention Highgate, Princess?" Ash asks me, handing the phone back to Loki, then pulling me in close again and tucking me under his arm.

"No," I reply, frowning. "But she didn't tell me about my uncle either, so..." I trail off, still feeling hurt at the things that she withheld from me, a painful tightness in my throat.

"Your uncle came to Highgate, didn't he, Lilly?" Kai inquires, rubbing his chin as he looks at me.

"Yes, he did."

"So, maybe she was just visiting him?" Loki suggests, taking another sip of his drink and wincing when it hits his split lip. "He was in our parent's class, wasn't he?"

"I think so, although I don't think he's ever mentioned them, or anything really," I tell them, pursing my lips in thought.

"Well, it's probably that then," Ash says, not sounding convinced at all, and when I look up at him, his own brows are dipped, and he's sharing a look with the others.

"What?" I question, sitting up so that I can see him fully, his arm dropping from around my shoulders. "You think that it doesn't quite add up?"

"I just don't trust my dad, or any of the board, as far as I could throw them," Ash tells me, reaching out to brush some hair out of my face. "And your safety and well-being are my top priority. *Our* top priority."

He leans in and places a gentle kiss on my lips, leaving me feeling all fuzzy and tingling whilst helping to lessen the unease that I was starting to feel. It doesn't disappear completely, though, and I can't help wondering what else my mother has kept from me.

---

The rest of the journey is pretty uneventful. We have some dinner; steak cooked medium rare, small buttered potatoes, and a colourful salad. Don't ask me how we got this on a plane, apparently, it's what you get for being rich bastards.

After dinner, I take a long nap with Ash once he's made me explode several times on his tongue and fingers. I fall asleep, exhausted before I can return the favour.

We land some hours later, although because of the time difference, it's only eight in the evening, which is all kinds of mindfuckery. Feeling slightly discombobulated, we exit the jet to find a car waiting for us on the tarmac. It's another black limousine with a smartly dressed Balinese guy, who looks about our age, waiting by the open door.

"Good evening, sirs, miss. Welcome back," he greets us, his speech slightly accented as he puts his hands in a prayer position and gives us a shallow bow, then straightens up. All the guys follow suit, bowing, so I do the same. "Your package is in the back, Master Matthews."

"Thank you, Nengah," Kai responds with a smile, indicating with a hand that I get in first.

I smile at Nengah, then climb in the back. The boys follow me in, and soon we're on our way. Kai hands me a paper bag, and I open it to find a box. Opening that, I find a single white tablet inside. The morning after pill. My heart does a little flip, which is stupid because there is nothing to worry about either way. He hands me a bottle of water.

"Thanks." I smile tightly at him, aware of three pairs of eyes on me as I pop the pill on my tongue and take a mouthful of water, swallowing it down. "So, when do we see Jax?" I ask them, wanting to move on from that shitstorm.

"We're headed to the port now, and from there we'll take the yacht to Cempedak Island, which should take just over an hour," Ash informs me, looking down at his phone briefly. *Of course they have a fucking yacht.*

The car journey feels like it whizzes by, and takes an age at the same time. I'm so excited to see Jax, to have all my boys together with me again. It feels so wrong to be apart from any of them. Anxious butterflies flutter around my stomach. I'm worried about how we'll find him. What state he'll be in, and how he's coping with his withdrawal. I know there will be side effects from the withdrawal, that he may be suffering from all sorts of things, but I'm desperate to see that he's okay. That's he's still my He-Man.

By the time we reach the port, I'm practically vibrating, much to the irritation of Ash.

"Bouncing in your seat won't get you there any faster, Princess," he comments, looking at me with slightly narrowed eyes, his tone surly and sounding a tad jealous as he waits for Nengah to open the door.

"Don't be a dick just because you've got blue balls, Ash," Loki teases, earning a whack in the chest from the Ice Knight himself.

"I can sort those out for you on the boat, if you like?" I offer, my voice dropping huskily without conscious thought, and his frown lessens slightly. That is, until Loki opens his mouth again as we exit the car.

"That's the rub of it. No sexual intercourse for the man, for six to eight weeks, right *Lucifer*?" Loki tells us like the shit stirrer he is, a wide grin on his face. That earns him a punch to his gut this time.

"What? Why?" I ask, looking at Ash and frowning. He raises his brows, and then it dawns on me. "The dare!" I hiss, my eyes widening as we walk towards the docked boat, which is fucking huge.

"A Vanderbilt never reneges on a dare or bet," he tells me casually, not making eye contact, and acting like he's not talking about a dick piercing as we board the yacht. Nengah and some other guys bring our luggage behind us.

I'm momentarily distracted from that revelation by the sheer beauty of the craft we've just stepped onto. It's all sleek lines and polished light wood and has several levels, or I guess decks. On the side, in scrolling script is the name *The Princess Lilly* and my heart stutters to see it. *Did they name a boat after me?* There's soft lighting everywhere, and as I look around, I find all three boys looking at me intently.

"Do you like it, Pretty Girl?" Loki asks, his uncertainty completely adorable. He bites the edge of his lip and shuffles his feet on the wooden deck.

"Did you buy a fuck off massive boat and name it after me?" I ask, slightly aghast. Obviously, Her Vagisty preens at the show of adoration.

"We've had the yacht for a while, but decided to rename her after you," Kai tells me in his lovely melodic voice, and I can feel myself turning into girl goop. I've missed the sound so much over the past couple of weeks.

"Thank you," I tell them, deciding to embrace the romantic gesture for what it is, and not letting my ideas over the unfairness of wealth get in the way. "I mean it. This is one of the most romantic things anyone has ever done for me."

I notice a smartly dressed older man, in a crisp white uniform, waiting on one side of the deck to greet us.

"Welcome aboard, Mr. Vanderbilt, Mr. Matthews, Mr. Thorn," he says in cultured tones, with a wide smile. "Nice to have you back with us."

"Thank you, Wayan," Ash replies. "May I present Lilly Darling. Lilly, this is Captain Wayan."

"Ah, the name change makes sense now. A pleasure, Miss," Wayan says, inclining his head in my direction, his grin getting even broader. Then he turns back to Ash. "We're just loading up, and then we'll be ready to set sail. If you'll excuse me, Ketut here will see that you are settled." He indicates with a hand towards another smartly uniformed man, younger this time. Then Captain Wayan turns and walks off.

"This way please, sirs, miss," he tells us, holding his arm out, and the boys seem to know where we're going as they stride ahead into the interior.

I follow behind, gaping at the plush decor. We are led down some floating wooden stairs to a huge seating area with cream leather sofas and armchairs surrounding coffee tables. At the far end is a huge dining table next to semi-circular French doors that open onto another deck.

"Some drinks, please, Ketut," Kai orders. "I'll take my usual. Lilly?" he asks me, looking at me as I stand at the base of the stairs, trying and failing not to show how out of my depth I am.

"Um, just some iced tea, please, if you have any?" I ask, feeling overwhelmed.

"Of course, peach or lemon?" Ketut responds with a polite professional smile.

"Lemon, please."

He takes the others' orders, then leaves to get our drinks, and some snacks Loki asked for.

"Come sit, Pretty Girl," Loki orders, grabbing my hand and dragging me over to the sofas. He sits down, then pulls me into his lap, the others joining us seconds later.

"So, can I see?" I ask Ash with a raised eyebrow as soon as we're settled.

"He won't even tell us what he got," Kai tells me, a slight smile on his face.

"Good things come to good girls, Princess," Ash says with a sexy as sin smirk on his face.

"I am a good girl," I whine, pouting to see if that works. He just shakes his head.

"Well, keep being good, and I might show you." I stick my tongue out at him, and he narrows his eyes. "Brat," he says under his breath, although there's a heat turning the silver molten, and a tilt to his lips that tells me he loves my brattish attitude.

Ketut comes over with our drinks and snacks; all kinds of yummy things from sweet potato fries, to golden crispy calamari, and nutty satay chicken. We spend the next few minutes talking and catching up with what we've all been up to in the two weeks that we've been apart.

Kai remains pretty quiet throughout our conversation, a pensive frown on his face as he stares into his wine glass, full of what I assume is sake. I get up from Loki's lap, walk around the low table and reach out to Kai. As my fingers brush the side of his face, he flinches so hard that his drink sloshes down the side of the glass, dripping over his hand. Lightning quick, his hand shoots out, grabbing my wrist in a bruising grip that sets my heart racing.

His eyes are wild, and he looks into my panicked gaze, his own clearing as confusion crosses his features.

"Fuck, Lilly! Are you okay? You scared me," Kai exclaims, abruptly letting my wrist go, and reaching over to grab a napkin whilst setting his glass onto the table. I can't help rubbing at the bruised skin, and his eyes dart down, tightening in the corners when he sees what I'm doing. "I'm so sorry, darling."

"What the fuck, Kai?!" Loki snarls, coming to stand next to me, taking my hand in his grip, and inspecting the joint. I wince when he moves it a certain way, and he growls.

"Kai, I'm so sorry," I rush out, a little breathless from the adrenaline rush. "You looked sad, and I wanted to, I don't know, give you a hug," I tell him, still standing and shrugging my shoulders.

His own droop, and look of desolation flits across his eyes, making tears spring unbidden to my own, before he looks down to the napkin in his hands, his fingers slowly shredding it. Ordinarily, I'd go to him, but his reaction to my touch just then has left me reeling.

*What the fuck happened in the past two weeks?*

"Shit, I'm sorry if I scared you," he says gruffly, dropping the shredded napkin and clawing through his hair.

I shake my head in disbelief.

"You have nothing to apologise for, Kai," I say, trying to assure him, but he doesn't bother to look at me. "Kai, you're scaring me now. What happened?" I murmur, swallowing thickly.

Ash and Loki have gone quiet, Loki still grasping my arm and taking a step closer as if he doesn't trust his friend, but I don't pay him any attention. I've only got eyes for the man who looks so broken before me.

He sighs again, and when he looks up at me, his eyes are a maelstrom of swirling emotion, it's hard to pinpoint them all. There's an aching sadness, anger, and his lip curls up a little as if in self-loathing.

"Nothing, darling," he tells me after a deep breath. "I just hate going back *home*," he spits the word as if it's poison on his tongue.

I know that he's not telling me the whole truth, that there's more going on here. My heart pounds with the knowledge.

"I've got some work to do," he tells us in a monotone voice, before getting up, and walking off into the depths of the yacht.

Something is terribly wrong.

---

KAI

*Fuck!*

The flash of pain in Lilly's hazel eyes haunts and excites me in equal measure. That's how I know I'm broken, beyond repair. The fact that inflicting pain on her gives me a semi, even when we're not in a sexual situation, when she's not enjoying it tells me all I need to know about how fucked up I truly am.

*How can she ever love someone as terrible as me?*

I stalk off, heart pounding and limbs shaking. I don't see my surroundings as I try to outrun the demons that always rear their heads after I've been home for any length of time.

*Home*, what a fucking joke. It's not been a home since the night my parents were placed into the ground when I was ten years old.

Sounds from the past try to push their way to the surface; the muffled cries of a child, the comforting touch that turned unwelcome.

I shake my head, my hands reaching up to cover my ears, as I begin to pick up my pace, coming to an abrupt halt at the railings surrounding the deck. Looking down, the churn of the dark water below soothes my erratic thoughts, hypnotizing me and calling to me like a siren song.

Briefly, I wonder what it would be like to let the waves take me into their watery embrace, thoughts of sinking to the depths swirling in my mind.

*Would the sea be cold, or warm? Would it hurt? Or would it be a blessed relief from this torture, this crippling shame that I've lived with since that night?*

I come to with a ragged gasping breath, my knuckles white on the top rail, and my upper body leaning precariously over the edge.

Taking another deep inhale, I can feel the salty spray hit my face and burn my lungs. I can't let him win.

I'm not fucking stupid. I've done my research. I know that keeping this secret, even from my best friends, my brothers, isn't healthy. But how can I tell them the darkest shame of my life? I know that the part of me that believes it was my fault, that I deserved it, that I must have wanted it, is full of shit. That I shouldn't feel so worthless.

But knowing something in theory, and believing it are two very different things.

My head drops into my hands, suddenly feeling far too heavy to hold up.

I can feel myself unravelling at the edges, the darkness threatening to overtake for good.

And there's not a damn thing I can do to stop it.

# CHAPTER FOUR

LILLY

We don't see Kai for the rest of the journey, and there's an uneasy roiling in my stomach that has nothing to do with the rough motion of the boat. I can see the worry in the others' faces, in the wrinkling of their brows, and the tightening of their muscles.

Although the yacht put down the anchor about twenty minutes ago, the island can only be reached by a smaller craft such as a jet-ski, which is exactly what we shall be using.

"You're with me, Princess," Ash tells me as we step onto the lowest deck. There's an open panel in the side of the yacht, Ketut waiting off to one side, and four jet-skis already bobbing in the water next to us.

Ash passes me a life jacket, as Loki strolls past us, grumbling about not being quick enough.

"Thanks, but where are yours?" I ask, seeing Loki get off the boat sans life jacket.

"Put on the jacket, Princess," Ash the Ashhole orders me, a smirk firmly in place. I roll my eyes, earning the narrowing of his, but do as he says. I really want to see his dick piercing, so compliant Lilly it is!

Kai comes down the stairs, drawing all eyes to him as he walks past Ash and I with a tight smile, climbs on a jet-ski, waiting for Ketut to unhook it, and then it roars off, carrying him off into the dark night with a spray of salt water.

"Something's not right, Ash," I say, rubbing my arms, feeling cold all of a sudden.

"I know, Princess," he replies, taking one of my hands and squeezing it gently, before leading me to the water. "Fuck, he reminds me a little of Luc before..." he trails off, his shoulders tight and his jaw clenched as he watches Kai disappear into the darkness.

I reach out and cup his cheek with my free hand.

"It won't come to that, Ash. We won't let it," I tell him vehemently, and his jaw eases a fraction at my declaration.

"I hope so, beautiful. I really do," he sighs a great heaving sound, then rolls his shoulders before putting a smile back on his face. "Come on, get on."

He lets go of my hand, stepping away to get onto the jet-ski, then holds his hand out to me. I take it, my pulse racing as I step behind him and sit pressed up against his back, my hands wrapped around his trim waist. It's my first time on a jet-ski and excitement fizzles through my veins.

"The first one there gets Lilly for dessert!" Loki yells, before gunning his engine, and zooming off.

"Fucker!" Ash shouts over the roar, then we're off at breakneck speed. I grip tighter as my heart leaps, and my stomach flip-flops as we race in the dark, the stars and moon our only light.

"Are you sure that this is safe?!" I shout, leaning closer so that Ash can hear me. My fingers instinctively curl tighter into his linen shirt, uncaring if I leave it all crumpled.

I feel him chuckle, his back vibrating against my front as he just guns the engine more, making us go faster, and a squeal leaves my lips. I'd be lying if I said it wasn't exhilarating as hell. My whole body feels alight with nervous excited energy, my heart thrashing in my chest as we speed through the night.

Within minutes, we are pulling up beside a wooden pier, Loki leaning against one of the tall wooden posts, arms crossed over his chest, and a smug as fuck grin on his face. I look around, noting with a frown that Kai is nowhere to be seen.

There are several posts, torches on every other one lighting up the way along the boards. They lead right up to a huge bush, standing at least ten feet into the air, with an archway carved into it. Peeking above the bush, is the outline of a peaked thatched roof, which must be the villa and as with most things of theirs it looks fucking huge. *Snort.*

Ash kills the engine, then grumbles as Loki takes the rope he throws, and helps guide the ski, tying it off. Loki then reaches out his hand, pulling me up and into his arms in a single smooth move.

Helping me out of the jacket, he pulls me close, and then leans in, whispering into my ear, "I'll claim my prize once Jax has said hello." He bites my lobe, sending shivers rippling across my body, like the trails we left in the water with our jet-skis.

"Lilly," a voice deep as the waters that surround us says, and my head whips round to see Jax strolling down the jetty. My eyes drink him in for a second, noting that he's trying to test my sanity by wearing loose grey sweatshorts, and nothing else, which is obvious by the tantalising outline of his huge cock.

I tear out of Loki's arms with a half sob, half laugh, and run to Jax, throwing myself at him. Luckily he catches me, wrapping his huge arms round me, although he does stumble back a step, which makes me begin to pull back in concern.

"Shit, Jax, I'm..." Before I can finish my sentence, one of his big hands comes up between us and grasps my throat, using his grip to pull me in for a searing kiss.

He forces his tongue into my mouth straight away, leaving me no option but to open up to him and let him plunder my mouth. I gladly give him full access, loving the taste of his kiss after all this time without him, the intense worry, making the wait extra fraught. He tastes like the safest place in the world, like being wrapped up after being out in the cold.

My hands claw at his biceps, trying to get even closer, and his grip on my throat tightens just enough to let me know that he's in charge of this reunion.

Warmth pools in my centre, dampening my knickers as my whole body feels alight, even though there is a slight chill in the night-time air that pebbles my skin. I want to, no, *need* to feel him everywhere, and I let out a frustrated moan at the clothes that separate us.

His hardness presses into my lower stomach, letting me know that he's on the same page, and when he grinds his dick into me, I break the kiss with a gasp.

"Jax, fuck. I need you, Jax. So bad," I pant, feeling wild in my desire.

He leans back with a smirk, and I notice the tiredness in his eyes, even though they're sparkling with lust as well. I almost hesitate, but his other hand leaves my waist to snake round the front of me, dipping into my harems, and under the waistband of my underwear.

A rumbling growl sounds in his throat as he makes contact with my slick folds, his pupils going wide when more juices flow out of me at his simple touch. I'm so wound up, so fucking needy for him, that I'm almost climaxing from his fingers alone.

"Jax..." I plead, my hips moving and seeking more. I hear groans behind me, looking up to see Ash and Loki, their eyes blazing heat.

My attention returns back to Jax when he pinches my clit, a sharp cry leaving my lips at the addition of pain. I'm like a bitch in heat, needing to reassert our bond and mark him, having him mark me in return. My nails rake lightly down his arms, his whole body shivering as they leave red trails in their wake. I can't help the purr that sounds in my own throat as my eyes follow the lines.

A deep chuckle tumbles from his kiss-swollen lips, his fingers continuing their dance around my nub and along my slit, but never going deeper, leaving me desperately wanting.

"I wanna hear you beg, Baby Girl. Beg for my fingers, for my cock," he orders gruffly, still teasing me, and denying me what I desperately need.

"Jax, please. Please give me your fingers. I need your cock so deep inside me that I can't fucking breathe," I rasp, looking him straight in the eyes. His smile turns positively feral, but he doesn't relent, still tantalising me until I feel like crying.

"Loki," he rumbles. "Condom."

"Why the fuck do you all assume I have them on me at all times?" Loki asks in exasperation, but when I turn to look at him with a—*are you serious?*—look, he's pulling a foil packet from his chino shorts pocket. He walks towards us, then holds the condom out to Jax.

"Take it, Baby Girl," Jax commands me, his tone telling me that if I want what he's not currently giving, I best follow orders.

"Yes, sir," I say, a touch of snark in my tone as I do as he says. I just can't help myself, clearly.

His eyes narrow and his nostrils flare.

"For that, you'll get one clit orgasm, but no prep for my, what do you call it?" he asks, looking all kinds of smug. "Oh, that's right, my *monster cock*."

I swallow hard, but I can feel wetness seep from me at the threat, even though given my experience with that cunt, Robert, I know how fucked up it is to get turned on by consensual non-consent. Although, the keyword here is consensual.

"Oh, you like the idea of me forcing my cock inside your tight pussy, do you, baby?" he questions huskily, and I whimper.

He's still not giving me what I'm craving, and as he's maintaining eye contact, he sees every glimmer of frustration that crosses my face. Fuck, at this stage, he'll brush my clit and I'll fucking come all over him. I nod my head.

"I want to hear you say it, beautiful."

"Yes," I murmur, my mouth dry.

"Good girl. Put the condom on my dick, Baby Girl," he tells me, licking his lips.

It takes me a couple of tries to open the packet, my hands are trembling that much. Finally, I take the rubber out, and after checking it's the right way up, I look down between us to Jax's massive erection, straining against his shorts. There's a spot of dampness on the fabric, right over the top of his cock, which I know is precum, and if Jax didn't have such a tight hold of my throat, I'd drop to my knees and lick the salty drops that are bound to be smeared all over his tip.

I lick my own lips at the thought, earning dark chuckles from all three boys, Ash behind me and Loki in front.

"Don't worry, baby. Plenty of time for me to choke you with my cock later," Jax assures me as I lift the waistband of his shorts up and over his hard length, leaving them to drop to the floor.

Taking his solid member into my hand, I relish the silky soft feel as I wrap my fingers around him, the tips not touching because he's just that big, and pump up and down a couple of times. I moan at the same time he does. *God, I've missed this cock!*

"Keep that up and I won't make it inside you. Baby Girl," Jax rasps, his hand flexing on my throat, tightening so I can no longer move my head.

Although tempted to torture him a little more, I want to feel him push his way inside me, so I stop playing and roll the condom on. He's breathing pretty hard, and before I can ask if he's okay, Loki, the wind-up merchant, pipes up.

"Sure you're fit enough, big guy? I can always take over for you if you're struggling. We all know blue balls over here ain't of any use."

I hear two low growls simultaneously, and I look up to give Loki a *cut it the fuck out* look.

"Eyes on me, Lilly," Jax tells me. My attention snaps back to him, at the same time his finger picks up speed, circling ever faster but avoiding my nub until I'm a squirming, panting mess.

"Jax..." I plead in desperation, begging with my eyes for him to let me come.

Without any warning whatsoever, he presses down hard and gets exactly what he ordered moments ago. I fucking shatter with a cry, soaking his fingers, my knickers, and I suspect my harems, as the mind-blowing orgasm sweeps over me, making the stars overhead shine brighter.

Before I can come down from the heavens, Jax lets go of my throat and is tugging my harems and knickers off, helping me to step out of them and my flip-flops, my legs trembling. With a strength that is reassuring given his withdrawal, he picks me up, his huge hands under my thighs, my arms instinctively wrapping around his thick neck, my legs round his waist. He walks us to one of the huge wooden posts, slamming my back against it with a jarring thud.

I barely have time to take an inhale when he's nudging my entrance with his bulbous tip. He lets out a hissing growl, pushing forward and I can feel my pussy walls stretching almost painfully to accommodate him. Due to the lack of prep, there's a sharp sting as he keeps surging, and I gasp and squirm in his arms, my legs clenching around his waist.

"Stay still, woman," he snarls as he goes deeper, and my fucking eyes roll when finally, he bottoms out.

"Fuck, Jax," I moan low, my body relishing the fullness that only he can give. It's almost too much when he's fully seated inside me, I swear he touches my cervix, but I love it.

"Jesus, I've missed being inside you, Baby Girl," he confesses, his voice raspy like sandpaper as he starts to withdraw, mindful of my comfort even though he threatened force.

"Show me, Jax," I urge, grabbing his man bun in my fist and yanking, looking directly into the swirling depths of his blue eyes that flicker in the light from the torches. “Show me how much you’ve missed my cunt.”

His answer is a growl, and he thrusts hard, filling me up and making me scream with the hint of pain and the overwhelming pleasure that follows. My arse is still throbbing from Ash’s attention earlier, the rough wood chafing the marks that he left, and just adding to the delicious sensations that are running all over my body.

True to my request, Jax shows me how much he’s missed my pussy. With every powerful thrust and animalistic sound that leaves his lips, he tells me that I am his, and he is mine. I take all that he has to give me, feeling him deep inside me, rubbing and massaging my inner walls, until the wonderful burn of an orgasm builds in my core.

“Jax…” I gasp, my hands letting go of his hair, nails digging into the back of his neck.

“I got you, baby,” he rumbles out.

Without missing a single thrust, he leans in and bites down so hard on my neck, I know that he’s broken the skin. I throw my head back, hitting it on the post as my climax tears through me with the force of a riptide, my mouth open in a soundless scream. My whole body shudders and convulses, my pussy clenching and fluttering around Jax’s huge member, gripping him so tightly that I’m surprised he can continue.

But he does, not letting up, and sucking my neck so that my orgasm keeps rippling over me, almost becoming too much. Finally, after a few long minutes, he thrusts deeper than he has done so far, a whimper leaving my lips just as a roar leaves him, and he stills.

We stay connected, panting and trying to come back to the pier, the Indonesian night wrapping around us in a comforting embrace, the sound of the waves lulling us into a trance-like state.

I feel a cool drop on my overheated skin, landing on my shoulder. For a moment, I panic, thinking that Jax is crying for some reason, but then another lands on my knee, and another on my head, until all of a sudden the heavens open, and rain pelts down on us.

A joyous laugh tumbles out of me, my head still tipped back and my eyes closed, letting the rain cool me and wash over my body. Jax nuzzles my neck, a spike of pain flaring where he bit me.

"We should probably get inside, Baby Girl," he raspingly says into my ear, and I shiver at the sound combined with the feel of cool rain.

He pulls out, helping me down and stabilising me on unsteady legs. Looking down, I can see he's still pretty hard, the condom filled with his cum, slightly dangling off the tip. I smile as my idea from earlier pops back into my mind.

As Jax reaches down, I grab his wrist, halting his movement. He looks up at me in confusion, then a heat enters his lust filled eyes as I sink down onto my knees before him. Carefully, I take the rubber off, holding it upright, then roll my eyes back up and watch him as I lick his dick clean. He twitches like he wants to pull away, but instead, he wraps his hand in my hair.

I finish with a final lick to the tip, noticing that he's almost fully hard again. Then, keeping eye contact, I bring the condom up to my lips and tip it so that his cum flows into my mouth. His eyes widen, nostrils flaring, and the hand in my hair tightens, as I lower my hand, opening my mouth so that he can see the salty liquid on my tongue before I close my lips and swallow.

I hear two groans next to me.

"Did you just..." Loki trails off, and I look over to see him with his dick out, his own cum glistening on the tip.

"We should get in from the rain," I hear Ash order, his voice husky, but sounding pissed off.

"Just because you've got frozen blue balls, Vanderbilt," Loki grumbles, putting his dick away.

"Or it could be because Lilly is shivering and her lips look blue," Ash deadpans, stepping up to me and holding out his hand. I can't help but notice the boner he's sporting, poor man.

His words set the guys in motion, Jax's hand falling from my hair as he pulls up his shorts. He reaches down, grabbing my knickers and harems, then frowning when he realises how wet they already are. Ash helps me up, having taken off his shirt and wraps me in it. It reaches to just below my arse so I'm somewhat covered, and he tucks me under his arm, all of us tramping down the jetty towards the entrance to the villa whilst the tropical rain pours down on us.

---

## JAX

I pull the sleeping beauty closer to me, wrapping myself around her soft, naked body and taking a deep inhale of everything that is Lilly as I listen to the rain that still pours outside the open window. My body starts loosening up as her smell settles into my soul after the past two weeks of hell.

I breathe a sigh of relief that Lilly and the guys weren't here to see the more serious withdrawal symptoms. An image of lying on the floor, curled up into a ball crying with the pain in my joints and muscles flashes across my mind, my arms pulling her even closer as I bury my face in her ginger scented hair—*fucking Ash.*

The symptoms have eased, the only reason that I agreed to seeing everyone, although as tonight seems to be proving so far, the insomnia is still going fucking strong. I've been swinging between being wide awake to sleeping for what's felt like days. And the mood swings have been off the charts.

Part of the other reason for seeing the guys, especially Lilly, is my hope that it'll help to stave off the depression that's been looming over me the past few days. I can already feel Lilly's magic working, weaving over me like a spell of protection. Ash was right when he called her a pixie, and I am willing to surrender myself to her fae powers.

"Jax..." she moans sleepily, and it's so damn sexy that I can feel my dick stirring against her ass. At least reduced libido is one symptom I'm not suffering from. "I can practically hear the cogs in your mind whirling."

"Sorry, Baby Girl," I mumble in her ear, loving the way her back arches into me. "Can't sleep," I tell her with a sigh.

She turns around so that she's facing me, her face outlined in the soft light that's filtering in from the hall. God, she's so fucking beautiful. It blows my mind that she's even in my bed, let alone that she loves me. I am the luckiest fucker alive, even if it's not felt like it the past few weeks.

"You look tired, love," she says, a cute as fuck frown creasing her brow. I swear my heart skips a beat when she calls me that. I want to hear it on her lips for the rest of my life.

Her hand comes up to cup my face, and my breath stills gazing into her hazel eyes, seeing the love shining in them. Before Lilly, no one had ever touched me with affection, not that I can remember anyway. Maybe my mom used to, but my sperm donor soon beat that out of her, telling her it would make me soft.

Suddenly, an idea springs to mind, and my skin gets itchy with the need to be outside with my girl.

"Will you come with me, baby?" I ask her softly, watching every thought that crosses her stunning face. "I want to show you something."

"Of course," she says with a smile. "I'd go anywhere with you, Jax."

The truth of her words hits me square in the chest, the trust that she's placed in me makes me feel as though I'm ten feet tall. I give her one last squeeze, placing a quick kiss on her lips, then get up and help her out of bed, grabbing some clean sweatshorts and pulling them on whilst she dresses in a tank and tiny shorts that have me rethinking my plans.

I grab my phone, then pull her out of the room and head towards the front door. The lodge is quiet, everyone else having gone to bed long ago and giving me some alone time with her.

She gives me a quizzical look as I lead her to the door, opening it, the sound of the hammering rain filling the quiet space.

"Jax!" she hisses through her teeth, and I pull her out into the downpour. "What the fuck are you doing?" she asks, laughing as I tug her faster, heading for the pier.

A chuckle of pure happiness rolls out of me as we walk along the wooden boards, and I stop in the middle, turning to face her. Her usually bouncy brunette hair is plastered to her head until she resembles a drowned cat, but she's never looked more beautiful to me. I probably look similar given that she pulled my hair out of its tie earlier.

"One of the few positive things that my shitstain of a sperm donor insisted on growing up, was that I had to keep in touch with my Southern roots," I tell her, scrolling through my phone until I find the song I'm after. Thank fuck for waterproof iPhones.

There's that cute frown line again as she looks at me, the beginning of *Hard To Love* by Lee Brice starting to play. Walking over to one of the posts, I place the device down, then stroll back to her, stopping a step away.

"Dance with me?" I ask, my heart drumming for some inexplicable reason. I've never shown anyone this; not even the guys know my love for country swing dancing.

She beams, water cascading down her face as she steps towards me, taking my outstretched hand. We begin to move, slowly at first with a two step, but she quickly picks up the steps, following my lead. She sways her hips like a pro, unsurprisingly, a delighted giggle falling from her lips when I back slide into a pivot and spin her, in front and behind me.

I basically dip her like Prince fucking Charming, and her laughter fills my ears as I bring her back up, stealing a quick kiss. Beaming back at her, I keep leading us, twirling her around me, swinging my hips in time to the beat, the rain falling around us as we dance.

We get lost in our own world, partners in perfect synchronicity until all too soon the song starts to come to a close. I finish the dance, dipping her several times, then pulling her close and slow dancing, our hips pressed tightly together.

As the song ends, I capture her lips with my own, kissing her until I'm lightheaded and we break away, gasping.

"Jesus, Jax," she pants, her pupils blown and chest heaving, her nipples hard and pressed against the thin fabric of her tank."How did I not know you could dance like that?"

I shrug, smiling like a loon at her.

"It was my escape growing up," I confess, my voice low as if worried we'll be overheard. "Something my father encouraged that I loved doing."

I suddenly feel shy, exposed, in a way that I've never let myself be before and I look out towards the sea, the rain obscuring my view. I feel her hand on my face, bringing me to look back at her.

"It was an escape for me too. Dancing," she tells me when I give her a questioning look, a soft, gentle smile on her face. "We all need at least one thing that we love doing, Jax. It's nothing to be ashamed of."

I can't help myself, I lean down and kiss her fiercely again. *Could this girl get any more fucking perfect?*

Bending down a little more, I pick her up under her thighs, which wrap around my hips, not breaking our kiss as I start to stride back to the lodge.

"Phone!" she gasps, breaking our kiss with a laugh.

Turning back around, I walk to the post, letting Lilly grab my phone, and then turn us back, walking up the pier with her tight in my arms.

"Looks like I've made you all wet again, Baby Girl," I say, trying and failing to hold in the smirk.

"Jax Griffiths," she laugh-scolds. "Was that a dirty joke coming out of those lips of yours?"

"Sure sounded like one," I tease, releasing one hand to swat her hard on the ass for being a brat.

She squeals, laughing as I jog the rest of the way up the pier, back to the shelter of our island home.

"I love you, Jax," she tells me, giving me all kinds of chills as we reach the door.

"I love you, Lilly," I reply, the words coming easier than breathing as I open the door, walking through and kicking it shut behind me.

And I spend the rest of the night showing her just how much she means to me.

# CHAPTER FIVE

LILLY

I wake up with a delicious ache between my thighs and a warm lemon scented body wrapped round my naked back. There's also something hard and unyielding, poking into my arse, and a throaty chuckle escapes me.

"God, I missed waking up next to you, Baby Girl," Jax rumbles in the sexiest voice known to man, all gruff and husky from sleep. His arms tighten round me, pulling me against him even more, and he nuzzles into my neck as his hand starts drifting south.

Just as I'm about to reply, though he's already turning my mind into mush with his touch, the door flies open and with a sense of déjà vu, Loki strolls in. Jax groans, pausing in his attentions.

"The fuck you want?" he growls at the angel faced intruder, who smirks in return.

"Merry belated Christmas!" Loki shouts, darting to the bed and grabbing my hand, yanking me away from Jax who snarls like a wolf and lunges to grab my other hand, missing by a hair. "Need to be quicker next time, *He-Man*!" Loki cries triumphantly, pulling me out of the bed.

"Hey! I am not a fucking dog toy!" I scold as Loki pulls me close, grabbing a handful of my arse as his lips descend onto mine.

I get lost in his kiss, drowning in all things Loki. My hands rub up and down his bare chest, teasing his nipple bar with my fingertips, eliciting a deep moan from his throat.

"Much as I would love to take this further..." he murmurs against my lips. "Ash and Kai want to give you their presents."

"Presents?!" I screech, pulling away and starting to walk towards the door. "Why the fuck didn't you start with that?"

"Um, Baby Girl?" Jax questions, so I stop and turn back, brow raised. "Not that I'm complaining, but you may want to put some clothes on, otherwise I don't think it'll be just gifts that are exchanged."

"Fair point, well made." I nod seriously, looking down at my naked, slightly flushed body. Turning back into the room, I head over to my bags, which are on a stylised carved wooden chair.

I do a quick pit sniff, decide I'm not too fruity given that Jax and I had a shower when we got in last night. I hear manly chuckles behind me.

"What?" I ask, my forehead creased as I turn to face them, one hand on my popped out hip.

"Need me to sniff your pussy to make sure that's okay too?" Loki asks, trying and failing to keep a straight face. Jax outright barks a laugh, and then, I kid you not, they fucking high five like children.

"Fuck off, Loki," I tell him, sticking my tongue out, then smirking as a diabolical idea comes to mind.

Reaching my other hand down, I use a finger to swipe between my folds. Both boys go deathly silent as I bring the finger up to my lips, darting my tongue out and licking the digit before sucking it into my mouth. My own flavour bursts on my tastebuds, musky, but not unclean.

"I'm all good, ta," I tell them, turning back to my bag, and pulling out some underwear and clothes for the day. I go for red lace—*obviously, given the festive theme*—and a light cotton rainbow sundress with a full circle skirt.

Before I can so much as take hold of my knickers, strong hands spin me round, throw me over a huge shoulder, and then deposit me on the bed with a bounce and a squeak.

"Jax..." I warn, and he smirks down at me, getting to his knees on the bed. His smile grows wider as Loki joins us. "Ash and Kai will be mad..."

"Don't worry, Pretty Girl. I'm sure you'll enjoy their punishments," Loki tells me seconds before they descend on me like lions on a kill.

Suffice to say, we are late, and all need a shower after all.

---

Once we're clean and dressed, we walk into the living room area, where I get to appreciate the guy's island villa that it's daytime. It's stunning. The far wall is floor-to-ceiling glass doors, revealing a stunning view over the water. There's a swimming pool set into the deck with one of those disappearing edges so that it looks like you are swimming out to sea. We're on a higher level, so the view goes on for miles, with small specks in the distance that I assume are other islands.

The room is all light wood, carved in an Indonesian style. There are brightly coloured textiles everywhere, making my inner creative very happy, and comfy looking light grey sofas, with throws and blankets, again in bright colours, thrown over the backs and sides.

On one side is a wooden open style kitchen, with wooden countertops and all the modern conveniences one could wish for. To the left of the glass doors is a beautiful carved wooden table and dining chairs, enough to seat eight people comfortably, and let them enjoy the view whilst dining.

"Merry Christmas, Lilly," I hear Kai's melodic voice, and I look to the side to see him approaching me.

He has dark circles under his eyes, his hair in its usual disarray, and my eyebrows draw together with concern.

"Merry Christmas, Kai," I say back, a catch in my throat as he stops in front of me, holding a thin, long deep red box in his hands.

"I'm—" he starts.

"Kai—" I say at the same time, then we both chuckle ruefully. "You go first," I offer, desperate to reach out to him, to wrap myself around him, but a little nervous given his reaction last night on the boat.

"Lilly, darling, I'm so sorry about last night. I—" he cuts himself off, one hand running through his hair and mussing it more as he sighs. "Going back home...it brings up bad memories for me. It takes me to a dark place, and well, I guess I was still there, even though I was with you."

He looks up at me, his eyes full of torment, and I know that I'm not getting the full story. I know that things were bad with his uncle, his training horrific and brutal. I'm starting to think that it is worse than we all thought, and my stomach churns at the idea of him suffering even more at the hands of that evil man.

"Kai, there's nothing to apologise for. You can't help instincts, love," I tell him, not able to help taking a step forward, my hand reaching out to cup his cheek automatically. I pause in the movement, and he huffs, closing the distance.

The relief that floods my body when my palm makes contact is so strong that tears sting my eyes. I blink them away, seeing his whole body relax as he steps closer, our bodies flush. A deep exhale comes rushing out of me. I can feel his warmth through our clothes, and my soul sings as his hand alights on my own cheek, his thumb rubbing it.

"Fuck, Lilly," he whispers, leaning in further until his lips hover over mine. I can taste his breath, a mixture of mint and the green tea he favours, and I breathe him in until he's once again a part of my very being. "Don't give up on me," he pleads, and his words make the breath catch in my lungs.

"I will never give up on you, Kai. On any of you," I assure him, my own fingers moving into his hair and gripping tightly, pulling him closer until I no longer know whose breath is whose. "We are bound together, you and I, Kai. And nothing in this world, or the next will be able to keep us apart."

His lips slam down on mine, swallowing my moan as he kisses me with such desperation I can barely keep up. It's as if I am all that lies between him and the darkness, a darkness that is threatening to overwhelm him completely.

He breaks away panting, his eyes a little wild. Clearing his throat, he holds out the box in trembling hands.

"This is from all of us," he tells me, a slight tremble in his voice.

I take it, a small smile on my lips, my heart still thudding from our kiss. Looking down, I see it's wine red velvet, beautifully soft under my fingertips, and tied with a black ribbon in a bow. I pull one of the ends, the knot unravelling, and the ribbon falls free. Opening the box, I gasp as a platinum silver charm bracelet winks back at me. It's already got several silver charms, which I take to represent the guys and me; a lily, a sugar skull for Ash, a koi for Kai, an angel for Loki, and a Norse style wolf for Jax. There's also some more; a silver Big Ben to show my birth city, a fairy to represent my favourite Shakespeare play, and a silver American flag for my senior year.

I swallow hard, the lump in my throat making it hard to say anything.

"Do you like it, Princess?" Ash asks, his low voice sending a shiver across my skin like the caress of a night-time breeze. I look up with a watery gaze seeing that the others are all standing in front of me, all four of them waiting to hear my answer.

"I love it, thank you," I manage to whisper out, kissing Kai on the cheek, then stepping to Ash and Jax, doing the same. Loki, my wonderful Loki, breaks the serious moment by polishing his cheek and presenting it to me, making all of us laugh.

"Can I give you guys your gifts?" I ask, excited anticipation running through me as we all go to sit down on the sofas, picking up drinks from the side tables as we pass. They're all soft drinks or juice, as Jax's doctor said to lay off alcohol for a bit too, just to clean out his entire system, and make sure that he doesn't slip from one addiction to another.

"I thought you'd never ask, Pretty Girl!" Loki exclaims, his arms along the back of one of the sofas.

I get up, walk over to the palm tree that has been decorated like a Christmas tree including twinkling lights, and grab the four black gift bags, bringing them over and handing one to each of the guys. They are specific, so I wrote gift tags to make sure they each got the right one—*See! Not just a pretty face!*

They all look up, and when I nod in encouragement, they tear into them, and for a split second, I wonder if they've ever received a real gift before. One with no expectations or strings attached. The thought makes me frown until I hear Loki roar with laughter as he pulls out a bright pink fluffy bunny onesie.

A grin splits my lips as Jax holds up a huge Incredible Hulk onesie, his lip twitching. Kai takes out a stormtrooper one, a boyish grin on his handsome face, and all traces of darkness gone for the moment. Finally, Ash takes out a red devil one, and they all look at me with adorable confusion.

"Are we going dogging?" Loki asks, and all eyes swing to him.

"What the fuck is 'dogging,' dude?" Jax grumbles, throwing a cushion at him, which Loki dodges like a wanker.

"'Dogging is a British English euphemism for engaging in sexual acts in a public or semi-public place, or watching others doing so,'" Kai interjects, reading off his tablet.

"For fuck's sake, Loki!" I exclaim, my jaw dropping at his suggestion. "How did you even come to that...No, we're not going dogging, Jesus. Just keep going."

They do as I say, pulling out the large black boxes, and I watch as they each open them up and take the top layer of black tissue paper out.

"Fuck yeah!" Loki shouts, pulling out the paintball gun, aiming at Ash, and pulling the trigger. *What a cuntcake!*

Ash just raises a black brow, not even flinching as nothing happens. Loki looks down, pouting at the gun.

"You need to get the ammo at the centre, fucking imbecile," Ash says, rolling his eyes and setting his bag and box aside on the floor.

He gets up, all leisurely insouciance, and stalks towards me. He's wearing some grey linen trousers without a shirt, and all of his inked up muscles are on display, distracting me to no end.

"Thank you, Princess," he says once he reaches me, stepping close and pressing a light kiss against my lips.

"How long until you're healed again?" I ask against his lips, his kiss setting a fire in my core. Having to wait for him is like the most delicious torture I've ever been through.

He chuckles, the sound seeming to vibrate right down to my clit, and a moan escapes my lips, passing into his.

"Another five weeks, maybe four. I'm a fast healer."

I let out a shaky breath as he pulls away, stepping behind me to the palm-Christmas tree. The others have all gotten up, and they too thank me, pressing kisses on my lips and making me feel so loved up it's almost sickening.

"We each got you some other presents too, Princess," Ash tells me as Loki takes my hand and leads me to take a seat on the sofa once more. From there, I spend the next forty-five minutes being absolutely spoiled rotten.

Kai gives me a book of American poetry, plus a huge bag of Bordelle lingerie; basques, harnesses, bras, bodies and thongs. I squeal, throwing myself in his arms, scraps of lace and straps flying everywhere.

Loki presents me with five—*yes, fucking five!*—Irregular Choice shoe boxes, all new arrivals including yellow Shirley Bass rainbows, rainbow dinosaur Nick of Time's, and red Full House boots with gold stitching that reads 'Queen of my own destiny.' He also gets a shriek and a full tackle hug.

Jax gives me a gold pair of boxing gloves with matching wraps. The gloves have 'Baby Girl' written across the wrists, and Jax tells me that training starts when we get back. I'm a little more careful with his praise, sitting in his lap and kissing him when he growls that he's not, and I quote, 'a fucking pussy invalid.' He also gives me several sets of silk cami and shorts PJs with a knowing smirk and a comment that they should see me through the next term. *Ballbag.*

Then, finally, Ash kneels in front of me, a medium-sized black velvet square box in his hands.

"If I didn't know you better, *Ice Knight*, I'd say you have a flair for the dramatic," I tease him, earning a small tilt of his lips as he opens the box so that I can see the gold collar and matching cuffs nestled in red silk inside. There's a chain that links the cuffs, although they look like they can be separate too.

"Something to look forward to," he tells me with a devilish grin that sends shivers cascading down my spine and causes my nipples to harden.

By the time we're done, it's lunchtime, and although it's not a full Christmas dinner—it's way too hot and all of us, bar Jax, are suffering from jet lag—there is a wonderful buffet laid out on the table for us by Mama Dewi as they call her. She's an older Balinese lady, with a face as wrinkled as a walnut, and a wicked dirty laugh.

She lives with her family on the next island over, and the guys give her several gifts and kiss her weathered cheeks before she leaves. Ash tells me that she has been taking care of the Vanderbilts since he was in nappies, so when Julian let her go some years back, Ash employed her. Apparently, Julian owns a different island—*fucking rich peple*—but Cempadek belongs to all the guys outright.

Loki helps her down to the pier where a grandson is waiting with a boat to take her home for the day. When he returns, we all sit round the table and begin to tuck into the feast that she left for us.

Obviously, I show my appreciation for her cooking by way of moans and groans about how fucking awesome the food is, earning heated looks from the guys. Deciding to tone it down, otherwise I'll never get to finish my meal, I turn to Jax who's sitting next to me.

"How's it all going, Jax?" I ask, looking him over and seeing that he's not digging in like the rest of us, but is pushing his food around his plate which is unlike him. I worry my lower lip, a move which has Jax reaching out and tugging it from under my teeth.

"I'm okay, Baby Girl. Just not as hungry as I usually am at the moment, I guess," he tells us, his thumb still brushing over my bottom lip. "Loss of appetite is normal. And I've been sleeping a lot. Again, all normal, so nothing to worry about."

I still can't help looking him over, in his loose sweatshorts and tank top. Is he looking slimmer? Maybe he's not eating enough, and he does look really tired...

"Lilly," he growls out, and the sound of my name in his deep voice is enough to shock me out of my spiralling thoughts. "Come here," he tells me, scooting his chair out a little and patting his thigh, which still looks huge, to my relief.

I get up, grab my plate, and sit down on his lap, wiggling until I'm comfortable. His big palm comes to rest on my waist, and the tension flows out of my body at his touch. I'm completely lost to all these guys, dependent on them like I've never been before. A part of me knows it's dangerous, especially given their families and the violent nature of their lives. But it's too late now, we complete each other in a way that few ever get to experience, and if the sudden horrific death of my mum has shown me anything, it's that life is too short not to take every blessing, every piece of love and hold on to it fast.

Taking a piece of satay chicken in my fingers, I twist in Jax's lap until I'm facing him, holding up the morsel to his lips.

"Eat," I command in a firm tone. He raises a brow, one side of his lips tilting in that almost smile of his, but does as I ask and opens his mouth, letting me slip the chicken in. "Good boy," I tell him with a smirk of my own.

His fingers tighten on my waist, his other hand coming to rest on the apex of my thigh, over my dress. He applies a little pressure, enough to make my eyes widen and my breath catch. I can see by the gleam in his blue eyes that he's letting me know who's the boss here.

"Kai, any luck on finding out more about that picture?" Ash asks, interrupting our stare-off.

“What picture?” Jax enquires, turning his head to look at Ash, his forehead wrinkled.

“There’s a picture of Lilly’s mom in Chad’s study, with all of our moms at a Black Knight Corp gala,” Ash tells him, that look of unease back in his eyes.

“What? Why?” Jax asks, looking up at me.

“I don’t know, she never mentioned even coming to America,” I say, placing another bite into his mouth. “Let alone having any connection to your company.” And yes, I’m still a little pissed at being so out of the loop where she’s concerned.

“So, interestingly, I managed to get the guest list from that gala,” Kai informs us, pausing to reach over and grab his iPad, bringing up a list of names. “Your uncle is on there Lilly, Adrian Ramsey, but his plus one is someone called Violet Rochester. No mention of a Laura Darling on the list at all.”

I can feel my eyebrows drawing together, my stomach fluttering, as he looks up at me.

“So I did some digging into Violet, and it turns out she and your uncle were engaged, and then she disappeared completely, about nineteen years ago. Never to be found again.”

“What?” I murmur, my whole body suddenly feeling overheated, and sweat trickles down my spine, even though we have the air con on.

“That must be the heartbreak the newspaper articles were talking about when we looked up Ramsey,” Loki adds, and my head whips in his direction.

“I’m sorry, what? You looked into my uncle?” I ask, my tone a little caustic and my body stiff. Loki rubs a hand across the back of his neck, looking away as his cheeks flush.

“Hey, Baby Girl, it’s okay. Take some deep breaths, baby,” Jax says in a soothing tone, his palm leaving my waist to rub comforting circles on my back.

His words make me realise that I am indeed panting, so I do as he suggests and close my eyes, taking some deep, long inhales and exhales until I feel better.

“I’m just so confused,” I tell them when I open my eyes again, my gaze immediately finding Ash’s grey ones. His eyes are hard, brows dipped, but there’s a softness there that I know is for me. “Your parents don’t seem the sort not to have everyone’s names on the list. And it seems so strange that

Violet disappeared around the time my mum was pregnant with me." My head is swirling, and I can feel a headache coming on, the food lying all but forgotten in front of me.

I feel Jax's hands alight on my tense shoulders, rubbing and kneading them until I'm relaxing and trying to hold back moans at how good it feels.

"We'll work it all out, Princess," Ash tells me, his tone resolved, letting me know that he's taking this seriously. "Trust us."

# CHAPTER SIX

LILLY

After lunch, Loki suggested we go down to the beach, so we spend the rest of the day on the golden sand or in the beautiful turquoise waters, relaxing and listening to music, because of course, Loki has a playlist. He told me that you need a playlist for every occasion; from torture to chilling on the beach. I mean, he's not wrong.

Although this time of year in Bali and the surrounding islands is often quite wet, the rain holds off, and the temperature is balmy and the perfect amount of heat. I can feel my troubles and worries melt away as the sun warms my skin, and the sea breeze kisses my body.

Kai is still a little distant, yet I can see him trying to act normal, to hide the darkness that has surrounded him since that night on the boat. But even though he is a part of our group, sitting on a colourful outdoor rug on the warm golden sand, he's lost in his own mind, gazing out over the water. His face is a blank mask of indifference, his eyes intense, staring at the horizon. It's frightening to see him so...closed off. I'm sure the others notice. I see Ash looking Kai's way as much as I am, a frown marring his brow.

"We'll get to the bottom of it, Ash," I tell him, reaching out for his hand as he sits next to me.

"If anyone can, it's you," he replies, squeezing gently as he wraps his inked fingers around mine. His faith in me is warming, and I can only hope that it's not misplaced.

He looks mouthwateringly good, positively edible, in just some loose black swimming trunks and his ink covered skin. Her Vagisty is going all kinds of crazy, the horny bitch!

As I look at Kai once more, a wicked, bratty idea comes to mind, which will hopefully lighten the mood a little and chase some of that darkness from Kai's eyes. A flutter of nervous anticipation alights in my stomach; *what if he rejects me?* I brush it aside. I'll take the risk if there is even a small chance that it'll help him.

Letting go of Ash's hand, I get up, going over to the bluetooth speaker and Loki's phone, scrolling until I find the song I'm after. The beginning of *Sexual Healing* by Azee starts to play, the slow sensual beat washing over us like the caress of the waves on the shore.

Ash's grey lust filled eyes are fixed on me, and I glance over to see Loki and Jax who are in the water. They look up, pausing their game of catch—*I know, boys, eh?*—watching to see what I'm up to. Turning, I fix my stare on Kai, who's still looking out at the sea, his arms draped on his bent knees, and I walk towards him, coming to stand in front of him as he sits in his koi fish print swim shorts.

Finally, he looks up, his honey eyes dark, and gives me a small smile that makes my heart ache, and butterflies flutter in my stomach all at once. It's such a beautiful, lost, sad kind of smile that I have to hold in the cry that wants to escape my soul.

Keeping eye contact, I reach behind me, undoing the string securing my cherry print bikini top. Moving up to my neck, I do the same to that tie, letting the fabric drop between us on the rug. I reach for the strings at my waist next, undoing them one at a time until I'm standing before him, our toes touching, fully naked, and the sun licking every inch of my body.

I close my eyes briefly as a fragrant breeze teases my nipples, hardening them to tight nubs, and pebbling bumps all over my skin.

"I will risk sand in Her Vagisty, Kai, if that's what it takes to make you smile," I inform him, my lips lifted in a smirk. I open my eyes as a husky laugh falls out of his own lips, transforming his face into something worthy of the gods. "There he is," I say, my voice a rusty whisper, full of swirling emotion.

"Lilly, I'm sorry..." he starts to say, frowning, but trailing off as I get to my knees, one thigh on either side of his lap, my bare pussy hovering over his crotch.

His hands come up, caressing my thighs in a touch that leaves me shivering and aching, his eyes lowered as he watches his hands. Pausing at my arse, his fingertips dig into the flesh until I gasp, desperate for more despite the lingering sting from Ash's punishment yesterday.

"Please don't apologise, love," I tell him in a slightly breathy voice, and a bright smile lifts his lips at the endearment. "Talk when you're ready, but until then, use me as you need to."

My own hands embrace either side of his face, tilting it upwards so that our eyes meet, and we're gazing into each other's souls. I let him see all the love I have for him, hoping that he knows it's unconditional, and won't change regardless of what is going on in his head.

"You are too good for me, Lilly Darling," he murmurs, his own voice catching as his eyes glisten slightly, and my heart bleeds for him.

"No," I murmur back, leaning down so that the next part is said against his lips. I want him to take my words inside of himself, to taste their truth. "I am just right for you, as you are for me."

He pauses, his hands tightening even more on my lower cheeks before he closes the distance between our lips. The kiss starts out slow, a tentative exploration of each other, a rediscovery. I let him take charge, opening myself up to him as our tongues tangle and caress. Soon our embrace becomes heated, the sun above us eclipsed by our passion for each other, as we devour one another.

Kai pulls me tighter to him, my core lining up with his hardness. A groan leaves both our throats at the contact, and we start to move in unison, seeking more of that delicious friction. I shamelessly grind down on him, unable to help myself as Kai uses his firm grip on my arse to guide my core, so that it rubs up and down his shorts covered shaft. It feels as though the sun has somehow come down from the heavens, and is now in the centre of me, burning me up from the inside, making me desperate for more of Kai.

"Kai, love, sir...please," I moan when Kai's lips leave mine to trail a blaze of fire down my neck.

His head dips, capturing one of my hardened nubs into his warm mouth, teasing it with his tongue. My hands pull his head closer, trying to show him what I want, what I need. He pops off immediately, looking up at me with hard, hot lust in his eyes.

"Ash," he says, voice soft yet commanding. "Hold Lilly's hands behind her back."

His stare doesn't waver from mine, and I feel Ash's hot skin press up behind me, my breath shuddering out of me at the touch. I was so wrapped up in Kai that I didn't even hear my dark knight's approach. His smooth palms glide down my arms from behind, leaving a cascade of shivers in their wake. Placing a soft kiss on my bare shoulder, he grasps my wrists, then brings my arms behind me, holding both in one hand.

I whimper as he slowly, torturously, smooths the other hand around to cup one of my breasts, squeezing hard enough to turn the whimper into a gasp. Kai gruffly chuckles, then lowers his head once more. I watch as his tongue darts out, teasing my nipple again, his teeth occasionally grazing the sensitive nub.

His hands leave my hips, and I watch as he pulls the waistband of his shorts down, freeing his beautiful, fully erect cock. It stands straight up, and a moan escapes my lips at the sight of his piercings glinting in the sun. Bringing his hands up to guide my hips once again, he closes the distance between our bodies so that I'm grinding on the underside of his hard length, his metal adding a layer of sensation that's driving me wild. Ribbed for her pleasure as they say!

I rest my head back on Ash's shoulder with a deep breathy sigh, and Ash uses the access to pepper kisses and nibbles along the column of my neck. A sharp pain makes me jolt, and I look down to see Kai using his teeth to pull my nipple taut. He lets it go, then begins on the other side, Ash holding both my breasts out like an offering, massaging the one that Kai has just released.

I can feel the familiar burn of an orgasm begin in my core, and I start to move faster, desperately chasing the elusive pinnacle. But I need more.

"Please..." I murmur, my head once again on Ash's shoulder, my arms still trapped behind me in his strong grip. My eyes are closed, the rays of the sun making even the darkness bright.

Ash ceases his assault on my neck and breast, clearly waiting for Kai's instruction. Kai pauses, leaving us in stillness, me panting and exquisitely aching.

I crack my eyes, just catching Kai's nod, and a thread of excitement sizzles through me as Ash's hand leaves my aching globe, making its way slowly down the front of my body.

"Are you going to come on my fingers with just a touch like you did so prettily for Jax last night?" he asks me in a husky whisper.

"Yes...Ash..." I beg, almost crying with need as Kai resumes the movement of my hips, building me up again so that I'm on the edge of the precipice, looking down, but needing a push.

"When Kai says you can, Princess," he tells me, and I part moan, part cry with the need for release.

I open my eyes and look down at Kai to see he's leaned back a little, his eyes focusing on the way my pussy is rubbing up and down against him. There's precum glistening on his lower stomach, and my mouth waters for a taste.

Kai picks up the pace, rubbing me along his length furiously, sending jolts of sharp pleasure up from my core, his body at the perfect angle. I can't tear my eyes away from the sight of us, with Ash's tattooed fingers waiting to one side but not obstructing our view.

"Now," Kai growls out, and I watch as Ash's fingers finally make contact and pinch my clit hard.

That's all I see as the world detonates around me, my eyes closing with the force of my climax, my fingernails digging into my palms behind me as wave upon wave of intense pleasure rolls over me. My cunt clenches around empty air as I come, my release definitely soaking the front of Kai's shorts, which are pooled beneath me.

I hear his guttural moan moments later, his body going rigid underneath me, and I look down with a satisfied smile to see that he has climaxed too, ropes of glossy cum covering his stomach, my pussy, and Ash's fingers.

"I don't blame him, Princess," Ash whispers in my ear, nipping my lobe as he pushes his own hard-on into my arse crack.

"Fuck, Ash," I gasp, pushing back but stopping when he takes a sharp breath.

"Trust me, Princess. If I wasn't still sore, I'd fucking destroy this pretty ass and cunt right now," he tells me, pulling back a little. His words cause a full body shiver to whisper over me.

Finally, he lets go of my hands, and I roll my shoulders back, enjoying the tingling feeling of being unbound. I grab Ash's hand, the one covered in Kai's cum, and bringing it to my lips, I suck each finger, then lick anywhere that still has the salty liquid on it. Both men give a low moan, and I look down to see a satisfied heat in Kai's amber eyes.

I give him a cheeky grin, then push gently on his shoulders so that he lies back on the rug. Bending over, and shuffling down on my knees, I force Ash to back up until my face is hovering over Kai's cum covered stomach and crotch. With long sure strokes, I lick his seed off, loving the burst of salt on my tongue.

A soft warm tongue runs up my slit, an animalistic groan falling from my lips as Ash begins cleaning me with his own tongue. I'm still so sensitive, and the idea that Ash is also tasting Kai on my cunt is so arousing that it doesn't take long for him to build me up again until I'm quivering and shaking, and on the brink of a second climax.

Kai's abs tense, and I roll my eyes up to see his hooded gaze staring down at me as I squirm and gasp. His hands come up into my hair, gripping it between his fingers and forcing me to look at him as I get closer and closer to release.

Suddenly, Ash's lips seal around my clit, sucking hard and then biting down, and with a cry, I explode once more, my whole body flushing hot then cold. My arms give way, and I collapse on top of Kai, his fingers releasing their grip. I'm panting and sweaty, my heart pounding as I lay my head on his damp stomach and relearn how to breathe.

I hear Ash's deep rueful chuckle behind me. "Never thought I'd taste your cum, bro. It's not that bad."

Kai's stomach moves with his own gruff laugh, and I lift my head to look up at him through heavy lids. There's a wonderful sated look on his face, a smile gracing his lips as he looks down at me.

"I love you, Lilly Darling," he murmurs, and the heat from the sun's rays on my skin are nothing compared to how his words make me feel.

Delicious warmth floods my body, and I know that he'll be okay. We've not lost him, and hopefully, he'll feel comfortable enough to share whatever it is that's bothering him soon.

"I love you, Kai Matthews," I tell him back. "More than I knew was possible."

---

We spend the next few days in utter bliss, playing and lounging on the beach, or in the crystal clear sea. We eat delicious food made by Mama Dewi until we're fit to burst, and we make love as if there'll be no tomorrow. Well, apart from Ash who, although drives me wild with his fingers and tongue, won't even tell me what his piercing is, let alone show me. I don't hold it against him too much, seeing as he's currently healing, but still, it's a dick move, pun intended.

I know that it's not all about sex, but it's part of our bond, it's how we heal and work through things. And I don't care if people say it's not healthy, screw them. Seriously, sex is a completely natural way to express your feelings for someone and to connect in the most primal way. Not to mention, orgasms are great for your health and wellbeing so...yeah. I'll be carrying on, thank you very much.

I'm awoken in the middle of the night by the vibrating of my phone on the bedside table. Grumbling, I try to ignore it, but it starts up almost immediately again.

Untangling myself from the angel on one side of me, and the viking on the other, I scramble out of bed to grab the offending device, intending to hurl it out the window. Looking down at the flashing screen, I see it's a British number, from London, I think.

My brows draw down as I contemplate for a moment who would be calling me from the U.K. with a number that I don't know, but coming up blank, I decide to answer. If it's a cold-call, they can pay the fucking extortionate overseas call rate.

"Hello?" I ask, voice low and croaky, sitting down on the edge of the bed.

"Is that a Miss Lilly Darling?" a well spoken British male voice asks.

"Y–yes, I'm Lilly Darling. Who are you?" I query, sitting up straighter on the side of the bed, and blinking more sleep away whilst rubbing my eyes with my free hand.

I feel the rustle of bedsheets behind me, then a warmth presses against my back, and the comforting smell of vanilla washes over me. Leaning back into the embrace, Loki's arms come around my naked body, and I tune back into what the man on the phone is saying, just in time to hear his reply.

"Firstly, can you please confirm your date of birth, and the address that you were living at until January of last year?" he enquires, and because I'm still half asleep, I give him the information.

"Thank goodness. You are one hard young lady to get hold of, Miss Darling," he says with a rueful and relieved sounding chuckle. "I'm Richard Payne, from Payne & Sons Solicitors, in London."

Confusion wraps around me like a foggy blanket. *Why have solicitors in London been trying to get ahold of me?*

"Oh...I wasn't aware of any solicitors trying to get ahold of me?" I say aloud, wondering why my uncle has never mentioned it. *Perhaps he doesn't know?*

"Well, we've been trying to reach you since January of last year, but with no forwarding address, it's been quite a challenge. Especially as your mother was most insistent that only you were to know that we were even looking for you."

"My mother?" I question, my brows lowering even further and my heart rate picking up. Loki pulls me closer so that my entire back is touching his front, as if he can sense that I need comfort.

The bed dips next to me, and my hand is taken into a huge one. I look up to see Jax sitting next to me, a look of confusion over his face too. Both guys don't say anything, just lend me their strength and support, letting me know that they're here if I need them.

"Yes, I'm calling about her will, as you are the sole beneficiary."

I feel a wind rushing in my ears, and my hand tightens in Jax's grip. Taking a deep shaking breath, the room comes back into focus.

"My mother's will?" I ask, my voice quivering. Loki's arms around me tighten, and Jax starts rubbing my knuckles in a soothing motion.

"Yes, her last will and testament. Would you be able to come to the office in London? We really need to verify your identity, and talk this through in person," he asks. "I'm free tomorrow, anytime if that's convenient?"

"Ummm...I'm not sure, I'm in Bali, but maybe..." I trail off, not quite knowing what to say, and looking to Jax. "Can you hold on a second, please?"

"Of course, Miss Darling," he replies.

Bringing the phone away from my ear and looking down, I press the mute button on the screen.

"What is it, Baby Girl?" Jax questions when I look back up at him. He's all washed out in shades of grey, the tattoos on his arm standing out in stark contrast in the predawn light.

"A guy claiming to be a solicitor in London," I tell him and Loki, who snuggles even closer to my back. "He says my mum left a will, and he wants to see me tomorrow to talk through it." My mouth feels dry saying the words, my tongue darting out to lick my lips. My head is spinning with all the possibilities, with even more secrets that she must have kept. *Why could no one else know about this?*

"Hey," Loki says gently from behind me, bringing his face round so that he's looking directly at me in the dim light. "If you need to go to London, we can go to London."

"Really?" The sense of relief that floods through me at his words is palpable. My whole body sags into his embrace, which tightens further.

"Absolutely, baby," Jax replies, squeezing my hand reassuringly, and I turn to give him a small relieved smile.

Bringing my phone back up, I take it off mute and bring it up to my ear.

"Mr Payne?" I enquire.

"I'm still here, Miss Darling," he responds kindly.

"Can I give you a call when we land? I'm not sure when that will be, what with the time difference and the flight, but maybe we can arrange a time to meet then?"

"That sounds like a grand plan, Miss Darling. I shall ping over my personal mobile, and this is the office number. Just drop me a line, and provided it's not after midnight, I shall answer."

"Thank you, Mr Payne," I say, feeling lighter now that we have a plan.

"You are most welcome, Miss Darling. I shall speak to you soon. Goodbye."

"Goodbye," I return, ending the call.

I sit staring at the screen for a moment, my head swirling with the phone call, and what it all means.

"Let's go wake the others," Loki suggests, kissing my cheek. "One step at a time, Pretty Girl."

I nod. "One step at a time."

# CHAPTER SEVEN

ASH

We step out of the plane to drizzle and grey skies. *Ah, England in the winter, nothing quite like it.* Especially after leaving the tropical climes of Bali.

But I promised myself that I would be everything that Lilly needed, and she needed to come to London, so here we are, on a private airstrip just outside of the metropolis, freezing our nuts off.

Pulling our coats tighter around us—*thank fuck we brought them when we left Colorado*—we hurry over to a black Mercedes V Class, our private transfer provided by Claridge's Hotel. We could have stayed at the London home, but it belongs to my shitstain father, and I try to avoid anything to do with that waste of life. I also like showing off for Lilly, stupid I know. But what's the point of wealth, if you can't experience the luxuries of life? Or share it with those that you care about?

Our driver is standing there in the rain, holding the door open for us as we approach. No umbrella poor fucker.

"Thanks," I say as we climb in, the others getting in behind me.

Loki and Jax are quicker than me and manage to sit on either side of Lilly, facing myself and Kai. *Bastards*. This sharing thing definitely can be a challenge at times. It takes getting used to, although, it's easier because it's them, my best friends in the whole world.

We all buckle in and are driving off toward the motorway within minutes.

"Breakfast at Claridge's first, then Paynes," I tell Lilly, glancing down to see her wringing her hands in her lap.

The boys take one hand each, intertwining their fingers with hers, and she visibly relaxes at the contact. I feel a spark of sharp jealousy, wishing it were me sitting next to her. Holding her hand. Comforting her. But then the sticky feeling passes as I see the way her shoulders relax a little at their touch.

The voice of my cunt of a father tells me I'm letting her make me soft. But as with most things he says, I ignore it.

My eyes land back on the road, noticing the traffic building up as we get closer to the city. *Fucking rush hour.*

Eventually, we make it to Claridge's, which isn't far from our home in Mayfair. The car drops us off outside the red brick facade of the hotel, the flags looking bedraggled in the rain. The Head Concierge, Martin, comes out to open the car door and direct the bellboys towards our luggage in the trunk.

"Welcome back, Mr. Vanderbilt," the older man greets me as I exit the car, holding an umbrella up so that I don't get wet from the rain that is falling harder now.

"Thank you," I reply as he hands it to me.

"Mr. Matthews, good to see you again," he says as Kai emerges, handing him an umbrella too. Kai nods in return, and a pang of worry shoots through me for him. He's been unusually quiet since Christmas, and I bet his fucking uncle is to blame. "Mr. Thorn, a pleasure as always," the man smiles wide at Loki, giving him an umbrella too.

Martin goes to help Lilly out, but I step back towards the door, cutting him off and holding out my hand for her to take. She grasps it and a fissure of electricity shoots through me at the touch, as she places one heeled foot onto the wet pavement. She's wearing the new boots Loki bought her, and she looks hot as hell in them.

I pull her towards me so that she's under my umbrella, and even though I can see that she's nervous by the tightness of her eyes, she still gives me a smile so warm, that it makes it feel as though we are still on the beach in Cempedak.

I can't help but lean in and place a kiss on those luscious lips of hers, sucking gently on her lower lip and swallowing the gasp that escapes. I release her before things can get heated, or more heated, between us.

"You must be Miss Darling," Martin says warmly. "Welcome to Claridge's."

"Thank you," Lilly replies, looking up at the art deco frontage with slightly wide eyes, that sparkle and gleam even in the dull winter light.

"Mr. Griffiths, welcome back," I hear the man say as I tuck Lilly's hand into the crook of my arm and lead her towards the glass doors.

A pair of smartly dressed doormen open the doors at our approach, nodding in welcome. As we step through, I hear Lilly sigh as warmth envelops us, and I look down, unable to stop myself from taking in her every reaction to the elegance that surrounds her.

Her troubles are clearly forgotten as she gawps at the entryway with her lips parted, and eyes widening further, wonder written across her face. She's fucking mesmerizing, and it's all I can do not to sweep her up and run to our suite.

"This is...this is incredible," she whispers, looking around at the black and white tiled floor, the white columns, and shaped mirrors that are all around us.

Lilly has this ability to make you see things as if for the first time, and I feel a stirring, a lightness in my chest as I take in the entrance. It really is the pinnacle of refined elegance. I can't wait until she sees our suite.

"Your bags will be taken to your rooms, Mr. Vanderbilt," Martin informs me, having caught up to us. "Would you like to freshen up first, or head straight to breakfast?"

"Breakfast!" Lilly interjects before I can say anything.

It comes out a little loud, unintentionally so, if her blush is any indicator. I chuckle at her slight outburst, earning a small glare from her, which only makes me smile wider.

"Breakfast first it is then, Miss," he says with an indulgent smile. This girl has some magic power over men, I swear. We all become her slaves, fulfilling her every whim, just for a smile in return. "If you'd care to follow me to The Foyer, your table awaits." He indicates with one arm down the hall.

We follow him, Lilly's hand still clutching my elbow like we're in *The Great Gatsby* or some shit. I place my hand over the top of hers, loving the contact of skin on skin. *Just three, maybe four more weeks*, I say to myself, then we can have all of our skin touching. It can't come fucking soon enough, any longer and I think my balls will legitimately explode.

Loki and Jax are shooting some shit behind me, and I can see Lilly smile as she glances over her shoulder at them. Kai is still pretty quiet, walking at the back of our group, and my brows droop to see him still so withdrawn.

I feel Lilly squeeze my arm, and I look down to see her soft smile.

"He'll talk to us when he's ready, Ash," she reassures me, and I squeeze her hand back in gratitude, looking ahead once again. She really is too good for the likes of us, taking time to reassure me, even though I know that she's stressed about seeing Payne.

I hear her intake of breath as we step through the doors into The Foyer. Like the entrance hall, it's all cream walls and mirrors, only with silver and sage accents instead of black.

"Your table, sirs, miss," Martin says, leading us to a table in the corner that's a little more private than the others, as it's set back into an alcove.

It's the one we usually like to sit at, and I must remember to leave him a good tip for remembering again. He gets one of the servers to take our coats, then he pulls out Lilly's chair, waiting for her to lower down before starting to push it back in.

We all take our seats, the servers bringing us a selection of breakfast foods. Pancakes, fruit platters, and even what they call a full English, which consists of sausages, bacon, eggs, mushrooms, and tomatoes. It's all delicious, although Lilly mostly picks at her plate, which is very unlike her.

I can see the others glancing at her, worried frowns on their faces.

"I– Do you think we could get there early?" she suddenly asks, looking up from her mostly untouched plate. "I just...really want to get this over with, you know?" She looks at me, and I smile gently while nodding.

"Sure, Princess," I reply, getting up and holding my hand out for her to take.

She grasps it, a grateful smile on her own lips as she stands up. The others stand as well, and Martin rushes over, his face creased with concern.

"Is the breakfast not to your liking, Mr. Vanderbilt?" he asks.

"Oh, I'm sorry, it's my fault," Lilly rushes in, drawing his eyes to her. "You see, I've a very important appointment that I'd just like to get to, and I'm too nervous to eat. It really looks amazing," she assures him, and my love for this girl, this angel, increases at the pains she takes to make sure Martin doesn't think that he, or his team, has done anything wrong.

"I quite understand, Miss Darling," he tells her with a fatherly smile, his eyes soft as he looks at her. *You and me both, dude.* "I'll get them to put some in containers for you to take with you in case you feel peckish later."

"That would be wonderful, thank you," she replies, darting forward and kissing his cheek.

The poor man blushes scarlet, clearing his throat as he indicates for a member of the serving staff to take some of the food for wrapping, and instructing another to bring back our coats. If she hadn't caught him before, she certainly has now as he turns to her with stars in his fucking eyes.

"I'll get them to bring the car around," he tells us, still looking at Lilly. "This way to reception, and it'll be along in a jiffy."

He turns on his highly polished heel, and we follow behind, Lilly still holding my hand.

"A bit old for your harem, Pretty Girl," Loki murmurs from Lilly's other side as we head down the hall. I growl like an animal at him, which just makes the shithead laugh that roaring laugh of his.

"Shut up, Loki." Lilly sighs, playfully whacking him in the chest with her free hand. Again, he just laughs, taking that hand and placing a kiss onto the back of it. *Fucking smooth kiss ass.*

We arrive in the entrance hall once more, one of the doormen coming over to let us know that the car is waiting out front. The server comes over, handing us our coats. Martin guides us to the glass doors, telling us that our food is already in the car.

We step out into the drizzle once more, umbrellas ready for us and being held by a bellboy each. A quick few steps to the waiting vehicle, and we're once again inside the Merc. This time, I make sure to sit next to Lilly, much to the annoyance of Jax who grumbles as Loki takes her other side.

Buckling up, we're driving off in a matter of minutes, Lilly's hand still firmly in my grasp. I sent Martin our itinerary before we landed, so the driver heads towards Buckingham Palace. Victoria Chambers, where Payne & Sons is located.

Looking across at Lilly, I can see she's worrying her lip between her teeth, so I reach over and pull it out.

"Only one of us gets to bite that lip, Princess," I tell her, my voice firm.

It may make me an asshole, I mean more of an asshole, but I feel the need to control her. Especially when she's doing something that may hurt her at all. Her pain is all mine. And I guess, the others' too.

She gives me a small glare, which reassures me that she's not too anxious, and I can see the temptation to bite it again, just to test me, written all over her face. I arch a brow at her, and it seems she accepts my challenge, as I knew she would, because her bottom lip starts to disappear into her mouth again, all while holding my gaze.

Glad that my distraction is working, I swoop down, my hand grabbing a fistful of her hair as I capture her bottom lip in my own teeth, biting hard enough to bruise, but not break the skin. I swallow her gasp as my mouth closes over hers, my tongue forcing entry inside, to tangle and stroke hers.

She leans into my kiss, her body relaxing as my tongue coaxes hers.

"We're here, sirs, miss," the driver informs us as we come to a stop.

I release her mouth, loving the fact that her pupils are blown with lust, and her chest is heaving. Her lip has the beginnings of a purple bruise, and I want to fucking growl in appreciation at seeing my mark on her. *Yep, I'm fucked.*

"Let's go, Princess," I order gruffly, a smirk on my face as I let go of her hair and open the car door before the driver can.

I give her my hand again, helping her out onto the sidewalk. Thankfully, it's no longer raining, and we look up at the row of white buildings before us. I look back down at her to see her straighten her shoulders and taking in a deep breath as the others come around us. My chest swells with pride. *That's my beautiful, brave girl.*

"Let's go." She nods, taking a step towards the building with a brass plaque that reads *Payne & Sons, Solicitors.*

She lets go of my hand, stepping forward, and as we all follow behind, I'm reminded that although we may be Knights, she's our Queen, and we will follow her wherever she leads.

# CHAPTER EIGHT

LILLY

I walk up to the navy panelled front door, pressing the brass bell, my muscles quivering with a nervous rolling in my stomach. All my senses are heightened; I can hear a faint birdsong above the sounds of traffic, smell the mixture of dirt and wet leaves from the damp pavement.

It's strange being back here in London. Feeling this mixture of homecoming, yet a little like a stranger at the same time. Like this is no longer my home at all.

"Paynes and Sons," a female voice crackles over the intercom.

"Hi, um, Lilly, um, Darling here, to see Richard Payne," I stutter back, cursing my nerves. A warm hand lands on the small of my back, Ash's ginger scent washing over me and instantly calming me.

"Ah, come in, Miss Darling," she replies, the door buzzing, and I push it, stepping away from Ash's comfort and missing his touch immediately.

We walk into a brightly lit reception area, a Georgian window on the same wall that the outside door is situated, letting in some winter daylight. There's a crystal chandelier hanging down from the incredibly high ceiling, and a dark wooden desk sits at the base of a curving staircase. Behind it is an attractive older woman, with a neat blonde bob streaked with grey, looking at the screen of an iMac.

She looks up at our approach and smiles widely at us, not faltering when her eyes flick to the guys behind me.

"Good morning, Miss Darling, and guests," she says. "Mr Payne is expecting you and will be down shortly. Can I check your documents, please?" she asks, and I hand over my passport. She takes it, looks at the back page, then nods. "Please take a seat if you wish." She indicates a plush Chesterfield sofa in teal velvet, that's opposite her desk.

"Thank you," I murmur back, feeling nauseous, and wishing that I had eaten breakfast back at the hotel. We walk over to the sofa, but I can't sit down, nervous energy making me too jittery.

"Hey, Pretty Girl," Loki murmurs gently, taking one of my hands in his and stopping me from picking at my corduroy pinafore dress. I chose the mustard with a bee print, in the hope that it would make me feel cheerful. It's not working. "It'll be okay, promise," he assures me as I look into his beautiful green eyes that are sparkling as the weak sunlight hits them.

Just having him, all of them, near is helping to ease some of the tension inside of me. This whole thing has bought up feelings about my mother's death that I thought I'd dealt with. Foolish really, to think that the trauma would just disappear.

I nod, not knowing what to say, but stepping into him until I can rest my head on his strong chest, my arms wrapping around him and his own coming to pull me into a tight hug. Closing my eyes, I take a deep inhale, breathing him in, and being surrounded by Loki's familiar vanilla scent calms me further, until the nausea abates.

"Good morning, Miss Darling," a cultured man's voice calls out, and I open my eyes to see an older gentleman reaching the bottom of the stairs, a broad smile on his face.

He's of a slight build, and to be honest, he doesn't have many defining features, he'd be quite unmemorable. I recognise his voice from our phone call yesterday though, or maybe it was the day before with the time difference? Fucked if I know.

I take a step back, but keep hold of Loki's hand, and give Mr Payne a small smile.

"Good morning, Mr Payne."

"Richard, please," he replies, stepping towards me but keeping a respectful distance. "I'm so glad you could make it."

"Me too, although, I'm still a little confused and frankly in shock," I tell him honestly.

"Of course, that is to be expected. If you follow me, we shall get down to business and keep you in suspense no longer," he says kindly, stepping to one side and sweeping his arm towards the stairs he just came from.

He starts forward, and Ash immediately steps up next to him, striking up a seemingly casual conversation.

"So, Richard, being a solicitor is a bit of a change from police work," Ash says, and Mr Payne's, Richard's, steps falter slightly, although his smile doesn't drop.

"I'm flattered that you took the time to look into my background, Mr Vanderbilt," he replies, heading up the stairs.

I just stare at the exchange, not surprised that Ash looked into him, but I am impressed that Richard knows who Ash is given that I didn't mention it in any of our communications.

Ash nods. "I like to protect my interests, Richard. I'm sure you understand."

I bristle at being referred to as an 'interest,' and Loki must notice as he leans in to whisper into my ear.

"Don't worry, Pretty Girl. You can punish him later when we make him watch you ride my cock." I shiver at his words, whilst also being appalled that he just said that here, in the offices of what looks like a pretty high-end solicitor. *Fucking piss artist!*

Deciding that the only reaction that comment deserves is an eye roll, I look around to see several panelled wooden doors lining a carpeted corridor. We head towards the first one, and I catch a glimpse of his name on a brass plaque before Richard opens the door and ushers us in.

A large dark wood desk sits in front of double windows, the same multi-paned ones as downstairs, with a view of St James' Park filling them. The whole office is not quite what I expect, with box files stacked everywhere haphazardly, and the chaos makes me like Richard more.

"Now, before we begin, Miss Darling," Richard says, closing the door softly behind him and coming around to sit behind the desk. He gestures to the two leather chairs in front of it, so I sit down, Ash beating Loki to the other chair. Loki stays beside me, and I can sense Jax and Kai flanking me, creating a wall of protective comfort at my back. "I need to check that you are happy for these boys to be present too?"

"Absolutely," I say with no hint of hesitation in my voice. That is one thing about today that I am certain of, their presence.

"Excellent. So, as I briefly mentioned in my phone call, your mother entrusted Payne and Sons with her last will and testament."

At his words, my breath hitches, and I feel Loki's hand come down onto my shoulder, squeezing gently and lending me strength. My hand comes up to grasp his, our fingers intertwining.

"Yes," I manage, my voice a little raspy. He nods, then looks down at a sheaf of papers.

"I shall read it now for you.

"Last Will and Testament of Laura Darling

**I, Laura Darling, presently of Newland House, England, hereby revoke all former testamentary dispositions made by me, and declare this to be my last will."**

I can't help the way my body tremors at hearing those words, knowing that my mother most likely sat in this chair and filled this out.

He continues reading some legal shit that I don't understand at all. He then goes on to list my mother's estate, and a lump fills my throat at the mention of a small sum of money, and our flat, which I'm pretty sure I am going to sell because I can't bear the idea of living there or even going back there.

**"I also bequeath Lilly Darling the bonds and shares that I own pertaining to Black Knight Corporation in their entirety."**

The entire world stops spinning, the universe holding its breath as those words sink in.

"I'm sorry, what?" I squeak. Richard looks up from the document at my interruption.

"I beg your pardon?" he asks, an open, if slightly confused look on his face.

"You said bonds and shares in Black Knight Corporation?" I reply, feeling Loki's hand gripping my shoulder tightly, his body stock-still.

"Yes, that's right," he says, shuffling the papers on the desk and bringing out one to read. "The bonds each give you an annual yield of one hundred and fifty thousand dollars, currently just over one hundred and twelve thousand pounds, plus an additional one hundred and fifty thousand upon their maturity, in eighteen months time. The shares make you the majority stakeholder, or shareholder, in the company."

My eyes widen at this causal impartation of information, my chest tingling and a sense of lightheadedness coming over me as I take in what he has just said.

*What the ever-loving fuck is going on?*

"I guess this helps to explain the photo," Loki says with a rueful chuckle, and my head whips up to look at him.

"What do you mean?" I ask, brows furrowed.

"Well, your mom was obviously a shareholder from the start, so it makes sense that she was at the gala," he reasons, and I just shake my head at how crazy this all is.

I turn to look at Ash, who has deep frown lines marring his brow as he looks at the papers on Richard's desk.

"Did you know?" I ask him, a flash of unease spiking through me. "Is this why your dad is so interested in me?"

His own head turns to look at me, his eyes hard.

"No, I didn't fucking know, Princess," he replies, his tone scathing and cutting like the steel of his eyes. I take a sharp breath in at his words. "And I have no fucking idea why my dad is interested in you. Although, this would help to explain it." He says the last part almost to himself as he looks at Loki standing next to me, then the others behind me.

"Ahem," I hear Richard clear his throat in front of me, so I turn in my seat to face him once more. "Your mother had the forethought to register everything in your name, so there's no sticking point there," he tells me reassuringly.

"Oh, okay," I mumble back, my head spinning still from the majority shareholder bomb.

*I own a fucking company! And not just any company, either. The guys' company.*

"Now, that concludes the reading of your mother's Will. Here are the documents that outline everything that we've discussed, including bank account details, how many bonds you have, etcetera," he says, handing me a manilla folder, which I take, my movements on autopilot. "I can see that you're a little surprised by what you've heard today, so can I suggest you take a few days to let it all sink in, and then if you have any questions or need of my services, just make an appointment with Sammi downstairs?"

"Y–yes, that sounds good," I stammer out, getting up and clutching the folder to my chest with slightly trembling hands. "T–thank you, Mr Payne, uh, Richard."

"You are most welcome, Miss Darling," he smiles kindly at me, getting up and coming round to open the door for us. The guys each shake his hand as we leave, but I can't seem to make my hands let go of the folder to do the same, so I just smile and leave the room.

We walk down the stairs silently, Loki holding my elbow, providing a steadying grip as we descend. Reaching the bottom, we make our way across the foyer, leaving the building. I take a huge lungful of the damp London air once we're outside, feeling like it's the first time I've taken a proper breath in hours.

"You realise what this means, right?" Loki says as we wait for the car, and I look up at him to see an achingly familiar gleam in his eye.

"What's that?" Jax asks, and his low voice sends the usual delicious shivers over my body, like the caress of a warm breeze in the heat of summer.

"We're officially fucking the boss," Loki quips back, barking out his sexy laugh at his own joke.

I can't help it, my face splits into a wide grin that soon turns into a full belly laugh until tears stream down my face. Before I realise it, I'm sobbing, tasting salt as tears drip down my cheeks. Someone gently takes the folder from my grasp, then I'm surrounded by my guys in a group embrace that is so full of love and support, the tears flow faster until it feels as though there are none left.

"It wasn't that bad of a joke," Loki says as I lift my face, his thumbs brushing the remnants of my tears away. I shake my head, unable to speak just yet, although I do manage a watery smile.

"Let's get you back, Lilly," Kai murmurs from my side, and I startle a little at hearing his lovely melodic voice. He's been pretty much silent thus far. I turn to face him, Loki's hands falling away to be replaced with Kai's as he cups my face, bringing his forehead to mine. "It'll be okay, my darling," he whispers, placing a gentle kiss on my lips. "Promise."

# CHAPTER NINE

LILLY

As we step towards the idling car that has been waiting for us, I hear an achingly familiar voice call my name.

"Lilly!"

My stomach drops. You know, like when you are at the top of a roller-coaster and start to descend? It's like that but about a million times worse, like my heart skips a beat and the world stops spinning for a moment. I turn around in what feels like slow motion.

"Lexi?" I whisper as the gorgeous brunette woman comes towards me, wearing killer heels and a tan Burberry mac that showcases her curves to perfection.

My eyes flit to the hulking man coming up behind her, and my breath stills as I take in his huge form, tattoos peeking out of his shirt around his wrists and neck. He could definitely give Ash a run for his money in terms of the amount of ink that covers his skin. I'm speechless, not able to say anything as they reach our little group. *What the fuck are they doing here?*

"Lilly. My little Lilly Bear," Lexi croaks, voice full of emotion as tears fill her green eyes. They're not emerald like Loki's, but more of a spring green like newly sprouted leaves covered in dew. "Oh, Lilly love, I've missed you so much."

She goes to close the distance between us, but a blond Viking steps in her way, completely blocking her from my view.

"Who the fuck are you," I hear Jax rumble as the others close ranks, until all I can see is a wall of muscled backs.

I mean, the view is fucking awesome, but, yeah, I need to see what's going on in front of them as well.

"Guys, it's okay. I know them," I assure them, trying to push between Loki and Jax but not getting very far. "Fucking move!" I hiss out in frustration, ready to start shit if they keep ignoring me. I feel a desperation to make sure that they're really here begin to stir in my chest, my pulse pulsing in my ears.

They move aside slightly, leaving just enough of a gap for me to squeeze through. Fuckers. As I step through, I see Ryan squaring up to Jax, both practically snarling and vibrating with the need to let their beasts loose. I roll my eyes.

"Can you guys do the whole my muscles are bigger than yours shit later please?" I huff, stepping in between the fucking giants, causing Ryan to back up a step.

Jax brings a hand to my waist, pulling me closer to his body until his heat feels like it seeps into me, regardless of our clothes and outside coats. It's really bloody distracting, but I manage to keep Her Vagisty under control to deal with the matter at hand. *Ho-bag!*

Ryan's gaze flicks down to Jax's hand, then over the other boys, all of whom look a little scary with scowls on their faces. It's pretty adorable, and I have to rein in the smile that wants to spread on my face. Turning back to look at Lexi and Ryan, the almost smile drops as I wonder what they're doing here, and how they knew I'd be here.

"Damn, girl! You got yourself one of those reverse harems that you were always reading about, huh?" Lexi laughs, taking in all the guys with a glittering twinkle in her eyes.

It helps break the whirlwind of thoughts swirling in my mind, whilst also causing me to blush scarlet. She always knew what was going on with me, so I'm not surprised that she guessed correctly what is between me and the boys.

Her eyes come back to rest on me, and the soft look of pure love that shines in them makes tears spring to my own.

"Oh, darling," she says, her own eyes filling up as she holds out her arms to me.

I don't think about the fact that I haven't heard from them in almost a year. I just tear out of Jax's grip and throw myself at the woman who was as close to me as my own mother. Her arms wrap tightly around me, surrounding me in her floral perfume and love as she holds me close. Tears track down my face, dripping onto her mac and darkening the fabric. My own arms band around her, holding on for dear life.

I feel Ryan step up behind me, and his own arms come around both of us, adding his scent of sandalwood that feels so much like home that even more tears fall. I soak in their embrace for several moments, letting the comfort wash over me and soak into my bones.

Finally deciding that I need some answers, and need to explain to the guys what the hell is going on, I straighten up, untangle myself and take a small step away. Immediately, Jax is at my back again, pulling me against him, and I draw from his strength to ask what has been silently eating away at me for almost a year.

"Why did you disappear?" I ask, swallowing the lump that is still in my throat. Ryan's brow dips, his jaw clenching.

"We didn't disappear, little one," he tells me in his gruff voice. His chestnut hair is peppered with grey, more than when I last saw him a year ago, and his jaw is covered in a light stubble that really suits him.

"I haven't heard from you in almost a year! What the fuck else do you call it?" Anger washes over me in a wave at his words, the feelings of rejection and abandonment roaring to the surface.

"Lilly lovely, he's right. We've been trying desperately to get ahold of you, but seem to be blocked at every turn," Lexi rushes in, stepping towards me and taking hold of one of my hands. "We tried everything. All the socials, email, and even sending bloody letters! But we never heard a dicky bird," she tells me, her eyes pleading and her East London roots showing with the use of Cockney slang.

"I–I don't understand..." I trail off, looking between her and Ryan whilst being held by Jax with the others on either side of us.

"It's the truth, little one," Ryan assures me, his hazel eyes boring into mine. “We didn’t even get invited to the funeral, so we couldn’t talk to you then.” His jaw works like his teeth are clenched tight, a shimmer of tears in his own eyes that he tries to blink away.

“W–what?” My breath whooshes out of me, and I suddenly feel light-headed, leaning into Jax more who tightens his grip.

I never got to go to her funeral. I was too drugged up, basically under sedation for several weeks after Mum’s death. Whenever I was awake, I would be an absolute mess. Screaming, rocking, and unable to cope. My uncle said that anytime the funeral was mentioned, I would fly into a mindless rage, and they’d have to sedate me yet again. I have very little memories of that time, more a feeling of pain and terror, but then, I guess that’s what trauma and heavy drugs will do to you.

Although I wasn't able to attend, I’d assumed that Lexi and Ryan would have been there.

Before I can even formulate a response, Ash steps in.

“Can I suggest that we take this indoors somewhere? Before it starts raining again. This seems like a conversation to have in private.”

“Y–yes, that's a good idea,” I stammer out, seeing the concern in Lexi’s and Ryan’s eyes, their gazes pained as they look at me. “We’re staying in Claridge’s, can you meet us there?”

“Of course, Lilly Bear,” Lexi replies, squeezing my hand. “We’ll be right behind you.”

I watch as they walk away until Jax takes a step back, and turns me back around to face the car, his huge hands on my upper arms.

“Come on, Baby Girl. Let’s get in the car, and you can have some breakfast,” he softly suggests, letting go and grasping my hand in his warm one. I follow him, my mind a maelstrom of emotions and thoughts.

We settle inside the plush interior, the luxury lost on me as Jax buckles my seatbelt, and Ash opens one of the food containers that he got from somewhere. It’s full of fruit and those small caramel Stroopwafels, and although it feels as though my stomach is churning, when he brings a waffle to my lips in silent command, I take a bite. My appetite returns full force as the sweet flavour hits my tongue, and before I know it, I've finished them and the fruit, leaving the container empty.

I must have eaten quickly, because we pull to a stop outside the hotel as I swallow my last mouthful.

"Good girl," Ash praises, using his thumb to wipe a crumb from the corner of my mouth. "Right, before we go in, can you tell us who Lexi and Ryan are?" he asks, and I'm shocked to realise that I didn't even introduce them. I take a deep breath.

"Lexi was Mum's best friend, she worked at Grey's too," I tell them, looking at Kai who gives me a small smile that warms me more than the heating in the vehicle. He's putting his stuff aside to help me deal with mine, and my chest feels like it's going to burst, my heart so full as I look at him and then the others. "Ryan was Mum's long-term boyfriend, practically a father to me although she never made it official for some reason."

Ash nods, Kai obviously filled him in on our conversation by the lake last term, then the door opens and he's stepping out, holding out a hand for me to take like a gallant Knight.

I look around to see Lexi and Ryan walking up to us, tentative smiles on their faces as they take in the hotel. Like Mum, Lexi earnt well, but this is next-level shit.

I step away from Ash, taking hold of Lexi's hand and her face lights up with a brilliant smile, the very reason why she had the best tips at Grey's. It feels so comforting to be holding her hand, and we walk like that, following Ash and Jax with Kai, Loki, and Ryan coming up behind us.

Once inside, Martin, who was there to greet us, takes us over to the Art Deco style lift, ushering us inside. He leaves us to it, only after Ash assures him that we know where we're going several times. Apparently, The Prince Alexander suite is their usual, and they've stayed here quite often before.

We take the lift up to the third floor, the male uniformed lift attendant making sure we get where we need to be, because heaven forbid we press the damn button ourselves.

Our personal butler, Edwards—*I know, what the ever-loving fuck has my life become?*—greets us as the gold lift doors open. He's of middle age, dressed in a smart dove grey uniform with white gloves.

"Good morning, Mr Vanderbilt, Mr Matthews, Mr Thorn, Mr Griffiths, and Miss Darling," he says politely as we step out of the lift onto the carpeted hallway floor. "This way, please." He indicates with an outstretched arm, and we follow after him to the end of the corridor where he opens white wooden double doors. "We've added a slightly larger table to seat five, as per your request, Mr Vanderbilt," he tells Ash as he ushers us through into an entrance hall.

Yep, you heard me right. Our suite has an entrance hall, complete with black, white, and grey marble tiled flooring, a crystal chandelier, and mirrors reflecting the space making it feel light and airy.

"Thank you, Edwards," Ash replies, and his American accent is stark against the butler's upper class British one. "Can we have a light buffet lunch sent up, please, enough for us and our guests."

"Of course, sir," Edwards bows his head, opening one of the doors and revealing the living room space before holding his arm out to take our coats. Once he has them all, including Lexi's and Ryan's, he hangs them up on an antique coat stand, then turns away to presumably fulfil Ash's request.

My steps falter, alongside Lexi's, as we take in the room before us. We seem to be in a corner of the hotel, because there are floor-to-ceiling windows draped in white gauze, and framed with duck egg blue watered silk curtains on two sides. Coordinating silk cushions are scattered on the navy blue velvet sofas, walnut side tables situated next to them. Other silk upholstered chairs are dotted around the room, and there's a small dining table, plus a fucking baby grand piano. To top it all off, there's another crystal chandelier. *Jesus.*

It's not quite Buckingham Palace, but it wouldn't be out of place in a stately home.

"Drinks?" Ash queries, snapping me out of my room-fest.

"Whiskey, single malt," Ryan says gruffly, and I arch a brow at him. "Please."

Loki chuckles, obviously remembering all the times I pulled him up on poor manners.

"Lexi?" Ash asks, and I think it takes her a little by surprise as she jumps.

"Same, please..." she replies, raising her perfect eyebrows at him.

"Asher Vanderbilt," he says, heading over to what looks like a drinks cabinet. *He's such a cuntwaffle sometimes!*

"You can call him Ash," I tell her, earning a raised brow from the devil himself, although he doesn't say anything further as he turns and starts preparing drinks.

I pull Lex towards one of the sofas, heaving a sigh of relief as I sit down in the soft cloud-like seat.

Loki and Jax come to sit opposite us on the other sofa, taking up the whole fucking thing. *Bloody massive bastards.*

"Loki Thorn," my fallen angel announces, leaning forward. "And this hulking piece of real estate," here he pauses to wink at me, and although I roll my eyes, my face heats fifty shades of crimson, "is Jax Griffiths."

Jax just nods at Lex, then at Ryan who grabs his drink off Ash and comes to stand behind me. Ash brings me over a fruit juice mocktail, and I'm touched that he somehow knew I wanted to keep a clear head for this.

"Thanks," I say, and his grey eyes soften ever so slightly, his lips twitching in response.

Kai hands Jax an orange juice, which makes Jax rumble something that no doubt was rude under his breath, and passes Loki a bourbon. He sits down on one of the cream silk chairs with a wine glass of clear liquid, which I'm guessing to be sake.

"Kai Matthews," he tells Lex and Ryan, giving them a small smile.

Finally, Ash returns with what I think is whiskey for himself, and sits on my other side, even though there is a vacant chair to my left.

I take a sip of my drink, loving the burst of pineapple and coconut on my tongue.

"So," I begin, taking a deep breath and setting my drink down on the walnut coffee table in front of me, and turning to face Lex with Ryan in my peripheral vision. "How did you know where I'd be this morning?" I ask, as it's been bothering me since I first saw them.

"Sammi told us," Lex replies breezily. "She used to work at Grey's, remember?"

And suddenly it hits me, my eyes widening. I knew I recognised Richard's receptionist.

"Shit! I thought I'd seen her before," I exclaim, inwardly rolling my eyes at the fact that I didn't guess who she was.

"Wait, Payne's receptionist told you we were there?" Ash cuts in darkly. His warm hand comes to rest on my neck, his fingers lightly playing with that sensitive spot between my neck and shoulder, sending tingles racing across my skin straight to my now pebbled nipples. *Twatwaffle.*

"Please don't be cross, Ash," Lexi begs, her eyes flitting over my shoulder before coming back to rest on me. "We've been so desperate, and she knew that. I know she probably shouldn't have told us, but I can assure you she didn't tell anyone else. She's one of us."

Ash just hums in response behind me, so I decide to try and focus on something else.

"Why weren't you at Mum's funeral?" I ask, feeling a chill as I look at her. There's a sharp pain on my hand, and I bring my finger up to see that I must have been picking at my cuticles, my index finger is bleeding around the nail bed.

Lexi tuts, grasping my hand and inspecting my finger. She reaches into her trouser pocket, pulling out a tissue to wrap around it, all while keeping my hand in hers.

"We didn't know," she tells me sadly, her eyes glistening and making the green colour shine like grass after it's rained.

"The first we knew was when we finally managed to get hold of Adrian's secretary who told us that it had already happened and was a quiet, family only affair," Ryan cuts in, his voice rough. I glance at him to see his jaw is tightly clenched, his fist gripping his glass.

"I don't understand," I tell them, my confused gaze fliting between the two of them, then settling on my hand in Lexi's. "I wasn't there either," I admit softly, a tear escaping my eye, and slowly making its way down my cheek, my throat thick. "I was too...fucked up, sedated for three weeks, and by the time I was compos mentis, it was weeks later."

It's the one thing, apart from the argument I had with her, that I am ashamed of. I was too lost in my grief to attend my own mother's funeral. But to know that she may have been...alone. *Why would Adrian do that?*

I feel Ash shift closer to me, his warmth caressing my back as his hand moves to rub soothing circles on my upper back.

"Oh, Lilly Bear," Lex murmurs, squeezing my hand. "Don't blame yourself, love, it's not your fault. Any of it." More tears drip into my lap at her words, yet I know that what she is saying is true, and a small part of me is beginning to let go of the blame. "Do you, do you know where she's buried?" Lex asks gently, and my head snaps up, my heartbeat thrashing in my ears.

"I–I, n–no," I stutter, realising that I truly have no idea where she is, or what happened to her after the funeral. Nausea fills my stomach, my fingers going cold.

"Highgate Cemetery," Kai tells the room in his melodic voice, my head turning in his direction as I let out a huge breath, my muscles going weak. I catch his eye, giving him a wobbly smile, which he returns, pushing his glasses up his nose. I've never been more thankful for his research skills.

"How do you know that?" Ryan asks suspiciously, and I turn my head back to look at him with a slight glare. He's staring at Kai, eyes narrowed.

"Cool your heels, Ry," Lex scoffs. "If Lilly trusts these boys, then so do we. End of."

Ryan grumbles, but backs down, looking at me again a little sheepishly.

"Did Sami tell you that Richard was reading Mum's will to me today?" I ask her, and her eyes go wide, mouth falling open a little.

"No, she gave us no details. Just said that you were going to be there, and what time," Lex replies.

"Did you know Mum had stocks, shares, and bonds in Black Knight Corporation?" I question, suddenly desperate to know more about this part of my mum's life. Lexi's arched brows dip.

"Isn't that the big company who used to bring clients into Grey's?" she turns to Ryan and enquires. He also frowns.

"Yeah. And come to think of it, Laura was never there when they came...I don't think, apart from maybe once..." he responds in an uncertain tone.

I look round at the guys, but if their furrowed brows are any indication, they are just as confused as we are.

"I wonder if that Mr Black guy would know more..." Lex muses aloud, and I catch Kai sitting up straighter, leaning forward.

"Did you say, Mr Black?" he quizzes her, his tone urgent. Jax and Loki sit forward in their seats too.

"Yeah, he's a regular," Lex tells him, then looks at me. "He was your mum's biggest fan," she says, flashing a small smile. "Why?" she asks, looking back at Kai.

None of the boys say anything, just exchange glances. I let go of Lex's hand, turning so that I'm facing Ash, knowing that the others will follow his lead.

"What's going on, Ash?" I ask firmly. He darts a look to Ryan and Lex, and I can't help but roll my eyes at him. "I trust them as much as I trust you. They were at my birth for fuck's sake!"

He waits a beat, then sighs, taking a sip of his drink.

"Well, apart from apparently you, a Mr Black is the second largest shareholder of Black Knight Corp."

# CHAPTER TEN

LILLY

After that bombshell, which poses more questions than answers, we all eat a light but delicious lunch of finger sandwiches, more fruit, and some divine mini cakes.

The boys leave Lexi, Ryan, and myself to catch up, sitting on the sofas as we sit round the small table. I tell them all about Highgate, about the crazy amount of schoolwork, and the beautiful Colorado scenery. Lexi almost chokes when I tell her in hushed tones the story of Ash's party, when I danced for the guys using all the moves she taught me—obviously omitting being tag teamed afterwards by Loki and Jax whilst Ash watched.

She makes me promise to have a girl's night whilst I'm here, and I just know she's going to ask me all about the guys, because she's always been a dirty bitch!

As they're getting their coats on, Lex suddenly turns, a huge smile on her gorgeous face.

"What are you doing tonight?" she questions, practically bouncing on her toes.

"Um, I don't think we have any plans..." I start, but she interrupts with a squeal.

"Yay! It's the Grey's New Year's Eve party, you must come!"

"Wait, it's New Year's Eve?" I ask, my head spinning as I try to work out what day it is. She rolls her eyes at me.

"You always were clueless, Lilly Bear!" she laughs, pulling me in for a hug. "I'll tell Grey to reserve you a table. You remember *Bom Bidi Bom* and *Candyman*, right?" she whispers in my ear, and it suddenly dawns on me what she's saying.

A grin takes over my face, which she returns with a wink as she pulls away, and leans back in to kiss my cheek. "Let's show those boys what you can really do, huh?" she murmurs.

---

## LOKI

We find ourselves standing in the entrance hall of one of the most exclusive gentlemen's clubs in London. The walls are painted a soft grey, with matching velvet drapes, and black and white tiled flooring.

A thrill runs through me at being here. I mean, it's fucking Grey's! This is where deals that change the course of the world are made, all whilst sipping the finest alcohol, and watching the most gorgeous girls dance, although the latter no longer interests me now that I have the most beautiful woman in my bed nightly. In all our dealings and preparations to take over our roles at Black Knight, we've never been invited inside Grey's until tonight.

"Welcome, and Happy New Year," a stunningly attractive redhead greets us, beaming but not overly familiar. "Let me show you to your table, Lilly will join you shortly," she tells us, leading the way to a dark wooden staircase and down to a basement level.

The lighting down here is more typical of what I would expect from a strip joint, albeit a high-class one, being dark and moody, with clearly expensive furnishings, a clean woodsy smell and twinkling lights on the ceiling that I think are in the patterns of star constellations. The redhead leads us to a set up in the corner that has dark grey semi-transparent drapes surrounding it, a large circular table in the center, and is surrounded by deep red leather chairs. There are steps that lead up to the table, and I notice that each of the tables are set up the same, all with identical drapes to create a more intimate feel. I like it and my heart beats faster with anticipation of the unknown.

She takes our drinks order, leaving us to seat ourselves. I look around as we take our seats and grin, excited to see what Lilly thinks of our attire. Being an exclusive joint, Grey's demands high standards from its guests, so we are all wearing black tie outfits, as is the expectation here, and look fine as fuck.

Lilly left this afternoon, not long after Lexi and Ryan, as she said she needed to prepare for tonight. Whatever the fuck that meant. Our drinks are brought to us, and I peer around, fingers tingling with the night to come, whatever it entails.

"Where the fuck is Lilly?" Jax growls out, sipping his soda like it did him wrong. I can't help chuckling at him, earning a glare which only makes me laugh harder. "Fuck off," he grumbles, but the corner of his lips lift ever so slightly.

We appear to be the last people to arrive because we've not long sat down when suddenly the lights go out, plunging us into complete darkness. My heart starts racing again as the familiar opening beat of *Bom Bidi Bom* by Nick Jonas starts to sound over the speakers. Spotlights appear in front of the tables, one by one, illuminating girls wearing a variety of black lingerie, standing there clicking their fingers in time to the beat. A wicked smile comes across my lips as I get an idea of where Lilly might be. The naughty minx.

The light in front of our table goes on, and I swear I stop breathing, my heart pausing in its thumping rhythm. *Holy fuck.*

Lilly stands in front of us, wearing...well, fuck me. My eyes peruse her body slowly, giving me the best kind of torture as I take her in.

She has a jeweled halter bra of sorts on, the jewels swirling around her gorgeous fucking tits, with a small part, just over her nipples, covered with black cloth. There are ropes of sparkling crystals dangling down from her bra to her hips, and I bite my knuckles at what lies there. A jeweled belt lies low on her luscious hips, so fucking low that I'm not sure how the fuck it's staying up. The sparkling gems swirl, creating a heart type shape right over her pussy, where black silk, that is almost fucking transparent, flows to the ground, scooping down so that her bitable thighs are exposed, and presumably just covering her ass in the back. More ropes of jewels hang from the belt, decorating the outside of her thighs.

I manage to tear my eyes away for a brief second to glance around at the guys. They are all in a similar state to me, devouring her like she's a meal and we are starving men.

My gaze flits back to her as she ascends the steps, the curtains coming to close behind her of their own accord, creating a magical world where only she exists. The beat changes and she begins to dance for us.

*Jesus fucking Christ.*

The way she moves her body hypnotizes us, like a snake luring its prey. We are her willing fucking sacrifices, eyes following her every move as she dips and turns, running her hands all over her delectable body. I'm hard as a fucking rock right now, almost ready to blow my fucking load watching this goddess perform for us, and only us.

It suddenly feels very warm even though I can feel the breeze of the air conditioning against my neck, and I pull at my shirt collar, knowing that it's no good, it's the fire inside me that burns for this woman that's raising my temperature.

She catches my eye, giving me the sexiest fucking grin, and a groan slips from my lips when she moves her leg and her skirt splits, revealing a creamy inner thigh. Ash hisses a breath to my right, and I can hear Jax's growl over the music to my other side.

She turns around, giving me a view of her silk-clad ass as she winds down to the tabletop, going on her knees then spinning round, facing me and moving her body the way she does when she's riding my fucking cock. Instinctively, my hand goes to my crotch, rubbing my hardness to try and get some relief from this inferno inside of me.

Suddenly, hazel eyes have caught mine, darting down and becoming hooded when she sees what I'm doing. Licking her lips, a wicked, naughty smirk comes over her plump lips, and I just know that what she has in mind may get me in trouble. *Fuck it!*

Her eyes come back up, and she mouths, *"I dare you,"* at me. She fucking knows I can't resist a dare, so holding her hazel eyes with my own, I lower my zipper. She looks down, still moving her body, kneeling on the table. A gasp leaves her lips, that I want so desperately wrapped around my cock, when my dick springs free. I lean back to make sure she has a good view as I spit into my hand, grabbing it in my slicked palm. *Shit, that feels good.*

Pumping my fist a few times, I can't help but close my eyes at the rush of pleasure that skitters up my spine. My lids jerk open when I feel something brush my tip softly, to see Lilly leaning over me, her fingers outstretched. She catches my eye.

"Stand up," she orders, and although I raise my brow, I'm not objectionable to being ordered around in the bedroom. Or well, exclusive strip club.

I do as she says, glancing around to see that with the drapes, you can barely see what's happening at the tables. All thoughts are cut off when smooth lips give me what I want, wrapping around the tip of my aching cock.

"Fuck...yes..." I hiss, my hand coming up to tangle in her hair, grabbing a fistful and using it to push down slightly.

She follows my lead, taking me all the way to the back of her throat and holding me there, swallowing around my length until my legs fucking twitch. Looking down, I watch as she starts to pull back, taking a breath before sinking down again.

I look up at the others, seeing that they all have their dicks in their hands, stroking to the same rhythm that Lilly is sucking. Even Ash has his out, and I finally get to see what metal he got. Fuck, he doesn't do things by halves! I catch his hooded gaze, smirking, and he puts his finger to his lips, clearly asking me to keep my mouth shut.

Before I can think of a smartass remark, Lilly does something with her tongue that she knows drives me fucking wild, and I snap my hips forward, burying deep inside her throat.

"Jesus, Pretty Girl," I exclaim in a whisper-growl, drawing my hips back so that she can breathe before snapping them forward again. I repeat the move until I'm fucking her mouth, and she relaxes, letting me use her.

Shooting stars of pleasure light up my whole fucking body until I feel the familiar burn of my orgasm fast approaching. The possibility of being caught any moment, in one of the most exclusive clubs in the world, has me climaxing so fucking hard I swear I black out.

Ropes of cum coat the back of her throat, and I pull out so that it covers her tongue and fills her mouth too. She looks up at me, eyes watering with her makeup smudged. But to me she's never looked more beautiful, especially when she opens her mouth to show me my own cum before closing her lips and swallowing it down.

The guys groan around us, and I see Ash quickly put his dick away before Lilly turns her head in his direction. Her chest heaves as she looks at him, and her eyes narrow when he holds his cupped hand out.

"Drink, Princess," he smirks, his voice a little breathless.

I swear my dick starts to get hard again when she crawls towards him, grabbing his hand and bringing it to her lips. Not taking her eyes off him, she starts lapping at the cum in his palm like a cat with fucking cream, only stopping when it's all clean, his palm glistening.

"Good girl. Now the others," Ash commands, stroking the side of her face tenderly.

My breathing quickens as she does his bidding, turning to go over to Kai who holds out his jizz filled palm to her. She drinks that, then moves on to Jax where she does the same thing one more time. Even I hear his growl of approval as she licks his big palm with sure strokes of her pink tongue.

She finishes with one final lick, and I regret not putting my dick away sooner as he's pretty much hard again. But I guess I can't spend the whole night with him out. Shame.

*I Feel Like I'm Drowning* by Two Feet comes over the speakers just as Lilly straightens up and the drapes around our table begin to slowly open.

"That's my cue," she tells us, giving me a cheeky wink, then walking down the steps, scurrying off across the polished floor towards a door that Ryan is guarding. He gives us a nod.

"What the fuck is she up to now?" Ash muses aloud, his eyes narrowed on the door that our brunette pixie vanished through.

A devilish smirk lifts my lips, my own eyes going back to the door as I remember the feeling of her plump lips wrapped around my cock, which twitches at the visual.

"Whatever it is," I start, grabbing my drink and leaning back in my seat, "you know it'll be good," I tell him. "And besides, you can punish her later, brother."

---

## LILLY

My mouth still tingles from the pounding that Loki gave it earlier, my throat a little sore and my pussy damp and fluttering, Her Vagisty demanding satisfaction.

"Did they enjoy *Bom*?" Lexi asks, leaning over and helping me to pin the army-style navy blue garrison cap into my forties styled hair.

My lips twitch, and that's all the answer she needs. She chuckles that throaty laugh of hers, and I get up, surveying my costume in the full-length mirror for the next dance. I'm looking damn fine if I say so myself!

A navy and cream striped bra, which gives me awesome cleavage, with red sequin trim; high waisted navy shorts, with gold buttons that end just along my arse cheek line, with red sequin suspenders; black fishnet tights, and red sequin heels complete the look. My makeup is on point with cherry red lips and sharp cat eye eyeliner.

"Your mum would have been so proud of the stunning young woman you've become, Lilly Bear," Lexi tells me as she comes up behind me, wrapping her arms around my waist. Tears sting my eyes at her words, my heart beating double time.

"Do you think so?" I ask, a slight wobble in my voice as I catch her eye in the mirror.

"I know so, gorgeous," she assures me, straightening up. "And I think, for what it's worth, that she would approve of your harem," she adds with a wink.

"Lexi!" I scold, my cheeks flushing as she just smirks at me. "Thanks for convincing Grey about tonight," I say in a more serious tone. "I know he doesn't usually let underage girls perform."

"No worries, darling. You're practically part of the furniture here, and he, like the rest of us, was just so relieved to have finally found you," she replies, dropping an air kiss on my cheek then sauntering off in her own red sequin heels.

My mind takes me back to entering the club earlier this afternoon, the squeals and tears from the girls, and the way that Grey's eyes glistened slightly as he looked me over. He's a man of few words, and when he does speak, people tend to listen, so when he said "Welcome home, Lilly," I got so choked up I could barely breathe.

Lexi's right, I basically grew up at Grey's; apparently, I used to nap the best in a corner during rehearsals with the music turned up full volume. These people are my family, and I'm ashamed that I forgot that fact for a time.

"Time to go, girls!" Justin, who's been at Grey's for-fucking-ever shouts, clapping his hands and breaking into my thoughts.

We all start to exit the doors, down the performers' staircase to the basement, and I can just hear the faint sound of the current song coming to an end as I reach the bottom step. Nervous butterflies flutter in my stomach as the door opens into darkness, and I bounce on my toes in anticipation of what the boys will think when the lights go up.

They looked utterly drool worthy in their tuxes, so much so that it was hard to remember my steps when I danced for them earlier. I don't have any more time for thoughts of my hot as fuck guys, as the opening bars of Christina Aguilera's *Candyman* starts playing, the lights go up, and I run to my table, along with the others, in order to get there on time to start the dance.

I can't keep the wide smile off my face as I step up onto the table and see my guys' faces. Loki's jaw is hanging open, Jax is biting his lip in the most distracting way, Ash is rubbing his jaw, his eyes molten, and Kai's eyes are full of fire as he takes me in from my cap to my heels.

It's a quick paced dance, a mix of sensual burlesque moves, pausing in provocative positions, and lindy hop, with some good old sexy dancing thrown in. The true beauty of this number is that we dance in unison, some moves even in perfect synchronicity following on from one another, and as the curtains around the table are open, I see the other girls all dancing with me.

I'm not sure the Knights notice though, their eyes glued to my body as I dance in time to the beat. The look in each jewelled orb is positively feral, like wolves that have spotted their next meal, and my heart starts racing from more than just the dancing. We come to the part of the dance that's floor, or table work, our legs in the air opening and closing in time to the music.

As the number begins to draw to a close, I keep Ash's eye, unable to look away as I perform the closing moves. I can't help the smirk that lifts my cherry lips when he reaches down to adjust himself. I'm still pissed that I clearly missed seeing his dick earlier, and the mystery piercing. And I bet Loki won't tell me later! *Jizzfucker!*

My chest is heaving when the song finishes, leaving me in a classic pin-up pose; standing with my knees bent, arse out, and hands on my thighs. I vaguely register the applause around us, watching as Ash slowly brings his hands together, keeping eye contact.

Our stare off is interrupted by two of the serving girls bringing over what looks like chocolate fondue. I look back to Ash, registering his devilish smile as they set it down.

"Thank you," he says to them, and they bow their heads in return.

The curtains that surround us start to whisper closed, encasing us in our own world again. I look over to Loki, seeing a look of delighted puzzlement on his face that probably matches my own.

"What's going on?" I question, locking eyes with Ash as he reaches over to grab a strawberry.

"Lie down, back on the table, Princess," he orders, and his hard voice lets me know that I best obey. Of course, my inner brat decides to make an appearance, unable to help herself.

"Why?" I query. His nostrils flare, but a delighted gleam enters his steel eyes. I hear Kai growl behind me, just as *Twisted* by Two Feet starts to play.

"For that, you don't get to come until the stroke of midnight," Ash informs me casually, taking off his jacket.

My gaze is focused on his hands as he achingly, slowly undoes each silver cufflink, setting them on the table. Then, he rolls the sleeves of his shirt up his forearms and to his elbows, showcasing his beautifully inked arms, leaving me breathless and my cunt dripping. I swallow hard at the arm porn show he's giving me, hearing his low chuckle.

"Now. On. Your. Fucking. Back," he orders, all traces of humour gone, and my gaze snaps up to see his grey orbs are hard and unblinking, his jet black brows lowered over them, screaming that he's the hunter and I'm the prey.

Unable to keep standing, even if I wanted to, I sink shakily to my knees, careful to avoid the desert that surrounds me. Sitting back, I finally lie down, looking up at the dark ceiling that resembles the night sky, with glittering crystals and twinkling lights.

Kai's face comes into view, and I notice that he too is without a jacket, his sleeves rolled up. The top two buttons of his shirt are undone as well, and his bow tie is missing.

"See," he whispers seductively as he leans further forward. "You can be a good girl." He pulls back, bringing his hands up, and I notice that he is holding his undone bow tie in them. "Lift your head up, darling."

This time I do as ordered straight away. I wouldn't put it past them to withhold orgasms all night. He wraps the cloth around my eyes, plunging me into darkness, only the slight glitter of light appearing along the edges of my blindfold. My head jerks slightly as he knots it to one side so that the knot isn't pressing on the back of my head when I lower it back down.

"Arms up, Baby Girl," I hear Jax rumble, and my head turns towards his low voice, again doing as I'm told without a fuss.

My heart rate picks up, my breathing coming in short pants as I feel my wrists being bound, presumably with his own bow tie. My thighs rub together, desperate to ease the ache that is building in my core, soaking through my thong and shorts.

"Naughty, Lilly," Loki croons, grabbing my foot, and bringing my leg up, placing a gentle kiss on my inner ankle that sends shivers skittering across my skin. The move effectively stops me from even attempting to ease the throbbing between my legs, and I whimper.

"Oh, Princess," Ash tsks, and my head turns to look down, but obviously with the blindfold, I can't see what he's doing. "You've got forty-five minutes until midnight yet," he chuckles like the cuntmuffin that he is. "Loki, take her shorts off, expose her pretty pink pussy."

My breath hitches at his words, a flash of nervous anticipation flooding through me. I mean, I know I just gave Loki head, and there aren't any more dances planned for me to take part in, but someone could interrupt us at any moment. The thought of getting caught has a rush of liquid seeping out of my cunt.

What I assume are Loki's hands brush the bare skin at my waist, my skin tingling at the touch.

"Lift your hips, Pretty Girl," he orders once he's undone the side zip, and I obey.

Slowly, he pulls them down my legs, managing to get them over my heels without taking the shoes off. I swear that boy has as much of a shoe fetish as I do!

*He'll have to take them off to take the tights off...*I start to muse but the fucker just has to prove me wrong. With a tearing sound, that I hope the music covers, he rips open the crotch of my fishnets.

"Don't you fucking dare!" I hiss, but it's too late as I feel the crotch of my knickers rip, Loki snapping the thong.

Before I can curse him out, I hear a growl, then feel a wet tongue lick my damp folds from opening to clit, and my hips buck off the table as a deep moan leaves my lips. The action causes more liquid to seep out of my lower lips, earning another Loki growl.

"She's fucking soaked," he groans, and I can feel cool air as he blows on my overheated sex.

"Such a pretty pink pussy," Ash coos in appreciation. "Now, there's some melted chocolate up there that I'm sure Kai will enjoy," he tells me, and a fine tremble begins in my limbs at the idea of the burning hot chocolate dripping on my body. "But I prefer my strawberries with cream, don't you, Loki?" he asks.

I whimper as I feel the cool round fruit being dipped into my dripping cunt, just as someone moves the cups of my bra aside, exposing my pebbled nipples to the air. Ash hums in approval from near my feet, just as my left nipple is tweaked hard, and I cry out.

"What's your safe word, Lilly?" Kai asks, his voice gruff and full of desire.

"Red," I whimper back just as I feel a hot tongue slide through my folds again, not sure if it's Ash or Loki.

"Good," he replies, seconds before I feel the burn of the molten chocolate hit my sensitive nipple.

I gasp, which turns into a moan as a mouth seals over the bud, a tongue swirling over the sensitive flesh, then sucking the chocolate off. Another burn on my other nipple leaves me panting, a cool strawberry dipping into my cunt at the same time.

I lose all sense of time as I'm consumed, lost in the sensations of hot tongues, cool fruit, and burning chocolate until I'm quivering so close to the edge I can feel myself beginning to fall off.

"Not yet, Princess," Ash's husky voice growls out, and I cry out in alarm as all of them stop, leaving me untouched until my thrashing heart starts to slow.

Then, they begin the sweet torture once more, building me up only to stop as soon as I near climax. They repeat this process several times over, swapping places, until I'm a sweaty, sticky mess, aching and pleading for release.

After what feels like a lifetime, the music quietens, and a countdown begins.

"Ten!" voices from outside our bubble shout.

"Ten seconds, Princess," Ash whispers in my ear, and I jump thinking he was at the other end of the table. He pinches my nipple, tugging it until I groan.

"Nine!"

I can feel myself edging closer as a hot mouth covers my other nipple and a tongue dips inside me.

"Eight!"

My whole body starts to tingle, from my toes to my teeth in sweet anticipation of the release to come.

"Seven!"

"Not yet, Pretty Girl," Loki cautions, his musician's fingers teasing my side as he peppers my neck with gentle kisses. He must have swapped places too.

"Six!"

God, I'm so fucking close, my entire body trembling with the need to come.

"Five!"

"Are you going to squirt for us, Princess?" Ash's husky voice asks in my ear. *Fucking hell.*

"Four!"

Ten seconds have never felt so fucking long!

"Three!"

"Almost there, darling," Kai's melodic voice sounds from the bottom of the table, his fingers teasing my clit. "You're doing so well, beautiful."

"Two!"

"I want you to come all over my face, Baby Girl. On the one," Jax orders, his husky voice and naughty words bringing me so close I can taste freedom.

"One!"

Thick fingers slam into me as four mouths descend on my body at the same time.

I.

Fucking.

Shatter.

My whole body lights up, only being held down by strong hands as I explode like the fireworks that are no doubt covering the sky in multicoloured lights at this very moment. Wave upon wave of intense pleasure crashes through me, and I obey Jax's command coming all over his face as my liquid release gushes out of me.

Happy fucking New Year.

# CHAPTER ELEVEN

LILLY

We spend the next couple of days enjoying the sights of London, doing the whole tourist thing. We take an open-top bus, something I've never done before even though I grew up here. Lexi and Ryan join us every day, and it's wonderful to have them back in my life again, as if they were never out of it.

Ryan is still a little unsure of the guys, casting suspicious looks their way every so often until one day, Jax and him start talking and discover that they both spent time in South Africa training. Although I'm not sure what that means for either of them. I know that it can't be good if Black Knight was involved, which they would have been given that Jax mentions it as part of his training. It hurts my soul that they went through that, especially Jax. I can see a newfound respect in Ryan's eyes after that, and I'm glad that they've found some common ground.

We have two days left, and I wake up in an empty bed, wondering where Loki and Jax, who spent the night exploring my body in the most mind-shattering ways, are. Coming out of the bedroom, dressed in just Loki's T-shirt, I sleepily stumble into the living room area to find a wonderful breakfast laid out for me, and all four guys sitting round the small dining table with *Slow*

*Hands* by Niall Horan playing softly in the background. They all stop talking when I enter, looking up at me as I walk towards them, their eyes drinking me in and causing a blush to spread across my cheeks.

"Morning, Princess," Ash greets me, getting up and pulling out the chair in between his and Kai's for me.

He kisses my cheek sweetly when I reach him, then motions for me to take a seat, pushing the chair in as I lower myself down. He resumes his seat, and it's then that I notice they're all still looking at me intently. I can't help narrowing my eyes at them.

"What's going on?" I ask, raising a brow as I watch Kai begin to fill up a plate with pancakes, fruit, greek yoghurt, and then drizzling it all with syrup.

"We thought, Pretty Girl, that you might like a girls' day with Lexi, so we organised a spa day in town with lunch and champagne," Loki tells me, pouring me a large glass of fruit juice, most likely tropical, as he knows that's my favourite.

"Oh," I respond, my lips lifting at the thoughtfulness of these men. "That sounds wonderful, thank you," I tell them, accepting the plate from Kai and the glass from Loki.

I take my knife and fork, cutting some pancake and piling on some strawberries and yoghurt, and bring my fork to my lips just as Ash speaks.

"And then tomorrow, we're visiting your mom's grave, Princess."

His tone is gentle, but even so, my hand freezes, my appetite vanishing. I've been avoiding the subject, knowing that I have to face it soon, but unable to bring myself to even think about it, about going there.

With measured control, I lower my fork down, the food uneaten on it. Looking up and round at the guys, they've all paused in their eating, and are looking back at me with varying degrees of love and concern etched on their faces. Taking a deep breath, I turn to face Ash.

"Okay," I say with a nod.

His hand comes up, his warm, dry palm cupping my face in a gesture so loving and sweet that the tears I've been trying to hold back spring to my eyes, and a lump forms in my throat.

"Good girl," he says softly. "Now, eat your breakfast, and drink your juice."

Part of me knows that I should probably bristle at his dominating ways. That my inner feminist should be burning her bra and screaming 'down with the patriarchy!' But I just feel a sense of relief at following his orders, at not having to decide anything. There's something so freeing about relinquishing control to another person. Ash knows that I need to eat, even if I don't feel like it, so he's not saying it just to be a controlling dick. He's just taking care of me in the only way that he knows how

Before I can pick up my fork again, Kai's slender fingers grasp the silver handle and bring the morsel to my lips. His honey eyes capture mine sans glasses, encouraging me to open up, which I do, letting him place the fork on my tongue. I take the food off with my teeth as he pulls the fork out, a smile lifting his lips as I begin to chew, the sweetness of the fruit and syrup bursting on my tongue and making me realise how hungry I am.

"Mmmm...thanks," I mutter, swallowing it down and reaching for my juice.

I take a big gulp, smiling when the tropical flavour fills my mouth. I can feel my forehead crease as I see that darkness is still there in his amber depths. I hate that it looks a lot like pain and inner turmoil. Reaching out, I take his hand, twining my fingers with his, marvelling for a second that although he's slighter than the others, his hand is still bigger than mine.

"I love you so much, Kai Matthews," I whisper to him, catching his gaze so that he can see the truth of my words.

*Afterlife* by Hailee Steinfeld starts playing softly in the background, and his hand tightens around mine, his breath leaving his chest on a shaky exhale.

"I wish I deserved it," he murmurs back, his demons rising to the surface so clearly I can almost see them gazing back at me, eyes full of self-loathing.

My heart drops at his words at the same time that a fire lights inside of me, determined to make him believe that he is worthy, regardless of what happened to him to cause this doubt.

Getting up out of my chair, I let go of his hand and manage to squeeze myself onto his lap without knocking anything off the table—*go me!* His hands immediately go to my bare thighs, the touch sending a shiver running through me that goes straight to my core. Placing my hands on his cheeks, I run them up the sides of his face and into his hair, gently tugging until he's looking up into my eyes again. His pupils are blown, a mix of lust and self-deprivation swirling in his eyes.

"You are worth everything, my love," I tell him fiercely, feeling his fingers digging into my thighs as I speak. "Every drop of love, every-fucking-thing. You are mine, Kai, as I am yours, and nothing on this earth will change that.

Understand?" I'm practically snarling at him, my grip tight as I force him to feel my truth. I'm so fucking angry at a world that would make this incredible man feel undeserving.

A small growl sounds in his throat when my fingers pull his hair more, the sound making a rush of wetness leave my pussy that's pressed up against his rapidly hardening dick. I can't help but grind against him, inwardly cursing the silky material of his pyjama trousers that acts as a barrier.

Abruptly, I let go of his hair and reaching down, I pull Loki's T-shirt off my body, dropping it to the ground next to us.

"Now, show me you deserve me by taking what you want," I command him, knowing that it'll make his dominant side sit up and take notice, and hopefully help to draw him out of this pit of self-despair.

A breath hisses out of him as he takes in the sight of my naked, flushed body. My nipples peak even more when his hungry eyes alight on them, and one of his hands leaves my thigh, pinching the nub between his thumb and forefinger hard enough that I cry out as another rush of wetness coats my inner thighs.

The sound must be his undoing as in the next second, my feet crash to the floor as he stands up, his chair falling on the wood with a thwack. I'm spun around and pushed down, my breasts squashed into his plate of food, the sweet smell of crushed fruit and syrup filling my nose. I hear other items crash to the floor seconds before a hand cracks across my arse so hard that I scream, my cunt clenching on nothing but air as my fingertips claw at the wooden tabletop.

"Dude," I hear Loki say, his tone uncertain just before a second punishing hit lands, causing another shriek to leave my lips.

"I'm okay," I rasp out, my heart pounding in my chest. I trust Kai, even now. He won't hurt me, not ever.

Kai growls at Loki, low and loud in return, and this time a moan leaves me, my hands grasping at the tabletop on either side of my head. It's such a fucking sexy sound that I can't help but squirm, seeking relief for the desperate ache that has built so suddenly in my core.

"Do. Not. Move," Kai rumbles behind me in a voice so unlike his own that I immediately obey.

I hear the rustle of foil, then suddenly my legs are being kicked apart wider seconds before I feel the tip of him nudging at my entrance. An animalistic keen sounds in my throat as he pushes inside me, forcing his way into my tight channel with no preparation, his metal hitting me in all the right places. A hand wraps around my messy bun, pulling me up sharply, my palms supporting my weight as I finally look round me, both of us moaning when he bottoms out.

All three guys are now standing, watching us with a mixture of lust and worry, yet their sweats are tented. I meet each of their stares, giving them a small smile to show that I'm okay. My heart rate picks up because even though I trust Kai completely, this is uncharted territory for us.

His monsters are riding him hard, and I've laid down a challenge that he's unable to resist. However, I'd be lying if I said that the fear is not turning me all the way on, and if the grunt behind me is any indication, Kai can feel my pussy clenching around him in excitement.

Kai presses us forward, taking something from the table that I'm unable to see due to his tight grip on my hair.

"Kai!" Ash exclaims, stepping forward with his eyes wide just as I feel cool metal pressed against the top of one of my breasts.

"Tell him your safe word, darling," Kai purrs in my ear, his breath hissing as my inner walls tighten round him.

"Red," I whisper, holding Ash's worried gaze. I've an idea of what Kai might be doing, and if I'm correct, I can totally understand why it may be triggering for Ash. "I'm okay, Ash. Truly."

He gives a brief nod, but I can see his hand shake as it sweeps through his hair, even as his gaze fills with lust, his inner Dom enjoying watching me in fear. Kai chooses that moment to use his grip to tip my head down so that I can see that my guess was correct. He's holding a small fruit knife with a wooden handle, and a wicked sharp, slightly curved blade, the tip indenting my flesh just above my areola, but not cutting it. Not yet.

Even though I knew it was there, seeing the blade pressed against my skin causes my heart to start drumming in my chest even more, something that Kai must feel as he thrusts forward, burying himself even deeper inside me, which feels fucking amazing.

"See how fucked up I am, Lilly love," he growls in my ear, nuzzling the side of my neck with his nose, a gasp falling from my lips as I shudder. "Your fear turns me on like nothing else, and I want to hear you scream in pain as

I'm buried deep inside you. I want to see your blood running red when I'm using you like you're nothing but a hole."

"Kai..." I moan, my voice low, letting him know how much his words are affecting me in all the right ways, which is probably the complete opposite of what he thinks they would do. "Please."

His grip on my hair turns punishing, pulling until tears sting my eyes. The room wavers, and although I know the others are there, everything else fades away apart from me and the broken man behind me, holding a knife against my soft skin.

*Bad Drugs* by King Kavalier, ChrisLee begins to sound in the room, and I gasp as a sharp pain stings my right breast. I'm still at an angle that I can look down and see a bead of red well at the knife point. Fascinated, I watch as it drips down the globe of flesh, trailing a path towards my cleavage. A hiss of pain falls from my lips, my fingers flexing as he draws the blade down, creating a shallow cut, and more drops of blood drip down over my pale flesh.

*Jesus fucking christ. Who knew Diesel Viper had it right all along?*

The fear, mixed in with the pain, and having his thick, pierced cock inside me is a heady combination, leaving me gasping as the familiar burn of an orgasm begins to build in my centre.

"Fuck, Kai," I groan, as he takes the knife away, the acidic fruit juices coating my skin stinging the cut, and just adding to the myriad of sensations that are assaulting my senses.

Suddenly, I hear the clatter of the knife against the table as he withdraws, leaving me bereft. For a moment I worry that he's going to leave me unsatisfied, covered in fruit, yoghurt, and my own blood, but before the thought can settle, he twirls me round, picks me up under my thighs, roughly lifting me onto the tabletop. Giving me no time to adjust to my new seated position, he pushes my chest roughly, my back landing amongst the spilled breakfast as he forces me down.

He snarls, leaning over me to lick and lap at the cut, the sharp pain from his tongue leaving me squirming and desperate for more, my fingers trying to find purchase on the smooth wood I'm lying on.

"Sir," I plead, hoping that he won't leave me unfulfilled for long.

His head snaps up, and I'd laugh because the tip of his nose and his chin are covered in a mix of squashed fruit and yoghurt, but the sight of my blood on his lips stops me, as does the feral look in his eyes. He bares his teeth, which are also tinged red, in a smile that sends shivers running all over me as fire races through my veins.

Straightening up, he reaches over for the knife once more, picking it up as he stands between my open thighs. I watch transfixed, my heart racing, as he brings it to my inner thigh, gasping sharply as he makes three shallow cuts in quick succession. With a wicked smile on his lush lips, he places the knife carefully down beside my hip on the table, then brings his hand back to my leg. Wiping his finger along the cuts, the sting intense, he gathers my blood on his fingertip, seemingly hypnotised by the drops of glistening ruby.

His eyes flick up to mine, the amber almost entirely swallowed up by black, before they look back down, and with barely a touch, his finger alights on my cunt, rubbing my own blood on my clit.

I'm so wound up with the pain, fear, and the taboo nature of what he's doing, that one brief touch is enough to detonate an earth-shattering orgasm that rips through me, my liquid release gushing out of me as I yell his name.

I crack my lids just in time to see Kai kneel down, eye level with my still pulsing pussy. Before I can even think about coming down from the heavens, his hot warm tongue licks my clit in a firm hard stroke.

"Fuck! Shit! Fuckity shit!" I whimper, as he licks me again, and again, and again, until I'm squirming, whining, and panting, not sure if I'm trying to escape or get closer as wave upon wave of pleasure rolls over me.

Suddenly, he stops and I yelp like a kicked puppy.

"Hold fucking still!" he bellows in a rough voice, making me jump, the remaining crockery on the table rattling. My heart feels like it's pounding hard enough to escape the confines of my chest, a slight tremble in my limbs.

"Kai!" Ash snaps behind us, and I hear Jax's growl sound in warning.

"I'm okay, Ash," I say, not taking my wide eyed stare off Kai.

My eyes meet his, dark and drowning as he gets up, my gaze darting down to see his beautiful cock rock-fucking-solid, and begging to be buried deep inside me once more. I look back up to see his chin glistening, and a dangerous smirk on his lips.

"You still deserve me, my love," I pant, watching as his eyes widen and nostrils flare.

With a roar that leaves me quivering and snatching my arms onto my chest, he sweeps his hand across the tabletop to my right, sending dishes of food crashing to the floor. He repeats the move on the other side before stopping to look down at me, his chest heaving, hands and arms covered in breakfast foods.

I lie there, the slight shivering of my body the only outward sign of the effect his behaviour is having on me. And part of that is pure, unadulterated lust. This uncontrolled wild side of his is turning me on. A lot.

With a snarl, he grabs my thighs, spreading them even wider to the point of pain, and I gasp. A malevolent grin takes over his lips, and he catches my hand, wrapping it around my leg, and then doing the same with the other until I'm holding myself completely open for him.

The next thing I know, he's grabbing his dick, lining it up with my soaked entrance before he slams inside of me, hard and fast. An animalistic groan leaves his lips as a scream of pleasure-pain leaves mine, then he starts pounding into me, using me like I'm a hole to be filled, just as he promised. I know I'll be aching later, but I currently have no more fucks to give because it feels so damn good, my whole body lights up with pleasure that has an edge of exquisite pain.

I look up to see his face creased in a frown, his hands holding my hips in a bruising grip as he thrusts harder and harder, impaling me on his cock, the sound of our bodies, moans, and grunts louder than the music in the background.

Sparks ignite in my core, my climax rushing towards its peak with the force of two atoms colliding until I'm screaming his name, uncaring if the whole fucking hotel hears, my nails digging into my thighs as I come. Stars burst, and new galaxies are formed as my orgasm tears me apart, leaving me utterly spent.

Moments later, I hear the roar of a thousand lions as Kai finds his own release, jerking inside of me, then collapsing on top of me, his weight a welcome heaviness.

We lie there, panting and breathless as the world rights itself around us. Slowly, I begin to hear the sound of someone clapping. Opening my eyes, I look to the side to see Loki standing there, his rapidly softening dick hanging out. Clearly he enjoyed the show. His emerald eyes are alight with sated satisfaction, as well as the usual shit stirring mischief.

"Bra-fucking-vo, my friend!" he shouts. "Nice to finally see you let go, dude," he adds, continuing to clap until Jax steps into view, and cuffs him on the back of his head.

“That was...a little fucked up,” Jax tells Kai, a feral grin on his face, and he, too, obviously liked what he saw, especially if his flushed cheeks and post orgasm glow are anything to go by. “But so fucking hot.”

Kai lifts his face off my chest, a huff of laughter escaping as he turns to look at me.

“Are you okay?” he asks, concern filling his honey eyes as he lifts himself off me even more, looking down to the cut on my breast, a flash of predatory satisfaction gleaming in his eyes.

“I’m peachy,” I reply, still breathless and my voice all kinds of husky. “Are you?”

“I—” he starts, biting his bottom lip adorably. “I do feel better,” he tells me, a blush staining his cheeks as he stands up, holding out his hand for me to take.

I can’t help but chuckle softly, then wince as I sit up, Kai noticing the move and frowning. Her Vagisty, for once, is quiet, probably hiding after the pounding we just got.

“Good,” I say, using his help to stand. I wobble, and he catches me, bending down to pick me up bridal style. “I can walk,” I tell him, although that may be bullshit if my still quivering legs are any indicator.

“I know,” he says softly, nuzzling my cheek. “But I need to take care of you,” he whispers in my ear, giving me all the warm and fuzzies as he turns and walks off towards the main bedroom.

I look over his shoulder to see the others starting to clean the mess up. Catching Ash’s eyes, I raise a brow, hoping he knows I’m asking if he’s okay. Placing a hand on Kai's pec, I halt his movement so that Ash can come towards us. My dark Knight, my big daddy Dom—*fucking snort*—cups my face with his warm palm, looking deep into my eyes as Kai stands there holding me close.

“You okay, Princess?” he asks, his voice rough. There's a fine tremor in his hand against my face, and a spark of worry tinged with guilt alights in my stomach. With Ash's history of self-harm, that must have been all kinds of triggering for him.

“Yes,” I murmur back, rubbing my cheek into his hand. “I'm sorry if that was triggering for you, love,” I tell him, loving the way his breath hitches at the term of endearment.

“Shit, dude, I didn't fucking think,” Kai says, obviously upset if he's cursing so much.

“It's cool,” Ash replies, looking up at Kai briefly. His steel grey gaze comes back to mine, swirling with love, and lust, and a hundred other things. “Maybe, in the future, we keep the knife and blood play to a minimum when I'm around?”

“Sure,” I reply at the same time as Kai does, also agreeing.

Ash gives me a soft smile before he leans down to place a gentle kiss on my lips, then goes back to clearing the mess of shattered plates and squashed food. I’m seriously impressed that they’re actually bothering to clean. Being the rich bastards that they are, I had expected them to just call for one of the maids to come and deal with it.

Carrying me back into the main bedroom, Kai walks over to the en suite, switching the light on as we pass. He takes us to the enormous shower, setting me carefully down onto the chaise that’s next to it as he turns it on, waiting a few moments for the water to warm up.

I watch as his back muscles bunch and cord as he goes about his tasks. Turning to face me, he stops, going to push his glasses up his nose then realising that he’s not wearing any.

“I love you, Kai,” I say with a smile as he leans down to help me up. He pauses, his hand coming to cup my jaw.

“I love you, Lilly,” he whispers gazing into my eyes with such intensity it’s a wonder the world doesn’t stop spinning.

Then he proceeds to make good on his promise, taking care of me thoroughly and showing me that he is a man of more than just words.

If only he would believe mine.

# CHAPTER TWELVE

LILLY

We take a long, gloriously hot shower, where Kai washes me from top to toe until I'm squeaky clean all over, using my new favourite ginger shampoo and conditioner to wash my hair. Wrapping me in a huge white fluffy towel that he prewarmed on the heated towel rail, he grabs a medical first aid kit Ash brought in whilst we were showering. Lifting me up, he places me on the sink countertop, setting to work wiping my cuts with antiseptic and covering them with gauze, bandages and tape.

"You are amazing, Lilly," he tells me softly, placing the last bit of tape on my inner thigh to hold the gauze in place. "I don't know why I thought I could scare you off with my darkness," he adds, looking up at me, his eyes holding equal measure of wonder, awe, and pain. "The light you have in you shines so brightly, is so strong, that you can take any amount of darkness, and burn it away. People often mistake goodness as a weakness, but you are stronger than all of us, my darling. We would truly be lost without you."

I don't realise that I'm crying until I taste salt on my lips, his thumb coming up to wipe my tears away as he leans in closer, his hand then moving up into my wet hair, his fingers tangling in the brunette strands.

"You are my light, Lilly. My soul. Everything that I am, or ever will be, is yours and yours alone. And when we take our final breaths on this earth, our souls will remain bound, travelling the winds together for all eternity."

"Oh, Kai," I say in a broken whisper against his lips as he presses them to mine in a kiss so tender and sweet that the stars sigh.

"I promise that I will tell you everything soon. I just need some time," he murmurs, pulling away and looking into my eyes once more, his hand still in my hair.

"Take all the time you need, my love," I tell him, his eyes closing and a beatific smile comes over his features at my words. "I'm not going anywhere."

I lean in, placing my head on his damp chest and wrapping my arms round him in a tight hug, sighing in pure bliss and contentment when he returns the embrace. We stay that way until Loki pops his head past the door, an indulgent and relieved smile on his lips as he looks at us.

"Time to get ready, Pretty Girl," he tells me. "Your carriage awaits!"

I can't help giggling when he waggles his eyebrows in that goofy way of his before disappearing again. Kai helps me off the counter, holding my hand as he leads me to the bedroom, exiting wearing only a towel to go to his room and get dressed.

On the bed I find black lacy underwear, a navy cropped T-shirt, and some new mustard yellow Run and Fly dungarees with a bee print. There's a piece of the hotel notepaper with Ash's elegant scrawl over it.

*Wear these today*

I can't help beaming down at the note in my hand, loving the sweet yet commanding gesture. He knew I was eyeing these very dungs up. I do as he says, pairing them with the yellow and rainbow Irregular Choice Shirly Bass shoes that Loki bought me for Christmas. I walk back into the main living room area to, once again, find all the guys waiting for me, and my gaze immediately connects with Ash's grey one, the corner of his lips lifting to see me wearing what he laid out for me.

He walks towards me, stepping so close that I'm completely consumed by his spicy ginger scent. Leaning down, he takes a deep inhale, a low rumbling sigh escaping his lips.

"I fucking love that you use my shampoo," he says so that only I can hear as his hand finds the bare skin on my side that the crop top leaves exposed.

Tingles and goosebumps spread from his touch as he glides his hand upwards, a hissing breath leaving him when he discovers that I didn't quite follow his instructions. He groans as his fingers skate across my bare breast, my nipple pebbling as his thumb rubs over it.

"Why do I need underwear for a spa day?" I ask in a saucy whisper, my voice slightly breathless, loving the way he almost splutters when he realises what I'm implying.

"Sorry to cockblock you, Blue Balls," Loki sniggers like a wankstain at Ash's responding growl. He grabs my hand and pulls me out of Ash's grip. "But the car and Lexi are waiting."

I blow Ash a kiss, laughing at the frustrated outrage on his face as Loki leads me to the front doors of the suite. I blow both Jax and Kai kisses as we pass, managing to grab my coat as Loki pulls me out of the door and into the lift.

"That was mean," I mock scold, my eyebrows raised as he pushes me up against the mirrored back wall of the lift, his hand wrapping around the top of my throat, ignoring the poor attendant who stares straight ahead.

He doesn't reply, just closes the distance, covering my body with his as he gives me a bruising kiss that makes me forget where we are, or that we have an audience. He pulls away, leaving my head spinning and my heart racing just as the doors ding open, an evil grin on his face.

"I wanted to make sure you thought about me all day," he says with a smirk, taking my hand once again and leading me out of the lift and across the bright foyer.

"Do you know why Ash was so frustrated this morning?" I ask, a grin to rival his on my own lips.

"Why? His balls about to drop off, they're so blue?"

"Maybe," I start, glad I grabbed my coat, wool scarf, and beanie hat before we left the suite as the biting January temperature hits my exposed face. It may be brilliant sunshine, but it's still winter in England. We stop in front of the open car door, and I turn to face him. "Or maybe it's because I didn't quite follow his instructions about what to wear today and left some bits on the bed."

Giving him a quick peck on his still lips, I climb into the car and shut the door, immediately engulfed in a hug from Lexi.

"Why did Loki look so confused?" she asks, and I chuckle.

About ten minutes later I get an incoming text.

> Angel: ::devil emoji:: You naughty minx! He'll spank you when you get back! Xxx

A laugh leaves my lips even as my thighs clench with the thought of the punishment that awaits me upon my return.

---

I spend a wonderful day at a high-end spa with Lexi, drinking champagne and being pampered to within an inch of my life. We have full body hot stone massages, pedicures and manicures, mud wraps, facials with the most wonderful smelling products, and spend time in the hot tub and pool.

The car that picks us up takes us to The Hard Rock Cafe, where the guys and Ryan are waiting. We gorge ourselves on burgers, fries, and milkshakes, all whilst listening to nineties rock music, and admiring the memorabilia lining the walls.

Yawning, we head to the car that'll take us back to the hotel, Lexi kissing me goodnight, saying that we will see them tomorrow. I must fall asleep on the way home because the next thing I know I'm being carried into our suite.

Looking up, I give Jax a bleary-eyed smile as he holds me effortlessly, even though he still looks pretty tired himself. He sets me down gently on the bed, helping me to strip off, and then we crawl under the covers, Loki joining us a moment later.

I fall back asleep surrounded by warmth and love, feeling so safe sandwiched between two of my guys, like nothing can ever touch me as long as they are near.

---

I wake up, unsure at first what woke me, then hear the hint of a piano melody caressing my skin being played somewhere nearby. Gently extracting myself from the sleeping men in my bed, I pad naked across the plush carpeted floor and out the door, heading towards the main living area and the haunting sound.

My skin tingles, a tentative smile drawing my lips upwards as I gaze at

Ash sitting at the instrument, the lid down so to quieten the sound, wearing only light coloured sweats. His tattooed hands are on the keys, his eyes closed as he plays a piece that makes my soul ache. It's utterly beautiful whilst also being desperately sad, and moisture stings my eyes as I watch him shrouded in darkness, the only light in the room coming from a streetlight outside that casts everything in an eerie orange glow.

I remember the story Kai told me, about when they were thirteen or so, and Ash had tried to run away to become a concert pianist, but then his father had found them, and by the sounds of it, punished him severely. I thought he no longer played, that was the impression Kai gave me anyway. But as his fingers effortlessly move over the keys, my heart swells to know that he must have found a way. He wouldn't be this good if he hadn't played all these years.

As the piece draws to a close, he looks up, his hands not faltering even as a banked heat enters his grey orbs when he spots me leaning against the door-frame, naked, watching him.

"It's called *Opus 38*, by Dustin O'Halloran," he explains, his voice gruff as the last note resounds in the still night air. "I learned it after Luc...died."

My feet carry me closer to him without conscious thought, the need to comfort him overwhelming.

"I had no idea that you still played," I whisper, not wanting to disturb this moment, this suspended time we are currently inhabiting.

I come to a stop next to him, my hands reaching out and running through his dark, silky hair, loving the feel of the strands as they move through my fingers.

"It's not something that I can broadcast," he tells me, his own voice quiet. He leans into my touch, resting his head on my stomach, his arms coming around my hips. His breath sends shivers racing across my body, my nipples becoming hard points even though the room is warm. "My father, well, you've met him, does not approve of his son playing a musical instrument. Thinks music is for, and I quote, 'queers and faggots.'" He practically spits the words, clearly disgusted by his father's bigotry. "But fuck him."

I smile at that.

"Yeah, fuck him," I echo, smiling wider and feeling all kinds of warmth inside when a manly chuckle falls against my skin.

Lifting his head, he looks up at me.

"Can I play something for you?" he asks, biting his plush bottom lip as he studies me intently.

"I'd love that," I tell him, heat radiating throughout my body at his soft expression and bright glossy eyes that shine in the darkness.

He smiles in return, his whole body relaxing. I start to turn, intending to sit on a nearby chair, when he stops me, his arms banding tighter. Looking back down, there's a devilish glint in his eyes that I'm more used to seeing on Loki's face.

*This is either going to be really good...or really bad. Maybe both?*

"Up here, Princess," he orders, leaning back and releasing one of his arms, patting the top of the baby grand piano lovingly.

"What? No!" I exclaim, shaking my head and trying to take a step back.

Of course the wanktrumpet tightens his grip with the arm still around me.

"I don't like to repeat myself, Princess," he tells me sternly, a threat clear in his voice.

"Fine," I grumble, looking at the instrument with a huff. *How the fuck am I meant to get up there?!*

As if reading my mind, Ash scoots back the bench he's sitting on, grabs my waist, and in a single panty melting—*you know, if I had any on*—move, lifts me up, depositing my bare arse on the cool surface of the lid, right on the edge.

"Ash!" I hiss, squirming as Her Vagisty tries to escape the temperature of the lacquered wood.

With just his signature Ash-hole smirk, he sits back down, pulling the bench closer to the keys. Flushing, I suddenly realise that he's in between my legs, getting an eyeful so to speak. I begin to close my thighs when he chuckles in that sexy way of his, making Her Vagisty perk up and twitch. *Greedy bitch.*

Grabbing one ankle, he places my foot on his shoulder, doing the same to the other leg until I am literally spread wide open for him, having to prop myself up with my hands behind me for support so that I can still look down at him.

"Much better," he comments. *Cuntcake.* "I learned this not long after we met you," he confesses softly, looking down at his hands hovering over the keys. "It's called *I Love You,* by Jurrivh."

My breath stills, my heart thudding as my fingertips tingle at his words.

And then he starts to play.

I stop breathing entirely for several moments as the music flows over and through me. I can feel the vibrations of the notes running through my body, making my core ache for this man. This man who feels so much, but hardly ever shows it, has been trained not to show it, but it's all there. And it's the most beautiful thing I've ever experienced.

He doesn't look at me as he plays, his eyes closed, his fingers flying across the instrument in a gentle, loving caress. Taking a large, deep breath, I am grateful that I'm not standing. I don't even think that I could, not with my knees weak and my heart hammering like it is. I'm hyper aware of my entire body; the coolness of the wood that I'm sitting on is warming under my body heat, the notes as they flow through me, letting me feel the music in my very core like never before.

The sounds pour into my ears, teasing moisture to my eyes when I think about what he told me. He learnt this not long after he met me. He's loved me since then, almost from the start.

All too soon, the final notes are sounding in the room, leaving their lingering song in the air like the sweetest perfume. Ash's hands still, his head still bowed and his chest rising and falling with heavy breaths, like this moment was difficult for him.

He's made himself vulnerable in a way that he hasn't done before, and I feel so blessed to have been witness to it.

"Ash," I murmur, my voice raspy with all the love that is desperate to break free, like a caged bird.

"I feel like I've loved you for my whole life, Lilly," he whispers back, his own voice just as choked as mine. "I just needed to find you."

He lifts his head, his eyes shining, and I watch, spellbound, as a single bead of glittering moisture breaks free and glides down his cheek. I move my feet off his shoulders, shuffle-sliding down off the piano and eliciting a jumbled sound as I hit the keys until I'm in his lap, my legs on either side of him. Reaching my hand out, I use my thumb to swipe the tear from his face, bringing it to my lips and tasting his love.

His confession.

His declaration.

A moment later, I feel his hand grab the back of my neck as he pulls me in for a kiss that obliterates a past where we weren't together. A kiss that makes up for all the lost time, for all of the pain that we've been through without one another.

His tongue dominates mine, showing me his love with every stroke, telling me without words his truth. I let him in freely, matching him caress for caress as I repeat back my truth. My love for him. My need for him.

He pulls away, both of us panting. I can feel his hardness directly under my aching pussy, and it takes everything in me not to grind down, to try and seek relief, remembering that he's still healing. His eyes drill into mine, his pupils wide with lust and longing that I know my expression mirrors.

"Fuck it," he rasps out, his voice gruff and lips swollen.

Before I know what's happening, he's lifting me up, his fingers digging into my arse cheeks in a deliciously maddening way. The bench falls to the floor, making a dull thudding noise as it hits the carpet, and he stands, carrying me to the side of the piano.

"Ash, what—" I start, hissing as he none too gently places me back on the lid of the instrument, my arse on the edge of the side. Silencing any further questions that I might have, he slams his lips back onto mine, his hands holding my face captive.

I get lost in his taste; like winter nights, sin, and darkness. But not the kind of darkness that you're afraid of, the kind that protects you and hides you from all harm. He breaks away once more, kissing down my neck, pausing at my breasts to take each nipple into his mouth, his hands cupping and stroking them whilst he sucks and bites the tender globes until I'm a squirming mess. He pushes me down, not pausing in his ravishment so that I'm lying flat on my back, my legs hanging off the edge.

"Ash," I moan, when he goes lower, kissing, licking, and nipping my abdomen. Then lower still, teasing me all around my slit, my cunt fluttering, and Her Vagisty begging for some attention. "Ash," I whine this time, scowling and grabbing his hair in clenched fists when he just does that stupid sexy man chuckle again and carries on with his exquisite torture.

"Impatient tonight, aren't we, Princess," he teases, breathing along my folds, making my breath hitch and my hips buck towards him as I desperately try to bring his head closer with my grip.

He clearly takes pity on me, or can't help himself, because in the next moment, sublime bliss fills my entire being as his warm tongue licks me from opening to clit, and I explode on his tongue, crying out with the force of my release.

Yep, one lick is all it took to make me come. That man can play me just as well as the instrument that I'm lying on, no doubt about that.

I hear a growl of approval, my eyes closed, still riding that orgasm wave, when I hear the rustle of a foil packet, then feel a nudge at my opening. I snap my eyes open and lift my head, only to find him standing between my thighs, pushing his hard dick inside me, his hands holding my thighs open.

My inner walls clench and flutter around him—*that damn dick obsessed butterfly is back*—as I watch him thrust gently, feeling his new piercing massage my passage until he's fully seated inside me. We both groan at the sublime sensation, and I watch, enraptured at the look of pure bliss on his face, his eyes closed as he savours the moment.

"But—" I start, my voice husky as I push up onto my elbows. His eyes open when I speak. "You're not fully healed."

"I'm healed enough, Princess," he informs me in a rough voice, and I study his features to see if there's any pain in his expression, willing to stop this if there is.

He doesn't give me more than a moment, though, a breath, before he pulls almost all the way out, then plunges back in hard. My eyes fucking roll, and I drop back down with a thud and he repeats the move again. And again. And again, until I lose count and all ability to think coherently as he bombards me with his passion, gyrating harder and going deeper.

"Shit, Ash!" I cry out, my nails scraping the smooth surface of the instrument that I'm lying on, uncaring if I scratch it, as electric currents zap and zing across my body with every surge of his, the new metal in his dick adding a layer of sensation that has me seeing stars.

"Christ, Lilly," he hisses through clenched teeth. "I'd forgotten how fucking good your pussy wrapped around my cock feels." His shallow thrusting rubs my G-spot with the piercings on every stroke. "That's it, baby, come for me, come all over my dick," he orders as I start to clench around him, my climax hitting me with the force of a fucking freight train.

He pulls all the way out, causing a squirt of liquid to shoot out of me, covering his lower abs and chest as I scream. I look down just in time to see him pull the condom off, blowing his load all over my stomach and breasts, a deep groan falling from his perfect lips. More moisture leaves me at the sight and knowledge that I'm covered in his hot seed. We've marked each other in the most primal way and I fucking love it.

My eyes catch on glinting silver, and I gasp.

"You got a fucking magic cross!" I exclaim, sitting up to get a better look, uncaring of his cum dripping down my body.

Just beyond the mushroom head of his dick are four small metal balls, creating the impression of a cross with the bars hidden inside.

"How did it feel?" he asks, his voice a touch breathless.

Tearing my eyes away from his new jewellery, I look into his eyes.

"Fucking incredible," I beam at him, and he smiles right back, looking all kinds of pleased with himself.

"Good," he replies, holding out a hand and helping me off the piano. "Now, let's get cleaned up. You've got a big day today and need to get some more sleep." My heart sinks when I remember what we're doing later; visiting Mum's grave. "Hey, it'll be okay. We'll be with you the whole time," he tells me gently, pulling me to him in a tight hug, the warmth of his naked body seeping into mine.

# CHAPTER THIRTEEN

LILLY

Blinking my gritty eyes open, I wake to weak morning light, cocooned in a spicy ginger warmth that I snuggle into. Catching movement across from me in the corner of my eye, I'm captivated by honey amber eyes. Kai smiles softly at me from his bed, looking far more awake than how I feel. Yet still, he has bags under his slightly bloodshot eyes and exhaustion coats him like a fog, as if he hasn't slept well in months, years.

I frown as it suddenly occurs to me that we've never slept in the same bed. I've never woken up with Kai wrapped around me, and that bothers me. Is it due to an accident, the others getting in bed with me first? Or has he purposefully pushed me away in that regard?

"Why the frown, darling?" His melodic voice, a little gruff this morning, breaks into my tumultuous thoughts. "Worried about today?" he enquires gently, and my frown deepens, my breath stuttering out of me at the thought of what's to come this morning.

"Yes," I reply in a whisper, my empty stomach rolling. I decide not to press the issue of our lack of bedsharing just yet. I'll wait until he's ready to talk.

He gives me an understanding nod, his head moving on the soft fluffy pillow he's resting it on.

"You're not alone, Lilly," he soothes. "We will be there every step of the way."

I swallow hard, my eyes filling as the arm holding me from behind tightens, pulling me closer to the hot naked body at my back.

"And if it gets too much, just say the word and we're outta there," Ash murmurs in my ear, nuzzling into my hair and sending welcome shivers skipping over my body. "But you need to do this, Princess. Trust me, you need closure."

"I know," I mumble back, gripping his arm tightly as I continue to gaze into Kai's eyes, my breath shuddering out between my lips.

At that moment, the door flies open, and Loki strolls in, completely naked—*obviously*. His emerald eyes find mine, and in the next minute, he leaps onto the bed in front of me, somehow managing to lie down underneath the covers as I'm bounced back into Ash, who gives an oomph sound at the impact.

"Loki!" I cry, a giggle escaping my mouth as he wriggles closer, successfully dispelling the sadness that was building in the room. He smells like vanilla and musky man, a scent that I am addicted to, his hair all mussed from quite clearly having just woken up.

"Dude, what the fuck?" Ash grumbles behind me, shuffling back to make room for the fallen angel that's landed in our bed, which luckily is a double, although it's still a squeeze with these two lumps in it.

"Jax is not a good snuggle bunny," Loki pouts, and it's so adorable, sexy, and ridiculous that I lean forward and plant a kiss on his lush lips. "And his morning wood should be classed as a fucking weapon of mass destruction."

We all snort at that, which turns into full belly chuckles when Jax walks in, proudly sporting said weapon of mass destruction.

"What's so fucking funny?" he asks, his deep voice gruff from sleep as he settles at the end of the bed. "It's like the ass crack of dawn."

I fucking lose it, laughing so hard that my stomach aches, and tears stream down my face.

"I fucking love you all, so much," I choke out, looking around me to see matching grins on all their faces, their expressions soft.

---

We decide that as we're all awake, arse crack of dawn or not, we might as well get up and get ready. Ordering breakfast, we lounge around in the living room until it arrives. I surprise myself by eating a healthy serving of bacon—*crispy because anything else is just plain wrong and sacrilegious*—toast and poached eggs, all washed down with my favourite tropical juice.

We leisurely eat, talking about everything and nothing. Then Loki and Jax join me for a shower, which helps to kill some time as they coax orgasm after orgasm from my poor abused pussy. *I lie, Her Vagisty fucking loves it!* We take our time getting dressed, using up more time until we're ready to leave.

We're due to meet Lex and Ryan at Highgate Cemetery at ten, so we order a car for twenty-past nine to leave plenty of time to get there. Once we're seated in the car, I look around at my guys, my soulmates. We're fairly colourful, Mum hated black so I decided that we'd be as brightly coloured as possible. The guys, all apart from Loki, struggled a little as they mostly wear dark colours.

Kai found some mustard yellow chinos, which he paired with a red check flannel shirt, a forest green cashmere v-neck jumper, and a matching green bow tie. He epitomises geek chic by topping it off with a green tweed coat and a red cashmere scarf. Jax chose dark grey jeans and a sky blue T-shirt that makes his eyes pop, with a darker blue hoodie and a sports-type wool jacket. Ash has gone for a suit, of course, but in a navy pinstripe instead of black. He paired it with a vibrant Liberty print shirt, no tie, and a navy wool long coat. He looks like every woman's wet dream, sophisticated yet devilish with his black tattoos peeking out at his neck.

Loki, wonderful, marvellous Loki, somehow without my knowledge, bought himself a pair of black rainbow dinosaur Run & Fly dungarees. He wears them with an emerald green T-shirt, just to prove that his eyes are as good as Jax's, red Converse Chucks, and what looks like a vintage brown sheepskin bomber jacket, complete with tan fluffy wool at the wrists and collar.

I went for my Run and Fly rainbow pinafore, sparkly glitter rainbow heels, and a red wool short coat, with a beautiful Peter Pan collar and ruffles at the wrists. It arrived at the suite this morning, along with a note:

*Saw this and thought of you. Wear it today, Little Red.*

## *Ash*

I stroke the beautiful soft wool as we make our way through the early morning London traffic, having been driving for about twenty minutes already. I notice my hand shaking moments before Loki's larger warm hand covers mine, intertwining our fingers. His other hand moves my hair over my shoulder, popping an air bud into my ear. The opening of *Steady Now* by Nilu begins to play, the words and gentle swell of the music perfect for calming my nerves.

My hand grips his as we journey on, the lyrics of the song flowing over me, encouraging me to take deep breaths, and know that this is just one moment in my history. It doesn't define me, and it won't be like this forever. The world keeps spinning, new things on the horizon.

The song ends, and I breathe a contented sigh. *Too Sad to Cry*, by Sasha Alex Solan starts to play next, and tears spring to my eyes.

"Shit," Loki hisses under his breath, reaching into his pocket to change the song.

"Leave it, please," I murmur, turning to look at him, his face wavering as the tears spill down my cheeks.

"Pretty Girl," he replies, voice pained, his palm coming up to cup my cheek and bring our foreheads together. "I hurt when you do, baby."

His words make the tears flow faster, and it's a bittersweet relief. I didn't cry for a long time after Mum passed, too terrified to even think about what had happened. Then, that night, when Ash made me recount it all in detail, it was like a dam had been broken inside me as I was able to start my mourning of her.

Now I'm glad to cry, even though it hurts, because it shows that I'm not too scared. We travel the rest of the way like that, Loki holding my face to his, and gently kissing away the steady stream of tears that fall down my cheeks. Jax rubs my back in soothing circles, Ash and Kai leaning forward to take a hand each, surrounding me in their love and support as I quietly cry.

"Hey," Jax says from my other side, his hand stilling in its movements. "We're there, Baby Girl." His voice sounds gruff, and I look over my shoulder, Loki releasing my face, to see his own eyes glistening. "We all hurt when you do," he tells me simply, and I turn, letting go of the others' hands to cup his face in my palms and place a gentle kiss on his lips.

Ash and Kai get out first, then Loki, leaving just Jax and I in the car. My heart rate picks up as the moment draws closer, the moment when I will have to face what happened.

"I'm scared, Jax," I whisper, pulling back and looking at him with wide eyes, my hands moving to grasp his own.

"I know, Baby Girl," he responds, a frown drawing his brows together. "But we're all here for you, and we're not going anywhere. Nothing bad will happen to you," he assures me.

His words calm me a little, enough that I can take a deep inhale and nod. He flashes me a minute smile. "That's my girl," he praises, keeping hold of my hand as he gets out, then helping me to exit the car.

I see Lexi and Ryan, holding a bunch of flowers each, waiting near the ornate black cast iron gates to the beautiful cemetery.

"Hey, Lilly Bear," Lex greets me softly, and I let go of Jax to give her a hug, then do the same with Ryan. His jaw is clenched tightly, and deep lines are etched on his forehead.

"You doing okay, big guy?" I ask him, my own brows dipping in concern for him. Mum's death wasn't just hard on me. Ryan was practically her husband in all but name. They loved each other deeply.

He gives me a tight smile in response. "I'll be fine, little one," he reassures me, giving my hand a brief squeeze.

"Shall we?" Ash asks, and I notice that each of the guys holds a huge bouquet filled with different coloured lilies, Mum's favourites. A lump forms in my throat as I step towards Ash's outstretched hand.

"How did you know they were her favourites?" I ask, my voice a little wobbly.

He gives me one of his Ash-hole looks, raising an eyebrow. Right, I am named after her favourite flower after all. He kisses the top of my head, then leads the way through the gates and along the winding paths of the cemetery.

We're surrounded on all sides by gravestones, monuments, and beautiful statues, with bare trees dotted here and there. We've lucked out on the weather again today; it's chilly but sunny. Turning off down a more narrow path, we come to a stop underneath an oak sapling with a simply carved headstone in front of it.

*Laura Darling*
*Beloved mother and sister*
*18th September 1980 - 21st February 2025*

The ground surrounding the grave looks freshly cleared, only a few dead leaves litter the space, with nothing but neatly clipped turf covering the site. Glancing around, frowning, I see that the surrounding graves are not as well kept as Mum's.

"We came here yesterday to tidy it up a little." Ash's ginger scent washes over me as he leans down to speak. "Apparently, wild violets grow here in the spring," he tells me.

I squeeze his hand in silent thanks, letting go when he passes me his bunch of flowers. They're simply tied with natural string, no cellophane, and I step forward to place them on the grass, a tremor in my hands.

"Hi, Mum," I whisper, tears springing to my eyes again as they trace the simple lettering carved into her headstone.

And then it hits me. I'll never be able to tell her about the guys, about how wonderful they are, and the fact that they're helping me to heal. She'll never meet any children I may have one day, never hold her grandchildren in her arms and sing them lullabies like she did to me as a child. We'll never dance to awful eighties pop songs on the radio, never make another Christmas cake together. I'll never be able to tell her how sorry I am about that stupid argument. Never tell her how much I love her.

I don't realise that I've collapsed, my nails digging into the turf, sobbing as my heart breaks for all the things I'll never get to do with her again until strong arms wrap around me, lifting me and turning me round so that I can bury my face into a ginger scented cashmere covered chest.

I fist the soft material, tears tracking down my cheeks and soaking into his no doubt stupidly expensive coat. He just holds me, his arms banded tightly around me, keeping my pieces together whilst I fall apart under the winter sun.

Some moments later, I lift my tearstained face towards the sky, closing my eyes and letting the sun dry my cheeks. Taking what feels like the biggest breath I've taken all year, I look back down and find Ash's steel eyes on my own.

"Thank you," I whisper, my voice cracking slightly.

"Of course," he says back.

Looking to the side, I'm met by Jax's piercing blue gaze. I give him a watery smile.

"Thank you, Jax," I tell him, wetting my dry lips.

"Always, Baby Girl," he replies gruffly.

I turn to the other side to find Loki studying me.

"Thank you, Loki."

"No need, my heart," he says, reaching out to stroke my slightly damp cheeks. "I'd do so much more without even a thought," he adds, fresh moisture stinging my eyes at his heartfelt words.

I turn my head to find Kai's honey amber eyes watching me with such love it steals my breath for a moment.

"I told you, darling," he says, stepping closer to my back until I can't see him as he's right behind me, his scent of fresh woods after the rain mixing with Ash's. "Everything I am, or ever will be, is yours," he whispers in my ear, placing a soft kiss on my neck that sends tingles racing over me, despite my sadness.

I stay surrounded by my guys, my warriors, my Knights, for several minutes, breathing them in under the winter sun, the sounds of birds chirping in the background.

Inhaling deeply, they give me the strength to look round, remembering that Lex and Ryan are here too. I find Lexi's green eyes, not far from where I stand, swimming with tears as she looks at me surrounded by my guys.

"Your mum would have been so happy to see you with them, Lilly Bear," she tells me in a choked voice.

Fresh tears well in my own eyes at that. Kai steps back and to one side, and I turn in Ash's arms so that I'm facing Lex and Ryan.

"For what it's worth," Ryan begins, stepping closer to us, glancing at each of the guys in turn. "You have my approval and blessing. They are good guys, little one." He gives the guys a sharp nod, which they return. *Men.*

Kai takes a step forward, looking at me as he takes a piece of paper out of his pocket.

"I have a poem that I'd like to read, if that's okay with you, Lilly?" he asks, and I give him a wobbly smile.

"I'd love that," I say, my heart swelling.

He turns to face the grave, but still so that I can see him in profile and begins to read.

*"'Do not stand at my grave and weep.*
*I am not there. I do not sleep.*
*I am a thousand winds that blow.*
*I am the diamond glints on snow.*
*I am the sunlight on ripened grain.*
*I am the gentle autumn rain.*
*When you awaken in the morning's hush*
*I am the swift uplifting rush*
*Of quiet birds in circled flight.*
*I am the soft stars that shine at night.*
*Do not stand at my grave and cry;*
*I am not there. I did not die.'"*

He turns to look at me once again, his features soft as he takes in my tearstained face.

"It's called *A Thousand Winds*, by Mary Elizabeth Frye," he tells me.

"It's beautiful and perfect," I whisper, reaching out to take his hand, bringing it up to my lips and placing a kiss on his knuckles.

Looking back up, I glance round at the people who I love, and who love me in return without condition. It feels as though my heart swells to twice its size, threatening to burst from my chest as I drink them in, the winter sunshine wrapping its chill around us but unable to touch us.

Stepping forward, I walk to Mum's grave, kneeling down to place my hand on the headstone.

"I'm going to be alright, Mum," I tell her, my eyes welling up once more. "They'll look after me."

Closing my eyes, I stay there for a few moments, hearing the breeze rustling in the trees, the birds chirping around us, the sunshine warming my face as the world keeps spinning.

Standing up, I take one last breath, gazing down at the stone.

"Bye, Mum," I whisper, then turn around to face the others, focusing on my guys. "Let's go home."

They all break out into blinding smiles, obviously realising that I don't mean the hotel, but back to Colorado. Back to Highgate Prep.

Although, they do say that home is where the heart is. And my heart is standing before me, kept safe in the bodies of four beautiful men.

# CHAPTER FOURTEEN

LILLY

We arrive back late, stepping off the plane into the crisp winter Colorado mountain air, the stars shining brightly above us, our breath coming out in puffs of steam. Luckily, there are a couple of days before the new term, or semester starts because my body is all kinds of fucked-up from the three different time zones.

I sleep for a solid fourteen hours, my Viking on one side, my fallen angel on the other, and wake up groggy, but feeling less exhausted as afternoon sunshine filters around the edges of the curtains in Loki's dorm room. Stretching, I notice that the bed is empty either side of me, Jax and Loki clearly having left some time ago if the cold sheets are any indication.

Getting up, I grab a navy blue T-shirt from the floor, Loki's vanilla scent all over it as I take a whiff before throwing it on, and heading out of the room and down the stairs towards the bathroom. My brows draw together in a frown as I register how quiet it is, and looking around, I can see that the guys aren't down here.

I take care of business, flushing and washing my hands before coming back out and looking around again. Spotting a piece of paper on the kitchen island, I make my way over and grab it.

*Got called away to a Black Knight Corp. meeting, be back this evening.*
*Your breakfast is in the fridge, make sure you eat it all up and drink your juice, Princess.*

An empty feeling lies in the pit of my stomach as I read the note, my appetite gone as thoughts race across my mind. *What Knight meeting? Did they only just find out about it? What if they have to...hurt someone?*

Closing my eyes, I take a deep, calming breath, although nausea still swirls in my stomach at the thought of them being forced to do awful things at the hands of those that are meant to care for and protect them. They'll tell me what happened when they get back. I can't do anything to change things now anyway, so I might as well try and distract myself until they get home.

I decide to follow Ash's instructions and have something to eat, opening the fridge to find a yummy bowl of Greek yoghurt, and a glass of juice on the shelf. Fresh granola flapjacks and syrup are waiting for me on the counter, with another note next to them.

*I made your favorite, chocolate chip*

Oh, Kai, you wonderful human!

Tucking in, I moan at the buttery oat-y taste, the flapjacks still warm from the oven. Finishing up, I put my bowl and glass in the dishwasher, and go to take a shower, then head back upstairs to get dressed.

Suddenly, I crave fresh air and looking out the window, although it's a little cloudy, it's not raining. A walk around campus sounds perfect to help blow these cobwebs away, and just what the doctor ordered.

Twenty minutes later, I'm heading out of the front doors of the Academy, wrapped up in my wool coat, hat, and scarf, with super cute mittens on my hands, and wearing my favourite Run and Fly rainbow dungarees. Taking a deep inhale, a smile lifts my lips as the frigid air hits my lungs. This is exactly what I needed.

Rounding the corner of the building, my lips drop into a frown when I hear girlish jeering and laughing up ahead. Narrowing my eyes, I come round a large topiary bush to find Amber Cuntmuffin—*surprise, surprise*—and her two fanny flap sidekicks surrounding a girl I've not seen before.

I can't see much of her, as they have her completely surrounded, but what I can tell from the ugly twists of their faces is that whatever they are saying isn't nice. Frowning harder, I approach them and catch Amber sneering at the poor girl, who looks close to tears.

"Why don't you go back to the gutter that you came from, charity case."

What the ever-loving fuck is wrong with this cumdumpster?!

"You know," I start, having stepped up right behind her. She whirls round, eyes bulging unattractively when she sees that we're almost face to face. "Just because you have a cunt, doesn't mean you need to act like one all the time." I smile sweetly at her, tilting my head to the side in a fake gesture of innocence.

"Oh look, here comes the other English bitch." Her lip curls back as she practically snarls at me. "She's the school whore, so you guys should get along just fine, Trash," she says, looking over her shoulder at the new girl, spitting out the insult and making the other girl flinch. Her name-calling just washes over me, and I smirk at her. "Let's go, Bianca, Tina." Ah, so those are their names. I guess I couldn't call them fanny flap one and two forever. *Snort.*

Amber takes a step away from me, her clones on either side of her. I swear they used to have different hair colours, but they're all varying shades of blonde now.

"Yeah, we wouldn't want to catch something," sneers Fanny, I mean, Tina. Or maybe Bianca. Fuck if I know, they all look the bloody same.

"What, like a personality?" I ask with a smile, earning more sneers from all three of them. "Run along, Fanny, your master is calling." *Whoops, guess Fanny it is!*

She vibrates with fury, like a little bunny boiler ready to explode. I can't help the chuckle that escapes at the visuals of bunny fluff flying everywhere when she detonates. Fanny aka Tina takes a step forward, but Amber lays a hand on her arm.

"She's not worth it, Tina," she growls out, then looks at me with a smug smile that makes my heartbeat thump in my chest uncomfortably. "She'll be put back in her place soon." Then, with perfectly executed hair flips, they turn on their heels and walk off.

"Well, that was ominous," a soft British accented voice says next to me, and I startle, having forgotten all about the new girl.

"Ah, don't mind Cuntmuffin. She's just sore because I'm with the guys that she wants," I tell her, finally able to take her in.

She's a petite blonde, barely reaching my shoulder, and I'm not exactly tall at five-six. Her pale blonde hair sits close to her head in tight curls, and with her sparkling blue eyes, all big and round like a bushbaby, she definitely looks like she belongs in the forest behind us. She's wearing jeans, Doc Martens, and a massive green puffer jacket with fake fur round the hood that practically drowns her. She smiles mischievously at the nickname I have for Amber, holding out her hand, the gesture drawing my lips up.

"Willow Anderson," she states as I grasp her tiny hand in mine, shaking it. She really is like a fairy.

"Lilly Darling, pleased to meet you, Willow," I reply. We let go of each others' hands with a chuckle, and I can see that she's eyeing me up as much as I did her. "Out with it," I say with a laugh, turning and indicating with my hand that we walk together.

"You said 'guys' that you're with, like there's more than one..." she trails off, a cute as fuck blush stealing over her cheeks as she looks at me from under her lashes. I can feel an answering heat in my own face, but I'm not ashamed of my unconventional relationship.

"That's right, I have four guys, who are all best friends, that I'm seeing," I tell her, watching as her eyes widen slightly, but her steps don't falter, and instead, she tips her head to the side a little, a slow smile building on her face.

"My brother and his best friends are inseparable. I can't imagine them ever being apart," she says, looking up at me with a twinkle in her eyes. "I might have to drop some hints about Iris when I speak to them next."

"Iris?" I question, loving how this girl's mind works, similar to my own in that we carry on conversations that we're having in our head out loud.

"Iris Montgomery sponsored me to come here after... Well, after some shit happened back home," she informs me, looking away, her hands twitching by her sides.

"And where's home?" I ask, seeing that a swift subject change is in order.

"World's End Estate, Chelsea, in London. You?" Another slow smile tilts her lips upwards.

"Islington, then Wiltshire with my uncle after some shit happened," I beam at her, and her grin grows wider. "And Iris sponsored you to come here?"

"Yeah, well, she persuaded her dad to pay for a sponsorship for me. I just...needed to get out, you know?" She looks at me then, and I can see pain so similar to my own swimming in her deep blue eyes. Although, my heartache is less now than it was when I first arrived.

"Yeah, I know," I reply softly, and we continue to walk a little ways in comfortable silence.

"So," she begins, that mischievous look back in her baby blues. "Wanna tell me all about your four guys? I'm gonna have to live vicariously through you. My brother and his friends, the fuckers, scared off any prospective boyfriends I may have had before I even got to say hello." She chuckles in a frustrated way, her blue eyes taking on a haunted look for just a second, but then she blinks and it's gone.

My heart aches for her, knowing that feeling so well. The feeling of being so overwhelmed with your trauma that you daren't even think about it. I can only hope that she'll be able to talk about what happened one day and start to move on.

"Well," I say, knowing that right now she needs a distraction, "there's Loki, Jax, Kai, and, of course, Ash."

"Oh shit!" she exclaims, stopping us and grabbing hold of my arm. "You're seeing the Black Knights?!" She's practically bouncing with excitement.

"You've been here, what? Five minutes? And you know about them already?" I shake my head.

"Girl, they're the hottest guys here. Not to mention the richest and the most dangerous." She fans herself ridiculously, and I laugh out loud at her antics. "Tell me, are they as incredible in bed as the rumours suggest?"

I like this girl, we are kindred spirits. Not afraid to get straight down to the nitty-gritty of a situation and all the good stuff. She is my spirit animal.

"Better," I say, a salacious grin pulling my lips up. She squeals, scaring some birds in the nearby trees who take flight, and we both chuckle.

"I knew it! Tell me everything," she demands, and a blush steals over my cheeks again thinking over all of mine and the guys' intimate times together.

"I could tell you, but then I'd have to kill you," I answer, faking a sigh. "But I will tell you how we met."

I spend the rest of the afternoon walking with my new fairy friend, talking about everything under the sun. I invite her back to our dorm, and we get pizza delivered from the kitchens, eating the cheesy goodness whilst she regales me with tales of her own misspent youth.

It's the perfect distraction, and although I get twinges of worry, I'm also full of happiness at having met Willow. I can't wait for the guys to meet her.

---

LOKI

Worry swirls around us like a dark storm cloud as we step inside our dorm. Fatigue washes over me as I take my Chucks off, trying to be quiet so as not to wake the sleeping beauty upstairs, who is hopefully in my bed, waiting for me.

A need for her crashes over me with the force of a sledgehammer, and before I know it, my feet are carrying me towards the stairs.

"Loki," Ash quietly calls out as I reach the bottom step. I turn to look at him, seeing the unease in his eyes reflecting my own. He won't sleep tonight. "They're up to something. Stay sharp."

I nod, seeing Kai and Jax head for the drinks cabinet. I can't blame the big guy for going against the doctor's orders after a visit with our folks. BL—*before Lilly*—I would have joined them. Now, I just want to lose myself in her softness. In her. Ash is right, the cunts at Black Knight are up to something, inviting us all for a Knight dinner this Friday, instructing us to bring Lilly. I just hope that they don't know how important she is to us, otherwise, they really will have us by the balls.

I look up to find that I'm in front of my door, my hand on the brass knob and no recollection of how I got here. Turning it slowly, all thoughts of my parents, the company, and anything that is not Lilly Darling fly out of my mind as the hall light casts a soft glow on Lilly's sleeping form.

She's on her back, the sheets tangled around her waist, her glorious naked tits left exposed. I stand and watch her like a total fucking creeper for several moments, following all of her delicious curves with my gaze.

Deciding that I can't stand not touching her for a second longer, I walk in, leaving the door open as usual. Those fuckers downstairs can enjoy her cries when I'm balls deep inside of her. Stripping, I place one foot in front of the other, careful to be silent as I approach the bed. *Guess my training is good for more than just sneaking up on my marks.*

I take a condom out of my jeans pocket before taking them off, and slowly roll the rubber on my already hard dick. I also grab my phone, scrolling until I find the song that I've been obsessing over for the past few days. Setting the volume on low, I connect it to my sound system, but don't hit play just yet.

With my heart beating fast in anticipation of what I'm about to do, I gather saliva in my mouth, before quietly spitting in my palm. Watching Lilly sleep, I bring my hand down, wrapping it around my hard cock and spreading my spit over the surface. My eyes roll as I repeat this twice more, pleasure exploding along my length as I make sure I'm nicely lubed up for my girl.

I reach over and carefully pull back the comforter, exposing her beautiful pussy to me. My breath hitches as she gives a gentle moan, shifting her legs, then settling back down. I pull the covers right off her, happy to see that her thighs are parted enough that I can get between them.

Flicking my eyes up to her face, I watch her features as I climb onto the bed, gently pushing her legs wider apart until I can see her glistening cunt, open and ready for me. My dick twitches at the sight and a part of me wants to dive in between them with my tongue and teeth, making her scream my name. But the need to be surrounded by her, her body gripping mine, is too overwhelming to ignore. Lowering myself down, I move so that my tip is notched at her entrance. Fuck, I know that this is wrong. Forcing myself inside her whilst she sleeps. That doesn't stop me from surging forward though, grunting as her unprepared walls clamp around me. I quickly hit play on my phone, dropping it beside us just as she wakes with a gasp.

"Shit, Loki!" she rasps out, ending on a moan as I keep moving, thrusting until her body accepts mine and I'm fully seated inside her.

"Shhh, baby," I murmur, my voice strained with how fucking good it feels to be inside her, lightning tickling my nerves as her inner walls grip me exactly as I hoped they would.

Pausing, which is sweet agony, I wait until Khalid starts singing *Better*, and then sing along, crooning in her ear as I begin to move, our bodies flush together. It takes everything in me to keep my voice steady as I thrust inside her wet heat, her walls already fluttering around my cock.

"Loki," she moans when I hit that sweet spot inside her over and over again. Her nails rake down my arms, back, and ass, and I fucking love the edge of pain just as much as she does.

"You love it when I force my way inside you, don't you, naughty girl," I say, grabbing her wrists and bringing them up over her head, pinning them to the mattress.

She moans, a rush of wetness coating my dick as I pick up the pace, starting to fuck her hard, just the way she likes.

"Yes! Fuck, yes, Loki!"

I knew she would love it. She likes it as rough as we can give, and I'm more than happy to oblige. Transferring both her wrists to one of my hands, I move the other to wrap around her neck, like Jax often does. As soon as I start constricting her airway, her pussy walls clamp down so hard I almost shoot my load then and there.

"Uh ah, Pretty Girl. You don't come until I tell you to, understood?" I question through gritted teeth, stopping completely and gazing down at her. Her cheeks are flushed, her nipples peaked as they press against me. *Fuck, I'm not gonna last long at this rate.*

"Please..." she whispers, opening her eyes and looking into mine, begging me to allow her release.

"Soon, my heart," I reply, capturing her soft lips with mine and kissing her deeply. She tastes like every hope I've ever had, every good thing, and all the happy days rolled into one.

Unable to help myself, I begin to move once more, starting off slowly again.

"Keep your hands there, baby," I order, letting go of her wrists. Using my free hand, the other still wrapped around her slender neck, I hook her leg over my arm, and we both fucking groan at the new, deeper angle.

"Harder, please, Loki," she asks, her eyes closed, a look of pained bliss on her face as I fulfill her request.

I begin pounding harder, faster, until I'm impaling her on my cock. Letting go of her throat, I move to grab her other leg, and go up on my knees to get an even deeper angle. *Fuck.*

I feel like my entire body is on fire, my teeth clenched so tightly I'm surprised they don't crack as I fight my release. Feeling my balls draw up, I know that I can't hold it back anymore.

"Come now, baby," I growl out, pulling out of her completely. I watch enraptured as she squirts all over me and herself, her release even reaching her shoulders. She cries out in ecstasy, her whole body going rigid as her legs shake in my grip and her hands claw at the mattress. *Jesus, that is so fucking hot.*

Releasing her thighs, I whip the condom off, pumping my cock in my fist until I, too, explode, seeing stars as I cover her pussy, stomach, and breasts with my climax. I stay kneeling, panting, watching our combined essences cover her glorious body. *It's enough to make any man hard and ready for round fucking two!*

She opens her eyes, a lazy smile on her lips as she glances at me with a look that sets my heart racing all over again. Her whole body practically glows in the darkness, highlighted by the light coming in from the hall.

"I love you so fucking much, Loki Thorn," she whispers, her voice husky and satisfied.

"I love you, Lilly Darling," I reply huskily, leaning down to capture her lips again, tingling all over at the contact of our bodies, not giving a fuck about getting my cum all over me. "Now, let's go downstairs, and you can show the guys how pretty you look covered in my cum," I tell her, nipping her lip then getting up and holding a hand out.

"Fucking wankstain," she chuckles, rolling her eyes at me, but taking my hand anyway.

Wrapping my arm around her, I pull her close, kissing her hair and savoring the just fucked smell that is all Lilly. The first moment I caught it wafting off of her, like spring after the darkest of winters, I knew she would be our fresh start. Our new beginning.

Shit, I would make a fortune if I could bottle that scent, but she's all ours, only we are allowed to cover ourselves in her bounty. And we don't share with anyone else; they can all live in despair for all I care. As long as she's by our side, in our beds, the rest of the world can fuck off.

# CHAPTER FIFTEEN

LILLY

The next morning, Loki and I head downstairs to find the others sitting round the table, eating breakfast. I sit down to a plate of pancakes, crispy bacon, and eggs, all drizzled with syrup, with a glass of fresh orange juice and ice.

I look up to catch Kai's amber stare.

"Thank you. For this, and the granola bars yesterday," I tell him, a feeling of lightness descending over me. I love that they take care of me.

I know that in this day and age of feminism and equality between the sexes, it's not necessarily the most popular view, but there's something about being cared for by a man, or in my case four men, that feels right. Like it's meant to be this way. And anyway, we look after each other, just in different ways.

"It's my pleasure, darling," he replies with an upturned face, his beautiful smile lifting my spirits further. There is still that darkness in the depths of his eyes, like something is eating away at him from the inside. A fissure of worry skitters through me.

"I'm sorry we weren't here yesterday, Princess," Ash says to my left, and I turn to face him, my heart beginning to race as I suddenly remember why they were gone.

"What happened? Did you have to..." I trail off, swallowing hard, unable to finish my sentence. Ash grimaces, pausing with his coffee cup partway to his plush lips.

"No, just usual training stuff, and a meeting afterwards," he tells me, and I just know that there's more to it. I want to know what the meeting was about, but I want to find out about their training first.

"What does your training entail?" I ask hesitantly, watching him intently. His face starts to shut down, then he sighs, closing his eyes and setting his cup down.

"Well," he starts, opening his lids and locking me in his steel gaze. His brow is wrinkled, his hands clasped on the table, his cheeks tight with the force of his clenched jaw. This isn't easy for him, and my heart aches for this strong man who's seen such horrors. "There's the usual self-defence and offence training," he tells me.

"Basically, we learn how to beat the shit out of people," Loki interrupts, Ash snapping his head towards the redhead and snarling. "Don't fucking sugarcoat it, man. Just tell her, she can handle it," Loki argues, looking my way with a small smile as he says the last part.

"Hey," I say gently, resting my hand on Ash's arm which is vibrating with tension. He turns to look at me, his eyes pained. "I will not think any less of you, my love. Or any of you," I tell them, looking at each one in turn. "I love you. It's a forever kind of thing," I joke, loving the stunning smile that graces Ash's lips once I look back at him.

"Loki's right, we learn to beat people up. As you know already, we extract information from them and often have to get physical. So we practice to prepare, and *they* like for us to keep up with our skills," he practically spits out. "We also have different roles that we train specifically for. Loki specializes in stealth and espionage, blending into different situations seamlessly."

I can't help my snort at that, Loki being subtle is not something I'd imagine him capable of. He looks at me, with one auburn brow raised as if to remind me of exactly how stealthy he was last night, and my cheeks heat with the memory of waking up with him pushing his way inside me.

"Jax trained in South Africa, learning how to patch people up in appalling conditions, so that he can better..." Ash pauses here and swallows.

"Torture people," Jax simply states, his low voice sending shivers across my skin as always, although not just the usual lust filled ones. I look to see his blue eyes are hard, no doubt remembering all the pain that he's doled out over the years.

I reach across and grasp his huge hand, giving it a squeeze. His eyes brighten, a small tilt of his lips letting me know that he received the message of acceptance and love I was trying to give. I don't blame any of them for what they've been forced to do, forced by the very people who should have been protecting them.

"Kai specialises in tech, as you know," Ash carries on, and I study Kai, who gives me a tight smile. "He's trained in online warfare, hacking, and pretty much any way to take someone down, ruin a life or business, all from the comfort of home." I give Kai a reassuring smile, and he nods in return. But his deeds clearly trouble him too as I see his jaw is clenched and hands are nervously picking at the food on his plate.

"And you?" I ask, turning back to Ash. His jaw is steel, rock-solid, his stare faraway, avoiding eye contact.

"As our leader, Ash has to make hard, impossible decisions, and they test his commitment regularly," Loki once again interjects, his voice full of pain for his friend, and Ash's eyes go dark, his brow furrowed.

"Like what?" I whisper, my mouth going dry as my grip tightens on Ash's arm.

"Like whether someone lives or dies," Ash tells me, voice lacking any emotion, his eyes empty and staring just over my head, like he's recalling all of those lives he's been forced to take.

Tears sting my eyes as I let go of his arm, and use both hands to guide his attention back to me. His grey eyes find mine, and they are haunted, full of ghosts that no eighteen year old should have following them around.

"I'm so sorry, my love," I murmur, feeling moisture spill down my cheeks. His whole face softens, his own hand reaching up to wipe away my tears with his long pianist fingers.

"Don't cry, Princess. Please. I can't bear to see you cry over me," he pleads huskily, leaning down and placing our foreheads together.

"I told you, you are worth every tear of mine, Asher Vanderbilt. You all are. My tears are not mine anymore but yours, as the rest of me is yours."

He takes a sharp inhale, his large chest rising, and I know that it will take time and persistence for him, for all of them, to believe that they are worthy of my love. I will tell them a thousand times a day if that's what it takes. Closing the distance, I place a gentle kiss on his lips, tasting the salt of my tears mingled with the coffee that lingers on his. He kisses me back, his whole body relaxing as he seeks entry with his tongue. I willingly give it, loving the taste of him in my mouth as we explore each other, like discovering a new place just off a well known path.

He ends the kiss with one last sweet peck on my lips, pulling away and looking more at peace than he did before.

"I love you so much, Lilly," he confesses, staring into my eyes with such intensity, I know that I should be scared. But I'm not. I meant what I said. We are a forever type of thing. "Now eat up, otherwise, we'll be late for our first day back."

I begin to cut into my pancakes, heaping my fork with eggs and bacon too, and moaning when I place the food in my mouth. *Fucking yum!*

We finish breakfast in a comfortable silence, although I do catch the others giving Ash funny looks every so often. After the fifth time, where Jax actually elbows Ash in the side, I turn to face the man in question.

"Out with it, Lucifer," I tell him, his lips quirking at the nickname. He sighs, setting his own cutlery down.

"At the meeting last night, Julian told us that we're having dinner this Friday with all the Black Knight families," he tells me, peering at me. He rubs the back of his neck whilst biting his lip in a way that would be very distracting if I didn't suddenly feel butterflies take flight in my stomach. "And we've been told to bring you."

"W–what?" I ask, my stomach dropping. "W–why?" I look at the others, but they all have matching looks of worry on their faces.

"We don't know, Pretty Girl," Loki answers, taking hold of my suddenly cold hand. "But we will be there, and I promise we won't leave you alone, not even for a moment," he tells me vehemently, rubbing his fingers across my knuckles.

"Do they...do they know about the bonds and shares?" I question, turning to Ash. His brow is once again deeply furrowed. Poor guy will have terrible frown lines soon if this keeps up.

"I'm not sure how they can, although that thought did occur to us, too," he muses. "I looked at the papers. Laura was, and now you are, silent investors. Completely anonymous."

"But I wouldn't put it past them to have found out," Kai states, his melodic voice full of concern.

"Maybe it's just dinner, you know?" I say, feeling unconvinced. "I mean, Julian seems to have a bit of a...thing for me, right?" My nose wrinkles remembering his inappropriate looks and touches.

Ash's upper lip peels back.

"I hope that you're right, Princess," he says, looking round at the others before settling back on me.

But as chills spread over my skin in the warm room, I can't help the feeling that I'm wrong.

---

The first day back in class flies by, and before I know it, it's lunchtime. Willow shared my last class, Interior Design, so we head to the dining hall together. I open the wooden doors, hearing a gasp next to me as Willow takes in the beautiful, light-filled space with a slack-jawed expression.

"We're not in Kansas anymore," I say with a chuckle, thinking back to the first time I stepped foot in here, and the awe I felt seeing it.

"We are definitely not in World's End, that's for sure." She ruefully laughs as we make our way to a table next to one of the floor-to-ceiling windows.

"Did you not come here for breakfast?" I ask as we take our seats, Willow facing the door, whilst I choose one looking out at the breathtaking view of the mountains and forest.

"I was too nervous to eat," she admits, looking a little lost as a waiter, Gerald, comes over.

"Good afternoon, Miss Darling, Miss Anderson," he greets us, Willow's eyes going wider than even I thought possible.

"Hello, Gerald," I reply, beaming at him. "Have a good Christmas and New Year?"

"Yes, thank you. And yourself?" he politely enquires. I decide against telling him that I went to Bali to see one of my boyfriends who's recovering from steroid abuse, discovered that I'm rich in my own right, have stocks and shares in a company of dubious intentions, and visited my mother's grave for the first time.

"Lovely, thank you," I say instead.

"Do you ladies know what you want today?" he asks, looking from me to Willow.

"Ummm..." she starts, looking all kinds of flustered as her cheeks heat up.

"I'll take the steak, chunky fries, and side salad please, and a glass of full-fat coke with ice," I tell him. My intention was to have a salad, but I'm suddenly craving meat. *Snort. Not that kind of meat. Although...*

"Of course. And you, Miss Anderson?" he questions Willow, who looks like a rabbit in headlights.

"Uh, I'll take the same," she quickly replies, breathing out a relieved sigh.

"I'll put the order in and bring your drinks back shortly," he tells us with a smile. I grin back, I like the old man. Not like that butler, fucking Crow. Speaking of, I haven't seen him around for a while.

"What kind of school canteen is this?" Willow hisses at me, interrupting my thoughts, and I laugh at her.

"I know, right. The day's menu choices are on your iPad. Or you can just order what the fuck you like, and they'll make it for you," I inform her with a roll of my eyes. *Rich pricks.*

"Jesus," she murmurs, going still as the whole place goes quiet. Her eyes widen again, and it really is adorable.

I turn round, a huge smile lifting my lips as my Knights walk in looking all kinds of dark and dangerous. My core twinges at the sight of them. They spot me and head towards our table. Having spent the past few weeks with them, I'd forgotten just how imposing they can be.

Ash in his usual pristine black suit, tie, and smoothly styled jet hair, his eyes the colour of steel. Jax dressed head to toe in black, his bulging muscles threatening to rip his T-shirt in a Hulk moment. His lips twitch ever so slightly when his sparkling blue eyes meet mine, and I savour that almost smile that's meant for me alone. Kai is the epitome of geek chic in green chinos, a chequered shirt, navy bow tie, and a mustard cardigan. He looks so damn hot I can feel my temperature rise just watching him. Loki struts in like a fucking peacock, his auburn hair artfully disheveled, his low slung jeans hugging his toned legs, his white T-shirt sculpted to his torso in the most mouth-watering way. Today his shirt has a drawing of an eye in black ink, an anatomical heart in red, and an etching of a cockerel.

A delighted laugh tumbles from my lips as my hands cover my mouth, and his face lights up with an arrogant as fuck smirk. When they finally reach our table, he swoops down, capturing my lips in a bruising kiss that leaves me breathless and tingling.

"I missed you, Pretty Girl," he says, his lush lips turning down in a pout as he sits in the seat next to me and pulls my chair closer to his.

Jax sits on my other side, scooting his chair closer, then leans in and tangles his hand in the hair on the back of my head. Using his grip, he turns my head until I'm facing him, then proceeds to decimate my lips with his velvety ones. Her Vagisty is panting like a bitch in heat by the time he pulls away, and my heart races seeing the look of wild hunger in his blue eyes.

"I missed you, too, Baby Girl," he rumbles against my lips as he pulls away, his own lips lifting as he sees my dazed look.

"Shit, girl! That was hot!" Willow blurts out, and all eyes turn to her, Ash and Kai having sat down too, making her squirm in her seat.

"Who the fuck are you?" Jax growls, letting go of my hair and levelling her with his piercing stare. She swallows audibly.

"Hey!" I scold, whacking his pec with the back of my hand. *Fuck! When will I ever learn that their muscles are hard as fucking rock?* "That's Willow. She's my new bestie, so play nice."

Bad bitch that she is, she holds her hand out, waiting for Jax to shake it. To his credit, he does and doesn't pull a dick move like squeezing too hard either. *Brownie points, Jax.*

"Jax Griffiths," he introduces himself, letting go of her hand with a small nod.

"Nice to meet you, Jax," she replies politely, holding her hand out to Loki next, then Kai, who both introduce themselves. Finally, it's Ash's turn.

"Asher Vanderbilt," he states, shaking her outstretched hand. His voice is cold, but not unfriendly. "Your brother is Hunter Anderson, co-leader of The Shadows crew, based in the World's End Estate, Chelsea. And Iris Montgomery convinced her father to sponsor your senior year here."

I look at him with wide eyes, almost as round as Willow's.

"That's right," she says, her voice a little shaky. "How did you know all of that?" she questions, suspicion laced in her tone.

"I make it a point to know things, especially if they involve my girlfriend," he tells her, and my heart does a little pitty-pat at the term. Stupid really, given all that we've gone through.

"Good to know," Willow murmurs, just as Gerald comes back with our drinks.

He takes the guys' orders, then heads off again, leaving us in a slightly strained silence.

"Fuck's sake," I huff out, turning to Willow and ignoring the brooding arseholes around me. "How was your first morning?"

She proceeds to tell me all about it, and before long Loki joins in, with the odd word from Ash and Kai. Jax remains quiet, but that's no surprise given his usual engagement level with strangers being zero. Our food arrives, and we all eat, continuing to chat. I invite Willow back to our dorm for dinner later, both of us silencing any arguments by offering to make shepherd's pie for the guys.

I'd call that a successful introduction.

After all, they didn't threaten to kill her.

# CHAPTER SIXTEEN

LILLY

The rest of the week is over in a flash, and before I know it, it's Friday, and I'm getting ready for dinner at the Vanderbilt's mansion. I've chosen an original nineteen-thirties bias cut gown in wine coloured velvet. It has a high scoop neckline, and is strapless, with a silk waist tie and a short train. The pièce de résistance is the back, which is completely open, the fabric gaping on either side of the opening to give tantalising glimpses of my sides as I move.

I've put my hair up, wisps teasing around my face and neck, and my makeup is all smokey eyes and dark red lips. And of course, my feet are in Irregular Choice heels, emerald green sequin ones with a matching bow on the toes.

"Jesus, Pretty Girl," Loki rasps, and I look up from applying the finishing touches to my face to see him devouring me with his stare, leaning in the open doorway of his room. Luckily, the fabric is fairly thick so it hides my pebbling nipples, and I watch him in the mirror with bated breath as he stalks towards me, a predator's gleam in his eyes.

When he's behind me, he reaches out and runs a single finger down my spine. I can't hide the full body shiver that races across my skin at his touch.

"Fuck, if we didn't have somewhere to be..." he trails off, swallowing and biting his lip as his other hand goes to his crotch, adjusting himself, the outline of his dick clear through his dress trousers.

He's looking fucking edible himself in black trousers and a matching jacket, with a crisp white shirt and black bow tie. My whole body is suffused with heat, my nerve endings tingling as I stare at his reflection. I watch as he brings his hand up to my face, and lean into his touch when his finger brushes me from temple to jaw, leaving a blazing trail behind.

"You keep eye fucking me like that, Pretty Girl, and I won't be held responsible for my actions," he whispers in my ear, his voice low and sinful, his breath tickling my skin and stirring the hair around my face.

"Loki..." I whine, my whole body alight, my skin suddenly feeling too tight to contain the fire that is burning inside me.

"Time to go!" Jax calls from downstairs, breaking the tension that's threatening to drown Loki and I.

Loki heaves an enormous sigh. "Come on. Let's get this shitshow over with."

The fire suddenly goes out, his words effectively dousing the flames and leaving me feeling nauseous. I turn with my own sigh, and he grasps my hand in his warm one, looking down as my charm bracelet tinkles. A beautiful smile tugs at his lips as he leads me out of the door, grabbing my clutch like a true gent, and down the stairs.

"Ash and Kai went ahead..." Jax starts, trailing off as he spots us. "Fuck."

I can't help but chuckle at his awestruck look, his eyes like blue flames as he takes me in. I'm sure mine are just as heated as his, my stare devouring him. He, like Loki, is also in a tux and bow tie, and damn, does it look fucking incredible on him. His hair is tied up in the usual sexy as fuck man bun, his beard neatly trimmed. Her Vagisty is practically weeping at this point, begging me to take them both back upstairs and get lost in their arms.

"It gets better, bro," Loki tells him, a sexy yet pained smile on his face. *Same, Loki, same.*

He takes a step away from me, holding our hands up, encouraging me to do a slow twirl. A satisfied smile tilts my lips when I hear Jax curse behind me.

"Fuck," Jax repeats, and I turn back to see him rubbing a huge hand over his face. "We best leave now before I change my mind, Baby Girl, and take you back upstairs."

My breath hitches at the promise in his eyes, sweet anticipation making my core ache, mixing with nervous butterflies taking flight in my stomach as we leave the safety of our dorm, and head towards the lion's den.

We walk out of the front doors to be greeted by a valet holding out Jax's truck keys to him, the truck idling on the drive in front of us.

"Shotgun!" I cry, quickly making my way to the front passenger side and sticking out my tongue at Loki, who pouts back.

We all get in and buckle up, the butterflies flapping their wings furiously and increasing my heart rate. I don't know why I'm so nervous. Perhaps because the boys are? Or maybe it's just instincts. Whatever it is, I need to calm down before I explode. What I need is a distraction. Luckily for me, I've a hulking Viking who's sporting a semi sitting next to me in the driver's seat.

"How far until we get there?" I ask, an idea forming in my mind as we start to drive off. I grab Jax's phone, which is wirelessly hooked up to the speakers and scroll, selecting *Night Drive* by HENRY and hitting play, putting the phone back on the magnetic charging port.

"About fifteen, maybe twenty minutes," Jax says, eyes flicking to me, driving through the ornate gates. "Why do you have that look on your face, Baby Girl?" he asks as he focuses back on the road, his brow furrowed.

"What look?" I say innocently, unbuckling my seatbelt.

"What are you doing, Pretty Girl?" I hear Loki question from the back, but my attention is all for the big guy next to me. Leaning over, trying to avoid the gearstick, I open his suit jacket, popping open the button on the waistband of his trousers.

"Baby Girl..." Jax warns in a growl, which I ignore as I carefully undo the zipper, my breath coming in a sharp gasp as we take a bend at high speed.

"Eyes on the road, big guy," I tease with an evil smile.

"Shit," Jax gasps as his huge, beautiful erect cock springs free.

*Commando in all situations, huh?* I muse as I wrap my hand around it, barely able to get my fingers to meet, it's just that big. I pump his silky length up and down, making Jax moan low and deep, and the car lurches as his foot presses a little too hard on the accelerator.

"Jesus Christ!" Loki hisses from the back, and I glance over into the back-seat to see the glint of his pierced dick, which he has out and palmed. "You are something else, Pretty Girl," he moans, pumping his own fist up and down in time with my movements, his eyes locked on my hand wrapped around Jax. I whimper at the sight, my pussy fluttering as I take both these beautiful men in.

"Fuck. That feels so good, Baby Girl," Jax moans, and I can see he's struggling to keep his lids open and on the road, his hands clenching on the steering wheel, his knuckles white.

Taking my other hand, I start to gently massage his balls, every so often hitting that sweet spot just behind them. As I stroke and tease his member, I can feel him getting impossibly harder in my hand, his balls getting tighter and starting to draw upwards.

"Fuck, Lilly," he growls, his husky voice making my thighs clench. "I'm gonna come!" he gruffly shouts, and that's when I lower my head, taking his tip into my mouth and sucking hard whilst my fist keeps a tight grip, pumping harder and faster.

Hot salty cum shoots into my mouth, coating my tongue as he orgasms with a roar, and the car jerks to the side. I swallow every mouthful, loving how I can affect this strong man so much that he loses control.

Seconds later, I hear Loki gasp out his own release with a curse. Sitting up, there's a satisfied smirk on my face when I notice the lipstick marks on Jax's cock.

"Jesus, Baby Girl." His voice is a husky rumble, deeper than usual, which I didn't think was possible. I just beam back, almost preening at his tone of sated disbelief as I tuck him back into his trousers, lipstick marks and all. Grabbing my clutch, I drop down the sun visor, using the mirror to fix my lipstick.

"Hey, Pretty Girl, grab the wipes from the glovebox for me, please?" Loki asks from the back. "I didn't have that naughty mouth to catch my load."

My cheeks flush as my thighs clench together with the thought of wrapping my lips around Loki's cock, using my tongue to play with his piercing. *I swear I'm in a permanent state of horniness whenever I'm around any of these boys!*

I take a deep shuddering breath, grab the packet of wipes, and reach back to hand them to him. Loki keeps my stare for a moment more before taking them and cleaning himself up. He looks up again as he leans forward, his thumb wiping the side of my mouth, then he brings the digit to his own mouth, sucking off the drop of Jax's cum that sits on the tip.

My heart fucking stops, my stare locked on his mouth as he slowly withdraws his thumb, the heat in his emerald orbs sparking and flickering like a flame.

"Not bad," he whispers, a sexy as fuck smile on his plush lips. Fire roars around my body, consuming me with lust and creating an ache so intense I feel like I may pass out from need. "Touch yourself, baby. I know that you need to. Ease that pressure," he commands me, and I whimper, my breath stilling in my chest.

"Loki! Fuck, dude, I'm hard again," Jax grumbles, kickstarting my breathing once more.

But my hands move of their own volition, reaching for my hem and drawing my skirt up my legs, the soft velvet making my whole body tingle as it slides up my skin. Loki's now sitting so far forward, he's in between the front seats, staring down as I inch the garment up my thighs. Lifting my arse, I make sure to pool my skirt around me so that I'm not sitting on it. Wouldn't want a wet patch.

"Good girl," Loki croons as I expose my black lacy thong, moving it aside to show him my glistening pussy lips. I hear a manly gasp as he takes in my bare cunt. "You've been busy," Loki comments in appreciation. I had a full Hollywood wax after class, driving into town with Willow.

"Wha–" Jax cuts off, swearing as he looks down and sees the view Loki has.

"Keep driving, *big boy*," Loki teases, earning a snarl in return, to which he just chuckles.

*Love Is a Bitch* by Two Feet comes over the speaker, the beat heightening my senses, as my hand drifts down of its own accord, to swipe between my slick folds. A low moan falls from my lips as pleasure bursts across my closed eyelids, my head falling back to hit the headrest with a dull thud.

"Such a good fucking girl," Loki praises as Jax groans beside me, my fingers dipping inside my aching pussy and coating themselves in my wetness. "Now tease your cunt, baby."

"Fuuuuck..." I murmur as I go deeper, circling my opening with my middle finger, my lower lips fluttering and desperate to be filled. "Please..."

"Push two fingers in, nice and slow, Pretty Girl," Loki commands, his voice low and full of dark deeds done at night. "And open your fucking eyes."

I obey immediately, my greedy pussy demanding more as I slowly slide two fingers inside myself. My lids lazily stutter as my mouth falls open on a gasp, emerald eyes dark as a raven's feathers staring back at me, full of fire. Movement catches my eye, and I look down to see Loki's hand wrapped around his fully erect cock, gripping it tightly as he moves once again in time with my own hand. Though this time, my fingers are buried in my pulsing cunt.

"Tell me how your pussy feels," Loki demands, and Jax swears, the car speeding up once again as we wind our way down dark mountain roads.

"Wet," I rasp out, breathless with the exquisite pleasure that rolls over me as my fingers start to thrust harder and faster. "So fucking wet."

"Isn't she perfect, Jax?"

"So fucking perfect," Jax grinds out between clenched teeth, and my hooded gaze turns to him to see him once again white-knuckling the steering wheel.

"Loki, please. I'm so close," I say, begging him for release as I turn back to him.

"Add another finger," he orders, his voice harsh as he, too, is close to another climax. I can hear it in the strain of his voice, see it in the way his hand furiously pumps his cock, precum glistening at the tip.

"Shit, yes," I say on a gasp as I do as he says. The sounds my pussy makes, wet and sucking, are obscene, filling the car with the scent of sex. "Loki, yes!" I scream as I fracture into a thousand pieces, my release coating my hand and the leather seat beneath me.

I slump down, my entire body liquified as I ride my orgasm, my fingers slowing, leaving my pussy twitching in the afterglow. I hear Loki grunt, and watch as he catches his climax in his hand, his face blissful.

"Give Jax a taste, baby," Loki commands breathlessly, and I manage to rouse myself to follow this one last order.

Placing my wet fingers against Jax's lips, I sigh as he opens his mouth, his tongue licking my fingers from base to tip, before he takes them into his mouth one at a time, sucking them clean.

"I fucking hate you both," he grumbles once he's finished, fixing his pissed off stare at me then Loki. "We're here, and I've got a raging fucking hard-on."

I giggle, reaching over for the wipes that Loki is holding out and cleaning up, then straightening my dress. My laughter is short-lived, however, when I look past Jax's head, up at the imposing mansion. It's not the grandeur of the building that kills my humour, but the man standing at the top of stone stairs.

In the low light, shadows play across his face until he's nothing but a wraith, a monster, the kind that lives in the darkness and comes out to steal the souls of innocents. I see out of the corner of my eye, both guys turn to look in the direction that I am, but I'm unable to take my glower from that of the man standing there, a demon's smirk on his face.

"Well, there goes my boner," Jax ruefully sighs, and the joke is so unexpected coming from him, that it breaks the spell I'm under, and I turn back to him, my brows raised.

"Jax Griffiths, I love you," I say, leaning over and placing a kiss on his lips, tasting myself on him.

"I love you too, Baby Girl," he mumbles into my mouth, his words flowing into me and giving me strength for the night ahead.

I hear the back door open and shut, then a blast of cold air hits my back as my door is opened. Turning, I see Loki, lined in moonlight and the yellow glow of the outside lights.

"Come, let's go dine with the devil and his minions," he says, his hand outstretched.

Here's hoping we have long enough spoons.

# CHAPTER SEVENTEEN

LILLY

The winter chill hits my skin, goosebumps pebbling all over my arms and back as I take Loki's hand, and he leads me up the front steps. They look like marble, grey veins running through them until they have the appearance of bone in the moonlight. When we reach the top, the devil himself is there to greet us, columns of marble on either side of him.

"Welcome to Vanderbilt Manor," Julian welcomes me, all charm and lethal smiles, his hands outstretched to encompass the grand home behind him.

The mansion reaches up so high that I can't see the top and is made from the same bone coloured marble. It stretches either side of us, seeming to disappear into the distance, it's that vast. I can appreciate the beauty in its history, but it's austere, all hard lines and harsh decoration. There's nothing soft and welcoming here.

He walks towards me, stepping right into my personal space, his hand going around my waist as he tries to pull me away from Loki, who keeps a firm grasp of my hand. I shiver, and not from the cold when his thumb traces the bare skin at my back.

"Exquisite, as always, Darling," he whispers against my cheek, placing a soft kiss there that leaves bile in my throat. I don't know if I misheard, or if he purposefully left off the 'Miss,' but I've never disliked my surname before now. He cheapens it, making it sound like an endearment he has not, will not, earn the right to use.

His lips linger on my cheek for a second too long, his hand too, before he steps away and frowns down at Loki's hand, still clutching mine as he steps forward beside me, Jax coming up on my other side. They encase me in their scents, vanilla and citrus, lending me the strength to shake off Julian's inappropriate touch.

"Boys," he says dispassionately, nodding at them both. "Shall we?" Holding out one arm, he indicates that we follow him as he heads inside, a butler closing the door softly behind us.

The grand entrance hall is huge, but dark despite all of the lights, of which there seem to be hundreds. The walls are painted a deep navy, adding to the dark and gloomy feel, and huge portraits of presumably the Vanderbilt ancestors line the walls. The floors are black and white chequered marble, and there's a double staircase, also in marble, leading to the next floor. We pass by several dark wood doors, all closed, and although there must be heating somewhere for the air feels warm, shivers climb up and down my body at the coldness of the interior. There's no life here, only pictures of the long dead.

Julian stops in front of a set of wooden doors, which open from the inside as if by magic, although as we pass through, I see more liveried servants. We enter a vast dining room, panelled in dark wood with more portraits lining the walls and a huge marble fireplace on one wall.

An impossibly long table sits in the middle of the room, lit candelabras along its centre, and sparkling glasses, plates, and silverware in front of each chair. It looks as though we are the last to arrive, as most of the chairs at the far end are full with whom I assume are the guys' parents and members of Black Knight Corporation. Everyone looks up as we enter, and I find myself wanting to shift under their scrutiny. Julian leads us past the empty chairs, stopping in front of the head of the table.

I find Kai sitting ramrod straight next to an older, distinguished looking gentleman, with salt and pepper hair and a very eighties moustache. *Gross.* Kai's honey eyes are dark, and when he meets mine, it takes everything in me not to react. Not to run to him and drag him away, never to return. He has the look of a man who is drowning, desperate for air but unable to reach the surface. My hand tightens on Loki's, and he follows my gaze, a frown drawing his perfect brows together.

"Lilly, may I introduce Stephen Matthews, Kai's uncle," Julian says, and I look to the side, finding eyes similar to Kai's staring back at me. "He stepped up when Kai's parents tragically lost their lives in that fatal car accident, all those years ago."

Stephen nods his head, his eyes devoid of…anything. There's no warmth there, or even dislike. There's nothing, and I feel cold all over. It's like being stared at by a shark who doesn't care if you live or drown in the watery depths.

"A pleasure," he says, his voice a cruel hard thing that sends unwelcome shivers over my skin.

"P–pleased to meet you," I manage to murmur, taking a deep inhale when I feel Jax stroke my free hand, stepping up close behind me.

"Loki, Jax, you know where your seats are. I can show Lilly to hers," Julian says, his tone curt and expression pinched.

Loki reluctantly lets my hand go, my fingers feeling bereft as he leaves me with a look full of worry. He goes to sit next to Kai, a beautiful woman with the same auburn hair tumbling over her shoulders, sitting on Loki's other side. I can see his features reflected in hers, although where Loki is warm and inviting, hers is a cruel beauty, sharp and unforgiving. She must be his mother, and on her other side is a blond man, with the same emerald eyes as Loki. They look me over, undressing me, and his tongue darts out over his lips as if he likes what he sees.

I can't suppress the shudder as Julian introduces us.

"This is Chad and Rebecca Thorn, Loki's parents."

"A pleasure, Miss. Darling," Chad says, his voice low like Loki's but lacking the sensuality of his son's timbre.

"Lovely to finally meet you, Lilly. I can call you Lilly, can't I?" Rebecca says, her voice sugary sweet, but like Snow White's apple, there's poison lurking in the depths.

"Of course, Rebecca," I smile saccharinely back, having to suppress the chuckle at the way she flinches and narrows her eyes when I use her Christian name. "Nice to meet you, Chad," I add, hating the oily feeling that slivers over my skin when he hears his own given name from my lips. *Fucking Chad.*

I look over when I hear a chair scrape on the marble floor, to see Jax sitting next to a tiny blonde woman. She looks up at him with such love and sorrow in her eyes that it takes my breath away. He looks down and gives her an affectionate smile, taking her hand and kissing the back of it sweetly.

"Rafe and Jannet Griffiths, Jax's parents," Julian continues, leaving the top of the table and stepping next to me, taking my elbow. My heart rate kicks up a notch, knowing that I'm in the hands of a predator, but I shake my head when Jax looks ready to get up and knock Julian the fuck out.

"So, you're the cunt leading all our boys around by their dicks?" I hear a gruff voice say, and my head turns sharply to see a guy of similar, if slightly smaller, build to Jax; basically huge and hulk-like, sitting next to Jax. I don't miss Jax's mum flinch at his crude words or Jax's growl.

"That's me," I smile sweetly at him. "You must be the pathetic excuse of a man who beats his wife and child to make up for his micro penis." I hold his gawking glare, even as his face goes an unhealthy shade of purple, and I hear Loki covering up a bark of laughter with a cough.

"Why, you little bitch!" Rafe roars, shooting up from his seat, as if to make his way over to me, but Jax gets to his feet as well.

"Sit the fuck down, *old man*," he snarls, and warmth suffuses my limbs at his defence of me.

I smirk as Rafe does as his son orders, and takes his seat once more.

"You like to keep things interesting I see, naughty girl," Julian chuckles next to my ear, and I literally have to swallow down vomit at his words, chastising me like he's my sugar daddy. *Fucking hell.*

His blasted hand lands back on my bare skin making me jump, and he guides me to an empty chair next to Jannet Griffiths, Ash on my other side.

"And you know me and my wife, Samantha," Julian finishes, pulling out the chair for me as his wife doesn't even look up from studying something on the table.

"Nice to see you again, Samantha," I say, lowering myself in my chair as Julian pushes it in. She looks up, startled.

"Oh, Lilly," she starts, her voice soft and wispy like a puff of smoke. "I didn't know that you were coming."

"I told you, Mom," Ash says from beside me, his hand coming to my thigh and squeezing gently underneath the table.

"Silly me," she says breathlessly, then goes back to staring at her empty plate. She jumps when Julian claps his hands.

"Let's begin!" he calls, and the doors open to reveal servers in smart black tailcoats and white gloves, holding small plates, which must be our starters.

Ash leans in, his ginger scent calming me as it wraps around my body like a warm hug.

"Princess," he murmurs in my ear, the same one his father just spoke into, but the shivers I get this time are all from pleasure.

"'O, she doth teach the torches to burn bright!
It seems she hangs upon the cheek of night
Like a rich jewel in an Ethiope's ear;
Beauty too rich for use, for earth too dear!
So shows a snowy dove trooping with crows,
As yonder lady o'er her fellows shows.
The measure done, I'll watch her place of stand,
And, touching hers, make blessed my rude hand.
Did my heart love till now? forswear it, sight!
For I ne'er saw true beauty till this night.'"

My breath catches and my cheeks flush as he quotes Shakespeare at me, his tone hushed, reminding me of the first time he told me he loved me on Halloween.

"Whispering sweet nothings already, eh, boy?!" Chad shouts from across the table, my eyes darting up in time to see him lick his fucking lips again as he looks at me, and effectively dousing all my warm and fuzzies. *Wanker*.

"Chad," Julian snaps out, my head turning to see him with narrowed grey eyes, staring at the other man.

"Apologies, Julian," Chad murmurs, looking quickly down in an act of submission. *What the fuck is going on?*

"Let's eat," Julian announces, his tone light as if he didn't just tell off his business partner and long-term friend.

Ash squeezes my hand before letting go and picking up his cutlery to eat. I look at my plate, noticing a seafood starter, then stare panicked at my cutlery, having no fucking clue which ones to use.

"Outside in, sweetie," a soft voice says to my left, and I turn with a grateful smile as Jannet, Jax's mum, picks up her own smaller set of cutlery from the outside and pointedly looks at mine.

"Thanks," I chuckle, copying her. "I was a little lost."

"It's a small thing in return for the kindness that you've shown my boy," she whispers, her hands shaking, making the fork scrape lightly on the plate. "For helping him to...get clean." She speaks the last part so quietly, if I weren't already leaning in, I would have missed it.

My heart aches for her, tears springing to my eyes. Although I hope I would never be under the thumb of a man, to the point that I let him get my son addicted to drugs, I don't blame her for being unable to stop it. By all accounts, she is the victim of domestic abuse, and you can see it clearly in the way she holds herself, like her very soul is injured.

"I love him," I confess to her, just as quietly as she spoke to me. "I love them all, and would do so much more for them."

"I know," she whispers back. "And they clearly love you in return. I could see it the moment you walked in. For what it's worth, I'm sorry for what is about to come."

My heart throbs at her words, my breathing quickening as visions of a bloodbath fills my mind's eye. Before I can respond, Julian stands up, hitting his wine glass gently with a fork, the tinkling sound halting all speech in the room.

"Before we move onto the main course of the evening, I have a little announcement to make," he says, his face wreathed in smiles as he turns to look at me. Ash's grip on my hand becomes bruising at the same time my brows furrow. "Asher?"

Ash lets go of my hand, turning in his chair to face me as he reaches into his trouser pocket. He's wearing a tux like the others, but I barely register that as my vision zeros in on the small black velvet box that he's holding out in front of him.

"Lilly Darling," he starts, opening the box, and I see the twinkle of a diamond and ruby inside. "Will you make me the happiest of all men, and do me the greatest honour, of becoming my wife?"

# CHAPTER EIGHTEEN

LILLY

I stare at the unusual glittering diamond and ruby ring, nestled in deep crimson silk, dumfounded. The sound of a chair crashing to the floor behind me registers, along with a growled curse, but it's as if it's all far away, in some other place.

"Marry you?" I whisper, finally looking up into Ash's face. His steel eyes are swirling, a myriad of emotions running through them, but the overarching one is a plea, begging me to trust him. My brows draw down, my head shaking slightly. "Why?" I ask, but this time I look at Julian. After all, he's the one behind this, the puppetmaster. "Why do you want me to marry Ash?"

He smirks at me, and I want to fucking punch his perfectly straight teeth out of his devil's mouth.

"How was your little trip to London, Darling?" he asks instead, tipping his head to one side like a snake contemplating its prey. I hate that he uses my surname like a term of endearment. Shivers cascade over me as I'm trapped in his predator's leer, and in my peripheral vision, I see Ash stiffen further until he's become the Ice Knight everyone knows him to be. "You didn't think we wouldn't know about your jaunt, did you?" And then Julian tsks at me like a naughty wayward child, and my blood boils at the fucking audacity of this man. "That somehow, we wouldn't know about those bonds and shares in *our* company your mother had hidden away."

I can feel my face go cold, the blood draining from it, and no doubt leaving me pale and terrified looking. And I am. I'm fucking scared shitless at what this means.

"Now," he starts, stepping out from his space and coming slowly, menacingly, towards me, leering eyes holding mine. "We can't have a slip of a girl like you, who knows nothing about the work that has gone into Black Knight Corporation to make it the great enterprise that it is today, holding us to ransom. At first, I thought that we could just...dispose of you, like we usually do to things that get in our way," A growl sounds behind me—*Jax, no doubt*—but my eyes are full of the crazed grey of Julian's, unable to look away. "But then, everything goes to your uncle, as your next of kin, and that doesn't help us much either."

He steps fully behind me, and my relief at no longer being under his scrutiny is short-lived as his hands come down on my shoulders, gently like a lover's caress, his thumbs stroking the base of my neck. Bile fills my mouth, and it takes everything in me not to throw up all over the glistening silverware.

"Father," Ash grits out, jerking as if he wants to stand up and rip the older man's hands off me. *Please, Ash.*

"I'm not done, boy," Julian snarls, his grip tightening to the point of bruising, and a sharp gasp falls from my painted lips. "Where was I? Ah, yes. I had a better idea, so here is what will happen. You will marry Asher, be the happiest of brides, radiant on your wedding day, etcetera. Ash will become your next of kin, you will name him in your Will so that if anything unfortunate were to happen to you, he will inherit your stocks, shares, and bonds. Of course, you will remain a silent partner." He pauses, going back to caressing my shoulders lovingly, and I can't suppress the shudder that runs through me. "Oh, and they'll be no more whoring yourself out to the other boys. I will not have bastard grandchildren." His fingers dig in again, as if to reinforce his point, but I barely register the pain, my mind a maelstrom. Then I feel his breath against my ear as he leans down and whispers, so only I hear. "Although, if you ever want a real man between those pretty thighs, you only have to ask."

Dizziness washes over me at his words, my nails digging into my palms deep enough to break the skin with a sharp sting. I feel dirty, a sense of violation settling deep within my soul as he straightens up, giving me one last caress before my back is cold once more when he moves away. My eyes are unseeing, staring straight ahead as I think about all that he's just said. I can't see a way out, and panic starts to flutter at the edges of my vision, black dots appearing before me.

Suddenly, I feel a solid weight settle on my thigh, gripping me hard and bringing me back into the room. Slowly my head turns, as if I'm underwater, and I meet Ash's clear grey eyes. There's sorrow there, as well as a fierceness in the tight lines around his eyes that tells me we will get through this. He lets go of my thigh, taking my left hand in his, and bringing it in front of him. I don't look away as I feel him slide the ring onto my finger, the cool metal soon heating up with the contact of my overheated skin. There's a flare of...something, that flashes in his grey orbs. It's very close to possession, and my heart thuds in my chest with the knowledge that I am his now, officially.

"A toast!" Julian cries, his voice jovial and full of merriment, and waiting staff step forward with pre-opened bottles of the finest Dom Pérignon. *They must have known before I did.*

The thought flies through my mind as I continue to stare at Ash, letting his strength flow through me, bolstering my walls until they are solid enough to face these demons. He leans in, keeping his eyes locked with mine until he's no longer able to.

"I will not take them away from you, Princess. I promise," he murmurs in my ear, the same one his father spoke into mere moments ago. But this time, my shoulders droop with relief, moisture stinging my eyes.

"Thank you," I say back, my lips barely moving so as not to alert anyone else of our hushed conversation.

"Anything," he tells me, pulling away just enough so that I can see the vow in his words. "Anything for you, my love."

---

## ASH

I try to reassure her with my eyes, her own hazel ones swimming with a mixture of gratitude and devastation. I can't deny the asshole in me loves the idea of her being my wife. Of owning her, having my family's ring on her finger like countless generations of Vanderbilt women before her. The thought is enough to make me rock-fucking-solid, even with these jackals surrounding us.

But, cunt though I might be, I would never take her away from the others. I couldn't do that to them, to her. She's theirs just as much as she's mine, regardless of what a piece of paper may say.

I look past her to see Jax, hands clenched into fists on the table, his flute of bubbling champagne untouched as he vibrates with anger. Slowly, he turns his head and meets my gaze. *Fuck.* His eyes are full of piercing blue rage, his lips pressed together in a tight line.

Only years of training allow me to hold my ground, no outward sign of the fear that's taken root in my heart. In my soul. He has never, in our entire lives, looked at me like he wants to feel my insides slither between his fingers. And he could, he knows how to make someone's internal organs become external, all while keeping them alive.

I nod my head, the move barely perceptible. But like me, years of rigorous training allows him to see the movement. His brows dip slightly, a note of confusion entering his blue orbs. So I do the only thing that will assure him of my meaning.

The sounds of our parents' celebration and chatting around us fade as I stare into the blue depths of his eyes, and with an infinitesimal movement of my lips, I mouth the one word that will tell him all that he needs to know.

*Yours.*

His nostrils flare slightly, his shoulders loosening a small amount. He gives me a slight nod back, and I know that he'll give me shit later when we're alone, but at least he understands.

Turning my head, I look across the table to find Loki and Kai watching our exchange. Both have matching looks of rage in their eyes, all directed at me. I can't blame them, I would feel the same if one of them had been chosen. I just got lucky for once in my miserable life, my cursed Vanderbilt blood being good for something at last.

I catch Loki's eye, the emerald blazing as he tries to suppress his anger. People think that he's the least dangerous of us all, all smiles and flirtatious winks. But in some ways, he's the worst of our little group. You don't see the knife coming until it's buried in your chest, all while he smiles at you like you're the best of friends, and your death is a big joke.

His hand grips his dinner knife, and it takes a lot for me to suppress the twitch of my lips at the thought that he wants to stab me, right here and now. Last year, I would have begged him to do it too. Not so much anymore.

Staring into his eyes, just like with Jax, I mouth the word he needs to hear.

*Yours.*

His grip loosens on the piece of gleaming cutlery, although he doesn't let go of it completely. *Good.*

I meet Kai's narrowed honey scowl, and before I can mouth the same to him, he beats me to it.

*Mine.*

I nod and see his beast recede into the depths once more. It's always the quiet ones you have to watch out for. They'll dance in your blood, leaving crimson footsteps in the snow just because it looks pretty.

The servers lean in, taking away our starters and replacing them with plates filled with roast meat, golden roast potatoes, buttery vegetables, and lashings of gravy.

"In honor of my soon to be English daughter-in-law, I thought we'd eat a traditional British roast dinner," My father announces, looking at Lilly with far more than fatherly affection in his leer. My hand grasps hers, rubbing her knuckles as I bring it to my thigh and give him a death glare. "Are you pleased, Darling?"

*I swear if that cunt uses her last name like that one more fucking time...*

I don't realize that I've squeezed her hand tightly until she squeezes back, so I loosen my grip, turning to dip my head in apology at her. She gives me a weak smile that damn near breaks my black heart.

"T–thank you," she whispers, looking quickly down at her left hand, which is still in mine.

I let the sounds of everyone beginning to eat wash over me as I finger the sparkling antique jewel that now sits on her ring finger, the diamonds glinting in the candlelight. It's an antique piece, mid-eighteenth century, and has been in my family since that time. A Burmese ruby and rose cut diamond sit side by side in a heart shape, set in rose gold, with a crown of three smaller diamonds sitting atop them. On the side in enamel is the motto UNIS À JAMAIS which means 'united forever' in French. It suits her delicate hand, and a fissure of certainty runs through me, like she was always meant to wear it.

"Did you know that this ring has been worn by a Vanderbilt woman since the mid-eighteenth century?" I ask her, looking up from our hands to watch her reaction, drinking in every movement of her beautiful face.

"It's stunning," she whispers back, looking at her hand as if it's strange to have the weight of so much history on her finger.

"The story goes that several times great-granddaddy won it from a visiting Russian Tsar in a card game." A rare smile lifts my lips at the memory of my grandmother telling Luc and I the story as children. "Apparently, it belonged to his favorite courtesan, who threw a spectacular tantrum in the middle of the party when he lost it, where, much to the amusement of everyone present, the Tsar threw her over his knee and spanked her until she begged for mercy."

I watch as her eyebrows raise to her hairline, then drop as she sharply looks up at me when it dawns on her what I just said.

"You gave me a whore's ring?" she asks, lifting one eyebrow and giving me a scathing look.

God, she's exquisite when she's angry at me. It takes almost more strength than I have not to give her one of my signature smirks. I lean in, so close that my lips brush her ear as I whisper in them.

"You gonna make me throw you over my knee again, Princess? In front of all these people? Naughty minx." Then I nip her earlobe for good measure, relishing the hiss of breath that leaves her lips.

My smirk is fully in place as I pull away, although it drops slightly when I catch the look of pure unfiltered lust in her eyes. *Fuck, that backfired.* We both swallow hard, but luckily the sound of silverware on glass breaks us from our trance.

"Another toast!" my father cries out, and I turn to see him raise his champagne flute in the air. We all follow suit, waiting for him to speak like good little lapdogs. It makes me feel sick, following him like this. One day soon, just a little longer, and he'll be the one following orders. "To the beautiful Lilly, and my son, Asher. May you have a long and happy life together, a fruitful union..." He pauses here and gives her another lecherous look that makes my hand tighten around my glass to almost breaking point. "And above all else, continue the legacy that is Black Knight Corporation, as your heirs will after you."

Everyone raises their glasses higher, a chorus of "Here, here!" sounding around the table as we all drink the bubbling liquid that costs thousands per bottle, but tastes like nothing but ashes in my mouth.

# CHAPTER NINETEEN

LILLY

The rest of dinner—*orchestrated bullshit more like*—flies by, but I don't taste a thing of the delicious-looking meal, too busy trapped in my own head. It's not that I don't want to marry Ash, in fact, the idea fills me with an intense feeling of satisfaction. And there's something almost relieving about belonging to someone officially, body and soul.

But what about the other three pieces of my soul? The other three men that own my body? How can I be happy being the wife of one, and not the others? We are all entwined until there is no separating us, will this change things?

"Ash," Julian says, his voice finally breaking through my turbulent thoughts. "Why don't you take your lovely fiancée back to Highgate? Jax and Kai can go with you." Why not Loki too? I briefly glance at the cuntwaffle but decide not to raise a ruckus since the guys don't seem to be too worried about it.

I hate the way he orders everyone around, tells us all what to do, and expects us to jump and do it. I can see that Ash feels the same, his hands clenched into fists under the table, his eyes full of silver fire. Even so, he gets up, placing his napkin beside our dessert plates, his chocolate brownie untouched like mine.

"Shall we?" he asks in a low voice, holding his hand out for me to take.

I give him a brief smile, hating that I should be ecstatically happy, but am not. Most women are, I believe, when an impossibly beautiful man, who they love, proposes. Taking his hand, I, too, get out of my seat, feeling a gentle touch on my left hand. Turning to look down, I meet piercing blue eyes in a soft, round face.

"Congratulations, Lilly dear," Jannet says softly, giving me a smile full of warmth. "It was wonderful to meet you."

"You too," I whisper, a lump in my throat, squeezing her fingers back briefly before letting them go and turning to face Ash once more.

I hear the others scrape back their chairs, Loki, Kai, and Jax getting to their feet as we walk past, Ash's hand on my bare back a soothing warmth.

"Not you, Loki," Julian's voice cuts across the noise of our departure. "There's something we need to discuss."

Ash tenses up next to me, the hand on my lower back going completely still as we pause and I look back at Julian, then Loki who's jaw clenches.

"Just Loki?" Ash asks his father, whose face darkens.

"I'm not in the habit of repeating myself, boy," Julian replies through gritted teeth, all sense of joviality gone.

Ash simply turns back and urges me to carry on walking, even though I can feel waves of anger radiating off his taut body.

The mansion is a blur as we hurriedly walk through it, my heels clacking on the marble floors. I can't help the sigh of relief that leaves my lips as we step outside, pausing to breathe in the frosty Colorado air, a sigh of relief leaving my lips even though the freezing night air has my teeth chattering within moments.

"Here," I hear Kai say from behind me, and I'm suddenly engulfed in his woods after the rain scent as his suit jacket falls over my shoulders, still deliciously warm from his body.

"Thanks," I reply gratefully, a shiver of a different kind skittering over my skin as he places a gentle kiss on my cheek.

"Let's go," Ash commands, his tone hard. I know, like the rest of us, he just wants to get out of here as much as I do, plus is more than likely worried about leaving Loki behind. "Jax, I'm driving. Lilly's up front."

"You staking your claim already, *brother*?" Jax snarls, stepping up into Ash's face, glaring down at him. Ash grinds his teeth together so hard I'm surprised that they don't crack.

"That wasn't a request," he growls out. "Give me your damn keys, and get in the fucking truck."

They stare at each other for several moments, huge chests heaving, and a spark of guilt flashes in my chest. I don't want to come between them, to disrupt their bond.

"Hey," I say, stepping closer, placing a hand on Jax's forearm which is vibrating with tension. "Not here. Let's just get back, okay? Then you can go all caveman and throw me over your shoulder." The last part earns a small twitch from Jax's lips, a relieved smile falling from mine.

With a final growl, he tosses the keys at Ash, who deftly catches them, as he walks towards his truck, parked where we left it on the drive. Kai follows, jogging to catch up.

"Come on then, Princess," Ash says with a sigh, taking hold of my hand and leading us towards the vehicle.

A chilly breeze slips through Kai's jacket, and looking up into a starless sky, I can't help the feeling that this is just the start of something that will change us all irrevocably.

---

## LOKI

I sit there, surrounded by these people, monstrous shadows dancing around them in the candlelight, half drunk champagne glasses littering the table. I'm glad the others have left, especially Lilly.

*God, how am I going to tell her?*

"And if I refuse?" I ask, looking up into the eyes of a wolf, the devil himself, Julian Vanderbilt. He smiles his demon grin, all straight teeth and black lies.

"Then Ash may find himself a widower not long after his wedding day," he casually throws out, eyes hungry for any reaction I show.

However, I've learnt their lessons well, my cool façade not cracking as I stare right back at him. Inside is a different story, my heart rips apart, knowing that with what I must do to keep her safe, I will break her apart, too.

"And anyway, it's not such a bad deal, son," my cuntstain of a dad pipes in, and I turn to glare at him, showing exactly what I think of him. I smirk when he swallows hard. Good. Let him be scared of me.

I don't bother to reply, turning back to the master puppeteer himself, and giving a brief nod, I seal my fate.

*Forgive me, Pretty Girl.*

---

## LILLY

The next few weeks pass by, tension rife within all of us. When we got back the night after dinner at the Vanderbilt's, Ash, Jax, Kai, and I sat down and talked the whole thing over. Turns out that Ash had found out mere moments before we arrived, Kai, too.

But as Ash pointed out more than once, he had no choice. Julian and the others, bar Jax's mum, are all monsters with pitch-black souls. If Ash had refused to propose, they were going to dispose of me just like Julian had told me at dinner, whispering death threats in my ear like sweet nothings.

Jax relented with a growl, then threw me over his shoulder like the caveman that he is and took delight in making me scream his name over, and over, and over again whilst the Vanderbilt ring sat twinkling on my finger. *Fucking brute.*

Loki didn't join us in the night as he usually does, and hasn't since, although Jax and Ash have been keeping me more than occupied at night. In fact, I've barely seen Loki since the dinner, and a dark premonition fills my stomach. I know there is something going on. I know that it isn't good, and the feeling leaves me sick to my stomach constantly, and off my food with worry.

It doesn't help that Kai is also a little absent and looks exhausted, dark circles ringing his eyes, lines marring his forehead. Seems that his darkness has returned since that night, too.

Things feel like they're spiralling out of control, and I'm helpless to stop it.

It's the day before Valentine's Day, which also happens to be Loki's birthday—*I know, irony knows no bounds*—and I'm walking down the hall with Willow, heading to our yoga class. She's chattering away about some guy she's interested in, and I'm trying to listen, I really am, but sickness swirls in my stomach, making it hard to concentrate. It was so bad this morning that I couldn't face breakfast.

"Lilly?" Willow's sweet voice penetrates my thoughts. "Are you okay?"

I turn to face her, concern in her blue eyes as she takes me in. I'm obviously looking like shit, my face was especially pale in the mirror this morning as I was getting ready for the day.

"I'm just feeling a bit queasy. I have been since dinner at Ash's parents."

She, like everyone, knows about mine and Ash's engagement. However, unlike everyone else, she knows that it was forced by his parents. I gave her some bullshit about them finding out about us being together, so being kind of old-fashioned they expedited things and forced the proposal. I don't think she believed me, but being the beautiful human that she is, she didn't question it.

She doesn't know about the death threats, my standing in Black Knight Corp., or what the guys do. I'm almost certain that she suspects something is up, not wholly believing my excuses for not being over the moon about being engaged to Ash. And given her background, and her brother's involvement in running The Shadows—a notorious postcode gang in West London that even I've heard of—I think she would get it and not be surprised. She's not gone into details, as I haven't with her, but she's seen the darkness that lives in this world. Experienced it firsthand. It's in the haunted look in her blue eyes, and the slight tremble in her hands when she recalls vague stories from the past.

"Lilly, now, don't get pissed, but you've been feeling sick so much recently. Is there any chance you could be pregnant?" she asks, looking at me sideways as we continue to walk.

I stop dead in my tracks, as does she, a sinking niggle in my stomach.

"I can't be. I mean, there was a mess-up at Christmas, but I took the morning after pill a few days later..." I trail off, remembering what Kai had said about how it loses its effectiveness the longer you leave it.

"So there is a possibility?" she hedges, turning to face me full-on, lowering her voice as she quickly glances around. "When was your last period?"

My eyes flitter side to side as I try to recall the last time Aunty Flo came to visit.

"I–I don't think I've had one since before Christmas," I tell her, latching onto blue eyes full of sympathy.

“I’m popping into town later, so I’ll grab you a test. Then you’ll know for sure either way.” She reaches out, taking my suddenly cold hand in hers and giving it a squeeze.

I nod in thanks, swallowing thickly as we continue walking down the hallway.

*Shit, what if it’s positive? What will I do then? Fuck!*

Thoughts tumble in my mind until I feel queasier than ever, swallowing down bile as we approach a group of students standing around outside of the gym building. My eyes roll as I hear Amber Cuntmuffin’s nasally voice.

“I think a June wedding would be perfect, don't you?”

I huff a laugh under my breath, pitying the poor fool who’ll be shackled to her for the rest of his life. However, as we go past, I stop dead in my tracks for the second time this morning when I catch sight of who’s standing next to a beaming Amber, his face bereft of its usual flirty smiles.

“Loki?” I ask, my whole body flashing cold when I meet anguish ridden emerald eyes.

“L–Lilly...” he starts, taking a step forward, but is cut off by cuntface magee herself, who grabs his arm, the crowd before her parting as she drags him towards me.

“Oh, haven’t you heard?” she asks, a smug as fuck smile on her face as she holds out her left hand. “Loki and I are engaged.”

My whole world shatters, fine tremors wracking my body as I gawp at the garish bauble in the February sunshine.

“Loki?” I ask again, swallowing the lump in my throat, looking up at him. “What’s going on?”

His eyes burn with jade fire, but it’s soon replaced with a devastating sadness that seeps into my very bones, chilling my soul. His Adam’s apple bobs as he swallows hard, his lips moving, but no sound escapes as we stand in awkward silence.

“Aren’t you going to congratulate us?” Amber asks, her voice penetrating the haze that’s descended over me.

Anger, the likes of which I have never felt before rushes over me in a tidal wave, followed by an intense sickness that rises from my stomach, refusing to be ignored any longer. Without saying a single word, I spin and flee, just making it to the edge of the forest before tossing my bag aside, and falling to my knees, vomiting at the base of a tree.

"Shit! Lilly!" Loki cries and I hear footsteps approaching behind me. A hand alights on my back, rubbing soothing circles. "Fuck, Lilly, I'm so sorry. I should have told you sooner. I was a fucking coward. I have no choice about this, but I shouldn't have let you find out this way."

I finish heaving, acid stinging my throat as I spit on the ground once more.

"Water," I croak out.

Seconds later, a water bottle is pressed into my hand, and I gratefully swill my mouth out, before taking a tentative sip, then another. A tissue is passed to me, too, which I use to wipe my mouth.

My mind still swirls like a tornado with everything that has happened recently, twisting until I want to scream. One thing stands out clearly, though, like a beacon of light. Turning round, careful to avoid the puddle of vomit now behind me, I face Loki, both of us still on our knees. I'm relieved to see that cuntface hasn't followed him out, Willow either.

His brows are drawn together, and there are dark circles under his beautiful eyes, which are full of sadness and anguish.

Cupping his cheek, a move he leans his face into, I hold his gaze. "We will find a way through this, my love." His breath hitches and his eyes fill with moisture when I call him that. It's as if he thought I would have given up on him upon hearing this news. "Our fucking souls are merged, Loki. Nothing can separate them. Not cuntface, not Black Knight Corp., and certainly not Julian fucking Vanderbilt."

His own hand comes up to cup my cheek so that we form an unbreakable circle. "But they'll kill you, Pretty Girl," he whispers, horror entering his gaze as it trails across my face. "If I refuse, you will not live long past your wedding day."

A brief flash of fear lights up inside of me but quickly dissipates when I remember that we are not without power. In fact, we may have more than they do, now that I know about my inheritance.

"So we get them out of the way first," I tell him, fierce determination filling me up and I straighten my back as if preparing for war. "Even if that means permanently removing them from the picture."

His eyes go wide as he registers my meaning. And I do mean it, with all my heart. If we can't remove the rotten core of Black Knight Corp. by legal means, then we will kill them. They've done terrible things, horrific things, without once getting their hands bloody as they force their own flesh and blood to bear the stains of their sins.

And as the saying goes, if you can't beat them...then it's time to get the knives out.

# CHAPTER TWENTY

LILLY

It turns out Loki hadn't even told the guys—*stupid ballbag*—and received a few punches when we got back to the dorm after our various gym classes until I managed to calm everyone down with threats of my own brand of violence, i.e. Her Vagisty going on strike.

Grumbling, we all sit on the sofas, a fire roaring in the fireplace, the crackling of burning logs a soothing sound. The soft beat of Sinead Harnett and GRADES singing *If You Let Me* washes over us as we clutch mugs of hot chocolate made by Kai, who used freshly shaved chocolate and warm milk. He usually puts some kind of whiskey in them, but I told him to leave it out of mine, my conversation with Willow playing on my mind. Kai gives me a considering look, but doesn't say anything, doing as I asked. I should tell the guys, but I'm being a coward for now. I'll wait until I take the test tomorrow.

I snuggle up to Loki, loving his vanilla scent mixing with the cocoa scent of my drink. His arm wraps around me, pulling me closer and grabbing my legs until I'm draped across his lap. I decided that she can't have him, I licked him and he's mine now, so she can just fuck right off. Hence the reason he's here with me and not her, and I don't give a fuck if she doesn't like it. Plus, this is his dorm so she can't exactly stop him being here anyway.

"I fucking missed you too much, Pretty Girl," he murmurs, nuzzling the top of my head.

"Well, you've got no one to blame but yourself," I sass back, loving the way his hand tightens on my shoulder and the growl that sounds from his chest. *Got to love an alpha!*

"Right," Ash starts, gaining all of our attention. "Now that, thanks to Lilly, we have a majority share in the company, we need to start putting into place the removal of the current board." His grey eyes are the colour of flint, hard and unyielding, and a fierce sense of satisfaction floods my body at his words. "Kai?" he asks, turning to look at Kai, who unsurprisingly has his tablet in hand.

"The easiest way to do it is to set them up. Frame them with a crime, one so bad that they'll be locked away for a long time, and be forced to step down, giving up any rights, shares, and control of the company," he tells us, his voice hard, eyes unforgiving.

"And the crime?" I ask, having an inkling of where this is going, but needing to hear it from his lips.

"Murder," he replies, with no hesitation. "One of the board must die, the others proven to be the murderers, without doubt or question."

Chills skate across my body, my fingers tingling as they grip my mug, unfeeling of the heat coming from the drink. I look round at the others, matching looks of grim determination on their faces.

"Then we're in agreement?" Ash questions, asking the room. The guys all reply in the affirmative. "Lilly?" He turns to me, his face hard, but not without sympathy, a thoughtful expression on it. "Are you in?"

"Always," I reply, my heart beating a solid rhythm in my chest as the weight of what I've just agreed to settles on my shoulders.

Loki's grip around me tightens as Ash gives me a single nod with a gleam of what looks like pride in his eyes.

"Then it's settled. Any ideas on when? Where?" he asks, and once again, Kai speaks.

"The annual summer fishing trip at Flint Lakes," he says, looking up from his tablet. "It's a male-only trip, no wives or girlfriends," he looks at me apologetically. "So only your dads and my uncle will be there." I can see the others nodding at his words, but an objection rises in my chest.

"I want to be there, to help," I say firmly, sitting up straighter. "They've threatened my life, are forcing me to marry Ash, and have Loki engaged to that fucking cunt. I have a right to get justice, too. Maybe not as much as you all, but still."

"You're so hot when you're being all bloodthirsty, baby," Loki croons in my ear, and despite trying not to, I can't help the grin that takes over my lips.

"We've corrupted you good, haven't we, Baby Girl?" Jax comments next to us, and I turn to beam at him, too.

"Don't worry, Princess," Ash assures me, and I turn my head to look into his steel eyes. "You'll get your pound of flesh." I give him a sharp nod in return, his lips twitching in response. "So for now, we carry on as if nothing is happening. That means, Loki, that you continue with your wedding plans with Amber, keeping your distance from Lilly when out in public."

Loki and I both stiffen at his words, and even though I know Ash is making sense, it still stings like needles scraping along my skin. But then, I think, maybe this is just a new challenge. One I can definitely rise to.

As if by divine intervention, *White Lies* by Bolshiee comes over the speakers, the sensual beat and her haunting voice filling me up, leaving me feeling all kinds of wanton.

Breaking Ash's gaze with a devious smile, I hold my mug up as I swing my legs to straddle Loki's lap, and his hands immediately come to rest on my thighs. He squeezes gently as my knees come either side of his hips, placing my core over his crotch.

"Princess..." Ash starts, his tone stern. "We're not done here."

I just give Loki a suggestive smile, one brow raised, knowing that he'll be up for the challenge, too. His own lips respond with a devilish grin.

"Naughty, Pretty Girl," he murmurs with a chuckle, then licks his lips. I pluck at his T-shirt with my free hand.

"Off," I order, leaning back slightly so that he can comply. He places his mug on the side table, then takes his shirt off in that insanely sexy way guys always do—*what's with that?*

He throws the garment aside, giving me a 'what's next?' look. Taking hold of the spoon in my mug—Kai always tops my hot chocolate with lashings of whipped cream and a spoon to eat it with—I fill it with the still scalding liquid, and holding Loki's stare, begin to drizzle it down his bare chest.

It's hot enough that he hisses, the noise turning into a moan when I follow the path with my tongue, paying special attention to his nipple piercing. His sweats bulge, his hard length begging to be freed. *Patience, Lilly.*

Getting another spoonful, I trickle the drink down his chest once again, then proceed to lap the liquid up like a cat with a bowl of cream. Looking down, there's an obvious stain of precum on his sweats where the tip of his dick is, the outline of his piercing clear underneath the fabric, and I shudder at the sight. I'm faring not much better, my silk sleep shorts already soaked, and Her Vagisty practically shouting to be filled.

Settling back into Loki's lap, I can't help but grind down on his dick, capturing his mouth with mine, our tongues tangling. I can taste the whiskey from his own drink, and for the first time today, my stomach feels calm.

"Fuck, Pretty Girl," Loki rasps out, his fingers grazing my nipple through my silk cami top.

"Allow me," Jax says, taking the mug of chocolate from me, and setting it on a side table on his side.

My nipples start to pebble under Loki's attention, pressing against the silk of the top, zings of pleasure flashing through me. His hands start to trace along the lace hem, dipping underneath it and taking my top with him until he's lifting it up over my head and throwing it aside.

"So fucking beautiful," he rasps out before taking one of my tight buds into his hot mouth, my hips bucking, and his hardness pressing firmly against my silk clad core.

I move against it, creating a delicious friction that begins to drive me wild, and Loki growls, sending delicious vibrations across my breast and straight to my core.

His hands come around to the front of my shorts, and a deep groan sounds in his throat when his fingers find me already dripping.

"Such a good fucking girl, so wet for me already," he says huskily, making another rush of heat flood my aching pussy.

I'm confused for a second when he withdraws his hand, both hands moving to grip the crotch of my shorts, one in front of the other. Suddenly, I get an inkling of what he's about to do.

"Loki, don't you fucking..." I start to say, cutting off at the sound of ripping silk as he tears them in two, opening it up so that I now have two flaps of fabric hanging from my waist, instead of a pair of shorts. He looks up at me with a wolfish grin on his handsome face. "You fucker!" I scold, moaning when two of his fingers enter me.

I forget all about my ire as he moves them in and out of my dripping cunt, and I start to ride his hand, seeking him deeper, faster. One of his hands comes up to my throat, in a very Jax-like possessive move reminding me of the other night, and he squeezes gently.

"Oh shit, Loki!" I scream as I come hard and fast, coating his hand and lap with my release, letting go of everything that is going on, all of the shit that surrounds our lives currently, as I spiral into sheer bliss.

"That's it, baby," he says roughly, "come all over me like a good girl." His dirty talk and still thrusting fingers make me orgasm a second time, seeing fucking stars as I writhe and moan on his lap. Slumping down on top of him, completely spent, I hear his manly chuckle before he whispers in my ear. "We're only just getting started, Pretty Girl," he tells me, his voice giving me shivers at the sensual promise in his words.

He picks me up under my thighs, standing then turning round, all with me wrapped around him like a spider monkey. Encouraging my legs to go down, he then spins me round so that my back is to his front. Pushing down between my shoulders until I'm bent right over with my arms resting along the back of the sofa, he gives me all of half a minute, the crinkling of foil sounding behind me, before I feel him nudging my entrance.

He goes slow, allowing me to feel him inch by torturous inch before he's finally fully seated inside me, both of us groaning at how amazing it feels.

"Shit, baby. You feel so fucking good," he says through gritted teeth as he starts to withdraw before he slams back into me, causing a strangled cry to leave my lips. Picking up the pace, he begins to pound into me, the sound of our flesh slapping together overriding the music, and I can already feel tingles racing all over my body.

I feel a warmth on my face before a hand caresses the side of it.

"Don't forget about us, Baby Girl," I hear Jax growl out as I open my eyes to see him and Kai with their dicks out in their hands, right in front of my face.

*Holy shit! Two for the price of one!*

Jax is the first to guide his member to my mouth, and I open up, my hand wrapping around the base of him, wanting to taste him so badly, a small keen leaves my lips.

"So desperate to choke on my cock, Baby Girl." He chuckles darkly as I lick the tip, tasting the drop of salty precum.

I greedily take him in, my mouth stretching around his thick length as I look up at his face, loving the deep groan that leaves his beautiful lips. He watches me intensely as I start to bob up and down, sucking and licking him like he's my favourite ice cream. Loki is still thrusting inside me, hard and deep, making me take Jax deeper into my throat, which is not an easy feat given his size.

For a split second, I worry that it'll make me sick again, but my stomach seems to have settled for now, so I go to town, trying to swallow as much of his dick as I can, spit already dribbling down my arm as I pump what can't fit. My eyes water and I gag slightly when he hits the back of my throat, but I carry on, taking him deeper and shivering at his deep groans of satisfaction and pleasure.

I feel Loki wrap my hair around one fist as he pulls me off of Jax's dick with a pop.

"Don't forget Kai, baby. Show his dick the same love you just showed Jax's," he orders, angling my head towards Kai's waiting cock. My cunt flutters around his dick, the note of command in Loki's tone turning me on even more.

I don't have time to hesitate as Kai's hand takes over from Loki, and forces my head down by my hair, pushing his dick into my mouth. I take him in, moaning at the feel of his piercings along the bottom of my lips and mouth. They add a metallic taste to his musk, and I use my tongue to play with them as I sink further. Looking up at him and seeing the searing look in his eyes as he stares down at me, I decide to experiment a little. Bringing my teeth into the mix, I graze them along his length as I bob back up. A hiss leaves his lips, his hand tightening its grip until my eyes water even more with the pain of my hair being pulled, and his hips buck towards me, telling me he liked that. A lot.

I hollow my cheeks and glide down his length and back up using my teeth again, before letting it go. Immediately Jax's hand is in my hair, pulling me towards him, his cock back in my mouth, thrusting deep and hitting the back of my throat once again. I swap between the two of them, learning the differences between them with my lips and tongue as Loki starts to thrust even faster and deeper. One of Loki's hands comes around my front, rubbing my clit, pinching it every so often, and I cry out around Kai's cock in my mouth as his hand cups my jaw hard.

My cries must set him off because the next thing I know, his dick turns rock solid, and he thrusts all the way in, seconds before he pours his hot cum down my throat with a curse. As soon as he's finished, Jax's hand tightens in my hair and pulls me off, replacing Kai's cock with his own and fucking my face in earnest.

I relax my jaw and let him use my mouth like Loki uses my pussy, loving their dominance over me.

"Come for me now, baby," Loki growls out as he coats his thumb in my juices, taking it to my puckered hole and pushing it in.

*Jesus, fuck!*

I do as he orders, coming so hard that I whiteout, my whole body alight with electric fire. Vaguely, I hear Loki roar behind me, and Jax in front, as they both find release almost simultaneously. I can taste Jax's salty cum in my mouth, and I swallow every damn drop like it's the finest nectar.

I feel utterly boneless and totally blissed out. The boys pull out of me, a final gasp escaping my lips as they do. I slump, draped on the back of the sofa whilst panting when Kai's face comes into view as he crouches down in front of me.

"Such a good girl, my darling," he coos, pushing hair back off my sweaty forehead. "Let's get you all cleaned up." Leaning in, he presses his lips to mine in a kiss that is full of tenderness and love.

"Not quite yet," I hear Ash's deep voice say behind me, and turning my head, I look over my shoulder at him through hooded eyes. He's still sitting on his chair, his suit trousers straining as his fully erect dick pushes against them, his thighs wide.

A small whimper leaves my lips when he raises one hand, crooking his finger at me. Turning round, I get up, and on shaking legs, walk around the coffee table towards him. Stopping in front of him, my chest heaves and my body tingles with the aftereffects of multiple orgasms. Looking down, I stare into fathomless grey eyes, eyes full of fire, lust, and the threat of punishment.

"On your knees," he orders, his face almost blank, yet his eyes churn and swirl. I comply, my legs giving way anyway, landing on the plush rug with a thump. The heat from the fire tickles the right side of my body, a contradiction to my slightly cooler left side, my over sensitised skin pebbling with goosebumps.

"Undo my pants, *fiancée*," is his next decree, his nostrils flaring slightly and letting me know exactly how excited he is. You know, if the massive hard-on he's sporting didn't already give me a clue.

With trembling hands, my fingers fumble with his belt buckle, the metal clinking as I open the clasp. My breathing picks up as I pop the button open at his waist, then carefully unzip him, revealing his black boxer briefs, his rock-solid length pushing against the fabric. His new piercings are outlined, too, four little balls that make my aching mouth water.

I pause, waiting for his next instruction.

"Take me out, and suck me like the good little whore I know you can be," he instructs, and my eyes snap up to his, narrowing when I see his arsehole smirk and raised brow.

*Challenge accepted, bellend!*

"Oh, one second, Princess," he says, stalling my movements as his hands reach for his belt, pulling it from the loops of his trousers with a rustle as it passes through the fabric. "Kai."

Turning, I see Kai walking over, his navy sweats back in place, his nipple bars twinkling in the firelight. He takes the belt from Ash, a gleam of excitement in his amber eyes.

"When I tell you, whip her with this. She's been a naughty girl, not waiting for us to finish the meeting, so she needs to be taught a lesson on her knees," he tells him, and Kai's fingers tighten on the leather, a short inhale through flared nostrils showing his approval of my punishment. "Look at me, Princess."

I do as Ash orders, looking up at him as my whole body trembles with anticipation. I'm just as excited as they are for this, juices sliding between my thighs at the thought of what's to come.

"You may begin."

I don't move for a fraction longer, pushing his buttons just slightly, waiting for the telltale sign of his brows dropping before lowering my gaze and reaching for his boxers. A sigh leaves my lips when I pull his silky length out, and I can't help rubbing my thumb over the precum on the tip, delighting in the hissing breath that falls from his own lips.

With a smug smile, I lower down, holding him in my palm as I take his head into my mouth and explore the new metal with the tip of my tongue. His deep groan causes heat to flood my core and wetness to fill my pussy, so I do it again, rolling him around my tongue.

"Kai," Ash breathes seconds before I feel a sharp crack along my lower back, making me gasp aloud. A palm reaches down to soothe the hurt, tingles following the move. "Don't stop, Princess," Ash orders, his fist wrapping around my hair as he pushes me down.

I open wide, letting him fill my already abused mouth, then my throat, gagging when he hits the back.

"That's it. Be a good, dirty slut and take me all the way in like you did with Jax and Kai," Ash rasps out, his other hand coming to the back of my head as he forces my head down further.

I can do nothing but relax, trying to calm my panicking heart as he cuts off my air supply with his dick. He groans, and although he has complete control, literally deciding if I breathe again or not, a heady rush of power fills my limbs at being able to bring this man such pleasure that he forgets himself.

"Kai," he grits out, sounding pained, but I barely register it as another hit lands, this time across the back of my waist. I jerk, unable to cry out, but the pain turns to tingling pleasure when a hand strokes down my back, making me arch.

Just as black spots start to fill my vision, Ash lets me up, and I take a gasping breath of sweet air as his dick no longer fills my airways. My eyes are streaming, spit spilling down my chin as my back smarts, but my pussy pulsates, begging for some contact.

"Please," I croak, looking up at Ash as I let go of his cock. I'm begging him for something, anything.

He reaches down, gently caressing my face.

"You're doing so well, little slut," he croons, and I know that I shouldn't, but I shiver at the term. It's fucking hot as hell to be degraded by his words. "You can have a treat. Up on your knees, legs spread," he commands. "And get back on my dick."

I rush to do as he says, pushing up so that instead of sitting back on my heels, my arse is in the air. I shuffle to spread my knees as far apart as I can get them, thanking the powers that be that the rug beneath them is thick and soft. Lowering my head back down, I take his cock in my hand and mouth once more, lavishing it with my tongue and sucking until his hips buck.

“Kai,” he grunts out, one hand back in my hair, but letting me take the lead. “Whip her pussy.”

I take a sharp inhale through my nose, my heart rate spiking and a mewl sounding in my throat at his words.

*Yes! Fuck yes!*

No sooner does that thought flit through my mind, than I feel the sharp sting of the leather end of Ash’s belt hitting my soaking cunt. I scream around Ash’s dick, the jolt of painful pleasure so intense that I almost come from that one hit.

“Another!” Ash demands, taking over and holding my head whilst he thrusts upwards, fucking my throat.

A deep animalistic cry sounds in my throat as the belt lands on my core again, this time, causing liquid to shoot out of me, coating my inner thighs as I shiver.

“Again!” Ash growls, continuing to thrust harder and faster, so much so that I know I'll be sore in the morning.

I don’t feel it now as Kai whips my dripping pussy again, and again until I’m a quivering mess, only being held up by Ash’s tight grip as his thrusts become disjointed and frantic. Wave upon wave of pleasure rolls through and over me, my nerves tingling almost painfully as my pussy is whipped and my throat fucked.

With a mighty roar, Ash comes, thrusting so hard and deep that I don’t even taste his release. I see stars and fireworks all at once as an orgasm hits me full-on with one final whack from Kai.

Moments later, Ash pulls out, and a soft whine leaves my lips as I slump over Ash’s thighs, chest heaving and body covered in sweat. Kai places a gentle kiss on my shoulder.

“You are perfection, Lilly,” he whispers in my ear before setting the belt down on the arm of the chair.

“Our perfect Princess,” Ash murmurs, stroking my hair with languid movements. “Jax, come take care of our girl.”

Jax picks me up gently as if I am the most precious piece of china, and takes me to the bathroom, where Loki already has the shower running, and Kai walks in, placing a thick, fluffy towel on the heated towel rail. There's a brief argument about whose soap I'm going to use. I don't bother buying any as I love to smell like one of them every day. They settle on Kai's, I think using a game of rock, paper, scissors to decide, and a minute later, I'm in the shower with Jax washing me, coating my body in Kai's fresh woodsy scent.

The shower wakes me up enough to function slightly, but still, the guys get me out and dry me off. Loki has brought down a new silk PJ set, in navy blue with cream lace, and fluffy bed socks—*I get cold feet, don't judge!* They help me to dress, build up the fire, and we're back to snuggling on the plush sofa, Ash on one side and Kai on the other.

I fall asleep to the sounds of Ash's heartbeat lulling me to sleep, the crackle of the roaring fire my lullaby.

# CHAPTER TWENTY-ONE

LILLY

A moan escapes from my lips, my eyelids fluttering lazily open as pleasure unfurls in my core.

"Loki," I breathe, looking down between my parted thighs, and just making out the glint of his auburn hair in the sunlight filtering around the edges of the curtains.

"Shhh," he hushes me, his breath fanning out onto my inner lips, causing a shiver to cascade over me. "You're interrupting my birthday breakfast."

I can feel his smile against my pussy as I groan aloud, grabbing his hair in my fist and bringing his head closer to my dripping centre. Vaguely, I can hear *Birthday Sex* by Jeremih playing in the background, an amused smile drawing my lips up.

He decides that he really is hungry and eats me out with gusto, ruining me with his tongue. His hands pin my hips down as I begin to buck against his face uncontrollably, my moans growing louder and my nails raking his scalp.

"I see Loki's starting to celebrate already," Jax whispers in my ear, his voice all kinds of husky as his hand palms one of my naked breasts, squeezing it and adding a layer of exquisite pain that has me writhing for more. "Care to share, brother?"

"Fine," Loki grumbles, leaving me hanging on the precipice, panting and needy as he pulls away. "On your side, Pretty Girl."

Loki gets to his knees and helps me to turn so my back is to Jax's front, the sound of a condom wrapper being opened behind me, before my leg is pulled over Jax's hip. A long low moan leaves my lips as Jax pushes inside me, stretching my lower lips with a slight burn, but finding no resistance thanks to Loki's ministrations. *I must admit, I'm liking the way he keeps waking me up!*

"Fuck, baby," Jax hisses in my ear, pulling me close by wrapping his hand around my neck from behind. "You take all of me so fucking well."

Then he starts to move, causing fine tremors to wrack through my body at the delicious intrusion. I look up with hooded eyes to see Loki staring at us, his own dick gripped tightly in his fist as he watches Jax's cock disappear inside of me. His eyes flick up and catch mine.

"You up for a birthday sixty-nine, Pretty Girl?" he asks, his wide grin clear in the semi darkness.

"Yes," I murmur, uncaring that my throat is still a little sore from last night and the pounding that Jax and Kai gave it.

Slowly, Loki leans over me, grabbing my lower jaw in his hand, and turning my face so that I'm looking up at the ceiling. The pad of his thumb pulls my lower lip down, encouraging me to open my mouth. Hovering his lips over my now open mouth, I see his jaw working, then a long line of spit leaves his mouth and lands on my tongue. I can taste my own musk, although he won't let me close my mouth, holding it open.

"Don't swallow...yet," he instructs, his voice deep and full of decadent sin. My nipples harden, the pleasure from his naughty action and words adding to that of Jax's huge dick spearing me from behind.

I keep my mouth open, his saliva sitting on my tongue as he gets into position, lying on his side and lining up his hard member with my parted lips. One hand grips the base of him, helping to guide his length in my mouth, the other hand reaches between his legs, grabbing his balls and massaging them as I play with his piercing using my tongue.

"Shit, baby," he groans, pausing as he enjoys the pleasure that I'm clearly giving him. "Best fucking birthday breakfast."

My eyes close as his warm tongue alights on my clit, sparks flying from the connection as Jax keeps up his steady thrusting, the combination of them both making me moan around Loki's length. Loki picks up the pace as Jax does, working so perfectly together as they fuck the living shit out of me.

Suddenly, Jax stills, shudders, then resumes with renewed vigour, pounding into me.

"Dude, what the ever loving fuck?" he groans out, burying his face into my neck and nibbling it, his hand tightening around my throat, not enough to cut off my air supply...yet.

"I didn't want to end up with a black fucking eye from your massive balls," Loki replies, his breath tickling my clit. "Feels good though, huh?" And I can tell he's wearing a shit eating grin.

"Fuck off," Jax grumbles, but he doesn't stop. Whatever Loki is doing to him, fondling Jax's balls by the sound of it, he doesn't seem too bothered by it. In fact, it seems to spur him on, as he starts to fuck me hard, just like I love.

His punishing pace puts me off my rhythm with my birthday blowie, but Loki takes up the slack, fucking my mouth so that all I need to do is open up and give him access.

"Shit, I can feel you in her throat," Jax hisses, his hand tightening as Loki enters my throat, then withdraws. I move my hand from his base, allowing him to thrust his whole length inside.

I can only moan and keen deep in my throat as they fuck both my ends in tandem, somehow finding a matching rhythm. Their thrusts start to grow frantic just as a fire lights in my core, spreading throughout my entire body until I'm blinded by it, screaming around Loki's cock and clamping down around Jax's.

They both give one final, hard thrust, filling me utterly and completely as they find their own climaxes with growls. My whole body turns to jelly as I come down from the highest peak, gasping as Loki pulls out of my mouth, leaving a trail of cum on my tongue.

He flops onto his back, panting, as Jax pulls out from my still pulsing pussy, and falls onto his back too. I let out a raspy breath, my own chest heaving, a film of sweat covering my body.

"Shit, Baby Girl," Jax rumbles, his own breathing laboured.

"Best birthday wake up, ever," Loki chuckles.

---

I bite my ruby-painted lips, looking in the mirror as I finish putting my hair up in an elegant low bun, leaving some tendrils tickling my shoulders. A sigh leaves my lips as my hand lowers, the last pin in place.

We had a wonderful day in our dorm, celebrating Loki's nineteenth birthday exactly as he asked—; watching nineties films on the sofas, eating junk food, and generally hiding away from everyone and everything. I gave him the retro Chili Peppers T-shirt that I'd ordered, which he put on straight away, looking fucking edible in the faded red cotton.

"Loki will be pleased that you dressed to match his eyes," Ash tells me from the doorway, and I look into the mirror to see him leaning against the frame, dressed in black tie. *God, he's gorgeous.*

He's right, I'm wearing a nineteenth-thirties emerald silk dress that is the exact green of Loki's eyes. The top part is fairly loose, skimming over my bust, with thin silk straps that come up over my shoulders, falling all the way to my waist in the back, leaving my entire back exposed. There's a fitted silk waistband that wraps around me, making my waist appear smaller than it actually is. The skirt flows around me like water when I move, the front slightly higher than the back—which touches the ground.

I watch as Ash stalks into the room, a predatory gleam in his eyes, and I'm reminded of the night Loki did the same. The night that I was forced to get engaged to Ash. I frown at the memory.

"You look too beautiful to be frowning, my love," he whispers once he reaches me, his fingers trailing down my spine. My nipples pebble at the touch, a sigh escaping my lips.

"I hate this," I whisper back, meaning it. I hate the forced situation, the fact that it's tainted something that should be so beautiful. I hate that Loki isn't here, on his birthday, because he's having to escort his fiancée—an engagement that he's also been pushed into—also, to the Valentine's Ball.

"I know," he replies, his own brow marred with a frown. He heaves a sigh. "Time to go, Princess."

I turn to face him, looking up into those unfathomable grey orbs.

"For what it's worth," I begin, gazing deeply into the depths of his eyes, my soul trying to touch his. "A part of me loves the fact that I will be your wife."

I watch as his nostrils flare, a roaring fire blazing in his eyes, his hand alighting on my hip and pulling me closer.

"All of me loves the fact that you will be my wife," he responds huskily, his grip tightening. "Loves that I'll have you in a way they won't." And he takes a deep, pained breath, closing his eyes for a moment. I know he feels the same guilt that I do, the guilt that comes from liking this situation, even though it's been forced upon us.

"You ready, Baby Girl?" Jax calls out, striding into the room and breaking the moment.

I heave a sigh of my own, turning to face him and giving him a weak smile. He, like Ash, is wearing black tie and looks devastating.

"Yes," I reply, shaking myself and taking a step forward. Ash's hand falls from my hip as Jax holds his out for me to take.

"I might as well make the most of it," he tells me as we exit the room.

"What?" I ask, my eyebrows dipping as I turn to look at him briefly as we head down the stairs.

"Once we leave this dorm, we can't touch you, or be overly familiar with you," Kai says, waiting for us at the bottom of the stairs.

"Oh, yeah. I'd forgotten since we spend all of our time here," I reply in a quiet voice, biting my lower lip.

We descend into a weighty silence, no one quite knowing what to say.

"Come on, we may as well get this over with," Ash suddenly says, taking my hand and pulling me to the door. "The sooner we get there, the sooner we can come home."

We follow him, as we always do, squaring our shoulders as if going into battle. I suppose, in a small way, we are. We don't know how much our movements are being watched and reported back, clearly some are if Julian's knowledge of my love life is anything to go by.

*Chin up, shoulders back, Lilly.*

Let's show them that we're made of sterner stuff than they think.

---

Like the Halloween party, there are doormen waiting to let us into the ballroom. Unlike the Halloween party, they are dressed in tuxedos with no scary makeup. They open the double wooden doors with a flourish, and I can't help the gasp of breath and my widening eyes.

The room has once again been transformed. Huge bouquets of red roses sit atop white covered tables, red petals strewn across the surface of them, and golden chairs tied with red organza bows seated around them. One wall looks to be entirely covered in red roses, real not fake, and all above the huge buffet table are hanging branches dripping with pink and red flowers and glass globes with flickering candles inside.

"They really do not scrimp on this shit, huh?" I say aloud as we walk down the small set of steps and head towards a table in the front.

"You're only just realising this, Princess?" Ash scoffs, and I scowl at him, earning another chuckle. *Dickbucket!*

He pulls out my chair, pushing it in as I sit down, then calls over one of the waiters waiting staff who's holding a tray of rose champagne. Jax sits down next to me, a huge plate of food in front of him.

"I see your appetite has returned," I tease, a small tilt of his lips causing butterflies to erupt in my stomach.

"Here," Kai says softly, placing a plate in front of me, with a selection of some yummy looking foods.

"Thanks," I say, looking up and catching his gaze. He looks uncomfortable, which isn't unusual for him in these kinds of social situations. I can still see the darkness lurking in the depth of his amber orbs, the tight lines around his eyes giving away the strain that he's currently under. I just wish he was able to share his burden, knowing that it's what he needs. To exorcise his demons. Otherwise, they just fester, eating away at your soul until nothing is left but desperation and the pitch black of loneliness.

A hyena's laugh jerks me from my thoughts, and I clench my jaw when I see Amber the Cuntmuffin leading Loki to the dance floor. I'm staring so intently at them that I don't even know what song is playing, and if looks could kill, she'd be a pile of ashes and fake lashes on the floor.

Loki's whole body is tight when she starts grinding up on him, her skinny arse almost falling out of her dress, it's that short. I'm all for people wearing what they want, freedom of expression and all that, but what she wears is barely more than underwear and just reeks of desperation.

"Princess," Ash warns under his breath, and I take a steadying inhale, trying to relax my tense shoulders.

"Lilly!" I hear Willow call, and turning my head, I see her striding towards me, pulling a guy by his hand.

She looks stunning in a dress the same colour as her eyes, the shape a simple, elegant fitted bodice with a flared skirt that ends just past her knee.

"Hey, Willow. You look beautiful," I tell her, getting up to give her a hug. We've become close over the past few weeks, and it made me realise how much I was missing having a girlfriend.

"So do you!" she exclaims, giving me an appreciative once over as we pull apart. "Oh, this is Ben." She indicates the guy standing behind her.

He's cute, in a kinda All-American way, all thick brown hair and sparkling white teeth.

"Hey," he says, flashing a smile, which dims a little as Ash stands next to me, no doubt scowling. "Ah, h-hi man."

Ash remains silent—fucking rude twatwaffle that he is—until I elbow him in the ribs.

"Hello, Ben," he drawls in that low voice of his, and whilst it makes me shiver, poor Ben visibly swallows. I roll my eyes.

"Don't mind him, Ben. He was hit with the arsehole stick on the way up from Hell," I tell him, watching as his eyes widen, flicker to Ash, then look back at Willow, who's positively shaking with repressed laughter.

"You'll pay for that later, Princess," Ash whispers in my ear, his tone dark.

*Oh, I fucking hope so.*

"Uh, I-I'll go get some drinks," Ben squeaks out, practically tripping in his haste to get away. Willow sighs.

"Did you have to scare him off?" she asks Ash, hands on her hips as she scowls at him.

"If he was any good, he wouldn't have been scared off," Jax says behind us, and Willow gapes at him.

"Hang on a fuck, you speak?" she exclaims, her hand on her chest and her big eyes even wider with her fake sarcasm.

I hear a bark of Jax's laughter, which really does shock Willow if her 'what the fuck' look is anything to go by. I turn, planning on taking my seat again when I catch sight of Amber pawing at Loki like he's a fucking dog toy.

*Oh, I'm gonna cut a bitch.*

"Excuse me," I mumble, and without pausing to think through what I am doing, I march over to the DJ and demand the next song. There must be something crazed in my gaze because he nods, his eyes wide and palms held up in a placating gesture.

I set my sights on Amber, still fawning over a stockstill Loki. He catches my gaze as the opening beats of *The Boy is Mine* by Liv Lovelle come over the speakers, and his eyes go wide as I walk right up to them, invading their personal space.

Amber turns round, presumably to see what Loki is staring at, a smug as fuck grin coming over her lips when she sees me standing there. Unfortunately for her, Liv begins to sing, and I mouth along, holding her increasingly narrow gaze as the lyrics start to sink in. I start to dance, gyrating up against her, touching her with dismissive gestures as I successfully manoeuvre myself so that I'm standing in between her and Loki.

I keep her gaze and keep singing along as I start to grind my arse into Loki, his hands coming up instinctively to my waist, even as he leans down to whisper in my ear.

"What are you doing, Pretty Girl?" It ends on a groan as I move my body so that I'm rubbing up against the bulge in his trousers that is now very prominent. "Fuck, you are going to get us in a shit load of trouble, baby," he rasps, pulling me closer, his hands tightening their grip on me.

Amber's face is as red as the roses that surround us as she notes the move, standing there watching as her fiancé basically dry humps me on the dance floor.

"Get your dirty whore hands off of him!" she screeches, taking a menacing step towards me, fake nails ready to claw my eyes out.

"Touch her, and I'll fucking kill you," Loki growls out, continuing to dance with me, his words and the venom of his tone halting Amber in her tracks.

"B-but, you're mine!" she wails, angry tears filling her eyes. "We're engaged!"

"Oh, honey," I reply, my voice sickly sweet as my hand comes up into Loki's hair, pulling his face down into my neck. He places a kiss there, a small moan leaving my smirking lips as the spot tingles. "He will never be yours."

She stamps her foot—legit stamps it like a three year old—then spins on her shiny Louboutins, storming from the room.

"Are you quite finished fucking my fiancée on the dancefloor?" Ash's voice drawls from the side of us, and I turn my head to take in his affected posture of boredom. I'd believe it, too, if it weren't for the way his grey eyes spit with anger.

*Whoops.*

"Told you, baby," Loki sighs, placing one final kiss on my shoulder before straightening up, but not stepping back.

My eyes narrow, my body flushing hot.

"Fuck Black Knight Corp.," I hiss, loud enough for him to hear but no one else. Both Ash's brows raise at my ire. "And fuck Julian cuntish Vanderbilt."

I spin, slamming my lips on Loki's as my hands tangle in his silky hair. He remains still for a millisecond, clearly in shock, then with a deep, panty melting groan, he kisses me back, pulling me closer with a firm grip on my arse. I vaguely hear gasps from those that surround us, but I've no more fucks to give. Unless, of course, it's with my guys.

Although I long to give into Loki's demanding kiss, I break away, panting and trembling with a heady mix of lust and anger. Turning back, I find Ash still standing there. He looks less angry, a softness to his gaze, even though there's a tightness about his shoulders that tells me he's worried.

Stepping away from Loki, I step into Ash, cupping his face with my palm and bringing him down to my lips. He comes readily, his lips meeting mine in a kiss full of tenderness and understanding. There's definitely another gasp from our audience— *what, are we in some kind of teen movie?*— but like before, it's hardly on my radar as he destroys me with his soul aching kiss. It's sweet and beautiful, like the sun on your face after a long cold winter, and I bask in it.

Reluctantly pulling back, I look past him to see that Kai and Jax have joined us, encircling us in their protection, gazing on with heat in their eyes. I step away from Ash, Jax stepping towards me.

"Fuck Black Knight," he says, his voice fierce, his blue eyes wild and piercing. He grabs me around the waist, pulling me roughly towards him so that I fall into his huge chest.

His lips smash onto mine, his tongue demanding entry like this is a declaration of war. And it is. I will no longer be under Julian's rule. I'll marry Ash because aside from the fact that a part of me really fucking wants to, it makes sense just in case anything does happen to me. I want to make sure that my control over the company goes to them so that they can continue to work towards overthrowing the current regime.

But I will no longer let anyone tell me what I can and can't do. Jax breaks the kiss as abruptly as he started it, proud approval shining in his eyes, and as I turn to face Kai, who has come up behind me, a loud crack lands on my arse, the pain making me gasp alongside the rest of the students who are staring at us with eyes hungry for scandal.

"Lilly, darling," Kai murmurs, holding me captive in his honey gaze as he steps into me, his hands coming up to cup my face tenderly. My own rest on his chest, relishing in the fact that I can feel his thundering heart through the silk of his suit jacket. "You are a Queen, and we are your loyal Knights, ready to go into battle on your behalf, and bathe in the blood of our enemies," he tells me, his eyes boring into mine as he speaks of war like a love declaration.

His full lips lower, pressing onto mine as he holds my face, and my world rocks and tips under his caress. He worships me with his kiss, his tongue tasting like champagne and victory, or a war already won. The rest of the room fades away as we embrace, the music, the decorations, and other students becoming nothing more than a memory as our lips move together.

We part, taking a final breath of each other before separating. I look around at them—my Knights in tarnished armour—and my soul cries with joy at having found our mates. They look fierce, dressed to the nines in their black suits and bow ties, with matching expressions of determination on their breathtakingly handsome faces.

My gaze moves out into the room, seeing many have their phones out, no doubt recording this latest scandal to upload as soon as we leave. I stare into one device, my jaw set and shoulders back.

"The Black Knights are mine," I declare, my war cry carrying out across the suddenly quiet room as one song finishes. "Try to take them away from me at your peril."

My message isn't for the viewers of TikTok, or Instagram, but for Julian Vanderbilt himself. I know that he has eyes everywhere and is watching our every move. I want him to know that he's no longer calling all the shots.

"Let's go," I say to the guys, who continue to surround me as we start to make our way out of the ballroom.

"Lilly!" I hear just as we reach the top of the steps. Willow rushes towards me. "Aside from the fact that that was fucking awesome, even if I'm not sure why it was necessary," she says, and I flush, knowing that there is so much that I can't tell her yet, if ever. "You left your purse at mine yesterday."

I frown, not recalling having even been at hers yesterday, as she hands me a small green silk purse, long and thin. She gives me a look, and like a camera zooming in, it comes back to me. The pregnancy test. Clutching the small bag, feeling the hard edges of the box inside, I throw my arms around her in a tight hug.

"Thank you," I murmur in her ear. She hugs me back just as tight.

"What are BFFs for, huh? Good luck, babe."

My heart pounds as I let her go, turning to resume walking out of the doors which open as we approach. Dread swirls in my stomach, alongside fluttering butterflies, my thoughts swirling like a vortex.

*Did I just fuck up declaring war on Julian? Will he retaliate? What happens next?*

But a single burning question rises above all the others, repeating in my head until it's all that I can think about.

*What if I'm pregnant?*

# CHAPTER TWENTY-TWO

LILLY

"I just need the loo," I say, not even taking off my shoes as I rush into the bathroom.

I can feel their eyes on me as I close the door, but I need to do this alone. I just want to process whatever the result is before telling them. Kicking off my heels, green sequin Irregular Choice, of course, I tear open the purse, finding a digital test inside. Thanking Willow for getting the one that literally tells you if you're pregnant, I open the box, taking the test out of its wrapping.

*Now or never, Lilly.*

I set the test to one side whilst I hitch the silk of my dress up, tucking the hem into the top so it's completely out of the way—*I know! I am the epitome of ladylike behaviour*.

Grabbing the test, I sit on the loo and do as instructed, peeing on the stick then popping the lid back on. I set it to one side, washing my hands and untucking my dress as I wait.

And wait.

And fucking wait.

*Jesus! How long do these things take?!*

My breath catches as finally the screen changes.

**Pregnant.**

Fine tremors wrack my body, and I suddenly feel ice cold. At the same time, a strange surge of blissful elation fills me at the thought of carrying a child. Loki's child. I wonder for a brief second if this is how Mum felt when she found out she was pregnant with me. This bizarre mix of happiness and sheer terror.

*Oh god, Loki.*

I have to tell him. I look up at my shaky reflection in the mirror, noticing my wide eyes and flushed cheeks.

"You can do this, Lilly Darling," I tell myself, my voice much more confident than I feel.

Grabbing hold of the test, I walk to the door, pausing briefly with my hand on the handle for one final deep breath, before opening it.

The guys are all sitting on the sofas, the fire roaring as they swirl various liquids in glasses. They've taken their jackets off, loosened their ties, and Loki, Jax and Kai all have their shirt sleeves rolled up. I smile at the fact that Ash hasn't, although he has undone the first couple of buttons.

"Everything okay, Pretty Girl?" Loki asks, and my gaze snaps to him. Immediately, he gets up, setting his glass down and coming towards me as if he knows. "What's happened?"

I see the others stiffen behind him, straightening up, but my focus is on the auburn haired angel in front of me.

"I'm pregnant," I whisper, holding out the test for him to see.

His brows dip for a second, looking down at the screen which still shows that one word. I watch him intently, seeing the flush rise on his cheeks as his eyes widen. His gaze comes back up to me, and suddenly, I'm so worried about how he'll react.

"Christmas Day," he says, not as a question but as a statement. I nod, my throat tight, waiting.

"What the fuck is going on?" Ash demands, striding towards us.

"Lilly's pregnant," Loki tells him, not looking in his direction, keeping his gaze on me.

Ash stops like he's just been sucker punched. "What?"

I can see the others come up next to him, shocked expressions on their faces, but my gaze catches on Loki's, waiting for his reaction.

"It's not the end of the world, is it, Loki?" I whisper, pleading with him to anchor me, to tell me that it'll all be okay, regardless of how crazy this is.

"No," he answers, and my shoulders sag, my breath whooshing out of me at his answer. "It's really not the end of the world, Pretty Girl."

He cups my face in his palm, his emerald eyes full of such tender emotion that my own fill with tears.

"I couldn't imagine anyone else I'd rather be in this mess with," he tells me, his own eyes wet as he places a soft kiss on my lips. "Me and you are in real trouble now, Pretty Girl."

Then he drops to his knees, his hands framing my middle as he kisses over my flat stomach.

"Hello, little one."

My eyes close, the tears falling freely as I feel a sudden lightness wash over me. Fingers wipe the tears away, and I open my lids, turning my head to the side to see Jax looking at me, his gaze full of fierce protectiveness and love.

"We'll look after you both," he tells me simply, cupping my face and making more tears fall, my throat aching.

"Nothing will happen to you, I swear," Kai vows from my other side, and an uncomfortable shiver runs through me at his promise. I shake the uneasy feeling off, giving him a watery smile.

Loki stands back up, wiping his eyes, and my heart aches with love for him, for them all.

"Fuck, I'm gonna be a dad," he says, running his hand through his hair.

"Yeah, to my wife's child," I hear Ash snap out, and I look past Loki to see Ash standing there, a face like thunder.

Loki's face blanches. "Shit, that's a cluster fuck."

My attention returns to Ash, who's still standing there, looking lost. Stepping away from the others, still clutching the damn test in my fist, I walk towards him in a swish of silk. Dropping the test onto the side table with a clatter, I step right up to him, my hand coming to cup his jaw.

"Hey," I say softly, his blistering gaze landing on me. There's anger there for sure, but also a blinding terror. "I need you, Asher Vanderbilt. *We* need you," I tell him, taking his hand with my spare one and placing it on my stomach. I swear I almost feel something as his palm strokes me, his fingers twitching. "You will all be fathers to our baby."

"What if I'm no good?" he asks, the terror shining brightly in his eyes. "I don't exactly have a good role model to look up to," he huffs out a self-deprecating laugh that cuts me to the quick.

"You will be an awesome dad, Ash, and our child will love you for it," I say, my voice firm with conviction in that truth.

His eyes close for a moment, his head tipping forward until our foreheads are resting together, his hand still resting over my stomach, warming the area under his palm.

"I love you, Lilly," he says, his voice choked with emotion.

"I love you, Ash," I reply, placing a gentle kiss on his lips.

The others come to us, surrounding me in their loving protection as their hands come to my stomach, until there's not a space left untouched where our baby is growing.

---

A week goes by, then two, then three, and yet no word from Julian, or any of the other members of the board. I can't even bring myself to think of them as the guys' families, there's no familial love there, nothing that gives them the right to be known as such. The radio silence leaves a sour taste in all our mouths, distracting us from our schoolwork as we wait on tenterhooks for some kind of backlash.

Meanwhile, Kai works on the plan. The murder plan. I hate how right it feels, to be plotting someone's death and the downfall of several others. But this is one thing that they have earnt, and if that makes me a monster, then so be it. I'll embrace the darkness with open arms if it keeps us all safe and stops the abuse that my guys have gone through, and continue to go through.

The weather warms up, signs of spring in the air, although apparently, it's not officially spring until we get snow on the tulips that fill the Academy planters. Something eases in my heart, my breaths coming a little easier as winter starts to wane. It's silly really, bad things can happen at any time, regardless if the birds are chirping and the sun is shining.

We've decided to keep my pregnancy quiet for the moment, I'm only ten weeks or so along anyway, so it's not as if anything shows yet or will for a while. The sickness still plagues me, and reminds me of stories Mum told me of how morning sickness was a load of bollocks when you feel sick all damn day. How right she was.

Kai spends hours in our kitchen making me things to try and tempt me to eat, and he brings me lemon and ginger tea in the mornings which helps to settle my stomach enough for a plain breakfast of peanut butter on toast. He tells me he's stockpiling recipes for when I feel up for more and has researched the best diet during pregnancy to ensure that the baby and I are getting all that we need.

Jax has me on various vitamins and supplements, having done his own research into what I need. He's also planned an entire exercise regime suitable for pregnancy and has added a massage course which includes pre and post natal massage to his studies.

I've had to stop Loki on more than one occasion from buying up the entirety of the Frugi newborn store, an English company online that he found, which specialises in rainbow designs. He holds me close pretty much every night, hardly letting the others get a look in, telling me all the things that he plans to do for our child, the ways in which he'll care for us.

It's enough to make me cry, which I seem to be doing at random points now. Apparently, that's normal.

Ash is the only one that seems a bit reserved, a bit separate from us. I hate it, but I know that he's coming to terms with the situation, with his worry about what lies ahead, and what will happen when Julian decides to get his revenge.

We don't have to wait much longer for the first hit.

We're lounging on the grass outside, in the formal gardens of the Academy, Willow with us, when Jax's phone buzzes. He answers it, his face going deathly pale as his eyes lock onto mine, like a drowning man.

"What?" he growls, chills running down my spine at the danger in his voice. "When?"

I sit up from lying back on Loki, the others and Willow all looking at Jax with alarm. He ends the call, his hand still like the calm before the storm, as he looks at the now dark screen.

"What's going on, Jax?" Ash asks, casting a quick look at Willow, who flushes.

"I've, um, got some homework to catch up on," she says, getting up and giving me a quick peck on my cheek.

"Thanks, lovely," I whisper in her ear, and she just nods with an understanding smile. This girl really is the shizzle.

Jax watches as she walks off, waiting until she's disappeared into the doors of the Academy before he speaks, his voice low and pained.

"Mom's in the hospital," he tells us, and my heart stills, knowing it's not for something routine. "She was beaten half to death last night, supposedly by intruders, who left her for dead while they stole all the valuables."

"No," I whisper, my hand coming to cover my mouth as tears spring into my eyes, making Jax bob and weave in my watery vision.

"It was Dad, I fucking know it was!" he snarls, suddenly standing up and launching his phone at a nearby planter with a roar, shattering the device, and sending little pieces of plastic and glass flying. He turns to us, his eyes wild, and my soul breaks for him. "He's been beating on her for fucking years, always holding back under Julian's orders."

"What?" I ask, horror coming over me and filling me with its icy touch.

"It would look bad for the company if one of the board was found to be a wife beater," Kai spits out, disgust clear in his tone. A fine tremor begins in my muscles, and I wrap my arms around myself, in a bit to warm up my cold limbs.

Just then, my own phone vibrates in the pocket of my dungarees with an incoming message.

I take it out and gaze at the screen, my breath stilling as I read the words on the screen.

**Unknown: Do not test me again, daughter darling.**

"Oh god," I whisper, dropping my phone like it's just burnt me. I look up into Jax's anguished face, my body temperature rising as nausea swims in my stomach. "I'm so sorry, Jax."

My head drops into my hands as sobs wrack my body. It's all my fault. I was so fucking stupid thinking that I could basically send Julian a middle finger with no repercussions. *Stupid, so fucking stupid.*

"Hey, hey, Baby Girl, look at me," Jax says softly, his big hands cupping my jaw and lifting my head up so that I'm looking into his beautiful blue eyes. "This is not your fault, baby," he assures me, but I'm shaking my head before he's even finished.

"Read the message, Jax! It's all my fault for being a stupid fucking idiot! Your mum is in hospital because of me," I tell him, blinded by my anger and heartache. His eyes harden.

"Don't let him do this to you and fuck with your mind. You're smarter than that."

I want to believe him, so badly, but my stomach churns with guilt at what my reckless actions have caused.

"I'm so sorry, Jax," I whisper, my voice a sad, broken thing, more tears spilling down my cheeks.

"It's not you that owes me an apology, baby," he replies, placing a gentle kiss on my trembling lips. "You didn't order this. You didn't strike the blows."

*I might as well have.*

I don't say it out loud, but if the sigh that escapes from his lips is anything to go by, and the fact that he knows me better than I know myself sometimes, he sees it in my eyes. My self blame.

"We should go and visit," Ash says from behind us, already up and brushing off his suit. "I take it she's in Mount Vernon?"

Jax nods, letting go of my face and standing up. He looks down, holding his hand out to help me to my feet. My mind races with bloody images, the scene of Mum's murder flashing before my eyes, before I blink it away.

Jax refuses to let go of my hand as we walk to the student car park, throwing the keys to his truck at Ash, who deftly catches them, and opens the driver's side. Jax opens the back, ushering me into the middle, then getting in behind me, Loki on my other side. They buckle me in, my hands too shaky to be able to do it for myself.

"Drink this, Baby Girl," Jax orders, passing me some kind of sports drink. I bring it to my lips on autopilot, making a face at the tart fizzy taste. "Small sips, that's it, good girl," he praises as I continue to take small sips as he ordered.

Loki rubs my other hand, which is feeling a little warmer, and I no longer feel quite so dizzy.

"Thanks," I say, looking up to see Ash's furrowed brow and worried gaze as he looks at me in the rearview mirror.

"You went all pale and cold, Pretty Girl," Loki tells me, bringing my hand to his lips and kissing it. I turn to look at him, noticing that his shoulders are tight as he takes a deep breath.

"I think you went into shock, baby," Jax says, my head turning to look at him. He studies me with a professional eye, and I suddenly have the thought that he'd make an awesome doctor. "But your colour is returning, and you don't feel cold and clammy anymore."

"I'm sorry, Jax. I should be taking care of you after..." My voice trails off, unable to finish my sentence.

"Don't do that, don't blame yourself," he grits out through clenched teeth. "This is not your fault."

Fresh tears sting my eyes at his words. I know he's right, I only stood up for myself. I didn't hurt his mum. But guilt still slivers uncomfortably in the pit of my stomach.

"We're here," Kai says from the front passenger seat, and I look out of the front window to see that we're pulling into a circular drive.

The building that sits behind it doesn't look like any kind of hospital that I've seen before, more like an old style Golden Age mansion. It's all white columns and tall windows, with what looks like beautiful grounds and manicured lawns surrounding it.

We halt to a stop at the front entrance, a smartly dressed valet coming to greet us. Ash tosses him the keys once we get out, coming round to stand in front of me, taking my face in his hands.

"You okay, Princess?" he asks, the muscles in his arms strained as he studies me.

"I'm fine, Ash, just a little shaken," I tell him, feeling even warmer when he leans in and places a gentle kiss on my forehead.

"You went so pale," he murmurs into my hairline, pulling me close until his body is flush with mine. "Shit, I was scared, Princess."

And it's then that I realise that this must be bringing up awful memories for him, too, memories of finding a loved one covered in blood but too damn late to help.

He holds me for a moment, surrounding me with his spicy ginger scent, before pulling back but keeping hold of my hand as we head up the few stone stairs that lead to some imposing glass front doors.

"The hospital has valet parking?" I ask incredulously, stepping through the automatic doors that open with a quiet swish.

"Only the best for the Black Knight families," Loki drawls sarcastically on my other side as we walk on the marble floor towards the reception desk.

The inside feels a lot more like a normal hospital, with modern tech and the residue smell of antiseptic. It still has a glass chandelier, though, just to make sure we all know that this is not a place for the peasants. *Conceited fuckers.*

"Jannet Griffiths," Jax announces in a gruff voice to the young receptionist, who looks up slightly startled before she schools her features and puts on an award winning smile.

"Of course, she is expecting you, Mr. Griffiths," she says brightly, totally at odds with the situation. "Room two-oh-three, up the stairs, through the door, and third on the left."

Jax grunts his thanks, then turns, heading in the direction of the stairs.

"Thank you," I offer as I pass, giving her a smile which she returns tenfold. *That's just fucking creepy.*

"You're most welcome, Miss Darling," she replies, and both myself and Ash stop in our tracks, looking at each other with matching looks of concern, creasing our brows.

"Come on, Princess," Ash says, putting aside that fuckery for another time, as he leads me after the others.

We find the room easily, opening the door to see a huge space, filled with bouquets of flowers, which act as pops of colour in the dim lighting. The curtains are drawn, and as I look over to the bed, to the machines that beep, I can see why.

My breath leaves me in a gasp as tears fill my vision. She, Jax's mum, looks so small and helpless on the bed, her face a myriad of purple and blue, one arm in a plaster cast.

"Mom," Jax says, his voice shattered and broken, like a favourite ornament. He crosses strides to her bedside, picking up her hand that's not in a cast as he lowers to a seat next to her bedside.

Her eyelids flutter, her chest rattling with a deep, painful breath as she slowly turns her head to look at him.

"Jax?" she asks, only able to open her swollen eyes a fraction.

"I'm here, Mom," he says, the heartbreak clear on his face. "The guys and Lilly, too."

"Lilly?" she questions, her voice rough, turning her head to try and find me in the gloom.

"Hi, Mrs. Griffiths," I say softly, letting go of Ash and stepping forward, walking towards her bed. I pick up her cup of water, placing a straw in it before bringing it to her lips for her to drink. Jax gives me a grateful look, his eyes shining.

"Thank you, Lilly dear," she croaks, her voice less raspy than it was before. A lump forms in my throat, hating that she's thanking me when it is partly my fault that she's in this position in the first place.

"Was it him?" Jax bursts out, voice hard and cutting. "Was it Dad?"

An anguished look comes over her face then, and she doesn't take her eyes off me as she replies.

"I'm not as strong as your mother was, Lilly. She was always the bravest of us."

My world spirals, my breath whooshing out of my chest as I look into her familiar piercing blue eyes, and see the truth of her words, even if I can't understand them.

"What?" I whisper, but before she can answer, the door bursts open and a nurse strides in.

"Time for more...oh! I'm so sorry. I didn't realise that you had visitors," she fumbles, flushing as we all stare at her.

"Not to worry, my dear," Jannet Griffiths responds, a kind smile tugging her split lip, making her wince. "I could do with some more pain relief."

Jax leaps up, moving to one side so that the nurse can administer the meds. Before I can step away, Jannet grabs my hand, forcing my gaze back on her.

"You have formidable blood in you, Lilly. Don't let them make you forget it," she says, her voice quiet but intense, giving my hand one final squeeze, before letting it go as she closes her eyes.

I look up into Jax's eyes, finding him looking down at his mother as if seeing her anew. He definitely heard her cryptic remarks, and it's clear that he has no idea what she is talking about.

She's just confirmed that she knew my mum, and by the sounds of it, quite well. What did she mean she was strong, the bravest of them all?

Why does it feel like I'm getting more questions than answers, the more time passes?

And the biggest question of all?

*Who was Laura Darling?*

# CHAPTER TWENTY-THREE

JAX

I sit on the chair next to my mom's bedside, listening to the bleep of the machines and watching the rise and fall of her chest as she breathes. I'm all alone, having sent the others back to Highgate with Lilly, who looked dead on her feet.

I'm gonna fucking kill him, that cuntstain of a father of mine. My lip curls, a sour taste in my mouth as I think of him. I know it was him. I can practically make out that shitty signet ring he wears on his right hand in the bruises on her face.

My fists clench as I catalog her injuries once again, knowing that she won't tell me the truth, and she won't report him. I remember the time that I beat the shit out of him, a grim smile pulling my lips up with the memory of his blood coating my hands for once. Looks like he'll need a little reminder of the lesson that I thought he'd learned that day.

"Be careful, baby." I hear her rasping voice say, and I look up into eyes that reflect my own. Only hers are full of concern and worry. "I know that look, Jax. Nothing good will come from revenge."

I take her hand once more, so much smaller than my own.

"He won't get away with this," I vow, righteous fire filling my black soul until it's ablaze. "He will pay."

"Oh, baby," she whispers, shifting with a small moan, which only adds fuel to the fire of my anger. "And what if Lilly gets caught in the crossfire?"

The fire goes out, cold dread sitting like a heavy weight in my stomach.

"What you said to her earlier, about her mom..." I trail off, seeing her gaze turned pained and knowing that I won't get anything else out of her.

"I shouldn't have said it, but she looked so downtrodden, so broken," she replies, swallowing painfully. I reach for her cup, bringing the straw to her lips so that she can drink. "I can't say any more, Jax. I promised..." she starts, getting restless, and her heart monitor picks up slightly.

"Hey, don't worry, Mom. I won't force you, just rest," I assure her, feeling pleased as she relaxes into the pillows again. Suddenly, I have the overwhelming need to tell her about the baby. She's always loved children, and she desperately needs to smile. Plus, I know that I can trust her, she's clearly good at keeping secrets. "Lilly's pregnant."

Her whole body goes still as she looks at me, joy warring with desperate sadness in her eyes.

"Oh, baby. Is it, I mean, are you..." she trails off, looking away and blushing. I can't help the grin that splits my lips in a rare smile.

"Loki," I say, feeling a twinge of...something, at the fact that it's not my child she's carrying.

"I guess, it doesn't really matter," she surprises me by saying, my mouth hanging open. "I know that you'll all be fathers to that baby, and damn fine ones, too." Her eyes shine as my chest goes tight. "You'll take care of them both, my sweet boy."

"I will," I croak out, clearing my throat which feels tight all of a sudden. A part of me may wish that Lilly's baby was biologically mine, but Mom is right. It doesn't matter if we share the same genetics, that baby belongs to the five of us as we belong to each other.

"Julian has other things planned," Mom says into the weighted silence, the room filling with tension at her words. "I don't know what, but I think he's trying to teach you all a lesson for disobeying him. Be on your guard, son."

My stomach rolls, my heartbeat feeling sluggish as I take in what she's telling me. It seems that Julian's ire is not yet sated.

I just hope we're ready for his next move.

---

LILLY

Another week passes with Jax's mum still recovering in hospital. He told us of her warning, about Julian's reign of terror being far from over, and to watch our backs. We remain on high alert, tension surrounding us as we wait for his next move.

Jax visits every day after school, somehow managing to keep up with his studies, too. I would be woefully behind if the guys didn't keep on my arse, making me sit down to study, even though some days, I can barely keep my eyes open.

I'm approaching what I think is my twelfth week, sitting in the library with Willow when she leans over to whisper in my ear.

"Have you had your twelve week scan yet?" she asks, jerking me awake after I almost fall asleep in my calculus book.

"Huh?" I ask on a yawn, rubbing my eyes.

"You know, the scan you get at twelve weeks?" she questions me, brows raised.

"Ummm..." I trail off with a cringe, my hands fiddling with my pencil.

"You have seen a midwife, right?" I bite my lip, and her eyes roll so hard I'm surprised they don't get stuck. "Bloody idiots! The lot of you!" she hisses, packing up her stuff, then standing to do mine. "Come on," she orders, grabbing my hand and pulling me to my feet.

"Hey!" I whisper-yell as she drags me from the library, my Converse squeaking on the floor. My feet are just too achy at the moment for my beloved Irregulars, plus none of the guys will let me wear heels because of the baby- *le sigh*.

She manhandles me all the way to my dorm, holding her palm out when we get there.

"Key," she demands, and I can see a fire in her eyes that lets me know she's pissed. I obey, trying to placate her, which doesn't seem to work as she throws the door open once she's unlocked it, pulling me inside before slamming it shut.

"What the fuck?!" Loki exclaims, jumping up from the sofa, Ash and Kai doing the same.

"What the fuck is right, you prick!" Willow snarls, finally letting go of me. I watch wide eyed as she strides towards him, getting all up in his grill. She looks ridiculous, like a tiny fairy up against a giant, but she doesn't let that stop her, poking her finger in his chest. I wince, knowing how much that hurts from past experience. "I don't know what kind of shit is going on with you guys, but you need to get your heads out of your arses and take Lilly to a fucking midwife! She needs tests and a scan to check that the baby is okay. Plus, regular check ups and shit!"

Loki stands there, jaw clenched as his cheeks flush. He heaves a sigh, bringing his hands up to run through his hair. He turns to look at me, his eyes pained.

"Fuck, Lilly, I had no idea," he says, and I shake my head trying to tell him that neither did I.

"Of course, you bloody didn't! You're an eighteen year old guy for Christ's sake!" Will says, throwing her hands up. She turns to Ash, who stands there with a gleam of respect in his eyes as he looks at her. "Get on it, Vanderbilt," she orders.

One perfect black brow arches, his lips twitching with amusement that she probably doesn't spot otherwise she'd be spitting mad again. He reaches into his suit trousers pocket, pulling out his phone and scrolling until he finds what he's looking for. Holding my gaze, he brings the phone up to his ear.

"Dr. Richards? Yes, it's Asher Vanderbilt here," he says, cool as always, holding my gaze as he speaks. "My fiancée needs to see an obstetrician, do you have someone on your team?" He pauses. "Yes, thank you, we are very excited, but needless to say this is news of the utmost confidentiality." He says the last part in a hard tone, almost threateningly, and I wonder if he has something on this doctor that he doesn't want shared. "Tomorrow at ten, perfect. We shall see Dr. Kent then. Thank you."

Ending the call, he bypasses a smug looking Willow to come up to me, hand cupping my jaw.

"I'm sorry I didn't think of this," he whispers, swallowing thickly. "I'd never willingly put you, or the baby, in danger."

"I know, Ash. You weren't to know what I'd need," I tell him, my own hand palming his cheek, but I can see the regret and determination in the hard steel of his eyes.

"But I should know, and I will give you everything you need and more, my love," he whispers back, brushing a light kiss against my lips that gives me all the shivers.

"I'm coming, too," Loki says firmly, and I look to see he's also stepped up to us. "I want to be there, and I don't give a fuck how it looks." Ash just nods, looking over at Kai, who lifts his chin.

"I assume Jax will want to be there as well," he sighs, but not like he minds all that much. "Kai, email administration will you."

"Right," Willow pipes up, and I must admit I'd kinda forgotten that she was here. *Worst friend ever.* "Now that that's sorted, go run my girl a bubble bath, give her something yummy to eat, then an early night."

I love the way she bosses the guys around, and I love that when it comes to me, they all jump and do as she orders, Loki giving me a quick peck before heading into the bathroom, Kai coming over to do the same before heading to the kitchen.

"I'll see you later, babe," she tells me, nudging Ash out of the way so that she can give me a hug. "Let me know how it goes tomorrow, yeah?"

"Hashtag-obvs," I chuckle, squeezing her back tightly. "Thanks, hun."

"Always, boo," she replies, planting another kiss on my cheek before sweeping out of the door. I am coming to love that girl.

"She's growing on me," Ash declares, taking my hand and leading me to the bathroom. I chuckle, moaning as the smell of my favourite lavender, marjoram, and geranium bubble bath fills the air.

Ash kneels down, undoing my Chucks and helping me to slip my feet out of them. I can hear Loki swirling the water around and know that he'll be getting the perfect temperature for me. Ash starts to undress me, helping me out of my berry red Lucy and Yak dungarees, yellow cotton T-shirt, and lacy bra and french knicker set, until I stand before him naked.

"You are so beautiful, Princess," he murmurs, his hand reaching out to trail across my stomach. I swear it flips at his touch, even though I know that there's no way I'll feel anything until at least twenty weeks.

My breath hitches, thinking he'll continue south, but he just takes my hand in his and leads me to the bath, helping me climb into the huge tub. He helps me to get settled, Loki placing a glass of cold water on the side by my head. They both turn, starting to head out of the door.

*"'O, wilt thou leave me so unsatisfied?'"*

I quote at their backs, and they pause, turning around slowly, a smug grin on Ash's face.

"Did you just quote Shakespeare at me to get you off, Princess?" he asks, amusement clear in his tone, a wide grin pulling up his lush lips. I arch a brow at him, opening my legs in clear invitation.

"Don't have to tell me twice," Loki comments, coming back into the room and walking around the bath, kneeling on the floor. "Want us to take care of all your needs, Pretty Girl?"

"Yes," I reply, my voice breathy with sweet anticipation.

"Yes...what?" he teases, his hand dipping into the water, his fingers grazing my inner thigh and sending shooting stars straight to my core.

"Please," I moan, fingers capturing my jaw and turning my face so that I'm staring into grey eyes instead of emerald.

"Good girl," Ash praises, and my whole body flushes as he dips his head, placing his lips on mine.

His kiss is languid, a slow, torturous teasing of mouth and tongue that soon works me up into a frenzy of need, especially with the combination of Loki's fingers swirling just around my clit but not quite touching it.

"Ash...Loki," I beg, my voice a breathless whine, desperation clawing at my centre. "Please."

"Seeing as you asked so nicely," Loki replies, slamming two fingers inside me, the heel of his hand hitting my clit. My back arches out of the water, my hands grasping the slippery sides of the tub as pleasure explodes across my closed eyelids.

Ash holds my jaw firm in one hand, deepening the kiss, his tongue plunging into my mouth, somehow in time with Loki's fingers. I feel a sharp tug on my exposed nipple, and I cry out into Ash's mouth, but he doesn't release me, swallowing my moans as he destroys me with his mouth.

"That's it, baby," Loki whispers in my ear, voice strained and low as he continues to fuck my pussy with his fingers. "Let us take real good care of you."

My leg lifts, balancing my foot on the side of the tub so Loki can go deeper, hitting that sweet spot over and over again until I'm a writhing mess. Ash's hand slips down from my jaw to the top of my neck, tightening his grip so that I'm struggling to take a full breath as he continues to dominate my mouth.

"Come for us, Pretty Girl," Loki orders, adding a third finger just as Ash pinches my nipple hard.

I scream into Ash's mouth, my pussy clamping down on Loki's fingers as wave upon wave of exquisite pleasure rolls over me, lighting me up from the inside. They don't stop, not until I'm a quivering, twitching mess.

Ash finally releases my mouth with a final gentle kiss, letting go of my nipple at the same time as Loki pulls his fingers out, making me gasp.

"So fucking beautiful, Princess," Ash says, his eyes hooded and making my cunt pulse.

He stands up, his trousers tented in the most mouth watering way. I turn, and Loki does the same, adjusting himself in his grey sweats. He leans down, giving me a peck on my kiss-swollen lips, before straightening up, and walking back around the bath.

I watch, my brows furrowed as they begin to make their way to the open door.

"What about you guys?" I ask, my voice husky, when they start making their way out.

"We're taking care of you, Princess," Ash states, looking at me over his shoulder. "Now, wash up, and come get something to eat. Early night for you tonight."

And with that, they walk out, leaving me very much satisfied.

# CHAPTER TWENTY-FOUR

LILLY

I wake up after a gloriously restful sleep, mostly thanks to Ash who insisted I sleep with him to make sure I actually slept, and didn't, well, you know. I do live with four guys after all.

*Hashtag-firstworldproblems.*

*Or, perhaps it should be reverse harem problems?*

Either way, I feel much better this morning, especially when a certain ginger scented devil wraps his arms around me and pulls me closer, his morning wood digging into my lower back.

"Good morning, Princess," he rumbles out, his voice fifty shades of husky and making Her Vagisty perk up.

"Good morning, love," I reply, arching into him as he nuzzles my neck, sending shivers of delicious electricity skirting over my body. Naked as always when I'm in one of their beds, I actually should just bin all my pjs at this rate.

"You don't know what it does to me when you call me that, Princess," he growls out, his hand flexing on my stomach, before dipping lower, but not quite low enough, as he teases me.

"Ash, love," I say, squirming and trying to get his hand where I need it to be. He growls again at the term of endearment, thrusting his hard length against my back, making me moan. "Stop being such a cunt tease."

He huffs out a laugh against my neck, more tingles travelling over my skin as his warm breath caresses me. He moves his hand a fraction, then another, and just as he is about to reach the gold at the end of the rainbow - *oh yeah, I just referred to my vajayjay as a pot of motherfucking gold* - the door bursts open with a crash.

"Morning, campers!" Loki declares, strolling in with a swagger and a shit-eating grin. "I hate to stop what looks like a really fun time, but it's nine-fifteen and we have to be there at ten."

Ash groans behind me, the sound a match for my own frustration.

"Fine," Ash practically snarls out, pushing up abruptly and letting all the warm air out of our little cocoon of duvet. Comforter. *Whatever.*

"Don't give me that look, Pretty Girl," Loki admonishes me, still smiling like he's thoroughly pleased at being a cockblocker. And cuntblocker. *Bastard.* "Let's go meet our baby!" he shouts, and a flutter of anticipation alights in my stomach at the realisation that I will be meeting our baby for the first time today.

"Fine," I huff, sitting up, less cross than I was when he first stormed in. "I needed a piss anyway."

"Such a lady," Loki jokes, laughing when I give him the middle finger and follow Ash out of the room.

Jax and Kai are already dressed, waiting in the living room for us, so Ash and I get a wriggle on and somehow manage to get ready in fifteen minutes. As we're heading out of the door, Kai hands me a tupperware and a reusable thermos.

"Breakfast," he tells me with a smile, and my mouth waters at the thought of my ginger, lemon and honey tea, and peanut butter on toast. The same breakfast that I've eaten every morning for several weeks now thanks to Kai.

"You are a godsend, Kai Matthews," I tell him, planting a kiss on his cheek as we leave.

The journey to the obstetrician luckily doesn't take long, and soon we're pulling up to a modern looking wood and glass building, nestled in the forest.

*Swallows Birthing Centre* is engraved in elegant cursive on a brass plaque next to the glass door, which opens as we approach. We're met by a smartly dressed man, in his mid-forties with dirty blond hair and a square jaw. He's quite handsome for an older guy, if you're into the whole age gap thing. There's a younger looking woman next to him in light pink scrubs.

"Mr. Vanderbilt," he says in a soft, calming voice, a broad smile on his face, and I'm instantly put at ease by his calming tone. "Welcome. And you must be Miss Darling, our mother-to-be. Congratulations."

"Thanks," I reply quietly, a fissure of excitement running through me at his words. It's nice to have someone congratulate me, only the guys and Willow know that I'm pregnant, although we'll have to announce it at some point. I won't be able to hide it forever. *That's future Lilly's problem.*

"Welcome to Swallows. I am Dr. Arnold, and this is Lisa. She'll be your midwife, alongside myself as your OB," he tells us, the woman next to him giving a smile of her own. "Would you like your guests to sit in today, too?" he asks, looking from me to Ash.

"Yes, please," I reply as Ash gives a nod of assent.

"Excellent. If you'd like to follow me, let's have a quick chat about dates etc., then we can get to the scan so you can meet your baby."

My hand finds Ash's, gripping tightly as we walk after the doctor and midwife. Nervous butterflies flutter around in my stomach, threatening to bring my breakfast back up. We are taken into a large bright room with huge glass windows that look out into the forest.

"It's blacked out glass so no one can see inside," Lisa explains kindly, seeing my slight look of alarm.

"Thank goodness," I whisper, clearing my suddenly dry throat as we sit down. Lisa disappears briefly, opening what looks like a fridge on the other side of the room, then walks back over carrying a chilled bottle of water with her.

"Here," she says, handing it to me with another smile.

"Thank you," I say, tearing up a little at the kindness. *Bloody hormones.*

"Would anyone else like anything?" she asks the guys, who all shake their heads, or tell her they are fine.

"Right, just some information gathering first," Dr. Arnold says, looking down at a tablet in his hands. "When was your last period, may I call you Lilly?" he asks, looking up at me.

"Um, sure," I respond, feeling my cheeks flush at the question. "Well, um, as for my least period, I, uh, am not quite sure. But I only had unprotected sex on Christmas Day..." I trail off, my face burning and palms sweaty. Ash reaches over to grasp my hand, rubbing my knuckles soothingly, and I give him a grateful smile.

"Okay, let's work with that for now, and the scan will be able to confirm how far along you are," he replies. He then proceeds to ask me a whole bunch of questions, about myself and my medical history, then my mother's medical history. "Right, I think that's it." He beams at me. "If you could head over to the bed, and just get undressed enough so we can get to your stomach, we can do the scan."

"Okay," I murmur, more nerves flooding my system, my mouth once again dry.

Lisa pulls a curtain round to give me some privacy, and I take the top part of my yellow bee cord dungarees down, lifting up my T-shirt, then hopping up onto the bed.

"Are you ready, Lilly?" Lisa calls softly from the other side of the curtain.

"Yes," I answer, taking a deep breath to calm my thrashing heartbeat.

She opens the curtain, and Dr. Arnold wheels over a big machine with a screen on it, as well as a keypad and a scanner looking thingy.

"You can come over, too," Lisa tells the guys, clearly not sure who to address.

Ash is immediately at my head, Loki next to him, who takes hold of my hand in his warm one. Mine's a little cold, so he rubs it gently. Kai manages to squeeze in next to him, giving me a soft smile, as Jax stands behind them. Being the tallest, he can see over their heads.

"You ready?" Dr. Arnold asks, and all I can do is nod. He sits down on a stool, grabbing a bottle and squeezing some warm gel on my stomach. I watch as he picks up the scanner, rubbing it into the gel and pushing it down into my soft stomach.

Then I hear it.

The whooph-whooph of a heartbeat.

My gaze snaps up to the screen, seeing the unmistakable outline of a baby, white on a black screen.

*Fuck.*

"Loki," I whisper, gripping his hand tightly as my eyes try to take in every detail, and I am surprised by how much I can see.

"I know, Pretty Girl," he whispers back, his voice choked and cracking slightly. I briefly glance away from the screen to see his glassy eyes watching the screen enraptured.

My gaze flits to Ash, to see a similar expression of wonderment on his face, softening it until I can finally see who he was meant to be, without all the suffering and trauma he's been forced to go through. I next find Jax, looking at the screen with amazement on his face, his usually tight jaw slack even as a fire burns in his eyes. Always our protector. I finally come to rest my gaze on Kai, and he almost breaks me. There's a devastating sadness etched in lines across his face as tears drip down his cheeks. He quickly removes his glasses, swiping under his eyes, and my heart aches for him. Before I can say anything to him, though lord knows what that would be, the doctor speaks.

"All looks good, measurement wise," Dr Arnold states, my head turning back to him. "I'd say you're around the sixteen week mark. Shall we switch to 3D mode?" he asks, and I nod.

A gasp leaves my lips when my baby, *our* baby, suddenly appears on the screen as if it's right in front of us.

"Fuck," Loki breathes, dispelling the tension in the room and making the doctor and midwife chuckle. "Sorry," I hear him apologise, but my gaze is fixated on the screen, watching our baby twitch and turn.

I feel a hand stroke my hair, before lips press a gentle kiss on the top of my head, his ginger scent engulfing me in warm comfort.

"It's our baby, Ash," I whisper, my eyes stinging as I continue to stare at the wriggling baby on screen.

"It's perfect, just like its mother," he murmurs, and a tear escapes my lids, leaving a wet trail down my cheek.

And then it hits me with the force of a mack truck.

*I'm going to be a mother.*

My breath stills as the thought settles its heavy weight in my very bones.

*I am going to be a mother.*

A slight panic begins to flutter at the edge of my vision, the idea of being responsible for another being scaring the absolute shit out of me.

"Hey," Ash whispers, gripping my jaw gently and turning my head away from the screen so that I'm gazing into the depths of his grey eyes. "You will be a wonderful mother, Lilly Darling, soon to be Vanderbilt."

He gazes deeply into my eyes, willing me to believe this truth. And although I'm still mildly terrified - *yep, that's a legit phrase and makes complete sense!* - the weight on my chest lessens until I can breathe deeply again. Then the last part of his pretty speech registers.

"Hang on, I never said I was going to change my name," I hiss out, partly outraged at the assumption, partly preening at the idea of being Mrs. Vanderbilt.

"No wife of mine will be anything less, *Darling*," he informs me with his signature Ash-hole smirk. I narrow my eyes at him, deciding not to start an argument, especially when I'm not actually that objectionable to the idea.

"Well, that's us done here. All is normal and expected," Dr Arnold tells me, using a paper towel to wipe off the gel on my stomach. "Would you like some pictures?"

"Yes!" Loki blurts out, and we all chuckle then, an adorable blush covering his cheeks as Jax claps him on the shoulder whilst grinning.

As we exit the building, pictures of our baby safely tucked in pockets, I take hold of Kai's hand, drawing him back from the others who go ahead towards the parking at the rear where the truck is.

"Are you okay?" I ask him, biting my lip as I take in his red eyes and down-turned features.

"Yeah...No, shit, I don't know, Lilly. Sorry," he says in an exasperated tone, a hand coming to rub the back of his neck. "It was just seeing that baby, your baby. It's so innocent, so pure, and I guess it just reminded me of all that..."

He looks up to me, his gaze pained and full of guilt all at once. My soul aches for him, and I just want to take his pain away, throwing it to the four winds.

"Hey," I say softly, stopping us and cupping his jaw with my palm. It's slightly rough with stubble, and although it makes me worry that he's not his usual meticulous self, I can't help but like the rough look on him. "First off, it's our baby. All of ours, you included. And secondly," I continue, willing him to believe me, "it's okay to feel sad, resentful, and anything else. All your feelings are valid, Kai. This is a crazy situation, and it's bound to be difficult, and dredge up things from the past. Things that you'd rather forget."

A single tear trails down his cheek, and I use my thumb to wipe it away, even as my own eyes fill.

"You need to let this burden out soon, my love," I whisper, watching as he closes his eyes briefly, tipping his head back, my hand still cupping his cheek.

"I know," he whispers back, his voice broken and bone weary. He tips his head forward again, looking at me with desperation in his eyes. “I’m so fucking scared, Lilly. I’ve been keeping it in for so long, and I don’t know how to let it out.”

“Oh, Kai,” I choke out, pulling him to me and wrapping my arms around him in a fierce hug. I want to say something, anything, but no words come. Instead, I just hold him close, trying to show him how much I love him.

I just hope that it is enough.

# CHAPTER TWENTY-FIVE

LILLY

Several days later we're sitting in our dorm, studying on the sofas. Kai is next to me, tapping away at something uber complicated on his tablet, whilst I try to study for our latest Shakespeare assignment. We're looking at *Macbeth* this term, and it's not exactly a play full of rainbows and sunshine. Ash is on his chair, well, sofa, but he always sits on it, usually alone, and Loki is on the floor, flipping through some textbook. Jax is on the other sofa, his notes spread around him as he looks up something in a huge book, which looks like some kind of medical journal.

My phone buzzes beside me, and I pick it up to see a text. My heart stops as I see who the sender is.

**Unknown: Honesty is always the best policy, don't you agree, daughter darling?**

My heart pounds painfully in my chest. Does he know about my pregnancy? That we're trying to hide it from him?

An audio message pops up next, my stomach sinking as my thumb hovers over the play button. Whatever this is, it's not good, not good at all.

My pulse pounds as I hit the play button, my brow furrowing as the distinct sounds of rustling sheets and heavy breathing come over the speakers. I can sense the others still as the sound fills the room, followed by the sound of a young boy crying.

*"If you didn't like it so much, Kai, why are you hard?"*

My wide gaze snaps up to Kai, who's frozen next to me and deathly pale. Before I can say anything, the man's voice, Kai's uncle if I'm not mistaken, sounds again.

*"That feels good, doesn't it?"*

*"N-no."*

A young boy, Kai, sobs.

"Oh my God," I gasp out, my hand covering my mouth as the hideous truth of what I'm hearing registers. Tears sting my eyes, and my hand shakes, but I don't stop the recording, listening to Kai's sobs and laboured breaths, his uncle saying foul things, as he...as he abuses him.

There's a final cry, part pleasure, part pain, before the recording cuts off.

Tears stream down my cheeks as I look up, my whole body trembling.

"Kai?" Ash asks, voice cracking with pain. I turn my gaze to see that he, too, is pale, and looks ready to vomit.

"He stole my first orgasm," I hear Kai say in a voice devoid of all emotion, my head snapping back to him. "I didn't realise that he recorded it, sick bastard."

Then he leaps up, and with a roar like a wounded animal, he launches his tablet at the fireplace. He does the same to the laptop sitting at his side, then the coffee table, lamps, and side tables, until the floor in front of us is littered with debris.

I'm full on shaking now, silent sobs wracking my body as I watch him break, jumping every time he throws something at the wall. The others sit ramrod straight, staring at him with anguish across their faces, their fists clenched, breathing laboured.

Kai stops, like all the life has left him, and chest heaving, he sinks to the floor, unheading of all the shards of glass and pieces of wood that must be cutting into him. I lurch forward, as if to go to him, but Loki stops me, holding me to him as I struggle.

"He's hurting, Loki," I beg, pleading with him to let me go. I still as Kai begins to talk.

"The first time, it was the day that we buried my parents," he begins, looking at his trembling hands. "That night, he came into my room, climbing into bed with me, and–and what I thought was meant to be comfort, turned into something, sick and twisted. I was ten years old." He gives a sharp laugh, and I'm not the only one who flinches at the sound as it cuts into our hearts, leaving us bleeding. "He visited me every night from that night, mostly touching himself, then moving on to touch me. That recording was, I think, the first time I came, his–his hand wrapped around my dick. I was thirteen."

My breath stutters in my chest, horror leaving an acidic taste in my mouth at his words. The boys curse around me, but my eyes are fixed on Kai's bowed head, his limp hands.

"By my fifteenth birthday I was obviously too old for his tastes, probably helped that I'd been training hard, so he could no longer force himself onto me."

He looks up then, straight at me, his eyes those of a broken creature pleading for the pain to stop. My lip trembles, my heart racing as he speaks again.

"But he was right, you know. If I didn't like it, why did I keep getting hard? Why did I come?"

And this time, Loki can't stop me as I tear out of his grasp, uncaring of the pain in my feet as the sharp broken pieces of furniture pierce through my fluffy socks. I drop to my knees in front of him, useless tears coursing down my cheeks as I reach out to touch him, stopping short when I realise that he might not want to be touched.

"Can I touch you, please, my love?" I ask in a shaking voice, thick with sorrow.

"You want to touch me? After hearing that?" he questions, and this time my soul fractures into a thousand tiny pieces, scattering amongst the broken things that lay around us.

"I will always want you, Kai Matthews. Regardless of what some prick paedophile did to you when you were a child." My voice is strong, full of anger at a world that would let this happen. At Julian for obviously knowing about it, but not stopping it. "And as for you wanting it, it was clear as day that you didn't, Kai. That man took what was not freely given, and none of it was your fault, you hear me? None of it."

His lip trembles, tears tracking down his flushed cheeks, his glasses gone. A deep mournful sob falls from his lips, and like a dam breaking, it's followed by another, and another. Throwing my arms around him, I pull his body into mine, his own arms wrapping tightly around my waist as his body shakes with the force of his grief, his head buried in the crook of my neck.

My own vision is blurry as I look up to see Ash on his feet, tears falling down his own cheeks as he gazes at his friend, heartbroken. He comes towards us, wrapping his arms around Kai, who just cries harder. I feel Loki come up behind me, and I look as he kneels, his face wet as he, too, wraps his arms around Kai and me, adding his comfort. I look up as Jax approaches, dropping to his knees in front of us, his jaw working, his eyes brimming with tears. He wraps us all in his huge arms, and we stay that way, holding tightly onto each other, as if we are the only thing stopping the others from floating away.

Eventually, Kai's sobs subside, turning to quiet hiccups, then silence. Lifting his head up, he looks into our faces each in turn, his eyes red and his face tearstained. He looks at Jax last, who takes Kai's face in his huge hands, bringing their foreheads together.

"We will bathe in his blood, brother. You will take what is owed in flesh and blood," he tells Kai fiercely, and the tension leaves Kai's body, a small smile tugging his lips.

Jax's words should chill me. They should fill me with horror and disgust. But they don't. My darkness relishes the idea of hurting the vile monster who stole from one of my soulmates. Who took a child's innocence, and caused such pain and doubt in his heart.

We will all bathe in his blood, paint the walls red with it. And as I look around at the faces of the men I love, body and soul, I see the vow etched there like carving in stone.

Kai's uncle will die.

And we shall be the ones to do it.

---

We all help to clean up the living room, waving off Kai's apologies. Then I run him a bubble bath, getting in with him at his insistence, and letting him hold me as the warmth of the water surrounds us. After we've gotten out, we eat a simple meal of pasta with herby tomato sauce that Loki and Ash prepare, then I head upstairs with Kai, who takes me to his room.

I realise as I walk in, that I don't think I've ever really been in here before. It's tastefully decorated in burnt umbers, reds, and browns, like leaves in autumn. He has pretty much the same furniture as all the others, with the addition of a large dark wooden cupboard.

He gets dressed for bed in a pair of navy silk pyjama bottoms, leaving his chest bare. I put on my own navy silk nightdress, unintentionally matching him. Looking up at him, I'm suddenly unsure as to what happens next. I've never slept in a bed with Kai. Never stayed the night in his arms.

He looks at me, his brow furrowed, then he sighs, pulling back the covers and climbing into bed.

"Stay with me tonight, Lilly?" he says, the end sounding like a question. I heave a sigh of relief, a smile forming on my lips as I climb into bed next to him, surrounded by his refreshing woods-after-the-rain scent as we settle down, facing one another.

"Can I play you a song?" I ask, remembering a song that I heard recently, which is perfect for all I want to say to him in this moment.

"Sure," he replies, reaching for his phone and handing it to me. I've left mine downstairs. I can't bear to look at it right now, not after that message.

I scroll through Spotify until I find what I'm after, connecting the device to the bluetooth speakers in his room, then hitting play.

*Carry You* by Ruelle and Fleurie starts to play as we lie there, gazing into each other's souls. My lips move with the lyrics, Kai's hand cupping my face as tears spring in his eyes. My own smart and burn, and soon the pillow beneath us is damp. I keep mouthing the lyrics, telling him that I am here and that he's not alone.

We stay that way, letting the music flow through us, going some way to heal the cuts and gashes that the past few hours have inflicted on our souls and hearts. The song finishes, and we continue to gaze at each other, Kai's hand on my cheek, mine on his bare chest, feeling his heartbeat underneath my fingertips.

My eyes go wide as there's a sudden flutter in my lower stomach.

"What?" Kai asks, his body going stiff as he sits up slightly. I'm about to reply when I feel it again, like butterflies tickling me. A smile tugs my lips up.

"I can feel our baby, Kai," I whisper, my hand leaving his chest, placing it on my stomach where I can feel the movements. I wait for another flutter, and although I feel it on the inside, my hand remains still. “Only inside, but it’s moving, Kai.”

The smile that lights up his face is so beautiful that angels must weep in the heavens as he practically glows.

“Can I?” he asks, lifting his own hand off my cheek. “I know I won’t feel anything.”

Taking his hand in mine, I place it directly above where the flutters keep happening. As his palm warms the area up, the flutter happens again, three times in quick succession.

“It knows you're here,” I beam, not caring if it's bullshit as the quiver happens once more.

He smiles wide back at me, even though I know he can’t feel a damn thing. We fall asleep like that, facing each other, his warm hand covering the life that’s growing inside of me, smiles on our faces.

# CHAPTER TWENTY-SIX

KAI

For the first time in a long time, longer than I can remember, I sleep soundly, with no night terrors to plague my dreams. Perhaps my sleep these past few months would have been more restful if I'd slept in the same bed as Lilly sooner. But she was haunted by her own night-time demons. I didn't want to add mine as well.

I wake up slowly, beautiful hazel eyes gazing at me, soft with love and acceptance. My heart tightens painfully in my chest, but it's not an unwelcome sensation.

"Good morning, Kai, love," she whispers, a smile teasing those lush lips of hers as she continues to drink me in, as I do her.

"Good morning, darling," I manage to choke out, realising that my hand is still on her stomach, over where her baby grows.

Our baby grows.

*That is going to take some getting used to.*

But a fierce surge of protectiveness floods my body, settling in my soul as we lie there, my hand flexing on her stomach. I will defend this innocent until my last breath if need be.

"How are you feeling?" she asks, a cute as fuck frown line appearing between her brows as she brings her hand up to cup my face in that way of hers. Shivers run over my body at her touch, as they always do.

I pause before answering, really taking stock of how I'm feeling after everything that happened last night.

"Raw," I reply with complete honesty. "But lighter, now that it's out in the open. Like a weight has been lifted." She gives me a smile so bright, I'm surprised I'm not blinded forever more.

"I'm glad you're not having to carry it alone anymore, my love," she whispers, her voice thick and the shine of tears sparkling in her eyes.

"Me too," I murmur in response, closing my eyes and rubbing my face into her hand with a sigh.

"Kai?" she asks, her voice tentative and a little unsure. I open my eyes to see her biting her lip. My morning wood twitches at the sight.

"Yes, darling?" I reply, my temperature rising as a heat enters her gaze.

"Make love to me. Please?"

*Fuck.*

This girl. She's something rare. Something precious. And she's asking me to make love to her as if it would be a chore?

Her cheeks heat in that adorable way of hers, and she opens her mouth as if to say something more, but I don't let her. I pounce, loving the small shriek that leaves her lips as I land on top of her, sliding my achingly hard length inside her, the noise she makes turning into a husky moan. There's no resistance, she's already lubricated. It's something I've noticed about her recently, and apparently is quite common in pregnancy. Her legs come up, wrapping around me on instinct.

"Shit..." I rasp out. "You feel incredible without a condom." And she does, her wet heat surrounding me and warming me to my very soul.

"Kai," she moans, her fingers tangling in my hair as she pulls our mouths together. She kisses me like I'm the air that she breathes, and I do the same, trying to inhale everything about her as I begin to move my hips in a slow, teasing rhythm.

My hands take hold of hers, bringing them up above her and pinning them there, our fingers intertwined as I do as she asked me. Make love to her. Normally, I'd want to, crave to, give her some pain, in order to find my own release. But something about this morning is different. I don't need it. Oh, I still undoubtedly will punish her in all kinds of delicious ways, hearing her cries of pain as I'm buried deep inside her.

But today, I just want her cries of pleasure, which she gives me with abandon as I rock my pelvis, stroking her inner walls, and sending lightning bolts across my skin at the same time.

"I love you so, so much, Lilly Darling," I growl in her ear, hitting that sweet spot just inside her, if her pussy flutters are anything to go by. "You make me a better man. You complete me, make me whole, and I'm." Thrust. "Never." Thrust. "Letting." Thrust. "You." Thrust. "Go."

Her cries grow louder, until her nails dig into the backs of my hands where I'm still holding her down, and her cunt ripples around my dick. I can feel the heat pooling in my own core, racing up my spine as I head towards the pinnacle of my release.

"Kai, oh shit, Kai!" she yells, and warm liquid coats me as she comes, her pussy clamping down hard until I'm fighting for every thrust, grunting with the effort to push through.

My movements become frenzied, our hips snapping together with loud, wet sounds as I move faster, impaling her over and over again. With an almost agonised roar, I climax, shooting my seed deep inside her with one final, hard thrust. Stars flash behind my closed eyes, my breaths panting and my whole body alight as I bask in the glow of her. Of us.

Releasing her hands, my own run through her hair as I hold her close to me and find her soft lips with my own. I kiss her deeply, our bodies joined in the most primal way.

A knock sounds on the door.

"Time to get up. I can't hold Loki back for much longer," Ash tells us, his amused voice clear through the partly opened door. "And you'll be late for class."

I smile against her lips.

"What?" she asks, her own lips curving in a smile as I pull back slightly, but not out of her. Not yet.

"It's about time Loki had to listen to someone else fuck you, while he stands there with a raging boner," I chuckle, and she laughs, her pussy clenching around me, turning my laugh into a groan. "Don't laugh, darling. Otherwise we will never leave this bed."

"Sorry," she murmurs softly, a wicked gleam in her eyes.

"No, you're not."

"Not even a little bit," she replies, trying and failing not to laugh again.

*Naughty minx.*

I give her a smirk, her own eyes widening as she feels me growing inside her, my hips thrusting slowly once more.

We are definitely late for class.

---

LILLY

I'm bone-weary as I walk with Kai and Loki back to our dorm at the end of the day. I crack what must be my hundredth yawn, both guys chuckling.

"Come on, Pretty Girl," Loki says, pulling me closer and wrapping his arm around my shoulders. "Let's get you back, and I'll run you a bubble bath, while Kai makes you some ramen."

My stomach growls, much to both boys' amusement, as Kai unlocks our door, only to come to a standstill just inside.

"Dude!" Loki hisses, pulling us to a stop just shy of bumping into Kai's back. "What the fuck?"

Kai steps aside, and my blood runs cold, then boiling hot at the beaming face of Julian Cuntish Vanderbilt, standing with Ash and Jax by our dining table.

"Ah, is that Lilly I see with you boys?" Julian enquires, just like the perfect father-in-law. His eyelid twitches as he takes note of Loki's arm slug around my shoulder, but his smile doesn't falter. "Come give your papa-to-be a hug." He spreads his arms out wide, a challenge on his face as he looks at me.

Adrenaline rushes through me, chasing away any tiredness as I step out from Loki's embrace, and walk towards him. After what he did to Jax's mum and the audio message, I can't afford to antagonise the man. But I hate him with every fibre of my being. He quickly wraps his arms around me, pulling me inappropriately close when I step up to him. I hear him take a deep inhale *- did he just fucking sniff me? Gross!*

I catch Ash's gaze, which is full of suppressed rage, his cheeks flushed, as Julian whispers into my ear, holding onto me for far too long.

"You didn't heed my warning, darling. About staying away from the other boys. And now you must all learn your lesson, naughty children." He chuckles, like he is a doting father and just doing his job.

Finally, he lets go, taking a step back, but still with that fucking Cheshire cat grin on his face. *God, I want to smack it off.* I feel sick, a mixture of adrenaline, nerves, and revulsion churning my stomach until my hands shake. Ash steps up next to me, his hand coming around my waist and pulling me into his warm body. I heave a sigh as I snuggle into him, giving no fucks what Julian thinks. Ash plants a kiss on my hair, near my ear.

"You okay, Princess?" he asks, his deep voice laced with concern. I nod.

"Yeah," I whisper, turning my head so that I'm no longer staring into the eyes of *that* man. My blood boils again at the thought of what he's done over the past week or so. Just as my tight muscles relax into Ash, Julian speaks again, obliterating any calm I possessed.

"I hear congratulations are in order, son?"

Both Ash and I snap our heads up, going utterly still as we stare at Julian. I smell vanilla and Kai's wooded scent as I feel their warmth at my back, seeing Jax come up to Ash's other side.

"How far along are you, Lilly, *Darling*?" I shudder at the way he says my last name, like I belong to him.

"Sixteen weeks," Ash replies, my tongue unable to move as panic flutters at the edges of my vision. I feel a hand brush my back, my own coming up to my stomach, in an instinctive act of protection.

"Wonderful!" Julian calls. His smile grows wider, sending shivers over my skin, the hairs at my nape standing on end. It gets a hard edge to it, cutting like a knife. "Although, I do hope that it is yours, boy. I won't tolerate a bastard in the family."

My breath stutters in my chest, my stomach dropping at his words.

"It is," Ash says, standing a little taller, straighter. I look at him to see that he has transformed into the Ice Knight, something he does whenever Julian is around.

"Well, we can always get a paternity test when the baby is born, so not to worry," Julian informs us, like it's a foregone conclusion. Ash's hand tightens on my waist, reassuring me enough that I can take a deep inhale.

A knock sounds at the door, my brows dropping.

"Ah, that'll be Erica. Let her in, Loki," Julian says in a cheery voice.

Loki does as he's bid, and I turn to see a young woman with short buzzed hair walk in, pulling a small suitcase along behind her.

"Mr. Vanderbilt," she greets Julian, a small forced smile on her face. It's almost like she doesn't like him. *Interesting.*

"Erica. So pleased that you could make it on such short notice," Julian replies, stepping around us to air kiss her cheek. She shivers, but he doesn't seem to notice. Then he turns to me. "Erica will be your wedding planner, my dear."

My eyes go wide.

"My...wedding planner?" I question, my hands dropping from my stomach and finding Ash's hand waiting, our fingers intertwining.

"Of course." Julian is back to beaming again. "With your wonderful news, we'll need to speed things up so that you're married to Asher before you start to show fully." He chuckles again like the doting father that he is not. "And with your uncle not giving his permission for your nuptials to go ahead, I think May twenty-first would be a good date. Don't you?"

"But that's..." I trail off.

"Your birthday, yes. What a lovely way to spend the day," he says, his gaze open and oh so sincere. "It doesn't give us a great deal of time for planning, just over eight weeks, and to send invites, etcetera, but I'm sure with Erica's help, we'll manage."

I stare at him, unmoving and in shock. Ash's grip tightens, his fingers rubbing over my knuckles in a soothing gesture.

I'm getting married on my nineteenth birthday. *Shit.*

"Well, I shall leave you to it. Whatever she wants, Erica. No expense spared," he says, pausing beside me to drop a kiss on my cheek. His lips linger for a fraction of a second too long, his fingertips brushing my stomach. "Just think, you could have made me a father again instead of a grandpa," he whispers in my ear, so quietly that I know the guys don't hear.

Bile rises in my throat as he steps away, tears springing into my eyes as I stare straight ahead. I don't move as he leaves, my grip tight on Ash's hand. The door shuts with a loud bang, breaking me from the trance that Julian left me in.

"Excuse me," I rush out, bolting to the bathroom and slamming the door behind me as I throw myself down on my knees, just managing to get my head over the toilet bowl in time, as vomit spills from my lips.

Gentle hands hold my hair back as I retch and cough, a cool cloth placed on my forehead and a glass of water pressed into my hand when I sit back on my heels, my eyes closed.

"What did he say to you, Princess?" Ash asks, stroking my hair back from my sweaty face.

I look into his face, his grey eyes swirling with concern. It takes me a couple of tries before the words will come.

"That he could have been the f-father of my baby, instead of its grandpa," I tell him in a trembling voice, tears spilling from my eyes.

A curse sounds from my left, and I turn my head in time to see Loki punch the mirror, shattering it, shards of glass flying across the room.

"That fucking perverted cunt!" Loki roars, his chest heaving. I leap up, feeling a wave of dizziness that I ignore as I rush towards him, my shoes crunching over the glass.

"Hey, it's okay, my love," I tell him softly, taking his now bleeding hand in mine and tutting.

"None of this is fucking okay, Pretty Girl," he whispers back, placing his forehead against my own. "None of it."

"It will be soon, brother," Ash says, his tone serious as he walks towards us, placing a hand on Loki's shoulder. "They will hurt for what they have done to us, and we'll be the ones watching them bleed. Before the baby is born."

The boys exchange an intense look, Loki nodding as they seal the vow between them.

My eyes drift down to Loki's bleeding hand, watching the blood drip onto the shards of glass at our feet, and a shiver runs through me. There will be more bloodshed before this is over.

I just wonder how much of it will be ours.

# CHAPTER TWENTY-SEVEN

LILLY

The meeting with Erica wasn't that bad. In fact, it was actually kind of fun, once I got into the swing of it. After all, what girl doesn't dream of planning her wedding to one of the loves of her life?

Ash basically lets me decide everything, not batting an eyelid when I say that I'd like it outside, with the mountains as our backdrop and a party in the woods afterwards. And he just smirked when Erica asked about what colour theme we'd like, telling her that it would be rainbow themed before I'd even opened my mouth.

*Could I love him any more?*

We managed to get most of the details down, from the flowers, to the food and music, and she left, telling me that she'd made an appointment with the wedding dress shop in town for me this Saturday.

Two days' time.

My head spins with how fast things are moving, how much my life is changing in such a short space of time.

Friday morning rolls around, and as we leave the dorm, there's something in the air. I can't pinpoint it exactly. It's a feeling of foreboding that sticks to me like tar, leaving my heart rate up and my palms sweaty as we walk down the central stairs and into the main hall.

I see Willow rush up to us, her bush baby eyes wider than usual and her face tight. Her gaze briefly flicks to Loki at my side, before coming back to me, sympathy in her eyes.

"Have you seen?" she asks, holding her Academy iPad to her chest.

"Seen what, Willow?" I ask, my throat thick as her mouth turns down. My heart beats painfully in my chest.

"I'm so sorry, Loki," she replies, my brows dropping as she holds out the iPad and starts playing a video.

It takes a moment for my eyes to make sense of what is on the screen, but when they do, they must go as wide as Willow's.

"Is that...*Clarissa?*" I whisper, horrified as I watch a young, naked Loki, underneath an equally naked Clarissa, who's writhing on top of him. The sounds she's making are those of a cheap pornstar, and bile fills my throat when I realise just how young Loki looks. Maybe he's thirteen at the most. *What is wrong with these fucking people?*

I tear my gaze away to look up at him. His jaw is clenched so tightly, I can hear his teeth grinding together, his cheeks mottled, his whole body tight. I reach out to touch his rock solid arm, but he flinches away at the contact, like it burns him. My eyes sting at the rejection, even though I know he doesn't mean it.

"How many are there?" he asks through gritted teeth, not taking his eyes off that damn video.

"Um, I dunno," Willow answers, cringing slightly. "Maybe twenty or so. But I've not watched them."

My heart sinks.

"Loki..." I start, reaching out again, but he takes a step back.

"Just...leave me alone, Lilly," he replies, his hands shaking. "Leave me the fuck alone." Then he turns and storms back towards our dorm, his body tight and practically vibrating with rage.

Tears spring to my eyes as I watch him go, and I rub my chest with the pain suddenly there.

"Fucking Julian! This has his stench all over it," Ash snarls, watching Loki disappear. "Kai, can you take this shit down?"

"On it," Kai replies, his own iPad already out as he furiously taps at the screen.

"Good," Ash says, turning to look at me. "Go to him, Princess. And you, Kai. He needs you both." He strokes the side of my face, brushing away a stray tear that falls.

"When will it stop, Ash? Why would Julian share this?" I ask, begging him for answers that he probably doesn't have.

"To hurt us, discredit us. Show us that we are nothing compared to him and the board. Take your pick, Princess," he tells me, pulling me into him and surrounding me with his warmth. Kissing me on the top of my head, he lets go, encouraging Kai and I to go back to the dorm. "I'll explain to your teachers, don't worry."

I flash Willow a grateful smile, getting a sympathetic one back. I really must organise some time with her soon. Talk about the world's worst friend.

We hurry to the dorm, Kai finishing his task just as we open the door to devastation. I gaze with bated breath at the mess that lies in front of us. The new things that we'd just bought, replacing the stuff that Kai had broken, are all lying in pieces on the floor. Feathers float around us from the torn sofa cushions, as *Bad Child* by the Tones and I fills the air with its melancholy beats. My heart breaks for this beautiful boy, who only ever wanted love and affection, but instead was given neglect and abuse.

I hear a whimper, and my gaze snaps around to see Loki, sitting on the bottom step of the spiral staircase, his head in his hands. I approach slowly, cautiously, as you would a wounded animal, Kai behind me.

"Loki, my love?" I say softly, my soul hurting as he slowly brings his head up to look at me. His eyes are red, tears glittering on his auburn lashes, the emerald jewels dull and shattered.

"I was fucking thirteen when she came into my room, sent by my asshole father to 'turn me into a man'," he tells me woodenly, not breaking my gaze. My heart feels like it's a lead weight in my chest, falling to the pit of my stomach as he tells me his awful story.

"Oh, Loki," I breathe, unbidden tears falling from my eyes.

"I was young, stupid, and excited by the free pussy. The first time I was shit, it lasted less than three minutes." He gives a hard laugh that cuts me badly. "But she kept coming back, fucking me, letting me fuck her. Teaching me all about a woman's body."

He runs his hands through his hair, and my soul aches for him. He was so young, and yes, he may have enjoyed it physically, but she was still a predator. And his father...I knew something was wrong with that cunttrollop.

"She became possessive. Wouldn't let me see other girls. Driving any away that I brought home. It took me two years to get out from under her thumb. I'd bulked up a bit by then from our training, so I used that to scare her into leaving me alone. It's not something I'm proud of."

I rush to him as he hangs his head. Dropping to my knees in front of him, ignoring the sharp pain, and taking his face in my hands.

"Loki, she deserved everything she got. She was a predator, regardless if your father was the one to start it." I force him to look at me, to see that I'm not disgusted. That I don't love him any less for his past.

"We told you at the time, dude," Kai says, crouching down next to me, placing a hand on Loki's knee. "She's a grade A cunt."

Loki huffs out a laugh, looking from me to Kai.

"Yeah. I just...feel dirty, you know?" he confesses, his voice cracking as moisture fills his eyes. My heart shatters for him. He turns to Kai. "Kai, please."

My brow furrows in confusion as I turn to look at Kai, who's gone stiff.

"You don't need to be punished, Loki. You've done nothing wrong," he tells the other boy gently, his hand tightening on Loki's knee.

"I-I know...I just need..." Loki stutters, and I jump in, unable to bear the broken look in his eyes.

"What do you need, my love?" I ask gently, his gaze coming back to me.

"Pain."

My heart stutters as his emerald eyes bore into me, digging deep, pleading. I lick my bottom lip.

"Please, sir," I say, keeping hold of Loki's gaze, which widens slightly. Kai takes in a sharp inhale, and I know that his nostrils are flared, a raging heat in his eyes, even though I can't see him.

Suddenly, Loki's gaze is ripped away from mine, a fist in his hair, pulling hard enough that he winces as Kai jerks his head to the side.

"You do exactly as I say, understood?" Kai's voice is hard, his arm corded as he holds Loki's head in place.

"Yes, sir," Loki breathes, and my pussy flutters, a shiver cascading over me at his assent. I know some might say it's fucked up, but sex heals us, we heal each other with our touches. Both pleasant and painful.

"Safeword?" Kai asks, not letting go, his eyes roving Loki's face with a banked heat in the amber depths.

"Eggplant," Loki responds, not missing a beat, and a slight smirk tilts his lips upwards. My own lift in response. *Trust Loki.*

Kai's lips twitch, too, before he lowers them to hover just over Loki's, making my breath hitch. Loki's Adam's apple bobs, and he swallows hard, his head still pulled back and held captive by Kai.

"Good," Kai whispers, slamming his lips onto Loki's in a fierce kiss that sends shockwaves to my centre.

They kiss each other hard, Kai clearly dominating as he forces his tongue in Loki's mouth. My core floods with heat, my thighs trying to rub together as I watch them, lips locked and eyes closed. A low growl sounds in Kai's throat, a groan in Loki's, as Kai nips Loki's bottom lip, hard enough that a bead of blood drips down Loki's chin as Kai pulls away.

"You sure?" Kai asks, voice husky, chest heaving. "I'm not holding back anymore, Loki."

"Fuck, yes," Loki whispers, taking hold of Kai's hand, the one not still tangled in his hair, and bringing it to his bulging jeans. "I'm sure."

Kai's breath stutters as his hand makes contact, sliding his palm over Loki's clearly hard length. *Fuck me, it's gotten hot in here.* Loki groans, thrusting his hips into Kai's palm, who smiles and tuts. Kai turns to me, still gripping Loki's hair.

"And you, Lilly? Are you all in?" he asks, a slight look of uncertainty entering both boys' eyes.

"Fuck, yes!" I gasp out, my voice all kinds of husky and breathy after that show. "I'm all about the MM."

Kai looks adorably confused, until Loki whispers something about 'fucking romance tropes'. Shaking his head, Kai finally releases Loki's hair, stroking the side of his face in a tender gesture that has my heart melting. He takes a deep breath, closing his eyes, and when he opens them a moment later, Kai the Dom is back.

"Upstairs, my room, naked," he orders, standing up. "Now."

Loki and I get to our feet, rushing up the stairs and into Kai's room, panting with huge smiles on our faces. Loki grabs me, pulling me in for a blistering kiss as we strip each other in record time. He releases me with a wink, just as Kai walks in, shirtless, wearing only his navy chinos and glasses, his feet bare. We turn to face him.

"Good, pets," he praises, and I notice Loki's dick bobs as my nipples harden at the nickname.

Kai leaves us standing facing him as he walks over to the window, pulling the drapes closed, ensconcing us in darkness. A lamp flickers on, casting its warm glow over the room. Finally, music sounds, *Renegade (Slowed + Reverb)* by Aaryn Shah playing softly in the background, the sensual beat and lyrics thrumming through me.

Kai comes back into view, walking over to the large cupboard and opening it using a small key. After rummaging inside, he turns around, a pair of black padded leather cuffs slung around his neck by a gold chain, and holding a vibrating butt plug in one hand and a black play wand in the other. I can't suppress the smile that draws the corners of my lips up. Kai sees, turning a positively feral grin on me, which makes my smile falter.

"I got you a new toy," he says, voice low and suggestive, caressing my body with his words. "You can use it as you watch us," he tells me, stalking over to me and pressing the buttons, a low buzzing sound filling the room.

He places it against my clit, and I cry out, my knees threatening to buckle as waves of the most intense pleasure I've ever felt hit me with the force of a tsunami. A dark chuckle leaves him as he abruptly takes it away.

"But you aren't allowed to come until I tell you to."

A gasp leaves my lips, my eyes going wide as I look into his merciless face. He arches an eyebrow.

"Y-yes, sir," I reply in a murmur, heart pounding.

"Isn't she such a good girl, Loki?" Kai asks, stroking my face, then handing me the still vibrating wand.

"Yes," Loki replies, and I look at him to see his eyes ablaze with emerald fire.

"Yes, what, Pet?" Kai asks, his tone hard, and my head whips back to him.

"Yes, sir," Loki rasps out, and fuck me, if I don't drip a little at that.

"On the bed, darling," Kai orders, and I immediately obey, my heart pounding as I settle myself against his pillows. "The wand, use it on your clit."

A small whimper leaves my lips as I bring it in between my legs, the vibrations immediately setting all my nerves alight. *Fuck.*

"Face Lilly, Pet. Hands on the bed," Kai's low, slightly strained voice sounds behind Loki. Loki does as ordered, and I bite my lip at the drop of precum that glints on his tip, making his piercing glisten.

Loki swallows hard at the sight of me, spread eagled and pleasuring myself.

"Shit," he whispers, earning a sharp smack on his arse from Kai. Loki hisses, but not just in pain.

"I didn't say you could speak. Do not talk unless spoken to directly," Kai admonishes.

He takes something out of his pocket, and I hear the opening of a cap, followed by the squirt of liquid. Loki goes to turn round, but Kai forces him down further with a hand between his shoulder blades, pressing him into the bed as he seems to push something into Loki.

A deep, slightly pained groan leaves Loki's plush lips, his eyes closing in ecstasy.

"Do you feel the vibrations, Pet?" Kai asks in a husky voice, stroking Loki's arse with his palm.

"Yes, sir," Loki moans out, moving his hips against the bed, clearly seeking some relief. Another crack lands on his other arse cheek, making him groan again.

"Same rule applies to you, Pet. No coming until I say," Kai commands.

I taste copper as I bite my lip again, trying to ignore the climax that wants to tear through me. I hear Kai's dark chuckle, and look up to see his heated gaze on me.

"Do you like your new toy, darling," he asks me with a smug smirk.

"Y-yes, sir," I reply in a strained voice. "Thank you, sir."

His hands clench into fists, clearly liking the gratitude.

"Good. Stand up, Pet," he orders Loki, who obeys with a groan.

His dick is so hard it looks almost painful, and he has to use his arms to help him up. Kai strokes his palm down Loki's arm, making him shiver. When he reaches his wrist, he takes one cuff, buckling it on, then unclasping the chain that secures it to the other. Reaching up to the top corner of his four poster bed, Kai unhooks another chain, fixing it onto Loki's cuff so that Loki's arm is pulled up tight. Kai repeats this process with the other wrist, until Loki is standing with his arms spread wide above his head, his muscles corded. Although I can't see, it looks like he is on his tiptoes.

"Did I say you could stop?" Kai's sharp voice asks, my hand immediately resuming its tortuous task with the wand, electric ripples running through me.

"Sorry, sir," I mumble, shivering as the exquisite pleasure begins again.

I watch as Kai walks back over to the cupboard, taking something from the back. I gasp when he turns round and I see he's holding a beautiful wood handled leather flogger. The handle is carved and made from a stunning honey- coloured wood. Each leather strand that hangs from it is braided, with a small tab of leather on the end.

The song changes to *Sacrifice*, Black Atlass & Jessie Reyez, the beat pulsing through me, adding to the vibrations of the wand, and I groan, panting in order to hold off the pleasure.

Kai smiles at me, a grin full of promise, as he stalks towards Loki. Shadows play across his face as he walks, flickers of the demon inside of him coming to the surface. My gaze flicks to Loki, and my breath hitches as he watches me with hungry eyes.

Kai steps up behind him, taking the flogger and trailing it over Loki's back, then up over his shoulder, and across his chest. I watch enraptured as Loki's eyes flutter closed, a moan falling from his plump lips.

"Do you know what this is, darling?" Kai asks me, his honey gaze suddenly on mine.

"A flogger," I whisper, a small moan sounding in my throat as I hit a particularly sweet spot, my legs trembling.

"Close, it's a cat-o-nine tails. A leather one, and one of Loki's favourites, isn't it, Pet?" *God, I love it when he calls him that.*

"Yes, sir," Loki moans, opening lust filled eyes as he looks at me. I'm so fucking close I can feel the temptation to fall into bliss, my nerves on fire as the wand works its magic.

"Move closer to him, darling," Kai orders, watching as I scoot down the bed so that my toes brush Loki's thighs. "Good girl. I'm going to hit you five times with this, Pet," he tells Loki, caressing his back once more with the cat-o-nine tails. "Then, I'm going to wrap my hand around that hard, aching dick of yours, and jerk you off until I order you to come all over Lilly." Both Loki and I groan at that visual. "Count with me, darling."

Kai takes a step back, and I watch with wide eyes as he lifts his arm up, then brings it sharply down with a flick of his wrist. Loki's body jerks, a low moan escaping his lips when the strikes hit. My breathing speeds up, my pussy pulsing as I work the wand against me.

"One," Kai says.

"One," I breathe, locking eyes with Loki when he opens them and stares at me. There's pain in there, but also relief, pleasure, and lust all rolled into one intense gaze, that's hyper focused on me. His body jerks again, the sound of leather hitting flesh cutting through the air.

"Two."

"Two," I repeat, my voice barely above a pleasure-pained whisper. Lightning shoots across me, originating in my clit. I don't know how much longer I can last without disobeying Kai. Loki's body moves again, sagging a little in his restraints, before jerking again.

"Three."

"Three," I moan, Loki's heated gaze turning me on like nothing else. Another full body twitch as a hit lands.

"Four." Kai's voice is strained now, but I can't look away from Loki to see whether it's due to exertion, or passion.

"Four," I murmur, swirling that damn wand around my clit to try and give myself a breather.

"Back on your clit, darling," Kai commands, and tears sting my eyes as I comply.

It feels so damn good, it's just too much. Loki's whole body swings with Kai's next strike, the chains creaking with the force of it. Loki throws his head back, anguished rapture on his face as more precum leaks from his cock.

"Five," Kai pants, the thunk of the cat-o-nine tails hitting the floor sounding in my chest.

"Five," I repeat, gasping as Kai undoes his chinos, pulling them and his pants down to let his hard dick spring free.

Stepping out of them, he steps up right behind Loki, whose moans echo mine as Kai's hand glides down his sweat slicked chest and abs, wrapping around his hard member in a tight grip. Loki's hips jerk, his head falling back onto Kai's shoulder, and fuck me if that sight isn't burned onto my retinas for all time, my pussy clenching as I watch them.

"Did you like that, Pet?" Kai rasps out, licking the shell of Loki's ear.

"Yes, fuck, yes, sir," Loki breathes, hissing when Kai pumps his hand up and then back down.

"Such a dirty mouth, Pet," Kai chides, moving his hand in a slow and steady rhythm up and down Loki's cock. "Next time I will have to fill it with my cock to keep those naughty words in." Loki and I groan at the same time, the visuals of Kai's words making my empty cunt pulse and flicker. "But today, I'll make do with coming all over your back, as you come all over Lilly."

Again we moan in unison, and I watch Kai's grin turn feral. He starts pumping harder, his other hand clearly gripping his own dick as his arm moves in sync with the one playing with Loki. *Ambidextrous bastard.*

"Look at her, Loki. Look at our darling girl," Kai orders, and Loki tips his head up, hooded eyes meeting my own.

My own hand moves the wand faster, in time with Kai's, and I can feel the burn of my orgasm threatening to consume me, the fingers of my other hand digging into the sheets.

"Please, sir," I cry quietly. "Please, please, please."

Kai's lip hooks up, teeth gritted, sweat beading his brow as he moves both arms faster. Loki bares his own teeth, hissing breaths escaping him as he holds his own climax back.

"Just a little longer," Kai rasps out, his own hips bucking in time with Loki's. He's close. I can see it in the tightness of his jaw.

"I-I can't!" I moan, fire licking my heels as my whole body tries to light up. "Sir, Kai, love, please!"

"Now!" Kai roars, and we all let go, exploding into fragments of ourselves as we climax.

I watch as Loki spills his seed all over me, with such force that some lands in my hair, but I don't give any shits as I burn and burn with my own orgasm, screaming my pleasure. I feel my release pour from me, soaking my hand, my inner thighs, and the bed beneath me. I hear Kai grunt out his own climax, and just manage to open my eyes to see him bite Loki's shoulder as he comes.

Slumping back, I lie there, eyes closed, panting, sweat and cum covered, as I fall back into my own body, which tingles from the top of my head right down to the tips of my toes. My arms are outstretched, the wand still vibrating in my palm, but I couldn't move even if I wanted to.

There's the clink of a chain, then another, and a warm solid weight falls gently on top of me, settling between my spread thighs. Lush lips find mine, Loki's tongue sliding into my mouth as he kisses me with languorous strokes.

I manage to kiss him back, gasping into his mouth as his hips start to move, and I feel him getting hard again.

"Loki, no, I can't..." I trail off with a moan, and he slides inside of me, lighting me up once more when he begins to slowly gyrate.

"Blame Kai," he murmurs against my lips. "He forgot to take the butt plug out."

*Church* by Chase Atlantic begins to play, Mitchel Cave's sensual voice stroking my overheated skin. I shudder as Loki starts working me up again, my body so sensitive that it almost hurts.

"Naughty pets," I hear Kai chuckle, turning my head to the side to see that he's standing next to the bed, his hard dick in his hand, glistening with lube. *What the fuck are these boys eating to keep getting hard like this?!* "Flip her over so she's on top," he commands, and before I know what's happening, Loki rolls us so I'm on top, my knees braced either side of his hips. Somehow, he's still inside me.

I moan low as the new position allows him to go deeper, my pussy twitching and pulsing around his hardness. I feel the bed dip behind me, a hand running down the length of my spine, making my back arch.

"My beautiful darling," Kai coos, his hand moving down until it reaches the place where Loki and I are joined.

A stuttering gasp falls from my lips as his fingers push inside me, hearing Loki groan a curse at the same time.

"Such a good girl, isn't she?" Kai praises, his voice deep and satisfied sounding.

"Such a good girl," Loki rasps out underneath me. My head rests on his shoulder, my nose tucked into his neck, inhaling great lungfuls of his vanilla scent, mixed in with the musk of sex.

"Loki," I moan as his hands pull my arse cheeks apart, opening me up even more. Kai's fingers leave my cunt, to be replaced by the top of his hard dick. "Kai! It won't..."

"Shhhh, darling. You can take both of us in that sweet pussy of yours," he grits out as he slowly pushes forward, one hand gripping my hip.

The stretch burns, tears springing to my eyes as he continues to thrust forward. Neither guy is lacking in the girth department, and it feels as though I'm being stretched to breaking point. I wriggle, my body trying to escape, but

Loki holds me firmly, Kai's fingers digging into my soft flesh hard enough to bruise.

"Please, it hurts," I cry, but that's a lie. Yes, it does hurt, but it also feels incredible having both of them inside my cunt, and in amongst the pain is a tendril of pleasure.

"Just a little more, darling, that's it, breathe through it," Kai grits out, grunting as he thrusts one final time, his hips hitting my arse. "Fuck."

My whole body trembles, sweat coating my skin as we lie there, both boys deep inside my pussy.

"Shit, dude! I can feel your metal," Loki groans, his hands flexing on my arse. I shudder at the visual, both guys groaning as my cunt flutters around them. My hands grasp Loki's shoulders, my nails digging in as I adjust to them.

"Play with her clit, Pet," Kai orders, holding still inside me as Loki lets go of one arse cheek, wriggling his hand between us.

I cry out as his fingers make contact with my poor, engorged clit, electric fire racing across my skin when he starts rubbing it. Kai starts moving, making Loki's fingers falter as he starts to withdraw, only to slam back in.

I let out a choked sound as sparks fly through me, biting down on Loki's neck until I taste copper as the pleasure-pain rushes through me. Loki begins to pull out as soon as Kai's deep inside me, incoherent noises sounding in my throat as they find an alternating rhythm, not giving me time to breathe between thrusts.

"You take us so beautifully, Pretty Girl," Loki praises, his voice harsh and rough.

"Tell me what you can feel," I beg, my own voice sounding broken and raspy, shivers taking over my body as they thoroughly use me.

"I can feel your warm wet walls clamping and fluttering around my hard dick," Loki starts, and my inner walls clench at his dirty talk. "I can feel Kai's piercing rubbing against me, and fuck me, Pretty Girl. I get why you scream so much when he's inside you." He lets out a pained chuckle as Kai thrusts harder, eliciting a sharp gasp from my own lips.

"Let's make our darling come, Pet," Kai chokes out, clearly close to release. "Open your eyes, darling."

I do as he orders, watching as his face comes into view when he lowers himself down, his weight pushing me flush onto Loki. My breath hitches when his lips hover over Loki's, a sinful smile on them. His tongue darts out, licking Loki's lower lip before he presses down in a blistering kiss.

Loki pinches my clit hard, and I'm gone. My whole body flushes with fire, followed by electricity, as I come so hard I black out, unable to take a full breath. My whole body shakes uncontrollably, and I scream as I'm consumed by pleasure. The boys pick up speed, thrusting harder and faster as they chase their own releases, climaxing one after the other with deafening roars.

I come back to the world of the non-orgasmic panting, my poor abused pussy already aching and sore. I whimper as Kai pulls out, flopping next to us, his own body covered in a sheen of sweat, his chest heaving. Loki slips out of me at the same time, a moan leaving my lips, but he continues to hold me to him, my body moving up and down with his deep inhales.

"You are incredible, baby. Fucking incredible," he whispers, stroking a shaking hand over my damp hair, kissing my head.

"So incredible, darling," Kai repeats, breathless as he opens his eyes and locks gazes with me. His hand finds mine, our fingers intertwining as we lie there.

Warmth suffuses my whole being at their words and touch, sinking into Loki's body as I bask in the afterglow of our lovemaking, counting my lucky stars as I often do and thanking whatever gods that exist that we found each other.

# CHAPTER TWENTY-EIGHT

LILLY

The next morning I wake up in between Loki and Kai, my pussy sore but my heart full.

"Morning, darling," Kai whispers, his amber eyes gazing into mine as he reaches out to stroke down the side of my face.

"Good morning, my love," I beam back at him, feeling Loki stir behind me.

"Morning," Loki echos, his voice gruff and husky as he pulls me close to him. His hand reaches around, stroking my stomach. I feel those flutters again, tickling my insides.

A knock sounds at the door.

"Willow is waiting downstairs, Baby Girl," Jax says, opening the door and finding me nestled in amongst his friends. His lips quirk up in a smile. "Something about a wedding dress appointment?"

"Oh shit!" I exclaim, scrambling to get out from between the boys. "I'd completely forgotten about that!"

Yesterday I'd messaged Willow, asking if she would come with me today to look at wedding dresses. She jumped at the chance, so I rush around Loki's room, where we all stayed last night, grabbing my clothes and getting dressed. I had a bubble bath before bed, so I still feel fairly fresh, and frankly don't have the time to shower now.

"Catch you guys later," I rush over, kissing first Kai, then Loki. "Don't do anything I wouldn't do." I wink at them, both chuckling in response.

I'm only teasing them. We spoke about the new development in their relationship yesterday, and they both decided that they enjoy each other sexually, but would find it weird if I wasn't there too. I did assure them that if they wanted to play without me that was okay, but they just looked at each other, and shrugged, again saying they would rather I was there. I'm not going to complain, it's like having my own male on male porn show with front row seats. *Hot as fuck!*

I kiss Jax when I reach the bottom of the stairs, grabbing my thermos and a homemade granola bar that he holds out for me.

"The car is waiting for you girls," he tells me, Ash being with his parents again this weekend. I hate that he has to keep going there, especially with what I know about and have experienced firsthand with Julian.

"Morning, babe," Willow says, laughing at my no doubt flustered appearance. "I bet those boys kept you so busy with the D that you forgot. Tell me I'm wrong!" she laughs as my face goes red, remembering what happened yesterday.

"Something like that," I chuckle back, grabbing my phone and purse as we head out of the door.

"I need all the deets, like yesterday!" she begs, linking her arm through mine as we exit the front doors to find a limo waiting for us. *Nice touch, Jax.* "My love life is shit, nonexistent at best."

She huffs, and it's my turn to laugh. I know that she's waiting for the right person to lose her V card to, so she isn't actually that desperate to jump into bed with anyone.

I look up as the driver gets out, coming round our side to open the door for us. A blush steals across my cheeks as I meet the blue eyes of Tom, the driver that took Loki and I to the airport and...yeah. Willow gets in, but my steps falter as he continues to stare at me. Not in a creepy way, but there's an intensity to his gaze that makes me pause.

"Hello, Tom," I greet him, and he blinks as if from a daydream. "Can I, uh, help you with something?"

"Apologies, Miss Darling. You just remind me of someone I used to know," he replies, shaking his head and giving me a small smile. “Congratulations on your engagement.”

“Uh, thanks,” I say, ducking my head as I climb in the car, blinking that strange encounter from my mind.

As we make our way into town, I give her a rundown of what happened after we caught up with Loki, her eyebrows getting higher with each word.

“Fuck me,” she sighs, fanning her face. “Talk about hashtag-livingthedream.”

I smile, even though my face is hot and I know that I’m blushing redder than a whore in church. She’s right, though, I am living the dream.

The car comes to a stop, and I look out the window to see that we’re outside a very up-market-looking bridal shop. It also has a quaint feel about it, being in one of the older buildings, so it doesn't feel sterile like some I’ve seen and expected this to be.

A bell above the door tinkles as we open it, and a woman in her late forties approaches us, a kind smile on her face and a tape measure around her neck.

“Welcome,” she greets us, looking incredibly attractive in a grey pencil skirt, white blouse, and a red silk scarf tied around her neck. “You must be Lilly. My name is Jen, and I’ll be helping you today.”

“Pleased to meet you, Jen,” I smile back, butterflies taking flight in my stomach now that I’m here, surrounded by a sea of white and cream lace. “This is my friend and chief bridesmaid Willow.” I indicate Willow, who looks in shock back at me.

“I am?” she asks, her wide eyes a little misty.

“Of course, if you want to be, that is?” I ask, a little hesitantly.

“Abso-fucking-lutely!” she squeals, throwing her arms around me. She pulls away after a quick hug, wincing and looking over at Jen. “Sorry, mum always said I have a sailor’s mouth.”

Jen just laughs, holding her hand out towards a younger girl, who steps forward with a tray. On it sit two flutes of bubbling champagne.

“I’ve heard worse,” she chuckles. “Champagne? Our secret,” she says with a wink.

“Oh, um, I can’t, because, um, I’m pregnant,” I stutter out, her face showing no shock or judgement. A breath of relief whooshes out of me.

“Amelie, something soft for Lilly, please,” she asks the younger girl, who smiles, letting Willow take a glass before heading to the back of the shop, disappearing through a door. Jen looks back at me. "So, do you have any ideas of what you'd like?"

"Well, not really, no," I chuckle, feeling another blush steal over my cheeks.

"That's absolutely fine," she says, guiding us towards a rail of dresses. "Let's start here, at the empire line ones, which will be easier for you in your condition."

She starts pulling out the most beautiful dresses I've ever seen. Lace, tulle, sparkling crystals and beads, all in shades of white, cream, and champagne, a few even in light gold and blonde. She tells us that she designs them all, and with the help of a series of seamstresses, sews them in the workroom at the back of the shop.

But gorgeous as they are, none feel quite me.

"I'm sorry," I tell her, sitting down on a plush grey velvet love seat next to Willow. "They're just not..."

"You. I know. And no need to apologise," Jen reassures me with a smile, looking me over and no doubt noticing my rainbow patterned Run and Fly dungarees. Not exactly subtle and elegant. "I wonder...Amelie," she calls, and the younger girl comes out from the back. "Bring the dress you've been working on, please."

"W-what?" Amelie asks, her eyes wide. "Really?"

"Yes, please," Jen replies, smiling kindly at her, and I admit, I like this woman. Amelie turns around, heading out the back.

She returns a few moments later, and I sit up straighter, my heart thudding as I see the spill of colour across her arm. Standing in front of me, she lets the hem drop to the floor, and I gasp, completely lost for words.

It's an empire line, like the others, with an off white beaded lace covering the shoulders, coming down to cover the bust part as well. My eyes travel down the fall of plain soft white chiffon, that starts just under the bust and ends in a train at the back, the hem decorated with a matching beaded, lace pattern as that of the top.

But the thing that makes this particular dress perfection is that it appears to have been dipped into a sunset, the colours bleeding up the skirt, finishing probably around knee height. It starts as a deep indigo at the hem, turning into violet, then purple, magenta, pink, red, orange and finally, a deep yellow.

"I think, by that look, we've found your dress," Jen says softly, and I tear my eyes away, moisture filling them as I look at her. I swallow hard.

"It's perfect," I whisper, my gaze drawn back to it, loving how the colours shift and change tone as the light falls across it.

"Let's try it on then, although, I suggest we leave any alterations until closer to the time to account for your changing shape," she tells me, ushering me into a changing room and hanging the dress on a hook by its wooden hanger.

Stripping quickly, I reach out, feeling the softness of the material before slipping it over my head. It falls around me like a cloud, as I can't tear my gaze away from my reflection in the mirror, even if the dress isn't yet done up.

*I look like a bride.*

It hits me then, really hits me, that I am getting married. That I'm having another man's baby, the best friend of my groom to be. What a mess. But looking into the mirror, at the bride that I will be, it suddenly feels so real.

"Are you ready, Lilly?" Jen's soft voice calls on the other side of the curtain.

"Yes," I reply, taking a final look at the woman standing in the mirror before me.

*Ready as I'll ever be.*

---

After wowing Willow and Jen at the dress shop, both declaring that the dress was perfect and 'the one', Willow and I head to the tea rooms for a late lunch. Luckily, my sickness seems to be abating somewhat, so I'm able to eat a delicious cream tea, with finger sandwiches and mini cakes.

We head back to Highgate, deciding to spend the rest of the weekend watching Netflix and chilling. Kai and Loki join us, Jax appearing some time later, sweaty and delicious looking from a workout. After showering, he joins us, too, lifting me up and sitting back down, then placing me on his lap and pulling one of the blankets over us.

"Hey," I murmur, snuggling into him as he pulls me closer, a low rumble sounding in his chest.

"Hey, Baby Girl," he replies, and I feel his words vibrate against my ear. "Did you find your dress?"

"She found the dress to end all dresses!" Willow exclaims, gesticulating and sending popcorn flying. I chuckle at her antics, so pleased that she's here with us. "It's fucking incredible."

"I'm glad you found something, baby," Jax tells me, a smile clear in his voice even though I can't see his face. "I can't wait to see you in it, even if I'm not the one putting a ring on your finger."

My heart aches, and I sit up, pushing away so that I can look into his beautiful blue eyes. The light of the TV casts them in a kaleidoscope of blues, changing from almost navy to ice. My brows drop, my lips parting as I struggle to find the right words.

"I wish..." I start, taking a deep inhale, then releasing it slowly. "I wish I could marry all of you, officially. A part of me hurts having to marry only Ash. But it also feels so right at the same time, you know?"

He reaches out, cupping my face in his huge palm, and I can't help but nestle into it.

"I know," he rumbles back. "And none of us hold that against you, we know that you'd marry all of us if you could. Sure, I'm jealous as fuck that Ash drew the lucky straw, and I can't wait to get him in the ring to take a little bit of that out on him," he adds, an evil grin pulling up the corners of his lips that makes me worry for Ash a little. "But I'll get over it. We'll get over it, Baby Girl."

I lean in, placing a gentle kiss on his lips, a sigh caressing mine as I pull away again, aware of Willow being here.

"Thank you, my love," I whisper, his nostrils flaring and his grip around me tightening at the nickname. I love all of their reactions when I use it.

He pulls me close again, his hands stroking down my back in a soothing caress that soon has my eyes closing, his heartbeat lulling me to sleep.

---

## JAX

I hold Lilly tightly as her body grows heavy against mine, her breathing evening out as she falls asleep under my touch. I love how she's so comfortable now that she can do that. Trusting me to take care of her when she's at her most vulnerable.

I meant what I told her. I wish to God it was me she was marrying, but as long as I keep getting moments like this, I'll get over it. Especially if I can get Ash in the ring a time or two.

Willow looks over, seeing that Lilly is asleep, and quietly leaves, saying that she'll text Lilly tomorrow.

"How's Enzo?" Loki asks, careful to keep his voice low so as not to disturb Lilly. She stirs slightly, then settles back down when I keep rubbing her back.

"Good. Pleased about his wedding invite," I smile, remembering Enzo's knowing smile as he told me that he and Rosa will be there.

"Jeez, Erica works fast," Loki comments, sounding impressed. He's right to be, Ash and Lilly only gave her the list of invitees yesterday, and already she'd sent the invites by courier.

"How did training go? Did you get the fight moved?" Kai asks, the TV screen reflected in his glasses hiding his eyes.

"I'm almost back to where I was before," I tell them, feeling the ache of my muscles that I've been working hard on lately. "Enzo managed to get it postponed until May seventh, but they wouldn't do any later."

Loki whistles, and I glare at him as Lilly stirs again.

"Fourteen days before the wedding...better than the day before I guess," he comments, giving me one of his shit eating grins that tells me he's about to say something insulting. "At least the bruising will have a chance to heal a little so you don't look like shit in all the photos."

I growl, grabbing a pillow and launching it at his head. He ducks, which just makes me growl again as it flies past him.

"She'll want to come, you know that," Kai says, and I pull the girl in question tighter against me. "We won't be able to stop her."

"Fuck," Loki hisses, and I agree with him. Underground MMA fights are no place for a girl like her, especially not in her condition.

"You'll have to all keep her safe, away from the scum," I tell them, my lips twitching when Loki's jaw clenches and Kai grinds his teeth.

"Of course we will keep her safe," Loki all but snarls at me, Kai giving a sharp nod of agreement. "And if anyone so much as looks at her wrong..."

I know that my grin is as feral as both of theirs, as bloodthirsty. Some things in life are simple, at least that's what I've always thought.

If anyone goes near our girl, they won't see the sunrise.

# CHAPTER TWENTY-NINE

LILLY

I wake up smiling, still surrounded by the scent of sweet lemons, the warmth of Jax at my back. I love that I no longer spend a single night alone. Some might find it suffocating, but it brings me a sense of peace to know that one or more of my guys are with me all night, keeping me safe from monsters, both imagined and real.

Heading downstairs, I'm dressed in one of Jax's huge black T-shirts, which falls off one shoulder, and a pair of soft cotton boy shorts with pictures of unicorns all over them. I'm desperate for a wee, apparently this is most definitely a pregnancy thing, but it should start to ease a little now that I'm at the four month mark.

I startle when I see Ash sitting at the table, an espresso sitting in front of him, the faint light of pre-dawn casting its watery glow across his inked torso. He looks up, and I gasp when I see his face. One eye is puffy, there's a cut on his cheek, and his lip is clearly split on the same side.

"Fuck, Ash!" I exclaim, wanting to go to him, but my bladder is legit going to burst if I don't go right now. "Shit, I'm about to piss myself. Don't move."

His deep chuckle cascades over me as I dash to the bathroom, sighing in pleasure as I sit on the loo - *pissing has never felt so bloody good before!* Flushing,

I'm worrying the whole time I wash my hands. Hurrying back out, he's still sitting there, so I swing past the freezer, grabbing an ice pack and tea towel to wrap it in, before going over to him.

"Turn," I instruct, his lips twitching at the order. He complies, and I step in between his wide spread legs - *totally justified btw, he definitely needs the extra space, if you know what I mean.* "Dare I ask?"

"Julian surprised me with some extra challenges yesterday," he tells me, wincing as the ice cold wrapped pack alights against his puffy face. "Including about ten ex-Marines." *God, that man is such a ballsack cunt!*

Ash's hands come to my hips, pulling me closer. His fingers tease along my waistline, his palms resting over my now slightly rounded stomach. I seem to have 'popped' in the last couple of days, a small but definite baby bump visible.

"Oh, Ash," I sigh in a soft voice, wishing there was anything else I could say or do to help, but knowing that there isn't.

"Do you know how fucking jealous I am that it's Loki's child you're carrying, and not mine?" he asks me, rubbing my stomach. The baby kicks, but Ash doesn't react so obviously can't feel it yet.

"W-what?" I stammer, the subject change throwing me as I continue to hold the ice pack to his face.

"I've always been an asshole, Lilly. Possessive and controlling," he growls, hooking my knickers in his fingers, and drawing them down my thighs. My breath catches as his intentions become clear. He needs the distraction of my body, and I am helpless to deny him.

He lets my knickers drop to the ground, taking hold of the hem of my - Jax's - T-shirt, and lifting it over my head as he stands up. The ice pack drops to the floor with a heavy thud as it falls from my hand.

He takes a minute, studying my naked body in the dim light, his eyes caressing me, causing my nipples to peak and my breathing to quicken. An inked hand reaches out, tracing my curves, leaving a fire in its wake. He reaches the apex of my thighs, which I feel more than see with my stomach now in the way.

"Open," he commands, looking at his hand as I obey, shifting my thighs so that they are parted.

I cry out at his first touch, moisture leaking out of me as he traces a finger up and down my slit, swirling my opening and clit. I'm so responsive to these guys, and they know my body so well that it doesn't take much to bring me to the brink. He stops, leaving me panting and desperate for more.

"Turn around, hands on the table, Princess."

The cool wood soothes my hot palms as I follow his instructions, waiting. He kicks my legs wider, and a second later I feel his bulbous head pushing against my entrance. A hiss leaves my lips as he enters me, I'm still a little sore from the combination of Kai and Loki on Friday, but it soon turns to a pleasure filled moan when his piercings rub my inner walls. And the fact that his bare skin is inside me, no barriers between us, drives me wild, making me buck against him.

He pauses once he's fully seated inside me, a contented sigh sounding behind me as my nails scrape the wood of the table in pleasure. He starts to move, slowly at first, tingles racing up my spine as he gets faster, bringing me to the edge once more with his dick this time. I can feel the burn of an orgasm begin, my inner muscles fluttering around Ash's cock, begging him to keep going. Only he slows down and pauses before I can fall over into exquisite bliss.

"I'm so fucking close, Ash. Please," I pant through gritted teeth.

He reaches around, fingertips stroking over my slightly swollen stomach from behind in a loving caress.

"Next time, it'll be my fucking baby in your womb. Won't it, Princess?"

"W-what?" I question, my head spinning once more with his words. He starts leisurely pumping his dick in and out of me, quivers racing through my core, but not enough to allow me to climax. *He's fucking denying me my pleasure, the wankmonster.*

"The next baby to grow inside you will be mine, understand, Princess?" he asks, his tone condescending as fuck, as he continues teasing me with his slow strokes.

"Fuck off, Ash! It's my body, and I'll decide *if* I have another baby, and *who* the father will be," I inform him, all kinds of pissed off, and attempting to straighten up, having had enough of his jealousy.

But his hands on my hips tighten, holding me in place with a mocking laugh that should piss me off more than it does. *Jesus, I'm so fucking messed up that even his cruel laugh makes my pussy flutter.*

"That's where you're wrong, *fiancée*. This body." He squeezes my hips tighter, eliciting a squeak of protest from my lips. *Okay, it's part raw fucking pleasure too*. “This pussy.” He punctuates here with a sharp thrust, and a deep groan sounds in my throat. “All of you belongs to me. I may be gracious and share with the others. But don't mistake my kindness for anything other than that.” He's growling by the end of his speech and has completely stopped thrusting inside me, holding just the tip in my entrance. “So I'll tell you again. The next baby you carry, *Princess*, will. Be. Mine.” He thrusts hard in between each word, reinforcing his point physically.

I'm mewling underneath him, unable to move as he holds me in a bruising grip. He's building me up to a crescendo, my orgasm fluttering at the edges of my vision. Just as the wave is about to crest, he pauses, again with just his tip inside me.

“Ash!” I scream, clawing at the table, giving no shits about scratching it to buggery as I’m beyond frustrated.

“Well?” he asks breathlessly, and I just know that he has one perfect arrogant jet black brow raised. I also know that the twatterdick won't let me come until I agree to his alpha bullshit.

“Fine! Yes!” I shout in response.

“Yes, what?” The git asks back, his tone smug.

“The next baby I have will be yours!” I screech. “Are you fucking happy now?!”

“Ecstatic,” he replies, in a somewhat droll tone.

Then he thrusts so hard and fast that if he wasn't holding onto me, I would be flat on my stomach on the table. I cry out as he lets his inner animal take over and fucks me like a demon, snarling and snapping like a wild beast, the sound of his hips hitting against me, loud in the quiet.

I soon see fucking stars, screaming out his name as my whole body tightens, then liquifies with my release. He gives one final, punishing thrust, as if he's trying to impregnate me right now, finding his own climax with a deafening roar.

“Good girl,” he says, voice breathy as he pats my arse like a fucking dog.

I’d snap like one, too, you know, if I hadn’t just been fucked to within an inch of my life. So I just huff as he pulls out, feeling some of his cum slide out of me. He notices, a growl of what sounds like approval leaving his throat, then I feel his fingers push it back inside my abused pussy, as if he can’t bear for any of his essence to leave my body.

And I know that maybe I should take him to task over his alpha bullshit.

That it's a product of the time he's spent with Julian recently, that he's been moulded by Julian to crave ultimate control. It's a part of who Ash is, and I love all of him, the good and the bad, the beautiful and the ugly. It's the reason that I heave myself up onto shaky legs, turning to face him and wrapping my arms around his sweat slicked chest.

It's the reason why I kiss the side of his neck, and whisper gently in his ear.

"The next baby can be yours, my love."

His whole body shakes, his arms banding around me in a steel like grip as he buries his face into my hair, inhaling deeply and pulling me so close that it's difficult to know where I finish and he begins.

---

The others come down just as I step out of the shower, each placing a kiss on my damp head as I pass them on my way back upstairs to get dressed. Deciding to go with comfy, it is Sunday after all, I throw on some loose wine red harems and a new mustard yellow T-shirt that has a picture of a vintage rainbow with 'Bookish Vibes' in seventies bubble font on the front.

I pause as I catch a glimpse of myself in the mirror, turning to the side to admire my little bump. My hands come to cup my stomach, in a move that I'm sure so many women have made before me.

"You're such a MILF, Pretty Girl," Loki drawls from the doorway, and I chuckle as he walks towards me, wrapping his arms around me from behind.

He places his hands on top of mine, our fingers interlacing as we hold my stomach. I watch in the mirror as numerous emotions flit across his features, his gaze on our hands.

"I'm scared, Loki," I confess in a whisper, his eyes coming up to meet mine. "Not of giving birth really, but, shit. We're just kids, and with everything going on with Black Knight..."

His arms tighten around me.

"I swear to you, Lilly, I will never let anything happen to you. Or our child," he vows, his emerald eyes almost glowing with his conviction. "And as for the other thing, yes, we're young. And I'd be lying if I said I wasn't scared. But I know that you will make an incredible mother, you're able to love the four of us assholes." A choked laugh escapes me as tears fill my eyes. "And there are five of us, five people to love the shit out of this baby. That's all it really needs. Our love."

He pulls me closer as tears drip down my face. I'm so sad for him, for this beautiful boy who was missing the one thing he really needed growing up.

"You know, you're kind of wise sometimes, Loki," I tell him, sniffling. He turns me in his arms, wiping my face with his sleeve.

"Not just a pretty face," he tells me, winking. "Kai said we need to start carrying around tissues, you cry so often at the moment," he chuckles, causing more tears to fall even as I huff a laugh.

"Fucking hormones," I reply, making him laugh.

"Come on, baby mama." He takes me by the hand, and we start to walk out of the room. "Let's get you something to eat. Kai is making some bacon, eggs, and pancakes."

After eating a delicious breakfast/brunch, we decide to all go for a walk, as it's a gorgeous spring day. Heading out of the dorm, we make our way downstairs only to see the whole place littered with white pieces of paper.

I get a sinking feeling in my stomach, a shiver coming over my skin despite the sun streaming in through the huge windows. Highgate is nothing if not spotlessly clean, so this must be purposeful. Although, I'm still surprised that the admin staff haven't cleaned it up yet.

Loki bends down to pick up one of the papers, his face going pale as his eyes flit back and forth reading what's on the page.

"Ash..." he says in a tight voice, looking up with a haunted look in his eyes.

He hands the page to Ash while Kai and Jax reach down to grab their own copies.

"Fuck!" Jax snarls, just as Ash crumples the page in his fist, a flush creeping over his cheeks.

"What?" I ask, my heart pounding as I look at their faces, full of anger and devastation. "What is it? Tell me, please."

Kai hands me his copy, his eyes so sad behind his glasses that moisture stings my own. Looking down, my throat goes dry, my breath stilling as I read what's on the page in front of me.

It's a letter, addressed to Ash in a messy scrawl. The paper shakes the more I read, tears falling down my cheeks as Luc's final words swim before me.

. . .

*Dear Ash,*
*I can't fight you and dad anymore. I don't want to, and I don't want what he's offering. I just want peace, so I'm taking myself out of the game. The crown is all yours.*
*Luc*

"Oh, Ash," I gasp, looking up at him and remembering that day in front of the chapel, the beautiful voices of Pentatonix behind us as he told me about finding Luc in his room on the last day before summer, dead and covered in blood.

Anger floods my system, overriding the grief, as I realise that this is yet another of Julian's punishments. "How could he do this?!" I exclaim, my jaw tight. "You're his son, for fuck's sake! And so was Luc!" I'm so cross, my blood boils, scaling my veins and tinting my vision.

"Hey," Ash turns to me, letting the paper drop to the floor and taking mine out of my hand. "Don't get so worked up, Princess. It's not good for the baby." He takes my shaking hands in his, prising the paper out of my grip and dropping that too.

Pulling me into him, I'm engulfed by his spicy ginger scent, which calms me instantly. Wrapping my arms around him, I hold on tightly as the angry tears subside. Looking up, I see his jaw is still clenched, but his steel eyes are full of concern for me, and my heart hurts.

"I'm sorry, Ash. I'm such an arsehole for flipping out and then making you comfort me, when it should be the other way round."

He gives me a tight, almost vicious smile, with an edge of resignation to it. It sends a shiver down my spine, and I'm glad that I'm not the one he's pissed at.

"I'm used to this kind of shit, Princess. It's not the first time he's used Luc's suicide against me. And you're not an *asshole*." He gives me one of his trademark smirks, clearly making the point that I'm saying the word wrong. *Twatwaffle.* "Kai, organise a clean up crew to come in and deal with this mess. I want these gone stat."

"On it," Kai responds, his iPad in hand as he starts tapping away at the screen.

"Let's go for that walk, shall we?" Ash asks, letting me go, but tucking my hand into his arm like an old fashioned gentleman taking his lover out for a walk. You know, the lover who's pregnant with his best friend's baby, whilst his father forces an arranged marriage on the couple, not knowing that his grandchild will not be of his blood. *God, I'm living in a Mills and Boon novel!*

Despite the rocky start to our day, I soon settle with the gentle exercise, taking deep soothing breaths of fresh air as we make our way through the forest, leaving Highgate, Julian, and all the shit behind us.

We come to a break in the trees, a beautiful meadow full of delicate spring wildflowers spread out before us. I let the sun warm my face, closing my eyes as I feel its rays caress my skin.

My pocket vibrates with an incoming message, and sighing, I take it out, to see that it's from Julian.

**Julian Cuntish Vanderbilt: Just a lesson for the Princess left x**

Just like that, all the warmth leeches from my body, and I'm no longer able to feel the rays of the sun, even though there isn't a cloud in the sky.

"What is it, Princess?" Ash asks, brows furrowed, and I shiver at the nickname, hating that Julian just used it. I turn the screen to face him, and a curse falls from his lips as he reads the message.

"When will it stop, Ash?" I ask, my voice thick, suddenly so weary I lean heavily on him as my knees feel weak beneath me.

"When one of them dies," he tells me, a vicious gleam in his grey eyes. "And the others are rotting in jail."

I should feel revulsion.

I should feel horror.

But I don't.

I only feel a sick sense of relief at the idea of being free from the blackness that is Black Knight Corporation. Of finally being free from Julian's oppressive presence.

What sort of person have I become?

# CHAPTER THIRTY

LILLY

The next week goes by pretty quietly, Erica popping over on Wednesday after classes finish, to talk table settings and finalise the menu. I have never really agreed with the idea of forcing people to sit with complete strangers, so we decide to forgo the traditional wedding seating plan, letting people choose to sit where they like.

Sheer multi coloured sari tablecloths over white ones will cover the tables, bunches of rainbow-coloured flowers in ceramic jugs sitting in the centre, along with glass jars full of fairy lights. The marquee will be lined in colourful transparent fabric, making it appear like a rainbow tent, with swags of more flowers and fairy lights decorating the edges.

We decide to have a menu that represents both Ash and I; loaded hot dogs, pulled pork, as well as British cheeses with oat crackers, and a play on boiled eggs with soldiers for dessert. The guys looked at me with confused faces when I spoke about it, until I explained that for breakfast we'd often have soft boiled eggs, the yolks still running, with buttery toast cut into slices to dip into them.

There will of course be a rainbow sponge wedding cake, covered in fluffy buttercream as well as a donut cake, each tier being a different flavour of a very well known American donut brand.

She tells me that she'll organise tasters of everything, and we set a date of next Wednesday at some place in town to try all the food and make sure it's what we want. She lets me know that almost everyone who has received an invitation via email, we thought that this would be quicker than trying to post, especially to England, has accepted, and excitement runs through me at the idea of seeing Lexi, Ryan and Mr. Grey again so soon.

Friday rolls around and I find myself once again tired but less exhausted than I was last week. Willow informs me that it's because I'm now in the 'glowing' phase of pregnancy where I look radiant, no longer need to pee all the damn time, and generally will find things a little easier. I must admit that I don't feel sick all the time, although I have banned Kai from preparing any fish dishes in the kitchen, as the smell turns my stomach.

I'm walking back to the dorms with said bush baby fairy–totally a thing–when I remembered something that I wanted her advice on.

"If someone wanted to, say, get revenge on a predatory cougar, what, theoretically, would be the best way to go about achieving it?" I bat my eyelashes at her, causing a throaty laugh to erupt from her lips.

"Hmmmm," she murmurs, a serious look coming over her face. "One could, in theory, leak video footage of said cougar to the police, reporting the abuse," she answers, an excited gleam coming into her eyes. "Oooohhh! Could you also discredit her with Julian somehow? Like, make out that she's disloyal to Black Knight?"

I pause, my head tilted to the side as I think on her suggestion.

"It would be funny to see her carted away in cuffs," I muse, liking the idea. "And you're definitely onto something with casting her in a black light with Julian..."

"Lilly," she says, interrupting my internal plotting. I look at her, pausing when she lays a hand on my arm. "I know that there's more going on here, with Julian and Black Knight, than you can tell me, and that's okay. Just know that I will help you however I can. My brother...he has connections and I will use them."

My eyes soften as I gaze at her, my hand resting on top of hers and squeezing gently.

"You are an awesome person, Willow Anderson, and one of my favourites."

But then a fissure of worry runs through me, and I bite my bottom lip. "But how would Loki feel? To be exposed so publically?"

"You could ask," she replies as we resume walking. "It probably should be him who makes the final call after all."

She's right. It definitely should be his decision. He was the one that suffered the abuse. I just hope he goes for it, as I can't help feeling that it's the closure he needs to finally see that it wasn't his fault. That she was a predator, and he an innocent.

"I'll ask now," I tell her, reaching my door and turning to face her. "Wish me luck."

"Good luck you bad bitch," she says, darting in to kiss my cheek. "I'll catch you tomorrow?"

"Abso-fucking-lutely!" I respond, chuckling as she gives me a dorky as fuck wave, before walking off down the hall to her own room.

Miraculously, she managed to snag a room all to herself, all of the dorms being full after my arrival. She claims that palms were greased, which doesn't surprise me in the least given this place, and the way money seems to talk.

Taking a deep breath to still the butterflies suddenly fluttering in my stomach, I put my key in the lock and open the heavy wooden door. Pausing in the doorway, I take a moment to admire the guys. My loves. The other parts of my soul.

Kai's in the kitchen, preparing something that makes my mouth water and my stomach grumble, as *Nothin but a Monster* by Ari Hicks plays softly in the background. Jax and Loki are sitting on one sofa, Ash on another, all clutching gaming handsets, and playing what looks like a pretty violent game if the blood and gore on the screen are anything to go by. Loki shouts at the screen as something appears to kill his avatar, Ash's lips lifting in a smirk as Loki swears at him. Jax laughs, the sound deep and low, making my nipples pebble even from here.

"You're a dirty fucking cheat, Ash!" Loki shouts, throwing his controller down in disgust, getting up and finally spotting me as he turns. "Pretty Girl!" he exclaims, leaping over the back of the sofa and rushing towards me.

He wraps me up in a breath stealing hug, like he literally didn't see me just this morning. My arms go round him anyway, inhaling the vanilla scent that smells like home.

"I missed you," he whispers in my ear, nuzzling the side of my neck, goosebumps appearing across my skin where he touches me.

"I missed you too, love," I reply, finding his mouth with my own, and losing myself in his plush lips and soft tongue. My whole body relaxes into him as he kisses me back, all of the tension I didn't know I was holding escaping out of me with a sigh.

Reluctantly, I pull away, looking into his eyes. My lower lip slips under my teeth as I try to think of the best way to broach the subject of Clarissa.

"Out with it, baby," Loki tells me, keeping his arms around me as he arches a brow.

"I've been thinking about Clarissa," I blurt out, wincing at my own bluntness. His arms stiffen, feeling like solid marble as they hold me, but he waits for me to continue. "And, uh, how we should deal with her."

His lip twitches on one side, a mischievous glint entering his gaze.

"You planning to seek revenge in my honour, baby?" he teases, some of the tension leaking out of him.

"Yes."

"So fucking hot," he moans, thrusting his hips at me, and I feel his hard length pressed against my rounded stomach.

"Loki!" I chastise, shaking my head. "Focus man!"

"Why don't you two share with the class, Princess?" Ash drawls from the sofa, and I peer round Loki to see him sitting there still, game controller on the coffee table in front of him.

I step away from Loki, taking his hand in mine as I lead him to the others, Kai having sat down as well. I let go of him, placing a kiss on first Kai's, then Jax's lips, then walking over to do the same to Ash. Only, being the Ash-hole that he is, he pulls me into his lap, grasping my face in both hands, and kissing me soundly.

As usual he dominates with his lips and tongue, obliterating everything and everyone else with his touch. My body lights up under his caress, a whimper leaving me as he pulls away with a final peck on my now swollen lips.

"Now, what have you been plotting, Princess?" he asks, sounding cool as a motherfucking cucumber, whilst I'm a hot mess.

I go to get up, but he lets go of my face, encircling me in his arms and pulling me more firmly into his lap. *Guess I'll stay here then.*

"I've been thinking about how we can deal with Clarissa," I tell them, my voice firm and upper lip curling as I say her name. *She doesn't deserve a fucking name, cum guzzling slutbucket.*

Jax growls, but not at me, at the aforementioned slutbucket. Loki stiffens again, and Kai clenches his hands into fists. Ash, unsurprisingly, remains still and unmoving underneath me.

"And what do you propose?" he questions, voice level, letting me know that he's taking what I say seriously. This is what makes him a great leader. He may be an arsehole, but he will still listen to every opinion and suggestion, weighing it and considering it.

"Well, we start by leaking the videos to the police." I watch Loki take a sharp breath, but he doesn't interrupt. "Reporting her for sex with a minor. At the same time, we 'find' evidence of her betrayal of Black Knight Corporation, and share that with Julian, ensuring that she earns his ire, getting the maximum sentence, plus total public humiliation and annihilation."

Jax whistles, Loki's brows raising to his hairline. Kai is nodding, fingers tapping out a rhythm on his thigh as if he's itching to grab his tablet and start typing.

"It'll also have the added benefit of earning Julian and the board's trust, helping to show that you are the good soldiers they've trained you to be, and so can be trusted. That way, they won't see the knife coming when you stab them in the back."

Ash's fingers tighten against my hip, one hand lifting up to my face, grasping my chin and turning me to face him.

"Loki was right, Princess," he whispers seductively, his steel grey eyes boring into mine, banked heat in their depths. "You are so fucking hot when you're plotting revenge."

"So, you like the idea?" I ask, my pulse speeding up as I stare back at him.

"I fucking love it," he tells me, a gleam in his eye and a satisfied smile on his face. "Kai."

Loki doesn't let go of my chin, gazing into my eyes as I hear Kai get up, then sit back down, the gentle tap of his fingers on his tablet sounding soon after.

"I've just transferred several lump sums to her account, under the guise of being from the CEO of Wolfgang Security," he tells us, sounding distracted. My eyebrows raise to my hairline, a chill sweeping over me at the things Kai can do all from an iPad.

"Who?" I ask, still trapped in Ash's stare.

"Our biggest competitor in the security industry," he tells me.

"Also sent some incriminating emails to her from him that I've put in her deleted folder," Kai tells us.

I place my hand on Ash's, silently asking him to release me, which he does. Turning my head, I look at Loki.

"Are you okay with this, Loki?" I ask, looking intently at his reactions to see how he's feeling.

He rubs his hand over his face, drawing his fingers through his auburn locks, my own hand itching to do the same.

"Yeah, I guess. It's about time she paid for what she did," he says, his voice getting stronger as he finishes. Kai stops tapping to place a hand on his knee and squeeze it.

"In that case, Kai, can you send that too please?" I ask, and he looks at me with a cheeky grin which makes my stomach somersault.

"You ordering me around too now, darling?" he questions, his smile getting wider as I blush. He gives me a wink, then looks back down at his tablet, his fingers flying across the screen. Minutes later, he looks back up at me, his look sombre. "Done."

"And now we wait," Ash supplies, trepidation running through me at his words.

Kai sets his tablet aside, getting up.

"Dinner's ready," he announces, heading over to the kitchen and opening the oven.

"I'll help lay the table," Loki says, giving me a small smile, then following Kai over.

Jax stands too, walking over to me and holding out his hand. Grasping it, he helps me up, and we go to take over plates and cutlery to the table, Ash bringing glasses and a jug of iced tea. Loki helps Kai carry Asian baked chicken, veggies, and steaming fragrant rice.

We sit down to eat, as if we hadn't just planned the ruination of someone's life.

Just another day in paradise, I guess.

# CHAPTER THIRTY-ONE

LILLY

On Saturday morning we turn on the news to see Clarissa being carted away in cuffs, shoved into the back of a police cruiser, cursing and screaming like a fishwife. I can't help the evil smile that graces my lips at her public humiliation. *Fucking twatwaffle deserved it.* Loki gets a call an hour later asking him to go down to the station to make a statement. After a Facetime briefing with Julian, who rages at the betrayal of the company when the guys tell him about the 'payments', Loki heads into town with Kai, planning - and I quote - 'to bury her pedo ass'.

Classes ramp up a bit the following week, in preparation for more exams apparently, but I'm so used to the workload that I barely notice, spending most of my spare time studying. News of my pregnancy has spread, although everyone assumes that it's Ash's baby, and this is the reason for the rushed wedding.

Things have changed since Julian's 'punishments', there are definite whispers among the students, whereas before, people wouldn't dare to speak about the Knights at all. They still keep their distance, respect and fear mixed on their faces as they gaze at them, but there's an air of sharks circling as we walk through the halls.

Surprisingly, Amber has kept her distance, too, still sneering at every opportunity, but nothing more. She seems to have given up on Loki for the moment, and Julian hasn't pushed the issue either, which makes my skin itch, suspicion crawling down my spine.

With the extra school work and generally feeling tired from being four and a half months pregnant, I almost miss that Jax has started spending most of his time in the gym again.

I catch him heading out one night after dinner, his bag slung over his shoulder.

"Can I join you, Jax?" I ask, halting his movements as he goes to walk out of the dorm.

"Sure, Baby Girl," he rumbles. "I've got your new gloves so we can do some careful practice if you like?" I nod eagerly, and he waits by the door whilst I run upstairs to get changed.

I come down, wearing some maternity leggings, a sports bra, and a tank top. I've just invested in some maternity clothes, finding that even some of my dungarees are becoming a little snug.

We walk in the direction of the school gym, hand in hand, comfortable silence surrounding us.

"How are you, Jax? How's working out now, you know, since getting clean?" I ask softly, glancing at his profile as we walk. God, he is so handsome, with his close beard and blond hair, tied in that man bun.

"I think I'm almost back to where I was," he tells me, a smile on his lips. "I've been training hard, especially with the fight coming up..." His eyes go wide at the same time that mine do, and I pull us to a stop.

"Oh shit!" I exclaim. "Your fight! I'd completely forgotten." A cute as all get out blush steals across his cheeks, and I can't help but beam at him. "When is it?"

"May seventh."

"Oh, that's two weeks before...."

"Yep, it was the most Enzo could manage to get it postponed, otherwise I'd have to forfeit," he informs me, tugging my hand so that we start walking again. We stay silent for a moment, his warm hand in mine as we walk outside, heading round the school to the new state of the art gym and swimming pool building, which was built over Christmas. "I don't suppose I could convince you not to come?" he asks after a beat, and I see him giving me the side eye.

"To the fight? Not a fucking chance!" I laugh, seeing the rueful smile on his face.

"Yeah, that's what I thought," he sighs, gripping my hand tighter for a second. "Just, promise me you'll stay with the guys. These fights...they're not attended by good people, Baby Girl."

"I promise I'll be good," I reply, mostly telling the truth, and he nods his head, releasing a breath.

"Now, come and let me show you how to kick my ass."

I laugh, the sound surrounding us with its lightness.

"Please, we both know that I could have you pinned underneath me any time I choose," I sass back, and the grin he gives me in return is positively feral.

"Is that so, Baby Girl?" he asks, and my heart rate picks up when a decidedly naughty smile tugs his lips upwards. "We'll test that theory later. For now, we train."

"Spoil sport," I grumble, earning a deep chuckle as he leads me into the gym.

It's pretty empty tonight, only two other guys in there who are just finishing up as we walk in. Jax nods to them, leading me to the boxing ring in the centre.

"Now, we're only gonna use the pads, Baby Girl. No contact, just in case. And if you need to stop, just say, okay?" I grumble out an assent as he hands me my new gloves, the ones he bought me for Christmas, with 'Baby Girl' on the wrist straps.

Taking out his phone, he thumbs the screen, and the gym fills with the opening lyrics of *Him & I* by G-Eazy and Halsey. My head bobs with the beat, my lips tugging up as the lyrics flow over me.

We spend the next forty minutes practising boxing moves, until a sheen of sweat covers my body and I'm panting hard.

"I'm done," I gasp out, taking my gloves off and gratefully taking the bottle of water that Jax hands me.

"You did good, Baby Girl," he tells me, not even looking flushed as he stands there in a wifebeater and long shorts. *Fucking cockwomble.*

We leave the ring, and I sit down on the mats to do some stretching, whilst Jax goes over to the punching bags. He doesn't bother with gloves, or even wrapping his hands, as he starts to lay into them with unrestrained violence. My brows begin to dip, my heart pounding as he keeps hitting the bag, his breath hissing out with each strike. I wince as his knuckles split, the red of his blood dripping down his hands as he doesn't even pause, each strike now sounding wet and making the bag swing.

Looking up, his chest heaves with exertion, his face a mask of pain and anger, nostrils flared, teeth bared. I get up, pain lancing my own chest as I walk towards him, knowing that this is no ordinary training session. He's hurting badly.

"Jax, love?" I question softly, keeping back a little, giving him space. The thump of his hits keeps coming, and I bite my lip at how raw his knuckles now look. "Jax! Stop! Please," I beg, my voice choked as I step forward, my hand out.

He looks up at me, eyes wild, sweat dripping down his face.

"It hurts so good, Baby Girl," he rasps out, voice sounding broken. "I need to hurt."

"Oh, love." A sob escapes my throat, and I take another step towards him, and another, until I can place my hand on his quivering bicep.

"I failed them, baby. I failed them all." And my heart breaks as he hangs his head, his shoulders rounding forward in a posture of defeat.

"Failed who, darling?" I ask, my chest tightening. I've been so tied up with everything, that I didn't notice how much he was hurting.

"Mom, Loki, Kai, Ash...you," he replies, his head still hanging.

"What? No, sweetheart, you've not failed us," I try to assure him, but he just shakes his head at me, finally looking up, torment clear in his swirling blue eyes.

"I wasn't there when my mom got beaten up, ending up in the hospital. I couldn't do a damn thing when that bastard Julian was hitting on you. I didn't know that cunt was praying on Loki until afterwards, and Kai...Fuck!" He twirls, punching the bag again so hard that blood splatters his chest. My heart breaks for him. Our protector. "How did I not know, Lilly? How did I not see that he was hurting so bad, for so long?" Anguish is clear in his voice, and he looks at me, begging for answers that I'm not sure I have.

"Oh, love. You were in a hell of your own then. You all were. It wasn't your fault, none of it was your fault."

At my words he drops to his knees, his head in his hands as his shoulders shake, great heaving sobs leaving his body. I don't hesitate, dropping in front of him and wrapping my arms around his huge frame. His own arms band around me, and he buries his head in my chest, pulling me tightly against him. Tears stream down my cheeks as he cries in my arms, falling apart as I hold him.

*When will the torment end? When will we be free of the horrors that we've experienced?*

We clutch each other, his pain surrounding us like a dark cloud full of stinging insects. Gradually, the smoke lifts, Jax's sobs subsiding until his breathing is somewhat back to normal. He lifts his head, gazing up at me with red rimmed eyes, dried tears on his cheeks matching my own.

"Baby Girl," he croaks out, voice hoarse. "I'm so sorry..."

"Don't you dare apologise for being vulnerable, Jax Griffiths," I tell him sternly. "It's what makes you human, and just makes me love you so much more."

He gives me a smile, letting go of my waist and sitting up on his knees with his hands coming up to cup my face in his bloodied palms.

"I should be the one to apologise. I've been so tied up with everything, the pregnancy, the wedding, and the others. I haven't given you the time you needed, Jax. I'm so sorry." A sob escapes my lips this time, my vision blurring.

"Don't you dare apologise, Lilly Darling," Jax scolds, using my own words against me. "You've had so much happen, in such a short time. And you're the glue that sticks us together, the air that we all breathe. The others needed you more."

"But you needed me, too, and I didn't notice." It's my turn to hang my head, only his grip stops me, forcing my gaze to his.

"You are everything, Lilly Darling," he whispers, pulling back, and he gazes at me with swirling blue eyes, full of fierce love and adoration. "Never doubt that. And you noticed now." I take a deep breath, accepting his words and vowing to myself that I'll keep an eye on my gentle giant.

"There was something that I wanted to ask you," I say, nerves floating in my stomach as I look up at him. It's so silly, given all that we've been through, but I can't help being a little nervous at what I'm about to ask. Even so, I know that it's the right decision.

"Shoot," he tells me, still looking at me like I hung the moon, his blue eyes soft and a little less pain filled.

"So, I was chatting to Lisa the other day, and she, uh, said that she doesn't have to be the one to deliver the baby. So I was wondering if you would?" I say, stumbling over my words a little. He's stock still, blinking, his gaze blue fire. "Jax?"

"You want me to deliver your baby?" he asks softly, his voice holding a note of disbelief. I place my hands on his broad chest, feeling his hot skin through his sweat soaked tank top. His heart pounds hard, like he's just run a marathon.

"I can't think of anyone else I'd rather have, Jax," I tell him, my own voice sincere.

A small gasp leaves me as I see the blue of his eyes turn misted once more. His grip on my face tightens.

"These hands have brought so much death, Baby Girl," he rasps out, and my own breathing becomes painful. "I would be honoured to bring some life into the world for once. Thank you."

A tear escapes my eye, falling down my tear stained cheek as I lean up, too full to say anything, presenting my lips to him. He kisses me tenderly, as if I am the most precious thing in the world to him. As if I am the light to his dark, the good to his bad. The angel to his monster.

I try to heal him a little with my kiss, tell him that it doesn't matter what he's done before, what he might do in order to survive. I love him, flaws, sins and all.

And the room fills with our love as we embrace, chasing away the dark shadows of the past, bathing us in its glow.

I just hope that it's enough. Julian isn't finished yet. My punishment still awaits, and I've the sinking feeling that whatever it will be, will test us to our limits.

# CHAPTER THIRTY-TWO

LILLY

Before I know it, the night of Jax's fight is upon us, and I'm standing in front of my, well technically Loki's, mirror. Jax calls himself The Black Knight - *gotta love a theme* - I looked him up, videos of his fights are on YouTube. From what I can tell, he's good, really fucking good, his opponents unable to withstand his methodical attacks for very long. His fights are fast and brutal; he doesn't appear to have ever lost a match and seems to have become a bit of a legend in the underground MMA scene.

I cast my eye over my outfit for tonight, giving myself a smirk in the mirror. I'm soon realising that comfort is key where being pregnant is concerned. So I've opted for sexy loungewear, sporting some MagicStitch-Witch leggings, in their red astronomy print, my legs a kaleidoscope of reds, oranges, pinks, and electric blue. On my top half, I'm wearing a white tank top that I had printed especially for the occasion. The internet and express shipping really is amazing. For make-up and hair, I've gone with dark smokey eyes and messy, tumbling brunette waves cascading over my shoulders. As I'm not allowed to wear my beloved heels - *the guys banned them as soon as we discovered I was pregnant, the fuckturds* - I'm wearing a pair of Irregular Choice trainers that Loki bought me as a compromise.

They're not just any trainers, and I may have launched myself at him when I opened the box. They're platform high tops, covered in a crazy busy Care Bear print, with metallic rainbows on the heels, pink faux fur padded collar, and removable Care Bear plushies in front of the laces. *Oh, and they light up, motherfucker!*

A low whistle sounds as the man of the hour walks in, and our eyes meet in the mirror - *that seems to be happening to me a lot recently*. I take Jax in as he stalks towards me, from his black gym shorts, to the all black T-shirt that acts like a second skin, flowing over his muscles, and clinging to every ridge and line.

His lip quirks up as he takes in the design on the front of my tank. It's the Black Knight Corporation logo, only I changed the text to say 'The Black Night', in a font called Beast, which is, well, beast-like. I also included a splash of red in the form of blood splatter across the Knight's helmet that makes up the normal logo.

"You like it?" I ask as he steps up behind me, engulfing me in his lemon drizzle cake scent, his huge arms coming round and pulling me close.

"I fucking love it, Baby Girl," he rumbles, nuzzling his nose into my hair-line behind my ear, shivers skittering across my skin as he takes a deep inhale. A growl tumbles from his lips, vibrating through me straight to my core. "I'm gonna need you after the fight, baby. But you'll need to remember your safe-word. I won't be in control, so tell me now if that will be too much."

My whole body lights up, my breathing picking up as his words settle inside me, starting a flame in my centre.

"I'm fine with that," I whisper, watching his pupils dilate in the mirror.

"Hard limits?" he asks, watching me back intently. I think for a moment.

"Nothing that might hurt the baby, obviously," I say, and he gives a sharp nod. "And I think no choking, just to be safe. But you can still put your hand round my throat, just not restrict oxygen."

"Time to go, bro!" Loki calls from downstairs, interrupting us.

"Let's go, Baby Girl," Jax murmurs in my ear, taking another deep inhale before stepping back. He takes hold of my hand when I turn round, tugging me downstairs.

"You look hot as fuck, baby mama!" Loki exclaims, his eyes raking over my body. I roll my eyes at him and my apparently new nickname. I still check him out, and he looks mouthwateringly good. He's wearing a black form fitting T-shirt, too, and snug black ripped jeans, tucked into black biker boots, and what looks like a black bandana around his neck.

"You'll need a jacket, Princess. It's cold outside," Ash tells me from behind, and I turn round, my jaw dropping when I catch sight of him.

He's dressed identically to Loki, only his fully inked arms make it look like his sleeves are long, and ink peeps through the rips in his jeans. I've never seen him so casually dressed to go out before, and Her Vagisty practically weeps at the sight. Before I realise what I'm doing, I let go of Jax's hand, stride over to Ash, and grab the back of his neck, slamming my lips against his.

It takes him a second to get over the shock, but soon his arms are pulling me in, and he's kissing me back just as fiercely as I kiss him. It's messy, feral, and glorious. A cough sounds behind us, and I break away, panting and aching for more.

"What the fuck did he do to earn a kiss like that?" Loki whines, and I chuckle, my eyes darting to Ash's red swollen lips that are pulled up into his signature smirk.

"Here you are, darling," Kai's soft melodic voice sounds behind me, and I turn to see him holding out my vintage red and white baseball jacket.

"Thanks, love," I smile back, placing a gentle kiss on his lips and appreciating that his outfit matches the others, with the addition of his black framed glasses.

Putting the jacket on, I walk over to Loki, kissing him on his adorable pouting lips, pulling back before he can deepen it, then doing the same to Jax.

"There you are, everyone has had a kiss."

"Not the fucking same, Pretty Girl," Loki grumbles.

"Come on, grumpy gills," I tease, taking his hand in mine and leading him to the front door of our dorm. "Let's go watch Jax beat the shit out of some poor sap."

It takes about forty minutes to get to the fight location, and I'm surprised to see we're approaching what looks like an old abandoned warehouse in the middle of nowhere.

"What is this place?" I ask as we pull up at the end of a row of cars. There must be over a hundred parked up here.

"This is one of the homes of King of the Streets, an underground fight club," Ash says into the dark interior. He turns to face me from the front passenger seat as Kai puts Jax's truck into park. "Don't fucking wander off. Don't fucking speak to anyone. Understood, Princess?"

I glare at him, feeling a little bratty, but Jax grips my hand tightly next to me.

"Fine," I sigh, earning an eye twitch from my fiancé and a growl from Jax. "I'll be good."

I smell vanilla and cocoa before Loki whispers into my other ear.

"I won't be."

Before I can retort - *although, let's be frank here, what does one say to that?!* - chilled air hits me as he exits the truck, my nipples pebbling under my tank. The other doors open, and Jax keeps hold of my hand, helping me out of the truck. His arm practically vibrates with tension, and I can see him looking around like a predator, evaluating our surroundings.

We enter the building, the low hum of conversation blanketing us, drowned out by the sounds of *Ready or Not* by the Fugees, Ms. Lauryn Hill, Wyclef Jean and Pras. *Got to love a classic fight song!* Harsh floodlights highlight the ring in the centre of the vast space, although ring isn't quite accurate. It's cage-like, in that it's made up of metal fence panels, the kind with metal chain link for sides, so that a cage is created on the bare concrete floor. This is not UFC standard, not by a long shot, and I grip Jax's arm tightly with my free hand as worry floods my system.

As I look around, I notice that most of the people around me have bandana masks covering their lower faces, and a chill shivers down my spine at the eerie sight of so many devils, skulls, and scary clowns that surround me. I look at my guys, seeing them pull up their own bandanas, the lower part of their faces a print of a mediaeval Knight's helmet. Jax is the only one who leaves his face bare.

People take note as we walk towards the ring-cage, and I can see them giving all of us appraising looks. Jax's upper lip curls in a snarl as someone wolf whistles at me, his head whipping in the direction of the sound.

"Save it for the fight," Ash orders, placing a hand on Jax's shoulder, causing my Viking to pause and take a deep breath.

Jax doesn't speak, just resumes walking. I can see the scowl on his face, his eyes distant yet focused at the same time. Like he's not here with us at all, but with his opponent already.

One of the metal fences opens, and Jax leads us into the cage. My breathing quickens as I gaze around at the people surrounding us, fingers gripping the chain link and faces hidden by their masks. A guy comes up to us, his face also hidden, a grinning skull printed over the fabric, colourful ink decorating his arms in full sleeves.

"You ready, Knight?" he asks Jax, and Jax nods, then turns to face me.

His hand leaves mine, coming up to tangle in my hair, pulling my body flush against his. My heart thumps in my chest as he looks deep into my eyes, the blue of his own almost entirely swallowed up by black. Using my hair, he pulls my face to his, his lips dominating mine in a bruising, possessive kiss. I submit, not having any choice or desire to do otherwise, and a moan sounds in my throat as his tongue brushes mine.

A growl leaves him in response, and I swallow it greedily, my skin feeling too tight as his kiss wreaks havoc on me. He starts to pull back, but before he can completely break away, I bite down hard on his lower lip, the copper of his blood filling my mouth. Pulling back, I smirk up at him, then lick my lower lip where his blood started to drip down my chin. He leaves the trail of red to drip into his blond beard, his nostrils flared, and a feral look on his face. His beast is riding him hard tonight for sure.

"You just can't help yourself, can you, Pretty Girl?" Loki asks, stepping up behind me and nuzzling my neck in the same spot Jax did. "Don't worry, brother. I'll keep our girl warm for you," he teases, earning a loud growl from Jax that raises the hair on my arms.

"Seems like you can't either," I respond dryly, letting Loki pull me away and back out of the cage, Kai follows behind us, Ash hanging back for a moment, presumably to give Jax some last minute encouragement.

Jax keeps his gaze on me, until Ash physically grabs his face, obviously telling him to keep his head in the game if the scowl on both guys' faces is any indicator.

A moment later, the colourful inked guy comes back over, and Ash leaves, heading out of the ring alongside another guy. My eyes flit back to Jax to see him squaring off against a mean looking motherfucker. His face is a mess, nose squashed and scars running across it. He's about the same height and build as Jax, so they're clearly well matched.

"Who's he?" I whisper, stepping closer to the chain link fencing, Loki tight to my back but not squashing me. Kai is on my left, and Ash comes up to my right, caging me in a protective semi circle.

"He's known as The Crusher," Ash tells me, the worry courses through my veins when the guy smiles an evil grin at Jax.

"He looks...like a fucking psycho," I say at a loss for a better word to describe the maniac that Jax is about to fight. "And why aren't they wearing gloves?"

"It's an underground bare knuckle fight," Kai answers, his hand brushing mine. "No gloves, no rounds, no rules."

"What?!" I exclaim, watching and feeling sick as Jax and The Crusher step apart, the referee stepping back and signalling for the fight to begin.

The crowd around me goes wild, chanting and shouting, but it's as if I'm under water, hardly hearing them as Jax circles his opponent. The guy tries to kick Jax, but he easily brushes it off, throwing a brutal punch to the man's unprotected face. I wince as blood, and what looks like a tooth, flies across the concrete floor.

"Nice," Ash says beside me, but the madman facing Jax just laughs, then launches himself at my Viking, wrapping his arms round Jax's torso, looking like he's trying to squeeze the life out of him.

"Shake him off, Knight!" Loki shouts angrily as Jax gets pinned to the fence opposite us. Jax punches the guy in the side of the head several times, but Crusher holds fast, even though it looks like blood drips down the side of his face.

The two fighters grapple for what feels like hours, but realistically can only be a minute or two at the most. Jax's muscles strain, trying to get the upper hand, but he can't seem to untangle this crazy motherfucker from round his ribs.

"Looks like our Knight just needs a little more incentive," Loki whispers in my ear, and I startle, not having realised that he'd stepped up so close behind me, his front pressing to my back.

His hand comes round my front, making its way down over my top, shivers dancing over my skin as he lifts my tank and slips his hand under the waistband of my leggings.

"Loki," I grit out, his fingers dipping into my knickers, a husky laugh sounding in my ear as he discovers just how wet I am. In my defence, Ash started it, looking so fucking edible in those ripped jeans, then Jax's kiss added fuel to the fire.

"Looks like watching Jax beat the shit out of that guy is making our girl all hot and bothered," Loki says, loud enough for the other two to hear, and they step closer.

"Loki, what the fuck are you doing?" Ash growls out, tension in his tone. "Fucking exhibitionist."

Loki's fingers slip through my folds, and I moan low, feeling his hardness pressing against my lower back, as he leisurely strokes my clit, lighting me on fire.

"Loki," I groan this time, losing myself to his touch, those clever musician's fingers playing me like a maestro.

"Look at Jax, baby. Watch our boy as I make you come," he murmurs huskily in my ear, and my gaze focuses back on Jax, who's still grappling with his opponent. "Hey, Knight!" Loki leans back slightly and shouts, loud enough to cut through the din of voices around us.

Jax's head darts up, the loss of concentration earning him a sharp jab to the ribs, but he doesn't register it, his eyes taking in where Loki's hand is in between my legs. Loki thrusts two fingers deep inside me, and I can't help but cry out, watching as Jax's nostrils flare and his face fills with rage.

"You've done it now, bro," Kai whispers, amusement in his voice, when with an almighty roar, Jax manages to throw off the other guy, sweeping his foot in a move that sends The Crusher crashing backwards.

Jax is on him in a second, knees either side of the other guy's torso and pounding his head with his fists. Loki matches each strike with a thrust into my dripping pussy, and I gasp and writhe as ripples of pleasure radiate over my skin, building me higher. The crowd are going wild, screaming with bloodlust as Jax whales on his opponent, who can do nothing but try to cover his head with his arms.

Loki's pace picks up, the heel of his hand hitting my clit, and I watch, helpless to fight my impending climax, as the ref walks over and pulls Jax off, raising his arm and declaring him the winner. Loki bites down on my neck just as Jax's wild gaze finds mine, and I explode, my cries lost in the screams and jeers of the crowd.

But Jax sees me, watching with a ravenous hunger as I fall apart on his best friend's fingers. My chest heaves as if it were me in the ring, instead of him, and just as I'm coming down from my high, Jax tears out of the ref's grip, running towards us.

My heart pounds when he leaps at the fence, somehow managing to climb it and drop down beside me, Kai stepping back just in time to avoid being crushed. Loki turns us, pulling his hand out of my knickers, my release glistening on his fingers.

Jax stares at me, chest heaving, ignoring all of the shouts and hollers that sound around us. His gaze flits to Loki's hand as the mischief maker holds it out from behind me. Jax's nostrils flare, scenting the air like a wolf, and he takes a step forward, pressing his sweat soaked chest to mine. He leans down, taking an almighty sniff of Loki's hand, then in a move that shocks me and lights me up all at once, his tongue darts out and licks Loki's fingers, a low rumbling groan sounding in his throat as he cleans them.

My brain short circuits, Her Vagisty screaming *'Hells Yeah!'* as I watch him, his eyes closed and rapturous delight on his face. I can feel Loki's arm trembling, his other hand gripping my waist tightly, obviously affected by Jax's move.

"Maybe next time he'll join us and Kai, huh, Pretty Girl?" he whispers softly in my ear, and I whimper.

Jax's head snaps up at the sound, his pupils so dilated that only a thin ring of electric blue is visible. Loki steps back, leaving my back exposed, but although the warehouse is cold, I burn. I take a step away from Jax, kicking my trainers off and shrugging out of my jacket. I stare into his eyes and watch him like you would a wild animal, trying to anticipate when it'll strike.

He stays still, watching as I take another step back, my flight instincts screaming at me to run.

# CHAPTER THIRTY-THREE

LILLY

"Everyone out!" Ash shouts, giving no shits about the grumbling people round us. I don't take my gaze off of Jax, who stands there, completely still apart from the rise and fall of his chest. "Now!" Ash roars, and I feel more than see people scatter for the doors.

Within moments it's just us, and my fingers tingle at the sudden silence. Jax holds my gaze, then takes a slow menacing step forward. I take one back, not taking my eyes off him for a minute. His own eyes widen, sparkling with the chase, as he takes another step towards me, and I back up again, my heart pounding, breathing fast.

We repeat this dance until I round the corner, taking a few steps before bumping into something hard and solid, but warm. Ginger surrounds me, and I feel suddenly lightheaded with relief. It's short lived as Ash leans down, careful not to touch me.

"In the cage, Princess."

I swallow hard, seeing the opening into the cage-ring to my left. Jax growls, and my head whips to face him, seeing that he's almost reached me. So I do what every stupid female lead in horror movies does, backing into the cage, soon finding myself in the middle. Jax enters, the opening shutting with a clang that seals my fate.

Accepting my fate, I close my eyes, my other senses becoming heightened as soon as the darkness engulfs me. I hear Jax stalking towards me, the whisper of his trainers on the concrete loud in the quiet. I feel the tickle of air across my fingertips, smell the tang of blood and sweat in the air. My tongue darts out, and I taste the salt of my own fear on my lips.

The heat from Jax's body caresses my exposed skin as he steps right up to me, and I open my eyes to find his broad sweaty chest in front of me, his T-shirt gone, and his rune-like tattoos on full display. I track my eyes upwards, until I'm looking into his gaze once more, the blue still mostly swallowed up by black.

I tremble as he leans forward, his hand coming up to wrap round my throat, holding my head close and sniffing my hair and neck. Another whimper leaves my lips unbidden as his teeth graze the sensitive flesh where my neck and shoulder meet, and a low rumbling purr comes from him in response.

In a lightning fast move, he lets go of my throat, grabbing the underside of my thighs, and pulls me up so that my legs wrap round his thick waist. He drops to his knees, jarring us, then leans over until I'm lying flat on my back on the concrete, the cool surface making me hiss. Letting go of me, he makes his way down my body, sniffing every so often, his hands tracing my curves, purring as he reaches my rounded stomach. He pauses at the juncture of my thighs, and I cry out as he presses his face down, taking a huge inhale, then rubbing my scent all over his face. Fuck, that shouldn't be so hot, but it really is, liquid pooling in my centre as he marks himself with my musk.

His fingers grip the top of my waistband, pulling my leggings and knickers off and tossing them behind him. Within seconds his face is back at my pussy, eating me out ravenously, like I'm his last damn meal. I get no build up, no easing into it, and am still sensitive from Loki's attentions earlier, plus wound up from our chase, that my orgasm tears through me almost painfully. Liquid rushes out of me, which Jax greedily laps up, each flick of his tongue making me twitch.

I'm a panting, gasping mess, my entire body tingling, when he sits back on his heels, his huge erection straining under his shorts. He looks at me with a smug satisfaction, his beard full of my release. Leaning forward, he grasps my hips in his large hands, surprising me with his gentleness as he turns me over, bringing my hips up so that I end up on hands and knees, with him kneeling behind me.

A low keening moan leaves my lips as I feel him start to push his way inside me, my arms already shaking from the pleasure that whispers over and through me at his invasion. With a sharp snap of his hips, he bottoms out, a low rumbling purr sounding in his chest, as a cry tears through my lips, his hands rubbing all over my arse.

I feel him lean forward, the neck of my tank going taut before the tearing of fabric sounds in the air. My top falls down my arms, my bra following next, thankfully not torn - *cuntbandit* - a gasp falling from my lips as he rakes his fingernails down my back. The move sends tingles falling all over me, and I push back, feeling him hit my fucking cervix. I swear my eyes roll all the way back.

He grunts, wrapping my hair around a fist and pulling my head back at an angle that leaves my neck exposed. Clearly deciding that he's had enough of taking it slow, he pulls out, his free hand holding me in place by my hip, before slamming back inside me.

I scream with the pleasure-pain that being impaled on Jax's monster cock creates, my whole body shaking and jerking as he fucks me hard and fast. Snarls sound behind me, his grip on my hair and hip tightening, his thrusts wild in their ferocity. My nails try to bury themselves into the concrete, my cries and whimpers filling the room, as my body is assaulted by raw pleasure. I let go completely, submitting totally to his will, and the freedom of letting my instincts take over soon have me reaching an earth shattering climax.

My inner walls slam around Jax's cock so hard that he grunts and snarls louder, forcing his way inside me as my cunt clenches and grips him. Screams leave my throat raw as the orgasm reaches epic proportions, my whole body shaking violently with the force of it. Jax's grip is the only thing keeping me up as he keeps pounding into me, and with one final hard thrust, he comes with a roar, falling forward and biting the same shoulder that Loki did earlier, the sharp pain causing another wave of rapture to hit me.

My arms give way as he twitches above me, his dick still pulsing inside of me. He manages to cushion our fall, rolling us so that I end up half on top of him, my back to his front, my head resting on his enormous bicep and his dick still nestled inside my twitching pussy. We lie that way, panting, our skin covered in sweat, as the high recedes, leaving a feeling of utter euphoria.

"You okay, Baby Girl?" he rumbles out after a while, his voice husky and sending shivers across my skin.

"Yes," I croak out, "I'm amazing."

He chuckles, his hand moving down to cup my stomach. At that moment, the baby decides to do an almighty kick, and Jax freezes behind me.

"Was that?" he asks in wonder, then a delighted laugh sounds behind me as the baby kicks again.

"You can feel it?" I ask, excitement chasing away the lethargy that the incredible sex had left me in.

"Shit, yeah," he replies as another kick lands. "Guys!"

Within seconds, the others are crouched down next to us, looking a little worried.

"Is everything okay? Is the baby okay?" Loki asks, voice panicked, and I can't help the blissed out smile as I grab his hand, placing it over the spot where Jax's was just seconds ago.

Clearly indulging us, the baby gives another kick, and Loki's eyes go wide.

"Fuck, that's our baby."

I can only nod my head, my eyes misting as Loki's glisten, a laugh falling from his lush lips as the baby kicks him again.

"It's got your fighting streak, Jax, that's for sure!" Loki exclaims, making room for Kai, who chuckles when his hand is kicked, too.

"You clever beautiful darling," he murmurs, staring into my eyes with such love, that the mist turns to drops, and one slides down the side of my face, which is still pillowed on Jax's bicep.

"May I?" Ash's low drawl sounds, and Kai moves to one side so that Ash can kneel down and place his hand on my stomach.

For a moment nothing happens, and I hold my breath, begging our unborn child for one more so that he can feel it, too. It's clearly feeling very obliging, or is trying to impress its fathers, as Ash's hand jumps with another kick. His eyes snap up to mine, the steel in them soft.

"Strong, just like its mother," he whispers, and I swallow hard.

"Just like its fathers, too," I reply, another teardrop falling down my cheek.

I shiver as the cold air suddenly hits me, and Ash leans down, placing a gentle, reverent kiss on my lips.

"Come on, Princess. Let's get you home and into a nice hot bath," he says, leaning back, then helping me to my feet.

Loki whips off his T-shirt, pulling it over my head, and I nestle into its warm vanilla smell. Kai fetches, then helps me into my knickers and leggings, and Jax brings me my trainers, helping to slip them onto my feet. I bask in their attention, as they each take care of me, Ash wrapping his arm around me and pulling me close.

We walk out of the warehouse into the night, the stars twinkling behind us and the full moon lighting the way to Jax's truck. Getting in, I'm sandwiched between Ash and Jax, soaking up their warmth, and we start the drive back to Highgate. Back home.

Although, really, we're already home, as home is where the heart is. And mine is sitting around me, cradled in four bodies, in four men, the five of us bound to each other in ways that can never be separated.

# CHAPTER THIRTY-FOUR

LILLY

The two weeks after Jax's fight are a complete blur, what with exams - *which hopefully I don't completely fail at!* - wedding planning, and another appointment with Lisa, my midwife. Turns out I'm a teensy bit anaemic, which Kai takes as a personal affront, feeding me steak and green leafy veg until I can't stand the sight of it. Jax gets me some iron infused water, so I start taking that as well.

Luckily, Erica is incredibly good at what she does, organising a taster menu at a hotel in town, getting the marquee sorted and built, as well as contacting the registrar who'll perform the ceremony. She does all this and more effortlessly, which is a huge relief as I haven't a Scooby Doo - clue - what I'm meant to be doing.

She organsied a last minute fitting with the dressmakers, just to ensure that no adjustments need to be made due to my changing shape. A couple of minor alterations later, and it fits me to perfection. The dress hangs in its garment bag in Ash's room, in his woodland mansion, as I've named it. I'm getting ready here, along with Willow who is my maid of honour and only bridesmaid. She practically cried, throwing herself at me when I asked her, silly fairy.

The boys are staying at Highgate because according to a stupid tradition that no one knows the origin of, they can't be with me, as it's unlucky for the bridegroom to see the bride the night before the wedding.

My hand trails down the garment bag, my stomach turning uncomfortably with nerves as I pace the room. It's late, Willow already in bed and probably snoring away. I worry my lip, unable to settle. My mind races, like a pinball machine, landing on one thought, only to fly to another.

I'm excited for tomorrow, to become Ash's wife is a dream come true. But it also breaks my heart knowing that I can't marry the others, too. It almost feels like a betrayal, even though I know that they don't see it that way. I turn, my back to the open stairway, as I pace to the window.

And all this stuff with Julian, with Black Knight Corp., buzzes at me like a wasp. *How will we take them down? How can I help? What if we fail?*

A noise behind me has me spinning, only to come up short as I see my four Knights, dressed in grey sweatpants and nothing else, standing shoulder to shoulder. It's enough to still my swirling thoughts as my brain short circuits.

"W-what are you doing here?" I ask, a sudden lightness making me feel as though I could float away. Ash steps forward, his tattooed chest looking almost alive in the low lamplight as he walks towards me, stopping in front of me. As always, my heart rate picks up at his nearness.

"We both know that none of us would have gotten any sleep, Princess, if we'd spent the night apart," he murmurs, his voice low and deep, telling me that we won't just be sleeping tonight. At least not straight away.

"We'll be gone by the morning, darling," Kai tells me, stepping forward until he's standing to my left.

"No need to worry about bad luck, Baby Girl," Jax adds, stepping up to my left.

"And anyway," Loki drawls, sauntering towards us until he stands behind me. "We make our own luck in this world, Pretty Girl." My temperature skyrockets at being surrounded by them, being caged in by them. I shiver, my nipples becoming hard points underneath my silk nightdress when a hand trails down my bare arm.

"And the...outfits?" I say, my voice all kinds of breathy as the hand on my other side pushes down the thin strap of the nighty, the other strap quickly following until it pools at my feet in a puddle of rose pink.

"Loki told us that, according to your 'not-gangbang' books, this is lingerie for men," Ash informs me, a slight smirk tilting one side of his lips.

"He would be correct," I breathe, looking down and seeing the clear outline of Ash's, Kai's, and Jax's hard dicks pressed against the soft grey fabric. Not to be forgotten about, Loki pushes his hips against me, proving that he is in a similar state of arousal.

Loki's hands come round my sides, cupping and kneading my breasts, groaning.

"These have definitely gotten bigger," he sighs appreciatively, tweaking my nipples and making me hiss at their sensitivity. "Nipples are more sensitive, too."

Ash bends down, taking one bud in his mouth, sucking and flicking it with his tongue until I'm writhing against Loki. I feel Jax's hand on my left making its way down to the juncture of my thighs, quickly finding the bundle of nerves and circling it.

"So fucking wet for us already," he rumbles out, his finger moving faster until I cry out.

"And so responsive, darling," Kai whispers, his hand dipping below Jax's, two fingers sliding into me with ease.

I gasp as they work in synchronicity, playing my body like experts. Lights dance across my vision, my body going completely rigid as my climax crashes over me. My knees buckle with the force of it, but they hold me up, working me through my shudders and cries, until I'm a glowing thing, floating to the heavens.

"I think she's ready for us, boys," Ash chuckles, and suddenly I'm lifted up, my legs wrapping around a firm waist. I crack my eyes to see that I'm holding onto Jax, my eyebrows squishing together in confusion. *I swear Ash was just in front of me...*

Jax carries me over to the huge bed - *I'm sure it wasn't this big the last time I was here!* - passing me into a set of vanilla scented arms.

"Hey, Pretty Girl," Loki whispers in my ear, pulling my back flush against his front, his hot skin almost scalding me as I realise that he's naked beneath me.

"Hey," I murmur, as he lies down, with me still on top of his body.

"Loki, what..." I start to ask, as he grabs my thighs, bringing them up and over his hips so that I'm opened wide before Jax.

"Shhhh," he hushes, nuzzling my neck as he lets go of one leg, moving his hand so that it feels like he's grasping his hard cock.

"What a sight," Jax purrs, taking a bottle of clear lube that Kai passes him.

He squirts some into his hand, barely warming it up before he coats my pussy making me gasp at the cold, moving to rub some onto my rosebud. He slips a large finger in, and I moan low as he moves it back and forth a few times. I shudder as he pulls the digit out.

"Need a hand, bro?" he cockily asks Loki.

"Thanks, dude." My eyes are wide at this seemingly normal exchange, like Jax is offering Loki to help lift a heavy box, not to help him get his dick into my arsehole.

My eyes go wider still as Jax reaches between my legs, my view cut off by my baby bump. But I hear Loki groan, feeling his tip line up with my puckered hole.

"Loki," I gasp, the sharp sting of his thick pierced cock pushing past the ring of muscle making me squirm.

"That's it, Pretty Girl," he grits out, both hands back on my thighs pulling them apart wider. "Let me in, baby."

My nails dig into his forearms, hard enough to break the skin as he keeps pushing forward until he bottoms out - *pun intended.* Jax looks on with a lust filled gaze, his hand wrapped around his shaft, pumping up and down at the sight.

"Fuuuuck," Loki moans, moving his hips underneath me, pumping himself gently in and out of me.

"You ready, Baby Girl?" Jax asks in a husky whisper, leaning down and capturing my lips in his before I can answer.

He pulls away, taking one of my legs out of Loki's grip, putting my ankle on his shoulder. Loki stops moving when Jax starts to nudge his way inside my dripping pussy.

"Shit!" I cry out as he stretches me. "So full."

"That's it, baby. Take our cocks like a good fucking girl," Loki hisses in my ear, groaning as with a final thrust, Jax's hips make contact.

They start to move, one pulling out as the other pushes in, finding a rhythm that drives me wild, whipping my nerves into a frenzy. I feel the bed dip by my head, and look up to see an upside down Kai, stroking his glinting cock.

"Up on your hands, darling," he orders, and the guys pause to help me balance on Loki's chest. "Good girl. Now open up."

I do as ordered, moaning as Kai slides his thick length into my mouth, not even pausing as he pushes it down my throat.

"Look at that throat bulge," he coos, and Jax rumbles in appreciation, one hand coming up to my neck to encircle and squeeze my throat. Kai hisses, pulling out to allow me to take a breath, before pushing in again, cutting off my airway once more.

Loki and Jax start moving again, and all I can do is relax as they fuck me, waves of pleasure rolling over me.

"My turn," I hear Ash rumble, and I'm tugged off Kai's cock by my hair, his piercings clacking on my teeth. I hear Kai growl, and open my eyes to see Ash pressing the tip of his dick to my lips, painting them with his precum. "Open wide, Princess, and let me fuck that sassy mouth of yours."

I do as he commands, and he fulfils his promise, thrusting hard and fucking the back of my throat with sharp thrusts.

"Shit, dude. You want her to be able to say her vows tomorrow," Jax chuckles, groaning as my pussy tightens around him when he hits my G-spot over and over again.

Ash slows down, his thrusts gentling but still deep. I moan as fingers find my clit, rubbing circles around and over it, sending a fire sweeping through me. My hair is pulled, my lips releasing Ash's cock with a pop as Kai soon pushes his inside. I moan and writhe as the fire spreads, barely noticing Kai's rough moves.

"She's so close," Jax grits out, picking up speed, the sound of his hips snapping against me loud in the room.

Loki follows his pace, and I explode, hearing their grunts as I clench and clamp down around them. Loki is the first to follow me into oblivion, biting down on my neck, sending another orgasm crashing over me. Jax roars his release a second or two afterwards, his hand tightening around my throat and Kai's cock, causing Kai to pour his release down my throat.

He pulls out, Jax loosening his grip and letting go as he pulls out of me, causing Loki to slip out, too. I fall back onto Loki, lying there panting, my heart pounding as bliss coats every fibre of my being.

"My turn, Princess," Ash repeats, pulling me off Loki, my back landing on the cool sheets.

He climbs on top of me, his body flush with mine as he pushes inside my aching cunt. My legs automatically wrap around his hips, pulling him deeper and making us both groan.

"Ash," I whimper, his hands coming up to cup my face, his elbows either side of my head.

"You can come for me, can't you, beautiful?" he coaxes, his hips moving in a slow nerve tingling rhythm.

I vaguely register *Earned It* by The Weekend starting to play, the song bringing back memories of Loki buried inside me, singing, as I was tied to Ash's bed. As if sharing that same memory, Ash chuckles.

"I'll tie you up again soon, Princess," he whispers, bringing his forehead to mine as he starts moving his hips faster. "You were made for us, Lilly Darling. Every atom belongs to the four of us, just as every part of us is yours. You make us greater than the sum of our parts, until we become more than we ever thought possible. You are as vital as the blood that pumps in our veins, as crucial as the air that we breathe. You are our beating heart, and our souls are bound together for all eternity."

Ash may not be able to sing me to orgasm, but he can talk me into one. His words set off a chain reaction inside me, my pussy walls tightening around him as I come with a cry, clinging tightly to him. He thrusts a few more times, prolonging my pleasure, before he succumbs, coming deep inside me with a manly groan.

We stay locked together for several moments, breathing the same air as we hold each other, the high settling into our bones.

"Come, Princess, let's get you cleaned up whilst the guys change the sheets," Ash suggests, and I look around to see the others coming back into the room, shower fresh.

A small sound leaves me as Ash pulls out, then helps me up on shaky legs. He wraps his arm round my waist, walking me to the door, pausing as each of the others place a kiss on my no doubt swollen lips.

After showering, the warm water and Ash's ministrations making me all kinds of sleepy, I walk into the room, holding Ash's hand, to find the others waiting around the enormous bed, wearing boxers.

"Did you get a bigger bed?" I ask Ash, as he leads me to the side, indicating that I climb in.

"I figured that we'd all want to sleep with you sometimes, so it seemed like a good option," he tells me, voice matter of fact and completely unaware of the fact that I've just melted into a puddle of girl goo. "If that's okay with you?"

"It's perfect," I tell him softly, scooting into the middle.

"Shotgun!" Loki hollars, leaping onto the bed on my other side, Ash quickly climbing in beside me.

I giggle as Jax and Kai grumble, but climb in, too, Kai behind Loki and Jax behind Ash.

"I don't want your weapon of mass destruction waking me up, got it?" Ash deadpans, and we all burst into peals of laughter, tears streaming down my cheeks when Jax asks what the fuck he's talking about.

I fall asleep with a smile on my face, nestled in a bed of love, with my unborn child kicking away under two of its fathers' hands.

# CHAPTER THIRTY-FIVE

LILLY

I wake up the next morning, my body aching in the best possible way, the scent of my guys lingering in the bed with me. Lying there, I take a moment, the spring sunshine dancing across the ceiling.

*I'm getting married today.*

The thought fills me with giddy excitement, followed by a rolling feeling in my stomach as nerves settle in. *I wonder how Ash feels?*

"Rise and shine, you gorgeous bride!" Willow calls, stomping into the room and eyeing up the bed. "I'd join you in there, but Ash really needs to work on the soundproofing of this place." Her nose wrinkles even as her eyes twinkle with mirth.

"Oh God," I groan, my cheeks flushing as I hide under the duvet, which doesn't help at all considering it still smells like them.

"Come on, lazy bum!" she responds, way too cheery for this time in the morning as she yanks the covers off me. "The girls are already here to make you into a goddess for your harem."

"Urgh, fine," I grumble, sitting up then realising that I'm completely naked still. "Willow!"

She throws a silk robe at me, cackling evilly as she walks out the door.

Putting the robe on, I follow downstairs to find the large sitting room full of people. I pause, taking a deep breath before stepping into the fray.

Erica is the first to approach, an understanding smile on her face.

"How are you doing?" she asks, handing me a glass of juice with ice in it. I take a sip, giving her a grateful smile when I realise that it's tropical, my favourite.

"Terrified," I tell her with a huff of laughter. "Excited."

"As to be expected." She smiles warmly at me, guiding me to the table, one end of which has been set up like a dressing table, complete with a mirror with lights. "Now, Asher made it clear that my ovaries are on the line if you don't eat anything, so eat this up, then we'll get started."

I chuckle, not surprised anymore by Ash's dominating care of me. I do as ordered, finishing my homemade chocolate chip granola bar - *Kai, you legend* - and glass of fresh juice.

"Right, now comes the fun part!" Erica exclaims, leading me to the other end of the table, and sitting me down in front of the mirror. I'm kinda regretting my life choices right now, not having even put any knickers on.

For the next God knows how long, I'm primped, primed, and pampered to within an inch of my life. They even put rainbow colours in my hair to match the hem of the dress, pinning it in a complicated style that leaves the majority tumbling over one shoulder, my long lace edged veil pinned into place. When I look at myself in the mirror after I'm declared 'done', I hardly recognise the beautiful bride sitting before me.

Willow appears in the mirror, looking ethereal after her makeover, her eyes wide as usual.

"You look...wow," she whispers.

"You do, too," I murmur back, and her hand comes to my shoulder, mine coming up to grasp it.

"Dresses, ladies," Erica declares, ushering me out of my seat and up the stairs. "I'll leave you to get your underwear on, just shout when you're ready."

I step inside Ash's room once more, noticing that the bed has been made, a white gift bag sitting on top of it. There's a notecard inside, Ash's elegant scrawl over it.

*Wear this for me today, Princess*

I smile, taking the ivory silk lace out of the bag, impressed with his choices. Ivory silk and lace briefs, with a matching soft bralette with a low back so it won't be seen underneath my dress. Matching lace-edged thigh high hold ups—the kind that just grip without needing suspenders—complete the set.

There's a flat square box at the bottom, and I open it to find a beautiful lace garter, another note nestled in the lace.

*And wear this for the rest of us*

Smiling, I put it all on, marvelling at how comfortable it all is, and at how Ash clearly took that into account when buying it.

"Ready," I call out, looking in the full length mirror as Erica and the young dressmaker walk in.

"Excellent, now the dress," Erica claps her hands with glee as the dressmaker helps me into the dress, doing up the buttons that fasten it at the back.

Once secure, Erica brings over my new Irregular Choice heels, a wedding gift from Loki on the understanding that I only wear them for the ceremony, and wear flats for the rest of the day and night. They're the same style as my red sequin Dorothy heels, but are covered in white glitter, with a white bow on the toes.

"You look perfect, Lilly," Erica tells me softly, her eyes a little misted as we gaze at my reflection in the mirror. "Right, time to go."

My fingers tingle as I walk out of the room, my nerve endings firing all at once when I walk down the stairs to see Willow and Ryan waiting.

"Lilly, you look...astonishing," Ryan murmurs gruffly, his voice choked as he gazes at me.

He takes my hand in his huge one, his eyes misty, and I choke out a laugh.

"Don't get me started, my make-up took hours," I tell him, and we laugh. He leans in, pressing a light kiss on my cheek.

"Your mother would be so proud, little one," he whispers, and I blink furiously trying to keep the tears at bay.

"Time to get into the cars," Erica interrupts quietly, effectively dispelling the slight sadness.

Willow steps forward, handing me my bouquet of beautiful rainbow coloured flowers, and keeping hold of my hand, Ryan leads us out of the mansion. An old fashioned white car, with a ribbon wrapped around the flying lady on the front, awaits us, glinting in the sun.

"Where on earth did you get a vintage Rolls?" I exclaim, eyeing up the beautiful vehicle with appreciation.

"Your soon-to-be husband has his ways," Ryan tells me, a smirk of approval on his lips as the driver, who's in a very smart dove grey uniform, opens the door. "You ready?"

I take a deep breath of forest air, our luck holding as the spring sunshine beats down on us, lending its warmth for the day.

"As I'll ever be," I reply, stepping into the car, and towards my future.

---

## ASH

I stand gazing out at the stunning mountain view, beautifully framed by the floral archway. But I don't see a damn thing, waiting for Lilly, my bride, to arrive.

"You okay, bro?" Loki asks, clapping me on the back, his hand squeezing my shoulder. Kai and Jax are showing the final guests to their seats, and have been greeting people as they arrive.

"Why am I so fucking nervous, dude?" I ask, bewildered at the butterflies that have taken flight in my stomach.

"Because you're marrying the girl of our dreams, you fucker," Loki replies, and I know that he's only half joking, his hand tightening a little more on my shoulder.

"Yeah, I know, bro," I reply, turning to look at him, just as the musicians start playing the bride's piece of music.

My heart leaps in my chest as I face the aisle, and the sight that greets me stops my breath, the world pausing as she walks towards me. She looks...transcendent, her beauty surpassing everything in this universe and all the others. Her dress floats around her, hinting at her pregnancy, and I have to suppress a primal growl of satisfaction at her obvious fertility.

The dress is exquisite, and I follow down to the hem, which looks as though she's stepped into the setting sun behind us, bringing it with her. The timing of the ceremony now makes sense at least. She wears a long veil, but her face is free, her hazel stare locked on me when I tear my gaze back up to her radiant face.

I almost fall to my fucking knees at the smile she gives me, unsurety and nerves there but a happiness that I never knew I could inspire.

"I fucking hate you, bro," Loki grumbles in my ear, and I can't blame him. I would hate me, too.

Finally, Lilly is standing beside me, Ryan placing her hand in mine. She gives it a squeeze, a hint of amusement in her eyes as she looks at me.

"Great song choice," she comments, and I smile, wanting to laugh out loud.

I gave her free reign over everything, bar the music for today. And I didn't tell her either, as I wanted to keep it a surprise. The song being played on a baby grand and cello by The Piano Guys is a rendition of *A Thousand Years*, and I chose it after hearing that she went to see the Twilight films at midnight with a group of friends, and squealed when that werewolf took his shirt off. *Fucking amateur.* She laughed at me when I commented that I never understood why Bella had to choose between the two, although personally I was always team Jasper and Alice.

The piece comes to an end, those damn butterflies still flying around inside me.

"Dearly beloved..." The registrar begins, the rest of the ceremony passing by in a blur until suddenly I'm placing a ring, my ring, on her finger, and she's doing the same to me. Her hands don't shake, her words don't falter as she looks me dead in the eye and becomes my wife.

"You may now..." I don't wait for the fucker to continue, cupping her face with my hands and pulling her soft lips to mine.

It's the kiss of a new beginning, all fresh and sweet like the twilight mountain air that surrounds us. I kiss her as if she's the very air I need, the thing that keeps me breathing because she is. And she's so much more, to me, to all of us. She matches me stroke for stroke, her hands on my chest, gripping my morning suit and pulling me closer.

I vaguely register cheers and whoops, mostly coming from Loki behind me, but I'm lost in this woman, my fucking wife, and I don't ever want to be found. Reluctantly, I pull back, grinning when I see that she's just as affected as me, her pupils blown and lips swollen.

"Hello, wife," I murmur, tasting the smile on her lips.

"Hello, husband," she replies, and damn, if my knees don't go a little weak at hearing her call me that.

The registrar interrupts us, reminding me that we need to sign the register and marriage certificate, Loki and Jax following as witnesses. Once that's done, it's time for us to walk down the aisle, her hand tucked into the crook of my arm, man and wife. A delighted peal of laughter rings from her lips, echoing around us as the piano plays a version of *Earned It* by The Weekend. A blush coats her upper chest and cheeks, blooming under her skin, probably remembering what happened the two times she's heard this song.

"Naughty, husband," she teases with a smile as people throw rainbow petal confetti over us. I can't even be annoyed at the petals sticking to me, a shiver running through me at her words. I lean down, close enough to whisper in her ear.

"The next time you call me that, I'll be buried deep inside your sweet cunt, wife."

I watch enraptured as her nostrils flare, the red on her cheeks deepening as she licks her lips.

It's a promise that I intend to keep.

# CHAPTER THIRTY-SIX

LILLY

I sit back, stomach pleasantly full after eating our delicious mash up of British and American cuisine. We had scrambled egg and bacon on tiny pancakes, loaded hot dogs and chilli cheese fries, followed by a mango and cream dessert that looked like a boiled egg, and a selection of British cheeses and oatcakes to finish.

Patting my rounded stomach, I hear a deep chuckle either side of me.

"Full, Baby Girl?" Jax asks, his hand quickly dipping to ghost over my stomach in a protective gesture. Like Ash and Kai, Jax wears a light grey tailored morning suit, with a rainbow waistcoat and tie. Loki, my wonderful Knight of mischief, has gone for a full on rainbow suit, the fabric literally striped in rainbow colours. And he looks fucking stunning, as do the others, all tailored perfection and clean lines.

Because of our unconventional seating plan - *aka non-existent* - I'm sitting at a round table with all of my favourite people. Jax is on one side of me - *I dread to think how he won that privilege* - and Ash, my new husband, on the other. I'm not sure I'll ever get used to the fact that I'm now married. I'm now Mrs. Vanderbilt.

Kai is on the other side of Ash, Loki next to Jax. Willow is here with us, chatting to Lex and Ryan, who are also on our table.

I cast a glance over my shoulder and catch Julian's eye, shivering when he gives me a feline smile before turning back to talk to my uncle. Yep, Adrian turned up, and briefly congratulated Ash and I, although the smile didn't reach his eyes as he shook Ash's hand.

The sound of tinkling glass swings my gaze back to Ash, who rises in his seat, standing up and taking everyone in his sweeping steel gaze.

"Ladies and gentlemen, I'd like to start by thanking you for joining Lilly and I on our wedding day," he starts, briefly glancing down at me, a warm smile tugging his lips up. My own mimic him, my cheeks hurting from all of the smiling I've done today, most of which has been at my guys so I'll take the pain. "When Lilly agreed to be my wife, well, it truly was the happiest night of my life." He's staring at me as he says this last part, and my palms sweat, remembering that night at his parents' manor house, and how fraught with tension it was. But he means it, and I realise that really was a happy moment for him, one in a life full of sad moments. "My wife," he pauses, and takes a slight breath, letting me know that he's as affected by these new terms as I am. "My beautiful wife is a fan of Shakespeare, so I'd like to read *Sonnet 116* for her."

He looks back down at me, holding my gaze as he recites.

"'Let me not to the marriage of true minds
Admit impediments. Love is not love
Which alters when it alteration finds,
Or bends with the remover to remove:
O, no! it is an ever-fixed mark,
That looks on tempests and is never shaken;
It is the star to every wandering bark,
Whose worth's unknown, although his height be taken.
Love's not Time's fool, though rosy lips and cheeks
Within his bending sickle's compass come;
Love alters not with his brief hours and weeks,
But bears it out even to the edge of doom.
If this be error and upon me proved,
I never writ, nor no man ever loved.'"

I take a gasping breath as he finishes, realising that I'd held it the whole time that he spoke. His image wavers as I blink furiously, trying in vain to stop the tears from leaving my eyes. Cheers erupt around us as he bends down, capturing my lips in a kiss so tender and gentle that a small sob sounds in my throat.

"I love you, Lilly Vanderbilt," he tells me, his lips ghosting across mine as he pulls away so that I taste his words.

"I love you, Asher Vanderbilt," I whisper back, my voice raspy as I try to talk through the lump in my throat.

Another glass rings, and I look to see Ryan standing up, tugging at the neck of his shirt, his face going slightly red.

"I was there when Lilly came into the world, kicking and screaming as Lex passed her into her mother's arms. I was there when she learnt to crawl, then walk - at ten bloody months old mind, which I can tell you was a right nightmare!" He laughs along with us, then holds my gaze. "I was there when she started talking, when she went off to school for the first time, when she experienced a thousand other milestones that a young girl does. And some that she never should have had to." I bite my lip, Ash gripping one hand and Jax the other, his other hand wiping away the tear that escapes. Coughing, Ryan continues. "And now I'm here, standing in front of a beautiful woman, a beautiful wife, and wondering how I got so lucky to have such a wonderful daughter." He swipes his own wet eyes, Lex handing him a tissue whilst a cry-laugh escapes her. "And I couldn't be more proud of the young lady that you've become. We couldn't be more proud. And your mum, well, I just know that wherever she is, she's smiling and jumping around like a loon at how far you've come, at how much you've grown."

Tears track freely down my cheeks as I nod, unable to say a single thing to this man who is a father to me, in all but blood.

"You've found yourself good guys, little one. Good protectors, who'll take care of you for the rest of your life." None of us miss the way that Ryan gives no shits and includes all my Knights, not just Ash, and I couldn't give a flying fuck about the whispers from the other tables. "So, let's raise our glasses in a toast," he continues, a roguish look in his brown eyes as he lifts his champagne flute. "To Lilly and her Knights!" he cries, a shocked giggle escaping my lips as others at our table raise their glasses and make the same toast. The rest of our guests follow suit, a little delayed as no doubt they thought they ought to be toasting the bride and groom, not the bride and grooms. *Ah well, fuck 'em!*

"My turn," Loki leans over to whisper, standing up and coming up next to me, holding his hand out. "Come on, Pretty Girl."

I quirk a brow at him, but let him pull me from my chair and lead me over to the dance floor, a stage set up at one end. There's a band there, a beautiful quirky black haired girl smiling down at me, standing in front of a microphone. I don't notice much else as Loki leaves me standing in front of the stage, pressing a kiss to my cheek, then hops up onto the stage.

He confidently strides over to a high stool, which has an acoustic guitar propped up next to it, and a microphone in front of it. Grabbing the guitar, he sits down, giving me a panty decimating grin.

Then he opens his mouth and starts singing *If We Never Met*, by John K, and Kelsea Ballerini, and I just melt. He holds my gaze as he sings, and there's an intense look in his eyes, like although the song has a fun beat, he wants me to take it seriously. And I do. I take the message he's giving me into my very soul.

At one point, the girl starts singing, and Loki puts his guitar back onto the stand, hops off the stage, and grabs my hand, pulling me towards him and moulding his body to mine as we dance together. I'd somehow forgotten that this boy can move like he's making love on the dancefloor.

He picks up the lyrics, singing into my ear as he moves his hips against mine in a slow, teasing movement, and my knees go weak, a fire igniting in my core at the memories of the times he's been singing into my ear whilst being inside of me.

All too soon the song finishes, as does his movements, and I'm left pressed up against him, feeling just how affected he is with his heaving chest and hardness pressed against my stomach.

"You may be his wife, Pretty Girl," he rasps into my ear, nuzzling my neck like he just can't help himself. "But you're my soulmate, the mother of my child, and I will love you for my entire goddamn life, and then some."

"I fucking love you, Loki Thorn," I manage to choke out, my voice thick with all the emotions that are swirling inside of me.

A throat clears behind me, and I turn to see Jax standing there, waiting a step behind us. Loki laughs, and I glance back.

"Your other soulmates await," he tells me ruefully, pressing a kiss to the corner of my lip. Before he can pull away, I turn my face, kissing him full on, uncaring of our other guests as I kiss the shit out of him.

It takes a second, but with a groan he returns the embrace, matching my passion with his own. Reluctantly, he pulls away, and looks at me like I am everything in the entire world to him. Stepping away - *luckily he's managed to get himself somewhat under control so that he's not walking around at full mast* - he walks backwards, holding my gaze until I feel a warmth at my back, huge hands alighting on my upper arms.

"May I have this dance, Baby Girl?" Jax's rough voice whispers in my ear, the same ear that Loki murmured into. I shiver with the feel of it, all rough hands and long nights spent wrapped up in each other.

"Yes, always," I reply, turning and letting him hold me in his huge arms. It always feels like coming home whenever Jax holds me, like I'm in a warm room, safely tucked away from the raging storm outside.

The sounds of a country guitar start playing, and when a male voice starts singing, I recognise the song as *Die a Happy Man* by Thomas Rhett.

A happy shiver caresses my skin, and my lips split into a wide grin as Jax leads me into a slow country swing dance. He moves with a grace that only those of us who know him aren't surprised by, and we twirl around the dancefloor, uncaring that we're the only ones dancing.

We lose ourselves in the music and each other, the twist and twirl of the moves, the lead and pull. I know that he chose this song purposefully, telling me how much I mean to him through the lyrics, and the way that he holds me like I'm the most precious thing in the world.

All too soon the song finishes, and once again I'm being held close by one of my Knights.

"You are the greatest thing to have ever happened to me, Baby Girl," he mumbles into my hair, his voice rough with emotion. "And I don't care that you're a Vanderbilt, because you will always be mine as well."

"Jax..." I rasp out, my own throat thick. These boys are determined to make me bawl my eyes out and explode with happiness today.

He pulls back, gazing fiercely into my eyes, his own a swirling blue vortex. Achingly slowly he lowers his face to mine, his lips pausing a hair's breadth above my own, his warm breath teasing me. Tired of waiting, I close the distance, a deep vibrating chuckle erupting in his chest at my brazen move.

Jax's hand comes up to cup underneath my chin, his fingers on one side of my upper throat, his thumb the other. He deepens the kiss with one of his signature growls, the noise heating my core as his tongue decimates mine, leaving me breathless and wanting more.

Before I can do something embarrassing - *like climb him like a fucking spider monkey does a fruit tree* - he pulls away, placing a gentle peck on my lips.

"Two more Knights, baby," he whispers, taking hold of my upper arms and turning me to face away from him.

My head is still spinning from our kiss when honey amber fills my gaze.

"Hello, darling," Kai's melodic voice fills my ears, and even though my cheeks ache with smiling so much today, my kiss-swollen lips lift.

"Hello, my love," I murmur back, and his eyes close in bliss for a brief moment, before opening again. His hand reaches out, his fingers brushing my lips, heat making the amber glow like the setting sun.

The haunting voice of Aaron Smith comes over the speakers, singing *Unconditional*, and tears sting my eyes, knowing the lyrics and knowing that they are perfect for us. For Kai and I.

He holds out his hand, and I place mine in his warm grip, letting him pull me close, taking me in a formal dance hold, waiting a beat, then setting off in a waltz. My heart races as he spins us around the empty dance floor, the lights and colours of the marquee becoming a kaleidoscope as we dance.

The song swells and ebbs, guiding our moves, but Kai stares into my eyes the entire time, captivating me in his gaze as he expertly leads. Everything that has passed between us is there; the immediate connection, the brief doubt, the coming together again and every revelation. Every declaration. Every iota of feeling that exists between Kai and I flows between us, and I can almost see its light, moving between us until it becomes something continuous and everlasting.

My cheeks feel damp when finally, reluctantly, we slow, eventually standing there, still gazing into each other's eyes. His hand lets go of mine, his fingers brushing my tears away.

"You and I are the stuff that dreams are made of, my darling," he tells me, his voice strong yet there's a rasp to it, too. "We are what the stars envy, what the moon longs for, and what the legends of old tell tales of. Our love is more than this world, Lilly. More than a piece of paper with a new surname. And it will remain long after we are gone from the earth."

A choked sob falls from my lips, and I feel them tremble against his as he kisses me with a tenderness that makes the tears fall faster down my cheeks. He worships me with his kiss, his lips parting mine reverently, his tongue caressing the seam until I let him in. His hands cup my cheeks, holding me like the most precious gem as he fills me up with his love, making me taste the truth of his declaration.

My lips chase his when he ends the embrace, placing a tender kiss on my forehead, before taking a step back.

"One Knight left, darling."

Giving him what must be a very watery smile, I turn, my heart leaping and breath catching to see Ash standing behind me. He looks sinfully handsome, the grey of his suit matching his eyes to perfection, tailored to his incredible body beautifully. His ink peeks out at his neck and wrists, tantalising as it hints at what's underneath.

There's a devilish smile on his lush lips as he stalks towards me, all elegant grace with a touch of restrained destruction. He stops just in front of me, our chests just brushing, and I have to tip my head up to look into those grey orbs. *Cuntbucket.*

"Did you enjoy your first dances, Mrs. Vanderbilt?" he questions, his brow arched arrogantly.

"Immensely, husband," I sass back, noticing the glint of possession in his eyes when I call him that. I feel his hand reach around my waist, his palm warming the skin underneath my dress.

"It's about time that the bride and groom had their first dance, don't you think, wife?"

"I dunno," I can't help but tease, loving the flare of annoyance that flashes in his gaze. "You've got a lot to live up to after their performances, don't you think?" I repeat his own question back to him, and his smile turns positively evil.

He gives a small nod, not taking his eyes off me, and a piano starts to play the opening notes of *Young and Beautiful* by Lana Del Ray. My gaze goes wide as the singer starts to sing, and I twist to face the stage, seeing Lana Del Fucking Ray standing there in a beautiful gown, singing into an old fashion microphone as a miniature orchestra plays behind her.

"Shall we?" Ash asks, his voice full of smug amusement, and I face him once more, unable to say anything. "Not like you to be speechless, *wife*."

He pulls my compliant, still shocked body into his, one hand on the back of my waist, the other holding mine in a classical hold, and begins to waltz me around the floor. Years of dancing has my body moving on autopilot as I no doubt gape like a fish.

"T-that's..." I trail off, unable to finish my sentence.

"Lana Del Rey? One of your favourite artists?" he asks, full on smiling now, which doesn't help my short circuited brain. "I know."

"H-how?" I croak out, stealing a glance at the stage as we spin past.

"I have my ways, Princess," he replies, still sounding entirely too pleased with himself. I mean, he should be, so I can't hold it against him really. His face softens. "And I wanted to make today special for you."

"Ash, marrying you is special enough," I assure him, following his lead as he spins us. "You are an amazing man, and I'm proud to be your wife."

The smile he gives me after the words leave my lips would leave the sun in shadow. His hand tightens on my waist, drawing me in closer until our bodies are flush and I can feel his heat warming the front of me.

"Fuck, Lilly. I still can't believe that you're mine, let alone that you are now my wife," he tells me, and the look of slight disbelief on his usually assured face makes my chest tight.

"I still can't believe that you, all of you, are mine," I confess quietly. But he hears me, a fierce intensity entering his gaze.

"Forever, Princess. We will always be yours," he tells me, his deep voice strong and with no hint of hesitation. "We will always love you. Always be by your side, no matter what."

Tears well in my eyes again, and I blink furiously, whilst at the same time feeling a weightlessness in my limbs at his words. The song comes to a close, and Ash brings us to a sweeping stop, dipping me like a fairytale princess and kissing me like Prince Charming would. You know, if that pansy wasn't afraid to use tongue and make his princess all hot and wet for him.

My hands grip his lapels, uncaring if I crease them as I pull him closer, deepening the kiss until he growls and pulls me back upright, abruptly ending the kiss.

"Keep that up, wife, and the guests will get more of a show than they have already," he rumbles out, and I'm sorely tempted to take him up on that offer, but decide to save it for later.

After all, isn't that what a wedding night is for?

# CHAPTER THIRTY-SEVEN

LILLY

After that a DJ comes onto the stage, and Julian approaches, all feline grace and wicked intentions.

"A dance with my beautiful new daughter-in-law," he says, but it's not a question, more like a demand.

"Lilly?" Ash asks, and my heart swells, my knees a little weak at the concern in his eyes. He'd refuse his father, for me, and I love him all the more for it.

"It's fine, Ash," I reply with a saccharine smile, and one of his brows lifts. "Can you ask the DJ to play Lilly's request, please?"

"Of course," he assures me, his tone still laced with confusion as he leans down to place a kiss on my cheek. "I hope that you know what you're doing, Princess," he whispers into my ear before pulling away. With one last scolding glance at his father, whose eyes are trained on me, he turns and heads to the stage.

Julian steps closer, pressing his body against mine in a move that makes me shudder, swallowing bile. He pulls me into a hold, one hand just above the swell of my arse, the other gripping my palm.

"Quite a show you've just given your guests, *daughter*," he purrs into my ear, and I clench my teeth when I feel something beginning to harden against my lower stomach. *Fucking hell! He's turned on by calling me daughter!*

The opening bars of an upbeat pop song starts playing, and Julian falters just as a wicked grin spreads my lips. I hear Loki's braying laughter as he recognises *Fuck You* by Lily Allen that's just started playing. You see, I asked the DJ in advance if, when I gave the request, he would play it, as I knew that Julian wouldn't be able to resist being his cuntish self and trying to assert his disgusting dominance over me.

Julian's grip becomes bruising, digging into my soft flesh, but I'm uncaring as I lean away from him so that I can look up into his face.

"What's wrong, Julian? Don't you like the song?"

His face is like granite, all hard lines and cold planes, his eyes silver fire as they try to burn me up. I can't resist poking the bear.

"I've had my lawyers look into Black Knight Corporation, and imagine my surprise to learn that I own more of your company than you do," I tell him, my smile genuine and wide. His nostrils flare, and I have to forcibly relax my jaw when his grip becomes painful.

His jaw clenches, his teeth grinding together as he continues staring into my eyes, our silent battle starting to be noticed.

"Didn't you want to dance? You wouldn't want to let your adoring public down now, would you? Where are they?" I tip my head to the side, looking around as if searching for them. I catch Ash's worried gaze, his brows lowered over grey eyes just as Julian bends to whisper in my ear.

"I see that you learn your lessons slowly, *daughter*." This time he practically spits the word out, and I can't stop flinching, seeing Ash start to head towards us. "Enjoy your honeymoon."

And with that, he drops his grip, turning and striding away from me, shoulders tense. I look after his retreating back, worrying my bottom lip.

"Princess? Are you okay?" Ash asks, suddenly at my side, the others surrounding me in a protective circle. I blink, turning my confused gaze to Ash's.

"He told me that I learn my lessons slowly, then wished me an enjoyable honeymoon," I tell him, watching his forehead crease, his hand coming up to my lower back, resting exactly where Julian's did.

"You don't go anywhere alone tonight, Baby Girl," Jax rumbles, grasping my cold hand in his large, warm one. My eyes lock onto his, the blue churning with worry.

"Hey," I say gently, stepping closer to him and cupping his face with my hand. "He was just being an arsegoblin." I'm rewarded with a quirk of Jax's lips, an almost smile.

"All the same, Pretty Girl," Loki adds, brushing my cheek with his fingers, until I'm lost in emeralds. "Stay with one of us for the rest of the night, yeah?"

I look at Kai.

"I agree, darling. I don't trust him or any of the board," he tells me, taking my other hand in his.

"Ash?" I question, not quite believing that it's as serious as they're making it out to be.

"Better safe than sorry, Princess." His hand rubs the spot that I know will have Julian's bruises, like he knows that his father has hurt me already tonight.

I shrug. "Okay, sure. Now can we just dance?"

I give a little wiggle of my hips, earning relieved smiles from all of them, though there is still a tightness around each of their eyes that causes unease to unfurl in my stomach.

---

A couple of hours later, I'm sitting with Loki, a pleasant tiredness settling over me as I watch Lex and Ryan on the dance floor, having a great time. Willow is up on stage with the DJ, looking like she might score tonight, and when she glances over to me, I raise my glass of pink lemonade in salute.

Jax is standing with his mother, who insisted on coming today even though he was adamant that she still needed to rest. I can see him hovering, her small hand in his large one, as she smiles and taps her foot to the beat of the song that's currently playing. Kai was called to his uncle's side, something about talking to some new tech developers that Black Knight has an interest in.

"Should we rescue Ash?" Loki murmurs in my ear, his long fingers pushing back the hair from my neck and sending electricity skittering across my skin.

I look over and chuckle to see Ash being hounded by some older couple, apparently some long distance relatives.

"Nah, I need a piss," I tell him, heaving myself to my feet and grateful that I took my heels off some hours ago, replacing them with simple ballet pumps.

"I love it when you talk dirty, baby," Loki groans, laughing when I whack his rainbow covered bicep.

We make our way to the exit of the marquee, posh portaloos having been set up outside and to one side, nestled in the trees and a path lit by strings of bare bulbs in rainbow colours. As we approach the doorway, someone steps up to Loki, and I see that it's his father, Chad.

"A word, son," he says, voice cold, and ignoring me completely.

"Just give me a minute," Loki replies, his voice just as devoid of warmth as his father's.

"Now, boy," Chad hisses, grabbing Loki's arm and halting his steps. Loki glares, his gaze scathing.

"It's okay, Loki. I'll just be a moment," I assure him, unable to wait any longer as the urge to empty my bladder becomes desperate. I hurry off, not able to wait for a reply, and rush to the loos, making it just in the nick of time.

After taking care of business, I wash up and head back outside to find a man, partly in shadow, waiting for me.

"Adrian?" I ask, squinting, then straightening up as the moon emerges from behind a cloud, highlighting his features. His grey suit is tailored to perfection, his black hair littered with more grey than when I saw him back in England.

"Lilly, congratulations," he replies, his voice smooth, and a little detached, his dark eyes locked onto mine. I mean, it has taken him all night to approach me, to congratulate me properly, and a fissure of anger runs through me at how this man, my only blood family, cares less than my chosen family.

"Thank you," I respond tightly, stepping to one side to pass him and head back to the party. He steps with me, and the anger that had been coiling in my stomach turns cold.

"I hate to do this here, today of all days, Lilly. But I've had news. About your mom," he tells me, stopping me dead as ice travels down my spine.

"About mum?" I repeat, taking a step closer to him. My heart races, and my palms sweat as his words sink in. "Have they found who did it?"

Before he answers, something sharp stings my neck, and my hand flies to the spot to bat the bug away. Only my hand doesn't make it all the way there, suddenly feeling too heavy to lift as my knees go weak.

"What the..." I trail off, my lips unable to form the rest of the sentence as my tongue grows heavy in my mouth.

My legs give out, and I hit the forest floor with a thud, unfeeling of the twigs and stones that poke my body. A dark shape leans down, a soft touch brushing my hair from my face, as words caress my ears.

"Enjoy your honeymoon."

I vaguely recall someone else tonight saying those exact words to me, but my brain is sluggish, and I can't seem to make the connection. The sounds of the music from the party fade, the bright lights of the marquee dimming, before everything goes black.

Need to know what happens next? Download Released to find out!

Want to keep up to date with all my news plus a whole load of spicy bonus content with all your favourite characters? Sign up for my newsletter HERE.

CAN WE EMBRACE THE DARKNESS?

BOOK THREE

# RELEASED

HIGHGATE PREPARATORY ACADEMY

ROSA LEE

# CHAPTER ONE

LILLY

"*Enjoy your honeymoon.*"

A pained moan escapes my dry, cracked lips as I stir, my whole body feeling like it's been hit by a double-decker bus. The dull ache in my head turns into a sharp stab, sending another deep, pain-filled groan echoing around me.

Blinking gritty eyes open, a screaming wave of panic rushes in when all I see is darkness. My heart thumps in my chest when I close and open my lids again, but I'm still surrounded by the endless black of my nightmares.

"H–hello?" I croak out, my voice a broken thing, rasping among the shadows. Clearing my throat and winching at the dryness, I try again. "I–is anyone there?"

My breathing stutters as I'm met by silence, a full body shiver skittering over me at the cold that surrounds my body. Pushing up onto my elbows, I have to pause as my head swims and throbs all at the same time. Bile burns the back of my already sore throat, but I manage to breathe through it, waiting for the nauseating dizziness to subside. Clenching my hands into the soft bed underneath me, I focus on the cool linen sheets until I can sit up fully with only a slight waver.

Pausing once again, I'm able to concentrate a little more and see that the room is not as pitch black as I first thought. Soft moonlight filters through the cracks of what looks like wooden shutters across the room. *There must be a window over there.* The hair on the back of my neck lifts at the eerie sight of undefined shapes around the room, the lighting casting everything in a sickly yellow glow.

Gingerly turning my still pulsing head, I can see the dark outlines of various bits of furniture; a large wardrobe and a dressing table with a mirror that reflects a ghostly image of a pale, frightened girl back at me. I quickly move on from the sight to see that I'm in a lavish, chunky wood, four-poster bed with heavy drapes.

A sudden kick in my lower abdomen causes my hand to fly over my bump, a whooshing breath of relief rushing out of me when I feel another movement. I've no idea what has happened to me, but the thought that something may have harmed my unborn child brings forth a wave of anger so fierce that spots blur my vision and I have to go back to breathing deeply to calm down.

Taking one final inhale, I steel my spine and slowly shift across the linen, the whisper of the fabric against my bare thighs a comforting noise in the silence.

*Wait! Shit, I should be in my wedding dress...shouldn't I?*

Panic flares hotly inside me again, my pulse racing as I vaguely remember that I was wearing my wedding dress before...before everything went dark. Looking down, I touch the silk nightdress that kisses my thighs and furrows my brows as I try in vain to remember when I got changed. My hand clenches into a fist, wrinkling the fabric as useless tears fill my eyes, the memory eluding me.

Suddenly, a noise makes my head snap upwards, and I see the dark shape of a door across from me.

"H–hello?" I rasp, my chin trembling and hands shaking as I grasp onto the post and pull myself to standing. "Who's there?"

Silence.

A hatch in the bottom of the door springs open, and I almost lose my grip on the wood as my muscles violently jolt, soft light flooding the room for a moment as a tray is pushed through before the hatch closes again. I curse myself for being a coward, even as my heart pounds in my chest. *I should have fucking gone over there when it was open!*

Taking a step away from the bed, testing how steady I am, I notice a set of drawers next to the bed with an ornate lamp sitting on top of them. Walking over to it using the side of the bed for support, I switch it on, flinching and close my eyes briefly against the light as a sharp pain lashes through my head. I wait for the throb to subside before slowly blinking my eyes open and taking in the room properly.

It's decadent, with a beautiful, hand-painted bird wallpaper covering the walls, light walnut furniture, and cream and gold silk furnishings. The whole space reminds me of something out of a Jane Austen film, and only adds to the confusion.

Remembering the tray, I glance back over to the door and stare at the covered plate as if there's a severed head underneath the silver dome. *Fuck, for all I know, there might be.* My body shudders at the thought, and I debate whether I can just leave it there, that is until hunger makes its presence felt in my empty stomach.

Giving a firm nod of my head—though no one can see my act of bravery—I straighten up and make my way shakily over to the tray. Stooping down, I take an immense breath, grasping the cool metal handle in my only slightly trembling hand.

"Don't be such a fucking ballsack, Lilly," I hiss, because we all know pussies are the stronger of the two appendages.

Decision made, I pull the lid off with a small, very lady-like screech, a self-deprecating laugh escaping my lips when I see that it's only a plate of Welsh Rarebit—aka cheese on toast—with slices of cucumber and a bunch of red grapes. My mouth waters at the smell of melted cheese goodness, and I wonder how whoever made it knew that it was a favourite of mine. I'm not sure whether to be creeped the fuck out or comforted. I should probably be the latter.

Setting the lid on the plush, cream and gold Persian rug, I lift the tray and take it back to the bed, placing it on the top of the blankets and sit down next to it. Taking a piece of warm toast between my fingers, a pleasure-filled moan leaves my lips when the first taste of salty, melted cheddar hits my taste buds, and before I know it, the plate is clean and I'm licking my fingers.

I look around the room again and see that I'd missed a jug of water and a glass sitting on the table alongside the lamp. Taking the tray and placing it on the floor, I get up and pour a glass, glugging the cool liquid until that, too, is empty. Giving an almighty belch, the urge to pee hits me like a truck, and I desperately look round. Seeing a door next to the one with the hatch, I waddle-rush over there, trying to move quickly but not piss myself, as I hope with fanny flaps crossed that it's a bathroom.

Opening the door, I thank all the gods that exist when I spot a toilet and make a beeline for it, doing a hop jig as I pull my knickers down and sit. As I relieve myself, I look down to see that the knickers I'm wearing are at least the ones that Ash gave me on our wedding day.

Trying not to think about my fucked up situation too much and my pounding head, I wash up, my jaw cracking with a huge yawn. Making my way back towards the bed, another yawn that would make a lion proud takes over me, my body feeling heavy and sluggish as I drop down onto the soft mattress.

My vision goes hazy, and when my eyes blink open again, there's a dark figure framed in the now open doorway. My lids shut again, and I feel someone moving me tenderly on the bed, pulling the covers over my body, and smoothing my hair back before placing a kiss on my temple.

"Ash?" I ask weakly, but that can't be right. There's no spicy ginger smell. In fact, I can't smell any of my guys, just a sharp, almost overpowering, cloying cologne.

"Hush now, Violet. Time to get some more rest. We must take care of the baby," a deep voice whispers, and instead of being soothing, it sounds like nightmares and monsters in the dark, but also familiar somehow.

Before I can try and work out who it is, another wave of exhaustion crashes over me, drowning me in darkness once more.

---

## ASH

"It's been three fucking weeks! What do you mean there's no fucking sign of her?"

Rage unlike I've ever known fills me as I launch my phone across the room with a yell, the sound of it shattering against the fireplace filling our dorm moments later.

My chest heaves as I stare at the glittering shards lying in pieces on the carpet, my fists clenching at my sides when the thought enters my mind that it's my heart, my soul, lying there as well as my phone.

"What the fuck is wrong with you, Ash?!" Loki shouts as he rushes down the stairs. The wrath that I thought couldn't get any worse increases tenfold when I look at him, red mist coating my vision. My pulse pounds in my ears, and my ability to see my surroundings tunnels, until all I can see is his failure to protect Lilly.

With an almighty roar, I launch myself at him, meeting him as he steps off the stairs with a brutal punch to his jaw that has his head snapping to the side. Not giving him time to recover, I hit him again, this time in the stomach, satisfaction filling my veins as all the breath whooshes out of his lungs, his hand clutching around himself. He straightens up a moment later, and a twinge of guilt runs through me at the sight of blood trickling down from his now split lip. Lowering his arms down to his sides, he looks at me with broken eyes, making the red mist begin to dissipate.

"Fight back, you asshole," I snarl at him, panting, but my raised fists begin to droop as he just stands there, looking lost. "Fucking hit me!"

"No," he states, squaring his shoulders. "It's my fault she's gone."

I raise my fists once more, nostrils flaring at his words. It *is* his fucking fault. *He* was meant to be watching her when she disappeared. When she was clearly taken from us.

But it wasn't just his fault. We were all meant to be watching her, and we weren't there when she needed us. With that thought, all the strength leaves my body, my arms falling back down to my sides, and my chest rising and falling with my heavy breaths. The crippling guilt leaves my chest feeling painfully tight.

"It's not just your fault, Loki," I tell him, my voice like sandpaper; all rough and grating.

Moisture fills his eyes, and my broken heart cracks more when he swallows hard, ready to argue. I know that he's taken this harder than the rest of us because he was meant to be with her at the time, watching over her at the reception party. But then he got caught by his dad, and we all got distracted, which we now suspect was purposeful. I have to tamp down the fresh rush of anger at that thought. That somehow, this stinks of Julian, my *father*. Especially as he doesn't seem as upset as a father-in-law should be at the kidnapping of his pregnant daughter-in-law. He's made next to no effort, bar speaking to the press, to find her. He's carrying on, as usual, declaring that 'it's out of our hands.' He knows something, I fucking know he does. Nothing is beyond the reach of Black Knight. Especially not a missing family member.

Reaching up, I clasp one of Loki's shoulders in my hand, pulling him towards me and wrapping my arms around him. My own eyes moisten as he takes a great heaving breath and clutches me back tightly.

"I'm so fucking sorry, Ash," he whispers, his voice thick and rasping.

"I know, brother. I know," I reply, my own voice hitching slightly with the pain that we both feel like a knife in the gut that can't be removed.

I release him just as the door opens and look towards it to see Jax walking in, swollen and split knuckles wrapped around his gym bag. We're all a mess without our Lilly to keep us in line. He kicks the door shut behind him, looking up at us with red-rimmed eyes.

"Anything?" he asks, and it's the only word that leaves his lips now since Lilly vanished. I can't blame him, the urge to cut myself has been so strong, I've had to get the guys to hide all the fucking knives and anything sharp. Kai keeps the kitchen ones under lock and key, and the others have hidden their razors from my reach. I shake my head, and he just grunts, dropping his bag and heading to the bathroom.

Loki and I watch him in silence, and just as he gets to the door, the front door bursts open again, crashing into the wall and making all three of us spin around, fists raised. My heartbeat settles a little seeing that it's Kai, glasses askew and hair an absolute fucking mess. He's clutching what looks like an open yearbook in his hands, looking down at it, and there's a flush on his cheeks.

"Guys!" he shouts, then winces when he sees we're all there in front of him. "Sorry, but I think I found something."

We all step forward, my stomach doing an uncomfortable flip as my heart races again at his words.

"Well?" Loki asks from next to me, not even giving Kai a chance to say another word. Kai just looks at him, his gaze softening briefly.

"I was looking through all the old yearbooks, trying to see if the 'Ace' you told us about after your father's strange phone call ever attended Highgate," he tells us, looking at me. "And I fucking found him!" he cries out, voice full of weary triumph.

Before we can answer, he turns the book around, and the world falls down around me as I look at the image on the page, unable to make sense of it at first. It's a photograph of a couple, a darkly handsome man who looks vaguely familiar, but it's the woman that he's got his arm wrapped around that sends chills down my spine.

"Is that..." Jax begins, his rough voice startling me from my own thoughts, though years of training mean that I don't show it outwardly.

"Lilly's mom, I believe," Kai tells us, his voice low. My gaze takes in the thick, wavy brown hair that tumbles over her slim shoulders, slightly darker in colour than Lilly's, and the hazel eyes, the pixie shaped face. There's a thud in my chest, a longing for my own pixie princess, that has become a constant companion these past few weeks.

"Not just Lilly's mom," I say, finally tearing my eyes away from the picture to read the description below.

"Fuck," Loki breathes out on my other side.

**Couple destined for great things: Adrian 'Ace' Ramsey with his fiancée, Violet Rochester, pictured here at a gala celebrating the announcement of their engagement.**

Fuck is right, and the fact that it's not the name which we knew of her explains why we couldn't find out much about her to start with.

"Does this mean that her uncle is actually...her dad?" Loki asks, and I tear my gaze away from the page to look at him, his tired eyes brighter than they've been in weeks, his brow furrowed with confusion.

"I think so," Kai responds, and I turn to look at him.

"And if Ace is Adrian..." I start, the pieces slotting into place, though I still can't believe that we may have a lead. I don't trust it. How can I if it turns out to be another dead end. Another split in my soul. Another rupture of my heart.

"Then he has Lilly," Jax growls out next to me, and the beast inside me purrs at the violence in his tone.

"Well, what the fuck are we waiting for?!" Loki shouts, looking like he's ready to swim to England right the fuck now if he needs to.

"Wait, we can't just go rushing in." I throw my hand out, my palm landing against his chest to stop him from leaving.

"Why the hell not?" Jax rumbles from my other side, and I can feel him practically vibrating with anger.

"Because there is a good chance that my shitstain of a father is involved, and we don't want him to do anything rash," I grit out, a headache beginning to form behind my eyes. I reach a hand up and pinch the bridge of my nose as I try to think of a way forward. "Plus, we have no idea if Ace–Adrian even has her. Yes, it's sketchy as fuck, but we can't just storm in and torture him if he's innocent." I shiver as Jax looks at me with dead eyes, like his humanity has fled and all that's left is the monster within. "She wouldn't want you to, Jax."

He blinks, and just like that he joins the rest of us with our gray moral compasses.

"We need eyes on her first, to confirm that she is there to begin with," I continue, my mind racing.

I snap my head up and lock eyes with Kai, knowing that he just had the same idea I did if the twinkle in his amber orbs is anything to go by.

"Willow," he murmurs, and I nod.

"The Shadows," I reply, starting to think aloud. "We'll owe them a favor."

"I'll give them anything bar Lilly and my firstborn," Loki states, voice clear, and my stare leaves Kai's to look at my redheaded brother. There's a rod of steel in his green eyes that I've not seen before, a pledge that tells me he's not messing around. My hand alights back on his shoulder, giving it a squeeze.

"We're all in agreement then? We contact Hunter and The Shadows?" I ask, looking from Loki, to Kai, and finally Jax. The latter hesitates for a few seconds, and I can see the need to burn down the world to save our girl in the blazing cold fire in his blue eyes.

"But if they can't find anything by Friday, I'll go to England and get the information myself," he tells me, his lips twitching with an evil smirk that makes me glad I'm not at the receiving end of his information-gathering.

"Deal. We'll all go," I assure him, copying his nod of agreement.

"Right," Loki interrupts the serious moment, and I know that whatever will leave his lips next would have our girl glaring at him. My dick twitches at the thought. "Let's go get our girl back so we can spank her ass for being such a naughty girl and leaving us with blue balls for this long."

A bark of laughter leaves me at how indignant she'd be to hear that the worst part of her kidnap was its effect on our balls. I know that Loki is just deflecting, using humor to cover his worry at what our girl is going through without us at her side.

As we turn to go, Kai and I in front, I hear a sharp slap and Loki's protest behind me. My lips split into a grin at the sound.

"What the fuck was that for?" he asks Jax in a disgruntled voice.

"Disrespecting Baby Girl," Jax replies, and although Loki grumbles, he doesn't argue with the big guy.

"Don't worry, Jax," Kai says as we leave the dorm, walking down the hall towards Willow's. "By the time we finish telling Lilly about what Loki said, his balls will be frozen solid before she'll touch them again."

Jax, Kai, and I laugh then, and even Loki gives a little chuckle. The sound lightens something in my heart, perhaps healing a small fracture too. We may not have much to go on, but it's more than we had this morning. It's a start, and for now, it'll have to be enough.

*Just hold on, Princess. We'll find you.*

# CHAPTER TWO

LILLY

After a night plagued with visions of shadow men and swirling lights, I prise open my eyes, which are stuck together with sleep dust, to soft daylight that filters through the gaps in the wooden shutters. Groaning, my head thumping again, I look around and jump when I see a middle-aged woman waiting a little way away, a soft smile on her face.

"Sorry to startle you, dear, especially in your condition," she says, her voice gentle, and although I've never met her before, she puts me at ease instantly with her calming vibe. "I'm Jacky, and I'm going to be your nurse and midwife from now on."

I can't help the way my jaw suddenly gets tight at the fact that my autonomy has just been taken from me, but it's like I can't grasp my anger enough to throw it back at her creepy, smiling face. Gingerly sitting up, trying to ignore the dizziness and throbbing headache, I have to swallow a couple of times before I can answer.

"Um, sure, uh, do you know where I am?" I ask, my voice raspy. "Where is Ash?" She immediately goes over to the side table and fills a glass with water before handing it to me. I eye it for a minute, but I just can't grasp what my mind is trying to tell me, so I bring it to my lips and glug the cool water down in one go. "Thanks," I say, handing the glass back to her. Her brow is lowered, which makes my own dip down.

"You're in Wiltshire, dear, at your uncle's house. He's looking after you, and the baby," she tells me brightly, her arm coming round my upper back to help support me as I try to get up and out of the bed.

"Wiltshire?" I pause, feeling unsteady and wobbling slightly as I get to my feet. I'm not sure if it's the thumping headache or the news that I'm back in England, with my uncle, that leaves me stumbling. "Adrian's house?"

"That's right, dear," she replies, keeping her arm around me, and helping to guide me to the bathroom door, somehow knowing that I need a piss, like yesterday. "Right, let's get you washed and dressed, shall we? You'll feel right as rain then, and I can do some checks on the baby to make sure all is as it should be."

I should feel embarrassed that a complete stranger is helping me sit on the toilet, then helping me into the shower and to wash, and a small part of me is mortified, but it's like it's buried deep inside me, drowning and unable to make it to the surface. I can't seem to get my feet and legs to function normally. I'm like a newborn lamb, unable to get my feet underneath me enough to walk on my own. My head feels full of cotton wool, and all the colours of the room are dulled and lifeless like an old T-shirt washed too many times, so I'm mostly glad for the extra help.

After dressing me in a soft, cotton nightgown that she found in the chest of drawers, which, although clearly new and unworn, smells musty. Jacky supports me as I lie back on the bed then takes mine and the baby's vitals. She listens to the heartbeat which makes tears sting my eyes, the steady rhythm grounding me as it always does, calming my fluttering nerves at this new reality that I've woken up in. She also takes blood samples and all the other things that Lisa, my midwife back in Colorado, used to do. The tears threaten to spill at the homesickness which fills me up at the thought of Highgate and my guys. My Knights.

"Where's my husband?" I ask once she's finished up.

"Husband, dear?" she questions, her eyebrows dipped as she helps me up again and leads me to a small table near the window that has a covered tray similar to last night's on it. "I bet you're hungry, dear," she tells me, taking the lid off to reveal a large salad with fragrant marinated grilled chicken and buttered bread that looks and smells freshly baked. My stomach takes that moment to growl loudly, and she chuckles. "I'll open the shutters, shall I? It's a lovely day out."

I nod, sitting down, and immediately shove a forkful of the salad with chicken into my mouth, thinking that I'm sure I just asked her something, but now I can't remember what it was. The room is flooded with light seconds later as the shutters are flung open with a clatter, and once my eyes adjust, I see that she's right, the sun is shining and the sky is a beautiful light blue, not a cloud in sight.

My fork pauses on its way back down to my plate as I notice something that sits at odds with the beautiful day outside.

Bars.

There are metal bars outside my window, and as soon as I see them, a wave of claustrophobia washes over me, leaving my skin tight and itchy and my breathing shallow. My wide eyes look up into Jacky's brown ones, which are full of a gentle sympathy.

"Why are there bars?" I ask, my voice soft and small as I try to make sense of what is happening here, but my mind is too foggy, and I'm unable to grab hold of a thought for too long before it flies away like a petal on the breeze.

"Oh, dear girl," she says with a sigh, coming to crouch next to me as my gaze goes back to those lines of metal that are trapping me in this room. "Your uncle is just trying to take care of you and the baby. He doesn't want anything to happen to either of you, dear."

I look back down at her. "Where is Ash? Loki? Kai and Jax?" I question, my voice trembling, suddenly overwhelmed with the need to be held in familiar arms that chase all the nightmares away. Again, there's a flash of softness in her eyes that I can't work out the meaning of, the corners crinkling as she reaches out and takes my cold, shaking hand in hers.

"Why don't you finish your meal, and then I can take you back to bed? To rest. You look so tired, dear."

My eyes fill with tears. I don't want to rest, I feel like I've lost so much time already. Letting go of Jacky's hands, I, once again, pick up my fork and spear a piece of chicken, bringing it up to my mouth.

But as I continue to eat, washing it down with a glass of fresh fruit juice, I do start to feel so bone-weary that my fork clatters onto the plate as if I can't hold it up anymore.

"Come on then, dear. Let's get you back to bed," Jacky tells me, helping me out of the chair and back into bed, tucking me in like a child. I'm sure I hear her whisper something that sounds suspiciously like, "poor delusional girl," under her breath.

All too soon, I'm dragged under into blackness once more, unable to fight the crashing wave of exhaustion any longer or the nightmares that await me.

---

The next few weeks follow the same routine. Jacky is always there when I wake up, ready to aid me in getting up and dressed before taking me over to the window to look out at the manicured grounds and the woods in the distance of my uncle's estate. I can see quite far into the distance, being on an upper floor, and it's a mixed blessing as it taunts me as well as gives me something to gaze upon. Like a bird in a cage, placed next to an open window and being able to see freedom but not taste it.

I give up asking about Ash, my husband, or any of the guys as each time she expertly distracts me and avoids answering until I feel as though perhaps it was all a wonderful dream. Perhaps I dreamt of going to America, meeting the guys, and falling in love.

*Maybe I've been here all along?*

My mind clearly likes to torment me as I am plagued with nightmares of arms banded tightly around me which do not belong to any of my Knights. Of sweet words whispered in my ear, of being called Violet. The worst are the nights where I dream that I'm back in the library with cunt-face Robert, his hands in places that they have no right to be, and his breathing heavy in my ear.

After those nights, I wake up covered in sweat and feel sick to my stomach, my pillow damp and dried tears on my cheeks. I notice small bruises on my waist, hips, and breasts, yet I have no knowledge of how they got there.

My mind struggles to focus on even menial tasks. It's getting worse and increasingly muddled the more time passes until I can barely remember what my life once was.

Before this room.

Before the bars on the window.

The silence that surrounds me. The night terrors that haunt me.

One day I wake up, and after assisting me with washing, Jacky gets me dressed not in another nightgown but in a soft, blue pantsuit that looks like it's from the early two-thousands.

"Why am I getting dressed? In proper clothes I mean?" I ask, giving her a quizzical look.

"Well, your uncle and I agreed that you needed some fresh air and to stretch your legs," she tells me, her face split into a big smile as she takes me over to the small table, and I sit down, a bowl of creamy porridge in front of me. "So, after breakfast, I'm to take you out for a walk." She beams at me like this is her life's biggest achievement thus far. Shit, maybe it is for all I know. I hear a familiar masculine chortle that makes my head swivel, expecting to see Ash next to me. But then I remember that he might not even be real, just a figment of my imagination, otherwise he'd be here, right? Jacky would know about him, right?

Shaking my head at my apparent craziness, I feel excited flutters in my stomach at the prospect of leaving my gilded cell, and I rush to finish my food. I do pause as the depressing thought that this is what my life has been reduced to hits me.

Helping me to stand, as I'm still so fucking unsteady on my feet, we make our way towards the door, and I can feel my pulse becoming faster the closer we get to it.

Taking a small, silver key out of her pocket, she unlocks the door, opening it into the room. It's funny how an object so tiny can exert such control over my life. In front of me sits a wheelchair, and I baulk at the sight, halting our movements.

"It's just to help you get outside. You're very weak, dear," she tells me kindly, her face sincere.

Taking a deep sighing breath and nodding, we move forward once more, and she supports my arm whilst I sit in the chair, tucking a fluffy wool blanket around my thin legs. Even with all the food that I've been given, my muscles have started to waste away with inactivity, so I'm determined to at least try and walk a little today, in the hope that I'll build my strength back up.

Jacky begins to wheel me along the corridor, and I realise that I do recognise the light blue colour of the walls and the various old portraits and landscape paintings lining them. We go past the carved wooden staircase, stopping in front of a light-coloured panelled door that looks the same as all the others that we've just passed. Stepping away from me, Jacky presses a brass button, and a second later the door slides into the wall revealing a lift.

"That's new," I mutter, not remembering it from before as she pushes me in, pressing the down button. The doors close with a soft swish, and I feel a jolt as we descend. For a moment, the wild thought that I'm descending into Hell flashes across my mind. Then I remember I'm already there; too weak to walk, in love with dark Knights that may not exist.

"Your uncle put it in specially, thinking that you might need it, especially once the baby arrives," she tells me, her voice soft, interrupting my pity party.

"Huh," I reply quietly.

Chewing my lip, I think on her words. On the surface, they show my uncle as someone who's thinking of the comfort and ease of others, a selfless person who'd spend a small fortune ensuring that a relative has all that they might need. On the other hand, I can't help wondering why he'd think that, as a normal, healthy, young woman, I wouldn't be able to manage the stairs. Regardless if I'm pregnant or not.

We come to a stop, and the doors open with another quiet swish, disrupting my swirling thoughts. I realise with a start as we exit the lift, that today my mind feels clearer than it has in weeks. I'm able to hold onto thoughts, they don't slip through my fingers like sand as they did just yesterday or the days before.

As we approach the double front doors with their clear glass panels, the sunlight floods in, shining all around the large entrance hall, making it feel light and airy. Very un-Hell-like. The tight knot in my chest lightens the closer I get to freedom. I can practically taste the fresh, English countryside, like newly mown grass and daffodils. A wide smile takes over my face when the doors are opened by my uncle's butler, Smith, and I can take a deep lungful of the sweetest air I've ever tasted.

We pause at the top of the entrance steps, and my eyelids flutter closed, the sun warming my face and heating my blood as though I'm a cold-blooded creature that needs light to survive, or I'll waste away.

"Allow me, Miss, ma'am." An unfamiliar deep voice startles my lids open, and I'm staring into laughing, brown eyes the colour of fallen autumn leaves. I study him as he bends down to grab the front of the chair. He reminds me of a slightly older Jax—*if Jax is real of course and not a figment of my fucked up imagination*—with his dirty blond hair tied in a messy man bun, and his facial hair that's more than stubble but less than a beard. He's less stacked than my Viking, though still muscular. "Rowan, give me a hand, will ya?" he calls in a pure west London drawl, and I look to the side to see the same man walking towards us.

Doing a double take, I hear Mr laughing brown eyes chuckle.

"Are you…" I begin, looking back at him.

"Twins? Yes," he tells me as I feel the chair shift when they lift it and start to carry me down the steps.

"But I'm the better looking one," a smoky voice says behind me—Rowan—and a surprised bark of laughter slips from between my lips, my hand flying to cover my mouth. The guy in front just smirks, and I must admit, if I wasn't in love four times over with possibly imaginary guys, I'd be tempted to fall because of that smile alone.

"Thank you, boys, that was very gallant," Jacky flutters, coming up next to me with a blush on her cheeks as they set the chair down at the base of the steps.

"You're welcome, ma'am, Miss," the first twin says, straightening back up as Rowan comes to stand next to him. They look at me intently with an unreadable expression, as though they're studying me. "Anything else we can help you with?"

I interrupt before Jacky can say anything. "What's your name? And why are you here?" I ask, my eyes narrowing, noticing their all black clothing, and the radios attached to the belts at their hips.

"Apologies, m'lady," the first twin replies, hand on his heart, a boyish grin on his face that has my lips twitching, followed by a crippling twinge of pain that lances through my heart at the memory of another cheeky boy I know—*maybe know*—but with red hair instead of dirty blond. "My name is Roman Kent, this is Rowan Kent, and we are part of the security your uncle has hired to help keep you safe."

My brows drop at his words.

"Safe from what?" I ask, but before they can answer, Jacky clears her throat.

"Well, thank you once again, boys, I'll be sure to call if I need your assistance," she says, her tone not unkind but a little brusque. "Right, dear, let's take a turn around the house, shall we?" She starts pushing me in the damn chair, turning me away from the intriguing Kent brothers.

Feeling a prickling in my skin, a shiver that's completely at odds with the warm sunshine, I turn around, leaning past Jacky, only to find both guys where we left them, one of them with a phone to his ear, staring after us.

"Oh, just look at those lovely daffodils!" Jacky suddenly exclaims.

My head turns to face forward again, and though my eyes see what looks like a lawn of yellow flower heads cheerfully bobbing in the slight breeze, my mind is still wondering who Roman and Rowan Kent are.

And what could my uncle possibly need to protect me from?

# CHAPTER THREE

LOKI

HUNTER 'SHADOWMAN' ANDERSON:

Found her.

"Guys!" I shout, my heart pounding in my chest like it's trying to get to my girl right the fuck now, the sounds of *Gone* by Blake Rose playing in the background. Leaping up and ignoring the slight wobble due to the heavy night of drink and drugs I've still not recovered from, I rush out of my room, almost colliding into Jax in the hall. "Did you see?" I ask him, almost breathless in my excitement. *Of course he fucking knows, dumb-ass, it was on the group chat we have with the leader of the Shadows Crew.*

"Yes," is all our quiet, giant of a brother says as we pound down the stairs to find Ash and Kai already standing in the main room waiting, heads snapping up as we approach. Ash strides towards us, hands slightly raised in an almost placating gesture, and I just know that what he's about to say will piss me the hell off.

"I need you to remain calm and hear me out. Both of you," he tells us, his voice hard but not unkind. My eyes narrow, and I stop in front of him, arms crossed over my chest, which rises and falls with my heavy breathing. I can barely contain the swirling storm of emotion running through me, like there's a sandstorm inside of me, waiting to burst free and suffocate anyone who gets in my way.

Jax comes up beside me, mirroring my pose, and a flash of respect and admiration runs through me at Ash, our leader, not flinching under our heavy scrutiny. Many grown-ass men would be cowering by now. Many have, but not him. His monster recognises its kin.

"Fine," I grumble out through clenched teeth. Jax just grunts.

"I've just spoken to Hunter, and the Kent twins have seen her," he starts, and a breath rushes out of me, my whole body tingling at his words. I was so fucking worried that she was gone for good, like a beautiful ghost, never to be seen again. "They say she's weak, likely drugged up, and seems confused, but looks like she's being fed and has a nurse with her."

My vision clouds, the red mist of my anger obscuring the room until everything else fades away, and the pounding in my ears is so loud it feels like the drums of war are sounding all around us in time with my racing heart. Jax's growling snarl brings me back to the present; Ash is still standing in front of us, spine ramrod straight, facing down the demons that have surfaced within his brothers.

"That dickhead cunt is drugging her?" I question, my voice cold and measured as I plot all the ways I'm going to remove his body parts while keeping him alive. No one hurts my Pretty Girl and gets away unscathed.

"They think so, but don't know for sure." He grimaces, and I feel my face twitch, knowing that there's more that will enrage my beast. "The point is, we can't rush in and rescue her."

As soon as the words leave his lips, Jax's fist connects with his jaw, and Ash stumbles back but manages to stay upright. My arms lower, hands clenching tightly, itching to do the same, even though I know that he'll have a good reason behind his orders. Kai comes over, standing between the two men, though Ash shows no sign of retaliation, just rubs his jaw as a line of blood trickles down his chin from a busted lip.

"If we rush in, it could get Lilly killed!" Kai snaps, his outstretched hand trembling, as if that would keep Jax back. He lowers it when Jax just stands there, chest heaving, but makes no move to hit our leader again.

"Explain," I bite out, arms folded once more to try and curb the desire to destroy everything and everyone in my path.

"There is no way my *father* is not involved, and if we suddenly ride off on a rescue mission, he'll know what we're up to. All it would take is one phone call, and she's gone...permanently," Ash informs us, and I know that he hates this just as much as we do. His controlling nature won't allow anything less than everyone he cares about being within arm's reach, safe and protected by him. But more than that, our fearless leader loves our girl with all his dark and wicked soul. He needs her light, just as we all do. We can no longer survive without it.

I've slipped back into drinking and taking drugs every night, seeking oblivion, chasing her spectre. Jax is working out harder than ever, and I suspect he's been taking part in the more illegal fighting circuits if his own bruises are any indicator. Kai looks as though he hasn't slept in weeks, working all the hours he can trying to find a lead. Fuck, even his schoolwork has dropped off, and he's not been on us to keep our grades up either. And Ash, he got us to hide all the knives and shit, but I've seen bloody tissues and bandages in the trash can in his room.

We're falling apart without her, and I don't know how much longer we can go on.

"What do you suggest?" I ask, my very soul feeling bone tired. I just want my–our girl back.

"Kai's birthday is in three weeks. We will book flights to Amsterdam, it is his nineteenth after all, but once we get there, we fly back to England and meet up with the Shadows. We'll need their help. Meanwhile, we replace her current nurse with one of our own. Hunter knows someone, so we can keep a closer eye on her and try to help where we can and stop the drugging," Ash tells us, his penetrating gaze swapping from mine to Jax's, trying to gauge our reactions. It's what makes him not only a good leader but a great one. He takes our opinions seriously. It's the one reason why our monsters heel to him.

"Three weeks?" Jax murmurs, voice laced with the sweet taste of promised violence and bloodshed.

"Three weeks," Ash replies, a sharp nod in Jax's direction. The big guy's nostrils flare, taking in a huge inhale.

"Okay," he responds before turning around, grabbing his gym bag which has taken up permanent residence by the door, and leaving. Ash turns to me.

"Three weeks and not a day more," I state, nausea swirling in my stomach.

How will she forgive us for leaving her there, knowing that we might have been able to get her out sooner? How can we forgive ourselves?

"Not a day more," Ash vows.

"Not an hour more," Kai adds, and the promise settles on our shoulders, a weight that I know we will all bear until we're holding our soul safely back in our arms.

*Hold on, my love, we're coming for you. Just a little longer now.*

---

LILLY

The next few days establish my new routine. I wake up, and with Jacky's help, get washed and dressed. Then she takes me outside in the chair, and I practise walking, again with her help, getting a little steadier and stronger every day. It's fucking crazy, my new life, but maybe this is the way it's always been? And everything I think happened before was just a beautiful, wonderful dream?

My stomach frequently gives an almighty heave, my unborn child making its presence felt and making me think that it all couldn't possibly have been imagined. Otherwise, how did this one come into existence?

I often see the Kent twins and they always make me smile, reminding me of each of my potentially imaginary lovers in various ways. Their playful banter, their sense of brotherhood, and the darkness that lurks within them, waiting for an outlet.

One morning, about a week after my first trip out of my room, I'm outside, walking around the rose garden with Jacky and admiring the buds that are just waiting to burst into fragrant bloom. One of the boys—Roman, I think, as his face is a little fuller than Rowan's—rushes over.

"Thank fuck–I mean thank goodness I found you, Jacky," he says, his voice a little breathless, although the lack of colour in his cheeks gives lie to the picture that he ran all the way here. Or maybe he's just that fit. "Your mum is on the phone, something about your father having a fall and in hospital."

A pained gasp leaves her lips, and I stagger as she shifts forward, loosening her grip on me slightly.

"Oh goodness!" she exclaims, looking round trying to spot the chair to help me back to it. But it's nowhere in sight, I was trying to push myself today and managed to go further, meaning that we're inside an arched walkway, out of sight of the house and patio where the wheelchair sits.

"I can help Lilly if you want to go now. She sounded pretty upset," Roman adds, and although he looks sincere, I've had some experience—*I think*—with trickster boys, and there's something a little off about his expression. Almost triumphant. My eyes narrow at the same time as my skin prickles while looking at him, sure that he's up to something.

"I–I don't know. I'm not meant to leave her alone..." Jacky frets, and I'm sure she'd be wringing her hands if she weren't supporting me.

"I'll be fine," I assure her, feeling a pang at the thought of her dad in trouble and her mum all alone. "I won't be alone. You should go."

She takes another millisecond, chewing her lip, but worry obviously wins as she gives me a small nod, her gaze already back towards the house.

"I'll take good care of her," Roman persuades her, wrapping his arm underneath mine. He's taller than Jacky, around the same height as Ash I think, so he has to stoop a little, but seems to be okay. Then I shake my head. *Ash might not even be fucking real, Lilly.*

We watch as Jacky rushes off, and he doesn't speak until she's rounded the corner and is no longer in sight.

"They said you were like a pixie," he tells me, and my heart stutters in my chest, the world dropping away at his seemingly innocent sentence.

"W–what?" I reply, my voice a breathy, trembling whisper as I crane my neck and look up into his usually laughing brown eyes. Today they're full of seriousness, and a touch of melancholy.

He doesn't respond, and I catch movement in the corner of my vision. I look down to see that he's reaching into his pocket, my chest tightening painfully at the move, then flinch my head back slightly when he pulls out a white earbud headphone. Before I can utter another word and give voice to this fluttering in my stomach, he pops it in my ear with a kind, sad sort of smile.

"*Princess?*"

My limbs go weak, and Roman grunts quietly as he takes more of my weight, my fingers digging into his arm. I know that voice, dark as a moonless night, but the kind of dark that hides you from the monsters seeking to steal you away.

*"Princess, tell me you're there,"* the voice begs, a catch that I've not heard from my darkest Knight before.

"A–Ash?"

*"Fuck, Princess...Fuck, it's so good to hear your voice,"* he replies, a sort of hiccupping laugh sounding in my ear as tears rush to my eyes.

"You're...you're real," I state, not a question, more a breath of relief, the yearning in my soul increasing tenfold at just the sound of his voice.

*"Yeah, Baby Girl, we're real,"* another deeper voice tells me, a similar stutter to Ash's marring his usually gravelly tone.

"Jax," I rush out with a sob, my free hand flying to cover my mouth, the other wrapped around Roman's waist. The salt of tears drops onto my lips, letting me taste my relief, my sadness, my heartbreak at being apart from the other parts of my soul.

*"Don't cry, Pretty Girl,"* yet another voice pleads, one that's usually full of mirth and mischief.

"Loki!" I cry out, my palm moving to my rounded stomach, and our baby gives a kick, as if it knows that its fathers are on the other end of the line, and is desperate to meet them.

*"We don't have much time, darling,"* the final of my Knights says, the melody of his voice dulled slightly.

"Kai," I whisper, closing my eyes as a smile tugs the corners of my lips up, the shadows cast by the plants around us feeling like the caress of my men. My Knights.

*"I told you that we were bound for all eternity, my darling. We were always going to find you. You're our beating heart,"* Kai tells me, the strength of his conviction flowing into me until I can stand a little taller. I open my eyes, my mind clearing a little more with each word, each syllable they make.

"What happened? Why am I here?" I ask, desperate to know the truth.

*"Your...uncle...took you,"* Ash replies, seeming a little unsure of his words. *"And we think my father is involved too."*

"Adrian?" I question, my head giving a slight shake. "Took me?"

*"Yes, and we think that he might be drugging you to keep you compliant,"* Loki interrupts, a sound of pain followed after. *"What? She needs to know,"* he hisses, but I can barely hear him, my mind replaying all of the times that I ate, then felt so exhausted I had to sleep for hours. All of my confusion, all of my weakness suddenly made more sense.

My fingertips trace the fading bruising on my hips, the ones in the shape of fingertips. The nightmares, the visions of shadowed men, and dreams of Robert, the guy who tried to rape me. *Were they imagined too? And what about my baby?*

*"Princess?"* Ash asks, his voice laced with concern. *"You still there?"*

"Yeah," I reply softly, clearing my throat and blinking. *One thing at a time, Lilly.* " I think it's in my food. The drug, I mean."

Silence.

*"Shit,"* Ash curses, followed by the muffled sound of something smashing that makes me wince. *"Keep it together!"* Ash barks, but clearly, the comment is not aimed at me. *"I'll sort it, Princess. Don't stop eating."*

A fissure of pleasure rolls through me like a feline stretching at his commanding words.

"So, what's the plan?" I question, getting back to business, though the wonderful warming haze of knowing that they exist, that I didn't dream up our time together, settles over me in a comforting blanket. Roman's head is turned the other way, giving us as much privacy as he can, though I've got the feeling whatever happens next will involve the twins.

*"That's our girl,"* Loki praises, and I can hear his smile, lighting up the sunny day even though I'm hundreds of miles away from him as I stand in the rose garden.

*"My birthday is in two weeks,"* Kai interjects, and I can just picture him pushing his glasses up his nose as he speaks, my breath hitching at the thought of the gesture. *"We plan to fly to Amsterdam to celebrate."*

"Okay..." I say, trying to figure out what the next step is, but my fucking head is still so clouded.

*"Once we get there, we'll catch a plane to England, and with the help of our Shadow Crew friends, we'll come and get you,"* Ash adds, taking up where Kai finished.

"Oh." I look back up at Roman, seeing a smirk on his admittedly pretty face. "Oh!" I gasp when it finally clicks. "The Shadows, Willow's brother's crew!"

Roman winks, then looks over his shoulder, his brow dipping.

"Gotta hang up now, pixie girl," he tells me, his voice softening when he sees what must be my face falling.

*"I love you, wife,"* Ash murmurs in my ear, and if I close my eyes, I can pretend that he's the one holding me up instead of a stranger.

"I love you, husband," I whisper back, trying and failing to keep the tremor out of my voice.

*"I love you, Pretty Girl. Give our baby a rub from me,"* Loki tells me, his voice thick, and my lip trembles, tears freely dripping down my cheeks.

"I will. Love you too," I respond, my heart aching so fiercely that I rub at it, trying in vain to ease the hurt.

*"I love you, darling,"* Kai whispers, his voice etched with sorrow.

"I love you too, my soul," I tell him, feeling as though no truer words have ever been spoken. They are my soul as it no longer resides in me, and the pain of being parted is almost unbearable.

*"I swear to you on my blackened heart and all that is left of my soul that we will come for you, and fucking dance in the blood of those that have harmed you, my love,"* Jax vows, and his declaration is full of love and vengeance in equal measure, making my heart thrill.

"I love you with all that I am, Jax. All that I will ever be," I say in return.

*"Good girl,"* he commends, his deep voice a rumbling growl that sends a shiver to my core, lighting me up from the inside out.

Before I can say another word, I hear footsteps on the grass behind us, and Roman plucks the earbud out, pocketing it and turning us around as I wipe my tears off my face with my sleeve.

I see Jacky hurrying over, her face damp and eyes puffy, and the thought that maybe her father's accident wasn't so accidental suddenly occurs to me. I freeze for a moment, but then realise that although I feel sorry for her, it doesn't horrify me, nor the idea that my guys may have had a hand in the misfortune of an innocent bystander. I'm clearly not as lily-white as I used to be, and somehow, I'm not ashamed of that.

"My father has had a nasty fall, and I'll have to take over his care," she informs me, fussing as if she plans to take over from Roman, but he doesn't let go, instead, he helps to lead me down the walkway and back to that fucking chair. "So the agency is sending a replacement this afternoon. I'm sorry, dear."

"Tha–that's fine," I respond, trying to work out what this means. Roman gives my waist a little squeeze, and I think he means to assure me that this, too, is linked back to my guys.

We make it back to the chair, which waits innocently in a patch of sunlight, unknowing that it now represents everything that is wrong with my situation. *I wouldn't fucking need it if my uncle wasn't drugging me!*

Roman supports me as I get settled into it, and I grudgingly admit to myself that I'm feeling drained, both emotionally and physically, so it's a welcome relief to finally sit down. Jacky takes hold of the handles and starts pushing me back towards the house, unaware of the maelstrom of my thoughts and the swirling storm of my emotions.

Two weeks.

Fourteen days and I'll be in their arms again.

I just need to hold on.

# CHAPTER FOUR

LILLY

I'm left alone in my room for a couple of hours after that, the new agency nurse is not able to arrive for a little while. It's the first time I've spent in my own company for almost a month, and it's nice not having eyes on me the whole time, watching my every move. Although the feeling of being observed doesn't disappear completely and I glance around the room warily, wondering if there are hidden cameras in here. I wouldn't put anything past Adrian at the moment, and just because I haven't seen him yet, doesn't mean that he's not keeping tabs on me.

The plate of food that I arrived back to sits on the small table in front of the window, uneaten. I know it's going against what Ash commanded; that I keep eating. But I just can't force myself to, knowing that it's more than likely drugged by my wankstain of an uncle, and may be harmful to my unborn child. I'm not sure how soon Ash will be able to make good on his promise and ensure that it's not drugged, so for now, I'll hold off as long as I can. My stomach grumbles, reminding me that I've not eaten since breakfast, so I take a sip of water from the glass that I'd filled up from the bathroom tap—I can't trust the water given to me either.

What I can't seem to work out is why he would go to such lengths to keep me placid, unaware, and compliant. It's not as if I can escape from here anyway, being in the middle of bumfuck nowhere, and with my shit sense of direction I'd get lost or picked up even if I did try to run. And I don't have any way to contact the guys. Well, I didn't up until this point. Especially as I thought them to be a figment of my imagination.

The warmth that covered me when I was talking to my Knights fills me again, my entire being aching to be with them once more, to be ensconced in their arms, surrounded by their loving embrace. I burrow into the feeling, wrapping my blanket tighter around myself as I watch the rain of a sudden shower hit the window panes with a tinkling sound. The rain and birdsong are the only music I get to listen to now.

The sun begins to lower in the sky when I hear the lock of my door turning with a click, and I twist in my chair to see the door opening and a woman younger than Jacky but older than me steps into the room, the door closing softly behind her. Her wheat blonde hair is in a neat ponytail, and her slight frame is covered by pastel pink scrubs uniform. It's her laughing brown eyes that give me pause, plus the tray that she's holding in her hands.

"Hi, Lilly. I'm Mai and I've bought you something to eat," she tells me, carefully stepping towards me, and placing the tray on the table while making sure not to knock the plate already there off. "I made it myself, and no one else has touched it," she divulges, looking me straight in the eye with a frank and open look on her face. *She knows about the drugs, right?*

"T–thanks," I reply, looking down to see a bowl of steaming soup. It looks like chicken and vegetable, and my stomach growls loud enough to be heard over the drizzle outside. *Yum!*

I hesitate for just a moment, unsure if she is someone my guys have sent or another of one of my uncle's minions. She leans in closer, her light, floral perfume fresh rather than cloying.

"Ash told me to tell you 'rubber duck' if you had any concerns," she whispers in my ear, my eyes widening at the phrase. Only Ash and I know about it, no one else. My pulse spikes thinking about when he was meant to use it, if he was feeling the urge to cut, and worry floods my veins at the thought that he may have self-harmed and I've not been there to help.

*Worry about that later, Lilly. Just get through this first.*

Not taking my eyes off the bowl—just in case someone *is* watching us—I take the spoon, dip it in, and bring it to my mouth. The soup is delicious, clearly homemade, and full of warm comforting flavour. There's a bread roll to go with it, and before I realise it, the bowl is empty and I'm feeling full but clearheaded. A contrast to how I've felt after most meals I've had here.

"Thanks, that was amazing," I say with a sigh, seeing the corner of her eyes crinkle with a wide smile. "Have we met? Your eyes remind me of someone."

"The twins are my cousins, bloody reprobates," she answers, laughing as she hands me a bottle of water, then sits in the chair opposite me. That makes sense; she has Roman's eyes. "So, what do you usually do around here?" she asks me, another sigh leaving my lips as I play with the tassels on the blanket.

"Nothing really, mostly I sleep after eating," I confess, seeing the laughter leave her eyes as her jaw clenches, and a flush stains her cheeks.

"Well, how about a game of Go Fish?" she finally questions, pulling out a pack of cards from her pocket, along with a chocolate bar which makes my mouth water. "Winner gets this," she tells me, eyes alight with challenge.

"You're on!" I tell her, beaming as she moves the trays to the floor next to us, then deals the cards. "But fair warning, I was a champion back in primary school. I even won Sally Weston's favourite, pink sparkly headband, which pissed her off no end."

She lets out a peal of laughter, and suddenly the room feels brighter, the grey day less dismal as we begin to play.

---

I lie down, the sweet taste of victory still on my tongue as I savour the last cube of chocolate melting on my tongue. Mai left after dinner, telling me she'll be back tomorrow at breakfast, and it feels so nice to finally have an ally here. Three if you count the twins, which I think that I can, considering Willow and the guys know them.

I shut my eyes, waiting for the familiar blackness of sleep to descend, but it eludes me tonight. Maybe it was the conversation with my guys earlier, their voices echoing inside my head like a shout in a cave. Even now I can hear them, and for the first time in weeks, it feels as though I'm close to them once more.

It's the middle of the night, and the room is in complete darkness before I start to drift off, only to be startled awake when I hear the soft click of what sounds like the lock on my door. A shadow fills the doorway briefly before it's closed again, the lock sounding once more. My heart thuds painfully in my chest, my body freezing up as the figure approaches the bed. It pauses briefly in front of me before moving towards the bottom of the bed, out of my line of sight.

My breathing becomes shallow when cool air hits my back as the duvet is lifted, the mattress dipping as the figure gets in behind me. Nausea swirls in my stomach when the heat of a body hits my spine through my nightgown, fingers digging into my hips painfully as a hardness is ground against my arse.

"Violet..." a deep, male voice groans, his painful grip loosening, then his palm glides down my thigh, fingers searching for my hem and leaving a sickening tingling in their wake. All whilst his hot, alcohol-scented breath washes over the back of my head, making me want to throw up.

*Remember, Baby Girl, go in hard and fast, like you want to push through your attackers' body.*

Jax's voice sounds in my head, as if he's right in front of me, and before my brain has time to catch up, I'm throwing my head back with a yell. The satisfying sound of cartilage breaking sounds in the room, and warm liquid hits the back of my head, coating my hair.

"FUCK!" the male voice shouts, the heat of his body moving away from mine.

My head throbs, the dark room spinning as I struggle to sit up, my breaths laboured and sawing out of my chest.

"Lilly?! Everything okay?" a loud voice sounds from outside the door, the handle rattling.

"Rowan?" I croak, turning just as the dark shadow of a man flies across the room, pausing at the wall opposite the bed before disappearing through it. *What the fuck?*

"We're coming in, Lilly," Roman's voice calls this time just as I hear the lock click, and the door swings open, hitting the wall with a crash. The room suddenly fills with light, and I squint at the harsh brightness, my hand flying up to shade my eyes as I manage to sit upright. "Fuck, why are you covered in blood?"

Both boys rush over to me, Rowan kneeling on the bed next to me to inspect the back of my head.

"Ow!" I hiss when he touches a particularly tender spot.

"Sorry, pixie girl," he soothes, his fingers becoming a little more gentle. "It doesn't look like you're bleeding. What in the ever-loving fuck happened?"

"There was someone in my bed..." I shiver, tears filling my eyes and my cheeks reddening with shame at what I have to say next. "H–he was—he was touching me, so I headbutted him with the back of my head," I tell them, feeling a drop of liquid hit my hands which are resting in my lap. "He called me Violet."

"Motherfucker!" Roman curses, running his fingers through his shoulder-length hair. His all black outfit looks a little rumpled, but I guess it would be if he's been on duty all day and into the night. "Where is he now?" he questions, looking around as if he'll find him hiding under the bed.

"He disappeared through that wall," I tell them, lifting my trembling hand and pointing to the spot opposite me. I can see a very faint outline in the wall, the right size for a door. Roman walks over to it, running his hands along the tiny gap.

"Servants' door, all the old manors have them. Can't have the help cluttering up the hallways. Fucking elitist pricks," he mumbles as a small click sounds in the room, and a second later the door opens to reveal a dark passageway. "He definitely went this way," he tells us, stepping to one side and shining the torch on his phone onto the floor, highlighting spots of red.

"Check it out, I'll wait here," Rowan says, getting off the bed and holding out a hand. "I'll help get you sorted, Lilly."

"Just because you're four minutes older, doesn't make you the fucking boss," Roman grumbles, but does what Rowan says and heads into the gaping darkness, shutting the secret door behind him.

"Has anything like this happened before?" Rowan asks me, his voice laced with gentle concern as he helps me out of the bed, tucking my trembling hand into the crook of his elbow. My other hand strokes over the fading bruises on my hip.

"I–I think maybe, but I've been too out of it to know if it was just a dream or not," I confess quietly, pausing when his steps stop. I look up to see that his jaw is clenched, his face hard. I swallow thickly, trying to find the courage to ask a question in return. "D–do you know who it was?"

His eyes close, a deep exhale leaving his mouth before he turns, facing me, his hand coming over mine and tucking it further into the crook of his arm.

"We're not sure, but I wouldn't be surprised if your uncle has a broken nose and two black eyes tomorrow." His eyes soften, his hand squeezing mine gently.

"Adrian?" I whisper, but don't hear if he replies as I tear from his grip, making it just in time to throw up in the toilet. I heave until there's nothing left, stomach acid burning the back of my throat.

I hear the sound of Rowan talking to someone, but my mind is too full of what he just implied. My uncle has been stealing into my bedroom at night, touching me, sexually abusing me, whilst I was too drugged up by him to defend myself.

All of a sudden the walls feel like they're closing in, my breaths coming in short, sharp pants as the weight of that knowledge sinks in.

*"Hey, Princess,"* a deep voice I vaguely recognise sounds as if from far away. *"Look at me, Lilly,"* the voice commands, and I turn my head, finding familiar grey eyes full of worry looking back at me. *"That's it, my love, good girl. Now breathe with me, in and out,"* Ash orders, and it takes me a second to realise that he's on a phone screen and not actually in the room. A wave of almost crippling sorrow hits me, but I do as he orders and follow his deep breathing until the edges of the room go back to their usual place.

"Ash?" I rasp, my throat raw and tears dripping down my cheeks as I wrap my arms around myself, still sitting on the bathroom floor in front of the toilet full of my own vomit. "H–he touched me, Ash."

*"I know, Princess, I know. And I will personally chop off each and every one of his fingers for daring to lay a hand on you,"* he growls out as a deadly fire burns in his eyes, a fire that warms me enough to sit up straighter. *"I wish we could come and get you right the fuck now but we can't, Princess."* Frustration is clear in the way he says the last part through clenched teeth. *"If my father even suspects...shit, he may order Adrian to kill you, and I just can't live in a world that you are not a part of. That's not an option, Princess."* His eyes beg me for my understanding, for my forgiveness.

"I–I know, Ash," I reply softly, lowering my gaze as my throat constricts at the thought of spending one more second with the fucking pervert that is my uncle.

*"Look at me, Princess,"* Ash directs once more, voice hard, so I do as he says. *"You will not have to face him again. One of the boys will be with you, day and night."*

"How can you make that happen?" I ask, mind swirling with the game that we're playing, the tightrope that we're walking.

"We'll tell him that Julian has given us orders to," Roman tells me, and I look away from Ash into his laughing brown eyes, which currently are full of evil humour. It also confirms my suspicions that Julian has something to do with this.

*"He won't question it if it's my father's orders,"* Ash interjects, and I look back at him. *"Because then he'll have to admit what he's been doing, and Julian won't like that one bit."* His lip curls, and I shiver at his words. Not for the first time, I curse being a woman, curse the fact that these old men all want something from me that I am not willing to give them, so they will try and take it by force. *"We won't let Julian near you either, Princess. I swear."*

I gaze into his eyes, full of a fierce fire and love, and I nod, scrubbing my own eyes with my hand. "Okay," I say, my voice a little scratchy but stronger than before.

*"That's my girl,"* Ash tells me, pride making his eyes shine. *"Now, Mai is on her way to help you get sorted, and the boys will be with you until she gets there."*

"I love you, Asher Vanderbilt," I confess, beyond grateful for everything that he is doing for me.

*"I love you, Lilly Vanderbilt,"* he replies, voice soft. *"I'll see you soon, okay, Princess?"*

"See you soon," I respond, my heart dropping as he ends the call.

Somewhere, a clock chimes one in the morning.

Thirteen days. I'll see him and the others in thirteen days.

All I need to do is survive until then.

# CHAPTER FIVE

JAX

Pain explodes across my knuckles when my fist meets its target, wet droplets of ruby red hitting my face as my opponent's lip splits. A heady sense of euphoria rushes over me when he goes down, lightness suffusing my limbs at the sight of his crumpled, defeated form. It's followed by a sharp, edgy feeling, my nostrils flaring at the fact that he stays on the ground, forcing me to leash the demon inside that's desperate to break free. That needs to wreak havoc and cause bloodshed.

The sounds of the crowd filter back into my ears, a mixture of hollers and jeers as some win the bets they placed earlier in the night while others lose.

"The Black Knight remains undefeated tonight!" the ref shouts, my still clenched fist pulled into the air, blood dripping down my arm, much to the crowd's screaming delight. They don't call it bare knuckle fighting for nothing, and I relish the sting that throbs along the limb almost as much as the agony I forced upon the guy lying prone on the dirt floor. "Is anyone else brave enough to face this Goliath?"

Silence greets his call, the clear night's sky surrounding us, stars twinkling in the inky depths above. My lip curls at the thought of taking a second's enjoyment when my Baby Girl is trapped in a hell not of her making. My jaw tightens like it does every time I think about her, and how fucking useless we are at the moment, leaving her there. It feels too close to abandonment for my liking.

"I'll fight him," a familiar, deep voice states into the quiet, and the crowd parts like the red motherfucking sea to let Asher Vanderbilt saunter through, his signature smirk plastered on his lips.

"Think you can win, rich boy?" I snarl, baiting him, letting my gaze travel up and down his body. He's fit, and pretty stacked, but not a match for me and my bulk.

"Pot and kettle, *Black Knight*," he teases back, stripping off his white tee and exposing all that inked-up flesh. He's been wearing suits less since Lilly went missing, opting for sweats and T-shirts like the rest of us. My lip tilts at the thought of calling him out on it. That'll rile him up for sure.

"Well, don't complain when that pretty face of yours gets all bloodied up, *Vanderbilt*," I volley back, rolling my neck as he steps right up to me, his bare chest brushing my own sweat and blood-covered torso.

A fissure of guilt runs through me at the knowledge that either Lilly would hate this—us fighting—or really fucking love it. Kai and Loki told us all about how much she enjoyed their company. Fuck, I can't wait for her to be back with us. I'd even touch this asshole's dick if she asked me to, just to see that fire in her eyes again.

"You think I'm pretty, Griffiths? I'm afraid you're not my type, too much between your legs for me," Ash retorts, and I can't help the dark chuckle that falls from my lips at the comment.

"We both know that your wife certainly enjoys what's between my legs," I reply, grinning smugly when a dark flush creeps up his neck. "What does she call it again...oh yes, my monster cock. But I'm sure that you're...adequate, pretty boy."

It's a testament to our years of training that the only reaction he gives me is a clenching of his fists and flared nostrils. He's as unflappable as a statue, which is just one of the reasons that he's our leader.

"You two done flirting, or do you need a moment alone to jerk each other off?" the ref interrupts loudly, the crowd laughing and whooping in the background.

I spit blood at Ash's feet, a wave of probably unwarranted anger washing over me. He's part of the reason why I'm not holding my girl right the fuck now. Well, his cunt of a sperm donor is, and it's far easier than I like to admit to transfer that purple-tinged rage to the son instead of the father.

I can see his face shift, eyes burning molten with wrath as he gears himself up for the fight, and I know he's just as pissed at himself as I am at my own inadequacies with this situation. I have a moment of hesitation, knowing that I surpassed him a few years back in terms of sheer strength.

"Don't you dare fucking hold back on me, Griffiths," he grits out, still issuing orders.

"Don't worry," I assure him, a rare smile tugging my lips up. It must not be a nice one as I see him flinch ever so slightly. "I won't."

Wasting no more time, I throw a punch that lands a solid hit to his jaw, snapping his head to the side as the sound of his teeth clacking together fills my ears like the finest symphony. He recovers quickly, not like the other shit-bags I've fought tonight, whipping his head around and landing a closed-fisted strike to my gut that almost has me doubling over. Almost, but not quite, as my own training kicks in.

"You've gotten better," I rasp out, and he gives me a feral grin, his teeth covered in blood.

The next several moments blur into a violent dance, both of us exchanging blows, landing an almost equal number of hits. Blood paints our skin, streaking it with red until we look like demons that have stepped out of hell, covered in our sins. Panting hard, Ash has put up more of a fight than I expected, I'm a little tired from my previous three fights and pause for a millisecond to take a breather. But, unfortunately for him, it looks like I'm still stronger than he is as in the next second I land a solid punch to the side of his temple and he goes down like a sack of shit.

"The Black Knight wins again!" the ref calls, but I sidestep him, going to my fallen leader, kneeling down in the dirt, and giving him a shake. He groans as his long, black eyelashes flutter—*no wonder Baby Girl fell for him so hard, fucking pretty boy indeed*—and he rolls onto his back.

"Fuck you, Jax," he rasps, coughing and spitting blood next to my knee.

"Yeah, fuck you too, Ash," I reply, grabbing his hand and hauling him to his feet.

"Urgh, careful, you fucking neanderthal," he complains as I settle his arm across my shoulders, wrapping my own around his torso a little more tightly than necessary, eliciting a hiss of pain from his swollen lips. "You were the one that beat the shit out of me, what do you have to be salty about?" I look down into his grey eyes, one almost swollen shut, and just give him a look. "You're still sore about me marrying Lilly, aren't you?" he questions, a stupid fucking smile on his face. "I just did what I had to do."

Another sharp grunt of pain leaves his throat as I poke what I suspect is a very bruised rib.

"Sure you did," I reply, huffing as his smile remains fixed. People give us a wide berth as we exit, probably on account of the grinning idiot next to me who can barely walk but seems ecstatic about it. Luckily we rode together, as I doubt he'd be able to drive himself, stupid fuck.

Goosebumps pebble my skin as the high of my fights leaves my system, and Ash sighs next to me when we get to my truck. I open the door for him, and before he gets in, he turns to me, his bruised face weary.

"There's been a development," he tells me, eyes shrewd once more. My heart gives a painful thud in my chest

"What kind of development?" I question, knowing that it relates back to Baby Girl.

"I'll tell you when we get back to the dorm," he replies, and the metal of the car creaks when my fingers tighten on the edge of the door.

"I should have fucking hit you harder," I grumble, stepping away and making my way around the front to the driver's side.

"Yeah, you should have," I hear him mumble, before he steps in and closes the door behind him.

Hand clenching the door handle hard enough that my bloody knuckles turn white, I look to the star-freckled sky and send up a prayer to whatever motherfucker might be out there.

*Keep her safe for me.*

---

## KAI

I flinch as Jax throws the coffee table across the room, the tinkle of shattering glass at odds with the violence swirling in the room. Loki isn't faring much better, his fists clenched, breathing hard as he tries to remain in control of himself and his wrath. But I see it, clear as day, swirling in the depths of his emerald eyes. A fire that rages and burns, threatening to consume us all.

I can feel my own pulse spiking, Ash's revelation about his phone call with Lilly in the early hours calling to my own inner demon. Her situation is so similar to my own, her uncle is as much of a pervert as mine. More so if he is actually her father. Sick fuck. The blackness of my own rage threatens to consume me, eating at the corners of my vision, but I keep my head. Pushing it back until it simmers in the corner, waiting for its target; Adrian Ramsey.

"We have to get her now, Ash," Loki bites out through clenched teeth. "We can't leave her there, you must know that?" My heart thuds at his pleading tone, my spirit breaking that much more at the knowledge of what she's up against.

"We don't have any other fucking choice!" Ash shouts, throwing his hands out wide, an ice pack clutched in one. I wince at the bruises already marking his face, the purples and blues of them already visible. "If Julian even catches the slightest whiff of what we're planning..."

He doesn't need to finish his sentence, we all know what Julian Vanderbilt is capable of. The depths he will go to in order to gain more control over the company. Although...

"Are we sure that he'd order her death?" I question, Ash's head snapping to look at me. "I mean, he knows that we care for her and that if any lasting harm came to her, we'd rebel big time."

"But as far as he's aware, we believe that she's missing," Ash answers, rubbing his face then hissing when he hits a sore spot. "She could stay missing, he could move her or just cut his losses. Unless we confront him about it, which just feels too risky with her still there, I can't see any other way forward but to wait until it's too late for him to do anything about it."

I nod, hating his words but knowing them to be the truth. We can't give Julian any reason to hurt her, to kill her. And I've no doubt that he would if he felt so inclined. He may find her...appealing, but if she were to die, all her assets go to Ash and thus stay under Julian's control. For now anyway.

"So we just fucking wait?" Jax snarls, and at least he's calmed down enough to speak. "And leave her with that pervert?"

"I know, I fucking hate it as much as you do," Ash confesses, voice fractured and pain-filled. "But I'd rather that than not have her at all. We can help her get over this. We can't bring her back from the dead."

We all flinch at his last words, feeling them to the pit of our very tortured souls.

"Fuck!" Loki exhales, though with a sad resignation and not the anger of a few moments before. "How will she ever forgive us for this? We're leaving her in the hands of a monster."

"She'll have the Shadow twins," Ash assures us, as much as himself I think. "One of them will be with her twenty-four seven. Plus she's got Mai now, to make sure she's no longer drugged."

I clear my throat. "I've been able to hack into his security system," I tell them, narrowed eyes swinging my way. "We can watch her using the CCTV cameras and see for ourselves that she's okay." It's the only reason that I'm able to keep my beast in check right now.

"And you didn't think to tell us this before?" Ash questions, one brow arched, his voice cold.

"Not my fault you don't check your phones. The app has been on there all evening." I shrug, a small tilt lifting my lips when they all rush to take their cells out of their pockets, Ash cursing as his sore fingers fumble with the screen of his brand new iPhone. I walk over and snatch the device out of his grip, earning a feral growl. "Let me."

A couple of swipes later, the image of our beautiful girl pops up on the screen. She's sitting at a small table, eating a bowl of something with the sun filtering through the window, while who I assume is Mai talks to her from another seat across from her. My heart swells when Lilly laughs, the musical, joyous sound fills the room even though there's no sound on the feed. I can hear it clearly in my mind.

We watch, enraptured, as she finishes her meal, breakfast most likely given that it's early morning in England, and with Mai's help stands, her rounded stomach obvious in her thin nightgown.

"She's gotten so big," Loki whispers, and I look up to see his eyes glued to the screen, tracing every line, every curve of our girl. I look back down to see her go through what I assume is her bathroom door, which closes behind her. Mai waits outside, giving Lilly her privacy which I am grateful for knowing just how much her life has been monitored by that fucking scumbag these past few weeks.

"I've sent the twins a burner phone, so soon we will be able to communicate with her too," I tell them all, my voice soft as I watch the closed bathroom door on the screen, desperate for another glimpse.

No one replies, though I feel the tension leak out of Ash next to me as we continue watching, waiting for our next fix.

We stay that way for a long time, drinking in the sight of the girl who stole our hearts, our souls, before we'd even realised what she was doing.

# CHAPTER SIX

LILLY

The next couple of days are like a breath of fresh air, like I can finally breathe fully again for the first time in weeks. Each day that Mai brings me freshly prepared food that only she handles, my head clears until I no longer suffer the effects of being drugged after each meal, and so my strength returns. I still use the wheelchair when she takes me out, something telling me not to let my uncle know how much stronger I am now. Truth be told, I'm not quite at full strength yet anyway, having been so inactive for the past few weeks.

I'm getting bigger too, most noticeably my growing stomach now that I'm six months gone. My tits are bigger, and randomly my nipples too, which Mai says is all normal. Baby seems to be getting along well, though not having access to an ultrasound means that we can't check everything. But all the checks that Mai does are fine, and my blood levels are okay.

One of the twins is with me at all times, even at night. The day after 'the incident'—as I'm now calling it because I just can't process what happened right now—the boys moved the massive, wooden wardrobe in front of the secret door, blocking it completely. They could only just about manage it, so I doubt that my uncle could move it alone. And although I haven't seen my uncle, Roman told me that he left to go into Harley Street to see about a nose job after apparently being kicked in the face by one of his horses. *Like that's fucking believable!*

Several days after 'the incident,' Mai and I are walking in the rose garden, once again under the archway. Mai helps me in order to keep up the pretence of my drug-induced state. Can't have my uncle thinking that I'm not weakened by the drugs. Some of the roses are in full bloom now, their heady scent wrapping around me in a floral perfume. There's a soft breeze that plays with the tassels on my light shawl, the loose trousers I'm wearing fluttering around my ankles as we stroll along. It's the weirdest thing. The wardrobe and chest are full of brand new maternity clothes, some with tags still on, but they're all just a little out of date and slightly musty smelling. Like they've been shut away for a while. They're mostly comfy if a little upper-class-rich-woman-who-goes-to-lunch for me, so I can't complain.

As we walk towards the end of the arch, intending to head out towards the man-made lake today, someone calls my name. I turn and smile to see Rowan jogging towards me. Both boys have become like the brothers I never had, teasing me to keep my spirits up and fiercely protective when it comes to my safety.

"Good morning, pixie girl, sis," he greets when he reaches us, not even a little puffed out. Bloody bastard. "I've a present for you, Lilly," he tells me, a mischievous glint in his brown eyes.

Raising an eyebrow at him, he just gives me what I am coming to realise is one of the twins' signature naughty smirks, then he reaches into his pocket and pulls out what looks like a brand new iPhone.

"What's this?" I question, my heart rate picking up as I take the device from him and tap my thumb on the screen. Immediately, I see a message waiting for me.

KAI EVIL GENIUS MATTHEWS:

So we can keep in touch, darling xxx

I quickly open it, rereading the message again as a smile tugs at my lips. I startle when another message pops up.

LOKI YOUR FAVOURITE BOYFRIEND THORN:

*winking face emoji*

*Fucking cuntmuffin!*

Followed by another.

ASH OUR ALMIGHTY LEADER:

Who the fuck gave us these stupid-ass nicknames?
Hello, Princess xxx

A laugh tinkles out of my mouth at seeing his words, and I can just imagine his grumbling tone of voice as he says them. Another message comes in, and I can't help a bark of laughter that rings around the spring morning.

JAX WEAPON OF MASS DESTRUCTION GRIFFITHS:

I'm betting Loki, fucker. Baby Girl, you there?

LILLY SEXY AF BABY MAMA:

I'm here. And I like the nicknames *kissing face emoji*

LILLY SEXY AF BABY MAMA:

Are you sure this is okay? It's not going to be tracked? Xxx

I nibble my bottom lip as I wait for a reply, knowing that Mai and Rowan act as a lookout whilst I stare at the screen like the lifeline that it is. A reply soon appears.

KAI EVIL GENIUS MATTHEWS:

It's a burner, my darling. Untraceable, so just keep it hidden xxx

***Loki Your Favourite Boyfriend Thorn changed the group name to Lilly's Not Gangbang Boyfriends.***

My hand slaps over my mouth as a shout of laughter leaves my lips.

ASH OUR ALMIGHTY LEADER:

I'm her husband, dickhead *middle finger emoji*

I feel a small tap on my shoulder, and I tear my eyes away from the screen to look up at a beaming Mai.

"We probably should be heading back, it looks like it might rain," she tells me kindly, and I look up to see dark clouds beginning to cover the blue sky. I did not miss the changeable British weather when I was in Colorado.

LILLY SEXY AF BABY MAMA:

Got to go, I'll text later. Love you all xxx

I pocket the phone before they can reply, otherwise, I'll never put it down, and with Mai on one side and Rowan on the other, we make our way back to the chair on the patio.

My pocket buzzes—I must turn the vibrate feature off just in case—and a warm glow fills my being at the lifeline that I've been given, the connection to my guys the best kind of feeling.

---

Later that night, after a delicious dinner of creamy pasta that Mai cooked and brought up, I snuggle into bed with my new phone in my hands under the duvet, the screen's brightness turned low as it will go. I still suspect that my uncle has a camera in here somewhere, watching me, and although he's not visited me since that awful night, I'd rather not give him any reason to. Or lead to the discovery of my new phone.

The screen lights up with a message from Kai outside of the group chat.

KAI:

Having trouble sleeping, darling?

LILLY:

How did you know?

I narrow my eyes at the screen while those little bubbles tell me he's writing.

KAI:

There's a camera in your room…

*I fucking knew it!* My heart races as I poke my head up, looking again to see if I can spot it. The screen flares just before it was about to black out.

KAI:

Don't worry, darling. I've looped the feed so that it only shows your uncle you sleeping at night, and then doing your usual routine during the day.

A breath of relief whooshes out of me, my fingers tingling as I type my reply, not bothering to hide my phone.

LILLY:

What can you see?

Those damn bubbles are back, and for reasons unknown I hold my breath, waiting for his response.

KAI:

You…in bed…

KAI:

Wearing too many clothes…

I slowly release my breath as tingles race over my skin.

LILLY:

I can't exactly sleep naked, especially with Roman in the corner…

A moment later I hear shuffling, then my door opening as I look up to see Roman leaving the room, closing the door softly behind him. One of the brothers has been taking the night shift in here with me, and I've been sleeping better knowing that I'm watched over. I feel better now knowing that Kai has his eyes on me too.

KAI:

Problem solved, Pet…

A shiver runs down my spine at the nickname. Laying down the phone on the pillow beside my head, I slowly, teasingly, push the thick duvet down my body, kicking it to the end of the bed with my bare feet.

KAI:

Good girl, now that nightgown.

Sitting up, I gather the garment up and pull it over the top of my head, dropping it to the bed beside me. My nipples harden in the cool air, my breath leaving my body in a shaky exhale. The phone lights up, the group chat flashing up this time.

ASH OUR ALMIGHTY LEADER:

What are you up to, Princess?

Both nicknames bring a smile to my lips. Another message from Kai pops up outside of the group chat.

KAI:

Prop yourself up on your pillows, Pet, legs open.

A sense of breathlessness overcomes me as I get into position, my pulse becoming fast.

LOKI YOUR FAVOURITE BOYFRIEND THORN:

Naughty, Pretty Girl, giving us a show like such a good little slut.

I lick my dry lips, waiting for Kai's next instruction, my eyes glued to the screen.

KAI:

Such a clever, beautiful girl. Now, suck your fingers, two should be enough.

I do as he commands, bringing my slightly trembling pointer and middle fingers of my right hand to my mouth, pushing them slowly in. There's something so exciting about knowing that I'm being watched by my guys, but not where the camera is or being able to watch them in return.

KAI:

That's it, Pet, make them all nice and wet.

My muscles relax as a smile pulls my lips upwards, my fingers popping out of my mouth, glistening with my saliva.

JAX WEAPON OF MASS DESTRUCTION GRIFFITHS:

Baby Girl...fuck you're killing me here...

I can't resist one long lick up the side of my finger, swirling my tongue around the top just as I've done countless times to their hard cocks, hoping that they remember the move too.

KAI:

Take them to that beautiful wet cunt of yours, Pet. Rub your clit nice and slow for me.

I do as instructed, trailing my fingers down the centre of my body, coming round the side of my swollen stomach, using touch to locate my pussy. At this stage, I can no longer see it if I look down, but my fingers find it easily enough, and just as Kai described, it's already slick with my excitement.

A heady moan leaves my lips at the first touch, pleasure zinging over my body when my fingers make contact with my engorged bud. The phone lights up beside me, and I turn hooded eyes to read the message.

ASH OUR ALMIGHTY LEADER:

You are a fucking goddess, wife. I'm as hard as stone for you right now, Princess.

Using my other hand, a little awkwardly, I type out a reply.

LILLY SEXY AF BABY MAMA:

Grip your dicks hard for me, pretend it's my hand wrapped around them.

JAX WEAPON OF MASS DESTRUCTION GRIFFITHS:

Shit, baby…that feels so fucking good.

My fingers move faster on my nub, imagining my Knights tugging and pulling at their hard cocks, and trying to pretend it's one of them playing with my body.

KAI:

Dirty Pet, getting so worked up over their filthy words. I'll have to get Ash to spank you again when you're home.

The ache that's permanently in my chest flares at the mention of home, but I shove it down, focusing back on the electric pulses that are starting to shoot from my core.

KAI:

I would do such dirty, terrible things to your body, Pet. Indulge all of your darkest fantasies, and play with all of your fears until you don't know whether to beg me to stop or keep going.

Heat flushes over my entire body as I read his words, my other hand reaching down to my aching breast and squeezing it. A gasp falls from my lips, my teeth sinking into the bottom one as I bring my fingers down to my opening and thrust them inside myself, fucking my hand hard and fast.

The phone lights up on the pillow next to me, and I have to open my cracked eyes wider to read the message.

LOKI YOUR FAVOURITE BOYFRIEND THORN:

That's it, baby. Fuck your hand like you would my cock. I wanna see you come all over yourself.

I feel myself getting higher and higher, the pleasure almost too unbearable after so long without it. I've been craving a release, needing to rid myself of this pent-up energy and frustration that being incarcerated has left me with.

Adding a third finger and closing my eyes, I call to mind four pairs of hands on me, gliding over and inside my body as I grind down on my fingers. I give into the intense feelings racing over my skin, uncaring as cries leave my lips with abandon.

Feeling myself reach the cliff's edge, I pull my fingers out, hitting my G-spot on the way as an orgasm rips through me and sends me into the stratosphere. Wetness coats my hand and the bed beneath me as I writhe, letting the stars fill my eyes and waves of exquisite torture run through and over me, leaving me gasping.

Lying back, relaxing completely into the mound of pillows behind me, I let my breathing slow, languidly looking over at the phone to see several messages in the group chat.

ASH OUR ALMIGHTY LEADER:

That was perfection. You are perfection, Princess x

KAI EVIL GENIUS MATTHEWS:

Such a good little Pet x

JAX WEAPON OF MASS DESTRUCTION GRIFFITHS:

Fuck, Baby Girl. you are so fucking beautiful when you cum x

LOKI YOUR FAVOURITE BOYFRIEND THORN:

*eggplant emoji**three drops emoji*

I chuckle at Kai, messaging the group as if he didn't orchestrate the whole thing like a conductor.

LILLY SEXY AF BABY MAMA:

Show me. I wanna see what I do to you all.

An influx of picture messages arrives a moment later. Toned abs glistening with cum and still hard dicks that make my mouth water.

LILLY SEXY AF BABY MAMA:

Soon, I'll lick it all off. Every. Last. Fucking. Drop.

It takes a couple of moments, but a reply lights up the screen moments later.

LOKI YOUR FAVOURITE BOYFRIEND THORN:

Fuck, Pretty Girl! I'll hold you to that *purple devil emoji*

I get up on only slightly shaking legs, smirking at the power that I'd forgotten I wield when it comes to these guys. It goes some ways to soothing my feeling of entrapment, of vulnerability, and being completely out of control at the moment.

Gathering the now wet sheets, I leave them in a pile, rooting through the drawers until I find fresh ones. I put them on the bed, and then head to the bathroom to get cleaned up.

Eight days left.

Just over a week until it will be their fingers inside me, their cocks I come all over.

My unborn child gives a strong kick, my hand flying to rest over the spot and feel the push of a foot or elbow.

*Soon, love. We'll be with them soon, I swear.*

# CHAPTER SEVEN

LILLY

The next week passes by in excruciating torture, the days growing warmer now that we're nearing the height of the English summer. Sure, we still get a couple of dull, rainy days—this is Britain after all—but on the whole, we are blessed with blue, cloudless skies, a complete juxtaposition to the twisting storm that's spiralling inside me.

This nauseating mix of hope and despair swirls in my stomach like curdled milk; knowing that my time being held captive here is coming to an end, but that it won't be without bloodshed. I'm hoping that it'll be just my uncle's life-force staining the walls, but there's always the chance that someone I care about will be caught in the crossfire.

I manage to message the guys every day, and even a few whispered FaceTime calls late at night, Roman and Rowan leaving the room to allow us to talk in privacy. I find seeing my guys heartbreaking and comforting in equal measure. Feeling so close, yet so far away, leaves my soul keening when we hang up and I'm returned to my isolation.

The day of reckoning arrives, another beautiful, clear morning with the dawn chorus serenading the sparkling dew on the clipped lawns surrounding the house. I was ready before Mai even got here, my mind restless and unable to settle into a deep sleep last night, regardless of how tired my body was.

"Can we go outside?" I beg, and she laughs at my widened, pleading eyes.

"Sure, I mean, it's like seven in the morning, but what the hell!"

I grab her arm, almost causing her to drop my tray of granola and fresh juice.

"You must eat first," she orders, her voice stern yet a smile teasing her mouth. "Then we can go."

"Fiiine!" I pout, letting her arm go and rushing over to the table in front of the window where I take all my meals.

After a rushed shovelling of cereal in my gob, I'm practically hopping on my feet as I drag her to the doorway, a chuckle escaping her whilst she opens the door. Unlike Jacky, she's never locked it. The freedom the unlocked door offered was an illusion and one that I just couldn't force myself to fall for. My uncle could be around every corner, every turn, and I can't let him know that Mai is on my side. Plus, I don't want to face that jizzcheese wanker anytime soon, even with one of the twins by my side.

I questioned her about the other midwife, desperate to know if she was party to my uncle's plot, but as far as Mai knows, Jacky was told that I was a danger to myself and my unborn child due to 'mental instability,' hence the need for sedation and monitoring. Mai knows this because she was told the same, my uncle not realising that she was connected to The Shadows and put into place by my Knights.

Mai also told me that the drug I'd been given is a type of strong antihistamine, and it's basically an antihistamine that, if given in high enough doses, can cause nightmares, dizzy spells, plus feeling tired all the time and unsteady on your feet. It's used for insomnia, hence my tendency to knock out after I've eaten the drugged food. Luckily, it's perfectly fine for pregnancy. The overwhelming relief I felt that my baby hadn't been harmed was staggering, my whole body sagging with the weight that was lifted from my shoulders.

The damned wheelchair waits by the door, parked up against the wall like a silent spectator, waiting for my downfall. With a cursory glance, I stride past it, deciding that today I will remain on my feet. After all, I no longer need to keep up any kind of pretence that I'm weak. I want to be ready for when my guys come, to show them how strong I am.

Especially as when I suggested that I could try and escape sooner without them, they wouldn't hear of it, Ash ordering me to remain where I was or face dire consequences. *Arsegobbler.*

I was tempted to disobey, but when Loki mentioned the pregnancy and the possible harm the baby could come under were I to be caught, not to mention the stress involved, I relented. I can't jeopardise the life and health of our unborn child, not for my own pride.

"Are we..." Mai starts, indicating the wheelchair behind us with her hand as I head towards the stairs.

"We don't need it today," I calmly inform her, pausing at the top step and gazing into her kind eyes. "I won't need it ever again after today."

Her eyes widen a fraction, realising what I'm saying, then she pulls me into a tight hug.

"I'll stay with you the whole time, and afterwards. Make sure you and baby are okay and well," she whispers into my ear.

I cling back just as tight, tears pricking my eyes, soaking in her support and letting it shore me up for the trial ahead. It means so much to have her with me, beside me. I know that she can handle it, she's told me a little of growing up in The Shadows before Hunter paid for her to go to med school and train to be a midwife several years ago. She said that she owes him a debt, and not just in terms of money, but he refuses to let her pay a penny back, stating that knowing that she's 'out of the life' is more than enough. And this is the only time he's ever asked anything of her in return, and even then he gave her a choice.

Even though we spend a good portion of the day outside, having a picnic lunch on the lawn that Mai prepares, the day drags unbearably slowly, time mocking me with each tick of the clock in the main hall. Taunting me from afar. Eventually, after I've bitten my nails down to the quick, Mai suggests that we head inside and that I try to rest.

It's so frustrating not knowing exactly what's going to happen. Or even when they're going to get here, and I feel like a child waiting for their parents to return home after a trip spent apart, desperate to see them again, full of barely contained excitement. The guys refused to tell me the whole plan just in case something had to change, and I think because they didn't want me to worry about anything. But what they don't realise is that not knowing worries me more, and fills me with edgy anxiety until I'm ready to burst.

Once we're in my room, I find it almost impossible to settle, sitting at the chair then getting up almost immediately to pace over to the bed and back again.

"Lilly..." Mai scolds from her seat in one of the chairs by the window, and I pause, wringing my hands and drawing my bottom lip under my teeth. "This won't make them come any faster, you know."

I hear Loki's snort in my head at her word—*bloody, filthy-minded bastard!* —and I know that she's right, but the tension coiled up inside me refuses to be quietened.

Standing there, I look out of the window at the beautiful landscape that surrounds us; the trees swaying gently in a soft summer breeze, the sound of birds chirping as we move closer towards evening even though the sun is still pretty high in the sky. Taking deep, even breaths, I allow myself to soak in the beauty, the majesty of nature. The world keeps turning, regardless of what happens today, and we must accept that nothing will stop that. Life will go on.

My baby gives a small movement, my warm palm coming to my stomach over the floral maxi dress that I'm wearing today. Perhaps not the most practical attire for escape, but it makes me feel good and is really comfy, so I refuse to change out of it and my flip-flops.

Just as the sun sets below the horizon, I hear the opening strains of *'Ride of the Valkyries'* by Wagner fill the room, the entire mansion seeming to vibrate with the sounds of the violin strings.

"What the fuck..." I trail off as the wardrobe starts to rock violently, my heart beating faster with each tilt. Mai rushes to my side, pushing me slightly behind her as the piece of furniture comes crashing down with an almighty boom, the floor trembling and a couple of pictures falling off the wall, landing with a smash of glass.

Two black-clad figures emerge from the darkness as the music builds to a crescendo, and my heart stills in my chest as they look straight at me. A fallen angel with hair of fire and a Viking with piercing, blue eyes.

"Hey, Pretty Girl," Loki whispers, and I'm not even sure if I hear him over the music or if his voice sounds in my head, but the low sensual sound of it races across my skin, setting me alight and leaving me breathless.

"Baby," Jax rumbles, his deep timbre stroking my soul and wrapping me up in smoky notes, cutting through the music.

"You could have just used the door, fucking heathens," a familiar drawl sounds from across the room, and my head snaps in that direction as two more black-clad figures enter the room.

Grey eyes lock on mine, and before I can say a word, think a single thought, Ash leaps onto and over the bed in a feline move, gently pushes Mai to one side, grabs my face in both his palms and slams his lips onto mine.

His kiss is devastating, full of pent-up longing and desperate sorrow. Each stroke of his skilled tongue is begging for my forgiveness, every caress of his lips a declaration to never let me out of his sight again. I return his embrace, trying to breathe him in, absorb every part of him into my own being.

My fingers clench into his T-shirt, my cuticles ripping with a sharp sting against the webbing that seems to cover parts of him, no doubt holding weapons. But I don't care. It's been so long, too fucking long since I've been in my husband's arms.

He pulls back, albeit reluctantly, his grip on my face still firm as his eyes trace over my features, drinking me in like a dying man.

"Hello, wife," he murmurs, his voice thick with emotion. He swallows hard, his Adam's apple bobbing. "Fuck, I missed you, Princess," he confesses reverently, dipping his head once more to rub my nose with his in a gesture so heartbreakingly sweet that tears fall down my cheeks.

"Hello, husband," I choke out, holding him to me for another moment, knowing that it won't be enough. It'll never be enough.

But my soul needs to feel the others with my own hands and lips to know that they're real. As if sensing the direction of my thoughts, Ash lets me go, his hands slipping down my face when he steps aside to reveal Kai.

"Darling. God, you are a sight for sore eyes," he says, his gaze devouring me as he steps into Ash's space and engulfs me in his fresh, woodsy scent. His fingertips brush my cheek, coming away glistening with my tears, and he pops the digits into his mouth, tasting my overwhelming happiness leaving tracks down my face.

"Kai," I can't think of a single thing to say, my entire being thrumming with his nearness after being away from them all for so long.

"It's okay, love, we're here now, and it'll all be okay," he assures me, eliminating any space between us, his hand tangling in my hair and angling my face as he kisses my trembling lips.

Like Ash's kiss, there is sorrow and regret in Kai's, but also a deep possession and assurance that lends credence to his words of moments ago. His lips and tongue tell me that he, they, will keep me safe, and never again will I have to endure this horror. My tongue matches his, our movements in perfect synchronicity as we relearn what each other tastes like.

The embrace ends with a bittersweet final peck of lips, and Kai steps away with a deep breath, letting Jax take his place.

My protective Viking wastes no time on sweet words or gestures, his huge hand wrapping round my throat and pulling me to him, crushing his lips to mine with the same force that he undoubtedly pushed the wardrobe over. He decimates me with tongue, teeth, and lips, punishing me for my absence, then soothing me a second later as his other hand gently strokes the side of my rounded stomach.

As if in reproach of his barbaric behaviour, the baby gives his palm a vicious kick, and Jax's mouth abruptly leaves mine, a dark, pride-filled smirk on his lips.

"I will fucking chain you to my bed if I have to, Baby Girl, but you are never to leave us again. Got it?" he growls at me, and I can't stop the visceral reaction I have at the sound of his voice and his words. It's fucked up, but my cunt clenches at the raw dominance coming off him in waves, and he fucking knows it as his smile gets wider, flashing me his pearly whites in what might be considered a snarl. "Good girl."

He too steps to the side, releasing my throat, and my eyes land on the perfect beauty of my trickster. But unlike the others, Loki stays back a few steps, avoiding my seeking gaze.

"Loki?" I question, advancing towards him on unsure steps, coldness suffusing my limbs as I worry about what might be causing this strange behaviour. Stepping right up to him, I can feel the tension vibrating in his body, his muscles twitching. "Hey, what's wrong?" I reach out, cupping his strong jaw in my palm and turning him to face me. I startle when I see his eyes swimming, his face a mask of tortured pain that cracks my fragile heart clean in two. "Talk to me, my love. Tell me what's wrong, please?"

His head drops, then slowly rises as the breath rushes out of his chest. His emerald eyes study me, cataloguing all that has changed over the past five weeks. His jaw tightens as he undoubtedly notes the slight gauntness that I still have from all the meals I missed when I was in a drug-induced sleep, the purple bruises under my eyes from the sleepless nights, all those times that my nightmares consumed me, nightmares that may have been more real than I knew.

"Fuck, baby, I'm so fucking sorry...I—" he cuts himself off, his voice cracking, full of rage and self-loathing, his upper lip curling upwards. "I shouldn't have left you that night."

My own chest empties as the breath leaves me at his confession.

"Loki, no, none of this is your fault. None of it," I tell him firmly, my eyebrows dipped as I will him to accept my words for the simple truth that they are.

Before he can argue further, and I see the reply about to leave those lush lips of his, I brace my other hand on his firm chest, lifting myself up onto tiptoes, and press my own mouth to his. My eyes close as the sweetness that is Loki Thorn rushes over me. He freezes for a millisecond, then with a panty-destroying groan, he wraps his arms around me, pulling me tight into his hard body as he kisses me back. His tongue seeks forgiveness that I readily give, and I willingly drown in his vanilla scent, needing him with a desperation that rivals my need to breathe.

Our kiss is interrupted by the crackling of a radio, Roman's voice sounding in the now silent room, their epic entrance song having finished at some point during our reunion.

"The dirty rat has been trapped in the library, Conrad. I repeat, the dirty rat has been trapped in the library. Over and out."

"I'm destined to spend my days surrounded by fucking imbeciles," I hear Ash grumble, and a giggle escapes my lips.

"Come on, Pretty Girl," Loki tells me, turning and slinging an arm over my shoulders. There's still a look of haunting guilt in his eyes, and I've the feeling that it'll take a while for that to vanish completely. "Time to skin ourselves a rodent. I made a playlist especially for the occasion."

"Of course you did," I respond with a chuckle, and a fissure of adrenaline rushes through my body at the fact that I'm being included in what they have planned. There's no hesitation in him, no protest from any of them as Loki guides me down the small gap between the fallen wardrobe at the end of my bed towards the door.

I look behind me as we exit the room, the others and Mai following us as we head towards the stairs. Catching Ash's eye, he gives me a small nod, an affirmation that he believes in me and my ability to cope with what lies ahead. I also like to think that he recognises my thirst for vengeance.

I stride down the stairs, one Knight beside me with three others following behind, my steps sure and steady. I look inside myself and realise that I, too, don't falter, don't pause at what is undoubtedly about to be a very bloody end for my uncle.

A smile that is most likely quite terrifying in its peaceful serenity tugs up my lips as I reach the bottom step, knowing that my only living relative will not see another sunrise. The thought fills me not with horror, but with grim satisfaction, and with a sense that justice will be served in my name once more to a monster, doled out by monsters much bigger and more frightening than he is.

Not for the first time, I know that I am one of them.

And damn proud of it too.

# CHAPTER EIGHT

LILLY

We enter the library as a group, Mai heading off after the guys told her that she needed to leave and there was someone from The Shadows waiting to escort her home. She was pissed and didn't want to leave me, but once the boys assured her that I would be looked after and no harm would come to me, she reluctantly left saying that I'd hear from her tomorrow.

The soft glow of the lit wall sconces is the only light in the vast space, the heavy curtains drawn over the huge windows so the rest of the room is in shadow, and there's a solitary, high-backed wooden chair in the centre of the room. In the chair is my uncle, bound with cable ties cutting into his wrists and ankles, tying him to the arms and legs of the piece of furniture. It's a beautiful piece, all carved wood and looks antique, the triangular back reaching above his head and making it look more like a throne than an ordinary seat. A throne of death perhaps.

His eyes widen when he sees our group, and he thrashes around, his cries muffled by the piece of gaffer tape that covers his mouth. Two shadows push off from the wall, making my heart thrash a little in my chest until the Kent twins' faces are revealed, dressed in their usual black and with matching, maniacal grins across their faces. A third shadow disentangles itself from the corner, the hulking figure making his way towards us.

He, too, is dressed fully in black, tactical gear, his body stacked, giving even Jax a run for his money in terms of bulk. His dark blond hair is cut short to his head, his jaw square like a Disney prince. But the darkness that swirls in his green eyes leaves me sinking further into Loki's embrace, his arm tightening around me as the man comes closer. And he really is a man, older than the twins by maybe a couple of years if the lines etched around his dark eyes are any indicator.

"Hunter," Ash's deep voice sounds in the room, Jax and Kai coming to stand on either side of Loki and I, framing us. Ash moves just a little in front of me, giving his protection too.

"Asher," Hunter replies, his own voice as cavernous as the endless caves that can be found in nature. The ones that people disappear into and are never seen again.

The boys clasp hands and exchange a firm handshake, clearly testing each other's mettle. Hunter gives Ash a half smile and nods, slapping him on the back as if he'd just passed some sort of test. He then leans to the side, letting go of Ash's hand and ensnaring me in his piercing gaze.

"This is the pixie that's caused so much trouble, huh?" he teases, and I realise that he has Willow's smile. This must be *the* Hunter, Willow's brother. The boys tense round me, Jax issuing a growl that does inappropriate things to Her Vagisty given the current situation. "Calm yourselves, boys, I'm only teasing," he tells them, his tone light and unafraid. "My sister speaks very highly of you, Lilly Vanderbilt. Tells me you helped her out over there, over some cunt called Amber."

"That's right, Willow is my best bitch, and we look out for each other," I tell him, deadly serious and hoping he sees how much his sister means to me too. He gives me a nod.

"You have The Shadows' protection for life," he tells me, voice full of a heavy gravity, and by the way the guys take an inhale around me, I know that this is a big deal.

"Thank you," I whisper back, realising that I have more chosen family around me than I ever realised.

"Family takes care of itself, pixie girl," Roman tells me, giving a sly wink that makes Loki bristle.

"Speaking of..." Hunter interrupts with a roll of his eyes at the mischievous twin, turning to gesture with an outstretched arm at my uncle. I swear the room gets colder by several degrees as my guys swing their gazes towards him, tied up and helpless.

Anger burns in my veins at how helpless I was when I first came here, when he was drugging me and sneaking into my room at night. I can feel my expression tightening, my body tensing as I look at the man before us, usually so put together and suave. He's wearing silk pyjamas, his hair a mess, and his face red as he tries in vain to free himself from his bindings. I smirk when I see his still puffy nose, a strip of tape over the bridge of it and bruising along each side and under his eyes.

"Nice work, Baby Girl," Jax praises from beside me, and I preen at the attention.

Rowan strolls up to him, casually grabbing an edge of the tape and ripping it off with a sound that reverberates around the huge room.

"I should have known it was you fucking boys, especially Julian's spawn, behind all this!" he spits out, still tugging at his bindings. "Julian won't stand for this, you little shits! He'll have your balls for hurting me!"

"What Julian will, or will not stand for is not your concern," Ash tells him, tilting his head to the side and studying the man as one might an insect you are about to dissect. "What is your concern, however, is how you might be of use to us so that we don't end your miserable existence in the most painful of ways right now."

"Fuck you, Vanderbilt! I don't fucking answer to you! Or your father!" Adrian screams, spitting at Ash. The globule doesn't even come close, yet Ash's lip still curls in disgust. Ash heaves a great sigh, as if this is all just so tiresome, and I watch with bated breath as he lazily strolls towards Adrian.

"This can go one of two ways, you know," he tells my uncle, voice bored as he inspects his nails. "You can answer our questions in full, thus helping yourself. Or you can resist."

"I hope he resists, don't you, Pretty Girl?" Loki asks me, loud enough for Adrian to hear and squirm more. Loki's body thrums next to mine, full of pent-up energy. "It's always so much more fun when they do."

I look up into his shining, green eyes, twinkling like jewels in the lamp light, and see an evil smile sitting on his face as he gazes hungrily at my uncle. And I'm not afraid like I might have been once upon a time. I look at each of my Knights in turn, all of them with a matching hunger in their eyes, a need to dish out vengeance on this man who has wronged me.

"I'm not going to tell you shit, boy," Adrian snarls, his confident smile wavering slightly at what he must see on Ash's face. I can't see, as my darkest Knight's back is to me, but I can imagine that it must be terrifying if my uncle's expression is anything to go by.

"I was hoping you might say that," Ash's voice sends chills across my skin, his words a promise of pain, and I shiver with how much I enjoy the sound. "Jax."

My Viking steps forward, sparing me a quick glance and a devastating smile that leaves my stomach full of butterflies. Without any preamble, he draws his fist back and punches Adrian square in the face, snapping his head to the side and drops of red spraying across the floor. I wince when I hear the crack of bone as presumably, his nose breaks again.

"That was for being a fucked up pervert and for sexually assaulting your own daughter!" Jax screams in a guttural roar, his whole body shaking, his huge neck corded.

"Wait, what?" I stumble out, my mouth falling open. All the boys freeze, turning towards me with looks of regret on their faces. Kai steps in front of me, cupping my face in his warm palms, and I can't help leaning into his touch.

"Adrian isn't your uncle, darling. He's your father. We believe that your mother wasn't called Laura Darling, but Violet Rochester, and that she was carrying Adrian's child when she ran from him," he tells me softly, trying to soften the blow with the caress of his thumbs.

"Fucking worthless whore that she was!" my un-father-Adrian scoffs, his voice thick and a little muffled. "Couldn't even get knocked up properly, not for lack of trying on my part." I look past Kai to see Adrian's deceptively handsome face, the monster underneath finally showing in the swelling on one side with blood dripping down his chin. "You boys think you know everything! Well, I'll tell you one thing. That good-for-nothing slut got herself knocked up with some other cunt's baby. Lilly is no more my daughter than she's my niece. The paternity test last year proved that."

He looks at me, his lip curled in a sneer as my world tilts on its axis, and I try to process the information that I've just been given.

"Why take me in then?" I question, Loki's grip tightening round my shoulders as Kai keeps his hands on my face even when he steps aside slightly, both lending me their strength. “If we’re not related, why pretend that we are?”

“That’s the billion dollar question now, isn’t it, little whore?” He smirks, his head whipping to the side again as Jax delivers another punishing blow.

“Don’t you even look at her, you fucking piece of shit!” Jax barks, grabbing a fistful of Adrian’s dark hair and pulling his head back, snarling right in his face.

“Shit!” Loki exclaims next to me, dropping his arm from around me and fumbling in his pocket. My heart hammers in panic, my head whipping round to face him, Kai’s grip dropping from me as well.

“What?” I ask, voice breathy and high, my pulse pounding. He brandishes his phone triumphantly.

“Almost forgot the playlist! That really would have been a disaster,” he responds, the sound of another fist hitting flesh loud in the room. It’s so utterly ridiculous that a giggle escapes my lips, my hand flying to cover them as the tension feels like it drains from the room. “That’s the spirit, Pretty Girl!” Loki beams, scrolling, and in the next second *American Boy* by Estelle and Kanye West starts blaring from speakers hidden somewhere in the room, drowning out the sounds of the beating that Jax is currently issuing. “Dance with me!” Loki shouts, grabbing my hand, twirling me so that my back is to his front, and pulling me to him.

He moves us as I outright laugh, his hips gyrating with the beat and letting me know how happy he’s feeling right now.

“Loki, you are incorrigible!” I gasp out, his hands bringing my own up and draping them over his neck behind me. I glance over to see Jax hit my–Adrian again, and what looks like a tooth flies from his mouth, skittering along the polished wooden floor.

“Talk dirty like that again, baby, and I’ll show you the meaning of the word,” Loki whispers in my ear, shivers making my nipples harden which is so many shades of inappropriate it’s unreal. “Kai, join us!”

I look up to see Kai step back in front of me, a sexy smile fixed on his face as he moves in as close as my bump will allow. His palms trace the roundness, his hips moving to the beat as we dance while Ash watches on with a softness in his eyes. Jax pauses in his beating to look over, a rare smile lifting his lips when he sees us dancing. The twins and Hunter are standing in the shadows, the latter stoic as he watches us, the former bobbing their heads to the beat. I knew they were our kind of people.

"You are all fucking insane!" Adrian shouts, his voice clear during a lull in the song. Loki doesn't pause or falter, spinning me so that my back is to Kai, who presses his own hips snugly into my arse, his arousal grinding up against me.

"All the best people are!" I call back, laughing as the boys spin me between them until the song ends.

"Ready to answer some questions?" Ash inquires, bending over slightly as Jax uses his grip on the top of Adrian's head to lift his drooping head up to face Ash. The older man's face is a bloody mess, his eyes almost swollen shut, and ruby red liquid drips from his nose and lips.

"Fuck you, Vanderbilt," Adrian rasps out in a pained mumble, spitting blood into Ash's face. My husband doesn't react, and from my position, I see a terrifying grin spread across his face before he straightens up and turns to face me.

"I made you a promise, wife," he tells me, accepting something from Rowan. He holds them up for us all to see, the blades of the secateurs glinting, and Adrian gives a pained groan, but clearly no longer has the strength to fight his bindings anymore. Ash turns to him. "I promised my wife here that I would cut each and every one of your fingers off for daring to touch her."

Adrian finds some strength to begin his struggle, but it's futile, the cable ties too tight and numerous to allow him much movement. His first scream is cut off by a new song blaring over the speakers, *Bodies* by Bryce Fox filling the room with the strains of a guitar and the beat.

I watch as Loki engulfs me from behind, his vanilla musk mixing with Kai's fresh, woodsy scent as the latter wraps an arm around my waist from the side. I expect to feel sick, to feel something apart from a detached sense of numbness whilst watching Ash cut off all the fingers on one hand with the bolt cutters, each one landing at his feet.

But I watch Adrian's vain struggles with a sick satisfaction running through my veins, enjoying the fact that his screams become more strained and gurgling as each digit falls. Ash pauses, and Jax holds something under Adrian's nose to wake him up after he loses consciousness. Ash makes a gesture, and Loki lowers the volume so that we can all hear the conversation about to take place.

"P–p–please…" Adrian whimpers, his voice so full of pain that I should feel remorse, but I don't. I feel nothing as I watch him twitch and shiver in front of us, knowing that he drugged me and touched me without my consent.

"You ready to confess your sins, Adrian Ramsey?" Ash interrogates, the secateurs dripping blood from their now red blades.

"Anything, yes, I'll answer your questions," Adrian murmurs, voice laced with agony.

"Why did you take Lilly?" Ash asks, tone hard and unforgiving. I step closer, Loki and Kai letting me go, then following along behind me. I move until I can see the dull light in Adrian's eyes as he answers.

"Julian wanted to punish her, and I offered to remove her for a time to teach her a lesson. But I was under strict orders not to harm the baby, in case it really is Julian's grandchild," he tells us, his chest heaving, his voice grating and raw.

"Why offer?" Kai interjects from beside me. "Why did you want to take her?"

Adrian traces his cracked lips with a bloody tongue just as the song changes to *Way Down We Go* by Kaleo.

"Because her mother stole something from me, and I was angry. Initially, I planned to just kill the girl, taking what was owed to me as her next of kin. But your fucking father had other ideas and married her off so that I could never get my hands on what belonged to me by rights!" His anger gives him strength, and he levels a venomous gaze at Ash, then moves to me. "It was too late to ever get my shares in the company back, especially after she cashed in the bonds and bought more shares, but I wanted to see you suffer for the sins of your whore mother."

Before I know what I'm doing, my hand snaps out and slaps him so hard across the face that my palm stings.

"Watch your mouth, or Ash will start on the other hand," I snarl, dark rage filling my veins at this man and all his revenge plans.

"Not quite like her then, too feisty," he comments dryly, teeth missing and blood running down his chin, and Loki holds me back from slapping him again as I step forward.

"Why drug me?" I ask, my voice cutting with my disgust at his actions. "How many nights did you climb into my bed, you fucking waste of oxygen?" I can feel my heart racing, my palms sweating at how angry I am that all this really had nothing to do with me.

"You look so much like her," he replies, his eyes softening, and bile rises to my throat, a sickening thought occurring to me.

"The outdated clothes...you tried to dress me like her?" The room spins, Loki and Kai's touch the only thing centering me and bringing me back to the library, and the disgusting creature in front of me.

"I loved her, in my own way, and she betrayed me, stealing from me and letting another man touch what was mine," he seethes, the anger towards my mother still fresh.

"How did Violet escape from you?" Ash interjects, and the question takes me somewhat by surprise, the name Violet still somehow not seeming to belong to Mum.

"I have no fucking idea. She had outside help. She drugged me, fucking bitch." I don't get time to step forward as Jax punches him in the chest, Adrian doubling over as much as his bindings will allow.

"Watch your mouth," my Viking tells him, my chest swelling at his defence of my mum even though he never knew her. Coughing and spitting out more blood, Adrian continues.

"For years I fucking searched for her, without even a whiff. And then, almost eighteen years after she disappeared, a contact saw an article in a London newspaper of a girl who he said looked eerily similar to my Violet." He stares right into my eyes, and though his own are mere slits as the skin around them is so puffy he can barely see, I feel the horrible truth sink in like a terminal disease.

A rushing noise like a fast-flowing river sounds in my ears as I'm transported to that fateful day, my mum clutching that very article that I tried to keep hidden, knowing that she'd be pissed. It all makes sense now, not being allowed any social media accounts, not even being allowed to be on anyone else's. My mum was hiding from this vile monster, and I led him right to our door.

"Pretty Girl?" Loki's voice penetrates the spiral that I'm tumbling down, dragging me back up and into the present again. "Talk to me, Lilly."

His arms band tight round me, and I blink to see Kai has once again blocked my view of Adrian, my face once again cupped in his palms.

"Whatever it is, it's not your fault, darling," he tells me, his serious tone willing me to believe his words.

"B–but it was me in that article, Kai. Even though I knew Mum would be mad, I agreed to do it anyway as I was so damn proud to have won that stupid writing competition. I—" My voice cracks as tears stream down my face, tasting like despair.

"Kai's right, baby," Loki whispers in my ear, nuzzling the side of my face. "It wasn't your fault this fucking freak couldn't let go."

I try to draw comfort from them, I really do. But I know that this sickening guilt will stay with me for many years to come.

"What happened next?" I ask as a thought occurs to me, not taking my eyes off Kai's comforting, amber ones, his thumbs brushing the tears from my face. "When you found Mum."

Adrian laughs, and the sound chills me to the bone. I just know that something awful is about to leave his mouth, but like a train crash, I am powerless to stop it.

"I found her in the kitchen. She thought that I was you, and started to apologise for your argument earlier. That must hurt, knowing that your last words to your own mother were in anger." I would stagger under the blow of his words if my two Knights weren't holding me up. Another muffled grunt sounds out, followed by another sound of flesh hitting flesh.

"Let him finish, Jax," I say, cold dread filling my body up until I'm numb. Kai holds my gaze, lending me what strength he can.

"She refused to tell me where the bonds were, told me that I'd never get my hands on them and that they belonged to you. I laughed at her. The pathetic, useless woman thought that she'd bested me. And then I took a kitchen knife and drove it into her body over and over again, watching the life drain out of her eyes."

My knees give way, the room changing once more to my old kitchen, covered in my mum's blood. A low keening noise sounds around me, and it takes me a moment to realise that it's coming from my lips as Loki holds me in a crumpled heap in his lap, Kai stroking my hair.

A scream cuts through my mourning, and I look through bleary eyes to see Ash cutting off all the fingers on Adrian's other hand, blood pumping from the severed digits. Jax blocks my view of the tortured man, the sound of ripping fabric loud over the broken, pained whimpers. Ash hands him the secateurs, and a second later a garbled animal shriek reverberates round the room, a lump of flesh hitting the floor at Jax's feet.

I watch with a sense of numbness as Jax steps back, revealing a gaping wound in Adrian's crotch. I should feel sick, but I feel nothing for this man, this monster who stole my mum's life long before he killed her. Ash hands Jax a small blowtorch next, and Jax lights it just as Ash wakes Adrian up with smelling salts.

Adrian's eyes widen, incoherent wails falling from his lips as Jax lowers the torch, the wails becoming more anguished as the sweet smell of cooking meat and burning fat fills the room. Bile rushes into my throat, threatening to spill over, but somehow I manage to hold onto the contents of my stomach, forcing myself to watch as justice is served.

What feels like an age later, Jax steps away, dropping the now unlit blowtorch and wiping his forehead with the back of his hand, leaving a bloody trail. He glances over to me still on the floor, his piercing gaze pained, refusing to meet mine.

"Jax?" I question, his stare finally meeting mine, but he doesn't move, doesn't come closer. "Help me up?" He takes a deep inhale, his nose wrinkling at the smell as if he's only just noticing it now. He still hesitates. "Please?"

Heaving a great sigh, he steps towards me, holding out a bloody hand for me to take once he reaches me. I grasp it, knowing that his hand is covered in the blood of my enemy. He added another black mark to his soul for me, and I love him for it, even as my soul hurts for him.

"Thank you, my love," I whisper once he's pulled me up to standing, and I place my other hand on his chest, his T-shirt damp with sweat and blood underneath my palm. Leaning in, I kiss him, worshipping my Knight in tarnished, bloody armour with tongue and lips. My protector and saviour deserves nothing less.

"I would do all this and more for you, Baby Girl. I'd burn the whole motherfucking world to the ground if you asked me to," he confesses against my tingling lips as we part, his free hand coming up to cup my face, the blood staining my skin.

"And I will always love you for it, no matter what you do," I whisper back, pulling away slightly so that he can see the truth in my eyes. "You belong to me, Jax Griffiths, and I belong to you."

The song changes and *Serial Killer* by Moncrieff & JUDGE breaks the heavy tension in the room.

"Fucking Loki," Jax mumbles, his lips tilted in a half smile at his friend's choice of music.

"What?" the man in question asks, bouncing up to us and throwing his arms round our shoulders. "It's the perfect song!"

We laugh, Kai and Ash joining in, and some of the heady tension in the room easing.

"You're all fucking crazy!" an inhuman-sounding rasp cuts through our mirth, and we all look over to see the mess that is Adrian Ramsey.

"All the best people are," I tell him once again, smiling at my collection of dark Knights, my monsters.

# CHAPTER NINE

ASH

I glance over at Lilly, taking her in in all her majesty. She's a fucking goddess walking this Earth, looking over at that cunt with all the disgust a lady would look at the shit that dared to get on her shoe.

Her statement rings true down to my very soul. All the best people I know are in this room, including the Shadows lingering in the corner. And we're all as mad as hatters, psychos that delight in bloodshed, that thrive when the light leaves our victims' eyes.

I gesture for everyone to form a semicircle around the waste of space.

"Adrian Ramsey, you have been found guilty of being a murderer, a pervert, and a general waste of oxygen," I tell him, my voice grave with the edge of a sneer. I look up at the people surrounding me. "What punishment shall we give this monster?"

"Punishment?!" Adrian gasps, his voice that of a broken man, and my blood sings to hear it. It's been too long since I let my own inner demon out to play. "Haven't I suffered enough? You said there were two ways this could go! I told you what you wanted to hear," he babbles as snot, blood, and tears leak down his face. I'm actually kind of impressed that he's still with us. I guess shock is a great masker of pain.

I turn back to look at him, my face a blank mask of indifference.

"I lied."

"If I may make a suggestion?" one of the twins—Roman, I think—asks. I nod for him to continue, folding my arms to hear him out. "During the Troubles, in Ireland," he continues, eyes alight with fevered excitement, "traitors to The Cause were given a six pack. Six shots, one in each ankle, knee, and elbow."

My lips tilt upwards at the idea, liking the sound of it. Turning to the guys, I raise my brows in silent question.

"Sounds good to me," Loki answers, hand clasped in Lilly's.

"Me too," Kai adds from Loki's other side, turning back to look at Adrian with dark eyes. Adrian doesn't know how lucky he really is; if we'd let Kai loose on him, he'd be in much worse shape than he is now.

Jax grunts his approval, his big hand wrapped around Lilly's, Adrian's blood coating their hands.

"Princess?" I ask, looking directly at her and seeing that Jax has left a bloodied handprint on her cheek. It makes her look like an angel of death, and my dick stirs in my combat pants just seeing it there.

She gives a sharp nod, her beautiful, hazel eyes boring into mine with her own monster front and center, gazing out with approval.

Hunter steps forward, clicking the safety off of a handgun just as *Straitjacket* by Bohnes starts to play.

"Y–you can't do this, you fucking bastards!" Adrian seethes, his voice barely above a whisper and his movements slow and sluggish. "Julian won't stand for this!"

Hunter hands the gun to me, its weight a comforting familiarity in my hand.

"Ah, I'm afraid that's where you're wrong," I tell him, stepping up close and taking aim at his left elbow. "Julian will never know."

The sound of the shot is loud, no need for silencers when we're the only ones here. The twins made sure of that. A garbled cry leaves the older man's ravaged throat as he slumps in his seat. Jax immediately steps up and revives him with ammonia. I pass the gun to Hunter, who's stepped up on Adrian's other side. He knows the drill, we all have to have something at stake here. All have to be involved.

Another shot rings out when he shoots the right elbow, Adrian groaning and whining with the pain. Hunter passes the gun to Jax, who steps around and points it at Adrian's knee. I watch without flinching as another shot rings out, Kai taking Jax's place and shooting his other knee out. Loki is up next, coming to stand beside me and shooting out the now, almost unconscious man's ankle.

He goes to pass the gun back to me to finish the job, but a small, dainty hand reaches for it instead.

"Princess? You don't need to—" I start, but she cuts me off with a fierce look in her eyes.

"He took my mum's life long before he drove the knife into her body, Ash," she tells me, staring down at the gun as if it's an inevitability. "So yes, I do need to. Show me?"

The last is said with a thread of uncertainty, her eyes wide and pupils blown with the adrenaline no doubt coursing through her veins. I cannot deny her, now or ever. She owns me, body and pitch-black soul.

Stepping up behind her, I pull her in close until our bodies are flush. I can't help but nuzzle her hair with my nose, my fingers tightening on her hips.

"Focus, husband," she chastises, but I can hear the smile, and a small growl sounds in my throat at the term. I fucking love it when she calls me that.

I push my semi into her, thriving on the gasp that leaves her own lips when she feels me growing. Deciding to play with her a little more, I remove one hand from her hips, gliding it down her arm, goosebumps following in my wake. Wrapping her hand more firmly round the gun, I place my own on top of hers and use it to take aim at his other ankle.

"Such a good girl knowing not to put your finger on the trigger until you're absolutely ready," I praise, my breath tickling her ear, and I delight in the shudder that rocks her body. "Now place your finger on the trigger. Yes, that's it. Take a deep breath, let it slowly out, and pull when you're ready," I instruct, holding her aim straight so that it doesn't waver.

"P–please...Lilly..." the bastard whispers, and I look to see his eyes pleading with her, but my wife shows no mercy, ignoring him completely as she exhales and then pulls the trigger, just like I told her to. His ankle shatters, blood and bone flying from it. She doesn't flinch, just lowers her arm, taking her finger carefully off the trigger and letting me take the gun. I hand it back to Hunter, an unspoken trust passing between us. We are brothers in bloodshed now.

"Done like a pro, my love," I whisper, placing a soft kiss on her neck before letting her spin round and face me.

"What happens next? How will Julian not find out what happened here?" she questions, a cute as fuck frown marring her forehead.

"Now, we burn this shit to the motherfucking ground!" Loki crows, whooping like the fucking pyro that he is. A grin takes over my face before I can stop it, and I cast my glance down at Lilly to see how she's dealing with this.

"Where are the matches?" she asks, giving me the sexiest smile known to man that has my dick rock-hard in an instant.

Unable to hold back, I grab her face with my free hand and give her a bruising kiss, telling her how much I love her with my lips and every caress of my tongue. We break apart panting, the stinging smell of expensive brandy burning our nostrils as the guys smash bottles around the room, pouring it liberally on Adrian's prone form. He splutters awake, eyes unfocused as he tries to make sense of what's happening around him.

"Brandy?" Lilly questions as her nose twitches, and she turns to look around the room.

"The finest we could find in this dickhead's cellars," I tell her, slinging my arm across her shoulders and pulling her close. "And it's less suspicious than petrol."

She makes an impressed sound, her head bobbing, and my lips twitch to see her act surprised that we know what we're doing.

"Not our first arson, Pretty Girl," Loki tells her as he comes to stand with us, Kai, Hunter, and the twins following.

We all watch in silence as Jax picks up the blowtorch once more and lights it, flames racing across the books and curtains where the alcohol has seeped into them.

"I can't believe that you're burning all these innocent books," Lilly admonishes as we watch Jax make his way round the room setting the books and curtains alight, Adrian's futile attempts to escape boring by now. "Fucking heathens."

"Can't make an omelette without breaking a few eggs, pixie girl," one of the twins says with a grin, and I flash him a glower, which only makes him smile wider. *Fucker.*

We stand sentinel as Jax approaches the man in the chair, watching as the flames catch on the alcohol that was poured over him. His mouth opens in a soundless scream as he's engulfed in fire, and I feel nothing other than a swelling sense of satisfaction that he will no longer be alive to torment Lilly. That revenge has been enacted on behalf of her mother.

"Let's go," my wife says, my arm dropping as she turns around and walks towards the door.

We all follow her out, her Knights, her lovers, her soulmates.

# CHAPTER TEN

LILLY

Wearily, we pile into two cars, me and the guys in one and the Shadows in another. I'm so tired, so strung out and bone weary that even the excitement of finally being reunited with my guys isn't enough to keep my eyes open. I fall asleep sandwiched between Ash and Loki, each one of my hands tangled with one of theirs.

I wake up a couple of hours later as we arrive outside a warehouse-type building next to the river Thames, the late night sounds of London filtering into my consciousness when a blast of cool air hits my face from an open door.

"Where are we?" I croak out, rubbing my gritty eyes then grimacing when dried blood flakes off my fingers.

"A safe place that no one else knows about," Ash tells me, pushing some of my hair back, his fingers trailing down my cheek and sending tingles racing across my skin.

I look around to see that it's quiet, although it appears that the other warehouses have been converted into apartments, much like the one before me. Ash helps me out of the car, and I lean on him as Kai leads us up the steps to the large, solid, wooden door.

"Who else lives here?" I question as he opens it, the door making no sound.

"Just us, Pretty Girl," Loki grins, taking my hand and pulling me away from Ash just as the place floods with soft light when Jax hits a touch panel on the wall.

The place is breathtaking, all exposed brick and wood and industrial metal, a mezzanine level creating an upstairs, with the downstairs completely open-plan. It feels light and airy, yet homely and cosy all at once, and huge windows look out over the Thames, lights twinkling on the opposite bank. I can spy a pool in a large courtyard on the other side of some glass doors. There's even a lawn and what looks like raised flower beds made from railway sleepers.

"I love it," I breathe out, feeling like this could be a place I settled. A home for us all. Although, I would miss the mountains of Colorado.

"We hoped that you would, darling," Kai tells me with a smile. "That's why we bought it." I beam back, a yawn quickly overtaking my smile. "Let's get you cleaned up and to bed. Would you like something to eat?"

My stomach chooses that moment to grumble loudly, and he huffs a laugh, kissing my hand and passing me over to Ash, who guides me towards the stairs. Suddenly, Ash sweeps me up into his arms, carrying me bridal style.

"Ash!" I yell, laughing as he proceeds to carry me up the metal and oak staircase.

"It's not quite a threshold, but it's better than nothing, right?" he queries with a tilt to his lips that leaves the butterflies in my stomach all aflutter.

We walk down the open corridor, and he takes me through a huge bedroom with an enormous bed up against one wall. I don't get to see much of it as we quickly enter the en suite, where Jax already has the shower running and is beautifully naked, washing off the blood from earlier. The water is tinged pink as it runs off him, but I feel no revulsion knowing where it came from and how it came to be splattered all over my Viking Knight. Loki is dressed only in sweats, placing a towel on the heated rail and he gives me a cheeky smile and wink when he notices me staring at Jax. My mind goes back to the first time that I met him back in the bathroom at Highgate and he helped me dry off. Fuck, that feels like forever ago, but it's been less than a year. Jesus, my life is crazy.

*Here with Me* by Susie Suh plays softly in the background as Ash sets me down, his hands going to my waist, well, what was my waist before I was pregnant. It seems to be disappearing somewhat. With gentle, worshipping hands that are covered in dried blood, he starts to strip me of my maxi dress, the stretchy fabric sliding down my shoulders and pooling on the ground around me. Knowing that these were clothes which Adrian bought for my pregnant mother sends a shiver across my skin, and I feel the tension release from my body as they fall off me.

Next goes my maternity bra, a cute, navy blue one with lace, and matching knickers until I'm standing naked, looking out of the huge window that takes up a whole wall and shows me the river. His fingers skate down my side, goosebumps following in their wake as he caresses my skin.

"I missed you so fucking much, Princess," he whispers in my ear, his breath tickling me and making my nipples harden. I let the sensations wash over me, pushing aside what happened at my uncle's house, just focusing on the here and now.

"Time for that later," Loki chuckles when I gasp as he takes my hand once more and pulls me away from Ash yet again. A growl sounds behind me, which makes Loki grin wider, but Ash lets me go, and I hear the sounds of him undressing too.

I step into the massive, glass shower, Jax turning round and giving me one of his half smiles as he takes my hand and pulls me under the blissfully hot spray. He steps in close, the heat from his body warming my back as a huge arm moves past me to grab the bottle of shower gel from the built-in shelf. Squeezing a generous amount into his hand, I am surrounded by his sweet lemon scent as he lathers up and proceeds to run his large palms all over my body, washing me from top to toe.

I groan and squirm when he bypasses where I really want him to go yet again, as he gets up from washing my feet from behind, not letting me turn round once.

"Jax..." I groan, my core desperate for touch, my skin alight and pulsing.

"Yes, Baby Girl?" he questions with what I can feel is a smirk against my shoulder. I hear another shower start and look beyond Jax to see Ash start to wash under another shower head on the opposite side of us. "You were saying?" Jax reminds me, and I push back into his front, his hard length pressing into my lower back.

"I need you, Jax. Please," I beg, not above pleading, the band of his arms not allowing me to turn fully and give him puppy dog eyes.

"I'm here, baby, I'll always be what you need," Jax whispers in my ear, his rinsed hand sliding around the swell of my stomach, his whole frame leaning over me as his fingers play with my damp, lower curls.

I grasp his forearms, and he glides a single thick digit between my slicked folds, finding my clit instantly and circling it teasingly. A deep moan falls from my lips at the heady pleasure as he plays with the nub, the feeling of his long-awaited touch almost bringing me to climax then and there.

"Jax...fuck, Jax..." I murmur, my eyes closing and his finger strumming a tune that I never want him to stop playing.

The swipe of a tongue on my pussy has my lids snapping open again, and I look down but my bloody baby bump stops me from seeing whose head it is. His fully tattooed back is clear, however, and I know that it's my husband, my dark Knight on his knees in front of me. Looking to the side, I see Loki watching us with heat in his emerald eyes, his image wavering in the droplets that drip down the glass. He's got his dick gripped in a tight fist, and I swallow hard at the sight of him pumping his hand up and down, the metal of his Prince Albert piercing glinting.

Ash opens my legs wider, and I lean on Jax as Ash's tongue dives inside my cunt, shooting stars flashing in front of my eyes as pleasure overtakes me with every stroke. Jax growls his appreciation as his finger moves faster on my nub, my breaths panting out of me as the tingles from their combined attention race all over my body.

It doesn't take long for my climax to detonate, and they hold me as I shatter into a thousand particles, crying out incoherently when the pleasure consumes me. I stay in Jax's arms, Ash's tongue making me twitch as he gives a final few licks before getting up. He looks at me with a fire turning the grey of his eyes molten, and a second later his lips are on mine, his tongue delving into my mouth.

The taste of my own release on his lips and tongue has me mewling and squirming once more, my fingers tangling in his wet locks and pulling him closer, trying to inhale his very essence.

We break apart slowly and reluctantly, his forehead pressing to mine as his solid member presses into my stomach. The baby gives an almighty kick, causing him to jerk back with a laugh.

"All right, I'll leave your mother alone," Ash murmurs, his hand coming to rest over the place where the kick was. "For now, anyway," he tells me, looking up with a wink, and I damn near swoon.

He turns around, shutting the shower off, and Jax unwinds himself from my back, helping me out of the shower where Loki waits with the biggest, fluffiest towel that's toasty and warm.

"Thanks, love," I tell him, my eyes darting down to see that his dick is back in his grey sweatpants and no longer looks hard.

"Don't worry, Pretty Girl," he assures me, "he'll be back later."

I laugh as he leads me out of the bathroom still wrapped in the towel, feeling a lightness inside myself that I've not felt in weeks.

---

## LOKI

A piercing scream wakes me a few hours later, my heart racing as I bolt upright in bed.

Lilly struggles next to me, sheets tangled around her legs as she thrashes and whimpers, her head moving from side to side.

"Hey, Princess, shhhh," Ash whispers from her other side, his hand reaching out and stroking her face gently.

Another cry leaves her lips as she sits upright, her eyes wide like moons in the darkness. I can see her pulse beating a fast rhythm in her neck, her cheeks wet with tears that continue to fall down her face. She swallows, blinking, her eyes focusing on mine, and my heart shatters at the lost look in them.

"Loki?" she rasps, voice hoarse, and she coughs to clear her throat.

"I'm here, baby," I assure her softly, reaching out my own hand to brush the tears away. She flinches, and my hand stops, a lump forming in my throat. "You okay, Pretty Girl?" I ask, begging with my eyes for her to let me in.

"I–I'm fine, just a bit hot," she mumbles, awkwardly getting to her knees and crawling to the end of the bed.

"Lilly?" Kai questions from beside me, and I turn to see his forehead creased, his tired eyes dull with worry.

"I just need some air," she replies, getting out of bed and putting on one of

Jax's shirts, the huge, black garment covering her completely, though her rounded stomach is starting to push the fabric out.

"Want some company, Baby Girl?" Jax asks from the other side of Ash, his voice thick with sleep and an undercurrent of concern.

"I'll be fine," she says, racing out of the door, not even turning to look back at us.

We all watch her leave the room, and there's a tightness in my chest, an uncomfortable feeling slithering over my skin. The feeling increases as *Panic Attack* by Liza Anne filters up from the speakers downstairs.

"Ash?" I inquire, biting my lip as my throat constricts.

"She just needs some time," Kai interrupts, ever the peacemaker, his hand stroking soothingly down my arm.

"She needs us," Jax growls out, and I glance at him in time to see him run a jerky hand through his long hair.

"Ash?" I repeat, looking to our leader to see what he thinks, needing his calm control as I can feel the edge of my world spinning out of control at the thought of losing her again.

He looks up at me, the grey swirling in his eyes, his brows pinched and neck tight.

"Let's do as Kai suggests and give her time. She needs to know we're here for her, but have the space to process what she's just been through." He sounds more confident by the end of his speech, though the way he swallows and looks down tells me that he's not a hundred-percent certain.

We all settle back down, my arm going to the gap that should be filled by our girl, the bed cool and no longer as inviting as it was when we all lay down together several hours ago.

# CHAPTER ELEVEN

LILLY

The guys come down the next morning, looking clean yet anything but refreshed. My own eyes feel gritty and dry, my throat tight when I remember last night.

I woke up feeling suffocated, unsure where I was or who was in bed with me. I couldn't stand the heat from their bodies, something I've always found comforting but ever since that night when I awoke to my uncle getting into bed with me, knowing that he'd been doing it the whole time...

I look up, catching grey orbs full of concern. Ash's image wavers as moisture fills my own eyes.

"I–I'm so s–s–sorry, Ash," I whisper brokenly before burying my face in my hands. The sofa I'm lying on dips next to me as I'm gathered up, the achingly familiar scent of ginger filling my senses.

"Hey, there's no need to apologize, my love," he murmurs, his lips brushing against my tangled hair. "It's okay."

"It's not okay!" I wail, lowering my palms and catching piercing blue eyes as Jax crouches in front of me. "How is any of this okay?"

"It's not," he tells me, his deep voice a soothing balm to my hurting soul. "But we're here to look after you now, baby." He grasps my hands in his large ones, rubbing his thumbs over mine. My lip trembles as I try to contain my emotions.

"What happened last night, Pretty Girl?" Loki questions, the sofa on the other side of me dipping as he takes a seat, his hand rubbing my back.

I sigh, giving Kai a watery smile as he holds out a cup of peppermint tea, Jax releasing my hands so that I can take it. It's the perfect temperature, allowing me to wrap my fingers around the mug and absorb some of the comforting warmth.

"I had a bad dream I guess," I tell them, looking down at the surface of the tea, wishing that it held all the answers to the maelstrom that is my current mental health. "I woke up thinking...thinking..." My voice chokes, the surface of the drink rippling as a tear drops into it.

"Thinking you were back there?" Ash questions, the vibrations of his voice calming my pounding heart.

"Yes," I answer quietly, brokenly. I take a deep breath and look up to meet kind, amber eyes full of warmth and love. "And that he was the one in the bed," I say, my eyelids falling shut with shame.

A soft brush of fingertips has them fluttering open again, Kai's face wavering as more tears spring to my eyes.

"I understand," he says softly, a haunted look entering his stare, and my throat tightens at this hateful thing we now have in common.

Carefully thrusting my mug at Jax, I launch myself at Kai and wrap my arms around his neck, sobs wracking my body as I cling to him. His own arms band around me, pulling me as tight as my pregnancy will allow, and I feel wetness on my neck where his face is buried.

We cry together, the pain of the evil that exists in the world lessening now that we have another to share it with, to understand how much it hurts, how dirty and tarnished you feel.

---

We decide to stay in the apartment, snuggled together on the sofas until Mai arrives later in the afternoon to check on me and baby. She declares that everything is fine, but recommends an ultrasound scan as I missed my twenty-week one. Ash gets straight on the phone and books one for the following day on Harley Street, using his name to get the best paediatrician in the country to fit us into his busy schedule.

I feel a slight chill at the thought of having to deal with Julian, who no doubt will hear of my return soon enough. But for now, I decide to set it aside, enjoying this reprieve before we have to face reality again.

After Mai's visit, and with it being such a beautiful summer's day—*a rarity in England I can assure you!*—I feel the overwhelming urge to see what the pool is like and float in the water for a time.

Getting up from the sofa where we were all lounging, none of the guys follow me as I head to the glass doors, which are open, letting in the slight breeze and city noises that I find I've missed a little.

"Where you off to, Pretty Girl?" Loki asks lazily, and I spin round giving him a lopsided smile before whipping Jax's T-shirt over my head and shimming out of my yoga pants. The guys had bought me some of my clothes, placing them in the closet in our room.

"For a swim," I tell him, pulling my soft maternity bra off, and beaming as all four guys sit up straighter, heat brightening their eyes. This effect I have on them, their desire for me, is addictive and always sends tingles racing up my spine. "Coming?" I lift a single brow, smirking as I step out of my knickers, leaving them in a pile as I turn and walk out into the garden.

Looking around, I'm glad to confirm that we're completely enclosed by our building, the garden being in the middle and no windows overlooking us, telling me just how much this place cost given the price of real estate in London.

I smile as *Astronomical* by SVRCINA starts playing on the outside speakers, the pleasure of having music back in my life making my skin quiver. It pebbles for an entirely different reason as a hot, naked body presses up against my back, arms dusted with auburn hair and littered with tattoos wrapping around me, a hard length poking me in the back.

"I fucking missed you so much," Loki whispers in my ear, placing teasing kisses along the column of my neck that leaves fire pooling in my core.

"Loki..." I moan, my whole body feeling heavy and aching with need. His palms glide down my sides, over my stomach, and find my pussy already wet for him.

"Did you miss me, baby? Did you miss my fingers inside you? My cock inside your dripping cunt?"

Fuck me, this boy and his filthy mouth. Another deep groan of need sounds in my throat as I try moving my hips to direct his touch. Luckily, he doesn't seem to be in a teasing mood, his musician's fingers dipping inside my damp folds and finding my opening. He thrusts two inside me, and I swear I see stars, my knees almost buckling at the searing pleasure that threatens to cleave me in two.

"More, Loki," I beg, my voice deep and my nails raking down his forearms. "I need you to fuck me, please."

His masculine laugh rumbles through me, his nose nuzzling my neck.

"As you wish," he murmurs in a sexy as fuck, husky whisper that has my inner walls clenching around his fingers. He pulls them out and I whimper, frustration lancing through me like a lightning bolt.

Taking my hand, he leads me to a wooden table that's about waist height for him. Leaving me there, he walks over to a blanket box, giving me a magnificent view of his arse and back, and grabs out an armful of thick blankets and cushions. Stepping back up to me, my skin quivering at his nearness, he layers the blankets and cushions on the tabletop, creating a soft surface towards the side edge of the table with a cushion presumably for my lower back.

"Up you get, baby," he orders with a devastating smile that melts me that much more. With his help I climb up onto the table, my legs dangling off the edge. "Lie back," he commands, his voice dropping an octave as he gives me a searing look. I do as commanded, lying back under the shade of the umbrella, the gentle, warm breeze tickling my skin. I raise my hands up over my head, taking a slight stretch and loving the way my muscles pull.

Loki disappears from view, then one of my legs is lifted, quickly followed by the other as he places them over each of his shoulders. Anticipation lights me up, making my breathing quicken until the swipe of a warm tongue has my eyes rolling and a keen falling from my lips. My fingers curl into the blankets underneath me with the bliss that rolls across my body.

"Fuck, I missed the taste of this pussy, Pretty Girl," he growls out, thrusting his head harder between my legs, pinning them open as he proceeds to take me to heaven with his tongue, making my legs quake and tremble as I come over and over again.

A shadow falls over my closed lids, so I open my eyes and see a pierced cock surrounded by black ink in front of my face.

"Open up, Princess," Ash demands, a shining bead of precum dotting the head of his shaft.

I do as ordered, and the sound that leaves his lush lips as he pushes his way in as far as this angle will allow sets me alight again. I groan as the salty, masculine taste of him fills my mouth, my hand grasping his base and pumping what won't fit. Another deep moan vibrates around his cock as Loki pushes inside my dripping cunt, his own piercing hitting all the right nerves.

"Shit, you feel so fucking good," Loki hisses, filling me completely at the same time that Ash pushes in as far as he will go, a deep sound echoing in his chest.

I lose myself to the rhythm of their thrusts, my eyes closing as pleasure rolls over me in spine-tingling waves. My nerve endings fire like fuses, lighting me up over and over again until nothing exists apart from our bodies and the carnal dance we are performing.

"Fuck, Princess, I'm gonna come," Ash growls out, his cock growing impossibly hard in my mouth and hand. I open my eyes to stare up at him through watering eyes, watching his climax colour his face in pained ecstasy before his seed fills my mouth. I swallow every drop greedily, my tongue swirling and licking until I've captured his release fully.

Clearly not liking my attention straying from him, Loki starts pounding into me hard and fast, his hands gripping my thighs in a bruising hold, his pace relentless.

I quickly let Ash pull out of my mouth, my back arching as much as my bump will allow as Loki builds me up again. Stars begin to dance in front of my eyes, my muscles tightening as my climax crashes over me, my own pleasure coating Loki as I come hard. I'm barely over the peak when I feel Loki stiffen above me, a deep groan of satisfaction leaving his lips as he, too, finds release.

We stay locked together, panting, letting the summer breeze caress our sweat-covered bodies as we come down from our high. Fingertips trace my cheek, and I turn into the touch, looking up into calm, grey eyes.

"You are exquisite, my love," Ash praises, leaning down and placing a kiss on my swollen lips. "Jax and Kai missed you too." He looks at me, a question in the furrow of his brow, and I know what he's asking.

"I missed them, all of you, so much," I reply, my hand coming up to stroke his damp cheek.

He pulls back with a smile, and I look past him to see my two other Knights lying on wide sun loungers, their underwear-clad bodies tense, but dicks hard, waiting with an air of uncertainty.

Grumbling, Loki pulls out and there's a rush of wetness that seeps out after him, our combined releases dripping down my inner thigh. He places a kiss on my thigh, stepping away as Ash takes my hand and helps me to stand on wobbling legs, leading me over to where Kai is lying on the cast-iron lounger.

*All Mine*, by PLAZA comes over the speakers, the beat washing over me, my hips swaying automatically. Kai gives me a beatific smile as I gaze down at him, drinking in all his glorious ridges and dips.

"Lube up, Kai," Ash orders, and Kai raises a brow, but leans over and grabs a bottle of lube off the small table between him and Jax, because of fucking course there's lube there. "Princess, Kai's going to fuck that pretty, little ass of yours while Jax fucks your beautiful pussy," he tells me, his eyes shining with excitement and I notice his dick starting to stiffen at the thought.

"I–I'm not sure how that's going to work..." I reply, trying to work it out in my pleasure befuddled brain and coming up empty.

"Don't worry, I'll help get you in the right position," Ash assures me with a devilish smile that renders any protestations I may have null and void. "Hop up, reverse cowgirl style."

I give him a raised brow, telling him with my look that women who are six months fucking pregnant don't hop anywhere. He just smirks, keeping hold of my hand as I climb up on the lounger, thankful that it seems pretty fucking solid and doesn't shake under our combined weight.

Once I'm hovering over Kai's crotch, his shaft so hard that it's lying flat on his stomach, the piercings lining the underside glinting in the sunshine.

"Lube her up, Kai," Ash commands, taking my other hand and pulling me slightly forward to give Kai better access.

I'm about to tell him that I may look like a fucking whale but I object to being spoken about like one, but the words come out as a garbled moan as Kai spreads the lube around my puckered hole then inserting his thumb and sending sparks racing across my skin.

My heart races, my breaths coming fast as he pumps it in and out, his fingers reaching between my legs to toy with my clit.

"Shiiiit..." I breathe out, the sensations his thumb creates peaking my nipples.

"Up on your feet, Princess, knees bent," Ash directs next, taking hold of my other hand and helping me to get into a low squat, my feet on either side of Kai's hips.

Kai pulls out his thumb, using the new angle to guide the tip of his slicked-up cock to my puckered hole, gently breaching the ring of tight muscle and making me see fucking stars as his piercings rub along my walls. Ash lets go of one hand, leaning down to rub at my clit as Kai keeps thrusting forward, the pleasure from Ash's touch making me relax more into Kai's intrusion.

"Kai...oh my god, fuck," I rasp, uncaring that I'm not making any sense.

"That feels so fucking good, darling," Kai grits out, pushing the last inch inside me with a grunt. His swearing lets me know just how much this is driving him crazy, and I relish in the power that I wield over him.

Kai's other hand grips my hip, his fingers digging in as he starts to pulse his hips in shallow movements, both of us making low, desperate noises. Kai pauses, and lightning zings across my skin as I open bleary eyes.

"Lean back on your hands, Princess," Ash tells me, letting go of my other hand. Kai supports my waist as I do as directed, placing my hands behind me on the lounger so that I'm leaning back. Ash steps away and to the side near my head, Jax taking his place with one of his rare, delicious grins.

"Hey, baby," he rumbles, his huge shaft gripped in his hand as he kneels between Kai's legs. "Room for one more?"

I chuckle, hearing Kai groan under me as my inner walls clamp around him. "Always," I tell Jax, ripples of excitement flooding adrenaline through my veins as well as a shot of fear at whether his huge cock will fit.

He gives me another pussy decimating smile, then brings his leg up and over ours on one side so that he's propped on one knee and one foot. I can't see what he does next, but I fucking feel the stretch as he starts to push his way inside my slick cunt, Loki's cum helping to ease his way.

"Fuuuuck..." I murmur, my head tilting back as Jax impales me on his monster cock. "I'd forgotten how fucking big you were, Jax."

He gives a manly snort, which morphs to a deep growl as he bottoms out.

"A lesser man would get a complex, darling," Kai teases beneath me, enacting his revenge as he drags almost all the way out and then thrusts hard back into my arse.

A sharp gasp leaves both mine and Jax's lips at the move, Jax holding still to let Kai do it again. And again. And again, until I'm quivering and shaking, crying out his name. He pauses, panting hard, and lets Jax take control whilst he holds me still.

Jax doesn't hold back, reminding me of just how large and powerful he is with every hard, snapping thrust into my dripping pussy. I let them use me, giving myself over to them completely as they work in symbiosis, wrecking me in the best possible way.

I'm soon unravelling between them, my limbs shaking with the force of my orgasm. Yet they don't let up, fighting my body's tightness to keep pounding into me with devastating precision, knowing exactly the right spots to hit to keep me coming over and over again.

"Loki, let's show our girl what she does to us," I hear Ash say, voice strained and husky.

Opening my eyes, I see him still standing on one side, dick hard and gripped in his fist as he pumps it with furious speed. I turn my head to the other side to see Loki doing the same, and the thought that they will be covering me with their cum whilst Jax and Kai fill me up with theirs has me whimpering with need.

*Fuck, I am literally going to die from too many orgasms.*

There are worse ways to go, I suppose.

Kai and Jax speed up, the noise of our bodies slapping together loud in the quiet of the summer afternoon, the sound of the river and music a backdrop to our love-making. Moments later, Jax slaps the side of my arse before going rigid in front of me, the mixture of pleasure and pain forcing me to follow him into oblivion with a scream that accompanies his own roar.

Kai follows soon after, thrusting hard and deep as he pours his release inside me, a pained groan sounding in his throat. First Ash then Loki groan, the hot splash of their climaxes coating my breasts and stomach, triggering another rush of liquid to coat Jax's dick as I come again.

Utterly spent, I practically fall on top of Kai, Jax slipping out of me with a rush of warm liquid between my thighs. Panting, my heart beats a strong rhythm as I lie back, unapologetic that I could be crushing Kai beneath me. I don't have to worry for too long as he turns us on our sides, spooning me, his own now soft member slipping from my arse. He holds me to him, uncaring that I'm covered in his friends' cum, and hugs me close, whispering praise in my ear, melting me completely.

I close my eyes, snuggling into his embrace and letting his love wash over me in a comforting wave. This is where I'm meant to be, in the arms of one of my lovers, my soulmates. Being loved, protected, and cherished by them all.

A dark kernel tries to make its presence felt, trying to drag me back into the nightmare that I've only just escaped from. I push it aside, trying to claw back the happy, contented feeling of moments before, but it feels tarnished now, and I can't help but shiver in the afternoon sun, its warmth not reaching the place where I need it most.

# CHAPTER TWELVE

LILLY

The next morning we go to the clinic, and I'm filled with a dizzy relief when the image of my baby appears on the screen, wriggling and moving around like a loon. The doctor declares all to be well, and with a clean bill of health, we go back to the apartment.

The next couple of days go by, the guys showering me with affection and making love to me at every opportunity. I love it, truly, but a part of me yearns for the freedom that I've been denied for weeks. To be able to just leave the house and walk around the city, go shopping, or just live unconfined.

The boys try; Loki taking me shopping to all my favourite stores, including Irregular Choice on Carnaby Street, Kai taking me to some amazing restaurants, Jax coming on some walks through the city's parks, and Ash and I visit the big museums.

It's wonderful to be back with them, but I can't help feeling a little smothered as it becomes apparent that I'm not allowed to go anywhere by myself. I understand, hell, I'm worried about being taken again too. However, I feel like I can't even broach the subject, Ash quickly shutting down any ideas I might have of independence, citing my safety as a cause for concern.

The nights are awful.

I can no longer sleep with them in the bed, waking up covered in sweat and panting, their hands morphing into those of another, unwelcome touch. I take to sleeping in one of the other bedrooms, or on the sofa when sleep just won't come.

I know they're worried, the pinched brows and frowns telling me how much. But I can't find it in me to talk about it, any of it. I can barely think about it without my pulse rocketing and the black tendrils of panic clawing at the edges of my vision, and it gets worse knowing that soon, we have to go back to America. My time here is running out, and the thought of leaving fills me with equal parts relief and dread.

The night before we're due to return is particularly bad, sleep refusing to come no matter how many sheep I count. Eventually giving up, I head downstairs, the cool quiet of the night feeling oppressive and choking. Unable to stand it a moment longer, I grab my phone, bringing up Roman's contact and dialling before I can think twice.

*"Lilly?"* he answers, voice slightly croaky from sleep. *"Everything okay?"*

I open my mouth to say yes, as I have done for the past few days whenever one of the guys asked, but when tears spring to my eyes, I find that I can't lie. Not anymore and not to someone who was there.

*"Lilly?"* he asks again, voice laced with worry.

"I need to get out, Roman," I tell him, closing my lids as a single drop of sadness trails down my cheek. I hate myself right now, for not wanting them and wanting to escape. "Know any clubs open or parties happening?" He's silent for a beat.

*"Sure, you know Depravity? In Shoreditch?"*

I'm nodding before he's even finished, spying the bags of clothes that I hadn't yet taken upstairs and run through my outfit choices.

"Yep, I'll grab a black, taxicab. Gimmie, say, twenty, and I'll meet you there?" I reply, jamming the phone between my ear and shoulder as I rifle through the bags, spotting a floral mini dress that'll work for a club.

*"Alone?"* he questions, his tone guarded.

"I'll see you there, Roman," I respond, not answering his question then hanging up.

Grabbing the dress, I ignore the nausea floating around my stomach, the guilt trying to tighten my chest. *I'll leave a note, and I'll be with Roman, maybe even Rowan so it's not like I'm all alone,* I reason to myself as I strip out of my

PJs, grabbing a new bra out of the bag and getting ready. *I'm a grown arse young woman, why the fuck shouldn't I go out?*

---

LOKI

> *Gone out with the twins, back later*
> *Lilly*

I read the note, my stomach dropping. Ash is going to lose his shit when he sees this. Letting out a deep breath, I run my hand through my hair trying to decide on the best course of action.

"Lilly's fucking gone," Ash rasps out, his voice tight and panicked as he comes clattering down the stairs, the circles under his eyes prominent in the dark. *Aw, shit.*

With a resigned sigh, I hand over the note, watching his forehead crease and the paper crumple in his hand. I wince at the punishment Lilly will receive for this.

"She just needs—" I start, stopping mid-sentence when he looks at me with flared nostrils and swirling eyes. Beneath the rage is a desperate worry, his hand coming up to twist and pull at his hair.

"We're losing her, Loki," he murmurs, his shoulders slumping as his arms fall down by his sides. "I don't know how to bring her back and let her have her freedom."

"I know," I assure him, reaching out and clasping his shoulder. I have no words of comfort to offer, nothing that will fucking help us. We can't make her talk about what she went through.

Jax and Kai stomp down the stairs, the sound loud in the quiet of our misery.

"Lilly's at Depravity," Kai states before he's even reached us, and I notice that they've both hastily gotten dressed. "One of the Shadows' clubs."

"How do you know?" Ash interrogates, and even I grimace at his harsh tone.

"Roman sent a text to us all," Jax interjects, holding up his phone for us to see. Ash snatches it out of his grip, his eyes tracing across the screen.

"Maybe we should..." I suggest, and three sets of eyes land on me. "You know, leave her tonight?"

"No," Ash states, voice hard and jaw clenched so I know that I've already lost. "She can't just disappear, not again."

"Okay," I say gently, catching his eye and begging him to calm the fuck down. "Just let me talk to her first."

He doesn't respond straight away, his ink-covered chest rising and falling with deep breaths. Then he gives me a single, sharp nod, a slight dip of his head, and the breath leaves me in a quiet whoosh.

Pretty Girl, I hope you're ready for the wrath of your Knights.

---

LILLY

I let the haunting voice of Hannah Reid from London Grammar wash over me as I sway my body to the beat of *Wasting My Young Years*. The vibe is chilled tonight, indie pop being the music of choice currently by the very talented DJ up on stage.

I left the twins at the bar to weave my way through the crowd and lose myself to the music, to the press of hot, sweaty bodies, and the anonymity of being lost in a sea of people.

Suddenly, a hard, hot body presses to my back, strong hands grasping my hips and pulling me tightly against what is undoubtedly a man. I'm about to step away when aching familiarity washes over me with his vanilla and cocoa scent.

Not wanting to break the illusion of dancing with a stranger, I don't say a word, bringing my hands up to tangle in his soft hair and pull him closer. If his feel and smell didn't tell me who he is, the way his figure moulds to mine as we dance is enough to assure me that my trickster Knight is at my back, pressing his torso and pelvis flush with my back as we dance.

We move together, not saying a word, even when the song slows and we're barely more than swaying side to side. Although with Loki, it's never just a simple dance, his body is undulating like some kind of erotic dancer until I'm all kinds of flushed and panting from more than just the heat in the room.

The song changes into *Silence* by Marshmello & Khalid, and another body presses against my front, sweet lemon filling my senses and forcing my closed lids open. I see my gorgeous, Viking Knight reaching out for me and pulling me closer to him.

He looks devastating in a tight black tee that clings to every muscle and makes my mouth water, and I forget why I wanted to be alone whilst we dance together, our bodies moving like water over rocks. The song is perfect for us, the lyrics resonating in my soul. We've found peace in each other, and I love all my Knights fiercely, their violence calling to me and surrounding me in comforting protection.

Letting go of Loki's hair, I reach up and grab Jax by his luscious locks, messing his man bun up as I pull his face to mine and kiss him with all the desperation I feel in my soul. I tell him with every stroke that I'm sorry I ran, that I'm tired of staying silent about what happened, and beg him to show me the way out of this darkness that I've fallen into.

We break apart gasping, the lights from the club painting his face in changing shades of blue and purple. Before I can utter a word, Loki spins me around, planting his plump lips on my still tingling ones, my eyes closing on instinct. His kiss brings tears to my eyes, it's crushing softness gut-wrenching. He shatters me with his forgiveness, with his understanding as his palms reverently cup my face, and he pulls back, pressing his forehead to mine, my eyes still closed.

"Ash is pissed, beautiful," he murmurs, his breath tickling my face.

I heave a dejected sigh.

"Take me to your leader then," I reply, a wobbly giggle leaving my lips when Loki chuffs out a laugh at my terrible joke.

With a final kiss pressed to my lips, he takes my hand, Jax grasping my other as we thread through the still dancing crowd, Jax making sure I have enough room, to the bar where Ash, Kai, and the twins stand. I flinch under Ash's intense scrutiny, unable to hold his stare, so I find Kai's, feeling that sticky guilt when I see that his brow is furrowed deeply.

As soon as we get there, Ash grabs my wrist and drags me away towards the front doors, ignoring my protests like the jizzmuffin that he is.

"Ash! You're fucking hurting me!" I shout as we leave the club, the relative quiet of the night outside jarring after the pounding music of the club. He lets go, and I rub my wrist which aches with the remnants of his tight grip. He spins around, his eyes wild, and I brace myself, my legs widening in a defensive stance, ready for the verbal lashing that I know is coming.

"What the fuck were you thinking?!" he shouts, stepping close to me, using his height to try and intimidate me. "You can't just fucking disappear like that! We had no idea where you were, Lilly!"

"I left you a note," I reply petulantly, craning my neck to look up at him with a glare, not showing him that my heart is racing a mile a minute.

"A note!" He throws his hands up, a cruel look taking over his features. "Forgive me for worrying, *Princess*," he sneers, and the barb cuts deeply, his use of my nickname spoken like a curse. "After all, you left a note with no fucking information on it, so I must be some kind of cunt for not getting that you couldn't stand being with us. That you wanted to run after we'd only just got you back."

His voice cracks with the last of his words, and tears rush to my eyes at the unwitting hurt I caused him, caused them all, by pushing them away, emotionally at least. I lick my suddenly dry lips.

"I would wake up with bruises on my hips, my breasts, and have no fucking idea how they got there," I confess, the wetness spilling over and tracking down my cheeks as my voice grows thick. "He hurt me in ways that I'll never know, never remember, and every time I close my fucking eyes, I can feel him getting into bed with me that night, and I'm frozen under his grasping hands. I feel his breath on my neck, and his–his dick pressed up against me. I'm drowning, Ash, and I don't know how to swim to the surface."

"Shit, Lilly," he rasps, his own eyes filling as he stares into mine. He pulls me to him, enveloping me in his strength, in his familiar, ginger scent that helps to calm my racing heart. "I'll bring you to the surface, my love. Or drown with you. But you are not alone. You don't need to fight this by yourself."

I break down, letting all the dark rage and anger out as I sob into his chest, my fingers fisting his shirt until they tingle. Under the London night sky, I shed every tear that I've been holding in, every drop of misery that I've kept bottled up inside me ever since I woke up in that room all those weeks ago.

Ash holds me tightly to him the entire time, lending me his unwavering strength and wordless comfort as I shatter into pieces in his arms.

# CHAPTER THIRTEEN

LILLY

I make my way downstairs the next morning, after having slept in the bed with Ash and Loki, sleeping the rest of the night away in blissful slumber for the first time since they rescued me. I've no doubt that nightmares will still plague me, but I feel so much lighter confessing my struggles to the guys.

"Good morning, darling," Kai greets me as I approach the kitchen area. I can see, and smell, that he's in the middle of cooking something delicious for breakfast, a spatula in his hands as he turns to face me, wearing sexy as fuck navy sweats and a tight, white T-shirt. *Wicked* by Miki Ratsula plays in the background as Kai moves his hips to the sultry beat.

Without skipping a beat, I throw myself into his arms, the utensil clattering to the floor as his own come around me in a crushing hug.

"Kai, I—" I begin, my voice cracking as I remember the hurt in his eyes at the club.

"It's okay, darling," he shushes me, pulling me even closer as he places a kiss on the top of my head.

"No, Kai, it's not okay," I tell him, my voice firm as I pull back so that I can stare up into his eyes, my face reflected slightly in his glasses. "I'm so fucking sorry, my love. I was a first-class arsehole last night and should have just talked to you guys instead of running away."

He stares into my eyes, his face soft and his own full of so much love and understanding that they're practically shining.

"Apology accepted," he says, then his lips tilt up into a very Loki-like grin. "And yes, it was an *asshole* thing to do." He emphasises the word, pointing out that we say it differently, with a waggle of his eyebrows.

"Cockwomble," I grumble with no heat behind it, leaning in to press a kiss to his soft lips.

He groans in the back of his throat, one of his hands coming up to angle my face so that he can kiss me deeper, his tongue plundering my mouth. I whimper, letting him ravish me and feeling exactly like one of those fucking fairytale princesses, my foot wanting to pop just like in *Princess Diaries*. An acrid, burning smell tickles my nostrils, and I pull back, Kai chasing my lips before his nose twitches.

"Shit!" he exclaims, letting me go as he turns to the hob and pulls the pan off the heat, the remains of a charred, black pancake smoking inside it.

"Oops," I say with a giggle, my breath catching when he turns around, a look of hunger in his amber depths and his sweats tented.

I swallow hard as he stalks towards me, forcing me to back up until I hit the kitchen island behind me. His fingers caress my hips, a shiver cascading down from his touch, and then hooking into my sleep shorts he pulls them down, letting the garment pool at my feet. My breathing picks up when he grabs the hem of my vest top and yanks that off over my head when I lift my arms. He lets that fall too, his piercing stare setting my body alight as it roams over my naked body.

In a move that surprises me, he lifts me up under my thighs, placing me on the cool marble, a hiss leaving my lips at the frigid temperature against my heated skin. Before I know what he's doing, he sinks down onto his knees, placing one of my feet, then the other onto his shoulders so that I'm spread open for him.

"So wet for me already, Pet," he coos, swiping a finger down my exposed folds which are indeed already slick. "Your distraction made me ruin my breakfast, and while I can make more, I've decided I want something else to eat."

*Fuck. Me.*

Kai dirty talking does things to Her Vagisty which should be illegal.

"Lie down, Pet," he orders, and although I wince at the cold as it hits my back, I obey his command, fluttering anticipation filling my stomach as I wait for his next move.

He doesn't make me wait long, and without further ado, a warm tongue swipes across my lower lips, a deep groan leaving my chest as he does the move again.

"So fucking delicious," he purrs, his breath caressing over my sex and making me even wetter.

He sets to his task with a determination that I'd be astounded by if I wasn't writhing around losing my fucking mind as a tsunami of tingles race up from my cunt.

"Kai..." I moan, my fingers clawing uselessly at the smooth surface of the worktop.

He doesn't relent, doesn't even pause as he keeps eating me like I'm the most delicious thing he's ever tasted. I can feel my inner muscles clenching, the world around me shifting as I come with a scream, my body bucking off the marble. My whole being is alight, the pleasure almost painful in its intensity.

It takes several moments for me to even be able to open my eyes, and when they do, they immediately lock onto stunning, emerald ones filled with fire.

"Good morning, Pretty Girl," Loki rasps out, leaning over to kiss me deeply, then pulling away, turning to Kai. "Are we having Lilly for breakfast?"

Kai stands up, walking round to stand in front of Loki, his lips and chin glistening with my release.

"I was," he tells him, then grabs the back of Loki's neck and pulls him in for a blistering kiss. I gasp with the ferocity of it, my pussy pulsing in time with their tongues as Loki licks my juices from Kai's mouth. Kai pulls back, glances at me then turns back to Loki. "On your knees, Pet."

*Maybe, I* by Des Rocs starts to play and my mouth pops open when Loki does as ordered, looking up at Kai with wide eyes of expectation. I swallow, my pussy fluttering when Kai pulls his hard length out of his sweats, the tip glistening with precum. He paints Loki's lips with it before Loki's tongue darts out to taste it and a whine leaves my lips that I barely recognise.

Loki starts kissing and nibbling Kai's pelvis like he just can't help himself.

A moan sounds in my throat, this is really fucking happening and my eyes are glued to the scene before me, to Loki on his fucking knees about to give Kai a blow job.

*Holy shitballs.*

"Have you ever given a blow job before, Pet?" Kai asks in a deep voice as he stares down at my trickster, pulling Loki away by his hair. Loki's gaze flicks up.

"No."

"I'll let you take it slow this time then," Kai offers, his hand reaching down to trace his fingertips over Loki's jaw. "Open up, Pet."

I watch, enthralled, as Loki opens his mouth and takes Kai's rigid shaft inside, a deep groan sounding in Kai's chest at the move.

"Fuck," I whisper, my stare not wavering as Loki reaches up to grab hold of the base of Kai's dick, holding it steady as he bobs back up. He pulls off, licking the tip a few times before taking it in his mouth again and gliding back down.

"That's it, Pet. Right fucking there," Kai mumbles huskily, one hand fisting in Loki's auburn mane. His other comes up and runs through his own hair, an almost pained look on his face.

I rub my thighs together, the ache at watching the show they're giving building in my core until I'm filled with pulsing desperation.

"Need some help there, Princess?" a deep drawl sounds at my feet, and my gaze swings to look down my body and I find a smirking Ash and Jax near my dangling feet.

"Yes," I say with a gasp, need roaring through me. The two share a look, then Jax steps around the side of the island, making sure not to block my view of Loki and Kai.

His large hands travel over my body, reaching for my sensitive breasts and tugging at my nipples, sending jolts of lightning through me. He's distracting enough that I don't notice Ash until he's pressing inside me, that delicious, magic cross piercing of his rubbing my inner walls maddeningly.

"Yes, fuck yes," I groan out, my back arching when he bottoms out.

"You feel fucking exquisite, wife," Ash growls the words, pausing before slowly pulling out and then thrusting back inside me, hard, sending my whole body jerking on the smooth, stone top, only his firm grip of my hips keeping me in place.

That's the only pause he gives me before pounding hard into me over and over again, making me see double as I desperately try to keep my eyes open to watch the others. I grit my teeth, all my nerve endings tingling like electricity is passing over my skin.

"Swap," Jax grits out, and Ash stills, panting hard, his fingers digging into my soft flesh. He does as Jax demands, pulling out as I whimper at the loss.

Jax is there in a hot second, pushing inside me as I squirm at the burn of his massive cock, watching his brow furrow as he tries to take it slow and let my body accommodate him.

"Hand, Princess," Ash orders, and I look at him, extending my arm out. He grasps my hand in his, wrapping it around his shaft that's slick with my juices. He wraps his own hand over mine, and moves us up and down his length, his head tipping back in pleasure.

"Oh shit, Pet," I hear Kai rasp, and I look back in their direction, my panting breath stilling as I watch Kai basically fucking Loki's face. "Make yourself come when I do, Pet."

"Holy shit," I breathe out, watching enraptured as Loki brings out his own dick in his spare hand and starts pumping furiously.

Jax chooses that moment to give up the pretence of patience and thrusts all the way in, his hands grabbing my hips in a punishing hold as he fucks me hard and fast. My body moves on the worktop with the force of his thrusts, sounds that I barely recognise as my own falling from my lips at his violent love-making. Ash, too, picks up speed, and I glance at him to see sweat beading his brow as he watches my face whilst our hands wank him off.

Pleasure zings and sparks over my body like a high voltage wire is being passed over me. I can barely breathe, any sound I make becoming strangled and incoherent as I try to watch them all, all the while being fucked good and proper.

Kai is the first to erupt, snapping his hips forward as he comes down Loki's throat. Loki gags slightly but takes it like a champ as he, too, comes all over the floor, his eyes rolling as he spills his seed.

The sight sets me off, my cunt clamping down on Jax as I follow the boys into oblivion with a silent scream. He thrusts hard a few times then stills as he follows me, coming deep inside me with a growl. Ash is the last to achieve his release, his free hand landing on the marble with a slap as he spurts cum all over my stomach and breasts.

We stay that way for several moments, panting hard as we try to remember what our bodies feel like. My eyelids close as I lie there, completely spent and drowsy from the bliss I'm experiencing. Moaning when Jax pulls out, Ash lets go of my hand as they step away. I crack my lids to see Kai helping Loki up, planting a soft kiss on his lips and wiping away the tears that leaked down his cheeks during that epic BJ.

"Good boy," Kai whispers, then steps away with a lingering touch.

Loki looks over at me, his naked chest glistening with sweat and still heaving. He walks towards me on shaking legs, coming to stand in between my legs and pulls me up to sitting. Lowering his mouth to mine, he kisses me gently, his tongue seeking entrance. I moan when I taste Kai's essence on his tongue, my fingers landing on his pecs and digging in.

The kiss ends, and I look at him with heavy-lidded eyes.

"You okay?" I check, looking into his eyes for any sign that what happened with Kai was too much for him.

"Fucking amazing," he tells me with a smirk, his voice rough, his hand cupping my cheek. I beam back at him, nuzzling into his touch.

"That was hot as fuck, Loki," I tell him, and he gives a deep chuckle.

"Let's get you cleaned up, baby," he says, helping me to hop off the counter and catching me when I wobble.

"I love you, Loki Thorn," I confess, wrapping my arms around him and pressing close as I lean into him.

"I love you too, Lilly Vanderbilt." He says my new surname with a tilt of his lips, then gives me a peck. Without missing a beat, he picks me up under my thighs and carries me up the stairs to the bathroom, murmuring sweet nothings in my ear the entire way.

# CHAPTER FOURTEEN

LILLY

We clean up, eat a yummy breakfast of pancakes with all the trimmings, and pack all our bags, ready for our flights later tonight back to Colorado. I plonk myself down on the sofa next to Jax, snuggling into his huge frame and loving it when he wraps one of his big arms around me, pulling me closer.

"So, what's the plan for the rest of the day?" I ask, looking around at the others who all seem to be staring anywhere but at me causing a slight chill to slither up my spine. "What? What aren't you telling me?" I go to sit up straighter, but Jax keeps a firm grip around me so that I can't fucking budge. Stupid man muscles being used against me.

"Princess, Lilly," Ash starts, leaning forward in his own chair and resting his elbows on his thighs. He looks directly into my eyes now, his own grey and as unreadable as a cloudy sky. "When we discovered who your mother was, what her real name was, Kai looked into her family."

"Yeah?" I ask, glancing quickly over to Kai who's also now looking my way with a sympathetic softness to his face as he holds his iPad.

"Yes, and she has living relatives, Lilly. Well, lots of relatives, but her parents are still alive. Harold and Petunia Rochester, aged eighty-seven and eighty-four respectively," Kai tells me, and there's a slight whooshing in my ears at his news.

"I have grandparents?" I question softly, my fingers tightening into Jax's T-shirt for support, glad that he pulled me so close to him.

"Yes, you do, Princess," Ash interjects, and I swing my wide eyes back towards him. "And they live in London, Kensington to be exact."

"Kensington?" I repeat, my mind spinning with how close they are, how close they may have always been.

"Would you like to meet them, Pretty Girl?" Loki asks me as he comes to crouch in front of me, taking my suddenly cold and tingling hands in his.

"B–But the flight?" I enquire, my mind going straight to practicalities.

"Can be delayed," Jax rumbles underneath me, and I feel the vibrations against the side of my face that's resting on his chest. "If you want it to."

I momentarily flashback to when I first met Jax and how quiet he was, only speaking when necessary. He talks more now, and I love the sound of his gravelly voice.

"Do you?" Loki repeats, and I blink, trying to remember the question.

Ah, yes, my grandparents. *Shit, do I want to meet them?* My pulse increases as I chew my lip, thinking about the answer to what feels like a loaded question. My baby gives a small movement, reminding me that it's not just me anymore.

"Yes," I reply, looking into Loki's emerald eyes, then up at Kai's, and finally Ash's. "I would like to meet them. Today if we can."

"We've already made contact and told them that if you wanted contact or to meet we would take you there. They're waiting for you, as long as you're sure?" Ash questions, and although I'm slightly taken aback at how fast this is moving, I appreciate the way they've put things into place. Also, my grandparents are in their eighties, and I'm guessing if I just turned up, they may have a bloody heart attack given how similar I look to Mum.

"I'm sure," I tell him, finally sitting up straight, Jax letting me go. I take a deep breath. "Let's go now."

Ash gives me a blinding smile as Loki stands up and offers me his hand, pulling me to my feet. He uses his grip to pull me to him, nuzzling my neck until his lips are close to mine.

"You are so fucking incredible, Lilly," he murmurs, placing a kiss on my cheek. I feel tears prick my eyes—fucking hormones—at the compliment. He pulls back, a twinkle in his own eyes. “Let’s go meet your grandparents, older ladies fucking love me!”

I cringe, thinking back to Clarissa, and raise a brow in a *did you really just go there?* look. It takes a second, but his face drops, his mouth opening and closing in a grimace.

“Fuck— Shit...I didn’t mean— Shit,” he stutters, and I can’t help but laugh, covering my mouth with a hand.

“Come on, Casanova.” Ash chuckles, grabbing Loki’s shoulder and pulling him towards the door.

“Coming?” Kai asks softly, pausing in his own walk towards the door, his hand extended. I take a deep breath, square my shoulders, and put my best foot forward, as Mum used to say.

“Yes,” I tell him, grasping his warm hand in mine and letting him lead me to a family that I had no idea existed until today.

---

We park outside what can only be described as a Chelsea mansion in Upper Phillimore Gardens in Kensington. I look up at the imposing, white building, the sun making it sparkle and shine like it’s touched by heaven. It's an old building, Victorian I guess, with five stories, four bay windows, and white marble steps that lead to a double, painted front door, columns on either side holding up a substantial porch. Window boxes filled with colourful flowers sit on every windowsill, making the whole place feel homely and inviting.

The sounds of traffic are dulled here, birdsong ringing in the air but doing nothing to soothe the butterflies in my stomach or my racing heart.

“Are you doing okay, Princess?” Ash inquires, his hand resting on my waist. I have to swallow a couple of times before answering.

“What if they don’t like me?” I ask in reply, wringing my hands in front of me and not taking my eyes off the currently closed, front door. Ash lets go of my waist, stepping in front of me as the others crowd round, circling me.

“They will love you,” he tells me, looking deep into my eyes as his fingertips stroke my cheek. “Just like we do.”

“You’re fucking awesome, Pretty Girl!” Loki practically shouts, making a choked laugh escape my dry lips when I turn my head to look at him. "And sexy as hell," he adds with a waggle of his auburn brows.

"Lilly, what is there not to like, my darling?" Kai questions me, drawing my gaze to his, the sun hitting the side of his glasses and reflecting my image back at me. "You're smart, beautiful, funny, and a wonderful person who isn't afraid to take on four broken boys and make them into men."

A tear trickles down my cheek at his words, my lips forming a wobbly smile as I take a shaky breath. My eyes close of their own accord when a lemon-scented warmth coats my back, and strong, large hands grip my hips.

"And the bravest fucking person I've ever met, Baby Girl," Jax declares, his deep rumble invading my very soul and making my nipples pebble as it always does. "So get that beautiful *arse* up those steps and show them how fucking amazing you are," he orders, making me chuckle at his faux British accent.

I take another deep inhale, dropping my shoulders, and reopen my eyes, giving Ash a curt nod. He smiles a devilish grin at me, my knees going a little weak at the sight of it.

"Good girl," he praises, holding out a hand as he steps back.

I take it in a firm grasp, allowing him to lead me up the stone steps. Before we can knock or ring the bell, the door opens to reveal an elderly gentleman in a butler uniform, face full of the wrinkles of a life well lived.

"Good morning, madam, sirs. If you'd care to follow me?" he asks in a well-to-do British accent, stepping back and holding a steady arm out to indicate that we come in.

I step inside the brightly lit entrance hall, loving the bright and airy feel, the old Victorian, black and white tiles shining, and the pale, lemon-coloured walls covered in mirrors and some landscape paintings.

"This way, please, Mrs Vanderbilt," the butler says, and I startle at the name. I mean, I know that it's my surname now, but, I guess I'm just not used to it yet from anyone other than my Knights.

"Sure," I reply, following next to him, Ash holding my hand on the other side and the others following behind us. "What's your name?" I ask, needing to fill the silence with chatter as my heart rate picks up with every step that we take.

"Jefferies, ma'am," he says, dipping his head in respect which feels all kinds of weird. "I've been with the Rochesters since your mother was a baby."

He drops that small bombshell with a wistful smile, a faraway look in his eyes. He pauses when he realises that I've stopped walking. "Ma'am?"

"Oh, um, sorry," I rush out, Ash squeezing my hand and giving me a small reassuring smile as I start walking again. "I'd, um, love to hear any stories you have one day, Jefferies," I tell the old man, who beams back at me.

"I'd be honoured to share them with you, ma'am," he tells me, stepping towards a door on the right and reaching to open it. I place my hand on his arm, his head coming up to look at me with a quizzical, fuzzy, grey brow raised.

"It's Lilly," I tell him. "Please call me, Lilly."

His chin wobbles slightly like this is some great honour too.

"Your grandparents are waiting for you in here, Lilly," he tells me softly, and I release his arm as he starts to open the door. "They are so excited to meet you. All of you," he adds with what I would describe as a mischievous smile at the guys. *Huh.*

I'm momentarily blinded by the sunlight that streams from the room that we step into, and it takes several blinks for my eyes to get used to it. When I can finally see again, I see an elderly couple standing in the middle of the room, her hands clasped in a firm grip in front of her, his hand on her shoulder. I take them in, from their kind, lined faces, to her twinset, and perfectly set hair, and then to his dapper, fitted suit and moustache.

"Lilly, darling?" she says in a thick voice, stepping towards me. Her movements are like a little bird, she looks so small and fragile standing in the streaming sunlight, dust motes surrounding her like a halo. "You look so much like her," she adds, reaching me and stretching out a hand as if to cup my face, but then pauses, looking a little unsure.

"Grandma?" I whisper, seeing a familiarity in the shape of her face, and the thickness of her grey hair.

"Oh, darling girl," she murmurs back, her eyes glistening, and without thought, I let go of Ash's hand and step into her embrace, the scent of violets engulfing me as I wrap my trembling arms around her and hug her tight. Her thin arms go around me, encasing me in her loving embrace, and it reminds me so much of my mum that I burst into tears, sobs wracking my body as she holds me tighter to her. "My darling, darling girl," she whispers, stroking my hair and planting kisses on the top of my head. "You're back now, that's all that matters."

I feel another set of arms envelop us, and I look up with tears still running down my face to see my grandfather's cheeks wet as he holds us both. He leans down to kiss my cheek, mumbling in my ear, "Welcome home, Lilly."

Clearly not wanting to miss out on the reunion, my baby gives a mighty kick, causing my grandma to let out an oomph sound. She pulls back, looking down at my rounded stomach.

"Harold, oh, Harold, look!" she exclaims, more tears dripping down her cheeks as she laughs and places a hand over my baby. "We're going to be great grandparents! Oh, you clever, clever girl!"

I laugh as my grandfather loosens his arms and steps back to have a look, his face wreathed in smiles too. "And who's the lucky father?" he asks, looking behind me, and I can't help the slight cringe at the question. I'm not ashamed about our unconventional relationship, just the thought of trying to explain it to my newly-found grandparents...*eek*.

"I am, Mr. Rochester," Loki steps forward, hand out to shake my grandfather's.

"Congratulations, son," Harold says, pumping Loki's hand enthusiastically. "Pleasure to meet you, Mr Vanderbilt."

"I'm Mr Vanderbilt, Lilly's husband," Ash says, holding out his hand, and I bite my lips together at the confusion on the old man's face. Harold drops Loki's hand and automatically takes Ash's, shaking it with a befuddled frown on his face.

"Ash is my husband, Loki, Jax, and Kai are my..." I pause, trying to think of what to call them. Boyfriends doesn't feel like it adequately describes our relationship. "Soulmates. They're all my soulmates."

My grandfather's grey eyebrows go almost into his receding hairline, his eyes wide.

"Oh, don't look like that, Harold," my grandmother scolds, finally letting me go and stepping towards the guys. "Have you forgotten the Woodstock of sixty-eight?"

"Petunia!" my grandfather exclaims, a blush tinting his cheeks as he looks at his wife. She just gives him an innocent yet calculating look, one perfect, silver brow raised. Loki looks on amused, while I can't help wondering what she might be referring to. The nineteen-sixties were wild according to all the stories, a time of sexual freedom.

"Let he who is without sin, my love," she tells my grandfather, placing a gentle kiss on his lined cheek, grasping his arm in her hands. He looks down at her with such love that my heart swells, feeling like it'll break free from the confines of my chest.

He looks back up, taking in each of the guys in turn with a serious look.

"You take care of her? All of you?" he asks, tone firm and unwavering. I'm suddenly hit with the thought that he's asking out of concern for my well-being, that he would take them all on if their answer isn't satisfactory. Warmth suffuses my limbs at having more people in my corner.

"With our lives," Ash tells him solemnly, not breaking his gaze until my grandfather looks at Loki.

"And our hearts," Loki declares, and there goes my own heart again, trying to escape once more.

"She's our souls," Kai adds, glancing my way briefly before looking back at my grandfather, who nods, then looks towards Jax.

"And we're hers," Jax states in that gruff voice of his, and I'm nodding, my cheeks wet again. Fucking hell, I'm surprised there's any water left in my body at this rate.

"Well, all right then," Harold confirms, his head bobbing. "I would have hated to have had a chat with my friends down in Vauxhall," he adds, still looking at the guys. Ash gives a respectful nod, although fuck knows what the old man is waffling about.

"Harold!" my grandmother chastises, whacking him in the chest. "Don't threaten Lilly's beaus with MI6!"

*Oh shit.* My grandfather has connections with the British Secret Intelligence Service. Good to know, and possibly, dare I say it, may come in handy too?

"Well, now we all know where we stand, Petunia," my grandfather reasons, patting her hand, my grandmother rolling her eyes at him as they walk back to me. "Let's have some tea, shall we?" he asks, holding out his spare arm, and I slide my hand into it, a sense of lightness filling up my entire being at being here with them, my blood family.

# CHAPTER FIFTEEN

LILLY

Although I desperately wanted to stay a few more days to get to know my grandparents better, they insisted that I head back to Colorado and back to school, stating that education is the key to success. So reluctantly, I get back into the car after hugs and promises of meeting up again soon.

I clutch my rolling stomach as we get off the plane some hours later, nerves leaving a sour taste in my mouth and tiredness making my eyes feel gritty and my limbs heavy. I've no idea what to expect from school come Monday, luckily it's only Friday—actually Saturday—morning, so I have the weekend as a reprieve.

"Daughter," a snake's voice sounds as we approach the waiting cars, the balmy, Colorado night air teasing my damp hair. My head snaps up, my feet freezing on the tarmac, and adrenaline waking me up in an instant as I'm transported to the night of my wedding.

*"Enjoy your honeymoon."*

I start to pant, blackness edging my vision as I stare into the hard, grey eyes of Julian Vanderbilt, his devil's smile firmly in place, his arms opened wide and a calculated look of concern all over his lying fucking face. He was the one to whisper that to me before everything went black that night. He played an active role in my kidnap.

Spicy ginger washes over me as Ash pulls me to him, his long, beautiful, inked fingers grasping my chin and turning it so that I face him, breaking his father's curse.

"It was him, Ash. He was there when I was taken," I tell him in a broken whisper, nausea whirling in my stomach. His jaw clenches.

"You don't have to talk to him, Princess," he assures me, his own grey eyes just as hard as Julian's, but full of a raging fire that I know is aimed at the older man. "Or look at him, or even let him fucking breathe near you."

My lip trembles as his words leave the air rushing out of my lungs, my skin tingling with relief.

"Take me home, please," I beg my husband, my Knight. He gives a sharp nod, flicking his gaze behind me briefly. "Take her to the car."

Vanilla and lemon surround me as Ash steps away, and Loki and Jax sandwich me between their hot bodies, Jax wrapping a huge arm around my shoulders and pulling me close into his warmth. Loki grasps my hand, and they lead me to the car awaiting us, Jax's huge form blocking Julian from my sight as I hear Ash murmur to him in a tight voice.

"How did you know she was going to be with us?" Ash asks, his voice clipped and completely emotionless. Julian's dark chuckle scrapes across my skin like an unwanted caress, and a revolted shiver takes over my body. Both boys gather me closer, and their mingled scents are a comfort and help combat the way my skin itches around Julian.

"Oh, son, you really should learn that I know everything that concerns me. Especially when it concerns my missing daughter-in-law. It was lucky you boys were there to help, fated some might say. And poor Adrian, dying in that horrible fire. They still have yet to find the body, apparently, it burned so hot that only dust remains. I did warn him that old English manor houses always had faulty electrics. Does Lilly know?"

My heart thumps in my chest, and I'm straining to hear Ash's reply as Loki opens the car door, releasing my hand to get in, then waiting for me to follow.

"Yes, Lilly is aware and has been through enough, don't you think?" Ash bites out, clearly aware of the insinuations of Julian's tone and little speech. Jax releases me and places a hand on my back, leaning in to whisper in my ear.

"Ash will tell you everything later, Baby Girl. Let's get out of here."

Deciding that he's right and that I just want to be as far away as possible from that fucking cunt, I step into the car, scooting next to Loki as Jax gets in behind me.

"Good evening, Mrs. Vanderbilt," I hear from the front, and I look up to see Tom smiling warmly at me in the rearview mirror. "Welcome back."

His kind words and the genuine look of concern on his face make tears spring to my eyes, and I have to swallow hard to be able to reply.

"Thank you, Tom."

He gives me a nod and another warm smile, the divider screen moving up into place as the car starts to pull away. My breath catches, my stomach suddenly dropping.

"Wait!" I yell. "What about Ash and Kai?" I ask, looking frantically behind me to see Ash still talking to his father and Kai waiting off to one side.

"Hey, baby, it's okay," Loki soothes, grabbing my hand and rubbing my arm. "They'll make their way back when they're ready. We've other cars they can call."

"Oh," I mumble, my cheeks heating as I chew my lower lip. "You sure they'll be okay?" I ask, turning my head to be captured by his beautiful, emerald eyes. Shit, I missed them and will never grow tired of looking into their variegated depths. His lips tilt upwards, his hand coming up to cup the side of my face.

"Ash is the big, bad wolf, Pretty Girl, and Kai can more than handle himself. Don't worry about them." I nod, still chewing my lip, and he tuts. "You know what you need, baby?" he asks me, a decidedly wicked gleam entering the green globes as his lips tilt up in that panty-melting smile of his.

"If you say a distraction, I'll..." I reply sternly, fighting the pull of my own lips as his go up in a Cheshire cat-like grin.

"You'll come all over my face while you ride Jax reverse cowboy style? Okay, baby, as you wish," he tells me, and I lose the fight, my body heating as the grin splits my lips at his *Princess Bride* reference. I made them all watch it when we were holed up at the warehouse apartment, confessing my undying love for Westley which Loki takes every opportunity to tease me about.

Loki lets go of my face, taking his phone out of his back pocket and hooking it up to the car's sound system. *Tidal Wave* by Chase Atlantic starts to play.

"Loki," I chastise when he slips into the footwell, which luckily is deep because this isn't just your usual SUV, it's a Knight car with seats that face each other in the back and plenty of room.

"Don't worry, I made sure poor Tom can't hear your cries this time," he teases, grabbing my loose, harem pants and tugging them and my knickers down my hips.

I could fight, but fuck, I need the release, my body wound tighter than a spring. Lifting my hips, I let him take them off until I'm naked below the waist, only a tank top covering my torso. I shiver, but as it's warm in the car so I know it's not from the cold.

Heated lips caress my neck with a growl that hardens my nipples to aching points as Jax kisses my sensitive spots, setting my skin alight. I gasp when a hot tongue licks up my slit, glancing down to see Loki's head between my spread legs.

*Fuck, yes, please.*

I give in, closing my eyes, and just let sensation take over, feeling in the moment. Hands and tongues caressing my skin and dripping pussy, Jax pulling out my breast and showering that with attention too. I drown in ecstasy, my fingers gripping Loki's soft hair and pulling his face closer with a sharp tug as I come nearer to my release.

"Shit, Loki, don't fucking stop," I beg in a strangled voice, so bloody close I can taste the orgasm, my whole body trembling with my impending release.

And like the fucking angel that he is, he goes harder, licking and sucking, grazing his teeth on my clit until I explode, seeing white as I come hard all over his face. Jax slams his lips onto my own and swallows my scream of pleasure as fire races across my nerve endings, lighting me up like a firework.

I go boneless, slumping in the seat as I relearn how to fucking breathe again.

"One," Loki says, his voice deep and so fucking husky that I almost come again just from the sound. I crack my closed lids to see his shit-eating grin, his lips and chin glistening in the passing street lights.

"One?" I question, my own voice raw, heat flooding through me when he bites his bottom lip. *Why is that so goddamn sexy?*

"We're gonna make you come at least twice more before we get back, aren't we, Jax?" he replies, and I swallow hard at the dark promise in his eyes.

"Sure are, Baby Girl," Jax rumbles, his own voice fifty shades of fuck me now, it's so deep and growling. "Now, come sit on my cock like a good girl."

I take a deep, shaky inhale at his words, my heart still racing but Her Vagisty begging for round two. *Who am I to deny royalty?* I think as I glance over to see Jax has his pussy clenching dick out, leaning back against the leather seat as he leisurely pumps it in his huge hand. I sit up, intending to swing my leg over and ride him like Seabiscuit when Loki places a hot hand on my bare thigh.

"Facing me, beautiful," he instructs, his eyes dark and nostrils flared as he licks that plush bottom lip. "I wanna see you impaled on that monster cock."

I'd laugh at his use of my nickname for Jax's dick if he didn't look all kinds of sinful and horny as he speaks.

"As you wish," I whisper back, that biteable mouth tilting up in a smirk as I repeat his words from earlier back at him.

Unable to help myself, I lean forward, sucking his bottom lip into my mouth, my pussy clenching at the sexy as fuck groan that sounds in his throat. He grasps the back of my hair, pulling me forward more as he kisses the shit out of me, the sweet and musky taste of my release coating our tongues.

Firm hands grab my hips, manoeuvring me so that my legs are on either side of Jax's massive thighs, my feet on the floor of the moving car. I go to pull back from Loki, but he fists his hand in my hair, holding on tightly as he uses his grip to push me back, not breaking our kiss.

A low, deep keen leaves my mouth, and Loki swallows it down as I feel Jax begin to push into my opening. It feels like all my synapses are firing, my pussy walls stretching to accommodate him, although Loki paved the way with my first orgasm so that I'm nice and wet.

"Fuuuuck," Jax groans in his rough as sandpaper voice, and my already hard nipples pebble further at the sound. I love that I can bring these boys to ruin with my body, just as much as they regularly destroy me with theirs.

My breath hitches and my eyes roll behind closed lids as Jax bottoms out, sheathed inside my wet heat and touching my fucking cervix. Loki finally releases my mouth, and I gasp with the intensity of Jax inside me. Sitting back on his heels, Loki looks at us with hooded, bedroom eyes.

"Now that's a fucking beautiful sight," he states, and my eyes dart down to watch him undo his fly, his rigid member springing free and making my mouth water at the drop of precum beading at the tip. "Time for that later, Pretty Girl." He smiles smugly, pushing himself up onto the seat opposite and mirroring Jax's pose.

I whimper as Jax begins to lift my hips, sliding me up his shaft until just the tip remains. He pauses, the sound of my racing pulse loud in my ears and vying with the sound of the music that cocoons us. The flexing of his fingers is the only warning I get as he slams me back down, and I cry out with how fucking good that feels. He repeats the move again and again until I'm a quivering, gibbering mess, the windows all steamed up.

"Jax, oh shit–fuck, Jax," I pant, my nails digging into the backs of his hands as he relentlessly fucks me, harder and harder until I'm seeing stars for the second time.

"Two," Jax growls out, stopping his thrusts and letting me ride out my climax while I twitch on top of him.

"Lean our girl forward, brother," Loki grits out, and I raise my gaze to see him scooting forward on his seat, holding his dick in a firm grip.

*Hells to the fuck yes!*

I eagerly lean forward until I can place my lips around the head of him and lick the precum that's shining there.

"Oh, goddamn, baby," Loki rasps, and the way his voice hitches as I swallow him whole does things to Her Vagisty that should be on some kind of danger list. Jax grunts behind me as I clench around him, then he resumes his thrusting, pushing Loki's cock further into my throat.

I relax, letting them take control and allowing them to use my body like it was made for their pleasure. The rolling waves of ecstasy that capture my body, binding me up in ribbons of exquisite sensation tell me that no truer statement exists. We were crafted for one another, moulded to be exactly what the other needs.

The boys build me up again, one of Jax's hands coming around to my front and toying with my aching, engorged clit until I'm squirming around both his and Loki's cocks.

"Come for us again, baby," he orders, electric pulses racing across my entire body and leaving me tingling.

My jaw starts to ache with Loki's treatment, but the way he fucks my throat just winds me up tighter, my third climax fluttering just out of reach.

"One more, beautiful," Loki grits out, just as his balls tighten up and he thrusts so hard that my lips touch his base, and his hard member cuts off my air supply as he pours his release down my throat.

It's the push I need, and I come hard, bucking wildly as I shatter into thousands of pieces, spots of black coating my vision with the force and the air deprivation.

I milk Jax, hearing him roar behind me as he snaps his hips up, pushing Loki's dick further down my throat. Just as the dots start to join up, Loki pulls out, and I take a huge gasp of sex-scented air into my burning lungs. Loki helps to push me back onto Jax, who is still sheathed inside me, as my whole body flops, my chest heaving and sweat covering my skin.

"Fucking hell, baby mama," Loki gasps, flinging down beside us, his softened cock still out as he drops his head back onto the headrest.

I see Jax raise a palm, and Loki slaps it like a fucking wanker, but I'm too fucked out—*yep that's a legit state of being*—to call them out on their bullshit. Twisting around as Jax slides out of me, I snuggle into his lap, uncaring that his cum is dribbling down my inner thighs.

The sound of his rapidly slowing heartbeat lulls me into a blissed-out coma, and I feel Loki cleaning up some of the mess between my legs before sleep claims me in a warm and fuzzy embrace.

# CHAPTER SIXTEEN

LILLY

The next morning passes by in a blur, the guys cocooning me in their loving embrace that a week ago felt stifling, but now feels like a warm security blanket, protecting me from the harshness of life.

I'm snuggled on the sofa with Loki and Jax, the latter massaging my feet which feels like utter fucking bliss as he rubs the tension away, when a frantic knocking sounds at the door. My heart leaps, and I sit up, pulse pounding until I hear Willow's voice on the other side.

"Stop fucking those hotties and open up! I know you're back, Lilly!"

A small laugh barks out of me as Ash strides over to the door, opening it with a scowl. Willow, bloody awesome bitch that she is, just brushes past him without so much as a pause in her step and stops when she sees me, her eyes welling up.

"Hunter told me what happened, and–shit. I'm so glad you're back, babe," she hiccups before bursting into tears, and I rush to get up and get my arse over to her, wrapping her now sobbing, fairy form up in a tight hug.

"I missed your crazy, lovely," I tell her, my own voice thick with tears.

We hold each other for a few beats, and it dawns on me how much I needed her these past few weeks, my new bestie. And also how much I might owe her and her brother. Pulling away, I look into her crystal eyes, the tears on her lashes making them shine like diamonds.

"Willow, your brother. I owe you all so fucking much," I say, sincerity in my tone. I definitely would have gone mad without the twins and Mai. She scoffs at my words.

"You don't owe anyone shit, babe," she tells me, her blonde curls bouncing as she shakes her head. "You're family, Lilly, and family helps each other, no questions asked or debts owed."

It's Ash's turn to snort at that, and we both look over to him, a question in my expression, but Willow beats me to it.

"Something to say, Vanderbilt?" she sasses him, and I love her for it. I think even Ash approves as I see a hint of a smile on his gorgeous lips.

"We are clearly not family as the Knights owe the Shadows a favour, according to your brother," he states, crossing his arms and levelling her with his stern, grey eyes. I can't say that I'm all that surprised, isn't this how gangs work after all?

"Please," Willow says, rolling her eyes and turning back to me. "It won't be something that you're not willing to do. The Shadows aren't those kinds of monsters."

There's a darkness in her eyes at the end, like clouds that sweep over the sun, leaving you shivering, and I'm reminded that Willow has her own past, her own tale of woe that she's yet to share. I won't push her though. She'll tell me when she's good and ready.

"How about a movie?" I suggest, grabbing her hand and leading her to the sofa, making scooting motions with my other hand at Loki and Jax so they give us some space.

"I'll make some popcorn," Kai offers, putting down his iPad and getting up to go over to the kitchen.

"Sweet and salty?" I ask, giving him pleading eyes, and he chuckles, placing a kiss on my lips as he passes.

"Of course, darling," he replies softly, and I beam at him.

"Urgh, you're all so in love it's almost sickening," Willow mock-scoffs, and I stick out my tongue, knowing that she doesn't mean it.

"So, tell me all the gossip that I've missed out on," I command her, and she wrinkles her nose as she thinks for a moment.

"Honestly? Not much happened," she says, and then her eyebrows lift as she clearly thinks of something. “Oh! There was one thing now that I think about it.” She leans closer. “The ex-Governor’s daughter has gone missing, presumed kidnapped but no one knows for sure. Apparently, his son, R-something, used to go here but left shortly after Halloween last year, no one knows why.”

“Robert?” I ask, my heart beating fast at the mention of my would-be rapist.

“Yes! That’s the one! His sister went missing as it’s been all over the local news. She’s just vanished without a trace, kinda like you.” She winces as she says the last part. “Soz, babe.”

“It’s okay,” I reply absently, looking up at Ash whose jaw is clenched. “Did you know?”

“Of course,” he answers, arching one perfect brow in that way of his. “It wasn’t important, given the circumstances.”

Oh yeah, given my abduction he means. Fair point.

“Well, I hope that they find her soon,” I say to the room.

“I hope that they don’t,” Kai murmurs as he walks back, carrying drinks while the popcorn begins to ping in the pan. I look at him.

“Why?”

“The shit that we planted on the Governor’s laptop was nothing compared to the rumours of what he’d planned to do to his daughter. Word was that he’d put her virginity up for sale to the highest bidder, so long as they had good connections,” he sneers, and suddenly I feel sick, taking my iced tea from him but not wanting to take a sip after that.

“What?! But he went to prison, didn’t he?” I ask him, a coldness spreading across my limbs.

“Twelve-month suspended sentence provided he undertook psychiatric treatment,” Kai practically spits out, his nostrils flared. “He argued that he wasn’t well and needed help.”

“Plus, the Benjamins helped,” Loki adds, his upper lip curled in a sneer.

“Why is it always the rich ones? Why does their money make them untouchable?” I ask, my eyes stinging as I think about the things that I—and my mother—have had to suffer at the hands of these corrupt, despicable men.

No one can give me an answer, and we sit in silence for a few moments, each lost in our own morbid thoughts.

"So, how's the baby?" Willow finally asks, and I give her a grateful smile.

We spend the rest of the afternoon catching up a little—though Willow is careful not to ask about my time in England and mostly regales me with all the latest Highgate gossip—and watching terrible rom-coms on the massive TV. It's so normal that my skin begins to itch, and I fake exhaustion to go upstairs to Loki's room, well, my room too, as I don't want Luc's old room now even though Ash did offer it to me. I need some time alone, still not used to so much contact with different people. I get jittery seeing the tightness in Willow's and the guys' eyes as they glance at me. We all know something is up, I'm not the same girl as I was before, and I hate that they might think it's them that's the issue. It's not, it's me. I'm...broken.

And that pisses me off. The fact that cuntbag, Adrian, has made me feel uncomfortable with the people that I love. Has changed me irrevocably that I feel like I no longer know myself.

*Isn't the princess meant to live happily ever after once the bad guy has been slain by her Knights?*

Yet, he isn't—wasn't—the only villain of my story, was he? I only have to think of Julian cuntish Vanderbilt's wicked smile and lingering touch, Rafe Griffith's lecherous gaze, and Stephen Matthews'—*fucking paedo prick*—cruel words.

No, Adrian Ramsey was not the only evil that needed to be eradicated. There are still yet more waiting for their karma.

Sunday night rolls around and I can't sleep, slipping out from between Ash and Kai who did their best to exhaust my body with so many orgasms I lost count. But my mind won't settle, the sticky dread of what tomorrow morning will bring occupying my jumbled thoughts. It's the first day back in class, and I don't know how I'm meant to function, how I'm meant to be after all this time of being away.

I quietly pad downstairs and hook my phone up to the speakers, turning the volume down but needing the noise after the silence of my confinement. I pause as I realise with a start that I am now more like the guys than I was before. We can't stand the silence, needing music to drown out the demons that threaten to take over and pull us under. How fucked up is it that it's our trauma that binds us? That the people who were meant to take care of us scarred us instead so badly that we had to take refuge in each other, our broken pieces fitting together far better than our whole selves ever could.

*Far From Home* by Sam Tinnesz begins to play, the song expressing how I felt for all those weeks, trapped and unable to escape my beautiful prison.

"Can't sleep?" I hear from behind me, and I turn to see Kai standing there limned in the silvery moonlight that's filtering in from the window. I asked them not to draw the curtains, needing to see the glittering night sky of Colorado to remind myself that I wasn't in Wiltshire at my, I mean, Adrian's house.

"No, my mind is racing," I confess in a whisper, wrapping my arms around myself even though the air is warm. I've a feeling that this isn't the kind of cold that a warm jumper will be able to fix.

"A wise and beautiful, young woman once convinced me that keeping things bottled up would only allow them to fester," Kai says, his lips tipped up in a soft smile, and he steps towards me until his fresh woods after the rain scent caresses my nostrils. "Talk to me, darling." The end of his words lilts up so that it's almost a question, as if he doesn't want to push me but knows that I need to spill out my troubles. I sigh, closing my eyes briefly. It makes the words easier to say somehow.

"I'm so fucking angry, Kai," I grit out, my jaw tight and fists curled. I feel the flood of rage flow through my blood, making my heart pound like the sound of war drums. My eyes snap open, looking up into his eyes. "I'm spitting mad that all these men think that they can just do as they damn well please, taking and taking and never thinking about their own fucking evil. That what they are doing is wrong on so many bloody levels it's obscene."

My chest heaves, the frustration at everything and feeling so fucking powerless spilling over, sitting like oil on water coating everything in its path and suffocating all that is pure and good.

"My whole life has been dominated by men controlling it, and I'm just a fucking pawn being placed where they want me to be. Shit, even before I was born, I was running from a man!"

I move away, pacing as my hands run through my hair, but I can't stop the flow of words that blurt out of me.

"M–my mum was killed because of a man. A man forced me to marry Ash. A man fucking kidnapped me. All because of what, Kai? Why do they think they can just take and take, never bothering to let me make my own choices?" I know I'm practically shouting now, tears streaming down my cheeks as I throw my hands wide, then drop them down at my sides, defeated. "I just want to be able to make my own decisions, choose my own destiny. Is that too much to ask?"

I turn to him, my shoulders slumped as I sob quietly, feeling so beaten.

"And the worst part?" I ask, looking up at him through blurry eyes. He just stands there, jaw working as if it's taking a gargantuan effort not to rush over and hold me as I break. "It's not over. They're still out there. What fresh hell will be next, Kai?"

"Lilly—" he starts, losing the battle within himself and striding over to me, wrapping me up in his embrace and pulling me so close I can feel his pounding heart matching the rhythm of my own. "We are all fucking pawns to them, my darling," he tells me, his own voice growling with frustration. He pulls back a little, placing a finger under my chin and raising it to meet his gaze. "But I swear to you on everything that I am, you will get your pound of flesh. You will be free, we all will."

I stare up into his face, his eyes a savage amber flame with his vow.

"I liked hurting him, Kai," I confess in a whisper, saying aloud what I've barely even admitted to myself. "I liked taking that gun and making him bleed."

I watch his reaction intently, my heart racing for an entirely different reason now. What if, after all this time, this admission is too much? I'm not the same Lilly who walked into this dormitory less than a year ago, hurting but with clean hands. Yet if anyone can understand this craving for violence, it's my dark Knights.

His beautiful mouth curves up into a smile that may give some men nightmares, but I relish in its depravity.

"That's because you are a warrior queen, made to shed the blood of our enemies," he tells me, a fierce pride in his tone as one hand comes up to stroke down the side of my face. "And you are perfect, Lilly Vanderbilt. Just right for us."

A shiver runs down my spine at his words, my inner demon preening at his praise and acceptance.

After all, what better way to defeat the monsters that plague us than by becoming monstrous ourselves?

"Wait here," Kai orders, placing a soft kiss on my cheek, his fingers trailing down my arm and leaving goosebumps in their wake. Anticipation swirls in my lower stomach as I watch him walk across the room and up the spiral staircase.

I hear quiet murmurs from upstairs, my breath speeding up when multiple footsteps start to descend the stairs. All four of my Knights alight at the bottom, Jax, Ash, and Loki looking deliciously sleep rumpled as they surround me in a wide circle.

*It's A Man's World* by Jurnee Smollett-Bell and Black Canary begins to play over the speakers, and I take in a deep inhale as one by one they all sink to their knees.

"Use us, Princess," Ash says, his voice deep and husky, his tattooed chest bathed in moonlight.

"Take back control, Pretty Girl," Loki adds, his eyes twinkling in the dark.

I swallow hard, my breath leaving my lungs in a shudder as I fill with love for these men, men who are all naturally alpha but are willing to set that aside to give me what I need right now. Reaching down, I pull my tank over my head, my nipples hardening underneath their heated gazes. Next, I shimmy out of my panties, and I relish in the sharp inhales that sound around me as I stand naked before them.

"She's going to kill us," Loki rasps under his breath, and a bark of delighted laughter leaves my lips.

"Nah, I like your cocks too much for that, Pretty Boy," I sass him, and his lips tip up into a grin that turns salacious as I step towards him, running my fingers through his hair before grabbing a fistful and tugging his head back. "Lie back,"

Releasing my grip, he obeys, lying on his back with his head in the centre of the circle the others have created.

"Good boy," I praise.

"Sexiest fucking thing ever," he groans, adjusting his tented sweatpants.

"Glad that you think so," I reply, arching a brow at him and loving the sense of power I feel at bossing Loki around. I can only imagine what it'll be like to boss all of them. "Now, you're going to lick me out like you're starving, and the rest of you will watch but no touching yourselves." A thrill runs through me as I look at each of them.

"Yes, ma'am." Loki salutes, and I can't stop the grin that tugs my lips upwards.

"Anything you say, Princess," Ash drawls in a low voice, and my eyes dart down to see his sweats straining at the crotch.

I look at Kai, who gives me a disarming smile. "As you wish, darling."

"Yes, my Queen." Finally, I look at Jax as he answers, and a full-body shiver cascades over my skin at the term. I like that coming from his lips, a lot if the wetness seeping down my thighs is any indication.

"Good," I state, turning my attention back to Loki, lying there patiently waiting for me. I walk over to him, placing my feet just under his armpits and making my way to my knees, facing the others. It's not as graceful as it used to be, but with the noise of manly desire that he makes low in his throat, I don't care. He wants me, regardless if I'm becoming more whale-like with each day.

"Jesus, Pretty Girl, you smell fucking divine," he moans, his hands grasping the globes of my arsecheeks and pulling me closer to his waiting mouth.

I gasp as his tongue makes a slow pass from my opening to my clit and back again, delving inside my channel and swirling around.

"I can taste them inside you, baby," he rasps, his voice muffled.

"It's rude to talk with your mouth full," I say back, my voice low and husky with the pleasure that he's already giving me.

His chuckle vibrates across my core and a deep moan leaves my lips at the feel of him between my thighs. Without saying anything else, he dives in so to speak, licking and sucking like I really am his last meal on earth, and it's all I can do to hold on, my head thrown back in ecstasy. My knees dig into the rug beneath us, but I hardly feel the ache as I hurtle towards a climax that I know will shake my very being.

"Loki..." I whine, my eyelids fluttering closed as I lose myself to the please that his naughty tongue is giving me.

More quickly than I'd like to admit, he builds me up until I'm shaking above him, my hands curled into fists and stars begin to burst behind my closed lids. He doubles his efforts, and soon I'm hurtling down the rabbit hole, crying out and soaking his face with the force of my orgasm.

He stills underneath me whilst I pant and sweat drips down my spine. Moving back a little to give him some breathing space, I glance down to see his mouth and chin glistening in the moonlight.

"Good boy," I breathe out again, and he chuckles deeply once more, his hands flexing on my arse.

"I aim to please, my Queen."

His smile grows wider as he feels my thighs clench. I really do like that term.

I tear my gaze away from him, my eyes finding Jax's, his stare intense and making my already hard nipples tighten. An idea springs into my head, and suddenly I'm desperate to feel him inside me whilst I ride that monster cock.

"Your turn to watch, Pretty Boy," I tell Loki, crawling off him and over to Jax. "Lose the pants," I order, kneeling in front of him. One of his blond eyebrows raises at my command.

Without a word spoken, he does as I request, his huge dick springing free and my mouth waters at the sight of the bead of precum glistening at the tip. Unable to resist, I lean down and lick it off, the hiss of breath that leaves his lips making my insides flutter. Straightening up, I look him in the eye, the desire in his stare almost burning me with its intensity.

"Your turn to lie down, big boy. Same position as Loki so the others can see my face."

The song changes to *Right Here* by Chase Atlantic as Jax does my bidding, again remaining silent as he gets into position. I wet my lips as I watch him, marvelling that this powerful man, these powerful men, are so quick to obey me. It's a heady aphrodisiac.

On my hands and knees again, I crawl over his body, my knees settling on either side of his hips, my legs spread wide to accommodate his size. Taking his shaft in my hand, I give it a few pumps just because I can and I love the way his hips jerk when I do. Then I place him at my opening, using touch to feel my way as my stomach now prevents me from seeing what I'm doing.

His hands come up to rest on my thighs, his fingers digging in as I slowly sink down, a deep, keening moan leaving my lips as I take him all the way to the hilt.

"Fuck, baby," he hisses out, his eyes leaving the place that we're joined and rolling to the back of his head.

"I intend to," I quip, wasting no time and moving my hips in a way that has him massaging my inner walls.

"You look so fucking beautiful like that, Queen," Ash tells me, and I look up to catch his scorching stare as he watches us, his hand drifting to his clearly rigid member. My core tightens around Jax at the nickname, making him groan deeply.

“Same rules as before Vanderbilt, no touching,” I tell him and I pick up the pace, Jax helping me to move up and down more on him.

Turning my attention back down to the big man beneath me, I catch his gaze, my lips tilting up in what I know is an evil smirk.

“No coming for you yet, big guy,” I tell him, and he arches a brow at me again, but then just gives me a nod to let me know that he’s agreeing to my request.

I start to move faster, the tingling tell of a second orgasm starting up in my core. My breath pants out of my chest, my breasts swinging as I begin to slam my hips down, the bite of pain as he hits me deeply, sending me closer to that edge. But there's something I want to try before jumping off.

Leaning down, I stretch my arms out until my hands can wrap around his thick throat. His eyes widen a fraction as he holds my stare, and a part of me can’t believe that the idea of choking Jax as I fuck him has a rush of liquid pooling between us.

“Oh shit.” I hear Loki whisper as I press tighter, feeling Jax’s pulse beat wildly underneath my fingertips.

Jax’s hands grab my waist, and he uses his grip to start pulling me up and down hard and fast so that I don’t lose the rhythm.

Fuck.

It feels so fucking good, his dick pounding into my dripping cunt, my hands around his throat, choking him. My inner walls start to tighten, and I’m gasping and whimpering as my orgasm threatens to overwhelm me. Just before I fall off the edge, Jax pulls me off him and fuck me, he hits something on the way out that has a literal fountain squirting out of me, coating his abs and lower stomach. I scream, my nails digging into the side of his neck as I convulse over him, wave after wave of pleasure crashing over me with the intensity of a stormy sea.

He lowers me down and I slump, panting and everything practically glowing as I tingle from one of the strongest orgasms I’ve ever had. His large palms smooth down my thighs, his deep whispers of how fucking beautiful I am settling deep into my soul and soothing the anger inside me that’s been present since my capture.

After a few moments, I lift my head to look around at the others and see the look of adoration and lust present on all of their faces. I feel sated, and I know exactly how I want this to end.

Pushing up to sitting, Jax's hard length trapped under my swollen pussy lips, I look down at him and then back up at the others.

"I want to taste you," I say to them. "All of you."

Some people believe that being on your knees for a man, his dick in your mouth is a place of submission, but I don't. It's a place of power, a place where you can be in control of how much pleasure, or pain, you give him, and I want to watch as they all come undone on my tongue, coating my mouth and upper body with their seed.

"Are you sure, baby?" Jax asks as he curls upwards, his arms banding around me and pulling me flush to his body.

"Yes."

Ash is suddenly there next to us, holding out a hand to help me up on shaky legs. He, too, pulls me close, placing a kiss on my lips. He steps back, keeping hold of my hand and leading me to the centre of the space, where Kai has placed a large throw pillow to cushion my knees.

Still holding Ash's hand, I lower once more to my knees, my head level with his bulging crotch. Letting go of his grasp, I pull his sweats down, freeing his rigid shaft, and watching as it bounces slightly then, begging to be touched. I grab the base, rolling my eyes upwards and watching as I open my mouth and take in his head, playing with his magic cross piercing before pushing forward until he's hitting the back of my throat.

"Fucking hell—" he groans, his hands coming to tangle in my hair and hold me as I sink deeper, breathing through my gag reflex until my lips meet the base of him. I pull back, my eyes on his almost pained expression as I bob my head up and down, coating him in my saliva and tasting the precum that's leaking from his tip.

Pulling back with a gasp, I turn to find Kai's cock ready and weeping precum. I take him in my slick hand, pumping slowly as I take him in my mouth but only playing with the tip, swirling it around my tongue, sucking and grazing it with my teeth until I feel him shake.

"Jesus...Lilly..." He gasps as I'm relentless in my pursuit of his pleasure, my other hand stroking Ash.

I let go of both of them, taking their hands and wrapping them around their own shafts, with a silent instruction to keep pumping. Shuffling around, I find Jax's cock in front of me next, glistening with my release and I waste no time in taking him into my mouth, my lips stretching wide to accommodate his girth.

"That's it, Baby Girl," he murmurs, his hand coming up to the back of my head and gripping my hair. "Right. Fucking. There."

His hand pushes down, forcing me to swallow more of him, my throat working around his shaft as I breathe through my gag reflex. Tears stream from my eyes as I gaze up at him, my hand fondling his balls and massaging the space behind them.

Someone takes my free hand, wrapping it around a hard member and guiding the stroking. My thumb finds the tip and I realise from the piercing that it's Loki, my hand working him in a steady massaging motion that I know makes his knees weak.

I keep fucking Jax's dick with my mouth and throat, his thighs beginning to tremble and his shaft goes rock-hard moments before a roar escapes his lips and hot, salty cum fills my mouth. I swallow some down, pulling away as he's still squirting so that the rest dribbles down my chin and breasts.

As soon as he's finished, a hand tangles in my hair, and Loki pulls me to him, thrusting his dick inside my mouth, Jax's release acting as lube as Loki face fucks me. I relax, letting him take his pleasure as both of my hands are wrapped around Kai and Ash who have stepped up close next to Loki. I look to the side as much as I'm able to, watching the pleasure on their faces and then Loki's, and I feel my own body begin to react at the power that comes from bringing these men to the brink of insanity.

"Fuck!" Loki yells, pulling out and coating my lips, chin, and chest with his climax, hot spurts of cum hitting me and coating me.

I'm panting as he steps back, letting Ash and Kai close ranks. I smile up at them, my chest heaving as our hands continue to move on their hard lengths.

"You look so fucking beautiful like that, Queen," Ash grits out between clenched teeth, his fingers coming under my chin and angling my head towards him. "Open up for me, tongue out."

I decide to obey him this time as that's exactly what I wanted to do, and so I hold his stare as I open my mouth, sticking my tongue out and waiting for him to finish on me.

It doesn't take long, his jaw ticking as a deep groan escapes his lush lips seconds before his warm release hits my tongue, dripping down onto my chin and chest.

As soon as he's finished, he pulls me off and turns my head to face Kai who weaves his fingers in my sweaty hair.

"I want to pour my release down that beautiful throat of yours," Kai tells me, his hand wrapped over mine, our grip punishing. "May I, my Queen?"

My thighs clench at that name again, wetness seeping down them.

"Yes, please," I whimper, gasping when I feel something wriggling between my slick thighs. I look away from Kai to see Jax with his face underneath me, his hands pulling me down until his hot breath fans over my lower lips.

Kai feeds me his dick, the piercing on the underside clacking against my teeth, at the same moment that Jax thrusts his tongue inside me. I cry out at the spark of lightning that shoots up from my inner channel, Kai taking the opportunity to push the rest of the way in until I'm choking on his dick.

A deep animalistic sound leaves his throat as he pulls out a little, only to snap his hips forwards and thrust back inside, my eyes streaming as I gag.

"So fucking precious," he coos, and I whine deep in my throat when hands grasp my breasts, pinching my nipples and smearing the cum all over them.

"Such a beautiful Queen," Ash praises, his hand coming up to the front of my throat and wrapping around it, making Kai hiss as Ash tightens his grip.

"And all ours," Loki adds, his scalding tongue flicking my cum covered nipple in time to Jax tongue fucking my cunt.

*Fucking hellballs.*

I'm consumed by them all, another orgasm building in my core as they build me up to a raging inferno. I become a shaking, quivering mess, and my hands grasp Kai's thighs, my nails digging in until I feel wetness seep from the wounds as I race towards the explosive finish that I know is waiting for me.

"Fuck! Lilly!" Kai shouts, thrusting deep as he does exactly what he asked and pours his hot seed down my throat.

It triggers my own climax, and I cry and tremble as electricity makes my limbs go rigid, more wetness shooting out of me as I come, and come, and come. I swear I black out for a while there, as the next thing I know I'm being lifted into strong arms, Jax's, I realise as I crack my eyes open.

"Thank you," I croak out, my voice raspy as only a good face fuck will leave it.

"You don't need to thank us, Baby Girl," Jax replies, walking us into the bathroom, the soft lighting around the mirror coming on.

“It’s what we’re here for, Pretty Girl,” Loki adds, placing a kiss on my cheek as he strolls past and opens the shower. The sound of water falling fills the room, alongside steam.

“We will never take your control, my love,” Ash tells me, his palm cupping my cheek as he presses our foreheads together, uncaring that I’m covered in his friend's cum, and held in the arms of one of those friends.

“And we will always love you, no matter what,” Kai finishes from my other side, and I twist my head to see him standing next to us, his own fingers grazing my damp cheek.

“And I will always love you,” I reply, pressing a kiss to his fingers.

The tender moment is interrupted, as usual, by Loki singing *I will Always Love You* by Whitney Houston, using the shampoo bottle as a mic, and I turn to see his hair sticking up and covered in bubbles. He obviously changes the words so it’s not about leaving someone, and his terrible rendition, sung in key, has me laughing so hard I think I might pee myself.

*Fucking bellend.*

# CHAPTER SEVENTEEN

LILLY

It's my first day back, and I feel sick to my stomach, chewing my lip nervously as I walk down the wide, sweeping staircase with my guys around me. As we reach the bottom, Jax tugs my lip from between my teeth with a small rumble.

"You don't need to be afraid, Baby Girl," he tells me, pausing and turning me to face him, his clear, blue eyes piercing into my very soul. "You are the strongest fucking person I know, these cunts are nothing."

Tears sting my eyes, and I swallow hard as his words sink in, coating my insides like a life-giving elixir. I hear the others murmur their agreement as I'm enclosed in their circle, the mixed scents of ginger, vanilla, lemon, and fresh woods soothing my fractious nerves. I take a deep breath, inhaling their strength into myself until my heartbeat calms and the black claws of panic recede.

"Okay," I tell them, turning my head so that I can look at each of them in turn. "I'm ready."

"That's our girl," Jax praises, leaning down to place a soft kiss on my lips that sends tingles all the way to Her Vagisty. He catches my slight gasp, and the sexiest smirk graces his lips as he pulls away. I clear my throat, trying to tell Her Vagisty that we can't just spend the rest of our lives with their dicks balls deep. She doesn't believe me and fuck if my knickers don't look like the bottom of a bird cage most days.

"I need to freshen up," I inform them, Jax's smirk blooming into a full-blown smile that does nothing to help my underwear situation. I'm a lost fucking cause by this point. "Fuck off," I grouch at him, stomping—*okay, there's a bit of a waddle going on*—to the girl's bathroom.

I feel them all at my back, not leaving me alone for a second, though thankfully none of them follow me into the lav. Part of me wishes they had when I look up as the door closes to see Amber and her two Cuntmuffins applying lipstick to already perfectly made-up faces.

She spots me in the mirror, her gaze narrowing, and her lip curling as she takes me in. I go to make a snarky comment about the fact that her make-up clearly isn't vegan and I'm pretty sure the brand that she's using was involved in an animal testing scandal a couple of years ago.

But then I just stop. I'm so fucking tired of all the drama.

"Why are you so afraid of me?"

"What the fuck?!" Amber scoffs, spinning to glare at me, crossing her arms and curling her upper lip. "Why would I be afraid of orphan trash like you?"

"I have four amazing men who will love me no matter what. I'll never be alone, never be lonely. I'm married to Ash Vanderbilt, heir to a billion-dollar empire. I have majority shares in that billion-dollar company. My future is secure and full of love."

A thought occurs to me then and gives me pause. Maybe Amber and I have more in common than I first thought. We are both pawns in a game of chess played by greedy men.

"You don't have to do as he says, you know," I tell her, looking her directly in the eyes, even as she raises her chin. "You don't have to be a pawn in your father's game. You are a strong woman, Amber. Don't become what he wants you to be."

Her facade cracks a little, like the fine lines of a porcelain cup that's been left out in the frost. Her lip wobbles ever so slightly, and her crossed arms appear more like they are hugging her and protecting her from this cruel world. Then I watch as she straightens her spine, adopting that mean girl persona once more like armour.

"Fuck you, Lilly," she spits out, turning on her Birkenstock heel and sweeping out of the bathroom, her clones giving me a confused look before following after her.

Well, that could have gone worse I suppose.

# CHAPTER EIGHTEEN

LOKI

I watch from the couch as Lilly comes down the stairs with heavy-lidded eyes. But the fact that she's here and not asleep in the middle of the night tells me that she, too, is having trouble sleeping. I know that she's been this way since we got her back. Restless, unable to relax.

And who can fucking blame her after what she went through. I want to bring that cunt back to life just to torture him all over again for hurting our girl, and don't get me fucking started on Julian.

She spots me sitting in a shaft of moonlight, her lips tilting upwards, and my heart pitter-patters in my fucking chest at her smile.

"Can't sleep either?" she asks in that beautiful voice of hers. It's like music to my love-struck ears, and I never want to stop hearing it.

She comes over to me, sitting next to me on the couch and snuggling under my arm. Shit, I still can't believe that we got her back and she's now here. Prickly guilt stabs into my chest, the blame of her being taken still raw for me, no matter how many times she tells me that it wasn't my fault.

Shaking my head, I wrap my arm around her and breathe the sweet scent of her hair in. Well, Ash's ginger scent as she's still using his shampoo, which the asshole lords over the rest of us at every opportunity. I'm waiting to point out to him that she may use his shampoo and be his wife, but I was the one to put a baby in her. Not sure I'll be able to run fast enough when I do remind him of that little fact.

"Did I ever tell you about the fallen angel tattoo?" I ask her, wanting to distract her from the worries that are creasing her brow as I look down at her.

"No," she replies, eyes alight with curiosity.

"Well," I begin, pulling her closer to me so that I don't have to look into those stunning eyes of hers. It's funny how I can torture and kill a man without a shred of fear, but talking to this goddess about my past fills me with fucking dread. "I got the piece done after Luc..." I swallow, the wound of his suicide still a sharp pain, though it is duller than it used to be. "After Luc killed himself. I felt like I'd let him down. Fuck, we were close, and I didn't see it coming at all. At the time, I blamed myself for not seeing the signs of how badly he was hurting, thinking that I could have stopped it somehow."

"It's not your fault, Loki, love," she interrupts, and I smile into the darkness at just how fucking good this woman is. She's always trying to help us, assure us, and I fucking love it. I squeeze her tighter.

"I know that now, Pretty Girl. But then, I was fucked up. Turning to drugs and pussy to try and forget. I think that the fact that my parents didn't give a shit about me also contributed to feeling like I wasn't enough," I confess, feeling a lessening in the tightness that I always carry around in my chest. She doesn't interrupt this time, other than to snuggle into my chest. "I wanted to mark my skin, to see the wound I was carrying inside on the outside. I looked up fallen angels. They have been thrown out of heaven. Lost the battle and are a symbol of pain, suffering, and sadness. Of shame," I whisper the last part into the darkness, taking another deep inhale of her scent. I love how it's often a mixture of all of ours, plus her own fresh spring smell. It calms my raging emotions.

"They are also a symbol of rebellion against society's rules," she tells me, pulling out of my grip and swinging her leg over mine until she straddles my hips, her hot, panty-clad core right over my rapidly hardening shaft. Fuck.

She reaches a hand on either side of my face and tips it up until I am staring right into her beautiful eyes.

"So, maybe your ink is about your future as well as your past?" she asks, and my hands tighten on her hips, my throat thick with emotion for this girl.

She has this ability to make me find the light when I'm drowning in fucking darkness.

"I fucking love you, Lilly," I tell her, speaking around the lump in my throat. She leans in, her breath, sweet and minty, fanning over my lips as she replies.

"I fucking love you too, Loki."

With a deep groan, I close the minuscule distance between us, pressing my lips to her soft, pillowy ones and devouring her with my kiss. Fuck, I would go all Hannibal on her if cannibalism didn't mean that she'd be dead.

She kisses me back just as hotly, her hips moving and grinding down on my now rock-solid cock.

"Loki," she pleads, breaking the kiss and rewarding me with a gasping moan as my lips travel down her neck, biting and sucking, and fuck loving the marks that I leave there.

"Yes, beautiful?"

She answers me by pulling off her tank top, and it's my turn to groan as her full, heavy tits are revealed, her pert nipples calling me like a fucking siren song in the moonlight. I lean into her, ducking my head to close my lips around one of the buds and suck, her hips bucking in time to the movements of my tongue.

"Shit, Loki," she says with a moan, grabbing fistfulls of my hair and pulling me forward. Her confidence in demanding what she wants sends a bolt of lightning straight to my dick, and I reward her by biting down on her flesh, making her cry out.

Moving one hand down the swell of her stomach—shit, there's something about knowing that the baby growing inside her is mine that makes me fucking crazy—I dip into the top of her panties, hissing when I feel just how fucking wet she is.

"Such a good fucking girl for me, baby. Wet and aching already."

She whimpers, and the sound does things to me that the devil would blush at. Grabbing the crotch of her panties, I give a quick tug, smirking at her gasp and the ripping sound as I tear the fabric to grant me the access that I need.

"Fucker," she scolds, but I can hear the smile on her lips.

I soon make her forget all about the damn things as I insert two fingers into her wet heat, not fucking around and rubbing at that spot just inside that drives her fucking crazy.

"Shit, Loki, fuck, I'm coming!" she gasps, moments before a rush of liquid leaves her cunt and soaks my hand and sweats underneath.

As she pants and shivers, I remove my hand, using it to pull my hard length out and slicking it with her release, groaning at the feel of her juices already coating me. Taking both of her hips in my hands, I lift her, hovering her over my dick as I let go with one hand and guide my cock to her opening.

"Loki," she moans in a deep, husky voice that has me almost coming as her still pulsing cunt grips my dick as I push inside her.

Fumbling for my phone on the cushion beside me, I hit play on *You're Special* by NF, the song filling the quiet and I sing along, knowing by the way her breath catches and her fingernails dig into my chest that she loves it when I do this. Moving my hips to the beat, I fuck her slowly, savouring the feel of her inner walls gripping me like she never wants me to leave.

It feels so fucking good that I lose the words of the song, my movements speeding up even as I want to prolong this pleasure for as long as humanly possible.

"Fuck, Lilly, baby. Your pussy feels so fucking good gripping my cock," I grit out, and her inner walls flutter around me, her hips matching my thrusts with movements of her own as she rides me hard and fast. "That's it, Pretty Girl. Ride my dick like it will never be enough."

And I know that my words are fucking true; it will never be enough. I will always want more. More of her, more of this.

Tingling begins at the base of my dick, and I feel my balls drawing up as I get as solid as fucking marble. Reaching between us, I start to pinch and rub her clit, a husky cry leaving her throat as her head falls back and she moves even faster. Just as I feel cum surge up my shaft with the force of a fucking rocket, her pussy clamps down around me like a vise, and she climaxes with a scream, her nails raking bloody furrows down my chest.

But I'm beyond caring as stars fill my eyes, an animalistic groan ripping from my chest when I thrust hard to the hilt inside her, growling like a goddamn wolf as I come inside her, filling her up with my seed.

"Loki, you are more than enough, my love. You brought me back to life," she whispers in my ear, her body draped over mine and my cock still buried deep inside her.

I pull her closer, marvelling that she came into our lives just a few months ago, and now none of us can live without her. She's our harbour, our refuge, and these past weeks, when she was gone, were legit the hardest of my fucking life.

"I can't breathe without you, Pretty Girl. I no longer exist when you are not there," I confess, peppering her neck with kisses and smiling when I feel her pussy walls spasming around my rapidly hardening cock. "You brought us all back from the dead, baby." I punctuate my words with the movements of my hips, holding her close to me as I shallowly thrust into her. Fuck, this will never get old, having her wrapped around me.

I spend the rest of the night showing her the truth of my words, worshipping her body until we fall into bliss over and over again and eventually pass out, still connected in every way.

# CHAPTER NINETEEN

LILLY

One week.

One week is all I have until finals and then graduation. That is if I've enough credits, which I'm not certain I do given the time that I've missed.

Shitballs. I'm royally fucked, and not in the good, four peens at once kind of way.

The week goes by in a whirlwind of revision classes and trying to catch up with almost two months of missed work. Luckily, Kai and the guys help me on that front, plus all the teachers seem suspiciously accommodating, giving me only a few extra projects even though I must have missed a fuck ton more.

I'm ready to leave campus when Saturday rolls around, desperate for some space from the silent judgement and curious stares of the student population that have made my skin prickle for the past five days. They don't dare say anything, but I know they all whisper about me, my disappearance, and my pregnancy. *Fuck them all to hell in a handcart.*

"Why don't we go paintballing?" I ask hopefully as we all finish up breakfast, remembering the Christmas presents I'd gotten the guys and suddenly thinking that we all just need a bit of fun.

Ash gives me what can only be described as a withering Ash-hole stare, and I want to slap him for it, my fists clenching around my cutlery.

"You can't go paintballing in your condition," he states with an eye roll as if that was the stupidest thing I could have said.

Suddenly my lower lip wobbles and before I know it, I burst into tears, throwing my knife and fork down with a clatter and shooting up to my feet. They're not delicate lady-like tears either, but great heaving sobs that rack my chest, and I'm sure snot slides out of my nose.

"Shit–Princess–fuck–I—" Ash stammers, his eyes wide and hands raised, and it would be funny if, you know, I wasn't crying so hard. Fucking hormones.

"You fucking asshole!" Loki hisses, shoving a still floundering Ash in his chair, and Kai gives him a chilling death glare across the table.

Jax whacks him upside the head, causing Ash to wince, getting up and then my Viking strides over to me and wraps me up in his huge, comforting embrace. Immediately, my sobs lessen as I inhale his warm, lemon scent. All the guys make me feel safe and secure, but Jax is like my refuge, my security blanket. He holds me, rubbing a huge palm up my spine until I quieten, my fists tight in his black tee.

He pulls back a fraction, just enough so that he can look deeply into my no doubt, puffy eyes.

"It's not safe for the baby for you to play paintball, Baby Girl," he tells me gently in that deep, husky voice of his, his thumb brushing the tears from my face. I heave a sigh, knowing he's right, but hating that there feels like so much I can't do, or eat because I'm growing a baby. "But," he adds, a mischievous twinkle in his ice blue eyes, "if you want to watch from the viewing platform, I'll shoot Ash in the dick just for you."

"I'd like to see you fucking try," I hear Ash grumble, and it pretty much seals his fate as I let a positively evil smirk tug my lips up.

"Deal."

---

Getting dressed, I decide on a cute as fuck denim, mini dress with a brightly-coloured, vintage scarf tied in a knot at my neck fifties style, and some brand new, red, sequin chuck-style high tops by my favourite shoe brand.

Apparently, after the guys discovered where I was, Loki went on a shopping spree and bought me a shit ton of maternity clothes in my style as well as several pairs of flats which he brought back with us from England. God, I love that boy.

I grab my sunglasses and phone, heading out of the room I share with Loki, bumping into Kai in the corridor.

"Jesus, Lilly, darling," he rasps, his eyes travelling down the expanse of my bare legs and his lips quirking at the glittering shoes. "You are so beautiful."

He steps into me, his fresh scent filling my nostrils as his hand snakes around my thickening waist and pulls me closer. My pulse speeds as he nuzzles my neck, kissing his way up to my ear and leaving me breathless and my knickers damp.

"Come with me, Pet."

I take in a sharp exhale at the name, my whole body feeling like a live fuse wire as he pulls me to his room, opening the door and then closing it behind us. He leads me to the bed, but instead of pushing me down onto it as I expect, he turns me around sharply so that my back is to his front. I groan as he grinds his hardness into my lower back, and I arch into him, telling him with my body what I want. He tuts, biting my earlobe hard.

"Naughty, impatient, Pet," he says, chuckling huskily as his hand slides down my side and his fingers hook under the hem of my short dress. "Hands on the bed, ass in the air."

I do as he commands, feeling him take a step back as I move, pulling the back of my dress up and over my arse. He laughs, no doubt at my choice of rainbow and unicorn patterned knickers. "Cute." He pulls them down to my knees, leaving them there and not taking them off.

I frown when a moment later my back is cold, and turning my head, I watch as he walks over to his cabinet of curiosities, aka toys to fuck you with. I can't see what he takes out, but he's soon turning back, stalking towards me with a wicked fucking smile on his lips. With his glasses, and hot nerd look, he's like a filthy Clark Kent, and I am fucking here for it.

He stops in front of my face, leaning down and opening his fist to show me a gleaming, metal butt plug in rainbow colours and with a pink jewel on the end. My breath catches, and I look to see a wide smile on his handsome face.

"I thought that you'd like this one, Pet. On account of your underwear choice," he tells me, running the plug up and down my bare arm. Goosebumps rise on my skin from the cool touch. "You'll wear this all day. Only I'm allowed to take it out, understand?"

"Yes, sir," I breathe, shivering slightly.

"Such a good Pet," he praises softly, straightening up and going around to my arse.

I hear the top of a lube bottle opening, then gasp as his fingers, coated in the cool lubricant, start to rub all around my back door, spreading it around. A groan leaves my lips as one finger enters me, then a second as he works the lube inside my hole.

"Kai," I moan, rubbing my forehead on the soft, cotton duvet cover as pleasure starts to build in my core, which flutters, desperate to be filled.

He withdraws his fingers, only to replace them with the cool metal of the plug, and I breathe in through my mouth as he pushes it inside me. There's a sharp pain as the wider part breaches my tight muscles, and he coos, stroking my arse as he coaxes me to take it all.

I'm a shaking, hot fucking mess, sweaty hair sticking to my forehead when he's finished, and I just lie with my cheek pressed to the covers of his bed as I get used to the delicious feeling of intrusion. Kai pulls my knickers back up and then my dress down before he encourages me to stand.

I quiver with the movement, the plug making its presence felt in the most distracting way.

"Good girl," he whispers, pushing my hair off my forehead and placing a kiss on my lips. "Let's go downstairs, the others are waiting."

Taking my hand in his, holding his other, slightly shining hand by his side, he leads us out of the room and down the stairs and I feel every. Damn. Step.

When we reach the bottom, he excuses himself to go wash up, and my cheeks burn as three sets of jewelled eyes lock onto me, assessing and narrowing.

"What's wrong?" Ash asks, striding over to me and taking my face in his palms, tipping it up to look into my eyes, worry creasing his forehead.

"N–nothing," I stammer out, feeling my cheeks heat up even more as the burn of the plug in my arsehole makes a lie of my words. I hear Kai chuckle and look over to see him casually sauntering over to us.

"Turn round, Lilly," he commands, and although he doesn't use his pet name for me, I feel my body wanting to do as he orders.

Ash lets go of me with a curious look in his eye, one jet-black brow raised, as I do what Kai says.

"Raise your dress and show them your new accessory," is Kai's next order. With my cheeks heating even more, I turn around, lift up the back of my dress, and pull my knickers back down before bending over.

"Fucking Christ," I hear Ash exclaim in a low voice, then a sharp sting hits my arse cheek as a cry of pleasure mixed with pain leaves my lips as he smacks me. It jostles the plug, and I feel the effects deep inside me, wetness slicking my thighs.

"Fuck me, that looks so pretty sparkling in your ass," Loki groans out, and Jax makes a growl of agreement.

"Right, time to go," Kai interrupts firmly. "Lilly, get dressed."

Swallowing, unsure how in the ever-loving fuck I'm going to get through this day with a butt plug inside me, I do as instructed. Taking a deep breath, I turn back around to find all of my Knights with hungry, almost desperate looks on their faces. It's then I realise that I'm not the only one who is affected by it.

"Ready," I announce unnecessarily. I stride past them, each step sending waves of sensation through me as I walk, my nipples hard and pussy aching by the time I reach the door. "You guys coming?" I ask, turning back to see them blinking, and I can't help the chuckle that falls from my lips.

They spring into action, grabbing various items before we all head out of the door and down to Jax's truck which sits idling by the front doors. A valet gets out, handing the keys to Jax with a nod, and disappears into the building behind us.

"Huh," I say aloud as we climb in and grit my teeth as that move sends sparks from my arsehole through me.

"What's up, beautiful?" Jax asks, turning in his seat to look back at me in the backseat. I'm sandwiched between Loki and Kai, both of whom have a hand on my exposed thighs.

"I've not seen Mr Smythe, that crow who showed me to the dorm my first night around for a while," I state, frowning. My gaze flits from one boy to another as they all look elsewhere. "You know something!" I accuse, turning to Loki who is staring out of the window. I grab his face, physically turning him to face me. "Tell me."

He grimaces, his eyes flicking to Ash in the passenger seat before coming back to me.

"Well, when I told the guys how he'd treated you when you got here," he starts, his free hand coming up to rub the back of his neck, and I hear Jax growl from the front as he starts the engine.

"You didn't fucking kill him?!" I shout, looking away from Loki to Ash who is turned towards me with an evil fucking smirk on his pretty lips. If fairies come with Jax's voice, they die with that smile of Ash's. I mean, the butler was a complete cumbucket, but I'm not sure he deserved to die because of it.

"We're not amateurs, Princess. Give us some fucking credit," Ash tells me, rolling his eyes like I'm being overly dramatic and didn't watch them castrate a boy or torture then kill a man, both of whom had wronged me. "We just made him see the error of his ways and had him relocated."

"Relocated to where?" I ask, looking at the amused smiles on each of their faces.

"He's now a semen collector for the Tailors' racehorses," Loki tells me, his face split into a wide grin.

"What?!" I question, my hand flying to my mouth to stifle my chuckle.

"He holds an artificial vagina for the studs in order to collect the semen so that they can inseminate the female horses and ensure good cross-breeding and stronger stock," Kai informs me, his face completely straight and deadpan. A slight twitch of his lips tells me he is holding in a laugh too.

"He's a horse wanker?" I enquire, my lips trembling with the effort to hold in my laughs.

"We thought that it was a job suited to his talents, being a *wanker* anyway," Ash replies, turning back to face the front.

"And he always did have a *stable* hand," Loki adds, and I fucking lose it, a bark of laughter bursting out of me, and then a groan as the plug shifts around. After a few chuckles, I manage to calm down enough to ask another question that has just popped into my head.

"Aren't the Tailors one of the gangs caught up in that turf war in Whetstone?"

"Yep," Ash answers, looking back around at me. "And Aeron Taylor owed us a favor."

I'm about to ask more, wondering who this Aeron is and why I'm only now finding out about him, but Loki squeezes my thigh, and when I turn to look at him, he shakes his head. So I leave it, deciding that it's not worth the hassle of getting pissed when Ash refuses to tell me. He'll open up about it eventually if it's important.

# CHAPTER TWENTY

LILLY

The rest of the drive to the paintballing site is spent quietly, listening to *Ain't No Sunshine* by Black Label Society as we drive through the summer morning. Soon after, we pull into a driveway carved into the woods, a warehouse-looking building nestled amongst the trees. Getting out, we head inside, Loki's hand wrapped around my own, the guys all carrying their bags of kit.

We're welcomed by a young-looking guy, maybe a few years older than us who, to be honest, looks like a bit of a stoner with his faded band tee and long hair. He seems to know what he's about though, shaking each of my Knight's hands professionally and telling them that they're up against a group of eight Navy Seals.

"Excuse me?" I interrupt, all eyes turning my way. "Did you say Navy Seals? Eight Navy Seals?" I question, thinking that I must have misheard him.

"Uh, yeah. Is that a problem?" stoner dude—*Mark, maybe*—answers, looking at the guys with a raised brow.

"It's no problem," Ash informs him, not looking away from me with a devilish smirk on his face. He steps closer to me until the front of our bodies are pressed together, and I shiver as he tucks some loose hair behind my ear. “Are you doubting our abilities, Princess?”

I swallow, my throat dry with the sexual tension that thrums in the air between us.

“N–no,” I whisper, taking a sharp inhale as his fingers trace down the side of my neck and across the scoop neckline of my dress.

“Good,” he mumbles back, placing a small kiss on my pulse point, and I feel him smile against my neck when he feels how much it’s racing. *Fuck-crumpet.* “We’re going to get changed. Wait here with Mark, and we’ll see you in a minute.”

He steps back, and they all head to some changing rooms on the far side of the entrance space. Mark gives me a friendly smile, opening his mouth to say something, then flicking his gaze behind me when we hear the door open. There’s the sound of male camaraderie, and I turn to see what must be the Navy Seals if their matching buzz cuts are anything to go by.

“Excuse me,” Mark apologises, going over and greeting them, with a similar talk that he gave my guys.

I cast my eyes over the new arrivals, wincing when I see that they’re all pretty stacked, although maybe not quite as big as Jax. They give me curious looks in return, clearly wondering what a pregnant teenager is doing here. I see the disbelief on one of their faces, then the wide grins and laughs as all of their attention shifts behind me, so I turn back and my own laughter rings out as my Knights walk towards me.

I’d completely forgotten about the costumes that I’d bought them to go with their paintballing equipment, and I must admit they look fucking hilarious.

Ash and Jax frown as they spot the guys behind me, but Kai and Loki just grin widely at me. I devour them with my gaze, admitting to myself that they still look fucking hot enough to eat, regardless of the onesies each of them wears. Ash is in a skintight devil costume, complete with a forked tail. His ink peeks up his neck and wrists, and the costume just highlights the valleys of all his muscles.

Jax looks almost like he might burst out of his bright green, Hulk onesie, and he’s left it open all the way to his belly button, making my mouth water at the delicious pecs and abs on display. He catches me licking my lips as my eyes dip below his waist and I notice how tight the costume really is over his crotch. Fucking hell, he's not even hard and I can practically see all the veins on his dick.

My gaze flicks over to Kai, his Stormtrooper onsie fitted and showing off his ripped physique, his glasses adding to this fuck me now geek vibe. He's left off the helmet and gives me a cheeky grin and wink as he catches me perving.

And of course, Loki steals the show and fucking knows it too. He's dressed in a bright pink, fluffy, bunny onesie, complete with hood and attached ears, and Jesus have mercy on my cunt because he looks fine as fuck. The zip is open to just above his crotch, his happy trail on full fucking display, and I've never wanted to fuck the Easter bunny so much.

"Keep looking at me like that, Pretty Girl, and I'll have to fuck that pretty mouth of yours," he tells me, and I snap my gaze back up to see the cocky as all get out grin splitting his lips wide.

Deciding that I need to gain the upper hand in this dickfest, I sashay up to him, running my hand down his exposed chest and pressing myself closer to his hot body. Running my hand back up, I grasp his furry ear as I lean in, placing my lips against his actual ear.

"Maybe I'll grab these whilst I ride *your* pretty mouth."

His hand comes up to my side, squeezing tightly, and he takes in a deep breath.

"Fuck, baby. Now I'm gonna go out there with a boner that'll be fucking easy to spot. Why don't you take that beautiful ass of yours over to Jax and give him a matching one? They'll see him a mile off with that monster standing to attention."

I shout a laugh as the man in question tells Loki to fuck off, then pulls me away from Loki's touch, wrapping a hand around the front of my throat and pulling me in for a searing kiss. I wrap my arms around his neck, pulling him close—or as close as my pregnancy will allow anyway—and give as good as I get, kissing him stupid until we break apart, panting. I lift a corner of my lips, my eyes flicking down between us.

"Done," I say, loud enough that Loki hears and chuckles. Jax's own lips lift in an almost smile at my comment.

"Give the others a good luck kiss, baby," he orders me, and I raise a brow in a semblance of protest, but we both know that I'm going to do it regardless.

Loki grabs me anyway, and I laugh into his kiss when I hear one of the

Seals make a comment about 'that kid's smuggling an anaconda in his pants.' Loki swallows my amusement, pulling me closer with a hand on the back of my neck as he deepens the kiss and makes my knees go all weak.

"Good luck," I manage to breathe out, shivering when I feel someone at my back, pressing me into Loki. Kai's fresh scent washes over me as he kisses my neck, his hands on my waist turning me around.

Ever so gently, he places his lips on my now swollen ones, teasing me with his light kisses and swipes of his tongue in moves that I know he's used on my pussy before, leaving me begging for more. Like he has all the time in the world, he deepens the kiss, everything around me disappearing beneath his touch. He ends the kiss just as gently, pulling away, and I open my eyes to stare into his amber ones, full of warmth and heat as they flick down my body.

I shiver and have to bite my lip to stop the moan that wants to escape as the feeling of the plug rushes over me, my inner walls clenching around it. Kai gives me a rare smirk.

"Wife," Ash calls, disrupting our moment, and I hear the Navy guys behind us splutter and whisper. Rolling my eyes at Ash's blatant attempt to shock them, and his Daddy Dom need to claim me, I saunter over to where he stands a few steps away.

Tilting my head to look up at him, I see the mischief glinting in his grey eyes.

"Yes, husband?" I ask, my tone laced with fake sweetness as I give him a brilliant smile, batting my lashes up at him.

"Were you planning on wishing me good luck too?" he questions, standing there, arms folded across his broad chest.

"As you asked so nicely," I sass back, pulling his arms open as I lean into him as if I'm about to kiss his lips.

Coming within touching distance, I bypass his lush mouth and instead dip down to his neck, dropping my mouth to it and beginning to suck. A deep, surprised groan sounds above me as I keep sucking, and his hands alight on my hips, clenching tightly. I can feel a hardness growing between us, which leaves me grinning against his neck.

"Fuck, Princess," he breathes in a rasp. "I'm going to come in my pants if you keep that up."

Deciding that as funny as that may be, I want him to come inside me or all over me later so I release my grip, beaming when I see the large hickey on the side of his neck, visible for all to see even through the black ink that covers him to his jawline.

"Good luck," I tell him, my tongue darting out to trace my moist lower lip at the dark fire which burns in his steel eyes.

"Where's Willow?" he asks instead of responding to my challenge, and my phone vibrates at that exact moment.

"Why?" I question, lifting it out of my pocket and looking at the screen. It's a message from the girl in question, apologising about not being able to make it today due to horrible period cramps.

"She's unwell," I tell him, glancing back up, having worked out that he'd organised her to keep me company whilst they played. His mouth draws into a straight line. "I'll be fine, Ash. Go have fun, and I'll watch you get your arses kicked from the viewing platform."

I point to the stairs that lead to a large lounge-like area and bar where people can watch the game below in the woods.

Ash just smirks at my taunt, his eyes promising retribution for that little slight. I hope it's in the form of his hand on my arse, but I guess I'll have to wait and see.

We all turn and head in the direction of the large doors that lead outside to where the game will take place. The Seals head that way too, and we end up walking next to one who gives Ash and I a curious look.

"So she's your wife?" he asks, clearly letting his curiosity get the better of him.

"Yes," Ash replies, giving the man a cursory look, his fingers linked with mine as we walk across the warehouse.

"But you let her kiss your friends?" the Seal continues, and I have to give him some credit for having the balls to ask. There's no judgement in his tone, just curiosity. Before Ash can answer, I do.

"Didn't your mummy ever tell you that sharing is caring, soldier?" I ask with a grin, and his jaw drops as my guys snigger. After a moment, he roars with laughter, the others all following suit, clearly having heard our conversation.

"Touché," he replies, still grinning as they start to head out and my boys pause at the door.

"Go," I tell them, letting go of Ash's hand and giving them each a shove.

With a final look and goodbye kisses from each of them, they do as I say, and a pang of disappointment hits me at not being able to join them.

# CHAPTER TWENTY-ONE

LILLY

Giving myself a mental shake and pulling my big girl panties up, I walk towards the stairs and bar area, consoling myself with the thought of all the fried food that I plan to order and my latest read just waiting on my kindle app.

After ordering at the bar, impressed by the setup even though I'm the only one currently occupying the space aside from the guy behind the bar, I settle into a soft, worn, leather sofa that faces a wall of windows which overlook the battleground. Music fills the space, *Dancer in the Dark* by Chase Atlantic giving the room an eighties feel. I smile and give my Knights a small wave when they look up and spot me, then they turn back to each other and put their heads together, clearly planning their strategy.

The ground is wooded with many areas open but also plenty of obstacles as well as hiding places. From my vantage point, my view is unobstructed, and I look to the right, spotting the Seals in a similar position to my guys, heads bent and obviously planning their strategy as well.

A loud horn blares, making me jump and then chuckle to myself at being a scaredy-cat. I watch the game, my book forgotten as I trace Ash, Loki, Kai, and Jax as they split up and start stalking towards the area that the Seals were in.

Their opponents stick together in teams of two, and my heart begins to race at the idea that it's two Seals to one Knight.

"Don't worry, daughter darling," a voice that haunts my nightmares whispers behind me as hands alight either side of my neck. "We trained them well."

I freeze as he strokes my pulse points, chuckling as he no doubt feels my frantic heartbeat, my body turning arctic cold. The black claws of panic scratch at the edges of my vision, and I can't move, can't fucking breathe, as Julian Vanderbilt continues to caress me from behind. Bile rises in my throat when I realise that his groin is level with my head, the rapidly increasing hardness of his erection pressing into the back of my skull.

I no longer see the bright sky outside, or my guys playing paintball below me as my vision swims, the badass bitch who shot my fake uncle gone as terror fills me. I don't know why Julian makes me feel this way, what sway he has over me, but I can't fight him, my head screaming at me to do something, anything, but my body just freezes further. It's like my subconscious recognises the predator within him, the danger that he possesses, and thinks that if I only stay still and quiet, he'll go away.

"Are you okay, miss?" a concerned voice asks, snapping me out of my panic enough to take in a deep breath, sweet air filling my empty lungs once more. Julian's hands tighten on my neck.

"Y–yes," I manage to stammer out. The young guy, the one I ordered from at the bar, flicks his gaze up to Julian, then back down to me.

"If you need anything else, I'll be right over there. Okay?" he questions, his eyes trying to give me a message that I appreciate but just can't respond to. Not verbally anyway. I dart a look behind him to my guys below, then look back at him, hoping that he may get the message to somehow get my guys up here.

"Thank you," I reply softly.

"That'll be all," Julian says over the top of me, his voice hard and cold. One of his hands leaves my neck, and I breathe slightly easier. His hand appears over the top of my head, a folded wad of notes held between his fingers. "My daughter and I would like some privacy."

The young man's eyes widen, looking at Julian's outstretched hand and then back down to me. He must see the sheer terror in mine because he hesitates a moment.

"Now," Julian snaps out, and the boy visibly flinches, his hand shooting out and grabbing the notes. He scurries away after that, and trembles take over my body when I hear the guy's steps echoing down the metal stairs. "Alone at last, *darling*."

I hear the slight creak of his leather shoes as he crouches behind me, seconds before his breath whispers against my ear, and I can't stop the shudder of revulsion that I feel with his nearness.

"Did you enjoy your little visit back home?" he murmurs in my ear, his fingers playing with the neckline of my dress. "I must say, you seemed to enjoy the nights when Adrian joined you, thrashing under his touch like the wanton whore your mother was."

My lips wobble, and a hot tear burns a path down my cheek at his words. It's all I can do not to vomit all over the floor, knowing that he witnessed my abuse and knows what happened more than I do. But I hold it in, not wanting to give him the satisfaction of a reaction. I bite my lower lip, tasting copper. He growls, his nails digging into the flesh just under my neckline, and I whimper, inwardly cursing the sound of weakness as it falls from my lips.

"It's a shame that he didn't have sound on the feed, but I still gripped my cock as I watched you shatter around his fingers, darling—"

"Father!"

Relief floods me as I turn at the sound of my husband's voice, his tone sharp and cutting as he strides across the room, his face full of rage. Julian gets up from his crouch unhurried, his fingers leaving one last caress that lingers on my skin like an acid burn.

"Son," he replies, with no hint of shame or anger in his tone at being interrupted accosting his son's wife. "I came to tell you about the board meeting next week."

"And you needed to tell me in person?" Ash replies, coming to a stop right in front of me and crouching down.

His steel-coloured eyes lock with mine, dismissing Julian completely as he takes in my trembling state. One hand still holds his paintball gun, and the other reaches out and grasps my cheek, his thumb brushing away the wetness there. His eyes narrow, the vein on his neck bulging, and he looks back up at Julian with murder in his eyes.

"Email me the details, and I'll make sure we are there," he states coldly, quickly looking back down to me and dismissing his father once again. That must really piss Julian off, and I almost smile at the thought, then remember what Julian said, and my head dips, heat burning my cheeks as tears fill my eyes. "Anything else?" I hear Ash ask.

"I've said all that needed to be said," Julian states back, and I know that his words are aimed at me, his words hitting their target as I want to curl into a little ball and break down. Vaguely, I hear Julian's footsteps as he walks away, the sound getting quieter when he gets further away from us.

More footsteps rush towards us moments later, and I tense up, only to relax when Loki speaks.

"Why the fuck was your father here?" he asks. "Lilly?"

"What happened, darling?" Kai questions, and I flinch, a sob tearing from my throat at that nickname. It's tainted now. I can only associate it with that vile man.

"Don't call me that," I mumble quietly, my voice thick and muffled. I lift my head and stare directly into amber eyes full of worry and concern. "Never call me that again."

"I–I'm sorry, love," he replies, hurt flashing in his eyes, his hand reaching out and stroking the cheek that Ash isn't still cupping.

"What. The. Fuck. Did. He. Do?" Jax snarls, each word bitten out like he's struggling to contain his rage, and my gaze finds his eyes flashing blue, his neck thickly corded, and his hands clenching and unclenching around his gun as if he's considering using it on Julian.

"Take me home, Jax," I plead, tears rushing to my eyes, and Jax doesn't hesitate, throwing his gun at Loki and pushing the others aside to pick me up. Wrapping my arms around his neck, I bury my face into it, shutting my eyes as sobs threaten to overwhelm me.

Jax holds me steady as he strides down the steps, his boots loud on the metal. I hear the others following behind us and then Ash's voice.

"Thank you for coming to get me," he says, and I look over Jax's shoulder to see the young guy from earlier looking after me with concern.

"She looked like she needed help," I catch him saying just before Jax walks out of the door and into the bright sunshine.

The warmth of its rays doesn't touch me, shivers wracking my body as we head towards Jax's truck. Without missing a beat, or letting me go, Jax gets the keys from somewhere and tosses them to Kai, the truck unlocking with a click.

Loki opens the door, and Jax doesn't even attempt to pry me off as he somehow manoeuvres us into the vehicle, keeping me on his lap as he settles into the seat. I nuzzle back into his neck, my shivers getting worse, and I try to take some of his warmth into me.

"She's in shock," I hear him rumble against me. "Grab a can of Nos from my bag, Loki," Jax continues, and I hear the rustle and slide of a zipper from next to me. The sound of a ring pull is next, followed by the hiss of a fizzy drink.

"Here you go, baby," Loki coos, and I lift my head enough to see him holding out an orange can, with the word 'NOS' on the side. "Drink some of this."

He holds it to my lips, which is a good thing as my hand is shaking too much to even think of holding it without the drink spilling all over us. Tilting it ever so slightly, I part my lips as fizzy, sweet mango fills my mouth. Swallowing slowly, I drink, pulling away when I've had enough. I do feel better, and my shaking has quietened down to a slight tremble now.

"Good girl," Jax soothes, his hand stroking down my back as I snuggle back into him, letting his scent of warm lemon mixed with fresh sweat calm me further. My eyelids droop, the adrenaline leaving my body exhausted, and Jax's touch and the motion of the car soothing me to sleep as I give into the darkness, welcoming it like an old friend.

# CHAPTER TWENTY-TWO

LILLY

I wake up as Jax carries me into our dorm, and for a moment, I just relish being held in his strong arms, his sweet, lemony scent washing over me in a comforting whisper. Ice fills my veins as the memory of what happened today at the paintballing centre rushes over me.

"I can walk, Jax," I tell him softly, placing my hand on his pec. His heart thuds underneath my touch, and there's tension in his muscles as his arms tighten around me. "Please."

He heaves a sigh but gently lets my legs down until I'm standing on my own two feet.

"What did he say to you, Princess?" Ash asks, standing in front of me, his tone gentle and not the demand that I expected to hear from him. Kai and Loki are on either side of him, all with matching looks of concern on their faces, eyebrows drawn and foreheads wrinkled.

Shame heats my cheeks. My skin feels too tight, and my hands are clammy as I wrap my arms around myself in a tight hug, stepping away from Jax, his hands falling from my waist where they had come to rest.

"I need a shower," I tell them, swallowing hard and unable to meet any of them in the eye.

"What did he tell you, Pretty Girl?" Loki asks, and he takes a step towards me.

Tears blur my vision, and a lump forms in my throat that's so big I don't know how to swallow past it. How can I tell them that I came, that I climaxed over Adrian's fingers? That my body enjoyed his intrusion, even if my mind was absent?

I shrink further into myself, my head dropping to my chest as the wetness overspills and traces down my cheeks.

"Adrian—" I begin, clearing my throat and feeling the vibrations as my body trembles. "Julian told me that I orgasmed for Adrian. That I came all over his fingers, a–and that he watched it all. M–masturbated over the footage."

There's a ringing in my ears, and lights dance in front of my eyes as the words leave my lips. Warmth is at my back suddenly, the lemon scent of Jax mixing with the spicy ginger of Ash at my front, followed by Kai's fresh, woodsy musk on one side and Loki's vanilla-cocoa perfume on the other. They surround me, grounding me and comforting me with their presence, lending me their strength.

A hand grasps my chin, bringing my teary gaze up to meet swirling, grey eyes.

"You have nothing to be ashamed of, my love," Ash tells me, his voice as fierce as I've ever heard it. "We do not blame you for your body's reactions."

A sob tears through my chest, more tears flowing at his words. He knew my deepest fear, that they would somehow reject me for this. Stupid, really, as I know our bond is stronger than that. I turn my head to the side as fingers trace over Ash's touch. Loki's emerald gaze is full of fire and conviction.

"You are not to blame, beautiful," he tells me, and another breath catches in my throat as I realise that he's talking from experience. His time with Clarissa and what she did evident in his assurance.

More fingers turn my face to the other side, Kai's kind, amber eyes full of pain and hurt for what I've been through.

"It was not your fault," he whispers, and another sob rips through me, this shared trauma we have cutting me to the quick.

Large hands wrap around my throat from behind, tilting my head a little so that I am looking, once again, at Ash as Jax murmurs in my ear.

"We will never stop loving you, Baby Girl," Jax tells me, his fingers grazing my pulse point. "That dead man cunt does not own any part of you. Julian does not own any part of you. We do. We own all of you, just like you own all of us, and that will never change, precious."

I shiver as one hand leaves my throat, tracing a path to the zip at the back of my dress.

"And you're going to give each of us an orgasm to prove that, aren't you, Baby Girl?" His voice is louder this time, and I see Ash raise a brow while feeling Kai and Loki stiffening either side of me.

A whimper passes my suddenly dry lips, my shame transferring to raging desire. Jax clearly realising that I need to get rid of this taint that Adrian and Julian have left behind.

"Yes," I whisper, my hands coming up to the zip in Ash's devil onesie and pulling it down as Jax pulls down my own zipper. Ash keeps one eyebrow arched, but he doesn't stop me, letting me push the garment off his muscled arms and revealing his inked-up torso. Gods, this man is too beautiful for words, all dark swirls of ink and hard lines.

My dress hits the floor, breaths hissing out of them as they see my teal, lace bralette. It doesn't match my knickers, which are the rainbow and unicorn patterned one they saw earlier, but I'm beyond caring right now as three sets of hands caress my sides, rounded stomach, and enlarged breasts.

"Have I told you how fucking hot I find you being pregnant is?" Jax growls in my ear, hot palms stroking over my bump. I groan, my eyelids fluttering as Kai and Loki hook a finger each in my knickers and draw them down.

"Eyes on me, wife," Ash commands in a thick voice, and I obey, shivering as his heated gaze runs all over my body. "Good girl," he praises, taking a step closer and pressing our naked bodies together, he must have taken off the onesie and his boots whilst I was distracted. His hand comes up into my hair, and he angles my head upwards.

Another moan leaves my lips to tickle his as he slants a gentle kiss over them, feathering his lips teasingly over mine until I'm mewling like a fucking cat, desperate for more.

"Please..." I beg, my own hand clinging onto his inked arms, my nails digging into his skin.

"Please what, Princess?" he asks just as Kai places a kiss to one shoulder, Loki to the other, and Jax nibbles and sucks my neck.

"Please make me come," I ask, my voice a breathy moan. "Please bury yourselves so deep inside me that I forget my own name."

Four groans fill the air, my words making them as desperate as I am as they all step even closer, their hot bodies a fever against mine.

"Upstairs, my room," Ash orders, picking me up under my thighs and pulling me from the others, who all snarl and growl like animals.

"That fucking plug is still there," Loki says with a drawn-out moan.

My arse clenches as Ash carries me, and I feel it, having somehow forgotten its presence.

"She'll be more than ready for us then," I hear Kai respond as I look over Ash's shoulder to see them all stripping out of their own onesies, dicks hard and bobbing as they undress, and what a fucking sight it is.

My pulse skyrockets when Ash kicks his door open, striding over to his bed and dropping me down on my back with a bounce. Before I can utter a sound, he's covering my body with his and sliding inside me in one hard thrust. I scream, the burn delicious as he pulls out almost all the way and pounds back inside my tight channel, his piercing rubbing along my inner walls, jolting the plug and sending tingling waves of euphoria all over my body.

"Fuck, Ash."

"I want your first orgasm before they get up here, Princess," he grits out, thrusting hard and fast, barely pausing between. "And you will give it to me."

One palm holds my hip in place, the other encircling my throat and squeezing as he fucks me so hard the whole bed shakes. The feel of him inside me, the movement of his hips brutal and snapping against my body, and the plug still lodged in my arse has me screaming and clawing as stars blind me and I come so hard my legs shake uncontrollably.

I peel open my closed lids when his pace slows, but he's still fully erect inside me, letting me know that he didn't come. Not yet.

"Good girl," he purrs, nuzzling the side of my face and peppering my jawline with soft kisses.

"You gonna share now, Vanderbilt?" a drawl comes from near the door, and I peer around Ash to see the others waiting, Loki's arms crossed over his naked chest. *Drip* by Asiahn begins to play, courtesy of Loki's playlist obsession no doubt, the sensual sound making my inner walls clench around Ash.

A surprised squeak leaves me as Ash switches our position so that I'm on top, his cock still buried deep inside me.

"Have at it," he lazily replies to my trickster, his hands on my hips and guiding me to move, both of us groaning at the new angle.

I love this position with him, he hardly ever lets me go on top, his need for control in the bedroom is no less than in his life. I tell him with my eyes how grateful I am that he's given me dominance, knowing that he understands my current need is greater than his. His own expression softens, his palm cupping my face and bringing me down into a kiss that sets my soul alight. A kiss that tells me he will always give me what I need, without question, and without needing to be told or asked.

A body warms my back, a large hand skating down my skin in a tender caress. My eyes go wide as a lubed-up finger pushes inside my already filled pussy, alongside Ash's hard length.

"Shhhh, baby," Jax soothes when I whimper and squirm, pumping his finger and leaving me gasping.

Ash distracts me with his soft lips once more, and I lose myself in his kiss, gasping into his mouth when another finger enters me. Ash groans, his hips taking over my movements with shallow thrusts. One hand tangles in my hair, the other coming between us to rub and tease my clit, making my hips buck at the extra sensation.

"Such a good fucking girl," Jax praises, adding another of his thick digits, and I make a sound in my throat that would be embarrassing if I gave a shit. But right now, I have no more fucks to give as Jax finger fucks me and Ash cock fucks me from underneath, his finger dancing over my clit.

A sound of protest leaves my throat when Jax withdraws his finger, and my eyes almost bug out of my head as he replaces them with the head of his monster dick.

"You can take him," Ash assures me through clenched teeth, his fingers finding my clit and rubbing circles around it. "Just relax, Princess."

I try to do as he says, relaxing under his expert touch as he plays with my swollen bud, Jax slipping in another inch.

"So fucking tight," he groans, his hands gripping my hips tight enough to bruise.

"Fuuuck," Ash curses when Jax keeps pushing. I whimper as the burn of being stretched by them both threatens to overwhelm me.

"Lilly," Kai's soft voice calls from the side, and I look over, gasping when I see Loki on his knees, Kai's hard dick in his mouth as Kai guides him with a firm grip in his auburn tresses, their bodies turned to the side to give me the perfect view.

Wetness floods my core, letting Jax slip all the way in, and I cry out at having both men inside me whilst I watch my other lover give head to Kai.

"Shit, Baby Girl," Jax groans, Ash cursing again as they give me a minute to get used to them. "I can feel the plug inside you too."

My eyes threaten to roll at the reminder, and I gasp when Kai forces Loki to take him deeper, Loki's fingers digging into Kai's arse.

"Shit, I can feel her fluttering around us just watching you two," Ash grits out, his finger still rubbing and playing with my clit, driving me crazy.

"Please," I ask, my voice full of desperate need. "Please, fuck me," I beg them, needing to feel them move inside me, even though I'm not completely convinced that they won't tear me in two.

They don't question me, don't ask for clarification, and settle into a rhythm of thrusting inside me that soon has me mindless with pleasure. I can't think, can barely breathe, and just feel as they fucking destroy any intelligence I may possess with their hard cocks and gripping hands.

"You feel incredible stretched over both our dicks," Ash grits out, and I open heavy-lidded eyes to see sweat glistening all over his inked skin, dripping down the side of his face.

"So perfect, baby," Jax murmurs behind me, his hand snaking up the column of my throat to wrap around just under my chin. "And you're gonna come for me like a good little girl, aren't you?"

I whimper as his grip around my windpipe tightens, making it harder to breathe.

"Yes, sir," I croak out, my voice barely above a breathy whisper as his hand tightens further, and his hips move faster.

Ash puts more pressure on my clit, moving his finger in a way that has my eyes rolling.

"Now, baby," Jax commands in a strained tone. "Come all over our dicks right. Fucking. Now."

I'm helpless to disobey, my body following his order as I explode, a silent scream leaving my mouth as I bask and writhe between them both. Fire races across my body, my nerve endings tingling and fizzing like a live wire is brushing across my body as I keep coming. I drag them under with me with animalistic roars, both thrusting to the hilt as they pulse inside of me, filling me up with their seed and prolonging my own release until I'm crying for it to stop. Begging for a reprieve.

I droop over Ash's chest, my rounded stomach making me arch my back a little, both of us panting and groaning when Jax slides out and flops beside us, also breathing hard. The bed shifts behind me, hands stroking down my body, and I feel the tug of the plug being pulled out of my arse, leaving me hissing into Ash's neck.

Moments later, the tip of a hard, pierced cock pushes against my rosebud, and I moan long and low as it slides in with ease.

"God, I love this fucking ass, Pretty Girl," Loki moans as he pushes all the way in, his teeth nipping my shoulder.

Ash's arms are wrapped around my slick body, holding me for Loki who wastes no time in finding his rhythm and fucking my arse with firm strokes. Exquisite pleasure rolls across my skin from inside me, and it's all I can do not to pass the fuck out with how good it feels.

"Loki," I whimper, the tingles returning as Ash begins to harden inside my pussy. "Ash..."

"Do you like it when I fuck you over your husband, baby?" Loki asks in a husky voice, grunting when Ash begins to move his hips too, both of them filling me up with their hard members.

"Yes, God, yes, I fucking love having your cock buried inside me," I reply, my nails digging into Ash's large shoulders as the intensity of what they are doing to my body overwhelms me.

"I love it when you talk dirty, baby," Loki growls out, picking up the pace, the sound of his hips slapping my arse loud in the room.

I become lost to the sensations once more, the push and pull as they take me to the edge and demand that I jump, their movements becoming frenzied as they chase their own releases.

"Fuck, baby," Loki breathes against my ear, stilling deep inside me as he climaxes. Ash pauses, but I hardly notice as I fall into oblivion with Loki, my whole body trembling with the force of my orgasm. The world stops moving, the planets aligning as waves of pleasure roll over me, dragging me under a sea of bliss and drowning me in ecstasy.

I groan as Loki pulls out, only to be replaced by another solid shaft pressing against my used hole.

"I c–can't," I plead, my voice hoarse and stuttering as Kai ignores me and continues to invade my arsehole.

"You can and you will, Pet," Kai tells me firmly, thrusting all the way in with a hiss. "You still owe me an orgasm."

Ash cups the side of my face in a tender gesture, and I look into his beautiful, grey eyes which are full of love and lust, his cheeks flushed and his hair stuck to his sweat-slicked forehead.

"You can give us one more can't you, Princess?" he asks, and I find myself agreeing with a slow nod just as Kai starts to pull out. "Good girl, I knew you could. You're our perfect treasure."

Holy fucking hotness, Ash praising me does all the things to my body, and when he starts moving too, I relax into their possession and let myself go under once more. Ash continues to hold my face, demanding I keep my eyes on his as they fuck me.

"Ash–fuck–Kai—" I babble incoherently, the intensity in my dark Knight's gaze undoing me just as sure as the movements of his hips. His other hand is gripping my hip, yet I feel fingers wiggle between us to play with my clit, and I look away for a second to see Loki's arm disappearing between our bodies.

"Eyes back on me, wife," Ash demands, and I do as he says, holding his gaze as they work to build me up once more.

I feel a large palm wrap around my throat, and I don't need to look to see that Jax is the owner.

"Just once more, angel," he tells me, his thumb caressing my racing pulse. "Come all over Kai and Ash, Baby Girl. Show them who owns that pussy and ass."

At Jax's dirty words, I explode, tears springing to my eyes when my orgasm hits me like a fucking sledgehammer. I can feel myself clamping around the guys, demanding that they join me in the abyss as my body tries to milk them. Their growls and rumbles, combined with the sudden stillness, tells me that they indeed followed me over the edge.

I feel weightless, my whole body liquifying as I give myself over to the exhaustion that only incredible sex can bring. We lie together, tangled in a heap of limbs, and the last thought to float through my mind before sleep takes me under is that Jax was right.

My Knights own me, body and soul, and no one can take that away from me.

# CHAPTER TWENTY-THREE

LILLY

The next week is finals week and passes by in a blur of frantic revision and nervous, frenetic energy. Apparently—and luckily for me—Highgate holds its exams later in the year than most, some shit to do with giving its bright, young students the best possible start in life. I guess it worked out for me as I didn't actually miss my finals, so at least I have a chance to pass.

I've no idea how well I'll do, or if I even stand a hope in hell of passing any of them. When I mention this to the guys one evening, Ash just gives me a mildly condescending look and calmly declares that I don't need to worry about failing, as I won't. When I jokingly state that he can't just buy me a high school diploma, his answer, without missing a beat is, "Why not?"

With the week finally over, we spend the weekend lazing around the dorm and just relaxing before the graduation ceremony the following week. It's Sunday evening now and we are watching Marvel on the huge TV, Ash on one side of me and Kai on the other as we snuggle while eating hot, buttered popcorn, homemade of course.

Ash's phone dings with a text, and I watch as he picks it up off the arm of the sofa before he frowns as he reads the message, his lips set in a grim line.

"What's up?" I ask, not able to see the screen but shifting so that I'm sitting up straighter and facing him. Someone pauses the film as Kai keeps a hand on one thigh, Ash still holding the other. His grey eyes lift up to me, and the set of his brow tells me that he's not happy with the content of the message.

"There's a Black Knight board meeting on Monday morning, first thing," he begins, still looking at me intently. I shake my head slightly, holding his gaze.

"And?"

"And my dad requires your presence, Princess. As the majority shareholder."

My jaw loosens, a hot flush creeping over my skin like ants crawling across my body.

"She's not fucking going anywhere near him!" Jax growls from across the room, and I look away from Ash to see Jax sat bolt upright, his lips flattened and his huge arm muscles flexing, which in any other situation would have me drooling.

"I know she can't go. I just don't know what his game is," Ash answers, and my gaze swings back to him as he grips my thigh tighter.

"He likely just wants to fuck with us," Loki adds, and I look over to see him sitting forward. "We can just say that she's sick or something."

My spine stiffens, eyes narrowing as they continue to discuss the subject as if I'm not in the room. Warmth coats my back as Kai leans closer to me, sensing my tension.

"Enough!" I yell, all conversation halting, and three sets of eyes swing my way. "For fuck sake, you talk about me as if I'm some weak and feeble female who needs coddling, and I'm fucking done!"

I get up—Kai and Ash letting me go—and begin to pace in front of them, the red of my ire colouring my vision. I pause in my steps, taking a deep breath and closing my eyes as I try to formulate in my mind what it is I want to say.

"I've been controlled my entire life, not trusted to make my own decisions, even though I wasn't given all the facts in order to make sensible ones," I tell them, my eyes still closed as I unburden my mind. "Even coming here was Adrian pushing me more than my own free choice. The first thing I truly ever decided for myself, was loving you all." I open my eyes then, looking at them, and my forehead creases as I look into each of their faces. Jax has his fists clenched, his gaze on the floor as his jaw works. Loki looks poised to leap up and wrap me in his warm embrace. Kai gives me a pained smile, an apology in his amber depths, even though he remained quiet before. I look at Ash last, his face an unreadable mask, his shoulders tense as I catch his eye. "Don't take my control from me too. I couldn't bear it."

"Shit, Princess," he grunts out, standing up and stepping up to me until I have to tilt my head to look at him. *Tall fuckwallop*. He lowers his head down, pressing his forehead to mine and tangling his fingers in my hair. My lids drift shut once more at his touch. "I'm an asshole, and I swear I will never leave you out like that again."

My throat goes thick, and I have to swallow hard.

"I know it came from a place of concern, Ash, but I need to be in charge of my own destiny," I tell him softly, my lips almost brushing his.

"What would you like to do, Lilly?" Kai asks, and I tilt my head to look over at him, giving him a grateful smile.

"I want to go," I reply in a firm voice, and I feel Ash heave a sigh against me.

"Fine, wife," he relents, straightening up, and I give him a wide grin as I glance up at him. His own lips twitch. "But you will not leave my fucking side, do you hear?"

"Yes, sir," I tease, and his fingers tighten in my hair as a low growl escapes him.

"I mean it. One of us is to be with you at all times," he insists, and I just can't help myself and roll my eyes. His grip on my tresses becomes punishing, and god if it doesn't make me wet between my thighs.

"I think my wife needs a lesson in obedience, boys," he states with a devilish grin that has my knickers dampening to soaking point and my thighs clenching.

---

## JAX

*I don't fucking like this,* I think as we all pile into the elevator at Black Knight HQ, a modern glass building as cold and unfeeling as the fucking cunts who run the crooked company. I catch a glimpse of my reflection in the mirrored walls, large arms crossed, forming a barrier as I feel the walls that I have to erect whenever I have anything to do with these bastards slam into place.

I see Lilly move, reaching for my forearm as she goes on tiptoes clearly intending to whisper something in my ear. I lean down, not unfolding my arms so that she can reach, and the warmth of her palm on my bare skin lights a fire under it. God, she's so fucking tiny, even with the sexy swell of her belly.

"Just imagine how amazing it would be to fuck in this lift, seeing my naked body from all angles as you pound into me from behind," she whispers in that sweet voice of hers.

*Fuck. Me.*

Just like that the walls come crashing down under a wave of lust that threatens to buckle my knees. Blowing out a low, steady breath, I straighten back up, ignoring the massive semi-chub I'm now supporting in my slacks. We all have to dress smartly for these bastards. I watch with a single raised brow as she faces the front, holding my stern gaze and giving me a wink and a fucking devastating, secret smile.

Great. I'm now going to walk into that boardroom with a raging hard-on.

"You alright, man?" Loki asks from my other side, and I just nod, not trusting myself not to slam my palm on the emergency stop button if I repeat what our naughty, little pixie just whispered in my ear. Jesus, Loki is just as likely to push that button as I am if he knew.

All too soon, the elevator comes to a stop, the doors opening with a ding to reveal a white, impersonal foyer. God, I hate this fucking place. It's so cold and sterile, but worse than that, it's all a fucking lie. The pure, clean look is just a cover up for the dark and depraved nature of the demons that run this company. It's a veneer covering up all the rot, the sweet, sickly air freshener trying to disguise the stench of decay.

I step out with my brothers in arms, all of us slipping into a formation that surrounds and protects our woman.

"Ah, boys." A tall, leggy blonde stalks towards us on black stilettos, the look in her blue eyes predatory as she rakes her gaze over each of us before settling on Ash. "How wonderful to see you. It's been too long," she purrs, running a hand down Ash's arm.

"Do you make a habit of touching what doesn't belong to you?" I hear

Lilly ask in a tone that would freeze your balls off, and see Michelle pause and her smile falter.

"Excuse me?" she asks, looking as Lilly steps between us and wraps her hands around Ash's other arm, tugging him away from the other woman's grip.

"I asked, do you always touch other women's husbands and lovers?" Lilly replies, her voice light but sharp, and my cock twitches in my slacks at the possessive note in her tone.

"I–um—" Michelle stutters, her cheeks flushing as she's called out.

"Sorry, Mrs Vanderbilt. I will never touch what belongs to you again," Lilly prompts, face expectant, and I have to cover a laugh with a cough, Loki copying me as we gaze upon our Queen.

"S–sorry, Mrs. Vanderbilt. It won't happen again," Michelle responds, dropping her head and sinking into herself.

"Good," Lilly states. "Oh, and just so we are crystal fucking clear, all these men belong to me."

Michelle's wide eyes fly up for a moment then drops back down.

"Of course," she says quietly, clearing her throat and nodding her head. "This way, please."

She takes off down a corridor, and we follow after her, Ash keeping a tight hold on Lilly's arm which is still wrapped around his.

"That was so fucking hot, wife," he murmurs, loud enough for us to catch what he says. "I'm so hard for you right now."

"Welcome to the fucking club," I grumble, and Loki gives a bark of laughter, coming up on Lilly's other side and linking arms with her.

"You can piss on me any time, Pretty Girl," he states, and I see Michelle stumble in front of us as she reaches a pair of grey double doors.

We pause, and Kai steps up behind Lilly, bending down to whisper in her ear, this time just us to hear.

"I like being claimed by you, Lilly Vanderbilt." I hear her gasp as he presses his hips into her lower back, clearly feeling his hardness too. At least I won't be the only one walking in there with a stiffy.

Michelle opens the doors, and we step into a light boardroom that has floor-to-ceiling windows on the wall opposite us, giving us a view of the town below and the mountains beyond.

I glance around the huge table, noting my cunt of a father, Julian Vanderbilt, Chad Thorn, and Stephen Matthews all seated and staring at us. It takes a huge effort not to curl my lip or let my fists fly at their smug fucking faces. I know they were the reason Lilly was taken, and have no doubt that they were all involved or at least aware.

Taking a deep inhale, I try to calm the rage that's threatening to overspill. It's then that I notice another figure, a man of similar age to our parents, his hair and eyes dark and his tailored suit clearly expensive.

"Boys," Julian greets, a lying smile on his lips. His grey eyes take us all in, pausing on Lilly, and his grin widens. A pounding starts in my ears, and I can feel my lips pulling back as I step closer to her. "Lilly, darling."

He doesn't get up, and it's a good fucking thing, as I don't doubt that I wouldn't be the only one to do him harm if he came near her again. Pictures of having him at my mercy while I take my blowtorch to his eyeballs for daring to even look at her like that flit through my mind, and I know that my snarl turns to a feral grin. He sees it too when he looks back at me, his face paling ever so slightly at the promise in my eyes.

*Oh yeah, fucker, I'm coming for you.*

Movement interrupts our stare off, and I see the dark stranger get up and move towards us. He stops in front of our group, in front of Lilly, and she lays a hand on my arm when I make a move to step in front of her.

"Mrs Vanderbilt," he says, and I'm surprised by his cultured British accent. "A pleasure to finally meet you. I knew your mother, and I must say you are the spitting image of her."

"You knew my mum?" Lilly asks, the hand that is still resting on my forearm frozen.

"Yes, I met her not long after she arrived in London and began working at Grey's. She was captivating when she danced, even more so when her pregnancy began to show." He looks down at Lilly's rounded stomach then, but not in a leering way. More like a fatherly way, his face soft and wistful.

"Mr Black?" Lilly asks with a gasp, and it suddenly clicks into place. This is the man who has the second biggest stakeholder claim in Black Knight Corporation. I look at the other guys to see matching looks of interest on their faces, though Ash still has a hard jaw and a possessive grip around Lilly's waist.

"Now that this little reunion is done with," Julian interrupts in an annoyed tone, and again images of committing violence against Ash's father pop into my head. "Shall we start the meeting?"

Glaring at him and the rest of the scum that sit at the oval table, we take our seats opposite them, Mr Black resuming his chair at what might be considered the head of the table.

“Right, let’s get started, gentleman and lady,” Julian begins, and I really don’t like the way his eyes keep raking over Lilly. It makes my hackles rise, my shoulders vibrating with tension. “Shall we begin with our plans for our heirs to take on more responsibility?”

# CHAPTER TWENTY-FOUR

LILLY

*What a fucking waste of time!*

That meeting wasn't about the boys taking on more responsibility. Julian and the others may have tried to present it in that way, but they were giving the guys crumbs, nothing more than what you might get a work placement student to do. *Fucking joke.*

And any suggestion I made was shot down straight away, and I was treated like the silly, little woman who didn't know how the big men ran things. *Fucking cockwombling knobheads.*

It was interesting the way Mr Black sat back and took it all in, then made a few suggestions that I could see Julian didn't want to consider but had to because they were the best thing for the business. Like expanding the software development arm of the company by looking at recent graduates from top Ivy League colleges.

He also put forward a proposal that Black Knight Corp start to use a company based in the city of London called Cavendish Brothers' Investments as our wealth managers, taking over how we invest our profits. It's run by two brothers, one of whom is the Marquis of Bath no less, and apparently, since they took it over from their parents several years ago, the company has made billions for its clients across the globe.

I could tell that Julian hated taking anyone else's suggestions on board, but the gleam in his eyes when Mr Black talked about the money to be made told me that he did take the recommendation seriously. When we all voted, it was a unanimous affirmative in favour of hiring the brothers.

The meeting dragged on after that, and most of what they were saying went completely over my head. I'm just not used to business speak, and I fucking hated feeling so stupid and lost. I had to keep suppressing yawns by the time it came to a close, and I barely managed to hold back a sigh of relief when all business was concluded and we were finally allowed to go.

Ash kept me close the whole way back to the car, Mr Black giving us a warm goodbye before stepping into his own waiting vehicle. I wondered about him, having a very vague recollection of Mum talking about her biggest fan. She never seemed to think he was a sleeze like some of the others could be. In fact, I do remember that he would scare off anyone who made her even the slightest bit uncomfortable when she was performing.

I'm too tired to ponder much more as we drive back, and soon am lulled to sleep, resting against Ash's chest with Loki on my other side as the guys talk quietly. I wake up when we arrive back at Highgate, the sun casting the old building in a beautiful, mid-afternoon glow.

"I need a shower," I declare, my muscles aching a little after the long drive and needing to wash off Julian's lecherous gaze. Leaving the boys to do whatever they feel like, I make my way to the bathroom and strip off the blouse and stretchy, cotton jersey, navy skirt I'd worn in a bid to look professional. I fucking hated it, the lack of colour and boring maternity clothes making me feel frumpy and unlike myself.

I leave them in a disgusted pile on the tiles, stepping into the shower, and groaning at the wonderful heat of the water cascading down my body. Looking down, I sigh as I find that my toes are completely obscured by my rounded stomach. My baby gives a little 'fuck you, bitch' kick, and I huff out a laugh.

"Sassy womb monster," I murmur, reaching for the shower gel and deciding to use Kai's fresh, woodsy-scented one today.

*Collide* by Justine Skye and Tyga starts to play over the bluetooth speakers, and my body begins to move to the sensual beat as I soap myself up, turning when I hear the snick of the bathroom door.

Giving my dark Knight a sultry smirk through the glass door of the shower and needing to feel sexy and see the heat in his grey eyes, I continue to rub my hands up and down my soap-slicked body as I move, revelling in the way his eyes stare at me hungrily.

I dance facing him before stepping back into the running water, and letting it cascade over my body and tease my peaked nipples. My smile grows wide as I watch him snap, striding up to the shower and stepping in fully clothed in sweats and a T-shirt.

"Do you know how fucking hard I was when I walked into that meeting earlier, Princess?" Ash drawls, voice low and like another sensation caressing my now sensitised skin.

"Oh really?" I reply, giving him wide, innocent eyes as I continue to move to the beat. He stares at me, water soaking through his shirt and letting me see all of his inked up muscles, my breath catching at his masculine beauty. He doesn't speak, just waits, staring at me with a ravenous hunger and building the tension until I feel like I might break this time.

With a movement that I should have seen coming but didn't, my back is hitting the shower wall and Ash is dropping to his knees in front of me, gazing up at me, his black hair plastered to his stunning face.

"I'm going to make you as hot as you made me," he whispers, moving his face closer to my aching pussy. His fingers skirt up my thighs, both hands grasping my hips, and he huffs a breath against my wet folds. "As desperate for my cock inside you as I was to fill up this delicious cunt when you claimed me as yours in front of that secretary." I groan at his dirty talk, knowing that he will make good on his promise and I'll be a wreck by the time he's through.

Using my hips, he guides me towards the other end of the cubicle, still on his knees as we move away from the spray.

"Turn around, hands on the bench," he orders, and I do as he says, placing my palms flat on the marble bench seat, excitement making my skin itch. "Fucking perfect."

Without another word, I feel his tongue lapping my slit from clit to opening, and I groan loud and low, my fingers flexing on the smooth surface of the marble.

"Ash," I breathe out, the expert movements of his tongue causing flutters in my lower belly and sparks to fly across my skin.

He destroys me with his tongue, and I go fucking wild when he starts to circle my puckered hole with it, pushing two fingers into my wet heat as he laps at my tight hole. He works me into a frenzy, his fingers and tongue obliterating me until my limbs shake and I can barely hold myself up.

"Come for me, Princess," he demands, reaching round and pinching my clit with his other hand so fucking hard I combust, screaming my release as I break apart. The noise of the shower becomes dull as I go blind and deaf all at once with the strength of my climax, my body convulsing around his still pumping fingers.

He gives me no break, and the next thing I know, he's pushing his hard pierced cock inside my still pulsing cunt, his fingers gripping my hips in a firm hold as he fights against my clamping inner walls.

"Fucking hell, Princess," he grits out, his voice tight and strained. I almost come again from the sound, knowing how much I affect him is the strongest aphrodisiac.

He starts bucking his hips hard and fast, just how I love it, and I'm soon tumbling towards a second orgasm, my pussy walls vice-like around him. Heat suffuses my limbs, and I have just enough brain cells left to squeeze my inner walls tighter.

"Come with me, husband," I demand, and he groans his sexy as fuck sound that shivers down my spine and pushes me closer towards bliss.

Thrusting hard once, twice, and a third and final time, he comes with a roar, his fingers digging into my hips hard enough to bruise, the bite of pain making me see sunshine and fucking rainbows as I scream for him. My whole body lights up like I'm the personification of electricity, my limbs twitching with the strength of my orgasm.

He pauses, buried deep inside me as we stay there and just breathe, the shower still running and steam filling the bathroom as we soak in each other.

Without pulling out, he bends over me and kisses my spine, wrapping his arms around me and standing us up so that my back is to his chest. I whimper when he slips out, and he chuckles in a self-satisfied, manly way.

"Don't worry, wife," he rumbles in my ear as he walks us backwards under the spray of the still hot shower. "After we wash, I'll get you all dirty again," he tells me, letting go with one hand as the other reaches for the soap, his this time, and brings it in front of us to squeeze a dollop into his other hand. "And again," he murmurs as he soaps up my breasts. "And again." My rounded stomach gets attention this time. "And again." His hand dips between my legs, and I can already feel the need burning in my core.

*Jesus, sex addict much?*

I mean, can you really blame a girl when she's surrounded by four, hot as fuck guys who all want to fill her up with their cocks?

# CHAPTER TWENTY-FIVE

LILLY

We get two days to chill out after that shitshow and spend it wrapped up together, listening to music and enjoying each other's bodies, making up for lost time.

The night before graduation comes all too soon, and the guys are all called away for Black Knight business. It leaves my stomach in knots, as they don't know if they're being summoned to deal with a competitor or just some more training.

"It'll be alright, sweetheart," Kai assures me, pulling me close as the others head out the door after kissing me goodbye.

"I hate this," I whisper into his chest, gripping his T-shirt in my fingers. "I hate that you have to keep doing this."

"I know, my love," he murmurs into my hair. "But it won't be for long. The summer hunting trip is coming up, and after that things will be different."

His words don't reassure me though, knowing that the plan to deal with their parents and Kai's uncle will be bloody and potentially dangerous. I pull back, my forehead creased, and stare deeply into his warm, amber eyes.

"Just, stay safe tonight. Keep each other safe."

"Always, love," he replies, placing a soft, parting kiss on my lips before leaving and locking up behind him. I'm reminded of Ash's stern words to not open the door for anyone as I stare after them, feeling a little bereft.

Trying to shake off my trepidation for the guys, I head into the bathroom and start to run myself a bubble bath. I'll grab my kindle and continue reading about those poor souls who are trapped in an insane asylum, loving each other despite all of the fuckery going on around them.

Surprisingly, the evening passes by quickly, mostly due to getting absorbed by my current read. I get up from the sofa where I was snuggled in one of Jax's huge T-shirts, intending to head to bed when a knock at the door to the dorm sounds, and I freeze, my heart pounding as I glare at it. My phone dings with an incoming message at that moment, making me jump out of my fucking skin, and I look to see a message from Ryan, Mum's old boyfriend and the closest thing to a father I had growing up.

**Ryan: Surprise!**

I look to the door again, and then back at the message. Hesitantly, I step towards the front door, peeking through the peephole, and then squeal in delight at what awaits me on the other side.

Unlocking the bolts, I throw the door open, a wide grin on my face.

"Ryan!" I shriek, throwing my arms around him and eliciting an oomph sound from his chest.

"Hello, Little One," he chuckles, steering us back into the dorm and softly closing the door behind us. I pull back to look up into his smiling face, noting a slight tension in the lines around his eyes. He lets out a sigh, his smile faltering before saying, "Apparently, I've come to kill you."

---

## ASH

Fucking bastards keeping us out all night and then making us attend a debrief so that we have to head straight to the graduation ceremony. I guess we should count ourselves lucky that it wasn't a mark this time, just some intel gathering and boring-ass surveillance.

I look at my phone again as we wait in our seats for the ceremony to start, biting my lip when I see that Lilly still hasn't replied to the message I'd sent this morning letting her know that we would meet her here.

"Still no reply?" Loki asks from my left, and I turn to see his tired eyes full of the same concern that I have, his cap and gown an artful mess. *Douche.*

"No," I reply curtly, glancing back down at the blank screen that's taunting me, like the empty space to my right where my wife should be sitting. I don't fucking like this, and my stomach churns with a feeling of unease.

The principal starts to speak, some shit about us being the best and brightest, but only half my attention is on him, my mind wondering where the fuck Lilly is and if something is wrong. He's halfway through his speech when my phone buzzes in my hand, and I look down with a small smile on my lips which freezes as I see it's a picture message from my cunt of a father. I glance back to find him in the rows reserved for parents behind us, and he looks at me with a cruel smirk on his lips that leaves me sick.

I look down at my phone, opening the message, and at first, my eyes don't make sense of the image before them, the color red causing me to blink a few times to try and focus. When I do, I wish that I hadn't, as my whole body goes ice-cold and a buzzing sounds in my ears.

It's Lilly, my beautiful Lilly, sprawled out on the floor and covered in so much crimson I can't tell where the wounds are. I can see her glassy eyes, sightless, her body in a pool of blood that surrounds her.

"No—" a strangled whisper escapes my lips before I can clamp them shut. My vision blurs, and for the first time, I understand why Luc found solace in the choice to no longer live. For there can be no life without her. Pain unlike any I've ever experienced wracks my body and threatens to double me over, only sheer determination and years of training hold me upright in my seat as I continue to stare at my worst nightmare come to life.

"Ash?" Loki whispers next to me, and I clutch my phone to my chest as I turn to face him, my movements sluggish as if my body is underwater. "Was that from Lilly?"

"N–no," I instantly reply, my mind racing as I try to work out how to tell him, how to tell them all that we've just lost our light. Lost our soul and reason for living. Before I can utter another word, our names are being called for us to go up and collect our diplomas.

Taking the reprieve, I practically leap to my feet, earning a curious look from Loki as I follow behind him to the stage. I have no recollection of what happens next, and I'm suddenly striding from the area outside where the ceremony is being held, rolled up diploma in one hand and my phone in the other as I round the corner of the building and lean against it, breathing hard.

Footsteps pound after me, and I look up through a haze of tears to see the concerned faces of my brothers by choice surrounding me.

"Ash, what's happened?" Kai demands, his voice unusually hard as his eyes take me in.

I open my mouth to speak, then close it, shaking my head as the tears fall from my eyes, scalding a path down my cheeks, and I close my eyes, willing the devil to strike me down so that I no longer have to breathe the air that she doesn't.

"Ash?" Loki asks, his voice trembling. "Ash, man, you're scaring us."

Opening my eyes, tears glistening on my lashes, I look at each of them and prepare to break their hearts and rip out their souls.

"Lilly's—" I start, my chin wobbling, and I have to pause to take a deep inhale, unable to look any of them in the eye when I voice the truth that is breaking me apart. "Lilly's dead."

Silence.

"That's not fucking funny!" I hear Loki yell, and I turn to watch him shaking as he clenches his fists.

"Fuck, I wish it was—" I start, feeling sick as I drop the diploma and bring up my phone, unlocking the screen to be faced with that fucking picture again. I don't say anything else, just turn the phone around and show them.

Silence.

Then I watch them all shatter, and I'm too broken myself to help them.

Loki drops to his knees, his face deathly white as tears stream down his cheeks and he shakes his head. "No, no, no, no," he whispers over and over again.

Kai shuts down, his whole face blank as he studies the image on the screen with an air of detachment that would piss me off if I didn't know that he's retreated inside himself.

Jax explodes, turning his back and walking over to a huge stone urn full of plants. With the pained roar of a wounded animal, he lifts it up and throws it onto the stones lining the path, the urn cracking and spilling soil and brightly-coloured blooms all over the path.

I watch them all, my brothers in arms, and I don't know how to fix this.

Even the great Asher Vanderbilt can't fight death once the grim reaper has taken a soul, and I fucking hate myself for it.

My phone buzzes once more, and it's pure instinct that makes me turn the device so that I can see the screen. My eyes narrow as I see it's a message from Enzo this time, and I unlock the phone to read it properly.

**Enzo: Need you all at the gym. Now.**

I look up to see Kai has his phone out too, presumably reading the same message from Enzo as he sent it to us all. He glances up a moment later and catches my eye. A glint of something enters his gaze, pushing through the deadened look that has taken over his features.

Looking down at Loki, I see that he, too, has his phone out, and I flinch when he raises his head and his agony-filled eyes find mine.

"We need to go," I tell him, reaching out my free hand to help pull him to his feet. It's a testament to his loyalty to me that he places his hand in mine and lets me help him to stand. I give his hand a squeeze, then look up to see Jax panting and staring at us with dark eyes. "Enzo needs us," I tell him, and although his brow dips slightly, he knows like I do that Enzo wouldn't call us if it weren't an emergency. Doesn't mean that I'm not torn between answering his summons, or going over to my father and stabbing him in the fucking eye where he sits back at the ceremony.

We head to the parking lot, stripping out of our gowns and caps just as we hear cheers from where the rest of our class is celebrating graduation. We leave our caps and gowns on the path, graduation doesn't matter, nothing does anymore. Silently, we all climb into Jax's truck, Jax having wordlessly handed over his keys to me when I held out my hand. He's in even less of a position to drive than I am.

The drive to Enzo's gym is also silent, just the sound of Jax's heaving breaths and Loki's occasional sniffle accompanying us as we weave through the mountain road towards town. My mind races, and I can hear Kai tapping away at his tablet, likely trying to discover the origins of the photo, desperate for anything to tell us that it's fake. That it's not real. That she is still alive.

It should worry me that I don't remember how we got here as we pull up outside the gym, the inside unusually dark for the middle of the day, but I just can't find it in me to give a fuck, so we get out and make our way up the steps to the front doors. A memory of bringing Lilly here hits me with such force that I actually stagger, Kai reaching out to steady me as Jax goes to push the doors open.

They don't budge, but a moment later they open a sliver as Tom, our driver and Enzo's brother-in-law, peeks out, and upon seeing it's us, opens the door further.

"Hurry," he instructs in a low voice, shutting and locking the door as soon as we step inside. His strange behaviour breaks through the fog of my grief, and I step forward to ask him what the fuck is going on when someone throws themself at me.

My body starts to react before my mind has a chance to catch up, my fist lifting, but before I can do my attacker any harm, I catch a voice that forty-five minutes ago I thought I'd never hear again.

"I'm so fucking sorry, Ash," Lilly says through her sobs, her slender arms wrapped around me so tightly I can hardly breathe. "It was the only way, but, fuck... I'm so, so sorry."

I grab hold of her biceps and yank her back, staring into her beautiful fucking face and watching the life shining in those stunning, hazel eyes. I can't speak, just drink her in as tears track down her cheeks.

"Fuck, Princess," I choke out, pulling her in close again and crushing her lips to mine in a desperate kiss. She kisses me back just as fiercely, my fingers digging into her arms as I try to inhale her into me.

She's suddenly torn away from me, and I snarl at whoever thought they could take her, only to come up short when I see that it's Loki, and he has fresh tears falling down his cheeks.

"You're not dead?" he asks, his voice full of wonder as he drinks her in just as I did moments ago.

"No, Loki," she replies with a sob. "I'm not dead."

"Thank fuck," he exhales, pulling her in for a kiss of his own. I watch them, enraptured and unable to take my eyes off her as I assure myself that this is no dream. That we didn't crash on the way over and this is not heaven.

She pulls away when Kai touches her shoulder, his own face full of so much emotion that it's hard to look at.

"I'm so sorry, Kai, my love," she whispers, turning to face him and stepping into his open arms. He brings her in close, wrapping his arms around her and taking in a deep inhale as his eyes close in ecstasy. I know that fucking feeling.

Pulling away just enough so that he can lower his lips to hers, they kiss, more tears falling down her cheeks as they embrace. The sweet kiss comes to an end as Kai places his forehead to hers.

"Shit, sweetheart," he murmurs, still holding her to him.

"I know," she replies, glancing away, and I see the moment she finds Jax, her whole body stiffening.

Stepping away from Kai, who reluctantly lets her go, she steps towards our silent brother who stands glaring with his arms crossed over his huge chest.

"Jax?" she questions, reaching out a hand and laying it on his forearm. "I'm so sorry, I can explain, love."

He grunts, opening his arms so suddenly that even I flinch. I take a step towards him, but stop when he just pulls her to him and encases her in his massive arms.

"It better be a good fucking explanation, Baby Girl," he grumbles. "My soul was broken when I saw that picture," he confesses, and I realise then just how much she's changed us all. Before she came into our lives, we could barely get Jax to talk to us, let alone tell us his darkest feelings.

"It is, I swear," she answers, looking up into his eyes. As if her lips are a magnet and he can't resist, he lowers his own and kisses her roughly, all of the worry and anger for what we have just been through spilling out into her mouth.

As the Queen that she is, she takes it, every last drop. Her kiss is an apology, an assurance that she's still here, and I can see it calm the beast within him until he almost slumps in her arms, his muscles relaxing as their kiss comes to a close.

"Come," she says, taking his hand as she steps out of his arms and looks at each of us, settling on me last. "Ryan is here and can explain everything."

# CHAPTER TWENTY-SIX

LILLY

I cast my eyes around the guys that surround me, my own Knights, all within touching distance. We're in Enzo's office, and I'm seated on the worn, leather sofa, sandwiched between Jax, who refuses to let go of my hand, and Ash, who has a possessive grip clamped tightly on my thigh. Loki and Kai are on the floor, refusing the chairs offered in order to sit at my feet, both with warm palms wrapped around my ankles, Loki's massaging and rubbing them, making it very hard to concentrate on what is being said.

"Julian put a hit out on Lilly," Ryan starts, no fucking build-up whatsoever, and I feel each of my guys stiffen.

"How did you find that out?" Ash asks, his voice laced with suspicion, and I cast him an annoyed look. *Surely he doesn't think that Ryan can't be trusted?* Although, I was wondering the same thing myself, and Ryan wanted everyone here before he explained. The man in question gives me what can only be a sheepish look, a blush staining his rugged cheeks.

"Being the bouncer at Grey's isn't my only occupation, just the one I have on paper," he tells me, and it takes a moment, but when it clicks, my eyes go wide and I sit forward suddenly.

"You're a fucking mercenary?!" I all but screech, and he winces but nods.

"Jesus. Since when?" He rubs the back of his neck and dips his head, looking away.

"Always, Little One," he says. "It's one of the reasons why your mother and I never got married."

"Well, shit," I huff out, feeling a twinge of guilt for always blaming Mum for not taking that step with him.

"How did you find out about the hit on Lilly?" Kai interjects, and all of their grips tighten on me. My heart thuds, a surge of pain in my chest flaring at the thought of receiving a picture of them lying broken and bleeding, and I grip Jax's hand back tightly.

"I'm one of the best at what I do, so I get the pick of jobs," Ryan tells Kai unabashedly. "As soon as I saw who the mark was I took the job, anonymously of course, and came straight here. The payout was high enough that I knew it would attract attention, so I needed to fulfil the terms as soon as possible."

We all sit in silence for a moment, processing what he's just told us. Julian wanted me dead, offered up a huge amount for someone to come and take my life. And the life of my unborn child, his grandchild for all that he knows. My hand comes up to caress my stomach, feeling my baby move inside me, and my breath hitches at the thought of how close he or she came to never having been born at all. Water fills my eyes, and a huge palm comes to cover my own. I look to the side to see Jax staring at me, his blue eyes full of a fierce fire.

"I will never let anything happen to you or our child," he vows in his gruff voice, and a tear escapes at the way he's claimed my baby as his own. I sniffle, clearing my throat and removing my hand from underneath Jax's to wipe the moisture off my cheek.

"What happens now?" I ask, turning to look at Ryan, then Enzo, and finally Tom. Enzo assured us that Tom will not breathe a word to Julian or any of the others on the board. Tom is loyal to his family, to Enzo, first, and the guys seemed happy with that.

"You stay dead," Ryan tells me, an apology in his eyes but his lips set in a grim line.

"I have a new identity for you, cara mia," Enzo states, stepping forward with a large, manilla envelope that he holds out to me. "Lilly Vanderbilt will be buried and no longer lives."

I take the package, opening it to find all the documents that I will need;

passport, birth certificate, driver's licence, medical documents, all in the name of Lilith Taylor.

"But you have to remain hidden for now, Little One," Ryan states, and I look up from the papers into his pleading eyes. "No one can know that you're alive. Not until Julian and the others have been dealt with. I assume you have a plan?" He turns to Ash as he says the last part.

Ash stiffens for a moment, then heaves a sigh.

"Yes."

"Care to share with the room?" Ryan asks, one brow raised and the corner of his lips tilted upwards, as though he finds Ash's distrust amusing. Ash waits for a beat more, eyes narrowed at the three men before us.

"Kai," he says, clearly giving Kai permission to divulge their plan. Kai sits up straighter, though doesn't remove his hand from my ankle.

"Every year we have to go on a late summer hunting trip with the rest of the board," Kai starts, pushing his glasses up the bridge of his nose in a cute as fuck gesture. "Well, with their fathers and my uncle," he clarifies. "It's in a cabin in the mountains, on private land, no neighbours." I lean forward, eager to hear the full plan. "We will drug their drinks on the first evening there, kill my uncle then frame the others, leaving prints on the weapon, shoe marks in the blood, and other forensic evidence that will point to them as murderers."

I sit there, and I'm stunned by my lack of horror at the casual way that Kai talked about murdering his uncle and setting up their fathers to take the fall. A grim sense of satisfaction fills me, and I think that my reaction should worry me, but it doesn't.

"Regardless of the forensic evidence, why would anyone believe that they wanted him dead?" Ryan asks, and my forehead crinkles when I consider his question.

"Kai is due to take over from his uncle, who only held his position until Kai came of age and graduated," Ash states and all eyes turn to him. "We've been laying a trail to show that his uncle is unhappy relinquishing his power and has been syphoning off more than his fair share from company profits."

"Plus leaking important confidential business information to leading competitors," Loki adds, and a small, tentative smile spreads on Ryan's face.

"Very thorough, boys," he praises, and I can see my guys perk up, chests pushing out at his approval. "How will you keep the suspicion off yourselves?"

"Easy, we drug ourselves too, with a smaller dose of course," Loki adds, and I can hear the devious smirk in his voice.

"And how are you going to stop them from hiding the body? Sweeping it all under the carpet?" Enzo asks, his Italian accent lending a beauty to his words that really shouldn't be there when plotting a murder and frame job.

"There's where you come in, coach," Jax rumbles from my side, and I turn to see a dark, wicked grin on his face that should scare me. Of course it doesn't, it just makes Her Vagisty sit up and fucking purr, the horny bitch.

Enzo just nods, so Kai continues.

"An anonymous tip-off from a lost hiker who heard all the screams and called the feds," Kai tells Enzo, who just nods again.

"And where will I be?" I question the room, holding my spine straight when they all swing their eyes to me.

"I have a cabin just over the state lines in Utah. No one knows about it, it's in a false name," Tom speaks for the first time, and I turn to look at him. He looks back at me with softness in his eyes, and not for the first time I wonder who I remind him of to make him look at me like that. "It's about a three-hour drive from here, so far enough away from everything."

My heart sinks, my stomach feeling hollow at the thought of being separated from my guys again.

"I hate having to be apart from you, Princess," Ash says in a low voice, his hand guiding my face to look at him. "But I think that this is the best plan to keep you safe. Julian needs to think that you're dead, otherwise, he'll keep gunning for you."

"I know," I murmur back, moisture filling my eyes once more, and I blink furiously to try and clear them away. "I just... I hate being without you all when I feel like I only just got you back." A hot tear falls then, and I can see the pain in Ash's eyes. The knowledge that just an hour or so ago he thought that he'd never see me again hurts something deep inside me.

"We'll be together soon, my love," he tells me, pulling me close so that our foreheads rest together, and I close my eyes as his warm palm cups my cheek, rubbing my tears away. "I swear it."

I let myself bask in his warmth, breathing in his ginger scent as if trying to memorise it for the time ahead without him.

"I don't want to be all alone," I confess after a few moments, pulling away and looking around the room, my chin wobbling.

"I've already messaged Rowan and Roman," Loki tells me, letting go of my ankle to come up on his knees and grasping my face in both of his hands. "They're coming with Mai. We just need to give them an address, and they'll be there."

More tears fall at that, at the relief that washes over me with his words. I'm glad that it'll be them, the twins keep my spirits up, and Mai was like the older sister I never had.

"We'll wait for nightfall, then head to the cabin," Ryan tells me, and I tear my gaze away from Loki's emerald ones to stare at the man who was like a father to me.

"Tonight?" I ask in a soft voice, and Ryan gives a heavy sigh, his mouth downturned.

"I'm sorry, Little One, but we need to get you out of here," he softly tells me, coming closer. My head moves up and down in a nod in Loki's grip, even as my soul feels like it's being torn into four pieces.

"Why don't you all go upstairs?" Enzo asks us, and I look over to him, frowning.

"Upstairs?" I question, and he gives me a small smile.

"I have a spare apartment above the gym, cara mia," he informs me, stepping towards us and handing Ash a key. "It's yours until you have to leave."

If I didn't feel like my heart was breaking, I'd blush. Enzo, Ryan, and Tom know what's likely to happen between the guys and I in his apartment, but I'm too heartsore to feel anything other than my own pain.

How can I bear to say goodbye after only having just gotten them back?

# CHAPTER TWENTY-SEVEN

LILLY

The door shuts quietly behind us, and I gaze around at the clean and neat apartment above the gym. It's a studio with a large bed in one corner, a small kitchen in another, and a living-dining space between. There's a door that I assume leads to a bathroom, and a bank of windows—blinds drawn—along the wall opposite the front door. The apartment can be accessed from the inside of the gym, and there's also a door that leads to a fire escape down the outside of the building.

Soft music starts to play, and I recognise the song as *Lifts* by Lia Marie Johnson. I close my eyes as one of the guys comes up behind me and sweeps my hair away from my neck, his hot breath tickling my skin before his soft lips place a gentle kiss there.

"Kai," I breathe out and sink into his arms that wrap around me, pulling me into his embrace, his fresh, woodsy scent enveloping me.

"When I saw that picture, sweetheart," he murmurs against my skin, and I tense up when I realise what picture he is talking about. The staged one of my death. "My world ended, and I wanted no part in a new world without you."

I melt back into him, fresh tears springing behind my closed lids as his arms move and he starts to unbutton the front of my shirtwaister maternity dress.

"Kai— I—" I stutter, lost for words at the raw pain of his and the rasp of his voice. A warmth in front of me has my eyes fluttering open to find Loki standing before me.

"I didn't want to believe it," my trickster Knight tells me, his own eyes glistening as he steps closer and helps Kai to push the dress from my shoulders. "I didn't want to believe that I might have to live in a world where you no longer breathed."

"Loki—" My voice catches on a sob, tears running freely down my cheeks as he dips his head, placing his lips above my trembling ones.

"But when I realised that it was really you downstairs, fuck, Pretty Girl. I thought I was gonna pass out," he confesses against my lips, closing the distance and kissing me so sweetly, so reverently, it's all I can do to not break down here and now in a sobbing mess.

I hated not being able to tell them, knowing that they would see that picture and assume the worst, but we needed believable reactions. We needed Julian to think that I was dead.

"Wait—" I pull back, my heart thudding as I turn to find Ash leaning against the back of the sofa, watching us with dark eyes. "Where does Julian think you are now?"

"He knows that we're here, blowing off some steam," Ash tells me, his arms crossed across his broad chest. He gives a small, devious smirk, his words not a lie, but I'm betting not the whole truth either.

"Doesn't he expect, I don't know, you guys to retaliate?"

Ash's smirk drops, his jaw clenching. "He thinks, because it's what we want him to think, that we are too well trained, too under his thumb and afraid of what he might do to us to seek revenge."

I slump a little, a slow breath leaving me at that confirmation of their safety. I don't even startle when I realise that Kai and Loki have stripped me naked, my clothes in a crumpled heap on the floor. Loki steps to one side, and Ash straightens up, stalking towards me with a predatory gleam in his silver eyes.

Two pairs of hands trace every curve, every dip and hollow of my body, and I'm shuddering under their touch alongside Ash's heated gaze.

"I finally understood why Luc wanted to die," Ash says, continuing the conversation Loki, Kai, and I were having, and I can't help the flinch, knowing that I would have felt the same if it had been one of them. "There's nothing without you, Princess," he confesses softly, stepping right up against me so that I can feel the heat of his body through his shirt against my skin. "I do not exist without you."

My face must crumple then as he reaches out and draws my mouth to his in a bruising kiss. He worships me with his lips and tongue, showing me how desolate he felt, how broken the news of my death made him. I kiss him back, letting him take everything that I have to give, an apology in the way that my tongue soothes his, my lips caressing him.

I jerk away as the door opens and shuts, turning my head to see Jax walking in with something in his hands. His brows are low, his jaw tight as he storms towards me. Ash steps aside to let Jax stand before me in all his vibrating ire. Taking in a sharp breath, I hold my ground as I look up at him, aware that I am the only one naked in the room.

"You know how I felt about that picture," he tells me gruffly, his eyes hard and his muscles corded. "I get why it had to be done that way, but I'm fucking furious at you, Baby Girl."

My eyes widen, and I open my mouth to say something, to argue with the twatwaffle, but he places a finger against my parted lips.

"I'm not going to kiss you now," he tells me, and my pulse picks up speed when he opens his other hand and I see coils of red cotton fabric. "Not until you've been punished for breaking all of our hearts."

My lips drag against his digit as they close, and I look up into his stormy gaze and see the pure, unadulterated need burning there. He can't do anything about what happened, knows it needed to happen that way, but needs to punish someone now to exorcise the rage that's running through his veins. I lick my lips, catching his finger in the process, and a shudder runs over his skin at the contact.

Wordlessly, I bring my hands in front of me, wrists together in offering. He waits a beat, then moves his finger away to grab the fabric and stretch it out until I see what it is.

"These are my wraps, Baby Girl," he tells me as he works to bind my wrists tightly together. "I haven't washed them since I last wore them, the blood from my split knuckles and my opponent is still on them."

My thighs clench, and I gasp as he pulls tight. I give an exploratory tug, but my wrists don't move. Deep chuckles sound around me, and I look up into Jax's eyes first to see the dark gleam of satisfaction there. Turning, I can see a similar expression on Ash and Loki's faces. Kai is still behind me, and I shiver to think of his amber eyes full of heat. He always likes me bound.

I jerk as a tug pulls me forward, and I turn my head to see Jax has the ends of the wraps in his grip and is pulling me towards the bed.

"Loki, on the bed," Jax orders, and my trickster Knight obeys, going ahead and pausing at the side of the bed. He holds my stare as he strips out of his clothes; a printed T-shirt and smart jeans that hug his body and hang criminally low.

My breath stutters out of me when he drops his clothes to the floor, standing there naked and hard, and my tongue darts out to lick my dry lips again at the sight of his pierced member standing to attention.

"Don't worry, Pretty Girl," he teases, reaching down and giving his dick a stroke, the pink tip glistening with precum that I'm desperate to lick up. "You can choke on my dick once Jax is finished with you."

I rub my thighs together once more, trying in vain to soothe the ache that's building in my core, but it's not what I need. I need them inside me to truly satisfy my craving.

Jax tugs the binds again as Loki climbs onto the bed, lying back and watching me with a need to match mine in his emerald eyes.

"Your turn, baby," Jax tells me, keeping hold of the end of the wraps and walking along the side of the bed to the metal-framed headboard. "Thighs either side of Loki, on your knees."

I do as instructed, my heart thudding and flutters filling my belly as I get into position, my bound hands on his chiselled abs.

"I'm liking the view, Pretty Girl," Loki compliments huskily, his hands coming up to frame my hips and his hips flexing slightly so that his hard length rubs against my folds, and we both groan at the zing of pleasure.

"Dick inside our girl, Loki," is Jax's next command, and my eyes widen as a smile tugs my lips upwards. This isn't seeming like a punishment so far.

"Yes, boss," Loki answers, lifting my hips up and then using one hand to line his head up with my already slick entrance.

The song switches to *Call Out My Name* by The Weekend just as Loki thrusts forward, seating himself to the hilt in one sharp move.

"Loki!" I cry out, the slight pain of his sudden invasion quickly overtaken by the pleasurable fullness of having him inside me.

Before Loki can move, Jax gives a tug on my binds and my arms jerk forward, Loki's grip moves up my body quickly so that I don't faceplant into his chest. My head snaps up to glare at Jax, but he just looks at me with a hard, unreadable expression on his handsome face as he keeps pulling, forcing me forward until I'm lying chest to chest with Loki, my breasts and round stomach pressed against him. Seemingly satisfied with the awkward way my arms are pulled above my head, I watch as he ties the ends of the red fabric to the headboard, effectively immobilising me.

I have some movement, my pregnant stomach preventing me from being squashed up against Loki completely, but it's minimal, and I can't help pulling against my bindings, testing them out. The bed dips behind me, and I arch my back when a large, warm palm caresses my arse lovingly.

"For forty-five minutes we believed that you were dead," Jax tells me in his rough voice, still stroking my backside. "But I'm feeling generous, so Ash, Kai, and I will each give you ten spanks." I gasp as his words register and feel the vibration as Loki huffs out a dark laugh beneath me. "And you're going to count them."

"And what about Loki?" I question, raising my head enough to look at the flamed-haired man beneath me. He gives me a devilish smile, his hands caressing my sides, coming around to cup my breasts and brushing his thumbs over my nipples, making my eyes roll.

"Oh, I'm here to make sure that it feels good, baby," he answers, punching his hips upwards and leaving me gasping. "I'm going to make you come again." Thrust. "And again." Thrust. "And again, until you beg me to stop," he informs me, leaning up to nibble at my lower lip. "And then I'm going to make you come some more."

My whole body shudders, goosebumps pebbling my skin as my nipples go rock fucking hard. *Death by orgasms is a fine way to go*. I open my mouth to say something along those lines when a sharp crack lands on my left arsecheek, making me yelp and Loki groan as my inner walls clench around him.

"One," Jax says, voice hard and unforgiving.

"O–one," I repeat, arching my back when Loki nibbles and sucks at my neck, his fingers rolling my peaked nipples and sending shocks of electricity across my body.

*Crack.*

"Two," I breathe out, moaning when Loki bucks his hips upwards, sinking deeper inside me.

*Crack.*

"T–three."

"Shit, she clenches around my dick like a fucking vise when you do that, brother," Loki grits out, one hand leaving my nipple to snake between us and find the engorged bundle of nerves between my legs.

Another hit lands at the exact moment that his fingers press down on it, and an orgasm rips through me with such force that I cry and buck, my nails digging into my palms as sparks shoot across my vision.

"What number was that, Baby Girl?" Jax asks, his voice strained and breathless.

"Uh...Four," I stutter out, my climax still zinging through me.

*Crack.*

"Fuck! F–five," I snarl, the mixture of pleasure that Loki's fingers, mouth, and dick are giving me mixing with the sharp stinging heat that's covering my arse.

My head rests on Loki's chest as smack after smack lands across my lower cheeks, my mouth counting the hits even as my brain becomes a fog of pleasure and pain.

Dimly, I register the bed dipping as Jax must get off and someone else gets on, and I open my bleary eyes to see Jax crouch at the side of the bed, his long arm reaching over and his blue eyes soft.

"Such a good fucking girl, baby," he croons, his hand stroking sweat-slicked hair from my face. "You did so well, Baby Girl."

*Crack.*

"E–eleven," I croak, twitching when a hand rubs the sore spot.

"That's it, sweetheart," Kai's melodic voice soothes from behind me, telling me that he's taken over my punishment. "Loki, our girl deserves another orgasm, don't you think so, Pet?"

"Yes, sir," Loki replies, his voice deep, and the rumble makes me shiver as Jax keeps stroking my face, his blue eyes boring into mine.

*Crack.*

Loki begins to rub my clit again, moving his hips so that every time he thrusts upward, Kai lands another blow on my glowing backside in a slightly different place to where Jax landed his hits. My eyes close as the pleasure builds to a crescendo, the tingle all over my body telling me that another climax is fast approaching.

"Open your eyes, Baby Girl," Jax commands, and I instinctually obey, immediately getting caught up in his piercing gaze. "Look at me while they make you come."

*Crack.*

Another few hits from above and thrusts from below and I'm screaming out my pleasure, tears filling my eyes at the intensity of my climax. Jax grips my hair and forces my eyes to remain on his as I shudder and writhe with Loki still buried deep inside me.

"Fuck, baby," Loki hisses, his fingers digging into my soft flesh as he holds me still. "Your pussy is trying to strangle my dick."

I can't answer him; I just pant, my lids heavy with post-orgasm bliss. The bed dips, and I groan as I realise that my punishment is not over yet.

"You going to scream for me too, Princess, when I bury my cock inside that tight asshole of yours?" Ash's deep voice crawls across my skin from behind. I shiver with the promise his words give, but he doesn't give me a chance to answer, landing a punishing blow to my already pulsing arse.

"T–t–twenty-one," I rasp, my throat dry from all of my cries.

"Here, sweetheart," Kai says from my other side, Jax letting me twist my head to see him holding out a bottle of water with a straw in it. "Drink."

Lifting my head as much as I can, I do as he says, the cold water a balm to my parched throat and mouth.

"Thank you," I say, placing my head back down on Loki's sweaty chest.

*Crack.*

"T–twenty-two," I say, my words stronger even though they still stutter out of me.

Ash doesn't take his time, landing blow after blow so quickly that I barely have time to count out loud. Loki also renews his efforts, and I'm soon screaming out another release as stars explode behind my closed lids and I strain against my binds as I come and come and come, just like Loki promised me I would.

Panting, I finally call out the final smack, and no sooner do the words leave my lips than a cold pack is being pressed to my throbbing cheeks. The instant relief it gives me has me sighing and crying in relief

I gasp as something cold and wet slicks down my crack, a finger massaging around my puckered hole, then slipping inside.

"Oh, god," I groan as the digit slowly pumps in and out, my hips gyrating with the movement, eliciting a moan from Loki below me.

The finger pulls out only to be replaced with the pierced tip of Ash's cock, and I suck in a sharp breath as he breaches the tight ring of muscle, pushing in until his hips meet my throbbing arsecheeks, the ice pack having been taken away.

"That's it, Princess," he gasps out, voice tight and strained as his fingers dig into my hips. "Take me all the way in that sweet ass of yours."

Incoherent noises leave my lips as he withdraws a little only to push back in, Loki alternating his thrusts from below until they are both pounding into me. I'm jerked upwards, a firm grip in my hair, and I open my eyes to find Jax kneeling, holding his cock to my lips, the tip shiny with precum.

"Open up, baby," he commands, and I do, taking his bulbous head into my mouth as Ash and Loki continue to fuck me.

Jax quickly takes over, thrusting all the way to the back of my throat and holding himself there until I can feel my lungs screaming for air.

"Damn, baby," he says with a grunt, pulling me off, and I gasp in sweet air. "Your mouth feels so fucking good."

"Care to share, big man?" Kai says from my other side, and Jax uses his grip in my hair to turn my head so that Kai's dick is in front of my face, all his piercings glinting in the low lights.

"Open up for him, baby," Jax orders, and once again I obey him, Kai's hand holding his dick as he guides it into my open mouth.

"Jesus, sweetheart," he exclaims as I suck and lather his hard member with my tongue, paying close attention to the piercings that run along the underside of his dick.

The song changes to *Into It* by Chase Atlantic, and Kai holds my throat as he glides his dick in and out of my slick mouth. Heat builds between my legs, Ash and Loki pumping in and out of me and Kai using my mouth is getting me so fucking slick that the wet sounds of our fucking can be heard alongside the sensual rise and fall of the song.

Jax grips my hair, turning me once again as he pulls me off of Kai and thrusts into the back of my throat with a vengeance. I relax into their combined embrace, letting them use me as our bodies move in a dance as old as time, my climax climbing as they build me up. I can feel them getting close too, their movements becoming frenzied and animalistic noises leaving their throats as they don't hold back and fuck me hard.

Loki is the first to break, slamming into me so hard that it pushes me over the edge once more, and a muffled cry sounds around Kai's cock as I come so hard I almost implode. Wetness slicks my inner thighs, the sound of Loki's continued thrusts obscene as my inner muscles clench around him and Ash in a stranglehold.

"Shit, Princess!" Ash yells, thrusting deep as he's dragged under, and I can feel him pulse into my arse as he holds me still and shoots his release deep inside me.

I'm still twitching as Kai pumps once, twice, and then pours his climax deep into my throat, forcing me to swallow every drop as his hands grip my jaw. Pain lances my skull as I'm ripped away, Jax slamming his dick into my mouth seconds before hot, salty cum coats my tongue, and I greedily swallow that too.

When his dick stops pulsing, he pulls out, and I collapse onto Loki, his softening dick still buried in my pussy as we all pant and gasp for air. After a time I feel my wrists being unbound, the ties loosening, and it's all I can do to flex my fingers as I lie in a blissful, exhausted heap on top of Loki.

I hiss as a cool gel is rubbed into my sore arsecheeks, realising that Ash must have withdrawn when I collapsed.

"How the fuck," I say, my voice fifty shades of husky, "am I meant to sit in a car for god knows how many hours it takes to get to Utah after that?"

Masculine guffaws and chuckles fill the room. *Fuckers.*

But, they are my fuckers, quite literally, and I press closer to Loki as my words sink in.

I think a better question is how am I going to survive without them for the next few weeks?

# CHAPTER TWENTY-EIGHT

LILLY

All too soon a knock on the door interrupts our post-orgasm bliss, and Ryan's deep voice tells me that we'll be leaving in twenty minutes.

As if on cue, *Lost Without You* by Freya Ridings starts to play, and tears spring to my eyes, the words of the song expressing exactly how I'm feeling at the thought of being separated from my Knights once again.

Silently, I get up and have a quick shower, Ash and Loki following me in and washing me so tenderly that the tears fall and mingle with the water that cascades over my skin.

Knowing that we don't have much time left, I step out of the shower to find Jax there with a towel, ready to dry me. Once he's finished, he leads me back into the main room where Kai waits with my clothes.

"We'll send the rest of your things as soon as we can," Kai murmurs softly to me as he helps me to get dressed, his touch lingering as if he, too, is dreading what's to come.

"How will you get them out?" I question in a quiet voice, finding Ash looking at me, eyebrows lowered.

"There'll be a funeral," he tells me, and I wince, freezing as I put my cardigan on.

"A–a funeral?"

"We have to go through with a burial," he tells me, moving closer and helping me into the garment. "I'm sorry, Princess, but we need to keep up with the pretense."

"I–I understand," I reply, and I do. I get that this has to look real, and if the look of sadness on each of my guy's faces is anything to go by, people will believe that I've died.

"It's time, Pretty Girl," Loki mumbles, reaching out and taking my hand in his. I look up to him, willing my face not to crack, and show him how much my heart feels like it's breaking. His pained expression tells me that I've failed, and he pulls me against him, wrapping his arms around me in a fierce hug. "I know, baby. I know." His voice breaks, and I can't stop the sob that rips free from my chest as my pain overwhelms me.

"It's only three weeks until the hunting trip," Kai adds, but his voice is flat like he's trying to convince himself that it won't feel like an eternity. "And here's a burner phone so we can keep in touch."

I lift my head from Loki's chest, my arm unwrapping from his torso as I reach out for the new iPhone that Kai is holding out for me.

"You ready, Lilly?" I hear Ryan ask from the other side of the door, and taking a deep breath, I step out of Loki's arms, wrapping our fingers together as I step towards the doorway.

We head down the stairs inside the gym, following Ryan's broad back as he leads us to a side exit that opens onto a dark alley that runs alongside the gym. It's night out, and the cool air soothes my hot face a little.

"I'll give you a minute to say your goodbyes, Little One," Ryan tells me, squeezing my arm and then going around to the driver's side of the car.

I've still got Loki's hand in a tight grip, and he pulls me into another crushing hug, squeezing me tightly. I don't care though, I need to feel him for the next few weeks so that I know I'm not back at that manor house in England, all alone and doubting the existence of my Knights.

"It's not goodbye," he whispers into my hair. "Just see you later, Pretty Girl."

He pulls back enough to dip his head and capture my lips with his own, and I taste the salt on his lips as he must do on mine, our sadness spilling down our cheeks in the summer moonlight. I cling to him as he tries to step away, but I don't want to be released, not now or ever.

"I fucking love you, Lilly," he says against my lips, giving me one last kiss before prising my arms from around him and stepping away.

"I fucking love you too, Loki," I choke back, a sob stuck in my throat as I watch his angelic features crease with despair.

Jax suddenly blocks my view, taking Loki's place and grabbing me by the back of my neck, pulling me into a soul-searing kiss. I grip his arms tightly, more tears tracing their hot path down my cheeks as I fall into his kiss. It's painful in its softness, in the way he teases my mouth and tongue, the touch of his own at odds with the way he grips me tightly, possessively.

I'm gasping when he pulls back just as suddenly as he grabbed me, looking into my eyes with his piercing blue ones.

"You are my fucking light, Baby Girl. My soul." He places my hand over his thumping heart. "My heart. I'll do whatever it takes to keep you, *both* of you, safe." His other palm caresses my stomach, our baby pushing against it and making him smile in that way that only Jax can.

"I love you, Jax," I tell him, watching that small smile brighten until it outshines the moon above us.

He places a gentle kiss on my forehead and then lets me go for Kai to take his place. My lips wobble, sheer determination the only thing keeping my knees from buckling under me.

Kai steps into me, so close that the heat from his clothed body spreads to mine, and I want nothing more than to bask in it. Both hands come up, palms cupping my cheeks as he brings our foreheads together.

"You are my freedom, sweetheart," he confesses softly, and I love the new nickname, something that only he calls me.

"And you are mine," I say back, closing the distance between our lips this time, desperate for one final taste.

We kiss as though it will release us from the tyranny that still holds us hostage, as though it will kill the monsters that lurk in the dark waiting to spill our blood and devour us.

"I love you," he whispers against my kiss-swollen lips, pulling away but keeping hold of my face for one final moment.

"I love you," I repeat back, swallowing hard when he lets go and steps away to stand back with Jax and Loki.

My darkest Knight, my husband, steps up to me next, and I hate the turmoil churning in his silver eyes.

"We will come for you soon, my love," he tells me, invading my personal space so that I crane my neck to look up at him and his fierce expression. "I swear on my cursed life that we will do what needs to be done, and then we can all finally be free to live."

He doesn't give me time to answer, to say a single damn thing before his lips are on mine and he's kissing the life out of me. It's a kiss that sends warriors into battle, that gives soldiers something to fight for, and I give freely, pouring all of my love and adoration for him into it.

We end the embrace softly, lingering for just another touch, another second more, trying to stave off the inevitable. He heaves a great sigh, like the weight of the world is on his shoulders.

"You are my everything, Lilly Vanderbilt," he says against my lips.

"You mean Lilith Taylor," I try to joke, but it falls a bit flat, and no one laughs, myself included.

"Regardless of your name, you are fucking mine, Lilly, and I am yours," he says vehemently, angling my head with his hand gripped under my chin so that I'm looking into his hypnotic, grey eyes. "We are fused and nothing can tear us apart. Not my father. Not the rest of the board. Not even the devil him-fucking-self."

Fresh tears sting my eyes and fall as I nod my head.

"I love you so much, Ash," I tell him, my own palms coming up to cup his stubbled cheeks.

"I love you too, Lilly."

The engine starts behind us, and the pain in the back of my throat intensifies as I try to swallow but can't. Taking a shuddering breath, I pull the last vestiges of strength I have and take a step away from Ash, then another, my hands falling away from him as his fall from me.

"I'll see you soon," I tell them all, indulging in one final look at my Knights, the moonlight casting them in its glow until they appear like vengeful gods, ready to wage war, all hard lines and corded muscles.

Turning around, I give them my back as I open the car door and get inside, wincing slightly as my sore arsecheeks hit the seat. But I welcome the pain, the reminder of my lovers, of the other parts of my soul that are waiting to be reunited with me.

I just hope that it's not too long before we can once again be in each other's embrace.

---

The drive to Utah is mostly silent. As much as I want to talk to Ryan, to find out more about his mercenary jobs, I just can't bring myself to make conversation. My soul aches so damn bad, like pieces are missing, and there's a heavy weight on my chest, as if I'll never be able to take a full breath again.

Ryan must sense my reluctance because he just puts some classical music on the radio and drives, leaving me to be lulled into a restless sleep full of broken hearts and dark shadows.

I wake as we pull up in front of a wooden cabin surrounded by forest, the predawn light fading from a deep purple to orange on the horizon behind it.

"Let's get you settled, Little One," Ryan suggests softly, switching the engine off and opening the door.

Taking a deep inhale, I follow, breathing in the fresh, damp air as I exit the vehicle. Looking up at the wooden structure, it reminds me of the hunting cabin that the guys took me to on Halloween, and I pause as I wonder if that's the cabin that they'll be going to in a few weeks. Seems fitting that the place we took revenge on Robert all those months ago will see justice served once more.

This, too, is double-storied, and as I walk inside, I notice that it has a much more homely feel, with cosy sofas covered in blankets facing a huge fireplace. Unlike the guys' cabin, there are no dead animals on the walls, which I am grateful for.

"Lilly, come look at this," Ryan's voice calls from the other end of the room, and I turn, gasping as I see that the entire wall is windows, letting the rising sun filter into the space.

Walking over to where Ryan stands by some open bi-folding doors, I can see there's a deck, and we have an uninterrupted view over the mountains and the valley below, all bathed in the beautiful dawn. Birds are singing, and tears spring to my eyes with the majesty of it all.

"There's always a new day, Little One," Ryan says softly from beside me, his big arm wrapping around my shoulders and pulling me into his side.

"Mum used to say that." I sniffle, breathing in his familiar scent and letting it comfort me, even as my heart fractures at being so far from my soulmates.

"She was a wise woman, your mum," he replies, his own voice a little thicker than usual.

I wrap my arm around his waist in a side hug, and we stay that way, watching the sunrise and letting its rays fill us with light, chasing away the darkness.

# CHAPTER TWENTY-NINE

LILLY

I sleep in late, waking up alone and bereft as I remember all that has happened in the last day or so. Ryan faking my death, those wonderful few hours in the apartment, the drive to the cabin.

My stomach growls just as the scent of bacon fills my nose, and I can hear low voices downstairs which confuses me until I remember who is coming to stay with me. With more energy than I thought I possessed, I throw back the covers and clamber out of bed, not stopping to cover my maternity vest and knickers as I rush from the room and down the wooden staircase.

"Mai!" I shout when I see her blonde hair at the dining table.

A huge smile splits her face as she stands up and hurries over to wrap me up in a tight hug.

"Lilly! It's so good to see you, girl," she tells me, laughing when my bump gets in the way. "Look at you!" She steps back and holds me at arm's length to admire my pretty big stomach. "You are positively glowing."

I blush, then shriek when twin blond heads poke around the French doors from the deck, wide grins on their faces.

"Roman! Rowan!"

I launch myself at them, both wrapping their arms around me in a hug.

"Jeez, pixie girl. You need to hold off on all those pies," Roman jokes, earning a poke from Mai.

"Fuck off," I tell him with a smile, all of us laughing when my stomach lets out a huge growl.

"Sounds like someone is hungry," Ryan says from the doorway, carrying two huge platters full of crispy bacon, fried eggs, and toast.

"Fuck, yes," I groan, practically attacking him in my bid to get to the deliciousness.

He chuckles as I pile my plate high, pouring myself a huge glass of tropical juice that was already on the table.

The others join us, filling their own plates, and we each take a seat, catching up on everything that has happened since we last saw each other.

"And I thought our lives were fucked up," Rowan comments, softening his words with a boyish smile.

"Yep, things are pretty messed up at the moment," I say, sighing as I set down my cutlery on my empty plate. I sit up straight, eyes focused on Ryan as I feel the colour drain from my face. "Shit, Ryan, my grandparents! They'll be devastated when they find out."

I'd told Ryan and Lexie about meeting Harold and Petunia last time we had a FaceTime call, and they were unsurprised to learn that Mum was using a fake identity.

"I'll pay them a visit when I get back home, explain the situation and the need for the current pretence," he assures me, reaching over and taking my hand in his, giving it a squeeze.

"Won't that put Lilly in danger?" Rowan asks, and warmth suffuses me at his concern.

"Her grandfather has ties with MI6, he knows how to keep a secret or two," Ryan explains, and I see both boys' brows raise, a grudging respect in their blue eyes.

"Right, Lilly," Mai says, turning to look at me. "I've bought some bits for you, the guys said you wouldn't have much, and I'd like to do some checks on baby, if that's okay?"

"Thanks," I reply, a lightness filling my soul at the thought that this isolation might not be all bad.

I have friends, am in an amazing location, and my guys are on the end of a phone. It could be worse.

---

That night I climb into bed, the mattress soft and the room cosy. I leave the curtains open; my room has a view over the valley below, and the sight is breathtaking as the dying rays of the sun kiss the land.

My burner phone buzzes next to me and reaching over, I smile wide as Ash's name appears on a FaceTime call. Swiping my finger across the screen, I answer.

"Ash!" I practically squeal, giggling when he winces slightly, but the smile on his face tells me that he doesn't mind my enthusiastic greeting.

*"Hello, Princess,"* his deep voice cascades over me, and I snuggle deeper into my pillows at the sound. *"How are you settling in?"*

"Mai and the twins are here," I tell him, launching into a description of our day spent unpacking all of the things Mai bought me, including some brightly-coloured fun maternity dresses and dungarees. Ash listens, an indulgent half smile across his lips as I talk. "How was your day?" I finally ask, and he heaves a great sigh.

*"We met with the funeral home,"* he tells me, bringing a glass of amber liquid to his lips and taking a deep swallow. *"Finalised arrangements."*

"Wait, do they have a...body?" I question, no longer quite as relaxed as I was when I answered the call. Another deep exhale passes his lips.

*"Yeah, some unknown Jane Doe."* He winces as he says it, and my own face scrunches at the thought of some poor girl taking my place.

"Make sure she gets the best," I say after a moment, and he looks up at me, his face full of wonder.

*"You really are too good for us, Princess,"* he says softly, and the need to be wrapped up in his arms is almost overwhelming. Searching for a distraction, I look behind him to see that he's not in the dorms.

"Where are you?"

A small smirk tilts his full lips.

*"I'm at my house, in the woods,"* he answers, moving to the side so that I can see the room he's in. It's dark, the only light from the setting sun filtering through the huge window. It's not a room that I recognise though. *"I wanted to play you something."*

My heart skips a beat, anticipation rushing through me in an electric wave. There's a bit of a wobble on the screen as he props the phone up, I assume on the lid of the piano, as he sits back down in front of it. I have to bite my lips to stop from making an excited noise as he cracks his fingers, looking at the camera with that sexy as fuck half smile that he only gives me.

*"Ready?"* he asks.

"Ready."

My mouth drops open when he begins to sing, his fingers playing *Love me Like you Do*, the Boyce Avenue acoustic version. I watch, enraptured as he sings for me, his voice husky and with an incredible range. His eyes are closed, his face bathed in the light of the dying sun, and tears fill my eyes at the raw emotion in his voice.

My pulse races, and I'm grateful that I'm lying down, as my knees are weak as fuck. I told him once that I loved this song, and I can't help feeling that he's learnt it just for me, pouring his soul into it and letting me know that he, too, understands the meaning of the lyrics. It's about an all-consuming love, love that defies the ages, and about the fact that you need to grasp it with both hands. It's our love, our journey.

By the time he's softly playing the final notes, hot tears are tracking down my cheeks, and I can't even blame the damn hormones. He pauses with his hands over the keys, then looks up, his own eyes glistening.

"A–Ash," I stutter out, no idea how to follow that up. How to convey to him all that I'm feeling right now.

*"I know, Princess. I know,"* he replies, his voice gruff. He clears his throat. *"Let me play some more while you go to sleep. You need to rest."*

"Yes, sir," I tease, snuggling down and grinning at his arched brow.

I try to keep my eyes open, try to watch him as he plays soothing classical music, but my body is exhausted, and I fall into the darkness with the sound of his sweet music comforting my soul.

# CHAPTER THIRTY

KAI

The three weeks since Lilly's 'death' drag and pass by in a blur all at once. The funeral happened a week after she arrived at the cabin in Utah, and we didn't have to fake the anguish at being parted from the love of our lives. We did have to hold back our anger at the fake sadness that Julian and the rest of the board—excluding Mr Black—showed, Jax visibly vibrating with the rage that flowed through his veins. I couldn't blame him, I, too, felt the need to maim and hurt, holding my darkness close. I'll get to unleash it soon. I just need to bide my time until then.

Something comes up at Black Knight Corp, the elders keeping it a secret from us, but the hunting trip gets postponed until late August. I'm not the only one worrying that it's closer to Lilly's due date than we'd like, only two weeks away in fact, but there's nothing we can do but wait, and comb through our plan to ensure that everything is perfect, every possibility accounted for.

Lilly's own disappointment is clear when we tell her, but like the Queen that she is, she accepts it for what it is and moves on. We are some lucky bastards to have found her.

Finally, the day of reckoning arrives, and we run through the plan one final time at Ash's house.

"Jax, you have the GHB?" Ash asks as we sit around his glass dining table, our packed bags by the door, *99* by Elliot Moss playing quietly in the background.

"Yep," Jax replies. He's withdrawn a little since Lilly went into hiding. Not as much as he was before her arrival, but he's not talking as much anymore, preferring his silence and only answering in single words.

"And you'll get it into their drinks this evening, with enough left over to give us each a mild dose?" Jax just nods this time. Ash sighs, noting Jax's silent affirmation with a head bob of his own. "Kai, are you ready?" He settles his steely gaze on me, and my senses heighten, a slight roiling in my stomach making me aware of my nerves.

"Yes," I answer, not elaborating. They've given me free rein over what I'm going to do to my uncle, the revenge that I'm going to carve into his skin. He gives me a tight nod.

"And I have the playlist," Loki adds, lightening the mood as Ash rolls his eyes, but there's a smile on his lips.

"Excellent," Ash deadpans, adding, "Enzo will come to help with cleaning ourselves up and take our clothes to be burned. But he'll be close the whole time in case we need him."

"Then we're all sorted," I state, each of us looking at the others with steel in our spines, jaws locked tight.

"One for all!" Loki cries, leaping to his feet and thrusting his hand into the centre of the table. I can't help the grin that splits my face, even as Ash gives a long, suffering sigh. Loki wiggles his hand, clearly growing impatient. I get up, placing my hand on top of his.

"All for one," I answer, my smile widening at Loki's beam of delight. He really is a ray of fucking sunshine sometimes. Ash sighs, copying my movement and putting his own palm on top of mine.

"All for one," he repeats in a bored tone, but the tilt of his lips shows his amusement.

"Come on, big guy," Loki cajoles Jax, waggling his eyebrows. "We need our fourth Musketeer."

Jax sits with his arms folded for another beat, then huffing, gets up, and thumps his hand hard on top of ours like a dick.

"Say it," Loki insists, and Jax holds his stare. A lesser man would wither under his intense scrutiny, but Loki holds his ground.

"All for fucking one," Jax rumbles, and Loki fist pumps with his free hand.

All for fucking one.

---

The irony of being back at the cabin we meted out justice to that scum, Robert, is not lost on any of us as we pull up in Jax's truck, parking at the end of the row of expensive SUVs.

"Let's get this shitshow started, shall we?" Ash asks, getting out of the passenger side, and we all follow him, grabbing our bags from the trunk and walking towards the front door.

It opens before we reach the bottom step, and my jaw aches as I grit my teeth at seeing Julian standing on the threshold. I did suggest that he is more deserving of death for all that he's put us through, but the guys wouldn't hear of it, saying that his punishment will be to watch as his world crumbles all while he rots in prison. My uncle on the other hand deserves a slow and painful death for what he did to me all those years ago.

It still rankles that we can't just kill them all and bathe in their blood as we watch the life flow from their eyes, but we have to be smarter and play the long game. Anyways, sometimes death is too kind, the lesser of a punishment.

"Boys," Julian beams as if he really doesn't know our hatred for him. He must though. Julian Vanderbilt may be many things, but stupid is not one of them. "Come on in."

He ushers us into the cabin, and I'm once again reminded that it's a place of dead things, the animal heads on the walls from previous kills reinforcing the impression that this is not a place for the living. Just as well given our plans for tonight.

"Son," Rafe addresses Jax, who grunts back. Neither goes to shake the others' hand, they just size each other up like male lions ready to do battle.

"Loki," Chad greets his son, stepping forward to give Loki a man hug, slapping him on the back. "You would have liked the fine piece of ass I had last night, big juicy tits and a tight cunt." Loki visibly shudders, passing it off with a laugh.

"I'm sure I would have, Dad," he replies, and I can see the cringe in his eyes, the skin around them tight.

"Kai," my uncle's voice sounds next to me, and I turn to face him, steeling my spine to face the monster of my childhood.

"Uncle," I respond. Like Jax and Rafe, there are no hugs or back slaps, just a wary recognition of a familial tie.

"Right," Julian's voice booms, taking centre stage as always. "Now that we're all here, let's have a bite to eat, and then we can do a spot of hunting before dinner."

"Let's kill some shit!" Chad cries, his tone excited, and the bloodlust already in his wide eyes.

Let's kill some shit indeed.

# CHAPTER THIRTY-ONE

LILLY

I wake up with a groan, a sharp pain tightening like a band across my stomach. It's so intense that all I can do is lie there and breathe, just like Mai has been getting me to practise for the past few weeks.

Once it passes, I get up and head to the bathroom, sitting on the toilet. It's when I wipe myself and notice the jelly-like, pink-tinged substance on the paper that I realise what is happening.

"Mai!" I yell, staring at what can only be my plug, or show as Mai kept calling it. Its presence tells me that the pain I experienced this morning might be my labour starting.

The door is flung open, and I look up with wide eyes as Mai rushes into the room, sleep tousled and still in her cotton PJs. I thrust the stained toilet paper in her direction, and she blinks, then straightens up and looks wide awake when she realises what it is.

"No need to panic, Lilly," she tells me in a soothing tone, stepping closer and around my still-held-out hand. "This doesn't necessarily mean that your labour will start today. Let's get you cleaned up and put some food in you, okay?"

"O–okay," I reply, finally putting the paper down the toilet and flushing whilst Mai starts up the shower.

Getting to my shaky feet, my heart feels like it's trying to fly free.

"Hey..." Mai takes my arm, helping me out of my sleep shirt. "Even if baby does decide to come today, we can handle it, okay?"

"Okay," I repeat once more, stepping under the warm spray and instantly feeling my shoulders relax under the water.

After I get dressed and eat something, we decide to go for a gentle walk, the pains coming fairly regularly but not that often. The twins follow us, both with wrinkled brows and stiff necks.

"Oh, for goodness' sake!" Mai exclaims after Roman hovers so close I almost trip. "Plenty of babies have been born a little early, Lilly is not about to keel over, so give her some bloody space."

I giggle as, chastised, they step back a bit, and a pang of intense sadness hits me when I realise that my guys would be far worse if they were here.

"The guys will be at the cabin by now; they won't be able to come here if things do ramp up," I pause as an intense pain shoots across my stomach, making it go rock-hard.

"That's it, Lilly, just breathe in and out," Mai encourages, rubbing my back in soothing circles until the pain eases and I can straighten up once more. "Let's head back, shall we?"

We turn to walk back, my arm linked in Mai's, and I worry my lip as we walk.

"I think that maybe we shouldn't let them know. I don't want them distracted," I tell them, and although I can see the twins scowling at that, they nod.

"It's shit, but probably for the best," Rowan says grumpily.

He's right, it is shit. I want my guys here with me. Jax was meant to help deliver our baby, but we can't always get what we want; I know that more than most.

Looks like this night may be one to remember in more ways than one.

---

## ASH

We all take our seats on various couches in the main living room after a long day of hunting elk and a meal of freshly caught elk heart. My father likes the idea of eating the heart of our enemies, and it doesn't taste too bad once you get over the idea. The staff that cooked it have gone home as planned, so it's just the eight of us.

Jax hands out glasses of scotch, catching my eye and giving an imperceptible nod to let me know that he's done his part and, at most, we have half an hour before the effects of the GHB kicks in.

The elders talk about business, lots of bullshit back slapping and congratulatory talk about this or that company that has been made bankrupt. I watch, sipping my drink and trying not to sneer at the devil's these men have become. It turns my stomach the amount of lives they've ruined, have forced us to take, all in the name of getting richer.

This isn't how the world is meant to work. Lilly has shown me that with her light and goodness, and her caring for others. We're meant to help people, help to pull them up, and not knock them down for our own gain. How many families have struggled because of us? Because of my father's insatiable greed?

"Asth—" the man in question slurs, grimacing as his eyes try to focus on me. Seconds later his glass slips from his hand, landing with a dull thud on the rug as he slides to the floor, eyes closed and slack-jawed.

Similar noises sound around the room, and I look up to see all four of them lying in a comatose state.

"Stephen won't be out for long," Jax informs us, going over to Kai's uncle and giving him a vicious kick. A small moan leaves the man's lips, but he stays down. Jax leans down, grabs Stephen under the arms, and hauls him in the direction of the basement.

"You ready?" I ask Kai, pausing him with my hand on his bicep. He turns to face me, and it takes more effort than I'd like to admit not to flinch at the sight of his cold, dead eyes, all the warmth drained away.

"Yes."

I loosen my grip, letting him go, but the stiffness in my shoulders remains as I watch him.

"Let's get this show on the road, brother," Loki says, his usual, teasing tone gone and replaced with the hard Knight that we've all been moulded into.

Taking one final, deep inhale, I draw my own darkness to the front, letting my inner demon take over for this bloody night's work.

One last life to take.

---

LILLY

The pains increase steadily as the day wears on, becoming more intense and frequent as evening draws in. When we returned from our walk, Mai helped me to set up the main living area as my birth space; placing affirmation cards around the room, and plugging in fairy lights that she'd brought with her. The twins helped to set up the bluetooth speaker, and the classical playlist that Loki and I had created specifically for the birth is playing softly in the background. There's a sharp pain in my chest which has nothing to do with my labour and everything to do with my missing Knights.

I keep walking round the space, pausing and breathing every time a contraction hits me. It's full night-time now, the moon shining through the French doors, the curtains left open at my insistence. I'm looking out into the darkness as another pain tightens my abdomen, and I grab hold of the back of a chair in a tight grip as it washes over me.

"That's it, just breathe through them, Lilly," Mai soothes, rubbing my back in circles. "You are doing so well, sweetheart."

Tears sting my eyes at the endearment. It's Kai's new nickname for me, and I would give anything to have him here. To have all of them here.

"They're getting stronger," I pant out, straightening up once it passes and resuming my pacing, Mai giving me the space to walk.

"And closer together," she says with a smile. "Baby is growing impatient to meet its mama."

"Here," Rowan says, holding out a bottle of some kind of sports drink. "You need to keep your energy levels up, especially as you haven't eaten much."

I take a sip, my heart aching when mango fills my mouth and I remember

Jax taking care of me in his truck after Julian had said those awful things at the paintballing centre.

I gasp as another searing pain hits me, and Rowan quickly grabs the bottle before I can accidentally drop it. I grasp his arm, digging my nails in as I pant, this pain stronger than the last and much sooner.

A cool cloth smelling of lavender is pressed to my forehead as the contraction subsides, and I sigh, breathing in the relaxing scent. It reminds me of all the bubble baths the guys ran for me.

"Sorry." I wince when I see the crescents in Rowan's forearms left from my nails digging in.

"No worries, pixie," he assures me with a grin.

The next hour or so is more of the same, walking and panting through the pains, time slipping away as I get lost in my own body and the war that is raging inside me.

I come to realise that's what birth is, a war with only one outcome. Your body is literally being ripped apart, and all you can do is ride the waves of agony, praying that you both come out of the other side.

---

## JAX

Agony contorts Stephen's face as the cat-o-nine tail lands on his torn-up back, blood spraying over Kai holding the whip. *Can You Hear Me Now* by The Score plays loudly in the background, Loki dancing around like a fucking insane person as the lyrics ramp us all up to a state of fury.

I lift my gaze to Kai, watching as he observes his handiwork with a cold detachment that's fucking scary. His chest is bare and glistening with crimson drops and splatter covering his face as he brings the whip down again.

Stephen struggles against his binds, crying out around his gag, but Ash tied him up good, hanging from the basement ceiling as Kai requested, so the fucking paedo isn't going anywhere. The beast inside me purrs in approval at the bastard finally getting what he deserves. Kai meting out the punishment that his uncle gave him all those years ago is the icing on the cake.

Tears track down the man's face, fucking pathetic sack of shit. He's saying something, and Ash steps forward, removing his gag.

"What was that, Stephen?" he asks, and a dark bark of laughter bursts out of me at Ash's tone. It's like we're in one of those shitty board meetings at Black Knight HQ, his tone bored and unemotional.

"P–p–please," Stephen rasps out, the whites of his eyes showing as he looks at Ash.

"Did you listen to a small boy's pleas, Stephen?" Ash questions and his voice is fucking arctic, his hand fisting in Stephen's hair. He holds his grip as another hit lands on the man's back, and we all relish in his loud scream, the sound unhindered by the gag.

Roughly, Ash lets go, stepping away and leaving bloody shoe prints on the concrete floor. Luckily, he's wearing his father's shoes, we all are except Kai who has plastic shoe covers over the top of his. Gotta keep up appearances and all that, footwear marks are evidence after all.

There's a loud sound of wet leather and metal hitting the floor as Kai drops the whip out of his gloved grasp. Casually, he strolls over to the workbench, and I watch, my arms folded as he picks up a pair of bolt croppers, a small blowtorch, and pliers. Turning, he catches my gaze, and there's no warmth there. A demon stares back at me, calling to my own, and when he holds out the blowtorch in a gloved hand, I don't hesitate.

I walk up to my brother, and with my own double-gloved hand, take it from him, knowing what he wants. Giving the pliers to Loki as he walks past, Kai strides to face his uncle, the man broken and bleeding, sagging in his chains before him. Stephen lifts his head, his wide eyes taking in his nephew and the bolt croppers he's holding.

"You forced your disgusting dick inside me when I was a child, when I thought that you were my savior, but soon discovered you were nothing but a monster," Kai tells him, his voice deep and rough, and my hand tightens around the blowtorch at his words. "So I thought that I'd cut it off."

Stephen struggles, and I wrinkle my nose as piss springs out from the appendage, the smell adding to that of blood in the room. Fucking disgusting.

"Y–you won't get away with t–this!" he cries, his voice hoarse and cracked.

"Yes, we will," Kai answers. "Loki."

Loki steps forward, grabbing the end of Stephen's dick with the pliers, and Stephen lets out a cry of pain as Loki pulls it out. It doesn't go far, small dicked motherfucker. Although, I guess if someone had my cock in pliers, I might not be showing them all I have to offer.

"Doubt you'll miss this much, Stephen," Loki comments, clearly thinking the same as me.

I light the blowtorch, Stephen's eyes darting to me as I step up close.

"You didn't think we were going to let you die that easily, did you?" I ask him, my voice low and dark. I laugh.

*Rest in Peace* by Dorothy starts to play, and I arch a brow at Loki.

"It's the perfect song for revenge torture!" he argues, his head bobbing with the rock music.

"Fucking madman." I chuckle, turning my stare to Kai.

"This," Kai tells Stephen, opening the cutters and placing them around the base of Stephen's dick, "is going to hurt."

---

LILLY

"Aaarrrggghhh!"

My scream echoes around the room as wave after wave of agony rips through my body, barely letting me breathe.

The pads that Mai placed on the floor cushion my knees as I kneel, my upper torso resting on the seat of the sofa as I grip Roman and Rowan's hands so tightly I'm surprised I've not broken them.

"That's it, Lilly!" Mai encourages me from behind. "I can see baby's head, breathe deeply and let your body do its thing."

I manage to follow her instructions, breathing through gritted teeth as I feel my vagina being stretched to an impossible size. Fuck, I thought Jax and Ash together down there was a lot, but it has nothing on this. This burns like nothing I've ever felt before.

"Good girl, that's exactly it," Mai praises, and it's all I can do to focus on just breathing.

Shit, I wanted to be all zen earth mother, and here I am screaming like a fucking banshee. Some things never change, a brief flash of meeting Loki for the first time flits through my mind before the overwhelming urge to push fills me.

"I–I need to push," I gasp out, sweat dripping down the side of my face.

"Then push, my lovely," Mai encourages, and I take a huge inhale, pushing as I breathe it out through another loud scream.

A rush of liquid and something else expels from between my legs, and my muscles feel suddenly weak as all tension leaves them. Seconds later the most wonderful, unexpected sound of a baby's cry sounds behind me, and I straighten my back as Mai passes a wriggling slick bundle between my legs.

*Oh shit.*

Instinctively, I grab my baby and bring it in close, marvelling at the miracle that I'm holding.

"Congratulations, Lilly," Mai says, her voice thick, and I sit back on my heels twisting to look at her.

"Is it a boy or girl?" one of the twins asks, and I look down at the bundle in my arms, the cord still attached and pulsing slightly.

"A girl," I whisper. "She's a girl."

I look up at them with tear-filled eyes, my forehead creasing as another slight pain hits me followed by more slickness between my thighs.

"That's the afterbirth," Mai informs me, and I do an awkward shuffle to see a large blob of red on the sheets we put down, the cord flowing from the placenta to my baby. My baby girl.

My eyes trace her tiny body, taking in every detail, and a choked laugh falls from my lips when I get to her head.

"She's ginger!" I exclaim, delight filling me as I look at her mop of red hair, just like her dad. "And has so much hair."

"She's beautiful," Mai tells me, coming beside me and wrapping her arm around my shoulders. "The cord has stopped pulsing, so let's cut it and you can have a lie down with her."

Mai orders the twins to get me something to drink and eat then helps me onto the sofa that's been pulled out to create a sofa bed. She helps me clean up after she's checked me over to make sure there were no tears, all the while I hold my baby girl to my chest and just fucking marvel at her existence.

"Does she have a name?" Roman asks, and I look up to find him and Rowan waiting with snacks and a drink.

I look back down at my baby, who's happily taking her first feed, and I can feel my lips lift up in a soft smile, warmth suffusing my entire body.

"Violet," I reply, not taking my eyes off her, my hand gently stroking her soft head. "Her name is Violet."

# CHAPTER THIRTY-TWO

KAI

I watch as the life drains from my uncle's eyes, leaving them dull and lifeless, and what was left of his blood drips down the slit in his neck. Lowering my arm, I still clutch the knife in my hand and look down briefly to see blood dripping on the already crimson-splattered floor.

I'd expected to feel something, relief maybe, but I'm still lost to my darkness and all I feel is numbness. I feel nothing for this man that was meant to take care of me but instead abused me for years. There's nothing but an emptiness inside of me as I look over his dead body.

"Come, brother," Jax says, placing a hand on my shoulder. "Time to get cleaned up."

Slowly blinking, I turn to face him, and the darkness recedes enough that my hands begin to tremble and a slight lightness infuses my limbs. Without saying anything, I hand the knife to Ash.

Walking over to the door that leads to a bathroom, I step inside and then strip my gloves and remaining clothes off, bagging them up to be taken away and burned by Enzo before the Feds arrive.

Footsteps sound on the basement stairs, and my heart ricochets in my chest until I hear the Italian trainer's voice. I turn the shower up high, stepping under the almost blistering spray and watching the pink water running down the drain, my head bowed.

A blast of cool air hits my back, then a warm body steps into the shower with me a moment later, muscled arms wrap around me from behind in a comforting embrace.

"Let me show you that you're alive, and not the monster he tried to make you into," Loki's husky voice whispers into my ear, his hard dick pressed into my ass.

A breath stutters out of me as I watch one of his arms reaching beyond me to grab the shower gel. I look down as he squeezes a dollop into his palm and then coats my thick length, the breath hissing out of me as he moves up and down in firm strokes.

"See how good that feels, sir," he rasps in my ear, his hips moving in time to his hand. A few weeks ago I would have freaked the fuck out at his dick near my asshole, but now it just feels incredible and I want more.

"I want you to fuck me, Pet," I say, my voice thick with lust, and his hand stills.

"Are you sure?" he asks, his voice breathless.

I twist my head, my hand coming to the back of his neck, and I pull him to me, slamming my lips against his. Wasting no time, I thrust my tongue into his mouth, and with a groan, he kisses me back just as fiercely.

Red hot lust pours through me, coating my insides and making me rock-fucking-solid in Loki's grip. His deep moan matches my own and reaching behind me, I wrap my hand around his own cock, nipping his lip as I grip him hard. Pulling away from his lush, kiss-swollen lips, I look him dead in the eye.

"I want your fucking cock in my ass, Pet," I tell him, my voice hard and full of command. "And I won't ask again."

"Yes, sir," he replies, placing his hand around my hip and tugging me back. One hand goes between my shoulder blades and pushes ever so slightly so that my ass is sticking out, ready for him as my chest is pressed against the cool tiles. A shiver races over my skin at the mix of cold from the tiles and hot from the water and Loki's hand caressing my ass.

I hear him spit in his hand, then feel the prod of a digit entering my back hole. A deep groan leaves my throat as he pumps in and out a few times, then the head of his cock replaces his finger when he pulls it out, the metal of his piercing cool against my fevered skin. I hear him spit again, feeling the wet glide of it between my cheeks as he pulls them further apart.

My heart races as he slowly pushes against the tight bud, and my fingers claw at the tiles that they are resting against when the burn of him entering me becomes almost too much. Before he thrusts in any more, he drapes his body over mine and reaches around to grab my dick in his palm, resuming his firm stroking.

"Fuck, Kai, you feel— Godamn," he gasps as he pushes in more, and my eyes roll at feeling him inside me, his hand pumping my dick.

Tired of waiting, needing him to be inside me all the way, I snap my hips back until his pelvis is pressed against my ass, and we both cry out at the feel of it.

"Fuuuuck," I hiss, and we pause there, just absorbing the intense sensation of being connected like this.

I needed him to fuck me like this not just to feel alive again and chase the darkness away, but to finally rid myself of the ghost of my uncle's abuse. The memories of his depravity don't try to take over because all I feel is Loki, his lips on my shoulder as he kisses me softly, telling me how good it feels to be inside of me.

Tears sting my eyes at the sheer relief which courses through me, knowing that I can embrace this side of myself with Loki without fear of my trauma rearing its ugly head.

I quickly get lost in sublime pleasure when Loki starts to move his own hips in a sensual dance. The push and pull of his hard dick inside me, his hand jerking me off at the same time, it builds me to a new kind of high.

"I want to fuck you harder, sir," he growls in my ear, waiting for my permission.

"Do it," I snarl, and he takes one of my hands, wrapping it around my own dick, both of his hands grabbing my hips in a bruising grip.

He starts fucking me hard and fast, and Jesus, it feels so damn good it's all I can do to stroke my dick as waves of ecstasy flow over me. The sound of our wet bodies slapping together is loud in the room, our breathing and grunts adding to the cacophony of sound.

"Fuck, Kai, I'm going to come in your ass—" Loki cries out, his words cut off with a deep groan as he slams himself deep inside me and pours his release.

He drags me with him, my balls drawing up and lightning shooting up my spine as I come all over the tiled wall. Lights dance in front of my eyes, my whole body alight with tingles as my climax races through me with a spine bowing effect.

Panting, I release my spent cock, and gasp when Loki pulls out. He grabs my shoulders and spins me around, cupping my face in both palms and lowering his lips onto mine. He kisses me with such tenderness that tears once again sting my eyes, and a sob stutters from my lips. He keeps kissing me, even as I cry into his mouth, my own hands tangling in his hair and pulling him closer.

The kiss comes to an end, Loki placing his forehead against mine, and we stand under the spray as my heartbeat returns to normal.

"Lilly's gonna be pissed she missed watching that," Loki jokes in a rough voice, and I huff a laugh.

"We'll have to do it again for her then," I reply, moving to place a soft kiss on his lips. "Thank you."

He steps back so that we can look in each other's eyes, his hand still clutching the back of my neck.

"Always."

"Let's get cleaned up," I say with a sigh, feeling lighter than I have in years.

One step closer to our new lives.

---

LOKI

Once we're all cleaned up and dressed in clothes that we'd placed there before the fun began, Kai and I exit the bathroom to find Ash and Jax carrying Julian down the stairs, Rafe and my sperm donor already situated, slumped in chairs. Sweat drips down the side of my temple, the heat on full blast to confuse the time of death.

It seems so strange to have shared such an intimate moment with Kai, our relationship moving up to the next level, one moment, then being faced with the remnants of our revenge plan. My fingers tingle in Kai's grip, his hand in mine as we approach the others, careful to avoid the blood on the floor, plastic covering our shoes.

After heaving Julian in the final remaining chair, Jax goes about putting their shoes back on their feet while Ash carefully carries the various tools that we used on Stephen to each of them, wrapping their hands around the handles of different ones so that it'll be their fingerprints that the Feds find.

Fingerprints on a murder weapon is a surefire way to earn a conviction, plus with the other evidence we've planted; footwear marks in the blood and the digital trail of my uncle betraying the company, there's no way they'll be able to avoid rotting in jail for a very long time.

We watch as Jax takes the blood that we collected from Stephen's slit throat, and using the knife, dips it into the container and flicks it over the three comatose men, before wrapping his own father's hand around the murder weapon.

"We'll get cleaned up, then join you guys upstairs," Ash informs us, stripping where he stands and dropping his clothes in the open bag that Enzo will take to be incinerated.

We'd brought clean sweats and shirts down before the torture party got started, leaving them in the bathroom, ready for this phase of the plan.

"Sure, I'll take these up," I reply, snapping another pair of gloves on and grabbing the bag.

Kai remains silent as we make our way upstairs, but it's a relaxed quietness, and a light-hearted feeling fills me up to think that, just maybe, he exorcised his demons tonight.

"It is done?" Enzo asks as we step into the living room from the basement, and I nod.

"Yep," I answer, for once no jokey comeback on my tongue.

"Good," he replies, glancing over at Kai with a shrewd look before taking two big steps and pulling him into a hug. "You did well, caro mio."

I watch as Kai takes a shuddering breath, wrapping his own arms around the older man and hugging him right back. A sense of calm washes over me at the sight of Kai not only accepting an embrace but returning it. He'll be alright.

"Right, boys," Ash states, jogging up the stairs with damp hair. "We're on the home stretch. Enzo, you take that final bag, burn it with the others. Give us thirty minutes, then call the cops."

"Si," Enzo agrees, taking the bag from me and then heading out of the door. He pauses when he reaches the threshold, turning and looking back at us. "I'm proud of you, boys, and honoured to watch you become the men you were always meant to be."

My throat tightens at his declaration, and I notice the others shift and stand a little taller at his words. With that, the older man walks out, leaving us to implement the final part of the plan. The part that I'm dreading if I'm being honest.

"Come on, let's get this over with," Ash says with a sigh, clearly feeling the same reluctance as the rest of us.

We enter the living room once more, collecting the glasses that our elders dropped, and Kai takes them to the kitchen to rinse them out. Jax sorts us new drinks, this time with enough GHB to knock us out for an hour or so, just enough time that if all goes to plan, we'll wake up in hospital after the cops have found us all. If it doesn't go to plan...well, who the fuck knows what happens then.

Jax hands us our glasses, giving Kai his when he returns.

"Bottoms up," I toast, raising the glass and slugging the measure back in one go. Best to just rip that band-aid off, I always think. I grimace with the burn of good quality scotch, wincing slightly at not taking the time to appreciate it fully.

"See you on the other side," Ash comments, drinking his next, not even making a face as he swallows. He's used to drinking this shit more than any of us, his father practically bottle-fed him on it.

Jax doesn't say anything, just throws his back like a badass before setting his glass down on the side table. Kai is the final one to bring his glass to his lips.

"Here's to a new life," he says, drinking it down.

The drug doesn't take long to take effect, and I feel a pleasant buzz start to loosen my limbs just as we hear a door crash open.

"Whath the fuckth?" Ash slurs, all of us unsteadily rising to our feet as the door to the basement flies open and Jax's dad is just fucking standing there, blinking and weaving around, gun in hand.

Everything happens too fast then, his unfocused eyes catching my gaze as I'm the closest to the door. The gun raises, and all I can do is watch as he levels it at my chest. My ears register the loud bang, my body jerking, and I watch as Rafe topples back down the stairs.

My ears are ringing, and I sluggishly shake my head, catching the red that's spreading across my left pec.

"Wellth, f–fuck," I stutter, looking back up to see horrified looks on the faces of my brothers before their eyes roll and they fall to the floor. I follow them down, darkness taking me in its embrace before my head hits the floor.

# CHAPTER THIRTY-THREE

LILLY

I wake up with a jolt, my heart pounding and a feeling that something isn't right making the hair stand up on my arms. A snuffling sound next to me brings my head down to see my baby, Violet, snuggled next to me, my body curled around hers protectively. Taking a deep inhale of her addictive baby scent, my panic subsides somewhat, but I can't shake that feeling of unease.

Needing the toilet and something to drink, I decide to get out of bed, but can't bear to leave Violet behind, so I pick her up and take her with me. She stirs a little but soon settles into my embrace, and it feels as natural as breathing to carry her in my arms, but also weirdly alien. I can't believe that she's here.

Padding quietly downstairs, I'm surprised to hear the murmur of voices, and even more so when I round the staircase and find the twins and Mai in the living room, all with concern written across their faces.

"What's wrong?" I ask, my voice lowered but my mouth really dry with all the possible scenarios running through my head. "Tell me."

"Loki's been shot," Roman states and my body goes ice-cold and numb, instinct alone making sure that I don't drop Violet, pulling her small body closer as if to protect her from the news.

"W–what?" I rasp, sinking down on the same sofa that I leaned on a few hours ago to give birth.

"We don't know all the details, just that something went wrong and Loki got caught with a bullet," Rowan elaborates, his knee bouncing.

"W–where is he?" I ask, pulling Violet closer to me, breathing in her scent which is the only thing helping me to stay calm right now.

"The private hospital, back in Brompton Lakes."

"We have to go there then," I say, standing back up and turning to head towards the stairs to get ready.

"Lilly, you only gave birth a few hours ago," Mai interjects, a note of concern in her tone. "It's a three-hour drive."

"Plus," Rowan interjects, "you're meant to be dead."

"He's Violet's father, and my soulmate," I say, needing them to understand that any discomfort I feel is secondary to my need to make sure that he's okay. Mai sighs, then gets up too.

"Luckily, we bought a car seat for Violet, just in case you had her whilst we were here," she tells me, giving me a small smile. "Let me take her while you get ready."

"Thank you," I reply, handing over Violet, careful not to jostle her.

I rush up the stairs, well, as much as my aching body will allow, and say a prayer to anyone who's listening that my baby gets to meet her father.

---

## JAX

Ash, Kai, and I sit around Loki's bedside, watching his still form lying there, and all I feel is sick with the thought that our freedom may have cost him his life. The doctor said that it was a clean entry and exit wound, the bullet passing through his shoulder, and although he may have limited use of the limb for a few weeks or months, with physical therapy he should make a full recovery.

But fuck, that was too close for my liking.

A groan pulls my worried gaze back up to my brother's face, finding his eyes blinking as he struggles to open them.

"Fuuucck," he rasps out, his voice cracked and painful sounding, and I leap to my feet, grabbing him a cup of water that the doc left for him.

"Shit, it's good to have you back," I say, holding the cup to his lips when his gaze finds mine. He drinks deeply, finishing the whole thing before resting his head back on the pillow with a long exhale.

"I feel like I've been hit by a fucking truck," he comments dryly, closing his eyes and wincing, then opening them and looking around the room. Ash and Kai are on the other side of the bed, both with grins on their faces, their previously tight shoulders slumped.

"You were shot," Ash tells him, and Loki's forehead creases, then his eyes widen as he remembers.

"By Rafe!" he exclaims, though his voice is no more than a cracked mumble.

"Yeah," I reply, then give a smile that I know is pure evil as I recall what the cops told us when we woke up a couple of hours ago. "Turns out he fell back down the basement stairs, cracked his head open like Humpty fucking Dumpty, and died in a pool of blood and piss at the bottom."

I mean, I wish I'd been the one to put a bullet in his brain after I beat the shit out of him, but I guess, this way at least, he's no longer walking the earth. Perhaps it's not the way a son should feel about his father's death, but I'm glad the bastard is dead.

"Talk about silver linings," Loki jokes, and we all chuckle, the tension dropping away from my limbs.

My shoulders tense once again when I hear a commotion outside, a harried woman's voice sounding in the hall.

"You can't go in there, miss!"

"Fuck off!"

"Is that Lilly?" Kai asks in a confused tone, but before we can answer, the door to the room bursts open, and in strides the woman herself, looking exhausted but beautiful in her wildness.

"Loki!" she exclaims, rushing across the room and practically pushing me out of the way as she flings herself on top of him.

He lets out a pained groan, but what makes me really pause is what sounds like the cry of a baby.

"Oh, poppet, I'm so sorry, shhhh," Lilly coos, pulling back and rocking the bundle in her arms that I'd somehow missed when she came in.

"Lilly?" Loki asks, his eyes wide as he, too, takes in the squirming bundle she's holding.

"Loki, guys," she says, her eyes swimming with tears as she looks around at our stunned faces. "This is Violet, our daughter."

She pulls the blanket away to reveal a beautiful baby with a shock of red hair on her head. I stare, stunned at the perfection of this infant, a wave of such intense love almost bringing me to my knees.

"Here," Lilly says, placing the baby in Loki's good arm, and a moment of panicked terror flashes across his face before he looks down at his daughter and he just fucking melts.

"S–she's perfect," he whispers, bringing her in close and nuzzling her hair. "Look at her hair!"

"I know," Lilly beams, and I wrap my arms around her from behind, taking her weight as she sags into me.

"Fuck, Baby Girl, you should be resting," I scold, trying to direct her to my chair, but she resists.

"Jax, I just spent the past few hours sitting in a car, feeling like my fanny was going to fall out every time we hit a bump, I really don't want to sit down right now."

I wince at her description, my respect for this woman increasing tenfold when I think about her having to give birth without us, or without full medical attention.

"But you're okay? Nothing went wrong?" I can't help but ask, pulling her closer as my heart beats wildly at the thought of her pain.

"I'm fine, fucking exhausted, but fine," she tells me, her arms wrapping along the length of mine. "More to the point, Loki, how are you and why the fuck did you get yourself shot?"

"It wasn't a choice, Pretty Girl," Loki murmurs back, not taking his eyes off Violet. "But I think I'm okay."

"He'll be fully recovered in a few weeks with some physical therapy," Ash answers softly, coming round the bed to draw Lilly into his arms and out of mine.

As much as I don't want to, I let her go and watch with a warm feeling in my chest when she nuzzles into him and he kisses the top of her head.

"I'm so fucking proud of you, Princess," he says, pulling away slightly to look into her eyes. "You are incredible."

Violet makes a little squeak then, and Lilly steps away from Ash, taking her from Loki, planting a quick kiss on his cheek, and then turning around to face us. She steps close to me, holding her arms out, and automatically, I take Violet from her, feeling a little awkward with this tiny bundle in my huge arms. She looks so small and breakable, but Lilly helps me to support her head, then steps back to give Kai a hug.

I look down, Violet's eyes closed, yet when I bring my finger up to her hand, her fingers grasp onto mine with a tight grip.

"She's strong, just like her mother," I marvel, my throat tight as I look up into Lilly's tired gaze, her lashes damp with tears but her smile wide. "Perfect like her too."

"I'm sorry you weren't there, to help with her birth I mean," Lilly says, her mouth downturned, Kai's arms wrapped around her from behind like mine were moments before.

"I'm sorry too," I say, and fuck, I hate that we weren't there when she needed us. One look at my brothers and I know they're feeling the same.

"D–did it all go to plan?" she questions, looking at each of us, settling on Loki last. "Well, apart from Loki getting shot."

"Yeah," Ash answers, taking a step towards me and brushing Violet's hair back, placing a soft kiss on her tiny head. "Everything else went to plan, and Chad and my father are in police custody."

Reluctantly, I hold Violet out for him to take, and he reaches for her with a gentleness that surprises me. None of us are soft men. We are hard and full of scars, our bodies built to hurt and take life, not to nurture it, but maybe we could be something more than what we were raised to be.

Ash kisses Violet's head again before turning and handing her back to Lilly when she starts to fuss, Kai's arms coming round both of them as we all stare at the miracle of new life before us.

Yeah, we are definitely more than what our fathers trained us to be. Life is not black or white, but a mixture of greys, and looking down at my brothers and our woman and newborn daughter, I know that they will help us to become what we were always meant to be.

# CHAPTER THIRTY-FOUR

LILLY

The next few weeks pass by in what can only be described as a hazy bubble of life with a newborn. The lack of sleep would be crippling if it weren't for my guys taking turns rocking and holding Violet so that I can get some much-needed rest.

Violet takes to the breast in a big way, Mai exclaiming how well she's doing when she comes to check us both over, assuring me that Violet spending hours at a time feeding is normal to start with as she encourages my milk to come in. When I'm still not convinced, she points out the full nappy bin—Kai had organised getting cloth nappies, citing that not only is it better for the environment, but also for Violet. When my milk does come in, my boobs become what Mai calls 'porn star breasts,' aka huge as fuck.

The guys, obviously, think that they're great, Loki lamenting that Violet is the only one currently enjoying them, perving on my feeding sessions until Jax smacks him upside the head for sexualising something which is completely natural and beautiful. Loki sheepishly apologies, telling me it was only my breasts he'd ever accost, making me laugh, then cry because, well, hormones are still a thing.

We recover in Ash's woodland house as I like to call it, and being surrounded by the forest in the late summer is perfect, the trees providing coolness to what might be oppressive heat. Kai takes Violet and I on walks in the late afternoon, carrying Violet in a stretchy baby wrap that he watched many YouTube videos to learn how to tie correctly. There's something about him carrying her that makes me all hot and bothered, and I look forward to our daily walks more because of it.

The date of Julian's and Chad's trials fast approaches, and the night before I find myself waking up, Jax asleep on one side and Violet on the other. We put a wooden bedside guard on the bed, making sure that whichever side Violet is on, she can't fall out. Sleeping with her in the bed, and feeding her lying down has saved my sanity because I often fall asleep with her happily sucking away, and sleep is precious at the moment.

Carefully getting out of the bed, I pop to the bathroom down the hall, not wanting to use the en-suite in case it wakes Violet up. As I leave the room, I hear the faint sound of a piano being played, a smile tilting my lips upward. I make my way down the corridor, pushing open the door to Ash's music room to find Ash shirtless at the piano, Loki sitting not far away with his guitar on his lap. He's also in a state of undress, wearing just sweatpants, his sling having been discarded even though he should still be wearing it. Men.

*Jesus H Roosevelt Christ, how is a girl meant to function when they walk around topless?*

Ash finishes up the song he was playing, an instrumental version of *7 Years*, just as Loki looks up and catches my eye, giving me a panty-melting grin.

"My turn to play for you, Pretty Girl," he tells me, and I remember back to the first night in the cabin when Ash called me from this very room and sang to me for the first time. "Why don't you hop up onto the piano there, let Ash take care of you for a bit."

I glance at Ash to find he's turned to face me, his heated stare on me, taking in my sleep vest and knickers.

"Come here, Princess."

Slowly, I walk further into the room, coming to a stop in between his splayed thighs, and his hands skim up mine, grabbing my arse and pulling me closer.

"I—" I start, biting my lower lip, unsure how to tell them what's swirling around in my mind. I want them, I am desperate for them; we haven't had sex of any kind since Violet's birth, all the guys allowing me to heal. But, although my body has now healed, it's not the same as before. It's soft and well, wobbly in places that were toned, and I've stretch marks all over my breasts from how big they've gotten. Not to mention the fissure of worry that it'll hurt, or be painful. I did push a baby out of Her Vagisty, and I'm not sure she's forgiven me yet.

"What is it, baby?" Loki asks, and I look over my shoulder at him, before looking back at Ash, then over his shoulder, not able to keep eye contact with either of them as I voice my worries.

"I'm not the same as I was before," I haltingly tell them, and tears sting my eyes, fucking hormones. "I'm soft and wobbly and marked, and I'm scared that you won't find me sexy." I say the last part in a whisper, but I know by the way that Ash stiffens, he heard it.

"Look at me, Princess," he demands, his voice unyielding as his hands tighten on my hips. I look down, swallowing hard and chewing my lip again. "You are more gorgeous now than you have ever been. This stunning body brought Violet into our lives, and continues to nourish her every fucking day." He skims his palms up my sides, cupping my breasts and sending delicious tingles across my skin. "I will never not find you sexy as fuck, marks and all."

Tears spill over onto my cheeks as a small laugh leaves my lips, and Ash stands up, his hand cupping my jaw to guide my lips to his.

"You will always be beautiful to us," he whispers the words over my lips before closing the distance in a kiss that reaffirms everything that he's just told me. He kisses me as though I am something to be savoured, something that he can't believe he is allowed to touch.

He manoeuvres us so that my arse hits the side of the baby grand, his hands coming to the hem of my vest and tugging it upwards, breaking our kiss so that he can pull it over my head. Lowering his head, he kisses each new mark that covers my tits, and I gasp as his lips worship my new body.

Loki begins to strum his guitar, singing *Thinking Out Loud* by Boyce Avenue, and fresh tears fall as he holds my gaze. My attention is stolen again by Ash when he hooks his fingers in the side of my knickers and pulls them down my legs, encouraging me to step out of them.

I squeak as he lifts me under my thighs, hissing when my bum hits the cold surface of the piano lid as he sets me down on top of it. Placing a hand on my sternum, he gently pushes me down so that I'm lying back on the lid, my legs hanging over.

"I'm scared it's going to hurt," I blurt out, and he gives me a soft look, his long, inked-up fingers trailing down the centre of my breasts, over my soft stomach, to the apex of my thighs.

"I'll make sure you're too wet for it to hurt, Princess."

Ash drops to his knees, and a low moan falls from my lips as his tongue licks my damp core.

"Still fucking delicious," he murmurs, his hot breath over my lower lips making me shiver and my nipples peak.

He doesn't say anything, just returns to my core, slinging my legs over his shoulders as he proceeds to eat my pussy like a man starved. His tongue explores every inch of my cunt, from my swollen clit to my opening, thrusting it inside my channel and licking me as if I'm a well that he's desperate for a drink from. Lightning trails up and down my body, my breath coming out in quick pants and gasps as my orgasm approaches embarrassingly quickly.

"Ash–shit–Ash—" I moan, glancing over at Loki who's still playing, his eyes burning into my skin as he watches us.

"That's it, baby, come all over my face like the good girl I know you can be," Ash commands, resuming his tongue fucking, and I can feel my body succumbing to his order, my legs shaking as my climax rips through me with a force that should shatter all the glass in the room.

I lose myself to it, to the pleasure that rolls me over and under until I'm floating, and Ash doesn't stop, his tongue licking, his mouth sucking, and his teeth nipping until I'm begging him to stop, my hands clawing at the surface of his precious instrument.

Finally, he relents, and I crack my eyelids to watch him stand up, his erection pressed against the front of his sweats as he looks at me with a predatory gleam. His chin glistens with my release, and I watch, shivering as he swipes the back of his hand over it, just to lick my cum off like he can't get enough. Loki has finished playing, the room quiet apart from my panted breaths.

"Perfect, Princess," he praises, pushing his sweats down and palming his thick cock. "Loki, do you have a condom?"

"I got an IUD last week," I say, my flushed cheeks heating. "Mai fitted it. I couldn't stand the idea of anything being between us."

Ash gives me a Loki-worthy smirk, stepping closer as he spits into his palm, Her Vagisty fluttering as he rubs it all over his cock to lubricate it.

"Are you ready for me, Princess?" he asks, his voice deep and husky.

"Yes," I answer without hesitation.

"Good girl," he replies, lining himself up to my slick opening and slowly pushing in. I wince at the slight sting, and he pauses. "Are you still good?"

"It's a bit sore, I guess," I murmur, and his brow wrinkles.

"Loki."

I turn my head to watch Loki come swaggering up, *Dusk Till Dawn* by ZYAN and Sia playing softly over the room's speakers.

"Yes, boss?" Loki gives Ash a shit-eating grin, and it makes me smile.

"Play with those tits you've been lusting after," Ash orders, and my smile drops as Loki's grows wider.

"Yes, sir."

Loki's eyes ravish my body, focusing on my huge tits that are leaking milk all down my sides. I can feel it pooling underneath me on the lid of the piano, and I flush, grimacing.

"You can blame this next part on my lack of being breastfed as a child," Loki tells me, dipping his head and lapping up the spilled milk, his hot, wet tongue making my heated skin pebble and small moans escape from my lips.

"Fucking yum," he says between groans, bending over me to give the other side attention. The more he sucks and licks at my breasts, the more milk leaks out, and I'm soon writhing and squirming.

"Fuck, that's making her wet," Ash growls out, and I gasp as he begins to push inside my heat, Loki distracting me from the slight discomfort. "Shit, Princess, that feels so fucking incredible."

His fingers grip my hip hard, and then I feel his touch on my clit, my cry loud as he starts to play it as skillfully as he does the instrument we're fucking on.

"Ash–oh god–Loki—" I gasp the words, my fingers tangling in Loki's hair as his tongue swirls around my sensitive nipple, drinking the milk that's flowing from me.

I get lost in a myriad of sensations; Ash's thick cock thrusting in and out of my now drenched cunt, his fingers toying with my tight bud, and Loki lavishing his affection onto my breasts. A maelstrom begins swirling inside me, heating me up from the inside out and incoherent noises fall from my lips as they build me higher, bringing me closer to what is promising to be a mind-blowing climax.

"You're so close, aren't you, baby?" Loki asks, and I crack my lids to see him hovering over my nipple, his mouth wet and his pupils blown with lust.

"So fucking close," I whimper, my whole body tingling with my impending release.

"Don't worry, we got you," he tells me, and I watch as he opens his mouth, lowers it over my stiff peak, and sucks. Hard.

I explode and implode all at once, my body going impossibly rigid as my climax takes me in its thrall, electricity zinging out to all my limbs. Milk shoots out from my breasts, and I feel Loki drinking all that I give him, the thought prolonging my pleasure. My pussy clenches around Ash, dragging him down with me as he orgasms with a snarl, burying himself so deep inside me that it triggers a second wave of flutters in my core.

Suddenly Loki's lips leave my nipple, and I open my closed lids to watch him gripping his dick, stripping it in a punishing rhythm. Seconds later, hot cum hits my body as he covers me in his seed, and that triggers a third orgasm, Ash groaning as my cunt grips him again, more wetness leaking out of me.

Loki raises his hand, his own cum glistening on his fingers, and brings them to my lips. Instinctively, I suck them into my mouth, licking his salty release off with a moan.

"Good girl," he says in a breathy voice, withdrawing his fingers and leaning down and kissing me, his tongue invading my mouth.

My hands stay limp at my sides as I kiss him back, my whole body sated and relaxed. He pulls away, and I glance down my body to see Ash giving me one of his beautiful smiles that used to be so rare.

"You are everything we could ever want or need, Princess," he tells me in a gruff voice, his own body loose. "Don't ever fucking forget it."

"I love you, all of you," I tell them, gasping as Ash finally pulls out, and Loki helps me to sit up.

Ash wraps his arms around me, kissing my forehead and pulling me in close so that our sweaty bodies are pressed together.

"I love you too, Princess."

Loki trails his fingers down my side, kissing my neck and cheek.

"I fucking love you, Lilly."

"Should you guys still call me that, you know, given my new name?" I ask, and they pull back to look at me, considering looks on their faces.

"You'll always be Lilly to us," Ash states, running his palm down the side of my face. "And we can always say it's your nickname."

"Although," Loki starts, and when I look at him he has a shit-stirring grin on his lips so I know that whatever will come next may earn him a black eye or two. "Technically, she is now free to marry whoever she wants, given that your wife died."

Ash growls, and it's only my arms still wrapped around his waist that stops him from lunging at the trickster.

"Only if I get to marry all of you," I blurt, realising how right that feels as the words leave my mouth.

Both pause, barely even breathing as they look at me, a mixture of consideration and hunger on their faces. Before anyone can say another word, the sound of Violet crying, then Jax's deep, soothing voice can be heard down the hall.

"She probably wants feeding," I tell them, the sound of her cries hitting me hard in the chest. Ash steps away immediately, he knows how a sense of panic washes over me when she's upset, and he helps me down off the piano and Loki pulls up his sweats and grabs my PJs.

"Go get cleaned up, Jax can soothe her for a minute," Ash tells me gently, pulling his own sweats up and intertwining our fingers, leading me from the room as Loki follows.

We walk into the big bedroom to find Jax rocking Violet in his huge arms, wearing only boxer briefs, and the sight stuns me for a moment before Ash gives a chuckle and pushes me into the bathroom.

"Clean up first, fuck him later," Loki says with a quiet laugh, and Jax looks up with a smirk, his blue eyes heating as he takes in my nudity and freshly fucked appearance.

Kai walks in then, carrying a tray of freshly baked cookies and a thermos of mint tea that I know will be the exact right temperature to drink straight away. I place a kiss on his cheek, his own eyes growing warm.

"You look stunning, sweetheart," he murmurs in my ear, and I shake my head with a giggle.

Reluctantly, I head to the bathroom, turning around as I reach the door to see all four of them cooing over the small baby in Jax's arms, and my heart feels so full it might just burst out of my chest.

# CHAPTER THIRTY-FIVE

ASH

Guilty.

That one word holds such weight. A word that signals our freedom.

Both my father and Loki's are charged with first-degree murder, life in prison with no parole as their punishment, and we've made sure that they won't be able to bribe their way out by getting there first.

We drive the new mini bus that Jax picked up yesterday back to my place in the woods, Violet asleep in the back with Lilly at her side and Loki next to Lilly. *Lost My Mind* by Alice Kristiansen plays quietly over the speakers, and I can't help feeling that this is our song. All five of us lost in each other.

"I can't quite believe it," Lilly whispers, resting her head on Loki's shoulder as we drive through the fall afternoon. "Is it really over?"

"It's really over, Princess," I say from the front, craning my neck to look back at her.

"And what happens now?" she asks, a small smile playing on her lush lips.

"Anything we want, sweetheart," Kai tells her, and her smile grows, rivaling the sunlight filtering through the trees alongside the road.

"I'd like to invite my grandparents over, and Ryan and Lexie," she replies.

"I'll message them now for you," I say, pulling out my phone and sending an email to them all asking if they'd like to visit, an idea forming in my mind of what we could all do while they are here.

We sit in comfortable silence for the rest of the journey, letting the fall sun wash over us as we drive home, unencumbered for the first time by the shackles that our parents put on us.

We're finally free to live, and I intend on doing just that with my brothers and our woman and child.

# CHAPTER THIRTY-SIX

LILLY

*TWO MONTHS LATER*

"Motherfucker!" Ash roars as he storms into the living room, the morning sunlight casting his inked-up body in a soft glow. I wince, glaring at him as Violet starts wailing at the noise.

I rock her in my arms, shushing her and trying to settle her as he looks devastated at upsetting her.

"I'm sorry, darling one," he tells her gently, coming up next to us and stroking her head in the way that always calms her down.

Once she's fallen back asleep, I pass her over to a waiting Jax, who continues to rock her in his huge arms because she has him wrapped around her tiny finger and he adores her sleeping on him.

"What happened?" I ask Ash quietly, Loki and Kai having come into the room, Kai handing me a hot chocolate with a kiss on my cheek.

"Somehow, my father has managed to change his sentence to some bullshit and is getting out on parole later today," Ash seethes, his whole body vibrating with anger. "Apparently, he has proven that he was coerced or some shit."

"What the fuck?" Loki exclaims, his voice lowered as he glances over at a sleeping Violet. "How the ever-loving fuck did he manage that?"

"He's Julian fucking Vanderbilt," Kai responds in a tired voice. "We should have known that something like this would happen."

"We did," Ash argues, running his hands through his hair and leaving it messy. "That's why we spent a small fortune bribing every goddamn official we knew."

"Do you know what time he's being released?" I ask, and they all look at me then, even Jax, blinking.

"Uh, midday I think," Ash answers. "Why, Princess?"

"We best be there to greet him, don't you think?" I answer, not saying anything more as I stride from the room and up the stairs to get changed.

"Why do I feel like there's something she's not telling us?" I hear Loki ask the others, and a smirk curves my lips as I make my way upstairs.

A lady never divulges all her secrets now, does she?

---

## LOKI

I can see the others watching our girl as we make our way to the prison that Ash's cunt of a father is due to be released from, even Jax is casting suspicious glances her way in the rearview mirror. She won't spill her secrets, no matter how much we press her, just telling us that we'll see with a sexy fucking smirk on those kissable lips.

Violet is making cooing noises as we pull up outside the prison gates, and just as Jax turns the engine off, the devil himself comes striding out of the gates, shaking the hand of the officer in charge, a big, stupid-ass smile on his lips.

My blood boils at the sight of him, at his smug fucking grin as he spots us getting out of the car.

"Boys!" he beams, strolling over to us looking pristine in a tailored suit, and it just pisses me the fuck off. Ash's fists clench at the sight, his back ramrod straight.

"How did you convince them to let you go?" Ash grits out, asking the question that has been plaguing us since we discovered the news. Julian's smile widens, and I'm reminded of the Cheshire Cat, teeth gleaming and ready to pounce.

"It always pays to have friends in high places, you know that, son," he tells Ash, holding his gaze, and I can see the sick enjoyment he gets from ruffling Ash's feathers.

The noise of the van door opening sounds in the quiet standoff, and Julian's gaze flickers over Ash, his eyes widening as he takes in what's behind us. I turn to see Lilly holding Violet, standing to the side of us.

"I–it c–can't be—" Julian mutters, his face pale as he looks at her smiling face. "–you're dead."

"Am I?" she asks, taking a step closer, that serene smile still on her lips. "I don't feel dead." She laughs then, like this is all a big joke, and the beautiful sound is so at odds with the conversation that tingles race up my spine.

Jax comes around the other side of her, his forehead creased, standing close enough to jump in if Julian tries anything. But as I look back at the man in front of us, he just stands there, slack-jawed, and his eyes dart all over her, clearly trying to work out what the fuck is going on.

"H–how?" he questions, narrowing his eyes in a way that makes me take a step closer to her, standing on her other side.

"How does anything happen, Julian?" she volleys back, and I watch her with wide eyes as she takes on our biggest adversary with an ease that fucking astounds me and makes my dick hard. "Ah, just in time."

I look beyond Julian to see more cars have pulled up, official-looking ones, and my mouth drops as federal officers step out of the vehicles, all heading our way. They have 'FBI' emblazoned in yellow letters on their vests and jackets.

"Julian Vanderbilt?" an older officer asks as Julian finally turns around to see what is happening. Lilly takes a few steps to the side too, and Jax and I follow her so that we all have a perfect view of Julian's face.

"Yes, who are you?" the man in question demands, still an arrogant prick.

"I'm Special Agent Sawers, and you are under arrest for the murder of Lilly Vanderbilt. Anything you say can and will be used against you in a court of law."

Another officer grabs Julian's wrists and cuffs them behind his back before Julian can even formulate a sentence.

*Fuck. I did not see that coming.*

I glance over at Lilly who looks smug as fuck, kissing the top of Violet's soft hair as she looks over the scene before us.

"She's right there!" Julian screams, struggling against his cuffs as he's led away. They don't even pause, dragging him to one of the cars and roughly shoving him inside.

"Care to share what the fuck that was all about, Princess?" Ash asks, arms crossed and a scowl on his face as we watch the cars drive away. Though, even I can see a small tilt of his lips, and respect shining in his eyes.

"Fingerprints on the murder weapon will really screw a guy over, don't you think?" she sasses Ash, stepping towards him after handing Violet to Jax, and placing a soft kiss on Ash's cheek.

"You had this planned all along, didn't you, Pretty Girl?" I question, stepping behind her so that she's sandwiched between Ash and I. I grin as her body shivers.

"Ryan suggested it," she tells us, her voice breathy and hitching when I push her hair aside and begin to nuzzle her neck. "When we faked my, well, you know. Better to be prepared and all that."

"What happens when he tries to pay them off again?" Kai asks from the side, and I glance over at him, his forehead creased as he tries to think all of the options through. *Sometimes he's cute as fuck.*

"He's not the only one with friends in high places," Lilly murmurs, and I look down to see Ash kneading her waist.

"Harold," Ash guesses, saying Lilly's grandfather's name as a statement more than a question.

"Yes, Harold," she answers, tipping her neck to the side so that I can access it more. I oblige by sucking a mark into her peachy skin, and she moans, the sound going straight to my dick.

"We best get back, Violet will be hungry soon," Jax interrupts, and just like that we all sigh. I love our baby, fiercely, but damn if my dick doesn't miss the opportunity to just bury itself inside our girl anytime we want.

"I'll feed her before we set off again," Lilly says, stepping from between Ash and I and taking Violet off Jax to go and give her a feed in the bus.

I look at my brothers and see matching looks of sheer fucking awe on their faces that I know is reflected in mine.

She's a Queen alright, and we best not forget it.

# CHAPTER THIRTY-SEVEN

LILLY

"I don't see why I'm coming to Enzo's with you. I can hardly do a proper workout so soon after birth, and as far as I know, Enzo doesn't offer any kind of post-natal program," I grumble, Violet snoozing in the back while I ride up front, Jax in the driver's seat of his minivan.

I like to call it the sunshine bus, and much to Jax's annoyance but to my delight, Loki paid some kid—Jude Taylor I think his name was—to cover the outside with suns, rainbows, and unicorns one night. Jax was so pissed when he saw it in the morning I thought he was going to strangle Loki until I begged him not to as I loved it. I also may have burst into tears at the idea of it being painted over, so here we are, driving in the sunshine bus, complete with motherfucking unicorns.

"Trust us, Sweetheart, it's a surprise," Kai tells me from behind, and I look to see Loki and him holding hands and snuggling in the middle seats. It makes my heart warm to see them openly sharing affection. Plus you know, they always let me join in, and fucking hell, watching them fuck each other, feeling them fuck me at the same time as each other, is something I am here for always.

"Fine," I relent, folding my arms across my chest, or at least trying but failing because porn star boobs are still a thing. *Codswallop!*

Soon we're pulling up outside the gym, Ash taking Violet who woke up as we arrived. We walk in to find it empty and quiet, with only Enzo and his wife, Rosa, standing there. She's stunning, tall and slender, with tumbling blonde hair falling in a waterfall down her back.

Rosa rushes forward, enveloping me in a tight hug, and the breath rushes out of me at the way she pulls me close. My arms automatically go around her, and my brows lower when I feel her whole body shaking. Shit. She's crying.

"My beautiful, beautiful girl," she says, pulling away and gripping my face in both her hands. Then, after a lingering look, she apologises, letting go to take a step back whilst I look on in utter bewilderment.

*What the ever-loving fuck is going on?*

"Principessa," Enzo says roughly, his own eyes wet.

"What's going on?" I finally ask, looking around at the guys who've come to stand in a loose semicircle around me. Everyone seems happy, smiles on their faces, but there's definitely an edge of sadness, and an air of melancholy, like something has been missing, or time wasted.

"Princess," Ash starts, handing Violet to Kai and taking my hands in his, turning me to face him. "Enzo helped your mom escape Ace. He gave her a new identity, just like he did for you, and got her out of the States. He's also your uncle by marriage."

My head whips back to Enzo, then Rosa.

"Rosa is your aunt," Ash continues gently, his grip on my suddenly cold hands a warm comfort. Rosa nods, her face wet but split into a big grin. "And Tom, he's Rosa's brother. He's your father, Lilly."

My world freezes as Tom, the Black Knight driver steps forward. His image wavers as my own eyes fill, and I can see the glistening of tears swimming in his blue gaze.

It all suddenly makes sense. The way he said that I reminded him of someone, the way he always looked at me as if he recognised me. I look so much like her after all. Like my mother.

We stand there for a moment, staring at each other, drinking the other in. He's handsome, with dirty blond hair that's getting a little grey at the temple, bright blue eyes, and scruff on his jaw.

"Lilly, I..." he begins in a rough voice, but before he can say another word, I'm throwing myself into his arms, wrapping my own around him tightly.

*He's my fucking dad.*

He catches me with a gruff sob, returning my embrace tenfold, and we just cling to each other for what feels like forever. There are so many years we've missed out on, so many hugs to catch up on.

"H–how?" I ask, pulling back to look at him, then around at the rest of them. "How did you find out?"

"Ryan, Principessa," Enzo says, stepping closer. "I thought that I recognised your last name, the one that I gave to your mamma, and so I asked Ryan what her name was." He wraps his massive arms around Tom and I, Rosa coming to do the same, all of us weeping happy tears as we cling to each other.

Violet gives a cry, and I disentangle myself to rush over and take her from Kai with a quick kiss to his cheek. I walk over to the little group, my dad, uncle, and aunt.

"Violet, meet your grandpa, and great-uncle Enzo, and great-aunt Rosa," I tell her, giving her a kiss, then holding her out for Tom.

Eyes wide and glistening, he takes her from me, immediately starting to rock her in his arms and kissing her soft head. She quietens in his embrace, and my cheeks hurt with how wide my smile is as I watch Enzo and Rosa reach out and stroke her on opposite sides of her face, both taking turns to kiss her lightly on top of her head.

Large arms wrap around me, lemon filling my nostrils as I lean into Jax's body behind me.

"Happy?" he asks, his voice low and gruff as usual.

"So fucking happy," I reply, hugging his forearms to me.

We stand like that for a moment, soaking in each other's embrace, and as I look at my daughter, father, aunt, and uncle, then around at my Knights, I feel like I'm about to burst with sheer happiness. My family is finally all together. Both my biological and chosen family.

We're all together now, and my heart has never felt so full.

# EPILOGUE

*EIGHT MONTHS LATER*

LILLY

A sense of déjà vu hits me as I glide my hands down the silk of my dress, only this time, instead of a white dress with an ombre that reflects the sunset at my hem, my whole dress is a rainbow. It's in a Grecian style, gathered at my shoulders and waist, flowing in soft silk to pool on the ground. A golden, jewelled belt glints around my waist, a gift from the guys, and I'm praying that it's not real gold or stones, but knowing them it just might be.

And the best bit? It starts as a lilac strip on my right side, moving through pastel rainbow colours all the way round, and when I twirl, I feel like I'm the pot of gold at the end of a rainbow. The gold sequin heels probably help with that too.

"You look so beautiful," Willow tells me, voice soft, and I look up into the mirror to see her elfin face beaming back at me. It took time, but she forgave me for the whole faking my own death and having to attend my pretend funeral thing. "Again."

We both crack up until I scold her for almost making me cry, and we end up wrapped up in a tight hug.

"You are the best bitch a girl could ever have," I whisper, my voice a little thick as I fight to hold back happy tears.

"You too, babe."

"Come on, Lilly Bear," Lexi calls, striding into the room and looking fucking stunning in a form-fitting, gold dress. "You don't want to keep them waiting, otherwise they'll come up here and you'll never get to the ceremony with you looking so gorgeous."

We're in the main bedroom at Ash's—I guess our—house in the woods. We've made it into a home, somewhere away from the hustle and bustle of a town or city. Somewhere peaceful, and full of fresh air for Violet. Plus, the crazy security that the guys have installed means that we all feel safe here.

"You're right, bloody cavemen," I answer with a chuckle, picking up my skirts because I always wanted a dress that I had to do that with, and what better day than now? "Is Violet okay?"

"She's with Ryan and Enzo. I swear those men are wrapped around her little finger," Lexi chuckles as we make our way downstairs, and I pause when I see who's waiting for me at the bottom.

"You look beautiful, Lilly," Tom states, his eyes glistening as he gazes at me in wonder. I'm sure I look back at him with the same expression. I still can't believe that after all this time, I know who my biological father is, and he's here to give me away to my soulmates.

"Thank you for today," I tell him when I reach the bottom step, a lightness suffusing my limbs as I take his hands in both of mine. "It means...a lot."

"I am honoured to walk my daughter down the aisle," he answers, his voice thick with emotion and laugh lines etched into his face. "I never thought that I'd experience it."

I squeeze his hands, once again fighting those damn tears, otherwise, Willow will scold me for ruining my makeup.

"Ready?" I ask him, and he chuckles.

"Isn't that my line?"

Laughing, we walk out of the front door into the late afternoon sunshine, and the feel of it caressing my skin has me sighing in bliss. Butterflies start flying around in my stomach as we walk down the floral-decorated path to the clearing, and the sound of a piano being played reaches my ears. My breath catches when we arrive and I see Ash sitting at the instrument dressed in a beautiful, light grey linen suit that showcases all his glorious ink.

He looks up, and just like that first night at the cabin, he starts to sing. I recognise the song as *Infinity* by Jaymes Young, and the world stops spinning as he holds my gaze, telling everyone in the clearing how he feels. My breath catches, and I just watch enraptured as he serenades me with his beautiful, husky voice.

I don't know how we arrive at the end of the aisle, only blinking when the song comes to a close as I realise that the others are all there too. Loki in a floral shirt covered in lilies, suit trousers, and a waistcoat, the shirt and waistcoat unbuttoned to reveal his delicious, inked chest, his nipple bar twinkling in the sun. Jax is next to him, looking positively delicious in his signature black; black shirtsleeves rolled to the elbow, black trousers, and black boots, laces undone. Kai is on my other side, gorgeous in mustard chinos and a green, chequered shirt with a forest green waistcoat. Ash comes up next to him, his gaze intense as he takes me in. I do the same to them all, drinking them in as if for the first time, my heart thudding in my chest as I realise that this is really happening.

"Take care of her," Tom tells them, pressing a kiss to my cheek and stepping away.

"Always," they reply together, and I would giggle if they didn't look so serious. Kai takes one hand, Loki the other, and we turn to face Oleta, our celebrant, the sounds of the woods tickling our ears.

"Gentlemen, Lilly, shall we begin?" Oleta asks, and my cheeks ache with my wide smile. We all nod. We decided that we'd use my real name, I just couldn't stand the idea of doing this under a false name, and we trust everyone present, they all know who I am after all.

"I'd like to start with a poem by Rev. Daniel L. Harris. It's one that Asher suggested as it encapsulates what he, Loki, Jax, and Kai feel for Lilly and what this ceremony means to them. It's called The Blessing of the Hands.

***'These are the hands of your best friend, young and strong and full of love for you, that are holding yours on your wedding day, as you promise to love each other today, tomorrow, and forever.***

***These are the hands that will work alongside yours, as together you build your future.***
***These are the hands that will passionately love you and cherish you through the years, and with the slightest touch, will comfort you like no other.***
***These are the hands that will hold you when fear or grief fills your mind.***
***These are the hands that will countless times wipe the tears from your eyes; tears of sorrow, and tears of joy.***
***These are the hands that will tenderly hold your children.***
***These are the hands that will help you to hold your family as one.***
***These are the hands that will give you strength when you need it.***
***And lastly, these are the hands that even when wrinkled and aged, will still be reaching for yours, still giving you the same unspoken tenderness with just a touch.'***

Tears fill my eyes at the words, and I have to swallow hard to stop them from falling, my grip on Loki and Kai's hands tight. My whole body feels alight with feeling, my heart so full that it's a wonder it's not exploded.

"And now, your vows and the handfasting," she continues, smiling broadly at us.

Loki lets go of my hand, Kai using his grip to turn me to face him. We place our hands between us, and Oleta brings out a beautiful woven rainbow cord, made up of ribbon, the colours matching my dress perfectly.

"You were my light when there was only darkness, Sweetheart," Kai begins, and my eyes stare into his honey brown ones, the image wavering at the edges with my unshed tears. "You showed me that there was something to hope for, that I could be loved. You are my soul, my heart, and my light."

As he speaks, Oleta wraps the cord around our hands binding us together. The tears fall by the end of his speech, tracing a hot path down my cheeks, and he reaches up with his spare hand to wipe them away, his smile beatific.

Loki steps up next to us, placing his hand over the top of ours.

"I knew that you would change my life, our lives, from the first moment that you stepped out of that shower," he tells me, his emerald eyes glowing in the sun. "I just never knew how much you would become a part of me. You are buried so deep inside, Pretty Girl, that if they were to cut me in half you would be there too, in every part of me."

I bite my lip, my breath hitching as he speaks, the cord wrapping around his hand and binding him to us. Jax is next, the massive bastard stepping up behind me and reaching around to lay his huge palm on top. He's so close I can feel every ridge, every outline of him, and it sends a heat searing to my core when he leans down to rumble in my ear, letting only me hear his declaration.

"You are mine, Baby Girl, and I am yours until we draw our last breaths on this cursed earth. And even then I'll fucking hold your soul to ransom and I dare anyone to take it away from me."

Gods, this man. When he makes a love confession, he doesn't do it by halves. My body aches for him, my heart soaring, and I don't know if I'm more emotional or turned on right now. Grey eyes capture mine, as Jax's hand is bound to mine, Loki's, and Kai's. Ash steps to the side of Kai who shifts a little so that my dark Knight can stand in front of me.

"You are the best part of me, Princess. You taught me how to love again, how to live again, how to breathe again. You arrived like a shooting star, burning all the bad that came your way and leaving only good. We were destined, it was written in the stars that we would be together, and I will never stop worshipping you, never stop thanking whatever god decided that I was worthy of you."

Ash always had a way with words, and he's just proven it to all our friends and family. I stare into his intense eyes, full of swirling emotions, and feel a completeness deep in my soul. His hand, too, is wrapped in the cord.

And then it's my turn. Taking a deep shaking inhale, I look at each of them in turn, my lashes dotted with tears.

"You all gave me love at a time when I'd lost everything. You gave me hope when I felt hopeless. You gave me back the parts of myself that I never knew were missing. You captured my heart, we are all bound together for eternity, and I never want to be released from your love."

I pour all that I have, all that I am into my words, and know that they affect my Knights as much as they do me when I look into jewelled eyes, all glistening. Jax pulls me closer, and I feel the shudder of his shaky breath.

The final knot is tied, and Loki pulls our clasped hands upwards to a cheer of the crowd behind us. Laughter falls from my own lips as tears drip down my cheeks, my body feeling weightless with happiness. I glance over and see all of our loved ones here; my grandparents, Ryan and Lexie, Enzo and Rosa, plus Tom who's holding our daughter, who seems delighted by the whole thing and is beaming a huge, gummy grin.

Jax's mum is here too, standing with Loki's sisters who whoop and cheer. Ash's mum is in rehab, undergoing a withdrawal from years of being drugged by his dad. Loki's mum has fled the country, having emptied the family bank account upon hearing of her husband's arrest. I'm glad, I never did like her, so we're looking after the twins too, our woodland home full of life and laughter.

"Well, I believe you have rings you'd all like to exchange?" Oleta asks, her own smile wide, and we all laugh again as we almost forgot that part.

I manage to place simple bands of platinum on each of the guys' left ring fingers, Willow holding them out for us. Kai then takes the puzzle ring that they had made for me; four intertwining bands of rose gold, platinum, gold, and white gold. One band for each of my men. He places it on my left ring finger, Loki taking over to push it down a little, then Ash follows, and Jax pushes it the rest of the way. The cool metal warms quickly to my skin and having taken off my wedding ring and engagement ring when I 'died,' a sigh of relief leaves me at having the familiar weight back on my finger.

"And that concludes our celebration," Oleta says. "All that's left for me to say is—"

She's cut off by Loki grabbing the back of my head and slamming his lips to mine. I laugh into his kiss, soon having to hold back a moan as his tongue caresses the seam of my lips, begging me to open to him. He kisses me soundly, my toes curling in my shoes when Jax's free hand wraps around the front of my throat, clearly not giving two fucks about our audience.

Loki pulls away with reddened lips pulled up into a shit-eating grin, and gives me a roguish wink. I just shake my head, my movement stopped by Ash grabbing my jaw and pulling my lips to hover millimetres from his.

"My turn," he says in a low voice, the words caressing my skin before his lips close the distance and he destroys me with his kiss. It's all Ash; hard, controlling, demanding yet full of tender worship, and I give in to him completely, my free hand resting on his chest, feeling his heart beating underneath my fingertips.

He pulls away with a lingering peck, and my eyelids flutter open to find Kai waiting. His free hand cups my cheek in a gentle gesture, and I nuzzle into the touch, my eyes briefly closing at the comfort. Achingly slow, he brings our mouths together, peppering light kisses over my lips, a small whine leaving mine. I can feel the smirk just before he finally deepens the kiss, plunging his tongue into my mouth and stealing my breath. His kiss reinforces his vows, tells me how much he loves me, and I return it, confessing my truth into his own mouth until we part, both gasping and needy.

Jax moves his grip from my throat to my jaw, turning my head to an almost uncomfortable angle before he lowers his lips and presses a soft, chaste kiss to my own. He pulls away just enough to stare into my eyes, his own filled blue fire.

"I'll get a proper kiss between those sweet thighs later, Baby Girl," he murmurs, stroking my lower lip with his thumb.

*Fuck.*

*Me.*

Boom, there goes my knickers. Grinning with a look that tells me he knows exactly what state he's left me in, he lets go of my jaw, but moves his palm to the top of my collarbone, holding me in such a possessive way that I can feel how ruined my panties really are. *Fannymuncher.*

"Time to party!" Loki shouts, and another cheer goes up as *Dancing in the Moonlight* by Jubël and NEIMY starts to play over speakers placed around the clearing.

"I love this song!" I cry, quickly untangling myself from our binding, the guys chuckling at my enthusiasm.

Once free, I then drag them all to the dance floor that's been set up to one side of the clearing behind us, a buffet table and bar on the other, beautifully decorated tables dotted around, glass jars of fairy lights twinkling on their surfaces.

We dance together, wide smiles splitting our faces, and as I look around to see all the people we love here with us, Jax holding our daughter who squeals with delight as he twirls around.

I can't help but think that maybe, just maybe, it was all worth it. All the pain, all the uncertainty, all the heartache and trauma.

Because all of that led me to them. To my Knights. To the other parts of my soul.

And I wouldn't be without them for any-fucking-thing.

## *SOME HOURS LATER...*

## LILLY

I'm still laughing as Loki drags me into the woods, the sounds of the party dying down the deeper into the trees we go. Moonlight surrounds us, lanterns lighting our way down a narrow path.

"Where are we going?" I giggle, clasping his forearm which feels fucking delicious as it flexes under my grip.

"Can't ruin the surprise, Pretty Girl," he chides me, his own teeth gleaming in the moonlight as he grins back at me.

Suddenly, I can see more lights between the trees, and we come out into another small clearing, a huge yurt covered in fairy lights sitting in the middle.

"Loki—" I gasp, pulling him to a stop. "What about Violet? She hasn't spent a night away from me yet and I—" He cuts me off with a finger to my lips.

"She's with Lexi at ours, and we won't be sleeping here so we'll be back with her before she wakes up. They have some expressed milk just in case," he assures me, stepping closer until his body is flush with mine and I can feel his heat through my thin dress. "Just for an hour...or three, maybe four." He gives me a wink and a cheeky grin that I just can't resist. *Cockwomble.*

"Okay," I agree, excitement making my fingers tingle, and my heart rate picking up. I love our daughter more than life, but having some time to be me again, to be us again, feels right and important. So that I remember that I'm still Lilly, as well as a mum.

"Good girl," he praises, and I shiver, but not with cold as he drags me the rest of the way.

He pushes open the flap, and I step inside, taking a sharp inhale at the beautiful sight before me. Colour is everywhere; bright rugs and cushions dotted around, plus an enormous bed in the middle of the floor, and it's all lit up with soft candlelight coming from countless tea lights in jars as well as more fairy lights in the roof space.

"Do you like it, Princess?" Ash asks, stepping from the shadows, and I swallow as I take in his naked, tattooed chest, his linen trousers slung low on his hips, and his feet bare as he stalks towards me.

"It's breathtaking," I tell him, not taking my eyes off his stunning body, tilting my head upwards as he gets nearer so that I can look into his beautiful, swirling grey eyes.

"I'm glad that you approve," he replies, one side of his lips tilted up in a half grin that he knows drives me crazy. His long fingers reach out to hook under the shoulder of my dress.

The belt falls to the ground with a soft thud, the sound of the zipper at the back being undone fills the quiet as Loki undoes my dress, Ash pulling first one shoulder down, then the other. The dress pools at my feet in a rainbow puddle on the floor, and I watch as Ash's face goes slack when he takes in my white corset, matching lace thong, and white suspenders and stockings.

"Do you like it?" I ask, parroting his own words back at him, my voice low and husky at the hunger in his eyes.

"You're breathtaking," he repeats my words back to me, reaching out again to run his musician's fingers across the top of my breasts. My skin pebbles as I shiver under his touch. "I believe that Jax owes you a kiss."

My breath stutters, heat flooding my core as Jax's words from earlier fill my mind.

*"I'll get a proper kiss between those sweet thighs later, Baby Girl."*

The man himself emerges from the shadows, and Ash steps aside to allow Jax to stand before me, also shirt and shoeless. His body practically thrums with power, and something in me preens at the sheer masculinity that rolls off him in intoxicating waves. The soft sounds of music fill the air as he sinks to his knees, *365* by Mother's Daughter, and I know it's Loki's doing as I've been obsessed with this artist recently.

I squeak when Jax grabs my arse, his huge hands squeezing my cheeks to the point of pain, and he yanks me closer. He buries his nose in my lace-clad cunt, taking a massive inhale, and heat floods my core, ruining my knickers further as he rubs his face in my scent like a cat. A big, fucking gorgeous cat.

"You always smell so fucking good," he growls the words, his hot breath brushing over the dampness and leaving me trembling.

"Yes, you fucking do," Loki murmurs, nuzzling into my neck and sending sweet vibrations straight to my nipples which peak under my corset. His hands come around, dipping into the top of my corset, and pull first one breast out and then the other. The heat from his now bare chest sizzles up my back where our skin touches.

Kneading my breasts in his palms and rubbing my sensitive nipples between his thumb and forefinger, he distracts me until the sharp sting of ripping fabric tells me that another pair of knickers has joined the many others that Jax has ripped off my body. I can't even be cross anymore, he replaces them all anyway, and as his mouth descends on my aching pussy, all thoughts of calling him out for it vanish.

"Fuuuck—" I groan out low and long as Jax's hand leaves my arse to grab my leg and place it over his shoulder so he can go deeper.

What he then does with his tongue should be fucking illegal, making low appreciative noises in his throat as he licks, sucks, and nibbles my dripping cunt. Fire begins to burn under my skin as Loki starts sucking my neck, mimicking Jax's movements until it feels like I'm in a tug of war with one man on either end, pulling me closer towards release.

"You look so fucking perfect like that, Princess," Ash's low drawl has my closed eyelids opening to see him standing behind and to one side of Jax. I follow the movement of his arm, sucking in a sharp breath when I see his inked-up hand wrapped around his dick, the magic cross piercing glinting in the low light. "Doesn't she, Kai?"

"Beautiful," Kai answers, stepping from the darkness at the edges of the yurt, shirtless and shoeless like the others. His own hand strokes his hard length, and my breath stutters as my eyes flit between him and Ash, watching as they pump their fists.

I yelp as a sharp slap lands on my pussy, wetness immediately following the sting.

"Stop getting distracted, Baby Girl," Jax admonishes in a low voice full of threat. "Or I won't let you come." I make a keen noise at the threat.

"Maybe she needs to be punished," Loki suggests, and I whimper, a full body shudder making me tremble in his arms.

"You have something in mind?" Jax asks him, and I feel Loki grin against my neck.

"Let go of her," he says, and when Jax does, Loki twists us around, my back still to his front, and pulls me backwards, towards where the bed was. He drops down, dragging me with him and scooting us back until his back hits the headboard.

"Loki!" I protest, gasping when he arranges me on his lap with my legs over his forearms, my bare pussy completely exposed.

“Now take out that monster cock of yours and whip her with it,” Loki tells Jax, ignoring me completely.

Lightning races up my spine at his suggestion of my punishment, and my core clenches so hard I’m almost coming from the thought alone.

“Oh, she liked that,” Kai comments darkly, his gaze fixed on my slick opening, his lips pulled up into a grin.

“You want me to whip that dripping cunt of yours with my big dick, baby?” Jax asks as he stalks towards me, unzipping his trousers when he reaches the end of the bed and stepping out of them. His dick is thick and full, so big that I always have a flutter of fear when it’s near me. I nod. “Use your words.”

“Yes, please.”

He gives me a full, masculine smirk, kneeling on the bed and grasping his cock as he gets into position, his knees spread so that his dick is hovering over my pussy.

“Count for me, Baby Girl,” he commands, then brings his hard length down. Hard. I cry out, my back arching as wetness seeps out of my lower lips.

“O–one,” I gasp, my core contracting with the force of his hit. Fuck, that felt incredible.

“She really likes that,” Ash comments and I twist my head to see him to the side of us, on the bed, his stare fixated between my legs. “Again.”

“Yes, boss,” Jax teases, bringing his cock down again, harder this time, and the wet sound of his flesh hitting mine is obscene, louder than the music playing in the background.

“T–two,” I rasp out, my whole body shaking in Loki’s grip.

“Again,” Ash orders and Jax obeys, giving me three slaps in quick succession leaving me writhing in Loki’s arms.

“What number are we on, Baby Girl?” Jax pants, and I crack my eyelids to look at him. His face is flushed, his chest slick with sweat. His dick is covered in my cream, precum leaking from the tip as he grips it hard at the base.

"U–uhum.." I stutter, my mind a fucking mess, just like my body is.

“Five, Pretty Girl,” Loki whispers in my ear, flexing his hips, and I can feel how hard he is beneath me.

“Five.”

“Good girl,” Jax praises, trailing his fingers up my thigh. “Five more I think, or until you come. You’re so close aren’t you, baby?”

"Yes," I moan, feeling my climax fluttering at the edges, leaving the world hyper-focused.

"Then come for me quickly, and I'll fuck you hard with my monster cock," Jax tells me, and Jesus fucking Christ his dirty talk is something else that needs to be a crime.

The hand not gripping his cock skates up my body, gripping the front of my throat tightly until I can barely get any air into my lungs.

"Eyes stay on me," he orders, and I look into his blue orbs as I feel another hard slap of his hard dick against my sensitive folds.

*Shit.*

My body jerks with the movement, more wetness seeping out of me and splashing my thighs as he does it again.

And again.

And again.

The next hit has me screaming his name as my fingernails claw Loki's arms to shreds when my orgasm slams into me, stealing my fucking breath and soul as I soar into the stars.

Wave upon wave of hot pleasure smashes into me as my whole body feels like it goes rigid and liquid all at once. Loki holds me still, telling me what a good fucking girl I am as Jax starts to fight against my pulsing cunt and pushes inside my fluttering channel.

"Fucking hell," he growls out, sinking deeper into me and prolonging my climax as I writhe and buck beneath him.

He gives me no time to adjust, my wet body accepting his intrusion easily as he bottoms out, then immediately starts to pound into me with such force that I hear Loki grunt behind me.

"Shit, bro, I'm glad that's not my asshole you're fucking right now," Loki exclaims as his grip tightens on my legs, holding me open for Jax to fuck even harder.

"You wish," Jax teases, his hand still gripping my throat as he destroys me with his dick, and I am fucking here for it, my tits bouncing painfully with each surge of his hips.

"Jax–fuck–shit—" I mumble, unable to say much when his grip around my throat tightens and only lets a trickle of air into my lungs.

I can feel a second release fast approaching, Jax building me up again every time he slams inside me and his pubic bone hits my clit. Pleasure zings up from my core, making my entire body tingle with the impending explosion.

"That's it, baby," Loki murmurs in my ear, licking up sweat that drips down my temple. "Come for him, cover him with your release."

Jax picks up the pace, then suddenly pulls out, and I squirt all over him as I come with a scream. His own release covers my corset and breasts, the hot cum dripping between them as ropes of it shoot out of his tip.

"Shit, Baby Girl," he rasps, falling to the side only for Ash to take his place.

"As much as I like this," he indicates my heaving chest that's covered in lace and Jax's climax. "I want to feel those breasts more as I fuck you and fill you with my cum."

Reaching forward he undoes the clasps at the front of the garment, undoing the suspenders that hold my stockings up.

"You can leave these and the shoes on," he tells me, pulling the corset off and tossing it behind me. I can feel some of Jax's cum slide down between my breasts, and Ash's eyes trace its journey down my body. "Fucking perfect."

Loki keeps hold of my legs, bringing them up more as Ash lines up his pierced cock with my opening then starts to push inside. My eyes roll, my thighs already quivering as he thrusts further inside me until he's all the way in.

"Ash," I say with a gasp, his hand cupping my cheek as he presses our foreheads together, my own gripping the back of his neck.

"I know, Princess," he whispers, his hips moving in an undulating rhythm that has me seeing stars at the edge of my vision. "It feels so fucking good, so fucking right when I'm inside you."

He keeps our foreheads pressed together while he fucks me slowly and deeply, a contrast to Jax's frantic fucking. *Call Out My Name*, also by Mother's Daughter, begins to play as Ash whispers sweet, love declarations in my ear all the while bringing me closer to the edge.

***"'When in disgrace with fortune and men's eyes,***
***I all alone beweep my outcast state,: And trouble deaf heaven with my bootless cries,***
***And look upon myself and curse my fate,***

***wishing me like to one more rich in hope,***
***Featured like him, like him with friends possessed,***
***Desiring this man's art, and that man's scope,***
***With what I most enjoy contented least;: Yet in these thoughts myself almost despising,***
***Haply I think on thee—and then my state,***
***Like to the lark at break of day arising***
***From sullen earth sings hymns at heaven's gate;***
***For thy sweet love remembered such wealth brings,***
***That then I scorn to change my state with kings.'"***

Tears fill my eyes and track down my cheeks at his recitation of one of Shakespeare's sonnets, and I remember all the other times that he quoted my favourite poet's words at me, using them as our own love language.

"Come for me, beautiful," he demands, his voice raspy and deep with how close to his climax he is. "Show me that you are mine."

One hand keeps cupping my cheek as the other comes between us and starts playing with my swollen clit, rubbing it in a rhythm that has the stars at the edges of my vision exploding and covering my body with stardust as I cry out his name. My limbs feel as though they are heavy and weightless all at once, like the stars really have come to earth and are filling me up with their light.

"Lilly—" he grunts out as he thrusts deeply a final time, filling me with his climax, his whole body rigid.

Panting, he stays buried inside me, our breaths intermingled as we share each other's air, unwilling to part just yet.

"I love you, Ash. So much," I whisper against his lips.

"I love you, my Lilly," he replies, placing a kiss against my lips before pulling away and out of me. I hiss as he leaves my body, but Kai gives me no time to mourn the loss as he moves up between my thighs.

"Kai–I–I can't," I whimper, my whole body aching as Loki finally lowers my legs, which tremble and shake.

"Yes, you can, Pet," he tells me, his voice a hard command. "And you will take Loki and I beautifully, because you're our very special girl, aren't you?"

I shudder as I feel Loki taking off his trousers beneath me, watching as he kicks them off his feet and Kai throws them off the bed. Someone hands Kai some lube, and he squirts some into his palm, reaching between my legs. Loki groans underneath me, dropping his head to my neck and biting me as Kai lubes his dick up.

"Shit," Loki curses, his palms squeezing my thighs. Contrary to what I believe, my body reacts as my pussy pulses with the harsh touch.

"We're both going to fuck this sweet pussy, aren't we, Pet?" Kai asks, and I'm not sure which of us he's talking to, but we both moan. "Lift up a little, Sweetheart." And I know that command is for me, so I place my feet on the bed and lift my hips, gasping when I feel the metal of Loki's piercing against my swollen channel. "Good girl, now sink down."

Again, I do as commanded, and a small whimper sounds in my throat as Loki's dick goes all the way in, impaling me on his hard length.

"Fuck, you feel epic," Loki rasps out, his hand hooking around my thighs and opening me further as he scoots us down a little.

I watch as Kai slicks up his own cock, the metal of his piercings sparkling in the candlelight. Loki groans as I clench around him, his hips making small movements that make me gasp and groan in turn. Kai leans over us, positioning himself at my opening which is full of Loki.

"Deep breaths, Pet," he instructs, surging forward and slowly pushing himself alongside Loki.

*Fucking hell.*

There's pain, but Loki quickly overrides that with his fingers playing my clit like he plays his guitar, and wetness that I didn't think was possible given how much I've already come, seeps out of me.

"That's it, baby. Take us both like the good fucking girl you are," Loki moans in my ear, and I pant as Kai pushes in further, all of us groaning when he finally bottoms out.

"That's so fucking hot," Jax comments, and I glance over to see his solid dick in his hand which is pumping up and down at the sight of us before him.

"Eyes my way, Pet," Kai orders, and my gaze snaps back to him as he slowly starts to withdraw, only to thrust back in hard, making Loki and I cry out.

"Fuck, your piercings—" Loki exclaims, and I can imagine how good they feel rubbed up against him inside me.

After that, I'm lost to the push and pull of Loki and Kai as they find a rhythm that leaves me breathless and shaking all over, sweat covering my skin as I ride out the pleasure that they are giving me. It takes surprisingly little time for another orgasm to sneak up on me, and I'm crying by the time the wave crests and drags me under in sheer bliss.

My whole body goes limp between them as they continue to use me, finding their release inside me together and filling me up with their seed. I hear Jax grunt, and then Ash as their release hits my torso and breasts, marking me as theirs.

"We are your Knights," Ash states, and I open my closed lids to look at him above me.

"But you are our fucking Queen," Jax adds, his fingers caressing my cheek until my head turns to him.

"And we will always love you," Loki whispers beneath me, placing a kiss on my neck, my cheek, and my temple.

"And we will always be yours to command," Kai adds, and I gasp as he pulls out of me, Loki slipping out at the same time.

"And I will love you for all eternity," I tell them in a breathless whisper, gazing around at the three Knights above me, Loki pulling me closer to him beneath me.

We stay in our tent, making love and dozing until the sun kisses the horizon and it's time to go back to the last piece of us; our daughter.

After cleaning up, we walk through the forest, the sound of the dawn chorus serenading us as we make our way home. I look at my soulmates, my lovers and husbands, and am filled with a sense of peace as I walk, seeing a similar expression on their faces.

Somehow, we found each other, and amongst all of the terrible things that have happened to each of us, we found ourselves too. We discovered a love that defies all the monsters of the world, that dares them to try and rip us apart, to break our bond. We brought new life into a world that was full of darkness, and now as the sun rises I can't help but think of all the light that is to follow, chasing away the dark, until it is all that is left.

We have been released from our shackles and bound ourselves together, our hearts captured in a love so strong that it can never be broken.

The Motherfucking End!

Are you intrigued by Hunter and the twins? Well, don't you worry because I have their story right HERE for you.

Not ready to let Lilly and her Knights go yet? Click HERE for a little steamy bonus scene.

If you enjoyed my Highgate Preparatory series, you might like Addicted to the Pain, book 1 in my Dead Soldiers vs Tailors Duet. But be warned, it's much darker than these books, and just like Lark and her Tailor boys, you may end up ruined...

# AUTHOR NOTE

If you enjoyed *Conquered*, please consider leaving a review. They help our books get in front of new readers as they teach the algorithm that we're bloody awesome. You have that power, so use it wisely my fellow smut slut.

How are you feeling after that? I can't quite believe that it's the end of Lilly and her Knight's story. Talk about all the emotions!

But here it is, all done and I'm so fucking pleased and proud of myself for getting it done and finishing my debut series!

And now onto the next project...be on the lookout for what's coming (*snort) next, but I can promise you it's dark and oh so fucking delicious!

# ACKNOWLEDGMENTS

I wouldn't be here, writing all the extra bits without the help of many simply wonderful people.

My gorgeous alphas and betas who give me incredible feedback, help the story to grow and tell me there is never too much sex. You are all so appreciated and your comments are more precious than gold.

My wonderful editor Polly who literally gives me life with her comments! She makes these books shine and I honestly would be lost without her.

I'd also be totally lost without my wonderful assistants, Tara, Amy and Lexi who do so much more than they get paid for!

And my lovely Rosebuds and Darlings, my Arc readers and Street Team. You guys don't know how much you do giving me awesome reviews and recommending my books. I love you all!

And of course, my amazing husband who supports me in all that I do, and enjoys the benefits of being married to a steamy romance author (you all know what I'm talking about!). I genuinely wouldn't be where I am today, as a person, craftsperson or author without him.

# ABOUT THE AUTHOR

About Rosa

Rosa Lee lives in a sleepy Wiltshire village, surrounded by the beautiful English countryside and the sound of British Army tanks firing in the background (it's worth the noise for the uniformed dads in the local supermarket and doing the school run!).

Rosa loves writing dark and delicious whychoose romance, and has so many ideas trying to burst out that she can often be found making a note of them as soon as one of her three womb monsters wakes her up. She believes in silver linings and fairytale endings...you know, where the villains claim the Princess for their own, tying her up and destroying the world for her.

If you'd like to know more, please check out Rosa's socials or visit

www.rosaleeauthor.com

Rosa's Captivating Roses

Linktree

# ALSO BY ROSA LEE

Also by Rosa

**HIGHGATE PREPARATORY ACADEMY**

*A dark whychoose romance*

Hunted: A Highgate Preparatory Academy Prequel

Captured: Highgate Preparatory Academy, Book 1

Bound: Highgate Preparatory Academy, Book 2

Released: Highgate Preparatory Academy, Book 3

**DEAD SOLDIERS VS TAILORS DUET**

*A dark whychoose enemies to lovers romance*

Addicted to the Pain

Addicted to the Ruin

**THE SHADOWMEN**

*A dark gang & mafia whychoose romance*

Kissed by Shadows

Claimed by Shadows

Owned by Shadows

**STANDALONES**

*A dark whychoose Lady and the Tramp(s) retelling*

Tainted Saints

*A dark whychoose stepbrother Cinderella retelling*

Tarnished Embers

*A dark whychoose mafia romance Co-written with Mallory Fox*

A Night of Revelry and Envy

www.ingramcontent.com/pod-product-compliance
Lightning Source LLC
Chambersburg PA
CBHW070340220726
48292CB00022B/4

* 9 7 8 1 9 1 7 3 3 2 0 9 5 *